Twentieth-Century

BRITAIN

PETER LANG
New York • Washington, D.C./Baltimore • Bern
Frankfurt am Main • Berlin • Brussels • Vienna • Oxford

Twentieth-Century
BRITAIN

AN ENCYCLOPEDIA

Revised Edition

EDITED BY
Fred M. Leventhal

PETER LANG
New York • Washington, D.C./Baltimore • Bern
Frankfurt am Main • Berlin • Brussels • Vienna • Oxford

Library of Congress Cataloging-in-Publication Data

Twentieth-century Britain: an encyclopedia /
edited by Fred M. Leventhal.—Rev. ed.
p. cm.
Includes bibliographical references and index.
1. Great Britain—History—20th century—Encyclopedias. 2. Great
Britain—Civilization—20th century—Encylopedias. I. Leventhal, F. M.
DA566 .T835   941.082'03—dc21   2001050262
ISBN 0-8204-5108-8

Die Deutsche Bibliothek-CIP-Einheitsaufnahme

Twentieth-century Britain: an encyclopedia /
ed. by; Fred M. Leventhal:—Rev. ed.
−New York; Washington, D.C./Baltimore; Bern;
Frankfurt am Main; Berlin; Brussels; Vienna; Oxford: Lang.
ISBN 0-8204-5108-8

Cover art: *View of Houses on Parliament seen across Westminster Bridge at dawn, for story
re poet William Wordsworth* ("composed upon Westminster Bridge")
Courtesy of Nat Farbman/Timepix

Cover design by Lisa Dillon

The paper in this book meets the guidelines for permanence and durability
of the Committee on Production Guidelines for Book Longevity
of the Council of Library Resources.

© 2002 Peter Lang Publishing, Inc., New York
275 Seventh Avenue, 28th floor, New York, NY 10001
www.peterlangusa.com

Printed in the United States of America

Contents

Topical Contents

Preface

When I was invited to edit an encyclopedia on twentieth-century Britain, my initial response was one of mingled skepticism and derision. The task seemed monumental and perhaps ultimately self-defeating. Was it possible within the span of a single volume to encompass enough of the history and culture of the century for it to be useful to its intended audience of university students, academics, and general readers? After initial hesitation, I accepted the challenge and have been grateful ever since for the opportunity to compile my own version of twentieth-century Britain. This revised and considerably shortened edition, commissioned by Peter Lang Publishing, has enabled me to remedy omissions in the original volume, to correct a few errors, to revise the bibliography, and to update a number of the entries. My task as editor has been, above all, to select the topics and contributors, recognizing—as reviewers of the encyclopedia noted—that another editor might well have chosen differently. The range of subjects covered has been partly determined by my own interests in social and cultural history, in the history of the labor movement, and in music and art. However, while I am ultimately responsible for the contents of this work, I have not sought to impose a uniform style on authors, preferring to encourage diversity of approach and independent judgment. I have, however, attempted to standardize spelling and capitalization.

Certain editorial policies that might appear idiosyncratic to the reader warrant explanation rather than apology. Many of the articles may be loosely described as biographical, but no effort has been made to insure that they include all the factual information provided in *Who's Who* or in the *Dictionary of National Biography*. Instead they have been intended as interpretive assessments, including whatever biographical detail authors deemed pertinent. Writers, artists, and politicians whose careers were mainly in the nineteenth century but who lived on into the twentieth have largely been excluded. Thus, there are no entries on Thomas Hardy or Henry James, on Lord Rosebery or Lord Salisbury, on Alfred Marshall or John Singer Sargent. At the other end of the century it seemed advisable to exclude some contemporary figures whose ongoing careers preclude full retrospective assessments.

The encyclopedia is arranged alphabetically, but with occasional accommodation to enable readers to find articles more easily. Wars and battles are referred to by their most familiar designations: the Boer War, not the Anglo-Boer War or the South African War; the battle of Passchendaele, not the Third Battle of Ypres. The First World War and the Second World War, which figure so prominently throughout this work, are identified consistently in that way rather than as World War I or World War II, although occasionally the First World War is noted in articles as the Great War. Individuals appear under the name by which they are best known: Lord Beaverbrook, not William Maxwell Aitken; Samuel Hoare, not Viscount Templewood; George Orwell, not Eric Blair, Margot Fonteyn, not Peggy Hookham.

Although the title *Twentieth-Century Britain* has been chosen deliberately to connote a concept broader than England, I have certainly not given equal space to all the components that lay claim to the term "British". Some attempt—admittedly inadequate—has been made to include Scottish, Welsh, and Irish literature, to discuss the rise of nationalism in constituent parts of the United Kingdom, and to recognize that economic and social developments have had distinctive impacts on different parts of the British Isles. This may appear to disregard the current debate over what constitutes national identity, but it seemed a reasonable solution to the problem of keeping the volume within manageable dimensions. In the case of writers, in particular, emphasis has been placed on individuals, e.g., Bernard Shaw, W.B. Yeats, and Dylan Thomas, who became part of a metropolitan British culture, partly because they left Ireland or Wales to live in London, but mostly because they are major figures within twentieth-century English literature. This has also justified the inclusion of the American-born T.S. Eliot and American-born artists like Jacob Epstein, whose professional work has largely been identified with England. Little attention has been paid to the Empire and Commonwealth except insofar as it affected developments in Britain.

A single volume imposes constraints not merely on the number of subjects permissible but on the amount of space that can be allocated to each. These articles range from 500 to 3,000 words, and my own judgment has largely determined the length of each entry. It has been an intriguing process to decide whether a particular politician or event merited a 1,000-word or a 2,000-word entry and to persuade contributors that such limitations needed to be imposed. This has not been done with the intention of slighting any individuals but in the recognition that certain events or professional lives warrant greater attention than others.

Within articles, words in small caps cross-reference other articles, but I have limited the use of "see also" to an absolute minimum. The topical contents at the beginning of the book organize most of the entries within nineteen categories to provide the reader with an alternative method of discovering the range of subjects. Each entry contains a short bibliography—generally books rather than articles—of critical, biographical, or related studies to enable the reader to pursue further investigation of the topic. In the case of literary figures it seemed sensible to avoid listing their own collected works, even where an authoritative edition exists. A brief guide to research material at the end of the encyclopedia indicates other sources for locating books and articles on the period, as well as general studies.

In the process of editing this volume I have had the rewarding experience of becoming acquainted with large numbers of scholars working on aspects of twentieth-century Britain. In selecting authors I have inevitably drawn on old friends both in the United States and Canada and in Britain, but I have had to depend on the generosity of others in locating scholars with whose work I was not familiar. I relied extensively on my Associate Editors for the first edition of the encyclopedia, Robert Caserio of Temple University, Chris Lawrence of the Wellcome Institute for the History of Medicine in London, and Peter Stansky of Stanford University, for suggestions as to topics and contributors. My greatest debts are to three individuals, without whose assistance the completion of the project would have been unimaginable. Gary Kuris, then at Garland Publishing, who commissioned the original encyclopedia, proved to be a model editor, offering wise counsel and sustaining my occasionally flagging spirits. James T. Dutton, my friend and department administrator at Boston University, provided technical assistance on a wholly voluntary basis, converting diskettes, devising a data base, and solving unforeseen computer problems, which enormously facilitated my task. My son David proved an invaluable editorial and research assistant, word-processing dozens of articles and checking innumerable bibliographical references. Finally, I am indebted to Phyllis Korper of Peter Lang Publishing who had sufficient faith in and enthusiasm for this project to encourage me to undertake a revised version of a work that had all too rapidly gone out of print.

Fred M. Leventhal

Chronology

1900

Labour Representation Committee established in February
Relief of Mafeking in May
Conservatives win October "khaki" election
W.G. Grace ends cricket career
George Cadbury founds Bourneville Village trust
Joseph Conrad, *Lord Jim*
A.T. Quiller-Couch, ed. *Oxford Book of English Verse*
Edward Elgar, *The Dream of Gerontius*

1901

Queen Victoria dies 22 January; Edward VII becomes King
Taff Vale judgment
Commonwealth of Australia established
First British submarine launched
Order of Merit established
Ronald Ross wins Nobel Prize for Medicine
Rudyard Kipling, *Kim*
Seebohm Rowntree, *Poverty: A Study of Town Life*
The World's Classics reprint series started
Edwin Lutyens, The Deanery Garden

1902

Treaty of Vereeniging concludes Boer War in May
Arthur Balfour becomes Prime Minister
Education Act abolishes school boards; transfers powers to local authorities
Anglo-Japanese treaty
Committee of Imperial Defence formed
British Academy incorporated
Arthur Conan Doyle, *The Hound of the Baskervilles*
J.A. Hobson, *Imperialism*
The Times Literary Supplement begins publication

1903

King Edward VII visits Paris
Emmeline Pankhurst creates Women's Social and Political Union
Albert Mansbridge establishes Workers' Educational Association
Letchworth developed as the first garden city

Universities of Liverpool and Manchester founded
W. Randal Cremer wins Nobel Peace Prize
Samuel Butler, *The Way of All Flesh*
Bernard Shaw, *Man and Superman*
G.E. Moore, *Principia Ethica*

1904

Anglo-French Entente
London Symphony Orchestra gives first concert
Rolls-Royce Company founded
J.W. Strutt, Lord Rayleigh wins Nobel Prize for Physics
William Ramsay awarded Nobel Prize for Chemistry
James Barrie, *Peter Pan*
G.K. Chesterton, *The Napoleon of Notting Hill*

1905

Henry Campbell-Bannerman becomes Prime Minister after Balfour resigns
Aliens Act attempts to curb immigration from Eastern Europe
Austin Motor Company formed
Opening of Piccadilly and Bakerloo Underground lines in London
Bernard Shaw, *Major Barbara*

1906

Liberals win 400 seats in February election victory
HMS *Dreadnought* launched
J.J. Thompson awarded Nobel Prize for Physics
John Galsworthy, *The Man of Property*

1907

Anglo-Russian Entente
New Zealand becomes a dominion within the British Empire
United Methodist Church established
SS Lusitania and Mauretania launched
Baden-Powell launches Boy Scout Movement
Rudyard Kipling awarded Nobel Prize for Literature
Joseph Conrad, *The Secret Agent*
Edmund Gosse, *Father and Son*

1908
H.H. Asquith becomes Prime Minister
Old Age Pensions Act
Olympic Games in London
Lord Northcliffe buys *The Times*
Ernest Rutherford awarded Nobel Prize for
    Chemistry
Arnold Bennett, *The Old Wives' Tale*
Graham Wallas, *Human Nature in Politics*

1909
David Lloyd George's People's Budget
Forcible feeding of suffragette prisoners
    introduced
Morley-Minto Reforms in India
Anglo-Persian Oil Company formed
H.G. Selfridge opens department store in
    Oxford Street
Minority Report of the Poor Law
    Commission issued
H.G. Wells, *Tono-Bungay*
William Beveridge, *Unemployment: A Problem
    for Industry*
Frederick Delius, *A Mass of Life*

1910
Liberals win February election with reduced
    majority
King Edward VII dies 6 May; George V
    becomes King
First labor exchanges open
Conciliation Bill on women's suffrage fails
Liberals win second 1910 election in
    December over Peers vs. People
Roger Fry organizes Post-Impressionist
    Exhibition in London
Arthur Evans completes excavation of
    Cnossus, Crete
Norman Angell, *The Great Illusion*
E.M. Forster, *Howards End*
John Galsworthy, *Justice*
Ralph Vaughan Williams, *Fantasia on a
    Theme of Tallis*

1911
Parliament Act limits powers of the House of
    Lords
Canadian-born Andrew Bonar Law replaces
    Balfour as Conservative leader
National Insurance Act provides health and
    unemployment insurance
Ford begins manufacturing automobiles in
    Manchester
Rutherford formulates theory of atomic
    structure
Official Secrets Act becomes law
First London season of Diaghilev's *Ballets
    Russes*
Max Beerbohm, *Zuleika Dobson*

1912
Escalation of suffragette violence
London dock strike
Marconi scandal
Lilian Baylis assumes control of Old Vic
    theatre
Robert F. Scott reaches South Pole
SS *Titanic* sinks after colliding with iceberg
    on maiden voyage
Royal Flying Corps established
Second Post-Impressionist Exhibition

1913
"Cat and Mouse" Act for temporary discharge
    of suffragette prisoners
Suffragette Emily Wilding Davison dies after
    being trampled by King's horse at Derby, 9
    June
Miners, Railwaymen, and Transport Workers
    form Triple Alliance
Trade Union Act allows unions to finance
    Labour Party through political fund
New Statesman founded by Sidney and
    Beatrice Webb
D.H. Lawrence, *Sons and Lovers*
Bertrand Russell and Alfred North
    Whitehead, *Principia Mathematica*

1914
Mutiny at Curragh garrison in March
Britain declares war on Germany, 4 August
H.N. Brailsford, *The War of Steel and Gold*
Compton Mackenzie, *Sinister Street*
Robert Tressell, *The Ragged Trousered
    Philanthropists*

1915
Gallipoli campaign
Rupert Brooke dies of blood poisoning en
    route to the Dardanelles
Douglas Haig becomes British Commander-
    in-Chief in France
Edith Cavell executed in Brussels
W.H. and W.L. Bragg share Nobel Prize for
    Physics
Ford Madox Ford, *The Good Soldier*
W. Somerset Maugham, *Of Human Bondage*
Dorothy Richardson, *Pointed Roofs* (first
    volume of *Pilgrimage)*

1916
Military Service Act imposes conscription
Battle of Jutland, 31 May
Lord Kitchener drowns when HMS
    Hampshire hits a mine, 5 June
Battle of the Somme, 1 July–19 November
Lloyd George replaces Asquith as Prime
    Minister
Summer Time introduced

James Joyce, *Portrait of the Artist as a Young Man*
Gustav Holst, *The Planets*

1917
British royal family adopts the name Windsor
Battle of Passchendaele (Third Battle of Ypres), 31 July–17 November
Leonard and Virginia Woolf establish the Hogarth Press

1918
Labour Party approves new constitution
British troops intervene in Russia against Soviet government
Wilfred Owen killed in action in France, 4 November
Armistice signed, 11 November
Lloyd George leads coalition to victory in December "Coupon" election
Universal male suffrage and votes for women over 30 enacted
Education Act raises school-leaving age to 14
Lytton Strachey, *Eminent Victorians*
Marie Stopes, *Married Love*

1919
Nancy Astor takes seat in Parliament as first woman MP
Massacre at Amritsar in April
Sankey Commission on the coal industry
London dockers refuse to load munitions for Poland on the *Jolly George*
John Maynard Keynes, *The Economic Consequences of the Peace*
Bernard Shaw, *Hearbreak House*
W.B. Yeats, *The Wild Swans at Coole*
Edward Elgar, Cello Concerto
Paul Nash, "The Menin Road"

1920
British mandate over Palestine
Government of Ireland Act partitions island
General Council of the Trades Union Congress formed
Communist Party of Great Britain founded
Women admitted as full members of the University of Oxford
Medical Research Council chartered
Royal Institute of International Affairs (Chatham House) begun
Agatha Christie, *The Mysterious Affair at Styles*
D.H. Lawrence, *Women in Love*
H.G. Wells, *Outline of History*
Stanley Spencer, "Christ Carrying the Cross"

1921
Parliament approves treaty creating Irish Free State

Threatened Triple Alliance strike abandoned on Black Friday, 15 April
Frederick Soddy wins Nobel Prize for Chemistry
R.H. Tawney, *The Acquisitive Society*

1922
Washington Treaty establishes Anglo-American parity in capital ships
Conservatives win November election with majority of 88
Bonar Law replaces Lloyd George as Prime Minister
Formation of Transport and General Workers' Union
Francis Aston awarded Nobel Prize for Chemistry
Archibald Hill shares Nobel Prize for Medicine
New tennis stadium opened at Wimbledon
T.S. Eliot, *The Waste Land*
James Joyce, *Ulysses*
Ludwig Wittgenstein, *Tractatus Logico-Philosophicus*

1923
Stanley Baldwin becomes Prime Minister after resignation of Bonar Law
Conservative Party lose majority in December election fought over issue of free trade
First Football Association Cup Final played at Wembley
John Macleod shares Nobel Prize for Medicine
W.B. Yeats awarded Nobel Prize for Literature
Bernard Shaw, *Saint Joan*

1924
Ramsay MacDonald becomes Prime Minister in first Labour government
Britain grants diplomatic recognition to Soviet Union in February
John Wheatley's Housing Act increases state subsidy for rental housing
Foreign Office publishes Zinoviev Letter, 25 October
Conservatives win October election with majority of 221; Baldwin returns to Downing Street
British Empire Exhibition held at Wembley
British Imperial Airways begins operations
Noel Coward, *The Vortex*
E.M. Forster, *A Passage to India*

1925
Chancellor of the Exchequer Winston Churchill restores gold standard
Britain signs Locarno Pact

Government offers subsidy after threat of
united trade union action on behalf of coal
miners, Red Friday, 31 July
Samuel Commission on coal industry
convened
Austen Chamberlain shares Nobel Peace Prize
Bernard Shaw awarded Nobel Prize for
Literature
T.S. Eliot, "The Hollow Men"
Virginia Woolf, *Mrs Dalloway*

1926

British Broadcasting Corporation chartered as
public corporation
Imperial Chemical Industries formed
General Strike, 3–12 May
T.E. Lawrence, *The Seven Pillars of Wisdom*
A.A. Milne, *Winnie the Pooh*
Beatrice Webb, *My Apprenticeship*

1927

Trade Disputes Act bans sympathetic strikes
W.H. Auden and C. Day Lewis, eds. *Oxford
Poetry*
Rosamond Lehmann, *Dusty Answer*
Virginia Woolf, *To the Lighthouse*

1928

Britain signs General Pact for the
Renunciation of War
Representation of the People Act lowers
voting age for women to 21
Scottish Nationalist Party founded
Alexander Fleming discovers penicillin
Owen Richardson wins Nobel Prize for
Physics
Radclyffe Hall, *The Well of Loneliness*
Aldous Huxley, *Point Counter Point*
D.H. Lawrence, *Lady Chatterley's Lover*
Evelyn Waugh, *Decline and Fall*
W.B. Yeats, *The Tower*

1929

Neville Chamberlain's Local Government Act
abolishes Poor Law Guardians and
restructures public assistance
Labour emerges as largest party in May
election; Ramsay MacDonald forms
second Labour government; Arthur
Henderson becomes Foreign Secretary
Robert Graves, *Goodbye to All That*
Lewis Namier, *The Structure of Politics at the
Accession of George III*
J.B. Priestley, *The Good Companions*
I.A. Richards, *Practical Criticism*
R.C. Sherriff, *Journey's End*
Virginia Woolf, *A Room of One's Own*
John Grierson's *Drifters* initiates British
documentary film movement

Alfred Hitchcock's *Blackmail*, the first British
talking movie
Henry Moore, "Reclining Figure"

1930

First Round Table Conference on India
London Naval Conference sets limits on
cruisers
Pilgrim Trust started with £2 million grant
from American E.S. Harkness
Siegfried Sassoon, *Memoirs of an Infantry
Officer*

1931

Naval force at Invergordon mutinies over pay
cuts
Second Labour government collapses after
Cabinet rejects cuts in rate of
unemployment benefit
Tory-dominated National government formed
under Ramsay MacDonald; confirmed in
landslide election victory with majority of
497
MacDonald expelled from Labour Party
Britain abandons gold standard
Statute of Westminster defines dominion
status
Vic-Wells Ballet begins performing at Sadler's
Wells Theatre
Virginia Woolf, *The Waves*
William Walton, *Belshazzar's Feast*
Jacob Epstein, "Genesis"

1932

Disarmament Conference opens at Geneva
under Henderson's presidency
Free trade ends as Government introduces
import duties and imperial preference
Lytton Commission on Japanese invasion of
Manchuria
ILP disaffiliates from Labour Party
Oswald Mosley forms British Union of Fascists
John Galsworthy awarded Nobel Prize for
Literature
Edgar Adrian and Charles Sherrington share
Nobel Prize for Medicine
Shakespeare Memorial Theatre opens in
Stratford-upon-Avon
Thomas Beecham founds London
Philharmonic Orchestra
Aldous Huxley, *Brave New World*
John Strachey, *The Coming Struggle for Power*
Charles Holden, Senate House, University of
London

1933

London Passenger Transport Board created
Paul Dirac wins Nobel Prize for Physics
Norman Angell awarded Nobel Peace Prize

Oxford Union "King and Country" debate, 9
   February
Vera Brittain, *Testament of Youth*
Walter Greenwood, *Love on the Dole*
Oxford English Dictionary
Alexander Korda, *The Private Life of Henry
   VIII*
Frank Lloyd, *Cavalcade*

1934
Unemployment Act imposes means test on
   family basis
Britain ceases war debt payments to United
   States
Fascist rally at Olympia, London, 7 June
Road Traffic Act introduces driving tests
Arthur Henderson awarded Nobel Peace
   Prize
Canon Dick Sheppard organizes peace pledge
   campaign
SS *Queen Mary* launched
John Christie establishes opera festival at
   Glyndebourne
J.B. Priestley, *English Journey*

1935
Peace Ballot organized by League of Nations
   Union
Baldwin succeeds MacDonald as Prime
   Minister, 7 June
Clement Attlee becomes leader of Labour
   Party
Conservatives win November election;
   National government majority of 247
Cabinet disavows Hoare-Laval Pact on
   Abyssinia
Anthony Eden succeeds Samuel Hoare as
   Foreign Secretary
Government of India Act provides for greater
   provincial autonomy
British Council founded
Allen Lane launches Penguin Books
James Chadwick wins Nobel Prize for Physics
T.S. Eliot, *Murder in the Cathedral*
Christopher Isherwood, *Mr. Norris Changes
   Trains*
Sidney and Beatrice Webb, *Soviet
   Communism: A New Civilisation?*
Alfred Hitchcock, *The Thirty-Nine Steps*

1936
King George V dies on 20 January; succeeded
   by Edward VIII
Oswald Mosley leads anti-Jewish
   demonstration in Whitechapel
Britain signs Non-Intervention Agreement,
   pledging neutrality in Spain
Ellen Wilkinson leads Jarrow unemployed
   march to London in October

Left Book Club founded by Victor Gollancz,
   Harold Laski, and John Strachey
King Edward VIII abdicates on 11 December;
   succeeded by King George VI
Henry Dale shares Nobel Prize for Medicine
A.J. Ayer, *Language, Truth and Logic*
Winifred Holtby, *South Riding*
John Maynard Keynes, *General Theory of
   Employment, Interest and Money*
Terence Rattigan, *French Without Tears*

1937
Neville Chamberlain succeeds Stanley
   Baldwin as Prime Minister in May
Duke of Windsor marries Mrs. Wallis
   Simpson
Matrimonial Causes (Herbert) Act extends
   grounds for divorce
Mass Observation founded
George Thomson shares Nobel Prize for
   Physics
Walter Haworth shares Nobel Prize for
   Chemistry
Viscount Cecil awarded Nobel Peace Prize
W.H. Auden and Christopher Isherwood,
   The Ascent of F6
George Orwell, *The Road to Wigan Pier*
Dorothy L. Sayers, *Gaudy Night*

1938
Anthony Eden resigns as Foreign Secretary
   over appeasement policy
Munich Conference, 29 September
A.R.P. implemented in England
National Marriage Guidance Council
   founded to promote marriage and family
   life
Women's Voluntary Services founded by Lady
   Reading
Edward Hulton launches *Picture Post*
Elizabeth Bowen, *The Death of the Heart*
Graham Greene, *Brighton Rock*
Henry Moore, "Recumbent Figure"

1939
BOAC founded
Radar stations in operation
White Paper pledges end to Jewish
   immigration to Palestine
King George VI and Queen Elizabeth visit
   the United States
Evacuation of children from cities begins, 1
   September
Britain declares war on Germany, 3
   September
Myra Hess organizes lunchtime concerts in
   National Gallery
Council for the Encouragement of Music
   and the Arts (CEMA) formed

Christopher Isherwood, *Goodbye to Berlin*
James Joyce, *Finnegans Wake*
Ellen Wilkinson, *The Town That Was Murdered*

1940

Winston Churchill succeeds Neville Chamberlain as Prime Minister, 10 May
British troops evacuate Dunkirk, 26 May–4 June
Churchill offers France union with Britain
Local Defence Volunteers formed
Battle of Britain begins in August; London Blitz continues until May 1941
SS *City of Benares* sunk in Atlantic, killing 73 evacuated children
Coventry bombed in November
Oswald Mosley imprisoned under Defence Regulations
"Cato", *Guilty Men*
Graham Greene, *The Power and the Glory*

1941

Virginia Woolf commits suicide, 28 March
Roosevelt introduces Lend-Lease
Churchill and Roosevelt issue Atlantic Charter, 14 August
Britain declares war on Japan, 8 December
Conscription of women introduced in December
Michael Tippett, *A Child of Our Time*
Henry Moore, *The Shelter Sketchbook*
Paul Nash, "Totes Meer"

1942

Singapore falls to Japanese forces in February
British North African victory in battle of El Alamein
Beveridge Report calls for comprehensive social services
Cripps mission to India; Gandhi demands independence
Noel Coward, *In Which We Serve*

1943

British Eighth Army reaches Tripoli
Churchill confers with Roosevelt at Casablanca, Quebec, Cairo, and Teheran
T.S. Eliot, *Four Quartets*
Humphrey Jennings, *Fires Were Started*
Michael Powell and Emeric Pressburger, *The Life and Death of Colonel Blimp*
Henry Moore, "Madonna and Child"

1944

Education Act provides secondary education for all in tripartite structure
Allied landing in Normandy on D-Day, 6 June
V-2 rocket attacks in September

William Beveridge, *Full Employment in a Free Society*
Joyce Cary, *The Horse's Mouth*
G.M. Trevelyan, *English Social History*
Francis Bacon, "Three Studies for Figures at the Base of a Crucifixion"

1945

British bomb Dresden, 14 February
Montgomery's forces cross Rhine, 23 March
VE-Day, 8 May
Family Allowances Act
Labour wins 393 seats in July election landslide; Attlee becomes Prime Minister
Lend-Lease ends after Japanese surrender; Keynes negotiates American loan
Ernst Chain, Alexander Fleming, and Howard Florey share Nobel Prize for Medicine for discovery of penicillin
George Orwell, *Animal Farm*
Evelyn Waugh, *Brideshead Revisited*
Benjamin Britten, *Peter Grimes*
Noel Coward, *Brief Encounter*
Laurence Olivier, *Henry V*

1946

National Health Service Act
Bank of England, coal, and civil aviation nationalized
Anglo-American Palestine Committee favors visas for 100,000 Jewish immigrants
"Britain Can Make It" Exhibition
Sadler's Wells Ballet reopens Covent Garden with *The Sleeping Beauty*
Arts Council established by royal charter
BBC Third Programme begins broadcasting
Cabinet mission to India fails to reconcile communal divisions
Burma gains independence
Frederick Ashton, *Symphonic Variations* (for Sadler's Wells Ballet)

1947

Convertibility of sterling restored in July
Indian independence proclaimed on 15 August; Communal strife compels partition into India and Pakistan
Town and Country Planning Act applies planning control to entire country
Railways nationalized
Edinburgh International Festival launched
Edward Appleton wins Nobel Prize for Physics
Robert Robinson awarded Nobel Prize for Chemistry

1948

Bread rationing ends
Marshall Plan

Representation of the People Act abolishes university seats and plural voting
University of Cambridge admits women to degrees
London Olympiad
P.M.S. Blackett awarded Nobel Prize for Physics
T.S. Eliot wins Nobel Prize for Literature
F.R. Leavis, *The Great Tradition*
Terence Rattigan, *The Winslow Boy*
Michael Powell and Emeric Pressburger, *The Red Shoes*

1949
Britain joins North Atlantic Treaty Organization
Britain devalues pound from $4.03 to $2.80
John Boyd Orr awarded Nobel Peace Prize
Elizabeth Bowen, *The Heat of the Day*
Christopher Fry, *The Lady's Not for Burning*
George Orwell, *1984*
Carol Reed, *The Third Man*
Henry Moore, "Family Group"

1950
Labour wins February election with majority of 6
British join United States in Korean War
Bertrand Russell awarded Nobel Prize for Literature
T.S. Eliot, *The Cocktail Party*

1951
Aneurin Bevan and Harold Wilson resign from Cabinet over imposition of health service charges
Festival of Britain
Labour outpolls Conservatives but loses October election; Churchill replaces Attlee as Prime Minister
Guy Burgess and Donald Maclean defect to Soviet Union
John Cockroft shares Nobel Prize for Physics
Benjamin Britten, *Billy Budd*
Anthony Powell, *A Question of Upbringing* (first volume in *A Dance to the Music of Time* series)
C.P. Snow, *The Masters*
"The Archers" first broadcast on BBC Light Programme
Robert Matthew and Leslie Martin, Royal Festival Hall

1952
Death of King George VI; Accession of Queen Elizabeth II
British atomic bomb announced
Archer Martin and Richard Synge share Nobel Prize for Chemistry

Samuel Beckett, *Waiting for Godot*
Agatha Christie, *The Mousetrap*
Evelyn Waugh, *Men at Arms* (first volume of *Sword of Honour* trilogy)

1953
Edmund Hillary climbs Mt. Everest
Winston Churchill awarded Nobel Prize for Literature
Hans Krebs shares Nobel Prize for Medicine
L.P. Hartley, *The Go-Between*

1954
Advent of commercial television
Max Born shares Nobel Prize for Physics
Roger Bannister breaks four-minute mile record
Kingsley Amis, *Lucky Jim*
William Golding, *Lord of the Flies*
Dylan Thomas, *Under Milk Wood*

1955
Churchill retires in April; succeeded by Anthony Eden as Prime Minister
Conservatives increase majority in May election to 58
Hugh Gaitskell elected leader of Labour Party on Attlee's retirement
British forces battle EOKA in Cyprus
Mary Quant opens boutique in King's Road, Chelsea
Michael Tippett, *The Midsummer Marriage*

1956
Suez crisis
Cyril Inshelwood shares Nobel Prize for Chemistry
C.A.R. Crosland, *The Future of Socialism*
John Osborne, *Look Back in Anger*
Angus Wilson, *Anglo-Saxon Attitudes*

1957
Eden resigns in January; Harold Macmillan named as Prime Minister
Britain explodes thermonuclear bomb in central Pacific
Wolfenden Report on homosexuality and prostitution
Ghana becomes independent
Archbishop Makarios released from imprisonment
Alexander Todd wins Nobel Prize for Chemistry
Lawrence Durrell, *Justine* (first volume of *The Alexandria Quartet*)
Richard Hoggart, *The Uses of Literacy*
John Osborne, *The Entertainer*
David Lean, *The Bridge on the River Kwai*

1958

Campaign for Nuclear Disarmament launched
First Aldermaston march
Notting Hill riots
Life peerages introduced
Frederick Sanger wins Nobel Prize for
    Chemistry
Alan Sillitoe, *Saturday Night and Sunday
    Morning*
Raymond Williams, *Culture and Society*
Henry Moore, "Reclining Figure"

1959

Macmillan leads Conservatives to third
    straight electoral victory in October
Gaitskell challenges Clause IV of Labour
    constitution
Obscene Publications Act limits censorship
Alex Issigonis introduces Mini car
Philip Noel-Baker awarded Nobel Peace
    Prize
John Arden, *Sergeant Musgrave's Dance*
Boulting Brothers, *I'm All Right, Jack*

1960

Macmillan government abandons British
    ballistic missile, Blue Streak
Agreement allows U.S. to use Holy Loch for
    Polaris missiles
Military conscription ends
Formation of European Free Trade Area
Cyprus and Nigeria becomes independent
Obscenity trial of *Lady Chatterley's Lover*
Peter Medawar shares Nobel Prize for
    Medicine
New Left Review founded
Olivia Manning, *The Great Fortune* (first
    volume of *The Balkan Trilogy*)
Alan Bennett, Jonathan Miller, *et al.*, *Beyond
    the Fringe*
Robert Bolt, *A Man for All Seasons*
Harold Pinter, *The Caretaker*

1961

Britain application to join Common Market
    rebuffed by DeGaulle
South Africa expelled from Commonwealth
University of Sussex opens
Espionage trials of Gordon Lonsdale, George
    Blake, and the Krogers
Iris Murdoch, *A Severed Head*
Muriel Spark, *The Prime of Miss Jean Brodie*

1962

Commonwealth Immigrant Act restricts
    entry to Britain
Conservatives lose Orpington by-election
National Economic Development Council
    (Neddy) sets targets for economic growth
John Kendrew and Max Perutz share Nobel
    Prize for Chemistry
Francis Crick, Maurice Wilkins, and
    American James Watson share Nobel
    Prize for Medicine for research on
    structure of DNA
"Coronation Street" television serial begins
Anthony Burgess, *A Clockwork Orange*
Doris Lessing, *The Golden Notebook*
Arnold Wesker, *Chips with Everything*
Benjamin Britten, *War Requiem*
David Lean, *Lawrence of Arabia*
Basil Spence, University of Sussex and
    Coventry Cathedral

1963

Hugh Gaitskell dies; Harold Wilson elected
    Labour Leader
Kim Philby granted asylum in Soviet Union
Profumo scandal rocks Tory government
Macmillan resigns as Prime Minister;
    succeeded by Alec Douglas Home
Robbins Report on higher education
Kenya becomes independent
Alan Hodgkin and Andrew Huxley share
    Nobel Prize for Medicine
John Le Carré, *The Spy Who Came in from the
    Cold*
E.P. Thompson, *The Making of the English
    Working Class*
Joan Littlewood, *Oh What a Lovely War*
Tony Richardson, *Tom Jones*

1964

Labour wins general election with majority of
    4; Harold Wilson becomes Prime
    Minister
Mods and Rockers battle at seaside resorts
Dorothy Hodgkin awarded Nobel Prize for
    Chemistry
Terence Conran opens first Habitat store
Philip Larkin, *The Whitsun Weddings*
Peter Shaffer, *The Royal Hunt of the Sun*
Barbara Hepworth, "Single Form"
Peter and Alison Smithson, *The Economist*
    building, London

1965

Churchill dies at 90, 24 January
Edward Heath elected Conservative Party
    Leader
Labour government promotes comprehensive
    secondary schools
Abolition of death penalty
Race Relations Act tackles discrimination and
    racism
Ian Smith issues Unilateral Declaration of
    Independence in Rhodesia
Universities of Kent and Warwick open

Edward Bond, *Saved*
Kenneth MacMillan, *Romeo and Juliet* (for
    Royal Ballet)

1966
Labour increases majority to 96 in March
    election
England defeats West Germany to win World
    Cup in football
Paul Scott, *The Jewel in the Crown* (first
    volume of *The Raj Quartet*)
Tom Stoppard, *Rosencrantz and Guildenstern
    Are Dead*
Richard Seifert, Centrepoint Tower, London

1967
Abortion legalized
Sexual Offences Act decriminalizes
    homosexuality
Wilson government application to join
    Common Market rejected
Devaluation of the pound
Milton Keynes designated as a new town
Ronald Norrish and George Porter share
    Nobel Prize for Chemistry
Alan Ayckbourn, *Relatively Speaking*
The Beatles, *Sergeant Pepper's Lonely Hearts
    Club Band*

1968
Restrictions imposed on immigration from
    India, Pakistan, and West Indies
Civil rights marches in Ulster

1969
Voting qualification lowered to 18
Barbara Castle issues *In Place of Strife* White
    Paper on industrial relations
British troops sent to Londonderry and
    Belfast
Divorce Act abandons principle of marital
    fault
Open University founded
Student unrest temporarily closes London
    School of Economics
Rupert Murdoch acquires the *Sun*
Derek Barton shares Nobel Prize for
    Chemistry
Samuel Beckett awarded Nobel Prize for
    Literature
John Fowles, *The French Lieutenant's Woman*

1970
Labour defeated in June election; Heath
    becomes Prime Minister
Conservative government introduces
    internment without trial in Ulster
Bernard Katz shares Nobel Prize for
    Medicine

1971
Industrial Relations Act
Dennis Gabor wins Nobel Prize for Physics

1972
Coal strike lasts 47 days
Northern Ireland goverment at Stormont
    suspended; replaced by direct rule from
    Westminster
Rodney Porter shares Nobel Prize for
    Medicine
John Hicks shares Nobel Prize for Economics

1973
Britain joins European Economic
    Community
Sunningdale Agreement proposes power-
    sharing arrangement in Ulster
Brian Josephson shares Nobel Prize for
    Physics
Geoffrey Wilkinson shares Nobel Prize for
    Chemistry
Nikolaas Tinbergen shares Nobel Prize for
    Medicine
Alan Ayckbourn, *The Norman Conquests*

1974
Miners strike in February; three-day work
    week imposed to save power
Conservatives defeated in February election;
    Wilson returns as Prime Minister
Labour wins October general election by
    narrow majority
Martin Ryle and Antony Hewish share Nobel
    Prize for Physics

1975
Margaret Thatcher succeeds Heath as
    Conservative Leader
First North Sea oil production
Referendum on membership in European
    Economic Community
David Lodge, *Changing Places*
Anthony Powell, *Hearing Secret Harmonies*
    (concluding volume of *A Dance to the
    Music of Time* series)
Margaret Drabble, *The Realms of Gold*

1976
Wilson retires; replaced by James Callaghan
    as Prime Minister
Denys Lasdun's National Theatre opens on
    London's South Bank

1977
Lib-Lab pact in Commons
Nevill Mott shares Nobel Prize for Physics
James Meade shares Nobel Prize for Economics
Margaret Drabble, *The Ice Age*

1978

Scottish and Welsh Devolution Acts
Peter Mitchell awarded Nobel Prize for
    Chemistry
David Hare, *Plenty*
Kenneth MacMillan, *Mayerling* (for Royal
    Ballet)

1979

Referendums on Scottish and Welsh
    devolution fail to win sufficient votes
Winter of Discontent: public service strikes
Conservative election victory in May;
    Thatcher becomes Prime Minister
Lord Mountbatten assassinated by IRA
    terrorists, 27 August
Geoffrey Hounsfield shares Nobel Prize for
    Medicine
Arthur Lewis shares Nobel Prize for Economics

1980

Michael Heseltine's Housing Act promotes
    sale of council housing
Callaghan resigns as Labour leader; replaced
    by Michael Foot
Zimbabwe becomes independent under
    leadership of Robert Mugabe

1981

Social Democratic Party founded; Shirley
    Williams wins Crosby by-election
Urban riots in Brixton, Southall, Toxteth
Prince Charles marries Lady Diana Spencer
D.M. Thomas, *The White Hotel*
David Puttnam, *Chariots of Fire*

1982

Falklands War against Argentina, May–June
Employment Act outlaws secondary strikes
    and restricts closed shops
Channel Four established as second
    commercial television channel
Terrence Higgins Trust launched to provide
    support for people with AIDS
John Vane shares Nobel Prize for Medicine
Richard Attenborough, *Gandhi*

1983

Falklands factor helps Conservatives win June
    general election with 144 seat majority
    despite mounting unemployment
Neil Kinnock elected Labour Leader in
    October
Graham Swift, *Waterland*
Richard Eyre, *The Ploughman's Lunch*

1984

Miners' strike
Privatization of British Telecom

Urban riots in Handsworth, Brixton, and
    Toxteth
Hillsborough Agreement in Ulster calls for
    Anglo-Irish consultation
Richard Stone awarded Nobel Prize for
    Economics
Julian Barnes, *Flaubert's Parrot*

1986

Local Government Act abolishes
    metropolitan authorities, including GLC
Heseltine resigns from Cabinet over Westland
    affair
Big Bang in City of London, 27 October
Privatization of British Gas
The Independent begins publication
Andrew Lloyd Webber, *The Phantom of the
    Opera*
Richard Rogers, Lloyd's Bank building

1987

Thatcher continues in office as Conservatives
    win third straight election
Britain signs Single European Act
Penelope Lively, *Moon Tiger*
James Stirling, Clore Gallery

1988

Community Charge ("poll tax") enacted
Section 28 of Local Government Act bans
    promotion of homosexuality
Social Democrats merge with Liberal Party to
    form Liberal Democrats
James Black shares Nobel Prize for Medicine
Stephen Hawking, *A Brief History of Time*
Salman Rushdie, *The Satanic Verses*
David Hare, *The Secret Rapture*
Mike Leigh, *High Hopes*

1989

House of Commons sessions televised for first
    time
Kazuo Ishiguro, *The Remains of the Day*

1990

Anti-poll tax riots in London
Thatcher fails to defeat Heseltine's
    leadership challenge in November;
    resigns Prime Ministership after 11-year
    tenure
John Major wins Tory leadership on second
    ballot to become Prime Minister
A.S. Byatt, *Possession*
Robert Venturi, Sainsbury Wing of National
    Gallery
Canary Wharf, Docklands, First Phase

1992

Major leads Conservatives to fourth straight

election victory in April with reduced
majority of 21
John Smith replaces Kinnock as Labour
Leader
Church of England votes to ordain women as
priests
Queen Elizabeth agrees to pay tax on private
income
Sterling crisis forces withdrawal from
European Exchange Rate Mechanism
Pat Barker, *Regeneration*
Michael Ondaatje, *The English Patient*
Alan Bennett, *The Madness of George III*

1993
Parliament ratifies Maastricht treaty on
European unity
Anglo-Irish Peace Declaration in Northern
Ireland
Black teenager Stephen Lawrence murdered
in South London
Richard J. Robers shares Nobel Prize for
Medicine
Tom Stoppard, *Arcadia*

1994
Opening of the Channel Tunnel ("Chunnel")
Multiracial government under Nelson
Mandela elected in South Africa; applies
to rejoin Commonwealth
Tony Blair elected Labour Party Leader after
death of John Smith
Conservatives suffer defeats in local
government and European elections
IRA declares cease-fire in Northern Ireland

1995
Collapse of Baring's, the oldest merchant
bank in City of London
Clause IV of Labour Party constitution
replaced
British Rail privatized
Seamus Heaney awarded Nobel Prize for
Literature
Hottest August since records began to be kept
in 1659
David Hare, *Skylight*

1996
European Union imposes ban on export of
British beef because of BSE scare

Divorce of Prince and Princess of Wales
Globe Bankside opens in Southwark
Scottish researchers succeed in cloning sheep
James A Mirrlees shares Nobel Prize in
Economics

1997
Election landslide gives Labour 418 seats for
overall majority of 179
Voter turnout of 73% is lowest since 1945
Hong Kong returned to China
New British Library opens in St. Pancras
Diana, Princess of Wales killed in automobile
accident
Scotland and Wales vote in favor of
devolution
William Hague replaces John Major as
Conservative Party Leader
John Walker shares Nobel Prize in Chemistry

1998
British and Irish governments sign Northern
Ireland power-sharing agreement at
Stormont
John Hume and David Trimble awarded
Nobel Peace Prize
Michael Frayn, *Copenhagen*

1999
Hillsborough Declaration proposes to bring
Sinn Fein into power-sharing Executive
Election of Scottish Parliament and Welsh
National Assembly
Unionist leader David Trimble becomes First
Minister of Northern Ireland government
Royal Opera House, Covent Garden reopens
after £214 million renovation
Richard Rogers Partnership, Millenium
Dome at Greenwich

2000
Ken Livingstone elected London's first mayor
Tate Modern opens in converted South Bank
power station
Queen Mother celebrates 100th birthday
Opening of the British Museum Great Court

Abbreviations

ANZAC Australian and New Zealand Army Corps
BBC British Broadcasting Corporation
BEF British Expeditionary Force
BMA British Medical Association
BOAC British Overseas Airways Corporation
BUF British Union of Fascists
CBE Commander of the Order of the British Empire
CEMA Council for the Encouragement of Music and the Arts
CH Companion of Honour
CHE Campaign for Homosexual Equality
CID Committee of Imperial Defence
CND Campaign for Nuclear Disarmament
CO Conscientious Objector
CPGB Communist Party of Great Britain
CWS Co-operative Wholesale Society
DBE Dame Commander of the Order of the British Empire
DIA Design and Industries Association
DORA Defence of the Realm Act
EC European Community
EMB Empire Marketing Board
ENSA Entertainments National Service Association
ETU Electrical Trades Union
EU European Union
FA Football Association
FBA Fellow of the British Academy
FRS Fellow of the Royal Society
GATT General Agreement on Tariffs and Trade
GCE General Certificate of Education
GCSE General Certificate of Secondary Education
GLC Greater London Council
HEFC Higher Education Funding Council
ICI Imperial Chemical Industries
ILEA Inner London Education Authority
ILP Independent Labour Party
IRA Irish Republican Army
ITA Independent Television Authority
KC King's Counsel
KG Knight of the Garter
LBC Left Book Club
LCC London County Council
LNU League of Nations Union

LPTB London Passenger Transport Board
LRC Labour Representation Committee
LSE London School of Economics and Political Science
MCC Marylebone Cricket Club
MEP Member of the European Parliament
MFGB Miners Federation of Great Britain
MI5 Security Service
MI6 Secret Intelligence Service
MOI Ministry of Information
MP Member of Parliament
MRC Medical Research Council
NATO North Atlantic Treaty Organization
NCB National Coal Board
NCF No-Conscription Fellowship
NEC National Executive Committee of the Labour Party
NF National Front
NFRB New Fabian Research Bureau
NHS National Health Service
NUM National Union of Mine Workers
NUR National Union of Railwaymen
NUSEC National Union of Societies for Equal Citizenship
NUWSS National Union of Women's Suffrage Societies
OM Order of Merit
PC Privy Councillor
PEP Political and Economic Planning
PPU Peace Pledge Union
QC Queen's Counsel
RAF Royal Air Force
RCA Royal College of Art
RIBA Royal Institute of British Architects
SDLP Social Democratic and Labour Party
SDP Social Democratic Party
SNP Scottish National Party
SSIP Society for Socialist Inquiry and Propaganda
TGWU Transport and General Workers' Union
TUC Trades Union Congress
UDC Union of Democratic Control
UGC University Grants Committee
UNESCO United Nations Economic and Social Council
WEA Workers' Educational Association
WSPU Women's Social and Political Union

Abortion

English abortion law is based on theological belief, and late abortion was always condemned on grounds that a fetus was a human life created by God. The stage at which the fetus was thought to be infused with God's spirit has, however, been a subject of controversy over the centuries. In 1803 abortion became an offense from the time of conception, but it was more severely punished after quickening in the second half of pregnancy. In 1861 the Offenses Against the Person Act was passed. This act laid down that attempted abortion at any stage was a felony with a uniform maximum punishment of life imprisonment. There were subsequent minor changes to abortion legislation, notably the 1929 Infant Life Preservation Act, which made it an offense, except to save the life of the mother, to destroy the life of a child "capable of being born alive," presumed to be at around twenty-eight weeks' gestation.

The practice of abortion continued to grow and reached epidemic proportions by the early twentieth century. In 1933 nearly 500 women were officially stated to have died in England and Wales as a result of abortion, a figure recognized in the Chief Medical Officer's Report for that year to be an underestimate. The social stigma attached to the subject ensured its systematic underreporting. The Abortion Law Reform Association was founded in 1936 by a group of radical women who campaigned to legalize abortion in the interests of the health and welfare of women. The following year the British Medical Association established a committee on abortion which also recommended reform of the law. In 1938 a celebrated trial took place after Aleck Bourne, an eminent gynecologist, carried out an abortion on a fourteen year old girl who had been raped by two soldiers. In this case, Rex v. Bourne, the judge ruled that abortion was lawful if the woman would otherwise die. He also argued that it might also be lawful if a woman's health were so adversely affected as to endanger her life. The government, under heavy pressure, set up its own inquiry, the Birkett Committee, which reported in 1939, recommending a measure of abortion law reform. Several subsequent legal cases seemed to confirm the legality of abortion to preserve the mental or physical health of the mother.

After the Second World War reformers became politically active in promoting private members' legislation in the House of Commons with the aim of obtaining clear statue law in this field. There were six such attempts between 1952 and 1965 to reform the abortion laws, all successfully resisted by ROMAN CATHOLIC MPs, who used all available parliamentary procedures to defeat reform. In 1967, however, David Steel MP, with the assistance of Lord Silkin in the HOUSE OF LORDS, piloted the 1967 Abortion Act to a successful conclusion. This permits legal abortion in England, Wales, and Scotland where it is necessary to preserve the mental or physical health of the pregnant woman, where a child would otherwise be born seriously handicapped, or where an additional child would affect adversely the health of the existing children of the family (the "medico-social" clause). The time limit derived from the Infant Life Preservation Act and was generally taken to be about twenty-eight weeks' gestation.

During the next twenty-five years Roman Catholic MPs, other MPs representing largely Roman Catholic constituencies, and right-wing CONSERVATIVE MPs made twenty unsuccessful attempts to amend, limit, or destroy the Abortion Act using all possible parliamentary procedural devices. In 1990 the Human Fertilisation and Embryology Act was passed to regulate multiple births. One of its clauses (Clause 37) slightly amended the 1967 Abortion Act. Abortion where the woman's life or health was at stake or where the child would be born handicapped was now legal without gestation limit (as it had always been in Scotland). Other abortions were now only legal within the first twenty-four weeks of gestation. Since non-urgent abortions had hardly ever been performed after twenty-four weeks, the practical effect of this amendment was negligible.

Legal abortions in Britain as a whole (excluding Northern Ireland where the Abortion Act does not apply) rose from 90,000 in 1970, to 170,000 in 1980, to nearly 200,000 in 1990. This included 11,000, 32,000 and 14,000 Irish and foreign women in those years respectively who came to Britain for legal and safe abortions they were unable to obtain in their own countries where abortion was still illegal or difficult to obtain. These numbers declined as countries overseas reformed their own abortion laws. Before the Abortion Act estimates of the extent of illegal abortion in Britain varied from 40,000 a year to 250,000 a year, with the government accepting a likely figure of about 100,000 a year. Whether there really is more abortion now than in the past, allowing for population growth, is a subject of some controversy. Illegal abortion seems to have been totally eliminated, and there are now no deaths from this cause. Nearly 90 percent of women who obtain abortion obtain them in the first trimester of pregnancy. Half obtain them free within the National Health Service. Others pay to obtain them in one of seventy private clinics which are licensed to carry out abortions. There are also non-profit consumer-oriented agencies that run their own clinics subject to government inspection.

It seems likely that attacks will continue to be made on the Abortion Act by extremist pressure groups but with diminishing parliamentary support. Public opinion surveys over many years have shown that between two-thirds and three-quarters of all electors support liberal abortion legislation.

Madeleine Simms

Bibliography

Brookes, Barbara. *Abortion in England, 1900–1967.* 1988.

Hindell, Keith, and Madeleine Simms. *Abortion Law Reformed.* 1971.

HMSO. *Report of the Inter-Departmental Committee on Abortion* (Birkett Report). 1939.

Office of Population Censuses and Surveys. *Abortion Statistics,* Series AB, No. 17. 1990.

Williams, Glanville. *The Sanctity of Life and the Criminal Law.* 1958.

Actors and Acting

British acting was dominated until the mid-1950s by actors who had made their names playing the great Shakespearean roles, although, in fact, the end of the actor-manager tradition, which had sustained most of the great Shakespearean actors since the eighteenth century, was signalled by the death of Henry Irving in 1903. While flamboyant and eccentric personalities like Herbert Beerbohm Tree and Mrs. Patrick Campbell were the stars of the Edwardian theatre, younger actors like Harley Granville Barker (1877–1946), Lillah McCarthy (1875–1960), and Lewis Casson (1875–1969) developed simpler and more colloquial acting styles in response to the new drama of Ibsen and SHAW which they championed for its progressive views of society and art.

The work of the actor-manager Frank Benson and the scholar William Poel had a major impact on the actor-centred, less spectacular Shakespeare productions at the Old Vic, which under the forceful management of LILIAN BAYLIS

between 1914 and 1937 became the breeding ground of the first generation of twentieth-century British theatre stars. The early reputations of Sybil Thorndike (1882–1976), Gwen Ffrangçon-Davies (1896–1992), John Gielgud (1904–2000), Ralph Richardson (1902–83), Peggy Ashcroft (1907–91), LAURENCE OLIVIER, and Michael Redgrave (1908–85) were made in Old Vic productions; Edith Evans (1888–1976), Charles Laughton (1899–1962), Flora Robson (1902–84), Alec Guinness (1914–2000), Paul Scofield (1922–), Richard Burton (1925–84), and many others achieved prestige through their appearances at the Old Vic.

Gielgud's first great success in Shakespeare was as Richard II (1929) at the Old Vic. He consolidated his reputation as the leading poetic actor of his generation with his great Hamlet (1930), a role he repeated several times until 1946 with enormous success. Gielgud is regarded as the finest verse speaker in the English language, excelling in roles which allow him to express his sensitivity, wit, and vocal agility. In the late 1960s he embarked on a career as a character actor in film and television, employing his patrician manner and brilliant timing to create cameos of rare distinction. The only real challenge to Gielgud's pre-eminence came from Olivier, a more virile and romantic actor, who was always determined to be as much an international film star as a great classical actor. A master of physical disguise, Olivier excelled in full-blooded impersonations of Romeo, Henry V, Macbeth, Coriolanus, Titus Andronicus, Richard III, and Othello. His vigorous style of vocal delivery was matched by his athleticism and charm. The very successful films of *Hamlet, Henry V,* and *Richard III,* which he directed and starred in, popularised Shakespeare for a cinema-going public.

Together with Richardson and John Burrell, he ran the Old Vic between 1944 and 1949 and became the first director of the National Theatre (1963–73). His performance as the seedy music hall comedian, Archie Rice, in *The Entertainer* made him the first actor of his generation to embrace the new drama of the 1950s. Troubled by ill health in the last seventeen years of his life, he continued to play major roles on film and television.

Richardson is usually regarded as the third in the triumvirate of pre-eminent male actors. Possessed of an endearingly eccentric stage persona, he had a unique gift for investing the character of the average man with transcendent qualities of spirit or imagination which brilliantly complemented the talents of his two peers.

Without doubt, Edith Evans and Peggy Ashcroft were the two greatest female stars of this generation. While Evans excelled at portraying upper-class characters who were either witty or poignant in their inability directly to express their feelings, Ashcroft's apparently artless performances were unparalleled in their capacity to illuminate the soul of a character, whether beautiful or malignant.

Donald Wolfit (1902–68) was a barnstorming eccentric whose heroic performances as a touring actor-manager occasionally achieved greatness. Redgrave and Guinness both learned a great deal from working with Gielgud in the 1930s. Redgrave, a handsome and intelligent actor who projected a quality of understated emotionalism, was a popular film star in the 1940s and 1950s. Guinness was a subtle character actor whose dry and self-effacing personality was unrecognizable beneath the mask of a given role. This talent, making him one of the most versatile actors in British films of the 1950s, guaranteed him enormous success in Hollywood films since the 1960s. One of the greatest actors to work at the Old Vic in the 1930s was Charles Laughton, an imaginative character actor of extraordinary intensity, who became the most successful British film star of his day in Hollywood. The most glamorous British star to achieve success in the classical theatre and in Hollywood films was Vivien Leigh (1913–67), who acted opposite her husband Laurence Olivier between 1937 and 1956.

Paul Scofield and Richard Burton appeared in the 1950s as the natural heirs of Gielgud and Olivier: each possessed a beautiful voice and fine physique, but although each gave a number of brilliant performances on stage and film, neither seemed able to sustain the consistent level of achievement of their predecessors.

The "throwaway" style of witty understated acting characteristic of West End commercial theatre was perfected by Gerald du Maurier (1873–1934) and given a tone of clipped 1920s modishness by NOEL COWARD (1899–1973) and his co-star Gertrude Lawrence (1898–1952). Coward's plays and his persona exerted a great influence on actors and playwrights until the 1950s, establishing a tradition of stiff-upper-lip reticence which was developed in films and television drama to produce the reserved and subtle naturalism characteristic of contemporary British television acting. Among the stars of British films who had mastered this understated style between 1930 and 1960 were Robert Donat, Celia Johnson, Trevor Howard, Rex Harrison, John Mills, Wendy Hiller, Dirk Bogarde, Glynis Johns, Richard Todd, Laurence Harvey, Kenneth More, and Richard Attenborough.

Britain has always had a strong tradition of comic actors, most of whom have performed successfully in legitimate theatre and revue, on radio, film, and television. Among the most memorable are Margaret Rutherford, Alastair Sim, Hermi-

one Gingold, Hermione Baddeley, Beatrice Lillie, Joyce Grenfell, Peter Ustinov, Robert Morley, Kenneth Williams, Beryl Reid, Peter Sellers, Peter Cook, Dudley Moore, John Cleese, Rik Mayall, Rowan Atkinson, and Stephen Fry.

Another tradition of serious acting reflecting a more egalitarian approach to social class was created in the wake of the "Royal Court revolution" of 1956 by young actors whose acting became associated with the work of contemporary dramatists (on stage and screen). Among those who achieved fame in the 1960s the most enduring have been Albert Finney, Peter O'Toole, Joan Plowright, Alan Bates, and Tom Courtenay.

Since the early 1960s inheritors of the great tradition of classical acting have usually come to prominence through the Royal Shakespeare Company or the National Theatre, although most modern British actors now establish their reputations with the public by appearing in television drama, which has consequently had a great impact on contemporary acting styles. Among the actors who achieved star status during Olivier's regime at the National are Maggie Smith, Anthony Hopkins, Derek Jacobi, and Robert Stephens; those who established or consolidated their reputations with the Royal Shakespeare Company include Vanessa Redgrave, Dorothy Tutin, Ian Holm, Judi Dench, Ian McKellan, Glenda Jackson, Janet Suzman, Alan Howard, Michael Gambon, Jeremy Irons, Antony Sher, and Kenneth Branagh.

Robert Gordon

Bibliography

Barnes, Philip. *A Companion to Post-War British Theatre.* 1986.

Burton, Hal, ed. *Great Acting.* 1967.

Findlater, Richard. *These Our Actors.* 1983.

Gielgud John. *An Actor and His Time.* 1979.

Tynan, Kenneth. *A View of the English Stage.* 1984.

Wardle, Irving. *The Theatres of George Devine.* 1979.

Adult Education

Many Victorian centers for adult education continued their work into the twentieth century. In LONDON the Working Men's College (founded 1854) and Morley College (1889) have survived to the present day; and Leicester's Working Men's College (1862) became Vaughan College, the extramural center of Leicester University College. Some cooperative societies carried on their tradition of devoting up to 2.5 percent of their profits to libraries, lectures, and other education services, although most branches spent little or nothing. The YMCA provided reading rooms, extension courses, lectures, and (during the FIRST WORLD WAR) army education. The National Home Reading Union (founded 1889) assisted autodidacts with reading lists and discussion circles.

Victorian QUAKERS had taught basic literacy through their Adult Schools; after 1899 the movement became more interdenominational and turned to teaching literature, current events, sports, arts, and crafts.

Every twentieth-century venture in adult education consciously strove to overcome the failure of the mechanics' institutes and the university extension movement to attract large numbers of working people. One of the more successful efforts was the Workers' Educational Association, created by Albert Mansbridge (1876–1952) in 1903, and governed jointly by committees of academics and workers. The pride of the WEA was the innovative tutorial class, first taught with brilliant success by R.H. TAWNEY at Longton and Rochdale in 1908. These three-year courses strove to attain a university-level schedule of reading and essay writing. The WEA also offered shorter courses and university summer schools, and from 1919 it provided classes for organized labor through the Workers' Educational Trade Union Committee.

In 1916 Mansbridge set up the Central Library for Students (later renamed the National Central Library) to loan out textbooks for adult classes. He went on to launch the World Association for Adult Education (1918) and the British Institute of Adult Education (1921). He founded as well the Seafarers' Education Service (1919), which offered libraries for merchant ships and, via the College of the Sea (1938), tutoring by mail for sailors.

In 1899 two Americans, Walter Vrooman and Charles Beard, set up Ruskin College at OXFORD to provide residential correspondence courses for working men. Some Marxist students at Ruskin, fearing that the college would fall under the control of the neighboring capitalist university, organized the Plebs League in 1908. The following year they staged a student strike and set up their own Central Labour College, which relocated to London in 1911. By 1921 the Plebs League had organized its local branches into the National Council of Labour Colleges. These groups offered a strictly Marxist program of classes, lectures, and correspondence courses explicitly designed to prepare workers for class warfare; and they continually attacked Ruskin College and the WEA for their more liberal approach to education.

Perhaps the most impressive ventures in worker-run adult education were the miners' institutes, which blossomed in the South Wales coalfields between 1890 and 1920. Though assisted by mineowners and local authorities, they were funded primarily by deducations from miners' wages and, after 1920, by the Miners' Welfare Fund. There were more than 100 such institutes by the Second World War, when the Tredegar Workmen's Institute (founded 1861) was offering courses, lectures, celebrity concerts; debating, theatrical, choral, operatic, and film societies; and a library issuing 100,000 volumes a year. By the 1970s most miners' institutes had fallen victim to the decline of the coal industry, competition from public libraries, and television.

Toynbee Hall, opened as the world's first settlement house in 1884, sponsored concerts, classes, literary societies, and (from 1901) the Whitechapel Art Gallery. By 1914 there were at least forty-six settlement houses in the United Kingdom, most of them offering courses for slum dwellers. Nonresidential settlements specifically devoted to education began in 1909 with Swarthmore in Leeds and St. Mary's in York. By 1918 there were also ten residential educational settlements in the Midlands and northern counties, including Woodbrooke (1903) and Fircroft (1909). Wales would be served by Coleg Harlech (1927), Scotland by Newbattle Abbey (1937). Hillcroft (1920) was the first residential college for working women.

Local Education Authorities subsidized university extension and WEA courses, and awarded adult bursaries and scholarships. They had their own Evening Institutes, which mainly offered classes in vocational subjects, crafts, homemaking, and athletics. The liberal arts were available as well, through such institutions as London's City Literary Institute. Some LEAs set up residential colleges, among them Grantley Hall (1949) and Wrea Head (1950).

The Women's Institutes, which emerged during the First World War, had almost a half million members by 1953. The WIs brought lectures and classes to rural areas, and sponsored dance, music, and drama groups. Their urban counterparts, the Townswomen's Guilds (1929), had a more feminist slant.

The University College of Hull set up the first department of adult education in 1928. By 1939 most English universities had a full-time director or department of extra-mural studies, usually working in cooperation with the WEA.

The universities and the WEA both contribued greatly to armed forces education during the SECOND WORLD WAR. The Army Education Corps, a tiny unit in peacetime, was expanded enormously. The Army Bureau of Current Affairs, begun in August 1941, introduced libraries, educational films, and compulsory classes for His Majesty's Forces. Leftist instructors and Conservative officers alike complained of political bias in the curriculum, and the large soldiers' vote for LABOUR in 1945 has been partly attributed to ABCA discussion sessions on post-war reconstruction.

The BBC had experimented with educational

broadcasting as early as 1924, initially with little success. With the OPEN UNIVERSITY radio and television have been used effectively in conjunction with correspondence courses and meetings with tutors. Since it took in its first students in 1971, the Open University has been open to any resident of the United Kingdom eighteen or over, regardless of academic qualifications. By 1990 it had awarded 100,000 B.A. degrees, as well as higher degrees, and it had a flourishing Open Business School.

Jonathan Rose

Bibliography
Blyth, John A. *English University Adult Education 1908–1958*. 1983.
Davies, J.H., and J.E. Thomas, eds. *A Select Bibliography of Adult Continuing Education*, 5th ed. 1988.
Goldman, Lawrence. *Dons and Workers: Oxford and Adult Education Since 1850*. 1995.
Jennings, Bernard. *Knowledge is Power: A Short History of the WEA 1903–78*. 1979.
Kelly, Thomas. *A History of Adult Education ih Great Britain*. 3rd ed. 1992.
Marriott, Stuart. *Extramural Empires: Service and Self-Interest in English University Adult Education 1873–1983*. 1984.

Ageing

During the twentieth century, for the first time in history, living into and beyond one's sixties became a normal expectation. This was due, of course, to reduced rates of mortality in younger age groups, especially among infants. Old people were not extreme rarities in earlier societies; over the 350 years before 1900 the median proportion of persons over sixty in various communities fluctuated between 6 percent and 10 percent, but many people of lesser ages were prematurely aged by poverty and hard-work.

Old age has long been more probable for females than for males. Life expectation at birth for WOMEN in the early 1990s was 77.4 at birth and for men 71.4 and both were rising. It is unhelpful in this context to compare life expectancy at birth over the whole century, because the very high infant mortality rates at the beginning of the century dramatically influence the figures. Those who survived the hazardous years of infancy had a very good chance of living at least well into middle age. It is more useful to point out that a woman of fifty in 1901 could expect to live to be about 71.6, a man of fifty to 67.5; in 1931 the respective ages were 74.1 and 71.6; in 1961 77.4 and 72.6.

The numbers living to very old age began to show a significant rise in the 1980s. In 1981 there were 400,000 women and 100,000 men over eighty-five, in 1991 600,000 and 200,000. In 1991 women over eighty-five made up 11.3 percent of the female population aged over sixty-five; men over eighty-five, 5.7 percent. As a percentage of the total population of England and Wales the over-60s were 7.6 percent in 1901, 11.7 percent in 1931, 16.8 percent in 1961, 20.7 percent in 1991. These rising percentages are largely attributable to the falling birth-rate over most of the century, though falling mortality rates obviously influence the absolute numbers.

Throughout the century class differences in life expectation narrowed only slightly. This is important to emphasize in view of the tendency to stereotype the old as an undifferentiated and usually marginalized category, as though differences of class, ethnicity, gender, income, power, and personal attractiveness ceased around sixty-five. If the old are often perceived as poor, it is partly because so many of them are female, who are more likely to be poor due to their lesser opportunities to accumulate wealth, other than by MARRIAGE or inheritance, when younger. Also social surveys of older people, which flourished from the 1950s, tended to focus upon and publicize the poverty, loneliness, and marginality of older people partly because social scientists generally seemed to find the poor more rivetting, or more vulnerable to academic intrusion, than the rich and partly due to a desire to improve their conditions through public exposure. The elderly are likely to be perceived as white because large-scale Black IMMIGRATION began only in the 1950s, and so only in the 1980s and 1990s were significant numbers of older BLACK PEOPLE becoming visible.

Cultural imagery of the old throughout the century has been generally negative and has occasioned little protest from older people in comparison with resistance to ageism in the United States. At the same time such imagery has steadily become less appropriate since fewer fitted the stereotype. As people age their physical and their material resources are inevitably depleted. But such depletion occurred at later ages as the century progressed. Better DIET, health care, and health awareness meant that by the early 1990s most people who survived past sixty remained fit into their later seventies; and most of those who survived into their eighties and nineties did not suffer a long period of severe ill-health and dependency before death. Research from the 1950s onwards persistently showed that most people could continue to be highly efficient at their accustomed tasks, both mental and physical, including surprisingly heavy labor, into their sixties and could acquire new mental skills even in their eighties. Financially over time, more older people acquired occupational in addition to state PENSIONS and owned property which could be converted into additional income. Retirement from work before the onset of physical decline, almost unknown for manual workers at any time before the twentieth century and uncommon before it, quite quickly became the norm in the 1940s and 1950s and, combined with greater prosperity, allowed more people a period of LEISURE later in life. The loneliness of old people is often "proved" by reference to the steadily increasing numbers living alone. But there is evidence that many chose to live alone in preference to the tensions of dependency upon their children. Nor does solitary living necessarily imply isolation from friends or kin. Old people in the 1990s were far more likely to have surviving children and to be in contact with them than in the days of high mortality and poor communications at the beginning of the century.

This is to stress the optimistic view to counter the stereotype. As more people live to be very old, more suffer from Alzheimer's or other incurable diseases. UNEMPLOYMENT in the 1980s and 1990s hit older at least as hard as younger workers, and large numbers were effectively retired in their fifties to face a very long period of marginality as a result of declining health and deteriorating public services. Among older as well as younger age groups there was discernible social polarization at the end of the century.

Pat Thane

Bibliography

Jefferys, Margot. Growing Old in the Twentieth Century. 1989.

Laslett, Peter. A Fresh Map of Life: the Emergence of the Third Age. 1989.

Thane, Pat. Old Age in English History. 2000.

Allen, (Reginald) Clifford (1889–1939)

Clifford Allen was a politician who never held elective office and who ended his career without meaningful party affiliation, an advocate for socialism who made his living speculating on the stock exchange, an enemy of the class system who became Lord Allen of Hurtwood (1931), a globe-trotting diplomat who was never accredited by any government, and a courageous martyr for peace who died prematurely as the result of a self-appointed mission in support of NEVILLE CHAMBERLAIN's cringing policy of APPEASEMENT.

When he crowned an impressive school career by winning an exhibition to Peterhouse, CAMBRIDGE in 1907, Allen seemed on the way to fulfilling the dream of his CONSERVATIVE Monmouthshire family that he become an ANGLICAN priest. At Cambridge, however, he read history, debated at the Union, and converted to socialism, joining and eventually presiding over both the University Socialist Federation and the University FABIAN SOCIETY. Allen's socialist creed cer-

tainly undermined his religious beliefs, and his political activism probably interfered with his studies, but a disappointing third class degree did not seem to dim his prospects. Upon leaving Cambridge, he was appointed secretary and general manager of the Daily Citizen, a short-lived Labour newspaper. Even before the prosaic Citizen's demise in 1915, Allen had become absorbed in the pacifist struggle against the FIRST WORLD WAR as one of the founders of the No-CONSCRIPTION FELLOWSHIP (NCF). Under Allen's leadership, the NCF, which drew most of its membership from the INDEPENDENT LABOUR PARTY (ILP) and other socialist bodies, became the largest and most effective anti-CONSCRIPTION, anti-war organization in modern British history.

As chairman and spokesman for the NCF, Allen acquired a national forum in which to display his considerable abilities as speaker, organizer, and leader of men; as an "absolutist" CONSCIENTIOUS OBJECTOR who endured over fifteen months imprisonment on account of his refusal to make any compromise with the warrior state, Allen achieved the status of left-wing martyr/saint. But while his obvious ability and courageous PACIFISM seemed to assure him a bright future in socialist politics, the tuberculosis he contracted in prison made him a semi-invalid who could never follow a normal working career.

Despite this setback Allen secured a place in left-wing politics. After returning from a Labour-sponsored trip to the Soviet Union, where he interviewed Lenin, lost his enthusiasm for Bolshevism, and nearly died of pneumonia, he was elected Treasurer, then Chairman, of the ILP. But by 1925 renewed ill-health had cost him the chance for a safe seat in the House of Commons, and ideological divisions had caused him to resign as leader of the ILP. For the next few years, Allen eschewed politics for Labour journalism as a director of the Daily Herald. Then, in 1931, he gained a peerage by supporting RAMSAY MACDONALD's decision to form a National government, but he also lost his credibility in the LABOUR PARTY as well as most of his former friends and allies.

Without party or influence (MacDonald effectively ignored him after 1931), Allen attempted to "plough my own furrow" as an independent representative for "progressive", non-party politics. With HAROLD MACMILLAN and others, he formed the Next Five Years Group (NFYG), which in 1935 published a much-praised scheme for inter-party cooperation to carry out a fully integrated domestic and foreign policy which could, according to its authors, lift Britain out of the economic doldrums while establishing a comprehensive peace settlement. When the

NFYG inevitably floundered, dragged down by political weakness and tactical disputes, Allen turned to personal diplomacy as a means of making his mark on Britain and the world.

During the inter-war period Allen had abandoned absolute pacifism for collective security under the LEAGUE OF NATIONS as humanity's best hope for peace. But as an inveterate activist (some like ANTHONY EDEN would say busybody) with sincere convictions and enormous confidence, Allen believed in bold initiatives. So, in January 1935 he used his status and charm to secure a personal interview with Hitler. In the course of their conversation Allen presented the German Chancellor with a plan for securing Nazi agreement to halt persecution of Jews and other minorities as *quid pro quo* for the satisfaction of all German grievances arising from the "wicked" Versailles treaty. This was to be the first step toward a comprehensive European peace settlement. Hitler feigned interest, and a second invitation from the Nazis inspired hope, but these were cynical ploys which, while they produced no results, encouraged Allen's illusions. Thus, even though by late 1938 Allen had lost faith in the efficacy of collective security under the League, he still believed he could use his German contacts to make a vital contribution to the best remaining hope for peace, Chamberlain's policy of appeasement.

In September 1938, in the midst of the Czech crisis and against his physician's advice, Allen undertook his final journey for peace, visiting Berlin and Prague and emphasizing to German and Czech officials the necessity for a four power conference to resolve the Sudeten question as the first step toward an all-round European settlement. Because the MUNICH agreement emerged from just such a conference, Allen went to his grave in March 1939 believing he had, at last, made a difference in the struggle for peace.

Sadly, for all of Allen's courage and devotion to sweet reason, his best efforts could neither shorten the First World War nor prevent the Second. Likewise, his belief in and work for the implementation of democratic socialism brought no personal or political triumphs. Yet, despite the ultimate frustration of his plans and hopes, Allen deserves to be remembered for the unselfish idealism and uncompromising honesty which made him a substantial contributor to the politics of conscience in twentieth-century Britain.

Thomas C. Kennedy

Bibliography

Gilbert, Martin, ed. *Plough My Own Furrow: The Story of Lord Allen of Hurtwood as Told Through His Writings and Correspondence.* 1965.

Kennedy, Thomas C. "'Peace In Our Time': The Personal Diplomacy of Lord Allen of Hurtwood, 1933–

38" in Solomon Wank, ed. *Doves and Diplomats.* 1978, pp. 217–39.

———. "The Next Five Years Group and the Failure of the Politics of Agreement in Britain," *Canadian Journal of History,* vol. 9 (1974), pp. 45–68.

Marwick, Arthur. *Clifford Allen: The Open Conspirator.* 1964.

Angell [Lane], [Ralph] Norman (1872–1967)

Norman Angell was a prolific anti-war writer and activist. Born Ralph Norman Angell Lane, he dropped Lane after his first book. He spent most of his life elaborating and promoting the idea that war would, in the modern world of economic interdependence, harm the victor as much as the vanquished. His most famous book was *The Great Illusion* (1909). In 1914 he helped to found the UNION OF DEMOCRATIC CONTROL and in 1920 joined the INDEPENDENT LABOUR PARTY. He served in Parliament in 1929–31, was knighted in 1931, and won the 1933 Nobel Peace Prize.

Despite a conservative, middle-class background, Angell was a restless and radical youth. At the age of seventeen he emigrated to the United States, where he worked as a farm laborer, cowboy, and journalist. In 1897 he took a job on a Paris newspaper, where he remained until returning to England in 1912.

Angell's public career began with the publication of *Europe's Optical Illusion* (1908). Lord Esher, the chairman of the COMMITTEE OF IMPERIAL DEFENCE, introduced it to many influential people, including KING EDWARD VII and Sir Richard Garton, an industrialist, who donated funds to establish the Garton Foundation in order to promote Angell's ideas. *War and Peace,* a monthly devoted to "Norman Angellism", was established in 1913. Politically, its contributors ranged from CONSERVATIVES to revolutionary socialists.

Angell's popularity plummeted during the FIRST WORLD WAR, partly because he was widely misinterpreted as having argued that war had actually become impossible, and partly because of his involvement (albeit limited) in the UDC, which opposed the government's war policy and advocated a negotiated peace.

Angell was one of the first critics of the Versailles treaty, which he thought embodied the fallacies he had exposed in his pre-war work and would lead to economic catastrophe. His views regained popularity—among leftists especially—as the international economy deteriorated. Angell moved sharply left immediately after the war, arguing, uncharacteristically, that capitalism was responsible for the flawed post-war settlement. These views took him into the ILP, but he soon gravitated towards LABOUR's moderate wing.

Between the wars he contributed to many journals and was active on a host of committees. He entered Parliament in 1929 on his fourth attempt and was disappointed not to be offered any government post by his UDC comrade RAMSAY MACDONALD. He was never comfortable in Parliament and was secretly relieved to lose his seat in the 1931 election. He spent most of the SECOND WORLD WAR in the United States promoting Britain's cause and urging American participation. After the war he moved further to the right, dismayed by many socialists' endorsement of Soviet expansionism.

Angell's theories influenced the outlook of an entire generation throughout Europe and the English-speaking world. They contributed to the growth of public hostility to the Versailles treaty and helped to create the climate of opinion which produced the generous settlement after the Second World War.

David Blaazer

Bibliography
Angell, Norman. *After All.* 1951.
Miller, J.D.B. *Norman Angell and the Futility of War.* 1986.

Anglicanism: see Church of England

Anglo-American Relations
During the twentieth century Britain and the United States became close allies. Their relationship stabilized before the Second World War, peaked during 1940s and 1950s, cooled during the 1960s and 1970s, and recovered during the 1980s.

As the century dawned, European imperial rivalries convinced Britain to improve relations with America in order to safeguard its Western Hemisphere interests. Britain urged negotiation to settle the Venezuelan border dispute; voted with the United States and against Canada in arbitration of the Alaska boundary dispute; supported the United States's open door notes on China; and recognized Washington's right to build and fortify a Central American canal. Britain maintained neutrality in the Spanish-American War of 1898, and Washington refrained from criticizing London during the BOER WAR. In 1906 Britain withdrew its military and naval forces from Canada and the Caribbean, signalling its reliance on the United States to police the Western Hemisphere.

The FIRST WORLD WAR threatened this rapprochement. From 1914 to 1917 President Wilson exhorted Americans to remain "impartial in thought as well as action," expressed disdain for British and German violations of American neutral rights, and equated Britain's war aims with Germany's. British officials fumed at Wilson's mediation efforts and resented American inroads into their trade and financial interests.

America entered the war in 1917, according to Wilson, associated, not allied, with Britain. He refused to integrate military operations as the Allies urged. Freedom of the seas, one of his Fourteen Points, challenged Britain's naval dominance. In late 1918 Wilson negotiated an armistice with Germany and compelled Britain to comply. At the Paris Peace Conference the British regretted Wilson's idealism, arrogance, and insensitivity to their wartime sacrifices. Rejection of the Versailles treaty by the United States Senate compounded British frustration.

During the inter-war years Britain and the United States only partially composed their disagreements. To avoid a post-war naval race, both powers signed the Washington treaty (1922) that established parity between them on capital ships. Negotiations in 1927, however, failed to limit non-capital ships, and mutual mistrust resulted. Limits on cruisers were set during the London Naval Conference of 1930, but the distance between the two states became evident in their incoherent response to Japan's invasion of Manchuria in 1931.

Financial problems also beset Anglo-American relations. Washington insisted that London repay wartime loans, rejecting pleas to forgive the debts as a contribution to victory over Germany. American approval of Anglo-French terms for collecting reparations from Germany and of the Dawes Plan to restore Germany's economy pleased London, and American and British bankers and industrialists cooperated in financial, petroleum, and communications enterprises. The Great Depression, however, strained relations. London blamed its general economic misery on Washington's collection of war debts, its record-high tariff of 1930, and the refusal of American banks to provide credits. Britain renounced the GOLD STANDARD in 1931, raised its tariff and developed the IMPERIAL PREFERENCE trade system, and defaulted on war debts payments in 1933. Britain organized the London Economic Conference in 1933 to restore world currencies, but President Roosevelt refused to abide in any agreement until he achieved domestic recovery. Bilateral negotiations from 1934 to 1938 failed to reduce tariffs, and the two powers traded mutual recriminations. In this atmosphere Congress passed neutrality laws to isolate the United States from political and military turmoil in Europe.

The discord in Anglo-American relations evaporated in the glaring heat of the SECOND WORLD WAR. In 1938 American and British naval officers secretly discussed joint tactics in the impending war in Europe. In 1939 Congress revised the neutrality laws to allow arms sales to London and Paris. The fall of France in 1940 convinced many Americans that they must fight against

Nazi Germany, and Roosevelt exchanged destroyers for rights at British bases, resumed selective service, and extended LEND-LEASE aid. The retreat from DUNKIRK shattered British illusions that the war could be won without American assistance. Prime Minister WINSTON CHURCHILL cultivated Roosevelt's friendship and encouraged him to enter the war. In late 1941 the two statesmen issued the Atlantic Charter and Roosevelt waged unofficial naval warfare against Germany.

From 1941 to 1945 the United States and Great Britain developed a special wartime relationship. They declared an alliance and agreed to follow a Germany-first strategy. American and British officials established the Combined Chiefs of Staff, integrated military commands, established joint boards for allocating resources, dovetailed intelligence operations, collaborated in the Manhattan Project, and cooperated in dispensing Lend-Lease aid.

Beneath the surface of the Anglo-American alliance loomed disputes over numerous matters. Despite the Germany-first strategy, American and British officers bickered repeatedly over how and when to take the war to Berlin. Americans suspected the British of designing war plans to recover their imperial interests after the war. Commercial issues such as control of Middle East oil, trade with Argentina, and post-war opportunities for American firms in the British Empire generated tension. Roosevelt frustrated Churchill at the Tehran Conference of 1943 by trying to mediate Anglo-Soviet differences. Debates over policy toward East Asia, the Middle East, and occupied Europe diminished Anglo-American harmony.

Relations cooled as the Axis peril vanished in 1945. The United States abruptly terminated Lend-Lease, dismantled the Combined Chiefs of Staff, and abolished the Middle East Supply Centre. Secretary of State James Byrnes refused to consult Foreign Secretary ERNEST BEVIN while preparing for Foreign Ministers' meetings. The United States offered Britain a generous loan but forced London to agree to make sterling convertible.

The escalation of the Cold War, however, convinced the United States to strike an alliance with Britain. In 1946, London and Washington jointly pressured Moscow to withdraw from Iran and merged their occupation zones in Germany. Washington declared the Truman Doctrine at London's invitation. Britain facilitated European acceptance of the Marshall Plan and gratefully accepted American largesse.

Ties became especially close on security matters. American and British military officers resumed wartime collaboration, shared contingency war plans, standardized weapons, traded intelligence, coordinated the Berlin airlift, and established the North Atlantic Treaty Organization (NATO) in 1949. They also coordinated covert operations against Iranian Prime Minister Mohammed Mossadegh in 1953. The weakest link in the strategic alliance developed when Congress passed the McMahon Act (1946), forbidding dissemination of atomic secrets abroad.

Despite Anglo-American unity regarding the Cold War in Europe, problems in other regions beset the relationship. Britain resented President Truman's pro-Zionism and American control of occupied Japan, and it recognized Beijing in January 1950 over American protests. Britain supported American military action in Korea but protested Truman's remark that atomic weapons might be employed and blocked an American plan to have the United Nations brand the Chinese aggressors. Washington excluded London from the Australia-New Zealand-United States pact and criticized Britain's response to the nationalization of the Anglo-Iranian Oil Company.

Problems continued to develop despite the accession to office of Churchill in 1951 and Dwight Eisenhower in 1953. London protested Washington's consideration of force to rescue French troops at Dienbienphu and negotiated the Geneva accords with the Soviets. Britain objected to American covert operations in Guatemala and handling of the Quemoy-Matsu crisis. Washington criticized London's policies toward the Buraimi oasis and Egypt. Anglo-American divergence peaked during the SUEZ CRISIS of 1956, when Britain attacked Egypt over American opposition and Eisenhower condemned his ally.

In the late 1950s American and British officials repaired their alliance. Strategic cooperation was reaffirmed at the NATO ministers meeting in December 1956. Prime Minister HAROLD MACMILLAN, a wartime associate of Eisenhower, met him at Bermuda in March 1957 to continue the healing. Eisenhower promised Macmillan sixty Thor missiles, the first time the United States ever provided missiles to another state. After Congress repealed the McMahon Act in 1957, Eisenhower shared nuclear secrets with the British and eventually exchanged nuclear components and Skybolt missiles for Polaris submarine base rights in Scotland. In addition, the British coordinated with the Americans their occupations of Jordan and Lebanon in 1958, backed Washington during the 1958–9 showdown over Berlin, and stood by Eisenhower during the U-2 debacle in 1960.

In the early 1960s Macmillan provided solace to President Kennedy after his unnerving experiences at the Bay of Pigs and the Vienna summit. When the United States cancelled development of the Skybolt missile system in 1962, Kennedy averted an Anglo-American rupture by selling London Polaris missiles. America embraced the Nuclear Test Ban Treaty of 1963, which Macmillan had advocated for six years.

The Anglo-American relationship cooled after 1963. Prime Minister HAROLD WILSON and President Johnson invested little in it. Britain's financial problems reduced its relative importance to many American officials, who encouraged London to join the EUROPEAN COMMUNITY (EC). Washington protested Britain's evacuation of military bases east of Suez and quarrels erupted over policy in Cuba and Malaysia. The Vietnam War seriously tested the Atlantic alliance. London refused Washington's pleas to send troops, disputed American assessments of Communist China's role in the war, eventually doubted that the United States could win and therefore questioned the destruction, and mediated between Moscow and Washington.

President Nixon tried but failed to restore closer relations because Prime Minister EDWARD HEATH practiced Europeanism in hope of entering the EC. Heath denied any special relationship with Washington and refused to serve as mediator between the United States and European powers after Henry Kissinger announced his "Year of Europe" plan in 1973. Nixon reciprocated by launching initiatives in China, the Soviet Union, arms control, and currency conversions without consulting London. During the 1973 Arab-Israeli War, London refused to participate in the airlift of supplies to Israel, criticized Nixon's alert of American forces, and endorsed EC negotiation of an oil deal with Arab states.

In the late 1970s President Carter tried with little success to improve relations with London. The British worried about his diplomatic naivete, evident in his alienation of Moscow over human rights; his consideration of a no-first-use pledge on NUCLEAR WEAPONS; his exclusion of intermediate-range missiles, the type aimed at British territory, from SALT II; and his excessive reaction to the Soviet invasion of Afghanistan. Anglo-American military ties remained close in the 1960s and 1970s despite the political disharmony. Both powers remained firmly committed to NATO, and London continued to welcome the American military presence in Britain while other NATO states pressed the United States to withdraw. Washington and London shared intelligence, integrated tactical military planning, and jointly developed the base at Diego Garcia.

Anglo-American political relations dramatically improved in the 1980s because Prime Minister MARGARET THATCHER sought to strengthen ties with America rather than the EEC. President Reagan backed Thatcher during the FALKLANDS WAR with weapons, supplies, sat-

ellite and signals intelligence, and access to the American airbase on Ascension Island. Washington sold London Trident missiles in 1982. Defying domestic opposition, Thatcher deployed Cruise missiles in 1983; participated in Strategic Defense Initiative research; allowed American aircraft to use bases in Britain in the raid on Libya in 1986; and supported Reagan's policies in Central America. Thatcher did not support the American effort to boycott construction of a Soviet pipeline, protest of the Soviet radar at Krasnoyarsk, and invasion of Grenada. Yet she remained close to Reagan, gained influence in American-Soviet arms control talks in the late 1980s, and emerged in the eyes of many as the senior partner of the alliance once Reagan lost prestige in the Iran-Contra scandal. The closeness of the relationship was revealed in the unity of purpose and action during the Persian Gulf War of 1990–1.

Peter L. Hahn

Bibliography

Bartlett, C.J. *The 'Special Relationship': A Political History of Anglo-American Relations Since 1945.* 1992.

Dimbleby, David, and David Reynolds. *An Ocean Apart: The Relationship Between Britain and America in the Twentieth Century.* 1988.

Dumbrell, John. *A Special Relationship: Anglo-American Relations Since 1960.* 2000.

Louis, Wm. Roger, and Hedley Bull, eds. *The 'Special Relationship': Anglo-American Relations Since 1945.* 1986.

Ovendale, Ritchie. *Anglo-American Relations in the 20th Century.* 1998.

Watt, D.C. *Succeeding John Bull: America in Britain's Place, 1900–1975.* 1984.

Anti-Semitism

Anti-Semitism, a hostility towards Jews as Jews, is often supposed to be absent from Britain. Commentators who celebrate British tolerance tend to underplay the presence of racial and ethnic conflict. However, hostility towards Jews has been a persistent feature of British social life in the twentieth century both in the form of ideas (written or spoken) and anti-Semitic behavior. Such hostility became more restrained after the Holocaust, but its tenacity meant that it did not altogether disappear. Even so, it is often difficult, both before and after the Holocaust, to identify such hostility, occurring as it often does under the more respectable facade of anti-alienism.

Anti-Semitism has been a constant feature on the fringe of British politics. It surfaced in the early twentieth century in the campaign mounted against the immigration of Russian Polish Jews. Some of the fiercest anti-Semitism expressed anywhere in Europe at this time appeared in Joseph Banister's *England under the Jews,* which was first published in 1901. It also remained an integral component in the ideology of the racial nationalist group The Britons, which was founded in 1919, as it did of the FASCIST groups which developed in the 1920s and 1930s. Among the Fascists, Arnold Leese of the Imperial Fascist League, offered a brand of racial, conspiratorial anti-Semitism which embraced a complete belief in *The Protocols of the Elders of Zion* and advanced older elements of anti-Semitic ideology such as the blood libel myth. However, the IFL was not the only extreme anti-Semitic organization in existence in the 1930s. The Nordic League was the most significant: one German observer regarded it as "the English branch of international Nazism". Anti-Semitism was also present in the 1930s within the larger Fascist group, the British Union of Fascists. Although OSWALD MOSLEY denied that he had ever been an anti-Semite, he articulated anti-Semitic sentiments under pressure. Other members of his organisation such as William Joyce, expelled eventually from the BUF in 1937, and A.K. Chesterton, an early biographer of Mosley, were more overt in their hostility towards Jews. At times the anti-Semitic sentiments of the Fascists could be translated into action, particularly in East LONDON.

It might be expected that between 1939 and 1945, with Britain engaged in war against Germany, anti-Semitism in Britain would not be advocated or tolerated. In fact, anti-Semitic beliefs continued to circulate in Britain throughout the Second World War. A number of Fascist and related organizations were proscribed by the government, but some anti-Semitic groups continued to function.

Following the war anti-Semitism in various guises has continued to appear in Fascist and racist speeches and publications despite the experience of the Holocaust. A move began in Britain and other countries to develop revisionist perspectives on the Holocaust, suggesting that it was a myth, manufactured by a powerful international Jewish community for political advantage.

This shadowy world of racial nationalism and Fascism, where psychopaths and fanatics operate, is inseparable from anti-Semitism in twentieth-century Britain. But hostility towards Jews has stretched into other areas of society. Before 1914 anti-Semitism, in what has been categorized as its "commonsense" rather than scientific form, circulated quite widely in the East End. Moreover, the violence directed against Jews in Tredegar in 1911 and the various examples of anti-Semitic discrimination reported at regular intervals in the *Jewish Chronicle* serve as reminders that anti-Semitism was reflected in forms of behavior towards Jews as well as in attitudes.

Following the Holocaust a greater degree of restraint has often been shown by the wider public in its response towards Jews. The persistence of stereotypes, evident in the recent treatment of the death of Robert Maxwell, is significant in revealing the continuity of anti-Semitic sentiment. The violence directed towards Jews in Lancashire in 1947 at a time of tension in the Middle East as well as the more recent attacks on Jewish cemeteries, property, and people, particularly in London, reveal the persistence of anti-Semitic conduct.

Nor has the state been entirely guiltless in condoning or perpetuating anti-Semitism, although official sentiment has often been masked as anti-alienism. Opposition to the naturalization of Russian Polish Jews, the policies of deportation which followed the 1919 Aliens Act, and the entry barriers erected against intending refugees from Central Europe in the 1930s, as well as the discriminatory policies pursued by the London County Council in the 1920s, all mitigate the benevolent image of official policy in Britain.

Whether the emphasis is on official or popular responses, anti-Semitic thought and behavior have been recurrent features of twentieth-century Britain. The fact that anti-Semitism has assumed greater significance in other countries should not be allowed to obscure its tenacity in Britain.

Colin Holmes

Bibliography
Cesarani, David, ed. *The Making of Modern Anglo-Jewry*. 1990.
Garrard, J.A. *The English and Immigration: A Comparative Study of the Jewish Influx 1880–1910*. 1971.
Holmes, Colin. *Anti-Semitism in British Society 1876–1939*. 1979.
Kushner, Tony. *The Persistence of Prejudice: Anti-Semitism in British Society during the Second World War*. 1989.

Appeasement

Broadly defined, appeasement refers to a method of diplomacy whereby a state engages in compromise and negotiation with a potential antagonist in order to alleviate grievances and preserve peace. But within the context of modern British history, appeasement has acquired a negative connotation and become a term of abuse and condemnation. During the 1930s appeasement was the label attached to the conduct of British foreign policy in regard to the Fascist dictatorships. According to critics, the appeasers totally misjudged the evil intentions of the Fascist leaders, negotiated with them out of fear and from a position of military weakness, yielded to diplomatic bullying and cravenly made unilateral concessions, rendering themselves vulnerable to charges of stupidity, cowardice, and moral bankruptcy.

Admittedly, British diplomats faced an unenviable task in the 1930s. FASCISM appeared to be the wave of the future, and Hitler and Mussolini demonstrated verve and energy as they furiously rearmed and launched an assault upon existing treaties and territorial boundaries. Despite their personal detestation of Fascism, British diplomats were determined to avoid another war, and acknowledging that the Versailles treaty had been too vindictive, they believed that the legitimate grievances of the Fascist states had to be met. Still, they might have moved more cautiously in view of Hitler's withdrawal from the Disarmament Conference and the LEAGUE OF NATIONS, and his subsequent attempted subversion of the Austrian state in 1934. Hitler's first major challenge to Britain came in March 1935, when he violated the Versailles treaty by announcing Germany's intention to rearm and reintroduce conscription. But Britain offered only tepid diplomatic protests and then proceeded to negotiate the Anglo-German Naval Agreement. This treaty allowed the German navy to exceed the limits imposed upon it by Versailles, thereby giving the impression that Britain was conniving with Germany behind the back of France in a major breach of treaty. In the autumn of 1935 Italy invaded Abyssinia, and Britain, anxious to keep Mussolini as a potential ally against Germany, was apparently willing to make extensive territorial concessions to Italy under the terms of the infamous Hoare-Laval pact, but when the terms leaked out an outraged House of Commons forced the government to scrap the deal. Economic sanctions were eventually imposed upon Italy by the League of Nations, but Britain along with most members did not pursue this policy with any tenacity or enthusiasm.

When Hitler remilitarized the Rhineland in March 1936, Britain condemned the action but showed no inclination to expel German troops from indisputable German territory, telling the French that no military assistance could be expected in the event of hostilities. When Hitler annexed Austria in early 1938 in a most brutal fashion, Britain showed a marked reluctance to get involved in central European affairs. The epitome of appeasement was reached during the Czechoslovakian crisis of 1938 when Hitler demanded the German-speaking portions of the Czech state. Britain readily accepted the principle of partition, gave France no encouragement to stand firm, and placed pressure upon the Czechs to accept this humiliating solution. The final agreement involving Czechoslovakia was signed at MUNICH in September 1938, and that name has since become synonymous with surrender and betrayal. It was only after Hitler occupied the remainder of the Czech state in early 1939 that the British government finally began to address itself with some urgency to rearming, negotiating alliances with allies, and taking a firmer line with Germany. Even then, the British CABINET hesitated to declare war upon Germany following its attack upon Poland in September 1939, thus giving the impression that appeasement had not been totally abandoned. Blame for this tragic series of events has fallen mostly upon a relatively small group of Tories, hardly surprising since the CONSERVATIVE PARTY commanded large majorities in the House of Commons during the 1930s. Two Prime Ministers, STANLEY BALDWIN and NEVILLE CHAMBERLAIN have been marked for special censure, especially the latter. Chamberlain was appeasement's principal architect and practitioner and has been savaged by critics as being vain, devious, reluctant to accept expert advice from the Foreign Office, and guilty of totally misjudging the personality of Hitler and the inner dynamics of Nazism. Perhaps the most serious criticism is that he continued to pursue appeasement after it became apparent that the policy was ineffective and that Hitler was not interested in honorable negotiations and reasonable compromises but only in diplomatic intimidation and military conquest. Other advocates of appeasement were LORD HALIFAX, the Foreign Secretary at the time of Munich, and two former foreign secretaries, SIR SAMUEL HOARE and SIR JOHN SIMON. A particularly notorious appeaser was Sir Nevile Henderson, the British ambassador to Germany 1937–9, who has been accused of exceeding his instructions in slavishly trying to accommodate the Germans. A shadowy figure in the appeasement drama was Sir Horace Wilson, the government's industrial adviser, but a man who had an important personal influence upon Chamberlain. Particularly useful to the Prime Minister was GEOFFREY DAWSON, who as editor of THE TIMES could use his influential newspaper to sway opinion. But it cannot be emphasized too strongly that support for appeasement, at least up to and including Munich, went well beyond a small clique of Britain's governing elites; this policy found wide acceptance among the general public, including pacifists, university dons, trade unionists, businessmen, newspaper editors, and elements of the Liberal and Labour Parties.

Since the Second World War, a vast amount of literature has been produced on the topic, generating much controversy and debate. In the immediate post-war period, historians and polemicists came down hard on the appeasers, sometimes indulging in personal vitriolic attacks. But during the 1960s, a newer generation of scholars came to the forefront, and more sober and objective scholarship began to assert itself. This was due partly to the release of important government documents as well as the fact that many of the participants began to write their memoirs or at least open their papers to established scholars. The results revealed a more complex situation, less amenable to simplistic analysis and banal cliches, and the end result was that there was now considerably more appreciation of the cruel dilemmas and hard realities facing the appeasers in the 1930s.

Much of this new scholarship revolved around the question of motivation: why did the appeasers appease? While there was vast range of answers given to this question and writers frequently hedged their conclusions with qualifications and exceptions, the collective response was that there were several reasons to account for appeasement, some admittedly reprehensible but most understandable under the circumstances. To begin with, there was the memory of the First World War with all its frightful slaughter and the fear that a future war, made more hideous by the addition of terrifying new weapons, might well destroy civilization. In this respect the appeasers faithfully reflected the sentiments of the general public, and it should be noted that anti-war sentiment was pervasive and peace organizations experienced much growth and popularity during this period. There was also considerable guilt over the harsh nature of the Versailles treaty, particularly in regard to its economic provisions and the questionable territorial arrangements of Central Europe. By the early 1930s it was inconceivable that Britain would go to war in order to defend such a discredited treaty, especially if the dictators invoked the Wilsonian principle of the self-determination of peoples in order to acquire territory.

Then there was the problem of allies. Historically, there were racial, religious, political, and dynastic bonds linking Britain and Germany, but the French were still viewed with suspicion. Ironically, Britain feared French aggressiveness and power in the 1920s, while by the 1930s France was seen as a nation lacking resolve and will power, riddled with pacifism, defeatism, and political factionalism. Nor could Britain automatically count upon the Empire and Commonwealth; in fact Britain's leaders were warned that if they got involved in a Continental war over questionable boundary disputes, they could not expect military assistance from the Commonwealth. The United States was viewed at this time as isolationist at best and untrustworthy at worst, too involved with its domestic economic problems to play a decisive role on the international scene. There was always the possibility of a military alliance with the Soviet Union, but aside from the Tories' ideological distaste for Bolshevism, it was believed that the Soviets were militarily weak after the ghastly purges of the officer corps, and that Stalin would demand too high a price for his support, mainly in the form of territorial annexations in eastern Europe. In turn, Marxist historians claim that the appeasers encouraged Hitler to move eastwards, seeing in Hitler a bulwark against Bolshevism and a valuable ally in maintaining the power of capitalism. Lacking reliable allies meant that Britain would have to look after its own defenses, and a rearmament program was launched, though rather belatedly. At the time of the Munich crisis, Britain was woefully short of almost every conceivable weapon, especially modern fighter aircraft, and the military chiefs informed the Cabinet that the armed forces could not prevent Germany from smashing Czechoslovakia in the event of war. Some historians have placed the blame for the nation's sorry state of defenses upon the stinginess of the Treasury, which feared that Britain could never recover from the Great Depression and might well experience an economic catastrophe if it spent vast sums of money on "unproductive" expenditures, such as armaments. Nor should it be forgotten that the LABOUR PARTY had consistently voted against defense expenditures up to the summer of 1937, mainly on the grounds that weapons were socially wasteful, economically disastrous, and likely to generate another armaments race with Germany.

Another way of understanding appeasement is to see it in larger historical perspective instead of confining the analysis narrowly to the 1930s. There are historians who argue that appeasement is a traditional policy, going back to the mid-nineteenth century when Britain, for selfish not altruistic motives, pursued a policy of peace and free trade as being the best guarantor of her continued economic and political predominance. Others taking the long view see Britain as a declining power since the nineteenth century; by the 1930s she was confronted by a menacing coalition of Japan, Italy, and Germany. Faced with such a perilous threat, lacking adequate armaments and allies, Britain either had to pursue a policy of peace at almost any price or risk defeat and disaster in a war. Another argument is that historically Britain never felt compelled to intervene in Central European affairs, the very areas where Hitler was particularly active; the areas of greatest concern to Britain, namely the Low Countries and the Suez Canal, were initially marginal in Hitler's scheme of things. Given these long range historical considerations as well as the specific forces at work in the 1930s, it is not surprising to find those who would argue that regardless of who was Prime Minister or what political party was in power, the outcome might well have been the same.

This vast amount of scholarship has produced no consensus, but in the midst of conflicting interpretations and partisan explanations, certain broad trends have begun to emerge. It is no longer fashionable to attack the appeasers personally as stupid, craven, or spineless; by and large even critics concede that the appeasers were decent, educated, and well-intentioned, motivated by a love of country and detestation of war, willing to risk personal unpopularity in order to avert the calamity of another conflict. Their guilt consisted more in misjudgment, self-deception, and bungling rather than unashamed cowardice or evil intent. There is also a greater appreciation of the constraints imposed upon the appeasers by strategic, economic, military, and political realities. But despite all this revisionism, few writers have sought to defend or approve what actually transpired during this period; explaining appeasement has not led to justifying it, and Munich will probably always be regarded as a national humiliation for Britain, a shameful surrender to brutality and force, a disgraceful betrayal of principles and peoples.

After the 1930s, politicians and nations tried to avoid the label of appeasement, believing correctly or incorrectly that the lesson of Munich was never to accommodate dictators but rather to confront their aggression immediately and directly, especially since they might well be bluffing. This led to a tendency among government leaders to draw historical parallels between Munich and a number of subsequent events. One of the most famous examples occurred in 1956, involving SIR ANTHONY EDEN, who was then Prime Minister and, significantly, had been a well known anti-appeaser during the 1930s. When Egypt's President Nasser nationalized the Suez Canal, Eden and some of his colleagues believed they saw a parallel with Hitler's bold diplomatic moves, and disdaining any compromise they launched an attack against Egypt with disastrous results for Eden's career and British diplomacy.

David C. Lukowitz

Bibliography
Adams, R.J.Q. British Politics and Foreign Policy in the Age of Appeasement 1935–39. 1993.
Crowson, N.J. Facing the Dictators: Conservatives and Appeasement. 1996.
Gilbert, Martin. The Roots of Appeasement. 1966.
Robbins, Keith. Appeasement. 1988.
Rock, William. British Appeasement in the 1930s. 1977.
Taylor, A.J.P. The Origins of the Second World War. 1961.

Architecture

Twentieth-century architecture in Britain is determined by the competing forces of design traditionalism, material and technological expression, and free style innovation which reflect both national and international developments in building. Late Victorian and Edwardian domestic design and public building extend nineteenth-century themes into the opening years of the twentieth century in late manifestations of the Arts and Crafts Movement, High Edwardian Baroque Classicism, Neo-Georgian design, and other traditional, especially classical, revivals which by late century found a symbiotic relationship with modernism in a phenomenon which architectural critic Charles Jencks has called POST-MODERNISM. Simultaneously, a restrained formalism affecting what Nikolaus Pevsner has called "pioneer modernism" prepared the soil for a more abstract and technological avant garde. During the 1930s both foreign and native practitioners of International Style modernism established a machinist aesthetic which by mid-century had manifested itself in significant housing, university, and multi-use complexes, evolved through a phase of "New Brutalism," and culminated in a High Tech expressionism of international acclaim and native royalist controversy.

A generation of turn-of-the-century Arts and Crafts architects rediscovered the free style designs of Richard Norman Shaw and the restrained "non-style" of Philip Webb and encouraged a veneration for the vernacular in domestic and occasionally commercial design. Webb's Standon (1891–2), East Grinstead, is rooted in local Sussex building traditions but characterized by a picturesque composition of traditional and innovative Arts and Crafts elements: grouped gables, exaggerated chimney stacks, variegated color and texture, individuality of expression, and a distinctly human scale effected by the diversity of forms and surfaces enriching this large and rambling country house. Stoneywell Cottage (1898–9) in Leicestershire discloses Ernest Gimson's unique translation of native building method and natural materials in a cottage so much a part of its locale it appears to have grown out of the ground several centuries ago.

Edwardian house designers would follow these traditions. SIR EDWIN LUTYENS' series of 1890s masterpieces of residential architecture continued after 1900 with Deanery Garden (1901), nestled behind aged brick walls in the heart of the Berkshire village of Sonning, while Marsh Court of the same year translates more historicist forms of Tudor architecture to its native Hampshire chalk walls with flint and red tile accents. This English reference of materials, which looks backward to John Ruskin and forward to New Brutalism and late-century High Tech architecture, finds particular expressiveness at the hand of Detmar Blow whose butterfly-plan composition for Happisburgh House (1900) in Norfolk com-

bines a roof of local Norfolk reed thatch with traditional wall patterns of local flint. Home Place
(originally Kelling Place) (1903–5) by Edward S.
Prior is a masterpiece of this local flint and
pebble-faced patterning, and of Arts and Crafts
artisan handicraft and pictorial colorism.

William Lethaby, at his Liverpool Cathedral
competition design (1903), envisioned concrete
forms of particularly expressive shapes. Lethaby
had just erected an experimental concrete vault at
All Saints' Church, Brockhampton (1901–2), a
Herefordshire church rich in symbolism, innovative in its use of materials, and traditional in its
exterior formal language despite its almost German Expressionist interior. Randall Wells' restrained Church of St. Edmund the Confessor,
Kempley, Gloucestershire (1903) appeared similarly proto-modern in its simplified forms, while
C. Harrison's Townsend St. Mary the Virgin
Church, Great Warley, Essex (1903–4) looked to
Art Nouveau decorative expression as the basis
for its displacement of traditional Gothic Revi-
valism with a history-free modernism.

Any move toward restrained surfaces and a
machine-efficient aesthetic at the expense of traditional architectural languages would be presaged in the rationalized traditionalism of C.F.A.
Voysey (The Orchard, Chorleywood, Hertfordshire, 1900–1) and C.R. Mackintosh (Hill House,
Helensburgh, Scotland, 1902–4). Although both
these architects, and these works specifically, were
viewed by spokesmen of the new modernism as
pioneers of the machine aesthetic, the works of
Voysey and Mackintosh more correctly embody
individualism, craftsmanship and a simplified traditionalism, and a morality linked to Ruskin and
the Gothic. At Upmeads, Stafford (1908), Edgar
Wood would cap a flat facade of banded and
grouped windows with a flat concrete roof in a
house which does look forward in its logical expression of structure and freer interior planning to
modern architecture. But Britain would await the
arrival of foreigners such as Peter Behrens, Erich
Mendelsohn, and Walter Gropius before a full-
blown European modernism was felt in England
in the late 1920s and especially 1930s.

The mood of the early century in Britain remained a free-style eclecticism, and nowhere was
this more imaginatively expressed within traditional formal elements than by the High Edwardian Baroque Classicism of A. Brumwell
Thomas and John Belcher. At both Belfast City
Hall (1897–1906) and the Stockport Town Hall,
Cheshire (1904–8), Thomas displays the Edwardians' admiration for the innovative English Baroque of Christopher Wren, John Vanbrugh, and
Nicholas Hawksmoor. The Belfast City Hall
places an elaborate dome on a French palace form
accented with corner towers based on Wren's

west towers at St. Paul's Cathedral. At Stockport
Thomas translates Wren's open, wedding cake
steeple designs into an extravagant Edwardian
Baroque. The Government Buildings at Parliament Square in Westminster, London (1898–
1912) evidence John Brydon's close reliance on
such details as Vanbrugh's towers at Blenheim for
source material for his own more English-
inspired Edwardian Baroque. Perhaps the most
extravagant of all is Belcher's tower for Royal
London House, Finsbury Square (1904–5) although his Ashton Memorial in Lancaster (designed 1904, built 1907–9) is a bombastic fanfare
of truly Edwardian splendor.

A continental European Baroque (more than
English Baroque) is reflected at Cardiff Hall and
Law Courts (1897–1906) by H.V. Lancaster and
Edwin Rickards, an expansive lay-out of Beaux
Arts planning. While Shaw's Picadilly Hotel,
Regent's Street (1905–8) may be said to be "free
Baroque," the slightly earlier Ritz Hotel (1903–6)
by Mewes and Davis is distinctly Parisian, and
their Royal Automobile Club, London (1908–11)
contained an entry hall reminiscent of Parisian
passages, a monumental public gathering place
embodying traditional French Neo-Classicism.
Davis redressed Luton Hoo (1903) and Polesden
Lacey (1906) in the new French fashion as well.

It was precisely this design method and historicist formalism, by which a popular architectural
dress was put on buildings like fashions of clothing, which disengaged the avant garde from the
practices of previous generations of builders. The
trend toward a more technological expression of
modern materials and methods was evidenced
earliest in Britain in works of the early 1910s. In
1914 the Trussed Concrete Steel Company built a
factory of three parallel blocks of reinforced concrete frame for the Birmingham Small Arms Ltd.
This work was preceded and then followed by
two functionally expressive designs behind classical facades: in 1910–11, John Burnet's Kodak
Building, Kingsway, London, and in 1916 the
Heal Furniture Store, Tottenham Court Road, a
steel frame structure by Dunbar Smith and Cecil
Brewer.

Even before the arrival in Britain of European
modernists, a more rational modern aesthetic
found a basis in the restrained free style classicism of such works as H.S. Goodhart Rendel's
1931–2 Hays Wharf and Charles Holden's monumental Senate House, University of London
(1932). Moreover, within the streamlined envelope of black and transparent glass of the Daily
Express Building (Ellis and Clark with Owen
Williams, 1931–2), Ronald Atkinson's extravagant lobby ornamented with Egyptian-inspired
wall relief sculpture provided London's best Art
Deco work of the period. The style, including its

streamlined moderne phase, is seen well in LON-
DON cinemas (the Leicester Square Odeon by
Harry Weedon dates from 1936−7), and found
particularly direct inspiration from transportation forms, as characterizes streamlined moderne,
in A. Pleydell Bouverie's 1937 Ramsgate Airport.
Some of the finest examples of the period's
Deco/modernist eclecticism were in factories of
the 1930s including Wallis Gilbert and Partners'
Hoover Factory (1932−5) and the superb row of
factories on the Great West Road out of London,
including Banister Fletcher's Gillette Factory
(1936) and two by Wallis Gilbert and Partners:
the Pyrene Factory (1930) and the Firestone Factory (1929).

Once transplanted European modernists arrived in Britain, the influence of the European
avant garde was immediately evidenced in a series
of classic British monuments of International
Style modernism. Behrens built the first modern
house in Britain at New Ways (1925−6) in
Northampton, and in 1930 the Russian Berthold
Lubetkin became the first European modernist
to emigrate to Britain. Lubetkin founded Tecton
in 1932 and built a series of innovative modernist
works from 1933 to late decade. His first projects
for the London Zoo include the Gorilla House
(1933−4) and the Penguin Pool (1934−5), the latter featuring steel reinforced concrete ramps of
structural expressiveness designed with the assistance of Ove Arup and innovative for their time.
Tecton's Highpoint I Flats (1933−5) displayed the
Le Corbusier five points of the new architecture
and manifestly presented to Britain what Le
Corbusier called "one of the first vertical garden
city of the future." It is significant, however, that
already by 1937−8 at Highpoint II (with its
Erechtheum caryatid casts at the entry), the
modernist block was marked by Mannerisms
which would later cause Jencks to include the
work in his defining essay on postmodernism.

Modernism was evidenced in private houses
(the first expensive London modern house was E.
Maxwell Fry's Sun House (1935) at 9 Frognal
Way), in blocks of flats, in factory design, and in
socialist experiments at health clinics of interest
both in and out of London. The machine aesthetic was immediately adapted for industrial and
transportation design and for at least one little-
known institutional design of precocious structural expressiveness reminiscent of August Perret in
France: the Royal Horticultural Society Hall,
Westminster (1929) by Stanley Hall & Easton
and Robertson displays a wide-span, reinforced
concrete construction to shape a monumental
interior space. Further, the reinforced concrete
and glass factory in Beeston for Boots Pharmaceutical Co. (1930−2) by E. Owen Williams rivals the noted Van Nelle Factory built by Brinck-

man and Van Vlugt outside Rotterdam in
1927−30 in its expression of frame and amount of
exposed exterior glass. While hints of the new
forms were evidenced in the work of Holden for
London Transport, particularly for such stations
as Arnos Grove (1932−3) built for the Picadilly
Line (1930−3), it would be Joseph Emberton who
would provide, in his Royal Corinthian Yacht
Club, Burnham-on-Crouch (1931) England's
only work recognized by Henry Russell-
Hitchcock and Philip Johnson as worthy of inclusion in their defining modern architecture exhibition and book *The International Style*.
Emberton's best known London work of the period is the 1935 Simpson Department Store which
he designed with engineer Felix Samuely and designer Lazlo Maholy Nagy. The year before Samuely had built the first all welded steel frame in
England for Erich Mendelsohn's famous pavilion
at Bexhill-on-Sea, the only portion constructed
of the De La Warr Resort Cure intended to include shops, a cinema, and hotel as well as the pavilion. The year *after* Emberton's Simpson Store,
Slater and Moberly (with W. Crabtree and
Charles Reilly) constructed on Sloane Square the
Peter Jones Department Store (1936−8), a work
which displays one of London's first glass curtain
walls in an expressive curved envelope wrapping
around its corner site.

As noted, Behrens introduced Britain to residential modernism at New Ways, and English architects were soon to follow with their own interpretations. The often traditionalist Oliver Hill
replaced Webb's 1873 Joldwynds in Surrey with a
Modern 1930 version, and the same year Amyas
Connell built Ashmole House in Amersham,
Buckinghamshire, both early expressions of the
stark, rectangular white concrete forms of high
modernism. Connell continued the language at
Grayswood (1931−2) and "High and Over" (1934),
near Ashmole, and in London, near Fry's Sun
House, at 66 Frognal Way (1936−8, Connell
Ward & Lucas). Modernist houses by Europeans
included Tecton's Six Pillars (1935), a house on
pilotis with roof terrace expressive of Corbusian
modernism and three works of 1936: Serge
Chermayeff's house for himself at Bentley
Wood, which included a Christopher Tunnard
garden, Walter Gropius's (with Maxwell Fry)
house for Benn Levy at 66 Old Church Street,
and Erich Mendelsohn's and Chermayeff's house
next door at 64. Gropius's best known work with
Fry was the Impington College complex in Cambridgeshire of 1936. Denys Lasdun, whose work
in cluster housing and university design would be
noteworthy in the 1960s, had been one of the
young English architects gathered by Lubetkin to
form Tecton, and at the age of twenty-four Lasdun built a surviving house in London at 32 New-

ton Road (1938), a work which echoes Le Corbusier's Maison Cook in Paris of 1926.

The socialist intentions of the new architecture were evident especially in blocks of flats and pioneer health centres, the most important of the latter including the Peckham Experiment (Owen Williams's 1934–6 Pioneer Health Center) and Tecton's 1938 Health Center at Finsbury. Among noteworthy designs by native British architects were Wells Coates's Isokon Flats (1933), Maxwell Fry's Ladbrooke Grove Flats (c.1933), Frederick Gibberd's (who would later build Heathrow Airport (1951) three and seven story picturesquely sited block of flats called Pullman Court (1935), and Wells Coates's 10 Palace Flats of 1938 based on Le Corbusier's Swiss Pavilion model.

The spatial potential of the new architecture was especially brought to public notice in the Royal Festival Hall (1949–51), South Bank, London, designed by Robert Matthew and Sir Leslie Martin. Its open riverfront facade (the exterior was later remodelled) revealed restaurant and gallery space and free circulation in a Modern expression of the new architecture. The later South Bank design by Lasdun for the National Theatre (1967–76) layers stepped terraces in a more form-giving architectural exercise. The exposed aggregate concrete panels and rough-shuttered reinforced concrete of the slightly earlier Queen Elizbeth Hall and Hayward Gallery (1964) are brutal reflections of a new dimension of late modernism.

"Brutal," indeed, was the telling label, as Britain had already initiated an international architectural movement, New Brutalism. The final period of British twentieth-century modern architecture is informed by this movement and produced noteworthy designs for HOUSING, new universities, cathedrals, and "Americanized" Late Modern office buildings and multi-use, large scale development (and redevelopment) including, at Canary Wharf in the late 1980s and 1990s, Europe's largest construction project.

With the work of Peter and Alison Smithson and James Stirling and James Gowan, designs based on the late career architectural languages of Le Corbusier, Mies van der Rohe, and to a lesser extent Alvar Aalto, informed a British-born movement known as New Brutalism. The Brutalists admired the *beton brut* of late-Corbu and the *art brut* of Dubuffet, the technologically expressive steel and glass of Mies, and the sculptural vitality and rough textural reality of Aalto's forms and brickwork at MIT's Baker House dormitory (1947–51). At Hunstanton Elementary School, Norfolk (1949–53) the Smithsons extended Mies' technological language to a steel-frame, glass, and corrugated metal construction which gloried in its "unfinished" interiors, crude

plumbing and electrical fixtures, and exposed heating, ventilation, air conditioning systems. Their Economist Building in London (1964) grouped three office buildings of varying height around a small piazza integrating pedestrian street life, the civility of adjacent Boodles Club, and a non-axial, more inviting contextual link of old and new. Stirling and Gowan's Langham House Flats (1958) were clearly based on Le Corbusier's Maisons Jaoul (1956) and paralleled the tactile, tectonic gruffness of mainstream Brutalism.

Between 1961 and 1965 seven new universities were built in England (Sussex, East Anglia, York, Lancaster, Essex, Warwick, and Kent) and an eighth in Scotland, Stirling. Basil Spence's designs for Sussex combined traditional and new materials and forms of concrete frame and brick in distinctly modern works of a classic monumentality, even reflecting beyond its sweeping arches the cloistered traditions of quadrangles. At East Anglia University Lasdun, on the other hand, turned to the late modern megastructure tradition in a linear arrangement of classrooms and administrative units: the complex picturesquely rambled across open Norfolk countryside and was distinguished especially for its stepped pyramid student dormitory blocks. Stirling's Andrew Melville Hall at St. Andrews University (1964) and the History Faculty Building at Cambridge (1965–7) were noteworthy, if not wholly successful additions to academic architecture.

During this same period an "Americanization" of the modern urban skyline began to be felt in Britain as elsewhere in Europe. The slab-on-podium model of Gordon Bunshaft's Lever House influenced both Andrew Renton's design for Thorn House (Basil Spence and Partners, 1957–9) and Sir Robert Matthew, Johnson-Marshall's New Zealand House (1960), the latter, one of the first completely air conditioned glass curtain wall office buildings in London. The more Formalist Centrepoint Tower (R. Seifert & Partners, 1967) stood vacant for over a decade, an unintentional monument to the failure of speculative development.

Finally, some noteworthy modern cathedrals continued Britain's historic line of noble ecclesiastical building. The Liverpool Anglican Cathedral, whose competition of 1903 was won by Giles Gilbert Scott with altered designs of 1910 by Scott, was modified again during construction throughout the mid-century. It is one of Britain's great Gothic Revival works. Guildford Cathedral (1932–66) by Sir Edward Maufe displays a cool, modern spaciousness, sharp profiles, minimal ornament, and more restrained neo-Gothic lines. Spence won the 1951 competition for the rebuilding of Coventry Cathedral (1956–62). Finally, a distinctly contemporary image for Christ the King Roman Catholic Cathderal, Liverpool (1960–7), by Frederick Gibberd, presents a pavilion as a symbolic "crown of thorns" in a highly derivative work borrowing from Oscar Niemeyer, Auguste Perret, and Marcel Breuer.

Robert M. Craig

Bibliography

Curtis, William J.R. *Modern Architecture Since 1900*. 2nd ed. 1982.

Jackson, Anthony. *The Politics of Architecture: A History of Modern Architecture in Britain*. 1970.

Jencks, Charles. *Late-Modern Architecture*. 1980.

Jeremiah, David. *Architecture, Design and the Family in Britain 1900–1970*. 2000.

Murray, Peter, and Stephen Trombley. *Modern British Architecture Since 1945*. 1984.

Service, Alastair. *Edwardian Architecture: A Handbook to Building Design in Britain, 1890–1914*. 1977.

Army

The BOER WAR dramatically exposed both Britain's diplomatic isolation and its army's inadequacy. The Anglo-Japanese Naval Treaty of 1902 and the Entente Cordiale of 1904 corrected the former; repairing the latter meant redesign of size, structure, command system weaponry, and mission of the army. In 1902 the COMMITTEE OF IMPERIAL DEFENCE was established to survey the strategic military needs of the Empire, giving Britain a singularly effective defense planning capability. In 1904 the Report of the War Office (Reconstruction) Committee, familiarly known as the Esher Committee, recommended an Army Council mirroring the Admiralty structure, a general staff, and redistribution of function in the War Office on clear and logistical bases. These and other reforms were carried out by Secretary for War RICHARD BURDON HALDANE, by whose name they are generally known. He saw to the production of field service manuals that set out regulations specifying staff responsibilities and procedures. His predecessors in the CABINET had variously envisioned a regular army of three corps (about 120,000 men) in addition to militia and reserves or a long-service regular army supplemented by a short-service home defense army. To rationalize the structure of the forces and save money, Haldane abolished the militia and reserves, creating in 1908 a Territorial Army of fourteen divisions, fourteen cavalry brigades, and corps troops for home defense. In addition to this force, whose members could volunteer for overseas service in wartime, the army now had an expeditionary force able to land in Europe in fifteen days from mobilization, as well as colonial forces. Introduction of khaki full dress, new weaponry, tactics and training methods completed the army's transformation. On the eve of the FIRST WORLD WAR the Regular Army numbered 247,432 with 209,280 reserves and the Territorial Army stood at 268,777.

At the outbreak of European hostilities the United Kingdom sent four divisions immediately to France to play a prearranged role guarding the left flank of the French army's planned advance into Lorraine. Within a few weeks the British had committed two additional divisions and sustained 89,000 casualties of the approximately 108,000 troops fighting. Territorial volunteers plugged the gaps: by December 69,000 of them were serving in France. LORD KITCHENER, who had been made Secretary for War at the outset of the conflict, set out to create a mass volunteer army known as "the New Army" or "Kitchener's Army." Nearly 1.2 million volunteers had come forward by the end of 1914, swamping the army's training and logistical capabilities. Huge difficulties in transport, supply, medical treatment, and troop welfare had to be mastered. In March 1916 CONSCRIPTION was introduced, and by June of that year the British Expeditionary Force in France numbered fifty-seven divisions divided into five armies. Though British army units were used in other theaters, the vast majority fought on the Western Front in a horrifying war of attrition. By war's end, 2.1 million men were serving outside the United Kingdom, nearly 1.4 million inside. Of 1.8 million casualties sustained, 744,702 were killed.

With the CABINET's insistence in 1919 that military planning should proceed on the basis that no major war was anticipated for a decade, the army lost its mission and reverted to a small force for putting down civil disturbances in places as disparate as Ireland and India, as well as guarding the ROYAL AIR FORCE bases by which the Middle East was controlled. This period of the ten year rule, during which the army had neither plans nor equipment and largely abandoned the professional orientation it had in the pre-1914 reform years, lasted until 1934. Despite the concepts and urging of the tactical visionaries, J.F.C. Fuller and Basil Liddell Hart, the army engaged in only desultory experiments in tank warfare, and, though these were enough to make it the world leader in that department, found it necessary to abandon such experiment after 1934 due to lack of budget and equipment. In that year the Cabinet set the course for military spending in austere times by deciding to maintain a first-class navy and develop a first-class air force. Fiscal retrenchment, belief in the efficacy of naval and air forces, and reluctance to commit a mass army to the risk of continental carnage experienced in the First World War combined to mandate an indefinite future for the army as a colonial police force. After MUNICH the mood changed rapidly, and in

February 1939 the Cabinet decided on an army of thirty-two divisions, six regular and twenty-six territorial, to be supplemented by twenty-three Commonwealth divisions. Conscription was introduced in May, and by July the army numbered 237,736 regulars, 212,000 reserves, and 249,000 territorials.

The coming of the SECOND WORLD WAR caught the army in the midst of an awkward and difficult expansion. As in 1914, it sent four divisions to France on mobilization and was able to add another half dozen by the time of the German attack in the west in May 1940. These were smaller than 1914 divisions, with three infantry brigades of only three battalions, a total of 13,600 men as against three brigades of four battalions, 18,073 men, in 1914. They were also better armed, with fifty machine guns to a battalion as against two in 1914, and where the earlier division had fifty-four 18-pounder field pieces, eighteen 4.5-inch howitzers and four 60-pounder field guns, the 1939 division had seventy-two 25-pound howitzers, forty-eight anti-tank guns, twenty-eight light tanks and forty-four Bren gun carriers. Yet the German breakthrough was swift and decisive: 199,000 British troops minus their equipment were evacuated from DUNKIRK by 3 June and the army was left without a toehold on the continent. This spared the British a repetition of the horrors of trench warfare and provided both the necessity and the opportunity for rapid recreation of the army as an offensive force.

The conflict saw not only huge expansion in the Regular Army's size, some of it achieved by incorporating the Territorial Army at the beginning of the war, but significant change in its shape and functioning. From an armored force of two armored divisions and one brigade in 1939, the army developed a total of twenty-eight armored brigades in 1945. Communications were largely switched from telephone and telegraph to radio early in the war; engineers added airfield construction and problems of amphibious warfare to their agenda; ordnance solved complex difficulties in supplying armies in deserts and jungles with millions of items; medical services became more flexible to accommodate the modern battlefield; and close air/ground cooperation was developed. The human problems of command, multiplied by resistence to mindless discipline by a more educated and sophisticated conscript, were addressed. As the war progressed, it became evident that the decisive theater was once again the west. Since the allied invasion of France came only after the German army had been thoroughly battered on the Russian front, the British army came out of the war with only 144,079 killed.

At the end of the war the potential for confrontation with the Soviets in Europe combined with unrest in the colonies presented a continuing complex mission for the army. In the immediate post-war years the British maintained an army in Germany, fought a full-scale guerrilla war in Malaya, and contributed a brigade to United Nations forces in the Korean War. To counter the effects of massive demobilization, conscription was retained, the term of service set at two years with the regulars and three-and-a-half years with the territorials or reserves. The Territorial Army was assigned the anti-aircraft defense of the realm and served as a strategic reserve, even though it was not at full strength until 1952. The beginnings of imperial retreat and the advent of nuclear weaponry made for widespread changes in the army in the mid-1950s. The Royal Air Force assumed complete responsibility for the air defense of Britain, and Territorial Army air defenses were scrapped with units reassigned or disbanded. Two territorial divisions were earmarked to flesh out NATO forces in wartime, the remainder being assigned to civil defense.

The SUEZ CRISIS of 1956 exposed the hollowness of Britain's pretense at being able to project force in pursuit of national interests and led to the Defense White Paper of 1957 that de-emphasized conventional land forces. Britain would rely on nuclear deterrence in major crises. Garrisons in the colonies were to be downsized, with flareups met by airlifting troops from the United Kingdom. Divisions were scrapped in favor of brigade-group organization. In light of this drastic change of mission and structure, conscription was ended in 1960. The Regular Army was limited thereafter to 185,000 long-service volunteers while the Territorial Army was pegged at 123,000, with a reserve of nearly 70,000. Through the 1960s the army experimented with organizational forms in an attempt to retain the tradition-laden regiments, cope with world-wide postings of troops, and deal with recruitment problems and fiscal retrenchment. This process produced first "administrative brigades" in which regiments constituted the battalions, the "administrative divisions" of eleven or twelve battalions. By the 1970s most of the historic regiments were no more. Moreover, the Territorial Army had disappeared into a Territorial and Army Volunteer Reserve of 50,000 created in 1966. Despite the presence in Germany of a British Army of the Rhine, the United Kingdom had abandoned the capacity for extended conventional land war in Europe, expecting any clash to be solved by diplomacy or escalate to a nuclear exchange in days. The collapse of the Soviet Union, the reunification of Germany, and progress toward European unity have validated the strategy just as the swift and successful FALKLANDS WAR justified reliance on deploying a highly trained and mobile force for small conflicts.

Joseph M. McCarthy

Bibliography

Barnett, Correlli. *Britain and Her Army, 1509–1970: A Military, Political and Social Survey.* 1970.

Barthorp, Michael. *The Armies of Britain, 1485–1980.* 1980.

Blaxland, William Gregory. *The Regiments Depart: A History of the British Army, 1945–1970.* 1971.

Crang, Jeremy. *The British Army and the People's War 1939–45.* 2000.

Strawson, John. *Gentlemen in Khaki: The British Army, 1890–1990.* 1989.

Arts Council of Great Britain

When the war came to an end in 1945 the COUNCIL FOR THE ENCOURAGEMENT OF MUSIC AND THE ARTS (CEMA) had not only earned its citation for meritorious achievement in fulfilling its original terms of reference to prevent the blackout of the arts in the wartime: it had shown that there was a continuing role in making the arts more accessible to the population.

On 12 June the Chancellor of the Exchequer announced in the House of Commons that the government would incorporate the Arts Council of Great Britain to be financed by the Treasury. The royal charter, dated 9 August 1946, constituted the Arts Council of not more than sixteen persons, selected by the Chancellor, after consultation with the Minister for Education and the Secretary of State for Scotland, together with separate and autonomous committees for Scotland and Wales. There is a separate Arts Council for Northern Ireland. The Council does not comprise persons representing other organizations, but members are chosen for their professional knowledge of, or concern for, one or more of the fine arts. Members retire on a system of rotation so as to prevent any solidification of interest.

Supporting the Council are advisory panels, initially for music, drama, art, and poetry, their membership changing every three years. These have since been extended to include advisory panels for dance, literature, photography, and film. No one taking part in this network of policy-making is paid for the work. The Arts Council is not a government department and bears little resemblance to those ministries of fine arts which exist in other countries. No minister directs policies or decides how, and to whom, its grants shall be made. There is no single instance on record of a minister requiring or directing, or even advising, the Arts Council to do this or not to do that: and when from time to time some action of the Arts Council is criticized in the House of Commons, successive governments have invariably declared that they will not interfere with the Arts Council's discretion.

This liberty of action carries with it the obligation upon the Arts Council to discharge its duties within the objects set out in its Royal Charter:

(1) To develop and improve the knowledge, understanding and practice of the arts;

(2) To increase the accessibility of the arts to the public throughout Great Britain;

(3) To advise and co-operate with departments of government, local authorities and other bodies to achieve these objects.

As a recipient of public funds, the Arts Council publishes an annual report, containing its audited accounts, to provide Parliament and the general public with an overview of the year's work and to record all grants and guarantees offered in support of the arts in England, Scotland, and Wales.

The first years's grant-in-aid from the Treasury totalled £235,000 (for 1945–6) and this has increased annually to £820,000 (1955–6), £3.91 million (1965–6), £28.85 million (1975–6), £106.05 million (1985–6), and to £221.2 million (1992–3).

The first Chairman of the Council was Sir Ernest Pooley who was succeeded by SIR KENNETH CLARK (later Lord Clark) in 1952. Sir William Emrys Williams, who had been a member of CEMA and the Arts Council from 1940 to 1951 was appointed Secretary-General in 1951, the start of the most significant period of development for the arts in Great Britain until his retirement in 1963. In 1965 the important appointment was Lord Goodman's as the Council's Chairman. Together with the appointment of Jennie Lee as Great Britain's first ever Minister for the Arts, the Council was granted a new Royal Charter of Incorporation by the Queen on 7 February 1967. This increased the membership of the Council from a maximum of sixteen to twenty and redesignated the Scottish and Welsh Committees as Councils. By the time Lord Goodman retired from the Council in 1972, the major national arts institutions in LONDON had been supplemented by the development of the arts resources to major regional companies throughout the rest of the United Kingdom.

The two most significant periods of office since then have been that of Sir Hugh Willatt as Secretary-General (1968–75), who was succeeded by Sir Roy Shaw (1975–83). As the most senior paid employees, both developed even more ambitious policies throughout these periods, placing great emphasis on supporting the work of creative artists, playwrights, and composers. Since 1983 appointments to the Council have tended to be administrators, accountants, academics, and lawyers rather than creative artists, and the

Council's officers have shifted policy from one of developing the arts and entertainments profession, maintaining and improving standards, and making the arts increasingly accessible to the population generally to a more value-for-money efficient business as required by government directives during MARGARET THATCHER's regime. This, in turn, has led to the Arts Council becoming a much less important force in the arts world since 1981, and in 1990 delegating increasing responsibilities to newly created Regional Arts Boards. It is yet to be seen whether this change in emphasis from central government subsidy to such funding as commercial sponsorship will enable Britain to maintain the high level of international earnings and benefits derived by the Treasury from the previous government investment in the arts.

The grant which Parliament annually votes to the Arts Council is offered in response to its application for funds based upon a precise appraisal of the needs of the hundreds of organizations it supports. It is important to note that the government grant invariably falls far short of the total Arts Council requirements but that if the Council were to decide to withdraw subsidy completely from any major organization, its total Treasury grant could well be reduced. It was originally hoped that the Council would be given a quinquennial grant, so as to enable its planning to be conducted on a long-term basis. Although a number of attempts have been made to institute at least a triennial grant, the national financial situation has obstructed that aspiration, and consequently for nearly half a century the Council has been compelled to practice hand-to-mouth policies.

One of the most fundamental changes of policy which has occurred in the Arts Council's history has been the diminution of directly-provided activities and the consequent development of self-governing, non-profit distributing companies, registered as charities, to provide the arts activities in Great Britain. This ensures that creative artists (playwrights, composers, choreographers, artists, sculptors, writers, poets and so on) are twice-removed from political control—once by the autonomous Arts Council, protected by its Royal Charter, and again by the independent producing companies.

The primary responsibility imposed by the Royal Charter is to preserve and improve standards of performance in the various arts. Thus, the Arts Council established the principal national institutions and helped preserve them with regular, annual subsidies: the Royal Opera, the Royal Ballet, the Royal National Theatre and the Royal Shakespeare Theatre Company. Next came the development of the Welsh National and the

Scottish Opera Companies and the major symphony ORCHESTRAS both in London and in the regions (in Liverpool, Manchester, Birmingham, Bournemouth and Glasgow). Finally, the establishment of the network of regional drama companies in all the main cities and towns, with the help of Housing the Arts funds to provide new and refurbished buildings.

Since 1980 there has been increasing encouragement to move towards a mixed-economy, so that the commercial world of the arts can help exploit subsidized activities to the benefit of both areas of work. For example, over half the West End theatre productions in recent years originated in subsidized companies. Further, most commercial productions, film, radio, and television programs, videos and cassette discs, and many British productions seen worldwide have been wholly dependent on talent trained and developed by subsidized drama, dance, and OPERA companies and orchestras.

Anthony Field

Bibliography
Harris, John S. *Government Patronage of the Arts in Great Britain.* 1970.
Hewison, Robert. *Culture and Consensus: England, Art and Politics Since 1940.* 1995.
Hutchison, Robert. *The Politics of the Arts Council.* 1982.
Sinclair, Andrew. *Arts and Cultures: The History of the 50 Years of the Arts Council of Great Britain.* 1995.
White, Eric Walter. *The Arts Council of Great Britain.* 1975

Ashton, Frederick (1904–1988)

Frederick Ashton, one of the handful of great ballet choreographers of the twentieth century, was largely responsible for formulating the British style of classic BALLET, in "chamber" ballets made for the tiny stage of Marie Rambert's Ballet Club, then in larger works for the company founded by NINETTE DE VALOIS and known first as the Vic-Wells, then as the Sadler's Wells Ballet, and finally in ballets on a grand scale that he created for that company after it moved to the Royal Opera House, Covent Garden, in 1946. In 1963 he succeeded de Valois as director of the company, which had become the Royal Ballet in 1956. He retired from that position in 1970.

Ashton had been inspired to become a dancer by seeing the great Russian ballerina Anna Pavlova in 1917, in Lima, Peru, where he grew up, but it was not until the early 1920s that he was able to pursue this ambition, when he began to study in London, first with the Russian choreographer Leonide Massine, then with Rambert. She encouraged Ashton to try his hand at choreography, and his first ballet, *A Tragedy of Fashion*, was presented in a London revue in 1926. Another major influence was Bronislava Nijinska, the sister of Vaslav

Nijinsky, who was the choreographer of a company formed by Ida Rubinstein in Paris in 1928, in which Ashton was briefly employed as a dancer.

Returning to London, Ashton continued to choreograph both for Rambert's dancers and for the Camargo Society, an organization formed to fill the gap left in London dance seasons by the disbandment of the Ballets Russes following the death of Serge Diaghilev. He also worked in the commercial theatre, staging dance numbers for musical comedy, revue, and cabaret, and for films. His first major successes were *Capriol Suite* (1930), a suite of court and country dances, and *Façade* (1931), which satirized various social and theatrical dance forms.

In 1934 he travelled to the United States to stage the Virgil Thomson-Gertrude Stein opera *Four Saints in Three Acts,* first in Hartford, then in New York. This gave him his first taste of international fame, but he returned to London, where in the following year he was invited by de Valois to join the Vic-Wells Ballet. He had previously worked for her as a guest dancer and choreographer, notably of *Les Rendezvous* (1933), which showed the beginnings of a personal neoclassical style, but now he was to be the company's resident choreographer. The association continued for the rest of his life.

During the rest of that decade Ashton created a series of ballets notable for the distinction of his collaborations with Constant Lambert, who, as musical director of the company, was responsible for arranging and sometimes composing scores; with designers such as Sophie Fedorovitch, Cecil Beaton, and William Chappell; and with the ballerina MARGOT FONTEYN, who emerged from the corps de ballet at the age of sixteen to become Ashton's muse for the next twenty-five years.

During the SECOND WORLD WAR British choreographers felt the need to celebrate the nation's literary heritage, as in Robert Helpmann's *Comus* (1942) and *Hamlet* (1942). Ashton also contributed to this trend with *The Quest* (1943), derived from Edmund Spenser's *The Faerie Queene.* But his first ballet at Covent Garden, *Symphonic Variations* (1946), was an affirmation of the supremacy of the classic dance. From then on dance was of primary importance in his work, even when he told a story, as he did in his first three-act ballet, *Cinderella* (1948), *Daphnis and Chloe* (1951), *Sylvia* (1952), and *Ondine* (1956), all of which were created with Fonteyn in mind.

Ashton also developed the talents of younger dancers, such as Nadia Nerina and David Blair in his new version of the old ballet *La Fille mal gardée* (1960), Lynn Seymour and Christopher Gable in *The Two Pigeons* (1961), and Antoinette Sibley and Anthony Dowell in *The Dream* (1964), each of them a masterpiece, as well as setting the seal on the new partnership of Fonteyn with Rudolf Nureyev in *Marguerite and Armand* (1963). The two trios that comprise *Monotones* (1965–6) represent the purest distillation of Ashton's classicism.

After his retirement Ashton contented himself for several years with choreographing small *pièces d'occasion*—small, that is, in scale, though *Thaïs* (1971) for Sibley and Dowell, *The Walk to the Paradise Garden* (1972) for Merle Park and David Wall, and *Five Brahms Waltzes in the manner of Isadora Duncan* (1975–6) for Seymour, are perfect works of art. In 1976 he returned to the larger scale with a long one-act ballet, *A Month in the Country,* based on Ivan Turgenev's play, also for Seymour, which showed no diminution in his powers.

His last major work was *Rhapsody* (1980), fulfilling a long-held wish to choreograph Serge Rachmaninov's "Rhapsody on a theme of Paganini," to which he made a piece that celebrated the virtuosity of Mikhail Baryshnikov and the Royal Ballet ballerina Lesley Collier. Ashton always felt that he was more appreciated in New York than he was at home, and for the opening of the 1983 Royal Ballet season at the Metropolitan Opera House he confected a *bonne bouche, Varii capricci.* He continued to involve himself in revivals of his ballets, such as the *Romeo and Juliet* he had choreographed for the Royal Danish Ballet in 1955, revived by London Festival Ballet in 1985, and *Ondine,* restored to the Royal Ballet repertory in 1988.

Ashton was a master of choreographic structure, building what he called the "scaffolding" of his ballets on the foundation of the musical score; in his realization of Igor Stravinsky's *Scènes de ballet* (1948), perhaps his greatest work, every step is related to the whole structure. But even a seemingly light *divertissement* like *Les Patineurs* (1937) can serve as an object lesson in putting a ballet together. Ashton may not have accomplished what the critic Alan M. Kriegsman called the "radical transfiguration" of the vocabulary of classic dance proposed by George Balanchine; his great contribution was to enlarge the use of classic dance as a poetic language, to encompass subject-matter of such subtlety and psychological complexity as he addressed in *Enigma Variations* (1968) and *A Month in the Country,* and yet preserve the autonomy of the dance itself.

David Vaughan

Bibliography

Dominic, Zoë, and John Selwyn Gilbert. *Frederick Ashton: A Choreographer and his Ballets.* 1971.

Kavanagh, Julie. *Secret Muses: The Life of Frederick Ashton.* 1996.

Macaulay, Alastair. *Some Views and Reviews of Ashton's Choreography.* 1987.

Manchester, P.W. *Vic-Wells: A Ballet Progress.* 1942.

Vaughan, David. *Frederick Ashton and His Ballets.* 1977.

Asquith, H(erbert) H(enry) (1852–1928)

As Liberal Prime Minister from April 1908 to May 1915 and head of a coalition government thereafter until December 1916, H.H. Asquith was the central figure in an era of intense political passion and turbulence. His premiership saw the breaking of the power of the HOUSE OF LORDS, the introduction of social reforms which laid the foundation of the WELFARE STATE, legislation for self-government in Ireland which brought the nation to the brink of civil war, and foreign and defense policies which ensured that Germany's war in Europe would not be quickly triumphant.

Asquith's parliamentary career from 1886 onwards was of such apparently ineluctable success that many students of his life were inclined to underestimate the ambition and application that had propelled him forward. His father, a Yorkshire wool merchant, died when he was eight. In spite of a much disrupted youth, the self-help, radicalism, and pragmatism of Yorkshire's business Liberals were deeply imprinted. A Balliol College fellowship followed a succession of academic honors at OXFORD and presidency of the Oxford Union. But politics was Asquith's vocation. The LEGAL PROFESSION had to be the path to financial security. While still a junior barrister, supplementing his income with lecturing and journalism, he married Helen Melland, the daughter of a prominent Manchester doctor. When she died fourteen years later, leaving him with five children, he had begun to recognize that she was "a restricting rather than a stimulating influence." His second wife, Margot Tennant, brought an appetite for society and politics that more than matched his own. Her father's wealth also relieved Asquith from the full burden of supporting the life-style of a prospective party leader.

Making his mark as Liberal MP for East Fife, he was invited to join W.E. Gladstone's last government as Home Secretary in 1892. In an increasingly discordant CABINET after Lord Rosebery succeeded Gladstone, Asquith was an effective departmental chief, a forceful debater, and a respected contributor to collective deliberations. By the time the government fell, he and many colleagues realized that it was only a matter of time and the avoidance of calamity before he reached the top.

The opportunity to step forward came when Sir William Harcourt relinquished the Liberal leadership in the House of Commons. But, foreseeing only years of dismal opposition ahead, Asquith resisted pressure to claim the prize. Expecting that SIR HENRY CAMPBELL-BANNERMAN would stand aside after the next general election, he set himself to put by funds sufficient to allow his undivided attention to party affairs.

Having allowed Campbell-Bannerman to come to the fore, Asquith showed him scant loyalty. During the BOER WAR and afterwards he did not hesitate to advertise their differences or to organize friends and followers to fight for control of the party. He conspired to have CB removed to the House of Lords in the event of a Liberal ministry being formed. But when the CONSERVATIVE government collapsed in 1905, it was unthinkable that he would decline the offer of the Chancellorship of the Exchequer. The compact he had made with SIR EDWARD GREY and R.B. HALDANE was dissolved, and these three Liberal Imperialists became key members of the new government.

On his unchallenged accession to the premiership in May 1908 he shifted the balance of the ministry by promoting DAVID LLOYD GEORGE to the Exchequer and WINSTON CHURCHILL to the Board of Trade. The Liberals were already in conflict with the House of Lords, yet no one foresaw the upheaval that was to be precipitated by the Lords' rejection of Lloyd George's 1909 Budget. The ensuring consitutional crisis tested all of Asquith's capacity to hold his Cabinet and party together, to withstand the robust bargaining of the Irish Nationalists who held the balance of power in the Commons after January 1910, and to face repeated onslaughts from a bitter Opposition.

Asquith relied on his colleagues for the initiatives and energy that sustained the government. He could declare policy emphatically but was rarely its creator. Nevertheless, the Liberal reform program—from the proposed abolition of plural voting to the introduction of national insurance against UNEMPLOYMENT and invalidity, from trades boards and labor exchanges to Welsh disestablishment and land taxes—could not have proceeded without his blessing and at times his decisive intervention.

Beset by growing industrial unrest, suffragette militancy, and vehement Conservative resistance to Irish Home Rule, Asquith's position as party leader was strengthened even as his ministry's hold on power grew more precarious. Liberal fortunes had not been helped by quarrels over naval estimates, incompetent preparation of the 1914 Budget, the continuing unpopularity of national insurance, and unresolved wrangling over Lloyd George's land campaign. But the German invasion of Belgium brought instant clarity to a political situation of ominous uncertainty.

Asquith's grip on power was progressively eroded as expected early victories did not materialize. The creation of a coalition with the Conservatives in May 1915 alienated many of his own party. It also set him on a path of compromise over manpower, CONSCRIPTION, and economic mobilization that continually dismayed a minority of Liberals while rarely satisfying a majority of their coalition partners.

In some respects more significant than policy difficulties in undermining the premier's authority was the manifest deterioration in his personal dedication and capability. Excessive drinking, noted a decade or more earlier, had by 1916 seriously diminished his capacity to cope with the unprecedented demands of wartime political management. An overlapping succession of friendships with younger women did not compensate for the lost companionship of Venetia Stanley, whose decision to marry his colleague EDWIN MONTAGU was a devastating blow. The final emotional trauma was the death in action of his eldest son Raymond in September 1916.

From the outbreak of the FIRST WORLD WAR Asquith had placed great reliance on the presence at the War Office of LORD KITCHENER. Kitchener's death in June 1916 robbed the ministry of a symbol of national unity. Meanwhile, Lloyd George was widely recognized as the embodiment of a spirit of full-hearted commitment to victory. Asquith was increasingly perceived as an impediment to overdue institutional changes and drastic policy solutions. There was enough truth in this to shake the loyalties even of some senior Liberal colleagues. When Lloyd George, AN-DREW BONAR LAW, and SIR EDWARD CARSON made common cause late in 1916 to insist on changes at the top, Asquith at first overestimated the strength of his own position. Concluding within a few days that he was likely to be reduced to a figurehead as Prime Minister, he resigned.

By refusing to take a subordinate place in the ministry while clinging to the leadership of the LIBERAL PARTY, Asquith ensured that the party itself would lose the benefit of association with the government in power when Germany was finally defeated. The next twelve years of his life were a melancholy coda. Rejected by the electors in 1918, he returned to the Commons in 1920 to lead a greatly depleted party. After the fall of the Lloyd George coalition in 1922 an uneasy reconciliation of Liberal forces was effected. Asquith retained the titular leadership of the Liberal Party after losing his seat in 1924 and accepting a peerage. He resigned at last in 1926 leaving Lloyd George to lead the Liberal remnant.

In retirement he wrote his *Memories and Reflections* (1928). Complementing earlier works on *The Genesis of the War* (1923) and *Fifty Years of Parliament* (1926), the autobiography was an austere but still revealing record. At the height of his powers Asquith had been a formidable parliamentarian. But there was no hiding the lack of vision to focus and sustain the outstanding qualities which had so impressed his contemporaries.

Cameron Hazlehurst

Bibliography

Brock, Michael and Eleanor, eds. *H.H. Asquith: Letters to Venetia Stanley.* 1985.

Hazlehurst, Cameron. "Herbert Henry Asquith," in John P. Mackintosh, ed. *British Prime Ministers in the Twentieth Century.* vol. 1. 1977. pp. 78–117.

Jenkins, Roy. *Asquith.* rev. ed. 1978.

Koss, Stephen. *Asquith.* 1976.

Searle, G.R. *The Liberal Party: Triumph and Disintegration, 1886–1929.* 1992.

Spender, J.A., and Cyril Asquith. *Life of Herbert Henry Asquith, Lord Oxford and Asquith.* 2 vols. 1932.

Astor, Nancy Witcher Langhorne (1879–1964)

American-born Nancy Langhorne of Virginia became, as Viscountess Astor, the first woman to sit in the House of Commons. Emigrating to Britain in her twenties as a young divorcee with a small child, she married the rising Conservative politician, William Waldorf Astor. Her 1919 victory in the by-election followed her husband's retirement from the Commons after inheriting his father's title and exemplified the success of the feminist movement in claiming women's political equality to men. She subsequently enjoyed a long career in Parliament, represented her Plymouth constituency for the CONSERVATIVE PARTY until her retirement in 1945. During that time, her tenacious and ebullient personality carved out a place for herself and the women who followed her in a seemingly irredeemably masculine institution.

Lady Astor's political achievements evidenced a deeply-felt, personal feminist commitment. Astor worked on behalf of the legislation that equalized the grounds for DIVORCE (1923) and lowered the voting age of women from thirty to twenty-one (1928). She consistently defended the right of married women to work and supported the principle of EQUAL PAY. She warmly welcomed women MPs of all parties who joined her in the Commons, creating a small community for them and encouraging their careers.

Nancy Astor's feminism exhibited a moralistic and socially conservative point-of-view, but it also reflected her own personal experience and her sympathy for human suffering. Her first marriage to an alcoholic and abusive husband gave her a lively appreciation of the plight of many women similarly circumstanced. Her interest in education issues, especially nursery schools, derived much of its energy from her experience as a mother and her love of children. She also continued to be an ardent champion of temperance throughout her life. Temperament, personal experience, and religious conviction—she was an unwavering Christian Scientist—underlay her views, but she lacked either a comprehensive political agenda or a coherent philosophical system.

Nancy Astor's political career manifested major

historical developments in two other respects. Her prominent position as a wealthy political hostess and her support of NEVILLE CHAMBERLAIN's policy of APPEASEMENT led the popular press of the 1930s to attribute to her and her social circle, known as the CLIVEDEN SET, undue influence on the course of British foreign policy. No substantive evidence supports this conspiratorial theory, although it enjoyed wide circulation at the time. Upon the outbreak of war Astor candidly admitted her misjudgment of the situation and became a staunch supporter of CHURCHILL's war CABINET, despite the notorious and long-standing antipathy between these two strong personalities of the Conservative Party.

Astor's close identification with her constituency in Plymouth, which suffered heavily during the BLITZ, and her work to bolster public morale defined the final stage of her public career. Seemingly tireless, her ubiquitous presence and jaunty manner became emblematic of England's continued will to resist attack and carry on the war effort to victory.

Nancy Astor's election to Parliament had great symbolic significance. She also enjoyed real, if limited, success as a parliamentarian. A prominent public figure throughout the 1920s, 1930s and 1940s, her influence had a decisive impact on developing and shaping the possibilities available to women entering the English political system after the FIRST WORLD WAR.

Gail Savage

Bibliography

Fox, James. *Five Sisters: The Langhornes of Virginia*. 2000.
Grigg, John. *Nancy Astor, A Lady Unashamed*. 1980.
Harrison, Brian. "Nancy Astor: Publicist and Communicator" in *Prudent Revolutionaries*. 1987. pp. 73–97.
Sykes, Christopher. *Nancy: The Life of Lady Astor*. 1972.

Atomic Weapons: see Nuclear Weapons

Attlee, Clement Richard (1883–1967)
Clement Attlee was Leader of the LABOUR PARTY between 1935 and 1955, Deputy Prime Minister during the SECOND WORLD WAR in the CHURCHILL coalition, and Prime Minister of the Labour government between 1945 and 1951. He became Earl Attlee in 1955.

Attlee was born on 3 January 1883, in Putney, the seventh child of a successful upper middle-class family. He was educated at Haileybury School between 1896 and 1901 and then proceeded to University College, OXFORD, where, in 1904, he took a degree in history. After spending a desultory period working in a law office, Attlee committed himself to settlement work among the poor in the East End of LONDON at Haileybury House, Stepney, which prompted his conversion to socialism. He joined the INDEPENDENT LABOUR PARTY in 1907, becoming parliamentary candidate for Limehouse. When the FIRST WORLD WAR broke out, Attlee joined the South Lancashire regiment, serving with distinction at GALLIPOLI and in Mesopotamia, where he was wounded, and ending the war with the rank of major.

In 1919, after Labour gained control of the Stepney council, he was co-opted as Mayor, his first political office. He served successfully in this post until 1920, joining GEORGE LANSBURY's Poplar campaign against tax cuts. In the general election of 1922 Attlee won Limehouse for Labour and was immediately given a post in the Parliamentary Labour Party, serving as private secretary to the Leader RAMSAY MACDONALD. He held his seat in the election of December 1923 and, when Labour formed its first government, was rewarded with a junior office, Under Secretary at the War Office. In 1927 MacDonald recommended his appointment to the SIMON Commission on constitutional reform in India. Despite some hesitations, Attlee served enthusiastically, gaining first-hand experience of India and becoming committed to a gradual move towards self-government. His position on the Simon Commission disqualified him for office when MacDonald formed his second government in 1929. But after OSWALD MOSLEY resigned in May 1930, Attlee replaced him as Chancellor of the Duchy of Lancaster. Though less aggressive in this post than Mosley, Attlee did use it to make a study of economic affairs, putting together his own memorandum on economic policy, which was duly ignored by the CABINET. In February 1931 he was shifted to his first administrative position, becoming Postmaster-General.

Attlee was on holiday in August 1931, when the government broke apart. In the election which followed in October, which cut Labour's parliamentary strength to a handful and decimated its leadership, Attlee retained his seat in Limehouse with a majority of only 551. He and STAFFORD CRIPPS, though both junior, were the only former ministers left in the Parliamentary Labour Party and were, therefore, natural choices to be lieutenants of the new parliamentary leader, George Lansbury. Attlee, who became Deputy Leader, worked tirelessly, making an enormous number of speeches both in Parliament and throughout the country. When Lansbury resigned from the leadership in 1935 over foreign policy disagreements, Attlee was made interim Leader for the election and, in November 1935, won the permanent leadership, against challenges from HERBERT MORRISON and Arthur Greenwood. Drawing upon the support of the core parliamentary party of 1931–5, Attlee took 58 votes on the first ballot, to Morrison's 44 and Greenwood's 33. Greenwood then dropped out, and Attlee won the second ballot by 88 to 48.

Attlee's style of leadership differed considerably from that of his predecessors. He was, first of all, ready to follow collective decisions, rather than initiate them. In the revision of domestic and international policy during the 1930s, for instance, Attlee certainly supported the shift in Labour's outlook, generally to the left in domestic policy and towards support for rearmament in foreign policy, but did not really leave his imprint on policy, as HUGH DALTON, ERNEST BEVIN, and Morrison did in different ways. Attlee did help ease Labour towards these developments but was not willing to sacrifice party unity for a clear lead on his part. This was particularly true over the question of non-intervention in the SPANISH CIVIL WAR. By 1937 and 1938, he was, however, taking a very firm line against the National government over Spain and the MUNICH agreement. He effectively articulated Labour's socialism in two works, *The Will and the Way to Socialism* (1935) and *The Labour Party in Perspective* (1937). Throughout this period his bland leadership within the party was questioned by those who envisaged Morrison or Dalton as inevitable successors.

It was the Second World War which strengthened his position within the party. First of all, Labour participation in Churchill's coalition from May 1940 gave him an opportunity to demonstrate his considerable administrative talents. Attlee may not have been a born leader, but he was a born committee man. Serving as Lord Privy Seal, Lord President, Dominions Secretary, and, unofficially at first, and then officially from February 1942, as Deputy Prime Minister, he proved his skills at running a Cabinet. In many ways, it was a dry run for his premiership in 1945. Attlee also showed his abilities at balancing the often volatile personalities of the coalition. His relationship with the party outside of Westminster was less happy, since he faced sustained criticism throughout the war from the Left, particularly from HAROLD LASKI, the most prominent left-wing intellectual. Through the war, Attlee contributed importantly to both the coalition and the party. Within the government he played an important role both in the shape of reconstruction policy, but also on such issues as India and post-war planning for foreign relations.

Attlee's strengthened position became evident during the 1945 election campaign, particularly in the contrasting image of calm he presented against Churchill's more hysterical stance. There was a brief and abortive attempt by Morrison to unsaddle Attlee after the election results, which was largely stymied by Bevin, a pillar of Attlee's strength. The experience of premiership between 1945 and 1951 demonstrated most of Attlee's virtues and some of his weaknesses. His choice of Cabinet was adroit, particularly in placing Bevin at the Foreign Office and ANEURIN BEVAN at the Ministry of Health. He also proved capable at drawing upon younger talent in the parliamentary party, such as HAROLD WILSON and HUGH GAITSKELL. Attlee quickly asserted his particular style of effective and clear Cabinet administration, generally following the drift of opinion within the Cabinet and using that to secure collective decisions.

In foreign affairs he lent considerable support to Bevin, his Foreign Secretary (and received Bevin's support at home). He shared the latter's opposition to the Soviet Union and his desire to bring the Americans towards commitment on the world stage, cemented with the establishment of the North Atlantic Treaty Organization in 1949. Attlee put much emphasis upon building up the United Nations; in this regard, for instance, he supported the use of military sanctions against North Korea in 1950. Attlee also took a controversial decision, with Bevin, in 1946, to build a British atomic weapon. His real triumph on the international stage, and one for which he can almost claim sole credit, was the independence of India, granted on 15 August 1947. Attlee's personal interventions in this sphere hastened the movement towards independence; replacing Wavell as Viceroy with EARL MOUNTBATTEN in 1947, setting a definite date for independence, and keeping the new republic within the Commonwealth, were masterstrokes. The speed with which independence was effected both in India and Burma after the war stands as the greatest testament to Attlee's skill at governing.

On the home front, Attlee was less obviously prominent, delegating responsibility to the relevant ministers. The economic crises of 1947 shook Attlee's position within the government and, in September of that year, he was faced with what amounted to a palace coup engineered by Cripps. Attlee's deceptive strength, and the support of Bevin, helped him foil the most significant challenge to his leadership during the years of government, defusing Cripps' threat with the offer of higher office. The dollar gap crisis, trade union unrest, and arguments over the NATIONALIZATION of the STEEL INDUSTRY during 1949 nonetheless helped to undermine Attlee's position and the reputation of the government.

In March 1950 Attlee called an election, which Labour won narrowly, its majority reduced to only fifteen. The following twenty months put a great strain on Labour and Attlee himself. He was, first of all, faced with a growing split which turned largely on a rivalry between

Attlee's favored successor for the leadership, the left-winger Bevan, and Gaitskell and Morrison on the right of the party. The conflict was precipitated by the Korean war. Though restraining President Truman and General McArthur in the escalation of the war, and, in particular, in the use of nuclear weapons, Attlee supported UN action in Korea and called for rearmament in Britain. According to Gaitskell, the Chancellor, this rearmament program called for charges to be imposed on certain provisions of the NATIONAL HEALTH SERVICE, something Bevan vehemently opposed. Though favoring Bevan, Attlee could not avoid a split within his Cabinet over the issue. Attlee and the party were serious weakened by Bevan's 1951 resignation and by the deaths of Cripps and Bevin. In 1951 Attlee called another election, which the party lost.

Between 1951 and 1955 Attlee remained as Leader of the Opposition, enduring a widening fissure within the Labour Party. Bevan and the "Bevanites" were the main cause of these splits, though the right wing, under Gaitskell and Morrison, were also culpable. Attlee was left in the middle, trying to keep the party together. Though often under attack from the Bevanites, Attlee attempted to protect them from reprisals by the Right and the unions. After four years of squabbling, Labour lost another election in 1955. Attlee wished to stand down from the leadership at this point, but was persuaded, largely by Bevan, to stay on in order to frustrate the leadership aspirations of Morrison. In December of that year, however, convinced that Morrison was no longer a contender for the leadership, Attlee resigned, to be succeeded by Gaitskell. It may be to Attlee's credit, in part, that his resignation was followed by a period of reconciliation between Gaitskell and Bevan. Upon retiring, Attlee was given a peerage and became Earl Attlee. He devoted his declining years to journalism and to the promotion of world government. He lived to see the formation of two Labour governments in the 1960s and died on 8 October 1967.

Attlee's achievement lies not only in the remarkable and record-setting twenty years he spent as leader of a fractious Labour Party, but also as the symbol in many ways of the Labour achievement of the 1940s—one of "sensible" socialism, bloodless, perhaps, but effective, democratic, and constructive. His role in granting India independence would alone guarantee Attlee's historical reputation, but his skills of administration and the quiet force of his personality within two dynamic governments, the coalition of 1940–5 and the Labour government of 1945–51, certainly mark Attlee as one of the most impressive politicians and Prime Ministers of the century.

Stephen Brooke

Bibliography
Attlee, Clement. *As It Happened.* 1954.
Burridge, Trevor. *Clement Attlee.* 1985.
Harris, Kenneth. *Attlee.* 1982.
Pearce, Robert. *Attlee.* 1997.
Tiratsoo, Nick, ed. *The Attlee Years.* 1991

Auden, W(ystan) H(ugh) (1907–1973)

W.H. Auden, one of the most distinguished and influential English poets of the century, was the third son of a cultivated doctor and a highly religious mother. He grew up outside Birmingham, attended the relatively progressive Gresham's School in Norfolk, and in 1925 went up to Christ Church, OXFORD, where he read English (thus incidentally becoming one of the first major poets to study English literature academically). Especially excited by the forms of Anglo-Saxon and Middle English poetry he read at Oxford, Auden rapidly established himself as a writer with a keen interest in the intricate mechanisms of verse. A pamphlet by Auden, *Poems*, appeared in 1928, the same year he received his degree. He spent ten months in Germany writing and reading widely in psychology, and in 1930 he published a full-length verse collection, again austerely titled *Poems*. Although Auden's taut, cryptic free verse poems were mostly about love, after 1930 he started to write a more public form of verse in which he castigated Britain's spiritual and public torpor. *The Orators* (1932) is a fusion of the love poetry and the public-minded stirrings. Despite his early work's obscurity, Auden was hailed as the leader of a group of left-wing poets that included LOUIS MACNEICE, STEPHEN SPENDER, and CECIL DAY LEWIS.

In the autumn of 1932 Auden started teaching at the Downs School in Herefordshire, and his poetry opened out, becoming more accessible. This is the start of the second phase in his career, the years when, drawing on Marx and Freud, he made uncanny connections between middle-class life and the political crisis gripping Europe. In 1935 the avowedly HOMOSEXUAL Auden married Erika Mann, Thomas Mann's daughter and a fugitive from Nazi persecution, so that she could obtain a British passport. The same year he left the Downs and worked briefly in DOCUMENTARY FILM. Then, for six years, Auden lived as a freelance writer. A second collection of lyrics, *Look, Stranger!* (1936), extended his fame, as did his plays. In the later 1930s he and one of his lovers, the novelist CHRISTOPHER ISHERWOOD, produced a string of dramas: *The Dog Beneath the Skin* (1935), *The Ascent of F6* (1936), and *On the Frontier* (1938).

The pre-war years were a period of continuous wandering. In 1936 he traveled with MacNeice to Iceland, a trip that resulted in *Letters from Iceland*

(1937). In January 1937 he went to observe the SPANISH CIVIL WAR. Although Auden was a leftist, he never joined the COMMUNIST PARTY, and he was shunted aside by the party bosses in Spain. In spite of being disturbed by internecine violence in the Republican ranks, immediately after he returned home, he wrote his most famous call to action, "Spain". In early 1938 Auden went abroad again, this time with Isherwood. They traveled to China to write about the Sino-Japanese War, but their *Journey to a War* (1939) became a parable about the difficulties of politically-engaged writing. The problem is developed in the volume's sonnet sequence, "In Time of War", which shows a change in Auden's moral imagination. Christian symbolism comes to the surface.

On their way back to England in mid-1938 Auden and Isherwood stopped off in New York. Returning to America in 1939, on the eve of the Second World War, was another turning point. The next period in Auden's career, initiated by a series of elegies and psychological portraits, is a phase of strenuous existential inwardness. He had fallen in love with a younger American writer, Chester Kallman, and his happiness released a flood of other feelings, including intensifying religious impulses. *Another Time* (1940) contains some of his best work, though, as the title indicates, the poems already seemed to him to belong to a vanished era. The book includes the celebrated "September 1, 1939", a poem that tries to come to terms with the failures of a "low dishonest decade". Auden became a practicing Anglican in 1940. The suggestions of a religious and poetic conversion are heightened in *The Double Man* (1941). "New Year Letter", a long neo–Augustan verse epistle, ends with a petition for aid from a numinous—though still unnamed—power.

Although Auden stayed a Christian for the rest of his life, he never was narrowly dogmatic, at least in his poems. In fact, his faith seemed to increase his intellectual curiosity. By inclination his mind was speculative, synthesizing, and eclectic—he was intensely acquainted with the advanced psychological, religious, and philosophical thought of his day—and Christianity allowed him to order this knowledge into a harmonious world view. But his reputation suffered in Britain during and after the war, partly because he was accused by fanatics of the Left and Right of abandoning his country, and partly because his writing developed in subtle and not immediately assimilable ways.

From 1941 to 1946 he produced three long poems, each of which addresses the situation created by the crisis of the war and by a breach in his relationship with Kallman (who nonetheless remained Auden's companion for the rest of his

life). Two of these long poems, "For the Time Being", a Christmas Oratorio dedicated to the memory of his mother who had died in 1941, and "The Sea and the Mirror", a commentary on *The Tempest* that Auden called his "ars poetica", were published in *For the Time Being* (1944). His final long poem, the ambitious *The Age of Anxiety* (1947), is an interior portrait of the average twentieth-century city dweller, cast in the form of a meeting between four New Yorkers in a bar on All Souls' Night.

In 1945 Auden spent a few months in Germany with the U.S. Air Force's Strategic Bombing Survey, studying the effects of aerial bombardment. Among the ruins of Darmstadt and Munich, his interest in the problems of contemporary civilization took on renewed urgency. The most important post-war works in this respect are the poem "Memorial for the City" (1949) and a series of lectures, *The Enchafèd Flood* (1950).

Like many of his generation, Auden was dissatisfied with the stagnant cultural and political life of Britain—he once compared his decision to emigrate to New York to the odyssey that lead his contemporary Guy Burgess to Moscow. In 1946 he became an American citizen. But he still wandered: from 1948 until 1957 Auden summered on Ischia, an island in the Bay of Naples. This period was inaugurated by the elegiac "In Praise of Limestone" in *Nones* (1951). The Mediterranean breathed a feeling of classical elegance into Auden's work, and renewed his interest in nature and history. This phase culminates in a pair of major sequences from mid-decade: "Bucolics" and "Horae Canonicae" in *The Shield of Achilles* (1955). The final pieces from the period were gathered in *Homage to Clio* (1960).

By this time Auden's verse had become very wry and conversational. His contrasting grand style continued its life, however, by finding an outlet in opera libretti. (He had already worked on an operetta, *Paul Bunyan*, with BENJAMIN BRITTEN in 1941.) He and Kallman wrote the words for Stravinsky's *The Rake's Progress* (1951) and later also collaborated on *Elegy for Young Lovers* (1961) and *The Bassarids* (1966), both by Hans Werner Henze, and *Love's Labours Lost* (1973), by Nicolas Nabokov. From 1956 to 1961 he was Professor of Poetry at Oxford. His late poetry came under the Horatian influence of Herbert and Dryden. His Horatian persona is represented in *About the House* (1965), which contains another major sequence, a poem for every room in his new summer home, outside Vienna, which he and Kallman had established in 1958. Auden's final books, *City Without Walls* (1969), *Epistle to a Godson* (1972), and the posthumous *Thank You, Fog* (1974) each contain important poems: restrained meditations in which extinction is a frequent subject. In 1972, feeling frail, Auden decided to leave New York and spend his winters back at Christ Church. On 28 September 1973 in Vienna he suffered a fatal heart attack.

Since his death, Auden's polemical aura, whether in its early political form or in its later High Church style, has faded. Towering over the mid-century's poetic landscape, he was a protean, didactic, virtuosic writer (he produced many distinguished prose collections), a restless, rigorously intellectual man who mingled a love of clinical exactness with an acute knowledge of human folly. In literary-historical terms his importance partly lies in his work's reaction against modernism's aesthetic of crisis and fragmentation, and in his far-reaching insistence that "The pious fable and the dirty story / Share in the total literary glory."

Nicholas Jenkins

Bibliography

Bloomfield, B. C., and Edward Mendelson. *W.H. Auden: A Bibliography 1924–1969.* 2nd ed. 1972.
Carpenter, Humphrey. *W.H. Auden: A Biography.* 1981.
Fuller, John. *A Reader's Guide to W.H. Auden.* 1970.
Hecht, Anthony. *The Hidden Law: The Poetry of W.H. Auden.* 1993.
Mendelson, Edward. *Early Auden.* 1981.
Osborne, Charles. *W.H. Auden: The Life of a Poet.* 1980.

Automobile Industry

In 1896 the Daimler Motor Company, housed in a converted cotton mill in Coventry, became the first commercial manufacturer of motor vehicles in Britain and began a process which would transform the economic and social contours of British society. The million people employed directly and indirectly in the industry by the late 1930s not only pioneered new forms of collective organization, but revised expectations of consumption levels. The 2 million vehicles in operation by 1938 required extensive public road works, which in turn altered the spatial configuration of British society. The size of the industry made it an obvious candidate for manipulation by the state in its attempts to implement Keynesian demand management schemes after 1945. More recently, the automobile has become the symbol of growing concerns regarding the environment and sustainable development.

In 1896 the industry had barely moved beyond the experimental stage. There was still resistance to the thought of mechanized vehicles propelling along British roads at excessive speeds. The Red Flag Act, which required a person to walk in front of any motorized vehicle, had recently been repealed, and the official speed limit had been raised to fourteen miles an hour. Initial technical breakthroughs came from Europe. Daimler relied on the German patents of Gottlieb Daimler for its early designs. The lack of standardization in the industry required the extensive use of highly skilled male fitters and turners using the techniques of the nineteenth-century craft worker.

By 1910 the technical lead in this industry had shifted towards the Americans. Their invasion of the British market began in earnest in 1911, when Ford commenced manufacturing vehicles in Manchester. Despite pre-1914 production levels of less than 10,000, Ford's Manchester shop implemented many of the labor practices perfected in Detroit. The influence of the trade unions was reduced after an extended STRIKE in 1913. Work tasks were simplified and made suitable for less skilled workers and the moving assembly line was introduced in late 1914. During this same period the hourly wages of Ford workers more than doubled bringing an example of the American high wage and high productivity strategy to Britain. By 1914 Ford was the largest producer of vehicles in Britain.

British producers responded quickly to the American challenge. New grinding and milling machines, developed in the United States, were widely adopted. These machines were less demanding of the skills of the operator but more precise in machining critical components such as pistons and blocks. New entrants such as Rover, Sunbeam, and Morris built on their experience in bicycle production, an industry which had implemented many of the principles of interchangeable mass production by the turn of the century. By 1914 many motor vehicle producers had reduced their dependence on skilled workers and had moved towards mass production.

The initial success of Ford in the pre-1914 era did not translate into American dominance of the British industry after the First World War. While the early British industry is best known for its luxury vehicles, manufactured by firms such as Daimler, Rolls Royce, and Sunbeam, there were a number of British firms producing less expensive cars, including Standard, Belsize, Swift, and Vulcan. But it was two other firms, Morris, who began producing the Morris Cowley in 1915, and Austin, who began producing the Austin 7 in 1922, who were the most successful in challenging Ford. Neither Ford nor General Motors, which began producing Chevrolets in Britain in 1924 and acquired Vauxhall in 1925, were able to match Austin and Morris. Designing cars better suited to British tastes, British roads, and especially British taxes, which penalized the high horsepower and fuel inefficient American designs, and sheltered by the McKenna duties, Austin and Morris captured 60 percent of the British market by 1929.

While British firms adopted much of the mass production system perfected in the United States, there remained important differences. Levels of output were in general lower and there was less emphasis on mechanization and sequential or moving assembly. On paper, skilled labor was still extensively used, but at least outside of body shops, the differences between the American and the British system should not be exaggerated. Firms such as Morris pioneered automated transfer techniques with their block and cylinder lines in the 1920s. These early automated lines failed in large part because of weaknesses in hydraulic clamping technology, but they were clearly precursors to the automated systems perfected in the United States during the Second World War.

The most significant difference between the British and American system of mass production was the continued reliance by British producers on shop floor workers to perform many of the duties which in the United States had been transferred to management. Operating under piece work payment systems, which closely tied earnings to output, British workers retained significant responsibility for preventive maintenance, chasing stock, and ensuring the smooth running of the shops. The pinnacle of this British combination of mechanized production techniques and continued dependence on shop floor workers for decision making came at Standard where the gang system of production was employed. Here, contrary to the overall thrust of Fordism and Scientific Management, workers retained control over staffing levels and task assignment and even played a role in selecting machinery and plant layout. Management dictated model design and output levels. In the early 1950s the gang system allowed Standard to earn above average profits and pay above average wages. In the 1960s and 1970s the shop stewards at Austin played a central role in overcoming sectional disputes and managerial incompetence to keep the plant running so as to ensure high bonus earnings for workers.

The 1950s were boom years for British producers. The European industry had been destroyed, and the American producers were preoccupied with satisfying domestic demand. British firms, encouraged by state rationing policies which rewarded exporters, dominated world export markets and enjoyed healthy profits. The strong position of producers provided openings for the resurrection of trade unionism in the industry which had been all but eliminated in the early 1920s. Motor vehicles had come to represent a major component of British exports and domestic demand and became the focus of government attempts to manage aggregate demand and stimulate regional development.

The period of success was short-lived. British manufacturers continued to follow conservative investment strategies, distributing much of their profits as dividends and expanding output by employing more labor rather than investing in new plant. By the late 1950s American advances in capital-intensive automated methods could no longer be ignored. British firms began the transition to this new system of production and by the early 1970s were facing bankruptcy.

Two problems surfaced in the transition to a more capital-intensive process. The first was the small size of British firms. Compared with the United States, where three companies dominated the industry, the British market had six major firms satisfying a much smaller market. The small British firms had difficulty raising the capital needed to finance the expensive new production systems and, even when the capital was found, had trouble producing at a level of output which justified the new investment. Equally serious, the still birth of managerial capitalism in Britain in the 1920s and the continued dependence on workers to coordinate shop floor activity made management vulnerable to labor slowdowns and stoppages. Unable to afford peace with labor in an increasingly competitive industry, but also unable to manage without the labor input which was a key to the inter-war success of the major producers, the transition to a more capital-intensive and managerial-directed system of production proved to be a disaster. A series of mergers, some under state pressure, were executed, giving birth to major new players such as the British Motor Corporation in 1952 and Leyland Motors in 1961, who in turn merged to form British Leyland Motor Corporation in 1968. Given the independent-minded British producers, they had limited effect in rationalizing product lines or capacity.

On the shop floor a wholesale shift from piece work to measured day work took place. Management was to take greater responsibility for coordinating production, a task at which they proved to be inept. The government was forced to bail out and effectively take control of what little remained of the British industry in the late 1960s and early 1970s, but the dominance of the British producers in their own market had ended. By the end of the 1970s over 50 percent of the British car market was satisfied by imports. The British-based operations of the American giants Ford and General Motors enjoyed new success. BL Ltd, which had absorbed most of what remained of the British producers, was forced to enter into a partnership with Honda to survive. By the early eighties and despite over a billion pounds of cash infusion from the government, BL Ltd. captured less than 20 percent of the British market and was a minor player in Europe. In 1988, in a deal that generated significant criticism from the EC, BL Ltd., now known as the Rover Group

was returned to private control under the ownership of British Aerospace, only to be sold in 1994
to the German automobile manufacturer BMW.

Wayne Lewchuk

Bibliography
Church, Roy, and Herbert Austin. *The British Motor
Car Industry to 1941.* 1979.
Dunnett, Peter. *The Decline of the British Motor Industry.*
1980.
Foreman-Peck, James, Sue Bowden, and Alan McKin-
lay. *The British Motor Industry.* 1994
Lewchuk, Wayne. *American Technology and the British
Vehicle Industry.* 1987.
Whipp, Richard, and Peter Clark. *Innovation and the
Auto Industry: Product, Process, and Work Organiza-
tion.* 1986.
Whisler, Timothy. *The British Motor Industry, 1945–94.*
1999.

Aviation

Britain is historically a world leader in the innovation and construction of both military and
commercial aircraft. Its factories and studios have
produced some of the most famous names in aviation history, and Britain has always been an important centre for civil aviation. In the 1990s Britain built large aircraft with its European partners
as well as smaller airplanes at home.

Early British aircraft were flown by many in-
ventors and builders who went on to form their
own companies. The FIRST WORLD WAR provided the real impetus for aircraft development,
and Britain produced war planes such as the Sop-
with Camel, DeHavilland DH4, and Bristol
Fighter. The wartime technical advances in both
land and seaborne aircraft led to the creation of
the ROYAL AIR FORCE in 1918 out of the previous
Royal Naval Air Service and Royal Flying Corps.

Commercial aviation in Britain began soon
after the war, using surplus war aircraft. A De-
Havilland DH4 operated the first true airline service, between LONDON and Paris, as early as 1919.
A number of small airlines grew up in the early
1920s as air travel became fashionable. Most of
these services were between London (especially
the new Croydon airport, opened in 1920) and
cities in France, Belgium, and the Netherlands.
In order to rationalize commercial aviation, many
small firms were combined into the new Imperial
Airways in 1924. Through Royal Mail contracts
and various other kinds of official support, Imperial Airways became Britain's international standard bearer of the inter-war years. It was most famous for its empire services, which by the 1930s
connected Britain to the Middle East, India,
Australia and New Zealand, and through Egypt
and East Africa to Capetown, South Africa.
Most of the commercial aircraft of the period, including the famous Empire flying boats, were

very cumbersome and slow, and their interiors
often resembled the ocean liners with which they
competed.

For a time airships seemed to provide a possible alternative to land aircraft. The British government experimented with airships in the years
after the First World War, and in 1924 the first
LABOUR government agreed to construct a large
airship in tandem with a similar design built by
Vickers. The two ships, the R100 and R101, were
completed by 1930, but the British airship program ended abruptly with the crash of the R101
in France on its maiden voyage to India, when 48
people, including the Secretary of State for Air,
were killed (1930).

British rearmament during the 1930s led to the
first of the monoplane fighter aircraft, the
Hawker Hurricane of 1938, that was the first true
departure from the biplanes of the 1914–18 era. Its
famous contemporary, the Supermarine Spitfire,
established an international standard for fighter
aircraft that was matched only by the German
Messerschmitt 109. The SECOND WORLD WAR
provided another opportunity for innovation, and
types such as the Mosquito fighter-bomber and
Lancaster heavy bomber were among the finest
and most versatile aircraft of their time. Advances
in aircraft design in the 1940s saw the introduction of the first British jet fighter, the Gloster Me-
teor, in 1944. British commercial flying effectively
ended with the outbreak of war, but in 1939 Imperial Airways was combined with a smaller, private
competitor to form a new national airline, British
Overseas Airways Corporation (BOAC).

BOAC reintroduced commercial services on
the empire routes in 1945, making use of old
converted Lancasters and flying boats that were
not competitive with new American transport
aircraft such as the Douglas DC-6 and Lock-
heed Constellation. The new Labour government also decided to create two new national
airline companies: British European Airways
(BEA) and British South American Airways
(BSAA), both in 1945. Britain led the way in developing new types of aircraft against fierce
competition from the United States. Although
large land aircraft such as the Bristol Brabazon
(late 1940s) were failures, the Bristol Britannia
and the Vickers Viscount (1950s) were successful medium and short range turbine-powered
airliners that enjoyed a speed and comfort advantage over their piston engine competitors. As
national airlines BOAC (which absorbed BSAA
in 1949) and BEA were expected to fly the new
British aircraft. The most innovative of these
was the DeHavilland Comet, which was the first
jet-powered transport aircraft in the world to
enter commercial service, with BOAC in 1952. A
series of fatal crashes led to the grounding of the

type in 1954, when investigations revealed metal fatigue. Although the Comet was totally revamped and re-entered service in 1958, the United States had by then developed jet transports that were able to take the lead in the world airline market.

Until the 1960s Britain was able to produce aircraft of every type in competition with American and European designs. The British government (both Labour and Conservative) was deeply involved with aircraft development and supported most programs. In an attempt to rationalize the aviation industry, the British Aircraft Corporation was created out of a number of smaller private companies in 1960; it later amalgamated with most of the remaining independents to form British Aerospace in the late 1970s.

The British government also supported collaborative projects with France, including the Jaguar fighter-bomber (1970s) and the Concorde supersonic transport. The latter began development in the early 1960s, but due to technical problems and vast cost overruns, did not enter commercial service until 1976. The Concorde is now the prestige aircraft of British Airways, the national company formed out of BOAC and BEA in 1973.

Due to persistent sterling crises and the decay of British industry, major British aircraft projects since the Concorde have tended to be in cooperation with partners. An Anglo-German-Italian consortium produced the Tornado fighter-bomber (1980s), and British Aerospace owns 20 percent of, and produces the wings for, the European Airbus series of airliners. Airbus has become the only major competitor for the powerful American Boeing Company.

The Conservative government of MARGARET THATCHER partially reversed the tradition of government involvement with the airline and aircraft industries by privatizing British Airways in 1987. British Aerospace is a highly diversified military and commercial aviation company and a profitable exporter. British commercial aviation and its supporting aircraft industry have returned to health in the 1990s, and British Airways maintains one of the world's largest route networks. British aviation expertise, alone or in cooperation with other countries, continues a long tradition of technical excellence.

David R. Devereux

Bibliography
Hayward, Keith. *The British Aircraft Industry.* 1989.
Higham, Robin. *Britain's Imperial Air Routes 1918 to 1939.* 1960.
Hudson, Kenneth. *Air Travel: A Social History.* 1972.
Hyde, H. Montgomery. *British Air Policy Between the Wars 1918–1939.* 1976.

Ayckbourn, Alan (1939–)

Alan Ayckbourn, the most prolific comic playwright currently working in Britain, was born in 1939 in Hampstead and educated at Haileybury. His first work in the theatre was as assistant stage manager in 1956, his career continuing in repertory theatre. His first four plays, produced at Scarborough, were written under the name of "Roland Allen". Among his fifty-six plays (as of 2000), the most popular have been *Relatively Speaking* (1967), *How the Other Half Loves* (1969), *Absurd Person Singular* (1972), *The Norman Conquests* (1973), *Bedroom Farce* (1975), *A Chorus of Disapproval* (1984), *A Small Family Business* (1987), and *Man of the Moment* (1990). He has won numerous drama awards, and in 1987 he was named a C.B.E. and was knighted in 1997. He remains based in Scarborough at the Steven Joseph Theatre-in-the-Round, where his plays are first performed before being staged in London, often at the National Theatre.

Ayckbourn satirizes contemporary middle-class society with a blend of astute observation and biting humor similar to that with which NOEL COWARD satirized the upper classes of an earlier generation. Stressing the need for theatre as entertainment, Ayckbourn has deliberately set himself apart from the political drama of the 1970s. Yet Ayckbourn has shown that farce at its most entertaining can also be profound. He describes his work as "black farce"—dark comedies which reveal pathos and tragedy beneath their ebullient surface. Ayckbourn speaks of "exploring attitudes to death, loneliness, etc.—themes not generally dealt with in comedy." His farce revolves around family rituals, dinner parties, birthdays, wedding anniversaries, reunions, and picnics, all of which teeter on the brink of personal and collective catastrophe. The forms of Ayckbourn's farces reveal a taste for experimental and symmetrical patterns: *Absurd Person Singular* has three scenes, featuring three married couples on three consecutive Christmas Eves, in three different kitchens. In *How the Other Half Loves* the separate lives and conversations of a middle-class couple and a lower middle-class couple are superimposed on each other. Thus the plays combine realistic and detailed observation of middle-class life in formally inventive and even surrealistic explorations of time and space. Sir Peter Hall justifies the inclusion of Ayckbourn's work in the National Theatre repertoire as an "accurate reflection of English life . . . [and] a very important social document."

Brian Pearce

Bibliography
Billington, Michael. *Alan Ayckbourn.* 1983.
Page, Malcolm, ed. *File on Ayckbourn.* 1989.
Watson, Ian. *Conversations with Ayckbourn.* 1981.

Ayer, A(lfred) J(ules) (1910–1989)

A highly influential twentieth-century British philosopher, A.J. Ayer was educated at Eton, where he was a King's scholar and at Christ Church, OXFORD, where he studied under the linguistic philosopher Gilbert Ryle.

On graduating, Ayer considered studying at CAMBRIDGE under the Austrian philosopher Ludwig Wittgenstein, but on Ryle's suggestion went instead to Vienna in 1932 to learn about the work of the Vienna Arde. Ayer endorsed the Logical Positivism of the Vienna circle and on his return in 1933 wrote *Language, Truth and Logic*, which was published in 1936. It became the manifesto of Logical Positivism and a classic of twentieth-century philosophy.

Ayer advocated the verification principle as a theory of meaning. This implied that all and only sentences expressing propositions are literally significant. A sentence expresses a proposition if and only if that sentence is (at least in principle) verifiable. All verifiable sentences are verifiable in only one of two ways: a priori (that is, intellectually) or a posteriori (that is, by observation). All and only a priori truths are analytic and all and only a posteriori propositions are synthetic and contingent (informative and although true, not necessarily true). In common with the other Logical Positivists, Ayer thought that the application of the verification principle to the sentences of metaphysics showed that they are meaningless. Hence a putative sentence such as "God exists" is nonsensical because it expresses no genuine proposition.

This in turn is because it is not even in principle verifiable.

In his moral philosophy Ayer was an emotivist. He held that ethical sentences are not literally significant but are expressions and excitements of emotion. It follows that contradictions may not obtain between different ethical positions because a contradiction may only obtain between a proposition and its negation and there are no ethical propositions.

In his philosophy of perception Ayer was a phenomenalist; he held that physical objects may be "reduced" to sense contents. This means that any sentence or set of sentences about physical objects may be translated without loss of meaning into a sentence or set of sentences about actual or possible sense contents.

Ayer was a radically anti-metaphysical empiricist philosopher, in the British empiricist tradition of John Locke, George Berkeley, David Hume, John Stuart Mill, and BERTRAND RUSSELL. He was Grote Professor of the Philosophy of Mind and Logic at the University of London from 1946 and Wykeham Professor of Logic at the University of Oxford from 1959. Ayer was knighted in 1970 and died in 1989.

Stephen Priest

Bibliography
Ayer, A.J. *Language, Truth and Logic*. 1936.
———. *The Central Questions of Philosophy*. 1973.
———. *Part of My Life*. 1977.
———. *More of My Life*. 1984.
Priest, Stephen. *The British Empiricists*. 1990.
Rogers, Ben. *A.J. Ayer: A Life*. 1999.

Bacon, Francis (1909–1992)

Irish-born Francis Bacon's paintings show the violence of life with an uncompromising relish and beauty that is often unsettling. Certainly, when the triptych *Three Studies for Figures at the Base of the Crucifixion* (1944, Tate Gallery, London) was seen at the Lefevre Gallery, London, in a group exhibition, "visitors," as John Russell recounted, "were brought up short by images so unrelievedly awful that the mind shut with a snap at the sight of them." At a time when the dominant stream in British art was a lyrical Neo-Romanticism exemplified by the work of GRAHAM SUTHERLAND, John Craxton, or John Piper, the directness of Bacon's triptych was seen as a violation of those aesthetic values.

Although the exhibition of this painting effectively marked the start of his career at the age of thirty-six, he had been painting since at least 1929. When he left Ireland for London in 1925, he had first worked as an interior designer, making abstract rug designs and tubular steel furniture. He took up painting in oils, after returning from a period in Paris and Berlin, and, rather than attend an art school, received advice from his friend the painter Roy de Maistre. Despite the inclusion in Herbert Read's *Art Now* of one of three versions of a *Crucifixion* (1933), he was largely unsuccessful during this period, and his painting received scant recognition.

It was with other painters and especially with Michael Andrews, LUCIAN FREUD, Frank Auerbach and Leon Kossoff—loosely termed the "School of London"—that Bacon has come to be identified. Even though these artists held no common set of preoccupations, beyond an adherence to the continued value of figurative painting, there was a pattern of friendship, signaled especially in the portraits that Bacon and Freud made of each other.

Portraits assumed a major part of Bacon's *oeuvre*, but rather than aim for a likeness he tried, as with all his paintings, to convey his perceptions of the nature of existence, which hinged on his pessimism about the condition of life. This attempt found a parallel in his general adoption of strategies of accident and chance, while his use of the unprimed side of a canvas, on which he painted directly without any preliminary drawing, along with his often unorthodox handling of paint testify to his attempts at unlocking images that could approximate this primal immediacy. Between 1946 and 1950 he lived mostly in Monte Carlo, where the lure of the Casino unlocked the urge to gamble that is all too apparent in his paintings.

Nevertheless, despite the distortions that Bacon wrought within his self-portraits or his portraits of friends and patrons, there remains a tangible likeness, not so much of that person's features (although the subject is always recognizable), but rather the likeness that derives from a contact between artist and subject, an event, a sense of existence distilled through memory. His paintings, apart from the portraits, rarely refer to actual narrative. The figures in *Three Studies for a Crucifixion* (1962, Solomon R. Guggenheim Museum, New York) are not intended to be read as being Goebbels or Himmler; neither is the swastika armband on one of the figures in *Crucifixion* (1965, Staatsgalerie Moderner Kunst, Munich) to be read literally in terms of Nazism. In this way his recurring motif of the Crucifixion is used as a potent image of the mechanics of inhumanity rather than a comment on Christ's Crucifixion; the paintings of popes are images of regression and alienation. Bacon's symbolism, vague rather than specific, is universal in its attack.

Similarly, although Bacon draws inspiration from a wide range of writers and artists, his attraction to such sources is a result of a recognition of the articulation of tragedy and extreme emotion rather than for the urge directly to transcribe a painting's external compositional and aesthetic values or a writing's sense of plot. The result of his 1957 series of paintings derived from a Van Gogh self-portrait was such as to de-particularize the source, *The Painter on the Road to Tarascon*, so that an image of solitary quest could stand on its own terms.

By the time of his death Bacon was widely held to be one of the world's most important painters. He had received two full-scale retrospectives at the Tate Gallery, London (1962 and 1985), quite apart from retrospective exhibitions at museums all around the world.

Andrew Wilson

Bibliography
Ades, Dawn, and Andrew Forge. *Francis Bacon*. 1985.

Alley, Ronald, and John Rothenstein. *Francis Bacon*. 1964.

Alphen, Ernst van. *Francis Bacon and the Loss of Self*. 1993.

Leiris, Michel. *Francis Bacon, Full Face and in Profile*. 1983.

Russell, John. *Francis Bacon*. rev. ed. 1993.

Sylvester, David. *The Brutality of Fact: Interviews with Francis Bacon 1962–1979*. 3rd ed. 1988.

Trucchi, Lorenza. *Francis Bacon*. 1976.

Baden-Powell, Robert (1857–1941)

Robert Baden-Powell was a British army officer who during the BOER WAR commanded the besieged garrison at Mafeking 1899–1900, holding out for seven months before being relieved. Back in Britain he was celebrated as the "Hero of Mafeking." He later founded the Boy Scouts in 1907 and the Girl Guides in 1910. A baronet from 1922, Baden-Powell became 1st Baron Baden-Powell of Gilwell in 1929.

Baden-Powell's father, who died when he was three, taught geometry at OXFORD; his mother, Henrietta Grace Baden-Powell would have a strong influence on him throughout his life. He attended Charterhouse School and then joined the 13th Hussars, serving in India from 1876 to 1883. He participated in the 1888 Zulu War, the 1895 Ashanti War in West Africa, and the 1896 Matabele uprising in Central Africa. In 1897 Baden-Powell was promoted to colonel, commanding the 5th Dragoon Guards, a cavalry regiment posted in India. From there, he went to South Africa to raise some cavalry and to organize the police forces along the frontier of Cape Colony. Then came Mafeking, which forever became linked with Baden-Powell, standing for British determination and "Pluck." To honor the hero, British composers came up with songs such as "Our Hero B-P", "The Hero of Mafeking Waltz", and "Major-General British Pluck". Baden-Powell capitalized on his fame to help establish and promote his great scheme for character building among the boys of the British Empire, scouting, which he started with a trial camp on Brownsea Island, off Poole, Dorset, in 1907. A year later he published his famous *Scouting for Boys* which went through many editions. He retired from the army in 1910 to devote himself full time to his beloved scouts.

The Boer War hero wanted above all to promote character, patriotism, and manliness through scouting, so that the British Empire could avoid the fate of the Roman Empire. In Britain the fear of the decline and fall of the British Empire gave scouting its initial stimulus. Just as the "Hero of Mafeking" had lifted sagging spirits during the Boer War, now after the war, with Britain's poor performance against an over-matched foe, Edwardian society seemed to be afflicted with pessimism and anxiety about the future. Baden-Powell's scouting seemed to offer to many in the middle class the hope of regeneration. The phenomena of Mafeking and scouting touched very deep nerves in British society, and both came from the complex personality of Baden-Powell. To a society wracked by fears of impending decline through a lack of virility, his program of character development had a potent appeal. Baden-Powell did not marry until he was fifty-five, taking a wife thirty-two years younger than he. Olave, Lady Baden-Powell (1889–1977), worked tirelessly on behalf of the Girl Guides, the female counterpart to the scouts, giving them the kind of strong authority figure that Baden-Powell was for the Boy Scouts. Throughout his life Baden-Powell wrote numerous books including *Quick Training for War* (1914), *My Adventures as a Spy* (1915), *Recovering to Success* (1922), *Life's Snags and How to Meet Them: Talks to Young Men* (1927), his autobiography *Lessons of a Lifetime* (1933), *Adventuring to Manhood* (1936), and *Paddle Your Own Canoe or Tips for Boys* (1939). Baden-Powell spent the last years of his life in Kenya where he died on 8 January 1941.

Richard A. Voeltz

Bibliography

Baden-Powell, Robert. *Scouting for Boys*. 1908.

——. *Lessons of a Lifetime*. 1933.

Hillcourt, William, and Olave, Lady Baden-Powell. *Baden-Powell: The Two Lives of a Hero*. 1964.

Jeal, Tim. *The Boy-Man: The Life of Lord Baden-Powell*. 1990.

Rosenthal, Michael. *The Character Factory: Baden-Powell and the Origins of the Boy Scout Movement*. 1986.

Baldwin, Stanley (1867–1947)

Baldwin was the dominant figure in British politics between the wars. He led the CONSERVATIVE PARTY from 1923 to 1937, establishing an image of moderation which contributed to its electoral success. He was Prime Minister three times, in 1923–4, 1924–9, and 1935–7, and played a crucial role during the National government of 1931–5. He retired from the premiership after the abdication crisis, and was created 1st Earl Baldwin of Bewdley in 1937. Baldwin's desire to promote social harmony and industrial reconciliation has been credited with the "appeasement of Labour" in the 1920s, while he has been accused of laziness, lack of resolution, and responsibility for the APPEASEMENT of the dictators in the 1930s. After Baldwin's death his reputation fell to a low ebb, but in more recent years he has become a symbol of "one-nation" paternalist Conservatism and his domestic achievements have received greater recognition.

Baldwin's political vision was formed by two factors during his early years in semi-rural Worcestershire. The first of these was industrial: the communal spirit between employer and worker in the family business, an ironworks of moderate size and prosperity. This influenced his quest to recreate this mood upon the national stage, and gave substance as well as passion to his oratory. The second element was rural: Baldwin developed an abiding love of the English countryside, and his ability to evoke this traditional heritage made a powerful appeal in a society gravely shaken by the FIRST WORLD WAR and the dislocations of the 1920s. His public image of the pipe-smoking English squire, honest but not clever, was both reassuring and popular. Baldwin was able to make a wide appeal across normal party lines, and was acknowledged to be his party's greatest electoral asset. He established cordial relations with the Labour opposition in the House of Commons, without which the formation or continuation of the National government of 1931 would have been unlikely.

Baldwin entered the House of Commons in 1908 for the seat formerly represented by his father and made little impact during his first ten years. In 1917 he was given junior office by ANDREW BONAR LAW, and in the April 1921 reshuffle following Law's retirement he came into the CABINET in the post of President of the Board of Trade. His rise from this position of relative obscurity to the premiership in the space of two years was both extraordinarily rapid and entirely unexpected. The cause was the revolt from below within the Conservative Party against the continuation of the LLOYD GEORGE coalition in 1922. Baldwin was the only Cabinet minister openly and vigorously to come out against Lloyd George: he expected this action to end his career, when in fact it made it. In October 1922 the coalition was overthrown, and into the wilderness with it went almost all the Conservative leaders. Bonar Law, who at the eleventh hour had consented to lead the revolt, became Prime Minister and had little choice but to make Baldwin Chancellor of the Exchequer. When in May 1923 Bonar Law's ill-health forced a final retirement with the party still divided, Baldwin succeeded him as both Prime Minister and Party Leader. Baldwin's image as the antithesis of anti-democratic reaction and his position in the House of Commons led to his selection instead of the more experienced Foreign Secretary, LORD CURZON.

Baldwin's rejection of the tarnished Lloyd George coalition had established his reputation for honesty. His determination to keep Lloyd George out of power and to thwart any revival of coalitionism was shared by his followers. Anti-

coalitionism was a dominant theme of the next decade, with the former coalitionists constantly suspected of intrigue and disloyalty. Ironically, such fears may have led to Baldwin's greatest blunder and the swift demise of his first premiership, yet also to have saved him from the consequences. In November 1923 he raised the banner of TARIFF REFORM partly to outflank Lloyd George, but slid instead into a general election in which the Conservatives lost their majority. He survived the period of opposition during the resulting 1924 Labour government mainly because no other credible non-coalitionist leader was available. Tariffs were dropped, and the moderate outlook known as the "New Conservatism" promoted in their place. In the election of November 1924 this pragmatism paid off, and Baldwin won a landslide victory.

Baldwin was at the height of his powers during his second premiership of 1924–9. During 1925 he established his authority over the CABINET in the "cruiser crisis" and over the parliamentary party with his appeal for "peace and goodwill in industry" in the Macquisten Bill debate. Baldwin was concerned during this period with the connected problems of educating the new democratic electorate, the challenge from the LABOUR PARTY, industrial strife, and UNEMPLOYMENT. He sought to buy time to resolve the conflict in the COAL INDUSTRY by providing a subsidy in 1925, to the dismay of much of his party. However, when that conflict spread to cause the GENERAL STRIKE in May 1926 his combination of firmness but fairness ensured that public opinion remained mainly on the government side. After the defeat of the General Strike, Baldwin's public reputation stood at its peak. The second half of the government was less successful than the first. The 1927 Trade Disputes Act was not harsh enough for many Conservatives, but aroused great Labour and trade union opposition. The Tory rank and file were alienated by the granting of the vote to women at twenty-one, by agricultural policy, and by failures to take action on protection for iron and STEEL and on HOUSE OF LORDS reform. The government gave much emphasis to social reform, with widows' pensions, Poor Law reform, and finally in 1928 the de-rating policy. In May 1929 Baldwin led a united if rather tired Cabinet into the election on a moderate platform which drew together all these themes. The most famous Conservative slogan from this campaign, "Safety First", was thereafter held to sum up Baldwin's approach to politics and all its supposed defects.

The Conservative defeat in 1929 led to the most serious crisis of Baldwin's career. There was great pressure from below to abandon the moderate pledges which had failed to secure victory, especially over tariff reform. Baldwin resisted this because he was aware that the Conservatives had to win back the industrial seats in the Midlands and north if they were to return to power, but this pragmatic approach led to great tensions in the party. During 1929 and 1930 his position came under sustained pressure from the Conservative strongholds, mainly in the south, where resentment was encouraged and vocalized by the "Empire Crusade" campaign waged against Baldwin by the press magnates Lords BEAVERBROOK and Rothermere. The crisis reached its peak in the summer of 1930, but the steam was taken out of the critics when Baldwin made a substantial move towards a "free hand" policy on protection in October. The press lords continued their attacks with little effect until their final defeat in the St. George's by-election in March 1931.

In the crisis of August 1931 Baldwin agreed to serve under RAMSAY MACDONALD in a temporary emergency cross-party team to save the pound, and then found himself locked into a permanent coalition. Baldwin had not sought this, but came to find the arrangement politically and personally agreeable. As leader of by far the biggest party in the National government, he was in many ways its most important figure without having the formal responsibility of the premiership. Baldwin concentrated his energies upon two areas. The first was keeping the coalition together, and especially coordinating its parliamentary work; the second was India. Between 1929 and 1935 Baldwin provoked further rebellions from the Conservative right wing, led this time by CHURCHILL, over his determination to follow the bipartisan line on India foreshadowed by the Irwin Declaration of 1929. The 1935 Government of India Act, placed on the statute book after a long struggle, though directly the work of SIR SAMUEL HOARE, is in many ways Baldwin's most concrete personal achievement.

In June 1935 he changed positions with Mac-Donald and became Prime Minister for the third time, winning a comfortable victory in the November 1935 election. The remainder of Baldwin's premiership was dominated by two crises: problems abroad with the Fascist dictators and problems at home with the new monarch. The hostile public reaction to the Hoare-Laval Pact in December 1935 gravely shook the government and the ditching of Hoare as Foreign Secretary reflected badly on Baldwin. In early 1936 he suffered a form of nervous breakdown, and the government drifted uneasily for several months. Towards the end of 1936 Baldwin recovered to handle the abdication crisis with tact and skill, to great public approval. He decided to retire at the coronation of GEORGE VI in May 1937, handing over to his heir-apparent for many years, NEVILLE CHAMBERLAIN.

Only one area of politics consistently aroused Baldwin's interest: threats to the general political stability enshrined in the parliamentary constitution. All his major battles were fought in this area, from the cynicism and corruption of the Lloyd George coalition, through the General Strike, the pretensions of the press barons, and the future of India to the abdication crisis. Once he shifted political conflict to this ground he was unbeatable, a fact found to their cost by apparently more able politicians such as Lloyd George and Churchill who constantly under-estimated his reserves of strength.

Stuart Ball

Bibliography

Baldwin, Stanley. *On England, and Other Addresses.* 1926.

Ball, Stuart. *Baldwin and the Conservative Party: The Crisis of 1929–1931.* 1988.

Campbell, John. "Stanley Baldwin" in John P. Mackintosh, ed. *British Prime Ministers in the Twentieth Century,* vol 1. 1977. pp. 188–218.

Middlemas, Keith, and John Barnes. *Baldwin.* 1969.

Williamson, Philip. *Stanley Baldwin.* 1999.

Balfour, Arthur James (1848–1930)

One of Britain's wealthiest and most powerful politicians, Balfour led the CONSERVATIVES in the House of Commons while his uncle, Lord Salisbury, served as Prime Minister. When Balfour held that position from 1902 to 1905, he enjoyed no great popularity in the aftermath of war in South Africa, demonstrating more initiative in foreign and imperial affairs than in domestic matters. Equivocating on TARIFF REFORM, Balfour tried to bridge deep divisions within his party until he resigned as Tory leader in 1911, later serving as a minister in coalition and Conservative CABINETS. As the Foreign Secretary from 1916 to 1919, he promoted closer ties with the United States and greater cooperation among the white dominions.

At the age of eight, when his father died, Balfour inherited a Scottish estate and fortune that his grandfather had amassed as a contractor in India. Balfour's mother, a sister of the Marquess of Salisbury, who served as Prime Minister intermittently from 1885 to 1902, inculcated religious devotion and bookish pursuits in her near-sighted, frail son. Balfour's years at Eton and Trinity College, CAMBRIDGE had less impact on him than the brilliant family circle of brothers, sisters, and their spouses, which broadened Balfour's philosophical and scientific interests. Unwavering in his religious and political beliefs, the skeptical Balfour had a low opinion of humanity's past and had little expectation that humans could do much better in the future.

Elected to the House of Commons in 1876, Balfour served his political apprenticeship under his uncle, Lord Salisbury, who first made Balfour his Parliamentary Private Secretary, then Minister in turn for Local Government, Scotland, and Ireland. Balfour used the carrot and the stick in Ireland, which gained him praise from Conservatives and Unionists, but the title "Bloody Balfour" from the Irish and their Liberal supporters. He led the House of Commons, serving as First Lord of the Treasury under his uncle in the 1890s and during the BOER WAR. Never an impressive orator, Balfour was more effective in parliamentary debate and in the Cabinet room.

When Salisbury resigned the premiership, Balfour moved into 10 Downing Street in July 1902. Balfour's party was weakened in the aftermath of the Boer War by LORD MILNER's employment of Chinese "coolie" labor in South Africa, by the conflict between Lords CURZON and KITCHENER in India, and especially because prices increased more rapidly than wages, all of which eclipsed Balfour's success in piloting his Education and Licensing Bills through Parliament. In foreign affairs, Balfour and his Foreign Secretary, Lord Lansdowne, negotiated an agreement with France and a treaty with Japan, both of which were designed to contain Russian expansionism. Balfour also established the COMMITTEE OF IMPERIAL DEFENCE, which brought together civilian, military, and bi-partisan figures to determine priorities. When the Unionist Joseph Chamberlain pressed for a scheme of tariff reform favoring the British Empire over other protectionist powers, Balfour tried to keep the free traders in the party, conscious that Tory protectionism had earlier been a liability and that Sir Robert Peel's free trade policy had split the Conservative Party. Balfour's efforts failed, and the Tories were badly defeated early in 1906. He even lost his own parliamentary seat in East Manchester but was soon returned for the safe seat of the City of London. Until 1911, when Balfour stepped down as Conservative leader, he had increasing difficulty in holding his party together in opposition to Liberal legislation, particularly their budget of 1909, advocacy of Home Rule for Ireland, and reform of the HOUSE OF LORDS. To "die hard" Conservatives, Balfour appeared weak, while others found him politically ineffectual.

The outbreak of war in 1914 gave Balfour a new political lease on life, when he was asked by H.H. ASQUITH, the Liberal Prime Minister, to serve on a war policy committee that had evolved from the Committee of Imperial Defence. In 1915 Balfour joined the Asquith coalition, taking charge of the Admiralty and reluctantly presiding over British evacuation from the GALLIPOLI peninsula. At the end of 1916 Balfour joined the coalition formed by DAVID LLOYD GEORGE, this time as Foreign Secretary. After the United States entered the war in the spring of 1917, Balfour visited Washington and promoted closer ANGLO-AMERICAN RELATIONS. Later that year he sent a public letter to Lord Rothschild, on behalf of the Zionists, affirming British support of a Jewish homeland in PALESTINE.

In the post-war years, Balfour assumed the mantle of "elder statesman" and left his mark on foreign and imperial affairs. He generally deferred to Lloyd George on Germany, Russia, the Middle East and Ireland, but played a bigger role in the settlement with Austria. Balfour also led the British delegation to the Washington Naval Conference in 1921. When Lloyd George's second coalition fell in 1922, Balfour was out of office until he joined the ministry of STANLEY BALDWIN. In 1926 he chaired a committee on inter-imperial relations, recognizing the equality of all British Dominions and paving the way for the Statute of Westminster of 1931, a year after his death.

Roger Adelson

Bibliography

Egremont, Max. *Balfour: A Life of Arthur James Balfour.* 1980.

Mackay, Ruddock F. *Balfour, Intellectual Statesman.* 1985.

Ramsden, John. *A History of the Conservative Party. vol 3: The Age of Balfour and Baldwin, 1902–1940.* 1978.

Young, Kenneth. *Arthur James Balfour.* 1963.

Zebel, Sydney H. *Balfour: A Political Biography.* 1973.

Ballet

A colorful hybrid of foreign influences and native talent, classical ballet in Britain traces its ancestry to the elaborate masques staged at the Tudor and Stuart courts and the riotous Harlequin pantomines of the eighteenth century. The academic classicism of France and Italy arrived in Britain during the nineteenth century, when the most acclaimed European dancers regularly performed at Her Majesty's Theatre, London. The greatest ballerinas of the Romantic era made their only joint appearance there, in the legendary *Pas de Quatre* (1845) Jules Perrot created for them.

At the beginning of the twentieth century British ballet was the sparkling centerpiece of the music-hall variety show and an enormous commercial draw at the Alhambra and the Empire theatres. The latter usually staged two extravagant new productions annually and ran them for six months, often with the delicate Danish ballerina, Adeline Genée, in the starring role. So many people wanted to see Genée dance that the Empire offered daily matinees for several months in 1907 to satisfy the demand for tickets.

Before the First World War England had its first glimpse of Russian ballet when Anna Pavlova and Mikhail Mordkin brought a small troupe to the Palace and Tamara Karsavina performed at the Coliseum. With the arrival of Serge Diaghilev's exotic Ballets Russes, ballet exchanged mere prettiness for primitive, dramatic, and sometimes shocking effects, and artists like Karsavina and Vaslav Nijinsky infused steps, mime, and characterization with passionate conviction.

Diaghilev's troupe also nurtured the founders of Britain's own ballet companies: NINETTE DE VALOIS (born Edris Stannus), Alicia Markova (Born Alicia Marks), Anton Dolin (born Patrick Healey-Kay) and Marie Rambert (born Cyvia Rambam) all danced for him, although Rambert was employed primarily to help Nijinsky, as choreographer, untangle the rhythms of Stravinsky's *Rite of Spring*. Inspired by the daring choreography and mesmeric performers of the Ballets Russes, and imagining a time when native dancers would make their own artistic impact, Rambert opened a ballet school in 1920, and de Valois did the same in 1926.

The Cecchetti Society was founded in 1921 to perpetuate the methods of the great teacher Enrico Cecchetti, and the Association of Teachers of Operatic Dancing (the Royal Academy of Dancing from 1936) was formed in 1920. Although the Ballets Russes continued to appear, performing opportunities for most British dancers during the 1920s lay in the commercial theatre, in pantomime or in revues, where two of Diaghilev's choreographers, Leonide Massine and George Balanchine, also found work before and after his death in 1929.

Part of a revue called "Riverside Nights," *The Tragedy of Fashion* (1926) marked the choreographic debut of FREDERICK ASHTON, whose works eventually formed the bedrock of the native British repertory. In 1930 the first public performances of Rambert's students, as the Ballet Club, marked the first steps of a native company. Led in its early seasons by Karsavina, the Ballet Club gave Sunday evening performances in the school's premises in Notting Hill. Markova succeeded Karsavina in 1931, and by 1934 the company had moved to the tiny Mercury Theatre and added weekday performances to the schedule.

Two extraordinary English choreographers created the remarkable repertory. Until 1934 Ashton provided a stream of short works stamped with the lyricism, eloquent musicality and sunny humor that would characterize his mature works and define the British style of dancing. Having made his debut with a comic piece, *Cross Garter'd* (1931), Antony Tudor discovered a unique and powerfully dramatic vocabulary from which he shaped his masterpieces, *Jardin aux Lilas* (1936) and *Dark Elegies* (1937).

Launched the same year as the Ballet Club, the Camargo Society was founded to further the interests of English ballet and fill the void left for both dancers and public when Diaghilev's company disbanded. Although it survived only until 1933 and produced only sixteen new ballets, it supplied another important breeding ground for British choreographers. Ashton made his witty *Façade* (1931), which is still widely danced today, and, having left Diaghilev to choreograph in Cambridge, Dublin, and London, de Valois created the starkly dramatic *Job* (1931).

She also made one piece, *Bar aux Folies Bergère* (1934) for the Ballet Club, but choreography was not her primary goal. In 1928 the producer LILIAN BAYLIS hired her to arrange the dances for the operas and plays at the Old Vic. With Baylis' support, in 1931 de Valois moved her school into the Sadler's Wells Theatre as the nucleus of a new company devoted exclusively to ballet. Called the Vic-Wells Ballet when it arrived, the miniscule troupe initially danced complete evenings of ballet only every two weeks. With Ashton as her resident choreographer from 1935 and the young MARGOT FONTEYN as her ballerina after Markova departed the same year, de Valois built a company of international stature at Sadler's Wells. It drew its strength from traditional productions of the nineteenth-century classics—*The Sleeping Beauty, Swan Lake,* and *Giselle*—and from the innovative choreography of Ashton, de Valois herself—*The Rake's Progress* (1935) and *Checkmate* (1937)—and, later, John Cranko and KENNETH MACMILLAN.

De Valois, Baylis, and Rambert created British ballet from a combination of vision, courage and tenacity. Until the Second World War, their fledgling efforts had to compete for an audience with several glamorous Russian companies, which visited LONDON regularly. But no foreign companies appeared in England between 1939 and 1946, and British ballet flourished as a result.

Ballet Rambert performed in factories and office cafeterias around the country and, from 1940–1, at the Arts Theatre in London, offering programs of "Lunch Ballet," "Tea Ballet," and "Sherry Ballet," along with the appropriate beverage. Tudor, who had formed the London Ballet in 1938, left England when the war broke out to join Ballet Theatre in America, where he spent the rest of his life, and his company merged with the Arts Theatre Ballet and shared performances with Ballet Rambert. Tudor's deliciously sardonic *Gala Performance* (1938) entered Rambert's repertory, as did new works by Andrée Howard and Frank Staff.

The Sadler's Wells Ballet, as the Vic-Wells was named in 1940, traveled outside the capital to civilian and military theatres and briefly visited Holland. It found a new home in the New Theatre, London, and a new, sometimes controversial choreographer in its *premier danseur* Robert

Helpmann, who created *Hamlet* (1942) and *Miracle in the Gorbals* (1944) after Ashton joined the ROYAL AIR FORCE.

Although CONSCRIPTION depleted the onstage forces and money was scarce, several new companies—International Ballet and the Anglo-Polish Ballet among them—emerged during the SECOND WORLD WAR and toured extensively for some time. Ballet Rambert closed down for 18 months (1941–3), but when it reappeared, it was supported for the first time by government funds. Under the direction of the economist JOHN MAYNARD KEYNES, the COUNCIL FOR THE ENCOURAGEMENT OF MUSIC AND THE ARTS (CEMA) financed and managed Rambert for four years (1943–7), during which time the company staged an acclaimed production of *Giselle* starring its compelling ballerina, Sally Gilmour.

Thanks also to the assistance of CEMA (the ARTS COUNCIL OF GREAT BRITAIN from 1945), de Valois' Sadler's Wells Ballet was invited to make the Royal Opera House its permanent home. Reopening the theatre in 1946, with Fonteyn in a splendid new production of *The Sleeping Beauty*, sealed the company's future at Covent Garden. Later that year, a second branch of the company, called Sadler's Wells Opera (later Theatre) Ballet, was established to foster new choreographic and performing talent for Covent Garden. In only fifteen years, de Valois had realized her dream of creating a company to represent the nation both at home and abroad.

Artistic triumph marked the post-war years. At Covent Garden, Ashton created a timeless masterpiece, *Symphonic Variations* (1946), and Massine appeared as a guest artist. Resident ballerina Moira Shearer starred in MICHAEL POWELL's film, *The Red Shoes* (1948), which introduced ballet to a vast new audience. And on its first transatlantic tour (1949), the company captivated the American public and press with its noble dancing and sumptuous full-evening productions of *Sleeping Beauty* and *Swan Lake,* then only known there in abbreviated versions.

Meanwhile, another important company was finding its feet in England. When Markova left the Vic-Wells Ballet, she and Anton Dolin organized their own company, the Markova-Dolin Ballet (1935–8). Having spent the war years dancing with Ballet Theatre in America, they returned to England to guest at Covent Garden in 1948 and founded a second small troupe with which they toured the country.

Encouraged by its touring success and backed by an experienced impresario, Julian Braunsweg, in 1950 the company adopted the name Festival Ballet (anticipating the FESTIVAL OF BRITAIN the following year) and gave its first London season. Markova left in 1952, but the Festival Ballet had quickly found an audience by offering international stars and an eclectic repertory at popular prices.

The company's artistic director until 1960, Dolin chose to concentrate on nineteenth-century classics—*The Nutcracker,* his production of *Giselle,* and eventually *Swan Lake*—and on the Diaghilev repertory; during the 1950s, Nicholas Beriosoff revived many of Fokine's works, and Massine revived his own in the 1970s. Led by an English *danseur,* John Gilpin, the principal artists hailed from Russia, Denmark, France, and Hungary.

Over the years the repertory grew rapidly with contributions by Balanchine, Harald Lander, Jack Carter, and Ronald Hynd, and new productions of the well-loved classics from Russia and Denmark. Renamed English National Ballet in 1989, the company still pursues Dolin's original policy, mixing choreographic novelty with classics and casting foreign dancers alongside British ones.

In 1956 the two Sadler's Wells companies were incorporated by royal charter as the Royal Ballet. They maintained their separate identities, however, and from the smaller company came the first memorable works of MacMillan, who changed the face of British ballet by reshaping the classical vocabulary in order to explore modern and psychological subjects.

Just as de Valois' enterprise took a firmer hold on the capital, a small regional ballet company was taking shape, and in 1957 Western Theatre Ballet gave its debut performance in Bristol. Directed by Elizabeth West, this group was interested, like MacMillan, in applying classical technique to contemporary themes. With the Arts Council's help, it toured Europe as well as Britain, often performing the topical ballets of co-director Peter Darrell, who took charge after West's untimely death (1962).

Having first visited Scotland in 1960, the company moved its home to Glasgow in 1969, took the name Scottish Theatre Ballet, and began building a community following for traditional dance and theatrical daring. By 1974, when the troupe was renamed the Scottish Ballet, it had developed an international reputation and was generally accepted as the national ballet of Scotland.

The spotlights of the 1960s focused on Rudolf Nureyev's matchless partnership with Margot Fonteyn and on the Royal Ballet's young stars: Antoinette Sibley, Anthony Dowell, and Lynn Seymour. Ballet Rambert made headlines in 1966 by abandoning classical ballet entirely and transforming itself into a contemporary company. Directed today by choreographer Richard Alston and called simply the Rambert Dance Company, it is the only British company that performs the seminal modern works of Merce Cunningham.

The second regional company to take root was the Northern Dance Theatre, which was founded in Manchester in 1969 by Laverne Meyer. Originally a lively blend of small-scale classical and modern works, the repertory now leans heavily on full-evening narrative ballets with a strong, theatrical slant and a broad popular appeal. Called Northern Ballet Theatre since 1977 and now operating out of Halifax, it was until recently the only classical English company based outside London.

But in 1990 the smaller Royal Ballet company, then known as the Sadler's Wells Royal Ballet, transferred its home base to Birmingham and changed its title to the Birmingham Royal Ballet. With that move, nearly sixty years after its founding, the national company represented the provinces and the capital equally at last, as de Valois always hoped it would.

Barbara Newman

Bibliography

Bland, Alexander. *The Royal Ballet: The First Fifty Years.* 1981.

Clarke, Mary. *Dancers of Mercury: The Story of Ballet Rambert.* 1962.

———. *The Sadler's Wells Ballet: A History and an Appreciation.* 1955.

Vaughan, Mary and David, eds. *The Encyclopedia of Dance and Ballet.* 1977.

White, Joan W., ed. *Twentieth-Century Dance in Britain.* 1985.

Battle of Britain and Blitz

The phase of the SECOND WORLD WAR known as the Blitz, from September 1940 to May 1941, followed directly upon the Battle of Britain beginning in July 1940. The Battle of Britain was a prolonged contest between the German Air Force (the Luftwaffe) and Fighter Command of the ROYAL AIR FORCE (RAF). In this battle, Fighter Command frustrated Germany's plans for a sea-borne invasion of England, a projected operation called Sea Lion by the Germans. The Blitz (German for lightning) refers to Germany's bombing of Britain, especially by night, from the climax of the Battle of Britain until the Luftwaffe had to turn its attention primarily to the Russian front in May 1941. The Blitz failed to achieve the destruction of Britain's economy or the collapse of public morale.

Hitler expected Britain to negotiate once her ARMY had been driven from the Continent and France had surrendered in June 1940. CHURCHILL's new government, however, vowed to fight on despite the weakness of Britain's post-evacuation army. Hitler therefore had to think of ways other than the existing submarine blockade to force Britain out of the War. A Luftwaffe bombing campaign might by itself, Hitler hoped,

cause the British to give up. If not, the German army would have to cross the English Channel for an invasion of Britain. An immediate crossing in June or July was impractical, but Sea Lion might be possible by September. Although the British army would not present much of an obstacle to such an invasion, Hitler had to worry about Britain's awesomely superior navy. Still, if the Luftwaffe could gain control of the Channel skies, then perhaps it could fend off the British fleet sufficiently for a crossing to be made. There was, however, a time limit on Sea Lion: the Luftwaffe had to win its battle with the RAF before autumnal gales would render the Channel impassable to landing craft, and Hitler had already wasted weeks of summer weather while hoping for a negotiated peace, his mind on his projected racial and ideological crusade against the Soviet Union.

Preliminary Luftwaffe operations against Channel shipping and naval forces began in July and continued into August with only partial success. ROYAL NAVY destroyers had to give up their base in Dover but could still dominate the Channel from other ports. Without a clear-cut victory over the Royal Navy, the Luftwaffe nevertheless shifted its attack inland against Fighter Command's bases and other facilities on 13 August.

The Luftwaffe seriously outnumbered Fighter Command, but the British enjoyed certain compensatory advantages. Hitler's bombers were extremely vulnerable to the RAF's Hurricane and Spitfire fighters; therefore the contest boiled down to a struggle between Fighter Command's Hurricanes and Spitfires and the Luftwaffe's Messerschmitt (BF) 109—the 109 being the only fighter plane the Germans had that could protect their bombers. The 109 was better than the Hurricane and at least as good as the Spitfire, but its operations were hampered by a number of factors. Its limited fuel capacity prevented lengthy patrols over England—Germany had neglected drop-tank technology—and the 109s' pilots had to remain at least relatively close to the bombers they were supposed to protect, thereby restricting tactical flexibility. Furthermore, since most of the fighting took place over England, British pilots who had to bail out could rejoin their units, while Germans who had to jump became prisoners of war.

Most important, the British had a well-developed RADAR and battle control system, enabling Air Chief Marshal Sir Hugh Dowding to utilize his limited resources to the fullest. The Germans did not entirely understand the British system and its importance and consequently did not make much of an effort to destroy it. This is usually regarded as a disastrous mistake on the part of Hermann Goering, Commander-in-Chief of the Luftwaffe; yet radar was hard to knock out in those days, and the British had several back-up systems—mobile radar stations and their CODE-BREAKING system, nick-named ULTRA, for example—so a prolonged anti-radar campaign might simply have wasted German resources and precious time before autumn.

Despite Britain's advantages, and despite the bravery of Dowding's pilots, the Germans appeared to be winning as of early September. True, German losses were very high, but Fighter Command was running out of experienced and rested pilots. On 7 September, however, Germany shifted her attacks primarily to LONDON, thereby giving Fighter Command's bases a much-needed breather. Goering did this for two reasons. For one thing, his planes had accidentally bombed civilian areas of London in August, provoking British retaliatory raids on Berlin, much to Hitler's and Goering's embarrassment; hence the revenge bombing of London beginning on 7 September. In addition, the Luftwaffe was convinced that Dowding was saving his limited resources by refusing all-out battle—which was true, although Fighter Command had not suffered as much as the Germans imagined; in any case, the Luftwaffe thought it could force Fighter Command into a final and fatal battle of attrition by attacking something Dowding would have to defend to the death, namely London. Yet still Dowding would not take the bait.

Seeing Fighter Command's relative inactivity as evidence of its debilitation, Goering expected total victory when he launched a gigantic raid on 15 September. To their unpleasant surprise, the Germans found Fighter Command full of fight, and Luftwaffe losses correspondingly catastrophic; at this moment of supreme crisis, Dowding had at last thrown in all that he could of his carefully husbanded forces. Hitler, dismayed by Fighter Command's apparent new lease on life, and increasingly worried about the weather, postponed and eventually cancelled Sea Lion.

Although speeches, books, and movies have ever since emphasized Britain's extreme peril in the summer of 1940, later reflection suggests that Sea Lion never had much of a chance. Even if the Luftwaffe had kept most after Fighter Command's bases, and even if that had led to Fighter Command's defeat, Dowding could and would have retreated beyond the Me 109's range and saved his remaining assets for invasion day. The RAF's Bomber Command could have destroyed much of Sea Lion's shipping in its German-held ports at night—and in fact did so even though Sea Lion was never launched. Most important, the Royal Navy could have operated in the Channel at night, safe from the Luftwaffe, tearing up Sea Lion's ports and convoys during the weeks it would have taken the German army to stage an adequate invasion, given the growing strength of Britain's army as of September. Thus, although Sea Lion was not merely a bluff, as some have thought, it seems unlikely that the Luftwaffe could ever have guaranteed its success even if it had reduced Fighter Command to a remnant; it is therefore unlikely that Hitler would ever have launched his projected invasion.

In this context, the Blitz must be seen as a poor substitute for Sea Lion. With invasion no longer possible after 15 September, the bombing of Britain lost most of its rationale. All that remained was the hope of crippling Britain's economy and/or terrorizing the British people into surrender. In retrospect, the Germans had little chance of achieving either objective. Air power enthusiasts before the Second World War had exaggerated the impact of bombing on both factories and morale. Moreover, the Luftwaffe's bombers did not carry bomb loads sufficient for an effective strategic bombing program. Besides, once Sea Lion was cancelled, the Germans could no longer justify the extreme bomber losses they had experienced in daylight raids during the Battle of Britain; therefore most of the Blitz was carried out at night, making it impossible to hit factories with any degree of accuracy.

Consequently, terror was the sole remaining purpose of the Blitz. Yet the British public did not panic and did not demand an end to the war. Instead, British civilians crowded in their underground and other bomb shelters at night and dug their cities out of the rubble by day, adding the story of their own bravery to that of Fighter Command, inspiring the admiration of the American public, helping to prepare Americans psychologically for their entry into the war on Britain's side. Frustrated, Hitler turned against Russia in June 1941, leaving an undefeated Britain in his rear.

Karl G. Larew

Bibliography
Collier, Basil. *The Battle of Britain*. 1962.
Fitzgibbon, Constantine. *The Blitz*. 1970.
Hough, Richard, and Denis Richards. *The Battle of Britain*. 1989.
Parkinson, Roger. *Dawn on Our Darkness: the Summer of 1940*. 1977.
Sansom, William. *The Blitz: Westminster at War*. 1947.

Baylis, Lilian Mary (1874–1937)

A unique figure in the British theatre, Lilian Baylis served as manager of the Old Vic for forty years, the restorer of the Sadler's Wells, and the woman responsible for bringing Shakespeare, OPERA, and later BALLET to ordinary people in LONDON at affordable prices. The eldest of ten children born to performing musicians, she received erratic and incomplete schooling, but solid musical training. She performed as a child prodigy on the violin, mandolin, and banjo in recitals and with the St. James' Ladies Orchestra. At seventeen she accompanied her parents to South Africa, where the Baylis family toured as a concert party known as "The Gypsy Revellers", Lilian supplementing the often precarious family income by giving music lessons. After being hospitalized in Johannesburg for a kidney operation, she returned to England to convalesce in 1897 and began to help her aunt Emma Cons to manage the Old Vic.

Seventeen years earlier Emma Cons (1837–1912), a protegé of Octavia Hill, had opened the Royal Victoria Coffee and Music Hall to provide uplifting, teetotal entertainment for the respectable poor at the former Royal Coburg, known for drunken rowdyism in an already blighted neighborhood. During its early years theatre offerings included lectures and concerts of opera excerpts, while part of the building was reserved for working men's ADULT EDUCATION in what became known as Morley College. Lilian Baylis became manager of the Old Vic in 1898, working in her aunt's shadow until 1912, when she assumed sole control over its operations.

After the death of Emma Cons, the Old Vic obtained a theatre license, which enabled it finally to present full-length operas and plays, although for some years it continued to intersperse lectures and temperance meetings in the weekly billings. Relying on wealthy benefactors and what she believed was her personal ability to intercede with God, the deeply religious, High Anglican Baylis survived recurrent financial crises to establish the foundations of a people's theatre with a loyal community following. Although she lacked commercial theatrical experience or private income, she managed by improvisation, frugality, and her domineering personality to keep the Old Vic open, however difficult it proved to combine artistry and philanthropy. Her tactlessness, explosive temper, and legendary stinginess were coupled with unremitting hard work and steely determination. Despite the minimal salaries, her initial reluctance to employ stars, and technically impoverished productions, often using borrowed costumes, her single-mindedness attracted many leading actors of their generation, who welcomed the opportunity to perform Shakespeare, under directors like Robert Atkins and Tyrone Guthrie, free of the commercial constraints of the West End. The Old Vic in the Baylis years produced all of Shakespeare's plays plus a range of other dramatic classics including Ibsen and Chekhov with, among others, Sybil Thorndike, Lewis Casson, Edith Evans, John Gielgud, Charles Laughton, and LAURENCE OLIVIER, acquiring an unmatched reputation for artistic integrity that widened its audience base.

In 1926 Baylis engaged NINETTE DE VALOIS to teach movement to Old Vic drama students, to choreograph Shakespeare productions, and eventually to establish a ballet school and company at the derelict Sadler's Wells, whose freehold Baylis acquired in 1925 with a grant from the Carnegie United Kingdom Trust. The slow progress of renovations meant that it was not until 1931 that the theatre re-opened as a North London version Old Vic. At first drama, opera, and ballet alternated at both theatres, but that proved impractical, and in 1936 the Sadler's Wells was reserved for opera and the so-called Vic-Wells Ballet, launched when the theatre opened. In their own building the ballet company and the Sadler's Wells Opera flourished, the latter performing in English many operas outside the restricted repertory hitherto attempted at the Old Vic.

In 1924 Lilian Baylis received an honorary MA at Oxford, and in 1929 she was named a Companion of Honour. She died suddenly of a heart attack at the age of sixty-three, having made a singular contribution to the arts in Britain and paved the way for what would eventually become the National Theatre, the Royal Ballet, and the English National Opera. A portrait of Baylis in the academic robes that became her trademark hangs prominently at the Coliseum in London.

Fred M. Leventhal

Bibliography

Dent, E.J. *A Theatre for Everybody: The Story of the Old Vic and Sadler's Wells.* 1945.

Findlater, Richard. *Lilian Baylis: The Lady of the Old Vic.* 1975.

Williams, Harcourt, ed. *Vic-Wells: The Work of Lilian Baylis.* 1938.

The Beatles

The Beatles were the first and perhaps most important global POP MUSIC group. They capitalized on the 1950s mass media explosion of rock 'n' roll, especially the star-making machinery which had catapulted Elvis Presley to fame. As the "fab four", they comprised John Lennon (guitar, vocals), Paul McCartney (bass, vocals), George Harrison (guitar, vocals), and Ringo Starr (drums, vocals). All came from Liverpool and consequently popularized Merseyside clubs, such as the Cavern, and guitar group music which became labelled "Merseybeat". They emerged into the media spotlight in 1962 and had a first British chart hit with "Love Me Do". Subsequent world wide chart single hits included "From Me To You", "She Loves You", "Yellow Submarine", "All You Need Is Love", "Strawberry Fields Forever", "Penny Lane", "Hey Jude", "Let It Be", and "Get Back". Numerous album chart successes were also notched up including *Beatles For Sale, Rubber Soul, Revolver, Sgt. Pepper's Lonely Hearts Club Band, The Beatles* (a double LP known as The White Album), *Abbey Road,* and *Let It Be.* Managed for a long while by Brian Epstein until his suicide and inspired by the arrangements and production of George Martin, the Beatles played live concert tours only until 1966, concentrating mainly on recording and songwriting. Their success is measured in later years by huge global record sales as well as controversial involvement in films (such as their own *Magical Mystery Tour*) and the 1960s "counter-culture", and the still prolific songwriting of Lennon and McCartney.

By the end of the 1960s the group was in turmoil as can be seen in the scenes recorded for the film *Let It Be* which chart the personal disillusionment of group members and the growing attachment of Lennon to Yoko Ono. The end came in 1970 amid threats of expensive legal wrangles over the group's affairs. All members subsequently embarked on variable solo careers and, despite constant media rumors over many years, the Beatles never played together again. Their last public performance was a famous free concert which included a rendition of "Get Back" played on the open-air roof of the offices of their company, Apple, in central London in 1970. The 1970s saw continuing coverage of their songs by many other artists and ever more intractable court cases over their financial affairs. In December 1980 Lennon, who had successfully applied to be allowed to live in the United States in the previous decade, was shot dead in front of the Dakota apartment building in New York where he and Yoko Ono lived. His killer, Mark Chapman, claimed he was a fan and had pursued Lennon for his autograph. Lennon had just finished recording a comeback LP after several years of musical inactivity. This was released to considerable commercial success. In November 2001, George Harrison died. The rest of the ex-Beatles continue their involvement in various branches of the entertainment industry to the present day, especially McCartney, who eventually received a knighthood.

Steve Redhead

Bibliography
The Beatles Anthology. 2000.
Lewisohn, Mark. *The Beatles: 25 Years in the Life.* 1987.
Norman, Philip. *Shout! The True Story of the Beatles.* 1982.
Stokes, Geoffrey. *The Beatles.* 1988.
Tobler, John. *The Beatles.* 1984.

Beaverbrook, Lord [William Maxwell Aitken] (1879–1964)
Beaverbrook was the leading "press baron" of the twentieth century and a maverick, but periodically influential Conservative politician. Born

William Maxwell ("Max") Aitken in Canada, he was created 1st Baron Beaverbrook in 1917. He was a personal friend of ANDREW BONAR LAW and WINSTON CHURCHILL, but vigorously opposed the leadership of STANLEY BALDWIN in 1929–31. He held ministerial office during both world wars, but his most significant contribution was as an energetic Minister of Aircraft Production in 1940–1.

In his early years in Canada Beaverbrook acquired the fortune which was the basis of his later business success. In 1910 he moved to Britain where he remained domiciled for the rest of his life, although he retained links with Canadian statesmen. An ardent believer in Joseph Chamberlain's crusade for TARIFF REFORM, Beaverbrook was elected as a Conservative MP in December 1910, mainly as a result of his developing friendship with Bonar Law. He made little impact in the House of Commons but acquired a reputation as a manipulator behind the scenes with a taste for intrigue.

There are three significant aspects to Beaverbrook's career. Typically, all revolved around a highly personalized form of political allegiance or antipathy. The first of these was Beaverbrook's role as confidant and supporter of Bonar Law from 1910 to 1923. He was among those who encouraged Bonar Law to maintain his candidature for the Conservative leadership in November 1911. Beaverbrook played a still more important role in bringing together Bonar Law and DAVID LLOYD GEORGE in December 1916 and thus precipitating the fall of ASQUITH from the premiership. Although Beaverbrook was also an intimate of Lloyd George after 1916, he encouraged Bonar Law to come out against the continuation of the coalition at the Carlton Club meeting of October 1922. Thus was his reputation as a political "kingmaker" established.

The second strand in Beaverbrook's life was of the most lasting importance: his preeminent position in the British national PRESS. In 1916 Beaverbrook acquired control of the *Daily Express,* which he built up during the inter-war years first to rival the *Daily Mail* and then to surpass it in the mass circulation popular market. The *Daily Express* formed the heart of Beaverbrook's press empire and remained the focus of his attention: he closely monitored both content and appearance, with a constant stream of instructions to his editorial staff. In 1918 he founded the *Sunday Express,* and in 1923 he completed his coverage with the acquisition of the London afternoon paper, the *Evening Standard.* Partly as a result of his media interests, he was made Minister of Information in 1918–19, but the appointment attracted press and parliamentary criticism. In the early twentieth century it was believed that the press wielded enormous influence over its readers, and thus politicians were both resentful and fearful of the power of press "barons" such as Lords NORTHCLIFFE, Rothermere, and Beaverbrook. After the Conservative election defeat of 1929, the latter two put this power to the test in an attempt first to force a protectionist policy upon the party and second to oust its unresponsive leader, Baldwin. Beaverbrook was the active force in their "Empire Crusade" campaign which enlisted members and contested by-elections. Baldwin found the press lords' attempt at "power without responsibility" to be an easy target for counterattack in the spring of 1931. However, rank and file support for "Empire Free Trade" had forced Baldwin to make substantial concessions on policy in October 1930: Beaverbrook's defeat was more apparent than real.

The final element of Beaverbrook's career revolved around his friendship with Churchill, which was especially close after 1940. Beaverbrook filled the vital post of Minister of Aircraft Production from May 1940 to May 1941, where his energy and willingness to innovate resulted in significantly higher output at a critical moment for national survival. He served as Minister of Supply 1941–2, but then left the government for eighteen months and campaigned vigorously for greater support for the Russian war effort and an early second front in Europe. He returned as Lord Privy Seal 1943–5, in which role he was regarded by many in the CONSERVATIVE PARTY as a mischievous and reactionary influence upon Churchill and was blamed for contributing to the 1945 election defeat.

Stuart Ball

Bibliography
Ball, Stuart. *Baldwin and the Conservative Party: The Crisis of 1929–1931.* 1988.
Beaverbrook, Lord. *Politicians and the War 1914–1916.* 2nd ed. 1960.
———. *The Decline and Fall of Lloyd George.* 1963.
Chisholm, Anne, and Michael Davie. *Lord Beaverbrook: A Life.* 1992.
Koss, Stephen. *The Rise and Fall of the Political Press in Britain: vol. 2: The Twentieth Century.* 1984.
Taylor, A.J.P. *Beaverbrook.* 1972.

Beckett, Samuel (1906–1989)

Samuel Beckett is one of the most significant writers of the twentieth century not only because of the originality and power of his work, but because his novels and theatre pieces, his one film (called simply *Film* (1965), starring Buster Keaton), and his plays for radio and television have had such a profoundly transforming effect on the various genres to which they belong. *Waiting for Godot* (1952) is the most striking example of this. A *succès de scandale* when it was first performed in

Paris in 1953, it quickly made its way round the world and changed the reigning conception of what theatre was, or ought to be, forever.

The elder son of Irish Protestant parents, Beckett was born in Foxrock, County Dublin, and died in Paris. He was educated at Portora Royal School, Enniskillen, and Trinity College Dublin, where he was greatly influenced by his French professor, T.B. Rudmose Brown, graduating with academic distinction in 1927. He was *lecteur d'anglais* at the Ecole Normale Supérieure in Paris for the years 1928–30, during which he was befriended by JAMES JOYCE. Beckett's first published text, the essay "Dante . . . Bruno. Vico . . . Joyce, " was written at Joyce's request. He returned to Ireland to take up a three-year appointment as Lecturer in Modern Languages at Trinity in 1930 but resigned abruptly in December 1931 and turned to writing, to which he devoted the rest of his life.

Beckett's monograph on *Proust* (1931) was followed by a collection of stories, *More Pricks than Kicks* (1934) and a novel, *Murphy* (1938), but none of these were widely read, and Beckett was still an obscure young writer when he took up residence definitively in Paris in 1937. It was there, between 1947 and 1950, that he wrote the trilogy of novels: *Molloy* (1951) *Malone Meurt* (1951) *L'Innommable* (1953), and the play that made him famous *En Attendant Godot* (1952). All of these works were originally written in French. (The first collected edition in English of the trilogy, entitled *Molloy, Malone Dies and The Unnamable,* appeared in 1959.) After *Molloy,* translated by Patrick Bowles in collaboration with the author and published separately in 1955, Beckett translated all his work himself, and it is the consistently bilingual character of his *oeuvre* that makes him unique among twentieth-century writers. (After the one-act play *Fin de partie* (1957), in English *Endgame* (1958), Beckett did most of his writing for the theatre in English, but continued to do his own translating.)

The austerity of Beckett's writing, and of the world-view it is believed to express, is legendary and is reinforced by the increasing brevity of his texts over the course of his career. Thus what has been called his "post-trilogy" writing consists of a series of short enigmatic pieces whose flavor is accurately conveyed by titles such as *Stories and Texts for Nothing* (1967)—the English version of *Nouvelles et textes pour rien* (1958)—and *Fizzles* (1976), as well as numerous plays for stage, radio, and television, among them, for the stage: *Krapp's Last Tape* (1960), *Happy Days* (1961), *Not I* (1973), *Rockaby* (1980), for radio: *All That Fall* (1957) *Eh Joe* (1965) *Lessness* (1970) and for television: . . . *but the clouds . . .* (1976), *Ghost Trio* (1977), and *Quad* (1980).

It is increasingly acknowledged by critics that Beckett's work is as much concerned with writing itself and with the relation of human beings to language as it is with depicting, in bleak, but by no means humorless terms, the human condition. It should be noted also, that for all his declared difficulty with writing as an enterprise, and his alleged desire for silence, Beckett was not only a prolific, but an unusually inventive writer. His willingness to explore different media and his great skill in exploiting the particular characteristics of each are quite remarkable, suggesting that far from being the reclusive figure he was often taken to be, he was thoroughly and happily a man of his time. Beckett was awarded the Nobel Prize for Literature in 1969.

Mary Lydon

Bibliography

Bair, Deirdre. *Samuel Beckett: A Biography*. 1978.

Brater, Enoch. *Why Beckett*. 1989.

Federman, Raymond, and John Fletcher. *Samuel Beckett: His Works and His Critics: An Essay in Bibliography.* 1970.

O'Brien, Eoin. *The Beckett Country: Samuel Beckett's Ireland.* 1986.

Trezise, Thomas. *Into the Breach: Samuel Beckett and the Ends of Literature.* 1990.

Beecham, Thomas (1879–1961)

Born in St Helens, Lancashire, 29 April 1879, Thomas Beecham became the most celebrated British conductor of the twentieth century, exerting a considerable influence over British musical life. He founded a number of organizations, some of which—the London Philharmonic Orchestra and the Royal Philharmonic Orchestra—were to become permanent and major institutions, and was associated with several British and foreign ORCHESTRAS and opera companies.

Beecham's father, Sir Joseph Beecham, owned a highly successful pharmaceutical business, and Thomas was educated at Rossall School and OXFORD. The family fortune enabled him to finance many of his early projects himself. His first important venture was the formation of the Beecham Symphony Orchestra in 1909. In 1915 he formed the Beecham Opera Company which performed in London and the provinces in the war years. The company became the British National Opera Company in 1923; by then it was no longer under Beecham's direction and was amalgamated with Covent Garden in 1929.

The formation of the London Philharmonic Orchestra in 1932 was intended to serve the joint interests of the Royal Philharmonic Society and the BBC. When it became a self-governing orchestra, reluctant to offer any conductor the exclusive status and rights that Beecham enjoyed, he founded, in 1946, the Royal Philharmonic Or-

chestra. This orchestra was the vehicle for his most conspicuous and meritorious achievements after the Second World War. Beecham's taste in music was eclectic. He championed the works of many composers before they had wide popular appeal, including FREDERICK DELIUS and Richard Strauss. He also brought to British audiences the work of foreign artists such as Diaghilev's Ballets Russes.

Many of Beecham's recordings testify to his understanding of orchestral and vocal textures; this is evident in his performances of works by composers as diverse as Mozart and Puccini. A figure of titanic energy, Beecham, who was knighted in 1916 for his contributions to British music, was frequently involved in controversy and was known for his caustic wit. More than any other figure in British musical life in the twentieth century, he was the subject of humorous quote and anecdote. Such reminiscences should not overshadow the lasting importance that his work had on British musical life.

Trevor Herbert

Bibliography

Beecham, Thomas. *A Mingled Chime: Leaves from an Autobiography*. 1944.

Cardus, Neville. *Sir Thomas Beecham: A Memoir*. 1961.

Jefferson, Alan. *Sir Thomas Beecham: A Centenary Tribute*. 1979.

Reid, Charles. *Thomas Beecham: An Independent Biography*. 1971.

Bell, Vanessa Stephen (1879–1961)

The daughter of the critic Sir Leslie Stephen and sister of VIRGINIA WOOLF, Vanessa Bell was brought up in a cultured environment (the photographer Julia Margaret Cameron was her great aunt, and Bell was an enthusiastic photographer for most of her life). She founded the Friday Club in 1905 after leaving the Royal Academy Schools as an informal art society. In promoting discussion through its meetings and as a social forum, it was modeled on the literary gatherings organized by her brother Thoby. It was in the interchange between these meetings that the BLOOMSBURY GROUP gained its cast of characters. From 1910 the Club became an exhibiting society based at the Alpine Club. In the same year she first met ROGER FRY, who included four of her works in the second Post-Impressionist exhibition.

During this period, when she exhibited with the New English Art Club, her painting did not contradict the prevailing orthodoxy; however, the effects of Fry's Post-Impressionist exhibitions affected her deeply. The formal simplicity and bold use of color that she discovered in paintings by Gauguin and Matisse, along with the sense of structure that she had already perceived in Cezanne encouraged her to paint in 1911–13 a series of paintings—such as *Studland Beach* (1911–12, Tate Gallery, London)—that were confident and uncompromising in their sense of purpose and originality. During this period Vanessa Bell was painting her most extreme abstractions, even though she was also painting more traditional themes such as still-lives at the same time.

Her abstract paintings also sprang from her involvement with the Omega Workshops, of which she was a co-director from 1913 to 1919, and indeed her first solo exhibition was mounted by Omega in 1916. In the same year she moved to Charleston in Sussex with DUNCAN GRANT, who as a CONSCIENTIOUS OBJECTOR worked on the land. There she continued her design work both privately, in creating with Grant the environment around Charleston, and publicly, designing decors for BALLET, textiles, and pottery, while with Grant and her son Quentin she collaborated between 1940 and 1942 on the decorative scheme for Berwick Church.

In 1919 both she and Grant joined the London Group, an exhibiting society of which they remained key figures until their deaths. The work of Matisse continued to exert an influence on her painting in terms of its color, simplicity, and unforced expressions of lyricism—all of which was emphasized especially in those paintings executed while traveling in France in the 1920s and 1930s when she regularly stayed in Cassis—and celebrated, as did Grant's paintings, the pleasure and sensuality of their life together. Such an outlook became less popular by the end of the 1940s, and her work (like Grant's) correspondingly fell from favor—her retrospective exhibitions being mounted posthumously. In her last twenty years her painting became tighter and less gesturally expressive although with an often high-keyed color.

Andrew Wilson

Bibliography

Bell, Quentin, and Angelica Garnett. *Vanessa Bell's Family Album.* 1981.

Spalding, Frances. *Vanessa Bell.* 1983.

Vanessa Bell: A Memorial Exhibition (catalogue). 1964.

Marler, Regina, ed. *Selected Letters of Vanessa Bell.* 1993.

Benn, Anthony Neil Wedgwood [Tony Benn] (1925–)

Tony Benn played a critical role in the policies and fortunes of the LABOUR PARTY in the 1970s and early 1980s. While he served in the WILSON and CALLAGHAN administrations of 1964–70 and 1974–79, Benn is best known as the standard-bearer of the party's radical left wing in the opposition years which followed both the 1970 and 1979 electoral defeats. In this guise he eschewed his earlier pragmatism and pledged himself to a standard of doctrinal purity on issues as diverse as public ownership, trade union rights, unilateral nuclear disarmament, and opposition to Britain's participation in the EUROPEAN UNION. His success in realigning the Labour Party was never completely successful, but his critics argued that he had done enough to ensure that the party was burdened with a "loony left" image which contributed to its electoral decline throughout the 1970s and 1980s. After 1983 a few of the radical causes Benn had espoused (women's and minority rights, environmentalism) did ultimately become entrenched in the party's ideological mainstream, but he became an increasingly marginalized figure, first NEIL KINNOCK and later TONY BLAIR insisting that Labour's recovery could only be secured by purging the party of the programs and spirit of "Bennery".

Anthony Wedgwood Benn was born on 3 April 1925 into an upper-middle-class radical family. His father William (created first Viscount Stansgate in 1941) was an Asquithian LIBERAL who joined the Labour Party in 1927, serving in both MACDONALD'S and ATTLEE'S Cabinets, while his mother, Margaret, was the daughter of a Scottish Liberal MP. His parents were both intensely religious, and, while Benn rejected formal Church dogma, his political philosophy was consistently informed by deeply held Christian principles. Benn attended Westminster School and New College, OXFORD, and his privileged upbringing was reflected in the public school accent which he retained throughout his career, even in his most populist phase. Appropriately, he entered Parliament in November 1950 as member for Bristol South East, a seat previously held by the equally patrician SIR STAFFORD CRIPPS. In the 1950s he was on the right of the Labour Party, although he was never esteemed in the same way by HUGH GAITSKELL as other young Oxford-educated socialists, such as ANTHONY CROSLAND or ROY JENKINS. Benn prospered much more under the leadership of Harold Wilson after 1963, and served in Wilson's first two terms as Postmaster-General (1964–6) and Minister of Technology (1966–70). His ideological position, and public persona, at this time was that of the technocratic socialist, his commitment to innovation signified by enthusiasm for developing the supersonic airliner Concorde, computerizing British industry, expanding the civilian nuclear power program, and attempting (unsuccessfully) to remove the sovereign's head from the design of postage stamps. Benn's self-conscious identification with "modernization" had already been registered in his epic battle to renounce the peerage which automatically passed to him on the death of his father in 1960, a struggle only resolved by his instigation of the 1963 Peerage Act which made it possible for him (and others) to disclaim a hereditary title.

Immediately after the 1970 election defeat, Benn was reincarnated as a populist guru of Labour's left wing. He condemned Labour's record in the 1960s as opportunist and demanded a radical commitment to socialist first principles, including more NATIONALIZATION and the unilateral renunciation of NUCLEAR WEAPONS. A key motif in his pronouncements at this time was a demand for greater democracy, both in the Labour Party and in society at large. He called for a greater role by the party conference in Labour policy-making, for greater public accountability from civil servants and the judiciary, and for increased workers' participation in the running of industry. Benn's ideology was not without contradictions. His devotion to grass roots democracy sat uneasily with a continued commitment to *dirigiste* and centralized forms of macroeconomic planning, while his hostility to Britain's entry into the European Community owed less to specifically socialist concerns than to a nostalgic attachment to the sovereignty of British law and Parliament. However, Benn articulated a growing sense of frustration among many Labour activists with the Keynesian-based vision of social democracy, which was apparently being called into question by the world recession of the early 1970s, and in 1971–2 Benn served as party chairman. Harold Wilson felt obliged to neutralize Benn's growing strength in the party by shackling him with the responsibilities of office, and he served as Secretary for Trade and Industry in 1974–5 and Secretary for Energy in 1975–9. An isolated, quarrelsome figure in the declining years of the Wilson-Callaghan governments, Benn appeared to relish the return to opposition after 1979 as an opportunity to remake the party on the lines of uncompromising socialist purity. However, that project ultimately failed when, despite its being held under the new electoral college system he himself had inspired, he narrowly lost the 1981 deputy leadership election to Denis Healey. While he remained an articulate standard-bearer of the left thoughout the THATCHER-MAJOR years (and a vigorous critic of New Labour after 1994), Benn became increasingly sidelined, his public image as an ideological zealot giving way in his seventies to that of the charming, eloquent, pipe-smoking elder statesman, albeit one who could (as over the Gulf War in 1991) still be roused to almost Gladstonian levels of principled moral indignation, "daring", in one of his father's favorite phrases from the Nonconformist pantheon, "to be a Daniel".

Martin Francis

Bibliography
Adams, Jad. *Tony Benn: A Biography.* 1992.
Benn, Tony. *Arguments for Socialism.* 1979.
———. *The Benn Diaries, 1940–1990.* 1995.
Higgins, Sydney. *The Benn Inheritance: The Story of a Radical Family.* 1984.

Bennett, (Enoch) Arnold (1867–1931)

Novelist, short story writer, playwright, critic, journalist, prodigious letter writer, Arnold Bennett was a multi-faceted celebrity in his day. At the height of his popularity, posters advertising his latest novel were plastered on London buses. He was offered and refused a knighthood. As he lay dying of typhoid, straw was spread around Chiltern Court to deaden traffic noise, a custom previously only followed for royalty. Since his centenary, some studies have begun to recognize Bennett's significance in the transition of the novel from realism to modernism. Of the thirty-six novels he wrote, the primary works are: *A Man From the North* (1898); *Anna of the Five Towns* (1902); *The Old Wives' Tale* (1908); *Buried Alive* (1908); the Clayhanger trilogy: *Clayhanger* (1910), *Hilda Lessways* (1911); *The Card* (1911); *These Twain* (1915); *Riceyman Steps* (1923); *Lord Raingo* (1926), and *Imperial Palace* (1930).

Bennett was born of potter's stock in Burslem, the Potteries, Staffordshire, England, although his father Enoch became a solicitor. The father's driving ambition was inherited by Bennett who, at twenty-one, abandoned his father's dream of a legal career for him and went to London. There his friendship with Frederick Marriott, an art teacher, spurred him to a succession of literary efforts culminating in his publishing the short story "A Letter Home" in the avant-garde periodical *The Yellow Book* and in his accepting an assistant-editor of a penny paper called *Woman*.

Within six years of his association with *Woman*, Bennett not only established the direction of his concern for serious writing, but also the pattern of frenetic productivity that was to astound and dismay his friends throughout his life. By September 1900 he had, beside his daily work, begun one sensational novel; published his first serious novel, *A Man From the North*; begun his first initial success, *Anna of the Five Towns*; published *Journalism for Women*; published three one-act plays called *Polite Farces*; collaborated on another play with his friend Arthur Hooley; and helped dramatize Eden Philpotts' novel, *Children of the Mist*.

By 1903, after the death of his father, he moved to Paris, became fluent in the language, acquired a mistress, became a close friend of the scholar, critic, and linguist Marcel Schwob, in whose circle Bennett met many continental artists. But he longed for marriage. At thirty-nine, during the course of a stressful eighteen months, Bennett planned to marry a young American, Eleanor

Green but, rebuffed, married his older secretary, Marguerite Soulié, who had theatrical ambitions. This marriage proved disastrous for both. They were legally separated in 1921, but Marguerite would never give him a divorce and outlived him. Nevertheless, in relative married content he had begun the major work he had been considering for four years. So inspired was he that in ten months of 1907 he completed the 200,000 word *The Old Wives' Tale*, written in a special calligraphy on special paper. Within the same period he produced two shorter farcical novels and a bewildering list of essays, short stories, dramatic writings, and popular philosophies.

His astounding fecundity was distinguished by its quality. *The Old Wives' Tale* won him the respect of discriminating critics and brought him requests for his work from prestigious literary journals, like FORD MADOX FORD's *The English Review*. The novel captures the impression of the passing of every day for a lifetime in the awareness of two sisters, one of whom lives a conventional life at home, the other of whom elopes to France, where she survives the Franco-Prussian War and the Paris Commune.

Some months before the publication of this novel, Bennett had begun to write articles headed "Books and Persons" for *The New Age*, another prestigious journal. His articles heralding the new Russian and French writers placed him unquestionably among the avant-garde and made him, at the midpoint of his career, a cultural leader for the aspiring young.

In 1909 he was exhilarated by the first full-scale production of *What the Public Wants*, starring Sir Charles Hawtrey and Ben Webster and praised by Max Beerbohm. He immediately wrote *The Honeymoon* which in 1911 starred Marie Tempest and was acclaimed for its humor. He also published the important first novel of the Clayhanger trilogy, a sensitive portrait of the growth of a loveable young man. Before he completed the second Clayhanger novel, he published *The Card* (in 1952 made into a movie starring Alec Guinness) and wrote, with Edward Knoblock, the play *Milestones* which, in 1912, ran for 600 performances.

Always restless, Bennett was persuaded in 1911 by his American publisher George Doran to visit the United States. He was acclaimed in New York, Washington, Chicago, Indianapolis, Philadelphia, Boston, and the universities of the New England states, and noted his experiences in *Those United States* (1912). His affluence now enabled him to buy Comarques, a country estate in Essex and a large yacht. He recorded his voyages at sea in *From the Log of the Velsa* (1914). But then the FIRST WORLD WAR broke out. Bennett, drawn back to London into close association with the newspaper magnate, LORD BEAVERBROOK, found himself forced into political activity in Beaverbrook's Ministry of Information. He wrote a series of weekly war articles for the *Daily News;* he became a director of the *NEW STATESMAN;* he toured the Western Front.

Within these years he completed the Clayhanger trilogy, wrote five more minor novels and three plays. By 1922 he had fallen in love with the young actress, Dorothy Cheston, who agreed to become his common-law wife and took his name by deed poll. He published *Riceyman Steps* (1923), a psychological study of miserliness which brought him the award of the James Tait Black Memorial Prize for the best novel of that year. In 1926 his only child Virginia was born and he published *Lord Raingo*, his depiction of the War Cabinet in action and a powerful study of melancholia in a good man in decline.

Bennett's last years were burdened by his young wife's unsatisfied theatrical ambitions, his need for more money to maintain his expensive living, and poor health. His productivity included the dramatization of an earlier novel *Mr. Prohack* (1922), which launched Charles Laughton's career. After travels in Germany and Russia with Beaverbrook, he began work upon his last completed novel *Imperial Palace* (1930), a tour-de-force about the hotel world and a sympathetic portrait of the "new woman."

Bennett's accuracy in locating, in his best work, the forms, the courses, and the strains in personal relationships link him with earlier writers like Anthony Trollope and contemporaries like Henry James, and helped pave the way for the fine discriminations found in younger writers like D.H. LAWRENCE and VIRGINIA WOOLF. Woolf's attack on Bennett in 1924 began the derogation of his work that still persists in academic circles.

Olga R.R. Broomfield

Bibliography
Broomfield, Olga R.R. *Arnold Bennett*. 1984.
Drabble, Margaret. *Arnold Bennett: A Biography*. 1975.
Hepburn, James. *Letters of Arnold Bennett*. vols. I–IV. 1966–86.
Lucas, John. *Arnold Bennett: A Study of his Fiction*. 1974.
Roby, Kinler E. *A Writer at War: Arnold Bennett*. 1972.

Bevan, Aneurin (1897–1960)
Aneurin (Nye) Bevan was a Labour MP and one of the key figures in CLEMENT ATTLEE's postwar Labour governments of 1945–51, being largely responsible for the formation of the free NATIONAL HEALTH SERVICE (NHS) in Britain, which came into existence in July 1948. His protests against the attempt of HERBERT MORRISON, HUGH GAITSKELL, and others in the government to impose prescription charges led him

to resign from office in 1951 and to act as the centre of a loose grouping of the socialist Left within the LABOUR PARTY which became know as the Bevanites, although he subsequently returned to the center of the party in the mid-1950s.

Bevan was born on 15 November 1897 in Tredegar, South Wales, was educated at elementary school and at Sunday school, and began work as a miner at the age of thirteen. He worked in the mines for nine years, during a turbulent period of industrial and syndicalist activity in South Wales, before winning a South Wales Miners' Federation scholarship to the Central Labour College, London, where he took courses on the history of socialism, Marxism, economics, and finance. On his return to Tredegar in 1921 Bevan became involved in the activities of the miners' union and was Chairman of the Tredegar Council of Action during the GENERAL STRIKE of 1926. Yet Bevan was mainly a political animal. He was returned as a member of his local District Council in April 1922 and was a member of the Monthmouthshire County Council from 1928 to 1929 before becoming the miners' MP for Ebbw Vale. He represented that parliamentary constituency from 1929 until his death in 1960.

In Parliament Bevan campaigned fiercely for the interests of the working classes, tirelessly championed the cause of the unemployed and strongly opposed FASCISM. He briefly supported OSWALD MOSLEY's New Party moves in 1931 because Mosley seemed to offer policies to deal with the unemployed, but quickly became disillusioned as Mosley moved in the direciton of Fascism and never actually joined the party. He opposed the Household Means Test, ranted against Fascism, and operated through the left-wing journal *Tribune* to attack a Labour Party, which was increasingly dominated by ERNEST BEVIN, the trade union leader. It was in 1934 that he married Jennie Lee, who, in her own right, became an influential force within the British Labour Left. During the SECOND WORLD WAR Bevan rejected the political truce which was agreed to by the major political parties and fought the war on two fronts—against the Fascists and against the Tory Party. Indeed, he was an unflinching critic of WINSTON CHURCHILL. It was during these years that he gained a reputation for being an orator reminiscent of fellow Welshman DAVID LLOYD GEORGE.

Yet Bevan's finest hour came when he became Minister of Health and Housing in the Attlee government of 1945. In that role he cajoled the private doctors and the British Medical Association, who referred to him as that "squalid nuisance", the "Minister of Disease" and a "Tito from Tonypandy", into working with the NHS which was formed in 1948. His remark that his Tory opponents were "lower than vermin" caused great controversy at that time. The NHS which he formed transcended the wartime reforms which were considered and the Labour Party's policy by effectively nationalizing the hospitals, creating a public general practitioner service, and by making the treatment of illness and the provision of medical treatment entirely free. In his book *In Place of Fear* (1952) he explained that it was ludicrous to expect patients to await a vital operation because they lacked the requisite number of self-contributions. But the NHS proved very expensive, and Morrison and other members of Attlee's Government decided to attempt to limit the expenditure and to introduce the prescription charges. Bevan fought off these attempts until the 1950 General Election, but then, on 17 January 1951, he was moved from Health to become Minister of Labour and National Service. The move coincided with the decision of Gaitskell, the Chancellor of the Exchequer, to impose health charges. Bevan's bitter row with Gaitskell led to his dramatic resignation from the government on 24 April 1951.

Between 1951 and 1955 Bevan became the figurehead of a loosely organized group of left-wing, Bevanite MPs, who advocated unilateral disarmament and challenged official policies. Indeed, it was Bevan's decision to oppose the Parliamentary Labour Party line of supporting the manufacture of the hydrogen bomb which almost got him expelled from the party in 1955. At this point, however, Bevan's position began to change. He lost to Gaitskell in the election for the post of Party Treasurer in 1954 and lost again to Gaitskell in the leadership contest of December 1955. From that point onwards he appears to have come to an understanding with Gaitskell, who made him Shadow Colonial Secretary, was positively patriotic over the SUEZ CRISIS of 1956, and rose in the party hierarchy by winning the post of Treasurer, which he held from 1956 to 1960. After his patriotic showing over Suez and the Soviet invasion of Hungary, he was made Shadow Foreign Secretary. With his rapprochement with Gaitskell, Bevan was soon to become a spent force for the Left. He effectively divested himself of the title "leader of the Left" at the 1957 Labour Party conference by attacking unilateral disarmament and eventually rose to become Deputy Leader in 1959. However, at the beginning of 1960 he went to the Royal Free Hospital for an abdominal operation. It revealed that he had a malignant cancer, from which he died on 6 July 1960.

Keith Laybourn

Bibliography
Campbell, John. *Nye Bevan and the Mirage of British Socialism.* 1987.

Foot, Michael. *Aneurin Bevan, 1897–1945*. 1962.
———. *Aneurin Bevan, 1945–1960*. 1973.
Hollis, Patricia. *Jennie Lee: A Life*. 1997.
Lee, Jennie. *My Life with Nye*. 1980.

Beveridge, William Henry (1879–1963)

If any one individual can be singled out as the architect of Britain's welfare state, then it must be William Henry Beveridge. He was born in 1879 into an upper middle-class family stationed in India, and in his youth he trod the conventional path of public school (Charterhouse) and OXFORD. However, Beveridge's youth was spent during years of social questioning in Britain, and while at Oxford he was influenced by the social reformist liberalism of Edward Caird, then Master of Balliol. On leaving Oxford, Beveridge worked as a leader-writer of the Conservative newspaper, the *Morning Post,* while living at the Toynbee Hall university settlement in East London.

UNEMPLOYMENT and casual labor were the scourges of Edwardian LONDON, and Beveridge believed that these problems could be remedied by limited state intervention which would adjust the supply/demand malfunctionings of the labor market. As he saw it, the answer was a system of labor exchanges, and it was his passionate advocacy of these that brought him to public attention. In 1908 Beveridge became a part-time, temporary civil servant with the Board of Trade to work on the planning of labor exchanges.

Gradually, therefore, Beveridge was being drawn into the complex world he was to inhabit for the rest of his active life: journalism, research, social administration, and academia. In 1909 he published a major study, *Unemployment, a Problem of Industry*. He became convinced that state social insurance, as represented by the 1911 National Insurance Act, could be extended to cover all the social risks that befell workers over the course of the life-cycle; simultaneously, the state could intervene at strategic points of economic activity and improve industrial efficiency.

During the FIRST WORLD WAR, Beveridge worked in the MINISTRY OF MUNITIONS and the Ministry of Food. In 1919 he was knighted and appointed Director of the LONDON SCHOOL OF ECONOMICS. Until he returned to Oxford in 1937 as Master of University College, much of his formidable energy was directed at the expansion of LSE into a social science institution of world standing. There were many forays into government-related work, notably as a member of the 1925–6 SAMUEL Commission on the Coal Industry and as Chairman of the Unemployment Insurance Statutory Committee (1934–44). The latter post confirmed his long-standing view (outlined, for example, in his pamphlet *Insurance*

for All and Everything [1924]) that social insurance could form the basis for a much more comprehensive social security system.

Thus by the time of the outbreak of the SECOND WORLD WAR Beveridge had amassed a wealth of experience and expertise in social questions that should have placed him immediately in a high position as a government adviser. That this did not happen was partly due to the lack of coordinated planning in the first year of war. But it also arose from Beveridge's rather difficult personality: immensely hard-working, widely read and intelligent, he could be insensitive, vain, and rude to colleagues, especially when crossed. These personality traits partly explain why Beveridge did not have more influences in the world of politics. But, paradoxically, they were indirectly to present him with the greatest opportunity of his career.

In 1940 Beveridge had been placed in charge of a rather insignificant Ministry of Labour manpower survey. Anxious to be rid of a rather troublesome colleague, ERNEST BEVIN recommended that Beveridge be appointed chairman of a proposed inquiry into the reorganization of social insurance and allied services that was to be part of the overall post-war reconstruction program set up in 1941. Accordingly, in June 1941 Beveridge was appointed chairman of an inter-departmental committee of civil servants established "to undertake, with special reference to the inter-relation of the schemes, a survey of the existing national schemes of social insurance and allied services, including workmen's compensation, and to make recommendations".

The last four words of the committee's terms of reference were to prove vitally important, for Beveridge's liberal interpretation of them resulted in a report that went well beyond what the government had expected. Beveridge was easily able to dominate his committee: in December 1941, for example, he composed a memorandum containing all the broad recommendations which were to appear in the subsequent Report. Thus, although there was considerable consultation and evidence-gathering from major organizations (such as the trade unions and the employers), the essence of the Report was Beveridge's.

In summary, the Report recommended that all the disparate state income-maintenance services which had grown up piecemeal since 1911 be pulled together, made universally available and comprehensive in coverage, and funded by state social insurance. Hence for the first time unemployment benefit was to cover the whole population and was to be supplemented by national assistance. Sickness benefit was also universalized and raised to the same level as unemployment benefit. Workmen's compensation was to be reformed, and new benefits for maternity and death were proposed. An important change was that the two OLD AGE PENSION systems (originating in 1908 and 1925 respectively) were amalgamated into one contributory scheme to which, for the first time, was attached a retirement condition. Three important assumptions underpinned the entire Beveridge plan: FAMILY ALLOWANCES would help alleviate child poverty, but more important to Beveridge was their role in preserving the gap between wages and benefit, and hence work incentives; a comprehensive preventive and curative NATIONAL HEALTH SERVICE would ensure that the social security system did not have to subsidise absence from work through illness; and full employment would both create a large enough tax base to fund the scheme and simultaneously would prevent it going bankrupt through an excess of claims. Beveridge's emphasis on the importance of these three assumptions shows how confident he was that the relationship between social security and economic growth could be symbiotic and mutually reinforcing.

Historians are agreed that Beveridge's personal contribution to the Report was enormous. To read the transcripts of oral evidence is to discover the extent of Beveridge's ability to persuade, cajole, or out-argue witnesses on highly complex questions. To read the Report itself is to understand why contemporaries were uplifted by the nobility of its language and its optimism for a better world.

Yet, paradoxically, historians now recognize that many of the recommendations made by Beveridge were already "in the CIVIL SERVICE pipeline" and that essentially his contribution was to rationalize these existing plans into one comprehensive whole. Family allowances had been considered by the Treasury at the start of the war (as an anti-inflationary, wage-control device: they would have protected the lowest-paid families from the full effects of a wage freeze), and had been the subject of a Treasury White Paper published in May 1942. Beveridge universalized unemployment benefit, but benefit levels were no higher—relative to wages—than they had been in the late 1930s. And in some respects, his recommendations almost seemed to mark a backward step. Full subsistence pensions were only to be attained after a twenty-year transitional period of slowly rising pension levels, and thus were to commence at a level out of line with the "subsistence principle" which was said to be central to the whole Report. Again, Beveridge's emphasis on state social insurance funding, with flat-rate benefits and flat-rate contributions (rather than a tax-funded, means-tested benefit system) meant that certain problems, such as varying expenditure on rent, were left unresolved.

However, these retrospective caveats cannot detract from the remarkable adulation that the Report received when it was published on 1 December 1942 from a public hungry for good news after three hard years of war. This was the first factor that made the Report appear more radical than its contents actually merited. The second was the reluctance of CHURCHILL's wartime coalition government to commit itself to implementing the Report—a reluctance that led to a heated House of Commons debate on 16–18 February 1943, at the end of which there was a substantial Conservative back-bench rebellion. Because of these background events, the Report was assured of a place in history.

Only in the very broadest sense did the Beveridge Report become the basis for the post-war welfare state. Beveridge's draft recommendations had been whittled down under Treasury pressure in the summer of 1942, and the Report was less than he had originally hoped for. Further paring down took place when a committee of civil servants under Sir Thomas Sheepshanks shaped the proposals into legislation in 1943–5. The principal relevant statutes were: the 1945 Family Allowances Act; the 1946 National Health Service Act; the 1946 National Insurance Act; the 1948 National Assistance Act. Together with the 1944 EDUCATION ACT, these founded what became known as the WELFARE STATE.

As author of a best-selling government report, Beveridge was showered with considerable public adulation for the rest of the war. All this he greatly enjoyed. He contributed to public debates about the post-war world, notably in *Full Employment in a Free Society* (1944), and was elected to Parliament as Liberal MP for Berwick-upon-Tweed in 1944. His political career was short-lived, however, for in the 1945 general election he lost his seat. Ever active, he accepted a peerage, continued his public career (for example, as Chairman of Newton Aycliffe Development Corporation), and died in 1963.

John Macnicol

Bibliography
Beveridge, Lord. *Power and Influence*. 1953.
Harris, Jose. *William Beveridge*. 2nd ed. 1997.
Social Insurance and Allied Services. 1942. Cmd. 6404 (The Beveridge Report).
Williams, Karel, and John Williams, eds. *A Beveridge Reader*. 1987.

Bevin, Ernest (1881–1951)

Shortly after the First World War, Ernest Bevin founded the TRANSPORT AND GENERAL WORKERS' UNION, which for long was the largest trade union in Britain. He was, with TRADES UNION CONGRESS General Secretary WALTER CITRINE, largely responsible for the direction the

British trade union movement took after the GENERAL STRIKE of 1926. After the financial crisis of 1931 he played a significant role in the reshaping of the LABOUR PARTY's policy that became the basis of the program enacted by the 1945 Labour government. In 1940 he became Minister of Labour, overseeing the wartime government's labor policies and in the process contributing to the creation of the post-war WELFARE STATE. After the war Bevin served as Foreign Secretary in the Labour government, helping to shape the international order that prevailed for the next forty years.

Born in Winsford, Somerset, on 7 March 1881, the illegitimate child of an agricultural labourer, Ernest Bevin had a childhood marked by poverty and insecurity. His mother died when he was eight years old, forcing him to move to his half-sister in Devon. When his formal education ended at eleven, he went to work for neighboring farmers. After two years of hard work for sixpence a week plus room and board, he moved to Bristol to live with his half-brother, eventually settling down as a mineral water delivery man. As a young man he became active in the Baptist church, then abandoned membership in the church, though not his religious faith, and became involved in the Bristol Socialist Society. It was at this time that he married Florence Townley, with whom he had one child, Queenie, born in 1914.

Because of his work for the unemployed, Bevin was asked in 1910 to organise the carters for the Dock, Wharf, Riverside, and General Labourers' Union, known as the Dockers' Union. He did this so well that he was then invited to work full time as a regional organizer for the Dockers' Union; four years later he was appointed as one of three national organizers. Bevin quickly concluded that increased organization provided the best defense for workers. He strongly supported the creation of a large general union, one which linked workers in different trades. During and immediately after the First World War the trend inside the trade union movement was toward greater concentration and organization. Using a plan suggested by Bevin, for example, the Trades Union Congress in 1920 created a new General Council to provide more centralized direction to the trade union movement. In that same year, after he had achieved national fame for his role in successfully presenting the dockers' case for a wage increase to an arbitration tribunal, the Shaw Committee, Bevin took advantage of his new prestige to help push for the creation of a new transport workers' organisation. His energy and practical ability proved decisive in overcoming the difficulties that had prevented previous amalgamation attempts and creating the

Transport and General Workers' Union out of fourteen different unions. It came into being on 1 January 1922, and Bevin was elected General Secretary, a lifetime appointment.

Although Bevin's central organizational goal as a trade unionist remained fixed, his strategies changed over time. Always angry at the exclusion of the working class from full membership in British society and at its failure to accept the trade union movement, he could often be belligerent and even at times flirt with direct action, the use of organized working-class power to secure political changes. Most notably, he supported the Council of Action that in 1920 opposed British intervention in the Soviet-Polish war. Until the General Strike of 1926, he sometimes thought that organized trade union power could compel changes in the way management treated workers. Increasingly, however, his need to deal with "facts as they are" led him to conclude that what was later called corporatism—the cooperation of business, the unions, and the state—provided the most effective route for working-class advancement. Particularly after the failure of the General Strike, which he had supported and helped lead, convinced him that capitalism was not about to give way to socialism, he, along with Citrine, successfully steered the TUC along this path.

Because the trade union movement had been so weakened by the growth of UNEMPLOYMENT and by the failure of the General Strike, Bevin concluded that trade unions had to work to change not just wages and working conditions but all social and economic policies that affected working people. Through his membership on the Economic Advisory Council and the Macmillan Committee, he tried, and failed, to influence the economic policy of the 1929 Labour government, which rejected his advice to do more to overcome unemployment. After Labour's disastrous electoral defeat in 1931, however, Bevin, particularly through his membership on the National Council of Labour, which coordinated relations between the Labour Party and the Trades Union Congress, worked to reshape Labour's domestic and foreign policies. In part because of his influence, Labour now developed a viable reformist program that endorsed NATIONALIZATION of a limited range of industries and Keynesian policies to regulate the economy. Bevin played an even more important role in reshaping the Labour Party's approach to foreign affairs. Opposed to traditional balance of power politics and suspicious of the ruling CONSERVATIVE PARTY, the Labour Party in the 1930s refused to support rearmament even in the face of a growing threat from Germany. In part once again because of Bevin's efforts, the Labour Party changed its position after 1937 and became a strong advocate of military opposition to Fascism, even though this involved support for a distrusted Conservative government.

Throughout the 1930s Bevin's corporatist trade union strategy had only partial success outside the confines of the Transport and General Workers' Union, signally failing to help unemployed workers or those who were not union members. At times, it also overrode rank and file activism and undercut the attempts of militants to expand trade union membership. But in May 1940 Bevin became Minister of Labour in the coalition government created at the height of the wartime emergency. Appreciating that the Ministry of Labour would provide him a key position from which to shape domestic policy, Bevin viewed the war as an opportunity to create the kind of industrial order that he had been advocating for over a decade. Corporatism had been problematic because neither the state nor business would cooperate fully with the trade union movement. Now, the war and his own position in the government ensured that cooperation. Bevin used this new partnership as the basis for the various measures he put in place to mobilize the entire country behind the war effort. He also took advantage of the moment to secure new institutional recognition for the trade union movement, which increased its membership by about a third. Believing that workers had a right to employment and security, Bevin converted the Ministry of Labour into a major policy-making department, greatly expanding its power to defend working-class conditions and STANDARD OF LIVING and in the process helping to prepare the ground for the creation of the welfare state after 1945.

After Labour won a massive victory in the 1945 election, he was appointed Foreign Secretary. Now he saw himself defending not just the working class, but all of Britain. For Bevin, the best way to protect British national interests—its world position, the basis of Britain's economic well-being, and the perceived threat from the Soviet Union—was to draw closer to the United States and pull back from Europe. In these years he played an important role in supporting the Marshall Plan, the aid plan to Western Europe that helped to revive its still lagging economy, and in creating in 1949 the North Atlantic Treaty Organization, which established a stable balance of power on the European continent. From the Foreign Office point of view, Bevin's work in these years was an immense success, preserving Britain's great power status and helping to contain the alleged threat from the Soviet Union, a judgment many historians have endorsed. It might also be said, however, that Bevin's determination to preserve Britain's traditional world position may have unintentionally hastened Britain's decline by delaying its coming to terms with its reduced power, tying it to an expensive military posture that interfered with economic growth, and turning it away from the most effective available path to economic modernization, membership in the emerging European community.

Bevin's legacy as Foreign Secretary remains a subject of debate. But his legacy as a trade union leader and Minister of Labour has endured and changed the institutional shape of Britain. Bevin created one of the largest unions in Britain, which continues to defend its members' interests in the ways he envisioned. His ideals of working-class rights to employment, adequate wages and working conditions, and social security were partially achieved by the 1945 Labour government. Even though they have been eroded since 1979, they remain a permanent achievement.

Peter Weiler

Bibliography
Bullock, Alan. *The Life and Times of Ernest Bevin*, 2 vols. 1960, 1967.
———. *Ernest Bevin: Foreign Secretary 1945–1951.* 1983.
Weiler, Peter. *Ernest Bevin.* 1993.
Coates, Ken, and Tony Topham. *The History of the Transport and General Workers' Union.* 1991.

Birth Control

The 1877 trial of freethinkers Charles Bradlaugh and Annie Besant for publishing a purportedly obscene edition of an American pamphlet on family limitation did not, as was once thought, initiate widespread use of birth control; it did coincide, however, with a European-wide transition in family fertility. By the early years of this century anxiety about the "racial" and imperial consequences of the declining birth rate had combined with the social hygiene crusades to make sex and procreation topics of worried discussion in the public press and, more discreetly, the journals catering to the intellectual elite. Yet even educated middle-class British women had little knowledge of birth control, and most physicians considered it harmful and were ignorant of effective methods. Nevertheless, it was clear from their birth rates that the middle classes had been using birth control for several decades. The preventives most commonly employed—*coitus interruptus* (withdrawal), abstinence, and the condom—all required male cooperation.

For working-class women, whose birth rates remained high, informal networks existed to pass on information about preventing conception, and there was a host of—more or less unsavory—commercial sources. Improved rubber pessaries (diaphragms and cervical caps) had been added to the older homemade douches, vaginal sponges, soluble pessaries, and other female barrier methods. Yet even working-class women who knew of their existence would probably have found most methods repugnant and impossible to use in homes lacking sanitary facilities and privacy. Many, if not most working-class women seem to have relied on ABORTION—either self-induced or performed by midwives, female relatives, or disreputable professional abortionists—long after safer, preventive methods were better known.

After the First World War MARIE STOPES's candid discussions of marital sex and birth control made her the most widely known figure working for women's access to safe, effective contraception. Her early writings carried a strongly feminist message of women's right to reproductive freedom and sexual pleasure within marriage. Moreover, Stopes argued that birth control would rescue the British "race" from biological degeneration and, by improving the health of mothers and babies through child spacing, replenish the population, not diminish it as opponents claimed.

In 1921 Stopes opened the Mothers' Clinic in North London to provide birth control to poor women and launched the Society for Constructive Birth Control and Racial Progress to pressure the Ministry of Health to offer birth control services at local maternal and infant welfare centers. In October of the same year the King's physician, Lord Dawson of Penn, strongly endorsed birth control in a speech to a lay Church congress. In November the Malthusian League opened the Walworth Women's Welfare Center; three years later the Society for the Provision of Birth Control Clinics (SPBCC) took over Walworth to train doctors and nurses and began opening clinics in London and provincial cities. Stopes's clinic and those of the SPBCC and of Dr. Norman Haire, an Australian sex reformer, provided birth control—usually the diaphragm or cervical cap and spermacide—free or at cost.

Throughout the 1920s eugenists, clergymen, scientists, feminists, socialists, and literary and intellectual leaders explored the scientific significance of birth control and its implications for Britain's national future. As controversies about birth control raged in the press, women's groups affiliated with the LABOUR and LIBERAL PARTIES organized to influence the Ministry of Health, members of Parliament, and the party conferences to support government-run birth control. Arguing that contraception improved mothers' health and ability to rear healthy children and would increase the self-sufficiency of the working class, Conservative MP NANCY ASTOR and Ernest Thurtle, Labour MP for Shoreditch, introduced resolutions and private bills; they pointed

urgently to evidence of the ill effects of too-frequent childbearing gathered in studies of maternal mortality and abortion.

In 1930, with the advent of a new Labour government, the birth controllers won a partial victory. The Ministry of Health quietly decided to allow local welfare centers, at their discretion, to dispense birth control devices to married women on strictly limited medical grounds. The same year the Lambeth Conference of Anglican bishops, long opposed to birth control, gave its limited blessing.

In the 1930s the voluntary birth control clinics, now federated as the National Birth Control Association (NBCA), concentrated on persuading the ministry to broaden its criteria to include social and economic factors and on convincing local authorities to provide birth control services at welfare centers. A number of local officials were actively supportive; where they refused to act, or interpreted the ministry's medical grounds too narrowly, the NBCA coordinated establishment of voluntary clinics. By 1939, 282 of 409 local authorities in England and Wales had made some arrangement to provide contraceptive services.

Although official medical opinion remained unfavorable, many individual doctors learned about birth control and began prescribing it for private patients. The findings of the clinical research initiated by Stopes, Haire, and (after 1927) the Birth Control Investigation Committee helped gain still more medical adherents.

In the mid-1930s, however, renewed fears of a dwindling population strengthened the always-vocal ROMAN CATHOLIC opposition to government sanction of birth control. The birth rate of all classes continued to decline in the wake of depression and high UNEMPLOYMENT, and predictions of depopulation converged with uneasy awareness of the population-enhancement policies being pursued in Italy and Germany. The SECOND WORLD WAR stripped the birth control movement of its momentum as doctors, nurses, and local and national volunteers found other vital assignments. By 1945 only about sixty clinics of the renamed Family Planning Association (FPA) were still operating.

The reproductive behavior of British couples, however, as documented by a postwar study, had moved toward a modern norm of deliberate family planning. Although relatively few women had actually visited a birth control clinic in the 1930s and 1940s, the 1949 report of the Royal Commission on Population showed that increasing numbers of couples of all classes wed during those decades used birth control—principally the condom and withdrawal.

While the acceptability of concerns about "racial" quality and imperial destiny receded after the war, the question of the ideal population for Britain continued to trouble political and social leaders. As it had after the First World War, the cultural climate encouraged married women to give up their jobs to returning veterans and devote themselves to bearing the children needed to ensure an adequate workforce. The national birth rate, declining since the 1870s, rose steeply right after the war and stabilized slightly lower in the 1950s before slowly rising again throughout the 1960s.

FPA leaders, fearing that the renewed push for population growth would limit birth control to medical grounds within the new NATIONAL HEALTH SERVICE (NHS), chose to continue running clinics on a voluntary basis. At no time during planning of the NHS did the Labour government contemplate providing complete contraceptive services, and FPA leaders made no attempt to persuade it to do so.

During the 1960s, however, perception of a world "population bomb," increased (non-white) IMMIGRATION, and higher birth rates turned British attention to the environmental and "quality of life" problems attendant on overpopulation. Conservative and Labour MPs and pressure groups outside government began to see family planning services as essential to a responsible population policy.

In the meantime, the contraceptive pill had come into being and was in general use in Britain by 1961. Much more than other female methods, the pill effected a revolutionary change in contraceptive behavior. In spite of concerns about side effects in the 1960s, by 1970 oral contraceptives were second only to the condom in popularity among women of all ages.

In 1967, when national birth rates were high and the trend toward women's participation in the labor force was both well established and conceded to be economically necessary to families and the nation, Parliament passed the Family Planning Act (preceded by the Abortion Act). The legislation, still permissive rather than mandatory, authorized local officials to offer birth control, at cost, to married and single women under NHS auspices; but it left many loopholes for recalcitrant or timid local officials. Only in 1974, upon reorganization of the NHS, was a fully effective, comprehensive program of birth control free to British women of all ages, classes, and marital status included in the National Health Service. It had taken more than fifty years from the opening of Marie Stopes's first birth control clinic. Since then, birth control, like other NHS services, has been subject to cutbacks but has remained firmly rooted in Britain's health and population policy.

Roberta A. Clark

Bibliography
Leathard, Audrey. *The Fight for Family Planning: The Development of Family Planning Services in Britain, 1921–74.* 1980.
Lewis, Jane. *Women in England, 1870–1950: Sexual Division and Social Change.* 1984.
———. *The Politics of Motherhood: Child and Maternal Welfare in England, 1900–1939.* 1980.
Soloway, Richard Allen. *Birth Control and the Population Question in England, 1877–1930.* 1982.
Szreter, Simon. *Fertility, Class and Gender in Britain, 1860–1940.* 1996.

Black People in Britain

In 1900, at the height of Britain's imperial power, the vast majority, some 366 million of Britain's 425 million subjects, were not white. Yet only a small number of Black people, perhaps several thousand, lived in the British Isles. In the course of the twentieth century British authorities and Black Britons themselves have included in the category "Black" or "coloured" an ethnically heterogeneous population, reflecting the geographical span of the Empire, and the racial hierarchies it fostered. Among them were East and West Africans, West Indians of African as well as Asian descent, British Indians and "Cingalese," [Sinhalese], Burmese, Arabs, Adenese and Berbers, British Somalis, Egyptians, Goans, East Africans of Asian descent, French Algerians, Portuguese, Hondurans, and Maltese. Interracial marriage and racially mixed children have further complicated the composition of this population.

Black people have lived and worked in Britain for centuries. In the decades before the Second World War, black people in Britain comprised two major groups: students and other relative elites who came to Britain for education and often returned to the colonies; and working people who more often settled in Britain, forming families and communities.

Some of the more prominent Black figures in early twentieth-century Britain included Duse Mohamed Ali (1866?–1945), editor of the *African Times and Orient Review* (1912–20); Dr. Harold Moody (1882–1947), founder and president of the League of Coloured Peoples; John Richard Archer (1863–1931), Mayor of Battersea in 1913 and Labour councillor for over twenty years; MPs Mancherjee Merwanjee Bhownagree (1851–1933), Conservative for Bethnal Green, 1895–1905; and Shapurji Saklatvala (1874–1936), Labour and later Communist for Battersea, 1922–9; cricketer Learie Constantine, Baron Constantine of Maraval and Nelson (1902–71); Satyendra Prasanno, Baron Sinha of Raipur (1864–1928); Indian Nationalist Vengalil Krishnan Krishna Menon (1896–1974); and a circle of Pan-Africanist intellectuals that included Cyril

Lionel Robert (CLR) James (1901–89), George Padmore (1902?–59), and Eric Williams (1911–81), who became the first president of Trinidad and Tobago in 1961.

The London-based League of Coloured Peoples was Britain's major Black self-help organization in the 1930s and 1940s. Although at times incorporating Indians, including long-time League officer K.A. Chunchie, and actively soliciting white patrons such as Lady Kathleen Simon, the organization was largely dominated by West Indian students and professionals and to a lesser extent by West Africans. Another major organization was the West African Students' Union, which published the journal *Wasu*. Marcus Garvey (1887–1940) spent his last years in London and published the journal *The Black Man* in the 1930s.

Most Black people in Britain were not celebrities, however, but working people, part of a global and multiracial colonized workforce whose labor was mobilized in service of the Empire. During both World Wars hundreds of thousands of colonial workers and soldiers served in Britain and Europe. But the most visible permanent settlements in the late nineteenth and early twentieth centuries were found in British seaports, shaped by the labor requirements of the British mercantile marine.

In the early twentieth century Britain's merchant shipping industry relied on the colonies for one-third of its workforce and paid them at colonial wage levels. Many Black seamen chose to migrate from the colonies to British and European seaports seeking better wages and working and living conditions. Black seafarers who migrated to Britain, transgressing the geographical barriers between colony and metropole, took refuge in multiracial communities in working-class dockside neighborhoods. The largest Black settlement, numbering several thousands, was Bute Town in Cardiff, notorious worldwide as Tiger Bay, but substantial settlements, numbering in the hundreds, existed in several other ports. These included Toxteth in Liverpool; Mill Dam and Holborn in South Shields; Kingston-upon-Hull; Salford, the port of Manchester; several Bristol Channel ports including Newport and Barry Dock; and, in LONDON, Stepney, Poplar, and Limehouse in the East End. Black seamen were also found in dozens of other British ports.

Among Black seamen as well as white, seafaring was a kin- and community-based occupation. Like migrants the world over, Black settlers in Britain lived with, worked with and relied upon networks of kin, co-villagers and compatriots to survive in Britain. In particular, many Black seamen relied on ethnic and kin networks for housing and maintenance between voyages. West Africans, Somalis, Arabs, and other Black settlers clustered in dockland enclaves linked or defined by kinship, culture, language, religion, and other common bonds. Here they had access to shops, cafes, social clubs, boarding houses, and religious institutions operated by fellow countrymen and by Black and white women. Women were active in this ethnic service sector, assisting in and managing cafes, acting as shills or informal agents for boarding houses, and operating brothels, market stalls and other local businesses. Although such businesses provided some employment ashore, most Black workers in Britain remained seamen. Because of this, Black women were relatively scarce, and interracial marriage was common. Although some interracial children experienced upward mobility through the schools, most tended to remain within these communities to work and to marry.

Of necessity, Black people in inter-war Britain enjoyed a measure of integration and mutual toleration with the white working people among whom they lived, worked, and married. Although class, ethnic, and religious divisions and even conflicts existed within as well as between Black and white groups, conflict and violence were not everyday occurrences. Black people maintained social and religious organizations and amenities which served their own while integrating them into the wider working class through MARRIAGE, work, and other activities and institutions.

In spite of or perhaps because of official mistrust and hostility, embodied in measures such as the Coloured Alien Seamen Order, 1925, these settlements maintained a surprising degree of geographical discreteness, longevity, and ethnic cohesiveness. Enumerations under the Coloured Alien Seamen Order suggest the relative size and proportion of different ethnic groups in the eighteen largest settlements remained relatively stable between 1925 and 1939. These settlements also sustained numerous religious, cultural and social institutions, among them the Islamia Allawia Friendly Society of Cardiff, the National African Sailors and Firemen's Union of Liverpool, the Somali Association of Great Britain, the Islamic Association of Great Britain, and the Improved Benevolent and Protective Order of Elks, a "Negro Friendly Society" active in London's East End. But race discrimination affected them all, prompting organization among Black seafarers "irrespective of creed or religion." Such organizations included the Cardiff Coloured Seamen's Committee, formed to combat union race discrimination, and its successor the Colonial Defence Association; and the Coloured Nationals Mutual Social Club of North Shields, formed to resist the British Shipping

Assistance Act, 1935, which effectively barred Black seamen from subsidized ships.

Thus Black settlements in early twentieth-century Britain reflected the multiracial and global character of Britain's still expanding Empire, and portended the Black immigration that accompanied the Empire's post-war implosion. They continued to exist on the eve of the Second World War, forming the nuclei of many post-war settlements.

During and after the SECOND WORLD WAR, Britain's global workforce was once again mobilized in aid of the mother country. Munitions workers, technicians, and other war workers were imported to Britain from India and elsewhere through the "Bevin Boys" scheme and other less publicized projects. The size and distribution of Black settlements in Britain altered as men from the colonies came to industrial centers to do war work or dispersed to the countryside like the "Honduranian" lumberjacks who harvested timber in Scotland. Thus began the post-war pattern of Black settlement in Britain's industrial cities as well as the ports. Yet port communities remained and became social centers for African-American GIs, colonial troops, and other Black war personnel.

The war and DECOLONIZATION produced a shift of focus among Black activists away from the metropole and toward the colonies, exemplified in the Pan-African Congress in Manchester in 1945. Yet the "Back to Africa" movement involved elites, while workers' migration from the colonies to Britain accelerated in the post-war period. After the war migration from the Caribbean and other colonized areas resumed, encouraged by the Nationality Act of 1948 which granted British citizenship to all imperial subjects. Frequently dated to the arrival in London of the Caribbean migrant ship *Empire Windrush* in 1948, the reconstitution and evolution of Britain's Black communities was actually an ongoing process. Since the Second World War the bulk of Black migrants have come from the West Indies, Pakistan, India, Bangladesh, and East Africa, but migration from other colonies and former colonies has continued. Large numbers of women as well as men have migrated, in particular from the Caribbean, to undertake medical training, or to work as typists, nurses, and domestic servants. In contrast to pre-war Black migrants who were usually seafarers, many Black migrants since 1945 arrived with technical or other occupational skills valuable to many British industries.

During post-war reconstruction, London Transport, British Rail and other industries recruited in the West Indies to fill jobs that white Britons rejected. Black migrants also came on their own, spurred by post-war depression in the colonized world and, in the case of the West Indies, the McCarran-Walter Act, 1952, which barred West Indian British subjects from entry to the United States under Britain's immigration quota. The NATIONAL HEALTH SERVICE absorbed nurses and other medical personnel who came from the colonies to train in Britain. Investigators in the early 1950s found many Black people were beginning to experience upward social mobility, and also found a wide range of experience and practice among different locales in Britain, and among different ethnic groups.

By the late 1950s, after a decade of highly publicized migration, there were approximately 192,000 Black migrants in Britain, constituting less than half of 1 percent of Britain's population: 107,000 West Indians, 50,000 Indians and Pakistanis, 5000 Nigerians and 30,000 others. Yet their presence provoked disproportionate alarm. When the British economy slumped in the late 1950s, the government sought to curtail Black migration, spurred by a series of white attacks on Black residents of St. Anne's Well, Nottingham, and Notting Hill, London, in August 1958. The Commonwealth Immigrants Act of 1961, essentially a "work voucher" scheme, backfired, prompting a wave of migrants from the colonies hoping to beat further restrictions. Continuing efforts to restrict Black migration between 1968 and 1981 were accompanied by increasingly embittered public debate of a racially charged character, and punctuated in the 1980s by inner city rioting by Black and white unemployed youth, events widely misconstrued in purely racial terms. Because of their concentration in public sector employment, Black Britons may also have been disproportionately affected by recent Conservative policies of privatization and cuts in state-supported services.

By the late twentieth century Black neighborhoods had formed in most of Britain's industrial centers, largely composed of Bengalis, Pakistanis, Indians, and West Indians, but also of Greek and Turkish Cypriots, Africans, and other formerly colonized people, including Asians expelled from Uganda, Kenya, Tanzania, and Malawi following Unilateral Declarations of Independence in the 1970s. Notable Black settlements include Handsworth and Sparkbrook in Birmingham, which has the largest Black population outside of London, Moss Side in Manchester, Chapeltown in Leeds, and St. Paul's in Bristol. In London, Notting Hill has become a center of Trinidadian settlement, site of the famous Notting Hill Carnivals, while Southall has attracted Indians and Brixton Jamaicans. In the late 1980s there were approximately 2.5 million Black people in Britain, amounting to perhaps 5 percent of the country's population. Of these an estimated 45 percent were born in Britain, and perhaps three-quarters of a million were Islamic.

Ethnic institution building and cultural and religious practices continue, coexisting with varying degrees of cultural syncretism or assimilation, and of interracial and multicultural activity. Second and third generation Black Britons are coming of age, transforming British cultural life. Mosques now inhabit abandoned churches, while Rastafarianism, a millenarian but politicized variety of pan-Africanism, has become widespread among youth of Jamaican descent. For the first time in decades, the 1987 elections returned four Black Members of Parliament, among them London activists Diane Abbott and Bernie Grant. They proceeded to form a parliamentary Black Caucus. The Islamic Party of Great Britain was formed in autumn 1989 and fielded candidates in the 1992 elections, most notably in Bradford.

The experiences of Chinese settlers in some ways resembled those of colonized Black people, but there were also significant differences. Before the Second World War most Chinese migrants to Britain came from Hong Kong and Kwangtung province in southern China, but since the war they have been joined by ethnic Chinese from Malaysia and the New Territories. Although many pre-war migrants were seafarers, Chinese businesses and communities were also well established ashore. Investigators have stressed Chinese settlers' maintenance of ties to China, including the remittance of wages abroad, the practice of importing brides from China to Britain as well as marital endogamy in Britain, and the training of British-born children in Chinese cultural practices. This, they argue, accounts for the persistence of distinctive Chinese communities in such places as the London docklands and Toxteth in Liverpool.

Laura Tabili

Bibliography

Collins, Sidney. *Coloured Minorities in Britain*. 1957.
Fryer, Peter. *Staying Power: the History of Black People in Britain*. 1984.
Green, Jeffrey. *Black Edwardians: Black People in Britain 1901–1914*. 1998.
Little, Kenneth. *Negroes in Britain*. 1972.
Sivanandan, A. *A Different Hunger: Writings on Black Resistance*. 1983.
Visram, Rozina. *Ayahs, Lascars and Princes: The History of Indians in Britain, 1700–1947*. 1986.

Blair, Anthony Charles Linton (1953–)

Tony Blair was the first LABOUR PARTY leader for a generation to become Prime Minister. From his election as the party's youngest-ever leader in 1994, he began a process of modernization, represented by the creation of "New Labour", which helped Labour to an electoral land-slide in the general election of 1997. As Prime Minister, he enjoyed unprecedented levels of popularity and presided over a strong economy and a reforming government. Although the late summer of 2000 saw the party move (briefly) behind the Conservatives in the opinion polls for the first time since 1992, there was still every expectation that he would go on to become the first Labour Prime Minister to win a full second consecutive term in office.

Born on 6 May 1953, Blair showed no early signs of a future in Labour politics. His father was a Conservative. Blair enjoyed a private education before going on to read law at St. John's College, OXFORD. Then he moved to London, where he worked as a barrister between 1976 and 1983. He trained in the chambers of Alexander Irvine, where he met fellow barrister Cherie Booth, who became his wife in 1980. They have four children, the youngest, born in 2000, the only child born to a sitting Prime Minister in modern British history.

Blair took little part in politics while at Oxford, although he did come under the influence of the ideas of communitarian philosopher John MacMurray. His involvement in Labour politics started when he moved to London, where he worked hard with others against the then powerful left. In 1982 he secured the candidature at a by-election in the safe Tory seat of Beaconsfield. He was heavily defeated but was fortunate to win the nomination for the safe Labour seat of Sedgefield (County Durham) at the 1983 election. Once at Westminster, he was rapidly promoted by party leader NEIL KINNOCK to a succession of front-bench positions and was elected to the Shadow Cabinet in 1988. Following the election of John Smith as party leader in the aftermath of the 1992 election defeat, he was promoted to the post of Shadow Home Secretary. This was an advantageous move. Despite the Conservative government's rhetoric, crime was rising sharply. Blair moved rapidly to claim law and order as a Labour issue; abandoning the party's hitherto progressive inclinations, he developed ideas on attacking crime which were summed up in his famous soundbite, "Tough on crime; tough on the causes of crime".

The sudden death of Smith in May 1994 inadvertently advanced Blair's political career. He and Gordon Brown, the Shadow Chancellor, were generally bracketed together as modernizers, with Brown perceived as the senior partner. However, Brown's popularity had waned alongside Blair. In addition, Brown was distraught at the leader's death, whereas Blair had felt no such closeness toward Smith, whom he had criticized privately for stalling on the modernization process begun by Kinnock. Key figures in the modernizing camp switched to Blair. Brown was persuaded that he should not stand, to avoid splitting the modernizing vote. In the election proper Blair easily defeated John Prescott (who became deputy leader) and Margaret Beckett to take the leadership.

Blair's inheritance was favorable. The Conservative government under JOHN MAJOR had been in the doldrums ever since Britain's forced departure from the European Exchange Rate Mechanism (ERM) in September 1992. The government itself was widely perceived as incompetent and riddled with corruption or "sleaze". Blair moved rapidly, however, to resume the modernization process. In early 1995 Clause IV of the party's constitution was rewritten to remove its historic commitment to NATIONALIZATION. Blair appeared to be influenced by communitarianism, by the American "New Democrats" under Bill Clinton, by ideas of a "Third Way" between free-market capitalism and state socialism, and by gurus of "stakeholding", such as the journalist Will Hutton. All this seemed to pay dividends: The party attained massive poll leads, and even the party's individual membership, which had appeared to be in permanent decline, rose sharply.

By the time of the May 1997 general election a Labour victory was widely expected, but its scale was not. In the event the party won 418 seats to the Conservatives' 165 seats, and had an overall majority of 179, larger even than that attained in its 1945 landslide. There were no Conservative MPs in either Scotland or Wales. The government he established contained strong figures from most segments of the party other than the far left (itself, by now, very weak). Brown became Chancellor; Robin Cook, Foreign Secretary; Jack Straw, Home Secretary; and Prescott was given charge of a huge new department covering Environment, Transport, and the Regions. By the beginning of 2001 all these men were still in the same posts, a remarkable level of continuity.

The government inherited a strong economy. Under Brown, "prudence" became the key word. Although taxes and expenditures rose somewhat, there was no return to the high tax regimes of previous Labour administrations, and value for money remained the key to public expenditure, as under the Conservatives. There was no wholesale reform of the WELFARE STATE. A general easing of benefits in some areas was combined with a determined effort to weed out the "undeserving". This brought a new hard edge to Labour's previously liberal rhetoric, which alienated some of the party's supporters. The same was true of Straw's tenure at the Home Office, where tough policies were implemented, although not always enforced with any great vigor. The government was more radical in promoting DEVOLUTION: following referendums, Scotland was given a Parliament with tax-raising powers, and Wales a weaker Assembly, and elective local government was restored in LONDON. Further constitution reform denied to hereditary peers their right to sit in the HOUSE OF LORDS, although early signs of interest in electoral reform soon waned. In foreign policy Blair struck a somewhat more cautious note over Europe than his immediate predecessors: It was clear that there were aspects of European welfarism that repelled Blair, who was keener to stress self-reliance and personal responsibility. Thus the question of Britain's joining the single European currency remained open. Blair's own inclinations were more Atlanticist, reinforced by his close personal relationship with President Clinton and his support for United Nations action in the Balkans.

Criticism soon followed the post-election euphoria. Blair was attacked for being a "control freak" as he pursued a presidential premiership. There were attacks on the use of "spin" and recurrent rows between leading members of the government (or at least their advisers). There were periodic allegations of "sleaze", which helped to bring down the Paymaster-General, Geoffrey Robinson, and which led to the temporary departure from the CABINET of Blair's key modernizing ally, Peter Mandelson, in December 1998. Perhaps more substantially, there were many who argued that New Labour was playing so much to the middle class that it was losing its core working-class support. Some of these criticisms were exaggerated. Repeated efforts to relaunch the CONSERVATIVE PARTY, under the erratic leadership of William Hague, brought more derision than support. Labour continued to win by-elections but on a reduced poll. Core voters in working-class areas might have been staying home simply because they saw no reason to vote when Labour had an impregnable majority at Westminster. In addition, the levels of sleaze encountered were, by contemporary standards, hardly startling.

At the party conference in September 2000 Blair stated that his second term in office would be more radical than the first, and this may well prove to be the case, following the Labour victory in June 2001. It seems clear that universalism in welfare benefits will continue to yield to targeting those most in need, and that market tests will still be applied to public services. No matter what happens though, it can be said that Blair has, through a combination of shrewd politicking, carefully honed rhetoric, and good fortune, led Labour to a position of ascendancy which, even a few years earlier, would have seemed inconceivable.

Andrew Thorpe

Bibliography
Anderson, Paul, and Nyta Mann. *Safety First: The Making of New Labour.* 1997.
Gould, Philip. *The Unfinished Revolution: How the Modernisers Saved the Labour Party.* 1998.
Rentoul, John. *Tony Blair.* Rev. ed. 1996.
Sopel, Jon. *Tony Blair: The Moderniser.* Rev. ed. 1995.
Thorpe, Andrew. *A History of the British Labour Party.* 2nd ed. 2001.

Blatchford, Robert Peel Glanville (1851–1943)

In the 1890s and early 1900s Robert Blatchford was one of the most widely-read socialists in Britain. His major book, *Merrie England* (1893), sold more than two million copies, while the newspaper he edited, the *Clarion,* was for many years one of the most important socialist publications in the country. Blatchford was a popular journalist and crusader on behalf of the socialist cause, although he was certainly not an original thinker. Moreover, his popularity was ephemeral, and his increasing jingoism and opposition to organized religion alienated many of his followers.

Born in 1851, Blatchford was apprenticed in his early teens to a brush-maker in Halifax before eventually joining the ARMY, an experience that made him a devout patriot and imperialist. In the 1880s he began a career as a journalist and became the leader writer for the radical *Sunday Chronicle* in Manchester. Writing about local SLUM conditions for the paper, Blatchford turned to socialism for a solution to the problems he encountered, influenced by the work of Henry George and William Morris. He launched his own newspaper, the *Clarion,* in 1891, a unique publication that explained the principles of socialism while entertaining its readers with a mixture of short stories, poems, and a healthy dose of humor. While it became the most widely-read organ of the socialist movement, the *Clarion* supported no single party or faction; rather, it deployed popular literary idioms in an attempt to disseminate a general message of socialist fellowship.

Throughout the 1890s Blatchford devoted his energy to encouraging various Clarion clubs—educational, social, recreational, and political organizations aimed at educating the masses in socialist principles by demonstrating that socialism had as much to do with how one lived one's life as it did with abstract doctrine. In 1893 he published *Merrie England,* through which he attempted to explain socialism to the general reader. It was Blatchford's most successful book, an effective piece of propaganda that was responsible for the conversion of many individuals to the socialist cause.

During the BOER WAR Blatchford lost credibility because of his support of British war aims. His enthusiasm for British imperialism, combined with his intense dislike of industrial capitalism, was a unique position for a socialist to hold, and it repelled those with more PACIFIST leanings. Nevertheless, the success of *Britain for the British* (1902) demonstrated that Blatchford could still attract many loyal supporters. Following the Boer War, however, Blatchford alienated many of them when he formally repudiated organized Christianity, which he had come to view as a barrier to progress and which he attacked in *God and My Neighbour* (1903) and *Not Guilty: A Defence of the Bottom Dog* (1905). During the early years of the new century Blatchford also wrote several novels, the most important of which were *Julie* (1900?), the story of a slum girl, and *The Sorcery Shop* (1907), a utopian novel that closely parallelled Morris's *News From Nowhere.*

In the early 1900s Blatchford campaigned for unity between various socialist organizations, as he had in the 1890s. Nevertheless, despite the electoral success of the newly-formed LABOUR PARTY in 1906, he continued to attack the policies and personal style of KEIR HARDIE and remained suspicious of Labour's electoral ties to the LIBERAL PARTY. Furthermore, his increasing warnings about German militarism fell on deaf ears in the socialist movement. Hence, when Britain declared war on Germany in 1914 and Blatchford swung the *Clarion* behind the government, many of his supporters deserted him.

During and after the war Blatchford remained an active journalist. He also began his drift to the Right, eventually considering himself a Tory Democrat. He was opposed to WOMEN'S SUFFRAGE and in the general election of 1924 voted for the CONSERVATIVE PARTY. Following his wife's death in 1921, he became a spiritualist and retreated from public view, abandoned by many colleagues after he repudiated his earlier socialist convictions.

For more than a decade few socialists were as popular with the British working class as Blatchford. Although he played only a minor role in the formal electoral struggles waged by the Left, and although his jingoism and disdain of parliamentary politics lost him support, Blatchford was a passionate critic of the social evils of capitalism, and his vivid description of those evils appealed to many who shared his own vision of what a transformed society might look like.

Chris Waters

Bibliography
Blatchford, Robert. *My Eighty Years.* 1931.
Thompson, Laurence. *Robert Blatchford: Portrait of an Englishman.* 1951.
Waters, Chris. *British Socialists and the Politics of Popular Culture, 1884–1914.* 1990.

Bloomsbury Group

The Bloomsbury Group, a coterie of intellectuals and artists, has a secure place in the cultural history of twentieth-century Britain, including as it does a writer of genius in VIRGINIA WOOLF and the century's most important economist in JOHN MAYNARD KEYNES.

Bloomsbury, the name attached to the group, derived from the Bloomsbury section of LONDON, near the British Museum, whose streets and squares were mostly designated with titles and family names associated with the Duke of Bedford, who owned much of the land. The area is respectable but unfashionable; it adjoins raffish Soho; and the two together might be taken to represent the combination of respectablity with a touch of bohemianism that Bloomsbury itself came to exemplify. The group had its beginnings foreshadowed when Sir Leslie Stephen died in 1904, and the Stephen children, Vanessa, Thoby, Virginia and Adrian—orphaned, but all in their twenties—moved away from the family house in upper middle-class Kensington to live on their own at 46 Gordon Square, Bloomsbury. There, they started to entertain on Thursday evenings, and out of these spirited informal gatherings the group emerged.

The origins of Bloomsbury go back to the early years of the nineteenth century: the group's essential seriousness, masked as it might be by wit and unconventionality, came from their Victorian forebears, even though they themselves were consciously in revolt against them. James Stephen, the great-grandfather of the Stephen children, was one of the most active members of the Clapham sect, a group of evangelical Anglicans, notable for their campaign against the slave trade. His son, also James, was a central figure in the administration of the British colonies, and his grandsons were FitzJames, a famous judge and conservative Utilitarian, and Leslie, a prolific literary critic, the founder of the *Dictionary of National Biography*, and well-known for his abandonment of the Christian faith. Less apparent was the importance of the feminine line. The Stephen children's mother, Julia Jackson, had the famous photographer, Julia Margaret Cameron, as an aunt. That generation was active in the upper-class artistic circles of late Victorian London.

The most immediate origins of the group go back to the young men who were friends of Thoby Stephen's at CAMBRIDGE at the turn of the century, among them John Maynard Keynes, LYTTON STRACHEY, and LEONARD WOOLF. Keynes, Strachey and Woolf were members of the secret Cambridge discussion society, the Apostles, at that time dominated by the philosophy of G.E. MOORE. Moore believed, and led his disciples to believe, that as he stated in the most famous sentence of his *Principia Ethica* (1903): "By far the most valuable things, which we know or can imagine, are certain states of consciousness, which may be roughly described as the pleasures of human intercourse and the enjoyment of beautiful objects." Two other crucial Cambridge contemporaries, not members of the Apostles, were Clive Bell and Thoby Stephen himself. Although Thoby would die of typhoid in 1906, he was the true maker of the group, having introduced his sisters, Vanessa and Virginia Stephen, to his Cambridge friends. Clive Bell would marry Vanessa and Leonard Woolf would marry Virginia. (Lytton Strachey's cousin, DUNCAN GRANT, was also an early member of the group.)

Before the First World War these young people felt that rationality had triumphed and they would be able to create a new modern world. They endlessly discussed all sorts of issues in their weekly gatherings in Gordon Square. They also believed in attempting to live sexual lives free of guilt and Victorian hypocrisy; perhaps even more unusually for the time, they enjoyed free and frank sexual conversations in mixed company.

Bloomsbury functioned most cohesively as a group in the years before the First World War. Its fame would come later, after the war, when they were no longer so sure that reason would conquer all and their original optimism had dimmed. (Yet Keynes became dedicated to ways that economics could be used to improve gradually the human lot.)

They had become even stronger as a group in 1910 when they were joined by two Cambridge men, both Apostles and both of a somewhat older generation: E.M. FORSTER and ROGER FRY. Fry was already a prominent art critic. That year he re-met Clive and VANESSA BELL, and with the assitance of Clive and others, he selected the paintings for the Manet and the Post-Impressionists exhibition in London at the end of the year. In effect, it was the introduction of modern art to England. For Bloomsbury, its immediate influence was upon its painters, Vanessa Bell and Duncan Grant. Years later, Virginia Woolf, with the exhibition in mind, made her famous observation in "Mr Bennett and Mrs Brown" that "on or about December, 1910, human character changed." By this she not only meant the new art in the exhibition, but the emergence of modernism in literature, especially as it came to full flower in the next decade in the works of JAMES JOYCE, E.M. Forster, D.H. LAWRENCE, T.S. ELIOT, and Woolf herself. She contrasted the modernists to the prevailing popular realism, singling out H.G. WELLS, ARNOLD BENNETT, and JOHN GALSWORTHY, decrying their unwillingness to see beyond realism to less literal and more imaginative truths of human character.

In the artistic world, modernism was represented in the theories of Roger Fry, and later by

Clive Bell. Both emphasized the formal values of paintings, which in effect meant turning attention away from representation to the shapes on the canvas, a precursor to abstraction. In *Art* (1914) Clive Bell put forth the doctrine of "significant form": One should not look for representational or symbolic aspects in art. The painter whom Fry and Bell most revered was Cezanne, and the Bloomsbury painters strove for something of his qualities in their work, particularly in the period 1910–18. Under Fry's leadership, Vanessa Bell, Grant, and other painters came together from 1913 to 1919 as the Omega workshop, to apply their ideas of abstraction and what would now be recognized as modern design to objects of ordinary life, such as screens and chairs. Bell and Grant continued to design and paint throughout their long lives. Charleston in Sussex, the house where they lived together until she died in 1961 (Grant died in 1978) is now a monument to their art in the paintings on the walls and the decorations of the rooms.

The giants of the group—and it is striking that one group of close friends should have included so many eminent figures—were Keynes, Woolf, Strachey, Fry, and Forster, although he was not at the center of the circle. Those figures, along with Leonard Woolf, were so important that they have separate entries in this encyclopedia and so it is not necessary here to outline their careers and importance. There were some further literary figures—less significant—who were more or less members of what was never a formal organization, such as the novelist David Garnett, who was Duncan Grant's lover and later the husband of Bell's and Grant's daughter, Angelica, indicating something of the sexual minuet that characterized their lives, and that has emerged in the modern biographies of members of the group. There was also Desmond MacCarthy, the literary critic. Among others, such writers as T.S. Eliot and the younger John Lehmann became good friends.

After the First World War the members of the group became increasingly famous. They remained close friends, frequently meeting in London and at Charleston as well as vacationing in France, the country outside of England which had their strongest allegiance. But their gatherings were less frequent than they had been before the war. Ever at the very center of the group were the two sisters, Virginia Woolf and Vanessa Bell. Deaths diminished the group: Strachey in 1932, Fry in 1934, the tragedy of the death of the Bells' son, Julian, in the SPANISH CIVIL WAR in 1937, Virginia Woolf by suicide in 1941, Keynes in 1946. All through their lives and accomplishments, there was a commitment to fight against what they saw as Victorian pretense and humbug, to penetrate below the surface to what might violate ordinary standards of reality but would nevertheless be something "truer", to follow ideas bravely wherever they might lead, not to forgo their middle-class comforts, but to work for a better world economically and artistically for others. They were crucial shapers of modernism in this century.

Peter Stansky

Bibliography
Bell, Quentin. *Bloomsbury.* 1968.
Palmer, Alan and Veronica. *Who's Who in Bloomsbury.* 1987.
Richardson, Elizabeth P. *A Bloomsbury Iconography.* 1989.
Marler, Regina. *Bloomsbury Pie: The Making of the Bloomsbury Boom.* 1997.
Rosenbaum, S.P., ed. *The Bloomsbury Group.* 1975.
Shone, Richard. *Bloomsbury Portraits.* 1976.
Stansky, Peter. *On Or About December 1910: Early Bloomsbury and Its Intimate World.* 1996.

Boer [South African] War (1899–1902)

The Anglo-Boer War ended the Victorian era and ushered in the twentieth century for Britain on a disquieting note. It demonstrated British diplomatic isolation in the days before the First World War and effectively dispelled the myth of British colonial invincibility. A preview of the war had occurred with a Boer victory in a skirmish in 1881 after which the British government was obliged to concede independent status to the Boer republics of Transvaal and Orange Free State. The uneasy tension which existed after 1881, however, exploded when gold and diamonds were discovered in the Boer territories in the latter part of the nineteenth century.

Gold and diamond discoveries were of little concern to the theocratic, agrarian Boer lifestyle. The Boers (farmers) were a dour Calvinistic people descended from seventeenth-century German and Dutch settlers; the *Volk,* as they called themselves, were fundamentalists in life as in faith. One of their strongest beliefs was that the white man was to be forever superior to the Black, who was scripturally ordained to be a permanent hewer of wood and drawer of water. One reason they had trekked north, away from the British Cape Colony in the 1830s, was that Britain abolished slavery in 1833. Their god-given right, they believed, ought not be tampered with. The increasing flow of *uitlanders* (Afrikaans for outsider, many of whom were British) scrambling into the Boer republics for the gold and diamonds was of growing concern to them, just as the harsh Boer treatment of *uitlanders* troubled the British.

Following the Jameson raid of 1895–6, that half-baked scheme for an *uitlander* revolt which had been concocted by Cecil Rhodes, an escalating series of events and fruitless negotiations exacerbated relations between the Boers and Britain. There is now creditable evidence that British Colonial Secretary Joseph Chamberlain and his representative in South Africa, SIR ALFRED MILNER, conspired to prevent any peaceful solution to the problem—both men probably influenced by the machinations of Cecil Rhodes. Milner in particular has been characterized as an intransigent obstacle to peace. Following a series of failed political negotiations, the Boers took the offensive, invading British Natal in October 1899.

Although superficially the war seemed a mismatch, in reality the Boers had several advantages. They were a hardy outdoors people, raised to horseback riding, hunting, and shooting. In addition, the Boers had used tax revenues they had raised from the hated gold and diamonds to purchase the latest armaments from German dealers; their weapons were, if anything, superior to the British. Furthermore, on the eve of the war the Boer forces comprised over 50,000 mounted soldiers, with rifles and ammunition for many more. In contrast, as late as September 1899, the British could muster no more than 14,750 men. Whitehall authorized a reinforcing contingent of 47,000, but not until 29 September.

In spite of this unreadied state, British public opinion ran high that this war would be no more than another of "Queen Victoria's little wars," quickly wrapped up once the fleet arrived bearing soldiers from the "thin red line." In truth the only European foes faced by the British ARMY since the Crimean War were the Boers themselves, who had in 1881 effortlessly trounced it at the battle of Majuba Hill. British confidence nonetheless was high when Sir Redvers Buller was sent out to command the forces.

Considering the Boer advantages, it is not surprising, therefore, that in the early days of the invasion there were several Boer successes, leading the British press to dub the week of 9–15 December as "Black Week." General Methuen was bested at Magersfontein, General Gatacre was repulsed at Stormberg, and commanding General Redvers Buller, defeated at Colenso, was forced to abandon his drive to relieve the Boer siege of the British military depot at Ladysmith. The Boers were able to sustain a multi-front campaign against the British and besiege, in addition to Ladysmith, the strategically significant towns of Kimberley and Mafeking. The scale of these disasters, as well as the inept defense he made of his actions, led to Buller's dismissal and replacement by General Frederick "Bobs" Roberts, Lord Roberts of Kandahar.

In time the British reinforced their garrisons and the weight of the full army turned the military tide. With their reinforced might, the British were able to relieve their forces, break the sieges of the three cities, go on the offensive and capture both Boer capitals by June 1900. The Boers refused to surrender, however, and fighting continued for two more years. By the time a British victory seemed certain, Lord Roberts was recalled for a hero's return to Britain, and General KITCHENER was left to mop up the remaining Boer resistance. The British government under Lord Salisbury now felt the time appropriate for elections and called what came to be known as the "Khaki" election. "Pro-Boer" LIBERALS such as DAVID LLOYD GEORGE attacked government policy, while the CONSERVATIVE administration wrapped itself in the flag, and the election was a victory for Tory war policy, maintaining their 130 seat majority and vindicating their war effort.

In the latter stages of the war the Boers abandoned full-scale encounters against the British and turned to guerrilla tactics conducted by small *kommando* units. Their defeat was a tedious process in spite of the British overwhelming military strength. Further, Britain proved to be friendless in Europe, jeered at by the European press for its inability to defeat an enemy it outnumbered twenty to one. After a century of enjoying "splendid isolation", the British found their diplomatic seclusion troubling and resolved after the war to shore up its diplomatic alliances. Finally, in a pique of anger over such untoward tactics as the *kommandos*, Lord Kitchener began a scorched earth policy, erecting miles of barbed wire quadrants with corner blockhouses, systematically sweeping for Boer units. In addition, Boer women and children were herded into concentration camps where many died of malnutrition and disease. Britain was criticized internationally while Liberal opposition leaders characterized government policy as "methods of barbarism."

By the spring of 1902 peace talks were begun, concerned in the main with the questions of Boer independence and white sovereignty. The peace of Vereeniging of May 1902 allowed the Boers a degree of political autonomy while retaining complete racial supremacy. The final twenty months of guerilla warfare had produced some strategic gains for the Boers, therefore. All British hopes for the Cape Colony color-blind voting policy applied to all South Africa were dashed. By the time of the peace negotiations the British public was so tired of the prolonged war that the government was ready to extricate itself by whatever circumstances. The Boers, in turn, fearing a Liberal victory in the next election, felt more comfortable negotiating with the Conservatives. The Boer republics were annexed and put under the direct rule of Alfred (now Lord) Milner. Britain also agreed to help repair damage to Boer territories by granting them interest-free loans.

British loss in lives was about 22,000, while Boer combat deaths exceeded 7,000. In addition, perhaps as many as 20,000 Boer women and children died in concentration camps. British performance was the subject of a Royal Commission investigation begun in September 1902. Chaired by the Earl of Elgin, the Commission issued a harsh indictment of the current system in July 1903, and reforms in the military were initiated that had implications for British performance in the First World War.

In the end, however, the Boers, though vanquished on the battlefield, were more calculating in defeat than were the British in victory. They reasoned that through the union of four African states that developed after the war (the Union of South Africa was created in May 1910), they might achieve dominion not only over their former two republics, but of all South Africa, and especially with the prerogative to treat their Black subjects just as the Old Testament seemed to suggest to them. Their strategy prevailed. Many Boers became tacit supporters of the Empire; Boer generals were feted as heroes in London following the war. The Boer conviction proved in the long run more intractable than was the British: the *het volk* survived Queen Victoria, and the Boers won the Boer War after all.

Newell D. Boyd

Bibliography

Farwell, Byron. *The Great Boer War*. 1976.

Kruger, Rayne. *Goodbye Dolly Gray: The Story of the Boer War*. 1959.

Pakenham, Thomas. *The Boer War*. 1979.

Smith, Iain R. *The Origins of the South African War 1899–1902*. 1996.

Warwick, Peter. *Black People and the South African War, 1899–1902*. 1983.

———. ed. *The South African War: the Anglo-Boer War, 1899–1902*. 1980.

Bonar Law, Andrew (1858–1923)

Although Andrew Bonar Law's tenure as Prime Minister lasted hardly more than six months, from 1922 into 1923, his career as a whole was of lasting significance. In particular, his accession to the CONSERVATIVE PARTY leadership in November 1911 occurred at a critical time for his party, battered as it had been by internal dissension and three successive electoral defeats. That it recovered its nerve and revived its prospects was in no small part due to his aggressive partisanship. During the FIRST WORLD WAR, however, Law assumed a more statesman-like role, collaborating successfully in a coalition with LLOYD GEORGE in administering the war effort and overseeing the subsequent transition, first to peacetime reconstruction and then to party government once again in 1922.

In many ways he was an unlikely choice for a party whose upper reaches remained so English, Anglican, and patrician. Law was none of these; born in 1858 in Canada, the son of a melancholy Presbyterian minister, and educated in Scotland, he began a career in the Glasgow iron trade. That experience disclosed no particular ambition or aptitude for political life, except for an undeniable effectiveness in debate that stemmed from his diligent preparation and exceptional memory. Those capacities stood him in good stead in his first parliamentary contest, in the Khaki election of 1900 when he benefited from a surge of wartime patriotic sentiment and was elected for a Glaswegian seat he had not been expected to win. Making his mark, appropriately enough, as a Parliamentary Secretary to the Board of Trade, it was not long before Law adapted his dry but formidable debating style to the realities of the Commons. Law's growing concentration on politics was probably accentuated by the death in 1909 of his wife, to whom he had been deeply devoted.

By 1910, through diligent application and a direct pugnacious style, he had earned a reputation within a Conservative Party shorn of much of its talent by the electoral debacle of 1906, and of much of its cohesiveness by the controversy over TARIFF REFORM. Law attracted further attention by his willingness to foresake his safe suburban London seat to contest an almost hopeless one in the free trade citadel of Manchester. Though he lost the election, he gained in stature, and returned to Parliament shortly thereafter in a by-election. Having earned high marks for his courage and selflessness, he was with some plausibility more than merely an idle spectator when the party met in November 1911 to choose a successor to ARTHUR BALFOUR, who had resigned as party leader. After a deadlock between the top two candidates, AUSTEN CHAMBERLAIN and Walter Long, Law emerged as the compromise choice, prompting Lloyd George to remark that "the fools have stumbled on the right man by accident."

For the next three years, however, Law did more to earn himself a place in Liberal demonology than in the good graces of constitutional scholars. Sensing that the resurgence of the Irish Question afforded an opportunity to restore Conservative Party unity, Law threw his weight against Home Rule and encouraged ULSTER separatist militancy to the point that he appeared to be condoning, even inciting, a direct challenge to parliamentary sovereignty. Whether Law's vehement "new style" was merely a tactical device to arouse the electorate for the anticipated campaign, or whether it was a reckless strategy born of despair and Ulster bigotry, is still unclear.

Irresponsible it certainly was, but whatever the verdict, Law had no doubt where his duty lay when the war broke out in August 1914.

Resignation in the face of duty dominated the remainder of his life. Law readily accepted the immediate suspension of partisan activity, and when ASQUITH broadened his government in 1915, he accepted without complaint a position (that of Colonial Secretary) beneath that to which his stature would have entitled him. With the further reconstruction of the government late in 1916, in which he was instrumental in forming a coalition with Lloyd George, he deferred again, accepting only the position of Chancellor of the Exchequer and leaving the prime ministership to his Welsh colleague. The strain of wartime administration, the onset of throat cancer, and the loss of two sons in battle all eventually prompted his retirement from politics, though it proved to be shortlived. His intervention in October 1922 brought the Lloyd George coalition to an end, but by then the ill and morose Law had little interest in doing more than returning public life to normal. In May 1923 he resigned as prime minister (being succeeded by STANLEY BALDWIN), having only some five months left to live. When Law was laid to rest in Westminster Abbey, Asquith is reputed to have quipped that it was fitting to "have buried the Unknown Prime Minister by the side of the Unknown Soldier." Apocryphal or not, the comment evokes Law's remoteness and failure to elucidate a constructive program with which his name would be associated. But he did not conceive of his role as a Conservative politician in that way. If his career had reflected the growing weight of business interests within the party, he too, like the Unknown Soldier, might be regarded as a victim of the war, having sacrificed his health, ambition, and family. And yet, he might also be regarded as one of its victors, having restored and then preserved the interests of his party.

Frans Coetzee

Bibliography

Adams, R.J.Q. *Bonar Law.* 1999.

Blake, Robert. *The Unknown Prime Minister: The Life and Times of Andrew Bonar Law 1858–1923.* 1955.

Ramsden, John. *The Age of Balfour and Baldwin 1902–1940.* 1978.

Bowen, Elizabeth Dorothea Cole (1899–1973)
Elizabeth Bowen's family came to Ireland in 1653 under Cromwell. Her early years were spent divided between Dublin and the family estate, Bowen's Court, in County Cork. After traveling in Europe, Bowen settled in London when she was in her early twenties and, under the tutelage of Rose Macaulay, began to write short stories. *Encounters,* her first volume of stories, appeared

in 1923, the year of her marriage to Alan Cameron, an employee of the BBC. After stints in Northamptonshire and Oxford the couple settled into a Regent's Terrace house and became part of a circle that included Cyril Connolly, John and Rosamond Lehmann, William Plomer, STEPHEN SPENDER, and VIRGINIA WOOLF.

During the late 1920s and the 1930s Bowen's short stories and novels appeared almost yearly. Her first novel, *The Hotel* (1927), was followed in 1929 by *The Last September,* one of her best works, which details the romance of a young Anglo-Irish woman with a British soldier stationed in Ireland during 1920–1. After *Friends and Relations* (1931) and the more substantial *To the North* (1932), she published *The House in Paris* (1935) and *The Death of the Heart* (1938), novels which made her widely known. These works express her view of the world as a tenuous and dangerous place; her characters are inevitably subject to betrayals both by other persons and by their countries.

During the SECOND WORLD WAR Bowen worked as an Air Raid Warden in London and as an employee of the Ministry of Information. In this capacity she made frequent trips to neutral Ireland to assess the state of Irish opinion regarding Britain. Both these occupations (and the bombing of her own London house) diverted her from writing, but made their way into her fiction in the short story collections *Look at All Those Roses* (1941) and *Ivy Gripped the Steps* (1946) and her brilliant novel of wartime love and espionage in London and Ireland, *The Heat of the Day* (1949). In this era Bowen also published two autobiographies: *Bowen's Court* (1942), the history of her family's tenure in Ireland, and *Seven Winters* (1942), the story of her own childhood.

After the war Bowen and her husband took up full-time occupancy at Bowen's Court, which she was the first woman to inherit. During these years she favored non-fiction: a gathering of essays and reviews, *Collected Impressions* (1950) and an eponymous study of *The Shelbourne Hotel* in Dublin (1951). Following her husband's death in 1952, Bowen embarked upon a more restless existence, one marked by struggles to keep up the estate. Her post-war fiction, *A World of Love* (1955) reflects her absorption in the problems of decay for the Anglo-Irish gentry still inhabiting southern Ireland. She traveled ceaselessly (often to American universities) and wrote eclectic articles for such publications as *Mademoiselle.* By 1959 she could no longer afford Bowen's Court and sold it to a neighbor who demolished it. 1960 marked the publication of *A Time in Rome,* her observations of various trips to Italy. Bowen spent the last decade of her life based in England, traveling and writing fragments of autobiography. These appeared in the posthumous *Pictures and Conversations* (1975). Her bizarre last novel, *Eva Trout: or Changing Scenes* (1968), reflects her difficult later years. She died of lung cancer in February 1973 and was buried in the family plot in Ireland.

Bowen embodied many paradoxes of this century: she followed in the English literary tradition, but insisted on her membership in the Anglo-Irish "race"; she wrote as a woman but denied being a feminist in any political or social sense; she claimed not to be a historian, but she often discussed past events in fiction and essays. Certainly cognizant of the modernist tradition, she preferred a more traditional style, combining her love of Jane Austen, Henry James, and Anthony Trollope with the Irish fondness for the ghost story. While she has often been viewed only as a brittle recorder of tea party concerns, she must be understood in the larger social context of the brutal history through which she lived: the "Troubles" in Ireland, culminating in the Irish Civil War, and the two world wars, which confirmed all that she detected to be wrong with the century she inhabited.

Heather Bryant Jordan

Bibliography

Bloom, Harold. ed. *Elizabeth Bowen.* 1987.

Gindin, James. *British Fiction in the 1930s: The Dispiriting Decade.* 1992.

Glendinning, Victoria. *Elizabeth Bowen: Portrait of a Writer.* 1977.

Jordan, Heather Bryant. *How Will the Heart Endure? Elizabeth Bowen and the Landscape of War.* 1992.

Lee, Hermione. *Elizabeth Bowen: An Estimation.* 1981.

Brailsford, H(enry) N(oel) (1873–1958)

As an author, journalist, and editor, H.N. Brailsford wrote about politics and world affairs for nearly sixty years, establishing himself as one of the most eloquent and incisive socialist commentators of his generation.

Born in Yorkshire, the son of a METHODIST clergyman, he grew up mainly in Scotland, attending the University of Glasgow, where he studied with GILBERT MURRAY and Edward Caird. After additional study at OXFORD and the University of Berlin, he embarked on an academic career, which he soon abandoned for journalism. In 1897 he resigned a position as subeditor of the *Scots Pictorial* to enlist in the Philhellenic Legion, a volunteer force fighting alongside the Greeks in their struggles against the Ottoman Empire, an experience he recounted in his only novel, *The Broom of the War-God* (1898). He soon won the attention of C.P. SCOTT, who sent him to Crete as a *MANCHESTER GUARDIAN* correspondent, the start of a long, but intermittent connection with that paper as a leader writer and foreign correspondent. This was followed by stints as leader writer and commentator on foreign affairs with a succession of Liberal periodicals: the *Morning Leader*, the *Tribune*, the *Daily News*, and, especially, the *NATION* throughout H.W. MASSINGHAM's editorship from 1907 to 1922.

During the first decade of the century Brailsford became involved with several groups agitating on behalf of liberal movements abroad and befriended Russian exiles living in London, like Prince Peter Kropotkin and Theodore Rothstein. Membership in the Balkan Committee and familiarity with the region made him a logical choice to lead a British relief mission to Macedonia in 1903–4 and later to serve on the international Carnegie Commission of Inquiry into the origins of the Balkan Wars. In 1906 he published his study *Macedonia,* which remained for many years the authoritative cultural and historical analysis.

Despite his professional and personal links with Liberal Nonconformity, Brailsford began to gravitate to the Left at the time of the BOER WAR, and in 1907 he joined the INDEPENDENT LABOUR PARTY in protest against the Liberal policy in Egypt. Liberal editors, like Massingham and A.G. GARDINER of the *Daily News,* did not attempt to curb his attacks on the Liberal government, readily publishing Brailsford's denunciations of the Anglo-Russian *entente* and his defense of Egyptian nationalism. In 1909, largely at the instigation of his first wife Jane Malloch Brailsford, Brailsford became involved in the WOMEN'S SUFFRAGE campaign, later serving as secretary of the ill-fated Conciliation Committee. In 1910 he was adopted as a women's suffrage parliamentary candidate for South Salford in opposition to Hilaire Belloc but withdrew in favor of a Liberal suffragist.

In much of his writing Brailsford sought to extend his friend and journalistic colleague J.A. HOBSON's economic analysis of imperialism to international diplomacy more generally. In his celebrated *The War of Steel and Gold,* published in June 1914, he deplored the covert relationship between finance and diplomacy that stimulated an armed competition between capitalist powers. Calling for more democratic control over foreign policy at home and concessions to Germany overseas to achieve a genuine Concert of Europe, he inveighed against the imperialist conspiracy against the public interest in the hope of averting international conflict. During the war he called for a negotiated peace, refuting allegations of Germany's sole war guilt. In addition he became the leading proponent of international government, pleading for an inclusive league of nations responsible for international trade and investment and empowered to enforce its decisions. His *A League of Nations* (1917) attracted attention among progressive internationalists, not only in England but in the United States.

After defeat in the 1918 general election, contesting Montrose for Labour, Brailsford traveled through Central Europe, reporting on the devastation in the aftermath of war. His graphic accounts, sympathetically depicting the plight of defeated peoples in Germany and Austria-Hungary, were published in the *Herald*, the *Manchester Guardian*, and the *New Republic* and later provided the material for two books, *Across the Blockade* (1919) and *After the Peace* (1920). In addition he offered expert advice on Central Europe in several reports for the LABOUR PARTY Advisory Committee on International Questions. One of the first Western journalists to visit the Soviet Union, he returned from a 1920 trip impressed by the economic strides being made, but critical of the suppression of dissent. He recorded his impressions in *The Russian Workers' Republic* (1921) and, after a second trip, in the more circumspect *How the Soviets Work* (1927)

In 1922 Brailsford was appointed editor of the *New Leader*, the restructured ILP weekly, which, over the next four years, he transformed into an internationally respected periodical. Mingling ideological exhortation with cultural enrichment, Brailsford offered a growing audience incisive analyses of world affairs and economic problems, as well as a literary section that included contributions by E.M. FORSTER, JULIAN HUXLEY, H.W. Nevinson, BERTRAND RUSSELL, and H.G. WELLS. In his own *Socialism for Today* (1925) and in the *New Leader* Brailsford helped to propound the ILP Living Wage program, which sought to increase mass purchasing power by compelling industries to pay wages sufficient for a civilized standard of life. Formulated for the ILP by a committee consisting of Brailsford, Hobson, E.F. Wise, and Arthur Creech Jones, the Living Wage became the focus of its policy for coping with UNEMPLOYMENT and a source of conflict with RAMSAY MACDONALD.

Dismissed as editor in 1926 by the dominant ILP Scottish contingent, Brailsford continued as a political columnist for the *New Leader* until he broke with the ILP in 1932, joining the dissident SOCIALIST LEAGUE within the Labour Party. In addition, he began to travel more extensively, to the United States and to India, to lecture abroad, and to write for the *Baltimore Sun*, *Reynolds's News*, and, most significantly, for the *NEW STATESMAN*, during KINGSLEY MARTIN's editorship. His books during these years, *Olives of Endless Age* (1928) and *Property or Peace?* (1934), recapitulated his views on internationalism and the links between capitalism and war, while *Rebel India* (1931) was an outspoken plea for Indian autonomy.

During the 1930s he continued to denounce the Versailles settlement and to call for disarmament, but after the outbreak of the SPANISH CIVIL WAR he came to recognize the need for collective security and offered one of the strongest indictments of CHAMBERLAIN's policy at MUNICH to appear in the British press. During the Spanish conflict he chaired the Labour-Spain Committee, raised money for Spanish relief, recruited volunteers, and assisted refugees. Early in the SECOND WORLD WAR he began to broadcast in the BBC OVERSEAS SERVICE and, in the book, *From England to America* (1940) appealed for American entry. He continued to work for the cause of INDIAN NATIONALISM, writing several pamphlets and his 1943 LEFT BOOK CLUB volume, *Subject India*. Late in the war he advocated the unpopular line of magnanimity towards Germany as a way of avoiding the pitfalls of Versailles. *Our Settlement with Germany* (1944) was widely attacked, notably by COMMUNIST PARTY functionaries.

After the war, in declining health, Brailsford undertook trips to India for *Reynolds* to cover the elections, to Germany in 1947, and to Yugoslavia in 1950. Among the very few honors he received in a long career was an honorary LL.D. from his own University of Glasgow in 1944. His last years were devoted to a long contemplated history of the Leveller movement, published posthumously as *The Levellers and the English Revolution* (1961).

Brailsford belongs to a long tradition of radical writers and pamphleteers, his intellectual links as much to Paine and Shelley as to Marx and Hobson. He was, above all, a dissenter, not in the religious sense—he rejected his Methodist upbringing—but as a radical critic of dominant institutions and values. Moving from Liberalism to a quasi-revolutionary socialism, he remained committed nonetheless to the ideal of political democracy. He was an internationalist who abhorred xenophobia, a socialist whose loyalties could not be confined within national boundaries. More than a journalist, he was, during his long career as a man of letters, an exemplary voice of reason, never wavering in his quest for international conciliation, social justice, and the liberation of subject peoples.

Fred M. Leventhal

Bibliography

Blaazer, David. *The Popular Front and the Progressive Tradition*. 1992.

Foot, Michael. *Debts of Honour*. 1980.

Leventhal, F.M. *The Last Dissenter: H.N. Brailsford and His World*. 1985.

Martin, Kingsley. *Editor*. 1968.

Taylor, A.J.P. *The Trouble Makers*. 1958.

British Broadcasting Corporation (BBC)

Founded in 1922 as a private monopoly regulated by the Post Office, the BBC became a public corporation in 1927 and rapidly established itself as a major institution of British national culture. JOHN REITH, the extraordinary figure who became its first Director-General, enunciated a paternalistic vision of "public service" that sought to counter the growing influence in Britain of Americanized mass culture. He rejected the notion that the public ought to be given what it wanted. Reith viewed culture as a form of self-improvement, a means of personal and social discipline. Painfully aware that the new medium of radio lacked respectability and tradition, BBC programmers constructed a schedule which reflected the most treasured cultural aspirations of the middle and upper middle classes. Symphony, OPERA, and chamber music occupied a privileged place on the broadcast schedule. Leading intellectuals provided "talks" on a variety of topics. Sunday was dominated by religious programs, followed by lengthy periods of silence. Announcers were expected to speak with a proper accent and wore full evening dress while broadcasting. During the 1920s Reith's ideal of public service uplifted the medium and the Corporation as much as the vast audience it sought to improve.

Yet middle-class cultural paternalism, like its aristocratic antecedents, could never completely divorce itself from public criticism and accountability. Although the broadcast schedule clearly gave disproportionate weight to the tastes of highly cultivated minorities, the BBC offered enough concessions to popular taste to escape broadcasting into a void. From the beginning a tension existed within the BBC between giving the public "what it wanted" and "what it ought to have". This tension became exacerbated as the audience rapidly increased in size. Between 1929 and 1933, for example, the number of license holders doubled, and by 1935, 98 percent of the population had some access to wireless programs. This increase reflected in part the ability of the BBC to provide a strong regional system of broadcasting that provided alternatives to the national programs from LONDON, but it also resulted in pressures on the organization, both external and internal, that exposed the contradictions of the Reithian ethos. The popular PRESS, though committed to the notion of the BBC's monopoly, hired radio critics who often deplored the organization's cultural elitism. Commercial stations on the Continent, such as Radio Luxembourg, beamed a steady stream of POPULAR MUSIC that captured a sizable British audience, especially on Sundays. As the BBC grew in size and moved to modern headquarters in Broadcasting House in 1932, Corporation offi-

cials began to modify the assumptions that buttressed Reith's cultural mission.

During the 1930s the BBC proved itself more responsive to public demand than its official rhetoric sometimes indicated. The number of variety and light entertainment shows increased dramatically; even jazz, which Reith abhorred, found its place on the schedule. Educational programing diminished and talks became more popularized. Gradually, the Corporation began to abandon its Sabbatarianism; the controversial "silent periods" on Sunday disappeared. After long opposition from some quarters, the BBC accepted the notion of systematic listener research and hired an expert from advertising to discover what the public wanted. The BBC still launched expensive operatic productions and continued to finance experimental dramas, but these and similar decisions regarding resources could not involve a rationale that listener research flatly contradicted. Even a monopoly committed to sustaining the arts could not ignore completely the sometimes subtle, sometimes brutal pressure of statistics. Listener research gradually became the box-office of the BBC.

There were other important changes during the 1930s. Technology and reception improved enormously; like the cinema, gramophone, and newspaper, radio became fully integrated into the everyday life of British citizens. The *Radio Times* sold over three million copies a week and *The Listener* enjoyed a circulation greater than both the *NEW STATESMAN* and *Spectator* combined. Empire broadcasting began in 1932, vastly extending the range of the BBC; for the first time, British subjects around the world could hear the voice of the King, including, most dramatically, during the abdication crisis of 1936. Freed from a series of restrictions imposed during the 1920s, the BBC became an important source for news, gradually overcoming the justified complaint by trade unionists that the BBC had supported the government during the GENERAL STRIKE. In 1936 the Ullswater Committee issued its report recommending renewal of the BBC's charter formulated by the Crawford Committee a decade earlier. In 1938 John Reith resigned to become Chairman of Imperial Airways, a decision he soon and forever regretted.

The SECOND WORLD WAR solidified the international reputation of the BBC, whose news and overseas broadcasts in a variety of languages became valuable sources of information. Although early in the war the Corporation sustained heavy criticism for its unimaginative broadcasts, the adoption of a Forces Programme especially designed for the troops became immensely popular among all segments of the population. During the BLITZ, two broadcasters in particular captured public attention: WINSTON CHURCHILL brought the cadences of eighteenth-century rhetoric to a twentieth-century medium; and the novelist J. B. PRIESTLEY, speaking in a distinctive Yorkshire accent once considered inappropriate for broadcasting, focused in his *Postscripts* on highly specific and concrete examples of the humane values which united the British. As the war progressed, the entertainment show *ITMA* included fictional characters whose catch phrases became part of everyday language, and perhaps less predictably, *Brains Trust* transformed intellectuals such as JULIAN HUXLEY into national personalities. Behind the scenes, the staff of the Corporation more than doubled, and the bureaucracy was reorganized to accommodate growth. F. W. Ogilvie, Reith's ineffectual successor, was eased out in 1942, to be replaced for a short time by a joint leadership. Although the BBC continued to distrust controversial political broadcasts, the discussion of war aims received more attention than Churchill would have liked. Throughout the war, correspondents broadcast vivid reports from the frontlines, including the beaches of Normandy.

From a background in the newspaper industry, William Haley became Director-General in 1944 and, until he resigned eight years later, committed himself to extending the Reithian ethos into the post-war era. In 1946, as part of a major reorganization, radio split into three distinct services. The Light Programme captured the vast majority of the audience; the Home Service, which emphasized the spoken word, proved a distant second; while the Third Programme, beloved by the cultivated elite, consumed one-third of the available airwaves to appease 1 percent of the listening public. In 1949 the BEVERIDGE Committee convened to review the BBC's charter and, after sifting through prodigious testimony, recommended that the monopoly continue, thereby overriding the objections of some members who argued for greater competition because of the rise of television.

Experiments with television began before the FIRST WORLD WAR. The pioneering figure John Logie Baird, like Reith a Scot, began to cooperate with the BBC in 1929, but his mechanical scanning system, for all its cleverness of design, eventually succumbed to its electronic rivals. In 1936 the BBC began broadcasting as the first regular high definition television service in the world. Audiences remained tiny, though appreciative, until 1939 when operations ceased for the duration of the war. In June, 1946 service resumed in an environment of rapid technological development and decreasing unit costs that helped assure the success of the new medium. During the 1950s, television came into its own, accelerating the decline of both radio and cinema. The telecast of the Coronation in 1953 reached over half the British population.

In a society that prided itself on free speech, centralized control over two powerful media of mass communication became increasingly anomalous. In the early 1950s criticism of the BBC's monopoly became more insistent, not only from well-organized pressure groups, but also from within the ranks of the CONSERVATIVE PARTY, which returned to power in 1951. In 1955, after complex negotiations, the Independent Television Authority began the process of awarding franchises to commercial television companies for designated regions of the country. Though ITV proclaimed adherence to the ideals of public service and remained heavily regulated, few doubted that it offered the public "what it wanted" rather than "what it ought to have". ITV's high salaries lured away some of the BBC's best staff. Audience ratings assumed a new importance.

The 1960s marked an important turning point in the history of the BBC. Hugh Greene, the Director-General for virtually the entire decade, modernized the Corporation to reflect the complicated social and cultural realities of a booming consumer economy. Greene welcomed more daring and controversial programing. The long-running *Z Cars* brought greater realism to the police show; the play *Cathy Come Home* exposed the problems of HOUSING; *Till Death Do Us Part* discovered unlikely sources of amusement in cranky characters. In these and similar programs, television audiences encountered personalities and situations that earlier, more paternalistic broadcasting routinely excluded. The satirical *That Was the Week That Was*, first broadcast in 1962, became emblematic of the decade's more open programing, not least because of its unpredictability.

The allocation of a new television channel to the BBC in the early 1960s allowed the Corporation to segment its programing according to audience, not unlike the division of radio into separate services after the Second World War. BBC 2, which began broadcasting in 1964, catered to a more cultivated viewer. Its dramatic programs, in particular, paid an unexpected dividend as the BBC entered the financially more troubled 1970s. The cost of licenses, a major source of income, failed to keep pace with the soaring prices of labor and new technologies such as color. For example, the license fee for color television, adjusted for inflation, did not increase between 1968 and 1985, even though from 1975 to 1983 the price of television soared 68 per cent in real terms. Like their counterparts in the FILM INDUSTRY, British television producers discovered that the international market, especially the

United States, offered a lucrative market for certain types of programs. *The Forsyte Saga, Civilization, The Six Wives of Henry VIII,* and *Elizabeth R,* all produced by BBC 2 in the late 1960s and early 1970s, sold internationally at considerable profit. In the United States public broadcasting and major oil companies eager to improve their tattered image during an era of rocketing prices especially welcomed prestige productions from the BBC.

Commercial competition also affected radio broadcasting. In 1964 Radio Caroline, a pirate station operating offshore, broadcast a steady diet of popular music that enraged BBC officials and captured the public imagination. Though government eventually cleared the sea of pirates, the BBC once again reorganized itself to accommodate its audience. Radio 1 devoted itself to popular musical programing; Radio 2 concentrated on more traditional light music; Radio 3 resembled the old Third Programme; and Radio 4 stressed current affairs and the spoken word. The introduction of commercial radio in Britain in the early 1970s terminated a half-century of BBC monopoly. Local broadcasting, in particular, expanded enormously both from the BBC and from various commercial franchises, not all of which proved financially successful. Listening habits also changed as the transistor and other technological changes such as the Walkman made radios more portable, especially for the young.

Broadcasting also transformed the nature of politics. The BBC had always played a major role in public affairs broadcasting, and during the 1950s introduced a number of widely-respected programs such as *Panorama* and *Tonight.* Beginning in the 1960s, however, politicians began to appreciate more fully the power of images on electoral opinion. HAROLD WILSON, for example, altered certain aspects of his appearance and speaking style to accommodate the viewing audience. In 1975, the House of Commons permitted its debates to be broadcast on radio; thirteen years later television entered the chamber. More and more, election campaigns revolved around television coverage, as commentators warned of the Americanization of British politics. During the 1980s MARGARET THATCHER's confrontational style of leadership not only became obvious to millions in her response to aggressive interviewers such as Robin Day, but in the vivid images emerging from the FALKLANDS WAR and the miners' strike. Increasingly, television shaped the political agenda and the BBC, like ITV, no longer became mere observers but active participants in the electoral process. If by the 1990s the BBC no longer commanded the "brute force of monopoly" that Reith defended with pride, its

ability to accommodate itself to changing audiences and technologies made it an integral part of twentieth-century British culture.

D.L. LeMahieu

Bibliography

Briggs, Asa. *The History of Broadcasting in the United Kingdom.* 4 vols. 1961–79.
———. *The BBC: The First Fifty Years.* 1985.
Carpenter, Humphrey. *The Envy of the World: Fifty Years of the BBC Third Programme and Radio 3.* 1996.
Nicholas, Sian. *The Echo of War: Home Front Propaganda and the Wartime BBC 1939–45.* 1996.
Scannell, Paddy, and David Cardiff. *A Social History of British Broadcasting.* vol. 1: *1922–1939.* 1991.
Seymour-Ure, Colin. *The British Press and Broadcasting since 1945.* 1991.

BBC Overseas Broadcasting

Though it went by different names as it evolved historically, BBC Overseas Broadcasting always helped shape the image of Britain abroad. The Empire Service began in 1932 as one of JOHN REITH's many contributions to the medium. Innovations in the technology of transmission combined with quality programing helped make "This is London calling" a familiar phrase throughout the world. In 1938 the BBC started broadcasting in foreign languages, in part as a response to similar initiatives on the Continent. Unlike the Germans and Italians, however, the Corporation eschewed more overt PROPAGANDA and often defined its public narrowly. In the Arabic Service, for example, the BBC sought an elite rather than a mass audience.

The SECOND WORLD WAR magnified immeasurably the significance of external broadcasting. The Overseas Service expanded to fourteen languages in 1939 and to forty-five languages by 1944. As country after country fell to the Nazis, Britain became a major source of news and inspiration for the occupied populations. In 1941 the BBC initiated the V for Victory campaign, an effort at propaganda that began modestly enough, but rapidly became so powerful an emblem of resistance in France, Belgium, and Holland that Germans adopted the symbol for their own purposes, thereby eventually blunting the campaign. Throughout the war external broadcasting constantly encountered difficult political problems. The British government's Political Warfare Executive, for example, pressured the Corporation to inject more propaganda into its international broadcasts, particularly the news. The BBC resisted these efforts by arguing that high standards of objectivity preserved the greatest asset of the Overseas Service, its credibility with foreign audiences. The Soviet Union permitted broadcasts in English to its territory, but balked at programs in Russian. The complex sectarian disputes of governments in exile forced BBC officials to become nimble diplomats, especially with the French. German jamming undermined some efforts at propaganda, but proved less effective when announcers especially selected for their low-pitched voices spoke in short, simple sentences. By the end of the war most commentators agreed that the BBC succeeded brilliantly in achieving superiority over the airwaves.

After the war external broadcasting suffered deep cutbacks in both staff and services. The government forced the BBC to surrender wavelengths and the number of languages broadcast diminished considerably. The advent of the Cold War, however, once again provided overseas broadcasting with a mission. The BBC carried less propaganda than the Voice of America, though both services struggled to overcome sophisticated jamming techniques. During the 1950s and early 1960s government continued to reduce the budget of overseas broadcasting as the BBC, like Britain itself, withdrew from Empire. In 1965, external broadcasting became known as the World Service, and projecting the image of Britain abroad entered a new phase. Radio continued to serve BBC enthusiasts around the world, but the export of television programs now became far more lucrative. BBC Enterprises, established in the 1970s, established complex co-financing agreements and sold television programs to international buyers, especially in the United States. Commercial television and the introduction of new technologies of transmission and reproduction during the 1980s made the BBC only one of many British voices in the global culture of the late twentieth century.

D.L. LeMahieu

Bibliography

Briggs, Asa. *The History of Broadcasting in the United Kingdom.* 4 vols. 1961–79.

———. *The BBC: The First Fifty Years.* 1985.

Mansell, Gerard. *Let Truth Be Told.* 1982.

British Council

The British Council is the organization which promotes cultural relations between Britain and other countries. Since beginning in 1934 as the "British Committee for Relations with other Countries," it has expanded to over eighty countries. Its programs promote an appreciation of Britain's culture and knowledge of the English language overseas by fostering personal contacts in the professional, educational, scientific, and cultural fields. The Council publishes and distributes literature, organizes classes, libraries, and exhibits, and provides technical assistance in fields such as health, agriculture, and literacy. Although the government supervises and funds the Council, it is technically an unofficial body. When it started, the Council sought to raise money from private contributions. The government granted it only £5,000, hoping that companies involved in foreign trade would become substantial contributors. However, business leaders were slow to support it, and it soon became too big to depend on voluntary contributions. In effect, it functions as an arm of the British government conducting what could be called cultural PROPAGANDA. Partly because it might be resented as a propaganda agency, the Council never established offices in the United States.

The Council's history reflects the changing requirements placed on British foreign policy since 1934. In the years before the SECOND WORLD WAR, when German and Italian propaganda was actively promoting Fascism, it was regarded as an indirect answer to this challenge, indirect because it avoided political attacks on Hitler and Mussolini, concentrating on the less controversial areas of culture and language. This was in keeping with the APPEASEMENT policies of British governments. This same reluctance to inflame relations with the Fascist powers also explains why the Council got little financial support. It was obliged to limit itself to a few modest programs in Europe and the Middle East.

The Foreign Office official who was the chief sponsor of the Council, Rex Leeper, and George Lloyd, who became its chairman from 1937 to 1940, both pressed for a more activist program. When the war began, the Council expanded rapidly. Despite the new Ministry of Information, which handled official press and propaganda programs, the Council still assumed many new tasks. From making films on cultural subjects to sponsoring classes in neutral countries and programs for American soldiers stationed in Britain, the Council showed its worth and prospered accordingly. By 1945 it was receiving over £2,000,000 a year to support these activities.

When the war ended, the Council initially faced some cutbacks and questions about its future. A new era brought different challenges: Britain's world-wide Empire was disintegrating and her status as a leading power was put in doubt by her crumbling economy. The Council's work in the colonies expanded as a way to reinforce allegiance to the Crown and then to ease the peaceful transition from colonial status to membership in the British Commonwealth. Even as Britain's military and economic fortunes declined, investment in the Council seemed to be a good way to enhance national prestige and promote exports. Although Eastern European communist regimes impeded Council activities, it still had a role to play in the Cold War. It conducted whatever cultural exchanges it could behind the Iron Curtain and kept alive contacts with the people in these countries.

By the 1980s the Council had become a vast organization with a budget of close to £300,000,000. Little known at home in Britain or in the United States, it still had an important presence around of the world. Much of its work was under contract from host countries and supported by payments: its English teaching program in Hong Kong held classes for over 10,000 fee-paying students, for example. Technical assistance work to developing countries has become an important task of the Council in this era. Through this work, and its network of libraries and institutes, it has enhanced Britain's influence and visibility around the world.

Donald S. Birn

Bibliography

Donaldson, Frances. *The British Council.* 1984.

Taylor, Philip M. *The Projection of Britain: British Overseas Publicity and Propaganda, 1919–1939.* 1981.

White, A.J.S. *The British Council: The First 25 Years.* 1965.

Brittain, Vera Mary (1893–1970)

Vera Brittain is best known as author of the autobiographical memoir *Testament of Youth* (1933), which deals with the personal and political significance of the FIRST WORLD WAR from a woman's point of view. *Testament of Youth* is generally considered to be one of the major British literary productions concerned with the Great War and is certainly the best known by a woman author. It was a best-seller both in Britain and North America when it first appeared and has enjoyed continued success ever since.

While her reputation as a major twentieth-century author rests on *Testament of Youth*, Brittain published more than twenty books and was a prolific journalist. The books include *Testament of Friendship* (1940), Brittain's memoir of her close friend and fellow writer Winifred Holtby, a second volume of autobiography, *Testament of Experience* (1957), nine novels, and several works of social commentary. In the inter-war decades her journalistic pieces appeared in a wide variety of publications, ranging from the feminist weekly *Time and Tide* to *Good Housekeeping*.

Brittain was politically active throughout her life as a FEMINIST and in the cause of peace. The peak of her feminist activity was in the 1920s and early 1930s, when she worked with the Six Point Group and the Open Door Council, two important inter-war feminist organizations. Brittain had been involved in internationalist activities from the mid-1920s, when she was a frequent speaker for the League of Nations Union. Her preoccupation with questions of war and peace deepened as the political situation worsened in the 1930s. In 1936 she became involved with the

Christian pacifist PEACE PLEDGE UNION. As she later wrote of her conversion to PACIFISM: "I had come to see the enemy . . . as war itself." During the SECOND WORLD WAR her outspoken criticism of the evils of war brought her opprobrium at the time but earned her a place in the history of British peace activism.

Born on 29 December 1893, Brittain was the daughter of a successful Staffordshire paper manufacturer. She vividly describes her upbringing in *Testament of Youth*, explaining that her education was designed to fit her for "provincial young ladyhood", but that she rebelled against conventional upper middle-class patterns for women and instead successfully fought to achieve admission to university. Brittain entered Somerville College, OXFORD in 1914 and completed her first year but then left Oxford for war service as a Voluntary Aid Detachment nurse. As the war was beginning, she had fallen in love with Roland Leighton, a school friend of her brother's, and in *Testament of Youth*, she movingly recounts the story of their love, Leighton's death in action, and the subsequent deaths of her only brother and two other close friends.

Brittain returned to Oxford after the war, completing her studies in 1921 with a degree in history. After Oxford she and Holtby, her Somerville contemporary, set up house together in London. In 1925 Brittain married the political scientist G.E.G. Catlin, and from its beginning their marriage was consciously and deliberately feminist. Brittain kept her own name—a significant symbolic statement during this period—and never allowed the marriage to interfere with her career. For many years Catlin was a professor at an American university, and the couple lived apart for extended periods in order to accommodate both careers. The marriage also accommodated the intimate friendship between Brittain and Holtby: from 1927 until her premature death in 1935, Holtby formed part of the Brittain-Catlin household.

From her early struggles to escape the fate of "provincial young ladyhood" to her later achievements as a writer and social activist, Brittain was representative of the group of educated middle-class women who brought to fruition the goals of Victorian bourgeois feminism in the years following the First World War. Throughout her adult life she was sustained by feminist convictions and driven by a fierce desire to achieve personal autonomy.

Deborah Gorham

Bibliography

Berry, Paul, and Alan Bishop. *Testament of a Generation: The Journalism of Vera Brittain and Winifred Holtby.* 1985.

———, and Mark Bostridge. *Vera Brittain: A Life.* 1995.

Bishop, Alan, ed. *Chronicle of Youth: Vera Brittain's War Diary, 1913–1917.* 1981.

Gorham, Deborah. *Vera Brittain: A Feminist Life.* 1995.

Britten, (Edward) Benjamin (1913–1976)

An English composer, pianist, and conductor, Benjamin Britten, together with MICHAEL TIPPETT, led the generation of composers following that of RALPH VAUGHAN WILLIAMS. The first performance of Britten's opera, *Peter Grimes* (7 June 1945), marked the revival of English OPERA, a revival sustained by Britten's subsequent eleven operas and those of Tippett. Britten's sympathy for the voice found further outlet in thirteen song-cycles, roughly half of which were written for his lifelong companion, Peter Pears, and in his writing for boys' voices. *On Receiving the First Aspen Award* (1964) contains an important statement of Britten's artistic beliefs, and these found particular expression in his music for amateurs, such as the children's opera, *Noye's Fludde* (1957), and in the creation of the Festival at Aldeburgh, where he lived from 1947. Among many official honors, Britten was awarded the Order of Merit (1965) and a life peerage (1976).

Born in Lowestoft, the son of a dentist, Britten enjoyed a musical upbringing. He began composing at the age of five, and such was his progress that Frank Bridge accepted the thirteen year old Britten as a pupil. Lessons with Bridge continued throughout Britten's school days, and both Bridge's professional instruction and Britten's formidable talent are well in evidence in the remarkable *Quatre Chansons Françaises* (1928). Britten's further development was somewhat frustrated by unsympathetic teaching during his period at the Royal College of Music in London (1930–3), although he gained more help from John Ireland's composition lessons than he was later to acknowledge. Despite opposition, he managed to secure a handful of prestigious performances while still at the College—his Op. 1, the *Sinfonietta* (dedicated to Bridge), was first performed at an Anne Macnaghten/Iris Lemaire concert (31 January 1933). A proposal to study composition further with Alban Berg was thwarted.

In 1935 Britten began writing incidental music for DOCUMENTARY FILMS produced by the General Post Office, which led to further requests for incidental music from the Group and Left Theatres. Such work was highly beneficial. Britten developed a technique for writing music of expressive immediacy often for restricted forces, a technique that he exploited subsequently when he turned to opera. Another advantage was his meeting and friendship with W.H. AUDEN, with whom he collaborated on several projects (*Coal Face,* 1935, *Night Mail,* 1936, both GPO; and *The*

Ascent of F6, 1937, Group Theatre with CHRISTOPHER ISHERWOOD). The bitter irony heard in the orchestral song-cycle, *Our Hunting Fathers* (Auden: 1936), and *Ballad for Heroes* for tenor, chorus and orchestra (Auden/Swingler: 1939) can be traced in part to Britten's developing political and social consciousness at the hands of Auden, although the latter's attempts to accelerate Britten's personal development met with little success. Auden's emigration to the United States in January 1939 was, however, an important factor in prompting Britten to follow suit the following April.

Britten's two and a half year residence in the United States (prefaced by a short visit to Canada) was a period of liberation. The grief occasioned by the deaths of his parents was objectified in the *Sinfonia da Requiem* (1940), dedicated to their memory, and Britten's commitment to Pears was consummated. Two song cycles, *Les Illuminations* (Rimbaud: 1939) and the *Seven Sonnets of Michelangelo* (1940), the latter Britten's first cycle written for Pears, mark the arrival of musical maturity, although the opera, *Paul Bunyan* (Auden: 1941), was not a success. The chance reading of an article by E.M. FORSTER on the Suffolk poet, George Crabbe, led Britten not only to realize how essential his native surroundings in Suffolk were to his well-being, but also provided him with the subject matter for *Peter Grimes,* the writing of which was facilitated by a $1,000 grant from the Koussevitzky Foundation. He returned to England in 1942, completing the *Hymn to St. Cecilia* (Auden) for unaccompanied chorus and *A Ceremony of Carols* en route. On arrival Britten registered as a CONSCIENTIOUS OBJECTOR and was subsequently exempted from military service on condition that he took part in concerts for the COUNCIL FOR THE ENCOURAGEMENT OF MUSIC AND THE ARTS (CEMA).

Following the success of *Peter Grimes* and the tragic chamber opera, *The Rape of Lucretia* (Ronald Duncan, after André Obey: 1946), Britten, with John Piper and Eric Crozier, formed the English Opera Group (1947), which was subsequently responsible for the artistic direction of the Aldeburgh Festival (1948). The comic chamber opera, *Albert Herring* (Crozier, after Maupassant: 1947), was succeeded by *Billy Budd* (Forster/Crozier, after Melville: 1951), with an all-male cast, and together with the chamber opera, *The Turn of the Screw* (Myfanwy Piper, after Henry James: 1954), continued to explore the theme, characteristic of many of his opera librettos, of innocence corrupted by evil. Sounds heard during a recital tour with Pears that included Java and Bali (1955), are recreated in the gamelan effects punctuating the ballet, *The Prince of the Pa-*

godas (1956), and a performance of the Japanese *noh* play, *Sumidagawa*, influenced the ethos and spare dimensions of the church parable, *Curlew River* (William Plomer: 1964), which heralds Britten's late style. Before this, however, both the full-scale opera, *A Midsummer Night's Dream* (Britten/Pears, after Shakespeare: 1960), and the *War Requiem* (Wilfred Owen: 1962) testify, on the one hand, to the richness and diversity of Britten's musical thought, and, on the other, to its seriousness of purpose, the requiem an impassioned indictment of war.

Much of Britten's instrumental as well as vocal music was composed for particular performers, and his friendship with the Russian cellist and conductor, Mstislav Rostropovich (begun in 1960) was celebrated in the Cello Sonata (1961), three Cello Suites (1964/1967/1971) and Britten's only major orchestral work to follow *The Young Person's Guide to the Orchestra* (1946), the Cello Symphony (1963). In 1967 the scope of the Aldeburgh Festival was enlarged with the building of the concert hall at the Maltings, Snape, and although Britten's penultimate opera, *Owen Wingrave* (M. Piper, after James: 1970), another pacifist work, was written for BBC television, his final opera, *Death in Venice* (M. Piper, after Thomas Mann: 1973) was first performed there. Britten was unable to conduct, having undergone open-heart surgery earlier during the year from which he never recovered fully. Only small-scale works were possible thereafter, most significantly the Third String Quartet (1975), linked both thematically and psychologically to *Death in Venice*, Britten seemingly identifying himself in the quartet with the opera's hero, Gustav von Aschenbach.

Trevor Bray

Bibliography

Carpenter, Humphrey. *Benjamin Britten: A Biography.* 1992.

Cooke, Mervyn, ed. *The Cambridge Companion to Benjamin Britten.* 1999.

Evans, Peter. *The Music of Benjamin Britten.* rev. ed. 1989.

Kennedy, Michael. *Britten.* 1981.

Mitchell, Donald, and Philip Reed, eds. *Letters from a Life: The Selected Letters and Diaries of Benjamin Britten 1913–1976.* 2 vols. 1991.

Palmer, Christopher. *The Britten Companion.* 1984.

White, Eric Walter. *Benjamin Britten: His Life and Operas.* 2nd ed. 1983.

Brooke, Rupert Chawner (1887–1915)

The poet Rupert Brooke was born at Rugby on 3 August 1887, the second of four children, all of whom died at an early age. His father was William Parker Brooke, Rugby schoolmaster, distinguished classics scholar, and Fellow of King's College, CAMBRIDGE. Rupert's mother, the dominant figure of the family, was the former Mary Ruth Cotterill, a niece of the Bishop of Edinburgh.

After attending the local preparatory school, Hillbrow, Rupert moved on to Rugby at the age of fourteen, which placed him under the direct supervision of his father, the new housemaster of School Field. Rupert was a model student who also excelled at CRICKET and rugby, but he suffered emotional conflicts, especially with his puritanical mother, on account of his HOMOSEXUAL orientation. Rupert's first recorded sexual encounter in 1909 was with Denham Russell-Smith, whom he had known at Rugby.

In 1906 Brooke went up to King's College on scholarship to read classics like his father. But from first to last Brooke was a vaguely rebellious, poor to mediocre student, known best only for his charm and physical appearance. He joined the FABIAN SOCIETY, but his socialism, which he combined with ANTI-SEMITISM and anti-feminism, mixed the aims and views of Edward Carpenter, Hilaire Belloc, William Morris, and H.G. WELLS. He found the "Simple Life" socialism of Carpenter was more appealing than the "scientific" socialism of SHAW and the WEBBS. It was through the Fabian Society that he met the most important young women in his life, Katharine ("Ka") Cox and the daughters of Sir Sidney Olivier, Noel and Brynhild. In the fall of 1908 James Strachey sponsored Brooke's election to the Cambridge Apostles. Although he barely managed a second on his classics exam, Brooke held his own with the more intellectual Apostles, including G.E. MOORE, James and LYTTON STRACHEY, and JOHN MAYNARD KEYNES.

By the summer of 1908 Brooke had become the center of a new group of Cambridge "Simple Lifers," soon to be known as the Neo-pagans. Philosophically, Neo-paganism amounted to little more than a mild rebellion against Victorian conventions and parental authority. In practice it meant bohemian dress, nude bathing, vegetarianism, and camping out unchaperoned in the summer. In 1909 Brooke left Cambridge for a rustic life in nearby Grantchester, determined to become "a BLOODY poet," rather than a conventional academic. But a strain of repressed sexual puritanism in Brooke had always been at odds with his boisterous bohemianism. He suffered a nervous breakdown in 1912 after an unsuccessful love affair with fellow Neo-pagan Ka Cox.

In late 1912 Brooke left Grantchester for London, where with Edward Marsh he launched the immensely popular *Georgian Poetry.* The "Georgian" poets were the subjects of considerable derision in the post-war years, but the five-volume

series included works of D.H. LAWRENCE, ROB-
ERT GRAVES, SIEGFRIED SASSOON, Isaac Rosenberg, and Edmund Blunden. In the summer of
1913, Brooke toured North America and the
South Pacific. A three-month idyl in Tahiti resulted in some of Brooke's most memorable
poetry. He returned to England in June of 1914.
When the FIRST WORLD WAR broke out, Edward Marsh arranged for Brooke to be commissioned in WINSTON CHURCHILL's Royal Naval
Division. He was never to see combat. Brooke
died of blood poisoning on the eve of the GAL-
LIPOLI campaign and was buried on St. George's
Day, 1915 on the Greek isle of Scyros.

Brooke's posthumous fame rests largely on the
timing of his death. He died while the war was
still thought to be a glorious adventure, before the
grim horrors of trench warfare had been brought
home to the volunteers and the general public.
His romantic war poetry captured the mood of
the early months of the Great War. Rupert
Brooke became the symbol of the heroic self-
sacrifice of his doomed generation and perhaps
something more. With the passage of time, he has
become known more as an image and a symbol of
an era than either as a poet or a "Neo-pagan".

Gordon B. Beadle

Bibliography
Delany, Paul. *The Neo-Pagans.* 1987.
Hassall, Christopher. *Rupert Brooke.* 1964.
Rogers, Timothy. *Rupert Brooke.* 1971.

Butler, R(ichard) A(usten) (1902–1982)
R.A. Butler, commonly known by the acronym
"Rab", was a leading Conservative politician of
the post-war period. As Minister of Education
1941–5, he created the post-war system in the ED-
UCATION ACT OF 1944. In opposition between
1945 and 1951 he played a key role in reshaping the
CONSERVATIVE PARTY. As Chancellor of the Exchequer 1951–5, he became a symbol of the post-
war economic and social consensus known as
"Butskellism". He served as Lord Privy Seal
1955–9 and was a reforming Home Secretary
1957–62. Butler was Chairman of the Conservative Party 1959–61, Leader of the House 1959–61
and Deputy Prime Minister 1962–3. He completed the trio of top CABINET posts as Foreign
Secretary 1963–4. In 1957 and 1963 he seemed to
be on the point of becoming Prime Minister, but
was thwarted both times by HAROLD MACMIL-
LAN. In 1965 he accepted a life peerage as Baron
Butler of Saffron Walden and became Master of
Trinity College, Cambridge, 1965–78.

Butler came from a family connected with both
CAMBRIDGE and imperial service in India, where
he was born. He was able to enter Parliament at
the age of only twenty-seven through his mar-

riage in 1926 to the heiress Sydney Courtauld. In
1929 he was elected for the safe Conservative seat
of Saffron Walden, for which he sat until retiring
in 1965. As Under-Secretary for India 1932–7 and
for foreign affairs 1938–41 Butler was at the centre
of the major political struggles of the 1930s. As
the Foreign Secretary, LORD HALIFAX, was in the
HOUSE OF LORDS, Butler became the principal
spokesman in the House of Commons during the
crucial pre-war period. Although not able greatly
to influence policy, his prominent role as a "man of
MUNICH" did him immense damage in the post-
war period and contributed to his failure to attain
the premiership.

Butler's two major contributions to the shaping of post-war Britain occurred before his long
service in high office in the 1950s. The measure
with which his name will always be associated
was the Education Act of 1944, which resolved
the long-standing religious complexities and
framed the system which has been in place ever
since. As Minister of Education Butler worked in
the background of the war effort, with little
interest or support from the Prime Minister,
WINSTON CHURCHILL. During the opposition
years of 1945–51 Butler, chairman of the Conservative Research Department, played a major part
in the reformulation of the party's philosophy, attitudes, and policies. He chaired the group which
drafted the Industrial Charter of 1947, and forced
its adoption upon an unwilling Churchill. The
Charter committed the Conservative Party to the
acceptance of Keynesian interventionism and of
the WELFARE STATE, and symbolised the determination to break with the image of the DOLE
queues of the 1930s.

In 1951 Butler became Chancellor of the Exchequer and presided over decontrol and the end
of RATIONING. His successful tenure of the post
culminated in a tax-cutting budget before the
1955 election which was widely credited with
helping the Conservatives increase their majority.
However, a sterling crisis and a revised budget in
the autumn of 1955 tarnished his reputation, and
ANTHONY EDEN moved him from the Treasury.
His role in the SUEZ CRISIS was regarded as weak
and indecisive, and when Eden resigned Butler
was found to have little support in the Cabinet.
He had a difficult relationship with the new
Prime Minister, Macmillan, who exploited his
administrative skills and prestige but also left him
exposed to humiliation. Butler was laden with a
mixed bag of duties, which were adroitly juggled,
and was shuffled from post to post. Even so,
when Macmillan resigned in 1963 Butler was the
favorite to succeed him. Macmillan promoted the
candidature of the Foreign Secretary, LORD
HOME, and Butler failed to press his claims, to

the disgust of some of his supporters. An urbane and feline character, Butler was always more of an establishment mandarin than a partisan political combatant. He was the ideal second-in-command, but many concurred in Macmillan's verdict that "he lacked the last six inches of steel" necessary for leadership. He remains, together with LORD CURZON and AUSTEN CHAMBERLAIN, the archetypal "best Prime Minister we never had", more fascinating in failure even than in success.

Stuart Ball

Bibliography
Butler, Lord. *The Art of the Possible*. 1971.
Cosgrave, Patrick. *R.A. Butler: An English Life*. 1981.
Howard, Anthony. *RAB: The Life of R.A. Butler*. 1987.
Thorpe, D.R. *The Uncrowned Prime Ministers*. 1980.

Cabinet

The modern Cabinet is the product of continuous historical development, shaped by the events of this century: no statute law governs its existence, although it has been several times mentioned in legislation. Thus it possesses no independent legal standing, although in political terms it may be succinctly characterized as the supreme coordinator of national policy, always provided it enjoys the confidence of a functioning majority in the House of Commons. In fact, a historical assessment of its role in this century involves the ways in which the various Cabinets have discharged that task of coordination, a responsibility collectively shared by the ministers who compose it; chosen by the Prime Minister, nearly all Cabinet ministers bear departmental assignments as well. Prior to 1900 the Prime Minister's standing among his Cabinet colleagues was universally accepted as *primus inter pares*, i.e. "first among equals."

Whether any measure of equality has survived these nine decades is open to question, in the main as a result of the roles played by and the powers accrued to by twentieth-century premiers, but also as a function of the heavier departmental responsibilities borne by his or her colleagues. Yet the Cabinet survives, at the very least, as an oft-consulted collective associate of the Prime Minister, and its individual members discharge essential tasks of government in executing the policies agreed to by Cabinet and accepted by Parliament. The Cabinet retains a key role in contemporary political practice, although its role is subject to the style of the Prime Minister, who need not involve the Cabinet in the resolution of all policy matters, including matters of great importance. Collective responsibility, entailing free discussion among Cabinet colleagues until a decision is reached, but thereafter mandating acceptance and defense by all, whatever their personal view, dictated that a veil of secrecy be draped over Cabinet proceedings, and provided one rationale for the Cabinet's refusal to maintain a record of its proceedings until late 1916.

Since the SECOND WORLD WAR as few as 16 – 18 ministers were included in Cabinets led by CLEMENT ATTLEE and WINSTON CHURCHILL, although after 1955 numbers were added; a typical post-1955 Cabinet would include 21 or 22,

considerably exceeding what is widely thought to be an optimal size of 12 –16. In 1992 Prime Minister John Major observed conventions, naming twenty-two in all: the premier (owing office to his leadership of the largest parliamentary party), two Treasury ministers—the Chancellor of the Exchequer and the Chief Secretary—the Lord Chancellor, the Leaders of the House of Commons and House of Lords, and sixteen others, most of whom bear the title of Secretary of State—Foreign, Home, Environment, Defence, Education, Transport, Social Security, Agriculture, Employment, Trade and Industry, Health, Northern Ireland, Wales, Scotland, Citizen's Charter, and National Heritage. Because of the vast expansion of government business, both at the departmental and Cabinet level, the twentieth century has witnessed the development of a far-reaching network of Cabinet committees, designed to ease ministerial burdens; in contemporary parlance, these committees reduce "overload" and enable the Cabinet to concentrate upon essentials. An inevitable result is that much business is settled without recourse to the Cabinet; nor is the "appeals" mechanism an easy one for dissenters from a particular Cabinet committee's decision.

Originally, the impetus for the committee system was the deadly business of war: in late 1916, DAVID LLOYD GEORGE essentially created both a new Cabinet system, including committees, and innovative Cabinet procedures; during the Second World War, Churchill presided over a major expansion of the extant Cabinet committee system. Both war premiers replaced the peacetime Cabinet model with a War Cabinet, designed to free a handful of leading ministers from departmental tasks in order to focus on basic tasks; Churchill involved himself in military matters to a much greater degree than had Lloyd George. In the interim, Lloyd George's innovative committee system had been scaled back, although—contrary to what is often asserted—it survived his own political downfall in 1922, as did certain other innovations which stamp him as the major Cabinet reformer of the century; for example, his establishment of a Cabinet Secretariat charged with keeping Cabinet Minutes and managing the flow of War Cabinet and government business. Indeed, S.S. Wilson has enumerated in excess of 850 Cabinet committees for the years 1922–39, although the vast majority were *ad hoc*, and some few never met.

In 1945 Attlee left no doubt that the committee system was there to stay, even as he returned to the larger peacetime Cabinet model. Thus Cabinet committees proved a permanent addition, although governments remain extraordinarily protective about their identity and functions. In 1983 MARGARET THATCHER went further than her predecessors in acknowledging four major standing committees (i.e., permanent for her regime), namely Home and Social Affairs; Legislation; Economic Strategy; and Oversea and Defence. The Prime Minister chaired the latter two; curiously, a sub-committee of the last had in effect functioned as a War Cabinet during the FALKLANDS WAR of 1982, although the full Cabinet continued to meet. Peter Hennessy reported that at least another 156 committees were in existence at this time; most were *ad hoc*, and apparently all were supported to some degree by the record-keeping mechanism housed within what is now known as the Cabinet Office. Cabinet committees can be differentiated functionally by composition: ministerial committees often include ministers outside the Cabinet as well as within; official committees are composed of civil servants, often working in parallel with ministerial committees but almost certainly in command of greater detail (they played hardly any role prior to 1939); mixed committees, drawing upon ministers and civil servants, were very few in number in 1983. Taken together, Cabinet committee activities constitute a well-hidden portion of contemporary Cabinet practices, although their records, for the most part, are made available with Cabinet records after thirty years.

Indeed, their ability to formulate policy at the sub-Cabinet level—even if the Cabinet does not review their decisions, they are binding under the terms of collective responsibility—constitutes a major plank in the arguments of those who contend that the Cabinet no longer plays the role of "hyphen-buckle" assigned it by Walter Bagehot. In broadest terms, they argue, Cabinet government has given way to what is characterized as "Prime Ministerial government," and the Cabinet itself has decayed into a "dignified" element of the English constitution. The "efficient" element is centered in the person of the premier, dominating his colleagues and supported by the administrative bureaucracy, specifically the senior civil servants—particularly the Cabinet Secretary, head of the Cabinet Office—who advise the Prime Minister and answer directly to him, or, unequivocally of late, to her. Well before Thatcher's long tenure, R.H.S. Crossman had all but single-handedly popularized the concept of

"Prime Ministerial government." Subsequently, Crossman drew upon his own experiences in HAROLD WILSON's Labour governments of 1964–70 to compile virtually a day-by-day account of how a much-weakened Cabinet functioned. Nonetheless, the concept of "Prime Ministerial government" stands independent of Crossman's account; the major scholarly work outlining its historical development had already been published by John Mackintosh in 1962, namely his authoritative *The British Cabinet*. It is fair to remark that scholarly treatment of the Cabinet over the past generation has embraced the notion that the dynamic between the Cabinet and the Prime Minister has altered—some say dramatically—towards the accretion of power in the latter's dealings with ministers, whether as individuals or collectively, in the Cabinet.

Yet it is also incumbent to acknowledge that several "insiders"—Crossman's own colleagues, including Harold Wilson—reject the contention that the Cabinet has been shorn of effective power and operates only as Downing Street proposes. Where Crossman reduced the present-day place of collective responsibility to that of "collective obedience . . . to the will of the man at the apex of power," Patrick Gordon Walker joins Wilson in insisting that the Cabinet discusses nearly all significant matters; further, since the Cabinet can influence, resist and in some cases alter policies initially formulated elsewhere, it remains a partner in government, collectively responsible for achievements and deficiencies. "Elsewhere" in this case is not only a reference to the work of Cabinet committees; it relates as well to the contentious work of both "partial Cabinets," charged with resolving matters that are conventionally not brought to the attention of the full Cabinet—NUCLEAR WEAPONS policy has been so handled since 1945, with only one exception—and "inner Cabinets," best understood as informal gatherings of the Prime Minister, a few favored Cabinet colleagues, possibly even advisers or senior civil servants, whose agreement preempts the Cabinet's role. Such alternative decision-making mechanisms are all the more important in light of the fact that modern Cabinets rarely (and, in some regimes, never) take formal votes; rather, the Prime Minister sums up the sense of the discussion and the Cabinet's decision. Obviously, the question of the Cabinet's collective responsibility remains a vital one, as is evident in Michael Heseltine's angry resignation from Thatcher's Cabinet in 1985.

It is sufficient to note that changes in the nature of twentieth-century politics and the tasks of government were bound to tell upon the pre-1916 relationship between the premier and the Cabinet; further, it is clear that the dynamic of that relationship has altered in favor of the former, whose power to command attention has become vitually "presidential." Finally, the disposition to command attention and to dominate proceedings is to a considerable degree a function of the personality and style of the premier: Lloyd George and Thatcher, for example, as opposed to Attlee and STANLEY BALDWIN. Although the controversy whether the Prime Minister remains "first among equals" or, instead, that the office has evolved into one different in kind from those held by Cabinet colleagues may continue, but the actual changes in their relationship are a part of the events of the past three-quarters of a century.

John F. Naylor

Bibliography

Gordon Walker, Patrick. *The Cabinet: Political Authority in Britain.* 2nd ed. 1972.

Hennessy, Peter. *Cabinet.* 1986.

Mackintosh, John P. *The British Cabinet.* 3rd ed. 1977.

Naylor, John F. *A Man and an Institution: Sir Maurice Hankey, the Cabinet Secretariat and the Custody of Cabinet Secrecy.* 1984.

Wilson, Harold. *The Governance of Britain.* 1976.

Wilson, S.S. *The Cabinet Office to 1945.* 1975.

Callaghan, (Leonard) James (1912–)

A pragmatic, temperamentally conservative man of shrewd populist instincts and great professional resilience, James Callaghan was Prime Minister from 1976 to 1979. He took over the leadership of the last LABOUR government before THATCHERISM changed the political landscape; the middle ground which had been his natural habitat was already breaking up as he reached the peak of his career. Unusually, Callaghan also held each of the other major offices of state: Chancellor of the Exchequer (1964–7); Home Secretary (1967–70) and Foreign Secretary (1974–6). Also rare among twentieth-century British leaders were his working-class background and lack of a university education. Raised by his widowed mother in a poor and strongly Baptist home, his work as a tax clerk drew him into trade union activity which in turn led to political ambitions. Elected to Parliament for Cardiff South in 1945, he held junior positions in the 1945–51 government. In the following decade he rose to prominence as a robust moderate, more at home with the party's grass-roots than intellectually with its left wing or personally with the "REVISIONISTS" led by HUGH GAITSKELL.

Callaghan's career briefly seemed destroyed by his Chancellorship. Although he did much for Britain's trade balance and currency reserves, and made several imaginative (if sometimes controversial) tax reforms, he was held responsible for the long, unsuccessful fight against devaluation and for the deflationary measures it required. He rebuilt his career at the Home Office. He addressed Northern Ireland's problems with compassion, showed less sensitivity to IMMIGRATION issues, and otherwise was largely indifferent to 1960s liberal opinion. He also cemented his closeness to the unions, and hence his importance to the parliamentary party, as a key opponent of the government's unsuccessful attempt radically to reform industrial relations.

As Foreign Secretary after Labour's return to power in 1974, Callaghan placed a conventional emphasis on the "special relationship" with the United States, tried with little success to deal with problems in Rhodesia and Cyprus, and oversaw the largely cosmetic renegotiation of terms preceding the 1975 referendum on continuing British membership of the EUROPEAN COMMUNITY. He succeeded HAROLD WILSON as Prime Minister in August 1975. Lacking a clear parliamentary majority, he faced a restless union movement, a divided party, and an inflationary economy too weak to sustain levels of public expenditure. His experience and tactical skills were severely tested. He is widely thought to have acquitted himself tolerably well in adverse circumstances, until the final months of an increasingly beleaguered three years. He maneuvered deftly to form a pact with the LIBERALS to secure a working parliamentary majority. He handled his CABINET skillfully, not least in securing agreement to a loan from the International Monetary Fund. The episode, however, was to many an emblem of Britain's economic decline and fading status. Callaghan was personally popular; his avuncular solidity contrasted warmly with Wilson's style. However, neither this nor his links to the unions prevented a bitter series of STRIKES in the "winter of discontent" of 1978–9 which led to an election defeat in May.

Callaghan retired from the party leadership to the backbenches in 1980 and was created a life peer (as Baron Callaghan of Cardiff) in 1987. He symbolized the passing of an era in party politics. His undoctrinaire Labourism was rooted in memories of the 1930s, a strong union movement, a mixed economy promising full employment, and an extensive WELFARE STATE. This political orientation was steadily eroded by economic and cultural changes, shifting intellectual currents, and a growing polarization of Left and Right which accelerated after the fall of his own government.

Steven Reilly

Bibliography

Callaghan, James. *Time and Chance.* 1987

Hennessy, Peter, and Anthony Seldon, eds. *Ruling Performance: British Government from Attlee to Thatcher.* 1987

Morgan, Kenneth O. *Callaghan: A Life.* 1997.

Cambridge, University of

In the twentieth century the University of Cambridge has become one of the world centers for scientific research and has been distinguished for its work in the fields of philosophy, LITERARY CRITICISM, economics, PHYSICS, and biological sciences. Despite genuine efforts to make the colleges of Cambridge accessible to less affluent students, the ancient university retains a measure of the ambience of social exclusivity and privilege that defined it in the years prior to 1918.

Before the First World War Cambridge was distinguished by the presence of philosophers G. E. MOORE, ALFRED NORTH WHITEHEAD, BERTRAND RUSSELL, and Russell's pupil Ludwig Wittgenstein. Russell was dismissed during the war for the publication of an allegedly seditious pamphlet, and Wittgenstein left Cambridge, to return in 1929. More than 2,100 Cambridge men were killed in the war, among them the poet RUPERT BROOKE, and 2,900 wounded. A disproportionate number of Cambridge men lost their lives, probably because they were commissioned as officers upon enlistment, and officers were more likely to perish than enlisted men.

The war was perceived as a turning point, after which Cambridge began to evolve into a modern, meritocratic research university. In 1919 three developments marked this evolution: the PhD degree was introduced, Greek was abolished as an entrance requirement, and ERNEST RUTHERFORD was appointed Professor of Experimental Physics and Director of the Cavendish Laboratory. The new degree marked the emphasis on graduate studies and original research that has characterized twentieth-century Cambridge, while the abolition of Greek made it easier for students from state schols or with training in scientific subjects to gain admission. Rutherford presided over a series of landmarks in experimental physics between 1920 and 1938, including the discovery of the neutron by James Chadwick, the splitting of the atom, and advances in theoretical quantum mechanics by Paul Dirac.

In 1920 a combination of misogyny and fear of admitting WOMEN to university governance allowed a repetition of the 1897 vote denying women degrees. In addition, places for women at the university were limited to 500, so that a man had a 90 percent greater chance of gaining admission than a woman. After 1920, when the UNIVERSITY OF OXFORD admitted women to degrees, Cambridge's position was widely viewed as reactionary, but it did not admit women to degrees until 1948.

In the immediate post-war period Oxford and Cambridge joined the other British universities in requesting state assistance to cover their finan-

cial losses during the war and the increased costs of instruction and research, especially in the sciences. A Royal Commission reporting on the colleges' finances in 1922 resulted in the modernization of university governance. Among other administrative reforms, pensions were created to allow the oldest members of the teaching staff to retire, and women became eligible for university teaching posts.

Between the wars the number of subjects proliferated, especially in the sciences, with new teaching posts in physics, metallurgy, mineralogy, zoology, entomology, geology and geophysics, physiology, and pharmacology, among others. In addition, the first Professor of Political Science was appointed in 1926, and the recently created English Tripos (or field) gained steadily in popularity. Classics flourished under Professor A.E. Houseman and history turned from the purely political and diplomatic to the study of social change under the direction of Regius Professor of Modern History G.M. TREVELYAN. In 1921 Geography became a recognized field, and the Scott Polar Institute for the exploration of the Antarctic was founded in the same year.

Throughout the 1920s student politics in Cambridge was largely conservative, and more than a quarter of the undergraduates served as volunteer strike-breakers during the GENERAL STRIKE of 1926. By contrast, student and staff politics veered to the left in the 1930s, with the participation of a small, but highly-visible number of Cambridge students in the SPANISH CIVIL WAR. A genuine concern for social justice resulted in an admiration for communism and in an atmosphere of greater seriousness in debate and student life.

In the 1930s JOHN MAYNARD KEYNES theorized the need for government to use public works to lessen UNEMPLOYMENT, and the study of macroeconomics developed at Cambridge. In the English Faculty F.R. LEAVIS began to develop his school of literary criticism and founded the journal *Scrutiny*. During the SECOND WORLD WAR Cambridge staff worked to break the German codes, and Cavendish physicists contributed to the development of RADAR and atomic energy.

After the war the university entered a period of rapid expansion. The number of students more than doubled between 1938 and 1984. New colleges were founded and existing colleges expanded: Fitzwilliam, Churchill and Robinson were new conventional colleges, Wolfson College was created to give a college affiliation to the university staff, while Darwin and Clare Hall were graduate colleges, catering to the numerous graduate students whose social and educational needs were poorly served by the undergraduate colleges.

The number of places for women continued to be inadequate, although two new women's colleges, New Hall and Lucy Cavendish College, were founded in the post-war period. Lucy Cavendish catered especially to mature women returning to university after an absence and, like Clare Hall, attempted to create a community of fellows and students by abolishing artificial distinctions such as separate dining areas for staff and students. The numbers of women at Cambridge at last rose in the 1970s, when the men's colleges began to admit women. By the 1990s all of the men's colleges were mixed, but three of the women's colleges, New Hall, Newnham, and Lucy Cavendish had chosen to remain single-sex.

Cambridge continued its tradition of excellence in scientific research after 1945: Frederick Sanger won the Nobel Prize for his work on insulin, FRANCIS CRICK and James Watson discovered the structure of DNA, and advances in radioastronomy resulted in the discovery of quasars and pulsars. The student revolts of the 1960s touched Cambridge but had little long-term effect apart from the establishment of the student union and increased student representation on committees. More important were the university's efforts to make access more democratic and student life more comfortable and informal. In 1966 Cambridge joined the Universities Central Council on Admissions (UCCA) which coordinated applications to all British universities and replaced Cambridge's complex admissions procedure. By the late twentieth century the university's efforts to admit the most talented students irrespective of social origin seemed to be having an effect. In 1990 the university admitted approximately 45 percent of its students from state schools, a considerable gain over the small minority admitted before 1914. The increase reflected the widening of access to PRIMARY AND SECONDARY EDUCATION as well as the universities' determination to recruit students on the basis of merit alone.

Despite its academic strength and its efforts to become more accessible, Cambridge has remained, in the public mind, the preserve of the privileged student. Together with other universities, it has come under pressure from government to operate at lower cost by raising the ratio of students to teachers, modifying or even abandoning the traditional small classes.

Elizabeth Morse

Bibliography
Brooke, Christopher. *A History of the University of Cambridge: vol. IV: 1870–1990.* 1992.
Fowler, Laurence and Helen, eds. *Cambridge Commemorated: An Anthology of University Life.* 1984.
Howarth, T.E.B. *Cambridge Between Two Wars.* 1978.
McWilliams-Tullberg, Rita. *Women at Cambridge: A Men's University—Though of a Mixed Type.* 1975.

Campaign For Nuclear Disarmament

Launched in February 1958 by a small group mainly composed of established public figures, the Campaign for Nuclear Disarmament (CND) quickly became a mass movement dedicated to ending British possession of NUCLEAR WEAPONS. CND's first peak of activity occurred within its early years; its second came twenty years later when deteriorating East-West relations, changes in NATO strategy, and the defense policies of the British and American governments stimulated a new wave of protest.

The movement began as a moral crusade. Many of CND's founders believed that unilateral disarmament would serve as an example to the super-powers and allow Britain to find a new role in the aftermath of its humiliation in the SUEZ CRISIS in 1956, which had revealed the nation's declining international stature. Support for CND often represented a fusion of morality and anxiety; the movement attracted thousands who were otherwise politically inactive. CND's leaders largely envisaged a pressure group pursuing conventional lobbying methods, and to many the LABOUR PARTY was a more plausible target than the CONSERVATIVE government of the day. The movement, however, rapidly grew into a more loosely-structured, broadly-based coalition. CND absorbed other recently-founded groups and inherited from the Direct Action Committee responsibility for a march from London to the Atomic Weapons Establishment at Aldermaston in 1958. Such annual marches, their direction reversed in later years, became a central unifying experience in the movement. Tensions were, however, often present; the founders of CND had no real wish to democratize the growing movement. For two years it lacked formal machinery for electing leaders or deciding policy; although decisions of its annual conference became in principle binding, the leadership was adept at remaining relatively autonomous.

In the early 1960s CND's annual marches and rallies attracted crowds of up to 150,000. Local groups and affiliated groups in trade unions and the professions flourished, and in 1960 the movement's influence was visible in the Labour Party's temporary conversion to unilateral disarmament. However, CND's appeal diminished as Cold War tensions eased and unused nuclear arsenals became a less considered aspect of life. By about 1964 CND had passed its first peak: it continued to exist as an organization but faded as a popular movement.

Events from the later 1970s stimulated a remarkable revival. A peace movement spread unevenly but powerfully across much of Western Europe: CND had the experience, status, and organizational framework to play the leading role in its British manifestation. The causes were several: President Carter's decision to develop the neutron bomb and to deploy Cruise and Pershing II missiles in Europe heightened fears that the United States envisaged fighting a "limited" nuclear war in Europe. The Soviet Union's invasion of Afghanistan in 1979 increased East-West tensions. The rhetoric and policies of President Reagan and Prime Minister THATCHER, described as "CND's best recruiting sergeants", contrasted sharply with the vocabulary of detente. Thatcher, determined to replace Britain's ageing Polaris system with the Trident class of nuclear-armed submarines, was seen by many critics as an aggressive, willing agent for American policy.

CND's national membership had dwindled to about 3,000 by the mid-1970s: it rose dramatically to over 50,000 in 1982 and a peak of 100,000 in 1984, with perhaps as many as 200,000 people belonging to affiliated and local groups. As in CND's first incarnation, membership was disproportionately from the educated middle class. Although the organization is officially non-partisan, a majority leaned to the left; the movement influenced the Labour Party's adoption of a unilateralist stance. Numerous protests and demonstrations attracted wide publicity, enhanced by advertising campaigns and the appeal of leaders such as Bruce Kent and Joan Ruddock. At Easter 1983 100,000 people formed a human chain between two nuclear weapons factories; in October 400,000 rallied in London's Hyde Park. The government was alarmed by changing opinion polls, and allocated a budget of £1,000,000 to counter CND's arguments.

However, CND was unable to transform government policy. Although public opinion about nuclear weapons was aroused and anxious, polls suggested that while new generations of weapons and American intentions were distrusted, a substantial majority remained convinced that Britain should possess a nuclear arsenal. CND had also to deal with complex relations with other more-or-less institutionalised groups, particularly the women who sustained a long protest at the US base at Greenham Common, whose fundamentalist views and unflinching determination were often caricatured by opponents as "loony Leftism". Tensions rose to a point which prevented CND organizing any large-scale demonstrations against the arrival of Cruise missiles in December 1983. By 1984 disputes over the way forward were dividing CND; many local groups believed that protests against particular weapons diverted attention from a more comprehensive opposition to nuclear arms. This emphasis underlay the 1986 "Basic Case" campaign, combining heavy advertising with much decentralised local activity. By then, however, the movement's impetus was fad-

ing. After the collapse of the Warsaw Pact and the Soviet Union, CND sought ways to avoid the slide into relative obscurity which had occurred in the 1960s. It continued to advocate that Britain abandon nuclear weapons and leave both NATO and the Western European Union. CND describes its ultimate hope as the achievement of "a world free of all weapons of mass destruction"; it consequently supports all attempts to achieve reductions not only in stockpiles of nuclear arms, but of chemical, biological, and "massively destructive" conventional weapons. The organization's national membership in 1992 was about 55,000: although much of CND's activity is decentralized, it retains a firm structure and claims to be one of the largest peace organizations in the world.

Steven Reilly

Bibliography
Byrne, Paul. *The Campaign for Nuclear Disarmament.* 1988.

Driver, Christopher. *The Disarmers.* 1964.

Marsh, Catherine, and Colin Fraser, eds. *Public Opinion and Nuclear Weapons.* 1989.

Parkin, Frank. *Middle Class Radicalism: The Social Bases of the British Campaign for Nuclear Disarament.* 1968.

Taylor, Richard K. *Against the Bomb: The British Peace Movement 1958–1965.* 1988.

———, and Colin Pritchard. *The Protest Makers: The British Nuclear Disarmament Movement of 1958–1965: Twenty Years On.* 1980.

Campbell-Bannerman, Henry (1836–1908)

Sir Henry Campbell-Bannerman led the LIBERAL PARTY to its greatest electoral victory in January 1906. His brief premiership launched a critical phase of British constitutional and social reform.

The Glasgow-born Henry Campbell, educated at the Universities of Glasgow and CAMBRIDGE, had twelve years experience in the family firm of warehousemen and drapers before entering the House of Commons in 1868. By 1871 he was a junior minister and had acquired a longer surname as the price of a substantial inheritance from an uncle.

C.B., as he preferred to be called, was an efficient and unspectacular administrator as Edward Cardwell's Financial Secretary at the War Office and at the Admiralty under Lord Northbrook 1882–4. Displaying an unexpectedly jaunty imperturbability, he further enhanced his reputation as Chief Secretary for Ireland and then as Secretary of State for War in successive Gladstone and Rosebery ministries.

C.B.'s great gift was his modest amiability. His radical political convictions were comfortably consistent with the post-Gladstonian Liberal agenda of Irish Home Rule, church disestablishment, and curbing of the HOUSE OF LORDS. Sociable and inclined to indolence, he looked no further than the Speakership by 1895. He expected H.H. ASQUITH and others to be "fully ripe" for leadership by the turn of the century, and he emphatically preferred a calmer life to the fighting vanguard role for which Lord Rosebery and other colleagues determined he should be reserved.

After the fall of the Rosebery government in 1895, the leadership of the Liberal Party as a whole was in abeyance. Several years of discord and jockeying for the succession preceded Sir William Harcourt's retirement from the Commons leadership. With Asquith declining to take up the task, C.B. was a near unanimous second choice for what most Liberals imagined was an interim leadership of the opposition. Lord Spencer, Asquith, and the ex-premier Rosebery all had stronger desires and better prospects of being the next Liberal Prime Minister.

In the event C.B. proved to be a remarkably effective leader of a deeply divided party. He survived electoral defeat in 1900 and the machinations of rival imperialist and radical factions during and after the bewilderingly protracted BOER WAR. When the CONSERVATIVE government was plunged into turmoil over TARIFF REFORM and education policy, C.B. skilfully focused his own forces on the weakened enemy.

In office from December 1905, in spite of manoeuvres by Asquith, SIR EDWARD GREY, and R.B. HALDANE, to deny him the premiership, he harnessed a wide range of old and emerging talent. Determined to implement a program of liquor licensing, educational, and electoral reform, he set the government on a course of conflict of the power of the House of Lords. His most acclaimed achievement was the magnanimous post-Boer War South African settlement. Domestically, his electoral generosity to LABOUR proved unnecessary in the 1906 election but of greater value in 1910.

No twentieth-century Prime Minister was more popular with either his colleagues or his opponents nor more trusted by the electorate.

Cameron Hazlehurst

Bibliography

Harris, Jose F., and Cameron Hazlehurst. "Henry Campbell-Bannerman" in Mackintosh, John P., ed. *British Prime Ministers in the Twentieth Century: vol. 1: Balfour to Chamberlain.* 1977, pp. 43–77.

Wilson, John. *CB: A Life of Sir Henry Campbell-Bannerman.* 1973.

Searle, G.R. *The Liberal Party: Triumph and Disintegration 1886–1929.* 1992.

Capital Punishment

Reduction in the number of crimes for which the death penalty might result to zero ended a long historical process that began in the early nineteenth century. In 1800 some 200 crimes (mainly against property) were capital offenses. At the beginning of the twentieth century the number of capital crimes had dropped to four: murder, treason, piracy, and sabotage. A death sentence was mandatory when an individual was convicted of murder; judges had no discretion in this matter. Clemency from the Home Secretary sometimes, but not always, commuted the death sentence into a prison term. From 1900 to 1949, 657 people were executed by hanging or approximately half of those convicted of murder. Application of the death penalty depended upon many factors including gender because only 10 percent of WOMEN convicted were actually executed; those found guilty of murdering a police officer had almost no possibility of reprieve.

The abolition of the death penalty in 1965 represents a case study in parliamentary lobbying, for throughout the century public opinions polls showed strong support for retention of capital punishment. In 1921 the Howard League for Penal Reform made abolition a principal objective. In 1925 the National Council for the Abolition of the Death Penalty was established to act as a coordinating body for those pressure groups dedicated to the cause. Many reformers pinned their hopes for success on the LABOUR PARTY as the vehicle for abolition. As a result, in the 1920s and 1930s the issue did not command a place among major public policy issues.

The advent of a Labour government in 1945 heartened those who believed that abolition was close. Debate about the issue rarely touched on the rationale of deterrence; it usually focused on the essential inhumanity of capital punishment as well as the possibility of error in its application. Although corporal punishment in prisons was abolished in 1948, the death penalty remained. Only in 1955 did this issue come to the forefront of British politics. Several notable cases had the consequence of questioning the wisdom of the death penalty. In December of 1952 two youths, Christopher Craig and Derek Bentley, were surprised breaking into a warehouse in Croydon, and Craig, aged sixteen, shot and killed a policeman. Bentley had already been in police custody for fifteen minutes at the time of the fatal shots. Bentley, aged nineteen, was convicted of murder under the felony murder rule and paid with his life. Craig, the killer, was too young for execution and was sentenced to life imprisonment. The most famous case of all, however, was that of John Christie, who in 1953 was found guilty of murdering six women including his wife. The problem was that four years earlier a lodger at the same address named Timothy Evans had been convicted of murder of his wife and child and executed. Many people came to believe that Christie, who had testified at Evans's trial, had committed all the murders and that Evans, an innocent man, had been wrongfully executed.

In 1955 a newly-formed National Campaign for the Abolition of Capital Punishment emphasized these cases to question the death penalty more strenuously than ever. As a result the Homicide Act of 1957, while not abolishing the death penalty, created categories of capital and noncapital murder. Not until 1965 did the Abolition of Capital Punishment Act suspend the death penalty completely for a period of five years; Parliament made this permanent in 1969. Attempts in 1979, 1983, and 1988 to reintroduce the death penalty for specific offenses have failed. The gallows, so fearsome a force in British society for so long, appears, for the moment at least, to have passed into history.

Richard A. Cosgrove

Bibliography

Blom-Cooper, Louis, ed. *The Hanging Question.* 1969.

Christoph, James B. *Capital Punishment and British Politics.* 1962.

Edwards, Ruth Dudley. *Victor Gollancz.* 1987.

Tuttle, Elizabeth Orman. *The Crusade Against Capital Punishment in Great Britain.* 1961.

Carson, Edward Henry (1854–1935)

Edward Carson, barrister, CABINET minister, judge, and ULSTER Unionist leader, was born in Dublin on 9 February 1854. A Trinity College, Dublin, graduate, he was admitted to the Irish bar in 1877 and the English bar in 1893, becoming Queen's Counsel in 1889. He was knighted in 1900. Carson served as a Conservative MP from 1892 to 1921, and as a minister in Convervative (1892, 1900–5) and coalition (1915, 1916–18) governments. From 1910 to 1921 he was leader of the Irish Unionist bloc of the CONSERVATIVE PARTY. Carson was a Lord of Appeal from 1921 to 1929, with a life peerage (Baron Carson of Duncairn). He died at Cleve Court, Kent on 22 October 1935.

Carson was an immediate success at the bar as both prosecutor and defense counsel. As senior crown prosecutor in Dublin (1889–92), he zealously enforced the Crimes Act of 1887. His devastating cross-examination of Oscar Wilde in the latter's libel suit against the Marquess of Queensberry (1895) led to Wilde's sodomy conviction and confirmed Carson's towering reputation. Carson's famous defense, in the Archer-Shee case (1910), of a naval cadet accused of theft was the subject of TERENCE RATTIGAN's play, *The Winslow Boy* (1946).

Carson's skill as a prosecuting attorney in Dublin, which attracted the attention of ARTHUR BALFOUR, led to his appointment as Solicitor-General for Ireland in 1892, and for

Great Britain from 1900 to 1905. After establishing his credentials as an uncompromising opponent of IRISH NATIONALISM and home rule, Carson in 1910 succeeded Walter Long as head of the Irish Unionist bloc in the House of Commons. Carson's certainty that Ireland's economy depended on ULSTER's heavy industry, and that freedom from British tariffs guaranteed the latter's health, strengthened his anti-nationalist beliefs. After declining to stand for the Conservative Party leadership in 1911, Carson committed himself to fighting home rule.

The ASQUITH government's introduction of a Home Rule Bill in 1912, after nullifying the HOUSE OF LORDS' veto by the Parliament Act of 1911, convinced Carson that only vigorous—and if necessary extralegal—measures would balk home rule. In addition to skillful obstructionism in the Commons, Carson took the lead in raising and training an 80,000-man armed forced of Ulster Volunteers (consisting mostly of Protestants) to resist home rule forcibly if it became law. Along with his Ulster lieutenant, James Craig, he made plans for converting the Ulster Unionist Council into a provisional government in Belfast. Carson persuaded ANDREW BONAR LAW, the new Conservative leader, to pledge support of his party for the Ulster Unionists.

Although Carson and his followers illegally imported guns from Germany and made other preparations for armed resistance to a prospective Dublin government, the Asquith Cabinet did not seriously interfere with them. The government's offer to exclude the six mainly Protestant northeast counties of Ulster from home rule for six years was rejected as a "stay of execution." There was a serious prospect of civil strife in Ireland, and possibly Great Britain, when the FIRST WORLD WAR began in August 1914.

Carson's offer of the Ulster Volunteers to the British army as a division was promptly accepted, although the same privilege was not extended to the largely Catholic National Volunteers. The Home Rule Bill became law in 1914, but its operation was suspended for the duration of the war. Carson joined Asquith's coalition Cabinet in 1915 as Attorney-General but soon resigned in protest against military policy. Following the Easter Rebellion in 1916 DAVID LLOYD GEORGE and Carson negotiated a plan for permanently excluding from home rule the six Protestant Ulster counties, but the scheme collapsed. Lloyd George included Carson in his coalition government formed in December 1916, initially as First Lord of the Admiralty until July 1917, subsequently as Minister without Portfolio in the War Cabinet until January 1918. At the Admiralty, Carson acted as spokesman for the naval professionals and disagreed with the Prime Minister over many issues, notably Lloyd George's decision to use warships to convoy merchant vessels threatened by German submarines.

After the war Carson realized that some form of Irish self-government was inevitable and concentrated on maintaining a British connection for the "Six Counties." In 1920 he threw his support behind the Government of Ireland Act, which established a separate government within the United Kingdom for Northern Ireland— ironically, a form of home rule. Carson retired from politics in 1921 upon receiving his judicial appointment.

Carson was a magnetic personality whom even his political enemies liked. Although a painstaking lawyer, Carson was not a successful administrator in public office. Historians dispute whether he was an effective leader of the Ulster resistance movement, or a figurehead for less prominent figures.

Don M. Cregier

Bibliography

Hyde, H. Montgomery. *Carson.* 1953.

Marjoribanks, Edward, and Ian Colvin. *The Life of Lord Carson.* 3 vols. 1932–6.

Stewart, A.T.Q. *Edward Carson.* 1981.

Catholicism: see Roman Catholicism

Chamberlain, (Joseph) Austen (1863–1937)
Born on 16 October 1863, the eldest son of the prominent Birmingham politician Joseph Chamberlain, Austen Chamberlain was groomed from an early age for a career in politics. He entered Parliament in 1892 as the Unionist member for Worcestershire East, and, after 1914, held his father's seat, as Conservative member for Birmingham West. Benefiting from his family connections, Chamberlain's political rise was rapid. He gained his first CABINET seat in 1900 as Postmaster General and went on to serve twice as Chancellor of the Exchequer (1903–5, 1919–21), Secretary of State for India (1915–17), Lord Privy Seal (1921–2), and First Lord of the Admiralty (1931). In a parliamentary career that spanned forty-five years, he came within reach of the premiership in the early 1920s but saw it slip out of his hands because of his support for continuation of LLOYD GEORGE's coalition government. Chamberlain's most productive period was his tenure as Foreign Secretary (1925–9) in BALDWIN's second government, during which he negotiated the Locarno non-aggression treaties (1925). After 1931 he assumed the role of backbencher and elder statesman.

Chamberlain's political career was conducted in the shadow of his famous father, an influential and powerful force in British politics in the decades before the FIRST WORLD WAR. Expected to follow in his father's footsteps, educated at Rugby and CAMBRIDGE, Chamberlain entered Parliament in the early 1890s and, benefiting from the family name, found rapid advancement to a post in the Cabinet. He nearly gained the leadership of the CONSERVATIVE PARTY in 1911 but gave way to BONAR LAW in the interest of party unity. The outbreak of war brought a seat in Lloyd George's War Cabinet. After the war Bonar Law's ill health led to Chamberlain's leadership of the Conservative Party and the House of Commons. Dissatisfied with Lloyd George's government, Conservative backbenchers met at the Carlton Club (19 October 1922) to vote against continuing the coalition. Chamberlain's support for its continuation cost him the party leadership and his chance at the premiership.

The rift that separated Chamberlain from the party was mended when he was asked by BALDWIN to serve as Foreign Secretary. Meeting with his French and German counterparts, Chamberlain played a central role in negotiating the Locarno treaties (1925). Britain and Italy guaranteed Germany's western frontiers with Belgium and France, while other non-aggression pacts were concluded between Czechoslovakia and Poland. Yet no similar guarantees were forthcoming for Germany's eastern frontiers. While pro-French in sentiment, Chamberlain was convinced of the need to bring Germany back into the community of nations. For his efforts, Chamberlain received a Nobel Peace Prize and a knighthood. Contrary to expectations, the Locarno treaties failed to have any lasting impact. The hopes of building a new concert in Europe were rapidly overtaken by the events of the 1930s.

The fall of Baldwin's Government in 1929 marked the decline of Chamberlain's political fortunes. With the formation of the all-party National government, he was offered the Admiralty rather than the preferred the Foreign Office. Chamberlain retired to the backbenches after the 1931 general election in hopes of clearing a path for the advancement of his half-brother (NEVILLE CHAMBERLAIN) to the Chancellorship. In the aftermath of the political debacle of the abortive Hoare-Laval Pact (1935), Baldwin offered Austen the Foreign Office, but he declined the invitation. He found consolation in the successful political career of his brother. Chamberlain's death on 16 March 1937 came just months before Neville succeeded Baldwin as Prime Minister.

Throughout his public life Chamberlain was dogged by unfavorable comparisons between himself and his father. While father and son bore a remarkable similarity in dress and outward manner, Chamberlain lacked his father's political ambition and skill. His aloofness and arrogance worked to prevent him from rising to the top.

While Chamberlain was noted for his sense of duty and loyalty, these same characteristics cost him the premiership in 1922 when he supported Lloyd George against the rank and file of the Conservative Party. Prepared for greatness, Chamberlain never managed fully to live up to expectations.

Van Michael Leslie

Bibliography

Chamberlain, Austen. *Down the Years*. 1934.
———. *Politics from the Inside: An Epistolary Chronicle, 1906–1914*. 1936.
Dutton, David. *Austen Chamberlain: Gentleman in Politics*. 1985.
Petrie, Charles. *The Life and Letters of the Right Hon. Sir Austen Chamberlain*. 2 vols. 1939–40.
Self, Robert C., ed. *The Austen Chamberlain Diary Letters*. 1995.

Chamberlain, (Arthur) Neville (1868–1940)

A Conservative politician associated with the policy of APPEASEMENT in the 1930s, Neville Chamberlain was educated for a career in business, entering local politics in Birmingham prior to the First World War. He served as Lord Mayor of Birmingham (1915–16) until he resigned to become Director General of National Service (1916–17) under LLOYD GEORGE. After the war Chamberlain entered Parliament and achieved a solid record as Postmaster General (1922–3), Paymaster General (1923), Minister of Health (1923–4, 1931), and Chancellor of the Exchequer (1931–7). After succeeding BALDWIN as Prime Minister (1937–40), Chamberlain confronted a deteriorating international situation. His response was the adoption of a dual policy of negotiation and rearmament. With the outbreak of war on 1 September 1939, he continued as a much criticized wartime leader. The failure of the Norwegian campaign galvanized opposition to Chamberlain's conduct of the war and led to his resignation on 10 May 1940.

Chamberlain was the second son of the noted Birmingham politician Joseph Chamberlain. Throughout his public life Chamberlain was influenced by family background that stressed politics and public service. While his older half-brother (AUSTEN CHAMBERLAIN) was groomed for politics, Chamberlain found himself sent instead into business. Educated at Rugby and Mason College, Birmingham, he began a career as an accountant, which was interrupted by his father's plan to recoup financial losses by growing sisal in the Bahamas. This scheme was doomed from the start by the poor soil of the islands and the low market value of sisal. Chamberlain's seven years as a planter on remote Andros Island reinforced his natural tendency toward aloofness.

On returning to England in 1897, Chamberlain took up the life of a successful businessman, managing a number of local companies in Birmingham. He served on the Birmingham City Council at the age of forty-two and was elected four years later as Lord Mayor. Chamberlain's time in municipal politics earned him a reputation for innovation and reform. He made important contributions in the areas of health care and TOWN PLANNING, a record that led to his appointment in Lloyd George's government as Director General of National Service in charge of mobilizing civilian manpower for industry. The ill-defined duties and powers of the post, combined with the personal hostility of the Prime Minister, led to his resignation and a lifelong animosity between Chamberlain and Lloyd George.

In 1918, nearing fifty, Chamberlain entered Parliament as the Conservative member for Ladywood, Birmingham. The fall of Lloyd George's coalition government in 1922 opened the way for rapid advancement under BONAR LAW and Baldwin. In little more than a year Chamberlain served as Postmaster General, Paymaster General, Minister of Health, and Chancellor of the Exchequer. He gained a reputation as a man who could get things done. Chamberlain was responsible for the Housing Act (1923) and the Local Government Act (1929). He reorganzied the Conservative Central Office and headed the Conservative Research Department. CHURCHILL referred to Chamberlain as the "pack-horse" of the administration.

In the National government that took office in 1931 Chamberlain returned to the Treasury, where he dealt with a range of difficult economic issues, sponsoring the introduction of a 10 percent general tariff and welfare reform. His position as Chancellor also placed him in the forefront of the debate over rearmament and foreign policy. Chamberlain urged an appeal to the country in the 1935 General Election on the issue of defense but was overruled by Baldwin. Arguing that rearmament must be selective and paced so as not to damage the recovery of the weak British economy, he pressed for expansion of the ROYAL AIR FORCE. Chamberlain's efficiency, energy, and willingness to give a lead on important policy matters marked him as the heir to Baldwin.

Once in office as Prime Minister, his plans for economic recovery and social reform were sidetracked by the need to deal with the growing threats to peace posed by the Fascist dictators and Japan. Chamberlain's appeasement policy stressed the removal of grievances through negotiation and the build up of an effective deterrence through selective rearmament. He tried to renew good relations with Japan and worked to separate Mussolini from Hitler. Faced with the need to defend a global empire with limited resources, Chamberlain viewed appeasement as a pragmatic policy in line with British interests.

The zenith of appeasement came during the crisis over the Sudetenland. After the absorption of Austria in early 1938, Hitler demanded self-determination for the German-speaking minority of the Sudetenland. Convinced that Britain was not prepared for war, Chamberlain made a series of sensational trips to Germany to attempt to end the crisis peacefully. Meeting with Hitler on 15 September, 1938, and then again on 22 September, he sought to reach a negotiated settlement. After the discussions broke down due to Hitler's demands that Germany annex the Sudetenland without delay, last minute efforts by Mussolini led to the Munich Conference. The Munich Agreement (30 September, 1930) saved the peace by turning over the Sudetenland to Germany at the expense of Czechoslovakia. While Chamberlain was hailed as the savior of peace, hopes were shattered by Hitler's invasion of the rump Czech state (March 1939). Britain responded by issuing ill-considered unilateral guarantees to the nations of Central and Eastern Europe threatened by German aggression while attempting to negotiate an alliance with the Soviet Union.

With the advent of war, Chamberlain continued to serve as Prime Minister with limited success. His war ministry was hampered by the refusal of the Liberal and Labour Parties to serve under him, although his harshest pre-war Conservative critics, Eden and Churchill, were taken into the government. Britain adopted a defensive strategy that called for the continuing build up of the armed forces and the avoidance of offensive action based in the belief that in a long war superior Allied resources would prevail over Germany. Confident of victory, Chamberlain proclaimed in April 1940 that Hitler had "missed the bus." But rising public and political pressure forced the government to adopt a more active strategy that led to Allied efforts to block the flow of iron ore from Scandinavia to Germany. The subsequent German invasion of Norway and the failure of British forces to stop the Nazi conquest of Norway opened the way for the fall of Chamberlain's government. Labourites, Liberals and dissident Conservatives came together to topple Chamberlain from power. After a series of heated debates, the government majority fell from 240 to 81. Chamberlain resigned on 10 May 1940, to make way for an all-party government under the leadership of Churchill. He continued in the government as Lord President of the Council and Leader of the Conservative Party until failing health forced resignation. Following a series of operations, Chamberlain died of cancer on 9 November 1940.

History has not treated Chamberlain kindly. Branding him as one of the "Guilty Men" of the 1930s, his critics have charged that he pursued an appeasement policy that only served to encourage aggression, led Britain into a war that it was unprepared to fight, and directed the war effort ineptly. While these charges all contain elements of the truth, Chamberlain's contributions to social reform, his role in building up the Royal Air Force, and the administrative efficiency shown in preparing Britain to wage total war, not to mention the successful transition from peacetime to wartime administation that laid the foundation for Churchill's success, mark Chamberlain as something less than the failure his critics have depicted him as. In retrospect, his greatest failure was the inability to grasp fully the nature of the threat posed by Hitler. Not even Hitler, Chamberlain believed, could contemplate a massive war of destruction that might leave Europe and Germany in ruins. But, if he had illusions about Hitler and the nature of the next war, his illusions were shared by the majority of the British people until the debacle of Dunkirk and the fall of France.

Van Michael Leslie

Bibliography

Charmley, John. *Chamberlain and the Lost Peace*. 1989.

Dilks, David. *Neville Chamberlain: Pioneering and Reform, 1868–1940*. 1984.

Feiling, Keith. *The Life of Neville Chamberlain*. 1946.

Macleod, Iain. *Neville Chamberlain*. 1961.

Parker, R.A.C. *Chamberlain and Appeasement: British Policy and the Coming of the Second World War*. 1993.

Chemistry

The history of chemistry in Britain in the early twentieth century, as in the world at large, was closely linked to the history of physics, and it would be difficult to classify some studies, such as those on radioactivity and atomic structure, as belonging solely to either domain. Nonetheless, British physicists and chemists have also had quite self-conscious professional identities, the chemists usually dating theirs to the founding of the Royal Institute of Chemistry in 1877. By 1900 several chairs of chemistry existed in British universities (the University of London B.Sc. in chemistry dates from 1858). University College London (UCL) and the Universities of Glasgow and Cambridge have had a worldwide reputation for chemical research and teaching throughout the century. In the first decade of the century British chemistry in virtually every respect was much less formidable than its Continental, especially German, counterparts, most British chemists gaining their degrees at European universities. Since the Second World War British chemistry, both industrial and academic, has stood somewhat in the shadow of American chemistry as evidenced by the fact that two of the Nobel Prizes for chemistry awarded to British nationals since 1945 were given for work done in America, notably that on chemical structure which earned Geoffrey Wilkinson the prize in 1973. In the second half of the century much of the most acclaimed British chemical work has been inseparable from biochemistry and MEDICAL RESEARCH. Frederick Sanger's Nobel Prize for chemistry of 1958, for instance, was awarded for work on the structure of insulin.

The FIRST WORLD WAR quickly illuminated the deficiencies of the British chemical industry. Dyestuff production, for example, was almost entirely dependent on German chemistry. In response, the wartime government promoted research into and manufacture of the basic chemicals used in dyeing and explosives. After the war the still shaky British industry witnessed a series of mergers, again in response to German developments (especially the creation of IG Farbenindustrie), of which the formation of ICI (Imperial Chemical Industries) in 1926 was by far the most significant. In 1927 ALFRED MOND at ICI set up a Research Council to link research in the universities and the chemical industries. The British chemical industry in these years was the parent to several significant synthetic medical compounds. In the 1930s May and Baker synthesized several of the first effective sulphonamides and in 1944 ICI produced Paludrine, an antimalarial. British chemists first established the formula of penicillin.

Radioactivity and atomic constitution were two areas before the Second World War which witnessed significant contributions by British chemists working in academic environments. In 1904 William Ramsay, Professor of Chemistry at UCL, received the Nobel Prize for his discovery of the inert gases, the same year that Lord Rayleigh received it for physics. Between 1904 and 1919 Frederick Soddy at the University of Glasgow and then Aberdeen was acknowledged as the world expert in radiochemical research. Soddy helped elucidate the nature of isotopes, work for which he received the Nobel Prize in 1921. The following year it was received by Francis William Ashton who, while at Cambridge, isolated more than 200 natural isotopes. In 1913 at the University of Manchester H.G.J. Moseley, using X-rays, first determined atomic number in terms of excess positive charge on the nucleus. This fundamental work revealed gaps in the periodic table leading to the discovery of new elements. At about the same time new ideas about atomic structure—the RUTHERFORD atom— were employed in the development of new theories of chemical bonding. The electronic theory of valency was largely developed by N.V. Sidgwick at the University of OXFORD. Also in the first two decades of the century the structure of chemical crystals was investigated by means of X-rays; a method developed by W.H. Bragg and extended by J.M. Robertson, Professor of Physical Chemistry at the University of Glasgow. Similar studies, but using electrons instead of X-rays, were developed in 1927 by G.P. Thomson, Professor of Natural Philosophy at the University of Aberdeen.

The inter-war years saw chemistry's expansion as an academic subject. Laboratory extensions were built and new buildings were erected at at least twelve universities including Cambridge, King's College London, and Birmingham. British university chemists also made important contributions to organic chemistry in these years. The acknowledged systematizer of twentieth century organic chemistry was Christopher Ingold. In the second decade of the century he worked with Jocelyn Field Thorpe at Imperial College and in 1924 became Professor of Chemistry at Leeds and then at UCL in 1930. By 1961, when he retired, the chemistry school at UCL was world famous.

The onset of the Second World War saw a British chemical profession five times the size it had been in 1914. A Central Register drawn up by various scientific societies at the start of the war recorded 6,000 persons working in pure or industrial chemistry. The chemical industry itself, at its peak of wartime expansion, employed nearly half a million people.

After the war, mainly because of developments in the petrochemical industry—the refining in the UK of Middle Eastern crude oil—the British chemical industry expanded at nearly twice the rate of other manufacturing industries. These years saw expanding employment opportunities for qualified chemists even though UK research expenditure was less than 2 percent of turnover compared with 5 percent in Germany and 4 percent in the United States. The 1960s and 1970s saw the results of this policy in pruning and mergers.

By 1970 a number of bodies represented the interests of British chemists, notably the British Chemical Society, the Royal Institute of Chemistry, the Society for Analytical Chemistry, and the Faraday Society. In 1980 the Royal Society of Chemistry was chartered incorporating all these previous groups. Post-war British chemical research has been dominated by large-scale expensive collaborative operations, although individual British chemists have continued to distinguish themselves and gain Nobel Prizes. In 1964 it went to Dorothy Hodgkin for her work at Cambridge on X-ray crystallography. For work on photochemistry, also at Cambridge, in the late 1940s, George Porter and Ronald Narrish received prizes in 1967. In 1969 it was given to Derek Barton for work on molecular structure. Barton was variously associated with Imperial College and Birkbeck College, London and the University of Glasgow, although the work for which he received the prize was done at Harvard in 1949–50.

Christopher Lawrence

Bibliography

Brock, William H. *The Fontana History of Chemistry.* 1992.

Findlay, Alexander. *A Hundred Years of Chemistry.* 3rd ed. rev. 1965.

——, and William Hobson Mills. *British Chemists.* 1947.

Russell, Colin A., ed. *Recent Developments in the History of Chemistry.* 1985.

Chesterton, G(ilbert) K(eith) (1874–1936)

G.K. Chesterton, a prolific and versatile man of letters, belonged to a circle of writers that included Hilaire Belloc, Maurice Baring, GEORGE BERNARD SHAW, H. G. WELLS, Charles Masterman, and Ronald Knox. He was born in London into a prosperous middle-class family, Liberal in politics and Unitarian in religion. After attending St. Paul's School, he studied at the Slade School of Art, but did not take a degree, directing his energies instead into journalism. He was employed as a free-lance journalist for the *Speaker, Daily News* and later wrote columns for *Illustrated London News* (1905–36) and his own *G.K.'s Weekly* (1925–36).

Growing out of his journalism, Chesterton's social criticism combatted the BOER WAR and the political corruption behind the Marconi scandal and opposed cosmopolitanism and utopianism, whether in the form of imperialism, socialism, COMMUNISM, FASCISM, or industrial capitalism. He defended the importance of social organizations small enough to avoid the imposed uniformity of empire but large enough to avoid rank individualism. As a professed liberal and democrat, Chesterton defended the "common man" against the collective state. He advocated, instead, a social model called "distributism" which maintained that the family was the fundamental unit of society and that the means of productive wealth, especially land ownership, should be widely distributed.

Between 1901 and 1936 Chesterton published over two dozen volumes of collected essays. But his most enduring works have been his novels and literary criticism. Among his best fiction is *The Napoleon of Notting Hill* (1904), a futuristic battle over a London neighborhood; *The Club of Queer Trades* (1905); *The Man Who Was Thursday:*

A Nightmare (1908), a proto-surrealist detective story; *The Ball and the Cross* (1909), a comical search by an atheist and a Christian for a place to duel; and the five volumes of Father Brown detective stories collected in 1951 as *The Father Brown Omnibus.* Among Chesterton's works of biographical and literary criticism, the most notable are *Robert Louis Stevenson* (1902), *Robert Browning* (1903), *Charles Dickens* (1906), *George Bernard Shaw* (1909), and *The Victorian Age in Literature* (1913). His poems range from the witty and whimsical to the religious, the best being, perhaps, *The Ballad of the White House* (1911), about King Alfred's successful struggle against Danish invaders. As a religious writer his most influential work is *Orthodoxy* (1908), written while he was an Anglican. This explanation of his own religious convictions followed upon *Heretics* (1905), a work which exposed the weaknesses in the reasoning of influential thinkers and movements of the day. Chesterton's important religious works after his conversion to ROMAN CATHOLICISM in 1922 include a biography of *St. Francis of Assisi* (1923); *The Everlasting Man* (1925), a study of Christ; and *The Thing* (1929), a collection of essays.

Andrew Tadie

Bibliography

Chesterton, G.K. *Autobiography.* 1936.

Corrin, Jay P. *G.K. Chesterton & Hilaire Belloc: The Battle Against Modernity.* 1981.

Sullivan, John. *G.K. Chesterton: A Bibliography.* 1958.

——. *Chesterton Continued: A Bibliographical Supplement.* 1968.

Ward, Maisie. *Gilbert Keith Chesterton.* 1943.

——. *Return to Chesterton.* 1952.

Children's Literature

Historically considered as a substandard literary canon, children's literature is difficult to define. Crossing generic boundaries, it is the only literary field defined by its intended *audience.* Because children's literature is not generally written by children, it seems to reflect adult conceptions of childhood rather than the concerns of children themselves. The past twenty-five years of increased academic attention to children's literature, related to the prominence of literary theory, has focused on the representations of the child and childhood in children's books.

Despite scholarly disagreements over Philippe Aries's hypothesis that childhood is a modern "invention," few would disagree that the idea of a separate children's literature is largely a legacy of Romanticism. If the golden age of children's literature—1860 to 1930—was predominantly British in character, the history of British children's literature throughout the twentieth century has become an increasingly complex story.

Critics like Jack Zipes and Alison Lurie point to the "subversive" nature of children's texts, speculating that they are quietly critical of the adult social order and that they reflect utopian aspirations. Other critics have seen the literature as formally and politically conservative, leading children to accept dominant Western and middle-class values. In most cases, however, the subversive and conservative element might be said to co-exist, as the works of RUDYARD KIPLING and E[dith] Nesbit (1858–1924) suggest. Kipling the imperialist wrote many of his most complex and inventive works for or about children, including *Kim* (1901), *Just So Stories* (1902), *Puck of Pook's Hill* (1906) and *Rewards and Fairies* (1910); the content of these books does not clearly endorse the Empire. Nesbit, the FABIAN socialist, revolutionized children's literature by eschewing both Victorian didacticism and manners; in her finest work, the Psammead stories—*Five Children and It* (1902) *The Phoenix and the Carpet* (1904) and *The Story of the Amulet* (1906)—she challenges Edwardian complacency; and yet, her fictional children can often seem middle-class youngsters on a fantastic holiday, visiting foreign cultures and times for an exotic thrill.

Drawing on a great Victorian legacy, fantasy seems the defining genre for British children's literature through much of the century, with nostalgic overtones. The impulse for adults who wrote for children before the FIRST WORLD WAR is often more regressive than it is exploratory, imagining childhood itself as the pastoral neverland of J.M. Barrie's (1860–1937) *Peter Pan* (1904) or Kenneth Grahame's (1859–1932) prepubescent male arcadia in *The Wind in the Willows* (1908). Perhaps only Beatrix Potter (1866–1943) might be said to have subverted the pastoral mode by means of her representations of aggression and violence in *The Tale of Peter Rabbit* (1901) and in her subsequent picture books for the very young.

The First World War and its aftermath appear to have brought an end to the explosion of children's books now considered classics. In contrast to the burgeoning institutional supports for children's literature in the United States, in Britain there was a general lack of interest in children's books. The notable achievements of the 1920s were the poetry and poetic stories of Walter de la Mare (1873–1956) and Eleanor Farejon (1881–1965) and the animated-toy stories of Margery Williams Bianco (1881–1944). A. A. Milne's (1882–1956) *Winnie-the-Pooh* (1926) and *The House at Pooh Corner* (1928) were not as sentimental as Bianco's work, but they recalled the pre-war pastorals of Grahame and Barrie.

The arcadian impulse before the war seems significantly watered down in its post-war manifestations. Though the great Edwardian fantasies were undoubtedly escapist, the 1920s gave rise to escapism of a more overtly commercial sort, exemplified by the career of Enid Blyton (1897–1968), the best-selling British children's author of all time and also the author most vilified by children's literature critics. Blyton began to flood the market with works like *Sunny Stories for Little Folk* (1926) and by 1950 had an annual income in excess of £100,000. More problematic is the *Doctor Dolittle* series (1922 onward) by Hugh Lofting (1886–1947). Lofting's experience in the trenches of Flanders gives a radical edge to the stories, but they are marred by racism and a contempt for the masses.

The influence of the *Swallows and Amazons* series (1930–47) of Arthur Ransome (1884–1967) has been far greater in Britain than in the U.S. The twelve novels resurrect the adventure stories popular at the turn of the century, but they are more domesticated and often set in the romantic landscape of the Lake District. Like earlier Edwardian fantasies, they take place in a world ostensibly without adults and evoke the idea of childhood as a holiday. But as Peter Hunt points out, there is a "subtle regulation" of the child's world by the adult world in Ransome's fantasies. Others have criticized the series's middle-class values. Still widely read in Britain, Ransome's novels anticipate the domestication of British children's fantasy in the 1940s and 1950s.

J.R.R. Tolkien (1892–1973), another veteran of the Flanders trenches, spent the major part of the 1930s writing *The Hobbit* (1937), widely regarded as the major work of fantasy between the wars. Tolkien's imaginary Middle-Earth undoubtedly influenced C.S. Lewis, who read the novel in manuscript. Lewis's *Chronicles of Narnia* (1951–6), an allegorical retelling of the Christian myth in seven novels, are more apparently didactic than Tolkien's novels. Tolkien's influence may be felt in the other major children's fantasy of the period, Mary Norton's (1903–) *Borrowers* series (1952–82), but with a distinctly post-war flavor. Miniaturized like the hobbits, Norton's Borrowers are depicted as a Victorian family attempting to escape the surveillance of the "human beans." Without the religious undercurrents to be found in Tolkien and Lewis, Norton creates a more social and political allegory in which her adolescent heroine, Arietty, negotiates postmodern dangers as well as crises of gender and sexuality. Norton's depiction of an old-fashioned domestic world under siege figures the enormous changes taking place in children's literature and the conception of childhood after the SECOND WORLD WAR. In recent decades children's writers have continued to explore alternative worlds, in high fantasy and in historical fantasy such as L. M. Boston's (1892–) *Green Knowe* series (1954–64), and Phillipa Pearce's (1920–) highly acclaimed *Tom's Midnight Garden* (1958). Darker psychological elements and a further mixing of genres become apparent in the works of Alan Garner (1934–) and William Mayne (1928–). Garner's metafictional experiments in books like *Red Shift* (1973) and Mayne's virtuosic use of subgenres of children's literature challenge historically conservative conventions. However, the fiction of this period is not unrelievedly dark: the comic novels of Roald Dahl (1916–90), notably *James and the Giant Peach* (1961), *Charlie and the Chocolate Factory* (1964), *The Witches* (1983), and *Matilda* (1988), are very popular with children. Dahl was the best selling children's writer living in Britain at the time of his death, despite adult objections to his works from both the Left and the Right. Perhaps such objections are not entirely disinterested, since adult hypocrisy is often the main target of Dahl's satire.

Though undoubtedly there are run-of-the-mill British "problem novels," the much touted "new realism" for children seems more of an American than a British phenomenon. The finest contemporary British children's texts are rooted in tradition, even as they test traditional generic boundaries as well as the boundaries between child and adult worlds. Innovators such as Joan Aiken (1924–), Nina Bawden (1925–), Leon Garfield (1921–), Jane Gardam (1928–), Aidan Chambers (1934–), and David Rees (1936–) are not so easily pigeonholed. It should be noted that Britain has produced the century's most innovative experiments in poetry written for children in the work of Ted Hughes (1930–98) and Charles Causley (1917–).

Richard Flynn

Bibliography
Carpenter, Humphrey, and Mari Prichard. *The Oxford Companion to Children's Literature.* 1984.
Hunt, Peter, ed. *Children's Literature: the Development of Criticism.* 1990.
Inglis. Fred. *The Promise of Happiness: Value and Meaning in Children's Fiction.* 1981.
Townsend, John Rowe. *Written For Children: An Outline of English Language Children's Literature.* 1983.

Christie, Agatha Miller (1890–1976)

Author of eighty-one novels, 149 short stories, thirteen plays, two autobiographical works (signed Agatha Christie Mallowan), some verse, and miscellaneous other writings, Agatha Christie may well prove the best-selling writer in English of the twentieth century. Although she wrote six "straight" novels under the name Mary Westmacott and nine romance thrillers and spy novels, and although several of her plays were successful, Christie's major achievement lies in her practice and development of the British DE-TECTIVE NOVEL. The British detective form (as opposed to the American tough guy detective form) follows a tradition set by Arthur Conan Doyle's Sherlock Holmes stories. That is, it underplays physical violence; it stresses cerebral riddle-solving; it preserves the tone of comedy of manners; and it affirms the existing social/moral order. The form is fundamentally Aristotelian in structure with a firm beginning, middle, and end. It engages readers by inviting them to compete with the detective in unraveling the mystery. It observes "fair play" rules that supply readers with clues they need in order to compete. Finally, it suggests that by means of intellectual apprehensions, productive social organization can be recovered and preserved. Christie wrote sixty-one novels in this highly formulaic genre, beginning with *The Mysterious Affair at Styles* (1920) and ending with *Elephants Can Remember* (1972). Her work is widely regarded as having set the standard against which other writers of whodunits must be measured.

No single Christie whodunit accounts for her special achievement. The sheer quantity of her writing is part of that accomplishment. So is the inventiveness with which she combined and recombined, mixed and remixed, elements of plot, characterization, setting, and ending, to create a long list of fresh-seeming, if familiar, surprising, if predictable, narratives.

Though she experimented with several central characters, her most popular series detectives were the Belgian-born, mustachioed Hercule Poirot, who solved problems by exercising his "little grey cells"; and Miss Jane Marple, the English spinster who solved them by applying the knowledge of human character she had acquired through observation of the villagers of St. Mary Mead.

Christie's novels, widely reprinted, often with variant titles, have been translated into 103 languages. Many of her novels and her short stories have been adapted for the stage, for the movies, and for television production. During her lifetime, Christie tended to object to such adaptation, but several of her plays, including *Ten Little Indians* (1945), *The Mousetrap* (1952) (the longest running play in British theatrical history), and *Witness for the Prosecution* (1953) were developed from her own earlier novels or short stories.

While some readers value her work primarily as one of the best sources of detail of British social history from the 1920s through the 1970s, she defined herself as merely "a tradesman in a good honest trade."

Mary Wagoner

Bibliography
Bargainnier, Earl F. *The Gentle Act of Murder: the Detective Fiction of Agatha Christie.* 1980.

Barnard, Robert. *A Talent to Deceive: An Appreciation of Agatha Christie.* 1980.

Christie, Agatha. *An Autobiography.* 1977.

Gill, Gillian. *Agatha Christie: The Woman and Her Mysteries.* 1990

Morgan, Janet. *Agatha Christie: A Biography.* 1984.

Wagoner, Mary. *Agatha Christie.* 1986.

Church of England

The Church of England, or Anglican Church, is the legally established national church of England (not of Scotland, Wales, or Northern Ireland). As England is, in turn, the largest constituent part of the United Kingdom, comprising over 80 percent of its population, its national church has long held a central place in Britain's public life. But in the twentieth century it has experienced an erosion of its membership and some loss of its general influence and stature. Nevertheless, it remains a large and important cultural, social, and political institution.

Its modern history can be traced back to 1534 when, during a wider religious turbulence on the Continent, ties with Rome were severed by Henry VIII, immediately occasioned by his need of a divorce. The Church of England emerged as an ecclesiastical hybrid—Protestant in that it was no longer under papal jurisdiction (the Crown now assuming the title of Supreme Governor), but claiming a Catholic heritage in its retention of the historic episcopate. This dual character has given the Church a theologically broad and comprehensive character, embracing both "Protestant evangelicals" and "Anglo-Catholics". This combination is sometimes referred to as a "via media", or middle way, between Western Christianity's two major camps.

The Church is divided into two provinces, Canterbury and York, each headed by a metropolitan archbishop. The southern province is the larger, comprising twenty-nine English dioceses which include Canterbury itself and the ancient diocese of London. It also contains a new (1980) Diocese of Europe which is the Anglican ecclesiastical presence on the mainland of Europe. The northern province is composed of fourteen dioceses, notably York and Durham. Most dioceses are in turn subdivided into archdeaconries (led by archdeacons), and thence into deaneries (led by rural deans).

The base organizational unit, covering the whole of England, is the parish, of which there are over 13,100. All have a parish church, some more than one. (In 1991 there were 16,500 churches). Most are served by a full-time priest (at present all male) paid a stipend out of national church funds. In 1989 these "incumbents" numbered (with assistants) 9,827, to which must be added 487 (1989) women deacons in full-time parish positions. Increasingly, such clergy serve more than one parish, especially in rural areas. In part this is a matter of necessity as inflation eroded financial resources. It also reflects a decline in church membership and clergy. Indeed, throughout the twentieth century clergy numbers have dropped to less than half their strength in 1901. Nevertheless, the Church's institutional and pastoral presence in every English village, town and city throughout England ensures a continued marked contribution to English society.

Among that population, though, the link with the Church has eroded over the years. Church statistics show that in 1988 infant baptisms, at 288 per 1,000 live births, and Easter communicants at 41 per 1,000 adults, were less than half the 1930 figures (699 and 85 respectively). Confirmations have fallen even more dramatically from 227,000 in 1910 to 62,000 in 1989. This represents an undeniably substantial attrition, reflected also in a 1989 English Church Census that indicates a membership of only about 1.6 million, or around 3 to 4 percent of the English adult population. This is slightly higher, at 5 to 6 percent in the rural countryside and suburbs but under 2 percent in the urban conurbations.

Nevertheless, recently the decline may have slowed. Church communicant rates, for example, are unchanged since at least 1976 (at 18–19 per 1,000 adults). In the same period, parish income has increased one third. Furthermore, the Church of England has a large penumbra, perhaps 40 percent of the population, who retain a residual Anglican identity. This reflects its historic cultural status as the national church. But this penumbra too has shrunk over time.

Secularization also affects the Church's contribution at the national level although the ties to the state, and its presence at state occasions, still give the Church of England visibility and a capacity to exercise some influence. State ceremonies include, for example, Remembrance Day ceremonies featuring the Bishop of London, and the coronation which is an Anglican liturgical act in Westminster Abbey. Formal ties between Church and monarchy are also strong. Thus, the monarch, as the Church's Supreme Governor, has the formal right to make appointments to all bishoprics (and many other Church posts). Since Victorian times, however, this right has been exercised in practice by the Prime Minister through a Patronage Secretary. In 1977, as part of a wider process of granting the Church a greater degree of self-government, a Crown Appointments Commission was formed in which the Church was given a greater voice in composing a short list (of two names). But the Prime Minister still makes the final decision, including the possibility of asking for further names to be submitted.

The Church of England also has an official presence within the HOUSE OF LORDS. Twenty-six bishops serve as Lords Spiritual, with full voting and speaking rights. The Archbishops of Canterbury and York, and the Bishops of London, Winchester, and Durham always have seats. Twenty-one of the other diocesan bishops serve according to seniority defined by the date of their appointment as diocesans. The Bishop of Sodor and Man, however, has an equivalent seat instead in the Manx Parliament, and the Bishop of Gibraltar in Europe (Diocese of Europe) is not eligible.

From this position, the Church of England makes an official contribution to the legislative process and gains informal access to the corridors of power. In practice, bishops nowadays give their Lords membership a relatively low priority. Attendance, therefore, normally devolves on one bishop by rota, and a few others by choice, usually including the Bishop of London whose office is adjacent to Parliament. On this limited basis, however, the bishops make a contribution as a respected Christian voice on a wide range of topics, briefed by an official from the Archbishop of Canterbury's staff at Lambeth Palace.

There is no equivalent presence within the more powerful House of Commons. Indeed, Anglican clergy remain barred from seeking election. Many members (predominantly Conservative) are active lay Anglicans, but rarely speak or vote as Anglicans. When parliamentary business in the Commons arises concerning the Church of England, it is often handled by a member who also serves as one of the Church Commissioners. In addition, there is an Ecclesiastical Committee, with members from both Houses, which liaises with the Church when parliamentary action is required.

That flow of ecclesiastical legislation has diminished in recent years through the gradual creation of Church bodies with devolved powers. In 1919 an Enabling Act established a Church Assembly which was in turn replaced in 1969 by a more powerful General Synod. The Synod is composed of a fifty-three member House of Bishops (all diocesans and nine elected suffragans), a House of Clergy (259 members elected from amongst archdeacons, cathedral deans and other clergy), and a 258 member House of Laity elected by active lay people from each diocese.

Although subjected to criticism as cumbersome, expensive, and bureaucratic, the General Synod has become the central policy-making body of the Church of England, to which important advisory committees and permanent commissions report. These include, for example, boards of Education (BE) and Social Responsibility (BSR). The BE develops policy for the Church's substantial investment in elementary (grade) and secondary (high) schools, which in turn entails dialogue with the Department of Education and Science. Equivalent links exist between dioceses and local educational authorities both of whom run schools directly. The BE also works closely with National Society for Promoting Religious Education, one of many semi-independent organizations associated with the Church of England. The BSR develops reports on a wide range of social and international issues, and publishes *Crucible*. Its range is indicated by its subdivision into committees for Industrial and Economic Affairs, International and Development Affairs, Social Policy, and Race and Community Relations.

Ecumenical relations are handled by the Council for Christian Unity. These include links with ROMAN CATHOLICS, the other major Church in England, and with various ecumenical agencies such as the World Council of Churches, the Conference of European Churches, the Council of Churches for Britain and Ireland, and Churches Together in England. Financial affairs are handled by a Central Board of Finance (created in 1914) which in 1991 had a budget of nearly £12 million. Like all the other central bureaucracy, it is based at Church House, Westminster, which is headed by a Secretary-General. However, a separate and independent agency, the Church Commissioners, handles clergy salaries and pensions. In 1991 its expenditure totalled over £200 million.

Besides these synodical and bureaucratic agencies, the other major focus of national authority in the Church of England lies in the office of Archbishop of Canterbury and his support staff at Lambeth Palace, London. Though lacking the powers and claims of the Pope, the Archbishop is the senior bishop and *de facto* leader of the Church of England. Officially the Archbishop (George Carey, 1991–2002) is Primate of All England (the Archbishop of York being merely Primate of England) and chairs the House of Bishops, an important leadership group in an episcopally-ordered Church. He is a very well-known public figure, having access to the Prime Minister, the House of Lords, and the media.

The Archbishop is also the focus of symbolic unity for the Anglican Communion, a grouping of twenty-eight self-governing Anglican Churches in 164 countries with a combined membership of around 70 million. They include the Episcopal Church in the United States, the Anglican Church of Canada and, within Britain, the Scottish Episcopal Church and the Church in Wales. Episcopal representatives of all the various Churches have been brought together approximately every ten years since 1867 by the

Archbishop of Canterbury at Lambeth Conferences. These have been supplemented in recent years by a London-based Anglican Consultative Council (1969) and a Primates' Meeting (1979), both also presided over by the Archbishop. The Archbishop has become an important international religious figure, dealing with the Pope, and leaders of other Churches, on a personal basis.

The traditional influence of the Church was conservative, reflecting its association with the state and its strength among the more privileged and rural sectors of society. Indeed, politically, it became known as the "Tory Party at prayer", and its episcopal leaders were seen as part of a dominant socio-political establishment having been predominantly nurtured in an ethos of elite public schools and OXFORD and CAMBRIDGE. Some of this conservatism remains, not least among its active laity, in regard to issues such as the monarch, Church establishment, and hostility toward labor unions. They reflect the wider views of relatively privileged suburban sectors. However, some shifts toward more centrist, liberal outlooks can be discerned in recent decades, particularly with the Church's synodical and episcopal leadership. In part this is the result of changed theological understandings, in part a broader recruitment process. The result has been some notable conflicts over public policy, especially involving Church leaders such as David Jenkins (Bishop of Durham) and Robert Runcie (Archbishop of Canterbury 1980–91), and the Conservative Government of MARGARET THATCHER. Issues included defense policy, discussed in the controversial Church report *The Church and the Bomb* (1982), and urban policy, scrutinized in *Faith in the City* (1985). Similar trends are found in Church reactions to the FALKLANDS WAR (1982) and the Gulf War (1991). Yet there are limits to this shift. The Church of England remains a church of the more privileged, and its lay membership reflects this. Institutionally, its conservatism can be seen in its reluctance to approve the ordination of women to the priesthood, although this changed in 1992 (and threatened to provoke a minor schism). But in all its diversity, the Church of England still embodies a uniquely English Christian heritage and thereby remains a influential institution throughout the land.

George Moyser

Bibliography
Brierley, Peter. `Christian` England: What the 1989 English Church Census Reveals. 1991.

Lloyd, Roger B. The Church of England: 1900–1965. 1966.

Machin, G.T. Churches and Social Issues in Twentieth-Century Britain. 1999.

Medhurst, Kenneth, and George Moyser. Church and Politics in a Secular Age. 1988.

Norman, Edward R. Church and Society in England: 1770–1970. 1976.

Welsby, Paul A. A History of the Church of England: 1945–1980. 1984.

Churchill, Winston Spencer (1874–1965)

Winston Churchill's political career spanned the first six decades of the twentieth century, and during almost all this time he was one of the best known and most significant of public men. He changed his party allegiance twice and was always suspected of being an ambitious adventurer, a diagnosis apparently confirmed by the political and strategic blunders that marked his progress. Between 1908 and 1929 he served as a CABINET minister for eight separate departments. The most important of these were his period at the Admiralty during the critical period of Anglo-German naval rivalry before 1914 and his less successful reign as Chancellor of the Exchequer in 1924–9. After a decade in the wilderness, he became the man of the hour in 1940, succeeding NEVILLE CHAMBERLAIN first as Prime Minister and later as Leader of the CONSERVATIVE PARTY. He served two terms as Premier, in the first and most important seeing the nation through to victory in 1945. He returned to power from 1951 to 1955, when he also stepped down as party leader. In later life he declined a dukedom, but in 1953 he accepted a Knighthood of the Garter. Churchill was also an accomplished military historian and biographer, especially of his illustrious ancestor, the first Duke of Marlborough, and of his father, Lord Randolph Churchill.

The crucial influence upon Churchill's early life was the legend left by the meteoric rise and fall of his father, a controversial and rebellious Conservative politician who died after a debilitating illness when his eldest son was only twenty. Winston Churchill's first career was in the ARMY, and he served in India and fought at the Battle of Omdurman (1898). Out of uniform as a newspaper correspondent during the BOER WAR, he was captured and then managed to escape. However, his military exploits and his journalism were only ever intended to be the prelude to a political career. After one unsuccessful by-election attempt (1899), he became Conservative MP for Oldham in 1900. He proved to be an awkward backbencher, more often a critic than a supporter of his own government. Relations were thus already strained before the bombshell of Joseph Chamberlain's campaign for TARIFF REFORM burst over the Conservative ranks in 1903. A strong commitment to free trade was to prove to be almost Churchill's only consistent principle for the next thirty years; in 1904 it led to his "crossing the floor" to join the LIBERAL PARTY. Churchill's pushiness had alienated many: after this apparently adroit quitting of a sinking ship, he became a figure of deep and lasting loathing for many Conservatives. Certainly, the rewards proved to be quick and great. After the Liberal landslide of 1906 Churchill was given a prominent junior ministerial post, and on H.H. Asquith's succession to the premiership in 1908 he entered the Cabinet as President of the Board of Trade. In this office and then as Home Secretary from February 1910 to October 1911, he was one of the government's most energetic reformers, forging a close friendship and radical alliance with the Chancellor, David Lloyd George. Two incidents only marred his reputation: the use of troops to quell industrial disturbances in South Wales, which led to two deaths, and his risky presence at the scene of the Sidney Street siege (1911).

In 1911 Churchill's career changed course when he was transferred to the Admiralty. The period was dominated by the naval challenge from Germany and the growing antagonisms which were to lead to war. Churchill rapidly became a convinced navalist, clashing bitterly with Lloyd George for greater funding for warship building. This was a characteristic feature of Churchill's career: he was a political chameleon who took on the colors of whichever ministry he headed, regardless of consistency or of any wider vision. Thus he had fought against naval spending as a radical social reformer in 1908–9, and was later to refight the same battle as an economizing Chancellor of the Exchequer in the 1920s. The coming of war showed Churchill at his best and at his worst. In the crisis of July 1914 he used his initiative to mobilize the fleet and avoid the risk of a sudden German coup, but alarm was caused by his reckless sending of naval troops to be captured at Antwerp. His constant interference in operational decisions led to strains with the professional head of the navy, Lord Fisher. This came to a head with the failure of the Gallipoli campaign (1915), a disaster that nearly broke Churchill and that hung over him like a pall for the next twenty-five years. When the first coalition was formed in May 1915, the Conservatives demanded Churchill's removal from the Admiralty, and after six unhappy months as Chancellor of the Duchy of Lancaster he quit Westminster to serve as a battalion commander on the Western Front.

When Churchill was recalled to office—over bitter Conservative protests—in July 1917, both the political situation and the internal health of the Liberal Party had been turned upside down by the fall of Asquith and Lloyd George's accession to the premiership. This fractured the Liberal Party into two warring factions, and during the next five years Churchill became Lloyd George's most important Coalition Liberal supporter. He served as Minister of Munitions from July 1917 until January 1919, as Secretary for War and Air for the following two years, and then as Colonial Secretary from February 1921 until the fall of the coalition in October 1922. Together with his close friend F.E. Smith, now Earl of Birkenhead, and R.S. Horne, Churchill was in the inner circle of coalition leaders whose loose commitment to party ties and hedonistic social life were mistaken by many critics for lack of principle and even honesty. When Lloyd George fell, Churchill was cast into the darkness with him, even losing his seat at Dundee in the 1922 general election.

This defeat was to lead to his first spell in the wilderness. During the following two years Churchill completed a passage back to Conservatism that had begun after 1918. On both the domestic front and abroad he had placed increasing emphasis upon the danger of socialism, and even of Bolshevism, and had been an advocate of Allied intervention in Russia. After 1923 he shed his Liberal affiliation for the guise of "Constitutionalist." He was adopted by local Conservatives for the safe seat of Epping, which he represented for the next forty years. The prodigal son was welcomed back to the fold in a manner that took many Conservatives' breath away when following the 1924 victory Stanley Baldwin appointed him to be Chancellor of the Exchequer. He remained at this post throughout the ministry, from November 1924 to June 1929. During this time, with some doubts, he restored Britain to the gold standard (1925) and also played a part both typically pugnacious and yet also generous in spirit in the General Strike and coal strike of 1926–7. Despite being Chancellor, he was never the second figure in the government, being still out of sympathy with his party over tariffs and constantly suspected of coquetting with Lloyd George.

Out of office after the Conservative defeat in 1929, he drifted out of touch with its Baldwinite leadership. In part, this marked the start of a dilettante period, which mixed foreign travel with journalism and biography. Churchill concentrated his attention upon his country house of Chartwell and sought to make his family financially secure and recoup money lost in the crash of 1929. He became an infrequent, and thus resented, attender at Westminster. His political crusades of the 1930s were in fact the product of deep convictions but only rendered his isolation all the greater. He appeared reactionary, in an uneasy alliance with the "diehard" Right, and was believed to be intriguing to bring down the National government. His opposition to Baldwin's bipartisan India policy had led to his resignation from the shadow Cabinet in January 1931 and his omission from the National Cabinet in August; for the next four years he led the India "revolt." In 1936 his support for EDWARD VIII in the abdication crisis led to his being howled down in the House of Commons: his career seemed to be over.

This apparent lack of balance and judgment inevitably colored views of Churchill's other theme during these "wilderness years": the danger of Nazi Germany and the need for rearmament, especially in the air. This stand was less marked or consistent than he and others later made it seem but was strongly critical of the government all the same. After MUNICH he gained in credibility, forging an alliance with ANTHONY EDEN and the younger anti-appeasers. On the outbreak of war in September 1939 Neville Chamberlain was forced to offer him a key post, and he returned to the Admiralty. As the stock of Chamberlain and other ministers dropped, Churchill's rose. He came to personify the "bulldog spirit" and was the only credible replacement for Chamberlain when the latter fell. LABOUR agreed to serve under Churchill, and he combined the posts of Prime Minister and Minister of Defense from May 1940 until July 1945; he also succeeded Chamberlain as Conservative Leader in October 1940. Churchill felt that all his life had been a preparation for this moment of supreme national danger and that he was "walking with destiny." His leadership was of vital importance after the fall of France, rallying the people behind the decision to fight on regardless. He was difficult to work with and for but was also inspirational and energetic, producing a stream of ideas that were then filtered through his immediate staff. He made a second vital contribution by forging a close relationship with the American President Roosevelt, which brought the United States almost into the war even before the attack on Pearl Harbor. The defeat of Hitler had absolute priority: after the German invasion of Russia (June 1941), Churchill welcomed the Soviet Union as an ally. However, he gave priority to the traditional British sphere in the Mediterranean theater, searching once again for the "soft underbelly" in order to avoid the costly frontal assault. This led to the Italian campaign after 1943, and the "percentages agreement" with Stalin on postwar influence in the Balkans (1944).

The Conservative Party had always been uneasy about their new Leader and resented his inner circle of cronies, mainly political outsiders like Brendan Bracken, Robert Boothby, and Lords BEAVERBROOK and Cherwell. However, with Churchill's prestige at their head, neither they nor he anticipated the Labour victory in the general election of May 1945. Churchill ran an ill-judged and over-confident campaign, but took the blow of rejection very hard. As Leader of the Opposition 1945–51, he tried to remain above domestic partisan politics. He was largely uninterested in the party's policy review but gave a general if reluctant endorsement. His main interest was in being a "world statesman." He opposed British withdrawal from Empire but also feared an American return to isolationism in the face of tightening Soviet control in Eastern Europe. At Fulton, Missouri, his "iron curtain" speech (5 March 1946) gave early warning of dangers of Communism and the onset of Cold War. In October 1951 the Conservatives returned to power, and Churchill served a second term as Prime Minister until April 1955. He attempted to reconstruct the closest thing possible to the wartime coalition, offering merger to the Liberals and including experts and other non-party figures. Churchill deliberately set out to show moderation in social policy. The NATIONALIZATION of iron and STEEL was reversed, but other Labour reforms left untouched, and the WELFARE STATE was shown to be safe in Conservative hands. The affluence of the later 1950s was heralded by the removal of controls and RATIONING, although the appeasement of the unions stoked inflationary pressures. Churchill again gave most attention to his attempts at superpower diplomacy, being after 1953 the only one of the "big three" wartime leaders still in power. Believing that he alone could achieve a breakthrough with Russia, he constantly postponed his promised intention to hand over to his heir-apparent, Eden. He made a good recovery from a major stroke in July 1953, but his powers were clearly fading, and he was eventually almost forced to quit in 1955. During his final years he was still subject to his "black dog" of depression and suffered further physical decline. In 1964 he retired from a House of Commons that he had barely attended for several years.

Churchill's was a long but erratic career, full of false starts and remarkable achievements, of insights and reckless impulsiveness, of early promise and dashed hopes. It was founded upon his extraordinary character and abilities, reluctantly admitted by his enemies, but was also hampered by the distrust which he continually aroused, at least until becoming war leader in 1940. If he had retired from politics in the late 1930s, his career would certainly have outshone that of his father, but otherwise would have deserved the verdict of Robert Rhodes James: "a study in failure." His stubborn and eventually triumphant leadership in the SECOND WORLD WAR, inextricably interweaving personal and national recovery, self-confidence, and success, was his greatest achievement. The "finest hour" in 1940–2, when total victory seemed to be almost within the grasp of

Nazi Germany, determined the course not just of British but of world history. Much else in Churchill's career was bronze or even lead, but this was golden, and upon this alone rests his scarcely challenged claim to be the most significant individual in British history, and one of the dozen most significant figures in world history, since 1900.

Stuart Ball

Bibliography

Addison, Paul. *Trust the People: Winston Churchill in Home Affairs, 1900–1955.* 1992.

Blake, Robert, and Wm. Roger Louis, eds. *Churchill.* 1993.

Churchill, Randolph. *Winston S. Churchill.* vols. 1–2. 1966–7.

Gilbert, Martin. *Winston S. Churchill.* vols. 3–8. 1971–88.

———. *Churchill: A Life.* 1991.

Pelling, Henry. *Winston Churchill.* 2nd. ed. 1989.

Soames, Mary, ed. *Winston and Clementine: The Personal Letters of the Churchills.* 1998.

Citrine, Walter McLennan (1887–1983)

General Secretary of the TRADES UNION CONGRESS (TUC) 1926–46, Citrine was an important force for moderation in the trade union movement. He went on to be a member of the National Coal Board before becoming Chairman of the British Electricity Authority, 1947–57. He was created first Baron Citrine of Wembley in 1946.

Citrine, who grew up in the Liverpool area, was of Italian extraction. Both his father and grandfather had been British seamen. Physically weak, he endured an unhappy period of hard manual labor in a flour mill before finding work as an electrician. Though from a Conservative working-class family, he became a member of the INDEPENDENT LABOUR PARTY around 1906. Joining the Electrical Trades Union (ETU) during the 1911 industrial unrest in Liverpool, he was elected the union's first full time district secretary in 1914. His eagerness for self-improvement included learning shorthand, a useful means of advancement in the world of trade union bureaucracy. His skills as an administrator took him to the Manchester headquarters of the ETU as Assistant General Secretary in 1920 and then in the same role to the Trades Union Congress (TUC) in 1924. Given the poor state of the health of his superior, Fred Bramley (1874–1925), he was soon taking additional responsibiliites and from October 1925 until September 1926, when appointed General Secretary, he was Acting General Secretary.

After the trauma of the GENERAL STRIKE (1926) Citrine worked hard to get the TUC and the trade union movement accepted as indispensable parts of British democratic society. He was a warm supporter of the talks between the TUC and influential industrialists—the Mond-Turner talks—which took place from January 1928 and which aroused strong criticism from both communists and right-wing industrialists. He also worked closely with the machinery of government when opportunity arose, serving in the 1930s on the National Economic Council, the Consultative Committee of the Treasury, a Royal Commission that investigated economic and social conditions in the West Indies (1938–9), and, during the SECOND WORLD WAR, in various important capacities.

In these endeavors his moderate and anti-communist views were very similar to those of other powerful British labour movement figures such as ERNEST BEVIN and ARTHUR HENDERSON with whom he worked. His acceptance of a knighthood in 1935 aroused much controversy. In fact he had declined this honor in 1932 and a peerage in 1930. Citrine also was a major moderate figure in international trade union affairs, being president of the International Federation of Trade Unions (1928–45). Attending its meetings in Berlin he witnessed the rise of the Nazis. He was a founder of the World Anti-Nazi Council and, from its inception in 1936, was chairperson.

With ATTLEE's post-war government, Citrine took senior posts in newly NATIONALIZED INDUSTRIES, accepting a peerage and leaving the TUC (1946). He served on the National Coal Board (1946–7), the Central Electricity Authority (1947–57), and (part-time) on the UK Atomic Energy Authority (1958–62). In retirement he wrote two volumes of autobiography, among the finest by any British trade unionist.

C.J. Wrigley

Bibliography

Citrine, Walter. *Men and Work: An Autobiography.* 1964.

———. *Two Careers.* 1967.

Lovell, John C., and B.C. Roberts. *A Short History of the TUC.* 1968.

Martin, Ross M. *TUC: The Growth of a Pressure Group 1868–1976.* 1980.

City of London

The City of London has remained throughout the twentieth century the pre-eminent world's financial center. Unrivalled before 1914, in competition with New York in the inter-war years, the City re-emerged at the top in the 1960s, overcoming the decline of the British economy. Along with New York and Tokyo, LONDON is today one of the the three main financial centers in the world and the leading one in the European zone. The City has played a key role in the British economy: its activities have been essential for the balance of payments and more recently, its world role has enhanced Britain's international economic status.

The golden age of the City of London started in 1870, following the defeat of France in the Franco-Prussian War, which ended the free convertibility of Bank of France notes. Its unrivalled financial position meant, in the first place, that the bulk of world trade was financed through the medium of bills of exchange drawn on London. With over 40 percent of the total exported capital of the world in 1913 raised on its financial markets,'London was the leading center for the issue of foreign loans and equities as well as the capital of international banking. There were more branches of foreign banks opened in the City— about thirty in 1913—and a larger number of multinational banks based in London—thirty-one overseas banks totalling 1387 non-UK branches in 1913—than in any other city. The nominal values of the securities quoted on the London Stock Exchange—over £11 billion in 1913—was larger than that of the New York and Paris stock exchanges combined. Insurance, another British speciality, was spreading its activities all around the world, with the emergence of large composite companies with offices in several cities in North and South America, Australia, and other parts of the Empire. London's dominance in insurance was also due to the unique role played by Lloyd's, first and foremost in the field of marine insurance, but also and increasingly from the early twentieth century through its capacity to ensure new risks. Many commodities were traded primarily, if not exclusively in London, and markets such as the Baltic Exchange for the chartering of ships, or the London Metal Exchange had no equivalent elsewhere.

This financial supremacy was primarily due to Britain's dominant position in the world economy: its share of world trade—25 percent in 1870 and still around 14 per cent in 1913, despite the emergence of its main rivals, Germany and the United States; Britain's Empire and position at the heart of the system of international payments centred on its deficit with industrialized countries and its net surplus with India; the role of the pound sterling in the smooth functioning of the international GOLD STANDARD. But this financial supremacy was also due to the development of the British financial institutions. The banking system was structured to manage the financing of world trade: the major London CLEARING BANKS, which by 1913 concentrated in their hands about two-thirds of the deposits of England and Wales, provided the necessary cash credit, while the MERCHANT BANKS' accepting business was the basis of world trade finance. The Bank of England, despite its loss of touch with the market, had by the beginning of the twentieth century devised methods to control the outflow of gold. The London Stock Exchange was the cheapest in

world for dealing in highly marketable securities. The business opportunities offered in London also attracted many foreign entrepreneurs and speculators who launched new ventures and enchanced the dynamism of the City.

The FIRST WORLD WAR terminated this supremacy, although not the prominent role of the City. Britain had to sell about 15 percent of its overseas investments in order to finance the war effort and, with the suspension of the pound's convertibility, the dollar started to replace sterling as means of payment for international commerce, in particular American foreign trade. But if New York was ready to challenge London's ascendancy, the City was no less determined to recover its former position. The restoration of the gold standard in 1925 at its pre-war parity was a deliberate effort in this direction. The City retained some advantages, in particular its expertise and experience, but its main handicap in comparison to New York was its lack of capital. In the 1920s the City was able to regain much of its pre-war international role, in particular as the centre for commercial credit and short-term funds, as well as in shipping and insurance, but in the foreign issues it was largely overtaken by New York. The disruption of international trade and the Great Depression of the 1930s, followed by the Second World War, undermined the City's overseas activities which, as a result, reinforced its links with the domestic economy. For example, while in 1910 foreign securities comprised 60 percent of all securities listed in the London Stock Exchange, this proportion had fallen to 30 percent by 1938.

The resurgence of the City of London after the Second World War, despite the comparatively poor general performance of the British economy, was primarily due to the opportunities it was able to seize in the 1960s and 1970s to become the center of new markets, in particular for Eurodollars and Eurobonds. The Eurodollar market developed out of dollars held outside the United States by banks, MULTINATIONAL COMPANIES, and others and traded entirely outside the United States. From $1.5 billion at the end of 1959, it reached nearly $50 billion in 1970 and $600 billion in 1980. The Eurobond market grew out of the Eurodollar market to provide longer term loans than was usual with Eurodollars, which were either lent short term, particularly in the inter-bank market or as syndicated medium term credits. The City was able to capture these markets because of its experience in international finance, the range of professional skills available, which had no equivalent in any other financial centre, and the concentration of foreign banks in the square mile. But the City was also able to supplant New York at the time of the undisputed financial supremacy of the United States because of the various regulations imposed by the American government, in particular the ceiling on interest rates paid on time deposits (known as Regulation Q) which made it more attractive to deposit dollars abroad and, above all, in London.

In the 1970s and 1980s Britain had the highest share of international banking activity, holding some 20 percent of the world's foreign assets in 1985; in the mid-1980s, London was also the principal market in foreign exchanges, with some 30 percent of a turnover which reached $600 billion a day in 1989. Although London's equities market was substantially smaller in volume than that of New York and Tokyo, it was more international and remained the largest in Europe. The City also retained strong international positions in various commodity markets, in insurance, as well as in such services as accountancy, law, or funds management. The difference from the pre-1914 or the inter-war periods was that very few of these transactions were now dealt in sterling and that much of this activity was undertaken by the foreign banks represented in London; their number rose to 521 in 1989, or twice the number in any other center.

The City of London is one of the success stories of the British economy. Nevertheless, it is often criticized for neglecting the domestic industry and diverting capital abroad, thereby contributing to the British economic decline. This is a matter of controversy since the City also has strong defenders. The clearing banks have been criticized for their reluctance to grant long-term credit to industry and for their lack of managerial role. The capital markets have been held responsible, particularly prior to 1914, for the huge volume of foreign investments—some £4 billion in 1913—which, critics argue, would have been better employed at home. More generally, the City has been accused of "short termism", from the company promoter of the early twentieth century, more interested in a fast buck than in the long term prospects of the company introduced to the market, to the mechanism of the takeover bid which prevents managers from taking a long-term view of the prospects of their company if this were to affect its immediate results. Finally, British monetary policy has been seen as systematically favoring the interests of the City to the detriment of industry, the most striking examples being the rejection of bi-metallism in the late nineteenth century, the return of the pound to gold at its pre-war parity in 1925, or monetarism in the early 1980s. On the other hand, it has been argued that there was no demand from industry for long term banking credit; that capital exports were the results of a rational behavior on the part of individual investors and ensured an efficient allocation of funds; that the City was always pre-

pared to support worthwhile long term projects while takeover bids ensured the replacement of poor management. As to the monetary options of the British government, there is no evidence that decisions were made in order to favor City interests.

Youssef Cassis

Bibliography

Kynaston, David. *The City of London. vol. 3: Illusions of Gold, 1914–45.* 1999.

McRae, Hamish, and Frances Cairncross. *Capital City: London as a Financial Centre.* 2nd ed. 1991.

Michie, R.C. *The City of London: Continuity and Change since 1850.* 1992.

Van Helten, J.J., and Y. Cassis, eds. *Capitalism in a Mature Economy: Financial Institutions, Capital Exports and British Industry 1870–1939.* 1990.

Civil Service

In England, as in other contemporary Western European states, the public sector employs approximately 30 percent of the work force. Those who work for the government departments directly accountable to Parliament, a useful definition of civil service, account for only about 10 percent of those paid out of public funds. At the beginning of the 1980s approximately 675,000 men and women held such positions. In 1960 the total stood at 719,000, a peak in civil service employment. Because of the difficulty posed by definition, statistics about the civil service should be treated with some caution. Nevertheless, until recent times the number of civil servants has generally followed an upward trend, except for a contraction during the years of depression and fiscal crisis in the 1930s.

The civil service has undergone considerable alteration in its composition during the course of the century. The industrial staff, for example, represented a majority of civil servants prior to the Second World War, but accounted for less than a quarter of the whole by the 1980s. As the size of the industrial sector grew smaller, the number of non-industrial civil servants increased, largely in response to the need to staff the expanding social services provided by the WELFARE STATE. As a consequence, many in the civil service today work in local and regional offices throughout the country and serve the public directly. Only about one-quarter of civil servants now carry out their duties in Greater LONDON.

The 1853 Trevelyan-Northcote Report set the terms of the modern discussion about the civil service. In this crucial document Sir Charles Trevelyan (1807–86) and Sir Stafford Northcote (1818–87) called for recruitment by open, competitive examination to a unified civil service that distinguished sharply between those engaged in "intellectual" (policy-making) duties and those engaged in "mechanical" (managerial) duties. In replacing a system of patronage with a system of merit, Trevelyan and Northcote envisioned departments of state headed by politically responsible ministers advised by politically anonymous officials.

Such ideas, representing a radical departure from previous practice, gradually garnered widespread acceptance, and, after 1870, successive governments took steps to implement these recommendations. The Civil Service Commission, established in 1855 to oversee competitive examinations, developed these along the lines of the classical curriculum characteristic of the public schools and OXFORD and CAMBRIDGE on the grounds that individuals of intelligence enhanced by the best "all-round" or "general" education would make the best civil servants. Consequently, men of high intellectual caliber but little or no training in particular areas of policy began to enter civil service careers. These developments took hold over a period of time. Not until 1919, with the appointment of Sir Warren Fisher (1879–1948) as Permanent Secretary to the Treasury and Head of the Civil Service and the imposition of open competition examination as virtually the only mode of entry into the higher ranks of the civil service did the so-called administrative class finally approach the unified, generalist elite proposed by Trevelyan and Northcote.

The large number of royal commissions and official government investigations dedicated to topics pertaining to the civil service since the Trevelyan-Northcote Report attest to the way in which the role of the civil service raises sensitive questions about good governance, social equity, and political access. Three issues in particular provoke debate. First, the disagreement about whether the generalist or the specialist expert makes the most efficient government official persists. Second, the class and gender biases that continue to mark civil service recruitment creates a perennial source of grievance. Finally, the extent of official influence on policy-making generates worry and suspicion.

The champions of the generalist civil service, most notably Warren Fisher, seemingly achieved the upper hand after 1919. The alternative view, which stresses the effectiveness and vigor of the expert and considers generalist knowledge as necessarily superficial, always had support in business circles and has attracted renewed interest in recent years.

Although ostensibly based on merit, open competition in practice tended to operate in a class-biased way. The type of education privileged by the examinations set by the Civil Service Commission was enjoyed mainly by the able children of the middle and upper classes, and the Administrative Class consequently became increasingly dominated by the products of public schools and Oxford and Cambridge, especially Oxford. This trend, already visible at the turn of the century, became even more deeply entrenched after the First World War. The need to recruit more widely during the Second World War went some way to counter this pattern, but it reasserted itself after 1945, proving remarkably resilient even as recruitment procedures underwent considerable revision.

The composition of the civil service exhibits gender bias as well as class bias. The first WOMEN to enter the civil service found themselves relegated to clerical positions and to positions in the inspectorate pertaining to women's issues. In 1894 the Treasury imposed a MARRIAGE bar, requiring any female who married to resign her position, which remained in force until 1947. After the First World War, the Civil Service Commission allowed women to sit for open competition examination, although they continued to be ineligible for positions in many departments, especially those dealing with foreign affairs and defense. Women also earned lower rates of pay than men, an inequity that successive governments refused to address until the 1950s. Today, women still dominate the clerical grades and rarely hold high-level positions.

The role of the civil service in governance has often come under harsh scrutiny by both left and right. The advice given by civil servants to inexperienced LABOUR ministers in 1924 and in 1929, for example, has been suggested as an explanation for Labour's failure to take radical measures to combat UNEMPLOYMENT and depression during this period. More recently, Thatcherite Conservatives have pointed to a left-liberal consensus among civil servants schooled in a post-war welfare state ethos as a source of entrenched obstruction within the government opposed to the implementation of significant policy changes.

The issue at stake here, the nature of the relationship between minister and official advisers, has been candidly explored by Richard Crossman (1907–74) in his The Diaries of a Cabinet Minister (1975–77). Political appointees who come to their positions with little or no background or experience suffer under some obvious handicaps managing departments staffed by those who can call upon a long experience in government service. This particular point of friction has roots in the very nature of parliamentary government, which depends upon CABINET ministers appointed to office for political reasons.

During most of the twentieth century the Whitley system of joint consultation governed civil service staff relations. Named for J.H. Whitley (1866–1935), who chaired the committee on industrial relations during the First World War that developed the concept, Whitleyism posited a system of committees composed of representatives of labor and management empowered to resolve disputes without recourse to strike action. Although intended to transform industrial relations in all economic sectors, the system took hold only in the public sector, with the foundation of the Civil Service National Whitley Council in 1919. Whitleyism placed a genteel stamp on labor relations in the civil service for fifty years. The rise in trade union militancy after 1969 profoundly altered this system. An effort to preserve the STANDARD OF LIVING of its membership in inflationary times led civil service unions to engage in a series of STRIKES during the 1970s. Although these achieved some measure of success at first, the 1981 confrontation between civil service unions and the THATCHER government ended with a government victory. This outcome upheld the constitutional authority of the government when the civil service carried its challenge to the point of undermining government policy.

Some developments in the character of the civil service since the Second World War have maintained the centralizing trajectory established under Fisher's leadership during the interwar years. The merging of the executive and clerical grades in 1947 followed by the addition of the administrative classes in 1971 exemplify this trend. The 1968 creation of the Civil Service Department also expressed government preference for a unified, centrally-controlled civil service. Even more recently, however, countervailing tendencies have begun to develop. Since the 1960s individual departments have taken primary responsibility for recruiting new entrants to their ranks. The Thatcher government abolished the Civil Service Department in 1981 and introduced new management systems at the departmental level to control costs and to assure efficiency in administration. With such initiatives Conservatives sought to reduce the civil service in size, curb its power, and increase its efficiency. The lengthy tenure of the CONSERVATIVE PARTY in office has given the government an opportunity to see to it that these changes leave a permanent stamp on the civil service. This development may not resolve the persistent political tensions that revolve around the civil service, since these often serve to express larger conflicts within the polity and the society at large.

Gail Savage

Bibliography

Chapman, Richard A. *The Higher Civil Service in Britain.* 1970.

Fry, Geoffrey K. *The Changing Civil Service.* 1985.

———. *Statesmen in Disguise: The Changing Role of the Administrative Class of the British Home Civil Service 1853–1966.* 1969.

Kelsall, R.K. *Higher Civil Servants in Britain from 1870 to the Present Day.* 1955.

Martindale, Hilda. *Women Servants of the State.* 1938.

Clark, Kenneth Mackenzie (1903–1983)

From the late 1920s onwards Kenneth Clark occupied a unique position in the world of the visual arts in Britain and exercised a major influence on wider cultural matters. His role is difficult to define, because he belonged to no single catagory or profession. His primary importance is as a critic working in the tradition of Ruskin and Pater. His best works in this vein, *The Gothic Revival* (1928), *Landscape into Art* (1949), and *The Nude* (1956) may all be said to have transformed the attitudes of general readers towards their subjects. They are characterized by a lucid power of synthesis and a coolly idiomatic prose style which sometimes disguise the fact that Clark was also a formidable scholar. His *Catalogue* (1935) of Leonardo's drawings at Windsor laid the modern foundations of Leonardo scholarship, and was followed in 1939 by a monograph on the artist which has never been superseded. At the outset of his career Clark was apprenticed to Bernard Berenson and aspired, like his master, to a life of scholarly contemplation, but he was distracted by his appointment to a series of public posts: Keeper of Fine Art at the Ashmolean (1931–3), Director of the National Gallery (1934–46), Surveyor of the King's Pictures (1934–44), Slade Professor of Fine Art at OXFORD (1946–50), Chairman of the ARTS COUNCIL (1953–60), Chairman of the Independent Television Authority (1954–57). He was also at various times a Trustee of the British Museum, member of the Advisory Council of the Victoria and Albert Museum, and Vice-Chairman of the Royal Opera House and National Theatre. After his resignation from ITA he embarked on a pioneering career as a television performer, culminating in the thirteen-part series *Civilisation*, first shown by the BBC in 1969. Alongside these public achievements Clark assembled a fine, eclectic collection of works of art and was a key patron of modern British artists, including Victor Pasmore, GRAHAM SUTHERLAND, John Piper, and HENRY MOORE. He was created KCB in 1938 and Companion of Honour in 1959. He received a life peerage in 1969 and the Order of Merit in 1976.

Clark came from a line of Scottish thread manufacturers who had amassed a considerable fortune. His parents moved between sporting estates in Suffolk and Argyll and the yachts, villas and casinos of the Riviera. Clark's father was eccentric, ebullient, and very often drunk. His mother was Quakerish, intelligent, and reserved.

This mixed heredity, artfully evoked in the first part of his autobiography, *Another Part of the Wood,* powerfully informed Clark's character in which an urgent desire to communicate enthusiasm mixed oddly with an aloofness that many found chilling.

Clark's neglected childhood offered one great consolation—the discovery of what he later described as "a freak aptitude" for responding to works of art. At Winchester he was neither happy nor distinguished, but his flair was spotted by an imaginative headmaster, Montague Rendall, who provided lantern lectures on the *quattrocento*. At Oxford Clark read history, but his real education took place in the Ashmolean, studying the drawings of Raphael and Michelangelo under the watchful eye of the Keeper, C.F. Bell, a connoisseur of the old school who also suggested the subject of his first book, *The Gothic Revival,* and took him to meet Berenson at I Tatti.

After Oxford Clark spent two years working with Berenson on a projected revision of *The Florentine Drawings*. The experiment was not an unqualified success—Clark was too independent to be a good apprentice—but it determined much of Clark's subsequent career, and the values of I Tatti with its mixture of intellectual endeavor and BLOOMSBURY manners were to shape Clark's life.

In 1927 Clark had married Jane Martin, an able and attractive undergraduate contemporary, who believed passionately in his talent. His career now underwent a meteoric succession of changes. He was invited to catalogue the Leonardos at Windsor in 1928; he helped to organize the great Italian exhibition of 1930 at Burlington House; and in 1931 he was appointed to C.F. Bell's post at the Ashmolean. Both Clarks moved easily between officialdom and high bohemia. They were young, fashionable, and widely courted. In 1934 Clark became the youngest ever Director of the National Gallery.

Clark's directorship was widely perceived as a success. He improved beyond recognition the hanging, lighting, and decoration of the Gallery, while also establishing a scientific department and making notable acquisitions, ranging from the seven Sassetta panels of St. Francis to Ingres' *Madame Moitessier*. His relations with his staff were less happy. His wealth, success, and confidence had attracted envy in the profession, and in 1937 he made a serious mistake, pushing through against strong curatorial opposition to the purchase at a Giorgione price of four small panels which were subsequently attributed to Previtali. Clark's discomfiture was widely relished, and the episode dimmed his appetite, never very keen, for institutional life. The advent of war reinvigorated his sense of public responsibility: the entire collection was evacuated to the Manod caves in Wales, but one great picture was brought to London each month throughout the air raids to console a public who also crowded to hear the lunch time concerts held in the empty galleries. Clark also worked in the film division of the Ministry of Information and was instrumental through the War Artists' scheme in helping to preserve the lives of most significant British artists, while at the same time commissioning at modest expense an invaluable record of the war.

Clark resigned from the Gallery at the end of 1945 in order to devote himself to writing and lecturing. For the next thirty years he was always in demand, and many of his best pieces were written to order. The lecture was the form which best suited him and, with the exception of *Piero della Francesca* (1951), all his best critical books grew from lecture series. Next to art he found his greatest enjoyment in the act of writing, and he developed a vivid, untheoretical style in which thought and feeling are closely and persuasively fused. His work is empirical and intuitive—he always proceeds by attempting to understand the individual genius of both artist and work of art. His achievement both in his writings and through television was to open the minds of ordinary people to the power of art, much as Ruskin had been able to do in the previous century. By a paradox of history, Clark attained his greatest fame and influence at a period—the 1960s—when his ideas and values were most under threat. His point of view was uncompromisingly male, Western, and bourgeois. His long career represents an unusual link between a near Victorian high culture and the world of mass communications. His success lay in communicating the idea of that culture to the widest possible audience without compromising either his beliefs or his material.

Fram Dinshaw

Bibliography
Clark, Kenneth. *Another Part of the Wood: A Self-Portrait.* 1974.
———. *The Other Half: A Self-Portrait.* 1977.
Secrest, Meryle. *Kenneth Clark: A Biography.* 1984.

Clearing Banks

The clearing banks, also called joint stock banks and High Street banks, are responsible for most of the commercial banking activity in the United Kingdom: they accept deposits, allow customers to use checks, grant credit in the form of loans and overdrafts, discount bills of exchange, and provide various other services for their customers. Founded mostly in the 1830s and numbering over a hundred in the mid-nineteenth century, they became dominated in 1918 by a small group of five giant banks, known as the "Big Five"—the "Big Four" since 1968: Barclays, National Westminster, Lloyds, and Midland.

The origins of the clearing banks date back to the Bank Acts of 1826 and 1833 which put an end to the Bank of England's monopoly by authorizing the formation of joint stock banks, the former outside a radius of 65 miles around LONDON, the latter in the capital itself but without the right of issuing notes. The joint stock form of ownership was at first considered, in particular by private bankers, as inadequate for the business of banking. However, the number of joint stock banks increased rapidly: their number reached 99 in 1850 and 122 in 1875. The London joint stock banks gained full recognition with their admission to the London Clearing House in 1854. The amalgamation movement which started in the 1860s and intensified in the 1890s reduced their number to 41 in 1913; among them a dozen banks based in London, with a network of branches covering the whole country, controlled about two thirds of the country's deposits. The apotheosis of this movement took place in 1918 with the almost simultaneous merger, two by two, of the ten leading banks, giving birth to the "Big Five": the Midland Bank, Lloyds Bank, Barclays Bank, the Westminster Bank, and the National Provincial Bank; they controlled 90 per cent of the bank deposits of the country in 1938. The National Provincial Bank and the Westminster Bank merged in 1968 under the name of National Westminster Bank, and the Midland, the largest bank in the world in the inter-war years, was taken over by the Hong Kong and Shanghai Banking Corporation in 1992, while continuing to trade under its own name.

The origins of these banks are diverse. Three main streams can be identified. Firstly, the London joint stock bank tradition, with the National Provincial Bank, established in 1833, and the Westminster Bank, established in 1834 under the name of London and Westminster Bank. Secondly, the provincial banks: Lloyds Bank and the Midland Bank. Both came from Birmingham— Lloyds Bank was established as a private bank in 1765 and converted into a joint stock bank in 1865, the Midland Bank was founded in 1836 under the name of Birmingham and Midland Bank—and were of a comparatively small size when they moved to the capital, respectively in 1884 and 1891. Through an aggressive amalgamation policy, they were to become the two largest banks in the country some twenty years later. Thirdly, the Quaker private banking tradition with Barclays Bank. Although its origins can be traced back to a private bank run by John Fraeme in the City of London in the 1690s, the bank was founded in 1896 by the amalgamation of twenty private

banks in London and the country, whose partners were all linked by family relationships and a former adherence to the SOCIETY OF FRIENDS.

Given the specialization of the English banking system, the role of the clearing banks has mostly consisted in accepting deposits and granting short term credit in the form of discounts, loans, or overdrafts. In the pre-1914 period this role was perfectly adapted to the requirements of the London money market. The bulk of world trade was financed through the medium of bills of exchange drawn on London. These bills were accepted by the MERCHANT BANKS, i.e. they promised to pay them at maturity, usually three months; they were then discounted by the bill brokers—also known as discount houses—and sold to the clearing banks which kept them as a self-liquidating investment. The clearing banks were therefore providing the cash credit which activated the entire system. These conditions were altered by the First World War as the national debt absorbed an increasing proportion of the resources of the clearing banks and international commerce was greatly disrupted during the Depression of the 1930s.

It has been questioned whether deposit banking as practised by the English clearing banks was as well suited for the requirements of British industry. Several committees inquired into that matter, in particular the Committee on Finance and Industry, also known as the Macmillan Committe, which published its report in 1931 and whose main recommendation was that the "gap" in the supply of long and medium term finance for small business—known as the "Macmillan gap"—should be filled.

The clearing banks have been criticized for their apparent failure to supply manufacturing industry with long term credit, whether in the form of long term loans or direct ownership of securities, on the model of the German banks. This criticism corresponds to the official banking orthodoxy; actual banking practices, however, varied over time. In the first half of the nineteenth century local bankers were closely linked to industrialists, and permanent overdrafts and rolled-over short-term loans were in fact equivalent to long term commitments. The intensification of the amalgamation movement in the 1880s and 1890s seems to have changed this attitude as general managers in London decided to put an end to what they considered as over-commitments. There is, however, no evidence that there existed a demand for long-term credit from industry. The situation changed again in the inter-war period. During the 1919–20 boom, the clearing banks abandoned much of their prudence and granted large overdrafts, particularly to the heavy and textile industries, which with the downturn of the 1920s often had to be converted into frozen loans and nursed for the remainder of the period. Although it can be argued that this long-term commitment was forced upon them by the prevailing circumstances rather than deliberately chosen as a new policy, the clearing banks appear on the whole to have adopted a positive attitude towards industry: their support was not exclusively dictated by security motives and advances meeting the banks' lending criteria were seldom refused. The clearing banks have also been criticized for their lack of managerial role and, especially during the inter-war years, for not using their position as creditors to encourage the rationalization of the basic industries. It is true that the banks did not play that role, not only because they did not want to, but because they lacked expertise in industrial finance and were primarily concerned with maintaining their interests of creditors. However, if they were unable to induce industrial reorganization, they used their position as powerful creditors to discipline and reconstruct management.

Contrary to their European counterparts, the English clearing banks developed only slowly into banking groups. Before 1914 they were unable to take a controlling interest in another company because they worked with a very small capital. A first move took place at the end of the First World War with the "affiliation" of some of the Irish and Scottish banks to the major clearing banks. The first of its kind was the affiliation of the Belfast Bank to the Midland Bank in 1917, making the former a subsidiary of the latter. A second step was the control of overseas banks, most notably by Barclays Bank which created in 1925 Barclays Bank D.C.O.—Dominion, Colonial, Overseas—after acquiring the capital of the Anglo-Egyptian Bank, the Colonial Bank, and the National Bank of South Africa. The first control over a merchant bank was not taken until 1967, when the Midland Bank took one-third share in Samuel Montagu. In the last twenty years, however, the number of subsidiaries of the clearing banks increased considerably.

The position of the clearing banks has been declining since the end of the First World War. The total amount of their deposits did increase, from £961 million in 1911–13 to £2.731 billion in 1936–8 at current value; at real value, however, they increased by only 60 percent. And although they rose from £6.4 billion in 1951 to £45.8 billion in 1979 at current value, they rose only by 12 percent in real terms. The clearing banks maintained a large share of banking deposits in the inter-war years, but they faced an increasingly strong competition from other financial institutions, in particular building societies whose proportion of bank deposits rose from 6 percent in 1923–5 to 23

per cent in 1936–8. After the Second World War the share of bank deposits held by the clearing banks fell from just under 70 percent in 1951 to 54 percent in 1965 and just over 18 percent in 1979. This was due to a large extent to the competition of the foreign banks in London, in particular in the wholesale deposits, i.e. deposits of large sums mainly by financial institutions and large corporations, including non-sterling deposits, on which the clearing banks have increasingly depended since the 1960s. The clearing banks have been partly responsible for this decline. Despite some innovations in their practices, they were content for decades to operate a price cartel and remain strictly within the frontiers of deposit banking. On the other hand, from the 1930s to the 1960s, the assets of the clearing banks have been dominated by the government debt, which represented about two-thirds of their deposits in 1950, and they have been, until the late 1970s, the main target of the financial authorities in their policy of credit control. The deregulation of the 1980s, the increased internationalization of financial services, and the revolution in information technology have presented the British clearing banks with new opportunities and at the same time forced changes upon them which brought them closer to the "universal banking" model.

Youssef Cassis

Bibliography
Collins, Michael. *Money and Banking in the U.K.: A History.* 1988.
Holmes, A.R., and Edwin Green. *Midland: 150 Years of Banking Business.* 1986.
Nevin, Edward, and E.W. Davis. *The London Clearing Banks.* 1970.
Winton, J.R. *Lloyds Bank, 1918–1969.* 1982.

Cliveden Set

The Cliveden Set was a term which came to be applied in the 1930s to the group of friends of Waldorf, Viscount Astor and his wife Nancy, who met at their Buckinghamshire country house, Cliveden. The term was coined by the communist journalist and editor, Claud Cockburn, in 1937 and was meant to refer to a small and highly influential secret cabal of wealthy conservative power brokers who enjoyed great, but unofficial influence over the government. The story of the political significance of Cliveden is really the story of the transplanted Virginian NANCY ASTOR, who inspired the political weekends at Cliveden and whose ideas set their agendas. With two active political careers in their Anglo-American family, Lord and Lady Astor turned their great estate of Cliveden into a regular meeting place for political discussion among public figures of many stripes of British public opinion. This interest in playing host to a cross section of politics was enhanced by the fact that Lord Astor owned the OBSERVER newspaper and his brother controlled THE TIMES, two of the most influential journals of the day.

By the mid-1930s, the most important international question which confronted Britain was how could war with the dictator powers, Germany, Italy, and Japan, be prevented? In 1937 NEVILLE CHAMBERLAIN had replaced STANLEY BALDWIN as Prime Minister and meant to seek a lasting peace through identifying the reasonable demands of the dictators and trying to meet them peacefully. This was the essence of the policy which came to be called APPEASEMENT. In this regard, LORD HALIFAX, Lord President of the Council and a close confidant of the Prime Minister, traveled to Germany in November 1937 to meet the Führer.

Cockburn, sole proprietor of a small journal called *The Week*, was violently opposed to appeasement. A communist and brilliant satirist, Cockburn opposed the Halifax visit and published a story which purported to reveal that one of the major seedbeds of appeasement thinking was the Astor country house. He soon coined the term "Cliveden Set" and popularized the idea that government policy was being made not in Parliament but in the luxurious Thames-side house of an Anglo-American millionaire and his politically-prominent wife.

It is true that the Astors supported the policy of appeasement and frequently entertained prominent appeasers such as Thomas Jones, GEOFFREY DAWSON, and Lord Lothian in their home. Cliveden also welcomed such anti-appeasers as ANTHONY EDEN, Lord Cranborne, and HAROLD MACMILLAN. The Cliveden Set, as a political entity, was a myth created by a clever and disaffected opponent of what was certainly a disastrous policy. Neville Chamberlain, however, took no orders from Cliveden.

R.J.Q. Adams

Bibliography
Cockburn, Claud. *Cockburn Sums Up: An Autobiography.* 1981.
Gannon, Franklin Reid. *The British Press and Germany, 1936–1939.* 1971.
Grigg, John. *Nancy Astor: A Lady Unashamed.* 1980.
Koss, Stephen. *The Rise and Fall of the Political Press in Britain: vol. II: The Twentieth Century.* 1984.

Clothing and Fashion

Clothing development is influenced by a complex web of social, cultural, and economic factors, none of which are unique to this century or to Britain. Indeed British clothing since 1900 has shared the same design influences as the rest of Europe and North America. The country has lost any notion of "Britishness" in its dress, although non-conformist street styles add a touch of independent styling within an otherwise international look.

A few national differences remain. Scotland retains its national dress based on the late eighteenth-century military kilt, coupled with early nineteenth-century Romantic styles, but the kilt is now worn regularly only by a small minority. Most Scotsmen only don them for their weddings, hired from the clothing rental shops. Welsh national dress was never anything more than a nineteenth-century fiction. The black steeple hats and red flannel cloaks are now restricted to Eisteddfods and bogus tourist amusements.

Thus a study of male and especially female dress in twentieth-century Britain, covers the same style trends as New York, Paris, Berlin, or Vienna. The befrilled S bend of the 1902–6 period gave way to the more upright slim line put forward in Paris by 1909. During the FIRST WORLD WAR hemlines shortened and became so flared that some mistakenly predicted the revival of the crinoline. However, following the dictates of Paris, British women took up the boyish "garçonne" look. Skirts shortened to the knee by 1926, breasts were flattened with corselettes, and to be fat became a social disaster. By the mid-1930s feminine lines, heightened by long bias cut skirts heralded a revival of womanly curves.

The restrictions of the SECOND WORLD WAR, however, did mark a uniquely British type of dress, as the government assumed control of the quantity and quality of both textile and garment production through its Utility Clothing Scheme. Women's styles remained virtually unchanged from 1940–6 with broad shouldered and neatly tailored, knee length suits and dresses. As soon as the long skirted, corsetted New Look was launched in Paris in 1947, British women once again adapted their styles to French lines. It was not until the mid-1960s, through the success of Mary Quant's generation of innovative young designers, that Britain regained any sort of fashion independence. This was retained thereafter through British youth sub-cult, street styles, though these are only worn by a minority.

The clothing of British men is epitomized by British traditions of excellence in craft tailoring. Saville Row and far cheaper local independent tailors or factories made up suits for all social classes. Conventional styles of the dark striped city suit and country tweedy jackets change slowly, with some business men still wearing Edwardian style overcoats with velvet collars. Bowler hats, however, disappear year by year. The mass of working class men wore shabby suits, flannelette shirts, and cloth caps from 1900 right through to the Second World War, saving their "best" for Sundays. Dramatic change came from the late 1960s with the mass adoption of American jeans, sneakers, jogging suits, bomber jackets, and sweatshirts.

Specific British influence on twentieth-century dress can be related to economic and social developments. The outstanding feature is the increasing diffusion of stylish clothes for women, trickling throughout British society, reaching to all levels by the mid-1950s. This is a reflection of the steady economic improvement in the lives of working class families. In 1900–20 most working-class women wore simple jackets, long skirts, and blouses. At home the ubiquitous apron or overall covered shabby working dress.

By the 1930s there was an increasing demand for cheap but fashionable clothes, especially in the more prosperous south, fed by the development of a larger ready-to-wear industry. By the 1950s the British teenagers became the newest fashion consumers. In the 1990s it is still possible to identify the really wealthy through their clothes, but it is also possible for the less affluent, but stylish to be just as "fashionable".

Against this background of socially expanding consumerism came a related technological response from the British textile and clothing industries. Viscose-based rayon, developed in the UK mainly by the firm of Courtaulds from 1906, was at first much despised for its glittering sheen and poor shrinking and wrinkling qualities, but by the late 1930s it was being widely worn, particularly in various creped finishes. From 1940s onwards the use of pure synthetic fabrics became widespread, starting with nylon in the USA and, by the 1950s, British polyesters—Terelene and Crimplene—together with acrylics—Courtelle. The British textile industry declined steadily under the weight of cheaper, rival imports. From the mid-1980s sports-influenced styles decreed blended and new synthetics—stretch Lycra, microfibers, Neoprene, and imitation rubbers—as well as a move toward more natural cottons, linens, and wools, a trend related to the fashionable "green" issues of the 1990s.

The technology of garment manufacture has changed less dramatically through the century. Men's wear has been manufactured on a highly mechanised production line basis since the late nineteenth century, largely based in the Midlands. By the 1920s Burton's and John Colliers were producing thousands of "made to measure" suits a week, in their factories. Women's wear, because the styling changes seasonally, has to be manufactured through more flexible processes—namely, in small factories. Chain stores like MARKS AND SPENCER made fashionable clothing at popular prices more accessible, and the importation of clothes manufactured in the Third World

has intensified competition among British retailers, styles changing with ever greater alacrity.

A major problem facing British fashion designers throughout the century has been the role of Paris as international arbiter of style. Thus wealthy British women bought their important clothes directly from Paris couturiers or from their LONDON annexes, while the London couture trade, centred in the Mayfair district by 1900, was forced to copy Paris styling. Compared to Paris with over 100 couture houses, London had only a dozen or so, and most were badly financed, relying for their clientele only on social elite, supplemented by a few actresses and film stars and sales to ready-to wear companies for copying. Styles related to the etiquette of the Court and social season—presentation, ball, dinner, and silk day dresses for weddings—all of a certain elegant, albeit conventional style.

Among these are two types of garments that can be identified as particularly British. Firstly, from the 1930s the full-skirted, romantic evening/wedding dress, usually in pale colours, revived again in the 1980s by Diana, Princess of Wales. Well-known London fashion designers in the 1900–14 period included Lucile (Lady Duff Gordon), Mme. Hayward, Reville and Rossiter, who dressed Queen Mary, Kate Reilly, who trained Madelaine Vionnet, and Sarah Fullerton Monteith Young. The great London department stores of Jay's, Harrods, Marshall and Snelgrove, and Selfridges dressed the rich and middle classes and had counterparts in every major British city. From the 1930s to the 1950s British couture shone on the international scene through the work of a talented generation of designers such as Norman Hartnell, Victor Stiebel, Peter Russell, Charles James, Hardy Amies, John Cavanagh, Ronald Patterson, and Michael Sherrard.

The second British style of international fame was the tailored suit. By 1900 walking suits were worn by women not only in the country but also for town expeditions. The most famous tailoring houses, Creeds and Redfern, were joined in the late 1930s by Lachasse, Digby Morton, and Hardy Amies and later by Vivienne Westwood and Paul Smith. In the mid-1930s top British tailoring ready-to-wear companies included Jaeger, Dorville, Dereta, Brenner Sports, and Windsmoor.

With these developments clients began to drift away from the couture houses. After the cancellation of the presentation of debutantes in 1958, the success of the British couture industry declined, retaining only an aging clientele, while the younger generation shifted to the new boutiques. By the 1960s many couture houses had closed, most, with the exception of Hardy Amies, failing to develop the lucrative ready-to-wear lines and perfume/accessory franchises which today keep the international couture system afloat. Even the house of Hartnell, which survived his death in 1979, finally closed in 1992. However, a new breed of designer was born out of the explosion of talent in London in the early 1960s, such as Mary Quant in Chelsea, John Bates, Barbara Hulanicki at Biba, Jane and Jane, Sally Tuffin, and Marion Foale, mostly graduates of London colleges of art and DESIGN. Their reasonably priced, boutique clothes, many sold in Soho for men as well as women, were ephemeral, young, and fun. Along with POP MUSIC, young London fashions took the international fashion world by storm. From this point on, young British designers and street/sub-cult styles exerted a dynamic influence on top designers the world over. Thus the old "trickle down" fashion diffusion system was finally broken, and mass-produced lines are now styled through a fusion of couture, *pret-a-porter*, street, and ethnic influences.

In a multi-cultural society many Britons of Asian descent dress in either traditional styles or modernized versions of them, shopping at specialist textile and fashion shops selling saris and Muslim dress. These, along with street dress and young Black British styles, are influencing mainstream fashion through the work of the new young generation of British designers, such as Helen Storey, Red or Dead, John Richmond, Rifat Ozbek, Workers for Freedom, Pam Hogg, John Galliano, and Body Map. It is within this strand of innovative design that a unique sense of "Britishness" in dress can still be found.

Lou Taylor

Bibliography

Arch, Nigel, and Joanna Marschner. *Splendour at Court: Dressing for Royal Occasions Since 1700.* 1987.

Bell, Quentin. *On Human Finery.* 1976.

McDermott, Catherine. *Street Style: British Design in the 80s.* 1987.

Mort, Frank. *Cultures of Consumption: Masculinities and Social Space in Late Twentieth-Century Britain.* 1996.

Wilson, Elizabeth, and Lou Taylor. *Through the Looking Glass: A History of Dress from 1860 to the Present Day.* 1989.

Coal Mining

Coal mining occupies a special position not only in Britain's economic history, but in its political development and the evolution of the role of the British state. In many ways its rise and decline represent crucial transitions in the the country's economic and political experience as an industrial power.

During the nineteenth century coal was central to Britain's industrialization, to the growth of its RAILWAY system, to its export earnings, and to ocean transport throughout the world. The major coal fields (in South Wales, the Midlands, the northeast, and in southern Scotland) had in turn become centers of heavy industries such as iron and STEEL, engineering, chemicals and shipbuilding. The resulting boom in output, exports, and employment, continued until the First World War, by which time there were more than 1,400 collieries and some 3,000 individual firms, accounting for one-third of Britain's exports and employing some 1 million men and boys—almost ten percent of the male labor force.

By the twentieth century the statistical significance of the coal industry was also associated with powerful social and political forces. The dependence of society on the supply of fuel, the concentration and coherent solidarity of mining communities, the self-consciousness and militancy of miners, and the sensitivity of the rest of society to an occupation which appeared at once dangerous, exploited, and heroic—all gave coal mining a special place on the national scene. And this was reflected in state intervention (to regulate working methods, safety, hours of work, and minimum wages) at a time when governments were otherwise very reluctant to intervene in business matters.

Ironically, the FIRST WORLD WAR both dramatized and eroded the importance and strength of the industry on the national scene. On the one hand, coal played a vital strategic role in what was the first great industrialized war. As a result, the miners were able to use their enhanced bargaining power to secure higher rates of pay and a direct role in wartime administration, while the government, with the aims of maximizing output, curbing profiteering, and avoiding inudstrial unrest, introduced controls over the finances, organization, and labor policy of the industry. On the other hand, however, the war led to a postponement of investment and modernization and a substantial increase in coal production in Britain's erstwhile export markets. After the war, and a temporary and artificial boom, the prosperity of the industry was undercut by high production costs, stagnating trade, increasing foreign competition, and economies in the use of fuel. The British coal industry now suffered from excess capacity, an unwieldy structure, antiquated equipment, and inflexible and high costs.

Given the history of poor labor relations and entrenched attitudes, the outcome was inevitable and uncomfortable. The mine owners pressed for the only form of cost-cutting—wage reductions—available in the short-run; the miners accused the owners of exploitation and a failure to pursue the sort of reorganization which would make the industry more competitive; neutral observers became profoundly depressed at the sight of an industry in need of rationalization but incapable of attaining it, and the government was confronted with industrial unrest, widespread

UNEMPLOYMENT, devastation throughout whole communities, and demands for financial help and an interventionist policy (e.g. to enforce industrial reorganization) which it found ideologically impossible to offer.

These problems were the more compounded —especially in the 1920s—by Britain's commitment to an orthodox monetary policy which established an exchange rate at which coal exports were even more uncompetitive. This was a point emphasized by JOHN MAYNARD KEYNES in 1925 when he opposed the return of the pound sterling to the GOLD STANDARD at a high rate of exchange. Soon after his warning, in 1926, the coal industry experienced its worst inter-war crisis. Resisting the owners' proposal to reduce wages and increase hours of work, the miners went on strike and were joined temporarily by other unions in a GENERAL STRIKE. The General Strike collapsed after a few days, but the miners held out grimly for six months, ultimately accepting defeat and wage cuts. But the reduction in labor costs helped little: economic dislocation continued for the rest of the 1920s, and from 1928 was aggravated by world depression. Suffering in the coal fields in the course of the great slump of 1929–32 was extreme, unemployment rose to over 20 percent (with figures of 40–60 percent in some important districts), and the industry appeared to stagnate, even at the lower level of output which it was forced to accept.

This prolonged and inevitable decline in one of Britain's erstwhile great staple industries was not, of course, steady. In the 1930s, along with the British economy generally, the coal industry experienced a recovery, which was accentuated by the needs of rearmament after 1936. After 1934, too, the government attempted to spur the rationalization of coal mining into bigger units under the aegis of a Coal Mines Reorganisation Commission. But neither industrial policies nor the forces of the market were able to revive the fortunes of coal to a significant extent.

The experience of coal mining during the SECOND WORLD WAR was in many ways a re-run of that of the First, although in 1939–45 government intervention was even more elaborate and the political leverage of the miners even greater. By the end of the war the industry's productivity, welfare, and future had become much more overt matters of national concern, and the numerous plans to use public intervention to restructure it, were capped in 1946 by the LABOUR government's surprisingly uncontentious move to nationalize coal mining with the device of a public corporation, the National Coal Board (NCB).

Over the next forty years or so the NCB had a checkered history (it was renamed British Coal in the 1980s). Massive investment and structural (ad-

ministrative) changes streamlined the industry and enhanced its productivity. At the same time, however, the monolithic scale of the corporation made for unwieldiness and inefficiency. More important, cheap alternative fuels (particularly oil) and technical changes among industrial and domestic consumers (using gas and oil to run transport, heating systems, and machinery) diminished the scope for expansion. The industry therefore continued its decline, at least as measured in terms of output and employment. By the late 1980s the vast majority of coal produced was used to generate electricity—and even that market was threatened by alternative fuels (gas, oil, nuclear). Moreover, in spite of NATIONALIZATION, the industry's instability continued—in large part owing to the centralization of labor bargaining, which increased the authority of the miners' union. And when there was a threatened shortage of oil, strike action for higher wages proved a powerful and disruptive weapon. This was the case, for example, in 1972 and 1974, when the miners gained large improvements in their wages (in 1974 their successful strike was even instrumental in bringing down the CONSERVATIVE government).

Table 1: Output, exports, and employment in British coal mining, 1913–93

	Number of pits	Employment (000)	Output (mn tons)	Exports (mn tons)
1913	3287	1118	287	98
1920	2851	1248	229	39
1929	2419	857	258	77
1938	2125	791	227	46
1947	958	705	195	5
1960	698	583	191	6
1975	241	245	125	2
1980–1	211	294	125	–2
1992–3*	50	44	80	–18

* A number of mines in 1992–3 were not producing coal, even though still "open". The major run-down of the industry which accompanied the move towards privatization came in 1993–4.

These gains, however, proved ephemeral. At one level the long-run stagnation in the market for coal, and at another level the political apprehension at the power and instability of the miners' union, were to weaken the miners and the industry. It was little wonder that the Conservative government which was elected in 1979 was determined to reduce both the power of the union and the significance of the industry, which, it felt, was excessive in relation to the demand for coal. This now-familiar situation provided the context for the major and violent miners' strike of 1984–5, when the miners claimed that the government was intent on closing large numbers of mines—a claim denied by the government, although later events seemed to justify it. In any event, the miners experienced a crushing defeat, thanks to the stockpiling of coal, the government's determination and planning, the reduced strategic significance of coal as an industrial fuel, and the fact that a large number of miners refused to join in the strike.

With the defeat of the NATIONAL UNION OF MINEWORKERS in 1985, the stage was set for further radical changes. One change was a major spurt in labor productivity: by the end of the decade the number of miners had been reduced by 50 percent, but the output had stayed the same. Yet in spite of this increase in productivity the industry continued to face economic trouble as the demand for British coal continued to stagnate. A degree of protection was afforded by favorable long-run contracts (originally signed under government pressure) with the then-nationalized electricity generating plants. But by the early 1990s the latter had been privatized and made more responsive to market forces alone, the government was unwilling to extend any form of subsidy to coal mining; and both the state and large consumers of coal had clearly decided that the political instability created by the past history of a powerful mining union was to be avoided by running down the industry even further. By 1994 the once great industry had been reduced to a dozen or so mines and some 10,000 miners, and was on its way into private hands. Coal mining had become an entirely negligible activity and as far as this staple industry of the initial industrialization was concerned, the nineteenth century finally came to an end in the last decade of the twentieth century. The process of decline—from both economic supremacy and political centrality—had proved long, poignant, and painful. It had been strongly resisted, but the effort had been unavailing. Economic forces had, inevitably, triumphed. And in the process coal mining, like Britain itself, had discovered that fundamental economic change cannot be divorced from political controversy, ideological debate, and social disruption.

Barry Supple

Bibliography

Ashworth, William. *The History of the British Coal Industry: vol. 5, 1946–1982: The Nationalized Industry.* 1986.

Buxton, Neil K. *The Economic Development of the British Coal Industry from Industrial Revolution to the Present Day.* 1978.

Kirby, Maurice W. *The British Coalmining Industry, 1870–1946.* 1977.

Supple, Barry. *The History of the British Coal Industry: vol. 4, 1913–1946: The Political Economy of Decline.* 1987.

Codebreaking

The interception and deciphering of secret foreign messages, in particular coded radio transmissions, were activities at which various British agencies excelled in the course of the twentieth century. Of particular significance were the forewarnings of German moves provided by British codebreakers during both world wars, most famously the intelligence gathered through access to the Enigma coding machine used by the enemy in the SECOND WORLD WAR.

Prior to the FIRST WORLD WAR reading foreign traffic, widely regarded as a highly ungentlemanly activity, was discouraged in government circles. The beginning of hostilities produced a major change of attitude; it nevertheless took time and a great deal of luck for the amateur cryptoanalysts working out of Room 40 at the Admiralty to be in a position to provide significant intelligence on enemy intentions. Central to the sucess of British signals intelligence was the fortuitous acquisition of a series of German codebooks in the first year of the war. Coupled with the interception of transatlantic cable traffic as well as wireless messages, this series of windfalls allowed the personnel employed at Room 40 slowly but surely to gain access to important enemy communications. The intelligence gathered was not always properly understood or disseminated (intelligence on the movements of the High Seas Fleet in the run-up to the Battle of Jutland in 1916 being a case in point), but in overall terms it was still of major benefit to the Allied cause.

Room 40 scored its greatest triumph in early 1917 by providing the British government with a copy of the famous Zimmerman Telegram—outlining German plans for a military alliance with Mexico directed against the United States—that helped to tilt Washington in favor of armed intervention on the Allied side.

The successor body to Room 40, the innocuously named Government Code and Cypher School (GC & CS), was run on a shoestring budget in the inter-war years. Nevertheless GC & CS, along with other intelligence sources, were able to provide the government of the day with translations of many Soviet diplomatic communications down through the mid-1920s—albeit sometimes of doubtful provenance—as well as copies of important Italian and Japanese naval signals in the early and mid-1930s.

The onset of the Second World War spurred renewed official interest in codebreaking, and GC & CS, now located at Bletchley Park, was progressively expanded to become the most vital arm of British strategic intelligence. (In 1939 the staff had numbered 150; by 1945 over 10,000 people were employed by GC & CS.) As in the days of Room 40, success was dependent on a mixture of human talent and acquired knowledge of enemy encoding techniques. The messages generated by the cipher machine the Germans employed—Enigma—were considered to be unbreakable in the late 1930s. However, thanks to the secret acquisition of examples of Enigma, lax enemy transmission security, and sheer hard work, the cryptographers at Bletchley Park were able from the spring of 1940 onward to provide vital intelligence—codename Ultra— on Axis movements and intentions. Senior field commanders made privy to Ultra did not always appreciate its significance, which, along with the need to keep the source absolutely secret from the enemy, meant that information available was sometimes ignored or not acted upon, in some instances at considerable cost, e.g., prior to the fighting on Crete (1941) and at Arnhem (1944). Nevertheless, the men and women at Bletchley Park, assisted from June 1944 onward by an early example of an electronic digital computer, generated an unparalleled amount of accurate and useful intelligence. Ultra proved particularly vital in fighting the Battle of the Atlantic and was a major factor more generally in the defeat of the Axis in the latter half of the Second World War.

Bletchley Park itself was wound up at the end of the war, but the interception and breaking of coded signals continued on a smaller scale at the renamed Government Communications Head-Quarters (GCHQ) at Cheltanham. Little is known as yet of the relative success or failure of post-war efforts to read Soviet and other traffic during the Cold War and after, though it is worth noting that since the late 1940s close and apparent productive ties have been maintained between GCHQ and its American counterpart, the National Security Agency.

S.P. MacKenzie

Bibliography
Andrew, Christopher. *Her Majesty's Secret Service: The Making of the British Intelligence Community.* 1986.
Beesley, Patrick. *Room 40: British Naval Intelligence, 1914–1918.* 1982.
Hinsley, F.H. *British Intelligence in the Second World War.* 5 vols. 1979–90.
———, and A. Stripp, eds. *Codebreakers: The Inside Story of Bletchley Park.* 1982.

Cole, G(eorge) D(ouglas) H(oward) (1889–1959)

Always known by his initials, G.D.H. Cole was a major intellectual figure on the British Left throughout the first half of the twentieth century. Along with such figures as R.H TAWNEY and HAROLD LASKI, he exercised an immense influence on the developing thought of the labor movement. His output was prodigious, including more than 100 books, and spanned a vast intellectual terrain. Associated first with the early century development of the doctrines of GUILD SO-CIALISM, a version of industrial self-government, he maintained this emphasis in his thought

thereafter but also wrote and campaigned on many other fronts too.

His background was an unlikely one for a socialist intellectual (his father, of appropriately Tory disposition, was in suburban real estate in London), but his conversion experience came at St. Paul's School when he encountered the work of William Morris. Henceforth he was a socialist, of an imaginative and uncompromising William Morris kind. From his OXFORD base, first as student then as teacher, he organized an assault on the prevailing WEBB version of administrative socialism and sought to substitute a more participatory model. In the decade which had the FIRST WORLD WAR as its center, Cole came to prominence as the major theorist of the new doctrine of Guild Socialism.

On one side he was influenced by the syndicalism and industrial unionism whose impact and meaning he interpreted in his first book *The World of Labour* (1913); on another side by the theoretical critique of state sovereignty by the political pluralists. When combined with his own understanding of the meaning of William Morris, this provided a basis for his embrace of the idea of National Guilds (as expounded in the pages of the *New Age* by A.R. Orage and S.G. Hobson) and his own development of this idea into the theory of Guild Socialism. Its root idea was industrial self-government by workers, but broadened by Cole into a general social theory. In a rapid succession of books (such as *Self-Government in Industry*, 1917, and *Guild Socialism Re-Stated*, 1920) he made and refined the Guild Socialist case, which became very influential for a time.

His prodigious industry also made him an indispensable figure in the developing institutions of the labor movement (including a period as the LABOUR PARTY'S research secretary following its 1918 reorganization). As interest in Guild Socialism declined with the arrival of economic slump in the 1920s, Cole turned his attention to wider matters and he became a one-man think tank for Labour as the party negotiated the problems of the inter-war period. Having become Reader in Economics at Oxford in 1925, he was well placed to offer a steady flow of policy advice and was one of those who provided a bridge between KEYNES and the Left.

He was an active participant in the politics of the Left over a long period, from a perspective he liked to describe as "sensible extremism." At Oxford the "Cole Group" was a home for young left-wing intellectuals and a place of passage for many who later became Labour politicians (such as HUGH GAITSKELL). In the 1930s his Society for Socialist Inquiry and Propaganda (SSIP) gave birth to the SOCIALIST LEAGUE, while he invented the New Fabian Research Bureau (NFRB) to provide Labour with an unofficial source of new policy ideas. He continued to produce an endless flow of books and pamphlets on a vast range of topics, including his series of weighty guidebooks for the Intelligent Man on current issues, and threw himself into the campaign for a POPULAR FRONT against FASCISM. In 1944 he became the first Chichele Professor of Social and Political Theory at Oxford, where he remained until retirement in 1957, producing his multi-volumed *History of Socialist Thought* (1953–60).

The influence of G.D.H. Cole is writ large over the whole landscape of the labor movement for half a century. All of its institutions—party, trade unions, FABIAN SOCIETY, *NEW STATESMAN,* workers' education—were shaped by his work. Yet he always remained unorthodox and maverick, his restless energy and radical imagination rubbing uneasily against the conservative anti-intellectualism of much of the British labor movement. ATTLEE's description of him as a "permanent undergraduate" captures some of this; as does Maurice Reckitt's famous ditty: "with a Bolshevik soul in a Fabian muzzle; Mr. G.D.H. Cole is a bit of a puzzle."

Yet Cole remains a formidable and, in some respects, a surprisingly contemporary figure. If much of his vast work was necessarily bound by the time in which it was written, interesting only for the historian, there is also much that remains of more enduring interest. The breadth of his work is extraordinary, encompassing several disciplines (history, economics, literature, social and political theory) and providing a monument to—as well as example of—impressive popular scholarship. Yet his distinctive legacy derives from his early engagement with Guild Socialism and his continuing sense that the Left had to devise a decentralized and participatory model of socialism, different from either welfare statism or COMMUNISM, if it was to find a future. That was an unfashionable view for much of Cole's life, but may not be so unfashionable now.

Anthony Wright, M.P.

Bibliography

Carpenter, L.P. *G.D.H. Cole: An Intellectual Biography.* 1973.

Cole, Margaret. *The Life of G.D.H. Cole.* 1971.

Wright, A.W. *G.D.H. Cole and Socialist Democracy.* 1979.

Committee of Imperial Defence (1902–1939)

From 1902 to 1914 and 1919 to 1939 the Committee of Imperial Defence (CID) was the British government's main advisory body on every aspect of home and overseas defense. It played a major role in formulating the underlying principles of defense policy and prepared plans to ensure that the armed services and their respective ministries would respond in a coordinated manner if war

were declared. At the end of 1916 its permanent secretariat, which recorded proceedings and communicated decisions to the appropriate departments, was transformed into an organization which served the CABINET as a whole and which subsequently became the Cabinet Office. This was one of the key innovations in governmental machinery to result from the FIRST WORLD WAR.

The CID was established in December 1902 as Britain began to modernize its forces and overhaul the machinery for the higher direction of military and naval policy in the light of the BOER WAR and the growing challenge of Germany. The old standing Defence Committee of the Cabinet was recast by ARTHUR BALFOUR, the Prime Minister, to include senior officers from the services as well as such Cabinet ministers as the Chancellor of the Exchequer, First Lord of the Admiralty, and Secretary of State for War. It was further remodelled in May 1904 along lines suggested by the influential Lord Esher (1852–1930), who saw it as the cornerstone of the structure supporting his proposed War Office reforms. The Prime Minister, previously an ordinary member, now became the chairman and, initially, the only permanent member, though Esher too was made a permanent member in 1905. The Prime Minister exercised absolute discretion in the choice of other members, so giving the body greater flexibility and authority. Simultaneously, the CID's ability to tackle problems in detail was vastly strengthened by the creation of a full-time secretariat. The first Secretary was Sir George Clarke (1848–1933), followed by Sir Charles Ottley (1858–1932) in 1907 and Captain Maurice Hankey (1877–1963) in 1912. However, the CID had no executive functions, its recommendations being submitted to the Cabinet or the departments concerned for action.

After 1906 much of its work was delegated to sub-committees. One, the Committee on the Co-ordination of Departmental Action, produced the War Book, a comprehensive list of the steps to be taken in the event of hostilities. While some tasks were eased by the formation of a general staff for the ARMY in 1906, the lack of a similar naval staff until 1912 hampered full integration of the policies of the army and ROYAL NAVY during this period and contributed to the Admiralty's poor performance at the crucial CID meeting on 23 August 1911, when the army's case triumphed and the shift towards future British involvement in a continental land campaign consequently grew more pronounced.

With the coming of war in 1914, the CID fell into temporary abeyance, its work being absorbed by other bodies. Britain's smooth mobilization showed the value of the War Book but the CID had failed to provide blueprints for the necessary expansion of the army, the conversion of industry to war purposes, or the additional reorganization of governmental machinery. A smaller body than the twenty-strong Cabinet was needed for swift response to the pressures of war so, in November 1914, Prime Minister HERBERT ASQUITH set up the War Council, a special Cabinet committee to review war policy and strategy. Hankey and the CID staff acted as a secretariat to the War Council and its successors, the Dardanelles Committee (June 1915) and the War Committee (November 1915). When DAVID LLOYD GEORGE replaced Asquith in December 1916, he combined the functions of the War Committee and the Cabinet by creating a five-man War Cabinet with its own secretariat under Hankey. Now, for the first time, a formal record was kept of Cabinet proceedings.

The CID was revived in 1919, with Hankey staying on as secretary to both the Cabinet and the CID. Before the War Cabinet was dissolved, it instructed the service departments to assume that the British Empire would not be engaged in another major war for ten years, a policy endorsed periodically by the CID until 1932. Nevertheless, the CID continued to advise the Cabinet as to how Britain's defense organization could best meet the changing conditions of the post-war world. To facilitate close consultation between the army, navy, and air force, the Chiefs of Staff Sub-Committee was established in 1923 and was soon the most important element in the CID. Subordinate to it were the Joint Planning Committee (1927), the Deputy Chiefs of Staff Committee (1932), and the Joint Intelligence Committee (1936).

Early in 1934 the CID recognized Germany as the potential enemy for the purposes of long-term planning. A significant rearmament program was introduced in March 1936 and, to remove some of the load of responsibility from the shoulders of STANLEY BALDWIN, then Prime Minister, Sir Thomas Inskip (1876–1947) was appointed Minister for the Co-ordination for Defence. In this new post, Inskip was to exercise, on the Prime Minister's behalf, the daily supervision of the CID, but he had no department and no executive authority.

In the years immediately before the SECOND WORLD WAR the CID was instrumental in establishing and developing the Cabinet War Rooms, an underground headquarters in Whitehall where the Cabinet and Chiefs of Staff could be protected from air attacks. At the end of July 1938 Hankey retired, and NEVILLE CHAMBERLAIN decided that Hankey's dual role had grown too large for one person. He therefore separated the two appointments. Edward Bridges (1892–1959) became Permanent Secretary to the Cabinet Office and Secretary to the Cabinet, while Colonel Has-

tings "Pug" Ismay (1887–1965) became Deputy Secretary (Military) to the Cabinet and Secretary of the CID. On the outbreak of war Chamberlain formed a small War Cabinet on the 1916 model and the secretariats of the Cabinet and CID were merged into a single War Cabinet Secretariat. The Committee of Imperial Defence ceased to have a separate existence on 5 September 1939 and was never resurrected.

Peter Simkins

Bibliography

d'Ombrain, Nicholas. *War Machinery and High Policy: Defence Administration in Peacetime Britain 1902–1914.* 1973.

Ehrmann, John. *Cabinet Government and War, 1890–1940.* 1958.

Ismay, General Lord. *Memoirs.* 1960.

Johnson, Franklyn A. *Defence by Committee: The British Committee of Imperial Defence, 1885–1959.* 1960.

Roskill, Stephen. *Hankey: Man of Secrets.* 3 vols. 1970–4.

Commonwealth

The Commonwealth—often still popularly called "British", though that qualifier was officially dropped in 1949—is a global association of states. There are currently 54 members, with a total population of 1.7 billion: roughly thirty per cent of the world's people. They range from India, with over 900 million inhabitants, to Tuvalu with about ten thousand; and from some of the world's richest countries to its poorest. Almost all are former British colonies, but since November 1995 they have included Mozambique, a former Portuguese possession in southeast Africa.

Emerging from the DECOLONIZATION of the British Empire, the Commonwealth is seen by its critics as little more than an imperial hangover, essentially irrelevant to the realities of modern global politics. In friendlier eyes, although it is a looser (and certainly a less British-dominated) association than its early architects had expected, it has successfully refashioned itself into a modest but positive example of internationalism, especially valuable to its smaller and poorer members. It has sponsored numerous programs of economic, educational, and technological cooperation, and an extensive network of non-governmental organizations (NGOs). It has also been seen to play a positive role in sustaining democracy, or aiding its restoration, in several member states during the 1990s.

The word *commonwealth* itself has a long and complex history, with its earlier usages carrying quite strong radical and even egalitarian associations. As it was revived by British statesmen in the late Victorian era (most influentially by Lord Rosebery in 1884), however, its dominant meaning was to describe a sub-system within the global reach of the British Empire. It meant those territories—primarily Australia, Canada, and New Zealand—whose majority populations were of British-Irish descent, which had achieved or were achieving parliamentary institutions, and a significant degree both of internal democracy and of control over their own affairs, increasingly codified as "Dominion" status. It was thus, in effect, a racially exclusive label distinguishing a British-diasporic "family of nations" from the peoples of the subject Empire.

In something like that sense, the designation "Commonwealth" began to be institutionalized after 1914. The Imperial War Conference in 1917 referred to an "Imperial Commonwealth". ARTHUR BALFOUR's 1926 report, and the 1931 Statute of Westminster, in defining Dominion status, also formally instituted the "British Commonwealth of Nations". Across the first half of the twentieth century, though, the label carried a bewildering and rapidly shifting variety of associations. Some politicians, perhaps especially Labour ones, increasingly used the word as a more benign semi-synonym for "Empire". Gradually, however, the dominant understanding came to be that the Commonwealth was neither a part of the Empire, nor another name for it, but rather Empire's successor. Such an understanding still carried considerable ambiguity: how far was it to be a continuation of Empire by other, less direct means, how far a genuinely free association of equals—and thus, in some sense, Empire's antithesis?

More substantively, as decolonization proceeded after 1945, the Commonwealth moved steadily from being a "white Dominions club" (including of course the white minority regime of South Africa) and toward multiracialism. India, Pakistan, and Sri Lanka became members on their independence in 1947–8. Ghana was the first black African state to do so, in 1957; followed rapidly thereafter by numerous African, Caribbean, and Pacific territories. As this process advanced, those British policy-makers who had expected, or even planned, that the Commonwealth would be the major focus for a continuing British global role—a kind of "informal empire," or of what opponents began to call "neo-colonialism"—were largely disappointed. The point at which this can be said formally to have been recognized came in 1965, when administrative control of the association passed from the British Commonwealth Office to an independent Secretariat. Although it was based in London, the Secretariat's staff and leaders were drawn from across the globe. The first Secretary-General was Arnold Cantwell Smith, a Canadian diplomat. His successors have been Sir Shridath ("Sonny") Ramphal from Guyana (1975–90), Nigerian Emeka Anyaoku (1990–2000), and New Zealander Donald McKinnon—all three former Foreign Ministers of their respective countries.

A few British colonies, on moving to independence, set their faces firmly against Commonwealth links: first and most importantly, Burma in 1948. For almost all, though, there were evident advantages in joining the association; even if there were also British pressures for them to do so, exercised during the transfer-of-power negotiations. Eventually, transition from colony to Commonwealth member became something almost to be taken for granted.

Intriguingly, none of the Middle Eastern countries which Britain had ruled under LEAGUE OF NATIONS mandates seems to have seriously considered, or been considered for, membership; not even those, like Jordan, where informal British influence remained very strong. In contrast, mandatory territories in Africa became near-automatic members, from Tanganyika in 1961 to Namibia in 1990. Behind the complexities of local politics and constitutional conflict, it might be suspected that the crucial differentiating factor was the degree of cultural—and especially linguistic—Anglicization that had taken place. The Commonwealth has no formal charter or criteria for membership, but English is the association's sole official language. By that measure, Mozambique's 1995 entry, and that of mainly Francophone Cameroon, were indeed mold-breaking—or perhaps merely anomalous. In the late 1990s Yemen, Rwanda, and the Palestinian Authority applied for membership. All would have been considered extremely unlikely candidates in earlier times; yet their applications were not rejected, but held under review. The idea that Burma, Jordan, Israel, and the Irish Republic might join or rejoin was also being floated in some circles.

There were nonetheless repeated controversies over criteria for membership, as decolonization advanced. Could states with republican constitutions be members, as Nehru of India demanded in 1947? (Ireland had already long been in this position, but it had always been seen as a special case, and in any event resigned its membership in 1949.) The eventual answer was "yes"; after much negotiation and via an artful compromise formula that republican members would acknowledge the British monarch as "symbol of the free association of the members, and as such the Head of the Commonwealth". Under this formula, eventually, a majority of members were republics: 33 in 2000, as against sixteen who retained the British monarch as their Head of State, and five which had their own indigenous monarchies. Could very small countries join, as Cyprus sought to do in 1960, without distorting the entire structure? Again the answer was decided to be "yes". Today,

24 of the member states have populations of under one million, making the Commonwealth probably the world's most important international forum for "mini-"—and even "micro-states".

By far the greatest issue of contention within the modern Commonwealth, however, was South Africa. Under increasing pressure from African and Asian members over its apartheid policies, South Africa left the association in 1961—in effect, jumping before she was pushed. Subsequently, the schism between Britain's continuing close relations with South Africa and most other Commonwealth members' abhorrence of the Pretoria regime strained relations close to the breaking-point, especially during MARGARET THATCHER's 1979–90 tenure as British Prime Minister. Her refusal to support sanctions against Pretoria left Britain isolated and embattled. A majority of member countries boycotted the 1986 Commonwealth Games in Edinburgh in protest. At successive Heads of Government meetings in 1987 and 1989, decisions were repeatedly recorded as "48 in favour, one against", with Britain as the solitary negative. After Thatcher's departure, the end of the Cold War, and, above all, South Africa's own transition to democratic majority rule, bridges were gradually rebuilt in the 1990s. South Africa rejoined in 1994, and the Commonwealth seemed rejuvenated. On re-entry, South Africa's new President Nelson Mandela came rapidly, near-universally to be seen as exercising a moral and persuasive force unequalled by any other Commonwealth leader.

Not all Commonwealth countries were democracies, not even by the least stringent definition: However in Africa, Commonwealth countries surrounded by the Pacific, and the Caribbean, proportionately more of them than of their regional neighbors fulfilled basic criteria of political freedom and human rights observance. By no means were all peaceful either; and there were even occasions of war between members, as with India and Pakistan in 1971 or Uganda and Tanzania in 1979. Widespread outrage at the internally repressive actions of some member states—as over Sani Abacha's Nigerian military regime in the later 1990s, with its ferocious crushing of Ogoni and other dissidents—did not translate into effective Commonwealth action against them. However, by the end of the century, there was a greater apparent willingness to act against members which flouted democratic norms. Some were suspended or effectively forced, for a time, to leave: as with Fiji after the military seized power there in 1987, or Pakistan in October 1999. The principles announced in the body's 1991 Harare Declaration, of commitment to democracy, good governance, and the rule of

law, were perhaps more widely honored—at least as aspirations—than ever before. Commonwealth advisers and monitoring teams helped supervise and ensure the integrity of elections in numerous member states, especially in Africa; including several which marked transitions to democracy from military, one-party or one-person rule.

Meanwhile, between the 1950s and the 1990s, the Commonwealth's importance to British foreign policy steadily declined. The crucial moment of change here was, obviously, Britain's entry into the EUROPEAN COMMUNITY in 1972. One consequence was that preferential trade agreements, which Britain had previously signed with several Commonwealth countries, had to be ended. For countries like New Zealand and several Caribbean islands which had relied on Britain as a major export market, especially for agricultural products, this was a serious blow. To some of them, it even seemed like a betrayal; though the 1975 Lome Convention and its successors retained or restored some of the trading links on a new, more multilateral basis.

On the constitutional level, the continued position of the British monarch as Head of State for many Commonwealth countries had certain consequences that seemed to critics anomalous or anachronistic. In Australia in 1975, the Governor-General Sir John Kerr used his powers as representative of the Crown to dismiss Gough Whitlam's Labor government, despite its parliamentary majority. The ensuing controversy fired calls for Australia to become a republic, which have recurred ever since. Elsewhere, it is said (and not credibly denied) that when American forces invaded Grenada in 1983, they carried with them a postdated letter to be signed by the Queen's representative on the island, Sir Paul Scoon, authorizing the intervention. Within Britain, there was recurrent discomfort at the fact that this constitutional setup made Britain's Privy Council the final arbiter of life-and-death decisions for Commonwealth states which retained the death penalty—even though Britain itself had long abolished CAPITAL PUNISHMENT.

It was no secret that QUEEN ELIZABETH II took her position as Head of the Commonwealth very seriously. In a British political system where the monarchy's role was otherwise both minimal and neutral, the issue of Commonwealth unity seemed to be something of an exception. In other respects, however, it appeared that the Commonwealth, marked by a stamp of past British influence it continued to bear, played a rather little active, continuing role in Britain's own political, cultural, or intellectual life. Even the once-ubiquitous label of "COMMONWEALTH LITERATURE" to describe (inaccurately) writing in English from outside the UK, had been generally replaced by the still less precise designation "postcolonial literature". Indeed, by the year 2001, the Commonwealth probably mattered less to most people in Britain than it did to those in many other member states. Almost everywhere, though, it was not so much the formal apparatus of ministerial meetings and communiqués which affected everyday life, as the numerous specialist agencies, informal associations, and NGOs the Commonwealth sponsored. These ranged from the Commonwealth Parliamentary and Universities' Associations, through the Fund for Technical Co-operation, to the four-yearly Commonwealth Games.

Undoubtedly the most profound, direct impact of the Commonwealth on Britain itself after 1945 came through IMMIGRATION. The history of such migration, and of the laws which regulated it, is complex and cannot be summarized here. Broadly, however, it shifted over time from almost unrestricted right of entry for Commonwealth and colonial subjects into Britain, to harsh de facto discrimination against them. Or rather, against those from "non-white" (the standard euphemism was "New Commonwealth") countries. Despite the ever-higher barriers, by 2000 migrants from such countries, with their descendants, numbered almost 3 million and were making their mark on every aspect of national life. Debate was vigorous over their relationship with Britishness and Englishness, and how their presence altered those ideas themselves. In counterpoint to this, such "Old Commonwealth" countries as Australia and New Zealand, with their own populations and cultural patterns becoming steadily less dominated by the British-descended, held their own intense enquiries into evolving national identity. The interconnections among these debates were rarely remarked. One obvious, continuing common thread, however, was that all the larger Commonwealth countries (except Canada) regularly played each other at CRICKET—and England was usually the loser.

Stephen Howe

Bibliography

Chan, Stephen. *The Commonwealth in World Politics.* 1988.
Commonwealth Secretariat Website: http://www.thecommonwealth.org
McIntyre, W. David. *The Significance of the Commonwealth, 1965–90.* 1991.
Mansergh, Nicholas. *The Commonwealth Experience.* 2nd ed. 1982.
Moore, R.J. *Making the New Commonwealth.* 1987.
The Commonwealth Yearbook.

Commonwealth Literature

The term Commonwealth literature acknowledges and celebrates the extraordinarily diverse literary productivity of the nations that emerged from the dissolution of the British Empire after the SECOND WORLD WAR. The specific wealth held in common is the English language, and the currency of the term Commonwealth literature draws the attention of a world-wide Anglophone audience to this body of work, which already includes three Nobel prizewinners: the Australian Patrick White (1973), the Nigerian Wole Soyinka (1986), the Saint Lucian Derek Walcott (1992).

In retrospect, WILLIAM BUTLER YEATS, Augusta Gregory, and John Millington Synge at the turn of the century were perhaps the first Commonwealth writers—the first to write out of the characteristically "Commonwealth" crossing of urgent nationalism and devotion to the tradition of the shared language (earlier Irish writers like Swift, Goldsmith, and Wilde had been agreeably assimilated to British literature). But the notion of a Commonwealth developed only in the 1930s as a description for the British Isles along with what would now be called the settler colonies: Canada, Australia, New Zealand, and South Africa. It was novelists from these regions, many of whom had spent considerable time in England, that after the war first began to be regarded as comprising Commonwealth literature. Among them were Patrick White, who had returned to Australia to write; DORIS LESSING, who came to England from Rhodesia (now Zimbabwe) in 1949, and immediately published her first book *The Grass is Singing;* Nadine Gordimer of South Africa; and Margaret Atwood of Canada. Their work was observant and generally realistic, making their farflung landscapes seem vivid and accessible to British readers. Yet from the beginning some of these novels address themselves particularly to the intellectual forum of the Commonwealth (rather than to either a specifically local or a "universal" audience)—as for example when Alan Paton's *Cry the Beloved Country* (1948) presents urgent South African issues before the tribunal of the Commonwealth.

The breakup of Empire induced an unprecedented migration back to the metropolis between the end of the war and the restrictive legislation of the early 1960s. One consequence was the discovery of authors from the "New Commonwealth"—the Indian subcontinent, Anglophone Black Africa, and the West Indies, and Malaysia. They were initially perceived as exotics; publishers responded to a taste for informative, almost ethnographic novels by offering the sights and sounds of the tropics in books like R. K. Narayan's *The Financial Expert* (1952), Chinua Achebe's *Things Fall Apart* (1958), and the genial early novels of V. S. Naipaul. But soon novels of all sorts began to appear, along with brilliant accounts of what it was like to *be* a Commonwealth writer: George Lamming's *The Pleasures of Exile*

(1960), Nirad Chaudhuri *Autobiography of an Unknown Indian* (1963), and C. L. R. James's *Beyond a Boundary* (1963).

Though fiction was the most widely disseminated genre, immigrant theatre was lively in London even in the 1950s; many plays were produced for radio and the stage, though they were only rarely published. Publishers favored playwrights engaged in active dialogue with the western tradition: from Nigeria, Soyinka rather than Duro Ladipo; from South Africa, Athol Fugard rather than Gibson Kente. As for poetry, in addition to public readings in London the BBC Colonial Service was an important medium. Several Commonwealth verse anthologies appeared during the 1960s, and in 1965 an extensive commonwealth arts festival was mounted at the Royal Court Theatre in London, coinciding with first issue of the *Journal of Commonwealth Literature*. Other periodicals in the field soon appeared, especially *Kunapipi, Ariel,* and *WLWE.* Beginning in 1969 the Booker Prize has honored a succession of Commonwealth authors, including V. S. Naipaul, Ruth Prawer Jhabvala, J.M. Coetzee, Michael Ondaatje, Salman Rushdie, as well as the Japanese-born Kazuo Ishiguro.

The sense that Commonwealth writing in some way constitutes a unified body of literature is grounded on the shared language, the relation (however attenuated) to its literary tradition, and more mundanely on the economic value of metropolitan publication, and on the alluring electronic simultaneity of the "global village" in the late twentieth century. Yet three distinct sorts of Commonwealth Literature can be identified: (1) new national literatures around the world; (2) new literatures of immigrant communities in England (for example, the novelist and screenwriter Hanif Kureishi was born in England, the playwright Mustapha Matura in Trinidad, but both write out of and for the communities of BLACK PEOPLE); (3) writing in England (as well as Canada and the United States) by self-styled exiles or expatriates who seem to participate in neither of the above categories. Unlike Sam Selvon or Wilson Harris who continue to write West Indian literature though they live in Canada and England, authors like Naipaul and Rushdie seem most comfortable addressing the Anglophone Commonwealth at large; behind them stand the examples of CONRAD and JOYCE.

The growing national literatures in English are not always well served by the umbrella term "Commonwealth literature", which invites a wider audience but tends to discount a work's relation to its indigenous languages, literatures, and culture. Particularly in Africa, India, and parts of Asia, literatures in English are sub-divisions of larger multi-lingual literatures, but in practice

"Commonwealth literature" refers only to the part of a nation's literary production both *written* in English and addressed to readers of English—that is, to an audience for the most part external to the place, unfamiliar with local language and custom. Amos Tutuola's novel *The Palm-Wine Drinkard* (1952), for instance, was widely praised for its vividly fractured language, but Commonwealth readers were unaware of the novel's indebtedness to Yoruba narrative (e.g. the novels of Daniel Fagunwa). Even in 1991 Ben Okri's hallucinatory novel *The Famished Road,* out of the same Yoruba tradition, was often characterized in terms of Latin American magical realism, a style from another hemisphere and another language which nevertheless has the advantage of being more familiar to Anglophone readers than Okri's own culture.

English is a global language, or a global family of languages, but accessibility to a wide readership seems an important criterion for any work's inclusion in "Commonwealth literature." So, for example, the extensive Onitsha market literature of Nigeria, pulp fiction written for a local audience in heavily creolized English, is not construed as Commonwealth; but neither is the impressive work of Jamaican "dub" poets like Linton Kwesi Johnson, even though they perform, record, and publish in London. In Britain itself, there is some danger that the designation "Commonwealth" serves as a code for minority literature; when, for example, Ishiguro's *The Remains of the Day,* a novel by a long-time British resident about a very British butler, is classified as Commonwealth literature, the term seems primarily to signal the author's ethnicity.

Indeed, because of its political implications the specific term "Commonwealth literature" is disputed; some cultural critics regard the notion of Commonwealth literature as an example of how Britain still lays claim to the products of its former colonies. Such critics prefer to speak of "post-colonial literature(s) in English". Other critics, noting that in practice "Commonwealth literature" means "non-British, non-American literature in English", prefer to speak of world literature written in English.

Laurence A. Breiner

Bibliography

Adam, Ian, and Helen Tiffin, eds. *Past the Last Post: Theorizing Post-Colonialism and Post-Modernism.* 1990.

Ashcroft, Bill, Gareth Griffiths, and Helen Tiffin. *The Empire Writes Back: Theory and Practice in Post-Colonial Literature.* 1989.

King, Bruce. *The New English Literatures: Cultural Nationalism in a Changing World.* 1980.

McCrum, Robert. *The Story of English.* 1986.

Riemenschneider, Dieter, ed. *The History and Historiography of Commonwealth Literature.* 1983.

Communist Party of Great Britain

For the first time since the 1920s there were no official Communist candidates at the British general election of 1992. The Communist Party of Great Britain (CPGB) had changed its name a year before at its 43rd Congress to the Democratic Left. It urged its few members (about 1,400) to support the candidates best able to defeat the CONSERVATIVES, whether LABOUR, Liberal Democrat, or Scottish National.

The fact that Karl Marx regarded Britain as a mature capitalist society ripe for revolution must have inspired some British workers and intellectuals to form a movement to realize his aims. A number of such organizations—among them the Social Democratic Federation, the British Socialist Party, and the INDEPENDENT LABOUR PARTY (ILP)—came into existence towards the end of the nineteenth century. As elsewhere, the FIRST WORLD WAR and the Leninist seizure of power in Russia in 1917 led to splits. Eventually, in July 1920 a small group of radicals, believing themselves to be the true heirs of Marx, founded the CPGB. They considered themselves to be the advance guard of the proletarian revolution. Their tactic was to seek affiliation to the LABOUR PARTY, which by 1918 had became the main opposition party, but its reformist leaders steadfastly refused to allow the CPGB to affiliate.

Affiliated as it was to the Communist International or Comintern, the CPGB was obliged to implement the policy decisions dictated by Moscow. As happened in other CPs, it lost members with each dramatic shift in policy. Although high turnover in membership was regrettable, it made it easier for the leaders to retain control over a party composed of inexperienced members. Leninist principles of democratic centralism and against factions compounded that control.

The CPGB operated through the trade unions and the Labour Party and sought to get its own members elected to Parliament. For most of its existence it denounced Parliament as a capitalist conspiracy, but one useful as a forum for party propaganda. Several Communists were elected to Parliament in the inter-war period. In 1922 J.T. Walton Newbold won the Scottish constituency of Motherwell. In the same year Shapurji Saklatvala, a middle class Indian, was elected at North Battersea (London) as a Labour MP although he was a member of the CPGB. Defeated in 1923, he was reelected as a Communist in 1924. In that year the Labour Party decided that no member of the Communist Party (or any other competing party) could be an individual member of the Labour Party. In 1935 William Gallacher was elected for the Scottish mining constituency of West Fife, the first Communist to defeat a Labour candidate. The only other CPGB candidate to stand, Harry Pollitt, was defeated. The fact that only two Communists stood in 1935 was in keeping with the changed party line. In the elections of 1929 and 1931 it had fielded twenty-five and twenty-six candidates respectively. In 1928, following Comintern instructions, the "class against class" line had been introduced and this meant fighting Labour as the "second capitalist party" instead of seeking affiliation with it. By 1935 the line had changed again into one of unity in the fight against FASCISM and war. Albert Inkpin, Party Secretary since 1920, fell victim to the change of line in 1929 and was succeeded by Harry Pollitt, who remained as Secretary until 1956.

The CPGB directed its campaigns before 1939 against UNEMPLOYMENT, colonialism, Fascism, and war and managed to extend its influence well beyond its ranks. JOHN STRACHEY, and to a lesser extent, Emile Burns, popularized Marxism during the 1930s when the attraction of Communism grew. Among the intellectuals identified closely with the CPGB were scientists J.D. Bernal, J.B.S. HALDANE, and philosopher John Lewis. Serious music was represented in the CPGB by Alan Bush and the FILM INDUSTRY by Ivor Montagu. Sean O'Casey was one of a number of writers supporting Communism. Two contributors to Marxist literary theory, Christopher Caudwell and Ralph Fox, were among the 526 British volunteers killed in the SPANISH CIVIL WAR on the Republican side.

When the Hitler-Stalin Pact was announced on 23 August 1939 shock waves registred throughout the CPGB. In the mistakenly-named Labour Monthly, its editor, CPGB theorist R. Palme Dutt, welcomed it as "logical." However, when war was declared on Germany, most CPGB members automatically assumed they would support it. The full implications of the Nazi-Soviet Pact had not yet sunk in. A pamphlet by Pollitt entitled How To Win The War stated, "The Communist Party supports the war, believing it to be a 'just war.'" After the Soviet invasion of Poland on 17 September, presented as an act of liberation, the CPGB was advised by its Comintern representative Dave Springhall that the war was imperialist and to be opposed. On 3 October this line prevailed in the Central Committee by twenty-one votes to three; Pollitt, Gallacher, and J.R. Campbell, editor of the Daily Worker, who remained unconvinced, were later persuaded to toe the party line.

Until the attack on the Soviet Union by Germany on 22 June 1941 the CPGB kept up its attack on the war. It lost some of its 18,000 members during this period but gained others from among the more militant trade unionists and some PACIFISTS. Exploiting the genuine grievances of ordinary workers under wartime conditions and Labour complicity in government policies, it called for the replacement of the coalition by a "People's Government" which would bring peace. It attempted to win support for this objective through a "People's Convention" held in London in January 1941, an event attracting delegates from a host of Communist front organizations such as air raid shelter committees, tenants groups, peace groups, factory committees, and anti-colonialist organizations. Although the government was authorized to intern individuals and ban publications deemed dangerous, it used its powers sparingly. It did arrest Sir Oswald Mosley, the Fascist leader, and more than 700 of his supporters. By contrast, hardly any Communists were taken into custody. The *Daily Worker* was banned on 21 January 1941, as was Claud Cockburn's *The Week*, but other Communist publications, such as *Labour Monthly*, were left untouched. The bans were lifted after the Nazi invasion of the Soviet Union.

Immediately after the attack on the Soviet Union Prime Minister Winston Churchill announced British support for the Soviets. The CPGB immediately swung round to supporting the war effort; it became super-patriotic, denounced strikes, and joined the political truce. This move meant that it did not field candidates in by-elections and resisted opportunities for criticism of government policies. It did however join with other groups to campaign for a Second Front. Admiration for the Soviet Union's war efforts was fostered by the popular media, which spurred a growth in membership. At the time of the German defeat at Stalingrad membership rose to an all-time peak of around 100,000, but it then began to decline. Common Wealth, a respectably radical, new political group critical of government policy, probably attracted some who might otherwise have opted for the CPGB.

In the election of 1945 the CPGB, fighting on a program close to that of Labour, put up twenty-one candidates. Only two of them were successful: Gallacher at West Fife and Phil Piratin at Mile End (London). In addition, D.N. Pritt, who followed the CPGB line consistently, as he continued to do until his death, was reelected as a Labour independent. Once the Cold War started, the CPGB attempted to promote trade union militancy against the Labour government. It had gained support during the war mainly in the firemen's union, the Electical Trade Union (ETU), the draughtmen's union, the National Union of Mineworkers, the Amalgamated Engineering Union, scientific workers, and some others. As it supported the Soviet Union unwaveringly, it became less and less popular. In the 1950 election it nominated a record 100 candidates, all of whom were defeated, including Gallacher and Piratin. Pro-Communist fellow travellers, standing as independents after their expulsion from the Labour Party, were also unsuccessful. Nor have any Communists been elected to Parliament since then.

Stalin's attempt to destroy Tito (1948), the invasion of Hungary (1956), the exposure of Stalin at the 20th Congress of the CPSU (1956), and the Soviet invasion of Czechoslovakia (1968) all contributed to the decline of British Communism. It also suffered from a ballot-rigging scandal by its members in the ETU. In 1951 the CPGB promoted a program labelled *The British Road to Socialism* which, in fact, advocated an East European-type system. John Gollan, who replaced Pollitt in 1956, could do little to revive the party's fortunes. In the 1960s it supported the CPSU in its dispute with Chinese leader Mao Tse-Tung and exploited opposition to the Vietnam War and nuclear weapons and left-wing disappointment with Harold Wilson's Labour government.

CPGB membership declined from about 34,000 in 1964 to under 20,000 in 1977. In that year it revised its program in a more reformist, Euro-Communist direction, provoking another split. The New Communist Party led by Sid French with a membership of 1,000 was established to advocate a more Stalinist approach. Meanwhile Trotskyist organizations such as the Workers' Revolutionary Party (1959) and Socialist Workers' Party (1976) were increasingly recruiting its potential clientele. In the 1980s Militant was the main standard bearer of this trend. The CPGB retained a residual influence in the 1980s, especially through its theoretical journal *Marxism Today* and to a lesser extent the daily *Morning Star* (formerly *Daily Worker*). It retained some prestige through one or two prominent trade unionists like Mick McGahey of the miners and Ken Gill of the engineers. On 9 December 1990 the CPGB decided to drop Marxism-Leninism in favor of Democratic Socialism. The collapse of Soviet Communism in 1991 led to the CPGB's decision to regroup under its new name of Democratic Left.

David Childs

Bibliography

Branson, Noreen. *History of the Communist Party of Great Britain 1927–1941*. 1985.

Childs, David. "The Communist Party and the War, 1939–41," *Journal of Contemporary History*, vol. 12 (1977), pp. 237–53.

Klugman, James. *History of the Communist Party*. 2 vols. 1968–9.

Laybourn, Keith, and D.L. Murphy. *Under the Red Flag: The History of Communism in Britain*. 1999.

Thorpe, Andrew. *The British Communist Party and Moscow 1920–43*. 2000.

Wood, Neal. *Communism and British Intellectuals.* 1969.
Worley, Matthew. "Left Turn: A Reassessment of the Communist Party of Great Britain in the Third Period, 1928–33," *Twentieth Century British History*, vol. II (2000), pp. 353–78.

Composers and Music

SIR EDWARD ELGAR's assessment of *A Vision of Life* (1907) by Sir Hubert Parry (1848–1918) as "fine stuff" is indirect evidence of his own debt to the nobility and grandeur of Parry's music, qualities the latter continued to explore during the Indian summer of his career in his Fifth Symphony (1912), the symphonic poem *From Death to Life* (1914), and the *Songs of Farewell* (1918) for unaccompanied chorus. In contrast, Elgar's view of the music of Sir Charles Stanford (1852–1924) as "neither fish, flesh, fowl nor good red-herring!" ignores the restrained ardor of Stanford's Clarinet Concerto (1902), the manly vigor of the *Songs of the Sea* (1904) for baritone, male chorus and orchestra, and the fiery passion that erupts intermittently in the Fifth Irish Rhapsody (1917).

However, despite the achievements of Parry and Stanford, neither composer could match Elgar; nor, indeed, could Sir Granville Bantock (1868–1946), although the novelty of the voluptuous harmonies and Straussian exuberance in his three-part cantata, *Omar Khayyam* (1906–9) and in *Sappho* (1906) for contralto and orchestra, led some of his contemporaries to think so. Bantock, close friend of Elgar and for a time of FREDERICK DELIUS, also supported Josef Holbrooke (1878–1958), like himself a pupil of Frederick Corder at the Royal Academy of Music, and the self-taught Havergal Brian (1876–1972). Each composer's large output is still being reassessed, but with Brian it is doubtful whether the centrality of his thirty-two symphonies, beginning with the immense *Gothic* (1919–27), will be displaced, or in the case of Holbrooke his Wagnerian operatic trilogy *The Cauldron of Annwyn* (1912/1914/1929). The greatest operatic success of this period was in fact the 216 consecutive performances of *The Immortal Hour* (1913) by Rutland Boughton (1878–1960), whose dissatisfaction with the London operatic scene prompted him to create at Glastonbury a center for opera performance supported by a commune of artists (1914–27).

Another prolific pupil of Corder, Sir Arnold Bax (1883–1953), self-confessed "brazen Romantic" and Celtic enthusiast, established his reputation with a substantial collection of tone poems including *In the Faery Hills* (1909) and *Tintagel* (1919). Subsequently he embarked on a series of seven symphonies, the First (1922), by turns aggressive and searingly elegiac, a bitter response to the events of the First World War and the Easter Rising of 1916. John Ireland (1879–1962), too, was

deeply affected by the war, the Edwardian pleasantries of his Phantasie Piano Trio (1906) being displaced by the sour harmonies of the Second Piano Trio (1917), written, according to Ireland, with "the boys going over the top of the trenches" in mind. Also like Bax, Ireland was an accomplished pianist, and both developed an individual pianism, Bax, for instance, in his Second Piano Sonata (1919) and in *Winter Legends* for piano and orchestra (1930), Ireland in his Concerto (1930) and in *Sarnia* (1941), three pieces celebrating Guernsey, one of Ireland's spiritual homes.

In contrast to Ireland's stylistic evolution, that of Frank Bridge (1879–1941) paralleled radical trends on the Continent more closely. As a pupil of Stanford (as was Ireland and the vast majority of English composers of his generation), Bridge's initial idiom was conservative, although invigorated by thorough professionalism as in the First String Quartet (1906) and Phantasy Piano Quartet (1910). However, in response to an increasing awareness of musical developments abroad and a deepening consciousness accelerated by his reaction to the war—Bridge was a pacifist—his late style, heralded in the monumental and sometimes systematically bitonal Piano Sonata (1924), was brought to fruition in the highly chromatic, aggressively energetic Third String Quartet (1927). The latter work, dedicated to the American patroness of chamber music, Mrs. Sprague Coolidge, who supported Bridge financially from 1923 onwards, was succeeded by further chamber works in a similar style, including the spacious Piano Trio (1929), before a partial relaxation was achieved in the partly neo-Classical Fourth String Quartet (1938). The centerpiece of these late works is the elegiac cello concerto, *Oration* (1930), a funeral address for the lost of the First World War and by implication a passionate indictment of all war.

For those intent on studying abroad rather than with Corder or Stanford, Iwan Knorr at the Hoch Conservatory, Frankfurt, became the preferred master, teaching Roger Quilter (1877–1953), Henry Balfour Gardiner (1877–1950), Cyril Scott (1879–1970) and the Australian Percy Grainger (1882–1961). Both Quilter and Balfour Gardiner were essentially Edwardian composers; their best works—in Quilter's case songs; in Gardiner's such orchestral pieces as Overture to a Comedy (1906) or *A Berkshire Idyll* (1913)—hardly transcend their period. By contrast, Scott, for a time, earned himself the reputation of a modernist. However, it was Grainger's openness to sounds, be they natural or man-made, heard in the music hall or produced by newly-invented instruments, that was indicative of a more radical aesthetic. Unfortunately, interest in his serious works has been eclipsed by the popularity of the folksong settings *Molly on the Shore* and *Country Gardens*.

Apart from Quilter, several other composers of his generation specialized in song-writing, including Ivor Gurney (1890–1937), whose considerable poetic talent was nurtured by an abiding love for English literature, particularly the Elizabethan and Georgian poets. Gerald Finzi (1901–56), too, could encapsulate the essence of the text he was setting in distinctive music, especially in response to Hardy's and Shakespeare's words, and in the ecstatic song cycle *Dies Natalis* (1926/1939), for high voice and strings, a minor masterpiece. Finally, the songs of Peter Warlock (1894–1930) exhibit a wide range of feeling, from the rumbustious "Rutterkin," via the jolly, uncomplicated "Pretty Ring-Time" and quietly introspective "Sleep," to the bleak despair of "The Curlew."

E.J. Moeran (1894–1950), who lived with Warlock for a time and whose song collection *Seven Poems of* JAMES JOYCE (1929) is influenced by him, expanded his style and technique during the 1930s to include a Sibelian thematic growth in his G minor Symphony (1934–7). The tough vigor of the Sinfonietta (1944) marks a further step towards modernism, although the outer movements of the Violin Concerto (1942), with their poetic dreaming, reveal the continuing strong influence of both Delius and RALPH VAUGHAN WILLIAMS on his style. Herbert Howells (1892–1983), too, was indebted to both composers, a ruminative pastoralism suffusing the String Quartet *In Gloucestershire* (1923), and a Delian sense of loss the *a capella Requiem* (1936), subsequently expanded into *Hymnus Paradisi* (1938). Each new recording of the neglected music of John Foulds (1880–1939) helps to fill out the incomplete picture of his achievement. His piano concerto, *Dynamic Triptych* (1929), can stand beside Vaughan Williams' (1931) without loss of face as can his ninth string quartet, *Quartetto Intimo* (1932), beside Bridge's later quartets.

During his lifetime, Foulds' reputation was based on his light music, the *Keltic Lament* (1911) catching the public's ear. Other composers, Haydn Wood (1882–1959), Eric Coates (1886–1957), and Frederic Curzon (1899–1973), specialized in this area. Coates' belief that music should play a vital part in everyday life became fact with the advent of broadcasting, and the choice of his music for signature tunes—the march, *Calling All Workers* (1940), introduced the radio program, *Music While You Work*, while another march, *Knightsbridge* (1933), heralded the TV program, *In Town Tonight*—introduced it to an enormous audience. The syncopated piano novelties of Billy Mayerl (1902–59), such as *Marigold* (1927) and the suite, *Four Aces* (1933), also became immensely popular.

For many composers of Vaughan Williams' generation, the progress of modernism on the Continent meant little or nothing. Nonetheless, Lord (Gerald) Berners (1883–1950), blessed with a talent for mimicry, could imitate Satiesque wit and satire in his *Trois petites marches funèbres* for piano (1914) and, by contrast, approach an almost expressionist idiom in another group of piano pieces, the *Fragments psychologiques* (1921). Influenced by Busoni, Bernard van Dieren (1887–1936), likewise approached expressionism in his Six Sketches for piano (1911) and in parts of the Chinese Symphony (1914), although in his later music he withdrew from such an extreme position. With WILLIAM WALTON's generation, some involvement with modernism was *de rigueur*. Thus Sir Arthur Bliss (1891–1975) originally drew for inspiration on the music of Ravel, Stravinsky, and Les Six as well as ragtime in, for instance, *Rout* for soprano and chamber ensemble (1920), its Gallic carnival atmosphere punctuated by the singer's nonsense syllables. However, by the time of the expansive and richly-scored Music for Strings (1935), an Elgarian Romanticism held sway. Constant Lambert (1905–51), pursued a similar course initially, but with the ragtime influence more pervasive, particularly in *The Rio Grande* for piano, chorus, and orchestra (1927) and the Piano Sonata (1929). The astringent, world-weary Concerto for piano and nine players (1931), which became a memorial to Warlock following his suicide, marked a new departure, although the balmy climate of *The Rio Grande* returned with syncopated rhythms and warm lyricism of the ballet, *Horoscope* (1937). Alan Bush (1900–95), like Bliss, changed course radically during his career, the dissonant counterpoint of his early string quartet, *Dialectic* (1929), giving way to a simplified idiom that could be used, as in the Byron Symphony (1960), to communicate with a wider audience and thereby give expression to his Communist beliefs.

A more sustained commitment to modernism can be heard in the music of other composers of Walton's generation. Sir Lennox Berkeley (1903–89), a pupil of Nadia Boulanger in Paris and a lifelong friend of Poulenc, found Stravinsky's neo-Classicism congenial. Unfortunately, Berkeley's reticence can sometimes lead to anonymity, but such works as the precision-crafted Six Preludes for piano (1945) and the grave, yet radiant, Four Poems of St. Teresa of Avila for contralto and string orchestra (1947) reveal a successful balance between emotional statement and restraint. In her series of thirteen string quartets, Dame Elizabeth Maconchy (1907–94) turned to Bartok rather than Stravinsky as a model—the five-movement design of her Seventh Quartet (1956) forms an obvious allusion to that of Bartok's

Fourth—but for Elisabeth Lutyens (1906–83), Humphrey Searle (1915–82), and Benjamin Frankel (1906–73) it was the twelve-tone works of the Second Viennese School that proved influential. As early as 1939 in her Chamber Concerto No. 1, Lutyens began to explore her characteristic brand of serialism, which became fully developed in *O saisons, o chateaux!* (1946) and reached a new level of intensity in *Quincunx* (1960), both vocal works with orchestra. Searle's preference for Schoenberg's emotionalism coupled with his enthusiasm for Liszt, made possible his one-movement Piano Sonata (1951), closely modelled on Liszt's and employing Lisztian thematic transformation but within a twelve-tone context. Frankel's development of an individual twelve-tone style during the 1950s bore fruit in his eight symphonies composed between 1958 and 1971, although the richly somber Violin Concerto (1951), written "in memory of the 'Six Million'" contains some of his most eloquent music. Another composer to draw on serial processes, if not a systematic twelve-tone technique, during the later part of his career was Alan Rawsthorne (1905–71), who made an initial impact with his Theme and Variations for two violins (1937) and the orchestral Symphonic Studies (1938). In these works his music's rapidly-shifting tonal centers, facilitated by inflecting major thirds to minor and vice-versa, created a distinctive idiom that he perfected in the Violin Sonata (1958). By introducing serial processes in his Quintet for piano and wind (1963) and Third Symphony (1964), Rawsthorne expanded the expressive scope of his style, adding to its variety and breadth.

During the 1930s British music benefited from the arrival of several émigrés intent on avoiding the horrors of Fascism. Egon Wellesz (1885–1974), Mátyás Seiber (1905–60), and Franz Reizenstein (1911–68), pupils of Schoenberg, Kodály, and Hindemith respectively, were all influential as teachers. Another Schoenberg pupil, Roberto Gerhard (1896–1970), was ignored for the first decade or so following his arrival, a time when he was consolidating his use of serialism; in the First String Quartet (1950–5) he developed his own technique of applying serial principles to rhythm. Subsequently he relinquished thematicism, leaving the organization of timbre as the prime structural factor in, for instance, his Concerto for Orchestra (1965) and the three final chamber works, *Gemini* for violin and piano (1966), and *Libra* (1968) and *Leo* (1969), both for small ensembles of contrasting instruments.

Sir Andrzej Panufnik (1914–91), another émigré (arriving in 1954 from Poland), together with Wellesz and Gerhard, bequeathed a considerable symphonic legacy. So too did such native composers as Edmund Rubbra (1901–86) and Wil-liam Alwyn (1905–85), while George Lloyd (1913–), Sir Malcolm Arnold (1921–), and Robert Simpson (1921–) continued to do so. In contrast to the vibrantly colorful symphonies of the Romantics Alwyn and Lloyd, those of Rubbra, propelled by contrapuntal thinking and muted in color, stand like ancient monuments, awesome in their totality, yet arising from very modest beginnings. A similar evolutionary process can be traced in Simpson's symphonies, although his model is not, as it was for Rubbra, sixteenth-century polyphony, but Beethoven, particularly for his dynamism and thematic development. While the symphonies of Arnold are outwardly more immediately attractive, the enigmatic juxtaposition of a popular, light entertainment tune within a non-popular context raises important aesthetic questions about the nature of stylistic unity, questions that have been increasingly highlighted by the enthusiasm of more recent composers for drawing on widely divergent models on which to base their style. Another precursor of this development is Ronald Stevenson (1928–), whose *Passacaglia on DSCH* for piano (1962) has a "global" range of reference, including the music of the work's dedicatee, Shostakovich, African drumming, and a Scottish Pibroch.

The free atonal style developed by Peter Racine Fricker (1920–90) acted as an influential antidote to British insularity during the immediate post-Second World War years, but was soon eclipsed by the avant-garde music of the "Manchester School," Alexander Goehr (1932–), Sir Peter Maxwell Davies (1934–), and Sir Harrison Birtwistle (1934–). Davies' earlier expressionist style, developed in such diverse theatrical works as the *Eight Songs for a Mad King* (1969), *Versalii Icones* for naked male dancer and instrumental ensemble (also 1969), and the opera *Taverner* (first produced in 1972), has been superceded by a calmer, more classically-oriented idiom as revealed in the First Symphony (1976) and the series of Strathclyde Concertos, works completed following Davies' move to remote Hoy in the Orkneys. Birtwistle's development has been similar in certain ways, the portrayal of frequently gratuitous violence in his ritualistic opera, *Punch and Judy* (1967), giving way to a more approachable scenario, the quest for self-knowledge, in *Gawain* (1991). Among more conservative figures, the fluent and adaptable character of the music of Richard Rodney Bennett (1936–), ranging from film music in various pastiche styles, via jazz, to a melodious twelve-tone idiom, attracted several commissions early during his career, including three large-scale operas, beginning with *The Mines of Sulphur* (1963) for Sadler's Wells. And the warmth and richness Nicholas Maw (1935–) derives from a mixture of radical and traditional elements has permitted him to produced a successful romantic comedy for Glyndebourne, the opera *The Ring of the Moon* (1970), and the expansive voyage of self-exploration for orchestra, *Odyssey* (1972–90).

For composers born during the 1930s, the range of styles a composer could adopt was wide; for those born during the next decade, the range was even wider. At one end of the spectrum, Brian Ferneyhough (1943–) has composed works like the *Sonatas for string quartet* (1967) on the knife-edge of intelligibility and playability, providing a model for younger composers of "The New Complexity" such as James Dillon (1950–). In contrast, composers belonging to the "English experimental tradition," often owing allegiance to Cornelius Cardew (1936–1981), who himself was influenced by Satie and Cage, can take the simplest of tonal materials but arrange them so as to undermine tonal music's onward momentum, as in *Lento* (1991) for orchestra by Howard Skempton (1947–). Another possibility is the "neo-Romanticism" of David Matthews (1943–), who has drawn on Mahler's alternately soaring and plunging lines (as well as TIPPETT's metric flexibility) in his Third Symphony (1985). Finally, an individualist such as John Tavener (1943–) lies outside the current trends, being dragged into the limelight as fashion dictates. Following an early success with the dramatic cantata *The Whale* (1966) at a Proms performance in 1968, a period of relative neglect has been succeeded by another Proms success, the ecstatic *Protecting Veil* (1987) for cello and strings, which has recently achieved something of a cult status.

Trevor Bray

Bibliography

Howes, Frank Stewart. *The English Musical Renaissance.* 1966.

Pirie, Peter J. *The English Musical Renaissance.* 1979.

Stradling, Robert, and Meirion Hughes. *The English Musical Renaissance 1860–1940: Construction and Deconstruction.* 1993.

Trend, Michael J. *The Music Makers.* 1985.

Compton-Burnett, Ivy (1884–1969)

The author of twenty novels, Ivy Compton-Burnett was a technical innovator and a devastatingly witty critic of the Christianized, patriarchal morality perpetuated in the novel proper.

After her first novel, *Dolores* (1911), an uneven parody of George Eliot, Compton-Burnett forged an original narrative technique in her subsequent nineteen works by writing the dialogue or dramatic novel, consisting primarily of conversation and of minimal commentary by a narrator. In 1925 *Pastors and Masters,* her first experiment in extended dialogue and her only novel set in contemporary times, was published to puzzled or awestruck reviews. After turning to the late Victorian and Edwardian country gentry as her chosen subject and setting, she brought to maturity her original voice and form in her third novel, *Brothers and Sisters* (1929), a tragi-comedy of inadvertent incest. Although all of her novels after *Dolores* are remarkably consistent in quality, perhaps the novels of her middle period best exhibit the searingly acute rationality that she trains on family life and human relations, as in the profoundly disturbing *Elders and Betters* (1943), a family drama of inter-generational carnage in which the wicked appear to flourish, and in *Manservant and Maidservant* (1947), in which children, a wife, a younger brother, and a servant strive to outwit and overthrow a family tyrant. Her later novels, including *A Father and his Fate* (1957) and *A God and his Gifts* (1963) became even more astringently dialogic as she continued to pare away extraneous exposition. In 1967, near the end of her long life, she was named Dame Commander of the Order of the British Empire. *The Last and the First,* probably her most conventionally optimistic novel because of the triumph of a wise and benevolent heroine over a tyrannical stepmother, was left unfinished at her death, pieced together from notebooks, and published posthumously in 1971.

A troubled family history provided her with much of the material and motivation for her fiction. The daughter of a renowned but controversial homeopathic doctor and an imperious mother, Compton-Burnett was born in Pinner, Middlesex and educated at home with her brothers in Greek and Latin, later receiving a degree in classics at Royal Holloway College in 1906. Her young womanhood was blighted by the FIRST WORLD WAR and a series of family tragedies— the death of her father, her two brothers, her mother, and the apparent double suicide of two younger sisters. After several years of emotional and physical prostration, Compton Burnett emerged as a distinctive novelist with *Pastors and Masters.* By setting up a quiet, orderly, but sociable life with the furniture expert, Margaret Jourdain, her companion for several decades and a member of the declining gentry about which she wrote, Compton-Burnett was able to draw upon her turbulent early life and produce a novel almost every two years.

Earlier assessments of Compton-Burnett's novels, while frequently laudatory, have been limited by a cultural resistance to Compton-Burnett's perspective as a woman writer who relentlessly satirizes hierarchical myth-making as institutionalized in the language that constructs religion, literature, the family, and society. Many readers have been daunted by the difficulty of her style, committed as it is almost exclusively to dialogue characterized by formal but simple diction and syntax and abundant clichés and aphorisms, but rendered complex by virtue of its unremittingly ironic tone. As suggested by her most clear-sighted characters, Compton-Burnett's novels propose the heretical views that God is "one of the best-drawn characters in fiction," that "the sight of duty does make one shiver . . . The actual doing of it would kill one, I think," that "there is horror in every heart, and a resolve never to be honest with anyone else," and that "we only oppress the weak." However, the novels also suggest that if we acknowledge sharing this flawed human nature, "to know all is to forgive all," and that through insight and intelligence, human beings can grow in tolerance and charity. Because Compton-Burnett's expansive moral perspective has been persistently misread as cynical, pessimistic, or deterministic, and because her dialogue technique has proven hard to imitate, her novels continue to be regarded as apart from the mainstream British novel. But Henry James's *The Awkward Age* is one of Compton-Burnett's predecessors; and Ronald Firbank, CHRISTOPHER ISHERWOOD, and MURIEL SPARK make similar exclusive use of dialogue in their notable novels.

Kathy Justice Gentile

Bibliography

Baldanza, Frank. *Ivy Compton-Burnett*. 1964.

Burkhart, Charles, ed. *The Art of I. Compton-Burnett: A Collection of Critical Essays*. 1972.

Gentile, Kathy Justice. *Ivy Compton-Burnett*. 1991.

Liddell, Robert. *The Novels of Ivy Compton-Burnett*. 1955.

Spurling, Hilary. *Ivy: The Life of I. Compton-Burnett*. 1984.

Conrad, Joseph (1857–1924)

Although probably the major English novelist between the Victorian and High Modern periods, Joseph Conrad [Jozef Teodor Konrad Korzeniowski], because of his Polish origins, densely formal style, and idiosyncratic tragic sense, is also an anomaly in the English tradition. His work has an enormous range of geographical settings—Malaysia, London, the Congo, South America, Russia. His mixed style fuses semi-popular romanticism, like that of Marryat's sea stories or KIPLING's colonial fiction, to political psychology, difficult syntax, deep moral skepticism, and intricate irony in the line of Flaubert, Turgenev, and James.

Conrad's father, Apollo Korzeniowski, was a gifted, volatile member of the Polish *szlachta* (or free gentry), whose literary work included translations from English (Shakespeare and Dickens), original plays, and political tracts. When he was arrested in 1862 for his political activism, his wife and four year old son went with him into forced exile in Russia. There Conrad's mother died of tuberculosis; his father died in Cracow when Conrad was eleven. The political-domestic themes, the scathingly ironic tone, and the even more caustic "sub-ironic"—Conrad's own term—bitterness in much of Conrad's storytelling may derive in part from these early deaths of his parents. He was, however, steered fussily and generously toward adulthood by his middle-class uncle Tadeusz Bobrowski.

For whatever reasons, the adolescent Conrad, no scholar, insisted on leaving Poland to become a sailor. Shipping out first from Marseilles and then England, he went to Malaysia, Borneo, Venezuela, and the Congo, among other places. As a twenty-eight year old foreigner he passed the English Master Mariner's examination in 1886—he later drew the scene of the examination in bold relief in *A Personal Record* (1912) as an instance of stern but benign bureaucracy. During this period his bilingual letters to Mme. Poradowska, a distant relative, express his pessimism and toy with mechanistic metaphors for the description of a brutal world. His "Up-river Book" (1890), kept while captain of the Congo steamer *Roi des Belges,* is a navigational notebook on the river, and is non-literary. Conrad had to overcome odds to gain British citizenship and status, among them the disapproval of those in Poland who regarded him as a deserter of his country.

In his late thirties chronic illness from his Congo voyage, along with belated marriage, decided Conrad to leave the sea and risk a novelist's career in English, his third or even fourth language. The first years of the writing career and the last of the sea life dovetail. *Almayer's Folly* (1895) and *An Outcast of the Islands* (1896) study mediocrity, isolation, and failure abroad in miserable "outposts"; the early, deservedly famous sea tales insist on the tedious, domesticated, laborious work-lives of sailors. With *The Nigger of the "Narcissus"* (1897), partly a study of crowd psychology, partly an analysis with Schopenhauerean and Nietzschean overtones of the limits of sympathy, Conrad broke through to a highly structured, formal, political-aesthetic style. That style owed something to collaborations on gradiloquent pulp novels with FORD MADOX [Hueffer] FORD, who accurately attributed to Conrad a supreme gift for the "architectonics" of fiction. Some of the ironic devices Conrad and Ford worked out together—delayed recognitions, sense impressions treated in stark isolation from each other, craftily scrambled time sequences, layered ironies of reported speech, studied non-answering in dialogue—were to influence later writers like VIRGINIA WOOLF and William Faulkner.

In Conrad, however, direct drawing of material labor governs the entire narrative, from events down to syntax, much more than in Ford, or for that matter in any other High Modernist. Persistent attention, for example, to the variety of breath-sounds—laughter, snores, whispers, coughs, and grunts—of the *Narcissus'* sailors links their bodies to the fact that the sailing ship itself depends for movement on the air of the material physical world. In *Heart of Darkness* (1899) a collective obsession with ivory, and in *Nostromo* (1904) an obsession with the silver of the national mine, lead to similar highly complex social organization around one material sign treated both as real and symbolic.

Conradian characterization is often founded on paradox and self-deception. The Black man aboard the "Narcissus," Jimmy Wait, believes himself to be a malingerer who is duping the rest of the ship by pretending to be ill, and turns out against his desperate denial to be in fact dying. This simple "knot"—pretending to oneself to pretend to others to be dying—is a typical structure of illusion in Conrad. By the end of the story, in addition, Wait also seems to stand not only for the fear of death but for the historically repressed memory of the slave trade, in process of being buried. This indefinite shadow of a political theme of slavery inside the inspired study of the sea, of the senses, and of a collective narcissistic fear of death is typical of the "problem" of Conrad: is he only a conservative moral psychologist or also a radically political psychologist?

Heart of Darkness employed the device Russian critics call *skaz:* a narrator inevitably tells more about himself than his ostensible subject. The mass death of African laborers in the Belgian Congo is made a journalistically real memoir, at the same time as it is a study in prose chiaroscuro. It begins the drawing of racial murder in modern literature. The story has recently been both attacked as racist and defended for its critique of racism. The narrator, Marlow—also a narrator in *Lord Jim* (1900), another work on later colonialism's intersection with personal illusions—observes the contrast between degraded managerial bureaucracy in the Congo and the grandiose insane imperialism of the famous character Kurtz.

Conrad's middle period saw the production of three clearly political novels. *Nostromo,* Conrad's "largest canvas," engages the theme of political psychology amidst pathetic revolutionary politics in a composite South American country. *The Secret Agent* (1907), Conrad's most burlesque tragedy, centers on Winnie Verloc, a Londoner who unwittingly marries a triple agent to secure a safe home for her idiot brother. In the novel's crisis she learns that her pathetic brother has been blown to bits carrying explosives in a mission to blow up Greenwich Observatory—perhaps in ef-

fect to destroy Time itself. (This "outrageous" story was adapted by ALFRED HITCHCOCK in the film *Saboteur.*) The last of the political novels, *Under Western Eyes* (1911) daringly rewrites *Crime and Punishment* in a more opportunistic, flat, and skeptical key, and is a remarkable modern exercise in belligerent revision of a literary predecessor.

During the First World War the Conrads worried about their son Borys in the war, while Conrad's craft became more deftly perfunctory and more saleable. *Chance* (1913) and *Victory* (1915) were his first books to sell well. The war seemed to him to confirm warnings he had made in such pieces as "Autocracy and War" (1905) about German and Russian sociology as seen from his Polish-English perspective. In his political views, Conrad assimilates the liberal traditions of the Polish *szlachta* class and of English constitutionalism to a virtually Hobbesian temperamental belief in the presence everywhere, not least in language and dialogue, of direct force as well as of subtler forms of coercion.

Some biographers define Conrad as having had three lives: the Polish youth, the French-English sailor, the English novelist. Conrad said he saw an intentional unity in his life, a movement towards England and writing. The different Conrads pictured since his death include the sea writer; the existential modernist and inventor of new degrees—zero of loneliness; the aesthetic-formalist-symbolist; the major ironist; the radical skeptic; the political novelist; the polyglot predicter of English's status now as a language inflected by non-native speakers. His works have survived interpretive storms a bit in the manner of his own taciturn, rigid sea captains. His greatest work fuses aesthetic and political themes with extraordinary tragic force and precise prose craftmanship.

Aaron Fogel

Bibliography

Fogel, Aaron. *Coercion to Speak: Conrad's Poetics of Dialogue.* 1985.

Karl, Frederick R. *Joseph Conrad: The Three Lives.* 1979.

Najder, Zdzislaw. *Joseph Conrad.* 1983.

Conscientious Objection

Historical examples abound, especially in the literature of certain Christian pacifist sects, of individuals refusing, even in the face of persecution, imprisonment, or death, to engage in military activities on the plea that conscience would not allow them to fight and kill fellow human beings. As a principle of British law, however, conscientious objection to military service is of recent derivation, initially recognized in a hastily-drafted clause to the Military Service (No.2) Act (1916), Britain's first comprehensive CONSCRIPTION measure. During the FIRST WORLD

WAR confusion over the meaning of this so-called "conscience clause" and inadequate administrative machinery for its enforcement created serious difficulties for both individual conscientious objectors (COs) and for the government which had attempted to make provision for them. The fact that the injustices and abuses imposed upon COs during the First World War were evoked to prevent their repetition in the Second was one of the shining victories for civil liberties and common decency in twentieth-century Britain.

The first conscience clause incorporated into British statute law was not concerned with the refusal to participate in warfare but with religious and medical objections to compulsory vaccination. Provisions of the Vaccination Act (1898) allowed exemption if parents could convince two justices that they believed vaccination to be harmful to the health of their children. In 1907 the government amended this procedure to permit exemption by means of a statutory declaration under oath. But while conscientious objection had thus been established as a legal principle before the imposition of conscription, the original procedures for establishing the *bona fides* of objectors proved to be inadequate for a society at war.

When Prime Minister H.H. ASQUITH decided in late 1915 that both military and political necessity had made compulsory military service inevitable, several LIBERAL members of his coalition CABINET expressed serious reservations about conscription; one of them, SIR JOHN SIMON, resigned in protest. Fearing that Simon might try to organize resistance in the House of Commons, Asquith hastily inserted a clause into the proposed Military Service Bill which recognized the right of exemption from military service "on the ground of a conscientious objection to bearing arms." Whatever Asquith's original motives for the inclusion of a conscience clause, his refusal thereafter to limit the right of conscientious objection to members of certain religious bodies which had traditionally opposed war established an important legal precedent. Despite the argument of many CONSERVATIVE politicians and most military officers that non-religious exemption would open a Pandora's box of unpatriotic and even subversive political resistance, Asquith held fast to the position that moral or intellectual as well as religious objections could be acknowledged as legitimate. Thus broadly interpreted, the British conscience clause became a pioneering model whose generous provisions were not matched in most other countries, including the United States, for half a century. Still, this vaunted reputation was only established after a number of sincere conscientious objectors had suffered considerable injustice or abuse.

Most problems in implementing provisions for conscientious objection during the First World War arose from the ambiguity of wording in the conscience clause and from the deficiency of the administrative machinery created to enforce it. When the act was introduced, statements by government spokesmen seemed to imply that while COs would be exempt from combatant service, they would be required, and for the most part would be willing, to "do something"—civilian work of "national importance" at the very least—in support of the war effort. This was a serious miscalculation which would cause no end of trouble. The burden of dealing with the question first fell upon members of local tribunals who were asked to judge the worthiness of applications for exemption filed in their districts. Few of the local citizens sitting on these voluntary bodies had either administrative experience or judicial training. Yet they were asked to sit in judgment of all pleas for exemption, including ill-health, serious economic hardship, and essential civilian occupation as well as conscientious objection, and to make the appropriate determination in each case. Their task was made doubly difficult by the murky directives from the Home Office and by the presence of a military representative who acted as a sort of devil's advocate on behalf of the ARMY, questioning the authenticity of nearly every applicant, especially conscientious objectors.

Between early 1916 and the end of the war over 16,000 men applied for exemption on the basis of conscientious objection. Local tribunals were expected to determine whether a CO's objections were genuine and, if so, whether his exemption should be absolute, temporary, or conditional upon his engagement in some form of military or civilian alternative service. Most COs received an exemption which satisfied their objection, but around 6,000 either declined to recognize the tribunals, refused to accept the kind of exemption they were granted, or were judged "not genuine".

At first, non-exempted conscientious objectors who did not respond to call-up orders were arrested by the police and, after a local court appearance, handed over to the military authorities. Once in military hands, COs were generally court-martialled for refusing to obey orders and sentenced to confinement in military prisons where they continued to be subject to the military discipline. After several sensational and highly publicized incidents in which COs were severely ill-treated while under military control, the army, anxious to be rid of a vexatious problem, issued Order X which provided that court-martialled COs be handed over to civil authorities for the execution of their sentences. The government, no less concerned than the army about filling the prisons with a new species of political prisoner, tried to accommodate objectors through the creation of the so-called Home Office Scheme which established work centers where COs were housed and given "civilian work under civilian control." Over 4,000 objectors availed themselves of this alternative to prison, but, in the end, the Scheme proved to be troublesome for the authorities, unsatisfactory for the COs, and unpopular with the public. Still, difficulties surrounding the Home Office Scheme were as nothing compared to the imbroglio created by 1,300 "absolutist" conscientious objectors who, as a result of their refusal to accept any compromise short of total exemption, were subjected to repeated sentences at hard labor for what was literally, although not technically, the same offense. Some of these individuals were stupidly or brutally treated, and a few died or became seriously ill as a result of their ordeal. Publicity arising from these exceptional cases, skillfully disseminated by war resistance groups, especially the No-Conscription Fellowship, caused the government embarrassment and exasperation far out of proportion to the number of individuals involved.

Eventually, after the socially-prominent Margaret Hobhouse had appealed to both Cabinet ministers and public opinion to secure the release of her absolutist son Stephen, a few seriously-ill absolutists, including Stephen Hobhouse and Clifford Allen, Chairman of the No-Conscription Fellowship, were released from prison through a special dispensation, but critics claimed that the government was merely resurrecting the old "Cat and Mouse" ploy used against suffragettes. Most absolutists refused to cooperate with any scheme for the mitigation of their sentences and were released only after the war ended, many of them in a seriously debilitated condition.

The story of conscientious objectors was one of the most irksome and least edifying chapters in the history of the Great War, but it was not entirely futile. Even before the war ended, administrative changes had been introduced which took the military establishment entirely out of the recruiting process. These reforms did not affect the treatment of COs before 1918, but they were a direct response to the difficulties that had been encountered in handling cases of conscientious objection. When compulsory military service was re-introduced in 1939, other changes, enacted to ensure that the worst problems and abuses of the Great War were not repeated, brought efficacious results. For one thing, after 1939 local tribunals were appointed by the Ministry of Labour and National Service, and their membership included individuals with legal training and experience. Furthermore, these

bodies, which dealt exclusively with conscientious objectors, were guided by clear and explicit directions allowing for various forms of exemption, including absolute exemption.

In practice, the choice for the nearly 60,000 COs who appeared before tribunals during Second World War was between conditional exemption on agreement to take up work of national importance under civilian control or entrance into military service as a non-combatant. There were, inevitably, cases of injustice or ill-treatment, but incidents of serious abuse were rare, and the ability of tribunals to provide a satisfactory exemption to most COs is clearly demonstrated by the fact that only 10 percent of Second World War objectors served any time in prison as compared with nearly one-third between 1914 and 1918. Improved machinery and sensible procedures were not the only reasons for the more efficient, and more humane, treatment of COs during the Second World War. Individuals on both sides of the issue made a significant difference. For the government, Ernest Bevin, Minister of Labour and National Service from 1940, showed sense and sensitivity in dealing with conscientious objectors, and the Central Board For Conscientious Objectors (CBCO), which acted on behalf of COs, generally cooperated with the state, unlike the resolutely hostile No-Conscription Fellowship during the Great War. An awareness of the worse problems and abuses of the First World War and a determination not to repeat them allowed Great Britain to set a standard for the treatment of conscientious objectors during Second World War that has never been surpassed and rarely equalled.

Thomas C. Kennedy

Bibliography
Barker, Rachel. Conscience, Government and War: Conscientious Objection in Great Britain, 1939–45. 1982.
Boulton, David. Objection Overruled. 1967.
Graham, John W. Conscription and Conscience: A History 1916–1919. 1922.
Kennedy, Thomas C. "Public Opinion and the Conscientious Objector, 1914–1919," Journal of British Studies, vol. 12 (1973), pp. 105–19.
Rae, John. Conscience and Politics: The British Government and the Conscientious Objector to Military Service, 1916–1919. 1970.

Conscription

Mandatory service (conscription) to raise military forces was unused in Britain after the end of the wars against the French Revolution and Napoleon. In the century that followed Britain relied upon a great fleet and a small professional volunteer army to police her worldwide Empire and protect her interests. The Crimean War, the Boer War, as well as numerous small imperial conflicts throughout the nineteenth century were all fought with volunteer forces. While by the early twentieth century there was a small pro-conscription movement in Britain—led by Field-Marshal Lord Roberts, hero of the Boer War, and his National Service League—it never succeeded in convincing either Parliament or the nation of the need for mandatory service.

The FIRST WORLD WAR, a conflict of unexpected size and scope, changed the way in which Britain raised her armies. The nature of that conflict—trench warfare punctuated by massive frontal assaults—required huge numbers of troops, and virtually the entire high command of the British ARMY and a growing number of politicians had by this time come to see compulsory military service as the only way to raise sufficient manpower for the Western Front once voluntary enlistments dropped off drastically after mid-1915. Conscription, however, was not popular among large elements of the public and many members of the LIBERAL PARTY who were supporters of the ASQUITH coalition government. As a stopgap measure either to gain the needed men or to prove the inadequacy of voluntarism, Asquith supported the so-called "Derby Scheme" (named for the seventeenth Earl of Derby, who chaired the effort) in the autumn of 1915 to exhort men voluntarily to "attest" that they would serve when called. Inadequate numbers came forward, and Asquith, caught between his anti-compulsion Liberal supporters and the determined pro-compulsion Tories who were angered by the troop shortage, brought in Britain's first mandatory service bill in January 1916. The law (the "bachelor's bill") applied only to unmarried men between the ages of eighteen and forty-one, and continued inadequate intake of men forced, in May, a general conscription bill which included married men.

Asquith's government fell in December, to be replaced by another coalition under the more energetic LLOYD GEORGE. The manpower problems of the British army on the Western Front were not overcome simply by the application of conscription, and, before the end of the war, further legislation was passed increasing the age of liability to conscription to age fifty and applying mandatory service to previously exempted Ireland. The Easter Rising of 1916 made its enforcement in Ireland virtually impossible, but even consideration of the possibility demonstrates the desperation of the government.

Britain's experience with conscription in the First World War offered a valuable lesson: during the seventeen months during which unrestricted voluntarism raised Britain's first army of continental size, many men possessed of the skills needed for the production of necessary military and export goods were gratefully enlisted by the army. Therefore, if conscription were to prove useful, it would have to be implemented at the outset of any prolonged struggle in order to allow the state the power to discriminate among men of military age, based upon their usefulness to the national war effort.

Another point worth noting is this: Britain was a liberal democracy with no tradition of mandatory military service, and, as a result, there were sizable minorities in the population who objected on moral, religious, or political grounds to the implementation of such legislation. This created the need to deal with large numbers of CONSCIENTIOUS OBJECTORS. Special regional tribunals had to be created throughout the nation with the power to exempt inductees from military service for reasons of conscience. Mandatory military service in Britain ceased in April 1920, and the army was demobilized. Thereafter there was no thought of peacetime compulsion: the idea was unpopular among the electorate, there was a general perception in and outside of government circles that Britain had no enemies to fear for the immediate future, and, finally, the military costs could be better spent on other needs in a time of tight budgets.

During the 1920s Britain was the only European power to disarm as promised at the peace conference. By 1935, with war raging in Asia and with Germany rearming openly in defiance of the treaty of Versailles, the British government announced modest steps toward rearmament. With Nazi Germany seen as the greatest and closest threat, the issue of conscription was again raised, though the three successive Prime Ministers of the so-called National government in the 1930s, RAMSAY MACDONALD, STANLEY BALDWIN, and NEVILLE CHAMBERLAIN all opposed its imposition.

By 1938, with Hitler threatening to annex the Sudetenland, Britain's French allies were pressuring Chamberlain to impose conscription. He opposed it, both for industrial and military purposes, as he felt it essentially inefficient and disruptive to labor-capital relations. The ultimate failure of the MUNICH CONFERENCE to satiate Hitler convinced many—if not the Prime Minister—that national organization both of industry and the military would be necessary for the war which was likely to come.

As the demand intensified for labor for munitions (especially aircraft) factories long understaffed during the years of disarmament and for volunteers for the increasing armed services, it became clear that voluntarism would once again be unable to supply the men—and ultimately women—needed. By April 1939 Chamberlain acquiesced and a modest conscription bill was introduced—the first peacetime law of its kind in modern times. It called only for only six months service for young men aged twenty and twenty-one.

War came in September 1939, and the liability of men to military service was broadened. WINSTON CHURCHILL and his all-party War Cabinet brought in even more precedent shattering legislation: in June a bill was passed which made all persons and property liable for wartime service. In March 1941 the "Essential Work Order" issued under this legislation gave the Minister of Labor and National Service, ERNEST BEVIN, the power to regulate and retrain labor as it was needed for the war effort. By the end of 1941 more than ninety percent of males between the ages of fourteen and sixty-four were either in the military or working in industry, and more hands were needed. Hence, in December the government responded with legislation which subjected all persons, regardless of sex, between the ages of eighteen and fifty years to some form of national service. At least in theory, the state had taken compulsory powers over the entire adult population.

In practice, industrial conscription was applied with great restraint and, in the main, was successful. In comparison to the First World War, trades disputes were fewer and less harmful to munitions production. By the close of the War Britain had almost 5 million men under arms, and her industrial establishments continued to be more productive than would have been predicted by even the greatest optimist in pre-war years. Conscientious objection continued throughout this war, too, though it attracted far less attention and drew less public support—and a number of the best known anti-conscriptionists of the 1914–18 conflict joined the war effort against Fascism.

Military conscription continued in Britain until 1962. Since then all British forces have been raised through voluntary enlistment.

R.J.Q. Adams

Bibliography

Adams, R.J.Q., and Philip P. Poirier. *The Conscription Controversy in Great Britain, 1900–18.* 1987.

Dennis, Peter. *Decision by Default: Peacetime Conscription and British Defense, 1919–1939.* 1972.

Hayes, Denis. *Conscription Conflict.* 1949.

Kennedy, Thomas C. *The Hound of Conscience: A History of the No-Conscription Fellowship, 1914–1919.* 1981.

Conservative Party

(Known as the Unionist Party c. 1895–1925; often referred to as the Tory Party, a name deriving from its eighteenth century origins).

The Conservative Party has been the principal force on the right of center in British politics since it emerged in its modern form during the first half of the nineteenth century. Despite periodic crises and divisions, the party has remained remarkably cohesive. No space has been left for any potential rivals on the right, a fact illustrated by the failure both of the BRITISH UNION OF FASCISTS in the 1930s and of the NATIONAL FRONT in the 1970s to draw off any significant amount of Conservative rank and file support. While rifts have occurred within the Conservative Party in Parliament and leaders have been overthrown, internal warfare has rarely been allowed to benefit opposing parties. In times of crisis the party instinctively draws together and rallies round the leader: a cliché of the period is that "loyalty is the Conservative Party's secret weapon". The foremost aim and function of the party is the winning of power, as much to prevent government falling into the hands of the Liberal or Labour Parties as to implement any specific Conservative program. In this the Conservatives have been spectacularly successful: since the Home Rule crisis of 1886 they have governed, either alone or as the predominant partner in a coalition ministry, for all but 37 years.

The party's electoral strength rests upon two foundations. In the first place, it has had the support of almost the whole of the upper class and of a large majority of the middle class. Middle-class support for the Conservatives grew after 1867, and increased still further with each of the three major rifts in the LIBERAL PARTY, which until 1918 was its principal opponent. The first of these was the Liberal split over Ireland in 1886, which led to a Conservative alliance with the splinter group of Liberal Unionists. Liberal Unionist leaders served in the CABINET in 1895–1905, and their group formally merged with the Conservatives in 1912: from this junction dates the present full official name of Conservative and Unionist Party. Second were the Liberal divisions during and after the FIRST WORLD WAR, and third the Liberal splits after the crisis of 1931, which culminated in the absorption of the National Liberal followers of SIR JOHN SIMON in the Woolton-Teviot pact of 1948. Conservative middle-class support had been traditionally centered upon the CHURCH OF ENGLAND, but as a result of these changes the middle class came to embrace many Nonconformists as well. However, even before the 1918 Reform Act this middle-class support would never have been enough on its own to win general elections.

The second factor on which Conservative electoral success has been based was the support of a very large number of working-class voters. Indeed, until 1945 it is clear that more working-class voters supported the Conservatives than the LABOUR PARTY, which from the early 1920s had displaced the Liberals as the alternative governing party on the left. The reasons for this voting behavior are not solely explicable in negative terms or by a simplistic concept of deference toward social superiors, though these factors may have played their part. The Conservative Party was always the party most sympathetic toward agriculture and to the self-employed, whether artisan, craftsman, shopkeeper, or small businessman. In addition they had a less puritanical approach to working-class lifestyles than Liberals and Labour on issues ranging from temperance reform at the beginning of the century to the sometimes unwelcome intrusions of the WELFARE STATE in the 1980s. Finally, the Conservatives were adept at exploiting national patriotism and pride, especially during Britain's period as an imperial and world power until the 1950s. Since then, accommodation to decline has produced a series of traumas for the party from the fiasco of the SUEZ CRISIS to the difficulties of membership of the EUROPEAN COMMUNITY, only briefly enlivened by the success of the FALKLANDS WAR of 1982. The success of the Conservative Party has often been partly attributed to the support it has attracted from women voters from all classes. Since 1918 WOMEN have provided a very large proportion of the party's local membership and its most active voluntary workers, although the parliamentary party has remained a mainly male preserve, and also exclusively a middle- and upper-class one.

The strength of the party organization has contributed both to its cohesion and to its electoral success. The Conservative Party organization has always had a powerful reputation, although its financial resources and its efficiency have often been exaggerated, not least by its opponents. The party organization consists of two complementary elements. The National Union (founded in 1867) is the representative body of the rank and file, with one recognized local association affiliated in each constituency. There is a regional tier, with England and Wales divided into 12 provincial areas: Scotland had its own separate structures. The National Union has an Executive which meets regularly, a Central Council (similar to but smaller than the Conference), and an Annual Conference. The National Union has influence but little formal power: policy is settled by the party leader, and the leader is selected by the parliamentary party. The second element in the organization are the professional salaried officials. At the national level these are located in the Conservative Central Office (founded in 1870), which is responsible to and directly controlled by the leader. Central Office provides a range of services to the leadership and MPs, but its primary role is to support the efforts

of local associations to win elections. The Conservatives' greatest asset has always been their extensive network of full-time trained local agents, which are employed by the individual local parties and not by the Central Office. The doctrine of local autonomy is paramount and jealously protected: the Central Office influences but does not dictate to the local branches. The ideal of an agent in each constituency was never attained, but the Conservatives have always had many more such agents than their rivals. However, their number has declined from 506 in 1959 to below 230 in 1994.

There have been three significant periods of reorganization since 1900, each responding either to defeat or to change in the electoral system. The first of these followed from the reverses of 1906 and 1910, which led to the establishment of the Unionist Organisation Committee in 1911. Under its recommendations the Chief Whip was relieved of the task of overseeing the party machinery outside Parliament, and a new position of Chairman of the Party Organisation, to be appointed by the leader, was established. The first such Chairman, Sir Arthur Steel-Maitland (1876–1935), modernized the organization in the period 1911–14. The second period of change followed from the provisions of the Reform Act of 1918. J.C.C. Davidson (1889–1970), Party Chairman 1926–30, gave a high priority to the development of branches for women and for working-class trade unionist members. The third period of reassessment followed the decline of the party machine during the Second World War and the defeat of 1945. Between 1946 and 1951 Central Office was reorganized, and large sums were raised under the energetic chairmanship of LORD WOOLTON. At the same time the Maxwell-Fyfe Committee (1949) recommended reforms in the National Union, in particular limiting the payments which constituencies had formerly expected from their candidates. Since the 1950s organizational developments have been of a minor but continual nature. Throughout the century the Conservatives have been the pioneers in political organization and in campaigning techniques, and have made innovative use of new media and technology from cinema vans to computerization.

The history of the Conservative Party since 1900 can be divided into several phases. The first of these was the period of defeat and disunity from 1900 to 1914. Under the leadership of Lord Salisbury (1830–1903) the Unionist coalition won a second successive victory in 1900, but the party's fortunes swiftly declined after ARTHUR BALFOUR succeeded his uncle in 1902. The principal cause of the problems of the following decade was the policy of TARIFF REFORM, first raised in 1903 by the second most powerful figure in the ministry, Joseph Chamberlain (1836–1914). His proposals to draw the British Empire closer together through IMPERIAL PREFERENCE captured the hearts and minds of the Conservative rank and file. However, tariff reform proved to be extremely divisive. It was opposed by a small group of free traders among the MPs and senior ministers. More seriously, it was a disastrous vote loser in urban areas, due to working-class fears that "food taxes" on cheap imported basics would raise the cost of living. Pragmatists in the party therefore sought to drop the commitment to full preference, leading to bitter conflicts with its "whole-hog" supporters. The internal divisions which resulted led to a Cabinet crisis in 1903 and largely contributed to three successive electoral defeats in 1906 and January and December 1910. The party was further divided over resistance to the Liberal government's Parliament Act (1911), and in 1911 Balfour resigned the leadership. His unexpected successor, ANDREW BONAR LAW, restored party morale with a series of vigorous attacks upon the government, especially in support of ULSTER's case during the passage of the Irish Home Rule Bill from 1912 to 1914.

The First World War transformed the position of the Conservative Party. As the "patriotic" party its advocacy of vigorous prosecution of the war led to increased popularity, and it also benefited from the splits and eventual decline of the Liberal Party. The Conservatives joined a coalition ministry under the Liberal Prime Minister H.H. ASQUITH in May 1915. This proved to be an unhappy arrangement, and in the crisis of December 1916 Bonar Law gave Conservative backing to the claims of DAVID LLOYD GEORGE. Although a Liberal, Lloyd George shared the Conservatives' priorities over the war effort, and his coalition of 1916–22 was a stronger and more cohesive government. When the war was won in 1918, Lloyd George was at the height of his popularity, and Bonar Law readily agreed that the coalition should be continued into peacetime to grapple with the problems of reconstruction. However, after economic depression and failures of policy in 1920 and 1921 the continuation of the coalition became increasingly unpopular amongst Conservative MPs and local activists. In March 1921 Bonar Law resigned for reasons of health, to be replaced by AUSTEN CHAMBERLAIN. Chamberlain was an inflexible and autocratic Leader, thought by his followers too closely committed to Lloyd George. The revolt from below against the coalition culminated in defeat for Chamberlain at a meeting of Conservative MPs, which he convened at the Carlton Club on 19 October 1922. Bonar Law led the victorious rebels, and thus ousted both Chamberlain as Party Leader and Lloyd George as Prime Minister.

The fall of the coalition was the formative event in Conservative politics between the wars. It marked a decision to return to normal party politics, with Labour replacing the Liberals as the main opposition. The events of 1922 also brought to the fore a group of anti-coalitionist junior ministers who were dominate in the leadership until 1940. The most important of these was STANLEY BALDWIN, who replaced the dying Bonar Law as Leader and as Prime Minister in May 1923. Despite leading his party into an unnecessary defeat in the December 1923 election and a serious assault upon his position between 1929 and 1931, Baldwin remained leader until 1937. Espousing a brand of moderate Conservatism and epitomizing traditional English virtues, he attracted widespread popular support. As a result of this and of the Liberal-Labour rivalry, the Conservative Party dominated the inter-war decades. Between 1918 and 1945 they were the largest party in the House of Commons for all but two and a half years. In the crisis of August 1931 they agreed to serve under RAMSAY MACDONALD in a National government in which they were by far the largest element. In 1935 Baldwin replaced Mac-Donald as Prime Minister, and in 1937 he handed on both the premiership and the Conservative leadership to NEVILLE CHAMBERLAIN. His period as leader was dominated by controversy over foreign policy, and his policy of APPEASEMENT led to the resignation of the Foreign Secretary, ANTHONY EDEN and to clashes with the group of anti-appeasers led by Eden and WINSTON CHURCHILL. Chamberlain exerted a much closer grip over the party than Baldwin had done, and while his policy appeared successful his critics were almost dragooned out of the party in the winter of 1938. However, the outbreak of war left Chamberlain discredited. After a substantial rebellion by Conservative backbench MPs in the Norway debate of 8–9 May 1940, he was forced to resign the premiership to Churchill. He remained party leader until declining health led to his resignation in October 1940, when Churchill was elected without opposition in his place. However, even the great war leader's prestige could not prevent the party receiving popular condemnation for the failures of the 1930s at home and abroad, and thus its second decisive defeat during this century in the 1945 general election.

The period in opposition to the 1945–51 Labour government saw the Conservatives not only energetically reorganizing but also engaged in a fundamental reappraisal of philosophy and policy. As a result, between the late 1940s and the early 1970s the Conservatives accepted the three pillars of the post-war consensus: universal free benefits in the welfare state, a role for government intervention in economic matters founded upon Keynesian theories, and some form of partnership in industry between trade unions and employers. Although Churchill remained rather unenthusiastic, these policies enabled the Conservatives to regain power in 1951 and then to remain in office continuously until 1964. The key figures in this period were Eden, who succeeded Churchill in April 1955 but retired after the Suez crisis in January 1957; HAROLD MACMILLAN, Prime Minister and Conservative leader from 1957 until November 1963; and R.A. BUTLER. Butler twice seemed on the brink of becoming Prime Minister, but in 1963 Macmillan manoeuvred to block him on personal grounds, and was instead succeeded by SIR ALEC DOUGLAS-HOME. Macmillan's sudden resignation had actually been due to ill-health, but since 1961 his ministry had been enmeshed by economic stagnation, public scandal, and diplomatic rebuffs. Therefore, by 1963 defeat seemed likely. Although his aristocratic lineage was an easy target for the meritocratic campaign of Labour, Douglas-Home managed to regain some lost ground, and the Conservatives only lost the 1964 general election by a narrow margin.

In August 1965 Douglas-Home stood down, and the first formal party leadership election by a ballot of MPs took place; it was also the first leadership selection while in opposition since that of 1911. The victor was EDWARD HEATH, whose lower middle-class background was thought more publicly acceptable than Macmillan's "Edwardian" style or Douglas-Home's "grouse moor" image. Heath survived the party's loss of further seats to Labour in the 1966 election, but never secured the affection of either the public or of his parliamentary followers. It was to general surprise that despite this and contrary to the opinion polls, he won the 1970 election and became Prime Minister. The failures of the Heath ministry of 1970–74 have been the catharsis of modern Conservatism. The reversals of policy, the failure to control inflation, or contain the trade unions through legislation on industrial relations, and two defeats at the hands of the miners led first to the fall of Heath and second to the rise and development of THATCHERISM. After losing the two elections of February and October 1974, Heath was forced to hold a ballot for the party leadership in February 1975 in which he was defeated by MARGARET THATCHER. Thatcher and Sir Keith Joseph (1918–94) had served in the Heath Cabinet, but since its defeat had raised the standard of a Conservatism founded upon the free market, rolling back government intervention in the economic and social spheres, and

leaving as much as possible to individual initiative. This was the core of Thatcherism, although in the 1980s this also came to stand for a style of government: authoritarian, centralizing, and secretive. Public concern over national economic decline and the power of the trade unions, symbolized in the "winter of discontent" of 1978–9, was receptive to this rejection of the post-war consensus, and led to Conservative victories in the 1979, 1983, and 1987 elections. Thatcher was the dominant personality in both the Conservative Party and national politics throughout the 1980s, and had the fervent support of the rank and file. However, failures in economic policy, the "poll tax", and her divisive approach to Europe led to her failure to win the leadership ballot forced by Michael Heseltine (1933–) in November 1990 by the 15 percent margin necessary under the rules. In the second ballot, JOHN MAJOR emerged as her successor.

Major had been endorsed by Thatcher, but he proved to be a pragmatist. At first this approach enabled him to distance his government from Thatcher's and to follow more popular policies, including abandoning the "poll tax". In the April 1992 election the Conservatives unexpectedly retained office, but with a slim majority of only 20 seats. This margin dwindled away through by-election defeats and defections over the next five years, and left the government dangerously vulnerable to the rebellion of a handful of rebel "Euro-sceptic" MPs. The Major government was beset by a range of problems after 1992. The continuing economic recession hit Conservative support in the south, and accelerated the problem of an aging and dwindling party membership. This had fallen from the peak of 2.8 million in the early 1950s to around 300,000 by 1997, and the decay of the organisation was accompanied by a financial crisis. The party's popularity slumped to record lows in the months after the sterling crisis of "Black Wednesday" in September 1992, and it was tarred with the image of "sleaze" after a series of personal scandals involving Conservative ministers and MPs. Disunity over the European issue became more serious and led to Major calling a leadership election in June 1995 to reimpose his authority. However, the Conservatives entered the May 1997 election damaged, discredited, and visibly divided; the result was a landslide defeat, with only 165 MPs being returned. Major resigned the next day, and the following leadership contest was won comfortably by the youngest candidate, William Hague. During the next four years he moved the party to a more Euro-sceptic position, ruling out joining any common European currency, but failing to capture public support.

Stuart Ball

Bibliography
Ball, Stuart. *The Conservative Party and British Politics 1902–1951.* 1995.
——, ed. *The Conservative Party Since 1945.* 1998.
Charmley, John. *A History of Conservative Politics 1900–1996.* 1996.
Francis, Martin, and Ina Zweiniger-Bargielowska, eds. *The Conservatives and British Society 1880–1990.* 1996.
Norton, Philip, ed. *The Conservative Party.* 1996.
Ramsden, John. *An Appetite for Power: A History of the Conservative Party Since 1830.* 1998.
Seldon, Anthony, and Stuart Ball, eds. *Conservative Century: The Conservative Party Since 1900.* 1994.
——, ed. *How Tory Governments Fall: The Tory Party in Power Since 1783.* 1996.

Cooperative Movement

The Cooperative Movement is a form of association for the purposes of trade, business, or agriculture, involving open membership, democratic control, dividends on purchases, and ownership by the members. The movement effectively began with the Rochdale Society of Equitable Pioneers in 1844 and enjoyed its greatest success in retailing and production. With some 12.5 million members by the 1930s, the movement represents an important aspect of modern British economic and social history.

By the late nineteenth century a federal structure was in place, based on the Co-operative Union (formed 1869) in Manchester, whose annual congress provided policy-making and educational leadership. This task of developing and promoting Cooperative enterprise was taken up in 1991 by the United Kingdom Co-operative Council, comprising twelve national institutions ranging from the Co-operative Wholesale Society (CWS) to the Co-operative Bank.

At its height, between the 1930s and 1950s, the movement owned some 29,000 retail shops, hundreds of factories, a bank, a building society, an insurance company, its own internal newspaper, *Co-operative News*, and, from 1929, a weekly, *Reynolds News*. From the early 1960s to the 1980s, however, there was an accelerating decline caused by factors including attempts to cater for nearly all consumer needs and tastes, the emergence of highly efficient and specialized commercial competitors, and a conservative management. By 1991 the number of societies had fallen to sixty-nine (from a maximum of 1,455 in 1903), with about 5,000 retail outlets. Trade volume stood at £7.333 billion, of which some 62 percent was in foodstuffs, but with significant activity in dairy production, pharmacy, motor trades, and funeral furnishing. Membership stood at 8.1 million. By this time there was clear evidence that the long-term decline had been stopped, following massive reorganization and the introduction of a new chain of superstores in the 1980s.

In the areas of distribution, production, and services, the CWS (established 1863) was dominant, accounting for many of its own products. This had initially been in goods such as footwear and biscuits, but later included insurance (the Co-operative Insurance Society), banking (the Co-operative Bank), and agriculture. In 1991 the CWS accounted for 27 percent of the movement's trade. Apart from the CWS, cooperative production has been insignificant in Britain. The Co-operative Productive Federation was established in 1882 to provide support, and by 1914 there were seventy-three small copartnership enterprises, chiefly in the clothing, footwear and printing trades. These declined to about thirty-five in the early 1970s, when there were several major attempts to promote worker cooperatives. Numerous worker takeovers followed the high level of business failures during and after the 1970s. The Industrial Common Ownership Movement, as it was known, was concentrated in wholefoods, radical bookselling and printing, although collectively employing only about 8,500 workers.

The movement, led by the Co-operative Union, has always been active in the area of education, running, for example, correspondence courses in such subjects as bookkeeping, and establishing the Co-operative College in 1922, based first in Manchester, and, from 1946, at Stanford Hall in Loughborough. Education was also a prime concern of the Guilds, the most significant of which was the Women's Co-operative Guild (WCG) founded in 1883. The WCG, an important pressure group, had 12,809 members in 1900, reached a peak of nearly 90,000 in the late 1930s, but declined to about 6,000 in the early 1990s.

While in theory the Cooperative movement is non-political, the Co-operative Congress decided in 1917 to establish a political arm in an attempt to bring direct influence on government on behalf of the consumer. One Co-operative Party candidate, A.E. Waterson, was elected MP for Kettering in 1918, but he immediately allied himself with the LABOUR PARTY. The fortunes of the two parties have been linked ever since. A formal understanding was reached in 1927, allowing cooperatives to affiliate locally with Labour, and from 1946 sponsored individuals ran as Co-operative and Labour candidates. The number of MPs reached a peak of twenty-three (from thirty-four candidates) in 1945. The credibility of the party was not helped by the defection of four MPs to the Social Democrats in 1981, and in 1983 only eight MPs (out of seventeen sponsored) were elected. In the election of April 1992 fourteen were elected out of twenty-three.

Brian Dyson

Bibliography
Bonner, Arnold. *British Co-operation.* 2nd ed. 1970.
Carbery, Thomas F. *Consumers in Politics.* 1969.
Cole, G.D.H. *A Century of Cooperation.* 1945.
Flanagan, Desmond. *A Centenary Story of the Co-operative Union, 1869–1969.* 1969.
Richardson, William. *The CWS in War and Peace, 1938–1976.* 1977.

Council for the Encouragement of Music and the Arts (CEMA)

The Council for the Encouragement of Music and the Arts, or CEMA as it was generally known, was the first experiment in state sponsorship of the arts and was the immediate forerunner of the ARTS COUNCIL OF GREAT BRITAIN. Launched late in 1939 under the aegis of the Board of Education but with funds from the Pilgrim Trust, CEMA was a direct response to the threat to the arts posed by the coming of the SECOND WORLD WAR. With theatres and concert halls closed in anticipation of bombing and with workers resettled in newly established industrial hostels, often isolated from urban amenities, access to entertainment was severely limited. In addition, the CONSCRIPTION of musicians and actors reduced the ranks of ORCHESTRAS and theatre companies, while restrictions on civilian transport, which made it difficult for groups to tour, eliminated employment opportunities for many artists. As early as September 1939 the Board of Education and the Treasury began to negotiate with a view to providing financial assistance to voluntary organizations involved in adult education. Officials recognized the need to preserve music, drama, and the arts during the emergency and to provide sufficient entertainment to sustain the morale of the civilian population. It was believed essential to show government concern about the cultural life of the country not only to reassure its own people, but for the sake of Britain's image abroad.

An ephemeral organization called the Art and Entertainment Emergency Council, including SIR KENNETH CLARK, who had already initiated lunchtime concerts in the National Gallery and the War Artists' Advisory Committee to employ artists to record the war, appealed to the government to utilize professionals in the arts, but CEMA stemmed instead from negotiations between Thomas Jones, Secretary of the Pilgrim Trust and Lord De La Warr, then President of the Board of Education, in December 1939. De La Warr envisaged a temporary expedient to aid beleaguered cultural pursuits during the emergency by encouraging amateur music and drama and by assisting unemployed performers. The Pilgrim Trust hoped to bolster the effort of voluntary agencies experienced in community arts by means of grants and by dispatching itinerant music and drama organizers to work with amateur groups. While CEMA's earliest policy formulations recognized the need to help unemployed professional artists, the initial orientation was towards amateur and educational activity of a distinctly populist sort, in which professionals might play an auxiliary role, but in which the emphasis would be on popular participation.

Yet even at the outset it was unclear whether the greater availability of culture would mean the provision of entertainment or the stimulation of amateur activity. Alongside the music travelers and drama organizers, CEMA funded concerts in canteens as well as orchestral performances, and by 1940 it began to sponsor tours by Old Vic troupes to Lancashire and South Wales. When the London BLITZ began, CEMA began to dispatch "flying squads" of musicians to air raid shelters, rest centers for the homeless, and, more extensively, to munitions factories, generating a rivalry with ENSA (Entertainments National Service Association). Generally, ENSA concerts featured a more popular genre of entertainment, while CEMA programs consisted mainly of classical music.

The Pilgrim Trust's initial grant of £25,000 was matched in the spring of 1940 by a Treasury grant, and for a time CEMA's funds derived equally from private and public sources. Eventually, however, it became wholly government-funded, and the original private administrative committee was transformed into a larger council appointed by the Board of Education and under its direct supervision. As its structure began to change, so too did its mission, with a shift away from the encouragement of music-making and play-acting by the people themselves to maintaining the highest standards of the arts in wartime and the rendering of assistance to performing artists.

The shift in emphasis from amateur to professional activity accelerated once the Pilgrim Trust withdrew at the beginning of 1942, after increasing its contribution to £50,000, and JOHN MAYNARD KEYNES was appointed as Chairman by the activist President of the Board of Education, R.A. BUTLER. During the four years of Keynes's dynamic leadership, CEMA became less populist, concentrating on quality and professional standards, but equally emphasizing entertainment more than education. Keenly interested in appointments to the Council and its panels, he demanded a high level of financial accountability from sponsored bodies, like the Old Vic and the British Institute of Adult Education. While eager to diffuse the artistic life of the country, he kept a tight reign on CEMA affairs, even when his Treasury responsibilities required lengthy absences in Washington. Keynes reversed the anti-metropolitan bias that dominated CEMA thinking during the Pilgrim Trust's more missionary phase by promoting a London Old Vic season and collaborating with a controversial, tax-exempt commercial company, Tennant Plays.

During Keynes's tenure the annual Treasury grant grew to more than £200,000, the administrative structure of CEMA was overhauled, with the appointment of regional officers in place of the music and drama travelers, and financial arrangements shifted from direct grants to guarantees as a way of encouraging local enterprise to become self-supporting. His aversion to bureaucratic red tape led him to streamline CEMA's often chaotic internal structure: full-time paid directors of music, drama, and art were appointed, and advisory panels were constituted in each of the three areas. At Keynes's instigation CEMA took over the management of the Theatre Royal, Bristol, in 1942 and began the complicated negotiations to restore Covent Garden as the home for a national OPERA and BALLET after the war. From 1943 on he and his colleagues were absorbed in transforming the CEMA into a permanent peacetime organization which would supervise state patronage of the arts. With minor structural changes the renamed Arts Council received a royal charter and began to function in 1946 as an autonomous agency carrying forward the work that CEMA had begun.

During its six years of existence CEMA had demonstrated that the receptivity of the public to the arts exceeded all expectations. By stimulating activity and providing entertainment, it had accomplished its initial goals of salvaging culture, raising morale, and providing employment for distressed professional artists. The Arts Council which replaced it at the end of the war bore the imprint of Keynes's conception of public patronage. His scheme was a compromise between private initiative and state control. Financially dependent on the Treasury, the Arts Council would determine how to appropriate its own funds, free from the intervention of Whitehall or the surveillance of Westminister.

Fred M. Leventhal

Bibliography
Glasgow, Mary. "The Concept of the Arts Council" in Milo Keynes, ed. *Essays on John Maynard Keynes.* 1975. pp. 260 –71.
Hutchison, Robert. *The Politics of the Arts Council.* 1982.
Leventhal, F.M. "'The Best for the Most': CEMA and State Sponsorship of the Arts in Wartime, 1939 – 1945," *Twentieth Century British History,* vol. 1 (1990), pp. 289 –317.
White, Eric Walter. *The Arts Council of Great Britain.* 1975.

Council Housing

Immediately after the First World War the government obliged local authorities to survey their HOUSING needs and to submit plans to address the problem of housing shortages. Exchequer subsidies were then made available to local authorities who by 1939 had built 1 million homes, equivalent to 10 percent of the housing stock. In so doing, council provision of accommodation assumed a central position in the housing market, and this was extended successively until 1982 when it represented 32 percent of dwellings. Between 1919 and 1987 14.2 million houses were built in Britain, 43 percent by councils. Of many regional variations, the greatest reliance on council housebuilding was in Scotland, where councils were responsible for 71 percent of all dwellings built in the years 1919 –87.

Explanations of the initial development of council housing vary. One view is that public housing was, like other areas of LIBERAL social welfare provision, a result of successful working-class agitation; another explanation is that state intervention was inevitable because of pre-1914 private enterprise failures to provide suitable low rental accommodation for workers; a third possibility is that disruptive wartime rental and building controls necessitated continuing public involvement in the housing sector after the war; and, though the "Homes fit for Heroes" election pledge is often thought to have prompted council housing, recent research shows that few "Heroes" were housed in this way, and that council housing was in fact, in LLOYD GEORGE's words, an "insurance premium" to placate a demobilized, disenchanted working class during the 1918 –19 period of intense industrial strike action.

The initial legislation, the Housing and Town Planning Act, 1919 was curtailed within months, once a degree of social stability was achieved; and in the face of rapidly escalating building costs, once the extent of the Treasury's financial commitment was realized. Housing subsidies were forthcoming from both CONSERVATIVES (1923) and the first LABOUR administration (1924), but there was an important philosophical difference in their approaches; the Conservatives accorded councils only a residual role where private enterprise was unwilling to provide homes, whereas Labour viewed municipal housing as central to the growth of the overall housing stock. When returned to power, and confronted with a dearth of private rented housing, the Conservatives continued the framework established by Labour. However, by focusing on aggregate numbers of council houses built in the 1920s, little account was taken of either regional variations, or the weekly rental levels fixed for council housing which were frequently beyond the means of the low paid. So, although 625,000 council houses had been built by 1929, when policy shifted in 1930 and 1933 towards Treasury subsidies for SLUM clearance and "de-crowding" initiatives, the underlying problem of an insufficient supply of working-class housing remained.

Between 1945 and 1955 councils constructed 1.6 million new houses, 50 percent more than between the wars, reflecting the political urgency of the housing issue. As the Labour minister responsible, ANEURIN BEVAN proposed an emergency program of local authority housebuilding, with the private construction sector limited to just 20 percent of total housebuilding. When in power between 1951 and 1964, and despite their ideological preference for private sector provision, Conservative politicians conceded a central role to council housing, though the emphasis of policy changed with the ending of general housing subsidies in 1956 and a move to more specific financial support for the demolition of downtown slums and the relocation of families in council houses, frequently on the periphery of the cities.

Local authorities dominated new rental construction after the Second World War, and by the early 1960s, the stock of council housing had overtaken the proportion in the private rental sector. Under Labour, returned to power in 1964, a national housing plan the following year proposed a further acceleration of council housebuilding. Output reached 180,000 in 1967, but public expenditure cuts in response to the devaluation crisis in 1967 meant central government reined in its financial commitment to local authorities. So 1968 was an important turning point; the age of mass council house-building, begun in 1945, came to an end in the early 1970s.

The housing shortage was much less by 1970 than formerly, and the political imperative for new housebuilding slackened accordingly. In addition, though high rise building accounted for a relatively small proportion of local authority housing, the image and reality of this type of dwelling contributed to a developing critique of council housebuilding and housing management. Changed housing priorities recognized "special needs", for example in dwellings for the aged and infirm, and together with an emerging awareness of urban environmental considerations, renovation and renewal meant that demand for council housing slackened and conversely, the retention of private sector housing was strengthened. In 1978, in a repeat of the foreign exchange crisis of the 1960s, stringent public expenditure controls were a condition attached to loans obtained from the International Monetary Fund, and capital projects such as housing were trimmed accordingly.

Since 1979 successive Conservative administrations have mounted a powerful critique of the public housing sector. The principal tactic has been to tap a rich seam of public disquiet regarding council housing management, drawing on tenants' complaints and housing departments' administrative complacency. Conservative politicians claimed that municipal landlordism was itself the problem. Restrictive monetary targets for public expenditure were another device developed to contain councils' capital expenditure on housing in the early 1980s. The main focus of policy was directed, however, at tenants' "right to buy" the property which they had rented from councils, normally on very favorable terms and at heavily discounted prices. This anti-collectivist or privatization strategy was given further impetus after 1986 by boosting private landlords, either as individuals through tax and investment incentives, or by means of encouraging housing associations as the builders and managers of rented accommodation. From 1988 existing council housing stock was de-municipalized by means of Housing Action Trusts and Tenants' Choice schemes whereby management and responsibility passed to local housing associations following ballot arrangements which have attracted considerable criticism. In one of the biggest transfers, almost 75,000 properties, the homes of more than a quarter of a million Scots, were removed from the public sector and transferred to a private agency called Scottish Homes in 1989 on the basis of a minority vote of the tenants involved.

The significance of council housing in Britain extends far beyond simple quantitative measures of additions to housing stocks. Developed on a mass-produced basis, often with experimental materials or methods, and concentrated on peripheral green field sites with highly standardized designs and minimal landscaping, council housing has become associated with second-class tenure. Council residents have also been stigmatized as second-class citizens, since unlike owner occupiers, tenants did not participate in the long run appreciation of house values. Excluded from capital accumulation, council tenants have also endured low quality health and education provisions. As a result, council housing has recreated the process of social segregation through the mechanism of residential segregation.

Richard Rodger

Bibliography

Daunton, Martin J., ed. *Councillors and Tenants: Local Authority Housing in English Cities 1919–1939.* 1984.

Dunleavy, Patrick. *The Politics of Mass Housing 1945–1975.* 1981.

Forrest, Ray, and Alan Murie. *Selling the Welfare State: The Privatisation of Council Housing.* 1987.

Lowe, Stuart, and David Hughes, eds. *A New Century of Social Housing*. 1991.

Merett, Stephen. *State Housing in Britain*. 1979.

Swenarton, Mark. *Homes Fit for Heroes: The Politics and Architecture of Early State Housing in Britain*. 1981.

Country Houses

The country house has enjoyed at least two dramatic reversals of fortune in the twentieth century. Traditionally the social and economic center of the great landed estate, it lost many of its former functions with the decline of agriculture from the 1870s onwards, and particularly after the First World War when so many of the great estates were dismembered. By the 1930s many country houses appeared even to their owners as relics of a bygone age, fated to be demolished, sold off, even exported to America. Since the Second World War, however, they have benefited from a sudden aesthetic and cultural revaluation not only among connoisseurs but also among the general public, and owners have consequently reaped enhanced economic returns through government grants and the commercial exploitation of tourism.

Before the First World War most of rural Britain was parcelled up into large agricultural estates, and most of these estates could claim a country house of some kind, ranging from the small manor houses of the parish gentry to great palaces like the Duke of Devonshire's Chatsworth. All of these houses would accommodate the owner's family and servants, when not in London for the "Season", offer entertainment for parties of friends staying for weekends or longer, provide working space for the managers of the estate, and serve as physical symbols of the landlord's local status and power. Some would be opened on ceremonial occasions to the local public, so that the interiors could be admired and/or envied. But public visitation of country houses had probably been declining since the early nineteenth century, as RAILWAYS made many houses accessible to too large a public, and owners sought to shield their possessions from the democratic franchise and rising taxation.

From the 1910s taxation and agricultural decline combined to dismantle many great estates, and their associated houses lost their commercial and symbolic functions. Could the country house survive simply as a house? Owners were on the whole dubious and unsentimental. If pressed, they would sell or lease the house even before selling off the estate. Between the wars there was still a lively market for country houses, as the automobile made entertaining in the country more popular. Failing a sale, owners might demolish, perhaps to rebuild on a smaller scale; something up to 10 percent of the nation's country houses

were destroyed before 1940. Although early twentieth-century taste valued the very oldest houses—medieval and Tudor—neither owners nor connoisseurs shed many tears over the loss of the run-of-the-mill country house built after 1660.

The SECOND WORLD WAR triggered another wave of sales and demolitions. Wartime shortages of servants, fuel, and building materials and requisition by government for evacuated schools, military uses, etc. had driven many owners out of occupation. After the war few people—neither old owners nor new rich—wished any longer to live in large, draughty, unmodernized houses in remote parts of the country. Consequently another 15 percent or so of the nation's country-house stock fell to the wrecking ball, and many more were gutted for institutional uses as schools, government offices, nursing homes, HOTELS, and the like. EVELYN WAUGH's *Brideshead Revisited* (1945) was a bestselling elegy to a country-house world that seemed dead and buried.

But in the late 1940s public interest in country houses had finally begun to stir, as sales of *Brideshead* suggest. Popular interest in ARCHITECTURE of all periods was booming, perhaps stimulated by the German bombing raids. A government inquiry into the fate of historic houses, chaired by Sir Ernest Gowers, reported in 1950 and focused its attention almost exclusively on the great country houses, recommending government subsidy to help preserve up to 2,000 of the best houses in private ownership. A limited grant system to help owners of historic buildings was in place by 1953.

Most important was the 1950s boom of motor tourism, both foreign and domestic. Already during the war, the NATIONAL TRUST, which had hitherto concentrated its efforts on the preservation of open space, had begun to acquire country houses with a view to opening them to the public. After the war, private owners began to contemplate commercial opening, as well. The pioneers were the Marquess of Bath at Longleat (1949) and Lord Montagu at Beaulieu (1952). Hundreds followed their example. As early as 1954, 150 houses had opened on a semi-commercial basis, drawing 2 million visitors; a decade later, 600 houses attracted over 10 million. Owners became tourism entrepreneurs, adorning their houses—now often "stately homes"—with safari parks, funfairs, motoring museums, garden centers, farming exhibitions, adventure playgrounds, whatever might give them the competitive edge.

In the 1970s the popularity of the country house broke through onto an even higher plateau. Economic downturn and cultural conservatism combined to generate a kind of mania for the preservation of these jewels of the national heritage. An exhibition about demolished country houses at the Victoria and Albert Museum in 1975 attracted much comment. Demolitions were halted entirely by firmer legislation. The LABOUR government was loudly berated, and not only by the right-wing press, for its failure in 1977 to buy and keep intact the Earl of Rosebery's house and collections at Mentmore. Books about country house life, fashions and architecture dotted the bestseller lists, notably Mark Girouard's series of sumptuous social histories and a raft of books produced under the aegis of the National Trust and *Country Life* magazine. There was even a spate of new country house building in the once despised neo-classical style.

This mania showed no signs of abating in the 1990s. What had seemed a world dead and buried in 1945 was full of life a half-century later. Taking tax benefits into account as well as grants and tourist income, public opening kept hundreds of houses in private ownership and decent repair. Hundreds more had never had to open at all, still maintained largely by agriculture or cannier investments. Three-quarters of all country houses extant in 1880 remained standing in 1980, over half in private ownership, perhaps a third with some public access, more than a quarter retaining some of their original estate land. The country house mystique remained buoyant and helped to sustain substantial fragments of the old country house world for those among the titled and leisured rich who held on through lean years.

Peter Mandler

Bibliography

Clemenson, Heather A. *English Country Houses and Landed Estates.* 1982.

Cornforth, John. *The Inspiration of the Past: Country House Taste in the Twentieth Century.* 1985.

Mandler, Peter. *The Fall and Rise of the Stately Home.* 1997.

Robinson, J.M. *The Latest Country Houses.* 1984.

Strong, Roy, *et al. The Destruction of the Country House, 1875–1975.* 1975.

Coward, Noel Pierce (1899–1973)

Playwright, actor, director, composer, librettist, and fiction writer, instrumental in the development of the English musical revue, Noel Coward wrote and produced over fifty dramatic works and was knighted in 1970 for his varied contributions to British theatre.

Born shortly before Christmas in 1899 in Teddington, Middlesex, Coward was encouraged early to pursue a life in the theatre. As a child he appeared professionally in several children's "fantasies." His earliest experiments in writing were all directed to the stage and eventually toward his own performance. Coward served briefly in the ARMY in 1918 but was discharged due to poor health. Years later he contributed to the war effort through active participation in the Entertainments National Service Association (ENSA).

Success came to Coward when he was still young: in the early 1920s he had four plays produced in both London and New York: *The Young Idea* (1923), *The Vortex* (1924), *Fallen Angels,* and *Hay Fever* (both 1925). Five Coward productions ran simultaneously in London in 1925, including *On With The Dance,* a musical revue commissioned by C.B. Cochran. Other contributions to revue included *Sirocco* (1927) and *This Year of Grace* (1928), which were a flop and a runaway success respectively. Coward elicited extreme reactions from contemporary audiences for his liberal portrayals of the social and sexual mores, but he often masked controversial subjects in witty dialogue. *Design for Living* (1933), one of Coward's most controversial plays, also became one of the greatest successes of his career. Other memorable productions from this period were *Bitter Sweet* (1929), *Private Lives* (1930), in which Coward starred with Gertrude Lawrence and LAURENCE OLIVIER, *Cavalcade* (1931), *Words and Music* (1932), and *To-Night at Eight* (1936).

The musical play *Operette* (1938) was followed by the hugely popular *Blithe Spirit* (1941), which ran for a record-breaking 1,997 performances in London. Coward produced other lighthearted works, including *Present Laughter* (1943) and *Sigh No More* (1945), before striking out in a serious vein with *Peace in Our Time* (1947). Coward returned to comedy with *Relative Values* (1951) and *Quadrille* (1952). *Nude with Violin* starred John Gielgud in 1956, and in the same year Vivien Leigh appeared in *South Sea Bubble.* Late in his career Coward wrote an adaptation of a Feydeau play entitled *Look After Luke* (1959) and a retrospective on acting, *Waiting in the Wings* (1960). His last original musical, *Sail Away,* was produced in 1963, and his last stage appearance was in his own *Suite in Three Keys* (1966), which hinted at his own HOMOSEXUALITY.

Coward also had a celebrated cinematic career, notably during the SECOND WORLD WAR, when he provided scripts, usually based on his plays, for such memorable films as *In Which We Serve* (1942), *This Happy Breed* (1944), *Blithe Spirit* (1945), and *Brief Encounter* (1945), all of which, in very different ways, extolled English virtues. He achieved some notoriety as a film actor as well, especially in *In Which We Serve,* where his portrayal of Captain Kinross was modeled on the career of LORD MOUNTBATTEN, and in later films like *Our Man in Havana* (1959).

Coward performed leading roles in the plays written by others, including Shaw's *The Apple Cart* (1953), and achieved success in the United States performing his own clever songs on the stage, in nightclubs, and on television. Throughout his career Coward found pleasure in the pursuits of watercolor painting and fiction writing. He produced two collections of short fiction: *To Step Aside* (1939) and *Star Quality* (1951), as well as two volumes of autobiography: *Present Indicative* (1937) and *Future Indefinite* (1954). His impact on the British stage, often deprecated by later playwrights, continues to be felt through the frequent revivals of his plays.

Martha A. Schütz

Bibliography
Fisher, Clive. *Noel Coward.* 1992
Lahr, John. *Coward the Playwright.* 1982.
Lesley, Cole. *The Life of Noel Coward.* 1976.
Mander, Raymond, and Joe Mitchenson. *Theatrical Companion to Coward.* 1957.
Morley, Sheridan. *A Talent to Amuse: A Biography of Noel Coward.* 1969.
———, and Graham Payn, eds. *The Noel Coward Diaries.* 1982.

Crick, Francis (1916–)

One of several British physicists to move into biology after the Second World War, Francis Crick's career has been dominated by the belief that complex biological phenomena can be explained using the laws of CHEMISTRY and PHYSICS. His role in the biological revolution of the 1950s and 1960s was crucial, starting in 1953 with the double helix structure for DNA (for which he shared the 1962 Nobel Prize for Medicine) and culminating in 1961 with the demonstration that the genetic code is read in triplets. Throughout this period Crick was a towering influence in molecular biology, formulating many of the basic ideas about how gene structure determines protein structure and coordinating an informal network of collaboration. More recently he has influenced fields as diverse as embryology and the structure of chromosomes. Since 1976 he has been interested in the workings of the brain and the problem of consciousness.

Crick entered biology in 1947, after spending the war in naval research, and two years later joined the Medical Research Council (MRC) unit in the Cavendish Laboratory, Cambridge. In 1953 a collaboration with James Watson (1928–), a visiting American postdoctoral fellow, resulted in the double helix model for the structure of DNA, an intellectual *tour de force* which combined information from X-ray crystallography and stereochemistry.

The double helix launched a decade of intense international activity in which the relationship between DNA structure and protein structure was worked out. The theoretical basis of this relationship was largely formulated by Crick: he proposed both the Sequence Hypothesis and the Central Dogma and deduced the necessity for adaptor molecules (transfer RNA) before any experimental evidence for their existence existed. It was the theoretical physicist George Gamow (1904–68) who suggested that the translation from DNA sequence to protein sequence could be treated as a formal coding problem, but it was Crick and his colleague Sydney Brenner (1927–) who established the rules by which hypothetical codes were tested against known protein sequences and showed, by an ingenious genetic experiment, that the code was read in nonoverlapping triplets.

In 1962 the MRC unit moved to a new research institute, the Laboratory for Molecular Biology, and Crick became head of the Molecular Genetics Division, a position he soon shared with Brenner. By the mid-1960s the genetic code had been broken, and Crick moved on to the problem of embryonic development and the role of the redundant DNA in multicellular organisms: in both areas his ideas have had a major influence on the direction of the field.

In 1976 Crick moved to the Salk Institute, California, and started working on the brain. The molecular biology which emerged in the 1950s resulted from the successful fusion of different traditions, and Crick is currently attempting to do the same thing to the neurosciences: bridging the gaps between neurophysiology, neuroanatomy, psychophysics, and computer modeling. He sees himself as a theoretical biologist, a role which is familiar to a physicist but rare in biology. There are many who would claim that he is the outstanding theoretical biologist of our age.

Guil Winchester

Bibliography
Crick, Francis. *What Mad Pursuit: A Personal View of Scientific Discovery.* 1988.
Judson, Horace. *The Eighth Day of Creation: Makers of the Revolution in Biology.* 1979.
Olby, Robert. "Francis Crick, DNA, and the Central Dogma," *Daedalus.* No.4 (1970), pp. 938–87.

Cricket

For more than 100 years cricket has been one of the most popular of British sports. Its capacity for uniting all social groups and virtually all regions of Britain resulted in its commonly being referred to at the end of the nineteenth century as "the national game," a title since claimed by soccer. Cricket's association with good sportsmanship and fair play gave rise to its being a symbol of civilized behavior. "It isn't cricket," in popular parlance, signified a lapse from the standards of decent conduct.

Though a game with a long history, cricket's specifically "modern" form was developed during the second half of the nineteenth century. An essentially southern English sport, with strong roots in both villages and towns, was disseminated to other parts of the country by middle-class men who had learned the game at public school. Its popularity was consolidated by the promotional activities of touring "circuses" of professional cricketers from the 1840s to the 1860s. By the following decade the predominant form of cricket was one sponsored by clubs based on the English counties. They had formed themselves into a competition (the County Championship) in 1864, the leading places being taken by Nottinghamshire, Yorkshire, Lancashire, Surrey, and Kent in the later years of the century. It was this branch of the game that came to be designated "First Class" and was governed by officials of the London club, Marylebone Cricket Club (MCC). But the existence of this level should not be allowed to mask the fact that much high quality cricket was played by clubs not part of the county circuit. Of particular note was the "League" cricket played in the industrial towns of the Midlands and north, which developed its own style and ethos.

In common with other sports, county cricketers were frequently paid professionals. By the end of the century professionals dominated the playing staffs of the leading counties in numerical terms, though (unlike soccer) the "all-professional" team was unknown. The amateur concept remained strong and many men from an upper class social background considered it beneath their dignity to play for money. Several of the game's leading players have been from this group, especially in the so-called "golden era" before 1914 when names such as A.C. MacLaren, G.L. Jessop, C.B. Fry, and F.S. Jackson often dominated proceedings. It was people of this social class who controlled the game both off and on the field of play. Few professionals became captains of county clubs before the 1960s, and no professional captained the England team between 1888 and 1952. Although eventually abolished in 1962, the distinction between amateur and professional carried immense social meaning, and it should be remembered that until 1962 the most prestigious non-international fixture in the cricket season was the Gentlemen v. Players match.

The leading cricketer from the 1860s until the turn of the century, the man whose name was synonymous with cricket, was W.G. Grace. Grace's importance was manifold. As a player his all-round achievements far outstripped those of his contemporaries. He thus helped to release some of the commerical potential of cricket, profiting from it himself (though, as a member of the country gentry, he played as an amateur, he nevertheless made far more money as a sportsman than he did from his profession in medi-

cine). And he established techniques of both batting and bowling that became the norm for years to come.

Largely because of Grace's stature, cricket also became an exportable commodity, taken up predominantly in the British Empire. By the 1890s, regular competitions among England, Australia, and South Africa were taking place. In the interwar period, the West Indies, India, and New Zealand joined this imperial club. Later additions were Pakistan (1952) and Sri Lanka (1988). The "Test Matches" among these countries represented the pinnacle of cricketing achievement, with those between England and Australia—the two oldest cricketing countries—producing especially keen contests. Australia had the better of these exchanges over the period (1920-53), when for much of this time they had the services of Don Bradman, a batsman whose achievements in consistently high scoring are unparalleled, even by the mighty Grace.

The duration of play in Test matches gradually increased to five days by the 1950s, but otherwise the game underwent few changes in organization or technique until the 1960s and 1970s. Two important innovations were then made to maximize the spectator and commercial appeal of the game. In 1963 a competition of one day matches (initially sponsored by Gillette) was introduced into the English county circuit. Its immense popularity prompted similar departures from tradition in 1969 and 1972, enhancing cricket as a television spectacle and stimulating improvements in some aspects of play, notably the art of fielding. Such one day cricket is now an essential part of the English game. The second innovation came in 1976 when the Australian media proprietor Kerry Packer launched World Series Cricket (WSC). This venture, aimed at bringing together a highly-paid group of the world's top players to perform in matches that would attract a vast television audience, had major effects on the English game. In the short term, but enabling the star cricketers to play off their employers against WSC and thus push up their earnings, it broke the long established hold of the MCC over English professionals and brought them better treatment. In the longer run, new methods of presenting cricket were adopted (mainly overseas) and the number of Test matches—the game's biggest money-making feature—was greatly increased. Though undoubtedly more commercial than ever before in the aftermath of the "Packer Revolution," cricket nevertheless still retains a social cachet and aesthetic quality lacking in most other British sports. It is, significantly, one of only a few British sports capable of generating a literature of "poetic" proportions.

Jeffrey Hill

Bibliography

Brookes, Christopher. *English Cricket: The Game and its Players through the Ages.* 1978.

Frindall, Bill ed. *The Wisden Book of Test Cricket, 1877–1984.* 1985.

Lewis, Tony. *Double Century: The Story of MCC and its Cricket.* 1987.

Midwinter, Eric. *W.G. Grace: His Life and Times.* 1981.

Sissons, Ric. *The Players: A Social History of the Professional Cricketer.* 1988.

Williams, Jack. *Cricket and England: A Cultural and Social History of England Between the Wars.* 1999.

Crime

Since it makes exciting copy, crime has been a popular subject with many sections of the British media throughout the twentieth century. However, from the mid-1950s general concern about crime became much sharper because of a steep and accelerating rise in crime statistics.

The judicial statistics, on which most assessments have been made, have as their basis crimes reported to the police. These statistics show that throughout the century the vast majority of serious crimes which could be prosecuted on indictment were offenses against property, in particular, different forms of theft and the handling of stolen goods. While property offenses consistently accounted for over 90 percent of recorded, indictable crime, those offenses which generated the most fear and the most publicity, namely violent and sexual crimes, only accounted for about 5 percent of the annual total. The homicide rate constituted only a fraction of violent crimes: at the beginning of the century the national rate was annually about 1:100,000 of the population; with some fluctuations this gradually fell to an all time low of 0.3:100,000 in the early 1950s, after which it began to rise just exceeding the rate of the beginning of the century in the mid-1980s. Serious crime as a whole remained constant between 1900 and 1914; thereafter it began a gradual rise, slackening in the decade following the Second World War, but soaring upwards from the mid-1950s. Allowing for the increase in population the figures show an annual rate of 249 crimes per 100,000 of the population in 1901, 2374:100,000 in 1965 and 6674:100,000 in 1984. An interesting implication of the pattern of these statistics is that the mass UNEMPLOYMENT of the inter-war years had little impact on criminal behavior; the sharpest increase in offending appears to coincide with growing affluence from the mid-1950s.

Yet while the official statistics continued to be used to justify political campaigns and policy making, and while their annual publication was commonly seized on by the PRESS, considerable debate developed over their value particularly in the last third of the century. The problem of the "dark figure", that is the number of crimes committed but never reported, had been recognized by the Victorians, but other difficulties were increasingly highlighted. Were more crimes listed because of an improvement in police recording procedures, including an end to the Metropolitan Police habit in the first quarter of the century of recording some reports of thefts as reports of lost property? Were more thefts being reported because of a growth in the insurance business and the need for a victim to make a report to the police in order to file an insurance claim? Was the marked increase in rape during the 1980s attributable to the fact that there was less stigma attached to the victim, a greater public awareness, and more sympathetic police interviewing? Were more crimes of violence reported generally because of a decline in public tolerance for rough and violent behavior? In the attempt to get a better understanding of levels and patterns of criminality victim surveys began to be conducted from the mid 1970s. The most comprehensive was the *British Crime Survey* first conducted for 1981 and involving one person aged sixteen years or above in each of 11,000 households in England and Wales, and 5,000 households in Scotland. In many respects the findings of the survey underlined the conclusions to be drawn from the official statistics, namely that violent and sexual offenses were few in number while much crime was extremely petty; however the survey did suggest that the increase in burglary was only a fifth of that shown in the official statistics during the 1970s.

While the statistics suggest that most crime in twentieth-century Britain has been petty and non-violent, such a conclusion would not be apparent from reading the popular press. The century has seen the creation of a succession of what, with reference to the portrayal of youth gangs during the 1960s, has been described as "folk devils". Indeed youth gangs often figured in this role: in the period before the First World War there was concern over the original "hooligans", in the inter-war period it was the razor-gangs, notably in Glasgow, and with the growth of youth culture after the Second World War, there came in succession, the Teddy Boys, the Mods and the Rockers, and the Skinheads. Offenders, given a generic name based on their *modus operandi*, were also popular with the press: the "motor bandit" and the "bag snatcher" of the inter-war years was replaced in the aftermath of the Second World War by the "cosh boy" and then by the "mugger". Individuals might also earn a new name signifying the horrendous nature of their crimes, furnishing the media with good copy and its readers or watchers with vicarious thrills: Peter Sutcliffe, even after his arrest and conviction, remained better known as "the Yorkshire Ripper".

Throughout the century most offenders were young males, often aged under twenty years. Though in the popular imagination youth gangs were the most public manifestation of youth deviance, offenses by youths were not always committed in groups, and youth groups were by no means all criminal. Older offenders might come together in gangs to conduct armed robberies, notably with the Great Train Robbery of 1963, but organized gangs of what might be termed "professional criminals" were responsible for only a small percentage of crime. In the first half of the century organized criminal gangs were most commonly connected with the more dubious bookmakers; the clashes between the Darby Sabini gang and the Brummagen Boys, and the Sheffield gang wars of the 1920s, all involved race-course rivalry between bookies. Organized gangs, notably the Messina brothers, established a hold over LONDON vice from the early 1930s; they treated their rivals with appalling brutality, but they also managed to develop links with respectable society. The Messinas' mantle passed, in the 1950s, to Peter Rachman who was as much involved with SLUM racketeering and gambling as vice, and who, shortly before his death in 1963, had a brief and unpleasant encounter with the most celebrated of the London gang leaders, the Kray twins. The Krays' business empire ran the gamut from vice to protection.

The majority of offenders processed by the courts during the Victorian period were from lower-class status groups. This contributed markedly to the postivist tradition in criminology which considered criminals to be members of an identifiable social group. From the 1920s the lower courts began to be clogged with individuals charged with contravening traffic legislation in motor vehicles; the popular notion remained that this was not "real" crime committed by "real" criminals, and positivist criminology with its continuing interest in sub-cultures, underpinned the popular view. In the aftermath of the Second World War and the subsequent IMMIGRATION of Afro-Caribbeans and Asians the positivist view of the criminal influenced the behavior of many rank and file police officers and in some instances, also police orders and tactics. Young Afro-Caribbeans were seen, particularly in the 1970s and 1980s, as particularly prone to street crime; the police response was often heavy-handed and this was a significant element in provoking the urban riots of the 1980s.

But also since the end of the Second World War positivist criminology has been subjected to considerable criticism. "Labeling" theorists urged that criminality is not something inherent in an individual but a label applied by society, and it is therefore as important to study law-makers, law-enforcers, and media campaigns as it is to study law-breakers. This, in turn, has been criticized from a radical perspective for not explaining why individuals offend, particularly the large numbers involved in property crime, and for implying that offenders are the victims of official labels. For the radical criminologists the key requirement is an analysis of the economic system which creates laws, thereby criminality, as a means of maintaining itself and its social structure; and they have stressed the contrast between the large number of lower-class property offenders prosecuted for the theft of goods of relatively little value, and the few white-collar offenders prosecuted for fraud and embezzlement involving hundreds of thousands of pounds. A series of scandals in the CITY OF LONDON during the 1980s, notably the Guinness affair of 1989–90 which led to the imprisonment of four well-known, highly respected businessmen, added weight to the radicals' arguments, yet "white-collar" crime has remained a much underresearched area.

Clive Emsley

Bibliography

Gatrell, V.A.C. "Crime, authority and the policeman-state" in F.M.L. Thompson, ed. *The Cambridge Social History of Britain 1750–1950*, vol. 3. 1990, pp. 243–310.

Hough, Mike, and Pat Mayhew. *The British Crime Survey: First Report*. 1983.

Howell, D.W., and K.O. Morgan, eds. *Crime, Protest and Police in Modern British Society*. 1999.

McClintock, F.H., and N.H. Avison. *Crime in England and Wales*. 1968.

Pearson, Geoffrey. *Hooligan: A History of Respectable Fears*. 1983.

Taylor, Ian R. *The New Criminology*. 1973.

Cripps, (Richard) Stafford (1889–1952)

Stafford Cripps (Richard was never used) was a prominent Labour politician. He joined the LABOUR PARTY in 1928, and in 1930, while still without a parliamentary seat, was appointed Solicitor-General on the sudden retirement of the incumbent. He was knighted as a customary dignity of his office, and entered Parliament in January 1931. He led the Labour Left from 1932 until he was expelled from the Labour Party in January 1939. During the SECOND WORLD WAR he served as ambassador to Moscow (1940–2); Lord Privy Seal and Leader of the House of Commons (1942); and Minister of Aircraft Production (1942–5). He was readmitted to the Labour Party in February 1945 and served in the post-war Labour CABINET as President of the Board of Trade (1945–7); Minister of Economic Affairs and Chancellor of the Exchequer (1947–50).

Educated at Winchester and the University College, London, Cripps began a promising career as a research chemist, but soon decided to follow his father and grandfather into the LEGAL PROFESSION, where both had been eminent. He became a barrister in 1913. His career was interrupted by war service and illness, but after he returned to the law in 1919 he quickly established a fine reputation and a lucrative practice, mainly in patent and compensation cases. He became Britain's youngest KC in 1927. His legal work for the London County Council impressed HERBERT MORRISON, who ultimately persuaded him to join the Labour Party. This decision was doubtless facilitated by the fact that Cripps's father, Alfred—a former Conservative MP—had, as Lord Parmoor, joined Labour in 1924, accepting RAMSAY MACDONALD's invitation to be Lord President. Like Parmoor, Cripps was a deeply commited Christian all his life, and his political concerns evolved from his work in Christian peace organisations.

After the 1931 general election Cripps found himself one of only forty-six Labour MPs, and one of a tiny handful with real parliamentary ability. He therefore became one of the triumvirate which led the Parliamentary Labour Party through this very difficult period. The political and economic crisis of 1931 convinced him that "gradualism" was dead, and his arguments that the next Labour government should assume emergency powers to deal with establishment opposition brought him opprobrium in the conservative press and rebukes from an embarrassed Labour leadership. Cripps was the effective leader of the SOCIALIST LEAGUE (the formal organization of the Labour Left) from 1932 until its support for the Unity Campaign led to conflict with the Labour Party and the League's dissolution in 1937. In 1938–9 he again incurred the wrath of the Labour leaders by campaigning for the POPULAR FRONT, which resulted in his expulsion. During the 1930s Cripps displayed considerable political naivete and tactical ineptitude. Despite this, and despite a dull platform manner, his parliamentary talent and overwhelming sincerity continued to inspire great loyalty.

The outbreak of war found Cripps with no obvious role. In 1939–40 he undertook a tour of India, China, and the USSR, acting as an unofficial government envoy. When Cripps returned, CHURCHILL appointed him ambassador to Moscow. The job was difficult and frustrating, particularly before the German invasion, and Cripps's independent approach caused some disquiet in the Foreign Office, but his mission was popularly regarded as a success. Assisted by his distance from the political parties, by the apparent vindication of his stance against APPEASEMENT, and by his identification with the Soviet alliance, Cripps returned home to enormous public acclaim, and was widely regarded as an alternative Prime Minister. Churchill had little option but to appoint him to the War Cabinet.

In March 1942 he was despatched to India to seek an accommodation with its nationalist leaders. They recognised his personal goodwill, but he was unable to offer acceptable terms and returned to Britain empty-handed. It has been argued that the India mission represented Churchill's attempt to discredit Cripps. If so, it was partly successful: his popular support declined, and after some disputes with Churchill and setbacks in the Commons he was moved out of the Cabinet to the important, if politically marginal post of Minister for Aircraft Production, where his technical and administrative skills made him highly effective.

By the end of the war Cripps had become an ardent proponent of a planned, mixed economy rather than wholesale NATIONALIZATION. His tenure in the key economic ministries was successful, although inevitably unpopular given the tremendous difficulties Britain faced. As President of the Board of Trade he had primary responsibility for RATIONING, which became more severe after the war. His lean frame, moralistic outlook, vegetarian diet, and simple lifestyle helped to identify him permanently in the public mind with the harsh austerity measures which he and the government were obliged to introduce.

During the severe winter of 1947 the government's popularity waned and its economic planning lost direction. Cripps and others therefore attempted to replace the Prime Minister, CLEMENT ATTLEE, with the Foreign Secretary, ERNEST BEVIN. Attlee met his difficulties by creating the Ministry of Economic Affairs under Cripps. Here Cripps displayed his usual efficiency, reinforcing his austere image with repeated exhortations to hard work. The new ministry could not really work effectively while separated from the Exchequer, and the forced resignation of the Chancellor, HUGH DALTON, provided the opportunity to combine the ministries with Cripps in charge. Ironically, his three deflationary budgets of 1948–50 marked the beginning of Labour's attempts to reduce welfare expenditure.

Cripps's health had long been troublesome, and the chronic overwork of the war and postwar years exacerbated the illness which led to his resignation in October 1950 and his death eighteen months later.

Cripps was a towering figure through two decades of British political history. Despite his inconsistencies he remained unswervingly devoted to the highest ideals of service. He served the Labour Party as its visionary conscience when it was at its lowest ebb and as a leading practical contributor in its years of greatest achievement.

David Blaazer

Bibliography
Burgess, Simon. *Stafford Cripps: A Political Life.* 1999.
Clarke, Peter. *The Cripps Version: The Life of Sir Stafford Cripps.* 2002.
Cripps, Sir Stafford. *The Struggle for Peace.* 1936.
Morgan, Kenneth O. *Labour in Power 1945–1951.* 1984.
———. *Labour People.* 1987.

Crosland, (Charles) Anthony Raven (1918–1977)
Anthony ("Tony") Crosland was one of the foremost British socialist thinkers in the post-1945 period. He was also a leading LABOUR PARTY politician, holding a series of ministerial posts—including that of Foreign Secretary—in the Labour governments of 1964–70 and 1974–9.

Born 29 August 1918 in Sussex, Crosland was educated at Trinity College, OXFORD where, after graduation, he took up the post of tutor and lecturer in economics in 1947. In 1950, however, he abandoned an academic career to become Labour MP for South Gloucestershire. He lost his seat in 1955, but exercised great influence within the party as a socialist thinker with the publication of his major work *The Future of Socialism* (1956). This was the most coherent statement of the "revisionist" position in the party debate on policy and strategy. From this point onwards Crosland became the principal intellectual exponent of LABOUR REVISIONISM.

In *The Future of Socialism* Crosland argued that Western capitalism had been transformed by important economic developments since 1945 and that socialism would therefore need to be reappraised. Like his friend and colleague HUGH GAITSKELL, Crosland regarded socialist aims as essentially ethical; they sprang from such ideals as liberty, fellowship, social welfare, and equality. The pursuit of equality required, in his view, a redistribution of resources and wealth in society by means of social expenditure and progressive taxation. Such measures would in turn, he stressed, depend on sustained economic growth. Crosland, like Gaitskell, offended Labour traditionalists by maintaining that public ownership should no longer be considered an indispensable part of socialist policy. Other methods—particularly educational reform and fiscal measures—were likely, he thought, to provide more effective means of attaining the ethical ends of socialism. He also invited the charge of doctrinal heresy by championing a mixed economy with a vigorous private sector.

By 1959 Crosland had returned to Parliament as Labour MP for Grimsby. During this period he strongly supported Gaitskell, the party leader, in his bitter struggles with the Labour Left over Clause IV and defense. When Labour returned to power in 1964, Crosland filled important ministerial posts, including those of Secretary of State

for Education and Science from 1965 to 1967 and President of the Board of Trade from 1967 to 1969.

With Labour unexpectedly in power again in 1974, Crosland was appointed Secretary of State for the Environment in HAROLD WILSON's second administration. Despite a disappointing result in the party leadership contest that followed Wilson's resignation in 1976, Crosland was promoted in that year to the post of Foreign Secretary in JAMES CALLAGHAN's new government. He held that post until his sudden death on 19 February 1977.

Crosland's last months in office were marred by a deepening economic crisis which culminated in the Labour government seeking loans from the International Monetary Fund in return for cuts in its public spending programmes. That episode challenged a major assumption underlying his revisionist analysis—that redistribution could be achieved by high social expenditure financed by continuous economic growth.

Nevertheless, Crosland will be remembered as an effective CABINET minister and, above all, as a major British socialist writer whose book *The Future of Socialism* must rank as one of the seminal expressions of democratic socialist thought in the twentieth century.

Tudor Jones

Bibliography
Crosland, C.A.R. *The Future of Socialism.* 1956.
Crosland, Susan. *Tony Crosland,* 1982.
Jefferys, Kevin. *Anthony Crosland.* 1999.
Lipsey, David, and Dick Leonard. *The Socialist Agenda: Crosland's Legacy.* 1981.

Curzon, George Nathaniel (1859–1925)
George Curzon, CONSERVATIVE politician, began his political career as MP for Southport 1886–98. Serving as Under-Secretary of State for India, 1891–2, and Under Secretary of State for Foreign Affairs, 1895–8, he showed considerable talent. Nevertheless the official announcement in 1898 that he would succeed Lord Minto as Viceroy and Governor-General of India was greeted with public surprise. Curzon took over as Viceroy in 1899 and served until 1905 when he resigned. He was then out of office until May 1915 when he joined ASQUITH's coalition War CABINET as Lord Privy Seal. When LLOYD GEORGE replaced Asquith, in December 1916, he became Lord President of the Council. In January 1919 Curzon was appointed deputy Foreign Secretary, and in October he assumed full control of the Foreign Office. Curzon remained Foreign Secretary until January 1924, serving under three Prime Ministers. Returning to office after the defeat of the LABOUR government in November 1924, he was given the lesser post of Lord President of the Council. He died after a short illness in March

1925. On being appointed to the Viceroyalty in 1898 he accepted an Irish peerage as Baron Curzon of Kedleston. He was an Irish representative peer in the HOUSE OF LORDS from 1908–16 and Leader in the Lords, 1916–24. In 1911 Curzon received an Earldom; in 1916 he succeeded his father as Baron Scarsdale; and in 1921 he was elevated to a Marquisate.

At thirty-nine Curzon became the youngest Viceroy in history. The viceroyalty, possessing enormous powers, gave ample scope for his considerable administrative ability. Many of his policies, especially tax reductions and restoration programs for India's neglected monuments, earned favor with the people of India. More importantly, he rigorously upheld the principle of equality before the law for both Indians and Europeans. Curzon's viceroyalty is generally regarded as the apogee of British rule in India. However, the partition of Bengal, as part of an effort to promote greater administrative efficiency, created an outcry within India that lost him much domestic popularity. At the same time the Conservative government in Britain was concerned by Curzon's autocratic methods, especially in his prosecution of a forward policy in British India's relations with Tibet, Persia, and Afghanistan. Moreover, Curzon had been involved since 1904 in a series of clashes with LORD KITCHENER over the administrative control of the Indian army. The row became increasingly acrimonious, and it was with a sense of relief that Curzon's resignation was accepted on 22 August 1905. He returned to England an embittered man.

On his return to England Curzon found himself without a seat in the House of Commons and, because his barony was in the Irish peerage, excluded from the House of Lords. He received no public honor for his Viceroyalty. It was not until 1908 that he entered the House of Lords after securing election as an Irish representative peer. He played a key role in the constitutional crisis of 1911, leading the "hedger" Conservative peers whose abstention allowed the passage of the Parliament bill to curb the veto power of the House of Lords.

The FIRST WORLD WAR brought a return to office for Curzon as a member of the War Cabinet of 1915. His concern about the prosecution of the war led him to participate in the conspiracy that toppled Asquith and brought DAVID LLOYD GEORGE to power in December 1916.

From January to October 1919 Curzon served as deputy Foreign Secretary under ARTHUR BALFOUR, who was fully occupied with the Paris Peace Conference. In October Curzon succeeded as Foreign Secretary, but his tenure was clouded by conflicts with Lloyd George, who sought to manage foreign policy, consigning Curzon to a surbordinate role. Members of Lloyd George's personal Secretariat, along with the Cabinet Secretariat, exercised functions that would normally have been discharged by the Foreign Office. In 1922 the tension between the two men came to a head during the Chanak crisis when Lloyd George's support of Greek ambitions against Turkey almost led to an Anglo-Turkish war. Curzon wrote out his resignation, which remained undelivered when on 19 October Lloyd George resigned. Continuing as Foreign Secretary Curzon helped Lloyd George's successor, ANDREW BONAR LAW, to form his administration, and when the latter resigned through ill health in May 1923, Curzon confidently expected to become Prime Minister. However, he was unpopular with many of his colleagues, and as a peer could not represent the government in the Commons. STANLEY BALDWIN formed a new government in which Curzon, his ambition thwarted, agreed to serve, belatedly gaining public acclaim for his skillful settlement of the Turkish issue by the Treaty of Lausanne (1923). Under both Bonar Law and Baldwin the problem of German reparations dominated government policy. In January 1924 the Baldwin government fell, and when the Conservatives returned to power in November, Curzon became Lord President of the Council instead of returning to the Foreign Office.

Curzon was a major political figure in twentieth-century Britain. As Viceroy, in opposition, and finally in government for all but ten months between 1915 and March 1925 Curzon played a very prominent role. Neither popular nor ideologically committed, he was intelligent and hard-working. He sought power for its own sake, while believing that the superiority of his abilities imposed the consequent public duty to serve his country and the British Empire.

G.H. Bennett

Bibliography
Dilks, David. *Curzon in India.* 2 vols. 1969–70.
Gilmour, David. *Curzon.* 1994.
Nicolson, Harold. *Curzon: The Last Phase 1919–1925.* 1934.
Ronaldshay, Lord. *The Life of Lord Curzon.* 3 vols. 1928.
Rose, Kenneth. *Superior Person.* 1968.

Dalton, (Edward) Hugh John Neale (1887–1962)
Hugh Dalton was a prominent LABOUR PARTY
politician and intellectual, a member of the coalition government during the SECOND WORLD
WAR, and first Chancellor of the Exchequer in
the post-war Labour government.

He was born near Neath in Glamorgan, the
only son of an Anglican cleric and tutor to the
sons of Queen Victoria. After attending Eton,
Dalton was an undergraduate at King's College,
CAMBRIDGE, studying economics under JOHN
MAYNARD KEYNES. He became involved in the
Cambridge FABIAN SOCIETY in 1907, converting
fully to socialism a year later. Upon taking his degree, Dalton briefly read for a law degree, but
turned instead to post-graduate work at the
LONDON SCHOOL OF ECONOMICS, all the time
committing himself further to socialist causes. In
1914, he married Ruth Fox.

During the FIRST WORLD WAR Dalton served
initially with the Army Service Corps, then
transferred to the Royal Artillery and fought in
Italy between 1917 and the end of the war. He recounted these experiences in *With Guns in Italy*,
published in 1919. At the end of the war, while a
full-time lecturer in economics at the London
School of Economics, he became involved in
policy work for the LABOUR PARTY. His search
for a parliamentary seat was unsuccessful until
October 1924, when he was elected for Camber-
well, Peckham, switching, in 1929, to the Durham mining seat of Bishop Auckland, which he
held, except for 1931–5, until the end of his career
in the Commons.

Dalton's expertise on economic affairs, cemented by studies on inequality, and his ease in
foreign policy, quickly caught the eye of the Labour Party leadership, and he was perceived
from an early date as a prospect for office. He
also found a place on the National Executive
Committee of the party as early as 1925. With
the formation of the second Labour government in 1929, he was considered for Cabinet
rank, but had to settle for the Under-
Secretaryship at the Foreign Office, under AR-
THUR HENDERSON. Dalton acquitted himself
well and avoided being tainted in the government crisis of August 1931.

In the election of October 1931 Dalton lost his
seat by a small margin, which damaged his

chances for the party leadership. He was, however, able to use the period between 1931 and 1935
to build a power base within the party headquarters at Transport House. In particular, he dominated domestic and foreign policy-making.
With HERBERT MORRISON, Dalton helped
shape Labour's commitment to economic planning in the 1930s. Dalton's views on domestic reform, drawn from a Fabian perspective, academic training in economics, and the
observation of experiments in the Soviet Union,
were best articulated in his *Practical Socialism for
Britain*, published in 1935. These views per-
meated the major party policy statements of the
1930s, *For Socialism and Peace* (1934) and *Labour's
Immediate Programme* (1937), for which Dalton
was largely responsible. He also helped turn Labour from a pacifist foreign policy to one which
favored standing up to the European dictators
through rearmament. With the help of ERNEST
BEVIN and WALTER CITRINE of the TRADES
UNION CONGRESS, Dalton had, by 1937, with the
party's adoption of *International Policy and Defence*, left his imprint on both foreign and domestic policy. In 1935 he returned to parliamentary politics, regaining the Bishop Auckland
seat. Despite his ill-fated support of Morrison
for the parliamentary leadership in 1935, he was
successful as party chairman. Throughout this
period Dalton also served as a patron to
younger socialist intellectuals, like HUGH
GAITSKELL, Evan Durbin, and Douglas Jay.

By the beginning of the war Dalton was a
prominent member of the Labour leadership. In
May 1940, with the formation of the CHURCH-
ILL coalition, Dalton was made Minister of
Economic Warfare, in charge, among other
things, of the economic blockade and subversion
of German-dominated Europe. He occupied
this post until 1942, a period characterized by
much intrigue over his running of the Special
Operations Executive, Britain's secret arm, dedicated to "setting Europe ablaze" with anti-Nazi
movements. In February 1942 he was moved to
the Board of Trade, becoming its President.
Here, Dalton displayed all his characteristic energy and exuberance, tackling such questions as
coal and clothes RATIONING and reconstruction.
One of his greatest achievements was the Distribution of Industry Act in 1945 which aimed at

relocating industry in depressed areas, a concern of his since the 1930s.

After Labour's election victory of July 1945, Dalton expected to become Foreign Secretary, a post he had long coveted. ATTLEE had doubts, however, and, instead, made Dalton Chancellor of the Exchequer. In the desperate economic conditions facing Britain at the end of the war, this was a key post and Dalton became an integral member of Labour's "Big Five": Attlee, Morrison, Bevin, and STAFFORD CRIPPS. His time at the Treasury was marked by achievement and crisis. His budgets were marked by a commitment to policies of "cheap money", inflating the economy, and to distinctively socialist planning through economic controls. He also nationalized the Bank of England, a central plank in Labour's platform. In this regard, Dalton was a successful Chancellor, a proponent of "socialist advance", who delighted his supporters in the Labour Party as much as he alienated his Conservative rivals. If Dalton was undone, it was by the weakness of the British economy. This began with the American loan, which he had supported, and continued through the arguments within CABINET about Britain's overstretched resources (Dalton demanding cutbacks in military expenditure), and ended with the crisis of sterling convertibility in the summer of 1947, demanded according to the terms of the American loan. After weeks of economic crisis following convertibility, Dalton was forced in August 1947 to suspend it, thus signaling Britain's diminished economic standing.

In November 1947, minutes before officially introducing the budget to the House of Commons, Dalton casually revealed its contents to a journalist. He was forced to resign because of this indiscretion. He was never again to exercise the same level of direct power he had enjoyed within the party and government before 1947. Dalton did return to the Cabinet, first in October 1948, as Chancellor of the Duchy of Lancaster (with responsibility for European affairs), then, between 1950 and 1951, as Minister of TOWN AND COUNTRY PLANNING. He remained active in the work of the National Executive Committee.

After Labour's defeat in 1951 Dalton moved into the role of elder statesman. He lost his seat on the National Executive in 1952 in the wave of Bevanite left-wing success. Once off the Executive, he concentrated on promoting his protegés, such as Gaitskell and ANTHONY CROSLAND. After the election of 1955 he resigned from the Parliamentary Committee to clear the way for younger members.

Dalton's contribution to the Labour Party was enormous. He played a profound role in shaping the policy assumptions which were adopted, in both domestic and foreign affairs, in the 1930s and brought to power in 1945. He may have been, as well, the most "socialist" Chancellor of the Exchequer the party has ever had, a symbol of Labour achievement between 1945 and 1947. No less importantly, Dalton fostered a generation of younger politicians, many of whom came to office in the 1960s. Finally, Dalton began a trend of lively autobiography in the Labour Party; his memoirs and now-published diary provide a fascinating and entertaining picture of the party between the 1930s and the 1950s.

Stephen Brooke

Bibliography

Dalton, Hugh. *Call Back Yesterday*. 1954.

——. *The Fateful Years*. 1957.

——. *High Tide and After*. 1962.

Pimlott, Ben. *Hugh Dalton*. 1985.

——, ed. *The Second World War Diary of Hugh Dalton*. 1986.

——, ed. *The Political Diary of Hugh Dalton*. 1986.

Dawson, Geoffrey (1874–1944)

Geoffrey Robinson (who changed his name to Dawson in 1917), one of Britain's most distinguished journalists in the twentieth century, was editor of THE TIMES from 1912 to 1919 and from 1922 to 1941.

Dawson was educated at Eton and Magdalen College, OXFORD, both institutions with which he maintained close links all his life. He was also the owner of a large estate in Yorkshire and, as such, occupied a natural place in the center of British social and public affairs.

He received his early political and journalistic experience in South Africa, where he served as Private Secretary to the British High Commissioner, LORD MILNER, and then became editor of the *Johannesburg Star*. He became one of a number of young acolytes of Milner, who later went on to form the Round Table group on their return to England, dedicated to the study of imperial and international affairs. In 1910 Dawson returned to London and in 1912 was chosen as editor of *The Times*, Britain's most influential newspaper, by the paper's proprietor, LORD NORTHCLIFFE. During his first period as editor of *The Times*, Dawson played a crucial role in the high politics of the FIRST WORLD WAR, particularly with his famous leader of 4 December 1916, which precipitated the resignation of ASQUITH as Prime Minister and his replacement by LLOYD GEORGE. However, in 1919 Dawson resigned as editor due to political disagreements with the highly opinionated Northcliffe, and from 1919 to 1923 he served as Estates Bursar of All Souls College, Oxford.

In 1923 Dawson returned to the editorial chair of *The Times* after *The Times* had been bought by

J.J. Astor on the death of Northcliffe in 1922. Dawson's second period as editor proved to be more controversial than the first, as he had to steer the paper through the series of domestic and international crises in the 1930s. His short-comings as an editor were highlighted by his involvement in the CHAMBERLAIN government's advocacy of APPEASEMENT from 1937 to 1939. Dawson enjoyed close friendship and political affinity with leading Conservative ministers of the inter-war years, notably VISCOUNT HALIFAX and Neville Chamberlain. This meant that under Dawson The Times was favored with a level of intelligence enjoyed by few members of the CABINET, but also that The Times thus became enmeshed in the policies of the government of the day, surrendering some of its independence for an active role in Chamberlain's pursuit of accommodation with Nazi Germany. Dawson's celebrated leader of 7 September 1938, for instance, presaged the dismemberment of Czechoslovakia at the MUNICH CONFERENCE.

During the first year of the SECOND WORLD WAR The Times regained some of its old reputation with constructive criticism of the War Cabinet, but Dawson retired in 1941 with his reputation nonetheless tarnished as one of the arch-appeasers of Nazi Germany.

Richard Cockett

Bibliography

Cockett, Richard. *Twilight of Truth: Chamberlain, Appeasement and the Manipulation of the Press.* 1989

The Official History of The Times, vols. IV (1912–48) and V (1939–66). 1952, 1984.

Woods, Oliver, and James Bishop. *The Story of The Times.* 1983.

Wrench, John Evelyn. *Geoffrey Dawson and Our Times.* 1955.

Day Lewis, Cecil (1904–1972)

Cecil Day Lewis was born 27 April 1904 at Ballintubbert, Ireland. His mother died when he was four, so the boy was reared in London by his father, an Anglican curate, and a devoted aunt. After attending Sherborne, he entered Wadham College, OXFORD in 1923. Sure of his poetic vocation from boyhood, he continued to write verse at college, where, in his third year he met another undergraduate, WYSTAN HUGH AUDEN, whose sheer intellectual assurance tended to overwhelm and reprogram Day Lewis. He and Auden together edited *Oxford Poetry 1927.*

Day Lewis's first volumes, *Beechen Vigil* (1925) and *Country Comets* (1928), are neo-Romantic and Georgian productions. In *Country Comets,* dedicated "To Her Whose Mind and Body are a Poetry I have Not Achieved," the chief tension is between philosophic universals and individual particulars. The poems ask if man is monad (part

of a system but without personal freedom) or a nomad (a free individual alienated from any coherent social system). *Transitional Poem* (1929) shows Auden's influence. The volume treats social problems and bristles with Audenesque images drawn especially from geology and other natural sciences. *From Features to Iron* (1931) makes symbolic use of the poet's wife's first pregnancy to urge the children of English privilege to develop cutting edges in an effort to become socially and politically useful.

Arising out of the many explorations of *Transitional Poem, The Magnetic Mountain* (1933) is a full-fledged work of prophetic urgency. The mountain is the new industrial revolution, drawing everyone into a workers' fellowship which alone is capable of building a new world. The fellowship is cast as a pilgrimage, a new Exodus from Egypt whereby the past must be abandoned so the future can be born. In 1935 Auden produced *Look, Stranger!* to force his generation to look analytically at the socio-economic crisis of the age. So Day Lewis wrote *A Time to Dance,* rejoicing that the little son whose birth is looked forward to in *From Feathers to Iron* would grow up in a different world as a result of proletarian calls to arms. Day Lewis extended the previous three volumes in the form of a verse drama, *Noah and the Waters* (1936). Previously invited to march to a mountain, the world's magnitudes are now urged, with new fervor, to get aboard the Ark before the Flood rises. *A Hope for Poetry,* his first book of prose criticism (1934) also offered this advice.

Barely supporting a growing family on a teacher's salary, Day Lewis turned to writing DETECTIVE FICTION under the pseudonym "Nicholas Blake". So remunerative was this new venture (he was eventually to write twenty volumes of such fiction, mostly centered on a detective named Nigel Strangeways) that he abandoned teaching and devoted his full time to writing and political activism. in 1936 he joined the COMMUNIST PARTY and helped establish the fledgling Gloucestershire party organization. His 1937 novel, *Starting Point,* expressed his political activism: ". . . all the comrades; in streets, in the country, in prison, in factories, in the little room above the tobacconist's shop and the May-Day Demonstration—they were with him and would be with him as long as he lived . . . they were the spies [history] sent forward into a hostile country . . . whose promise perhaps they alone could fully realize."

But by 1938 he decided he must choose between political activism and poetry. To make a clean break with the three previous years he moved to a thatched cottage outside Musbury in Devon. *Overtures to Death and Other Poems* (1938) lost the sure utopian vision of *The Magnetic Mountain*. The collection is about death: bombers with "iron embryos," laughing children slaughtered in the streets, and the drugged deaths of habitués of cinematic "dreamhouses." Living now in Thomas Hardy country, and making translations of Virgil's *Georgics* (1940), Day Lewis's *Word Over All* (1943) and *Poems: 1943–1947* exhibit his conclusion that the Ivory Tower of the secluded poet is superior to the Brazen Tower of Communist propagandist. As Auden had once influenced his poetic utterance, now echoes of Hardy sing out of "Brithday Poem for Thomas Hardy." But even in this flowering of his lyric gift he is troubled by irreconcilable choices and philosophic antinomies.

War brought Day Lewis's involvement first in a HOME GUARD platoon and then a return to London as an editor for the Ministry of Information (1941). It also produced emotional storms in the poet's previously quiet life. A passionate affair with the wife of a neighboring Musbury farmer produced a son, several poems, and—much later—the somewhat autobiographic Nicholas Blake story *The Private Wound* (1968). Day Lewis also developed a liaison with novelist Rosamond Lehmann. In 1949 he then fell in love with the twenty-four year old actress, Jill Balcon, whom he married in 1951 after divorcing his first wife.

His first marriage to Constance Mary King left two sons (one of whom wrote his father's biography), the second produced a daughter and a son, the actor Daniel Day Lewis.

In 1951 Day Lewis's translation of Virgil's *Aeneid* was broadcast by the BBC as part of the FESTIVAL OF BRITAIN. In the same year he was elected Professor of Poetry at Oxford. During the five-year period of incumbency, he became a public reader of his poetry, often in concert with Jill Balcon. He was awarded the C. Litt. honor from the Royal Society of Literature (1965) and in 1968 succeeded JOHN MASEFIELD as Poet Laureate, thereby becoming the first Irish-born laureate since Nahum Tate (1652–1715). But his final four volumes of verse, *Pegasus* (1957), *The Gate* (1962), *The Room* (1965), and *The Whispering Roots* (1970), received little critical attention for the work of an active Poet Laureate. The critical silence was all the more noticeable in that these volumes contained some of his best poems. After 1969 his formerly robust health declined. He died at Lemmons, Hadley Wood, Hertfordshire, the home of the novelists Elizabeth Jane Howard and Kingsley Amis, both bitter critics of the socialist welfare state for which Day Lewis once fought.

Elton Edward Smith

Bibliography

Cunningham, Valentine. *British Writers of the Thirties*. 1989.

Day-Lewis, C. *The Buried Day*. 1960.

Day-Lewis, Sean. *C. Day-Lewis: An English Literary Life*. 1980.

Gelpi, Albert. *Living in Time: The Poetry of C. Day-Lewis*. 1998.

Hynes, Samuel. *The Auden Generation: Literature and Politics in England in the 1930s*. 1976.

Smith, Elton Edward. *The Angry Young Men of the Thirties: Day Lewis, Spender, MacNeice, Auden*. 1975.

Decolonization

Within two decades of the end of the Second World War the British Empire was dismantled and transformed into the COMMONWEALTH of Nations. This whole process of decolonization did not have much effect on domestic politics or cause any major domestic political controversies. However, many of the colonies, especially in Africa, contained diverse ethnic groups that had maintained independent and often rival or hostile social systems before and during British rule. In many cases the British had deliberately kept them apart in a policy of divide and rule. On the point of independence, they were suddenly expected to share a sense of nationhood and a willingness to cooperate in friendly rivalry in a competitive electoral system. This did not always happen and many of them competed vigorously for office.

India was the most developed colony in the Empire both politically and economically, with British control beginning in the eighteenth century. The British introduced a series of reforms in 1909, 1919, and 1935 that gave greater responsibility for governing India to Indians while ultimately maintaining control. This was done in response to Indian pressure as well as the needs of the British to involve Indians in the running of the country. By 1939 the INDIAN NATIONALIST MOVEMENT was a highly organized one and had mobilized Indians throughout the subcontinent. It was led by Mohandas Gandhi and Jawaharlal Nehru for the Indian National Congress, founded in 1885 and overwhelmingly supported by Hindus; and Muhammad Ali Jinnah, who was mobilizing an increasingly large number of Muslims behind the All-India Muslim League, founded in 1906. By 1945 the LABOUR government was committed to independence for India; the Indian nationalists would accept nothing less. Gandhi and the Indian National Congress demanded that the government of India be turned over to its representatives at independence. This demand was rejected by Jinnah and the Muslim League, which, in 1940, passed a resolution calling for a separate country for Muslims. The League would not shift from its position, and Congress reluctantly agreed to the partition of India into states of India and Pakistan in August

1947. Freedom did not come without bloodshed in the northwest part of India when many Muslims migrated to Pakistan and Hindus to India. War was also to break out over the right to the state of Kashmir. In 1971 Pakistan was divided when East Pakistan seceded and became the new nation of Bangladesh.

With India independent the argument for maintaining a number of other colonies lost its force. Ceylon (Sri Lanka), smaller and with a prosperous export economy of tea and rubber, had an even more developed political system with a wider franchise than India. In spite of the division between the minority Tamils and the majority Sinhalese, independence was achieved very smoothly in 1948. Burma had received its independence a month earlier on 4 January 1948, and in general elections held soon after war's end, Aung San received an overwhelming vote of support for his call for independence. He was assassinated in 1947, but Burma became independent under Thakin Nu.

Malaya, an exporter of rubber and tin, played an important role in the Sterling Area. Before independence could be granted the British had to deal with communist guerrillas, mostly of Chinese extraction, who were soundly defeated. Tunku Abdul Rahman led the Federation of Malaya to independence in 1957. In 1963 Singapore, Sabah (the former British North Borneo), and Sarawak joined the federation, which then changed its name to Malaysia. Singapore, however, dropped out of the federation in 1965. The remnants of the British Empire in Asia were Brunei, which became independent in February 1984, and Hong Kong, which was returned to China in 1997.

While independence for India had long been conceded, the British had no plans for freeing their colonies in Africa, but within a decade of the Second World War they were also well on their way towards freedom. In West Africa independence began with the Gold Coast, which had a long history of protest, but was an apparently model colony. In 1946 the British introduced a new constitution that would set the colony along the slow road to freedom. In protest, however, the United Gold Coast Convention was formed in 1947. Riots broke out the following year and in 1949 Kwame Nkrumah founded the Convention People's Party. He instituted a policy of STRIKES, boycotts and demonstrations—"positive action" as it was called—that dramatically increased opposition to British rule. The British held elections in 1951, which only confirmed Nkrumah's hold on the country. Accordingly, plans were drawn up for independence, which came in 1957, when Nkrumah led the country to freedom under the ancient name of Ghana.

Once the Gold Coast became independent it became impossible for Britain to retain its remaining African colonies. HAROLD MACMILLAN recognized this in February 1960 when he said that the "wind of change" was blowing through Africa and that the British had to take account of the "growth of national consciousness." Nigeria was one of those countries where the British thought independence would come later rather than sooner because of its ethnic diversity, with Yorubas in the Western Region, Ibos in the Eastern Region, and Muslim emirates in the North. The British introduced three different constitutions in the complicated political situation before conceding independence in 1960 under the newspaperman Nnamdi Azikiwe as Governor-General, Abubakar Tafawa Balewa as Prime Minister, and Chief Obafemi Awolowo as Leader of the Opposition.

The other British colonies in West Africa were Sierra Leone and The Gambia, Britain's oldest colony in West Africa and the smallest on the mainland. Sierra Leone, which had been established in 1787 around Freetown as a settler colony for Blacks then living in England, and the hinterland was acquired during the late Victorian "scramble for Africa". Independence was granted in 1961, and internal tensions came to the surface in the 1967 army coup. The Gambia was pushed toward decolonization more by the British than by local politicians; elections outside the capital were not held until 1960. It became independent in 1965.

Of the non-settler colonies in East Africa, Tanganyika became independent in 1961, Uganda in 1962, and Zanzibar in 1963. Tanganyika, brought under German control in 1884, was taken over by Britain as a LEAGUE OF NATIONS trust territory in 1919. Unlike many African colonies, a united nationalist party had risen in Tanganyika under Julius Nyerere, and the country experienced more than twenty years of peaceful development under his leadership after independence. In 1964 it merged with Zanzibar—British territory from 1890 until independence—to become the United Republic of Tanzania.

Uganda was dominated by its largest kingdom, Buganda, which was opposed by the three smaller kingdoms of Bunyoro, Toro, and Ankole. As a result, no single nationalist party dominated the country. This has led to continuous political problems since independence with various coups, such as the 1971 one led by Idi Amin who instituted a particularly bloody dictatorship, only ended by invasion from Tanzania in 1979.

The situation in Kenya was even more complicated because it was also settled by Europeans and Asians who hoped to maintain power after independence. Administered since 1888 by William

Mackinnon's British East Africa Company and the British government, Kenya had the pastoral Masai people, the Kikuyu, and Luo as the dominant groups. The Kikuyu Association was formed in 1920, and the next year the more assertive Young Kikuyu Association (later the Kikuyu Central Association) was established. Other organizations were created before 1944 when the Kenya African Union was founded (mostly with the support of Kikuyus) and headed in 1947 by Jomo Kenyatta. A rival organization, the Kenya African Democratic Union, represented Luo and smaller groups. The nationalist movement in Kenya turned violent from 1952 to 1956, when a group of Kikuyu, the Mau Mau, took to the bush to fight for "Land and Freedom." It was led by a group of ex-servicemen and peasants who acutely felt the economic and social deprivation which gave rise to the whole movement. The British suppressed the movement, but independence came in 1963 under Kenyatta, who dominated the country until his death in 1979.

Northern and Southern Rhodesia were created by Cecil Rhodes and the British South African Company. The company ruled the south until 1923 and the north until 1924, when they both became crown colonies. In 1953 the prosperous Rhodesias and the poor Nyasaland were joined into a white-controlled Central African Federation. Opposing the Federation, Northern Rhodesia became dominated by Kenneth Kaunda, who led it to independence in 1964 under the name of Zambia. Kaunda created a one-party state in 1972 and ruled until 1991. Nyasaland's experience paralleled Northern Rhodesia's: it was dominated by an individual, Hastings Banda, who took the nation, renamed Malawi, to independence in 1964, and became its president for life in 1971.

Southern Rhodesia presented a problem to the British government because of the European settlers. The African nationalist party, the African National Congress, founded by Joshua Nkomo, split in 1963 into the Zimbabwe African People's Union (ZAPU) and the more radical Zimbabwe African National Union (ZANU). The white response came in November 1965, when Ian Smith and his government issued a Unilateral Declaration of Independence and instituted white minority rule. The British government, favoring majority rule, responded with economic sanctions, which proved ineffective. The struggle waged by ZANU and ZAPU finally led to the defeat of white Rhodesians, general elections, and independence in 1980, when the country, led by Robert Mugabe of ZANU, was renamed Zimbabwe.

In the Mediterranean the two islands of Cyprus and Malta, important as military bases, became independent in 1960 and 1964 respectively.

In North Africa, Egypt became especially important after the opening of the Suez Canal in 1869. In 1882 it was conquered by the British but became a protectorate in 1914. This ended with independence in 1922, but the British maintained troops there until 1956. Sudan, taken over in 1898, also became sovereign in 1956. PALESTINE came under British control in 1919 as a League of Nations mandate. A homeland for the Jews had been promised in this area by the British in the 1917 Balfour Declaration. Pressure from immigrant Jews in Palestine and the American government led to the establishment of the Jewish national homeland of Israel in 1948.

In the Caribbean and the Americas, Jamaica, Trinidad, and Tobago became independent in 1962, and Barbados in 1966. In 1967 Anguilla, Antigua, Dominica, Grenada, Nevis, St. Kitts, St. Lucia, and St. Vincent were linked with Britain as "Associated States", but Grenada became independent in 1974, Dominica in 1978, St. Lucia and St. Vincent in 1979, Antigua in 1981, and St. Kitts-Nevis in 1983. The Bahamas became independent in 1973, while Bermuda has, since 1968, been a self-governing British dependency. On the mainland, British Guiana became independent as Guyana in 1966, and British Honduras (Belize) in 1981.

Most of the newly independent states remained in the Commonwealth of Nations, which meets formally every two years. Political decolonization is almost complete with just a few territories around the world, such as Anguilla, Ascension Island, British Virgin Islands, Cayman Islands, Falkland Islands, Gibraltar, and others still ruled by Britain. Economic decolonization, however, is a burning question in many countries of the Commonwealth, raising talk of a "second independence."

Roger D. Long

Bibliography

Chamberlain, M.E. *Decolonization: The Fall of the European Empires.* 1985.

Darwin, John. *Britain and Decolonization: The Retreat from Empire in the Post-War World.* 1988.

Gifford, Prosser, and Wm. Roger Louis, eds. *The Transfer of Power in Africa: Decolonization 1940–1960.* 2 vols. 1982.

Hargreaves, John D. *Decolonization in Africa.* 1988.

Mansergh, Nicholas. *The Commonwealth Experience: vol. 2: From British to Multiracial Commonwealth.* 2nd ed. 1982.

Defence of the Realm Act (DORA)

Legislation in the form of the Defence of the Realm Act empowered the government to make temporary regulations necessary "for securing the public safety and the defence of the realm" during the FIRST WORLD WAR. DORA was really several acts, the initial legislation passed on 8 August 1914 being amended and extended several times.

DORA gave birth to hundreds of regulations. The public readily understood some curbs on normal activities: for instance, the ban on showing lights at night in large cities like LONDON and Birmingham in case this facilitated an airborne attack. They found others more puzzling: the authorities had to explain that shooting at pigeons must stop because someone might bring down an official "messenger". To prevent leakage of information useful to the enemy, the PRESS and international mail were censored through DORA. Newspaper reports on military campaigns could only repeat official bulletins. Giving unsanctioned details could bring fines or even closure of the paper. All letters to or from foreign countries, including military mail, were read and pruned by censors, and it was forbidden to enclose photographs or send picture postcards overseas.

Freedom of opinion generally did not suffer greatly under DORA. PACIFISTS, for instance, could still openly criticize the war. However, it was illegal to say or write anything that might disaffect the armed forces or harm recruiting. In 1918 the pacifist BERTRAND RUSSELL was sentenced to six months in jail under DORA for denouncing the presence of American troops in Britain. DORA was also used to curb behavior tolerable in peacetime but potentially hazardous in wartime. Heavy drinking, for example, was discouraged by shortening the opening hours of public houses and forbidding people to treat others to drinks. One regulation "protecting" the military effort that earned the scorn of women's groups was one that made it illegal for a woman with venereal disease to have sexual relations with a member of the armed forces.

DORA was more than just a policing tool. It also helped to extend state control over the economy. During the war the government established new ministries and departments to organize the supply of shipping, munitions, fuel, food, and other necessities. Heads of these units derived their authority from DORA powers delegated from the government. DORA allowed the requisition of any land, buildings, machinery, and materials required for the production of items vital to the war effort and for the management and housing of the labor force involved. The authorities could take over or nullify existing contracts and could control the pricing mechanism by setting fixed profit margins and prices at wholesale and retail levels. The Ministry of Food and Board of Agriculture used these powers, for instance, to take over the import of essential foodstuffs, fix prices, ration civilians, and issue compulsory cultivation orders to farmers.

Most of the DORA regulations ended with the armistice; a few in the economic sphere continued until normal trade could be resumed. Since the legislation was enacted for the duration of the war, DORA was automatically rescinded at midnight on 31 August 1921, the official end of the war for Britain.

L. Margaret Barnett

Bibliography

DeGroot, Gerard J. *Blighty: British Society in the Era of the Great War.* 1996.

Marwick, Arthur. *The Deluge: British Society in the First World War.* 1965.

Delius, Frederick Theodore Albert (1862–1934)
A contemporary of ELGAR, Frederick Delius fell more deeply under Wagner's spell, drawing on his chromatic harmony and thematic continuity, although the example of Grieg, Delius' friend and mentor, helped him to lighten his style. Delius drew inspiration from a limited number of ideas, notably the transience of love and nature.

In 1884 Delius' father, a German-born Bradford wool merchant, unable to interest his headstrong son in the family business, lent him sufficient money to emigrate and establish himself as an orange-grower in Florida. Delius could now immerse himself in serious composition, and a chance encounter with Thomas Ward, a gifted musician who lived in nearby Jacksonville, led to a concentrated six-month course of tuition. Subsequent study at the Leipzig Conservatory (1886–7) was less beneficial, although Delius met Grieg, who persuaded Delius' father to support Delius while he found his feet as a composer in Paris. Friends with Gauguin, Munch, and Strindberg, Delius led a bohemian existence for several years—he had already contracted syphilis. In 1879 he settled at Grez-sur-Loing, near Paris, together with the painter Jelka Rosen, whom he married in 1903, and lived there with few interruptions for the rest of his life.

Delius' sympathy for his surroundings can be heard in his third opera, *Koanga* (C.F. Keary, after G.W. Cable: 1897), set on a Southern plantation, *Appalachia* (Trad.: 1896/1903), a series of variations on an American slave song and the nocturne, *Paris* (1899), in which a Straussian sumptuousness and vitality suggest interesting possibilities that Delius did not, in the event, pursue. Stylistic maturity came with his next opera, *A Village Romeo and Juliet* (Keary, after G. Keller: 1901), which, although marred partly by undistinguished vocal melody, culminates in the ecstatic *Walk to the Paradise Garden*, after which the lovers scuttle the hay barge on which they are floating downstream. In *Sea Drift* (Whitman: 1904), for baritone, chorus, and orchestra, poignant regret for love's transience is captured in music of ever changing color and chromatic flow as a boy sorrowingly observes a seabird whose mate never returns. More positive feelings are explored in the monumental *A Mass of Life* (1905), a setting of texts from Nietzsche's *Also Sprach Zarathustra*, Delius identifying himself with Zarathustra's philosophy of living life to the full and of developing courage in the face of approaching death. The fortitude Delius himself had to muster as his health deteriorated was a contributory cause to a change in style in such works as the orchestral *North Country Sketches* (1914) and *Eventyr* (1917), where the sharper-defined sounds and uncompromising harmonies contrast with the sensuous sweetness of the earlier *Brigg Fair* (1907) and *In a Summer Garden* (1908). An unexpected turn to conventional forms in concertos for violin (1916), cello (1921) and violin and cello (1916), together with a string quartet (1916) and sonatas for violin (1914) and cello (1916), marks, in general, a period of flagging inspiration, and by the 1920s Delius had become an invalid, paralyzed in both hands (1922) and blind (1925). Eric Fenby came to his rescue, and, acting as his amanuensis, helped Delius complete a final handful of works, most notably the *Songs of Farewell* (Whitman: 1930) for chorus and orchestra.

Trevor Bray

Bibliography

Carley, Lionel, ed. *Delius: a Life in Letters, 1862–1934.* 2 vols., 1983, 1988.

Palmer, Christopher. *Delius: Portrait of a Cosmopolitan.* 1976.

Design

The history of design in twentieth-century Britain reveals both the continuing influence of the nineteenth-century arts and crafts tradition on the definition and the aesthetics of design, and the continuing reluctance of many British industries to hire professional designers. During the first half of the century design reformers within the government, education, industry, and the private sector felt that design had primarily a moral and social, rather than economic, import. Most industrialists, on the other hand, felt that design was not a significant factor in the marketability of their products, particularly given the relatively secure markets provided within the Empire; they also complained that "industrial artists" were not properly trained for the technical requirements of industry and were unwilling to subordinate their aesthetic goals to the more practical dictates of their employers. The impasse between design reformers and industry gradually changed as the design profession began to emerge in the 1930s, but even with the more specialized training for the "industrial designer" that began in the 1950s and the concomitant stress on the economic importance of design by the government, many

British industries continued to downplay the signficance of design.

The nineteenth-century arts and crafts movement might seem an unlikely foundation for the history of twentieth-century industrial design, as John Ruskin, William Morris, and many of their contemporaries disparaged the use of machines. By the turn of the century, however, several arts and crafts adherents (including Walter Crane and W.R. Lethaby, both of whom fashioned the design curriculum at the Royal College of Art at this time) argued that the machine could be understood as simply a new "artisanal tool" that ought to be employed by trained artists for the aesthetic, moral, and economic benefit of the community. British design reformers believed that their country's exports would not be competitive against those of Germany unless British industries hired artists to turn machine products into "industrial art." They argued that this was unlikely to occur unless industries were convinced that design increased product marketability, and that designers were trained to meet the requirements of industry. Despite their emphasis on training for industry, however, many design reformers believed that the fundamental basis for design education should be a solid grounding in the "fine arts" rather than a more specialized training in the manufacturing techniques of specific industries.

The Design and Industries Association, formed in 1915 to integrate art and industry, consisted of artists, educators, and businessmen, many of whom were imbued with the aesthetic and social ideals of Ruskin and Morris. However, the DIA did not share Ruskin and Morris' dislike of modern industry, believing that machinery and commerce were here to stay and must therefore be spiritualized by artists—resulting in the restoration of a merry (albeit mechanized) England. The organization's emphasis on simple, functional designs—their motto was "Fitness for Purpose," which was to become the rallying cry of virtually all design reformers during the inter-war period, including the Prince of Wales—was welcomed by important officials in government and education, many of whom also shared a similar allegiance to the moral and social visions of Ruskin and Morris. The DIA's aesthetic tended to be conservative, as was true of English design in general during the inter-war period: simple, plain, functional forms, with a modicum of decoration (frequently floral) were preferred over styles favored on the Continent, such as Art Deco or the more expressionistic variants of Art Nouveau.

Other organizations promoting the union of art and industry were formed in the 1920s, such as the government's British Institute of Industrial Art, and the Federation of British Industries'

Industrial Arts Committee. But these design reform organizations had little practical effect. Many British industries, rendered complacent by sales within the Empire, continued to downplay the importance of design as a significant factor in the marketability of their products. They also complained that artists were not properly trained to design for industry, a charge that had much validity and reflected the bias in British education that favored the liberal arts as opposed to vocational training. The course for industrial artists at the RCA, for example, emphasized training in the fine arts; artists were expected to acquire specialized knowledge of industrial techniques on the job. The other major training institution for industrial artists, London's Central School, had a more crafts-based curriculum, but neither school provided any training for design in the new light-metal industries (AUTOMOBILES, electrical appliances, etc.) that arose in the inter-war period. This situation remained true for nearly all British schools that offered courses in design (with the exception of Birmingham in the mid-1930s) until after the Second World War.

Design education in inter-war Britain thus remained oriented towards the crafts-based industries, such as furniture, clothing, jewelry, pottery, and textiles. As it was possible for so-called "fine artists" to become designers for these industries without much technical training, many of the most prominent designers during the period were painters or sculptors like PAUL NASH, DUNCAN GRANT, VANESSA BELL, GRAHAM SUTHERLAND, and BEN NICHOLSON. This new association between "fine art" and "design" was given further emphasis during this period through ROGER FRY and Clive Bell's aesthetic of "significant form," which they codified between 1910–14. For Fry and Bell, art's most fundamental quality was its design rather than its content. By emphasizing that art was more concerned with abstract design than with mimetic representation, Fry and Bell made it easier for fine artists to take up a career in design, which had formerly been associated with artisans. Thus, although Ruskin and Morris' goal of integrating art and industry was not accomplished in the 1920s and 1930s, one of their major objectives had been accomplished during this period: the hierarchical distinction between art and craft that had prevailed in the nineteenth century was essentially abolished through the widespread use of "design" as an inclusive term covering both art and craft. However, fine art and design were separated once again after 1945, when design became a more specialized, technical profession.

The Depression of the early 1930s brought renewed attention to the economic significance of design among government officials, educators, artists, and design reformers. The Boards of Trade and Education formed the Council for Art and Industry in 1934 under the direction of FRANK PICK, a chief executive of the London Underground whose own devotion to the principles of Ruskin and Morris led him to commission modern artists and architects to create a unifed design for the LONDON transport system. The Council argued that design should become a specialized profession, but they continued to think of the designer as an artist rather than as a technician, and to focus their inquiries on the training of designers for craft-based industries. A similar understanding of the nascent design "profession" as the province of artists was advanced by many writers on the design question, such as Herbert Read, Nikolaus Pevsner, and John Gloag; the first professional society of designers, the Society of Industrial Artists, was formed in 1930 primarily by artists (its first President was the painter Paul Nash).

While design reformers did look abroad to see how British design could meet foreign competition, most continued to express a conservative, provincial aesthetic. Many reformers professed allegiance to traditional "English" styles of design that emphasized "plain and good," organic, and functional forms in conscious opposition to more avant-garde styles derived from French surrealism or American "streamlining." And most British industries remained indifferent to the whole question of product design.

It was not until the Second World War that the government and industries recognized that the United States would be their primary competitor for export markets after the war, and that consequently more attention would have to be given to design for the light-metal industries. The government decided that British designers ought to follow the American model, established in the 1920s, of the professional "industrial designer." This spelled the end of the arts and crafts conception of the designer as a broadly-trained artists who needed little specialized knowledge to design for the crafts-based industries. Instead, the designer was redefined as a specialist versed in the technical requirements of a chosen industry.

The government established the Council of Industrial Design in 1944 to promote this new conception of the "industrial designer" as opposed to the "industrial artist." Similarly, design education at the RCA shifted from its inter-war emphasis on the union of the arts towards a more technologically-oriented training for the demands of the light-metal industries when Robin Darwin was appointed Principal in 1949.

The austere, functional forms favored by design reformers in the inter-war period gave way in the later 1950s and 1960s to a wide variety of style influenced by Continental and American designs. In the 1960s British design attained international prominence, not only through the works of individual designers but also through the promotional efforts of contemporary design reformers such as Terence Conran, who gave the field notable visibility through his own designs, the chain of Habitat stores he established in the 1960s, and the Design Museum he opened in 1988. But the history of contemporary British design is as much one of continuity as it is of change: while design aesthetics and approaches changed after the war, many British industries continued to remain relatively indifferent to design. The THATCHER government attempted to promote a closer integration of design and industry through its "Design for Profit" campaign of 1982: in this respect, at least, the Thatcher government resembled many that had preceded it.

Michael Saler

Bibliography

Heskett, John. "Industrial Design" in Boris Ford, ed., *The Cambridge Cultural History*. vol. 9. 1992. pp. 288–318.

Naylor, Gillian. "Design and Industry" in Boris Ford, ed., *The Cambridge Guide to the Arts in Britain*. vol. 8. 1989. pp. 254–93.

Saler, Michael. *The Avant-Garde in Interwar England: Medieval Modernism and the London Underground*. 1999.

Detective Fiction

The Anglo-American detective story typically displays three essential features: first, a serious crime, usually murder, must be committed early on; second, the identity of the criminal must not be revealed until the end; third, all clues, when finally assembled, must point to the criminal, and to no one else. There is considerable debate as to whether a detective story must include a detective figure, official or unofficial, but in Great Britain, as in America, the most important and lasting works in the genre have typically featured such a character. In addition, British detective stories, at least those written during the golden age of the 1920s and 1930s, generally take place within a relatively close and stable social milieu, usually rural or suburban, and seem to be concerned with restoring a pre-lapsarian societal innocence through the identification and scapegoating of the criminal.

At the beginning of the twentieth century British detective fiction was still dominated by the lean silhouette of Arthur Conan Doyle's (1859–1930) manic-depressive reasoning machine, Sherlock Holmes, who was given a new lease on life in 1901, in *The Hound of the Baskervilles*, after a hiatus of eight years and an (apparently) fatal plunge into the Reichenbach Falls. Conan Doyle would continue to write Holmes stories well into the 1920s, thereby sustaining the popularity of the short story form during a period of declining magazine sales. One beneficiary of Conan Doyle's example was G.K. CHESTERTON, who launched his own decidedly un-Holmesian, but quite popular, continuing detective hero in the short story collection, *The Innocence of Father Brown* (1911). Short, dumpy, clumsy, reticent, and intuitive, Father Brown took a fideistic and aleatory approach to the mysteries of crime that reflected Chesterton's own paradoxical, and Catholic, attitudes toward the mystery of life itself.

Detective novels were still being written during the first decade of the century, but not until the appearance of *Trent's Last Case* (1913), by E[dmund] C[lerihew] Bentley (1875–1956), did the detective novel regain a dominant market position. Like Chesterton, Bentley had set out to have some fun at the expense of the morose and coldly rational Holmes. His detective-hero, Philip Trent, an artist and occasional newspaper reporter with an avocational attraction to solving murder mysteries, owes more to Wilkie Collins' Franklin Blake (*The Moonstone*, 1868) than to Conan Doyle's creation. Trent would help to shape similarly dandyish breeds of sleuth, such as DOROTHY SAYERS' Lord Peter Wimsey and Margery Allingham's Albert Campion, whose most Trent-like turn appears in *Death of a Ghost* (1934).

The works of Sayers and AGATHA CHRISTIE, who together dominated the golden age, epitomize many of the generic features that became standardized during this period: that the circle of suspects must be closed early in the story (which was one reason for the recurrent country club, village, or manor-house settings), or that the criminal must be someone whose thoughts cannot be shared with the reader—a rule that Christie herself was the first to break. In general, detective fiction of the golden age is distinguished by its ingenious plotting, its close attention to physical setting and chronology, its playing with character-types, and its rather conservative bias toward the traditional values of class privilege and aristocratic noblesse oblige in a nihilistic post-war world. Yet this is not the whole story: Sayers' female sleuth, Harriet Vane, vindicates feminist values against tradition—for example, in *Gaudy Night* (1936).

Of the many detective writers that flourished during the golden age, a handful besides Sayers and Christie deserves mention. Margery Allingham (1904–66) first introduced the vaguely aristocratic and government-connected Albert Campion and his Cockney side-kick, Lugg, in *The Crime at Black Dudley* (1929). She continued writing well into the Cold War era, gradually humanizing her detective hero in the process. Ngaio Marsh (1895–1982), an actress and theatrical producer in her native New Zealand, was the creator of Inspector Roderick Alleyn, a professional rather than amateur sleuth but, like the Wimsey-ish Campion, of noble birth. Many of Marsh's stories unfold behind the scenes of a theatrical company or among theatre people. The series detective heroes of Michael Innes (1906–94) [the pen-name of John Innes Mackintosh Stewart] and Nicolas Blake (1904–72) [the pen-name of poet C. Day Lewis] owe much of their distinction to their connections with the aristocracy of letters rather than the peerage. Innes's Inspector John Appleby, who debuted in *Death at the President's Lodging* (1935), evinces his creator's donnish urbanity through his familiarity with such obscure tomes as the "fourteen bulky volumes of the *Argentorati Athenaeus*," while Blake's Nigel Strangeways, based loosely on the personality of W.H. Auden, is not above lacing his talk with allusions to T.S. Eliot and Emily Dickinson. Like Allingham and Marsh, however, Innes and Blake never let their interest in character, milieu, or literary allusion overwhelm the puzzle element.

Many golden age authors continued writing after the Second World War, but their idiosyncratic detective heroes began to apppear ever more brittle and prefabricated in the grim, harsh light of Britain's Cold War decline. Graham Greene (1904–91) had already, in thrillers like *Stamboul Train* (1932) and *Brighton Rock* (1938), begun to place less emphasis on the puzzle element and more on criminal motivation and the intricacies of moral reasoning than his golden age cohorts. Greene's example helped inspire other writers of crime fiction like Patricia Highsmith (1921–95), who, beginning with *Strangers on a Train* (1950) (later a well-known film by Alfred Hitchcock), ably advanced Greene's agenda. Highsmith, like many of her contemporaries, also began to include in her social tapestry ever coarser strands of post-war life.

From the 1960s to the present British detective fiction has evolved into a rather amorphous subclass of the realistic novel. The works of Ruth Rendell (1920–), animated by the eternally middle-aged figure of Sussex Inspector Reginald Wexford, display a keen ear for colloquial conversation and a fine aptitude for exploring the psychological nuances of sexual deviation. Colin Dexter (1930–) has continued in the classic vein of ingenious puzzlers while devising, in the irascible, pub-crawling Mozartian, Inspector Morse, something new in the tradition of the detective hero: an Oxford-educated prole. Sir John Mortimer (1923–), meanwhile, invented a new variation on the lawyer-detective in Horace Rumpole, a sort of Pickwickian Perry Mason.

One of the most talented of contemporary detective writers is P[hyllis] D. James—now Baroness James—(1930–), creator of the private detective, Cordelia Gray, and of Adam Dalgleish of Scotland Yard. James is clearly a practitioner of the old school in the ingenuity of her plotting and her fine-grained attention to scene, setting, and physical detail. These talents are in evidence in such works as *Innocent Blood* (1980), *A Taste for Death* (1986), and *Devices and Desires* (1989), where James seems to have pushed the boundaries of the genre as far as they can go in the direction of the realistic novel, with finely shaded studies of character and an emphasis on the complex nuances of moral decision-making.

Charles J. Rzepka

Bibliography

Haycraft, Howard. *Murder for Pleasure: The Life and Times of the Detective Story.* 1941.

Hubin, Allen J. *The Bibliography of Crime Fiction, 1749–1975.* 1979.

Murch, Alma Elizabeth. *The Development of the Detective Novel.* 1958.

Panek, LeRoy. *Watteau's Shepherds: The Detective Novel in Britain, 1914–1940.* 1979.

Symons, Julian. *Bloody Murder: From the Detective Story to the Crime Novel: a History.* 3rd ed. 1992.

de Valois, Ninette (1898–2001)

A pioneer of imagination, courage, taste, and inexhaustible energy, Ninette de Valois was the guiding force in the establishment of a classical ballet tradition in Britain and the founder of the company that is now the Royal Ballet. Pursuing her artistic vision with confident determination, she singlemindedly molded a ballet company to match her ideal conception of one.

Born Edris Stannus in Ireland and trained in England by ballet teachers of the French, Italian, and Russian schools, de Valois made her performing debut as a child, dancing on seaside piers, and her professional debut in a London pantomime in 1914. She was a principal dancer with Thomas Beecham's opera company at Covent Garden by 1919, and appeared later with a small touring company led by Léonide Massine and Lydia Lopokova before joining Serge Diaghilev's Ballets Russes in Paris in 1923.

Inspired by the extraordinary synthesis of the arts in Diaghilev's productions, de Valois returned to London and, in 1926, opened her own school, the Academy of Choreographic Art, which she knew could provide both a supply of dancers for her future company and a home in which a national style could develop.

Committed to giving her pupils professional experience, she offered her services and theirs to Lilian Baylis, director of the Old Vic Theatre, who bravely hired the students and their young teacher. For the next four years de Valois choreographed at the Old Vic and several other theaters, coaching the actors in stage movement and incorporating her dancers, and occasionally short ballets, into the plays and operas.

When Baylis reopened the Sadler's Wells Theatre in 1931, it became the cradle for de Valois' embryonic company. This tiny group—six women with de Valois as choreographer and leading dancer—presented its first complete evening of ballet on 5 May 1931. The historic debut took place at the Old Vic, and the entire program was repeated at Sadler's Wells Theatre ten days later.

Having moved her school and dedicated performers to the Wells, de Valois engaged Alicia Markova as a guest artist, fortifying her fledgling company with an established star whose presence anchored the first British stagings of the great Russian classics. Between 1932 and 1935, de Valois mounted complete productions of *Swan Lake, Giselle,* and *The Nutcracker* (called *Casse-Noisette* at the time). The backbone of her growing company's character, these challenging classical works educated the public and her young dancers simultaneously and set a performance standard they could all recognize and respect.

At the same time, de Valois began building a native repertory. FREDERICK ASHTON became the company's principal choreographer in 1935, and de Valois created her own finest works—*Job, The Rake's Progress,* and *Checkmate*—before the company mounted its first production of *The Sleeping Beauty* (then *The Sleeping Princess*) in 1939.

After leading many erratic tours at home and abroad during the Second World War, de Valois was invited to install her Sadler's Wells Ballet in the Royal Opera House, Covent Garden. Reopening that theater with a glittering production of *The Sleeping Beauty,* the company settled into its new, permanent residence in 1946, and de Valois quickly organized a second company to take its place at Sadler's Wells Theatre.

To attract the public, she collected a magnificent repertory of nineteenth century classics and masterpieces from Diaghilev's revolutionary Ballets Russes, and encouraged a succession of dancers to create new works: like Ashton, KENNETH MACMILLAN, John Cranko, and Robert Helpmann established their choreographic identity under her direction. To meet the demands of her chosen repertory, the dancers were trained as precise classical instruments, and the English style of dancing came to represent clarity of execution, lightness of attack, and sustained musicality.

Embraced as a national institution, the Sadler's Wells Ballet achieved international stature with its first visit to New York in 1949 and its frequent world tours during the 1950s. De Valois was made a Dame of the British Empire in 1951, and her achievement received its own accolade in 1956, when the two companies became the Royal

Ballet. She retired as director of the Royal Ballet in 1961, but continued to teach at its school, revive her own works, and serve the National Ballet of Turkey, which she founded in 1947. She was honored with the Order of Merit in 1992 and died nine years later at the age of 102.

Universally known as Madam, de Valois always claimed that "we shape no event as forcibly as events shape us." Yet in realizing her imaginative ambition, she herself shaped Britain's artistic life with sublime practicality and enduring wisdom.

Barbara Newman

Bibliography

de Valois, Ninette. *Come Dance with Me.* 1957.

Devolution, Scottish and Welsh

Devolution of government for Scotland and Wales was a long-delayed process. The idea of devolving authority, executive or legislative, to subordinate elected bodies in the Celtic nations, let alone federalism, seemed at variance with the broad centralism of English government since Tudor times. The Act of Union that absorbed the conquered Wales into the English governmental system in 1536 was an extension of this process. The Act of Union with Scotland in 1707 appeared to be a continuation of integrating Britishness, as indeed did Union with Ireland in 1801.

Nevertheless, the political distinctiveness of Scotland, at least, remained after the Union. The Scots retained their own institutions, the established Presbyterian Kirk, a separate education system, and, especially important, a separate legal system. A strong sense of Scottish culture remained, fostered by the writings of Sir Walter Scott in the early nineteenth century. The recreation of the Scottish Office in 1885, after pressure by the Whiggish Scottish aristocracy on Gladstone, further emphasized the Scottish national identity. In Wales, by contrast, while its distinctiveness in language and culture was apparent (if often deplored), there was a relentless process of absorption by Westminster and Whitehall, culminating in the abolition of the Court of Great Sessions in 1830. After 1867, however, the progress of franchise reform saw a radical Liberalism, symbolizing a buoyant political democracy with younger men like Tom Ellis and DAVID LLOYD GEORGE as its voices, raise a new range of Welsh issues. This trend resulted in separate Welsh legislation—the Sunday Closing Act (1881), the important intermediate Education Act (1889), and eventually the disestablishment of the Church in Wales (1919), along with administrative devolution in education (1907) and later health and agriculture.

Late-Victorian Britain, indeed, did accept Celtic pluralism—but not devolution. The movement for home rule in Ireland did lead to demand for "home rule all round" within the British Isles. However this concept was really an attempt by Joseph Chamberlain and others to circumvent IRISH NATIONALISM. Like a more full-blown federal solution, it never attracted enthusiasm among the dominant English. More crucial, neither Scotland nor Wales before 1914 showed the same passion for home rule manifested in Ireland. They sought national equality within Britain and the empire, not separation from it. During the BOER WAR, while the Irish Nationalists applauded British defeats, the Scots and (to a lesser degree) Welsh upheld the imperialist cause.

Devolution or modified federalism made no headway after the FIRST WORLD WAR. British politics remained firmly unionist, especially after the creation of the Irish Free State in 1922. The LABOUR PARTY, whose founding fathers, such as KEIR HARDIE and RAMSAY MACDONALD, had favored both Scottish and Welsh self-government, became as centralist as the CONSERVATIVES. The trade unions, class consciousness during the depression years, the commitment to nationwide central planning and national social standards killed off Labour sympathy for devolution. This trend was strengthened by the solidarity kindled during the SECOND WORLD WAR. Socialists like ANEURIN BEVAN derided separate policies for Scotland and Wales. Douglas Jay observed that "the gentleman from Whitehall knew best". The enhanced powers of the Scottish Office during the war did not appear to herald any wider constitutional rearrangement.

The modern history of devolution really begins in the mid-1960s. The Scottish National Party and the Welsh party, Plaid Cymru, both minor forces since their formation in the twenties, gained in support during the socio-cultural transformations of the 1960s, including the new radicalism of youth. Plaid Cymru saw both a revival of the language movement and the capture of its first parliamentary seat when Gwynfor Evans won Carmarthen in July 1966. The SNP won Hamilton through Winifred Ewing in November 1967, and scored heavily in local government elections. Much alarmed, the WILSON government set up the Crowther, later Kilbrandon, royal commission on the constitution, hoping that separatist feeling in Scotland and Wales would disappear. However, in 1973 Crowther came out with a majority recommendation for a Scottish parliament with a legislative role and an elected Welsh assembly whose powers would be executive only. The two general elections of 1974 resulted in the election of 11 SNP members and 3 for Plaid Cymru, while the Labour government shortly became a minority administration dependent on smaller parties. The CALLAGHAN government thus scrambled through Parliament separate bills for Scotland and Wales.

On 1 March 1979 referendums were held in both nations, but in the event devolution failed to progress. In Wales, where much of the Labour Party remained hostile to separatism, devolution was humiliatingly defeated by almost four to one. In Scotland it scraped home with a narrow majority on a lowish poll, but the vote for devolution was far short of the 40 per cent of voters needed for Scottish devolution to pass. Soon after, the Labour government was defeated. Conservative rule appeared to mean the end of devolution and a revival of strident Britishness under Mrs. THATCHER'S auspices. In Wales, devolution then made only slow headway, even though the growing role of the Welsh Office emphasized the distinctiveness of Welsh politics, while the nominated "quangos" appointed by the Conservatives led to talk of a democratic deficit.

It was Scotland, however, that triggered the success of devolution. Resentment at Tory rule from LONDON fostered the campaign for a Scottish parliament, notably among the dominant Labour Party, while the Constitutional Convention generated an all-party sense of potential citizenship among middle-class Scottish people. In the 1997 general election Labour won a huge majority under TONY BLAIR, committed to greater local autonomy, and with Scottish and Welsh devolution on the party manifesto. In referendums that September Scottish devolution, including powers over taxation, was carried by a two-thirds majority; in Wales, by contrast, devolution scraped home by only 0.3 per cent of the vote on a poll of barely 50 per cent. Donald Dewar became First Secretary for Scotland and Ron Davies for Wales. The latter, however, soon fell from grace after an obscure sex scandal, and Labour was attacked locally when it pushed through the election of the Blairite Alun Michael instead of the popular Rhodri Morgan.

The first elections for the devolved bodies took place in May 1999. Inevitably, given the modified system of proportional representation, there was no clear majority. In Scotland, however, Labour emerged as much the largest party, and Donald Dewar (who died in 2000) formed a coalition with the Liberal Democrats. In Wales, however, Plaid Cymru made remarkable gains, ending up with 17 members to Labour's 28. Labour decided to govern here as a minority administration. The first year of devolution in both nations had a mixed press. Popular enthusiasm was especially muted in Wales. Here, however, the eventual succession of Rhodri Morgan as First Secretary in February 2000 kindled local enthusiasm.

Clearly, despite teething problems, devolution had taken root. It might lead to regional governments in parts of England; electing a new mayor of London suggested that devolution was indeed a process rather than a series of discrete events.

There seemed very little sign of the break-up of the United Kingdom at the dawn of the new millennium. However, a combination of local devolution and regionalism, the assembly in NORTHERN IRELAND, along with the relationships struck with a more regional Europe indicated that the constitution would evolve further. Doctrines of parliamentary sovereignty and an incorporating union, once proclaimed by A.V. Dicey, were disappearing in the face of new polycultural pluralism.

Kenneth O. Morgan

Bibliography

Bogdanor, Vernon. *Devolution in the United Kingdom.* 1999.

Harvie, Christopher. *Scotland and Nationalism: Scottish Society and Politics 1707–1994.* 1994.

Keating, Michael. *Remaking the Union: Devolution and British Politics in the 1990s.* 1998.

Morgan, Kenneth O. *Rebirth of a Nation: A History of Modern Wales.* 1998.

Taylor, Bridget, and Katrina Thomson, eds. *Scotland and Wales: Nations Again?* 1999.

Diet and Nutrition

The twentieth century has seen great improvements in diet and nutrition in Britain. The mass of the population now eats a much more varied and healthful diet than it did at the turn of the century, consuming more meat, milk, cheese, eggs, vegetables, and fresh fruit and fewer starches. Previously, only the wealthiest could afford a diet so rich in protein and protective foods. Over the years, too, people in the lower income brackets increased their calories while those at the upper end of the scale consumed fewer. Patterns of food consumption, once highly differentiated by class in Britain, have thus become more homogeneous. A concomitant of this has been the fading of physical differences that existed between the income groups at the start of the century because of unequal degrees of nutrition. Advances in nutritional science and food technology, the spread of public awareness, a rise in real incomes, and government policy all contributed to these developments.

The government began to pay serious attention to the nation's diet at the start of the century. Two reasons for this were the high percentage of working-class recruits rejected for military service in the BOER WAR because of poor HEALTH, and the falling proportion of the nation's children being born to the middle and upper classes. About 80 percent of the population were considered working class before the First World War. If this group was increasing, it meant the future vitality and defense of the nation would depend even more heavily on those with the highest incidence of physical deficiencies. Cases of rickets had more than doubled in the past twenty years and other disorders such as anemia, muscular weakness, and tuberculosis were rife. Working-class people also tended to be shorter and thinner: there was an average difference of two and a half inches in height and sixteen pounds in weight between upper-class males and even the highest paid workingmen. Investigations showed poverty and diet, not genes, to be at fault.

In all countries, food accounted for a much larger share of the household budget earlier this century than it does today. In Britain before the First World War unskilled workers spent about two-thirds of their wages on food and still did not get enough calories or nutrients. Most working-class diets were deficient in protein, iron, calcium, and vitamins: fresh meat, milk, vegetables and fruit were expensive and were bought only in small quantities. People depended mainly on foods providing the highest number of calories for the least cost: bread, potatoes, sugar, jam, bacon, lard. In 1914 working-class adults ate an average of seven and a half pounds of bread and three and a half pounds of potatoes a week. In the typical family only the husband (the breadwinner) had meat more than once a week. Women and children subsisted largely on bread and jam consumed with strong, sweet tea. The fact that three quarters of all Britons were city dwellers in 1900 added to the problem, since most did not have gardens and bought all of their food from retailers. Changes in food technology towards the end of the nineteenth century, moreover, had rendered some shop-bought items less nutritious, with vitamins in particular lost. New milling methods had produced a popular but depleted white flour in place of stone-ground flour that contained some of the husk; a new vegetable margarine now provided a cheap alternative to butter; and canned vegetables and condensed milk had become commonplace. Free school meals (authorized in 1906 for children in need) and maternity and infant welfare centers (which counseled mothers on nutrition, among other things) were two ways by which the government tried to improve the diet of the working classes in the years before 1914.

By the standards of the day the middle and upper classes enjoyed a more than adequate diet in the opening years of the century. The discovery of vitamins in 1912, however, led by the 1920s to a reassessment of what constituted good nutrition. Previously, diets were judged in terms of calories, protein, carbohydrates, and fat. Now, in addition to calories, nutritionists focused on the protective quality of the food. Fruits and vegetables (other than potatoes), once dismissed as low value because they provided few calories and no known other nutrients, were publicized as essential for health. By 1938 the nation was eating two-thirds more vegetables and twice the amount of fruit than in 1913. Consumption of meat, milk, eggs, and fats also rose. The problem was that it was primarily the middle and upper classes who were adapting their diets to the new teaching. Dietary surveys made in the 1930s disclosed that although most people now got enough calories, food patterns among working-class families remained much the same as pre-war. Much of this was due to habit, but for at least 10 percent of the population, the prime reason was inadequate income—a factor hard to eradicate during the Great Depression.

Attempts by the government to raise the quality of the general diet met with mixed success in the 1930s. A campaign to increase milk consumption failed, and on the eve of the Second World War average intake of calcium in Britain was still only half what it should have been. Despite widespread publicity by a new Milk Marketing Board, few adults were convinced that they needed milk. The Milk Act of 1933 allowed elementary schools to sell subsidized milk, but only half of the children were enrolled in the program because families out of work still could not afford it. Advances in nutritional science offered the most satisfactory method of improving the national diet. By the early 1930s scientists could fortify commonly eaten foods to make them more nutritious: the government therefore ordered vitamins A and D to be added to milk and margarine and calcium, iron and vitamins to bread. Despite the continued monotony of many people's diets, the general standard of nutrition rose. In 1941 a study showed that children aged fourteen to fifteen were more than two inches taller than their counterparts twenty years earlier. The INFANT MORTALITY rate and the incidence of tuberculosis—also indicators of nutritional standards—had both fallen by 50 percent. This proved to be the beginning of a continuous improvement in national health associated with diet.

The war provided the opportunity for further change directed by the government and its scientific advisers. After January 1940 all foods except bread and vegetables were rationed, with equal shares of meat, dairy products, fats, and other foods allotted to each person. Children and expectant mothers received special supplies of milk, eggs, and juice; while factory workers and others in arduous occupations were provided with an extra, carefully planned, meal at the workplace. Subsidies and wage controls kept key foods within the purchasing power of everyone. Not only did health standards continue to rise, but the old unhealthful patterns of consumption finally began to give way. The general population was forced by food controls to draw more calories from milk and vegetables, and they became more knowledgeable about food values as the result of official publicity campaigns.

The WELFARE STATE established after 1945 ensured that wartime gains would be permanent. In 1948 all children became eligible for free milk at school. Infants were given orange juice and cod liver oil through clinics. FAMILY ALLOWANCES, paid to the mother, for each child after the first, were a method of increasing expenditure on food and other necessities for children. State PENSIONS and social security benefits covering the entire population meanwhile served to strengthen purchasing power and hence the amount spent on food by groups with low incomes. A rise in real wages after 1950 brought benefits to the general population. By 1981 Britons were spending on average only 15 percent of their incomes on food. Few now suffered from deficiency disorders: cases of malnutrition were more likely to stem from overconsumption rather than underconsumption. Free school milk was ended in 1970. Since the mid-1970s there has been a rise in popularity of health foods and diet plans. The same period has also seen a great diversification of diet linked to the spread of supermarkets around the country, the IMMIGRATION of large numbers of people from the British Commonwealth, Britain's entry into the EUROPEAN COMMUNITY, and an unprecedented degree of foreign travel among ordinary people. Tastes and expectations have broadened considerably and traditional British foods have lost ground to foreign cuisines. Ethnic restaurants now abound in Britain, and stores routinely offer a large selection of international foods that the younger generation, at least, no longer considers strange. Thus, as the century neared its close, a new revolution in diet was taking place that will make national eating patterns even further removed from those prevailing in 1900.

L. Margaret Barnett

Bibliography
Burnett, John. Plenty and Want: A Social History of Diet in England from 1815 to the Present Day. 3rd ed. 1989.
Dewey, P.E. "Nutrition and Living Standards in Wartime Britain" in Richard Wall and Jay Winter, eds. The Upheaval of War: Family, Work and Welfare in Europe, 1914–1918. 1988. pp. 197–220.
Driver, Christopher. The British at Table 1940–1980. 1983.
Drummond, J.C., and Anne Wilbraham. The Englishman's Food: A History of Five Centuries of English Diet. rev. ed. 1957.
Johnson, James P. A Hundred Years Eating: Food, Drink and the Daily Diet in Britain Since the Late 19th Century. 1977.
Oddy, D.J., and D.S. Miller, eds. Diet and Health in Modern Britain. 1985.

Divorce and Divorce Law Reform

The public dissolution of individual marriages has increasingly become a pervasive feature of contemporary life. In 1901 the Divorce Court granted 477 divorce decress, which constituted a divorce rate of .08 per 1000 married couples. During 1981 146,000 marriages ended in divorce, a rate of divorce of 11.9 per 1000 married couples. These numbers illustrate the transformation in marital relations witnessed by the twentieth century.

The inexorable upward trend in divorce during the past ninety years has not followed a simple linear path. Both the FIRST and the SECOND WORLD WARS stimulated temporary peaks in petitions for divorce. Although post-war divorce rates subsided, they did not return to pre-war levels. The divorce legislation of 1937 and 1969, which extended the grounds for divorce, also produced temporary peaks of divorce decrees that settled into higher rates of divorce than had previously prevailed.

The population seeking divorce has undergone important changes in composition during the course of the century. Today wives file most divorce petitions, more than 70 per cent of petitions in the 1980s. Prior to 1925, however, husbands filed a majority of divorce petitions. Husbands also more often initiated proceedings during the post-war surges of divorce in 1919–21 and 1945–47. The social profile of divorcing couples has also altered significantly. At the beginning of the century middle-class couples formed the majority of divorce petitioners. Estranged couples among the working class and the poor often had to make some informal and extra-legal accommodation to their situation, which might involved desertion followed by cohabitation or bigamous remarriage. Alternatively, they utilized the partial remedy of a legal separation that could be cheaply obtained in the magistrates' courts. Today working-class couples divorce in large numbers and, generally speaking, manual workers, both skilled and unskilled, exhibit divorce rates far higher then those seen among the professional classes, excepting the military and literary and artistic occupations.

Parliament passed legislation modifying the law of divorce in 1923, 1937, and 1969. The 1923 act equalized the grounds for divorces, although adultery remained the only grounds recognized by law. No longer constrained by the sexual double standard originally mandated by the 1857 Divorce Act, which had required wives to demonstrate that their husbands had aggravated their adultery by some additional matrimonial offense (i.e., cruelty, desertion), wives filed divorce petitions in increasing numbers, soon outstripping the number of those filed by husbands. The 1937 Herbert Act, named for A.P. Herbert (1890–1971), the humorist and MP who steered the legislation through Parliament, for the first time extended the list of legally recognized grounds for divorce beyond adultery to include desertion for three years, cruelty, and incurable insanity. The 1969 divorce legislation, in a radical departure from previous legal practice, abandoned the principal of marital fault. Instead the concept of "irremediable breakdown" served to justify the state's recognition of the end of a marriage. Important extensions in the provision of legal aid to the poor that took place in 1914, 1920, 1949, and 1960 enabled many previously deterred by the cost of legal proceedings to turn to divorce to mark an official end to their marriage.

Significant changes in social and cultural values prompted these legal reforms. From the turn of the century three distinct groups took a particular interest in the issue of divorce. Within the LEGAL PROFESSION, judges, and lawyers found themselves frustrated by the restrictive nature of the 1857 Divorce Act, which left so many outside the protection of the law. Women's organizations, both feminist and non-feminist, focused on the way in which the 1857 law enshrined the sexual double standard in statute. Finally, a small but active and vocal divorce law reform movement emerged. This group, predominantly male, envisioned MARRIAGE as a personal relationship invalidated by the failure of mutual affection between husband and wife. In their view, easier divorce would serve both the interest of the individual in leading a happy life and the interest of the state in freeing citizens to leave marriages devoid of love in order to form new, presumably happier and more productive, families.

Testimony before the Royal Commission of Divorce and Matrimonial Causes appointed in 1909 aired these and other competing visions of marriage. Although the Royal Commission found itself unable to reach unanimity, its 1912 Majority Report recommended an extension of the grounds for divorce beyond adultery, while retaining the principle of marital fault. The legislation of 1923 enacted the first installment of this program, and, after several failed attempts, the 1937 Herbert Act finally carried out the recommendations of the Royal Commission. The legal community and divorce law reformers greeted this success with more enthusiasm than did women's organizations, who worried about the disadvantaged economic position of divorced wives.

The Herbert Act settled matters for almost twenty years, but the question of marriage and divorce again became an important issue during the 1950s. The 1956 Royal Commission on Marriage and Divorce also failed to achieve consensus when confronted with a daunting range of opinion. However, the move to replace the concept of marital fault with a "no fault" divorce procedure, which culminated in the passage of the 1969 divorce legislation, received a full and sympathetic hearing.

England, which had the lowest divorce rate in western Europe at the turn of the century, today distinguishes itself by the highest divorce rate in the EUROPEAN UNION. The demographic path and trajectory of this preeminent feature of modern family life, as well as the development of the legal apparatus that permits its expression, stand out clearly. The larger-scale social and cultural changes that have fueled the spiraling demand for divorce include the idealization of marriage as an emotionally supportive relationship, the entrance of large numbers of WOMEN into the labor market and the ideologies of individual gratification and sexual equality. The psychological, social, and cultural consequences of mass divorce, understood in terms of the relationships between men and women, between parents and children and between the state and families, have yet to emerge with equal clarity. The impoverishment of women with dependent children and the separation of fathers from their children, troubling phenomena already associated with mass divorce, presage the complexities of the future reorganization of family life that will result from the working out of these processes.

Gail Savage

Bibliography

Phillips, Roderick. *Putting Asunder: A History of Divorce in Western Society.* 1988.

Rowntree, Griselda, and Norman H. Carrier. "The Resort to Divorce in England and Wales, 1858–1957," *Population Studies*, vol. 11 (1957), pp. 188–233.

Stone, Lawrence. *Road to Divorce: England 1530–1987.* 1990.

Documentary Film

Great Britain first acquired an international reputation for documentary filmmaking in the 1930s, although it was preceded by a tradition of educational and instructional filmmaking. The filmmaker John Grierson initially coined the term "documentary" to characterize the work of the American anthropological filmmaker, Robert Flaherty, who had made such films as *Nanook of the North* (1922) and *Moana* (1925). Thanks largely to Grierson's writings, "documentary" quickly became synonymous with cinematic realism and social amelioration. Initially, Russian filmmaking theory and technique were major influences on Grierson, particularly his beliefs about the purpose and social role of films. Grierson's own Calvinist background and his exposure to the United States were equally important. He saw Hollywood's dedication to escapism as a waste of a powerful new mass medium.

After the First World War Grierson had moved to the United States to study the mass media. He was particularly influenced by the ideas of Walter Lippmann, who argued that the new

mass media, so significant during the recent war, needed to be controlled by a responsible information elite. On his return to the United Kingdom, Grierson created a cadre of public servants who were media professionals. Largely through his guidance, the British government and big business both turned to film sponsorship as a public information and public relations medium and as a form of artistic patronage. He intended to use films as public education, while also challenging Hollywood, which often occupied more than 90 percent of British screen time. Beginning in 1927 Grierson produced both reports and films for the Empire Marketing Board (the EMB), a branch of the Department of Overseas Trade, intended to promote the British Empire's products to the British public. Grierson made his first film, *Drifters* (1929) for the EMB. *Drifters'* portrayal of the workers who caught, packaged and distributed Britain's fish harvest was a revelation. It was the first time that ordinary working people had appeared in a non-demeaning way in a British film. Like virtually all of Grierson's films, *Drifters* was seen primarily by non-theatrical audiences and was not shown widely in commercial release. Film societies, art theatres, and other elite venues were impressed, and Grierson quickly built a reputation and a following on the basis of this film. Over 300 documentary films were made in Britain in the 1930s, largely for the government and for big corporations such as Shell Oil and the public utility companies. A surprising number were socially critical and drew attention to a wide range of social welfare concerns such as poor HOUSING, malnutrition, pollution, and inadequate education. Grierson convinced big business and government alike that they gained from drawing attention to problems, and his writings soon transformed his small following into a coherent group.

This movement experimented with a range of forms. The early films, including *Drifters*, were essentially low budget versions of Russian style silent film montage. Later films experimented with dramatic re-enactments, including the famous *Night Mail* (1936) and *North Sea* (1938). These films often employed sets, scripted dialogue, and everything which appeared in the final cut was carefully structured. Nevertheless, in their use of actuality-based drama and non-professional actors, they were very innovative. At other times, Grierson's followers opted for a radical approach—to let ordinary people, speaking in their own words, address the camera lens directly and tell viewers about their everyday situations. This was particularly the case with *Housing Problems* (1935), which took viewers inside ordinary working people's homes in the East End of LONDON. Other films adopted a minimal style, using a simple combination of charts, voice over narration, and directly delivered testimony to let the facts speak for themselves. Films like *Enough to Eat* (1936), essentially illustrated lectures, were powerful indictments of social conditions.

First at the EMB and then, after 1933, at the General Post Office, Grierson surrounded himself with a group of young, mostly Oxbridge-educated men such as Basil Wright, Stewart Legg, Edgar Anstey, and Arthur Elton. There were other filmmakers, such as Paul Rotha, Harry Watt, and the Brazilian Alberto Cavalcanti, who were less directly aligned with Grierson, although they often collaborated with him. Grierson also attracted other artistic talents: W.H. AUDEN, DYLAN THOMAS, BENJAMIN BRITTEN, and the painter William Coldstream all worked with him at some point.

Britain's documentary filmmakers came into their own during the SECOND WORLD WAR. The Ministry of Information was a generous benefactor for documentary filmmakers, and some of their greatest films, such as *Target for Tonight* (1942) and *Fires Were Started* (1943) were made during this period. Many documentaries made during the war strongly resembled conventional fictional films. Their use of non-professional talent and their basis in real life events depicted in a non-heroic way, foreshadow the style and content of Italian neo-realist films made later in the decade. The war also allowed documentary filmmakers to get their work shown widely in commercial venues for the first time. *Target for Tonight,* which stoically depicted the British at war, was a huge commercial success. Another, more subtle tradition was best exemplified in the work of HUMPHREY JENNINGS, whose image-poems are moving snapshots of Britain at war. *Listen to Britain* (1941) and *Words for Battle* (1941) conveyed in a sophisticated way the cultural effects of the war, and its impact upon dance, music, and poetry in Britain. *A Diary for Timothy* (1945) dramatized the ambiguity and uncertainty surrounding the return to peace for many British people.

After 1945 British documentary filmmaking went into a hiatus. Grierson returned from Canada to work for the Central Office of Information and UNESCO before ultimately settling down as producer and host of *This Wonderful World,* a documentary show produced by Scottish television. Several of Grierson's protegés, including Watt and Cavalcanti, gravitated towards the feature FILM INDUSTRY, while others, such as Anstey and Elton, produced successful scientific and documentary films for organizations like Shell Oil and the Transport Film Unit. Their films continued to be associated with a social conscience and artistic flair, but they received far less attention than during the war.

British Free Cinema was a new filmmaking approach which emerged in the early fifties. Prominent figures in this group included Lindsay Anderson, Karel Reisz, and Tony Richardson. This younger generation of filmmakers owed relatively little to Grierson and their technique was quite different. Free Cinema was an attempt to go out into the streets and to capture reality on film. Burdened by cumbersome equipment and non-synch sound equipment, films like *Everyday Except Christmas* (1959) and *Momma Don't Allow* (1956) nevertheless managed to convey the sense of seeing the world for the first time. Many of their topics—teddy boys, jazz music, and coffee bars—show the transitions occurring in 1950s Britain. Free Cinema anticipated many of the ideas and methods of Cinema Verité and American direct cinema. Its films were structured around events as observed by the filmmakers, rather than being based on previously written scripts. Voice-over narration disappeared, as did scripted dialogue and most staged action. Filmmakers tried to make people behave as if the film crew was not there, interfering as little as possible with their film subjects' lives. The notion of attempting to capture events on film as they happened, a common practice in combat cinematography, but practically unknown elsewhere, was very innovative. The technology of the time was not up to the aspirations of these filmmakers: film stock was not fast enough, cameras were not light enough to be held by hand and had to be mounted on a tripod, and, above all, filmmakers did not have lightweight synchronous sound equipment. Even so, their best work compares very favorably with that of their French New Wave contemporaries.

In the 1960s British filmmakers experimented with dramatic forms which blurred the line between documentary and fiction. Peter Watkins in *The War Game* (1965) and *Culloden* (1964) and Ken Loach in *Kes* (1969) used non-professional actors and dramatic settings to convey social realities which would simply not be possible for conventional documentary or fictional forms. Watkins' work was so controversial that *The War Game,* originally made for BBC-TV, which dramatized the aftermath of a nuclear attack, was never broadcast. Television has become now the principal source of funding for documentary films in the United Kingdom, and documentary filmmakers such as Michael Apted and Roger Graef now look to that medium for support.

Paul Swann

Bibliography

Barnouw, Erik. *Documentary: A History of the Non-Fiction Film.* 2nd ed. 1990.

Nichols, Bill. *Representing Reality.* 1992.

Sussex, Elizabeth. *The Rise and Fall of the British Documentary.* 1975.

Stansky, Peter, and William Abrahams. *London's Burning: Life, Death, and Art in the Second World War.* 1994.

Swann, Paul. *The British Documentary Film Movement, 1926–1946.* 1989.

Dole, The

The dominant response to large scale and persistent UNEMPLOYMENT in inter-war Britain was to provide cash benefits to the out of work, pending a revival in the demand for labor. The legal and administrative apparatus deployed for the payment of unemployment benefit had its origins in the Edwardian period. Before 1911 there was no provision at national level for meeting the immediate needs of the unemployed. But with growing evidence from the turn of the century that unemployment and poverty were not determined primarily by individual moral failing but by economic forces, pressure mounted for a more systematic means of dealing with the involuntary unemployed. The resultant unemployment insurance scheme introduced in 1911 applied to only seven trades, with a workforce of about 2.25 million men in a total male labor force of over 10 million. This limited scheme was never intended to cover all periods of unemployment. It was designed as a remedy for fluctuations in employment, not as a cure for longer term unemployment. Nonetheless, it introduced the important principle that workers who made payments to an Unemployment Insurance Fund would be legally entitled to cash benefits of prescribed amounts and for limited periods should they subsequently become unemployed. The scheme was expanded during the FIRST WORLD WAR to cover munitions workers and more specifically in 1918 to provide state assistance to civilian workers who might face employment difficulties following the cessation of war work. Thus was born the Out of Work Donation scheme which provided unemployed adults with emergency benefit payments, including dependants' allowances, irrespective of their entitlement under the 1911 unemployment insurance scheme. The dole had arrived.

The unemployment insurance scheme proper was extended in 1920, but such was the increase in unemployment after 1921 that considerable numbers of workers found themselves unemployed long after they had exhausted their right to benefits by virtue of previous contributions to the fund. Many others had found it difficult to obtain sufficient regular employment to enable them to make the minimum number of contributions necessary to qualify for the payment of benefit. Depression and political expediency combined thereafter to breach the actuarial principles upon which the insurance scheme had been based. The Treasury allowed the Unemployment Insurance Fund to borrow money to enable workers who had exhausted their legal right to benefit, but who could prove to a local employment committee that they were genuinely seeking whole-time employment, to receive cash payments for a prescribed number of weeks. Such payments of non-contributory unemployment benefits pushed the Insurance Fund into increasing indebtedness during the 1920s and figured largely in the budgetary and financial crisis of the early 1930s. But they were continued in different forms down to 1930 because it proved easier for governments to meet the needs of the growing number of unemployed workers by redefining the conditions under which they could receive subsidized cash payments from the state than it was to devise ways of creating jobs. The expedient of providing payments to the unemployed outside of the rules of the insurance scheme was continued because of the government's politically naive, financially dangerous, and empirically unjustified assumption that the rise in unemployment during the first post-war decade was merely temporary and cyclical and could be countered by a series of ad hoc adjustments to existing regulations.

As the reality of structural and increasingly long-term unemployment slowly dawned, strenuous efforts were made to tighten the rules under which individuals could lay claim to non-contributory benefits. Although applicants had since 1921 been required to prove to local officials that they were "genuinely seeking whole-time work but unable to obtain such employment", from 1924 the onus of proof was put upon claimants to produce satisfactory evidence of their search for work. Local officials could refuse benefit if they were dissatisfied with a claim, without having to prove that an applicant could have found a job with greater effort. This "seeking work test" was not abolished until 1930. By that time government officials had become concerned to separate unemployment insurance from what in effect amounted to the payment of state relief to large numbers of the unemployed. Once the actuarial basis of the insurance scheme had been breached in 1921 to cater for those whose contributions record had collapsed, mass unemployment had effectively transformed the system into a publicly-funded state service. The root of the problem was the political decision to render the insurance scheme a substitute for, rather than a supplement to, the Poor Law, forcing it to undertake the task of relieving long term unemployment, for which it was unsuited, instead of allowing it to meet the needs of the short term cyclical unemployed. As a consequence, the basis of the unemployment insurance scheme had been transformed from one in which the principle of insurance predominated into a mixed system in which the insurance element had become subordinated to the element of relief.

Increasingly, the interests of the majority of contributors to the insurance scheme were being affected by a smaller but significant section of the workforce which had come to regard benefit without full contributions as a right. Moreover, the provision of maintenance outside the public assistance scheme, without any of the tests which normally accompanied either contributory insurance or Poor Law payments, made a mockery of denying benefits to those in agriculture and domestic service, who were not covered by insurance at all. Pressure mounted to find ways in which a distinction could be made between those eligible and those ineligible for the unemployment insurance benefit. The result was a cleansing of the system following the financial and budgetary crisis of 1931. The National government was determined to ensure that payments to the "industrial" unemployed who had exhausted their right to benefit would thereafter be subject to a test of need. The dole had given birth to the means test.

W.R. Garside

Bibliography

Garside, W.R. *British Unemployment, 1919–1939: A Study in Public Policy*. 1990.

Gilbert, Bentley B. *British Social Policy, 1914–1939*. 1970.

Drama

At the turn of the century the two most established dramatists were Arthur Wing Pinero (1855–1934) and Henry Arthur Jones (1851–1929), whose work looked back to French nineteenth-century conventions of the "well-made play", even though both were inspired by Ibsen. GEORGE BERNARD SHAW was the new voice in the theatre, an Irish Ibsenite, Wagnerian, and Marxist, championing a realism whereby character and dialogue were liberated from the conventional demands of plot. In Shaw's plays there is an emphasis on the discussion of ideas and social problems rather than action, leaving the audience with open questions: he describes *Major Barbara* (1905) as "A Discussion" and *Misalliance* (1910) as "A Debate in One Sitting". His plays debate and discuss politics (especially socialism and FEMINISM), science, and philosophy. But while Shaw's aims are realistic, his plays are often fantastic, and his later work moves towards deliberate self-reflexive theatricality. Shaw was to become the dominant intellectual force in early twentieth-century British theatre.

Other writers during the early years of the century whose work conformed to the realistic model were St. John Hankin (1869–1909), JOHN GALSWORTHY, and Harley Granville-Barker (1877–1946). Their works, along with Shaw's, gained a platform at the Royal Court Theatre, under Granville Barker's management, with Barker himself often playing the lead in Shaw's productions.

Granville-Barker's own *The Voysey Inheritance* (1905) and *Waste* (1907) and Hankin's *The Return of the Prodigal* (1905) and *The Cassilis Engagement* (1907) were concerned with moral and political issues; most notably, with the emancipation of WOMEN. Galsworthy's *The Silver Box* (1906), *Strife* (1909), and *Justice* (1910) examine class prejudice and the injustices of the legal system.

J.M. Barrie (1860–1937), author of *Peter Pan* (1904), was another important dramatist of the period. His plays are essentially fantasies, although they also include social commentary. In *The Admirable Crichton* (1902) he ironically attacks the class structure: shipwrecked on a desert island, a butler becomes a governor, while the aristocrats he has served are transformed into a working underclass.

In spite of the prestige of prosaic realism, the early years of the century witnessed attempts to re-establish the poetic tradition of drama. Verse plays by Stephen Phillips (1864–1915), Gordon Bottomley (1874–1948), J.E. Flecker (1884–1915), and JOHN MASEFIELD achieved some success. The most significant poetic dramatist of the period was W.B. YEATS. Yeats's "theatre of the mind" is influenced by the Symbolist movement, Irish folklore, and Japanese Noh drama; it anticipates in some ways the British avant-garde of the 1960s. The plays of J.M. Synge (1871–1909), whose work Yeats championed, incorporate both realism and poetic speech derived from the idioms of Celtic peasant life. Regarded as a major dramatist of the period, his most famous play is the satirical comedy *The Playboy of the Western World* (1907). The verse drama tradition continued in the 1930s with the emergence of T.S. ELIOT as a dramatist. Eliot's *Murder in the Cathedral* (1935) is about the martyrdom of St Thomas Becket. In Eliot's *The Family Reunion* (1939) the *Oresteia* of Aeschylus is given a modern setting.

During the first half of the century there was a surprisingly close relation between the novel and the drama. Galsworthy, W. SOMERSET MAUGHAM, and J.B. PRIESTLEY became famous both as novelists and dramatists. ARNOLD BENNETT had success with *The Great Adventure* (1913); JAMES JOYCE wrote *Exiles* (1915); and D.H. LAWRENCE wrote a number of plays.

In the 1920s distinguished comedies shared the stage alongside Shaw's new tradition of socially-conscious theatre. Maugham's comedies of the Edwardian period (four of them played simultaneously in London in 1908) were succeeded by those of NOEL COWARD. Good examples of the comedy of manners include *On Approval* (1927) by Frederick Lonsdale (1881–1954) and *Hay Fever* (1925) and *Private Lives* (1930) by Coward. At the Aldwych Theatre between 1925 and 1933 the farces of Ben Travers (1886–1980) exemplified the liberal mood of the period. Coward found it possible to mix high comedy and social observation of the post-war generation in *The Young Idea* (1923) and *The Vortex* (1924). Other plays during the period which explored social and moral themes include *A Bill of Divorcement* (1921) by Clemence Dane (1888–1965), Galsworthy's *Escape* (1927), and Maugham's *For Services Rendered* (1932).

Sean O'Casey (1880–1964) was another major playwright to appear during the 1920s. His Dublin trilogy—*The Shadow of a Gunman* (1923), *Juno and the Paycock* (1924), and *The Plough and the Stars* (1926)—shows the influence of Shaw, employs strong elements of realism and naturalism, and treats working-class life in relation to Anglo-Irish political events. His later plays, including *The Silver Tassie* (1929), *Within the Gates* (1934), *The Star Turns Red* (1940), and *Red Roses for Me* (1943) tend increasingly towards expressionism. Expressionism was also the dominant influence behind *The Dog Beneath the Skin* (1935) and *The Ascent of F6* (1936) by W.H.AUDEN and CHRISTOPHER ISHERWOOD. A movement away from realism is also exemplified in Priestley's career between *Eden's End* (1934) and *Johnson Over Jordan* (1939).

During the SECOND WORLD WAR revivals and escapism predominated. Such conditions continued for a while after the war, with drawing room comedies, farces, and popular thrillers holding favor. But TERENCE RATTIGAN emerged as a new and important voice. He examined troubled marital relationships in *The Browning Version* (1948) and *The Deep Blue Sea* (1952). At the same time Priestley and O'Casey continued to write significant plays—Priestley's *An Inspector Calls* (1946) and O'Casey's *Oak Leaves and Lavender* (1947)—and the verse drama tradition continued with Christopher Fry's (1907–) *The Lady's Not For Burning* (1948) and Eliot's *The Cocktail Party* (1950), *The Confidential Clerk* (1953), and *The Elder Statesman* (1958). However, the poetic revival was swept aside by a startling revival of realist drama, with strong political overtones.

The central figure in post-war theatre became JOHN OSBORNE, whose first play *Look Back in Anger* (1956) created a sensation when it was performed at the Royal Court, and gave rise to the phrases "angry young man" and "kitchen sink" drama. Osborne's play is conventionally realistic in form, but in exhibiting contemporary values and characters it appeared to be shockingly contemporary. In *The Entertainer* (1957), Osborne subsequently dramatized the failure of a music hall comedian, Archie Rice, tellingly set against the background of the SUEZ CRISIS and a decaying England.

The year 1956 also saw the first visit to London of the Berliner Ensemble which introduced the plays of Bertolt Brecht (1898–1956) to the British theatre. Brecht's epic theatre subsequently influenced the new generation of playwrights, including Osborne, Edward Bond (1934–), and John Arden (1930–). Arden's *Sergeant Musgrave's Dance* (1959), established him as a leading figure among the new generation of playwrights. The new English Stage Company at the Royal Court, formed by George Devine (1910–66), provided a platform for their work, as well as for N.F. Simpson (1919–), Ann Jellicoe (1927–), and Arnold Wesker (1932–). In Wesker basement bedsits take the place of the drawing rooms of Maugham and Coward, while upper-class accents give way to regional ones. Another important company to champion new playwrights was Theatre Workshop, under the direction of Joan Littlewood (1914–). Giving emphasis to proletarian culture, Theatre Workshop presented plays by Brendan Behan (1923–64) and Shelagh Delaney (1939–).

SAMUEL BECKETT has dominated British drama during the last thirty years in much the same way that Shaw did earlier in the century. When *Waiting for Godot* (1953) opened in London in 1955, its obscure dialogue and its unrecognizable plot seem to break every convention, yet it compelled attention. Beckett's drama is philosophical and abstract, symbolic, surrealistic, diametrically opposed to the realist tradition. His initial success was followed by *Endgame* (1957) and *Krapp's Last Tape* (1958). His influence became most immediately apparent in the work of HAROLD PINTER, but Beckett has influenced the whole course of modern British drama, by having established a precedent for theatrical experimentation.

One of the most remarkable plays to appear in the late 1950s was Pinter's *The Birthday Party* (1958). This dark comedy, which dramatizes the terrorization and destruction of an individual by two sinister men, was met with incomprehension and dislike. Pinter was soon to be categorized, along with Beckett and Simpson, as belonging to the "theatre of the absurd". Pinter's central themes—oppression, victimization, sexual and gender conflicts, and the destructiveness of language—can be traced through to his recent plays, *Mountain Language* (1988) and *Party Time* (1991).

The 1960s were a high point in British drama. In addition to Beckett, Pinter, Osborne, Arden, Bond, Wesker, important writers of the decade include Robert Bolt (1924–), David Rudkin (1936–), Peter Shaffer (1926–), Peter Nichols (1927–), TOM STOPPARD (1937–), Joe Orton (1933–67), and Christopher Hampton (1946–). Bolt's *A Man for All Seasons* revealed the influence of Brecht, as did Osborne's *Luther* (1961). One of Joan Littlewood's most famous productions was *Oh, What a Lovely War* (1963). Using a Brechtian style, popular songs from the First World War were juxtaposed with the stark reality of carnage. Orton wrote deliberately confrontational black farces, attacking bourgeois morality in *Loot* (1965) and *What the Butler Saw* (1969). The political comedy of Peter Barnes (1931–), in *Sclerosis* (1965) and *The Ruling Class* (1968), owed much to Orton's example. Stoppard established a tradition of philosophical comedy in *Rosencrantz and Guildernstern are Dead* (1966), which shows the influence of Beckett. Some of the other important plays of the decade include Pinter's *The Caretaker* (1960) and *The Homecoming* (1965), Beckett's *Happy Days* (1961), Shaffer's *The Royal Hunt of the Sun* (1964), and Bond's *Saved* (1965). The year 1968 saw the abolition of the censorship laws, established during the eighteenth and nineteenth centuries, which had hindered the work of modern dramatists from Shaw to Osborne.

The decade that followed saw the emergence of agitprop (agitation propaganda) theatre groups, which engaged the talents of young dramatists like David Hare (1947–), Howard Brenton (1942–), David Edgar (1948–), and Howard Barker (1946–). The 7:84 Theatre Company of John McGrath (1935–) is possibly the best representative of the movement. These small counter-theatre groups directly addressed working-class audiences, intending to mobilize them politically. Bond was a dominant figure during the 1970s and the early 1980s. His major plays, *Lear* (1971), *The Sea* (1973), *The Woman* (1978), and *Restoration* (1981), became increasingly radical and didactic. But by the 1970s agitprop had lost its momentum. The dramatists, with the exception of McGrath, were beginning to work on more conventional stages, including the Royal Shakespeare Company and the National Theatre.

The three most popular dramatists since the 1970s have been Michael Frayn (1933–), Simon Gray (1926–), and ALAN AYCKBOURN. Ayckbourn has been influenced by Stoppard. Trevor Griffiths (1935–) follows the example of Orton and Barnes in writing more politically-directed comedy. Since the 1970s an important tradition of FEMINIST theatre has also emerged in the plays of Pam Gems (1925–) and Caryl Churchill (1938–).

Brian Pearce

Bibliography

Barnes, Philip. *A Companion to Post-War British Theatre.* 1986.

Elsom, John. *Post-War British Theatre,* 2nd ed. 1979.

Innes, Christopher. *Modern British Drama, 1890–1990.* 1992.

Nicoll, Allardyce. *English Drama, 1900–1930: The Beginnings of the Modern Period.* 1973.

Taylor, John Russell. *Anger and After: A Guide to the New British Drama,* 2nd ed. 1977.

Worth, Katharine. *Revolutions in Modern English Drama.* 1973.

Dunkirk (26 May–4 June 1940)

Dunkirk is an English Channel port in northern France from which most of the British Expeditionary Force (BEF) was evacuated in May and June 1940 following the collapse of the Allied Front.

When the Germans attacked the Lowlands and France in May 1940, the BEF under General Lord (John S.) Gort moved into Belgium along with a portion of the French army according to plan. Unfortunately for the Allies, Germany's tanks broke through the French front in the Ardennes and split the Allied force in two, threatening the BEF and the French troops in Belgium with encirclement. The endangered Allied forces thereupon retreated to a perimeter around Dunkirk for evacuation. Germany's high command, fearful about wasting tanks in marshy coastal areas, called a halt to their advance, trusting the German Air Force (the Luftwaffe) to destroy the Dunkirk pocket.

It was a disastrous mistake: the Luftwaffe, drained from its previous battles, stationed far from the Channel, and suffering bad weather as well as ROYAL AIR FORCE harassment, could not prevent the evacuation; German planes were not equipped, nor their pilots trained to attack shipping in any case. By the time the German ground forces were allowed to move again, the perimeter was secure. The Luftwaffe and German artillery did force the ROYAL NAVY to conduct most of the evacuation by night, but that was enough: some 364,628 troops were removed, 224,686 of them British, the rest French plus some Belgians. The troops that escaped were disorganized and had been obliged to leave most of their equipment behind. Luckily the Germans were not capable of launching a cross-Channel attack for many weeks to come.

The vast armada of tiny, privately owned craft that assisted in the evacuation still symbolizes British self-sacrifice and pluck, although in truth most of the work was carried out by larger vessels. The legend has also obscured the fact that many British troops were evacuated later in June from other French ports. Nevertheless, the evacuation was a turning point in the SECOND WORLD WAR. Without it, the British would have been hard-pressed to find manpower for the rest of the war, and it was also the first occasion when Germany's armed forces failed to achieve an important goal. While it is true that wars are not won by brilliant retreats, the British people—and others—soon drew upon the Dunkirk legend as a source of inspiration and hope during the new crises that followed the fall of France.

Karl G. Larew

Bibliography

Barker, A.J. *Dunkirk: The Great Escape.* 1977.

Gelb, Norman. *Dunkirk: The Complete Story of the First Step in the Defeat of Hitler.* 1989.

Horne, Alistair. *To Lose a Battle: France 1940.* 1969.

Economic Performance

At the close of the nineteenth century Britain was an economic superpower. In manufacturing industry it was responsible for some 25 percent of the world's output and 40 percent of the world's trade. It controlled the largest empire in history, accounted for over 50 percent of all international investment, and dominated international trade and finance through the service industries of the CITY OF LONDON (banking, trade finance, insurance, transport, commodity and bill brokering). There was still widespread poverty in Britain, but the average STANDARD OF LIVING was among the very highest in the world, the strength of economic structures, and the achievements of British technology and enterprise were the object of curiosity and admiration in most other countries.

A century later Britain's relative economic position, its apparent industrial potential, and its national self-confidence—all presented huge contrasts. Britain was no more than a medium-sized economic power, other industrial countries had long outpaced its rate of growth and productivity, and its shares of world manufacturing output (about 4 percent) and trade (about 9 percent) had shrunk to modest levels. The country had slipped down the international league table of economic performance, whether measured in terms of levels and growth rates of gross domestic product (the national output of goods and services), of the sophistication of its technology and economic organization, or of the average living standards of its citizens. This, however, is to apply relative measures in the context of the most advanced countries. In fact, the economy continued to grow throughout most of the century (even if its growth rate has been exceeded by an increasing number of other nations), levels of material welfare have continued to increase, and by the standards of the overwhelming majority of countries in the world, Britain remained an advanced, rich, and buoyant economy.

Table 1 makes clear the extent to which Britain's modern growth rate has lagged behind that of other leading industrial nations (a fact which has been intimately associated with its diminishing share of world manufacturing output and trade). On the other hand, it also shows that Britain's economic "decline" has not been a matter of retardation or even stagnation, but rather of

TABLE I: ANNUAL GROWTH RATE OF GROSS DOMESTIC PRODUCT (%)

	1870–1913	1913–50	1950–73	1973–92
France	1.7	1.1	5.1	2.5
Germany	2.8	1.3	5.9	2.4
Japan	2.5	2.2	9.4	4.0
Netherlands	2.1	2.4	4.7	2.4
United Kingdom	1.9	1.3	3.0	1.9
Average	2.2	1.7	5.6	2.6
USA	4.2	2.8	3.7	2.4

other economies growing faster. Indeed, Britain's growth rate in the twentieth century has not shown a deterioration from that of the economy's halcyon days as the workshop of the world. Equally important, while latercomers undoubtedly overtook Britain, their growth rates have not continued to exceed Britain's by marked amounts. The contrast between Britain's economic achievement and that of other advanced countries is much less than that between the advanced countries as a group and poorer countries which account for the bulk of the world's population.

A striking feature of Britain's economic history has been the extent of "structural change"—the relative decline (in terms of output and employment) of manufacturing and the growth of services. To a large extent this has been the inevitable consequence of economic development as wealthier consumers spend more on HEALTH, education, LEISURE, and services generally; and as technical efficiency enables physical output to be produced with proportionately less labor. At the same time, however, the recent very rapid decline of old-established industries—especially the staple export industries of the nineteenth century, such as COAL, textiles, iron and STEEL, shipbuilding—but also of formerly important twentieth-century industries such as electrical engineering and electronics and, until the influx of Japanese enterprise and capital, AUTOMOBILES—implies an unhealthy erosion of the country's manufacturing base. And this, in turn, has weakened Britain's trading position, by narrowing the range of exports and making its consumers more reliant on manufactured imports.

Many of these problems did not emerge until relatively late in the century. Even though there was some anxiety about industrial competition, especially from Germany and the United States, well before the First World War, manufacturing industries were still powerful and British trade and finance were still supreme. It was, indeed, this strength which enabled Britain to endure the FIRST WORLD WAR so successfully, while its Empire was at its most extensive in the years immediately after 1918. Admittedly, the economic outlook became very clouded in the post-war decade. On the one hand, the industries which had brought so much employment and buoyant activity to South Wales, Scotland, northern England, and the Midlands, now appeared to have far too much capacity for the new conditions of world markets. Competition and the disruption of demand provoked crises, unprofitability, and widespread UNEMPLOYMENT in coal, textiles, shipbuilding, engineering, and metallurgy. On the other hand, the new frailty of the export economy and (even more) the dislocation of the world's economy, trade, and finance helped erode the international strength of the pound sterling.

From many viewpoints, therefore, the 1920s was an unhappy decade, troubled by inadequate economic performance and intense labor disputes. And it was followed by the severest depression of modern times (1929–32) during which Britain was forced to abandon both its traditional policy of free trade and the established value of the currency as sustained by the GOLD STANDARD. But, as with overall economic performance as measured by growth rates, the situation was not unmitigatedly bad. In the 1930s Britain's recovery from the slump was more widespread and rapid than in most other countries. And although unemployment continued at a high level and the reputation of the 1930s is not particularly admirable, the fact remains that through the inter-war period average living standards rose, many areas of the country (especially in the south) experienced a large measure of prosperity, and the economy proved very resilient as new consumption patterns and industries (electrical engineering, retailing, motor vehicles, chemicals, scientific instruments) flourished. As so often in British history, the benefits and costs of change were unevenly distributed geographically and socially.

The extent but also the limitations of Britain's continued position as an economic power were well exemplified in the SECOND WORLD WAR. The economy was sufficiently efficient to sustain Britain's role as a major belligerent, but insufficiently large to allow it to survive the war without the help of such powerful allies as the United States and the Soviet Union. For a decade or so after the war, and in spite of apparent austerity, the economy recovered rapidly and was able to contend against competition from other countries which had been even more exhausted, or devas-

tated, by war effort. But ultimately, and in spite of continued—even by its own standards, spectacular—growth, the British economy was outpaced by much of Western Europe and by the booming Japanese economy. Ever since the late 1950s therefore, the story has been a familiar, and occasionally contradictory, one: relative decline and a sense of unease and dissatisfaction, uncompetitive older industries and inadequate trade, disappointing productivity—but all joined with continuously rising living standards and a large measure of economic and social change as consumption patterns were modernized and new sources of wealth and jobs (especially in the service sector, but also in North Sea Oil production) transformed the reality of British life. By the last decade of the twentieth century, and in spite of much disappointment, Britain was still among the richest 10 percent of the world's nations.

Arguably, Britain's economic performance has been adequate when measured in terms of the continued positive growth in output and living standards. But the fact remains that it has failed to rival its principal competitors and continued to frustrate the private and public aspirations of its citizens.

In principle, then, the economy could have grown faster and become stronger. The fact that it failed to do so has been variously attributed to conservative social and entrepreneurial attitudes, to inadequate and hidebound education and training, to bad industrial relations, to a neglect of capital investment, to a reluctance to accept the personal and social costs of change, and to neglectful or inappropriate government policies. It is true that there is evidence for each of these presumed "failings" over the last century—although it is not always certain that Britain is alone among developed nations in exemplifying them, or that they are consistent with the long-run economic record. Three things, however, do seem clear. First, each of these "explanations" exists as part of a complex national situation which is very difficult to change by any conscious action. Second, the interdependence of these characteristics, and their conseequent resistance to manipulation, casts doubt on any "theory" which implies that there was a major and feasible alternative path to national prosperity. Third, in such a situation, economic performance and the attributes which determine it are the products of a long history: Britain's twentieth-century economy and growth record (including the attitudes, institutions, and behavior associated with it) are the products of its earlier development and its very success; and its recent experiences reflect as much maturity as failure. And in this respect it is not at all clear that the economies whose achievements appear to have so easily outstripped Britain's will not themselves experience the same retardative forces as emerged from Britain's own economic maturity.

Barry Supple

Bibliography

Crafts, Nick F.R., and N.W.C. Woodward, eds. *The British Economy since 1945*. 1991.

Dintenfass, Michael. *The Decline of Industrial Britain, 1870–1980*. 1992.

Kirby, Maurice W. *The Decline of British Economic Power since 1870*. 1981.

Middleton, Roger. *Government versus the Market: The Growth of the Public Sector, Economic Management and British Economic Performance, 1890–1979*. 1996.

Pollard, Sidney. *The Development of the British Economy, 1914–1980*. 1983.

Eden, (Robert) Anthony (1897–1977)

Anthony Eden, politician and statesman, was a Conservative Member of Parliament from 1923 until 1957. During these years he achieved increasing prominence in ministerial office (interrupted briefly from February 1938 until September 1939 when he sat on the back benches following resignation and from 1945 to 1951 when his party was in opposition). The posts he held were: Parliamentary Under-Secretary at the Foreign Office (1931–4); Lord Privy Seal (1934–5); Minister for League of Nations Affairs with a seat in the Cabinet (1935); Foreign Secretary (1935–8); Dominions Secretary (1939–40); Secretary of State for War (1940); Foreign Secretary (1940–5 and 1951–5); and Prime Minister (1955–7). In 1954 he was made a Knight of the Garter and was thereafter known as Sir Anthony Eden until he accepted a peerage in 1961 and became the Earl of Avon. His principal significance was as the architect of the ill-fated SUEZ policy in 1956, but he is also remembered for his resignation from NEVILLE CHAMBERLAIN's government in protest at the CABINET's wish to "appease" Italy and for his prominent role in wartime diplomacy symbolized by his attendance at summit conferences with the Americans and the Soviets at Teheran, Yalta, and Potsdam.

Every phase of Eden's career has provoked controversy among biographers and historians. So far as his period at the Foreign Office between 1931 and 1938 is concerned the question is whether he should on the whole be regarded as an "appeaser" or an "anti-appeaser." During his lifetime it suited him and indeed the CONSERVATIVE PARTY as a whole to emphasize evidence that suggested he had been a reasonably consistent opponent of the Fascist dictatorships and that his resignation in 1938 had been motivated by principled opposition to all that Chamberlain represented. In recent years, however, revisionist writers with access to relevant documents have

pointed out that he was much less hostile to Germany than to Italy and that this found expression, in particular, in his unwillingness to support French calls for armed resistance to the remilitarization of the Rhineland in 1936. Again, doubts have been cast on the extent to which he was consistently hostile to Italy given that he acquiesced in the lifting of LEAGUE OF NATIONS sanctions in 1936 despite the fact that Abyssinia had been totally conquered. And even his resignation can be seen as motivated less by high principle than by personal pique at Chamberlain's interference in his running of foreign policy.

Whatever the merits of these various arguments the fact is that he emerged in the 1940s as WINSTON CHURCHILL's principal lieutenant, and it was widely assumed at the time that they had an almost father-and-son relationship of great harmony of view. Recent revelations suggest, however, that at times Churchill and Eden were bitter rivals and disagreed about much during the latter's second and third terms at the Foreign Office.

During Eden's second term from 1940 to 1945 Churchill was at the height of his powers and almost invariably got his way when differences between the two men arose. But Eden robustly defended his opinions behind closed doors and may at times have been close to resignation. Above all, Eden was more willing than his chief to see the Soviets' point of view and to argue for concessions to be made to them. For example, Eden is usually considered to have been more eager than Churchill to promote the controversial policy of enforced repatriation of prisoners-of-war to the Soviet Union. These differences were further reflected in 1946 when Churchill, now Leader of the Opposition, gave a lead to the world in denouncing Soviet-style Communism in a speech in Fulton, Missouri. In private Eden made known his disapproval.

Increasingly Eden's quarrels with Churchill became more personalized. For the former believed that he should have been invited to take over as Conservative Party Leader in the aftermath of the general election defeat of 1945. But Churchill refused to stand down either then or following another defeat in 1950. The upshot was that when Churchill formed his peacetime administration (1951–5) great hostility existed between him and the impatient Eden. And now the latter, as the coming man, was often able to defeat his chief in Cabinet over major issues of foreign policy. It is, for example, not without irony that one of Eden's victories was to secure British withdrawal from the Suez Canal Zone in Egypt. And another strange twist arose when Churchill, hitherto so anti-Soviet, greeted Joseph Stalin' death in 1953 with the surprising claim that the new Soviet leaders were sufficiently different to justify the holding of a three-power summit. Eden, determined that his chief should not again be allowed to play the beau role on such an occasion, now conspired with the Americans to block Churchill's plan—though once Eden was himself Prime Minister he suddenly switched to supporting it with the result that a summit was held in Geneva in July 1955.

Eden's final term at the Foreign Office was marked by two other major events which are usually held to reflect credit on him. First, he had a key role in a conference held at Geneva in 1954 to arrange a compromise settlement necessitated by the French decision to withdraw from Indochina. Secondly, he played a decisive part in persuading France to agree to West Germany being allowed to rearm under NATO auspices.

Eden's premiership began auspiciously when he led the Conservatives to a general election victory in May 1955; and shortly thereafter he was able to bask in the world spotlight at the aforementioned Geneva summit. But soon stormclouds began to gather. First, economic problems (about which Eden was not particularly well-informed) multiplied, necessitating an emergency budget in October 1955. Then came increasing problems in the Middle East as Gamal Nasser led Egypt into an arms deal with Czechoslovakia followed by a sustained propaganda campaign against British influence in the region.

Eden's final months as Prime Minister were dominated by problems relating to Egypt, which brought matters to a head by nationalizing the Suez Canal—hitherto controlled by a company based in Paris. Though personally eager to take military steps to reverse this move, Eden in practice could not risk the hostility of the United States, the COMMONWEALTH, the United Nations, the LABOUR PARTY, part of British opinion and even some of his own ministerial team. Hence by mid–October it appeared that a humiliating diplomatic compromise was the most likely outcome. But then French representatives proposed to Eden that Israel be secretly induced to attack Egypt, thereby providing a pretext for an Anglo-French armed intervention to separate the combatants and to protect the Canal. The scenario was soon put into practice with catastrophic consequences. The United Nations, and the United States in particular, were not persuaded of the genuineness of Anglo-French proclaimed motives and brought overwhelming pressure to bear. The upshot was the the military operation was suspended with Anglo-French forces in occupation of no more than a third of the Canal. Eventually a humiliating withdrawal had to be accepted.

In the meantime Eden's health (weakened by a bile-duct operation that had gone wrong in 1953) was giving cause for concern. He accordingly resigned as Prime Minister and as a Member of Parliament in January 1957. Whether health was the sole reason for his departure at this time may of course be doubted, though this was his story and he stuck to it. But then he also stuck to the story to the end of his days that he had had no foreknowledge of the Israeli attack on Egypt— something that no historian nowadays could possibly endorse.

Eden's overall significance was recognized in THE TIMES obituary in 1977: "He was the last Prime Minister to believe Britain was a great power and the first to confront a crisis which proved she was not."

                                                    David Carlton

Bibliography

Carlton, David. *Anthony Eden: A Biography.* 1981.
Eden, Anthony. *The Eden Memoirs.* 3 vols. 1960–65.
James, Robert Rhodes. *Anthony Eden.* 1986.
Rothwell, Victor. *Anthony Eden: A Political Biography,* *1931–1957.* 1992.

Education Act of 1944

The 1944 Education Act established a system of education which lasted until the 1990s. It represents both the capacity of war to produce social change and to ensure that the change is not as radical as reformers have long wished. Some of the Act came from the 1938 report of the Spens Committee, which recommended that all children be divided at eleven into groups capable of receiving a secondary education of some sort. Division at eleven and SECONDARY EDUCATION for all were already established practice in many local education authorities by way of the selection through examination, the so-called "eleven plus", and a special places scheme which meant that the only children who could have the differentiated, more academic curriculum of secondary schools had to pass through the sieve of examination. Reformers had argued that all children were capable of some sort of education beyond the restrictive curriculum of the contemporary form of primary schooling, the elementary school.

In 1942 Board of Education officials began to argue that educational reform was an essential component of reconstruction. CHURCHILL, who had experienced divisive effects of earlier reforms was unenthusiastic, but R.A. BUTLER and ARCHBISHOP WILLIAM TEMPLE overcame some of his objections. Local authorities were already moving towards greater homogeneity of practice because evacuation and wartime mobility ensured some need for parity in the system. Bombing and alienation of buildings for military use meant that some improvement could be provided by replacement. All these factors encouraged reform, as did the poor physical quality of aging schools.

The White Paper which outlined the reforms established several key principles that went into the Act virtually unchanged. These were that children should be allocated to secondary education by age, ability, and aptitude at eleven; local education authorities should provide secondary education with parity between schools; primary schooling should start at five, and the school-leaving age should be raised as recommended in 1938 to fifteen. The contentious issue was the role of the churches in education. Eventually the Act left them with the voluntary aided schools, supported by the local authority but administered by the church authorities. All local authorities were to provide development plans which were both an audit of existing provision and a declaration of future plans.

The outcome of the Act in the short term set the pattern for the long-term effects. Selective schools, the grammar schools, continued to examine and select their pupils using the same examinations as before the Act. Across the country 20 percent of eleven year olds received this kind of education, but local authorities provided it for a range of five percent to 32 percent. Few technical schools were provided for craft training and few were built. Secondary modern schools, like the old higher elementary schools, provided for the majority of eleven year olds. The curriculum of the two main types of school was differentiated so that children left grammar schools and took the school-leaving certificate, the matriculation examination, which enabled access to higher education. The rest were discouraged from sitting the examination and encouraged to have a more sex-specific education for adult life with a slant towards manual jobs. Local authorities who wished to interpret the Act by providing a differentiated education for all under one roof, in the multi-lateral school, were turned down when they submitted their development plans by the Ministry of Education. A hard-fought political battle raised the leaving age to fifteen in 1947.

The Act confirmed the changes advanced by many local authorities before the war. Reform was limited by material deficiencies of long duration and consequent upon austerity. The curriculum was not centrally prescribed or much altered, and the segregation of the eleven year olds on academic lines was perpetuated. Historical debate has focused on the question of equality of opportunity and the secondary child, and the relative responsibilities of central and local government for innovation; primary schooling and curricular content remain virtually unexamined.

Deborah Thom

Bibliography

Gosden, Peter H.J.H. *Education and the Second World War.* 1976.

Jeffreys, Kevin. "R.A. Butler, the Board of Education and the 1944 Education Act," *History,* vol. 69 (1984), pp. 415–31.

Johnson, Richard *et al. Unpopular education: Schooling and Social Democracy in England since 1944.* 1981.

Thom, Deborah. "The 1944 Education Act—the 'art of the possible'?" in Harold Smith, ed. *War and Social Change.* 1986. pp. 101–28.

Edward VII (1841–1910)

The eldest son and second child of Queen Victoria and Prince Albert, Albert Edward was created Prince of Wales in 1841 and succeeded his mother in 1901. As future monarch, he was the object of the highest hopes of his parents who hoped to create in him an ideal king—a moral and intellectual paragon. They were to be disappointed. Albert Edward, unlike his elder sister, the Princess Royal, the future Empress of Germany, or his younger sister, Princess Alice, the future Grand Duchess of Hesse, displayed no leanings toward anything intellectual. As for morality, his standards were those of the more rakish element of the upper class. The efforts of his parents were nonetheless unsparing, and, in fact, may have had a result the opposite of what they intended. He had the advantage, however, of extensive travel; the most notable success was a visit to Paris with his parents in 1855. As a result, he developed a life-long love for France. He traveled as well to Canada and the United States, and extensively on the continent. He studied briefly at OXFORD and CAMBRIDGE, and joined the Grenadier Guards. After his father's death in 1861, it was thought that an early marriage was desirable, and in 1863, after considerable negotiation, he married Princess Alexandra of Denmark, daughter of the future King Christian IX of Denmark; her sister Dagmar was later to marry Tsar Alexander III of Russia, and her brother William was later to become King George I of Greece.

The Prince of Wales had a long apprenticeship. His mother, who mistrusted and disliked his style of life, would permit him virtually no role in her constitutional duties. As she suspected him of indiscretion, he was denied access to state papers until late in her reign. The Prince fulfilled a vast number of ceremonial functions, often with great success. He became, moreover, the center of much of England's social life; his London residence gave rise to the name of the Marlborough House set, admission to which was controlled by the Prince; for many persons he was the absolute arbiter of all things fashionable. He also became a frequent traveler, spreading goodwill for Britain in foreign courts. In 1871 he nearly died of typhoid on the tenth anniversary of his father's death. The Queen's dramatic rush to his bedside, and his seemingly miraculous recovery, restored the popularity of the monarchy which had suffered greatly because of Victoria's seclusion since Prince Albert's death. Republicanism, which had become a considerable force, was crushed, and the Queen was well positioned to become the symbol and embodiment of a proud and imperial Britain.

The private life of the Prince was a source of worry to many persons, above all the Queen. It was thought by some that he might not be fit to ascend the throne, and he was in fact involved in several scandals, testifying in a widely-publicized divorce proceeding and in a slander case and feuding with the members of the Churchill family. Respectable opinion, inspired by the PRESS, believed that adverse publicity and the Prince's irregular sexual life far outweighed in the public mind his many public duties, such as his intermittent service on the Royal Commission on HOUSING.

It is not surprising, therefore, that when he succeeded his mother in January 1901 his accession was greeted with apprehension. Yet he developed into an extraordinarily successful sovereign. He did not style himself Albert I, as his mother had hoped, and he immediately showed independence. He opened Parliament in state, something Queen Victoria had rarely done, and instituted a reign of considerable splendor and pagentry. The magnificence of his court pleased most Britons who found it reassuring in an age in which British power was increasingly challenged. Soon he became, even more than his mother, a comforting figure whose very presence on the throne seemed to assure continued British eminence. The state visit he and Queen Alexandra paid to Paris in 1903 was a triumph, and paved the way for the Entente Cordiale. He came to be regarded as a kind of uncle to all of Europe, and as one who could keep his difficult relatives in line, especially his nephew, the German Kaiser.

The result of his powerful personality was that his influence was exaggerated. He did not determine British foreign policy, but rather acted as one who would smooth the way for policies determined by others. As he was not industrious, he probably never acquired the knowledge that his mother did, but nevertheless his influence was felt particularly in military, naval, and diplomatic matters. He established good relations with his ministers, especially with the LIBERAL Prime Minister, Sir HENRY CAMPBELL-BANNERMAN, with whom he shared gourmet tastes. The King also seemed in tune with the twentieth century because of the breadth of his friendships, but he never let anyone around him forget his position. From one point of view the high point of his reign came in 1909 when his horse Minoru won the Derby, to the wild enthusiasm of the crowd.

Most of his reign was marked by bitter political controversy, in which the King played a role, often revealing a strongly Conservative prejudice. When the struggle over the Parliament Bill to limit the powers of the upper house intensified, he gave, but with great reluctance, an assurance that if the HOUSE OF LORDS did not pass the bill, he would create sufficient Liberal peers to get it through; and he did ask that an election be held in 1910. When the King died in May 1910 there were those who complained bitterly that he had been hounded to death by his government. But even those who did not hold such extreme views felt the loss of the King deeply, and the mourning was not only genuine but far more profound than had been the case in 1901. In a reign of just over nine years he had given his name to an era and had won the affection of his people. He had become a symbol of security in an increasingly dangerous world.

King Edward VII made a vital contribution to the evolution of the modern monarchy. If his mother had given the throne respectability, and if his father had played a vital role in distancing the monarchy from political controversy, King Edward gave it glamor and excitement. Much of the extravagance might have seemed inappropriate later, in a era of war and depression, but the magnificence associated with the King's court was later blended by his descendants with Victorian domestic virtues. Queen Alexandra, moreover, beautiful even in old age, was the perfect wife for King Edward; with her understanding and her lack of interest in almost everthing except her family, she was a model consort for her husband.

The King was survived by Queen Alexandra who died in 1925, and by his second son, KING GEORGE V. He was also survived by three daughters: Princess Louise, later Duchess of Fife; Princess Victoria, and Princess Maud, later Queen of Norway. His eldest son, Prince Albert Victor, Duke of Clarence, died in 1892, and his youngest son, Prince John, died in 1871.

Arthur Mejia

Bibliography

Lee, Sir Sidney. *King Edward VII.* 1925–7.
Magnus, Philip. *King Edward the Seventh.* 1964.
St. Aubyn, Giles. *Edward VII: Prince and King.* 1979.

Edward VIII (1894–1972)

The eldest son of the future KING GEORGE V and Queen Mary, Edward was created Prince of Wales (1910); succeeded his father as King (January 1936); abdicated (December 1936) and succeeded by his brother, the Duke of York (KING GEORGE VI); was created Duke of Windsor (1937).

Prince Edward (or David, as he was known to his family) was raised in an atmosphere of discipline and order. His father and mother gave the young Prince little affection, at least by modern standards, and he was subjected to the severe regimes of his nurses and tutors. In 1907 he was sent to Osborne and to Dartmouth in 1909, as his father was convinced that the NAVY would teach him everything he needed to know. Although this upbringing was often miserable, and although it certainly marked the future King for life, it was little different from the upbringing of other upper-class British boys. The education to which he was exposed, both at home and in the navy, was undeniably narrow, and strikingly nonintellectual. He was later exposed to a broader world at OXFORD and, under strict limitations, he was allowed to serve on the Western Front during the FIRST WORLD WAR.

It was after the war that he emerged as the center of attention for much of the world's press. His imperial tours, and his visits to the United States and elsewhere, made him a man who aroused passionate interest. His parents were often pleased by the good-will he inspired, but they were just as often distressed by his casual and informal manner which they thought inappropriate in the heir to the throne. They were also upset by his lack of interest in marriage and by his numerous affairs with unsuitable women. Generally these women were older and married, and with them the Prince lived a life which was basically self-indulgent and social; he showed little interest in affairs of state. During those years the adulation which surrounded the Prince led him to believe that he could always have his way, and his essentially frivolous life did not disabuse him.

The new King, although professing eagerness to reform the monarchy, soon reverted to his former style of life which was interrupted by a serious complication. For several years he had had as his mistress Mrs. Ernest Simpson, née Wallis Warfield of Baltimore, formerly married to Earl Spencer, an American naval officer from whom she was divorced in 1927. The King became determined to marry Mrs. Simpson, even though, by the time they would be able to marry, she would be twice divorced. As the King was the titular head of the CHURCH OF ENGLAND, which did not recognize DIVORCE, there was an obvious problem. Neither his private secretary, Alexander Hardinge, nor the Prime Minister, STANLEY BALDWIN, were able to dissuade him from his resolve to marry Mrs. Simpson.

The growing crisis was generally concealed from the British public by the self-censorship of the PRESS, but early in December the storm broke. The political implications were clear, as enemies of Baldwin hoped to form a "King's Party" which, in a wave of royalist enthusiasm, would sweep Baldwin from office and bring to power a government which, among other things,

would hasten rearmament. Among the leaders of this movement were LORD BEAVERBROOK, who cared little for the monarchy, and WINSTON CHURCHILL, who most definitely did. But Baldwin, who had far greater insight into the psychology of the British people, at least in peacetime, had come to the firm conclusion that the mass of the people would not accept as their Queen a twice-divorced woman whose background betrayed no sense of public duty. In this he was firmly supported by the LABOUR PARTY and by the Dominions. All halfway solutions failed to gain support, such as a morganatic marriage in which Mrs. Simpson would marry the King but not become Queen. When Churchill pleaded in the House of Commons that precipitate action should be avoided, he had an exceedingly hostile reception, for the country as a whole was clearly moving to the conclusion that the King must go. If Edward VIII had been willing to postpone his marriage to Mrs. Simpson for a year or two, or at least until after the Coronation in May 1937, there might have been a very slight chance that he could have established himself so firmly on the throne that he could have had both Mrs. Simpson and his kingdom. In any event, there was no possibility of marriage until Mrs. Simpson's divorce was final in April. But the King was impatient, and when he abdicated on 11 December, it was probably with considerable relief. He handed over the throne to his brother, the deeply distressed but far more suitable Duke of York, who became King George VI.

The King was not forced off his throne by a government embarrassed by his alleged concern with the unemployed, with whom he once expressed sympathy, or because of his supposed fondness for Nazism, based on an alleged statement to the German ambassador that as long as he was King there would never be another war between Germany and Britain. The King went, in part, because of a sense of his own inadequacy, but primarily because of the conservative (not in the political sense) nature of the British people. Although they were deeply loyal to the monarchy, that loyalty only extended to the monarch if he embodied that institution as it had been modeled by Queen Victoria and Prince Albert, and by Kings EDWARD VII and George V. King Edward VIII, however, most certainly did not represent the values of his family, as his mother, Queen Mary, who never forgave him, made very clear. The damage to the monarchy was thought to be great; as it turned out, the new King and Queen, and their daughters, rapidly repaired the damage.

In 1937 the former King was created Duke of Windsor by his brother, with the provision that neither his wife, nor his children, could bear the designation "Royal Highness." This was seen by the new Duke, correctly, as a snub, and was a principal reason why he and the Duchess, whom he married in June 1937, never lived again in England. The bitterness was compounded by financial problems, as the Duke negotiated with his brother over the sale of privately-held royal assets and about the Duke's allowance. The subsequent life of the Windsors was social, as it had always been; although there were events with political overtones, such as their visit to Adolf Hitler in October 1937. In 1940 a difficult problem arose concerning the safety of the Duke and Duchess, who fled to Portugal in advance of the Nazi conquest. There were rumors, probably unfounded, that the Germans intended to restore the Duke to the throne as a puppet king after their planned conquest of Britain. In the midst of the BLITZ, Churchill arranged for the Windsors, much to their displeasure, to go to the Bahamas. There the Duke remained Governor until 1945, after which they settled in Paris and resumed their previous style of life. Only rarely, such as on the occasion of his mother's death, did he return to England. He died in Paris in May 1972, shortly after receiving a visit from Queen Elizabeth II. He was buried in the royal burial ground at Frogmore. The Duchess attended the funeral, and was herself buried at Frogmore in 1986, still not a "Royal Highness."

Arthur Mejia

Bibliography

Donaldson, Frances. *Edward VIII.* 1974.

Windsor, Duke of. *A King's Story.* 1951.

Ziegler, Philip. *King Edward VIII: The Official Biography.* 1990.

El Alamein, Battle of

El Alamein is a town on the Mediterranean coast of Egypt, west of the Nile. Three SECOND WORLD WAR battles were fought in this vicinity in the summer and fall of 1942 during which the German drive into Egypt was stopped and finally thrown back.

In the spring of 1942 General Erwin Rommel's Axis forces, German and Italian, launched a new phase of the desert war, sending Britain's Eighth Army reeling back into Egypt to a position near El Alamein. Here the front became very narrow, hemmed in by the sea on the north and the Qattara Depression on the south. Thus it was an ideal defensive position for the British, apart from the fact that they were near their great bases in Alexandria and Cairo, while Rommel's supply line now stretched many hundreds of miles back into Libya. Nevertheless, Rommel attacked again on 1 July. General Sir Claude Auchinleck, Commander-in-Chief, Middle East, took personal command of the Eighth

Army and counterattacked the next day; after weeks of battle, the opposing forces settled down to a stalemate. Although Auchinleck had done well, receiving praise from Rommel himself, CHURCHILL believed that new commanders were needed for decisive victory. Therefore Auchinleck was replaced by General Sir Harold Alexander and the Eighth Army was given to General Sir BERNARD MONTGOMERY.

In the summer and fall of 1942 German commitments to the Russian front, British attacks on Italian convoys supplying Rommel, and large shipments of materiel (including American LEND-LEASE) to Montgomery all made Rommel's position increasingly precarious. He attempted to throw Montgomery off balance by attacking Alam Halfa ridge on 31 August, but failed to budge the heavily entrenched British. On 23 October Montgomery attacked with massive superiority in men and materiel, yet the narrow frontage now worked to Axis advantage, and it was not until 4 November that the enemy had been ground down enough by attrition to make their situation hopeless. Rommel, who had returned to Egypt on 25 October from sick leave in Germany, now defied Hitler's orders and began a skillful retreat back to Libya and ultimately Tunisia; Montgomery's pursuit was lack-luster.

El Alamein was celebrated by the British as a great and decisive victory, and it catapulted Montgomery to lasting fame. Yet it had been costly, and perhaps unnecessarily so: the Axis cause in Egypt would have been doomed with or without Montgomery's offensive because of the Anglo-American landings in French Northwest Africa beginning on 8 November, which threatened Rommel's supply ports from the rear. Perhaps if Montgomery had waited until just before 8 November to attack, Rommel's resistance would have been far less stubborn; still, Britain needed a victory of her own at that point in the war.

Karl G. Larew

Bibliography

Barnett, Correlli. *The Desert Generals.* 1982.

Carver, Michael. *Dilemmas of the Desert War.* 1986.

Lucas, James. *War in the Desert: The Eighth Army at El Alamein.* 1982.

Electoral System

At the beginning of the century about 60 percent of men over twenty-one had the right to vote. Most of them qualified under the householder franchise, which had given the franchise to adult male heads of households in boroughs in 1867 and in county constituencies in 1885. Because the older property qualifications still survived, plural voting by people who owned property in several places still continued, though the lodger franchise did mean that some relatively prosperous non-householders also had a right to vote. The redistribution of seats in the 1885 Act had taken a step towards "one vote, one value," though attention was still paid to the old idea of communities on which the House of Commons had been based ever since the thirteenth century. In the early years of the twentieth century the electorate was a little over 7 million, and the House of Commons had 670 members.

Between 1906 and 1918 the only change in the national electoral system was that the 1911 Parliament Act required a general election every five years instead of every seven years. Women gained the right to vote in all municipal elections, and pressure for them to gain the right to vote in national elections attracted more attention and caused more disturbance than any other franchise issue before the war, though plural voting, the position of unenfranchised men, and the disparities in size between constituencies were all discussed. Wartime pressure for votes for soldiers and sailors, and more generally for democracy in the sense of universal suffrage, led to the 1918 Representation of the People Act. It dealt with all these questions: it put men on the electoral register (to be drawn up twice a year, though retrenchment soon reduced this to once a year) at twenty-one subject to a simple residence requirement; it put women on the register at thirty subject to the slightly more complicated residence qualifications required for voting in municipal elections; it redrew the boundaries of seats in a way that recognized numerical equality as the basic principle for constituencies; and it provided for postal voting for men and women away from home on military service (and retained it for the universities).

Plural voting would have been greatly reduced by this residence-based system and by the new provision that all constituencies were to vote on the same day, but in any case no voter was allowed to vote in more than two constituencies; some people qualified for a vote for business premises, which produced about 250,000 additional votes, mainly for offices in the center of cities, and others received votes as university graduates, who numbered about 200,000 by 1945. To take account of the emergence of new universities, their total representation was increased from nine to fifteen (soon reduced to twelve by changes in Ireland). Other changes in constituency boundaries recognized that the population was continuing to move from city centers and from the countryside into the suburbs. Limits on spending were reduced to a level that made it unlikely that candidates even in the largest constituencies could spend much more than £1000, and the government relieved them from having to pay for the returning officers and other officials who ran the

elections, though they had to put up a deposit of £150 (refunded if they obtained 12.5 percent of the votes cast) to reduce the risk of freak or frivolous candidatures. This Act increased the electorate to 21 million and the seats in Parliament to 707, subsequently reduced to 615 by changes in Ireland. A separate Act passed later in 1918 enabled women to stand for Parliament on the same terms as men, and the differences in the age and residence requirements, originally introduced to ensure that women should not become a majority of the electorate, were ended in 1928.

In 1944 it was recognized that further changes in the distribution of population once more meant that the outer districts of large cities were under-represented. There was no time to do more before an election than create an additional twenty-five seats and set up a Boundary Commission to make changes for the future on a regular basis, within the limits of the representation given to the four countries in the United Kingdom by existing legislation, and with some regard for areas like Anglesey (as the present-day constituency of Ynys Mon was known), the Isle of Wight, Orkney and Shetland, and the Western Isles. Except for geographical areas like these, seats are not expected to have more than 25 percent more or 25 percent less than the average number of voters, and relatively few seats come close to so large a deviation from the average. At first it was thought that boundary changes could take place during the lifetime of each Parliament, but such frequent alterations would have been so great a strain on constituency organization that they were almost immediately based on the decennial census. The limits on spending were reduced once more and (in money terms) for the last time, though subsequent increases have not fully kept up with rises in prices. Campaigning in the second half of the century has focused more and more on the national activity of the central organizations and on newspaper and poster advertising before the election period has begun; neither of these developments was foreseen when limits were being placed on expenditures, and they are not subject to the constituency-based limits on spending that started in 1883. Parties are not able to buy broadcasting time for advertising, but as a public service free time is allocated to them for the period between elections and—with rather more argument about the allocation of the time—during elections.

After the war the 1948 Act abolished all plural voting and ended the university seats, and the House of Commons was reduced to 625 MP seats and it has remained quite close to that number in the decennial readjustments of seats. The Act also provided for voting by post for invalids and for those who had moved out of the constituency after the electoral register had been published. In 1969 the reduction of the age of majority to eighteen led on to a reduction of the age at which people received the right to vote.

In 1918 there was some discussion of changing the voting system to the Alternative Vote or the Single Transferable Vote, and the latter system was adopted for university seats. The question was considered by the government in 1929, when LABOUR was in office for the second time without any clear majority in Parliament or in the electorate, and the issue has been kept alive by subsequent elections in which minor parties like the LIBERALS have gained far fewer seats than their share of the popular vote suggests they might expect, but no steps have been taken along these lines in Britain. The United Kingdom has had eighty-one seats in the European Parliament since it joined the EUROPEAN COMMUNITY in 1973. Elections have been held for these seats since 1979, using the same first-past-the-post voting system in Britain for them as for national elections, despite the general European reluctance to use that method.

Although it became less common for individuals to move from municipal office onto the national stage, municipal elections became more and more a branch of national party politics in the first half of the century, and by 1950 all municipalities of any size were run on party political lines after elections in which voting was determined by the popularity of parties at Westminster. The same readiness to vote in response to Westminster politics has been visible in the first elections to the European Parliament. Voters' turnout in municipal and in European elections has steadily been lower than in general elections, and in national elections it has never matched the polls of over 80 percent recorded in 1950 and 1951. Since then it has fluctuated around 75 percent, with some tendency for turnout to be lower in solidly-held seats than in marginal seats; it is hard to tell whether this is the result of voter sophistication or of the parties' readiness to concentrate their full-time election agents in marginal seats. For the main change in the electoral activity in the twentieth century is the increased importance of the political parties; the role of the national campaign by the party leader has become greater, broadcasting is conducted on lines laid down by discussions among the parties, and the polling of public opinion, which has become so important a tool for devising party strategy, is too complex and too expensive to be carried out on anything other than a party basis. Apart from a few changes like allowing candidates to list their party affiliation on the ballot paper, much of the advance of the parties to the center of the stage has proceeded without official recognition

or restraint, and is accepted much more fully than is sometimes pretended.

Trevor Lloyd

Bibliography
Butler, David. *The Electoral System in Britain 1918–1951 Since 1918*. 2nd ed. 1963.
Cook, Chris, and John Ramsden, eds. *By-Elections in British Politics*. 1973.
Craig, F.W.S. *British Electoral Facts 1832–1980*. 1981.
———. *British Parliamentary Election Results 1918–1949*. 2nd ed. 1977.
———. *British Parliamentary Election Results 1950–1973*. 2nd ed. 1981.
———. *British Parliamentary Election Results 1974–1983*. 1984.
Kinnear, Michael. *The British Voter*. 2nd ed. 1981.

Elgar, Edward William (1857–1934)

One of the most important English composers since Purcell, Edward Elgar made significant contributions to most musical genres, bringing the Victorian cantata and oratorio to fruition and establishing the British twentieth-century symphonic tradition. Elgar was capable of writing popular music of distinction, and the central tune from his first *Pomp and Circumstance March* (1901), when linked with Arthur Benson's patriotic words, "Land of hope and glory," became England's second national anthem. Born at Broadheath, near Worcester, the son of a tradesman, Elgar was gentlemanly by nature, and, with the help of his wife Alice, became a gentleman in fact, counting royalty among his friends. Following an honorary doctorate from CAMBRIDGE (1900), Elgar received many official honors, including a knighthood (1904), the Order of Merit (1911), and a baronetcy (1931) and was appointed Master of the King's Music in 1924.

Although Elgar received some formal instrumental tuition including violin lessons from Adolf Pollitzer in London (1877–8), he was self-taught as a composer, absorbing what he needed from books and scores in his father's music shop at Worcester. He gained experience in performing and conducting in local music making, but his main livelihood was as a local violin teacher. Moving farther afield, he joined W.C. Stockley's orchestra at Birmingham, which performed his *Sérénade mauresque* on 13 December 1883, and the following year, *Sevillana* was given by August Manns at the Crystal Palace, London, a performance brought about by Pollitzer. Elgar's meeting with (Caroline) Alice Roberts, the daughter of a major-general, and his subsequent marriage to her (1889), brought him increased social status as well as confidence and spiritual support, but a move to London in 1889 to establish himself met with failure. The overture *Froissart* (1890), headed with an epigraph from Keats, "When chivalry lifted up her lance on high," was successfully performed in Worcester but not heard in London. Although Elgar, now in his mid-thirties, had to return to Worcestershire (Malvern) and to resume the modest career of a provincial music teacher, he did not abandon composition, testifying to his and his wife's strong belief in his latent genius. He wisely turned to the late Victorian market for festival cantatas and oratorios, and, returning to chivalry for his subject matter composed *The Black Knight* (Uhland, trans. Longfellow: 1892), to be followed by the short oratorio, *The Light of Life* (1896) and the cantatas, *Scenes from the Saga of King Olaf* (Longfellow/H.A. Acworth: 1896) and *Caractacus* (Acworth: 1898), the latter set partly in the Malvern Hills and Severn valley. Drawing on his expanding knowledge of the nineteenth-century orchestral and operatic repertoire, gained at the Crystal Palace concerts when living in London and on visits to Bayreuth and Munich to hear Wagner's later operas (1892–3), Elgar's developing style reaches an intensity in *King Olaf* that heralds maturity, as it does in the slow movement of the Serenade for strings (1892) and parts of the Organ Sonata (1895).

However, it was not until the orchestral Variations on an Original Theme ("Enigma") (1899), dedicated to "My Friends Pictured Within," that Elgar reached musical maturity, significantly in the company of his wife (Variation 1) and friends (Variations 2–13), with Elgar himself as the final variation. More enigmatic than the variations (but not titled as such) was the sacred cantata *The Dream of Gerontius* (John Henry Newman: 1900), its Catholic text (Elgar was Roman Catholic), unsympathetic to some music lovers and especially to those members of the ANGLICAN establishment who had the text's doctrinal infelicities expunged before performance in their cathedrals. Because of its difficulty and problems at rehearsal, the premiere at the Birmingham Triennial Festival (1900) was a failure, but a performance at the Lower Rhine Festival, Dusseldorf, in May 1902, conducted by Julius Buths, revealed the work's true stature. *Gerontius* was followed by the oratorio *The Apostles* (Elgar, after Bible: 1903), an advance on the former work in chromatic language and architectural grandeur, and *The Kingdom* (Elgar, after Bible: 1906), although the final oratorio in the planned trilogy was never completed. Elgar's faith wavered: his duties as the first Peyton Professor of Music at Birmingham University (1905–8) sapped his energy. Instead, building on his increasing mastery of purely instrumental music in the overtures *Cockaigne (In London Town)* (1901) and *In the South (Alassio)* (1904), and in the Introduction and Allegro for strings (1905), Elgar embarked upon two symphonies (A flat major: 1908; E flat major: 1911),

the first of which was performed nearly 100 times during its first year. The opening theme, typically marked *Nobilmente,* and returning several times during the opening movement and finale, acts as a unifying agent as does the idea of basing the third, slow movement, on a melody that is a thematic transformation of the second, the scherzo. Between the two symphonies came the richly expressive Violin Concerto (1910), unusual for its accompanied cadenza and inspired possibly by a temporary romance.

In 1912 Elgar's move from Hereford, near where he had lived since 1904, to Hampstead in London, was marked by the completion of an ode for alto, chorus, and orchestra, *The Music Makers* (O'Shaughnessy: 1912), which forms, with its use of self-quotation, a retrospective of Elgar's achievements to date. More backward glances followed in *Falstaff* (1913), an extended "symphonic study," where a return to knightly virtues, but not vices, reveals an Elgarian quasi-autobiographical interpretation of Shakespeare's character. The First World War, coming at a crucial moment in Elgar's creative development, stifled its impulse, although in *The Spirit of England* (Binyon: 1917), his last major work for soloists, chorus, and orchestra, the elegiac lament for the fallen is sustained with great compassion. A sudden efflorescence in 1918–19 produced three chamber works, the String Quartet, Violin Sonata, and Piano Quintet, all three also backward-looking to a certain extent, paying homage in part to Brahms. However, Elgar's late style is fully encapsulated in the Cello Concerto (1919), by turns poignantly elegiac, capricious, and passionate; in it, Elgar laments the passing of his own world. Following the death of his wife in 1920, Elgar completed no further works of substance, although a legacy of recordings of him conducting his own compositions was completed (1914–33). He returned to Worcester to live out his last years.

Trevor Bray

Bibliography
Gardiner, John. "The Reception of Sir Edward Elgar, 1918–c.1934," *Twentieth Century British History.* vol. 9 (1998), pp. 370–95.
Kennedy, Michael. *Portrait of Elgar.* 3rd ed. 1987.
Maine, Basil. *Elgar: His Life and Works.* 2 vols. 1933.
Moore, Jerrold Northrop. *Edward Elgar: A Creative Life.* 1984.
———, ed. *Edward Elgar: Letters of a Lifetime.* 1990.

Eliot, T(homas) S(tearns) (1888–1965)

Poet, essayist, playwright, critic, and "dictator" of literary taste, T.S. Eliot exerted an influence unequaled in Britain or the United States between the two world wars and after. Expatriated from the United States in his twenties, Eliot became a British citizen and embraced Anglo-Catholicism in 1927. His long poem *The Waste Land* (1922) seemed to mirror, if through a broken glass, the horror of post-war Europe. Its fragmentation and haunting musicality seemed apocalyptic in a world of shattered institutions and betrayed hopes.

A defender of tradition and orthodoxy, Eliot nevertheless led a poetic revolution. He denied the existence of *vers libre*, but was responsible for some of the most radical innovations in verse form of the century. He was fastidious and socially conservative, and yet was seen as a force for liberation by readers across the political spectrum.

Eliot's grandfather, a New Englander, chose a spiritual mission to the frontier: he established a Unitarian Church in St. Louis and in 1853 founded Washington University. Eliot's father was a successful businessman, a brick manufacturer, who was disappointed by his youngest son's choice of a literary vocation and did not live to see his success at it. His mother, a poet herself, nurtured his early literary interests.

Eliot entered Harvard University in 1906 and studied literature, philosophy, and history during what has been called Harvard's "glacial era" for its conservatism. He encountered there, among other luminaries, George Santayana, BERTRAND RUSSELL, Josiah Royce, and Irving Babbitt. The latter, whose lectures on the evils of romanticism complemented Eliot's own instinctive self-denial and rationalism, was especially influential. After a year in Paris (1910–11), Eliot began graduate school in philosophy at Harvard, eventually returning to Europe on a traveling fellowship in 1914. He completed his doctoral dissertation on the skeptical idealist philosopher F.H. Bradley in 1916, but never went back to claim the degree.

While at Harvard, Eliot studied Dante and Baudelaire intently and discovered, by reading Arthur Symons's *The Symbolist Movement in Literature*, the French poet Jules Laforgue. Eliot later described Laforgue as the poetic personality that had allowed him to find his own subject matter and voice—ironic, aloof, and disillusioned. "I learned," Eliot said, "that the sort of material I had, the sort of experience that an adolescent had had, in an industrial city in America, could be the material for poetry." The language, rhythms, and speech, he later wrote, of his immediate predecessors in the Anglo-American literary world were inadequate for the feelings of the poet writing of the "more sordid aspects of the modern metropolis."

The emotional expressiveness and power of Eliot's loosened verse form became clear in the poems collected in *Prufrock and Other Observations* (1917), a landmark of modernist writing. Eliot takes his reader into an urban phantasmagoria in these poems: ghastly streets and strange surrealized drawing rooms reflect the states of the passionless, isolated souls of his poetic characters. In "The Love Song of J. Alfred Prufrock" (1915), the cityscape—the cat-like yellow fog, the "muttering retreats," and "sawdust restaurants"— seems responsible for the narrator's psychological malaise, his inability to "force the moment to its crisis." Prufrock's problem is not just personal, but public and generational. This collection was followed by *Poems* (1920) with "Gerontion" (1920) as the leading item and *Poems, 1909–1925,* which included "The Hollow Men" (1925).

Eliot's marriage to an Englishwoman, Vivien Haigh-Wood, in the summer of 1915 after a two-month acquaintance was a disaster for both parties. They were two temperaments at odds, incompatible in personal disposition and in background. Financial difficulties, compounded by Vivien's frequent physical and emotional illnesses and the disapproval of his family, led to a nervous breakdown for Eliot in 1921.

While recuperating in Lausanne, Switzerland, Eliot completed work on *The Waste Land*. The double crushing weight of a sense of personal loss and of cultural disintegration are felt in this echo-chamber of historical significances. Disembodied voices are let loose like the furies on an "Unreal City," London as Dante's hell, doubling as every city in Europe. In this barren and dessicated land, sexuality has lost its fruitfulness. The poem is both a terrifying critique of a civilization and a passionate and lyrical cry of personal anguish. Lacking a single narrative center, the poem depends on fragmentation, a structural device that imitates the social deformations of the modern world. Eliot dedicated the poem to his friend Ezra Pound, whom he called "il miglior fabbro," the better craftsman, for his work editing the poem. The rediscovery of the manuscript of the poem in 1971 revealed that Pound had cut long narrative and dramatic sections and created the poem's montage effects of juxtaposition and contrast.

Eliot left Vivien Eliot in 1932 after years of acute mutual anguish. She died in a mental hospital in 1947. Eliot's second marriage in 1957 to Valerie Fletcher, his long-time secretary at the London publishing firm Faber and Faber, brought him comfort and happiness during the final years of his life.

Eliot's powerful, polemical voice as essayist set the intellectual agenda for several generations of critics. He shaped and manipulated his own career through his criticism, even as he revised according to his tastes the history of poetry in English. Among his most striking essays from his early career are "Reflections on vers libre" (1917), "Tradition and the Individual Talent" (1919), "*Hamlet*" (1919), and "The Metaphysical Poets"

(1921); from his late career, *Idea of a Christian Society* (1939), "The Music of Poetry" (1942), and "From Poe to Valéry" (1948).

Eliot's social and political conservatism became increasingly pronounced in his critical writing dating from the mid-1920s. In 1933 he delivered at the University of Virginia his most notorious lecture series, later collected as *After Strange Gods: A Primer of Modern Heresy* (1934). In these talks, he made disparaging remarks about "foreign races" and "free-thinking Jews." He later refused to have the collection reprinted because of his embarrassment about its content.

Eliot's embrace of Anglo-Catholicism ultimately moderated the tone of his conservatism. His "Ariel Poems," published between 1927 and 1930, and his lyrical meditation *Ash Wednesday* (1930) work explicitly within the framework of Christian symbolism and contend with the problem of Incarnation. "Burnt Norton" (1936), the first of Eliot's *Four Quartets* (1943), is a meditation on temporality and on intimations of the eternal, tested against the fragile beauty of the natural world. The remaining three *Quartets,* "East Coker (1940)," "The Dry Salvages" (1941), and "Little Gidding" (1942), were written during the Second World War. Eliot takes his measure of the "topography of pain" in these religious poems, not through doctrinal claims, but through the ruggedness of experience.

Eliot devoted much of his creative energy in his late career to the writing of plays in verse. The lyricism of the voices of the chorus, the "poor women of Canterbury," in Eliot's poetic drama, *Murder in the Cathedral* (1935), about the martyrdom of Thomas à Becket, represents the fulfillment of his ambitions to create a naturalistic theatre in verse. *The Family Reunion,* a complex psychodrama about marital guilt, was first staged in 1939. After the war he produced three more plays, *The Cocktail Party* (1950), *The Confidential Clerk* (1954), and *The Elder Statesman* (1959). Eliot's verses for children, *Old Possum's Book of Practical Cats* (1939) achieved posthumous notoriety in the celebrated stage musical *Cats* in 1981.

Eliot was awarded the Nobel Prize for Literature and the Order of Merit, the highest civilian award for a British subject, in 1948. At midcentury, his preeminence seemed unshakeable. Since then, he has come to seem more vulnerable—sometimes the subject of caricature—even as he still seems threatening. His star has fallen with, though not as far as, that of the "New Critics" he inspired. Eliot used avant-garde techniques for conservative ends. His politics were irrational and elitist. Yet he looked with unguarded eye at the "modern metropolis," and his social conscience dictated his decisions about poetic form. His monumental achievement can be measured not only in positive responses, but also in counter-attacks: many poets and critics alike, of his own generation and since, have honored him by defining their work against his strong influence. He captured the voices of a civilization in turmoil, and his taste defined an era. The pain and compassion of his poetry, and the strength of his critical imagination, remain compelling.

Elizabeth Muther

Bibliography

Behr, Caroline. *T.S. Eliot: A Chronology of His Life and Works.* 1983.

Bush, Ronald. *T.S. Eliot: A Study in Character and Style.* 1983.

Donoghue, Denis. *Words Alone: The Poet T.S. Eliot.* 2000.

Eliot, T.S. *The Letters of T.S. Eliot,* vol. I, 1898–1922. Valerie Eliot, ed. 1988.

Gordon, Lyndall. *T.S. Eliot: An Imperfect Life.* 1998.

Ricks, Beatrice, comp. *T.S. Eliot: A Bibliography of Secondary Works.* 1980.

Elizabeth II (1926–)

Queen Elizabeth is the fifth longest reigning monarch in British history, the longest serving since the death of her great-great-grandmother, Queen Victoria, in 1901. She celebrated her Silver Jubilee in 1977; in February 2002 she marked her Golden Jubilee.

The Queen was born on 21 April 1926 at Bruton Place, London, the home of her maternal grandparents, the Earl and Countess of Strathmore. Her father, Albert, Duke of York, was the second son of King GEORGE V (reigned 1910–1936), her mother Elizabeth, Duchess of York, was the former Lady Elizabeth Bowes-Lyon. From her early youth, Princess Elizabeth was the most famous little girl in the world: chocolates, china, and hospital wards were named after her, a popular song was composed for her, her face appeared on a Newfoundland stamp, and a slice of Antarctica became Princess Elizabeth Land. Yet at home in the nursery she developed into an orderly, self-contained, disciplined child, the responsible elder sister to Princess Margaret Rose (1930–2002). Her childhood was happy and secure, with fond parents and the opportunity to indulge her love of dogs and horses. But everything changed when, in December 1936, her uncle EDWARD VIII, abdicated in order to marry Wallis Simpson. Princess Elizabeth's father became King GEORGE VI, and she herself became Heir Presumptive to the British throne. The family moved into Buckingham Palace, surrounded by the panoply and restrictions of British royalty.

Princess Elizabeth and her sister spent the duration of the SECOND WORLD WAR at Windsor Castle where they were sent for safety. They were educated in the far from rigorous manner of upper-class children of the day by a governess, Marion Crawford, although Elizabeth, in view of her future role, was taught excellent French and had lessons in English constitutional history. Her parents saw to it that she met and entertained such important visitors as Eleanor Roosevelt and General Dwight Eisenhower as part of her future training, and on her sixteenth birthday she undertook her first ceremonial role, being installed as Honorary Colonel of the Grenadier Guards. In the last months of the war she took a course in the Auxiliary Territorial Service which involved learning to drive a truck, change its tires, and understand the working of the engine. She still prides herself on being a fast, skillful driver.

Princess Elizabeth's worldwide public debut came just before her twenty-first birthday on 6 February 1947 during her first tour outside Britain, a state visit with her parents and sister to the Union of South Africa, then still a self-governing Dominion. The post-war years saw the dissolution of the British Empire and the beginning of its transformation into the COMMONWEALTH, an association of former colonies and Dominions with the British monarch as its head. In what was to become her best-known broadcast, the young Princess dedicated herself to the service of the Empire and Commonwealth: "I can make my solemn act of dedication now," she said. "I declare . . . that my whole life . . . shall be devoted to your service, and the service of the great imperial family to which we all belong." The pledge which she gave that day in 1947 remained a constant for her. She is presently Head of the Commonwealth; her devotion to the organization is lifelong.

In November of that year she married the former Prince Philip of Greece, who became Duke of Edinburgh upon the marriage. Prince Philip, the son of Prince Andrew of Greece and Princess Alice of Battenberg, was related to Princess Elizabeth through both his maternal and paternal bloodlines. Through collateral descendants of George III he was her fourth cousin-once-removed. The marriage was popular as the first royal festival in post-war Britain still in the grip of austerity. WINSTON CHURCHILL called the wedding "a flash of color on the hard road we have to travel."

Within a year of her wedding Princess Elizabeth had produced an heir, Prince Charles, born 14 November 1948, and two years later, Princess Anne, born 15 August 1950. For two years she and her husband enjoyed the freedom of naval life in Malta, where he was a serving officer, but the grave illness of the King brought an end to this brief period of normality. Princess Elizabeth had to deputize for her father on many ceremonial occasions in the summer of 1950 and familiarized herself with State Papers. In the autumn of 1951 she and Prince Philip visited Canada and the United States for the first time: "Little Lilibet," the press reported, had "suddenly matured into the lovely young mother who one day is to be ruling Queen of England." An infatuated President Truman called her "a fairy princess."

But on that tour the Princess's private secretary, Martin Charteris, had traveled with the papers covering the Princess' accession under his bed. On 5 February 1952, as the Princess and her husband were in Kenya on the first leg of a tour of Australia and New Zealand, the King died suddenly in his sleep. His daughter succeeded him as Queen Elizabeth II and was crowned the following year as Queen of the United Kingdom of Great Britain and NORTHERN IRELAND, Queen of her other Realms and Territories and Head of the Commonwealth. Her coronation on 2 June 1953 was televised, sparking the beginning of a media revolution as millions in Britain and around the world watched the ceremony. There was huge public enthusiasm for the young Queen, who seemed to represent both a link with the historic past and a new future. Winston Churchill, her Prime Minister at the time, predicted a new Elizabethan age. Bernard Baruch called her "the world's sweetheart."

With her handsome husband and two young children, the Queen was held up as a moral example and the idealized representative of family virtues. The concept of the monarchy, which in later years was to rebound against it, was spelled out by THE TIMES, then still the voice of the Establishment, when in 1955 it thundered against the proposed marriage between Princess Margaret and Group Captain Peter Townsend, a divorced man: "Now in the twentieth century conception of the monarchy the Queen has come to be the symbol of every side of life of this society, its universal representative in whom her people see their better selves ideally reflected; and since part of their ideal is family life, the Queen's family has its own part in the reflection." Yet by the popular PRESS at the time, Princess Margaret's renunciation of Townsend on the grounds of duty and religion was seen as a forced sacrifice to outdated concepts which, by implication, included the monarchy.

Post-imperial disillusionment with the Establishment after the failed SUEZ expedition in 1956 brought the first criticisms of the Court and even of the Queen herself. In August 1957 Lord Altrincham attacked the Court for being "tweedy," failing to live with the times, and identifying the monarchy with a narrow aristocratic class. The same "second-rate" courtiers were responsible for the "prim little sermons" which the Queen delivered "in the style of a priggish schoolgirl, captain of the hockey team, a prefect, and a recent candidate for confirmation." No change had taken place in the Palace ethos, he (correctly) claimed, since the reign of the Queen's father. Yet in the prevailing atmosphere of royal worship, his sentiments caused national outrage, and he himself was physically attacked. The broadcaster Malcolm Muggeridge, who analyzed the current passion for the royal family as "the royal soap opera . . . a sort of substitute or ersatz religion," was banned from the BBC. Yet the social revolution that was taking place in late 1950s and early 1960s Britain could not fail to have its effect on attitudes towards an unmodernized monarchy. The Queen was shocked when in 1963 for the first time she was booed by left-wing demonstrators during the visit of the Greek King Paul and his German wife, Queen Frederika, who were regarded as unacceptably right-wing.

The same period saw the diminution of the royal prerogative in one significant area. In constitutional theory, the monarch has the right to appoint the Prime Minister, but by the end of the twentieth century this exercise of the prerogative had for all practical purposes ceased to exist. A succession of Prime Ministers have offered the Queen little choice. When Winston Churchill resigned in 1955, the fact that ANTHONY EDEN had long been regarded as his political heir apparent made it inevitable that the Queen would appoint him as his successor. Two years later the Queen's reluctance to enter the political fray left the choice in effect to her private secretary, Sir Michael Adeane, in consultation with ruling Conservative grandees. The LABOUR PARTY then announced that parties should decide their own leaders, an option later followed by the CONSERVATIVE PARTY (in 1965) which, although designed to save the Queen the embarrassment of having to choose between rival claimants to the leadership of a party, effectively removed the element of royal choice. This was prompted by the machinations of HAROLD MACMILLAN at the time of his resignation in October 1963 when, determined to block the succession of R.A. BUTLER, he put forward the candidature of the Earl of Home [ALEC DOUGLAS-HOME]. The Queen's acceptance of Macmillan's scheme to favor the aristocratic Home over the meritocratic Butler has been described as the biggest political misjudgment of her reign; she was seen as the instrument of a "magic circle" of Tory grandees.

The Queen's experience of public affairs has grown immeasurably over the half-century of her reign, so the most important aspect of her role—"the right to be consulted, the right to encourage, and the right to warn"—has not diminished. During the early years of her reign, her conversations with her first Prime Minister, Winston

Churchill (1952–5) often turned on their mutual interest, racing. Although the aristocratic, Foreign Office-trained Anthony Eden (1955–7) took a more aloof attitude, the Queen was kept informed of all aspects of the Suez crisis, including the secret agreements with France and Israel to attack Egypt. Harold Macmillan (1957–63) regarded her with reverence as well as affection. With her first Labour Prime Minister, HAROLD WILSON (1964–70 and 1974–6) her relations were of the warmest, and it was largely due to his fondness and respect for her that a potentially damaging crisis over the increase in the civil list was averted in 1975. The Conservative leader, EDWARD HEATH, who succeeded Wilson in 1970, demonstrated an undisguised disrespect for the Queen's cherished Commonwealth, downplaying her overseas role. In 1971 he effectively prevented her attendance at the Commonwealth conference in Singapore because of member-state attitudes on the questions of arms to South Africa. It is a truism that the Queen has got on better with Labour leaders than with Conservatives. JAMES CALLAGHAN (1976–9), another "old Labour" leader, had the utmost respect for the Queen's good sense in politics and world affairs, but the Commonwealth was once again a source of disagreement when MARGARET THATCHER (1979–90) became Conservative Prime Minister, principally over the question of sanctions against South Africa. Mrs. Thatcher was, nonetheless, the most loyal of Prime Ministers, even though it could be said that her assault on the established institutions of Britain turned unfavorable attention on the monarchy.

Undoubtedly the most difficult problem facing the monarchy over the last two decades has been its relationship with the media. From the adulation of the 1950s the mood of the 1960s turned to satire and indifference. The monarchy reacted with a popularity campaign, of which the most memorable images were from the film *The Royal Family* (1969), which for the first time presented the Queen and her children, of which there were now four—Prince Andrew was born in 1960 and Prince Edward in 1964—as human beings. Hugely popular at the time, the film was later criticized as destroying the mythic aspects of monarchy, "letting in daylight upon magic."

The public reacted to this presentation of the royal family with increasing interest which reached the point of obsession with the "fairytale marriage" of the Prince of Wales to Lady Diana Spencer, a world media event, in 1981. Princess Anne's marriage to officer and fellow horseman Captain Mark Phillips in 1973 had also been the occasion for a royal show, as was the Duke of York's marriage to Sarah Ferguson in 1986. But the image of the Queen's family as the ideal, which had been so assiduously promoted, imploded spectacularly with the successive scandals and divorces of the royal children in the 1990s. Andrew Morton's 1992 book, *Diana: Her True Story*, revealed the fairytale marriage as a sham of bitterness and adultery, offering a view of the royal family as "dysfunctional." The Queen herself described 1992 as her "annus horribilis." The revelations of the Morton book were followed by the publication of compromising photographs of the Duchess of York. In November fire ravaged Windsor Castle. Public reaction, prompted by a debate over the cost of the monarchy and the revelation that the Queen, alone of all her subjects, did not pay income tax, was that she should pay for the damage herself. When it was announced that the Queen had agreed to pay income tax on her private fortune, it looked as if she had been forced into it by events, although negotiations had been going on for months. In December Prime Minister JOHN MAJOR announced the separation of the Prince and Princess of Wales.

The breakdown of the marriage was accompanied by a media war between the estranged couple highly damaging to the image of the monarchy. In 1995 the Prince of Wales revealed in a television profile that he had committed adultery "after the irretrievable breakdown of his marriage." The program was accompanied by an authorized biography by the broadcaster Jonathan Dimbleby, in which the Queen was portrayed as a remote mother and the Duke of Edinburgh as an unsympathetic, bullying father. In November of that year the Princess of Wales retaliated with an emotional television interview in which she also admitted adultery and informed the public of her opinion that Prince Charles would never be King. The Queen, convinced that for the sake of the monarchy and the couple's children, Prince William and Prince Harry, the Wales's war must be brought to an end, wrote to each ordering them to divorce. The divorce became final in August 1996. Just over a year later, on 31 August 1997, Diana, Princess of Wales, was killed in a Paris car crash along with her lover, Dodi Fayed.

The impact of Diana's death on the British monarchy was even more revolutionary than her life had been. For a moment it seemed to observers that the dynasty tottered. It evoked a current of hostility towards the royal family, which was seen as culpable in its rejection of her. The Queen, as always cautious and reluctant to depart from tradition, was pressed by advisers and the Labour government led by TONY BLAIR into overt gestures, including a broadcast acknowledging Diana's contribution and example. Diana's brand of royal behavior, of a glamorous yet caring image, of reaching out to the people over the

heads of officialdom, set a new standard for the popular concept of the monarchy. Since then Buckingham Palace has worked hard to modernize itself, reducing the cost to the public; a "spin doctor" has been employed to handle presentation. The Queen is now seen as more approachable: she has visited a pub and taken tea with a family in public housing.

The Queen has reigned for half a century. She is widely respected for her dedication to what she sees as her job and her duty, her innate dignity and self-control. These may not be fashionable virtues, but they are enduring ones. While the Queen lives, there is no realistic chance of a British republic, despite currents of republicanism in the media and government, the abolition of the hereditary principle in the HOUSE OF LORDS, and the looming threat to the unwritten British constitution represented by the EUROPEAN UNION.

Sarah Bradford

Bibliography

Bogdanor, Vernon. *The Monarchy and the Constitution.* 1995.

Bradford, Sarah. *Elizabeth: A Biography of Her Majesty The Queen.* rev. ed., 1997.

Hennessy, Peter. *The Prime Minister: The Office and Its Holders Since 1945.* 2000.

Pimlott, Ben. *The Queen: A Biography of Elizabeth II.* 1996.

Emigration

Emigration from the United Kingdom in the twentieth century initially consolidated the pioneering impact of previous generations of settlers upon the world's demographic, economic, political and cultural geography. Since the principal destination of British emigrants also shifted early in this period from the United States to the white settler societies of Canada, Australia, New Zealand, and to a lesser extent South Africa, emigration strengthened for a while the British character of these original heartlands of the Empire-Commonwealth. Such a shift largely reflected altering economic opportunities overseas, but it was also affected by changes in government policy. In the early twentieth century governments in Britain and the COMMONWEALTH became more involved in determining the volume and character of migration, for example through the provision of assisted passages, which the British government financed after the First World War and formally maintained long after the Second. Nevertheless, emigration became demographically, economically and politically less welcome to the United Kingdom and immigration ultimately less significant to the former settler societies of the Commonwealth, which increasingly recruited elsewhere such immigrants as they needed.

Long-term comparisons of the volume of emigration by United Kingdom citizens are complicated because only after 1913 were emigrants distinguished officially in the records from other passengers leaving the country. Nevertheless, assuming for the earlier period the same ratio between emigrants and other passengers as existed for the later, we can be sure that emigration was high, even by nineteenth-century standards, in the decade 1901–10, probably amounting to over 1,816,000. In 1913 alone the recorded total reached a peak of 389,394. Figures after the war were never again so high, but they still totalled 1,811,553 between 1920 and 1929. True, in the Depression which followed, the total for 1930–8 was down to 334,467: indeed for the first time net IMMIGRATION was registered in that period. However, in the 1950s net emigration partly recovered to over 652,000 in the decade.

Compared with the population of the United Kingdom as a whole, emigrants were disproportionately young (mainly under forty-five) and included a more even balance of men and women and more young children than had been the case in the previous century (when single adult males had been more numerous). Studies of the social and occupational backgrounds and regional origins of twentieth-century emigrants have scarcely begun, although we can be sure that most (though less so the Irish) came from urban roots and had commercial and industrial occupations. Certainly, most were destined for urban employment overseas, in spite of repeated attempts to settle them in rural areas. What we cannot yet identify is the feature which distinguishes emigrants from those many more United Kingdom citizens of similar backgrounds who chose not to migrate. One distinguishing feature was probably the emigration of those with family or friends already overseas, so-called chain migration, a practice which would consolidate areas of existing British settlement. But such an explanation does little to account for the change in the direction of British emigration away from destinations in the United States towards the less densely settled societies of the British Empire, the so-called Dominions.

In the 1880s and 1890s less than one-third of British emigrants had sailed to Empire destinations, and most of the rest had crossed to the United States. But nearly half embarked for the Dominions between 1901 and 1910 and as many as two-thirds in 1911 and 1912. In the 1920s over 65 percent had chosen homes in the Dominions and nearly 47 percent even amidst the difficulties of the 1930s depression. After the Second World War opinion polls repeatedly showed a preference for Commonwealth instead of American destinations among those interested in emigra-

tion. The change largely reflected the expanding and more varied employment opportunities opening up in the Dominions by economic diversification, urbanization, and the development of speedier, safer, and more comfortable sea, and later air, transport between the United Kingdom and Australasia, virtually eliminating the ordeal of earlier emigration voyages to those distant Empire destinations. In addition, ideological factors may have been involved: it is probable that imperial sentiment achieved a deeper penetration of British POPULAR CULTURE in the first half of this century, and this may have induced more British emigrants to settle among those commonly described as "kith and kin".

But such a shift was also encouraged early in the century by British and Dominions governments either to increase or certainly to deflect the existing flows of emigrants leaving the United Kingdom to British territories overseas. It is true that some interest groups in the Dominions, such as labor organizations, Canadian nationalists, and the Afrikaners in South Africa, were often hostile towards the influx of yet more immigrants from Britain. But except in the last case or at times of local economic depression, they were normally unable to dent the prevailing popular and political sentiment that the immigrants needed for the further expansion of these British societies overseas should normally be drawn from the Mother Country. Certainly the governments of Canada, Australia, and New Zealand at various periods in the twentieth century, as earlier, attempted to attract selected immigrants from Britain, often with cheap sea passages or other inducements. It was, however, more remarkable when the British government first provided free passages to the Dominions for ex-servicemen and their families in 1919 and then passed the Empire Settlement Act in 1922. This legislation allowed for the expenditure of up to £3 million a year upon assisted passages for emigrants and overseas land settlement schemes, in financial co-operation with the Dominions. Imperial visionaries in the United Kingdom had been urging the British government to adopt such measures at least since the 1880s as a constructive response to the problems of poverty and social and political unrest at home and rising economic and political competition overseas: the redistribution of "surplus" British labor (including single women and orphaned or deprived children) in the underdeveloped territories of the Empire was popularly regarded as an important part of a process of imperial social and economic engineering. The onset of mass UNEMPLOYMENT in Britain after the First World War was, however, the immediate trigger, and the imperial enthusiast Leo Amery (1873–1955), seizing his chance, was the principal ministerial architect.

Between 1922 and 1936 the Empire Settlement Act provided assisted passages for 405,230 people, about 36 percent of the total who emigrated to the Empire in these years: 186,524 went to Canada, 172,735 to Australia and 44,745 to New Zealand (plus a mere 1,226 to South Africa). Substantial though these figures were in aggregate, they fell below the hopes of imperial visionaries. It is probable that the Empire Settlement Act increased the flow of emigration, encouraged the exodus of families, of single females and of children (for whom special schemes were devised), and diverted some emigrants away from non-Commonwealth destinations. Symptomatically, however, the British government never managed to spend all the money allocated to the scheme. Although the Act was renewed with less funding in 1937 (and again in 1952, 1957, 1962, and 1967 and only expired in 1972), doubts had grown by then about the merits of Empire migration which were never subsequently erased.

Demographic developments had made observers increasingly skeptical about mass migration. Birth rates were falling in Britain during the first half of the century, making the loss of young, fertile and perhaps more enterprising citizens a haemorrhage the country could not apparently afford to encourage. The implications for the British economy and society of a declining and AGEING workforce were worrying. Moreover, given the larger populations of the Dominions, their own natural increases (the excess of births over deaths) were proportionately more vital to further growth than immigrants. True, the threat of Japanese invasion during the SECOND WORLD WAR provoked a vigorous attempt subsequently to increase Australia's population through immigration, but by then the modestly growing size of the United Kingdom population finally required Australia (and other Commonwealth counties) to look outside the Mother Country and eventually even outside Europe for proportionately more of such stock as had to be imported. Commonwealth governments were also becoming yet more cautious about the immigrants they allowed in and certainly of those they assisted: increasingly, skilled workers only were required or those with capital or proven professional or entrepreneurial skills. These were, of course, also the personnel who in most cases could find attractive opportunities at home and whom the United Kingdom could least afford to lose.

In brief, since the Second World War the distinction between developed and developing economies, which earlier had encouraged mass migration from the United Kingdom to the United States and latterly to the Commonwealth, had largely eroded. At the same time, the self-interest which the British government had briefly seen in fostering imperial development by state-assisted settlement of "surplus" stock in the Dominions went into decline. A belief in the natural harmony between the parts of the Empire was giving way to increased competition for assets between the nations of the Commonwealth. Emigration, from a free society, could not be prevented, but it was no longer encouraged.

Stephen Constantine

Bibliography
Bean, Phillip, and Joy Melville. *Lost Children of the Empire.* 1989.
Carrier, N.H., and J.A. Jeffery. *External Migration 1814–1950: a Study of the Available Statistics.* 1953.
Constantine, Stephen, ed. *Emigrants and Empire: British Settlement in the Dominions between the Wars.* 1990.
Monk, Una B. *New Horizons: A Hundred Years of Women's Migration.* 1963.
Plant, G.F. *Oversea Settlement: Migration from the United Kingdom to the Dominions.* 1951.

Epstein, Jacob (1880–1959)

Jacob Epstein, Britain's most outstanding and innovative sculptor during the first half of the twentieth century, was born of Polish Jewish immigrants to America and brought up on New York City's Lower East Side. A mysterious childhood illness meant that even within his large family—he was the second son of eight surviving children—he was comparatively isolated and introverted, turning to reading and drawing. An art prize led him to the Art Students League, where he drew and painted, and he observed with great intensity the vivid life around him in the city. He also had a job in a bronze foundry. He came to Paris to study in 1902 and settled in London in 1905.

HENRY MOORE called him the father of modern British sculpture. With Henri Gaudier-Brzeska and ERIC GILL in England, Modigliani and Brancusi in Paris, Epstein was one of the leaders of the resurgence of interest in direct carving. It was his visits to the Louvre during his period in Paris that first aroused his interest in so-called primitive and enthographic sculpture, as well as in antiquities, an interest subsequently pursued at the British Museum. That interest was also expressed in two distinct fashions, both in his own sculpture and in a remarkably prescient collection that he made of such work (exhibited as the Epstein Collection of Primitive and Exotic Art by the ARTS COUNCIL in 1960). In much, if not all, of his monumental sculpture he was a carver and full of energy, occasionally crude; in his portrait sculpture, he was an exceptionally sensitive modeler. For much of his career he was controversial, and he made public sculpture an issue of debate within Britain, coming to embody within cartoon, caricature, and even in music hall jokes the popular idea of the Modern Sculptor.

Critical opinion has come to appreciate in particular his monumental carvings—Genesis (1931), Consummatum Est (1936-7), Adam (1938-9), Jacob and the Angel (1940-2), of which the last great free standing example is the bound figure of Lazarus, carved in Hoptonwood stone (1947) purchased in 1952 for the chapel of New College, Oxford where it still resides. His life long themes were evocations of the life force, with an emphasis on symbols of fertility and maternity, and the spiritual, evoking both specific religious imagery of both Old and New Testament, and a more generalized paganism.

The controversy over much of his public sculpture may have forced a retreat, and bound his imagination in much the way that Lazarus was bound. Public art in Britain suffered almost literally a monumental loss in the mutilation of the remarkable frieze of eighteen carved naked figures by Epstein commissioned in 1907 for the building of the British Medical Association in the Strand, London, by the architect Charles Holden (now the Embassy of Zimbabwe): the strength of feeling against these primal statues when the building became the High Commission for Southern Rhodesia led to the decay by neglect of the statues and their eventual semi-destruction *in situ* by a deputation led by the architect, partly on the grounds of safety. The campaign for their retention was controversial and totally failed. Another lost masterpiece, the Rock Drill, exhibited at the London Group in 1915 combined a helmeted, armored, and menacing figure—an extraordinary amalgam of stylized warrior, bird, and insect—surmounting a real piece of machinery, a drill. Other publicly sited masterpieces remain, including the fantastical and very affecting tomb for Oscar Wilde in the Père Lachaise cemetery in Paris, a sculpture in high relief of a winged demon angel, much affected by the absorption of Assyrian reliefs, particularly the Headed Bull in the British Museum. Here the dominant catalyst and influence was undoubtedly Eric Gill with his commitment to direct carving and truth to materials. Brancusi and Modigliani, both School of Paris artists and personal friends, were other readily assimilated influences, with their gift for simplification and understanding of ethnographic and antique art. Other lasting works include the highly energetic yet curiously charming monument to W.H. Hudson in Hyde Park, Rima (1925) also a carved relief, most strikingly influenced by the paintings of Gauguin, and the figures of Night and Day (Portland stone, 1928-9) on the facade of the headquarters of London Transport in St James. Even with these stylized primitive figures Epstein had to bow to public opinion by diminishing the size of the penis on the boy's figure in Day.

A fundamental aspect of Epstein's practice was the modeling of portrait busts, to be cast in bronze, and he sculpted some of the best known of the day. Outstanding examples include his portraits of JOSEPH CONRAD, Albert Einstein, GEORGE BERNARD SHAW, and RALPH VAUGHAN WILLIAMS, who said he could not see his own likeness in the Epstein, but could see his own father and grandfather.

From about 1911 portrait sculpture provided the main income for Epstein, always in need of funds for a grand life style, a huge studio in Hyde Park Gate, and his zeal for collecting; in pursuit of income, he was to execute many banal likenesses. The intense, impressionistic realism of his portraits was explored in parallel to his primitive, sophisticated stylizations of mythical and symbolic figures, and in his early career in England he was associated with the avant-garde, particularly the VORTICISTS. He was also to make many portraits of children, including his own; the best are lively, unself-conscious and totally unsentimental. A little known aspect of his work is a series of vivid, brilliantly imaginative flower paintings.

His last years were marked by official honors and commissions; Epstein was given an Arts Council retrospective exhibition at the Tate in 1952 (the same year that his Madonna and Child was sited on the Convent of the Holy Child Jesus, Cavendish Square), received an honorary degree from the UNIVERSITY OF OXFORD in 1953, and was knighted in 1954. In 1955 he was commissioned to create the major outside sculpture, St Michael and the Devil, for the facade of the new Coventry Cathedral designed by Basil Spence.

Marina Vaizey

Bibliography

Buckle, Richard. *Jacob Epstein, Sculptor*. 1963.

Epstein, Jacob. *Let There Be Sculpture: Epstein: An Autobiography*. 2nd ed. 1963.

Gardiner, Stephen. *Jacob Epstein, Artist against the Establishment*. 1992

Silber, Evelyn. *The Sculpture of Epstein with a Complete Catalogue*. 1986.

Equal Pay Movement

Throughout most of the twentieth century British WOMEN have been employed at lower rates of pay than men even when doing the same job. The government's rationale for this inequality changed during the century. Prior to the First World War government officials claimed women's output was less than men's, and that women were more expensive to employ because they were absent from work more often and had a higher turnover rate (partly due to the MARRIAGE bar). Later, as evidence emerged demonstrating that output was not linked to the gender of the worker, they relied on the family wage argument—i.e., male workers needed higher rates because they had families to support whereas women did not. But when reformers gathered data demonstrating that a significant minority of female employees were supporting dependents, usually elderly parents, whereas many male employees were bachelors supporting only themselves, opponents switched to a new argument.

The equal pay for equal work movement emerged in the CIVIL SERVICE and in teaching first because these were the areas in which large numbers of women were doing equal work. Female employee organizations in both areas began lobbying before the First World War but had little success apart from the 1914 Royal Commission on the Civil Service report, which recommended equal pay for equal work. Although the House of Commons voted in 1936 to grant equal pay to female civil servants and in 1944 to extend it to teachers, in both instances the government secured a reversal of the vote by threatening to resign. Fearing continued pressure for reform, CHURCHILL's wartime government appointed a Royal Commission on Equal Pay later in 1944 (with terms of reference forbidding it to make any policy recommendations) in order to prevent further action on the issue.

Following the war the FEMINIST Equal Pay Campaign Committee and the trade union Coordinating Committee on Equal Pay conducted separate campaigns that culminated in the presentation of two lengthy equal pay petitions to Parliament in March 1954. Shortly before this display of public and parliamentary support, the Chancellor of the Exchequer, R.A. BUTLER, had initiated a review of the government's policy; near the end of March he urged the CABINET to introduce equal pay in the public services. In winning Cabinet approval Butler, noting that Labour had pledged to introduce equal pay at once if they were returned to office, suggested that the CONSERVATIVES should proceed in order to reap the electoral benefits at the forthcoming general election.

There was little progress toward equal pay for industrial women workers until the June 1968 women's STRIKE at Ford's Dagenham plant. Claiming there would be continuing unrest unless the government acted, Barbara Castle, the Secretary of State for Employment, persuaded the Cabinet to allow her to introduce what became the 1970 Equal Pay Act. Since the Act only required equal pay for women employed on "the same or broadly similar" work, it benefited a minority of female industrial workers.

The Equal Pay Act's limitations resulted in new pressure for legislation to provide equal pay for work of equal value in order to extend the law to those employed on sex-segregated jobs. British governments resisted this change until the European Court ruled that Britain was not in compliance with the EUROPEAN COMMUNITY equal pay regulations. Under pressure from the court the Conservative government reluctantly introduced equal pay for work of equal value regulations in 1983, which broadened the scope of the law, but did so in a manner that hampered efforts to use it effectively. While some important individual cases, such as Hayward v. Cammell Laird (1988), have been won under the 1983 regulations, equal pay advocates have found them so inadequate as a means of eradicating pay discrimination that at the end of the 1980s the Equal Opportunities Commission was urging new equal pay legislation.

Harold L. Smith

Bibliography
Meehan, Elizabeth M. *Women's Rights at Work: Campaigns and Policy in Britain and the United States.* 1985.
Rubenstein, Michael. *Equal Pay for Work of Equal Value.* 1984.
Smith, Harold L. "The Problem of 'Equal Pay for Equal Work' in Great Britain during World War II," *Journal of Modern History*, vol. 53 (1981), pp. 652–72.
———. "The Politics of Conservative Reform: The Equal Pay for Equal Work Issue, 1945–1955," *Historical Journal*, vol. 35 (1992), pp. 401–15.

European Community: see European Union

European Union [*formerly*** European Community]**
Britain joined the European Community in 1973 though membership was first sought in 1961. Accession came after a long period of controversy within Britain, between those who saw Britain's future in Europe and those who sought to stress the special relationship with the United States and a continuing independent global role; and within the Community, between the French government of Charles de Gaulle and the five other members. He resented Britain's connections with the United States and wanted to move the European Community to a position of independence from the United States, especially in its foreign and defense policy, but also with regard to American direct investment in Europe.

By the late 1960s, however, both of the main political parties—Labour and Conservative—had come to accept the need to seek membership, and with the departure of de Gaulle in 1969, the Six agreed to reopen the question of British membership at their summit meeting at The Hague in December 1969. Negotiations were successfully concluded between EDWARD HEATH's

Conservative government and the Six in the summer of 1971, the principle of membership narrowly approved in the House of Commons in October 1971, with the LABOUR PARTY seriously split on the issue, and the Treaty of Accession was signed in January 1972.

Accession involved a commitment on the part of Britain to take part in what the founding Treaty of Rome (1957) referred to in its preamble as "an ever closer union of peoples," though there were disagreements about what precisely this meant. But Britain was unambiguously committed to the Common Agricultural Policy, to removing barriers upon her trade with other members of the Community, to accepting a system whereby money to finance the common activities went to the Community as of right, to a common commercial policy in relations with nonmembers, and to a legal system under which British courts would apply legislation agreed in the Council of Ministers that had not been approved in the House of Commons. Some commentators believed that this represented a challenge to British sovereignty, though others denied this since the whole arrangement rested upon a treaty between sovereign states, which had been approved by Parliament, and from which the British could withdraw without any constitutional or legal impediment.

In February 1974 the Heath government was defeated in a general election and replaced by a Labour administration under HAROLD WILSON which had by now moved into a position of hostility towards the Community and decided to renegotiate the terms of accession. It remained cautious in its approach to Europe throughout its period of office, which ended with MARGARET THATCHER's electoral victory for the Conservatives in May 1979. Renegotiation, which had insignificant consequences, led to a referendum about membership in 1975 when around 60 percent of those who voted said "Yes." Despite this, the left wing of the Labour Party remained hostile: in opposition in the early 1980s, the party's official policy was to withdraw. Labour MPs did not take up their seats in the European Parliament until 1976, and the trade union movement was unenthusiastic.

It was not until the late 1980s that the Labour Party shifted towards a pro-membership stance. In the 1987 election the issue was fudged, but by 1992 Labour had become much more positive in its approach to Europe than Mrs. Thatcher's Conservatives. It now supported more advanced forms of integration in the Community, such as the proposal for a European social charter, which would promote higher standards for workers, and membership in the monetary union, under which separate national currencies would be abandoned in favor of a single European Currency by the late 1990s—called the European Currency Unit (ECU)—under the management of a European Central Bank.

The CONSERVATIVE PARTY in contrast moved from a position of support for membership and a positive attitude towards involvement under Heath to a position of caution under Thatcher, with increasingly sharp divisions about the issue between the right and left wings of the party. Mrs. Thatcher made her position clear in a speech to the College of Europe in Bruges in the fall of 1988, when she explained her dislike of the Brussels bureaucracy, of what she saw as excessive centralization, and of socialism at the European level. She projected a policy of sentimental nationalism towards Europe, criticized European federalism, and strongly supported protecting Britain's sovereignty, freedom in international society, and links with the United States. When Thatcher came to office, she inherited a situation in which, because of Britain's need to import significant quantities of food and the way in which the Community was financed—through the so-called own resources system—Britain had a significant excess of contributions to, over receipts from, the Community. This was felt to be unreasonable as Britain was by now not among the richer European states. The European Community was the context of Britain's continuing economic decline. As a result Mrs. Thatcher was determined that Britain should contribute less, and this led to considerable acrimony between her and the other government leaders. It was not until June 1984 that this problem was settled, but the acrimony continued and became attached to other issues.

From the time of the settlement of the budgetary problem the Conservatives found themselves unwillingly taking part in an accelerating process of integration. The reasons for this were complex, but the main elements were the realization that unless concessions were made to the more supranational ambitions of the others, especially the French, Britain could be left behind on the margins of Europe and could miss out on the specific economic benefits resulting from the completion of the single market by the end of 1992. The main feature of the diplomacy between Britain and its partners after 1984 was, therefore, for Britain reluctantly to agree to increased powers for the common institutions, and increases in the level of regulation from Brussels, but to mitigate them as much as possible. Diplomacy leading to the agreement of the Single European Act in December 1985, which set out the procedures for completing the single market by the end of 1992 and gave greater powers to the European Parliament, showed clear signs of these tensions. A group of cautious states led by Britain, including Greece and Denmark, were forced to give ground to a group of more ambitious states, led by France.

The Maastricht Treaty also illustrated this tension, but for the British government there were other complicating factors. JOHN MAJOR, who succeeded Thatcher in 1991, was faced with the problem of negotiating the next stage in the development of the Community's arrangements, in particular those for Monetary Union, and for strengthening the Community's machinery for coordinating foreign and defense policies. It was probable that Major himself was more pro-European than his predecessor; he had, for instance, linked sterling with the other currencies in the Exchange Rate Mechanism of the European Monetary System when he was Chancellor of the Exchequer. But as Prime Minister, he now had the problem of keeping the right wing of his party in line. It was, therefore, necessary for him to appear to have fought fiercely against integration at Maastricht, the town in Holland where the negotiations took place. He won what he could claim was the important concession that Britain would not join the monetary union unless that was approved by Parliament and also succeeded in avoiding any commitment to the Social Charter. With the approval of the Maastricht Treaty by member nations, including Britain, in 1993, the European Community has been transformed into the European Union, although disagreement over the extent of monetary and other forms of integration persists.

Paul Taylor

Bibliography

George, Stephen. *Awkward Partner: Britain in the European Community.* 1990.

Gowland, David, and Arthur Turner. *Reluctant Europeans: Britain and European Integration, 1945–1998.* 1999.

Gregory, F.E.C. *Dilemmas of Government: Britain and the European Community.* 1983.

Kitzinger, Uwe. *Diplomacy by Persuasion: How Britain Joined the Common Market.* 1973.

Taylor, Paul. "The European Community and the State: Assumptions, Theories and Propositions," *Review of International Studies,* vol. 17 (1991), pp. 109–25.

Young, Hugo. *This Blessed Plot: Britain and Europe from Churchill to Blair.* 1998.

Fabian Society

Britain's oldest surviving socialist organization, the Fabian Society has been variously characterized as the world's first think tank and an intelligence corps without an army. Its members have been mainly middle-class London-based intellectuals, and have included every Labour Prime Minister. The Fabian strategy has been to conduct research into social and economic problems and to convey its recommendations to governing elites, thus promoting a gradual, rational, well-mannered socialism.

The society was launched 4 January 1884 at the home of Edward Pease (1857–1955), who would serve as general secretary from 1890 to 1913. Frank Podmore (1855–1910) suggested the name as an allusion to the Roman general Quintus Fabius Cunctator, who supposedly defeated Hannibal through delaying tactics. The early Fabians included GEORGE BERNARD SHAW, SIDNEY WEBB, and GRAHAM WALLAS.

All members had to subscribe to the Fabian "basis", drafted in 1887, but it was vague enough to accommodate socialists of all stripes. *Fabian Essays in Socialism* (1889), edited by Shaw, introduced Fabian thinking to a wide audience. In 1892 six Fabians, including Webb, were elected to the London County Council on a platform of "municipal socialism"—i.e., expanded social and educational services.

Although Fabians attended the founding conference of the INDEPENDENT LABOUR PARTY (1893) and the LABOUR REPRESENTATION COMMITTEE (1900), the society at first kept its distance from this emerging political force. Shaw and Webb preferred to "permeate" the LIBERAL and CONSERVATIVE parties, persuading them to adopt socialistic measures one reform at a time. The Fabian leadership had little faith in proletarian democracy, preferring government by altruistic "brain-workers" like themselves. To train such a corps of experts, Webb used Fabian money to found the LONDON SCHOOL OF ECONOMICS in 1895.

By 1906 many younger Fabians had grown dissatisfied with gradualism. H.G. WELLS attempted to transform the society into a militant socialist party and might have succeeded but for his childish personal attacks on the Fabian leadership. To reenergize the society, the Fabian nursery (for members under twenty-eight) was begun in 1906, the Fabian Arts Group and the first Fabian summer school in 1907, and the Fabian Women's Group in 1908.

In 1912 BEATRICE WEBB set up the Fabian Research Department, headed by G.D.H. COLE and William Mellor (1888–1942), to investigate how socialist economic management might work in practical terms. Later that year the Webbs founded the *NEW STATESMAN,* a weekly edited by Clifford Sharp (1883–1935). It would publish the work of the Research Department, along with polemics by Shaw, poetry by RUPERT BROOKE, and fiction by LEONARD WOOLF. In 1915 the Webbs assigned Woolf to prepare for the Research Department a plan for diplomatic machinery to prevent future wars. The result was *International Government* (1916), which outlined proposals that would be incorporated into the LEAGUE OF NATIONS.

By 1918 ARTHUR HENDERSON looked to the guidance of Fabian intellectuals to transform Labour into a governing party. He and Sidney Webb drafted a new LABOUR PARTY constitution, which significantly appealed to "producers by hand or by brain." In 1919 the Fabian Society formally became "a constituent of the Labour Party," but left open its options to work with other political movements.

Fabians were well-represented in RAMSAY MACDONALD's two Labour governments, but the society lost intellectual momentum in the inter-war years. Impatient at its failure to offer concrete solutions to the worsening depression, G.D.H. Cole formed the New Fabian Research Bureau in 1931.

Fabian activity revived during the Second World War. In 1940 Rita Hinden (1909–71) and Arthur Creech Jones (1891–1964) set up the Fabian Colonial Bureau, which established a cordial advisory relationship with the Colonial Office. The Bureau argued that Britain had an obligation to promote colonial economic development and gradual self-government for the benefit of native peoples. Its members included several future leaders of emerging African nations: Julius Nyerere, Kenneth Kaunda, Hastings Banda, Jomo Kenyatta, and Tom Mboya. The success of the Colonial Bureau inspired the formation (in 1941) of the Fabian International

Bureau, headed by Leonard Woolf, to advise on post-war reconstruction.

A majority of the Labour MPs elected in 1945 were Fabians, as were thirty-seven ministers in the ATTLEE government. The Fabians may have exaggerated their role in inspiring the British WELFARE STATE, which was mainly the work of Liberals like DAVID LLOYD GEORGE and WILLIAM BEVERIDGE, but Beveridge himself had been a Fabian back in the Edwardian years.

New Fabian Essays, edited by Richard Crossman (1907–74) in 1952, reflected a loss of intellectual direction: after six years in power, the authors could not agree on a coherent redefinition of socialism. HUGH GAITSKELL had invigorated Fabianism with a dose of Keynesianism, but his battles with ANEURIN BEVAN inevitably spilled over into the society, which lost members steadily throughout the 1950s.

Fabians again dominated the Labour governments of 1964–70 and 1974–9. The 1960s brought an influx of younger members, but membership fell off in the 1970s, when the society offered few answers to Britain's economic decline and trade union militancy. Linked as they were to the Labour Party, the Fabians were divided by the formation of the SOCIAL DEMOCRATIC PARTY in 1981. The SDP's founders included Shirley Williams (1930–), chairman of the Fabian Society, and three other Fabian officers. A membership ballot affirmed that members of parties other than the Labour Party could only be associate members of the society. The Fabians soon lost nearly one out of six members, but they survived to celebrate their centenary, as well as the election of Fabian NEIL KINNOCK as Leader of the Labour Party.

Jonathan Rose

Bibliography

Britain, Ian. *Fabianism and Culture*. 1982.

Cole, Margaret. *The Story of Fabian Socialism*. 1961.

McBriar, A.M. *Fabian Socialism and British Politics, 1884–1918*. 1962.

MacKenzie, Norman and Jeanne. *The First Fabians*. 1977.

———, eds. *The Diary of Beatrice Webb*. 4 vols. 1982–5.

Pugh, Patricia. *Educate, Agitate, Organise: 100 Years of Fabian Socialism*. 1984.

Falklands War

The Falklands Islands and the Falklands Dependencies—South Georgia, the South Sandwiches and the British Antarctic—were long disputed between Argentina and Britain and from 1966 to 1982 were the subject of ongoing negotiations. The Argentines made a *de jure* case for possession based on their inheritance of the sovereignty exercised over the Falkland (or Malvinas) Islands by Spain from 1767 to 1811; the British advanced a *de facto* claim based on continuous occupation in the nearly 150 years since the last Argentine had left, as well as upon the self-determination of the islands' population. Early in 1982 the Argentine government decided to mask internal problems of hyper-inflation and political repression by seizing the islands.

The first phase of the war began with the raising of the Argentine flag on South Georgia Island on 19 March by civilians landed by a navy transport and the landing of more than 100 Argentine troops a week later. On 31 March Prime Minister MARGARET THATCHER and her advisers were persuaded by First Sea Lord and Chief of Naval Staff Admiral Sir Henry Leach to begin assembling a large naval task force to counter Argentine moves. This force was in preparation when Argentines invaded the Falklands. Before dawn on 2 April, 120 Argentine commandos came ashore to seize Government House in Port Stanley and Royal Marine barracks two miles away. 800 reinforcements were landed that morning with more expected by air. On the following day the Argentines seized South Georgia.

The second phase of the war, a naval struggle in the waters around the Falklands, began on 5 April with the departure from Portsmouth of the first ships of a task force that would eventually comprise forty-four warships and twenty-two auxiliary craft under the command of Rear Admiral John F. Woodward. The British announced that as of 12 April, a 200-mile maritime exclusion zone would be imposed around the Falklands. On 16 April an Argentine task force including an aircraft carrier, the cruiser General Belgrano, two destroyers, and three submarines, put to sea. Nevertheless the British task force was able to take position off the Falklands. South Georgia was retaken on the 25th, and on 1 May aircraft from Ascension Island and the task force attacked Port Stanley airfield. On 2 May a British SUBMARINE torpedoed and sank the General Belgrano with a loss of 386 Argentine seamen. The debate over whether the Belgrano was inside the exclusion zone or not has almost obscured the fact that this sinking was the deciding event of the war. What might have been became evident on 4 May when an Exocet air-to-surface missile launched from an Argentine aircraft crippled a destroyer, H.M.S. Sheffield, which later sank. Masters of the sea, the British on 9 May began naval bombardment of Port Stanley. Only on 12 May were the Argentines able to begin major attacks by land-based aircraft. Though the Argentines had up to 216 fixed wing aircraft and 20 helicopters available as against British air units totalling a maximum of 55 fixed wing craft and 154 helicopters, the Argentine air strikes had little success until the British entered the narrow strait between East and West Falkland.

The third phase of the conflict, the ground engagement on East Falkland Island, began early on 21 May with raids on Port Louis, Goose Green, and Fox Bay as prelude to the liberation of Port San Carlos. Despite air attacks on fleet units in the vicinity, the British were able to land artillery, armored vehicles and surface-to-air missles, but four British ships were damaged at a cost of sixteen Argentine fixed-wing aircraft and four helicopters. In the next four days three more British ships were sunk and three damaged at a cost of fifteen Argentine aircraft and one helicopter. None of this stopped the invasion. Between 28 May and 4 June the British established the southern portion of a pincers on Port Stanley by capturing Goose Green despite adverse odds of four to one, then moving in to Fitzroy and Bluff Cove on the south coast. On 29 and 30 May the northern pincer was formed by the occupation of Douglas, Teal Inlet, and Mount Kent. British forces on the island now numbered about 9,500 and confronted nearly 8,400 Argentine defenders. The attack on Port Stanley began on 11 June with successful British assaults on Mount Longdon, Mount Harriet, and Great Ridge, followed by the capture of Wireless Ridge, Tumbledown Mountain, Mount Williams, and Sapper Hill. With the capital completely exposed to British artillery, General Menendez surrendered. When the British unilaterally announced the end of the conflict on 12 July, their losses amounted to 256 killed, 777 wounded, and 80 captured, while the Argentines had lost 746 killed, 1,336 wounded, and 11,400 captured. The British had lost six ships, 10 aircraft, and 23 helicopters, the Argentines three ships, 107 aircraft, and 10 helicopters.

Joseph M. McCarthy

Bibliography

Blakeway, Denys. *The Falklands War*. 1992.

Cordesman, Anthony H., and Abraham R. Wagner. *The Lessons of Modern War III: The Afghan and Falklands Conflicts*. 1990.

Hastings, Max, and Simon Jenkins. *The Battle for the Falklands*. 1983.

Middlebrook, Martin. *Task Force: The Falklands War, 1982*. Rev. ed., 1987.

Woodward, Sandy [John F.]. *One Hundred Days: The Memoirs of the Falklands Battle Group Commander*. 1992.

Family Allowances

A universal system of state-funded children's allowances was introduced in Britain through the passage of the Family Allowances Act (1945) by CHURCHILL's wartime coalition. The measure received bipartisan support, which was seen at the time to indicate a wide acceptance of its importance. In fact, family allowances have remained somewhat peripheral to both party politics and the WELFARE STATE in Britain and have often been neglected or come under threat. Although key to the prevention of child poverty, they remain an underfunded and much-misunderstood adjunct to a social insurance system organized primarily around the wage. Britain's family policies are among the least generous in the EUROPEAN UNION.

State aid to families with young children first became a matter of public discussion in the years before the First World War, as politicians worried about the "efficiency" and eugenic quality of the British population looked to programs like school meals to improve children's health. A few socialists and sex radicals like H.G. WELLS proposed that the state "endow" mothers as a reward for their "national service" of bearing children; some FEMINISTS also hoped that "endowment" would free women from direct dependence on men. Only after the First World War, however, when many saw the positive effects on child and maternal health of the extensive payment of cash "separation allowances" to soldiers' wives, did a wider campaign for the "endowment of motherhood," and later for family allowances, develop. A group of feminists and social reformers, including ELEANOR RATHBONE, established the Family Endowment Society, and in 1924 Rathbone published *The Disinherited Family*, the Bible of the movement, which combined a lucid exposition of the inadequacy of wages to meet family needs with a survey of family policies in other European and Commonwealth countries.

In the early twenties Rathbone and other advocates usually argued for family allowances on two grounds: as a measure of recognition to unwaged wives and as the only means of guaranteeing adequate support of children, given that wages were not be based on family needs. Such arguments were attractive to some feminists, although others feared that allowances would only deepen the identification of women with purely domestic roles. They also aroused interest among Labour's Women's Sections, and within the INDEPENDENT LABOUR PARTY, which included a proposal for children's allowances in its 1926 program, "The Living Wage." ILP enthusiasm did lead to a joint LABOUR PARTY-TRADES UNION CONGRESS inquiry into family allowances in 1928, but in 1930 the TUC rejected the measure, fearing that allowances might adversely affect wage rates.

After the failure of the Labour Party initiative, the campaign for allowances languished. Rathbone and other advocates continued to argue for improved benefits for children (whether in cash or kind) during the thirties; some politicians also saw a case for children's allowances for working men when they realized that, for men with many children, UNEMPLOYMENT allowances (based on family size) could exceed wage rates. Yet not until the SECOND WORLD WAR did a comprehensive national measure receive serious consideration. Many factors contributed to this new interest: growing cross-party parliamentary pressure; concern about the declining birth-rate; the fact that numerous children were already receiving allowances as the dependents of servicemen; government interest in avoiding an inflationary wage spiral; the TUC's reversal of its old opposition; and, finally, the endorsement of children's allowances by SIR WILLIAM BEVERIDGE in his famous Report of 1942. The 1945 measure established children's allowances at the rate of 5 shillings per week for each child except the first. After a determined campaign by Rathbone and others, the initial plan to pay the allowance to the father was overturned by a Commons free vote in favor of payment to the mother.

Family allowances received little attention and declined in value during the next twenty years. In the mid-sixties, however, when the work of Peter Townsend and other social scientists demonstrated that full employment and the welfare state had not rid Britain of poverty (and especially child poverty), family policy came back on the political agenda. For the next twenty five years, the Child Poverty Action Group [CPAG], under the successive leadership of Tony Lynes, Frank Field, and Ruth Lister, kept the problem of child poverty in the public eye. Support for a more comprehensive and generous family policy grew during the seventies, especially within the Labour Party, and in 1975 the WILSON government passed the Child Benefit Act, which envisaged replacing both the family allowance and the child income tax credit by Child Benefit, a new, universal, tax-free, non-means-tested cash benefit for all children, including the first. Yet the government, worried about the cost, refused to commit itself to a date for the commencement of the new scheme, and increasingly seemed likely to shelve the plan indefinitely. Minutes leaked from the Cabinet Office, and made public by Frank Field of CPAG, showed that ministers feared that trade unionists would object to the proposal to fund child benefit in part by abolishing child tax allowances disproportionately enjoyed by male wage-earners, and at least one section of the TUC did object to any transfer "from wallet to purse" even though aggregate family income would rise. The ensuing public scandal, CPAG's successful lobbying of some sympathetic trade unions and Labour organizations, and the persistence of Barbara Castle, then Secretary of State for Health and Social Security, did force the government to meet its commitment. Child Benefit became payable from 1977.

If Labour governments have sometimes exhibited more concern for working men than children, Conservative governments have been critical of the universal nature of Child Benefit altogether. The HEATH and THATCHER administrations consistently let the value of child benefit decline, preferring to build up new "targetted" programs for the low-waged, such as Family Income Supplement, introduced in 1971, and replaced by Family Credit in 1988. Critics such as CPAG charge that such programs tend to create a "poverty trap," since benefits decline as pay rises, and JOHN MAJOR to some extent broke with this tradition by raising child benefit substantially in his first budget. Yet child benefit remains contested; the best efforts of an alliance of feminists and poverty campaigners has not been able to compensate for the lack of party and union enthusiasm, and for a political tradition hostile to the identification of children as legitimate claimants on state resources.

Susan Pedersen

Bibliography

Macnicol, John. *The Movement for Family Allowances, 1918–1945: A Study in Social Policy Development.* 1980.

McCarthy, Michael. *Campaigning for the Poor: CPAG and the Politics of Welfare.* 1986.

Pedersen, Susan. *Family, Dependence, and the Origins of the Welfare State: Britain and France, 1914–1945.* 1993.

Rathbone, Eleanor F. *The Disinherited Family.* 1924

Fascism

In Britain, as in other countries, the ideological seeds of Fascism were sown before the twentieth century. However, the first organization in Britain which possessed a distinctively Fascist title did not appear until the 1920s. The heyday of British Fascism occurred in the 1930s with the emergence of the British Union of Fascists (BUF), under the leadership of SIR OSWALD MOSLEY. The identification of Fascism with Nazi Germany created difficulties for British Fascism during the SECOND WORLD WAR, and subsequently it has made little political progress. However, Fascist and related racial nationalist groups have continued to operate in Britain.

The British Fascisti, associated particularly with Rotha Lintorn Orman and reflecting the influence of Italian Fascism, began life in 1923. It was through the British Fascisti that William Joyce, who subsequently achieved notoriety as Lord Haw-Haw, became involved, later joining other organizations before departing for Germany in 1939. The Imperial Fascist League (the IFL), linked with Arnold Spencer Leese, was formed in 1928. Leese had spent many years in Africa before joining the British Fascisti on his return to Britain. There is a danger in regarding the IFL as a one-man band, but Leese's racial conspiratorial ANTI-SEMITISM became strongly stamped on the group.

In the 1930s various small groups sympathetic to Fascism, such as the Nordic League which had an overt anti-Semitic nature, began to appear. This period saw the emergence of the British Union of Fascists (BUF) under the leadership of Sir Oswald Mosley. The BUF, formed in 1932, was the vehicle through which Mosley hoped to fulfil his political ambitions. He had previously been a member of both the CONSERVATIVE and LABOUR Parties before launching his short-lived New Party in 1931. In the initial stages Mosley and the BUF garnered a fair measure of support for the Fascist cause. Men who had fought in the FIRST WORLD WAR and shared the comradeship of the trenches only to become disillusioned with post-war Britain, provided one important source of support. In addition the BUF appealed to young people, even without military service, who wanted to sweep away "the old gang" as the dominant political force. It appealed also to some conservative elements anxious about a perceived decline in Britain's role as a world power. In the early heady days of the BUF, the movement could count on the support of the Rothermere press through the columns of the *Daily Mail*.

An important turning point occurred in June 1934, when a meeting at Olympia in London generated considerable public violence and support for the BUF ebbed. In these circumstances the BUF soon became increasingly embroiled in the politics of East LONDON, where the tradition of anti-Semitism and HOUSING and labor problems became issues which Mosley hoped to exploit. The East End campaign turned violent and, in an attempt to control the para-military style of the BUF, the government passed the Public Order Act of 1936 which forbade the wearing of political uniforms (one hallmark of the BUF was the black shirt). By this time Mosley's organization was identified increasingly with Hitler's National Socialists, which limited the movement's appeal. Even so, on the eve of the SECOND WORLD WAR the BUF remained active, and Mosley, a charismatic politician and superb orator, continued to attract large audiences.

There is some dispute about the size of the BUF and whether or not membership had fallen in the course of the late 1930s. There is a greater agreement on the claim that the war led to the demise of the BUF as an effective political organization. Some members joined the armed forces, while leading figures, such as Mosley, Leese, Alexander Raven Thomson, the movement's leading ideologist, and Neil Francis Hawkins, its Director-General, were interned by the authorities for much of the war. Even so, certain fringe organizations sympathetic to Fascism continued to function.

By the end of the war Fascism had become associated with the excesses of Nazi Germany, and its post-war history in Britain was an anti-climax. Leese, retracting nothing, published a news sheet called *Gothic Ripples* but remained politically impotent. When Mosley revived his political activity and formed the Union movement, through which he campaigned for European unity based on racial criteria, he attempted simultaneously to distance himself from his earlier political career. However, election defeats at North Kensington in 1959 and Shoreditch and Finsbury in 1966 showed, however, that Mosley was generally regarded as beyond the pale.

When Leese died in 1956, his mantle passed to Colin Jordan, but his National Socialist Movement, active in the early 1960s, exercised a negligible influence. In 1967 Fascist and racial nationalist groups united to form the NATIONAL FRONT. Its embrace of an extreme nationalism, its anti-Semitism, its opposition to Blacks and Asians, and its involvement in violent street politics persuaded many commentators that it could be regarded as a Fascist organization. It seemed for a period in the 1970s that the NF might play a significant role in British politics, but its failure to achieve any success in the 1979 general election was followed by its collapse and eventual disintegration into a variety of warring factions. Such groups, small in number, still survive, and John Tyndall, the former leader of the NF, is one of the better-known activists.

Colin Holmes

Bibliography

Benewick, Robert J. *The Fascist Movement in Britain.* 1972.

Copsey, N. *Anti-Fascism in Britain.* 1999.

Lewis, D.S. *Illusions of Grandeur: Mosley, Fascism and British Society 1931–81.* 1987.

Lunn, Kenneth, and Richard Thurlow, eds. *British Fascism: Essays on the Radical Right in Inter-War Britain.* 1980.

Skidelsky, Robert. *Oswald Mosley.* 2nd ed. 1981.

Thurlow, Richard. *Fascism in Britain: A History, 1918–1985.* 1987.

Fashion: see Clothing and Fashion

Fawcett, Millicent Garrett (1847–1929)

Millicent Garrett Fawcett was the principal leader of the constitutional WOMEN'S SUFFRAGE movement in Britain during the period of its greatest activity, the years before 1914. Continuing her activities in changed wartime conditions, she presided over the movement's first and greatest success with the granting of the parliamentary vote to most women over thirty in 1918.

Born into a prosperous middle-class Suffolk family in 1847, Millicent Garrett entered political life in 1867 with her marriage to Henry Fawcett, the famous blind radical politician and CAMBRIDGE professor of political economy. Almost immediately she became active in many feminist causes, including legal reforms, employment, education, and a variety of moral issues. It was women's suffrage, however, that was from the start her leading interest. By the mid-1880s she was already the most important figure in a movement with many supporters but no real power. It was a movement divided by party political allegiance and weakened by the activities of politicians, few of whom wanted to do more than offer vague benevolence in return for electoral assistance.

Fawcett was intrumental in its unification and in the formation of the National Union of Women's Suffrage Societies in 1897. The NUWSS was in its early years a loose confederation of suffrage societies, without the strong central headquarters and executive created on its reorganization early in 1907, when Fawcett was elected it first (and only) president.

It was, however, the militant activities of the WOMEN'S SOCIAL AND POLITICAL UNION that pushed women's parliamentary suffrage into the forefront of political controversy. This second union, the WSPU, was formed in 1903, but it was not until 1906 that its unprecedented style of campaigning, characterized by verbal militancy, became a prominent feature of suffrage methods. Fawcett was in the early years among those NUWSS members who felt that the activities of the WSPU were to the benefit of women's suffrage, a sentiment that did not survive the WSPU's transition from militancy to violence in 1908–9.

Fawcett's domination of the constitutional movement, whose members, affiliated societies, and activities were more numerous though less newsworthy than those of the WSPU suffragettes, was not based on personal dynamism or autocratic methods of organization. In contrast to EMMELINE PANKHURST, the WSPU leader, her strengths lay in her writing and in personal contacts. The respect and loyalty with which she was held turned into veneration as the movement struggled to achieve its aims in the harsh pre-war political climate. Her role in these years was that of standard-bearer, manifesting optimism in the most adverse circumstances. To the interested public she was the most acceptable of suffragists, her personality making respectable a cause otherwise sullied by its connection with violence. It must be added, however, that if suffragette militancy failed to impress politicians, the constitutional methods of Fawcett and her friends equally failed to persuade them of the justice and good sense of granting votes to women.

The outbreak of war drastically changed the position of a woman almost universally respected among suffragists and known for her international suffrage links. Unlike the majority of her close colleagues, she expressed unqualified support for the conduct of the war, with a passion markedly at odds with the reasoned approach that had always characterized her advocacy of women's suffrage. After much uneasy private debate the NUWSS executive committee split openly at a special council of the union in June 1915. The majority of the more active committee members left their posts, and henceforward the NUWSS, at least nominally, supported the war as actively as its president.

In the context of a catastrophic war and the suspension of active suffrage work the passage of the Representation of the People Act in 1918, giving the vote to millions of women over thirty, was a somewhat hollow victory. It was, however, duly celebrated by the NUWSS and its allies, the evergreen Fawcett, still NUWSS president, taking the chair at a victory rally in March 1918. She was to live eleven years longer, during which period she continued her feminist activities on several fronts. One of the most important was the agitation to complete the suffrage victory by enacting equal suffrage between men and women, finally enacted in 1928.

In Fawcett the personality was easily overshadowed by the cause. A woman of strong passions, as her support for the First World War (and earlier, the Boer War) had shown, she excelled as a conciliatory and unifying force. Unique among her contemporaries for the longevity of her suffrage work and her achievements as a knowledgeable and witty writer, she did her best to conceal her personality from her colleagues and the public. To a later age she remains the principal, unwearying leader of the only mass movement inspired by British FEMINISM in the twentieth century.

David Rubinstein

Bibliography

Caine, Barbara. *Victorian Feminists.* 1992.

Fawcett, Millicent Garrett. *What I Remember.* 1924.

Rubinstein, David. *A Different World for Women: The Life of Millicent Garrett Fawcett.* 1991.

Strachey, Ray. *Millicent Garrett Fawcett.* 1931.

Feminism

Edwardian feminism was an influential if heterogeneous movement, one which encompassed a wide variety of organizations and made itself felt in many aspects of social life. Despite this variety, three principal aims can be detected. First, from the mid-Victorian period feminists had

consistently worked to improve WOMEN'S EDUCA-
TION AND EMPLOYMENT opportunities, in order
both to enrich women's lives and to free them of a
humiliating dependence on MARRIAGE and men.
Second, and again drawing on Victorian campaigns for DIVORCE reform and against the state
regulation of prostitution, feminists sought to reform sexual and moral standards: to raise the age
of consent, to increase the penalties for wife and
child abuse, and to apply to men the higher standards of chastity demanded of women. Finally,
feminists insisted that women be given a greater
voice in political life. Many tens of thousands of
women participated in the Edwardian campaign
for WOMEN'S SUFFRAGE, especially through the
militant WOMEN'S SOCIAL AND POLITICAL
UNION [WSPU] led by EMMELINE PANKHURST
and CHRISTABEL PANKHURST, and the constitutionalist National Union of Women's Suffrage
Societies [NUWSS] led by MILLICENT GAR-
RETT FAWCETT. By 1914 the "woman question"
had become a central issue in British social and
political life.

The outbreak of the FIRST WORLD WAR dramatically altered this situation. The question of
whether to support the war divided many feminist organizations, and decoyed many activist
women into either relief work or PACIFIST efforts.
The WSPU disappeared during the war, and
some members of the NUWSS's Executive left
the Union to found the British Section of the
Women's International League for Peace and
Freedom. Indeed, many pre-war feminists,
among them Kathleen Courtney (1878–1974),
Helena Swanwick (1864–1939), Margery Corbett
Ashby (1882–1981), and Emmeline Pethick Lawrence (1867–1954), as well as such later recruits as
VERA BRITTAIN, spent the inter-war years concerned as much with peace and international
cooperation as with sexual equality. The war also
shattered the remnants of Victorianism, making
way for a more explicitly modern sensibility, one
in which the high-minded rhetoric of feminism,
and especially its concern with sexual purity, was
increasingly labeled ridiculous, outdated, or
prudish. Finally, the war consolidated other political shifts that decisively weakened feminism's
political position. The strength of the LABOUR
PARTY lay not in those educational and philanthropic associations in which women had exercised such a important role, but rather in the
trade unions, in which women played little part
and which were committed to an ideal of a "family wage" deeply at odds with the goal of economic independence for women.

For all of these reasons the feminist movement
emerged from the war in a weakened position.
Yet the movement in the twenties also suffered
from serious internal conflicts. The extension of

the franchise to women over thirty through the
Representation of the People Act (1918) merely
exposed the extent of the disagreements. The
NUWSS, now renamed the National Union of
Societies for Equal Citizenship [NUSEC], split
repeatedly over such issues as protective legislation, BIRTH CONTROL, and FAMILY ALLOWANCES.
Although most feminists were agreed on (and
would unite to lobby for) complete political
equality, finally achieved with the Representation
of the People (Equal Franchise) Act of 1928,
there was little consensus in other areas. There
were four main groups, all of whom viewed the
old goals of economic independence and sexual
emancipation rather differently.

A first group exhibited the most consistency
with pre-war feminist demands. These "egalitar-
ians", working through the London Society for
Women's Service, led by Ray Strachey (1887–
1940) and Philippa Strachey (1872–1968), or the
Six Point Group and the Open Door Council,
both founded by Margaret Haig Thomas, Viscountess Rhondda (1883–1958), continued to insist on strict legal and economic equality between
the sexes, and to campaign in particular for improved economic opportunities for women, an
end to the marriage bar, an end to special "protective" legislation, and a more stringent interpretation of the ineffective Sex Disqualification (Removal) Act of 1919—all with little success. Yet
other feminists were skeptical that such
employment-centered efforts would ever affect
the lives of the majority of women, and especially
of unwaged wives. Such "new feminists," led by
ELEANOR RATHBONE, who succeeded Millicent
Fawcett as the President of the NUSEC in 1919,
lobbied for such "special" women's programs as
family allowances, arguing that such measures
would lessen wives' dependence on their husbands, and, by eroding men's claim for a "family
wage," make equal pay possible. Third, a number
of women, including Dora Russell (1894–1986)
and MARIE STOPES, denounced the old ideal of
sexual purity as repressive and indeed anti-
feminist, and supported birth control as an essential ingredient of women's emancipation—although such arguments were opposed by
feminists who feared that birth control would
merely increase women's vulnerability to men. A
final, moderate feminist presence can be detected
within the women's organizations of the labor
movement, which were concerned to improve the
lives of housewives and mothers—if not to challenge the sexual division of labor itself. The
Women's Cooperative Guild, and women in the
Labour Party and the INDEPENDENT LABOUR
PARTY thus campaigned vigorously in favor of
family allowances, improved social services, and
the provision of birth control information to

married women by public health authorities, sometimes in the face of serious party opposition.

By the 1930s, however, feminist organizations were small, divided and somewhat demoralized. The ideal of domesticity proved difficult to challenge during the slump, and the periods of wartime and of post-war reconstruction. The principle of EQUAL PAY was rejected by the National, CONSERVATIVE, and Labour governments in turn, and the WELFARE STATE set up after 1945 explicitly presumed a male breadwinner and nonworking wife. Although children's allowances payable to the mother were introduced with the Family Allowances Act (1945), they were derisory in amount. With the exception of the brief revival of feminist campaigns for equal pay and daycare provision during the SECOND WORLD WAR, women's political activism during the middle decades of the century took place largely within civic organizations which were by no means openly feminist, such as the Women's Institutes (which counted almost 500,000 members by the fifties) and the Townswomen's Guilds (250,000 members by 1945).

Feminism reemerged both as an important ideological force and as a political movement in the seventies. Yet the reasons for its revival, and indeed the goals of the movement, were not in the first instance economic—although the growth in women's labor force participation and a new sympathy within the trade union movement for women workers' concerns certainly helped to create a favorable environment for feminism. Lobbying by the older liberal feminist societies (the Six Point Group, the Fawcett Society) and pressure from the labor movement and especially from Barbara Castle together contributed to the passage and subsequent strengthening of the Equal Pay Act (1970)—which was made binding in 1975 and applied to comparable work in 1983—and of the Sex Discrimination Act (1975). Civil libertarian groups and the Fawcett Society also cooperated to ease passage of the Abortion Reform Act (1967), which legalized ABORTION during the first twenty-eight weeks of pregnancy. Yet the Women's Liberation Movement, as it came to be called, grew less out of the union movement or the old feminist societies than out of the protest movements and identity politics of the sixties. Women active in the peace, student, and anti-Vietnam movements became deeply disillusioned by the sexism and the organizational dominance of their male colleagues; they also discovered that the revolution in sexual mores and in contraceptive technology could be used not to "free" women but to pressure them into sexual activity. Feminists organized in small, woman-only, nonhierarchical groups, and concentrated on revealing and attacking the existence of sexism in personal and sexual life. National conferences of the Women's Liberation Movement held from 1970 until 1978 put forward a program of six demands—equal pay, twenty-four hour nurseries, free contraception, abortion on demand, legal financial independence for women, and the right to self-defined sexuality—but in 1978 the conference broke up over the question of whether a single resolution against violence against women should replace all other demands. Despite a lack of central direction, feminism in the eighties continued to bear fruit. Women's centers, battered women's shelters, rape crisis centers, women's studies programs, and campaigns against pornography and against violence against women survive in large part because of the diffusion of feminist ideas and the mobilization of feminist energies.

                                                                              Susan Pedersen

Bibliography

Banks, Olive. *Faces of Feminism: A Study of Feminism as a Social Movement.* 1981.

Caine, Barbara. *English Feminism 1780–1980.* 1997.

Dyhouse, Carol. *Feminism and the Family in England, 1880–1939.* 1989.

Harrison, Brian. *Prudent Revolutionaries: Portraits of British Feminists Between the Wars.* 1987.

Jeffreys, Sheila. *The Spinster and Her Enemies: Feminism and Sexuality, 1880–1930.* 1985.

Smith, Harold L., ed. *British Feminism in the Twentieth Century.* 1990.

Festival of Britain, 1951

Originally proposed as an international exhibition to commemorate the centenary of Great Exhibition of 1851, the Festival of Britain was devised as a nationwide series of exhibits and events from May to September 1951. Although eager to demonstrate Britain's recovery from the SECOND WORLD WAR, the LABOUR government in 1947, facing shortages and austerity, found itself unable to allocate sufficient resources for an international exhibition without making inordinate demands on scarce material and labor needed for reconstruction. Instead HERBERT MORRISON, the Lord President of the Council, called for a more modest national display illustrating Britain's contribution to civilization in the arts, science and technology, and industrial design. In contrast to earlier expositions, confined to a single site, like the British Empire Exhibition at Wembley in 1924, the Festival of Britain was planned as a series of events that would encompass the entire country. Whereas earlier exhibitions had celebrated Britain's far-flung interests by involving other countries or at least the Empire, the 1951 festival made a virtue of Britain's reduced stature by restricting its focus to the nation and emphasizing the vitality of British traditions.

The festival was planned by a group of young architects and designers under the direction of Gerald Barry, former editor of the *News Chronicle;* its centerpiece was a large multi-pavilion exhibit on the South Bank in LONDON organized around the theme of the land of Britain, the people of Britain, and British contributions to discovery. Rather than adopt the traditional formal geometrical pattern of great exhibitions, the festival planners designed an informal grouping of buildings on the twenty-nine acre site between County Hall and Waterloo Bridge, applying the ideas of the modern international architectural style to the temporary festival buildings, all of which were dismantled after the festival ended. The most dramatic of the structures were the Dome of Discovery, a vast aluminum saucer supported by forty-eight tubular steel struts and the graceful, vertical Skylon, a 250-foot high, elongated pod that appeared to be suspended in mid-air, but was actually supported by cables.

The official exhibitions also included a Science Exhibit at an enlarged Science Museum in South Kensington; a Live Architecture Exhibit in Poplar, where contemporary principles of town planning and modern building techniques were applied in the reconstruction of a badly blitzed SLUM neighborhood, renamed Lansbury; a book exhibit at the Victoria and Albert Museum; an exhibition of industrial power in Glasgow; and a farm and factory exhibit in Belfast. Scaled-down versions of the South Bank exhibits were transported to Leeds, Nottingham, Manchester, and Birmingham by the mobile Land Travelling Exhibition and to the principal seaports by the Festival Ship *Campania.* A large portion of Battersea Park was tranformed into a pleasure gardens and fun fair, where designers and artists created a fanciful imitation of the eighteenth-century gardens at Vauxhall and Ranelagh and a British version of Tivoli.

The ARTS COUNCIL sponsored a two-month London Season of the Arts, which focused on British music, painting, and literature and featured 200 orchestral concerts, performances of newly-commissioned OPERAS and BALLETS, and an array of classic British plays. Moreover, the Arts Council provided encouragement and financial guarantees to twenty-three arts festivals, including not only more established events at Stratford, Edinburgh, or Aldeburgh, but new ones in Liverpool, York, Norwich, Oxford, Cambridge, and other towns. Its commissioning of works specifically for the Festival of Britain acknowledged the importance of the artists in British culture, while enhancing its own role as arbiter of taste and official patron of the arts.

In addition some 2,000 villages and towns organized festival events on their own initiative, ranging from concerts to floral displays, from refurbishing ancient buildings to providing recreational amenities, adding an unprecedented dimension of popular participation to the more traditional exhibition format.

The Festival of Britain succeeded beyond the expectations of many of its planners, who had been skeptical about whether the project, dogged by STRIKES, budgetary cuts, and persistent inclement weather in the winter of 1950–1, would ever be finished. Supported by much of the PRESS, by the government, the royal family, which lent its patronage, and by the cultural elite, the festival opened at the beginning of May in a blaze of publicity, with a service of dedication at St Paul's and an inaugural concert at the new Royal Festival Hall. During the next five months the crowds at the South Bank continued to mount, attracted not only by the narrative exhibits themselves, but perhaps even more by the flowers, illuminations along the river front, fireworks, cafes, and nightly entertainment. Nearly 8.5 million people visited the South Bank and 8 million visited the Festival Pleasure Gardens, although attendance at other official exhibitions was considerably smaller.

The festival offered opportunities for younger architects, designers, and artists to expriment, providing the first occasion for a concentrated display of modern ARCHITECTURE in Britain. The exhibits, carefully controlled by a Presentation Panel, furnished evidence of British craftsmanship and good quality in industrial DESIGN, which may have helped to promote British exports. If it exaggerated the extent of British recovery from war, it did help to dispel some of the gloom and bleakness so pervasive in the late 1940s. The use of temporary structures reduced the demand on building materials, although the expenditure of £10 million still meant the diversion of resources that might have been used for housing or social amenities. Yet many felt that by injecting a note of gaiety and fun at a time of economic crisis and war in Korea, the festival played a vital role in restoring public morale and in demonstrating British resilience to the rest of the world. However modest its economic and aesthetic contribution, it did provide, in Gerald Barry's words, "a tonic to the nation".

Fred M. Leventhal

Bibliography

Banham, Mary, and Bevis Hillier, eds. *A Tonic to the Nation: The Festival of Britain 1951.* 1976.

Barry, Sir Gerald, "The Festival of Britain 1951," *Journal of the Royal Society of Arts,* vol. 100 (1952), pp. 667–704.

Conekin, Becky. "'Here is the Modern World Itself': The Festival of Britain's Representations of the Future," in Becky Conekin, Frank Mort, and Chris

Waters, eds. *Moments of Modernity: Reconstructing Britain 1945–1964.* 1999, pp. 228–46.

Frayn, Michael, "Festival" in Michael Sissons and Philip French, eds. *Age of Austerity 1945–1951.* 1964. pp. 330–52.

Leventhal, F.M. "'A Tonic to the Nation': The Festival of Britain, 1951," *Albion,* vol. 27 (1995), pp. 445–53.

Film Industry

Until the early 1950s Britain had a major film industry which made its money primarily from showing American films. British filmmakers, unable to produce enough films to fill British screentime, have always had to compete with the popularity of American films in the United Kingdom. British filmmaking seems to occur in cycles, with alternate bursts of crisis and activity. There has also been a traditional split between popular movies and elite art film.

Despite a long tradition of filmmaking, Britain has, more than any other country, been vulnerable to imports from other English-speaking countries. Hollywood has traditionally taken the lion's share of the British film market, often luring away many of Britain's most talented filmmakers.

Filmmaking began in Britain at about the same time it began in the United States. William Friese-Greene is recognized as the founder of British motion picture technology, his invention celebrated in the 1951 film, *The Magic Box* (Roy and John Boulting). British filmmaker Cecil Hepworth anticipated many of D.W. Griffith's technical and dramatic innovations, and in films such as *Rescued by Rover* (1903) demonstrated a sophisticated sense of film structure and narrative. The Brighton School constituted a lively indigenous fiction film tradition, but British filmmaking was disrupted by the First World War, and production went into a prolonged decline. In the 1920s British studios produced very few films, and the government attempted to legislate British cinema into existence by requiring exhibitors to show British films and offering tax incentives for producers to make films in the United Kingdom. These measures enabled a group of entrepreneurs and film makers, most of them, like Alexander Korda, foreign nationals, to revive British production, although most British accomplishments until the mid-1930s lay in the area of DOCUMENTARY FILM. By 1937 British filmmakers were once again very busy, making more films than in any other single year. Many were so called "quota quickies", inexpensive films intended to fill the bottom half of a double bill, produced by American-owned companies attempting to obey the letter, if not the spirit of the quota laws. The most commercially successful film in the 1930s was Korda's production, *The Private Life of Henry VIII* (1933), the first British

film which found a substantial overseas market. The small British studio system nurtured several directors, the most prominent being Anthony Asquith, Walter Forde, and of course, ALFRED HITCHCOCK. Gracie Fields and George Formby, both stars with a special appeal to working-class moviegoers were the decade's most popular stars, and light and musical comedies were the most successful genres.

The SECOND WORLD WAR was a wonderful time for British film, despite CONSCRIPTION of many performers and the scarcity of materials and studio space. For the first time the supply of American films was strictly regulated, and the United States even agreed to throw open its screens to British films. Films like *The Way Ahead* (CAROL REED, 1944) *Next of Kin* (Thorold Dickinson, 1942), and *In Which We Serve* (NOEL COWARD, 1942) dramatized the war for British cinema audiences in ways that Hollywood could not. Filmmakers like Coward and David Lean evolved a style which mixed stoicism and social realism to evoke a stirring image of the British at war. LAURENCE OLIVIER fought the war in allegories such as *Henry V* (1944), widely regarded as the definitive screen adaptation of Shakespeare. The Ministry of Information (MOI) was very active in commissioning films and shaping motion picture content. *The Life and Times of Colonel Blimp* (MICHAEL POWELL and Emeric Pressburger, 1943), one of the most expensive British films made during the war, clearly showed the influence of MOI policy, as did many feature films made during the war. Motion pictures were one of the few unrationed luxuries, and British theatregoers went to the cinema more often than ever before, despite the risks of aerial bombardment.

The war also enabled the Rank Organization to obtain a virtual monopoly within the industry. J. Arthur Rank, whose family fortune derived from flour milling, had moved into the film industry in the early 1930s. A devout Methodist who initially became interested in using films for religious and philanthropic ends, he soon became the major force in the British film industry. The Rank empire grew quickly and branched out into production and exhibition. By 1945 Rank had absorbed most of the country's studio capacity and first-run theaters, his empire becoming comparable in size to one of the American studios. The LABOUR government tolerated Rank's ambitions because he was felt to be the only real obstacle to American control of the British film industry. After 1945 American competition returned with a vengeance. Labour did not, as was widely feared, nationalize the industry, but it did provide financial support, anticipating that films would become a significant factor in international trade.

In the decade after the war British cinema acquired an international reputation for "literary" films, with David Lean's successful adaptations of novels by Dickens, beginning with *Great Expectations* (1946) and *Oliver Twist* (1947). Olivier continued to direct and star in screen versions of Shakespeare: *Hamlet* (1948) and *Richard III* (1955). Anthony Asquith directed several films adapted from stage plays, notably TERENCE RATTIGAN's *The Winslow Boy* (1949) and *The Browning Version* (1951), as well as *The Importance of Being Earnest* (1952). The partnership of Powell and Pressburger continued trimphantly with the widely-acclaimed *The Red Shoes* (1948). Carol Reed's work ranged over several genres, including the Irish political drama *Odd Man Out* (1947), the domestic melodrama *The Fallen Idol* (1948), the popular Cold War thriller *The Third Man* (1949), and an adaptation of JOSEPH CONRAD's *Outcast of the Islands* (1951). This did not constitute the bulk of British cinema production after 1945, which still consisted primarily of popular mainstream films. Filmmakers who catered to these mainstream tastes included Roy and John Boulting in films like *Brighton Rock* (1947) and Michael Balcon, the producer in charge of Ealing Studios, a part of the Rank Organization. Each year this studio produced a handful of films, the majority of them comedies, such as *Passport to Pimlico* (Henry Cornelius, 1949), *Kind Hearts and Coronets* (Robert Hamer, 1949), and *The Lavender Hill Mob* (Charles Crichton, 1951). These films echoed the problems of post-war Britain: diminished expectations and STANDARD OF LIVING, a lessened role in international affairs, and daily life encumbered by red tape.

In the 1960s British cinema moved towards social realism and away from the classics and cosmopolitan London. *Look Back in Anger* (Tony Richardson, 1959), the screen adaptation of JOHN OSBORNE's play inaugurated a series of films with working-class themes and settings. Other films in this mode included *Room at the Top* (Jack Clayton, 1959), *Saturday Night and Sunday Morning* (Karel Reisz, 1960), *The Loneliness of the Long Distance Runner* (Tony Richardson, 1962), and *This Sporting Life* (Lindsay Anderson, 1963). These films, often referred to as British "New Cinema", resembled the style and spirit of the French New Wave. Most were taken from plays or novels by young writers, like Osborne or Alan Sillitoe, who had tried to capture the feelings of dislocation and disillusion common among young working-class people in post-war Britain. Graphic and explicit, the language and actions of New Cinema's working class anti-heroes often shocked critics and audiences, but many of these films were critically and commercially successful. Other British filmmakers who emerged in the

1960s included John Schlesinger, whose films included *Billy Liar* (1962) and *Far From the Madding Crowd* (1967), and Richard Lester, whose BEATLES films, *A Hard Day's Night* (1964) and *Help!* (1965), were a vibrant upbeat rebuttal of the somber pessimism of British social realism.

At the same time American financing became increasingly important for the industry. Many of the bigger films made in the 1950s and 1960s, such as *Lawrence of Arabia* (David Lean, 1961), were co-productions which merged British talent and American money. The James Bond series, beginning with *Dr. No* (1962) carried this process further. American producers were attracted by Britain's skilled and relatively inexpensive work force and the favorable tax incentives and subsidies available for British filmmaking. Ultimately, many American films such as the *Star Wars* series and most of the Bond films were made in Pinewood, not Hollywood, although American production fled Britain in the 1980s, when the financial climate ceased to be as attractive.

During the 1950s and 1960s, largely because of competition from television, Britons lost the habit of going to the movies. Theaters closed in large numbers, and box office takings went into a decline only recently reversed. Without a substantial domestic market, British film production has always been precarious and is largely dependent today upon support from television. Since its inception in 1982, Channel Four, Britain's innovative second commercial television channel, has become the largest producer of independent features in Britain. This policy had led to a dramatic recovery of British filmmaking, with films like *My Beautiful Laundrette* (Stephen Frears, 1985) and *Letter to Brezhnev* (Chris Bernard, 1985) produced with Channel Four support. Britain also has a new generation of cerebral nonmainstream filmmakers, such as Derek Jarman (*Caravaggio*, 1986) and Peter Greenaway (*Prospero's Books*, 1992). Uncompromisingly intellectual, these filmmakers have international followings, but inspire only limited popular interest within the United Kingdom.

Paul Swann

Bibliography

Auty, Martyn, and Nick Roddick. *British Cinema Now.* 1985.

Barr, Charles, ed. *All Our Yesterdays: 90 Years of British Cinema.* 1986.

Dickinson, Margaret, and Sarah Street. *Cinema and State: The Film Industry and the Government, 1927–84.* 1985.

Landy, Marcia. *British Genres: Cinema and Society, 1930–1960.* 1991.

Park, James. *British Cinema: The Lights That Failed.* 1990.

Perry, George. *The Great British Picture Show.* 2nd ed. 1985.

First World War: Homefront (1914–1918)

The extreme demands of the first total war spurred major changes in British society on the homefront that included expansion of state control and government bureaucracy; an overall improvement in the standard of health despite the toll and tensions of war, long working hours, and eventual RATIONING; and significant intervention by the state in industry and conditions of labor. Some changes were only for the duration, while others left a post-war legacy. The government assumed such responsibilities as the formal takeover of the RAILWAYS by the Board of Trade; intervention in food production and distribution; and control of industries from munitions to shipbuilding to chemicals. In 1916 it adopted the unprecedented power of military CONSCRIPTION.

At first government food policy urged restraint in the consumption of bread, meat, and sugar as a patriotic duty. Following the shipping losses caused by the German submarine warfare, however, actual rationing was introduced by late 1917, beginning with localized rationing of coal and sugar. Queues became a standard feature of wartime life on the homefront, with popular frustration over shortages erupting into scattered protests and instances of looting. At one point the country had only four days' supply of sugar. But in early 1918 the government introduced comprehensive food rationing, queues disappeared, and the public gratefully accepted a system of remarkably equitable food distribution. National kitchens were established to supply ready-cooked meals to civilians, but they were only in certain areas and had little effect. The government urged Britons to grow as much of their own vegetables as they could. Garden allotments were cultivated on all kinds of plots, even around the Albert Memorial, and factories introduced allotments to grow vegetables for their canteens.

From August 1914 throughout the war the DEFENCE OF THE REALM ACTS (DORA) gave the government wide powers to regulate in the interests of public and national security. Initially designed to control the flow of information, and to protect communications and transport, these laws meant civilians were subject to military law. Under DORA, government adopted the food control measures, air-raid precautions, and the special policing of women accused of soliciting soldiers. PROPAGANDA and censorship were also undertaken within the powers of DORA. The British government used film, pamphlets, photographs, and posters as media of propaganda. Propaganda to inflame public opinion in Britain over atrocities supposedly committed by the Germans employed sexual imagery, particularly rape and the violent abuse of virgins; false accounts of supposed German outrages were widely circu-

lated. Poster images exhorted civilians to take up war work, economize on food, and buy war bonds. Government censorship filtered war news in multiple forms including film footage, letters from the front, and newspaper reports.

The state also adopted unprecedented forms of intervention in the management and control of industry, labor and conditions of work, and the provision of essential industrial supplies. As the major supplier of weapons and munitions to allied countries as well as to its own forces, British industry produced 250,000 machine guns, 52,000 aeroplanes, nearly 3,000 tanks, 25,000 artillery pieces and 170 million rounds of artillery shells. In March 1915 government representatives met with the principal union leaders, particularly from the Amalgamated Society of Engineers, and drew up the Treasury Agreement in which the unions agreed to the "dilution" of the skilled workforce (meaning substitution by unskilled and semi-skilled workers) for the duration, provided that the prewar status quo would be restored at the end of the war. In June 1915 the MINISTRY OF MUNITIONS was established with LLOYD GEORGE as its first minister. It oversaw a remarkable collaboration between government, industry and unions, with government intervention which contravened all principles of *laissez-faire* economics. The Munitions of War Act of July 1915 declared STRIKES and lock-outs illegal, quite ineffectively. It also introduced compulsory arbitration under a system of special munitions tribunals, and workers were restrained from leaving their jobs by a system of leaving certificates. The Ministry adopted control of wages and working conditions not only in government arsenals and factories but also in private companies which became "controlled establishments". By 1917 what had started as *ad hoc* interventions had become a total war economy. But not all ran smoothly. Increased participation in government by union and labor leaders backfired by creating a rift between union leaders and their rank-and-file membership. Syndicalist and socialist beliefs among workers were exemplified by the shop stewards' movement, particularly on Clydeside, which organized strikes throughout the war.

From mid-1915 there was virtually full employment. The war led to higher than ever levels of union membership, especially among women workers. The massive economic disruption, caused by the armed forces' draining of the industrial workforce simultaneous with the need for munitions, opened up employment opportunities particularly for women workers who had been confined to sweated jobs and low-paid domestic service before the war. From July 1914 to July 1918 the non-professional EMPLOYMENT OF WOMEN and girls in the United Kingdom increased by

1,590,000, of whom 891,000 were employed in industrial occupations. The Great War produced a proportional leap in the employment of women which took them from being 26 percent of all those employed in the United Kingdom in July 1914, to 36 percent in November 1918. While approximately a million women worked on all forms of munitions, women also took jobs in transport, as shop assistants, and in clerical work.

Despite shortages and food rationing, the higher average income among working-class families due to wartime employment and separation allowances for the families of servicemen, meant that the average DIET improved significantly. Although wartime inflation was high, the average increase in wages for working-class families maintained the spending power of most and increased that of some. Observers commented on the improved health of children in working-class areas, noting also that children were better shod.

A contributing factor to the improved diets of workers were the factory canteens which were a wartime innovation. Factories under government control as well as some private establishments instigated canteens with ovens for workers to heat their own food, or sold workers plain hot fare at reasonable prices, or both. Women workers were a particular target of this campaign to build the strength of the workforce, through the ministrations of women welfare supervisors. The Health and Welfare Department of the Ministry of Munitions conducted nutrition research and recommended menus for factory canteens and workers' hostels. A principal motive behind government sponsorship of canteens was the desire to keep workers sober; the drastic reduction of public house opening hours is a legacy of the war which contributed at the time to the decline in infant mortality rates.

Due to the improvement in diet, especially among the poorest paid, unskilled workers, the standard of PUBLIC HEALTH on the homefront actually improved despite the difficulties and the toll of warfare. There were, however, some countervailing factors. There was an increase in respiratory diseases, due to the effects of overcrowding at work and the strain of long working hours. More dramatically, the influenza pandemic of 1918–19 ravaged both the military and civilian populations, killing approximately 200,000 British people.

The war did come to the homefront, although it was nothing like the BLITZ would be in the SECOND WORLD WAR. Nevertheless, hundreds of civilians were killed and wounded by bombs in air raids by Zeppelins, Gothas, and Giants, particularly on the east coast and in the southeast. Other Britons lost their lives in industrial accidents of

wartime production; explosions in munitions factories killed hundreds of workers altogether, such as the 19 January 1917 explosion at a chemical works in Silvertown, London, which destroyed the factory and the neighborhood around it.

A strange new fact of wartime life were the ARMY camps that sprang up over the countryside, especially in the early stages of war as new recruits had to be drilled and trained. British, colonial, and dominion soldiers were to be seen everywhere: in streets, pubs, trains, cinemas, and parks. The attraction that troops exerted on some young women, and intermingling of soldiers and women in public places, led to concern about sexual morality and venereal disease, as well as innovations in policing. While police forces expanded to meet special wartime needs, women were granted semi-official status as members of the Women Police Service and the Women Patrols of the National Union of Women Workers. In this new capacity they patrolled streets, parks, and cinemas to prevent sexual liaisons and were employed by the Ministry of Munitions to control and discipline women workers. Fear of sexual promiscuity was fostered by changes in young women's clothing (shorter skirts and trousers at work), hair (shorter), and independent social behavior, such as dining alone in restaurants and smoking in public.

Within months of the outbreak of war the public presence of soldiers included the wounded, in wheelchairs, on crutches, bandaged, some missing limbs. Public buildings and large private houses were converted into HOSPITALS and convalescent homes. Factory workers and other groups organized entertainment and outings for wounded soldiers. Flag sellers and other patriotic charity fundraisers were a constant presence on the streets and in the foyers of public buildings; it was as though they had taken the streets over from the suffragettes, who had suspended their protests for the war but were partially victorious before it was over, when women over thirty gained the vote under the Representation of the People Act (1918).

Angela Woollacott

Bibliography

Braybon, Gail. *Women Workers in the First World War: The British Experience.* 1981.

Rubin, Gerry R. *War, Law and Labour: The Munitions Acts, State Regulation, and the Unions, 1915–1921.* 1987.

Marwick, Arthur. *The Deluge: British Society and the First World War.* 1965.

Turner, John. *British Politics and the Great War: Coalition and Conflict, 1915–1918.* 1992.

Wilson, Trevor. *The Myriad Faces of War: Britain and the Great War, 1914–1918.* 1986.

Winter, J.M. *The Great War and the British People.* 1985.

Woollacott, Angela. *On Her Their Lives Depend.* 1994.

First World War: Military (1914–1918)
According to pre-war plans, Britain would play only a minor part in a continental war. If forced into conflict with Germany, it would leave the land fighting to France and Russia. Britain would hold the seas, maintain exports, and so provide military material for its allies. This conception did not survive the onset of war. Britain's vital interests were too obviously in peril, its allies too fragile, the German onslaught too menacing. So Britain's authorities instantly set about raising a mass army, at first by voluntary means, from 1916 by compulsion.

Until that army could be trained and equipped, Britain's military participation was largely confined to its small regular ARMY. In accordance with pre-war arrangements—confirmed only after protracted discussions early in August 1914 among civilian ministers and their military advisers—five of the seven divisions of the Regular Army crossed the Channel and took up position on the left of the French (who numbered seventy divisions). They were hardly expected to be in the thick of the fighting.

This proved a miscalculation. The German attack through Belgium traveled much further west than anticipated before wheeling south so as to outflank and overwhelm the French left before descending on Paris. At Mons on 23 August, the German far right crashed into the British Expeditionary Force (BEF), who momentarily stayed the advance before falling back under weight of numbers. For thirteen days the Anglo-French left wing retreated, until it was over the Marne and within sight of Paris. There on 5 September General Joffre, the French commander, counterattacked and drove the Germans into retreat. The British and French kept up the pursuit as far as the Aisne, where (13–17 September) they were brought to a standstill by a combination of trenches, barbed wire, machine-guns, and artillery.

The French and German forces each swung north, seeking to outflank the other. Meanwhile the BEF, at the insistence of its commander, Sir John French, was plucked from central France and returned to the coast. French believed that in unoccupied Belgium he might maneuver his cavalry to effect. Instead his forces were beset by another massive German offensive, supported by heavy artillery and eager young recruits. At the first Battle of Ypres (October–November 1914) the numerically inferior and underweaponed BEF held—if at heavy cost—this onslaught: a futher demonstration of the defensive capacity of even rudimentary trenches.

By the end of 1914, therefore, the phenomenon of trench warfare was beginning to dominate perceptions of the Western Front. What signified was not trenches alone but the combination of trenches with the advanced weaponry thrown up by industrialization. Barbed wire, rapid-firing rifles, mortars, high-explosive and shrapnel shells, and machine-gun bullets bestowed upon defenders under cover great stopping power against an attacking force crossing open ground. That is, life in a trench might be a lamentable experience, with its constant accompaniment of rain, mud, lice, rats, and dismembered bodies, and its perils from shells and snipers. But it offered a much greater chance of survival than life in the open.

Here was a conundrum. If "trench warfare" gave so prodigious an advantage to the defender, how were the British and the French to liberate Belgium and humble the German military machine? In one view, the answer lay in resolute attacks on the Western Front supported by sufficient fire-power to batter down the opposing trenches. From this conviction sprang mighty offensives by the French in the spring and autumn of 1915, with supporting operations by the British at Neuve Chapelle, Aubers Ridge, and Loos.

That these endeavors were not based on entirely false premises is suggested by the partial success of the British at Neuve Chapelle on 10 March 1915. A considerable quantity of ammunition—considerable, that is, in terms of the small length of trench being attacked—overwhelmed the defenders and enabled British forces to seize the German front line (but not to go beyond that). Subsequent Allied operations during 1915, however, proved unrewarding. The objectives proved too ambitious, the support in guns and ammunition less than adequate.

Even at the beginning of 1915 some thoughtful men in Britain were expressing alarm at the potential trench stalemate on the Western Front. They drew the conclusion (which did not follow) that Britain, employing its sea power and ignoring the sentiments of its French allies, could do better elsewhere. They favored concentration against Germany's allies: either Austria-Hungary (in a process that DAVID LLOYD GEORGE quaintly described as knocking the props from under Germany) or Turkey (around which Sir Maurice Hankey vaguely hoped to "weave a web").

Little good came of these reflections. The Germans manifestly could send aid to Austria Hungary—which they happened to be propping up—faster than the Allies could mount an operation against it. And the projected demise of Turkey would hardly lessen Germany's potentiality for overrunning Western Europe. Anyway, Britain could not disregard the wishes of France, which for the moment commanded the only considerable army standing between Germany and the Channel. And Britain happened to possess no large surplus of warships or troops for major operations in distant parts.

Britain did in 1914-15 take some action outside the Western Front. Sensibly, it dispatched a force to southern Mesopotamia (then in Turkish hands) to safeguard oil supplies from Persia. Less sensibly, it then attempted to overrun all of Mesopotamia with a quite inadequate force. Again, late in 1915 the British (along with the French) landed troops in Salonika—in neutral Greek territory—in an attempt to rescue Serbia, but to no avail.

Best remembered of 1915's extraneous operations was the GALLIPOLI expedition. This did not originate in a decision to divert Britain's military effort from the Western Front. Only the NAVY, using obsolete ships, was to figure in the proposed penetration of the Dardanelles. (It was anticipated, without investigation, that a fleet bombarding Constantinople would cause all Turkey to surrender.) This "ships alone" scheme soon failed before the shore defenses of Gallipoli. So it was decided to land troops on the peninsula and so open the Dardanelles to the fleet. The military operation also failed. Landings on 25 April secured toe-holds on the shore but none on the high ground. Subsequent endeavors to press inland, despite a mounting commitment of military resources, availed nothing. By the end of 1915 the abandonment of the undertaking was well advanced.

For 1916, therefore, the nature of Britain's military activites seemed settled. The Western Front, whatever its perils, was the only region where some worthwhile purpose might be accomplished. Awareness of this coincided with a large development. The volunteers who had come forward at the outset were now trained and in uniform. Britain seemed able at last to participate fully in the war on land. Byt the appearance was deceptive. Whatever the accomplishments of industry and the MINISTRY OF MUNITIONS (formed in April 1915), Britain had yet to produce weaponry in the quantities and of the quality to support ambitious undertakings.

Planning for 1916 culminated in the Battle of the SOMME, a mighty Anglo-French (but predominantly British) offensive in central France. It began on 1 July and continued to 19 November. Its first day was an abysmal failure. The new British Commander-in-Chief, SIR DOUGLAS HAIG, hoped to rupture the German defenses at a stroke and pour his cavalry into open territory. Consequently, he spread his relatively meager supply of guns and ammunition over a wide area. This left the German defenses largely intact, and brought on his forces terrible casualties for pitiful gains.

The ensuing months on the Somme were a melange of major attacks (such as 14 July, 15 September, and 25 September), many weeks of sporadic and uncoordingated assaults by small groups, and finally a six-week period of struggle against rain and mud without discernible purpose. All told, the rewards for four and a half months of campaigning were meager. A ridge of elevated ground had been captured, the tank had been unleashed, artillery techniques had undergone important refinements, and many Germans had been killed. But there had been no breakthrough, the enemy still occupied secure defenses, and Allied losses exceeded those of their enemies.

This comparative failure helped to bring to power late in 1916 a new Prime Minister. Lloyd George took a dim view of British operations on the Western Front and Haig's apparent carelessness with his soldiers' lives. He also nursed an exaggerated respect for French commanders and believed that offensives should be launched in areas—such as Italy—where British forces would not be much involved.

Had Joffre and Haig had their way, the Somme campaign would have continued in 1917. But Joffre was sacked. And Haig was confronted both with a German withdrawal to new and formidable defenses (the Hindenburg Line) and with his own Prime Minister's disbelief in the Somme strategy. At conferences early in 1917, Lloyd George failed to convince anyone (least of all the Italians) of the merits of a primarily Italian offensive. So he switched his allegiance to the new French commander, General Nivelle, who promised in short order to rupture the German lines on the French sector of the Western Front. The BEF would provide only subsidiary support, at Arras. So enamored was Lloyd George of this proposal that he sought to place the British army under French Command.

Nivelle's offensive proved short-lived, as did his command of the forces of France (let alone those of Britain). The French army, disillusioned by the absence of swift success, mutinied. The only noteworthy gain from his operations, ironically, occurred on the British sector. Haig's forces on the first day of the Battle of Arras (9 April), aided by enhanced artillery, captured Vimy Ridge. But exploitation proved difficult. The weather was abominable, artillery could not be got forward with dispatch, and the enemy brought in reserves and threw up fresh defenses. The Battle of Arras continued for six weeks at heavy cost. But all potential had departed after forty-eight hours.

Nivelle's fall from grace, and the French army's lapse into mutiny, presented Lloyd George with a problem. He remained averse to predominantly British offensives on the Western Front. But France's forces were not at this stage capable of any great effort, the Italian option was unsaleable, and Lloyd George was strangely unresponsive to a strategy of set-piece, small objective offensives (like the capture of Vimy Ridge on 9 April and of Messines Ridge on 7 June). That left him with only one choice (which he affected to dislike): Haig's scheme for a decidedly ambitious drive out of the Ypres salient and towards the Belgian coast.

This undertaking (the third Battle of Ypres or PASSCHENDAELE) was the brainchild of the British command but could not have occurred without the consent of its civilian masters. Beginning on 31 July 1917 and continuing until 12 November, it remains notorious even among First World War operations as an exercise in futility. It was not as costly as the Somme, its first day yielded modest gains, and its middle month (September) witnessed three limited successes. But these positive aspects were overshadowed by Haig's repeated striving after distant objectives, and by his persistence in attacking during months of abysmal weather when ground turned to swamp, guns could not shoot with accuracy, and infantry were rendered almost immobile. The image of soldiers struggling in a sea of mud against unsuppressed opponents has haunted the imagination, and blighted Haig's reputation, ever since.

The year 1917 was not redeemed by the last military episode of the year, the initially much-acclaimed Battle of Cambrai (20 November–7 December). For the first time the British used a mass of tanks over good terrain, and (more importantly) fired a fully-predicted—and therefore surprise—bombardment. These enabled the infantry to make progress. But there was no breakthrough, and Haig's forces were left fairly exposed. A surprise German counter-attack ten days later recovered as much ground as had been gained.

The sorry events from July to December 1917 laid Haig open to dismissal. Lloyd George denigrated him but did not remove him. Instead, disregarding the Nivelle incident, he sought to diminish Haig's authority by elevating another Frenchman, General Foch. In time, Foch would become Allied Commander-in-Chief. But he never exercised large powers of control.

Yet, in practical terms, Haig would not in 1918 decide the fate of his army to the extent he had done previously. In the first half of that year, the actions of Britain's forces were mainly ad hoc responses to the initiative that the enemy briefly seized in the wake of Russia's collapse. And in the second half of the year, various elements throughout the British army responded creatively to the piecemeal but mounting opportunities offering in the aftermath of Germany's failure.

By 1918 Britain's home industry and financial resources and trans-Atlantic allies were providing the BEF with the weaponry to do battle effec-

tively. And the British army, in many departments but mostly important in its artillery branch, now possessed the expertise to employ guns and shells and tanks and airplanes to maximum effect. The consequence was noteworthy. By 1918, Britain (like its enemies) was scraping the barrel for infantrymen. Yet at this stage, thanks to an abundance of weaponry and the ability to employ it effectively, the terrible supremacy that defense had so far enjoyed over attack was receding. No trench system could long withstand a well-conducted, amply munitioned assault.

The year 1918, in consequence, falls into two phases. Between 21 March and 29 April, the Germans flung themselves on parts of the British sector, capturing many prisoners and some (fairly unimportant) ground. Having ceased to make progress, they then turned against the French, again with some success. This gave the British time first to recuperate and then to organize a succession of stinging counter-attacks. Beginning at Amiens on 8 August, the BEF—with increasing support by its allies—dealt unremitting blows upon its adversaries. By mid–September the Germans had been driven from all their gains of earlier in the year and were back on the Hindenburg Line. Here they intended to stand for the winter. But events had passed beyond their control. In great set-piece attacks on 18 and 26 September, employing large amounts of high explosive with the utmost skill, the British army overran first the ridge protecting the Hindenburg Line and then the central Hindenburg system. After that, a German surrender was only a matter of time.

The British military experience in the First World War is not remembered with favor. The prevailing image is of martyred infantrymen sacrificed by stubborn, unimaginative commanders. That perception is not wholly misguided. The war is noteworthy for an absence of inspired generalship and for many wasteful and culpable operations (even though some of them were the brainchildren less of benighted militarists than of "imaginative" civilians).

Yet the war's dreadful immobility was not the result of military stupidity. It sprang from a revolution in weaponry that bestowed great power on the defense. And it should be observed that just four years of mobilization and experimentation and growing expertise enabled this situation to be transformed. Four years, it deserves to be recalled, was significantly less time than it took to defeat Napoleon Bonaparte or Adolf Hitler.

Robin Prior
Trevor Wilson

Bibliography

Cruttwell, C.R.M.F. *A History of the Great War, 1914–1918*. 2nd ed. 1936.

Prior, Robin, and Trevor Wilson. *Command on the West-ern Front: the Military Career of Sir Henry Rawlinson 1914–1918.* 1992.

Wilson, Trevor. *The Myriad Faces of War: Britain and the Great War 1914–1918.* 1986.

Woodward, Llewellyn. *Great Britain and the War of 1914–1918.* 1967.

Fleming, Alexander (1881–1955)

Alexander Fleming, the discoverer of penicillin, was born in Scotland, the son of Ayrshire farmers. In 1901 he enrolled as a medical student at St. Mary's Hospital Medical School. Qualifying in 1906, he joined Sir Almroth Wright as an assistant in the Inoculation Department of the hospital, working initially on techniques for the diagnosis and treatment of syphilis. During the FIRST WORLD WAR Fleming turned to problems of wound infection, identifying infective organisms in battlefield casualties and their means of action. Most importantly, Fleming explored the reasons why the antiseptic techniques employed by surgeons did not work in war wounds. He showed that antiseptics could not only not reach the crevices where many microbes lurked, but were rapidly removed by the discharge of fluid and pus. He also found that antiseptics could destroy the patient's leukocytes—the body's defense against invading bacteria—while leaving the bacteria themselves unharmed.

After the war Fleming returned to St. Mary's and in 1921 made his first major discovery, that of a ferment (an enzyme in today's terminology) present in most body fluids that had the power to dissolve certain bacteria. Then in 1928 Fleming discovered penicillin almost by accident when a mold spore contaminated a plate in which he was growing staphylococci, a form of bacteria. What was different about this mold was that it appeared to dissolve the surrounding bacteria. More exciting still, when Fleming made sub-cultures of the mold he found that while the culture fluid was strongly antibacterial, it was non-toxic to human leukocytes or to laboratory animals. But Fleming failed to extract or purify the active principle in the fluid, and after a few tentative trials gave up using it as a therapeutic agent. The penicillin was too unstable and weak for treatment purposes. And there it might have remained, but for the work of Howard Florey and Ernst Chain in OXFORD. In 1940 Chain and Florey prepared enough partially purified penicillin for clinical trials which confirmed and extended Fleming's original findings. By the end of the Second World War the bulk of commercially produced penicillin came from the United States. In 1945 Fleming shared the Nobel Prize for Medicine with Florey and Chain for the discovery of penicillin.

Fleming is best remembered for his work on penicillin, and his name often unduly overshadows those of Florey and Chain. But penicillin was only a small part of his work. Most of his routine work was concerned with the production of vaccines, a lucrative project that made the Inoculation Department financially independent of St. Mary's, and on which Fleming relied for his salary. In 1921 Wright appointed Fleming to take charge of the production of vaccines. When Wright retired in 1946, Fleming took over the department, renamed the following year the Wright-Fleming Institute. Fleming resigned in 1955 and died later that year.

David Cantor

Bibliography

Macfarlane, Gwyn. *Alexander Fleming: The Man and the Myth.* 1985.

Fonteyn, Margot (1919–1991)

Prima ballerina of England's Royal Ballet and the embodiment of its flowing, lyrical style, Margot Fonteyn (born Peggy Hookham) was one of the greatest classical dancers of the twentieth century. Equally revered by the dancers she inspired and the public she enchanted, she endowed her dancing with elegant simplicity, seamless physical grace, and sensitive musicality, and her growth as an artist paralleled the growth of the company she led and crowned its many years of international success.

Fonteyn's career began in 1934, when she made her debut as a snowflake in *The Nutcracker,* and ended in 1986 with a guest appearance as the Queen in *The Sleeping Beauty.* Having made her mark quickly with the Vic-Wells Ballet (renamed the Sadler's Wells Ballet in 1940 and the Royal Ballet in 1956), she established herself as its brightest star in 1946, dancing Aurora in *The Sleeping Beauty* when it reopened the Royal Opera House after the Second World War. Aurora became her signature role, and when the company first toured America three years later, Fonteyn conquered the country with her joyous, radiant characterization and gentle, effortless expressivity.

A refined and subtle interpreter of the great nineteenth-century classics, like *Swan Lake, Giselle,* and *La Sylphide,* Fonteyn was also the constant muse of the English choreographer FREDERICK ASHTON, who created nearly two dozen roles for her. She was his ideal *Cinderella* (1948), his *Ondine* (1958), his Queen of the Air in *Homage to the Queen* (1953), and the luminous central presence in his masterpiece, *Symphonic Variations* (1946). His choreography and her poised and passionate interpretation of it together defined the Royal Ballet's illustrious style.

Fonteyn appeared as a guest artist with over thirty companies and created new BALLETS by

such varied choreographers as NINETTE DE VA-
LOIS, Roland Petit, John Cranko, and Martha
Graham. As the resident star of the Royal Ballet
until the early 1970s, she was partnered at home
and on the company's many world tours by its
noblest cavaliers, notably Robert Helpmann and
Michael Somes. When she was forty-two and
considering retirement, a new partnership with a
young Russian defector, Rudolf Nureyev, revived
and transformed her career. Fonteyn and Nureyev
became ballet's first international superstars; set
against his explosive energy and exotic ardor, her
exquisite purity and impeccable technique shone
with fresh authority.

Awarded a CBE in 1951 and a DBE in 1956,
Fonteyn was also President of the Royal Academy of Dancing (1954–91) and Chancellor of
Durham University (1982–91). Since modesty
and intelligence informed her character as completely as her dancing, no title or honor ever distracted her from her singleminded pursuit of artistic excellence. The greater her fame, the harder
she worked to perfect her natural gifts, until finally every aspect of her life reflected her love of
her art and her unbounded devotion to it.

Barbara Newman

Bibliography
Bland, Alexander. *The Royal Ballet: The First Fifty Years.*
    1981.
Clarke, Mary. *The Sadler's Wells Ballet: A History and an
    Appreciation.* 1955.
Fonteyn, Margot. *Autobiography.* 1975.
Money, Keith. *The Art of Margot Fonteyn.* 1975.

Foot, Michael Mackintosh (1913–)

A member of a dynasty of religious dissenters
and political radicals, Michael Foot had a career
as journalist, author, campaigner and, above all,
as a LABOUR PARTY politician. A long journey,
from backbench maverick to left-wing spokesman, then responsible "insider", and finally Party
Leader, ultimately did little good to his party.
Educated at a Quaker school and OXFORD, his
youthful conversion from Liberalism to socialism
led him to Parliament as Member for Plymouth
Devonport in 1945. For ten years a rebellious figure apparently indifferent to the attractions of
office, he lost his seat in 1955. Returned to the
House of Commons for Ebbw Vale in 1960, Foot
pursued his intense commitment to nuclear disarmament and otherwise often seemed content
to mix the irresponsibilities of dissent with the
world of letters. By 1970 he perhaps realised that
at fifty-seven he was too old to remain an *enfant
terrible*. He was elected to the Shadow Cabinet
and a year later unsuccessfully contested the
party's deputy leadership. An increasingly prominent voice of the Left, he became shadow
Leader of the House in 1972 and served as a

more self-disciplined bridge between wings of
the party. In 1976 his links to the Left and the
trade unions assisted his appointment as Employment Secretary, a post in which he was arguably too compliant in his dealings with the powerful union movement.

In 1976 HAROLD WILSON resigned as Prime
Minister. Foot survived as the final challenger to
the victorious JAMES CALLAGHAN in the struggle
for succession and became Deputy Leader of the
party. He and Callaghan represented its old
Right and Left, and joined in an effort to stabilise
it as divisions grew deeper. As Leader of the
House Foot was often more effective than critics
had expected in steering legislation through the
Commons; his skills reflected his deep affection
for and knowledge of the parliamentary process.
He also worked hard to protect Callaghan's left
flank until the latter's resignation in the wake of
Labour's 1979 election defeat. In 1980 Foot replaced him as Party Leader, combining some
center and right-wing support with that of the
ascendant Left.

Foot became Leader at a difficult, perhaps impossible time. The party's conflicts were intense,
public and bitter, its machinery archaic, its electoral base diminishing. He cannot be said to have
been equal to the job. He began an attack on Militant, but his memory of anti-Bevanite purges in
the 1950s would not allow him to carry it
through. He was unable to head off the party's
Left-dominated National Executive, which imposed policies repugnant to many moderate Labour voters. Above all, he could not persuade the
electorate that he was a possible Prime Minister.
His rhetorical style and frail, shabby appearance
let him be caricatured as more a mad prophet
than contemporary politician; although a cultivated man, he was accused of knowing more
about the eighteenth century than about his own.
In 1983 he led the party through a shambles of a
campaign based on an impossible manifesto and
a willful indifference to modern electioneering
techniques. When resigning, he passed to his
protegé NEIL KINNOCK a poisoned chalice, made
more toxic by his own limitations as a leader.

Steven Reilly

Bibliography
Foot, Michael. *Debts of Honour.* 1980.
Hoggart, Simon, and David Leigh. *Michael Foot: A Por-
    trait.* 1981.
Jones, Mervyn. *Michael Foot.* 1994.
Morgan, Kenneth O. *Labour People: Leaders and Lieu-
    tenants.* 1987.

Football

During the twentieth century football (soccer)
replaced CRICKET as Britain's national game. It
had more players and spectators than any other.

There were few parts of England, Scotland, or Wales where it was not the most popular sport. From September to April football was inseparable from Saturday afternoons; every town and village had their teams and leagues ranging from the most humble who played for fun to the semi-professional and the elite of paid players who performed before a paying audience for a living. By the 1930s the weekly football pool competition meant that the names of the leading professional clubs were familiar to many men and women who had never been near a football ground. Football had grown out of its regional origins in northern England, the Midlands, and Central Scotland and become part of the British popular culture. When England won the World Cup in 1966 everyone, except the Scots, rejoiced.

It was the football club that was the heart if not the soul, of the game. Both at the recreational and spectator level it was a site of sociability and the focus of local loyalties and rivalries. The English Football League, emulating American baseball, had its first season in 1888–9. The Scottish League began in 1890–1. By 1921 there were four divisions in England containing eighty-six clubs and two divisions in Scotland. This pattern has changed little since then. Promotion and relegation added to the excitement. Winning the first division became the prerogative of the big city clubs. In Scotland this meant the Glasgow "old firm" of Celtic and Rangers who were so dominant that in only four years during 1900–50 did one or other of them fail to win the championship. It was more open in England. Between 1900 and 1915 eight different clubs won the English First Division. All save Birmingham's Aston Villa were located in the north. By the 1930s Arsenal, from London, had become the dominant club winning five championships and in part reflected a shift in the economic strength of England from north to south. Arsenal remain a leading club, but Liverpool became the phenomenon of modern times, breaking all records with eleven titles since 1972.

But the most popular domestic competition is the Football Association Cup. This is a straight forward knock out first competed for in 1872. The final is usually in London, since 1923 at Wembley Stadium. If few can win the League, all can dream of winning the Cup, and big clubs are often knocked out by small fry along the way. It remains rare to win both English Cup and League. Only Tottenham (1961), Arsenal (1971) and Liverpool (1986) have done so this century.

The British not only invented modern football but persuaded most of the rest of the world to take it up. But there has always been a tension between British parochialism and international-ism. The British had their own international championship which lasted 100 years from 1883–4 to 1983–4. They refused to join the Fédération Internationale de Football Associations (FIFA) when it was established in 1904. They changed their minds after the First World War but left in 1928 following disagreements about what constituted amateurism. The British rejoined in 1946, and England first appeared in the World Cup in 1950, somewhat inauspiciously, as they lost to the United States.

The English League similarly lacked enthusiasm when the European Champions Cup began in 1955–6 and refused to allow the English champions to take part. The Scots were more sensible and their representative, Hibernian, reached the semi-finals. The following season Manchester United ignored parochialism and also reached the semi-finals. There was no British winner until Glasgow Celtic in 1967 but after that British clubs did well in what had become three European competitions. Aston Villa (1982), Manchester United (1968), Nottingham Forest (1979, 1980) and Liverpool (1977, 1978, 1981, 1984) all won the Champions Cup.

But this international success was marred by violence and hooliganism. English clubs were banned from European competition between 1986 and 1990 after crowd trouble at the 1985 European Cup Final in Brussels. Thirty-nine people, most of them Italian fans of Juventus, were crushed to death following a charge by a Liverpool section of the crowd. Violence by a small but nasty minority of young men had long disfigured the game in England. The main response was increased policing and supporter segregation.

Then came the Hillsborough disaster. Ninety-five Liverpool supporters died on the overcrowded terraces of Sheffield Wednesday before the 1989 FA Cup Semi-Final. The government set up an inquiry chaired by Lord Justice Taylor which highlighted the financial problems of the game as leisure patterns diversified. His report recommended all-seater stadiums for the leading clubs and was in tune with a growing tendency for football to become more commercialized. Sponsorship and a more affluent consumer were vigorously pursued. Large sums were obtained from television to screen live, mainly first division matches. In 1991–2 the leading twenty-two clubs broke away from the Football League to form the Premier League and to make an exclusive agreement with a satellite television company.

Tony Mason

Bibliography

Beck, P.J. *Scoring for Britain: International Football and International Politics, 1900–1939.* 1999.

Fishwick, Nicholas. *English Football and Society 1910–1950.* 1989.

Mason, Tony. *Association Football and English Society 1863–1915*. 1980.
——. "Football" in Tony Mason, ed. *Sport in Britain. A Social History*. 1989. pp. 146–86.
Walvin, James. *The People's Game: A Social History of Football*. 1975.

Ford, Ford Madox (1873–1939)

Novelist, poet and editor, art, literary and cultural critic, Ford Madox Ford (Ford Madox Hueffer until 1919) was the grandson of the painter Ford Madox Brown and, consequently, was reared on the rim of the Pre-Raphaelite circle. He repudiated it and embraced Impressionism during his years of collaboration with JOSEPH CONRAD. Ford and Conrad believed that a story could be told realistically only by rendering impressions, not by narrating events. Together Ford and Conrad wrote three novels, with *Romance* (1904) being the best known of them. Ford founded the *English Review* in December 1908 and edited it until December 1909, publishing established writers like JOHN GALSWORTHY, Thomas Hardy, W.H. Hudson, Henry James, H.G. WELLS, and Conrad, and giving voice to new writers like D.H. LAWRENCE and WYNDHAM LEWIS, both of whom Ford discovered and was the first to publish.

During this time he was involved in a notorious affair with Violet Hunt, which she commemorated in *The Flurried Years* (1928); it ended in 1919 when he was mustered out of the army, and moved to the English countryside with the Australian painter Stella Bowen.

Before joining the British Expeditionary Force to fight in Flanders and France, Ford wrote, among many other books, critical studies of Madox Brown (1896), Rossetti (1902), Holbein (1905), and the Pre-Raphaelite Brotherhood (1907); a trilogy on English culture published in the United States as *England and the English* (1907); pastiches in the manner of Henry James, of which *A Call* (1910) is most satisfying; satires on socialism and utopian thinking, the best being *The Simple Life Limited* (1911); and the historical novels of *The Fifth Queen* trilogy (1906–8) centered on Catherine Howard and Henry VIII. Ford praised James in his critical study of him (1913) as "the greatest of living writers and, in consequence, for me, the greatest of living men" just before writing his first undisputed masterpiece, *The Good Soldier* (1915), which rivals James's fiction with its elegance of form and its indictment of society. This novel of manners explores the sexual life of two upper-class couples and represents the perfection of Ford's idea of a novel: "the rendering of an Affair: of one embroilment, one set of embarrassments, one human coil, one psychological progression."

Ford published seven volumes of poetry before establishing a place for himself as a war poet in *On Heaven and Poems Written on Active Service* (1918). It answered his demand for a poetry that was at least as good as the best prose, a poetry that is written the way one speaks, expressing one's thoughts in the language of the day. Ford's final collection of poems, *Buckshee* in *Collected Poems* (1936), realizes this program completely in its concluding poem "Coda," a meditation on time.

Ford settled in France, shuttling between Paris and Provence, in 1922. He founded the *Transatlantic Review*, which survived for twelve issues in 1924, publishing such avant-garde writers as e.e.cummings, Ernest Hemingway, JAMES JOYCE, Ezra Pound, Gertrude Stein, and William Carlos Williams. At this time Ford began writing *Parade's End* (1924–8), a tetralogy (some insist it is a trilogy) on the Great War, which is arguably the best novel to emerge from the FIRST WORLD WAR. In the tortured relationships of Christopher Tietjens with his wife and lover, Ford realizes fully his constant theme of the anguish of sexuality, drawing modern human beings into love as uneasy compensation for modern war's witness that "man is to man a wolf." The completion of *Parade's End* coincided with the end of his relationship with Stella Bowen and the beginning of his association with Janice Biala, a Polish-American painter, which lasted until his death.

Parade's End made Ford a celebrity in the United States, where he traveled extensively and tirelessly promoted the works of young American writers. He continued to publish books until they numbered eighty-one at the time of his death. He completed a series of autobiographical memoirs that began with *Ancient Lights* (1911), continued in *Thus to Revisit* (1921) and *Return to Yesterday* (1931), and ended with *It was the Nightingale* (1933), all of which emphasize his literary, not his personal, life. Ford's last book was *The March of Literature from Confucius's Day to Our Own* (1938), written while he was teaching at Olivet College in Michigan, "a refuge for good writers who are down on their end-bones." He died in Deauville, France, on 26 June 1939.

Joseph Wiesenfarth

Bibliography
Green, Robert. *Ford Madox Ford: Prose and Politics*. 1981.
Judd, Alan. *Ford Madox Ford*. 1991.
MacShane, Frank. *The Life and Work of Ford Madox Ford*. 1965.
Moser, Thomas C. *The Life in the Fiction of Ford Madox Ford*. 1980.

Forster, E(dward) M(organ) (1879–1970)

E.M. Forster, known to his friends as Morgan, was a leading British novelist of the twentieth century, with his own special position, asserting his own point of view, more intensely English than those somewhat earlier residents, JOSEPH CONRAD and Henry James, who came to live and write in England, less of a realist than his immediate predecessors, the Edwardian novelists H.G. WELLS and ARNOLD BENNETT, less passionate than D.H. LAWRENCE. He was more of a modernist than Wells or Bennett, but less of a one than VIRGINIA WOOLF or JAMES JOYCE. He is a novelist and essayist who has much to say to the general reader as well as to any student of literature and of modern Britain.

Forster was the son of an architect, Edward Morgan Forster, who was descended from the Clapham Sect, a group of early nineteenth-century evangelical Anglicans who were devout philanthropists, particularly concerned with fighting the slave trade. Although in a formal sense, Forster abandoned their values, he maintained, in a modern version, and in a much more light hearted way, a good deal of their moral seriousness. Marianne, a daughter of Henry Thornton of Clapham, regarded Edward Forster as her favorite nephew and encouraged his marriage in 1877 to her protegee, Lily Whichelo. Their first child died at birth; the second, born on New Year's Day, 1879, was to be called Henry Morgan Forster but, at his christening, in a typical Forsterian confusion, his father provided his own first name by mistake. Edward Morgan he remained thereafter. His father died when Forster was twenty-two months old, and in his early years he was surrounded and doted on by women: his mother and her mother, and his great aunt Marianne. When she died in 1887, she left him a legacy of £8,000 which gave him enough financial security until he began to make a comfortable living from his writings. He published her biography, *Marianne Thornton*, in 1956, which concluded: "she and no one else made my career as a writer possible, and her love, in a most tangible sense, followed me beyond the grave." Hence in his earliest life, the theme of *Howards End*, money's ability to confer freedom, had been introduced. He had a happy childhood, living from 1883 to 1893 at Rooksnest, at Stevenage in Hertforshire, which served as the model for the house Howards End.

As was typical of literary members of the English middle class, happiness was much curtailed when Forster went to boarding school, at the age of eleven, to Kent House in Eastbourne, and then, an intensely unhappy eight years at Tonbridge, which he would pillory as Sawston in *The Longest Journey*. He then went to King's College, CAMBRIDGE in 1897, where he was supremely happy. His academic career was not particularly distinguished, but he made great friends there,

became a member of the secret discussion society, the Apostles, and was encouraged in his interests by two young dons, Goldsworthy Lowes Dickinson (whose biography he wrote in 1934) and Nathaniel Wedd.

Trips to Italy with his mother helped to liberate his imagination, and his first published story, "The Story of a Panic," (1904) tells of the central character, Eustace's, encounter with Pan in Ravello near Naples. It was there in 1902 that Forster became convinced of his vocation as a writer. His first novel, *Where Angels Fear to Tread*, was published in 1905. As in the story, Italy stands for the excitement of liberation, and its dangers, and is counterpoised to the restricted emotions of the English, and what Forster sees as their undeveloped hearts. Lila Herriton, a young widow, takes an extended trip to Italy, where she secretly marries Gino, a younger lower middle-class Italian. Forster gives such characters vitality and fecundity—they have a son—but he does not make them perfect noble savages. Lila's brother-in-law, Philip, one of Forster's Englishmen who thinks he understands, but doesn't, whose emotions have been curdled by thought, makes two trips to Italy to interfere, once to prevent a marriage that has already taken place, and second to kidnap the son of the union, an adventure that ends with an overturned carriage and the death of the baby.

His second novel, *The Longest Journey* (1907) is a less polished performance, and is more typical of a first novel, something of a *Bildungsroman*, appropriately dedicated to the Apostles. It tells of Rickie, whose lameness stands for his emotional limitations. He is an observer, but when Agnes Pembroke's fiancé, Gerald, dies, Rickie eventually marries her. The famous opening of the fifth chapter, "Gerald died that afternoon," demonstrates Forster's technique that CHRISTOPHER ISHERWOOD called "tea-tabling", a suggestion that violence can lurk beneath the decorum of English society. Like Gino in *Where Angels Fear to Tread*, Stephen Wonham, Rickie's illegitimate half-brother, stands for the more emotional side of life, uncontrolled and exciting. The novel ends with Rickie sacrificing his own life in order to save the drunken Stephen.

His third novel, *A Room with a View* (1908), made even better known through a very successful movie version (1986), tells a similar story but unlike the two previous novels, ends happily. Lucy Honeychurch has her feelings liberated by a visit to Florence, and being kissed in a field by George Emerson. Back in England, she attempts to turn away from her true feelings by becoming engaged to the prig Cecil Vyse, but with the proddings of George's father, and the manipulations of her cousin, the apparently unsympathic

Charlotte, she realizes the necessity to follow her true feelings and marry George.

These three novels, though charming and effective, might not have survived if Forster had not gone on to write his two major works, *Howards End* (1910) and *A Passage to India* (1924)—opinions are divided on which is the more important, with perhaps the latter having an edge. *Howards End* was a great success, established Forster's reputation as a major novelist, and was his first novel to be published in America. The story catches with uncanny and prophetic exactitude the growing conflict between the world of "telegrams and anger" and the idealism and vulnerability of the liberal tradition at the end of its tether. It preaches the message of the need to "only connect" the prose and the passion, the world of the Wilcoxes, those who make money, and the Schlegels, those who believe in the arts and the importance of personal relations. The details of the social novel, questions of property, the tolerated violations of conventions by men (Mr Wilcox has had a mistress) and the not tolerated violations by women (Helen has an illegitimate child) take a parallel course to more sweeping questions: the role of nature, permanence, abiding English qualities, and even a certain mysticism in the role of Mrs Wilcox, her house, and the wych elm that shadows it. The novel ends happily—the baby—Margaret's nephew, will inherit the house—and unhappily—Margaret is not able to save Henry Wilcox and make him see connections. Having written four novels in five years, Forster did not publish another novel until fourteen year later, and it would prove to be his last, even though he lived until 1970.

Since 1906 he had known Syed Ross Masood, and in 1910 he declared his passion for him, which was gently rebuffed. They remained close friends; Masood guided him in India in 1912, and would be the dedicatee of *A Passage to India*. In 1910 too he came closer to the BLOOMSBURY GROUP, and saw its members with increasing frequency. He started a novel, *Artic Summer*, but abandoned it. Inspired by a visit to Edward Carpenter, the apostle of socialism and HOMOSEXUALITY, in 1913 he wrote a novel of happy homosexual love, *Maurice*, but it was not published until 1971. He published one collection of short stores, *The Celestial Omnibus*, in 1911, and another, *The Eternal Moment*, in 1928. Before the war he also started to write short stories with erotic themes for his own amusement. These, and later stories, were published posthumously in *The Life to Come* (1972).

Forster started to write his Indian novel before the war, partially inspired by his trip, and after the war by serving as a secretary to the eccentric Marajahah of Dewas in 1921, an experience commemorated in his book *The Hill of Devi* (1953). During the First World War he worked in the National Gallery and then for the Red Cross in Alexandria, resulting in two publications, *Alexandria: A History and Guide* (1922) and *Pharos and Pharillon* (1923). He also has his first affair, with Mohammed el Adl, and from then on his personal life was much more fulfilled. For him, the war had represented the defeat of reason, and *A Passage to India* is a darker novel than his previous ones. Despite their efforts, the Indians and the English are not able to get along, life is reduced to the meaninglessness, and the possible transcendence, of the "ou-boum" of the Marabar caves where Adela Quested thought, and then thought not, that she had been molested by Dr Aziz. Connections are even less possible than they were in the world of *Howards End*. The Indians elevate Mrs Moore into a deity, and Fielding and Aziz mean to be friends. But nature—in the shape of the rocks that divide them on their horseback ride at the conclusion of the novel—will not permit it. In the novel the social and the visionary impulses are magically joined. Seldom has there been a more convincing portrait of decent men and women trapped in the impossibilities of the imperial situation. Seldom has there been a more haunting evocation of the irrationalism that underlies so much of human behavior.

He wrote as well a book of literary criticism, *Aspects of the Novel* (1927) and two gatherings of essays, *Abinger Harvest* (1936) and *Two Cheers for Democracy* (1951),("only Love the Beloved Republic deserves [three]"). In 1924 he inherited the house his father had built for his aunt Laura, and that would be his main home until he moved to King's College in 1946. There he would live until 1970, though dying at Coventry at the home of his long time lover and his wife. He used his authority against the suppression of literature, as when he defended *The Well of Loneliness* in 1928 and *Lady Chatterley's Lover* in 1960. He came to embody those virtues that we think of as peculiarly English: a firm belief in liberty, in fairness, in standing up for individual values, in refusing to be pompous, hieratical, self-adulating. In an intensely personal way he was not so distant from his Thornton forebears. Through his novels, and his other writings, he aimed to give pleasure, fulfill his aesthetic values, and also, to a degree, to improve the world and help the causes of private and public liberation.

Peter Stansky

Bibliography

Beauman, Nicola. *Morgan: A Biography of E.M. Forster.* 1993.

Crews, Frederick C. *E.M. Forster: The Perils of Humanism.* 1962.

Furbank, P.N. *E.M. Forster: A Life.* 1977–78.

Kirkpatrick, B.J. *A Bibliography of E.M. Forster*. 2nd ed. 1985.

Lago, Mary, and P.N. Furbank, ed. *Selected Letters of E.M. Forster*. 2 vols. 1983–5.

Stone, Wilfred. *The Cave and the Mountain*. 1966.

Trilling, Lionel. *E.M. Forster*. 1943.

Freud, Lucian (1922–)

Lucian Freud is widely regarded as Britain's foremost painter in the expressive figurative tradition, at least since the death of his one time mentor, FRANCIS BACON. With his psychologically charged, often theatrically posed, images of alienated naked figures in drab urban interiors, his moody, muted pallette, and "hard won" painterliness, Freud is an exemplary member of the "School of London," which also includes such painters as Frank Auerbach, Leon Kossoff, and the younger American-born painter R.B. Kitaj.

Born in Berlin in 1922, he was the son of architect Max Freud and grandson of Sigmund Freud, a lineage that has undoubtedly played a role in the exotic persona Freud has always managed to cultivate. He moved with his family to England in 1932 and was educated at progressive boarding schools. In 1939, the year he became a naturalized British subject, Freud enrolled briefly at the East Anglian School of Painting and Drawing, Dedham, his only formal training.

He first came to public attention with drawings published in the wartime literary journal, *Horizon*. Early works demonstrate a tentative Surrealism, with incongruous arrangements of objects such as a stuffed zebra's head, a battered chaise longue, and a cactus plant, but he was more closely associated with the Neo-Romantic group which thrived in London during and after the Second World War. Intense, bulbuous eyes, for instance, a characteristic of his early portraits, relate to the work of other artists in this group, such as John Minton, whose portrait he painted.

Freud made his own mark with meticulously executed realist works with a pervasive mood of alienation. Herbert Read dubbed him "the Ingres of existentialism," a perceptive remark in the context of an image such as *Interior in Paddington* (1951, Walker Art Gallery, Liverpool) which places an archetypal "angry young man" in dishevelled rain coat, cigarette in one hand, the other fist clenched, in claustrophobic proximity to a meticulously executed man-sized potted plant in an anonymous interior space. Later poses with comparable theatrical props include a male nude holding a rat (1977–8) and a female nude staring at a hard boiled egg halved in a dish (1980–1).

By the late 1950s Freud lost interest in the meticulous, Ingres-like sheen. He began to describe the face and body in terms of shape and structure, in *Pregnant Girl* (1960–1, private collection, United States) for instance; and often in female nudes the brushstrokes help to delineate shape. By the time of the monumental 1985 self-portrait (private collection) attention to tonal detail is so acute, however, that paint builds up in concentrations devoid of any compositional function.

A close relationship with sitters is said to be important for Freud and on occasion contributes to his mystique as an artist. His widowed mother sat for an extensive series in the early 1970s, while several of his daughters have modelled nude. The 1980s and 1990s were marked by increasingly ambitious compositions—both in terms of scale and complexity. The standard was set by *Large Interior, WII (After Watteau)* (1981–3, private collection) which involves five sitters (family members and his then mistress, the artist Celia Paul) arranged in homage to Watteau's *Pierrot Content* (1712).

A series of monumental male nudes from the early 1990s feature the transvestite performance artist Leigh Bowery. More "establishment" sitters have included Sir Jacob Rothschild, Lord Goodman, and Baron Thyssen-Bornemisza. Although the human form dominates his output, Freud has also executed cityscapes (viewed from his studio window) and obsessively detailed nature studies *Two Plants* (1977–80, Tate Gallery). These recall STANLEY SPENCER, who might also be considered a precursor for nudes where there is a macabre attention to blood vessels and veins. His artistic reputation was confirmed when he was named a Companion of Honour and later awarded the Order of Merit.

David Cohen

Bibliography

Feaver, William. *Lucian Freud* (exhibition catalogue, Tate Gallery). 2002.

Freud, Lucian, Nicholas Penny and Robert Flynn Johnson. *Lucian Freud: Works on Paper* (exhibition catalogue, South Bank). 1988.

Gowing, Lawrence. *Lucian Freud*. 1982.

Hughes, Robert, *Lucian Freud: Paintings* (exhibition catalogue, British Council). 1987.

Lampert, Catherine. *Lucian Freud: Recent Work*. 1993.

Friends, Society of [Quakers]

British Quakerism began the twentieth century in a state of considerable theological ferment. The Evangelicalism of the Victorian era, which had to some extent disfigured the distinctive Quaker identity during the previous century and made it difficult to distinguish the Society of Friends from many of the other Nonconformist denominations of the period, was gradually giving way to the intellectual liberation of the so-called "liberal theology" of the day. The first decades of the century indeed came to be regarded as a

Quaker Renaissance, when the energies and talents of a hitherto somewhat introspective Society were turned more firmly outward than ever before, and Quakers sought and attained for themselves an influential role in the public culture of the nation rather disproportionate to their relatively small numbers. Quakers were increasingly keen to realign their faith with contemporary Biblical scholarship, simultaneously undermining the place of Scripture in their corporate religious life while renewing the reliance on those "experiential" truths which were seen to be the hallmark of their seventeenth-century forebears.

A new emphasis on social responsibility and Quaker witness in national and international affairs gave rise to a generation of British Friends committed to bringing the historic values and testimonies of the Society more directly into public life. The work of Quaker thinkers and writers like Edward Grubb, John William Graham, and, most especially, John Wilhelm Rowntree helped shape an ideal of Quaker civic virtue and enlightened imperial citizenship. Quaker MPs like J. Allen Baker, T. Edmund Harvey, and Arnold Rowntree represented the Society's concerns about disarmament, international conciliation, and social justice in the House of Commons with eloquence and occasional distinction.

Educational endeavors assumed a heightened importance in the life of the Society, particularly with the foundation of Woodbrooke College at Birmingham in 1903. This institution, made possible through the generosity and vision of the irrepressible Quaker industrialist and philanthropist George Cadbury, aimed to raise the intellectual standards of Quaker ministry and provided the Society with sources of spiritual nourishment that continue to flourish today. Woodbrooke and the Summer School Movement out of which it grew, and the leadership of masterful Quaker teachers like Rendel Harris and John Wilhelm Rowntree, became the inspiration and formative influence for many of the most significant British Friends of the twentieth century.

The FIRST WORLD WAR prompted a comprehensive and sometimes painful re-examination of the Society's pacifist heritage. British Quakers were forced to re-interpret their historic Peace Testimony of 1661 for the new century, and a consensus on the appropriate response to the European conflict was often difficult to achieve. While some Friends were eager to hold to what might be called the purist line on Quaker pacifism—refusing to consider any form of service in the larger war effort on the grounds that even such non-combatant activity could be construed as participation in the militarist system—others felt that Friends had an obligation to commit themselves to some form of amelioration of the war's horrors. The Friends' Ambulance Unit, started in 1914 by the young Philip Noel-Baker (later to be awarded the Nobel Peace Prize in 1959 for his lifelong commitment to disarmament), provided less absolutist Quakers—including many CONSCIENTIOUS OBJECTORS after the introduction of CONSCRIPTION in 1916—with a new opportunity for humanitarian intervention which could also claim strong roots in Quaker tradition. However, other total objectors chose to demonstrate their convictions by enduring lengthy and harsh prison sentences for their refusal to perform either military or alternative service.

The defining fire of the First World War experience forged a new and more mature internationalism among British Quakers. This was exhibited in the work of the Friends War Victims Relief Committee and the Committee for International Service (founded in 1919 and subsequently absorbed into the Friends Service Council in 1927), both of which brought considerable distinction to the Society of Friends with their contribution to the European reconstruction effort. The eminent Quaker peace activist Carl Heath helped consolidate and expand this reputation with his proposal for the establishment of permanent Quaker Centers in a number of European capitals, several of which flourished throught the 1920s and 1930s and played a notable role in efforts to defuse inter-war tensions and to aid the victims of Fascism. With the founding of the Quaker Center at the LEAGUE OF NATIONS in Geneva in 1922 (now the Quaker United Nations Office), the Society embarked on a venture in international conciliation and alternative diplomacy that was to develop in the post-war United Nations era into one of the most respected non-governmental organizations working in the fields of disarmament, conflict resolution, and human rights. In 1947, at the close of the SECOND WORLD WAR (during which both the Friends Ambulance Unit and the Friends War Victims Relief Committee had again made significant humanitarian contributions), the British Friends Service Council and its counterpart body the American Friends Service Committee were jointly awarded the Nobel Peace Prize for their work.

Since the Second World War British Quakerism has grown into a far more heterogeneous community than at any other period in its history. The distinctly "universalist" flavor of much late twentieth-century Quaker theology has made the Society an active and much-welcomed participant in a wide range of inter-denominational and inter-faith activities, although the shift away from the Christo-centric basis of traditional Quakerism has met with a measure of opposition from those who fear the distortion of the Quaker inheritance into a recipe for a kind of bland ecumenism. Internationalism and the embrace of widely divergent Quaker traditions within the British Society of Friends had received a major boost with the establishment of the Friends World Committee for Consultation in 1937, a London-based body which continues to foster vital links among Quakers world-wide. Since 1945 British Quakers have consistently provided leadership, financial resources, and inspiration to a host of domestic initiatives promoting race relations, civil rights, and social and economic justice. Among British religious communities, the Society has made contributions to national debates about criminal justice, national security issues, education, and the rights of women and of homosexuals. In the last decade of the century the Society of Friends remains a vibrant and progressive spiritual forum, showing little sign of the decline which has stalked so many other British denominations in recent decades.

Brian Phillips

Bibliography

Kavanaugh, John, ed. *The Quaker Approach to Contemporary Problems*. 1953.

Kennedy, Thomas C. "The Quaker Renaissance and the Origins of the Modern British Peace Movement, 1895–1920," *Albion*, vol. 16 (1974), pp. 243–72.

Orr, E.W. *The Quakers in Peace and War, 1920–1967.* 1974.

Punshon, John. *Portrait in Grey: A Short History of the Quakers*. 1984.

Wilson, Roger C. *Quaker Relief.* 1952.

Yarrow, C.H. Mike. *Quaker Experiences in International Conciliation.* 1978.

Fry, Roger Eliot (1866–1934)

Roger Fry was, in SIR KENNETH CLARK's view, "incomparably the greatest influence on taste in England since Ruskin." Fry was described by the ARTS COUNCIL in 1952, on the occasion of an exhibition of his paintings, as a person of "legendary fame." He was a dedicated polymath, most anxious to achieve in just that area where he had in the opinion of many the least talent: as a creative artist, a painter. His paintings are relatively drab but are fascinating testimonials to his unceasing search for visual acuity and truth as he perceived it. His lasting legacy to the discipline of art history is the use of the term Post-Impressionist, in connection with the two major, revelatory exhibitions of Post-Impressionist French painting he curated in London at the Grafton Galleries in 1910 and 1912. The 1910 exhibition, called Manet and the Post-Impressionists, consisted over over 150 paintings, not only Manet, but focusing on Cezanne, Gauguin, and Van Gogh. He was savagely criticized for promoting such outrageous

art, and he himself referred to the storm of protest as an "outbreak of militant philistinism." Matisse was prominently featured in the 1912 exhibition, as were the Russian avant-garde and younger English artists (the second Post-Impressionist exhibition).

Fry was born in London to a distinguished Quaker family—his father, Sir Edward Fry, was a judge—and he studied science at King's College, CAMBRIDGE, where he took an outstanding degree (a "double first" in both parts of the natural sciences tripos). At Cambridge Fry was elected a member of the Apostles, the secret society credited with wielding a striking intellectual influence on English life. He also came under the influence of Professor J.C. Middleton, the art historian, who encouraged an emergent interest in drawing and painting. Fry went on to study painting and art history in Italy and Paris. Back in London in the 1890s he also studied art with the leading painter and printmaker, W.R. SICKERT. He not only began to paint with dedication but started a parallel career as a reviewer, critic, lecturer, and author. By 1901 he was the regular art critic for the *Athenaeum*. Fry was a lobbyist for the visual arts, involved in the foundation of the National Art Collections Fund (1903), which acquired works of fine and decorative arts for public collections in Britain, the *Burlington Magazine*, the preeminent periodical of art history, of which he was editor 1910–19, and the Contemporary Art Society in 1910. From the time he "discovered" Cezanne in 1906, he was aligned with Bloomsbury artists and writers, the critic Clive Bell and his wife, the painter VANESSA BELL, with whom he had a romantic liaison for several years—Fry was to have affairs with many women including Lady Ottoline Morrell, the alcoholic but talented painter Nina Hamnett, finally settling for nearly the last decade of his life with Helen Anrep. His own wife, the artist Helen Coombe, who was incurably mentally ill, outlived Fry by three years. Both VIRGINIA WOOLF and Quentin Bell were to write posthumous appreciative biographical memoirs of Fry.

Roger Fry had an unhappy period commuting to America as the curator of paintings for the Metropolitan Museum of Art in New York (1905–10). He had been offered the directorship of the National Gallery, London, just after he had accepted the offer of the Metropolitan and had felt morally bound to refuse; but his metier remained Europe. After difficulties with J.P. Morgan, the President of the Metropolitan, he left the museum; in 1911, he was to refuse the directorship of the Tate Gallery. He founded, with others of the BLOOMSBURY GROUP and WYNDHAM LEWIS, with whom he was to quarrel, the

Omega Workshops (1913) for the creation of objects for domestic use, decorated furniture, textiles, pottery, and the like. The Workshop has several purposes: to reform design in the applied arts and to offer opportunties to young artists.

In different ways Fry's activities have influenced the appreciation and understanding of art. His championing of the moderns—Cezanne, Van Gogh, Gauguin, the Fauves, Matisse, Picasso—brought their art to the attention of the British public. The breadth and depth of his interest, his passionate advocacy of Italian primitives as well as the most advanced art of his time, and his emphasis on the formal qualities of painting as more important than the ostensible subject all contributed mightily to new ways of approaching visual imagery. A volume of his lectures and reviews, gathered together in a collection called *Vision and Design* (1920), was one of the first Pelicans to be published and helped, along with his other books, to make his influence felt far and wide.

Marina Vaizey

Bibliography

Arts Council. *Vision and Design: The Life, Work and Influence of Roger Fry*. 1966.

Reed, Christopher. *A Roger Fry Reader*. 1996.

Spalding, Frances. *Roger Fry: Art and Life*. 1980.

Sutton, Denys, ed. *Letters of Roger Fry*. 2 vols. 1972.

Woolf, Virginia. *Roger Fry: A Biography*. 1940.

G

Gaitskell, Hugh Todd Naylor (1906–1963)

Hugh Gaitskell was Leader of the LABOUR PARTY from December 1955 until his death in January 1963. He was a Labour MP from 1945 to 1963 and served as Minister of Fuel and Power (1947–50) and Chancellor of the Exchequer (1950–1) in ATTLEE's post-war government.

Born 9 April 1906, Gaitskell was educated at Winchester and New College, OXFORD, where he was taught and influenced by the socialist theorist G.D.H. COLE. By the time of the GENERAL STRIKE in 1926 he had developed strong sympathies with the labor movement. After a brief but influential period as an ADULT EDUCATION tutor in the Nottinghamshire coalfield, Gaitskell became an economics lecturer in 1928 at University College, London, where he remained until 1939. Throughout the 1930s he was part of a small group of mainly Oxford-educated and London-based socialist intellectuals—the other members included Douglas Jay and Evan Durbin—who were eager to introduce Keynesian ideas on economic management into the Labour Party.

During the SECOND WORLD WAR Gaitskell, as a German-speaking economist, served with distinction as a temporary civil servant—first, in the Ministry of Economic Warfare and later at the Board of Trade as HUGH DALTON's personal assistant.

Elected to Parliament in 1945 as Member for Leeds South, Gaitskell was appointed Parliamentary Secretary and then Minister of Fuel and Power and efficiently supervised the NATIONALIZATION of the gas industry. He also played a key role in persuading the party leadership to accept the need for devaluing the pound during a sterling crisis in summer 1949. His evident grasp of the economic issues involved in that episode strengthened his claims to succeed SIR STAFFORD CRIPPS as Chancellor of the Exchequer. Appointed in 1950 at the age of forty-three, Gaitskell faced as Chancellor the central problem of how to finance a greatly increased rearmament program, which he favored, from early 1951 onwards. By that time he had become a fervent supporter of the Anglo-American alliance.

Another major area of controversy during his term as Chancellor concerned his decision to impose selective charges for NATIONAL HEALTH SERVICE patients. This led to the resignation from the government of ANEURIN BEVAN, the acknowledged leader of the Labour Left, and HAROLD WILSON. The subsequent struggle with Bevan and his supporters was the first of a succession of internal party conflicts in which Gaitskell was to be embroiled.

In December 1955 he succeeded Attlee as Labour Party Leader, easily defeating his main rivals, HERBERT MORRISON and Aneurin Bevan. His period of leadership was marked by fierce disputes and deep divisions within the party. At first, however, reconciliation seemed to be a major concern, with Bevan coming to the new Leader's aid by opposing unilateral nuclear disarmament at the 1957 Party Conference.

In the field of foreign policy Gaitskell proposed fresh initiatives for multilateral disarmament. He sympathized with the Rapacki Plan for a demilitarized zone, which would include the whole of Germany in Central Europe. He built, too, on Britain's pivotal role in the Commonwealth, forging new links with the Third World and with non-aligned states. In the SUEZ CRISIS of 1956 Gaitskell opposed the Anglo-French invasion of Egypt. His attitude was shaped by his preference for close collaboration with the United States as well as by his own moral commitment to the United Nations.

In domestic affairs Gaitskell soon became closely identified with the REVISIONIST position in the party debate over public ownership and its place in socialist policy and strategy. He shared the view held by TONY CROSLAND and others that the traditional identification of socialism with the public ownership of the means of production was no longer relevant in the post-1945 world. Instead, he favored a more ethical approach to socialism, which he viewed as "a collection of ideals towards which we hope to advance." Public ownership and NATIONALIZATION, its most commonly practiced form, were to be regarded merely as useful means of furthering those socialist ideals, rather than as fundamental. The central pillar of his socialism was equality, to be pursued through high social expenditure financed by steady economic growth and by redistributive taxation.

Following Labour's third successive general election defeat in 1959, the party was convulsed by bitter and divisive controversies. These centered around, first, the question of the party leadership, with Gaitskell an increasingly beleaguered figure; second, the future direction of Labour policy; and third, fundamental aspects of socialist doctrine. More specifically, deep divisions appeared over the issues of public ownership, nuclear defense, and the EUROPEAN COMMUNITY.

On the first of these Gaitskell raised the political temperature by attempting in 1959–60 to amend Clause IV of the party constitution. He believed that the clause was a source of misunderstanding and electoral unpopularity insofar as it implied a commitment by Labour to the public ownership of the whole—or at least the bulk—of the British economy. By 1959 Gaitskell had reached the conclusion that its amendment was necessary in order to remove that damaging misconception and to clarify, too, the party's broader socialist aims. However, his proposal, made largely without advice or encouragement from his friends, aroused deep suspicion and unease throughout the party. There was a widespread fear that his plans posed a grave threat to Labour's socialist identity and purpose.

Gaitskell's stance in this controversy was further undermined by the manner in which, throughout 1960, the Clause IV and nuclear defence issues converged. Most of the biggest trade unions, which had provided in the past vital support for Gaitskell, opposed his proposal to change the party constitution. Three of those unions—the Engineers, TRANSPORT WORKERS, and Railwaymen—at the same time declared their support for a unilateralist defense policy.

Faced by the hostility of the Left and by the indignation of the trade unionist center of the party, and caught up in a gathering onslaught against his defense policy, Gaitskell was eventually forced in 1960 to abandon any attempt to amend Clause IV.

In his simultaneous struggle with nuclear unilateralists in the party, Gaitskell was defeated at the 1960 Scarborough Conference where, in a celebrated speech, he displayed political courage in resolving to "fight and fight again". He did indeed fight back to overturn the 1960 unilateralist decision at the Blackpool Conference the following year.

On the European question Gaitskell broke with most of his closest supporters at the 1962 Party Conference by opposing British membership of the European Community. He succeeded, however, in what was to be the last great controversy of his political career, in uniting the bulk of the party on this issue.

By the end of 1962 it seemed to many that Gaitskell's leadership was unchallenged, with his public and party prestige at an unprecedented peak. He was then suddenly struck down by a rare collagen disease and died in London on 18 January 1963.

Gaitskell's premature and unexpected death, at the height of his powers, occurred at a time when Labour's electoral prospects seemed promising. Certainly his style of party leadership had been assertive and at times confrontational. His qualities—courage, determination, trustworthiness, intellectual honesty—were widely recognized. Yet in the eyes of his critics, these were offset by failings of stubbornness, intolerance, and inflexibility. His detractors claimed, too, that he lacked any real understanding of the labor movement.

Nevertheless, by the early 1960s Gaitskell appeared to his diverse admirers to be supremely well-equipped to serve as a distinguished British Prime Minister. Many have since concurred with Williams's judgment that, had it not been for a cruel twist of fate, Gaitskell might indeed "have been the great peacetime leader that twentieth-century Britain has badly missed, and sadly failed to find."

Tudor Jones

Bibliography
Brivati, Brian. *Hugh Gaitskell*. 1996.
Durbin, Elizabeth. *New Jerusalems: The Labour Party and the Economics of Democratic Socialism*. 1985.
Rodgers, W.T., ed. *Hugh Gaitskell, 1906–63*. 1964.
Williams, Philip M. *Hugh Gaitskell: A Political Biography*. 1979.

Gallipoli

The operations at the Dardanelles and on the Gallipoli Peninsula arose out of the desire of WINSTON CHURCHILL as First Lord of the Admiralty to use the ROYAL NAVY offensively and the willingness of the War Council to believe that seapower alone could exercise a decisive influence on the outcome of the FIRST WORLD WAR.

Turkey had announced its adherence to the Central Powers in October 1914, and Britain had declared war on it on 5 November. Churchill's scheme involved eliminating the forts protecting the Dardanelles and passing a fleet through the Straits to Constantinople. The Turks would then surrender, the Balkan States unite against the Central Powers, and a combined Balkan army under British leadership proceed up the Danube valley, attacking Austria and Germany from the rear and forcing their surrender. In the interim the Straits would be open to Russia, enabling that state to sell its wheat on world markets to pay for military supplies channelled to it by the British and French.

Naval operations against the Dardanelles forts began on 19 February 1915. A British fleet of twelve battleships eliminated the outer forts and entered the Straits to deal with those at the Narrows. Here the operation stalled. The ships could not get close enough to the forts to brings decisive fire to bear because of a series of minefields laid in the Straits by the Turks. These minefields could not be swept by the hastily improvised British mine-sweepers owing to heavy fire from mobile howitzers on the Gallipoli Peninsula. The howitzers could not be eliminated by the ships' guns. A major operation on 18 March by eighteen ships succeeded only in the sinking of three battleships and the crippling of three others.

LORD KITCHENER, Secretary of State for War, now decided that troops must be landed on the Peninsula to capture the forts, thus allowing the fleet through. On hand was a contingent of Australian and New Zealand troops training in Egypt. To these were added the British 29 Division, the Royal Naval Division, and a French division, making a total of 70,000 troops. Six weeks were required for the newly appointed Commander, Sir Ian Hamilton, to prepare this force, thus giving the Turks time to strengthen their defenses on the Peninsula.

The first landings took place on 25 April. The 29 Division landed on the toe of the Peninsula around Cape Hellas and a combined force of Australian and New Zealand troops (the ANZAC Corps) landed near Gaba Tepe opposite the Narrows forts. In the event, although successful lodgements were made in both areas, neither proved capable of much expansion. At Hellas British troops, reinforced later by the French, lacked the firepower in the form of heavy artillery to blow the Turkish defenders out of their entrenched positions. Three attempts to advance (1st, 2nd, 3rd Battles of Krithia) without such fire support were halted with great loss of life. In the ANZAC area the hilly and tortuous country, which as much as the Turkish defender, had thwarted progress inland on the 25th, continued to prevent even the launching of coherent operations. Through the months of May, June, and July, a stalemate occurred, while sickness began to take its toll of the attackers.

During this time the War Council in London resolved on an operation to break the deadlock. A new Corps (IX) composed of Kitchener Divisions was sent out, along with various other reinforcements for the Anzac troops. On 6 August a determined effort was made to outflank the Turkish positions facing the ANZAC perimeter and capture the Sari Bair Ridge which dominated the position. The plan proved too ambitious. Several small lodgements were made on the ridge but the small numbers involved were easily driven off by Turkish counter-attacks. A landing to the north of Anzac by the IX Corps at Suvla Bay managed to secure some ground that could be used as a base but was largely irrelevant to the main operation.

Following the August failure Hamilton was sacked and a new Commander (Monro) appointed. He recommended immediate evacuation. Kitchener refused to accept Monro's views but after visiting the Peninsula came to the same conclusion. The ANZAC position was evacuated on 19 December and Hellas on 8 January. This facet of the operation was well-planned and there were no casualties, the Turks seemingly unaware that Allied troops were leaving the Peninsula.

The Gallipoli operations cost the Allies 265,000 casualties (49,000 dead) and the Turks over 300,000 (90,000 dead). The strategic basis on which it was mounted was largely illusory. There is little evidence that the Turks would have surrendered to a British Fleet off Constantinople, less that the Balkan States would have sunk their ancient hatreds to combine against such a formidable foe as Germany. In any case their armies were little more than peasant levies—no match for the battle-hardened forces of the Central Powers. As for Russia, transportation difficulties to the ports and lack of shipping would have prevented the sale of wheat abroad. Nor did the Allies have any surplus munitions with which to supply their eastern ally. After Gallipoli the attention of the British returned to what was always the decisive question of the war—how to defeat the German army on the Western Front.

Robin Prior
Trevor Wilson

Bibliography
James, Robert Rhodes. *Gallipoli*. 1965.
Moorehead, Alan. *Gallipoli*. 1956.
Prior, Robin. *Churchill's World Crisis as History*. 1983.
Robertson, John. *Anzac and Empire: The Tragedy and Glory of Gallipoli*. 1990.
Wilson, Trevor. *The Myriad Faces of War: Britain and the Great War 1914–1918*. 1986.

Galsworthy, John (1867–1933)

In 1932, at the height of his fame, John Galsworthy was renowned the world over, a member of the Order of Merit, a founder and first president of PEN International, and a recipient of the Nobel Prize for Literature. Never out of print in either Britain or America, and translated into almost innumerable languages, his magnum opus, *The Forsyte Saga* (a trilogy including *A Man of Property* (1906), *In Chancery* (1920), *To Let* (1921), and two connecting stories) is the quintessential Edwardian work of fiction. In it, and in other novels and plays, Galsworthy captured and portrayed the values of British society of his time.

Galsworthy was born in Surrey, the son of a wealthy, property-owning solicitor and an unaffectionate mother twenty years her husband's junior. He attended Harrow and OXFORD without distinction, interested only in clothes and HORSE RACING, and learning to affect a monocle. At his father's insistence he studied law in London and was called to the bar at Lincoln's Inn, but never had a brief of his own. Instead, he collected rents from his father's SLUM properties. Galsworthy's interest in social reform stems from this activity.

In an attempt to motivate his son, the senior Galsworthy sent John on trips to different parts of the Empire. On one of them he met one of the two people who would influence him towards a career as a writer. JOSEPH CONRAD was first mate of the clipper ship *Torrens*, and the sailor-writer and the dilettante lawyer became mutually influential and supportive life-long friends. The other great influence on Galsworth's literary career was Ada Cooper Galsworthy, unhappily married wife of John's cousin Arthur. Ada, the model for Irene Forsyte, the beautiful heroine of the *Saga*, and John became lovers in 1895 in Paris, and she urged him to do something with his life. He obeyed by beginning to write. Fearing Galsworthy's father would disinherit him if she divorced and they married, the lovers waited until his death in 1904 to pursue her divorce. They were able to marry the next year, when Galsworthy had three apprentice novels and two collections of stories in print. Literary fame came in 1906 with the publication of *A Man of Property,* whose eponymous philistine antagonist, Soames Forsyte, based on cousin Arthur, became the central male figure in Galsworthy's fiction.

Other trilogies, replete with Forsyte characters, followed *The Forsyte Saga: A Modern Comedy* (1929) and *End of the Chapter* (1934). The best non-Forsyte novel is *The Country House* (1907).

Galsworthy's successful career as a playwright began with *The Silver Box* in the same year as the publication of *A Man of Property*. At his best, Galsworthy was a dramatist of conscience and a committed reformer. Between the two world wars he ranked second only to BERNARD SHAW, and on a par with J.M. Barrie, SOMERSET MAUGHAM, and J.B. PRIESTLEY. His most notable plays are the Ibsen-like thesis plays, *Strife* (1909), *Justice* (1910), and *Loyalties* (1922).

Although Galsworthy's reputation diminished after his death, his humanitarian concerns, his story-telling ability, and his deft portrayal of his social milieu, have insured a continuing readership throughout the English-speaking world. Critical and scholarly interest await a revival.

Sanford Sternlicht

Bibliography

Fréchet, Alec. *John Galsworthy: A Reassessment.* 1982.

Gindin, James. *John Galsworthy's Life and Art: An Alien's Fortress.* 1987.

Marrot, H.V. *The Life and Letters of John Galsworthy.* 1936.

Sternlicht, Sanford. *John Galsworthy.* 1987.

Garden Cities

Conceived by Sir Ebenezer Howard at the turn of the twentieth century, Garden Cities were inspired by currents of thought originating in the eighteenth century: one was concerned with the social basis of landowning and the economics of real-estate development, the other with the design of model settlements and decent working-class HOUSING. Similarly the Garden City movement fed corresponding, though divergent, streams of twentieth-century thought: one, concerned with land reform and the socialization of incremental land values, led nowhere; the other exercised great influence on housing design and TOWN AND COUNTRY PLANNING.

Howard saw land reform as the foundation of all reform: dividends from Garden City development were to be deliberately limited and surplus return on capital applied for the benefit of the tenant community, a principle applied when First Garden City Ltd. developed Letchworth from 1903.

The socializing of development profits was an old element of the Radical program fitfully revived by the LABOUR PARTY. Though there was nothing inherently partisan in Howard's ideas, it was thus natural that the social and economic ideals behind Garden Cities should have appealed to the Left, and Letchworth became a refuge for CONSCIENTIOUS OBJECTORS and others out of sympathy with national aims during the FIRST WORLD WAR. Just as nothing much came of Labour's efforts to tap development profits, so for many years neither Letchworth, nor Howard's second foundation, Welwyn Garden City (1920), made profits that could be socialized. Indeed even the necessary capital was not attracted. At Welwyn government loans, writing-off capital, and an end to dividend limitation were necessary between the wars, and in 1948 it was made a New Town to take LONDON overspill. Nor, but for parliamentary legislation in 1962, could Letchworth have survived the assaults of those who, attracted by the profits to be made from redeveloping low-density housing in the 1950s, took over First Garden City Ltd. The act transferred Letchworth's assets to a public corporation, thus safeguarding at a cost of more than £3 million, Howard's social and economic ideals.

Howard's work appeared when Britain was temporarily losing her lead in urban planning and design. Sir Nikolaus Pevsner concluded that Howard's Garden Cities were backward-looking, like the picturesque villages descended from New Houghton (1729) or Nuneham Courtenay (early

1760s) or the model industrial settlements and garden suburbs derived from New Lanark and Styal (1783–4). Circumstances disguise the novelty and fertility of Howard's ideas. One was the slow development of Letchworth and Welwyn, a consequence of Howard's unrealistic optimism concerning the economic "magnetism" of his land reforms: slow development produced architectural failure in the Garden City centers, and low-density building produced a "cottagey" rather than an urban scene. The fact that Letchworth's architects, Parker & Unwin, also worked at Earswick and Hampstead Garden Suburb obscured the real differences between that type of development and the Garden City.

Howard's essential originality derives from the scale of his planning. Earlier model settlements were small, rarely exceeding a few hundred inhabitants; their inspiration was local paternalism or PHILANTHROPY. Howard, however, intended nothing less than a profound alteration of the national settlement pattern, stemming the tide of rural depopulation and reducing the conurbations by groups of new planned Garden Cities of 32,000 inhabitants each, built around Central Social Cities.

Planning on such scale meant that those who carried on his work—organizations like the Town and Country Planning Association and influential town planners like Sir Raymond Unwin—had to work at theoretical questions of the first importance for post-war reconstruction planning in the 1940s. As far as ambitions on such a scale could ever have been carried out, they were realized in southeast England by Sir Patrick Abercrombie's Greater London Plan (1944), and it was Abercrombie's use of green belts, developed from the work of Howard and Unwin, that helped to reconcile the conservatively-minded Council for the Protection of Rural England to the plan, keenly supported by the Town and Country Planning Association. Green belts became part of general government planning policy from 1955. Industrial dispersal was also implicit in the Garden City, although it became part of government policy through the 1940 Barlow Report, which also owed much to academic geographers. Finally, the New Towns program can be discerned in embryonic form in the Garden City. Social balance and economic self-sufficiency were essential characteristics of both, and both (despite the appearance of England's first tower block at Harlow) were essentially low density developments. The good plain standards of early New Town housing may also be seen to derive from Garden City ideals and practice. Parker & Unwin, influenced by C.F.A. Voysey, designed and planned the best pre-1914 housing estates, eschewing the florid historical styles of Port Sun-

light and Bournville; their early achievements at Letchworth and elsewhere were carried forward by Unwin's work with the Tudor Walters Committee in 1918 and with the Ministry of Health to exercise a profound influence on the planning and design of housing estates and on the work of the post-war modernists who undertook Harlow and other early New Towns.

G.C. Baugh

Bibliography

Culpin, Ewart G. *The Garden City Movement Up-To-Date*. 1912.

Darley, Gillian. *Villages of Vision*. 1975.

MacFadyen, Dugald. *Sir Ebenezer Howard and the Town Planning Movement*. 1970.

Meacham, Standish. *Regaining Paradise: Englishness and the Early Garden City Movement*. 1999.

Miller, Mervyn. *Raymond Unwin: Garden Cities and Town Planning*. 1992.

Gardiner, A(lfred) G(eorge) (1865–1946)

Editor of the *Daily News* (1902–19), A.G. Gardiner was born in Chelmsford on 2 June 1865. He embarked on a career in journalism, first as a reporter in Bournemouth before moving to Blackburn where he joined the small *Northern Daily Telegraph*. As a skillful leader writer, Gardiner was promoted to editor of the weekly edition of the paper in 1886. When the proprietor of the *Northern Daily Telegraph*, T.P. Ritzema, became manager of the London *Daily News*, he recommended Gardiner to its new owner, George Cadbury, as editor of the troubled newspaper. Gardiner assumed the position in February 1902 at a time when the *Daily News*'s revenues and sales were at low ebb as a result of its stand against the BOER WAR and the fierce competition of the half-penny daily press. Gardiner, however, had an outstanding senior staff which included such very able journalists as J.A. Spender and H.W. MASSINGHAM (until he left to edit the *NATION* in 1906), who helped the young editor resolve the paper's serious problems. He proved to be a highly effective editor who not only achieved the respect of his editorial team, but recruited such new talent as G.K. CHESTERTON and C.F.G. Masterman and Robert Lynd (as literary editors), J.L HAMMOND, H.W. Paul, H.N. BRAILSFORD, and R.C.K. Ensor as leader and special feature writers. Following the LIBERAL election victory in 1906, Gardiner became a staunch supporter of SIR HENRY CAMPBELL-BANNERMAN's government and an ardent advocate of the reforms of DAVID LLOYD GEORGE and WINSTON CHURCHILL. Meanwhile, with his colleagues, Gardiner resuscitated the *Daily News* as an organ of the Radical Liberals and, equally important, as a paper interested in literature and the arts. He devoted much time to writing and achieved the respect of

Fleet Street for his knowledge of the British political scene during the pre-FIRST WORLD WAR era and for his success in converting the *Daily News* to a half-penny paper.

Unlike his friend Massingham, Gardiner accorded full support to his favorite Cabinet minister, Lloyd George, and Prime Minister HERBERT ASQUITH when Britain entered the war in 1914. But in 1916, when Lloyd George's intrigues ousted Asquith, Gardiner supported Asquith against Lloyd George. Like Massingham, he bitterly criticized Lloyd George's conduct of the war and even more so the Paris peace settlement which Lloyd George had negotiated. In fact, as a result of his relentless attacks against Lloyd George and his government and especially Gardiner's assertion that Lloyd George's Treaty of Versailles was a "blueprint" for the next war, the proprietor of the *Daily News*, Henry Cadbury, fearing that his editor's animus against the popular Prime Minister was inimical to the best interests of the paper, prevailed upon Gardiner to relinquish the editorship but to continue to contribute columns to the journal and other Cadbury papers. He was replaced in September 1919 by Stuart Hodgson and, in spite of his renown as a highly effective editor and polemicist, Gardiner did not seek another post and henceforth devoted himself to free-lance journalism and serious writing.

Gardiner's keen character sketches of prominent personalities, published collectively in *Prophets, Priests, and Kings* (1908), *Pillars of Society* (1913), and *Pebbles on the Shore* (1916), and special essays often signed as "Alpha of the Plough" were highly regarded even before his departure from the *Daily News*. As a free-lance, he published competent biographies of Sir William Vernon Harcourt (1923) and George Cadbury (1923) and a fine study of *John Benn and the Progressive Movement* (1925) and always found a good market for his articles and essays in numerous newspapers and periodicals. Often urged to write his autobiography and memoirs, Gardiner resisted the temptation and, even to the time of his death on 3 March 1946, at the age of seventy, maintained that all that needed saying about his life had already been said.

J.O. Baylen

Bibliography

Koss, Stephen. *Fleet Street Radical: A.G. Gardiner and the Daily News.* 1973.

Garvin, J(ames) L(ouis) (1868–1947)

J.L. Garvin was a distinguished journalist and editor of the *Observer* from 1908 to 1942. He was largely responsible for inventing the modern formula of modern Sunday journalism, as well as for the modern reputation of the *Observer*.

Garvin was born into considerable poverty in Birkenhead in 1868, the son of an Irish laborer who was killed at sea in 1869. He was educated locally and did not attend a university; his rise to the top of his profession was thus all the more remarkable. He left school to work as a clerk but in 1891 began his journalistic career as a reporter on the *Newcastle Daily Chronicle*. In 1899, after a rigorous apprenticeship in Newcastle, he moved to the *Daily Telegraph* as a leader-writer. It was during his years on the *Daily Telegraph* that he became a devoted follower of Joseph Chamberlain and a partisan supporter of his TARIFF REFORM campaign. Chamberlain's brand of Liberal Imperialism was to become Garvin's political creed for much of his life, and he also wrote three volumes of a massive biography of Chamberlain which were published in 1932–4. Garvin was briefly editor of the magazine *Outlook* (1904–6), before LORD NORTHCLIFFE appointed him editor of the *Observer* in 1908.

Northcliffe, the owner of a number of newspapers, had bought the *Observer* in 1905, when it was an ailing journal of little consequence. Garvin was brought in as editor to revitalize the paper, and he succeeded in doing this triumphantly. Particularly in his principled campaigns on political issues, such as naval rearmament against Germany from 1908 to 1911, he established the paper's reputation and influence, and became probably the best known journalist of his day. However, he clashed increasingly with Northcliffe, a man of equally strong views. Northcliffe declared his wish to sell the paper in 1911 but generously allowing Garvin three weeks to find a buyer for the paper himself. Garvin found William Waldorf Astor, who was willing to buy the paper, and the *Observer* remained in the Astor family until 1976.

However, it was William Waldorf's son, Waldorf Astor (husband of NANCY ASTOR), who took the principal interest in the paper from the start and under whose guiding hand that the Garvin *Observer* prospered, increasing its circulation to 200,000 by the early 1920s. Garvin probably reached the peak of his influence during the FIRST WORLD WAR, and his signed articles on the leader page of the paper became the most famous feature of the *Observer* throughout his editorship, required reading for the political classes. Indeed, during these years, it can be said that Garvin largely invented the tradition of modern Sunday journalism, describing his own creation as "half a newspaper; half a magazine or serial."

During the late 1920s, however, Garvin's influence began to wane as he grew increasingly isolated from the new political generation and, furthermore, lived in relative physical isolation at his home in Beaconsfield, cut off from Westminster and the small *Observer* office in London. During the 1930s he became an earnest advocate of a renegotiation of the Versailles Treaty, which he had always considered to be misconceived, and thus became labelled as an appeaser. To a certain extent this was true, but at least he came to these conclusions himself and refused to be used as a voice of government policy like some of his fellow journalists at the time. It was over APPEASEMENT that Garvin had his first serious political disagreements with Astor: after the MUNICH conference Garvin supported the Prime Minister, NEVILLE CHAMBERLAIN, as a symbol of national unity rather than out of conviction, whereas Astor tried, unsuccessfully, to persuade Garvin to argue in the *Observer* for a change of government throughout 1939 and 1940. When Chamberlain did resign in May 1940, Garvin and Astor found themselves similarly divided over the merits of WINSTON CHURCHILL as Prime Minister, whom Garvin supported unconditionally and Astor regarded with grave suspicions. This divergence of view reached a peak during the first two months of 1942, when Britain's military fortunes were at their lowest ebb, and Garvin's resignation was accepted by Astor after Garvin had written two articles in the *Observer* flatly contradicting Astor's known views on the higher conduct of the war.

Garvin's departure from the *Observer* left considerable bitterness on both sides, but he went on to enjoy a brief Indian summer as a columnist on the *Daily Telegraph* (1945–7), after having written with somewhat less success for the *Sunday Express* (1942–5). He died in 1947.

Garvin ranks as one of Britain's most important and influential newspaper editors of the century, both for the influence that he wielded through his weekly signed articles in the *Observer* and for his development of the Sunday newspaper as a distinct journalistic entity.

Richard Cockett

Bibliography
Ayerst, David. *Garvin of the Observer*. 1985.
Cockett, Richard. *David Astor and the Observer*. 1991.
Garvin, Katherine. *J.L. Garvin*. 1948.
Gollin, A.M. *The Observer and J.L. Garvin, 1908–1914*. 1960.

General Strike (4–12 May 1926)

To many Conservatives and some Liberals the General Strike appeared to be a challenge to constitutional government. To others it was simply a massive sympathy strike. Its failure brought to an end a century of talk of a "general strike" to bring down the capitalist system. The General Strike was also the concluding militant incident in a period of often tumultuous industrial unrest between 1910 and 1921. After it, industrial rela-

tions were less stormy and calls for widespread militant strike action were generally discredited.

The General Strike was essentially a mining dispute that spilled over. The problems of the British COAL INDUSTRY became very apparent once the post-FIRST WORLD WAR boom gave way to worsening conditions after 1920. The government, which had controlled the mines from 1915 to 1916, hastily decontrolled the industry on 31 March 1921. Resuming full responsibility for the industry at a time of tumbling international coal prices, the private owners demanded substantial wage cuts, the amount varying according to the profitability of the pits, thereby spelling an end to national wage agreements and to the minimum wage. The MINERS' FEDERATION OF GREAT BRITAIN (MFGB) expected reductions but was unwilling to accept cuts of the magnitude proposed. The MFGB was also insistent that a miner's wages should reflect the work put in and not the economic viability of his pit; for the union closing marginal pits was preferable to keeping them open by paying the miners less for their labor. Futhermore, the MFGB argued that, if it were in the nation's interest to keep unprofitable mines operating, the government, not the miners through low pay, should provide the subsidy. The Conservative-dominated governments of 1921–6 had no desire to subsidize industries, least of all coal which often was very profitable. Nevertheless in 1921 and 1925 governments did provide subsidies, and thereby raised expectations in the labor movement in 1926 that STANLEY BALDWIN could be pressured into doing so again.

Conflict in the mining industry became more serious when the TRADES UNION CONGRESS (TUC) supported the miners in 1925 and 1926. In 1925 the General Council of the TUC agreed to organize an embargo of the movement of coal when a coal dispute seemed imminent, following a fall in coal exports and a demand by the owners for an end to national collective bargaining, substantial wage cuts, and an additional hour (to eight) to the miners' working day. In July 1925 Baldwin's nine-month subsidy merely bought time.

During that time, the government made careful preparations to deal with a general strike, reactivating its emergency organization that had been ready to undermine strikes in 1919–21. The CABINET, for both political and economic reasons, was determined not to provide futher subsidy. Several on the Tory Right hoped for a showdown with organized labor, feeling it to be both necessary and electorally popular. While the miners, the COMMUNIST PARTY, and WALTER CITRINE, the acting secretary of the TUC, warned of a probable clash in May 1926, the trade union leadership generally was ill-prepared, probably hoping that something would turn up. Their best chance of a compromise settlement centered on the Royal Commission on the Coal Industry, appointed in September 1925 and chaired by Sir Herbert Samuel, which reported in March 1926. However, the owners were inflexible on the need for longer working hours, the MFGB was resolute behind the policy of "not a penny off the pay, not a minute on the day", and Baldwin refused to offer proposals, even about the reorganization of the industry.

The General Strike began at midnight on 3–4 May. At the start the TUC called out only certain key industries: railway, dock, and road transport workers; iron and steel; metals and heavy chemicals; the building trades; electicity and gas; and the printing trades. Engineers and shipbuilders, the "second line" of unions, were called out just before the strike was terminated on 12 May. Generally the strike was very well supported. Across the country trades councils enthusiastically ran the strike in their areas, with growing efficiency as the days passed. They were dismayed when the TUC leadership unreservedly ended the dispute.

The government had wide powers under the Emergency Powers Act (1921). Furthermore it could use a sizeable body of volunteers. It also had its news bulletins and official announcements broadcast by the British Broadcasting Corportion, and its case was also put, in combative style, in the *British Gazette*, edited by Winston Churchill, which had access to far more newsprint than the TUC's newsheet *British Worker*.

Within the Conservative Party, the General Strike strengthened the hands of those on the Right who wished for tougher trade union legislation, and Baldwin, who earlier had successfully resisted this, now took action with the Trade Disputes Act (1927). Under the Boards of Guardians (Default) Act (1926), the government could put commissioners in place of elected poor law guardians where it deemed that too generous relief was being given, a matter highlighted by the help given in some areas to miners' families.

The ending of the General Strike left the locked-out miners to struggle on alone. By late November they had been forced to return to work under whatever terms were locally available, leaving a residue of bitterness in mining industrial relations. Others also suffered, with many railwaymen, printers, engineers, and road haulage workers victimized by employers who ignored Baldwin's appeal after the strike that there should be no malice or vindictiveness. Trade unionism among miners and railwaymen fell by 26 and 22 percent by the end of 1927, though it is possible that sympathy for the miners helped the Labour Party in some areas in municipal and parliamentary elections in the following years.

After the General Strike the labor movement indulged in fewer recriminations than it might have done as it reunited to oppose Baldwin's trade union legislation. Under its president Ben Turner (1863–1942), the TUC, reverting to cooperation rather than confrontation in industrial politics, engaged in talks on a wide range of matters from January 1928 with a group of prominent industrialists led by Sir Alfred Mond. The General Strike has often been seen as a turning-point in British labor's history; but, perhaps, it is better seen as accelerating trends already underway after the post-war economic boom and the failure then of the more militant trade unionism.

C.J. Wrigley

Bibliography

Clegg, Hugh Armstrong. *A History of British Trade Unions Since 1889: vol. 2: 1911–1933.* 1985.

Laybourn, Keith. *The General Strike of 1926.* 1994.

Morris, Margaret. *The General Strike.* 1976.

Phillips, Gordon A. *The General Strike: The Politics of Industrial Conflict.* 1976.

Renshaw, Patrick. *The General Strike.* 1975.

Skelley, Jeffrey, ed. *The General Strike 1926.* 1976.

George V (1865–1936)

The second son of Albert Edward, Prince of Wales (later King Edward VII) and Princess Alexandra of Denmark (later Queen Alexandra), George became Duke of York (1892), Prince of Wales (1901), and succeeded his father as King (1910).

As a young man Prince George did not expect to become King, but the death of his elder brother, the weak and disreputable Duke of Clarence in 1892 put him in the line of succession. Shortly thereafter he married his brother's fiancée, Princess Mary of Teck, and adopted a disciplined domestic life far more in line with the standards set by his grandmother, Queen Victoria, than with the standards of his rakish father. Nevertherless, he always remained devoted to his parents. He was educated to be a naval officer, and the traditions, values, and principles of the navy were foremost in his character. Protocol and sartorial correctness were immensely important to him. His sons were brought up in the manner of the British upper class: stern regimens were imposed by parents, tutors, and nurses. The King found it difficult to treat his sons as adults until they married. In the case of the future Edward VIII, who was still unmarried at George's death, relations were never satisfactory.

George V was an exceedingly successful constitutional monarch. Although he fully understood that his basic prerogatives were limited, he did not hesitate, in private, to make his views known; his influence in several instances was marked. When he became King in May 1910, he was immediately faced with the crisis over the

Parliament Bill and, whatever his personal views may have been about the proposed limitations on the powers of the House of Lords, he supported the Liberal administration of Asquith. He did, however, request that a second general election be held in 1910, and later showed resentment that the possibility of a Conservative government was kept from him in that year. But at the height of the crisis he did all he could to make it clear to the Tory majority in the Lords that he would indeed honor his pledge to Asquith to create sufficient new peers to get the bill passed. He was most relieved when the passage of the bill saved him from that most disagreeable duty. He also did his best to cool passions during the crisis over Irish Home Rule, 1912–14.

During the First World War he was an admirable symbol of the nation, although, as a first cousin of the Kaiser, he was faced with some embarrassments. Eventually, in 1917, he gave the English name of Windsor to his dynasty. He and Queen Mary achieved considerable popularity during the war; they were among the few who took the pledge to abstain from alcohol for the duration of the war and lived up to it, although the King was given a dispensation after a severe riding accident in 1915 during a visit to the front. In military matters, the King played a significant role in his support of his generals, particularly Douglas Haig; royal influence was important in blocking Lloyd George's attempts to purge the higher command, many of whom, like Haig, had close personal associations with the King. Above all, he was highly conscious of the revolutionary implications of the war; he had only to look at the collapsed and collapsing monarchies of Eastern and Central Europe to see the potential danger to his throne, and he did all he could to distance the House of Windsor from many of his continental relatives. He played a key role, for example, in keeping his deposed cousins, the Tsar and Tsarina of Russia, out of England.

After the war the King continued to play his constitutional role with skill. In 1923 he made the important decision to deny the prime ministership to Lord Curzon and to give it to Stanley Baldwin. He carefully sounded out the leadership of the Conservative Party but the decision was essentially his. He realized that a peer, isolated in the Lords, would be inappropriate with Labour as the opposition; after all, Labour was virtually unrepresented in the upper chamber. And in 1924 he accepted a Labour government with good grace; one of his major concerns was whether the Labour ministers would wear court dress; assured that they would, he was relieved. He established close relations with many members of his Labour governments, often ap-

preciating their earthy humor. In 1931 he made his most controversial and dramatic political intervention when he persuaded Ramsay MacDonald not to leave office but to form a new national government of all parties to deal with the financial crisis.

In 1935 the King and Queen celebrated their silver jubilee and the affection which greeted them on their progresses through London was extremely impressive. The King seemed to have been genuinely surprised for he thought of himself as rather dull; in fact, the more fashionable elements of society so regarded him. But the warmth of the great majority of his people illustrated the enormous success and importance of his reign. King George, consciously or unconsciously, understood the role of monarchy in the modern world and how it personalized and humanized the extraordinary complexities of government and society in the twentieth century. The British people had not only come to see the King as a mystical figure representing the essence of the nation but also as the head of an actual family with whom they could identify. The King realized this and used modern technology to reach out to his people; his Christmas broadcasts, which started towards the end of his reign, were an enormous success and enhanced his role as a father-figure.

King George was the synthesizer of the various factors which constitute the modern monarchy. He understood that political power was no longer available to the sovereign but that political influence, wielded behind the scenes, could be very potent. This influence would stem to a great extent from prestige which, in turn, would come from the monarch's position and family life. It would also stem from knowledge, for if the monarch was diligent in reading the state papers sent to him, he would accumulate a vast store of information which could be translated into influence. King George understood what his grandfather, Prince Albert, had tried to impress on Queen Victoria: that the sovereign, in public, must be above or beyond politics, and thereby immune to political blame. He also understood what Queen Victoria so passionately believed: that the monarchy must be respectable. And he understood, as did his father, that the monarchy had to be exciting and splendid and glamorous. King George carefully maintained the pageantry that his father had revived, but fortunately, in light of the horrors of the war and the miseries of the Depression, he clothed it in an aura of Victorian respectability, domesticity, order, and duty.

King George died on 20 January 1936. He was survived by Queen Mary who died in 1953, and by four sons: King Edward VIII, later Duke of Windsor; Prince Albert, Duke of York, later

KING GEORGE VI; Prince Henry, Duke of Gloucester; and Prince George, Duke of Kent. His youngest son, Prince John, died in 1919. He was also survived by a daughter, Princess Mary, the Princess Royal, Countess of Harewood.

Arthur Mejia

Bibliography
Nicolson, Harold. *King George the Fifth.* 1952.
Prochaska, Frank. "George V and Republicanism, 1917–1919," *Twentieth Century British History*, vol. 10 (1999), pp. 27–51.
Rose, Kenneth. *King George V.* 1983.

George VI (1895–1952)

Second son of the Duke of York, later KING GEORGE V, and of Princess Mary of Teck, later Queen Mary, he was created Duke of York (1920) and succeeded his brother as king (1936).

Like his father, King George VI did not expect to be King and throughout much of his life lived in the shadow of his immensely popular older brother, the Prince of Wales, the future KING EDWARD VIII. Also, like his father, he was trained for the NAVY which he joined as a midshipman in 1913; he served at the battle of Jutland in 1916. Again, like his father, he was fortunate in his domestic life, marrying in 1923, Lady Elizabeth Bowes-Lyon, a daughter of the fourteenth Earl of Strathmore. In the 1920s he was most noted for his work with the Duke of York's camps, an idealistic effort, which continued until the war, to bring together boys of all classes in an informal setting, and thereby to lessen class tensions. The theme of his life was basically domestic; to a great extent the lives of the Yorks revolved around their daughters, born in 1926 and 1930.

The failure of his elder brother to accept the principles embodied by King George V was a matter of concern to the entire royal family, and in 1936 the affair of the new King with Mrs. Ernest Simpson increasingly became a growing threat to the life of the Yorks, for the Duke was his brother's heir. By the fall of 1936, the determination of the King to marry Mrs. Simpson led to his abdication in December, and the Duke, to his and his wife's dismay, ascended the throne; the bitterness caused by the abdication never entirely ended, and the new Queen was unable to forgive her brother-in-law. However, the King immediately set about restoring the monarchy's prestige. In order to emphasize continuity with his father's reign he styled himself George VI, foregoing the use of this own Christian name of Albert. He continued traditions such as the Christmas broadcast, a great effort, as the King had struggled all his life against a stammer which often made public speaking difficult. Above all, he reestablished the royal family as the center of domestic tranquility and virtue while at the same time he continued the formality and pagentry of his father's court. He resolved the difficult financial problems caused by the abdication and created his brother the Duke of Windsor, pointedly denying to the future Duchess the right to the designation of "Royal Highness."

The King and Queen were notably successful in their new roles. State visits to France in 1938 and to the United States in 1939, both undertaken in the expectation of war, were considerable triumphs. Although the King played a smaller role in politics than his father, he continued the tradition of familiarizing himself with the activities and policies of his governments, and his influence was occasionally felt, particularly in matters affecting the military. He would have preferred LORD HALIFAX to succeed NEVILLE CHAMBERLAIN in 1940 but neither exercised, nor tried to exercise, any influence over the outcome. During the war the royal family, second only to WINSTON CHURCHILL, became a symbol of Britain's resistance to the Nazis; the King's almost daily presence in London and royal tours of the devastated regions brought him great popularity and respect. After the war the King accepted, as his father had done, a LABOUR government, and he may have played a role in the selection of ERNEST BEVIN as foreign secretary. From time to time he queried the policies of the government and asked for detailed explanations, but he never deviated from his constitutional role. He set an example in the acceptance of post-war austerity, although the splendid marriage in 1947 of his elder daughter, Princess Elizabeth, to her cousin, Philip Mountbatten, was an immensely popular antidote to the grim life of the period.

The King's health started to deteriorate in the late 1940s, and he was eventually found to have cancer which necessitated the cancellation of a tour of Australia and New Zealand. The King died on 6 February 1952, and the mourning of the nation demonstrated the deep affection with which he was regarded.

Arthur Mejia

Bibliography
Bradford, Sarah. *The Reluctant King: The Life and Reign of George VI 1895–1952.* 1989.
Leventhal, Fred M. "Essential Democracy: The 1939 Royal Visit to the United States," in George K. Behlmer and Fred M. Leventhal, eds. *Singular Continuities: Tradition, Nostalgia, and Identity in Modern British Culture.* 2000, pp. 163–77.
Wheeler-Bennett, John W. *King George VI.* 1958.

Gill, (Arthur) Eric Rowton (1882–1940)

An accomplished and celebrated sculptor, wood engraver, and designer of type faces, Eric Gill is best known for his most conspicuous commission:

a series of stone reliefs placed over the principal doorways of the new headquarters of the BBC at Broadcasting House, Portland Place, London (1929). His main typefaces were Perpetua and Gill Sans produced in the early and mid-1920s for Stanley Morison, adviser to the Monotype Corporation. Many of his wood engravings, of which he produced more than 1,000, were published by St. Dominic's Press in Ditchling, Sussex; and in 1920 he was a founder member of the Society of Wood Engravers.

Gill was Britain's last thoroughly national artist, as well as being a proselytizer and writer with firm views on the role of an artist in modern society. His views were made known through over 500 articles, some of which were published as *Art-Nonsense and other Essays* in 1929. Although his views of consensus values were mostly critical, this never stood in the way of official commissions and honors, of which he received a number in the 1930s: an Honorary Associateship of the RIBA in 1935, for example, before being elected Associate of the Royal Academy in 1937. His national distinction was recognized in 1935 when he was commissioned by the British government to carve a large relief of *The Creation* for the League of Nations Building in Geneva. HENRY MOORE, who would take his place as national sculptor in the 1940s and after, was one of his assistants in the 1920s. The artist and writer David Jones was also subject to his influence—at Gill's Ditchling Community in 1921.

Gill was brought up in a CHURCH OF ENGLAND ambience, although he was received into the ROMAN CATHOLIC CHURCH in 1913. In 1914 he was commissioned to do a series of Stations of the Cross for Westminster Cathedral—his first major public work. He remained a religious artist, although his own definition of religion was broad, and he also associated his own work with primitivism and with the barbarian.

Gill, who defined himself primarily as a stone carver, trained as an artist and then as an architect between 1900 and 1903. In his spare time he studied monumental masonry, and lettering and writing, and it was as a letter-cutter that he established his independence in 1903. In all, 762 of his lettered inscriptions have been identified. An important early influence was that of Dr. Ananda Coomaraswamy, a botanist and geologist with an interest in the arts of India and Ceylon. Coomaraswamy helped him establish links between the true, the good and the beautiful, which involved the infusion of eroticism into his largely religious subjects. Coomaraswamy also put him in touch with C.R. Ashbee's Guild of Handicraft, thus pointing to the importance of cooperation and community, and drew his attention to William Blake as a possible role model. In 1905 Gill joined both the Art Workers' Guild and the FABIAN SOCIETY, from which he resigned in 1908, at the time of his meeting with Coomaraswamy. Although a founder member of the Artists' International Association in 1933, he had reservations about the constraints imposed by the systematic and the social. In his *Autobiography* (1940), written at a time when he was dying of lung cancer, he listed seven escapes: from art school, from the architectural profession, scientific materialism, the Arts and Crafts Movement, socialism, London, and the Fine Art World. His constant problem was one of reconciling his independence with involvement in society. His preference was for small-scale communities: in 1907 he moved from London to Ditchling in Sussex, where he remained until moving to Capel-y-ffin in the Black Mountains in Wales in 1924; then in 1928 he moved again, to Pigotts, near High Wycombe in Buckinghamshire. The Ditchling and Welsh years were given over mainly to design and engraving—in 1924 he received a government invitation to design postage stamps and new silver coinage; the move to Pigotts brought an increase in sculpture commissions. In 1928 he was asked by the architect Charles Holden to carve three stone reliefs of *Winds* for the outside of the new London Underground Railway headquarters at 55 Broadway.

His career as a public sculptor was advanced by the need for war memorials stemming from the carnage of the FIRST WORLD WAR, in which he served briefly in the RAF motor transport division. His major memorial, completed for the University of Leeds in 1923, was *Christ driving out the money changers from the temple*.

Although a moralist opposed to contemporary commercial culture, he was no ascetic. One principal piece of 1923 was of a naked female acrobat, *Splits*, and he often chose to depict scenes of love and coitus. The most tender of these love pieces is of the head and shoulders of *Tobias and Sara* (1926). His largest and most programmatic erotic tableau is of *Odysseus welcomed from the sea by Nausicaa*, completed for the Midland Hotel, Morecambe, in 1933. Originally considered as *High Jinks in Paradise*, it was finally described by Gill as a "holy picture," by which he seems to have meant that it epitomized Christian ideas of love as outlined in the Gospel according to St. Matthew. The women who welcome Odysseus give food, drink, clothing, and a helping hand. The same sort of conflationary process is evident in his *Prospero and Ariel*, one of his BBC pieces of 1931, where Prospero also takes the place of God the Father, and Ariel shows the stigmata on his hands.

Gill was an unusually powerful writer and expositor of ideas which validated his artistic practice. The importance of stone carving for him was that it represented a collaboration between the artist, who was partly responsible for the concept, and nature which contributed its materials and resistance. The artist's work was thus justified by nature. Copying from preliminary models was bad because it broke the connection with nature and with the moment of apprehension. Gill extended this insight to society at large, deploring disjunctions of the sort which separated laborers from the totality of their work. He was the last major British artist to act on such a root-and-branch opposition to the culture at large.

Ian Jeffrey

Bibliography

Collins, Judith. *Eric Gill: Sculpture.* 1992.
MacCarthy, Fiona. *Eric Gill.* 1989.
Skelton, Christopher, ed. *Eric Gill: The Engravings.* 1990.
Speaight, Robert. *The Life of Eric Gill.* 1966.
Yorke, Malcolm. *Eric Gill: Man of Flesh and Spirit.* 1981.

Gold Standard

The gold standard was an exchange-rate system, and adherence to it was one of the pillars of British economic policy through the first three decades of the twentieth century. The gold standard combined the free convertbility of the pound sterling with a stable rate of exchange. Thus the pound traded within just a few cents of the official parity of £1=$4.86 from 1900 to 1914.

The gold standard's appeal to British policy makers and their economic advisors was both economic and political. By assuring traders and investors that any pound balances they accumulated could be converted to the currencies of their choice or to gold at predictable rates, the gold standard promised to promote the international trade so important to Britain's prosperity. By subordinating interest rates and the money supply to the maintenance of the official exchange rate, the gold standard seemed to insulate domestic economic management from political pressures.

The FIRST WORLD WAR disrupted international trade and capital flows, altered domestic monetary requirements, and, consequently, forced Britain and most other gold standard countries to suspend free convertibility at the official exchange rates. Beginning with the 1918 report of the Cunliffe Committee on Currency and Foreign Exchanges After the War, successive official inquiries recommended that Britain return to the gold standard as soon as wartime dislocations had passed. In his budget speech of April 1925 the Chancellor of the Exchequer WINSTON CHURCHILL suspended the embargo on the export of gold and restored the free convertibility of the pound at the pre-war parity of £1=$4.86. This decision, which Churchill later judged mistaken, was made in the face of opposition from JOHN MAYNARD KEYNES who, along with a few dissidents in finance and industry, believed that this exchange rate overvalued the pound and that the downward adjustment of domestic prices that overvaluation necessitated would involve large-scale UNEMPLOYMENT, industrial unrest, and a sharp rise in bankruptcies. Churchill and the many economists, bankers, and manufacturers who supported him acknowledged that the return to the gold standard would be painful but claimed the long-terms benefits from an increase in international trade would ultimately outweigh the dislocations.

The Bank of England was only able to maintain the official parity of the pound in the second half of the 1920s by pegging the bank rate at levels higher than the sluggish state of the economy warranted. In the summer of 1931 the Depression, a banking crisis in central Europe, and domestic fears about the size of the government's deficit combined to cause a run on the pound. In late August the LABOUR government collapsed when it failed to agree on expenditure cuts that might have restored confidence or secured foreign financial support for the official exchange rate. The National government that replaced it was unable to stem the tide, and on 21 September 1931 Britain abandoned the gold standard.

Since 1914 the gold standard had been more potent in Britain as a myth than as an instrument of economic policy. To its proponents, the gold standard symbolized the stability and prosperity of the pre-war years, and their concern to restore it rested on the belief that doing so would return Britain to that golden age. To Keynesian critics of the gold standard, the reestablishment of the pre-war parity represented the sacrifice of British industry to the financial interests of the CITY OF LONDON.

Both the enthusiasm for the gold standard in the 1920s and the scorn were misconceived. The smooth operation of the system before 1914 had been the effect, and not the cause, of the buoyancy of the British economy. In the absence of an environment favorable to international trade, the gold standard could only reflect economic strains and dislocations, not overcome them. On the other hand, Britain's export industries suffered between the wars from deep-seated managerial and organizational deficiencies and from structural changes in the world economy. Even if the return to the pre-war exchange rate in 1925 did overvalue the pound, this only exacerbated problems that were independently causing British trade to decline and unemployment to mount.

Michael Dintenfass

Bibliography

Clarke, Peter. *The Keynesian Revolution in the Making, 1924–36.* 1988.

Kunz, Diane B. *The Battle for Britain's Gold Standard in 1931.* 1987.

Moggridge, D.E. *British Monetary Policy 1924–1931.* 1972.

Pollard, Sidney, ed. *The Gold Standard and Employment Policies Between the Wars.* 1970.

Golding, William (1911–1993)

William Golding's reputation rests largely upon his first novel, *Lord of the Flies* (1954), which has sold millions of copies, been filmed twice, and been studied by generations of students. While his critical reputation alternated between periods of disparagement and praise, he continued to write, publishing eleven volumes of fiction, as well as several books of essays, travel, and drama. In 1983 he received the Nobel Prize for literature.

Golding was born in Cornwall, the son of a schoolmaster at the Marlborough School. Throughout his childhood he was an avid reader, particularly of the adventure novels so popular for boys' reading. At Brasenose College, OXFORD, he studied science before specializing in Anglo-Saxon literature. After taking his degree in 1935 he began his career as a teacher at Bishop Wordsworth's School in Salisbury. During the SECOND WORLD WAR he served in the ROYAL NAVY, where he rose in rank from ordinary seaman to command of a rocket ship. Following the war he continued to teach until 1961, when his established reputation enabled him to write full-time.

It may be surprising that Golding, whose career stretched over thirty-five years, should be known best for his first novel. Yet *Lord of the Flies'* vivid narrative of marooned boys who try—and fail—to maintain the habits of civilization, along with the book's suggestive use of mythic symbolism, have made it an unforgettable experience for multitudes of readers both casual and academic. The novel adapts the shipwreck motif, reaching back through a long tradition including *Robinson Crusoe*, *The Swiss Family Robinson*, Jules Verne's *The Mysterious Island,* and Robert Michael Ballantyne's *The Coral Island* in order to reach conclusions more applicable to the ethos of the early Cold War. Whereas earlier shipwreck novels show civilization's consoling and enabling power, Golding's presents as an "inescapable recognition" the notion that "everything is a bad business."

The other novels of Golding's early career are variations on the themes proposed in his first. They examine characters in extreme situations in order to reveal the fragility of human existence. *The Inheritors* (1955), describing the life, struggles, and eventual destruction of a band of neanderthals who come disastrously into contact with a band of primitive humans, points out how the qualitites that underlie technological advance-

ment are not those of sensitivity or compassion. *Pincher Martin* (1956) shows how the spirit of technology fails an unscrupulous sailor who, washed overboard from his warship, creates a narrative of his own survival during the few moments before he drowns.

Golding's next pair of novels remains focused on individuals in distress and further explore the possibility of creative expression as a means of consolation. The narrator of *Free Fall* (1959) seeks redemption for his life as a user and abuser of others in the act of narration itself. In *The Spire* (1964), Golding's best novel, a work rich in historical detail and allegory alike, the dean of a medieval cathedral perseveres, in spite of obstacles both worldly and spiritual, to transform a mystic vision into the reality of stone.

After *The Spire* and through the 1970s Golding worked principally from earlier ideas, publishing *The Hot Gates* (1965), a book of essays; an unsuccessful novel of contemporary life, *The Pyramid* (1967); and a collection of shorter historical fictions, *The Scorpian God* (1971). During this period Golding's prestige declined substantially.

Darkness Visible (1979), an enigmatic fusion of allegory and contemporary issues that portrayed the forces of change and conservatism as equally incompetent, did much to restore Golding to the public eye, as did the next year's *Rites of Passage* (1980), a densely historical novel about a motley sea-voyage to Australia in the early nineteenth century, which won him the Booker Prize. Golding does not seem to have been able to sustain this resurgence, and later novels (*The Paper Men* (1984) and the sequels to *Rites of Passage, Close Quarters* (1987) and *Fire Down Below* (1989)), have been seen as flawed.

Golding's inability to sustain the success of his greatest work made him a controversial choice for the 1983 Nobel Prize in Literature. Nonetheless the strength of his best writing, its blending of historical models, themes and settings with modern ideas, its artful descriptions, and its mythic aspirations, remain significant.

W. Olin-Ammentorp

Bibliography

Biles, Jack I., and Robert O. Evans, eds. *William Golding: Some Critical Considerations.* 1978.

Crompton, Don. *A View from the Spire: William Golding's Later Novels.* 1985.

Dick, Bernard F. *William Golding.* 1987.

Oldsey, Bernard S., and Stanley Weintraub. *The Art of William Golding.* 1965.

Gollancz, Victor (1893–1967)

Publisher, political and social campaigner and writer, Victor Gollancz was founder (1928)—and until his death the driving force—of the highly successful publishing firm of Victor Gollancz

Ltd. Passionately political, in 1936 Gollancz founded the LEFT BOOK CLUB. During the SEC-OND WORLD WAR he supported the war effort and helped victims of the Nazis. A Jew, he worked for post-war reconciliation with Germany and organized Jewish help for Arabs; he fought too against CAPITAL PUNISHMENT, and for many charitable and progressive causes and published more than thirty books and pamphlets on moral issues, music, and himself. His awards included honorary doctorates from Trinity College, Dublin and the University of Frankfurt, the Glorious Star of China, the Grand Cross of the Order of Merit of the Federal Republic of Germany, and a knighthood (1965).

Gollancz was born in London on 9 April 1893, the only son of Alexander and Helena (née Michaelson) Gollancz, a family of Polish origin with a long rabbinical heritage. Alexander was a jeweller, two of whose brothers were knighted for academic achievements. Gollancz rebelled against his father's unquestioning Jewish orthodoxy and political conservatism. Educated at St. Paul's School, he then read classics at New College, OXFORD in 1912–14. His army service included a period of secondment to Repton School (1916–18), where he found his vocation as a political educator and was dismissed for fomenting political dissension among staff and pupils. In 1919 he married Ruth Lowy, with whom he had five daughters.

Gollancz entered publishing in 1921 with Benn Brothers Ltd. and in 1923 became managing director of a new general publishing company, Ernest Benn Ltd. Personality clashes led to Gollancz's departure in 1927 to set up Victor Gollancz Ltd. on a borrowed working capital of only £12,000. Within a few years he was acknowledged to be the most exciting general publisher in London. He had remarkable drive, energy, and belief in his own judgment, and, a rebel by nature, he delighted in shocking the publishing establishment by his bold advertising and his innovations (with Stanley Morison) in typography and jacket design. He made authors believe in his commitment to their work and in several instances transformed unknowns or the modestly successful into big sellers. By 1932 his bestselling authors included A.J. Cronin and DOROTHY L. SAYERS.

Success enabled Gollancz to begin the political publishing which he saw as the chief *raison d'etre* of his firm. The Liberal of youth and early adulthood had become a socialist, and in 1936 he founded the Left Book Club. Run with Gollancz's usual energy and flair for improvisation, and subsidized by the firm, the Left Book Club quickly became important in the movement for a POPULAR FRONT against FASCISM. By

April 1939 its membership was almost 60,000 and around two million books, half a million pamphlets and fifteen million leaflets had been distributed under its auspices. Communists were vitally important in the organization of the LBC, and Gollancz—though instinctively anti-totalitarian—was a fellow-traveler who later regretted his moral compromises over the political slant of the club's publications.

During the SECOND WORLD WAR Gollancz's main energies were devoted to trying to unite the ranks of the Left behind the war effort, but he also worked with the National Campaign for Rescue from Nazi Terror to secure government help for victims of Nazi persecution. Once the war was over, he vociferously challenged the view that all Germans were guilty and launched Save Europe Now in 1945 to assist suffering Germans materially and fight against vengefulness. A convinced Judaeo-Christian (though a member of a no religious group), he gave much assistance to Christian Action; with the outbreak of hostilities between Israel and the Arabs, he founded the Jewish Society for Human Service to help Arabs suffering from the effects of war and to annoy the leaders of the JEWISH COMMUNITY in Britain.

During the 1950s Gollancz's main crusade was as chairman of the National Campaign for the Abolition of Capital Punishment. He had become a convinced PACIFIST, who for the rest of his life continued to assist a wide range of charitable and progressive causes, including prison reform and nuclear disarmament. However as he got older and increasingly disillusioned with politics, he spent more and more time on metaphysical and religious reading, reflection, and writing and on his lifelong passion for serious music. He died on 8 February 1967.

Although the depth of his commitment to moral crusades and his writing occasionally distracted him, he was his firm's effective—though more and more erratic and old-fashioned—head until he suffered a stroke in autumn 1966. Highly egocentric, he was miserly with authors, his style was autocratic, his temper short and violent, and he could not take criticism. Yet his enthusiasm was infectious, his kindness and generosity to those in need legendary, and his flair and energy so apparent that those who could tolerate working with him often found him inspirational.

As a life-long opponent of the principle of private profit, he bitterly resented being described as a capitalist or businessman, yet among the many contradictions of his life is the fact that his most permanent achievement was his firm. His major importance was as a publisher of genius, but he also had an important role in British political debate. His political publishing was a key anti-Fascist force in the 1930s and helped to bring

LABOUR to power in 1945. Subsequent Gollancz campaigns—particularly those on behalf of post-war Germany and against capital punishment—had a powerful humanitarian effect on public opinion.

Ruth Dudley Edwards

Bibliography

Edwards, Ruth Dudley. *Victor Gollancz: A Biography.* 1987.

Gollancz, Victor. *My Dear Timothy.* 1952.

———. *More for Timothy.* 1953.

———. *Reminiscences of Affection.* 1968.

Hodges, Sheila. *Gollancz: The Story of a Publishing House, 1928–1978.* 1978.

Government of India Act (1935)

This Act marks the final legislative attempt by a British Parliament to create a constitution for India. Although the Act made important steps towards self-government for Indians, it proved to be a failure, largely because of antipathy to British measures on the part of important Indian political groups. At home, opposition was also strong on the part of Conservative back-benchers and imperially-minded segments of the British public. Only part of the Act's provisions were ever implemented because of the onset of the Second World War.

The Act emerged from the ruins of the Round Table Conference, which was an attempt to gain Indian cooperation in fashioning a new constitution for India. Unable to gain that cooperation, the National government pressed ahead with its own plans, which were presented in the White Paper of March 1933. The White Paper drew forth heated opposition from certain segments of the CONSERVATIVE PARTY, led by WINSTON CHURCHILL, who were greatly dismayed at what they saw as a retreat from empire, which could only weaken Britain's power and influence in the changing, troubling world of the 1930s. In India, opposition on the part of most nationalist politicians was no less intense. Largely because of these pressures, especially on the home-front, passage of the Act was delayed until August 1935.

The 1935 Act had several important features. At the center, there was to be a complex federal structure, with representation for British interests, the princely states, and the remainder of India. The central government's power in provincial affairs was to be limited. Self-government would be established at the provincial level, where assemblies would be elected by the general population, with only emergency powers reserved to the British governors. Special safeguards were established for the Muslim community, including the creation of new Muslim-majority provinces, reserved appointments to government posts, sep-arate electorates, and considerable autonomy for the provincial governments.

Indian opposition to the Act remained strong. The princes objected to their diminished legal status under the terms of federation and insisted upon safeguards for their future sovereignty. The Indian National Congress had for years been demanding complete independence and therefore rejected the Act as an imperialist smoke screen designed to prevent any real transfer of power to Indians. Under Jawaharlal Nehru's leadership the Congress decided in 1936 to contest the provincial elections scheduled for the following year, but then to refuse to form ministries, as a means of demonstrating both their popular support and their opposition to the new constitution.

Elections to the provincial assemblies were held in 1937. The results were an overwhelming victory for the Congress, which now claimed a mandate for rejecting the 1935 Act. Nonetheless, the Congress was persuaded to form ministries in those provinces where it had majorities or near majorities. Once in power, the Congress governments aggressively pursued nationalist agendas, which alienated both the Muslim minority and the Indian princes. Because of pressure from these two groups, the British were unable to implement the federal scheme for the central government before war broke out in 1939. The Congress ministries resigned that autumn, after the British unilaterally declared India to be at war with Germany. During the duration of the war the constitution created by the 1935 Act was held in abeyance, and India was ruled by the British authorities with little support, and much opposition, from most Indian nationalists. Only Muslim political leadership gave support to the British, with the hopes of getting a separate Muslim state after the war. Drastically altered circumstances in both Britain and India in the post-war period made impossible a return to the constitution created by the 1935 Act.

The 1935 Government of India Act was the final legislative attempt by a British Parliament to impose a constitution upon a unified India. Upon conclusion of the Second World War, British power in Asia was so weakened that the LABOUR government could do little more in India than beat as orderly a retreat from empire as possible. Communal divisions in the subcontinent had deepened as well, making any hopes for a unified, independent India impossible, even with a weak central government, as envisaged in the 1935 Act. The tragedy of partition which unfolded in 1947–8 was a stark monument to the inability of the British to legislate a constitution for an independent India that would be acceptable to most Indians.

Lynn Zastoupil

Bibliography
Moore, R.J. *The Crisis of Indian Unity, 1917–1940*. 1974.
Peele, Gillian. "Revolt Over India" in *The Politics of Re-appraisal, 1918–1939*, Gillian Peele and Chris Cook, eds. 1975. pp. 114–45.

Grant, Duncan James Corrowr (1885–1978)

Although Duncan Grant's reputation is tied up inextricably with that of the predominantly literary BLOOMSBURY GROUP—he is often regarded as its "court painter," having been welcomed into the group through his cousin LYTTON STRACHEY—this has served to obscure his major contribution to the introduction of modernism in Britain. In 1907, after a period spent at Westminster School of Art, he attended Jacques-Emile Blanche's Academie La Palette. After returning to England the following year, he cemented his friendship with future Bloomsbury Group members, especially JOHN MAYNARD KEYNES. However, despite having visited Matisse, Picasso, and Gertrude, Michael, and Leo Stein in Paris by 1909, he continued to paint in a fairly conventional manner until 1910 when his painting began to change following ROGER FRY's first Post-Impressionist exhibition (he exhibited six paintings in the second exhibition in 1912). However, even then the influences at work were as much the painters of the Sienese Trecento or the Florentine Quattrocento as Cezanne or even Maurice Denis, and this can be recognized in paintings from this period such as *The Dancers* (1910, Tate Gallery, London). Similarly, the mural panels executed in 1911 for the dining room at London's Borough Polytechnic—*Football* and *Bathing* (Tate Gallery, London)—reveal his adulation for Michelangelo as well as his fascination for Romanesque and Byzantine mosaic. Furthermore, paintings such as *The Tub* (1912) or *Head of Eve* (1913), both in the Tate Gallery, show the influence of work by Matisse and Picasso from 1906 and 1907 which he had seen in Paris in 1909.

What this emphasizes is the extent to which Grant's painting is formed not from doctrinaire belief in modernist theory or style but rather from a desire to fit the style to the purpose in hand. This open-minded attitude perfectly suited him for the demands of decorative projects, of which the commission from the Borough Polytechnic had been the first. In 1913 he was one of the founders of the Omega Workshops, under the direction of Roger Fry (Grant was a co-director until 1919), and this set the pattern that was to continue through his career for an interchange between his painting and his decorative projects that went both ways. His non-figurative paintings of 1914 and 1915 all have their genesis in much of his work for Omega. However, the best expression of this relationship within his work is

to be found in the environment created with VANESSA BELL after 1916 at Charleston in Sussex.

His work, following his first one-man exhibition in 1920 at the Carfax Gallery, continued to reveal the polarities that formed his art: between modernist experimentation and the traditions of the Italian Renaissance, between the literary and visual arts as well as between the fine and decorative arts. Within all this, the life that he made with Vanessa Bell at Charleston, London, and Cassis also came to be a major subject in his art. Not only did his paintings depict his surroundings and the many relationships between family and friends, but also the paintings—even when they are just still-lives—reflect the lifestyle he led; and this despite Bloomsbury's belief in the necessary distinction between art and life and his own belief in the significance of formal values over a painting's subject. This conflict is found not only in the decorations at Charleston but also more clearly in the various mural commissions he undertook, of which the most complex and accomplished in these terms are those made with Vanessa Bell and Quentin Bell for Berwick Church in Sussex between 1940 and 1942 and those for the Russell Chantry at Lincoln Cathedral from 1956.

It is the problematic nature of this closeness between his way of life and his painting that provides one explanation for the progressive decline in his reputation since the middle-1930s (along with that, for different reasons, of many of his contemporaries) as his work—along with its sensual depiction of his hedonist vision of life—was seen to be increasingly out of step with the times. Although he had shown at the British Pavilions for the Venice Biennale in 1926 and 1932, the thirty-three paintings that he was to have shown in 1940 in Venice were only shown in London because of the war. However, during the period between his retrospective at the Tate Gallery in 1959 and his death in 1978 his achievement was gradually rediscovered along with the reawakening of interest in the writing of the Bloomsbury Group even though his significance extends far beyond their predominantly literary concerns.

Andrew Wilson

Bibliography
Mortimer, Raymond. *Duncan Grant*. 1944.
Shone, Richard. *Bloomsbury Portraits: Vanessa Bell, Duncan Grant and Their Circle*. 1976.
Spalding, Frances. *Duncan Grant: A Biography*. 1997.
Watney, Simon. *The Art of Duncan Grant*. 1990.

Graves, Robert von Ranke (1895–1985)

During his lifetime Robert Graves published more than 120 volumes of poetry, fiction, criticism, translations, and studies of myth. He was born 26 July 1895, the third of the five children of Alfred Perceval Graves and his second wife,

Amalie (Amy) Elizabeth Sophie von Ranke. The Graves family was Anglo-Irish, tracing its lineage from John Graves, who was Sheriff of Limerick in 1719. The family included a variety of professionals, as well as John Crosbie Graves, first Commissioner of Police, Dublin, whose daughter married the German historian Leopold von Ranke, grandfather to Amy von Ranke Graves.

Robert detested his public school, Charterhouse, but was much influenced by one of the masters, George Mallory, who introduced him to the writings of BERNARD SHAW, Samuel Butler, RUPERT BROOKE, and JOHN MASEFIELD and personally to Edward Marsh, the organizer of the Georgian movement. His entry to St. John's College, OXFORD, was delayed because of the FIRST WORLD WAR. By joining a good regiment, the Royal Welch Fusiliers, he was doing what his birth and breeding required of him. His physical and psychological wounding during the war so affected him that he rejected the expectations of his class and ancestry, though he did receive his B.Litt. from St. John's. His first marriage to Nancy Nicholson, daughter of the painter Sir William Nicholson, produced four children, some poems that subverted the paradigms of Georgian poetry, and one of the most turbulent scandals in modern literature: his alliance with Laura Riding. She would dominate his life, end his marriage, and lead him into close understanding of the women of power whom he would portray in the novels *I, Claudius* (1934) and *Claudius the God* (1934), among others. Prose, including the novels and his autobiography *Goodbye to All That* (1929, rev. 1957), he described as "show dogs" he raised to support his "cat," poetry. Even his *Greek Myths* (1955), *Hebrew Myths* (1964) which he wrote with Raphael Patai, and his important Latin translations for Penguin were so termed. The exception among his prose writings was *The White Goddess* (1948, rev. 1952) in which he articulated his archetypal powerful woman, the goddess of the title, whose human expression is the muse, the inspiration and guide of every true poet.

Graves and Laura Riding had, at the suggestion of Gertrude Stein, moved to Deyá, Mallorca, in 1927. Forced to leave by the SPANISH CIVIL WAR, they finally settled in the United States in 1939, where they separated. Throughout the years of the Second World War Graves and Beryl Hodge, who would be his second wife, lived in England until they could return to Deyá. He was with Beryl Graves when he wrote *The White Goddess* and the poems that celebrated her. The rest of his life and writing would probe his experience of this archetype. T.S. ELIOT published *The White Goddess* at Faber, thereby continuing a friendship of years. (Originally, Eliot and Graves were to write the book that became *A*

Survey of Modernist Poetry, 1927, by Graves and Riding, a seminal text in New Criticism.)

Deyá was Robert Graves' permanent address after 1950, and he lived there until his death. He and Beryl had four children, the last of whom, Juan, is addressed in the poem "To Juan at the Winter Solstice," (1945) in which Graves states that there is "one story and one story only/ That will prove worth your telling": the story of the poet and the goddess who loves and destroys him. Though living on his island, Graves travelled much, to give the Clark Lectures at Cambridge in 1954–5 and to succeed W.H. AUDEN as Oxford Professor of Poetry in 1961–6.

Graves is often remembered for his refusal to compromise his moral or aesthetic sense in such controversies as his combat with W.B. YEATS over the exclusion of Laura Riding from the *Oxford Book of Modern Verse;* his revisions of biblical history in *King Jesus* (1946) and *The Nazarene Gospel Restored* (1954); his portrayal of Milton in *The Story of Mary Powell: Wife to Mr. Milton* (1943); and his turning *The Rubaiyat of Omar Khayyam* (1967) into a Sufi text.

Frank Kersnowski

Bibliography

Graves, Richard Perceval. *Robert Graves. The Assult Heroic 1895–1926.* 1986.

———. *Robert Graves. The Years With Laura 1926–1940.* 1990.

Higginson, Fred H. *A Bibliography of the Writings of Robert Graves.* 1987.

Kersnowski, Frank, ed. *Conversations With Robert Graves.* 1989.

Greene, (Henry) Graham (1904–1991)

Novelist, playwright, essayist, and writer of short stories, Graham Greene was born in Berkhamstead, England. Educated at Berkhamstead School, where his father was headmaster, and Balliol College, OXFORD, he became a staff member of *THE TIMES* from 1926–30. By 1930 three forces had begun to shape his career and would dominate it throughout: journalism, film, and CATHOLICISM. *Journey without Maps* (1936), the chronicle of Greene's walk across uncharted Liberia, and *Lawless Roads* (1939), a report on the condition of the Church in southern Mexico during the 1930s Revolution, were joined by a constant stream of journalistic reports on trouble spots and political crises in Latin America, Africa, and Asia. Greene established a rhythm in his career whereby reportage would become background material for a novel. Journalism taught Greene much about accuracy and style. Film also played a significant role in his career. During the 1920s and 1930s, Greene reviewed several hundred films, demonstrating a keen interest in and mastery of the form; later he wrote at least nine film scripts, including those for his own *The Third Man* (1949), *Our Man in Havana* (1959), and *The Comedians* (1967). He even appeared in one film, in François Truffaut's *La Nuit americaine* (1973). The influence of film, whether in the form of parallel montage, establishing shots, changing camera angles, or focused dialogue, is everywhere felt in his novels and stories. The third influence, Catholicism, entered his life in 1926 when he converted and in the following year married Vivien Dayrell-Browning. His conversion, he has said, was primarily intellectual, and intellectual problems and puzzles largely established and define the thematic issues in his writings: the nature of evil, the paradoxical nature of love, whether sacred or profane, the functions of suffering, "social gospel," the redemptive powers of sin, and the concept of spiritual and physical fatherhood. Paradoxes brought both attention and censure: attention paid by national news magazines, especially in 1948, censure from Vatican offices demanding that he revise *The Power and the Glory* (1940), *The Heart of the Matter* (1948), and *The End of the Affair* (1951) to make their handling of matters of faith less paradoxical, particularly so that they would not seem to imply that fornication, drunkenness, suicide, and adultery could be paths to sainthood.

Greene's career began promisingly. *The Man Within* (1929), a historical thriller set in early nineteenth-century Sussex and peopled with smugglers, sold well enough to justify Heinemann's confident £600 advance, but the promise was quickly squelched with *The Name of Action* (1930) and *Rumour at Nightfall* (1931), two historical novels which Greene later refused to reprint, claiming they were written too much under the shadows of JOSEPH CONRAD's later novels. He did not return to historical topics until *Lord Rochester's Monkey* (1974) and *The Return of A.J. Raffles* (1975), nor did he consciously allow Conrad into his world again until *A Burnt-Out Case* (1961), whose Congo setting made Conrad's presence inevitable, and *The Human Factor* (1978).

History in terms of the past simply was not Greene's area, though the workings of history in the contemporary world became the topic, after religion, most characteristic of his novels. From *Stamboul Train* (1932) until *Getting to Know the General* (1985), Greene's novels occupied themselves with political struggles throughout the world, whether post-Depression Europe, colonialist struggles in Indochina, the workings of social gospel in South America, or the shadowy actions of Cold War espionage. For the latter, Greene had particular knowledge, since he worked for MI5 and knew Kim Philby well.

Greene divided the ten novels written between *Stamboul Train* (1932) and *The End of the Affair*

(1951) into "entertainments" and "novels," but this classification has been of little use to readers and critics, and Greene himself dropped it later. It is more accurate to say that Greene was fusing mass culture (the DETECTIVE STORY, melodrama, and the thriller) with high culture (tragedy, the novel of ideas) in these works. The thriller's concern with public and often violent action and the tragedy's concern with problematic human decisions and their consequences met in a complex but often weak human being, who is marooned in a modernist wasteland. Some critics have labelled this bleak world "Greeneland," causing Greene to rage against their failures to confront the realities of his descriptions, but the settings form rich metaphors of a fallen world as much as realistic depictions of topography, customs, and milieu. *It's a Battlefield* (1934) and *The Power and the Glory* (1940) are representative of this period in his career. The former interweaves four plot lines, crosscutting as in the film *Grand Hotel*, involving individuals caught up in the economic, intellectual, cultural, and moral wasteland of London. *The Power and the Glory*, which takes its title from the *paternoster*, confronts a nameless Mexican lieutenant who believes suffering can be eliminated from his world through destruction of certain institutions, with a nameless priest who learns that suffering defines the human condition. Hunter and prey pursue one another across the harsh landscape of southeastern Mexico before the inevitable ending when the priest is captured by the lieutenant, but not before being captured by God. The novel ingeniously uses its Lent and Easter time-scheme to underline the religious themes of the novel, themes Greene pushed into the realm of sainthood and miracles in *The Heart of the Matter*, set in wartime Sierra Leone, and *The End of the Affair*, set in the wartime of the V-1 in London. Even in this period, though, there is another side to Greene, one often forgotten, which saw him writing children's books such as *The Bear Fell Free* (1935) and *The Little Steamroller* (1953).

The late 1940s and 1950s brought a serious mid-life crisis. Greene began to experiment with Dickensian first-person point of view, more consciously with Fordian time shifts, and to venture into other genres, particularly drama such as *The Living Room* (1953) and *The Potting Shed* (1957), further exploring the numinous world. He separated from his wife, though he would never divorce her, and moved to France, where he lived in Antibes for the rest of his life. In the novels of this period, *The Quiet American* (1955), Greene's warning to Americans and Europeans alike about attempts to re-establish colonial hegemony in southeast Asia, and *A Burnt-Out Case*, the tale of a famous architect, disillusioned with his work, who decides to visit a leper colony in the Congo, Greene meditated Hamlet-like over the superiority of detachment over involvement. Burnt-out himself, he felt that the story of Querry in *A Burnt-Out Case* would probably be his last novel.

Greene could not have known that he had almost three decades of creative life left, that he had seven more novels and two autobiographical volumes ahead of him. Much of his activity from the late 1950s on was retrospective in nature, especially the writing of the autobiographical volume, *A Sort of Life* (1971). Also, in planning a collected edition of his works, Greene extensively revised earlier novels: *Brighton Rock* (1938) lost its ANTI-SEMITIC references; a chapter was restored to *The Heart of the Matter* in an attempt to distance the reader from Scobie early in the work; and *The End of the Affair* was so extensively revised that its affirmation of miracles became a statement of the problematical and coincidental. Tone also changed, and from *The Comedians* (1966) on, rich veins of intellectual and physical humor moved from the shadows in which they hid in the earlier works into the foreground, a process seen quite clearly in *Travels with My Aunt* (1969), *Monsignor Quixote* (1982), Greene's postmodern redaction of Cervantes, and *Doctor Fischer of Geneva; or, The Bomb Party* (1980), a witty fable concerning human greed. Greene died in 1991, fully recognized as one of the major novelists of his generation.

David Leon Higdon

Bibliography

Allain, Marie-Françoise. *The Other Man: Conversations with Graham Greene.* 1983.

DeVitis, A.A. *Graham Greene.* rev.ed. 1986.

Greene, Graham. *A Sort of Life.* 1971.

———. *Ways of Escape.* 1980.

Sherry, Norman. *The Life of Graham Greene.* 2 vols. 1989, 1994.

Wobbe, R.A. *Graham Greene: A Bibliography and Guide to Research.* 1979.

Grey, Edward (1862–1933)

Sir Edward Grey was a Liberal politician and statesman. The son of an army officer, he belonged to a distinguished family, his ancestors including the Whig Prime Minister Lord Grey. Educated at Winchester and Balliol College, OXFORD, he was an undistinguished student and was sent down in 1884. This misfortune was really a stroke of luck, because under the influence of his parish rector, the church historian Mandell Creighton, Grey was inspired to give up rural pleasures for the responsibilities of a public life. In 1884 he became private secretary first to Evelyn Baring, the future Lord Cromer, and then to the Liberal Chancellor of the Exchequer H.C.E. Childers. Grey stood successfully as the Liberal

candidate for Berwick-on-Tweed in 1885, retaining the seat until his elevation to the peerage as Viscount Grey of Fallodon in 1916. He served as a junior minister in the Foreign Office during the Liberal governments of W.E. Gladstone and Lord Rosebery (1892–5) and became Foreign Secretary in the last Liberal government and the first wartime coalition (1905–16). He was made Knight of the Garter in 1912.

It was Grey who declared in 1895 that the French advance in the Sudan was unwelcome, a policy which led eventually to the Fashoda incident of 1898. In the disunion after the fall of the Liberal government in 1895, Grey followed Rosebery, becoming one of the leaders of the Liberal Imperialist faction of the party. He supported the CONSERVATIVE government during the BOER WAR of 1899–1902, even though many other Liberals were highly critical of the conduct of the war and some even sympathized with the Boers. Similarly, Grey supported Lord Lansdowne's foreign policy, including the alliance with Japan in 1902 and the *entente* with France in 1904. A believer in the value of continuity in foreign policy, Grey was swayed very little by Radical Liberal calls for the reduction of military and naval expenditures and the avoidance of Continental entanglements.

When the Conservative government resigned in December 1905, Grey joined his fellow Liberal Imperialists H.H. ASQUITH and R.B. HALDANE in an effort to dislodge the new Prime Minister, the Radical Liberal SIR HENRY CAMPBELL-BANNERMAN. This intrigue failed, but Grey joined the CABINET nonetheless. He soon made his mark as the first Foreign Secretary to orient British policy clearly around the single dominating fact of Germany's emergence as an aggressive power. Grey sought a balance of power and thus was not interested merely in an understanding with Germany. In 1906 he was able to reach a settlement of the first Moroccan crisis between France and Germany after making it clear that Britain would not abandon the *entente*. Unknown to most Cabinet members, this special Anglo-French relationship included secret discussions concerning a common military strategy. Grey recognized that Russia, weakened by defeat in its war with Japan (1904–5) and shaken by revolution, might exchange its alliance with France for one with Germany. Hence, he cemented the anti-German alliance of Britain, France, and Russia with the Anglo-Russian Convention of 1907. This arrangement involved more than an alignment against Germany, for Grey was also able to promote a relaxation of tensions between Britain and Russia over Afghanistan, Persia, and Tibet.

It would be a mistake, therefore, to see Grey's foreign policy as Liberal in any idealistic sense of the word. He was guided by Britain's security interests as a great power. As a result, he was the object of much criticism from Radicals and socialists opposed to normal relations with Russia and outraged by an international anarchy that seemed only to benefit the incipient military-industrial complexes of Europe. In domestic policy, Grey's stances were rather more Liberal. He supported WOMEN'S SUFFRAGE, land reform, and Irish home rule. He was prepared to go much further than many of his colleagues to accommodate the trade unions during the wave of labor unrest which swept over Britain and Ireland between 1910 and 1914.

Grey's claim to greatness rests on his struggle to maintain the peace of Europe before the outbreak of the FIRST WORLD WAR in 1914. Throughout these years Britain remained free of any formal treaty obligations to its French and Russian allies. In 1911 another German effort to strain the Anglo-French *entente* produced the second Moroccan crisis. Once again, the attempt failed. Significantly, Grey's policy had apparently gained such acceptance from his colleagues that none other than the Radical Chancellor of the Exchequer DAVID LLOYD GEORGE delivered the clear warning in July that further German interference invited war with Britain, and not just with France. Liberal unity was as yet more apparent than real, for in the narrow escape from war the whole Cabinet learned for the first time of the secret discussions with the French. This revelation led to some dissent among ministers, but in the end Liberal illusions about splendid isolation gave way to realistic appraisals, and the Cabinet became even more committed to France. Unfortunately, Grey was unable in the aftermath of the crisis to achieve an overall settlement of great power rivalries. With German help he was successful, however, in containing the Balkan Wars of 1912–13.

The assassination of the Austrian Archduke Franz Ferdinand in Sarajevo in June 1914 transformed the prospects for peace in Europe. Grey was unable to use Britain's formal freedom of maneuver to persuade Austria-Hungary and Germany to pull back from war with Serbia, Russia, and France. His great speech in the House of Commons on the coming war was not a rousing call to arms but a heavy-hearted account of his efforts in the cause of peace.

Once Britain had entered the conflict, Grey's diplomacy became part and parcel of the larger military struggle. He maintained good relations with the United States and succeeded in bringing Italy over to the side of the Allies (1915). While he seemed to appreciate emotionally that the war would change everything, Grey did not foresee that secret agreements and understandings might become dead letters or worse in the post-war turmoil in Russia, Europe, and the colonial world. Fortunately for Grey, who suffered from steadily worsening eyesight, his wartime responsibilities ended in December 1916 when Lloyd George replaced Asquith as Prime Minister of a reconstructed coalition government. Grey was raised to the peerage as Viscount Grey of Falloden and devoted most of his subsequent public activity to the League of Nations Union. He continued to play a role in the leadership of the LIBERAL PARTY and served as Chancellor of OXFORD UNIVERSITY (1928–33).

Grey resumed his country life, given up four decades earlier, especially his love of birds. Perhaps this return to a former life was a way of acknowledging that the basis for his foreign policy simply no longer existed, that the war had indeed turned the world upside down and left a man like him on unfamiliar ground.

Ian Christopher Fletcher

Bibliography

Grey of Fallodon, Viscount. *Twenty-Five Years 1892–1916*. 2 vols. 1925.

Hinsley, F.H., ed. *British Foreign Policy under Sir Edward Grey*. 1977.

Robbins, Keith. *Sir Edward Grey: A Biography of Lord Grey of Fallodon*. 1971.

Trevelyan, George Macaulay. *Grey of Fallodon: The Life and Letters of Sir Edward Grey, afterwards Viscount Grey of Fallodon*. 1937.

Guild Socialism

Guild Socialism was a political theory and movement which advocated workers' control of industry through a system of democratic "guilds" of producers. The idea was first elaborated in 1912 by S.G. Hobson and A.R. Orage in the monthly *New Age*. It was further developed by others including A.J. Penty, M.B. Reckitt, William Mellor, and G.D.H. COLE, who became its leading spokesman. A National Guilds League was founded in 1915, immediately after the Guildsmen's near-successful attempt to "capture" the FABIAN SOCIETY. Although its membership never exceeded 1,000, the League enjoyed influence among trade unionists, largely as a result of its control of the Fabian (later Labour) Research Department. A practical attempt to realize the guild idea in the building industry in the early 1920s collapsed after some initial success. The National Guilds League disbanded in 1924. Guild Socialism thus died as a movement, although there were subsequent attempts within the labor movement to rekindle interest in its ideas.

Guild Socialism was a reaction against the impersonalism and alienation of industrial capitalism, and, more specifically, against the state socialism of the Fabian Society, which provided the theoretical basis of much of the labor movement's political thought. Guild Socialists believed that the greatest injustice was not that the workers were poor, but that they were—to use Hobson's term—"wage-slaves": a condition which state ownership and control of industry would do nothing to change. They believed also that the root of capitalist power lay not in the state but in the workshop, and therefore could not be fundamentally challenged by political means alone. The latter view was the basis of the Guild Socialists' ubiquitous slogan, "Economic Power Precedes Political Power."

Some Guild Socialists, informed by the medieval movement of the late nineteenth century, were opposed to industrial civilization itself and proposed a return to handicraft manufacture in a medieval guild system. Their case was first argued by Penty in *The Restoration of the Gild [sic] System* (1906). The majority, however, accepted both the permanence and desirability of industrialism, maintaining that machine production, if justly organized, could reduce both drudgery and material want.

The modernist stream of Guild Socialism may be seen as an Anglicized and intellectualized version of the syndicalist ideas imported from France and the United States, which inspired many of the leaders of the strike waves of 1911–14. Syndicalism aimed—by means of an insurrectionary general strike—to replace the state with direct working-class power organized into "one big union." Unlike the syndicalists, most Guild Socialists argued that the state was necessary to represent people in those activities and interests which all had in common. Their view was deeply influenced by the pluralist theories of J.N. Figgis and F.W. Maitland, who had argued that the state was merely one of many forms of assocation into which the members of a given community might enter, and had no right to claim sovereignty over other assocations such as churches or trade unions. In Cole's adaptation of pluralism the guilds would represent the citizens in their capacity as producers on equal terms with the state, which would have the particular function of representing them as consumers. While most Guild Socialists broadly accepted Cole's view, others—most notably Hobson—held that an individual could not thus be in conflict with itself, and saw the state as embodying the spiritual, rather than the economic aspects of the citizens' personalities.

Guild Socialism's life as a political movement began within the Oxford University Fabian Society, in which Cole and Mellor were leaders. Although the attempt to capture the Fabian Society was conducted with the maximum possible abrasiveness, the core of the "old guard" Fabian leadership (BERNARD SHAW and SIDNEY AND BEATRICE WEBB) tried hard to keep the insurgents

within the fold. To this end, and in the hope that empirical research would cool their ardor, the old guard offered them a committee to investigate the rival proposed modes of social ownership. The strategy backfired: the committee almost immediately metamorphosized into the Fabian Research Department, which disseminated Guild propaganda among trade union leaders while providing them with information to assist in the practical conduct of industrial disputes.

The FRD's activities laid much of the groundwork for the founding of industrial guilds. The building guilds, which originated in Manchester in 1920 under Hobson's leadership, were initially favored by a government-sponsored boom in post-war HOUSING construction. Their collapse in 1923 was due to the end of government subsidies in the context of a general economic slump, the hostility of the building employers, and Hobson's financial mismanagement. Many Guild Socialist leaders had looked askance at the guilds from the beginning, arguing that they could not work on a piecemeal basis, and that control of the state was necessary to facilitate wholesale change.

The National Guilds League was another victim of the slump, which forced trade unions into a defensive posture. Its demise was hastened by a split over attitudes to the Russian revolution; the participation of some members in the formation of the COMMUNIST PARTY of Great Britain in 1921; and the CPGB's takeover of the Labour Research Department.

In the early 1930s two discrete efforts were made to revive guild ideas. A group around Hobson established the House of Industry League, which advocated replacing the HOUSE OF LORDS with a chamber of functional representatives. A group around Cole and Mellor formulated a set of proposals for workers' control of socialized industry. Some of their proposals were formally adopted by the LABOUR PARTY, but had no effect on the NATIONALIZATION policies of the next Labour government. The libertarian upsurge within the left in the late 1960s occasioned a further renewal of interest in Guild Socialism's hitherto neglected place in labor history.

David Blaazer

Bibliography
Blaazer, David. "Guild Socialists after Guild Socialism: The Workers' Control Group and the House of Industry League," *Twentieth Century British History*, vol. 11 (2000), pp. 135–55.
Briggs, Asa, and John Saville. *Essays in Labour History 1886–1923.* Vol. 2, 1971.
Carpenter, Niles. *Guild Socialism*. 1922.
Cole, G.D.H. *Guild Socialism Restated*. 1920.
Glass, S.T. *The Responsible Society*. 1966.
Reckitt, M.B., and C.E. Bechhofer. *The Meaning of National Guilds*. rev. ed., 1920.

Haig, Douglas (1861–1928)

Promoted to Field Marshal in January 1917 and made an Earl in 1919, Douglas Haig was Commander-in-Chief of the British Expeditionary Force (BEF) in France and Belgium from December 1915 until the end of the FIRST WORLD WAR. His performance during that period remains among the most controversial aspects of the 1914–18 conflict.

Born in Edinburgh of a prominent Scotch whisky manufacturing family on 19 June 1861 and educated at Clifton and Brasenose College, OXFORD, Haig entered Sandhurst in 1884, passing out first in order of merit. He was gazetted to the 7th Hussars in 1885 and served in India from 1886 to 1892. Taciturn and ambitious, Haig was nevertheless regarded as a capable administrator who emphasized the need for education and efficiency. The principles of war he absorbed at the Staff College in 1896–7 had a considerable influence on his conduct of operations in the First World War. Having won further recognition in the Sudan in 1898, Haig served with the Cavalry Division in the early stages of the BOER WAR, mostly as chief staff officer to Sir John French (1852–1925). The successful cavalry charge preceding the relief of Kimberley in February 1900 reaffirmed Haig's faith in the value of the mounted arm. In May 1901 he was given command of the 17th Lancers, combining regimental duties with those of a column commander.

Haig's career flourished after the South African War. From 1903 to 1906 he was Inspector General of Cavalry in India. Then, at the War Office, first as Director of Military Training (1906–7) and latterly as Director of Staff Duties (1907–9), he helped to shape and implement the ARMY reforms of R.B. HALDANE, including the transformation of the Militia, Volunteers, and Yeomanry into the Special Reserve and Territorial Force, as well as the creation of an expeditionary force and the Imperial General Staff. In 1909 Haig was appointed Chief of the General Staff in India, spending a frustrating two years trying, without total success, to prepare the Indian army for a wider role. However, in 1912 he took over the Aldershot Command, a post carrying with it the field command of I Corps when the BEF was mobilized for war against Germany.

On 25 August 1914, during the retreat from Mons, Haig's normally calm demeanor deserted him when German troops entered Landrecies, menacing his headquarters, but he quickly regained confidence, and on the Aisne in September his corps only narrowly missed seizing the Chemin des Dames ridge ahead of the Germans. At the First Battle of Ypres in October–November his resolute leadership of I Corps contributed to the blocking of German attempts to reach the Channel ports, even though the old BEF was thereby largely destroyed. As the BEF was reorganized, Haig was elevated to the command of its First Army on 26 December. In 1915, like many others, he was unable to find a solution to the trench deadlock and misread the lessons of the attack at Neuve Chapelle in March, opting thereafter for lengthy artillery preparation rather than hurricane bombardments. His disillusionment with his superior, Sir John French, increased on 25–26 September at Loos, where the late arrival of reserves prevented the First Army from exploiting initial gains, an episode which precipitated French's replacement by Haig as Commander-in-Chief of the BEF on 19 December 1915.

With Britain still the junior partner in the alliance with France, Haig could not attack in Flanders, as he wished, in 1916, being obliged to participate in a joint offensive on the SOMME. He envisaged a swift breakthrough, whereas Lieutenant-General Sir Henry Rawlinson (1864–1925), whose Fourth Army launched the attack, favored a more gradual "bite and hold" approach. Haig's failure to resolve such differences led to fatal ambiguities in the assault plan. Following the disastrous opening of the offensive on 1 July, Haig grew reconciled to a dour battle of attrition prior to another major assault at Flers-Courcelette on 15 September, when tanks made their operational debut. Haig has, perhaps, been unfairly blamed for using tanks prematurely yet, a decisive breakthrough having once more eluded him, he undoubtedly prolonged the offensive unnecessarily until mid–November.

DAVID LLOYD GEORGE, who succeeded HERBERT ASQUITH as Prime Minister in December 1916, was highly critical of Haig. However, he stopped short of dismissing him, and Haig managed to resist a move, in February 1917, to make him permanently subordinate to the new French commander-in-chief, General Robert Nivelle (1856–1924). Indeed, French army mutinies in 1917 caused the BEF to shoulder the main burden of Allied endeavors on the Western Front. While the BEF displayed marked tactical improvements in the assault phases of its battles at Arras (April), Messines (June) and Cambrai (November), Haig's performance in his offensive at Ypres from 31 July to 10 November was undistinguished, for he allowed the Fifth Army commander, General Sir Hubert Gough (1870–1963), to set unrealistic early objectives and again persisted with a costly battle too long in appalling conditions.

Recent studies suggest that Haig underestimated the threat to the Fifth Army in March 1918 and, at one stage of the German "Michael" offensive, was prepared to fall back on the Channel ports, away from his French allies. Even so, he supported the establishment of a unified Allied command under General Ferdinand Foch (1851–1929), and, during the German Lys offensive, showed commendable tenacity, exemplified by his "Backs to the Wall" order of 11 April. Later, Haig was one of the first to sense that the German army could be defeated in 1918. Moreover, in the final "Hundred Days" campaign, starting at Amiens on 8 August, the BEF won the greatest series of victories in the British army's history, achievements often forgotten in assessments of Haig. He returned home in 1919, was granted an earldom and appointed as Commander-in-Chief, Home Forces, retiring in 1921. In his last years he immersed himself in the cause of ex-servicemen, inspiring the formation of the British Legion and becoming its president. He died on 29 January 1928.

Peter Simkins

Bibliography

Blake, Robert. *The Private Papers of Douglas Haig, 1914–1919.* 1952.

De Groot, Gerard J. *Douglas Haig, 1861–1928.* 1988.

Terraine, John. *Douglas Haig: The Educated Soldier.* 1963.

Winter, Dennis. *Haig's Command: A Reassessment.* 1991.

Woodward, David R. *Lloyd George and the Generals.* 1983.

Haldane, J(ohn) B(urdon) S(anderson) (1892–1964)

J.B.S. Haldane was one of the most distinguished biologists of his generation, remembered above all for his contribution to the uniting of Darwinian evolutionary theory and Mendelian genetics in a series of papers published from 1924. These were collected and systematized as *The Causes of Evolution* in 1932, the same year that he was elected to the Royal Society. Haldane was a significant public figure and author of popular scientific essays. A man of strong convictions, he was for years a major figure in the COMMUNIST PARTY OF GREAT BRITAIN. After a succesful academic career at CAMBRIDGE and in London, in 1957 he moved to India to continue his work, becoming a citizen of that country in 1961. He was married twice and had no children.

J.B.S. was the only son of J.S. Haldane, a distinguished OXFORD physiologist; his sister was the novelist Naomi Mitchison (1897–1999). The Haldane family was of lowland Scottish noble extraction and politically illustrious: his uncle, RICHARD BURDON (LATER VISCOUNT) HALDANE, was a Liberal War Minister and Lord Chancellor. Haldane was educated at Lynam's School, Oxford and Eton, winning a mathematics scholarship to New College, OXFORD. He gained first class honors not only in that subject, but also in classics and philosophy (1914). During the FIRST WORLD WAR he served as an officer in France and Mesopotamia. From 1919 he worked in GENETICS and physiology at New College, Oxford, before joining Gowland Hopkins at Cambridge as Reader in Biochemistry in 1922. Parallel with this, he was put in charge of genetical investigations at the John Innes Horticultural Research Station (1927–36). In 1933 he moved to University College, London, as Professor of Genetics, then of Biometry. He made three trips to fight in the INTERNATIONAL BRIGADE during the SPANISH CIVIL WAR, gaining experience which led to his book *A.R.P.* (1938), a quantitative study of the likely bomb damage in the anticipated world war. He remained at U.C.L. until he took up a post at the Biometry Research Unit of the Indian Statistical Institute in Calcutta, transferring in 1962 to the Laboratory of Genetics and Biometry at Bhubaneswar.

Much of his work involved the application of mathematics to biological problems. His genetical and evolutionary researches were usually achieved not by experiment, but by re-analyzing established data about plant and animal populations. Mathematics, Haldane believed, was essential to Darwinian theory, because it was necessary to prove not only that natural selection could explain that species change, but, crucially, that it could have caused change at a sufficient rate to explain the variation observed in nature.

Along with his genetical work he undertook several series of physiological experiments. In 1939 he investigated the cause of casualties after the submarine *Thetis* sank, by observing the effects on himself and three others of being enclosed in a sealed chamber simulating submarine conditions. Later in the war he undertook similar work for the Admiralty on the physiological effects of gases at high pressure.

His works aimed at a general audience demonstrated a marked willingness to extrapolate from scientific to social principles. *Daedalus* (1924), for example, is a meditation on the deliberate directing of human evolution to enable the colonization of other worlds. *Callinicus* (1925) contains a robust defense of chemical warfare. *My Friend Mr Leakey,* a collection of children's stories, was published in 1937. He wrote more than 300 weekly columns for the *Daily Worker.*

Haldane will continue to be remembered as a biologist with equally strong convictions about society as about science, whose example inspired generations of students.

T.M. Boon

Bibliography

Clark, Ronald W. *J.B.S. The Life and work of JBS Haldane.* 1968.
Dronamraju, Krishna R., ed. *Haldane and Modern Biology.* 1968.
————. *The Life and Work of J.B.S. Haldane with Special Reference to India.* 1985.
Werskey, Gary. *The Visible College: A Collective Biography of British Scientists and Socialists of the 1930s.* 2nd ed. 1988.

Haldane, R(ichard) B(urdon) (1856–1928)

R.B. Haldane was a Liberal politician, jurist, educator, and philosopher. The second son of Robert Haldane, writer to the Signet, he was educated at Edinbugh Academy, the University of Edinburgh, and Goettingen University. He studied law at Lincoln's Inn, was called to the Bar in 1879, took silk in 1890, went special in 1897, and continued to practice in Chancery, the Privy Council, and the HOUSE OF LORDS until 1905. He stood successfully as a Liberal candidate for East Lothian in 1885 and held the seat until elevated to the peerage as Viscount Haldane of Cloan in 1911. His many honors included the Order of Merit (1915). He played a significant role in the last LIBERAL government, which enacted numerous social and constitutional reforms and confronted considerable domestic turbulence before leading Britain and the Empire into the First World War. Complicated and cerebral, he was capable of supporting such apparently divergent positions as military training for schoolboys and votes for women.

A Liberal Imperialist associated with Lord Rosebery, Haldane only entered the Liberal government with H.H. ASQUITH and SIR EDWARD GREY in December 1905 after they had failed to dislodge the new Prime Minister, the Radical Liberal SIR HENRY CAMPBELL-BANNERMAN. Haldane served as Secretary of State for War (1905–12) and Lord Chancellor (1912–15). As War Minister, he was responsible for crucial reforms which placed the ARMY on a sound footing for war in Europe. They included the establishment of a General Staff, later enlarged to an Im-

perial General Staff in 1909, and the formation of an Expeditionary Force, complete with transport and supply arrangements. In the Territorial and Reserve Forces Act 1907 the forces available to the Regular Army upon mobilization were reconfigured by transforming the Militia into a Special Reserve and organizing the Volunteers into a Territorial Force. The reforms were debated in an atmosphere of growing anxiety over the German threat to British naval supremacy and even the danger of invasion. Their enactment and implementation represented a triumph for Haldane over, on the one hand, Radical economism and PACIFISM and, on the other hand, CONSERVATIVE militarism and navalism.

Haldane was also responsible, in concert with the Home Secretaries Herbert Gladstone, WINSTON CHURCHILL, and Reginald McKenna, for the deployment of troops to maintain public order in Britain and Ireland. Although the Liberal government generally showed restraint during the labor unrest of 1910–12, some lives were lost in collisions between strikers and soldiers and worries were expressed about continued working-class adherence to Liberalism. In June 1912 Haldane became Lord Chancellor. He supported the cause of law reform, especially with regard to law of real property and conveyancing. Although limited in what he could do by the overlapping jurisdictions of the Home Office and the Lord Chancellor's Office, he also supported legal-administrative reform. In line with his predecessor on the woolsack, Lord Loreburn, Haldane tried to appoint and promote magistrates and judges on the basis of professional not party-political distinction. His greatest contribution lay in his efforts to improve the efficiency of the Judicial Committee of the Privy Council and the House of Lords, which handled important appeals from around the Empire.

Haldane's work for international peace and order included an unsuccessful mission to Berlin in 1912 for the purpose of seeking a reduction in the naval arms race and generally relaxing tensions between Britain and Germany. Haldane's admiration for German culture and philosophy became a liability during the FIRST WORLD WAR. He was forced to resign when Asquith formed the first coalition government in 1915.

A Hegelian who took a broad view of the state, Haldane did not allow his enemies to drive him from public life and administration. A life-long educator and one of the co-founders of the LONDON SCHOOL OF ECONOMICS in 1895, Haldane continued to take part in a wide variety of initiatives for the improvement of educational institutions and opportunities in both London and the provinces. He was President of Birkbeck College, University of London in 1919–28.

Haldane served once again as Lord Chancellor during the first Labour government in 1924. He subsequently led the Labour opposition in the House of Lords. He was probably the most distinguished Liberal leader to accept the LABOUR PARTY as the legitimate successor to Liberalism. His death in 1928, on the eve of the world slump, spared him the disappointments of the second Labour government and the larger political changes which made Liberalism all but redundant in British and European politics.

Ian Christopher Fletcher

Bibliography

Haldane, Richard Burdon. *An Autobiography.* 1929.

Heuston, R.F.V. *Lives of the Lord Chancellors 1885–1940.* 1964.

Koss, Stephen E. *Lord Haldane: Scapegoat for Liberalism.* 1969.

Maurice, Sir Frederick. *Haldane: The Life of Viscount Haldane of Cloan.* 2 vols. 1937–9.

Spiers, Edward M. *Haldane, An Army Reformer.* 1980.

Halifax, Earl of [Edward Frederick Lindley Wood] (1881–1959)

Edward Wood was born to wealth, privilege, and social status, and, upon the death of his father in 1934, he inherited the title of Viscount Halifax. He was educated at Eton and at Christ Church, OXFORD and was subsequently elected a Fellow of All Souls College, Oxford. A deeply religious Anglo-Catholic, he had considerable personal virtues, including an extraordinary ability to remain detached, objective, and fair-minded about highly contentious issues. A life-long CONSERVATIVE, he sat for years in both Houses of Parliament and held a number of important political and diplomatic posts, but he is primarily remembered as an arch-APPEASER who, as Foreign Secretary under NEVILLE CHAMBERLAIN, yielded to Nazi threats and abandoned Czechoslovakia in the infamous MUNICH agreement of 1938.

After holding several lesser ministerial posts, he was, as Lord Irwin, appointed as Viceroy of India (1925–31), a curious selection in view of his minimal knowledge of the subcontinent. India was then in a state of turmoil and near chaos, with nationalists demanding extensive political concessions from Britain. By nature a conciliator, he responded with dignity, calm, and fairness, eliciting respect from all parties concerned. He acted firmly but not brutally in trying to maintain law and order, publicly stated that dominion status for India was inevitable, and cut a deal with Gandhi in 1931 that temporarily reduced the violence and agitation. He could do little personally to affect the course of constitutional development or mitigate the communal violence between Hindus and Muslims.

After his return to Britain, he served briefly as Secretary of State for War (1935), becoming painfully aware of the wretched state of Britain's defenses. He also held a number of other posts, including Lord Privy Seal (1935–7), Leader in the House of Lords (1935–8, 1940), and Lord President of the Council (1937–8). But it was his appointment as Foreign Secretary (1938–40) that proved so fateful. Here he gained his reputation as a bungling appeaser, who shamefully agreed to turn portions of Czechoslovakia over to Hitler. In some respects the opprobrium is justified. He initially misjudged the Nazis, admitting after a visit to Germany that he personally liked many of their leaders and believed Hitler was sincere in not wanting war. He loyally supported Chamberlain during the Czech crisis, allowing the authority of the Foreign Office to be circumvented and usurped by some of the Prime Minister's personal advisors. Incredibly, he did not personally attend the three critical meetings that Chamberlain had with Hitler at Berchtesgaden, Godesberg, and Munich, to settle the Czech crisis.

However, more recent scholarship has partially rehabilitated his reputation. Unlike Chamberlain, Halifax saw Munich as a "horrible and wretched business", done out of dire necessity because of British military weakness, French indecisiveness, and the geographical isolation of Czechoslovakia. After Munich, Halifax encouraged Chamberlain to take a firmer line against Germany, pressed for more vigorous rearmament, gave military guarantees to Poland, Rumania, and Greece, and also attempted to negotiate an alliance with the Soviet Union, though with little enthusiasm and conviction.

Halifax was seriously considered as likely Prime Minister when Chamberlain resigned in May 1940, but he wisely recognized his unsuitability and deferred to WINSTON CHURCHILL. In December, Churchill asked Halifax to become ambassador to the United States (1941–6), a crucial posting since Britain desperately needed American economic and military assistance even though the latter was technically at peace and isolationist in tendency. Initially unenthusiastic, Halifax accepted out of a sense of duty and had what could be labelled a successful term. He got along well with President Roosevelt, committed no serious blunders, ran the large British Embassy staff with tact and efficiency, and educated the American public to Britain's dire peril and to her military needs.

Upon his return to Britain in 1946, he retired from politics and enjoyed playing the role of the country gentleman on his Yorkshire estate. He received numerous honors and took time to write his disappointing memoirs, *Fullness of Days*. Despite his intelligence and integrity, his deep sense of patriotism and religious piety, his unquestionable accomplishments, he will undoubtedly be primarily remembered as an "appeaser," although perhaps one less culpable than several of his colleagues.

David C. Lukowitz

Bibliography

Birkenhead, Frederick, Earl of. *Halifax: The Life of Lord Halifax*. 1965.

Charmley, John. *Chamberlain and the Lost Peace*. 1989.

Halifax, Lord. *Fullness of Days*. 1957.

Roberts, Andrew: *The Holy Fox: A Life of Lord Halifax*. 1991.

Hammond, J(ohn) L(awrence) (Le Breton) (1872–1949) and Lucy Barbara (1873–1961)

The Hammonds were pioneer social historians who are remembered especially for their trilogy: *The Village Labourer* (1911), *The Town Labourer* (1917), and *The Skilled Labourer* (1919). They gave an account of the condition of the English working class during the period of the Industrial Revolution which became a classic statement of the "pessimistic" case in a long-running debate over the STANDARD OF LIVING. John Lawrence Le Breton Hammond (known as Lawrence) married Lucy Barbara Bradby (known as Barbara) in 1901; they had no children. Their historical partnership developed in later years as their increasingly precarious health (hers tubercular, his mainly coronary) led to a steady withdrawal from an active participation in public affairs in London and the establishment of an even-paced life of authorship in the country.

Both of the Hammonds received a classical education, on which their literary work drew. They were as adept at painting the contrast between ancient Athens and modern Manchester as at elucidating the Homeric references in the discourse of Mr. Gladstone. Both came from professional families infused with moral and intellectual earnestness; his father was a clergyman of the CHURCH OF ENGLAND, hers the headmaster of a boarding school (Haileybury) which notoriously recruited CIVIL SERVANTS for the British Raj. The Hammonds gave this heritage a radical twist. Barbara made a striking impression in her youth as an early FEMINIST and became active in social work in London at the turn of the century. Lawrence began a career as a journalist associated with journals on the Liberal Left like the *NATION* and, increasingly in later years, the *MANCHESTER GUARDIAN*. He was prominently associated with the "NEW LIBERALISM", which took shape in the social reforms of the Edwardian period, until his appointment as as Secretary of the Civil Service Commission (1907–13). This meant that he had to renounce overtly partisan polemics—an initial impetus towards writing history instead.

With their first book, *The Village Labourer* (1911) the Hammonds established their reputation. Technically their work was founded upon Barbara's scrupulous research, especially in the public records, expounded in Lawrence's supple prose. Their account of how agricultural laborers fared under the enclosure measures of the period 1760–1830 opened up a far-reaching debate. They did not deny the economic rationality of the process, but pointed to the way that its costs were borne by the rural poor. The book culminates in an account of the laborers' revolt of 1830, which they took as the response to an injustice which could only have been perpetrated while the landed interest governed England untrammelled. This was indeed a study of class exploitation; but the Hammonds were neither Marxists nor determinists, but liberals who looked to the advent of representative government for effective remedy. Their work acquired immediate political overtones with the inception of LLOYD GEORGE's Land Campaign in 1913 which made the land the pivot of Liberal social policy.

In turning their attention next to the urban working class, the Hammonds reinforced the left-wing image of their oeuvre. *The Town Labourer* (1917) did not disparage industrialization as such but again asked the awkward question: who had paid for it? They regarded the Industrial Revolution as an exercise in exploitation which fitted the ideologies of an age which took social inequality for granted. Published at the end of the First World War, with revolution on the streets abroad and reconstruction in the air at home, their findings once more fed into current political debate. Their trilogy was completed with *The Skilled Labourer* (1919) which analyzed the impact of technological change in making skilled craftsmen redundant in the early nineteenth century. It presented the Luddite movement in an unwontedly sympathetic light, suggesting that it constituted not only an understandable response by the inarticulate in defense of their livelihood but also an excuse for repression by a reactionary government.

Other books followed, notably the study of the Chartist era which Penguin Books later published in an abridged—and bestselling—edition as *The Bleak Age* (1947). But the Hammonds' view of the Industrial Revolution remained their claim to attention—not all of it favorable. In the 1920s their interpretation was contested by J.H. Clapham, with all his authority as Professor of Economic History at CAMBRIDGE. He mounted an "optimistic" case on the standard of living by constructing a real wage index which showed substantial gains by industrial workers. Though the Hammonds publicly bowed on this point in face of the apparent weight of new statistical evidence, subsequent research was to show that Clapham himself had depended on a flawed price index.

Lawrence's own historical research in old age was devoted to the great Liberal statesman who had been the hero of his youth. In *Gladstone and the Irish Nation* (1938) he made brilliant use of the privileged access he had been given to Gladstone's diaries to render his Irish policy comprehensible in historical context. Again this is a book in which passion and elegance are counterpoised in giving form to a mass of arcane and rebarbative detail. The resulting portrait of Gladstone succeeds in conveying a sense of the man on which all subsequent scholarship has built. This was his last major contribution to historical scholarship. During the SECOND WORLD WAR he returned to his old job of leader-writer on the *Manchester Guardian;* but it was a valetudinarian life for the Hammonds thereafter.

The Hammonds have often been identified as socialist, yet their outlook throughout their joint career remained true to the nostrums of liberal reformism. Insofar as the Hammonds rested their interpretation of the Industrial Revolution upon a quantitative assessment, it was by no means overturned; and its main thrust, in fact, was qualitative in its concern for the impact of economic change on ordinary people's lives. While they depicted the bleak age of early industrialization, they also pointed to the civilizing process which urban life underwent from the middle of the nineteenth century. Though their work came to serve as a straw man, to be knocked down in a dismissive way by a new generation of professional economic historians, its scholarly credentials have survived with remarkable resilience.

Peter Clarke

Bibliography

Clarke, Peter. *Liberals and Social Democrats.* 1978.

Javurek, Teresa. "A New Liberal Descent: The 'Labourer' Trilogy by Lawrence and Barbara Hammond," *Twentieth Century British History,* vol. 10 (1999), pp. 375–403.

Thomis, Malcolm I. *The Town Labourer and the Industrial Revolution.* 1974.

Weaver, Stewart A. *The Hammonds: A Marriage in History.* 1997.

Hardie, (James) Keir (1856–1915)

Keir Hardie's career symbolized the emergence of Independent Labour politics. He was born in Legbrannock, Lanarkshire on 15 August 1856, the illegitimate son of a Scottish farm servant. Childhood poverty and underground employment in COAL MINING from the age of ten were formative experiences. His early involvement in trade union activities led to his effective exclusion from the industry in his mid-twenties. Alongside his agitational and rebellious tendencies he had a zealous devotion to self-improvement. After moving to Cumnock in Ayrshire in the early 1880s, he developed his journalistic talents, made am ambivalent compromise with middle-class radicalism, and keenly supported the LIBERAL PARTY.

Industrial and political pressures broke this allegiance. Hardie's outlook was radicalised in 1886–7 by another failed attempt to develop effective Scottish mining trade unionism. In January 1887 he established a newspaper, *The Miner,* and made links with socialists. Sixteen months later, in April 1888 he fought a by-election at Mid-Lanark as an Independent Labour candidate. In retrospect, this may seem a significant shift, although the extent of his ideological break with Liberalism remains controversial. His vote was 617, only 8.2 percent of the total in a three-cornered contest. Later that year he played a major part in the formation of the Scottish Labour Party, an alliance of radicals, land reformers, and trade unionists. This party's character illuminated the complexities of Hardie's own politics— assertions of independence, but a heavy legacy from his earlier Liberalism.

A symbolic moment came in July 1892 with his election to Parliament as the Independent Labour Member for West Ham South. Unlike two contemporaries and despite some local Liberal support, he retained his independence, attacking the subsequent Liberal government on labour questions, especially unemployment, and attracting criticism for his outspoken republicanism. Another crucial development came in 1893 when Hardie chaired much of the foundation conference of the INDEPENDENT LABOUR PARTY. From the following year he and the new party became almost synonymous. With the *Labour Leader,* his successor to the *Miner,* moving to weekly publication in March 1894. Hardie was emerging as a dominant figure in the socialist movement.

Yet the late 1890s proved difficult years. He lost his parliamentary seat in 1895, the ILP's early optimism faded. Together with other ILP leaders he defeated attempts to fuse the ILP and the Marxist Social Democratic Federation into a United Socialist Party. Instead he favored a broad labour alliance of trade unions and socialist groups. This strategy was consummated in February 1900, with the foundation conference of the LABOUR REPRESENTATION COMMITTEE, an achievement which owed much to Hardie's vision.

Alongside this organizational pragmatism, Hardie demonstrated principle and courage in his outspoken opposition to the British military campaign in South Africa. His outrage, although expressed frequently in the langauge of socialism, was fuelled more by liberal anti-militarism. Despite the widespread British support for the BOER WAR, Hardie won a parliamentary seat in the election of 1900. His return as one of the two MPs for Merthyr Boroughs owed much to quarrels amongst the Liberals who dominated this South Wales industrial seat. His victory meant that the LRC had one thoroughly loyal spokesman in the new Parliament. Alongside his robust assertions of independence, however, Hardie was flexible in his attitude towards electoral deals with the Liberals. This reflected his situation in Merthyr and also his blend of non–Marxian socialism and Liberal radicalism. The Liberal electoral landslide of 1906 brought thirty victories for Labour candidates, mostly the results of a secret pact with the Liberals. The LRC became the LABOUR PARTY and Hardie became Chairman of the Parliamentary Party.

Hardie's year and a half in this post attracted considerable criticism. Initially he led a parliamentary group that seemed to make a significant impact: for example securing the reversal of the TAFF VALE JUDGEMENT on trade union liability. Over time, the limitations of the Labour position became more apparent and frustration tended to focus on Hardie's leadership. Moreover he always faced a major problem in reconciling his awareness of organizational limitations with his agitational and propagandist instincts.

From his resignation of the Parliamentary Party chairmanship to the outbreak of the First World War, Hardie acted almost as an elder statesman with radical proclivities. He vigorously defended the Labour Party against critics from the Left who claimed that the compact with the unions was damaging to Socialist prospects, but he often felt unhappy about the caution of many Labour politicians. He had deep reservations about syndicalism, but he reacted to the industrial struggles from 1910 with bitter indictments of Liberal government policy. On the WOMEN'S SUFFRAGE question, his consistent and passionate advocacy of a liberal case for sexual equality led to tensions with many less committed colleagues. On all domestic issues in Edwardian Britain Hardie continued to work within the confines of Labour politics; often his attitudes were still informed by liberal values, but he articulated forcefully the emotions of the dispossessed and the disadvantaged.

The splendor and the tragedy of Hardie's career lay in his internationalism. An Empire tour in 1907–8 found him ambiguous on the White Australia policy, but he evoked a storm by his denunciations of British rule in India. His brief visit to South Africa brought riotous scenes as he condemned racial discrimination including the practices of white trade unions. Above all, Hardie became preoccupied with the threat of militarism

within Europe and placed increasing hope in the Second International as a means of averting catastrophe. The collapse of such hopes in August 1914 culminated for him in a bruising meeting in his constituency, cut short by patriotic disorder. The destruction of Hardie's political hopes was essentially the end of his career. Effectively a casualty of the war, he died on 26 September 1915.

An internationalist who was a thorough Scot, a pragmatist who was a romantic and a visionary, Hardie came for many to symbolize a radical political change. Yet he always remained an outsider, a loner through whose personality were reflected the achievements and the tragedies of the British Left.

David Howell

Bibliography

Benn, Caroline. *Keir Hardie.* 1992.

Hughes, Emrys, ed. *Keir Hardie's Speeches and Writings.* 1928.

McLean, Iain. *Keir Hardie.* 1975.

Morgan, Kenneth O. *Keir Hardie: Radical and Socialist.* 1975.

Stewart, William. *J. Keir Hardie.* 1921.

Health of the Population

The change in the incidence and distribution of disease and death among the British people in the twentieth century has been of such a colossal nature that it makes all other previous changes of this sort seem insignificant. The first half of the century saw a massive decline in morbidity and mortality from infectious diseases, especially among children. The second half witnessed a rising incidence of degenerative diseases in an increasingly AGEING population. Most, but not all, statistics point to the increasing health of the population. Statistics, however, are only pointers not definitive signs, since nearly all numbers used to indicate health are measures of the absence of disease, not measures of positive well-being.

At the beginning of the century, qualitatively speaking, the poor, and especially the children of the poor, suffered chronic, low-grade ill-health punctuated by episodes of severe, sometimes fatal, illness. Infectious diseases and nutritional disorders such as diphtheria, scarlet fever, osteomyelitis, and rickets were common. Undernourishment was the norm among the poor. In 1910 the report of the Chief Medical Officer on the health of schoolchildren described 10 percent as having serious defects of vision, 40 percent with bad teeth, 40 percent with "unclean heads or bodies" as well as noting that children were victims of a host of other complaints such as ring worm, enlarged tonsils, and adenoidal disorders. Crippling, if not fatal diseases, such as mastoid infection were common. In 1917 Professor Arthur Keith (1866–1955) found 70 percent of a sample of UNIVERSITY OF CAMBRIDGE students were above "full stature" (defined as 5ft 8ins). However, Medical Boards examining working-class recruits at almost exactly the same time, 1917–18, found only 36 percent were in this category. In contrast to this grim picture, by the year 2002, if current-trends continue, the overall portrait of the nation's health will show a well-nourished population relatively free of sickness in its younger age groups but containing a large proportion of elderly folk suffering from chronic degenerative disorders (mainly the arteriosclerotic diseases) and cancer. The hinge where the early pattern turns into the late one is roughly situated at mid-century.

The decline in mortality which was occurring in the late nineteenth century accelerated in the first half of the twentieth. In 1901 the crude annual death rate in Britain was about 18 per thousand; by 1960 it had fallen to 11.5. Thirty years later, in 1990, there had been little further gain and the figure was 11.2. Correspondingly, over the same period, life expectancy increased. In 1901 a man could expect to live to just over forty-five and a woman to nearly fifty. By 1960 these figures had jumped to roughly sixty-eight and seventy-four. By 1990 a further five years had been gained by both sexes. Scottish death rates, perhaps because of the comparatively late urbanization of central Scotland, have remained consistently higher than those of England. In general during the century regional differences in mortality have diminished. In the decade 1901–10 death rates in non-industrial areas were 25 percent lower than those for industrial areas in England and Wales. But by 1950 urban areas were offering definite advantages over the rural.

All of these crude figures, impressive as they are, simply disguise the site at which the greatest changes in twentieth-century mortality occurred. Practically every gain was made among children, and almost entirely among children born during the first half century. Of 1000 children born in 1900, 230, nearly a quarter, failed to reach the age of fifteen. By 1950 the figure was about 40. Even these figures disguise where the most significant changes took place. The fall in death rates occurred preponderantly among children under four, most notably among infants under one year. In this latter group mortality fell from around 160 per 1000 in 1900 to under 30 in the 1950s. This improvement was continued without remission through the distressed years of the 1920s and 1930s. The relation of these variations in mortality to occupation and class is an area of controversy. Nevertheless, it is indisputable that mortality, although it has fallen in all classes, has remained higher, at all ages, among the unskilled than among the professional classes.

These remarkable changes in mortality have been accompanied by a spectacular change in the pattern of disease. Between 1901 and 1971 73 percent of the fall in mortality can be attributed to a decline in deaths from infectious diseases. Children, as we have noted, were the principal beneficiaries of this reduction. Diphtheria, measles, whooping cough, scarlet fever, infantile diarrhoea nearly all disappeared as causes of infant and child mortality. In the population as a whole deaths from tuberculosis have shown the most notable decline. In the last decade of the nineteenth century nearly 1500 people out of every million in the population would die, every year, of respiratory tuberculosis. In 1971, 13 people in every million died of the same cause. Corresponding to the decline in mortality from infectious disorders has been a decline in the morbidity caused by these and other diseases. Again children have been the beneficiaries. The chronic disabling diseases of childhood, notably crippling infections of bones and joints, have become far less common. But even among the non-aged adult population the incidence of severe infectious diseases, such as lobar pneumonia, has declined considerably.

Many factors have played a part in the pattern of decline. Better HOUSING and better sanitation have continued to contribute substantially to the change, just as they did from the mid-nineteenth century onwards. Much prominence was given in the past to specific medical measures, such as inoculation and antibiotics. However, it is clear that although, in most instances, these technologies did make a small difference, they actually arrived late on the scene when curves were already making spectacular falls. The exact effect of medical intervention is thus problematical. Non-specific medical intervention, such as the provision of milk depots, district midwifery and nursing services have, presumably, been highly significant, but again their effect is hard to measure. The crucial factor seem to have been better NUTRITION. The benefits of a larger and more varied diet began to have an effect in the late nineteenth century, and these benefits accrued in the twentieth as the quantity and quality of food intake *per capita* gradually increased. Better nutrition made it possible for people to resist and recover from the diseases of childhood. Evidence of better nutrition is to be found in the trend towards earlier physical maturation and in the increase in heights and weights of schoolchildren. Such changes correlate extremely well with increases in the *per capita* national income. Besides increasing, this latter has also shown some reduction in inequality in the twentieth century. Nonetheless, throughout the century, the poor have remained smaller in stature than the rich.

The height of the poor was already increasing before the First World War and the inter-war years showed continuing gains. The SECOND WORLD WAR itself had beneficial effects; food distribution was more equitable and some groups were the beneficiaries of positive discrimination. By the end of the war 40 percent of school children had school dinners and 70 percent school milk. By the mid-1950s less than 2 percent of school children were in what the medical inspectorate considered an unsatisfactory condition. By the 1960s the slow increase in height, which had been going on since the nineteenth century, may have come to an end. Around this time doctors first began to comment on undesirable obesity in schoolchildren.

Such comments mark the turning point between the two parts of the century. Whereas childhood is the predominant theme in discussing the first half of the century, age and its diseases dominate the second. Between 1950 and 1990 the population of the elderly (over sixty-five years of age) grew by 3.7 million to 8.9 million, to represent 15.6 percent of British residents. But, just as crude figures for the early century disguise drastic changes among infants, so these later figures hide the rapid expansion in the population over seventy-five years. In 1948 at the start of the NATIONAL HEALTH SERVICE these folk numbered 1.7 million (3.4 percent of the population) by 1990 they accounted for 4 million (6.9 percent). This age shift and the disappearance of the childhood infectious disorders has been reflected in the causes of death. Of the total number of deaths registered in 1990 about 46 percent were related to the circulatory system, 25 percent to cancers (notably breast and lung cancer), and 10 percent to the respiratory system. Many of the people dying from these conditions were, of course, chronically sick before death. In fact expectation of life without disability has risen very little in the second part of the century. In 1988 expectation of life with "chronic disability" was fourteen years in males and seventeen in females. The geriatric hospital, it might be said, has replaced the sanatorium as a symbol of sickness in the adult population. Looking at specific disorders, ischaemic heart disease predominates as the main cause of death, even though the actual incidence has fallen since the 1970s. During the 1980s it claimed on average, 459 lives a day. Stroke is the second largest killer, followed by lung cancer. Scotland tops the age-specific mortality lists for the whole of Europe in all of these categories.

Measures of morbidity are much more difficult to achieve than measures of mortality, especially if the sickness does not come to the attention of a doctor. In a survey of sickness carried out between 1943 and 1952, two out of three people reported awareness of ill-health in the month prior to interview, females complaining of more ill-health than males. In spite of this high level of complaint, only one in four had seen a doctor, and only one in eight had lost time from work or been confined to the house. Similar surveys forty years later produced similar results. Although masses of statistics have been available since the advent of the National Health Service, measuring morbidity is fraught with problems. It seems certain, however, that in-patient hospital treatment has increased. Despite fewer beds, 9.1 million were treated as hospital in-patients in 1990–1 compared to 3.8 million in 1951. This surely does not indicate the deteriorating health of the people but, in part, greater public willingness to present for medical treatment. But how far curative medicine has improved the lives of the British people in the twentieth century is a moot point. Arguably the greatest medical benefits have not been in the most spectacular conditions, heart attack, kidney failure, cancer, which have been the source of some fairly spectacular but contentious therapies. For most people the great benefits of medicine have been at a much simpler level, in the use of drugs or surgery for disorders such as asthma, skin disease, hernias, varicose veins, and a whole range of other complaints which, while not life-threatening, are sufficiently intrusive to make normal life unpleasant or even impossible.

IMMIGRATION has also made a difference to the pattern of British health. In general ethnic minorities have poorer health than the rest of the population. For example, in the early 1990s death from heart disease was 46 percent higher among Asian women, and strokes killed 76 percent more Afro-Caribbean men than the average. Poverty, although significant, is not the only cause of the difference. For example, most ethnic groups smoke less than the population as a whole. As yet undetectable cultural factors also play a part. Schizophrenia is three times more common among Afro-Caribbeans living in England than among those in Jamaica. Tuberculosis is 25 percent more common among Asians than the white population.

Although, therefore, there are many indications that in general British people today are healthier than at the beginning of the century, there is still a problematic relation between health and the absence of disease. This is indicated, for example, by the increasing suicide rate among young men in the 1980s. The curve of drug addiction has also continued to rise, as has that of AIDS and HIV infection.

Christopher Lawrence

Bibliography
Barker, Theo, and Michael Drake, eds. *Population and Society in Britain 1850–1980.* 1982.

Berridge, Virginia. *Health and Society in Britain Since 1939*. 1999.

Floud, Roderick, Anabel Gregory, and Kenneth Wachter. *Height, Health and History: Nutritional Status in the United Kingdom 1750–1980*. 1990.

McKeown, Thomas. *The Role of Medicine: Dream, Mirage, or Nemesis?* 1979.

Heath, Edward Richard George (1916–)

Prime Minister from 1970 to 1974, Edward Heath led a CONSERVATIVE government initially determined to depart from many of the principles and policies of its recent predecessors. It foundered, however, on economic difficulties and a crisis in industrial relations. Heath's long career is also noteworthy for a strong commitment to the EUROPEAN COMMUNITY (EC) and for vehement criticism of MARGARET THATCHER's policies and manner after her 1979 election victory.

Unusually for a Conservative leader, Heath came from a lower middle-class family with no history of political involvement. More conventionally, he took his degree at Balliol College, OXFORD, was elected President of the Union, and served with distinction in the SECOND WORLD WAR. In 1950 he was elected to Parliament for Bexley, one of several promising newcomers who broadened the social and intellectual base of the party. Heath was not by nature an ideologue, a rebel, or a favorite with the party's grass-roots. His rise to prominence was as an insider: he joined the Whips' office when the party gained power in 1951, became Deputy Chief Whip the following year, and was promoted to Chief Whip in 1955. Despite his reputedly brusque manner, often later a disadvantage in his dealings with back-bench M.P.s, he emerged with some credit from the difficult task of managing party opinion during the 1956 SUEZ CRISIS. From 1959 to 1964 he held several government posts: as Lord Privy Seal he was widely praised for his handling of Britain's vetoed application for EC membership, and at the Board of Trade he showed an undoctrinaire approach to industrial policy.

Heath replaced SIR ALEC DOUGLAS HOME as party leader and Leader of the Opposition in 1965. Although he often fared poorly in parliamentary exchanges with Prime Minister HAROLD WILSON and showed little flair for the more combative, demands of his role, in some respects he became a commanding figure. He pursued a comprehensive review of party policy which formed the basis of the 1970 election manifesto and reflected his own vision of a modernized, flexible, more efficient economy as the nation's greatest need. The 1970 government broke with aspects of the "post-war consensus" which the major parties embraced for a generation. The "Heathites" put more faith in market mechanisms, less in state intervention in the economy. They disdained incomes policies and public funding of weak companies or industries; dismantled some interventionist agencies; pursued cuts in personal and corporate taxes to stimulate investment. Increased charges for some social services reflected unease at the growth of the WELFARE STATE. Heath's generally pragmatic search for efficiency, which often made him appear more comfortable with civil servants than with fellow politicians, extended to reorganizing parts of central and local government and the NATIONAL HEALTH SERVICE.

Also crucial to Heath's agenda was the reform of industrial relations by the creation of a tighter framework of labor law. The 1971 Industrial Relations Act, however, turned into a shambles. Effectively crippled by trade union opposition, it greatly impeded government-union relations at a time of mounting industrial unrest. The government, indeed, ran into trouble on several fronts. Inflation drove it to adopt a statutory prices and incomes policy; it moved to support failing companies; it passed the 1972 Industry Act to create extensive new powers of state intervention. The phrase "U-turn" became a cliche of the day: Heath seemed to have lurched towards a rough-and-ready form of corporatism, in which government sought the co-operation of business and organized labor in an uncomfortable triangle. In 1973 a mis-managed confrontation with the miners' union led to the imposition of a three-day working week to save power supplies. In an atmosphere of crisis Heath called an election for February 1974. He was unable to secure a renewed mandate; a minority Labour government was formed and won a slender majority in an October election. Heath had lost three of four elections; although reluctant to resign as party leader, he was replaced by Margaret Thatcher in February 1975.

The Heath Government left a legacy of high inflation, a large spending deficit and a weak balance of trade. Many of its non-economic initiatives proved short-lived, dismantled by successive Labour and Conservative administrations. Given Heath's abiding commitment, it is apt that at least his success in bringing Britain into the European Community survived. His decision to suspend the Northern Ireland Parliament and impose direct rule from London also set a course difficult to alter.

Assessments of Heath's career inevitably vary. His years as Prime Minister were marked by numerous failures, but at a time of acute difficulties. To many observers his essentially moderate and pragmatic approach, and the decency and humanity which underlay his famous reference to the "unacceptable face of capitalism", contrasts starkly with the tenor of the Thatcher era. The years after 1979 saw Heath, who continued to serve as an MP until 2001, as something of an exile in his own party, highly regarded abroad for his internationalist, pro-European outlook but shunned by the ascendant Thatcherites.

Steven Reilly

Bibliography

Ball, Stuart, and Anthony Seldon, eds. *The Heath Government 1970–74.* 1996.

Campbell, John. *Edward Heath: A Biography.* 1993.

Holmes, Martin. *Political Pressure and Economic Policy: British Government 1970–1974.* 1982.

Henderson, Arthur (1863–1935)

Familiarly known as "Uncle Arthur," Henderson was one of the three most important figures in the early history of the LABOUR PARTY, along with KEIR HARDIE and RAMSAY MACDONALD. Party Secretary for twenty-three years, intermittent Leader of the Parliamentary Labour Party, and CABINET minister in four governments, he made a major contribution to party structure and doctrine both before and after the crisis of 1931.

Born into poverty in Glasgow 13 September 1863, Henderson was the son of a laborer and sometime cotton spinner, who died when his son was nine, reducing the family to penury. Henderson left school shortly thereafter, working first in a photographer's shop. Although he resumed schooling when his stepfather moved the family to Newcastle, his formal education was limited, and at the age of twelve he was apprenticed as an iron-molder. It was also during his early Newcastle years that he underwent conversion to METHODISM, the formative moral and intellectual influence on his development, a faith he retained throughout his life. Like Keir Hardie, PHILIP SNOWDEN, and GEORGE LANSBURY, Henderson was to build his political doctrine on a strong foundation of religious conviction.

After Henderson qualified as a journeyman ironfounder in 1883, he became active in his local union, later becoming district organizer for Northumberland, Durham, and Lancashire. By 1892 his life as a manual worker had ended, and for the next eleven years trade union activity was the focus of his energy. Thus in addition to lay preaching and temperance reform activity, Henderson established contacts within trade unionism and the labor movement more generally, eventually becoming national organizer for the Friendly Society of Ironfounders, known for its conciliatory industrial policy.

What is notable about Henderson's politics in the 1890s is his unflagging Liberalism, a key factor in his appointment as agent to the Liberal MP for Barnard Castle and his election to the Darlington Town Council. Despite his identification with local Liberalism, he was selected in 1903 by the LABOUR REPRESENTATION COMMITTEE to contest Barnard Castle in the by-election precipitated by the retirement of Sir Joseph Pease and won the seat with the support of many Liberals who favored a Labour representative with orthodox Liberal principles. One of the initial band of five independent Labour MPs, Henderson remained suspect in the eyes of ILP militants. Yet the fact that Henderson appeared ideologically indistinguishable from the Lib-Labs in the House of Commons in no way vitiated his allegiance to the fledgling Labour group.

During the next years he collaborated with MacDonald on a handbook for election agents, and by 1904 was chosen as Treasurer of the Labour Representation Committee, succeeding David Shackleton as its Chairman in 1905–6 and subsequently assuming the role again from 1908–10. Ineffective at first in the Commons, he played a vital role in organizing constituencies in anticipation of the 1906 election, later serving as Chief Whip to the Labour contingent in the House. In 1911 he yielded the chairmanship to MacDonald to became Secretary, a position he held with consummate skill until 1934, exercising a domination over Labour Party machinery unmatched in its history. Admitting MacDonald's superior endowments, he recognized that his talents were organizational, not inspirational, gifts which complemented MacDonald's. Even though Labour did not improve its parliamentary position before the war, Henderson's efforts helped to transform it from a sectional pressure group to a national party.

In August 1914, when MacDonald resigned the chairmanship over Labour's decision to support war credits, Henderson was elected leader. Although he had been Secretary to the British section of the Second International, he abandoned his initial espousal of neutrality and endorsed British involvement in the FIRST WORLD WAR, situating himself in the mainstream of Labour opinion. His principal aims were to preserve party unity and to ensure that Labour cooperated in the national effort. More than anyone else, he was responsible for ensuring that the Labour Party, in contrast to European socialist parties, did not split. This implicated him in the government's recruitment efforts and led to a key role in the 1915 Treasury Conference to secure an industrial truce.

In May 1915 Henderson was invited to join the ASQUITH coalition as Labour's representative in the CABINET, nominally as President of the Board of Education, but effectively as adviser on labor matters. As the first Labour Cabinet minister, he enhanced his prestige in the movement, temporarily outdistancing MacDonald in reputation, while reinforcing his indispensability as LLOYD GEORGE's industrial conciliator, a task which sometimes incurred trade union enmity. He remained in the government when Lloyd George became Prime Minister, this time as part of the five-man War Cabinet, but was forced out in August 1917 when his colleagues disavowed Labour participation in a projected international socialist conference in Stockholm.

Abandoning the chairmanship of the Parliamentary Labour Party, he devoted himself to party reorganization with a view to extending membership, strengthening local parties, and devising a new post-war program. If he ceased to be Labour's most visible representative, a burden shouldered through the war, he relished his role as Uncle Arthur, expert wire-puller and reconciler of disputing factions. It was his control over the electoral machinery, deriving from close links with the unions and constituency activists, that made his authority unassailable. He was the principal architect of the new constitution, the mastermind of that precarious balance between a democratic, constituency-based mass organization, with individual membership, and a union-financed oligarchic structure.

Having abandoned Barnard Castle after fifteen years, Henderson was beaten at East Ham South in the 1918 election, re-entering the House for Widnes in 1919, but enduring prolonged absences from the Commons as a result of recurrent election defeats in the next few years. He represented Newcastle East in 1923, Burnley, 1924–31, and Clay Cross, 1933–5, but for most of that period his crucial activity was as party manager, supervising the selection of candidates, touring the country, setting up the advisory committees, and reorganizing the party into regions. He retained the secretaryship when he entered the first Labour government in 1924 as Home Secretary, a ministry MacDonald grudgingly conceded to him, despite Henderson's self-sacrificing efforts to secure MacDonald's return to the leadership two years earlier.

His brief tenure at the Home Office was unremarkable, but he served as a member of the British delegation to the London Conference on the Dawes Plan and later to the LEAGUE OF NATIONS, where he was one of the main proponents of the Geneva Protocol. After Labour left office, he continued to champion the cause of the League of Nations, while recognizing the need for effective sanctions as a guarantee of security, a stance initially abhorrent to much of Labour's PACIFIST opinion. In addition, he used his office as President of the Labour and Socialist International to enlist European working-class movements in the effort to secure peaceful settlement of disputes through the League of Nations.

In 1929 Henderson managed to wrest the Foreign Office from MacDonald, who had served as his own Foreign Secretary in 1924. The Prime Minister continued to keep exclusive control over ANGLO-AMERICAN RELATIONS, circumvent Henderson's authority, and barely conceal his growing suspicion of his longtime colleague. As the architect of a more responsible and realistic Labour policy, formulated in *Labour and the Nation* in 1928, Henderson was determined to implement specific goals, assisted by his able Foreign Office team—HUGH DALTON, Lord Robert Cecil, and Philip Noel-Baker. At his urging, Britain signed the Optional Clause of the League Covenant, prescribing compulsory arbitration for all justiciable disputes, as well as the General Act, extending arbitration and eliminating a nation's right to judge its own case. At the Hague Conference in 1929 he sought to reconcile French and German differences over reparations, and at Geneva he was instrumental in preparing the way for a general Disarmament Conference, which he was nominated to chair. Finally, in talks with the Russians he made significant progress towards the normalization of relations, including the exchange of diplomatic representatives and Soviet pledges to refrain from propaganda. In overcoming the resistance of the service chiefs and the defenders of national sovereignty to measures such as the Optional Clause and the General Act, he did more than any other figure in the party to foster the idea of collective security as the only way to make the League an effective agency for peace.

In the August 1931 financial crisis which brought down the second Labour government Henderson opposed MacDonald's efforts to impose cuts in UNEMPLOYMENT benefits, although he had originally accepted the need for projected economies. Once he realized the depth of TUC opposition to reductions, Henderson, always responsive to consensus, decided that the unity of the labor movement took precedence over the need to balance the budget. His resistance was crucial to swaying the majority of the Cabinet to his position, leading to an irreparable breach with MacDonald. Elected Leader of the Parliamentary Labour Party in opposition, he lost his seat in the 1931 electoral debacle and did not return to the Commons for two years.

He retained the presidency of the international Disarmament Conference, which opened in February 1932, although now only a private citizen rather than Foreign Secretary. His credibility deliberately undermined by the National government, Henderson refused to be deflected from the pursuit of multilateral concessions. If his single-mindedness prevented disruption in the proceedings, it was insufficient to galvanize competing powers into an accord, especially under the shadow of the Manchurian conflict. After months of laborious negotiations delegates conceded the principle of weapons reduction but refused to stipulate precise levels or to grant equality to Germany. Henderson's efforts at personal diplomacy in European capitals was equally abortive, and, once Hitler withdrew from the Conference, its failure was complete.

In 1933 Henderson was awarded the Wateler Peace Prize and the following year became only the third Englishman to receive the Nobel Peace Prize. Despite worsening health and disappointment over the collapse of the Disarmament Conference, he was reluctant to retire from politics, clinging to the party secretaryship until 1934, only a year before he died.

Never as charismatic as Keir Hardie or MacDonald, Henderson is too easily overlooked in the search for heroes of the labor movement. Leader only briefly and never Prime Minister, he devoted himself primarily to the party structure, which was largely his creation. More than any other figure he epitomized the alliance between trade unions and party that remained Labour's bedrock. His socialist ideology was a practical trade unionist view of incremental gains through parliamentary democracy, couched in laborist terms palatable to all elements. Transforming himself from an insular union official into a leader of European socialism and world statesman, he became the most prominent internationalist in the party during the 1920s, largely responsible for re-oreinting Labour's foreign policy to an increasing reliance on the League of Nations. An unflagging advocate of disarmament, he came closer to a conception of collective security than any British politician in those years, recognizing that only through the enforcement of peace, by military sanctions if necessary, could aggression be curbed. Architect of the modern Labour Party, he became by 1931 the tribune of peace for ordinary people throughout the world, eager to end the competitive armaments struggle.

Fred M. Leventhal

Bibliography
Hamilton, Mary Agnes. *Arthur Henderson*. 1938.
Leventhal, F.M. *Arthur Henderson*. 1989.
McKibbin, Ross. *The Evolution of the Labour Party 1910–1924*. 1974.
Winkler, Henry R. *Paths Not Taken: British Labour and International Policy in the Nineteen-Twenties*. 1994.
Wrigley, Chris. *Arthur Henderson*. 1990.

Hepworth, Barbara (1903–1975)

Barbara Hepworth, one of the leading British sculptors of the modern movement, was celebrated in her day as an exemplary female achiever, made a Dame of the British Empire and receiving numerous other honors. Born in Wakefield in 1903, Hepworth was a native of Yorkshire, a distinction she shares with HENRY MOORE, her senior by several years, as well as the critic and supporter of both sculptors, Herbert Read. Hepworth's and Moore's careers overlapped in several instances: they studied together at the Leeds School of Art and then at the Royal College in London; they belonged to the same avant-garde groups in the 1930s before going on to establish international reputations in the postwar period. Arguably, Hepworth has been unduly eclipsed by Moore, with his phenomenal institutional success, even though she anticipated Moore in certain formal respects, such as the piercing of holes through the sculpture.

From the start of her career Hepworth was devoted to the tenets of modernism, subscribing to the doctrine of "truth to materials" and direct carving. Her early torsos reveal an awareness of Maillol's simplified arcadian vision, while her animals and birds are indebted to Henri Gaudier-Brzeska, the pioneering modernist sculptor and VORTICIST killed in the First World War. Another influence in these pieces is that of her first husband, John Skeaping, an animal carver. ERIC GILL and JACOB EPSTEIN were also mentors, the influence of the latter clearly felt in her uncharacteristically "primitive" looking *Figure of a Woman* (1929–30), with its bulky limbs and clasped hands.

Hepworth was crucially involved in the development of abstraction in British art from the time she moved to Hampstead in the 1930s with BEN NICHOLSON, who became her second husband. She participated in such groups as Unit One, which set out in 1934 to represent "the expression of a truly contemporary spirit," and the international group, Abstraction Creation, and regularly visited Paris, where she befriended Brancusi, Mondrian, Miro, Arp, and Calder. Hepworth also contributed to the sole issue of the journal *Circle,* an international survey of Constructivism edited by Nicholson, Naum Gabo, and the architect J.L. Martin. In clean cut, sparse, sometimes minimal sculptural compositions Hepworth pursued simple geometric shapes such as the cone and the cylinder. However, in 1939, with the onset of war and the birth of triplets, Hepworth moved to St. Ives, where she, Nicholson, and Gabo formed the nucleus of an art colony which would span several generations and have a profound influence on the course of British art. Hepworth was deeply affected by the dramatic scenery of Cornwall, with the sounds of the sea and the glowing light for which St. Ives is legendary. The response was felt in her work as form became more complex and organic, retaining nonetheless a simple, compact rhythmic force. The scooped out inner sections began to be differentiated from the smooth outer forms either by rougher, more robust carving or by the introduction of color, often blue to signify sea and sky.

In a foreword to one of Hepworth's exhibition catalogues in the 1930s the scientist J.D. Bernal compared Hepworth's abstraction to megalithic art, whose break from neolithic naturalism, over many thousands of years, resembled the modern movement's break with Renaissance pictorialism. This foreword would prove prophetic in relation to Hepworth's carving. On an iconographical level, the prehistoric metaphor would intensify as Hepworth's reputation grew, and she was able to place works in more commanding and dramatic locations. Sculptures were actually titled "menhirs", and the late work, *Family of Man* (1970), consisting of nine bronze "figures"—comprising stacked geometric forms—is a Stonehenge-like arrangement. Bernal's foreword also anticipated a dynamic relationship between Hepworth and architecture which culminated in what is undoubtedly her best known piece, the megalithic twenty-one foot high pierced sculpture, *Single Form* (1964), installed in front of the United Nations Building in New York as a memorial to the late Secretary-General, Dag Hammerskjöld, who originally commissioned it. Although, like Moore, success encouraged Hepworth to engage assistants and cast enlarged pieces in bronze, carving remained more central to her aesthetic preoccupations.

Hepworth continued to live and work in St. Ives until her death in a studio fire at the age of seventy-two. The Trewyn studio and garden now serve as a Barbara Hepworth museum, in accord with her wishes.

David Cohen

Bibliography

Bowness, Alan. *The Complete Sculpture of Barbara Hepworth 1960–69.* 1971.

Gardiner, Margaret. *Barbara Hepworth: A Memoir.* 1982.

Hammacher, Abraham M. *Barbara Hepworth.* rev. ed. 1981.

Hepworth, Barbara. *A Pictorial Autobiography.* 1970.

Hodin, J.P. *Barbara Hepworth.* 1961.

Historic Preservation

Compared to its Continental neighbors, Britain was slow to develop a popular interest in the preservation of historic buildings and slower still to legislate effective protections for them. Practically until the 1960s it was possible to demolish or alter a privately-owned building without permission, whatever its historic value. Popular consciousness and eventually legislative protection made great strides after the Second World War, in tandem with a growing appreciation of the financial value of the architectural heritage, especially as a tourist attraction.

An influential minority, connected to the Arts and Crafts movement, did organize to promote the cause of historic architecture as early as 1877, when the Society for the Protection of Ancient Buildings was formed. But the S.P.A.B. soon developed a fusty, antiquarian reputation and restricted its interests pretty much to medieval and ancient monuments. Legislation of 1882, 1900, and 1913 gave government only limited powers to acquire (normally with their owners' consent) a handful of these older, usually ruined buildings. On the whole, the public remained suspicious of compulsory powers over private property and scornful of aesthetes' claims that older buildings gained in beauty what they lost in utility.

After the First World War, when state intervention in economy and society extended, the arts remained largely untouched and ARCHITECTURE—"the Cinderella of the arts", its lonely advocates complained—entirely. Rapid suburbanization, road development, and electrification effected a holocaust of historic buildings in the 1920s and 1930s. Public concern continued to focus on the oldest structures, such as Stonehenge and Hadrian's Wall. Local authorities were given compulsory purchase powers to protect historic buildings in 1932, but no money for the purpose, so the powers went unused. Huge chunks of Georgian townscape were pulled down, including John Nash's Regent Street in LONDON. That led to the formation in 1937 of the Georgian Group, originally as an offshoot of S.P.A.B., small but well-connected, with a genteel and aesthetic rather than scholarly tone.

The SECOND WORLD WAR wrought a great change. Patriotic feeling attached itself more clearly to the physical environment, built as well as unbuilt. The "national heritage" in buildings and landscape was coming into focus. Historic preservation also became part of the lively contemporary debate on the post-war reconstruction of cities and the development of TOWN PLANNING. A remarkably large audience suddenly appeared to interest itself in quite scholarly architectural topics. Not only popularizing enthusiasts like John Betjeman and Osbert Lancaster, but even architectural historians like John Summerson, J.M. Richards, and Nikolaus Pevsner became fixtures of the Sunday newspapers and BBC radio and television. Pevsner's *Buildings of England* series began to appear in 1951, sold well in Penguin paperback, and became instant authorities. Their catholic taste and very high level of scholarship represented an amazing leap over the Methuen *Little Guides* which had served as the standard county guides since late Victorian times. The Georgian Group began to score preservationist victories—Nash's Regent's Park was saved after the war—and already in 1958 there existed a Victorian Society, indicating how rapidly the public appetite for some historic buildings was spreading to encompass them all. Hundreds of community preservation groups popped up to protect less spectacular buildings and districts of local value, and they found a national mouthpiece in the Civic Trust, founded in 1957 at the instigation of Conservative minister Duncan Sandys. This mounting public awareness meant that the post-Second World War burst of state intervention would extend to historic preservation. Even in the midst of war (1944) government had undertaken the epic task of classifying all the best historic buildings of Britain into Grades I and II. From 1947 owners of these "listed" buildings were required to notify their local authority of intention to alter or demolish. After the Gowers Report on Historic Houses in 1950, Historic Buildings Councils for England, Wales, and Scotland were established (1953) to help private owners with grants for maintenance and repair. Yet government action lagged behind public opinion. Urban local authorities, in particular, were unwilling to forego the higher rateable values offered by redevelopment of their crumbling historic districts. At the center, CONSERVATIVE governments after 1951 were reluctant to use the powers or spend the money intended by their LABOUR predecessors for historic preservation. Most of the available funds were expended in the 1950s on a small number of COUNTRY HOUSES; cities were left to fend for themselves. Urban renewal schemes of the 1950s and early 1960s accounted for even more destruction, possibly, than the unplanned development of the 1920s and 1930s.

The consequence was a spectacular uprising of public opinion which began in the mid-1960s and continued into the 1990s. Local preservationist groups grew increasingly militant, and central government was gradually forced to match rhetoric with action. Conservation areas, offering protection for whole districts, were created by legislation in 1967. Listed building demolition became practically impossible in 1968. The Historic Buildings Council for England had its budget, virtually at a standstill since 1953, increased from £575,000 to £11 million in the course of the 1970s, with a growing proportion specifically allocated to urban sites. An old argument for preservation was now heard more widely: that Britain's bricks-and-mortar endowment was its most valuable national asset, uniquely able in the post-industrial world to draw dollars, marks, and yen from abroad.

In this atmosphere it was not surprising that political conservatism after 1979 manifested itself also in architecture. Popular affection for historic buildings built now not only on the buildings' own merits, but also on a negative anti-modernism. These feelings were stoked up both by Thatcherites, who approved of the "heritage industry" for economic reasons, and by more traditional conservatives (including the Prince of Wales), who had nostalgic and communitarian motives. Against these forces it proved impossible in the 1980s to replace the least distinguished Victorian building with the most distinguished modern design. By the late 1980s some cultural critics of the Left were worrying that the triumph of the "heritage industry" was symptomatic of a culture in terminal decline, though even they may secretly have preferred historic buildings to the POST-MODERN ARCHITECTURE of their own day.

                                                        Peter Mandler

Bibliography

Fawcett, Jane, ed. *The Future of the Past: Attitudes to Conservation 1147–1974*. 1976.

Hewison, Robert. *The Heritage Industry: Britain in a Climate of Decline*. 1987.

Lowenthal, David, and Marcus Binney, eds. *Our Past Before Us: Why Do We Save It?*. 1981.

Wright, Patrick. *On Living in an Old Country: The National Past in Contemporary Britain*. 1985.

Watkin, David. *The Rise of Architectural History*. 1980.

Hitchcock, Alfred (1899–1980)

Alfred Hitchcock was Britain's leading film director at the time he moved to the United States on the eve of the SECOND WORLD WAR. He briefly returned to Britain in 1944 to help with the war effort by making two short films for the Ministry of Information, and later to make *Under Capricorn* (1949) and *Stage Fright* (1949), to shoot locations for a re-make of *The Man Who Knew Too Much* (1955), and for his penultimate film, *Frenzy* (1972). A master craftsman, who pre-planned every detail of his films, he spent most of his long career frightening his audiences with a series of suspense thrillers.

Born in London to Roman Catholic parents, he began working for the British branch of Famous Players-Lasky in 1919, initially designing title cards for their films. He then served successively as script writer, set designer, assistant director, and finally director. In 1924 Michael Balcon's Gainsborough Pictures sent him to Germany, where he made his first two features, *The Pleasure Garden* and *Mountain Eagle* (1926) at Emelka Studios-Munich, much influenced by German expressionism and by Kammerspielfilme, or street realism.

Upon his return to England, the young Hitchcock gained a reputation as England's pre-eminent fiction director in a series of six silent suspense films, including *The Lodger* (1926). He made Britain's first talkie, *Blackmail* (1929), originally shot as a silent film, but then re-shot with sound. Hitchcock proved adept with the new sound medium: *Blackmail* uses sound motifs— the word "knife" is used rhythmically to haunt a young woman who is being blackmailed for having killed a would-be rapist. The film features a justly celebrated chase across the dome of the British Museum. As an employee of British International Pictures he directed adaptations of GALSWORTHY and O'Casey, the revue *Elstree Calling* (1930), and the sardonic *Rich and Strange* (1931), which portrays two young London suburbanites discovering life on a world cruise.

During these years Hitchccok was still finding his metier, but he subsequently signed a contract to make five films for the Gaumont-British Picture Corporation, which included several of the thrillers that established his reputation. *The Man Who Knew Too Much* (1934) and the adaptation of John Buchan's *The 39 Steps* (1935) are his best films from this period. Both feature the elaborate chase sequences that became his hallmark. The fast-paced *The 39 Steps*, which depicts Richard Hannay's attempts to elude Nazi pursuers, is structured around a series of escapes and chases. In contrast, the two subsequent films, *Secret Agent* (1936) and *Sabotage* (1936), ambiguous, narratively complex, and full of black humor, were less successful with audiences. Following the lightweight *Young and Innocent* (1937), Hitchcock made *The Lady Vanishes* (1938), which returned to theme of the Nazi menace and celebrated British amateur heroics. He made one more film in Britain, *Jamaica Inn* (1939) for Charles Laughton's Mayfair Pictures before moving to the United States, where he signed a seven-year contract with David O. Selznick.

Attracted to America by the availability of money and resources, Hitchcock promptly demonstrated his adaptability by winning two Academy awards with his first American film, *Rebecca* (1940), admittedly derived from a British novel. Working in the United States throughout the 1940s, he soon emerged as one of Hollywood's most skillful filmmakers with bizarre thrillers like *Shadow of a Doubt* (1942) and *Strangers on a Train* (1951), both of which featured aberrant personalities in quintessentially American characters. He returned briefly to Britain to make *Under Capricorn* in 1949, a critical and commercial failure set in nineteenth-century Australia. His next film *Stage Fright,* made for Warner Brothers in London, was also poorly received. Back in the United States, Hitchcock made a series of commercially successful films, employing popular male Hollywood stars, like Cary Grant and James Stewart. His choice of actresses from Madeleine Carroll and Margaret Lockwood to Grace Kelly and Eva Marie Saint reveals a preference for clever, but elusive women, frequently blonde, whose sexual-

ity was never blatant. The justifiably famous films of these years included *Rear Window* (1954), *To Catch a Thief* (1954), the remake of *The Man Who Knew Too Much* (1955), *Vertigo* (1957), *North By Northwest* (1959), and *Psycho* (1960). Hitchcock's powers seemed to wane during the 1960s with a succession of critical and commercial failures, although *Frenzy* confirmed that he was still a brilliant exponent of the psychological thriller. Hitchock, who became an U.S. citizen in 1955, was a familiar figure to American audiences, hosting his own television series from 1955 to 1965. He died in 1980 while working on a film about George Blake, the British double agent.

The leading studio filmmaker of his day, Hitchcock retained more creative control over his movies than any of his contemporaries. He had a sustained, often pessimistic, artistic vision, perhaps derived from his CATHOLICISM, which infused his work and moved his audience in a powerful way and a technical mastery that raised the psychological thriller to cinematic art.

Paul Swann

Bibliography

Kapsis, Robert E. *Hitchcock: The Making of a Reputation.* 1992.

Ryall, Tom. *Alfred Hitchcock and the British Cinema.* 1986.

Spoto, Donald. *The Art of Alfred Hitchcock.* 2nd ed. 1992.

———. *The Dark Side of Genius: The Life of Alfred Hitchcock.* 1983.

Hoare, Samuel John Gurney (1880–1959)

A CONSERVATIVE politician, Sir Samuel Hoare is remembered for his role in the controversial Hoare-Laval Pact (1935) and strong association with the policy of APPEASEMENT before the Second World War. Educated at Harrow and Oxford, serving as MP for Chelsea (1910–44), Hoare held several ministerial offices between the wars: Secretary of State for Air (1922–9, 1940), Secretary of State for India (1931–5), Foreign Secretary (1935), First Lord of the Admiralty (1936–7), Home Secretary (1937–9), and Lord Privy Seal (1939–40). His most notable achievement was the drafting of the GOVERNMENT OF INDIA ACT (1935). After the fall of NEVILLE CHAMBERLAIN's government in May 1940, Hoare became ambassador to Spain (1940–4). He was elevated to the peerage as Viscount Templewood in 1944.

As Foreign Secretary under STANLEY BALDWIN, Hoare negotiated the 1935 Anglo-German Naval Treaty that permanently fixed German naval strength at 35 percent of the level of British naval forces while allowing Germany parity in submarines. Coming only two months after Hitler's announcement of an expanded German army and reactivated air force, the naval treaty represented a bilateral revision of the naval clauses of the Versailles treaty that appeared to sanction German rearmament. Hoare later participated in the abortive Hoare-Laval Pact (1935) that called for the partition of Abyssinia in the face of Italian aggression. The news of the agreement came on the heels of an election year promise by the British Government to uphold the LEAGUE OF NATIONS and collective security. Negative public reaction to the plan led the CABINET to repudiate the pact and to ask for Hoare's resignation. The failure to deal forcefully with the Italian invasion of Abyssinia discredited the League and helped pave the way for war by encouraging further aggression by the Fascist dictators.

Prior to the Second World War Hoare was an influential member of Chamberlain's inner circle of pro-appeasement advisers with membership on the powerful COMMITTEE OF IMPERIAL DEFENSE. While Home Secretary, he took a constructive role in prison reform by insisting on more humane conditions and limiting the imposition of CAPITAL PUNISHMENT. Hoare continued after the outbreak of war as a key member of Chamberlain's War Cabinet, but after Churchill's accession to power, he found himself exiled to purportedly neutral Spain until 1944.

Although he was a man of ability and intelligence, Hoare's reputation for political intrigue, complicity in the Hoare-Laval Pact, and embrace of appeasement earned him disapprobation as one of the "guilty men" of the 1930s responsible for the disastrous course of British foreign policy. His political memoir of this period, *Nine Troubled Years* (1954), nevertheless stands as a cogent defense of Chamberlain and appeasement.

Van Michael Leslie

Bibliography

Cross, J.A. *Sir Samuel Hoare: A Political Biography*. 1977.
Templewood, Viscount. *Nine Troubled Years*. 1954.

Hobson, J(ohn) A(tkinson) (1858-1940)

J.A. Hobson was a leading liberal social theorist and economist whose ideas were disseminated mainly through his work as a radical author, journalist, and lecturer. He contributed importantly to the formation of British welfare thinking, his reputation resting on his writings in three main areas: an unorthodox economic theory of underconsumption, a major reformulation of liberal thought, and a trenchant critique of imperialism.

Hobson was born in Derby, where his father edited a local Liberal newspaper. After reading Classics and Modern Greats at OXFORD, he worked as a school teacher and university extension lecturer but inherited sufficient wealth to be able to choose a career of independent writing. His "heretical" economic views, originally developed in conjunction with A.F. Mummery in *The Physiology of Industry* (1889), brought him to public attention but occasioned dismissive criticism by the leading economists of the day. His consequent rejection by the academic world never ceased to rankle. From the 1890s onwards Hobson's radicalism was further developed through his activities as a journalist in leading Liberal forums, such as the *NATION* and the *MANCHESTER GUARDIAN*, which brought him into contact with other radicals such as L.T. Hobhouse, and through his editorial work on the *Ethical World* and the *Progressive Review*. In 1894 he became a founding member of the Rainbow Circle, a political and intellectual discussion group that included RAMSAY MACDONALD and HERBERT SAMUEL, and he lectured regularly for the South Place Ethical Society for some forty years. Hobson served as an expert adviser or witness for a number of committees and commissions of inquiry. During the First World War he was active in the peace-seeking UNION OF DEMOCRATIC CONTROL, and in 1918 he stood unsuccessfully for Parliament as an independent. After the war Hobson moved closer to the LABOUR PARTY and counseled on the formulation of their policies, while remaining a left-Liberal at heart and fostering the growth of a political middle ground. He published over fifty books and pamphlets and hundreds of articles.

Hobson's underconsumptionism, which received belated if qualified recognition by KEYNES in the 1930s, was both an economic and an ethical theory. It sought to explain the crises of capitalism and the prevalence of poverty and UNEMPLOYMENT as the result of insufficient spending power. Initially, Hobson believed this to be the consequence of over-saving by the rich; later, he expanded his views and located the cause of underconsumption also in a general maldistribution of wealth. In his earlier writings on poverty, unemployment, and the development of capitalism, low wages in particular were condemned for depriving large segments of society of the ability and will to consume. In *The Economics of Distribution* (1900) and especially in *The Industrial System* (1909) Hobson distinguished between a productive and an unproductive surplus, the former reflecting the co-operative contribution to production above legitimate costs and profits, and to which a society had a claim; the latter—unearned "improperty"—the reflection of the monopolistic and wasteful distortion of sectional and egoistic interests. The solution was an ambitious program of social reform, which entailed the redistribution of wealth, encouraged and directed by the state, including graduated taxation on incomes and inheritance and a system of state PENSIONS, a minimum wage, the regulation of the labor market, and social insurance. Though these ideas were not exclusive to Hobson, he played a significant part in including them in the new Liberal platform, through which they influenced the legislation of the 1906–14 Liberal administrations. Hobson has been criticized among others for failing to distinguish between saving and investment, but he nevertheless exercised influence on welfare economics. In particular, he repudiated the fairness of free, uncontrolled markets. He attempted to inject qualitative considerations into the narrowly quantitative "dismal science" of economics and to associate wealth with human flourishing in a manner inspired by the writings of John Ruskin. In the inter-war period he preached the virtues of rational economic planning as the democratic response to the rising dictatorships and as a policy that would maximize the efficient utilization of resources and humanize both producers and consumers.

It is as part of his larger opus, however, that Hobson's economic theories must be interpreted. He was, above all, a humanist and rationalist, a holistic thinker whose aim was to draw together the discrete fields of economics, political thought, social theory, international relations, and even psychology. Hobson's organic perspective suggested not only the interdependence of these areas but, in conjunction with Hobhouse, a view of society as an entity subject to evolutionary laws of development towards increasing rationality and self-regulation. As expounded in *The Social Problem* (1901), society was perceived as having needs and interests of its own that were not identical to those of its members. This allowed Hobson to posit a sophisticated theory of rights that identified both the individual and society as entitled to the property necessary to their co-ordinated development. Despite the potential authoritarian and conservative implications of an organic perspective, Hobson preserved a liberal outlook by insisting that the health of a society depended on allowing the free development of its members and by arguing that human diversity, when tempered by a consideration of the social nature of individuals, contributed both to individual and social utility. At the same time, he sometimes strayed into illiberal territory, exhibiting paternalistic tendencies, dallying with a mild form of eugenics, and falling prey for a while to ANTI-SEMITIC prejudices.

Hobson's organicism provides the key to his seminal modifications of liberal theory, best illustrated in his *The Crisis of Liberalism* (1909). He regarded the relationship between individual and society as one of mutual sustenance, and raised the ideal of welfare to co-equal status with that of liberty. Hobson abandoned the atomism and *laissez-faire* implicit in earlier liberalism, adopted a view of liberty as the unimpeded development of human potential, replaced the notion of competition with that of cooperation, and sought to break down sectional boundaries in an attempt to offer the underprivileged the full benefits of citizenship. He advocated a benevolent and impartial state which would attain humanist social ends and act as the democratically accountable agent of a rational social organism, when individual action alone could not secure civilized standards. Communitarian and collectivist ideas combined with a respect for individual development to locate Hobson at the heart of turn-of-the-century NEW LIBERALISM. The outcome was an ideology that laid the foundations for the British WELFARE STATE and increasingly attempted to marry the liberal respect for diversity with an insistence on greater equality and mutual obligation. During the First World War Hobson expressed disquiet at the growing state restrictions on civil and political rights, which he regarded as spreading the spirit of "Prussianism" into Britain. This led him to become more concerned with the irresponsible use of the power of existing states and attenuated his enthusiasm for too extensive state intervention, though he never abandoned his belief in collectivism.

Hobson's famous *Imperialism: A Study* (1902) was an application of his social and economic thought, later to be praised by Lenin. He saw imperialism not primarily as the wielding of political control over colonies, but as a product of sectional financial and business interests. Because underconsumption limited effective demand, those interests faced saturated home consumption and needed to find new markets for their surplus capital. In conjunction with aggressive anti-social military interests, they exploited subject peoples as well as perpetuating the domestically harmful social and political structure of the mother country and fanning irrational jingoistic support for imperialism. Hobson's views were strengthened by his 1899 experiences as a reporter on the South African BOER WAR (*The War in South Africa* (1900); *The Psychology of Jingoism* (1901). His solutions were to eliminate nefarious sectionalism, subject dangerous monopolies of economic power to social control, and appeal to the application of reason to public affairs.

In international relations Hobson combined an early regard for a Cobdenite breaking down of global barriers through free trade with an appreciation of the need for an international federalism and some form of international government. He wished to link the centralized supra-national regulation of the conduct of existing states with a respect for self-determination and diversity that allowed for the existence of national units (*Problems of a New World* (1921); *Democracy and a*

Changing Civilisation (1934). By the time of his death in 1940 Hobson had exercised an indirect but subtle impact on twentieth-century British politics, in shaping both progressive social thought and expectations of public policy. Since then, he has come to be recognized as one of the most versatile and creative British social thinkers of his times.

Michael Freeden

Bibliography

Allett, John. *New Liberalism: The Political Economy of J.A. Hobson.* 1981.

Freeden, Michael, ed. *J.A. Hobson: A Reader.* 1988.

———. *Reappraising J.A. Hobson: Humanism and Welfare.* 1990.

Hobson, J.A. *Confessions of an Economic Heretic.* 1938.

Townshend, Jules. *J.A. Hobson.* 1991.

Hockney, David (1937–)

Within the iconography of the "Swinging Sixties" in London the image of David Hockney held a special position. Walking down the street, dressed in a gold lamé jacket, with a shopping bag to match and with dyed golden blond hair, Hockney came to personify the image of the artist as celebrity. At the Royal College of Art, which he attended 1959–62 (and where he won the Gold Medal), he was at the center of a generation of students who are often associated with the emergence of Pop Art in Britain, including R.B. Kitaj, Peter Phillips, Derek Boshier, Allen Jones, and Patrick Caulfield.

Despite the clear evidence of the influences on Hockney's painting during this early period—from the work of Picasso, Alan Davie, FRANCIS BACON, or Jean Dubuffet—the strongest motivation was his desire to create a painting that would have a literary basis, be figurative in expression, and whose subject-matter would be personally oriented to his interests and obsessions. Although the work of Peter Blake (who had left the Royal College in 1956) would have provided one example of such an approach, it was the work of R.B. Kitaj—with whom he formed a close friendship—that encouraged him to embark on painting which had an overtly autobiographical dimension, or dealt with the issues raised in his mind by his own HOMOSEXUALITY. His suite of etchings *The Rake's Progress* (1961–3), executed after returning from a visit to New York in 1961 (at which point he also dyed his hair blond) provides an indication of the extent to which he took Kitaj's encouragement seriously, as well as underlines the extent to which his labeling as a Pop artist was misapplied.

After his first solo exhibition at Kasmin's Gallery in 1963 he made a visit to Egypt following a commission from the *Sunday Times* and then moved to Los Angeles until 1967. He was stunned by the quality of light and bright color that he found there, and that, coupled with clear architecture, manicured lawns, swimming pools, and roads, formed both subject and backdrop to his paintings of this period. Painted in acrylic rather than oil, Hockney's paintings started to assume first a flatter and then an increasingly photo-realist surface. His drawings similarly changed towards the use of a more detached and purely linear approach. This was especially apparent in his etchings. A comparison of *The Rake's Progress* with his *Illustrations for Fourteen Poems for C.P. Cavafy* (1966) emphasizes his evolution towards an unadorned clarity of line. What this later project also stressed was the importance that poetry held for Hockney as a source of inspiration. While at the Royal College he had discovered Walt Whitman as a model for his autobiographical approach to painting (*We Two Boys Together Clinging*, 1961, Arts Council of Great Britain, refers directly to Whitman's *Leaves of Grass*). Ten years after turning to Cavafy he made a suite of etchings inspired by Wallace Stevens' *The Man with the Blue Guitar.*

In 1975, the year before he returned to Los Angeles after a period spent living in London and France, Hockney designed the Glyndebourne Festival Opera production of Stravinsky's *The Rake's Progress.* This was the first of many such commissions—following his designs for Jarry's *Ubu Roi* in 1966—which recall, by virtue of their unified vision, Diaghilev's achievement in persuading artists like Picasso to design for the ballet, more than fifty years earlier. Such commissions also give an indication of Hockney's inquiring mind that has seen him create works with Xerox and fax machines as well as polaroid and other forms of photograph, in the same way as he has always sought out and investigated new and different forms of printmaking—often with startling results.

An understanding of theatrical artifice and a sense of spatial organization—demanded by the brief for his designs for the OPERA—have worked their way into his paintings of the last ten years. In a move away from the naturalism that had been found in his drawings and etchings, these new paintings like *A Visit with Christopher and Don, Santa Monica Canyon, 1984* (1984, the artist) have also been formed within the context of his continued fascination with the work of Picasso and his strongly held belief in the continuing vitality of a Cubist tradition.

Andrew Wilson

Bibliography

Glazebrook, Mark. *David Hockney: Paintings, Prints and Drawings 1960–1970.* 1970.

Livingstone, Marco. *David Hockney.* rev. ed. 1987.

Stangos, Nikos, and Henry Geldzahler. *David Hockney by David Hockney.* 1976.

Tuchman, Maurice, and Stephanie Barron, ed. *David Hockney: A Retrospective*. 1988.

Webb, Peter. *Portrait of David Hockney*. 1988.

Holst, Gustavus Theodore von (1874–1934)

An English composer and teacher of Scandinavian descent, Gustav Holst was a contemporary and close friend of RALPH VAUGHAN WILLIAMS, whom he met in 1895. They shared many enthusiasms in common, including one for folksong, and on "field-days" discussed each other's works in progress. Like Vaughan Williams, Holst took an active part in amateur music-making and directed annual informal festivals at Thaxted, Essex, from 1916. Being retiring by nature, he was bewildered by the success of *The Planets* and *The Hymn of Jesus*, and during the 1920s he developed a more astringent style in pursuit of his ideal of "tender austerity," best exemplified in the *Lyric Movement* for violin and chamber orchestra (1933), his penultimate work. He refused all official honors except the Howland Memorial Prize, for distinction in the arts, from Yale University (1924) and the Gold Medal of the Royal Philharmonic Society (1930).

Born in Cheltenham, the son of a piano and harp teacher, Holst received little encouragement to become a composer. Even at the Royal College of Music, London (1893–8), he found composition lessons with Charles Villers Stanford (1852–1924) unsatisfactory, although he welcomed his teacher's advice to develop self-criticism. While a student, he conducted the Hammersmith Socialist Choir, and in 1901 married the choir's youngest soprano, Isobel Harrison. On leaving the college, Holst earned his living as a trombonist before turning to teaching in 1903, and he became the Director of Music at St. Paul's School, Hammersmith in 1905, an appointment he held for the rest of his life, as well as Director of Music at Morley College (from 1907). He undertook additional teaching activities at the Royal College of Music and the University of Reading (both 1919), and was invited to become the Visiting Lecturer in Composition at Harvard in 1932.

An early, sustained addiction to Wagnerian chromaticism was finally cured by the discovery of English folksong, its integration into Holst's style clearly evident in *A Somerset Rhapsody* (1907). An interest in Hindu literature and philosophy, enlivened through learning Sanskrit, provided a different input, manifest in the economy and restraint of the opera, *Savitri* (from the *Mahabharata*, trans. Holst: 1908). This harbinger of his later style was overshadowed by the more conventional suites for military band (No. 1: 1909, No. 2: 1911), and especially Holst's masterpiece, the highly colorful orchestral suite, *The Planets* (1916), the war music of *Mars* acting as a model for countless film scores, and the sturdy, wholesome tune of *Jupiter* being subsequently (and regrettably) linked to a patriotic hymn-text. The expressive content of *The Hymn of Jesus* (Apocryphal Acts of St. John, trans. Holst: 1917), an unusual combination of wild dance and mystic contemplation, draws on the best elements of both *Savitri* and *The Planets*, but having created a successful alternative to Wagnerian opera in *Savitri*, it seemed regressive for Holst to resort to Wagnerian parody in his next opera, *The Perfect Fool* (Holst, 1922), the opening ballet of which acts as a summary of much of its most attractive music. Following the bracingly exuberant *Fugal Overture* (1922), the *Fugal Concerto* (1923), a rather bland neo-classical study in diatonic counterpoint, marks a new departure, more persuasively essayed in the *Terzetto* (1925) for flute, oboe, and viola, which is polytonal according to the different key signatures for each instrumental part, but in reality sounds at most only occasionally bitonal. The masterpieces of this new style, the bleak landscapes of the orchestral *Egdon Heath* (1927), a homage to Hardy, and *Betelgeuse* from *Twelve Songs* (H. Wolfe: 1929), numb the spirit. However, a return to human warmth in *Hammersmith* (1930) for military band and the *Scherzo* (1934) of a projected symphony suggest a final stylistic synthesis, but one that Holst was unfortunately unable to pursue further.

Trevor Bray

Bibliography

Holst, Imogen. *The Music of Gustav Holst*. rev. ed. 1986.

Short, Michael. *Gustav Holst: The Man and His Music*. 1990.

Home, Alec [Alexander Frederick] Douglas- (1903–1995)

Sir Alec Douglas-Home (later Lord Home of the Hirsel) had four main roles. As Prime Minister (1963–4) he oversaw a marked recovery in Conservative fortunes. As CONSERVATIVE PARTY leader (1963–5) he devised the present mechanism for electing party leaders. As Foreign Secretary (1960–3, 1970–4), he held office during Britain's two attempts to join the EUROPEAN COMMUNITY. As a retired party leader, he was the most influential elder statesman since ARTHUR BALFOUR.

Until 1960 he was unknown outside Scotland. Coming from a landed, non-political Scottish family, he was educated at Eton and Christ Church, OXFORD, where his interests were non-political. As Lord Dunglass, he was M.P. for Lanark (1931–45, 1950–1), social issues being his main concern. As NEVILLE CHAMBERLAIN's parliamentary private secretary (1936–40), he was briefly at the center of things.

Because of serious illness (1940–3) and electoral defeat, Home was largely outside national politics from 1940 to 1955. Even as a junior Scottish minister (1951–5), he was based in Edinburgh. In 1955, aged fifty-one, he joined the CABINET in the inconspicuous role of Commonwealth Secretary (1955–60). As such, he displayed quiet flair, but it was his becoming Leader of the HOUSE OF LORDS (1957–60) on the unexpected resignation of Lord Salisbury that moved him towards the Conservative inner circle.

His appointment as Foreign Secretary caused great surprise, which soon abated. Home's main task was to contain Soviet aggression, with crises in Berlin, Laos, and Cuba. Of all post-war Foreign Secretaries save ERNEST BEVIN, Home was the readiest to answer Soviet threats in language they understood. Elsewhere, Home played little visible part in the EC negotiations (1961–3), but the outcome, putting defence before economics, and Atlanticism before anti-American Gaullism, was in accord with his long-held principles.

Home's premiership was less controversial than the way he was chosen. After disasters in 1962–3, Macmillan fell ill and resigned suddenly. The obvious successors, R.A. BUTLER, Lord Hailsham, and perhaps Reginald Maudling cancelled out. After more systematic soundings of party opinion than ever before or since, Home emerged as the most generally acceptable figure, though no voting figures have ever been published. Of Cabinet colleagues, only IAIN MACLEOD and ENOCH POWELL refused to serve under him.

The public, the party, and Home himself, had not considered Home as a possible candidate until the week in which he took office. The Peerage Act (June 1963) allowed him to disclaim his hereditary earldom (1951–63) and enter the House of Commons, as Sir Alec Douglas-Home, at a byelection, sitting as MP for Kinross and West Perthshire (1963–74). These constitutional intricacies, his uncertain command of television and economics, and HAROLD WILSON's adroitness in public relations, all told against him. His strength in foreign policy, shown in effective handling of crises in East Africa and Cyprus, made little impact. The fashions of the day were against him, and he against them; yet the policy of his government emphasized liberal Conservatism, rapid economic growth, and an expensive social programme.

On 9 April 1964 Home announced an autumn election, a quietly prosperous summer ensuing, though Labour remained well ahead. By 29 September a poll put the Conservatives 2.9 percent ahead, Wilson however remaining much more popular than Home. In a neck-and-neck finish, Home lost by four seats, having been an estimated 100 seats behind on taking office.

In 1964–5, faced with the novel experience of opposition, he made an unconvincing parliamentary gladiator. Murmurings began in his own party, and EDWARD HEATH's star was rising fast. On 22 July 1965, unwilling to fight for position, Home resigned.

Unprecedentedly, he remained at the top, first as shadow Foreign Secretary (1965–70) and then as Foreign Secretary (1970–4). In this period his reputation and popularity grew markedly. His policies, except towards Russia, were not inflexible. He supported EC entry, and on Rhodesia he tried to steer a middle course. He chaired the party committee whose report *Scotland's Government* (March 1970) called for an elected Scottish Convention with limited powers. A firm Christian, he attacked the permissive society, but supported Wilson's abortive plan (1969) for reducing the House of Lords to 250 nominated peers.

His second Foreign Secretaryship was on predictable lines, combining firmness with reconciliation. He normalized relations with China and visited Peking. He increased British involvement in defence east of Suez, reversing Labour policies. He tried, and failed, to reach agreement on Rhodesian independence. Most strikingly, he expelled 105 Soviet spies, with only short-lived repercussions.

Home was more successful as Foreign Secretary, elder statesman, and symbol of integrity in public life, than as premier. Taking office at a period when aristocracy was fashionably linked with British decline, he was more unlucky than other post-war premiers in the timing of his premiership. In fact, in fourteen years in high office, he rarely put a foot wrong. In addition, as author of three books, a thinking Christian, a learned naturalist, and as one who reflected deeply on the fundamentals of international relations, he now appears as much of an intellectual as his former critics. Despite this, his premiership matters most as the last occasion, probably, on which a leader drawn from the old aristocracy will ever come to the fore.

Note on nomenclature:
Alexander Frederick Douglas-Home (1903–18) became, on his grandfather's death, Lord Dunglass (1918–51), a courtesy title held by him as a commoner. On his father's death, he became the 14th Earl of Home (1951–63), then disclaimed his hereditary peerages for life, being known as Sir Alec Douglas-Home (1963–74). In December 1974, he returned to the House of Lords as a life peer, under the new title of Baron Home of the Hirsel.

John Vincent

Bibliography
Churchill, Randolph S. *The Fight for the Tory Leadership*. 1964.

Dickie, John. *The Uncommon Commoner: A Study of Sir Alec Douglas-Home*. 1964. Home, Lord. *The Way The Wind Blows*. 1976.

James, Robert Rhodes. *Ambitions and Realities: British Politics 1964–70*. 1972.

Young, Kenneth. *Sir Alec Douglas-Home*. 1970.

Home Guard

Reviving a proposal made by WINSTON CHURCHILL in October 1939, ANTHONY EDEN proposed to the CABINET on 13 May 1940 the creation of a Local Defence Volunteers Force. He announced the project in a radio broadcast the following day. The first volunteers were trickling in to police stations before his speech concluded; 250,000 volunteered in the next twenty-four hours, 1.5 million by the end of June. Operational control of the force was vested in the Commander-in-Chief, Home Forces (General Sir Edmund Ironside), but selection of leaders proceeded locally on a democratic basis without formal ranks. On 23 July its name was changed to Home Guard by Churchill, who felt it would devour an invading army. In August the Home Guard units were affiliated to country regiments.

Volunteers had to improvise meeting places, uniforms, weapons and training procedures. In a given local group wearing business suits, coveralls and bits of FIRST WORLD WAR uniform, and bearing clubs, hunting rifles and homemade pikes, the only concession to uniformity was often a common armband with the initials "HG". The first shipment of 300 American rifles (eventually to total half a million) arrived in July, the first uniforms in the autumn. Training was remarkably various, from rudimentary close order drill to sophisticated programs of instruction in assassination and sabotage. One school, at Osterly Park in Middlesex, headed by Tom Wintringham, a veteran of the SPANISH CIVIL WAR, was so successful that it was taken over as War Office School (No. 1) for the Home Guard. Eventually there were four official schools.

By February 1941 ranks and commissions had been introduced and the age limit lowered to permit use of the Home Guard as a training ground for seventeen and eighteen year olds prior to their armed forces call-up. Professionalization continued in December with the National Services (No. 2) Act, which introduced CONSCRIPTION and compulsion. Those who had volunteered prior to the Act were free to leave while those who remained or were subsequently conscripted could be compelled to forty-eight hours of service per month. By summer of 1943 there were 1.75 million Home Guards organized into 1,100 battalions. Their average age was just under thirty and only 7 percent were ex-service personnel. Heavily involved in civil defense

activities in cities, elsewhere they were still oriented to local defense against sea or air invasion. From 1942 onward many of them were assigned to anti-aircraft defenses, with 140,000 in that role by September 1944.

Some historians, mocking the military abilities of home guards, have held that an invading German force would have made short work of them. Whether or not this was true, the Home Guard was of enormous significance in shaping and expressing civilian commitment to the war. In addition, it vastly extended the manpower of the armed forces by assuming ever greater responsibility for coast watching, guarding factories, landing fields and bridges, manning roadblocks, taking on anti-aircraft duties and assisting in civil defense, all of which freed regular military personnel for other tasks, especially in the months preceding the allied invasion of the continent in June, 1944. The success of that invasion and subsequent campaign eliminated the need for the Home Guard, and it was officially disbanded on 31 December 1944.

Joseph M. McCarthy

Bibliography

Brophy, John. *Home Guard: A Handbook for the Local Defense Volunteers*. 1940.

Calder, Angus. *The People's War: Britain, 1939–1945*. 1969.

Graves, Charles. *The Home Guard of Britain*. 1943.

Lampe, David. *The Last Ditch*. 1968.

MacKenzie, S.P. *The Home Guard*. 1995.

Homosexuality

In the late nineteenth and early twentieth centuries recognizably modern homosexual identities emerged in Britain. As these identities were slowly consolidated, the ground was prepared for the growth of a movement that would challenge popular prejudices and work for a change in the laws that prohibited sexual activity between men. While the 1950s and 1960s were dominated by cautious lobbying for legal reform, the 1970s and 1980s witnessed the development of a more radical gay and lesbian movement and the rapid growth of a gay urban subculture.

Although an underground homosexual subculture can be traced back several centuries, little was known about it in Victorian Britain. In the 1890s, however, following the passage of the Labouchere Amendment to the 1885 Criminal Law Amendment Act (which made male homosexual acts illegal), it was brought to the attention of the public through a series of scandals. Culminating in the trials of Oscar Wilde, they consolidated a public image of the homosexual and offered moral lessons about the dangers of deviant sexual behavior.

It was amid this "moral panic" about homosexuality that the first generation of sexologists began their work. In the face of older notions of homosexuality as a sin, they argued that homosexuality was an innate condition of certain individuals that could not be avoided and hence should not be persecuted. Edward Carpenter's study, *The Intermediate Sex* (1908), was central to the new thinking, as was the work of Havelock Ellis, whose *Sexual Inversion* was the first volume of his massive *Studies in the Psychology of Sex* (1896–1928). When the British Society for the Study of Sex Psychology was established in 1914, with Carpenter as its president, its work was inspired by Ellis. While it attracted a number of progressive intellectuals in the 1920s, the Society had little impact, either on attitudes or government policy.

Although no documented lesbian subculture existed in Victorian Britain, passionate, homoerotic friendships between women were common. Moreover, some women managed to "pass" as men in the public sphere. Both phenomena lasted into the new century, a period in which some women attempted to define themselves through the new language of sexology—an attempt that could backfire, given that the work of sexologists also served to render intense friendships between women suspect. Although Parliament tried to bring lesbianism within the scope of the criminal law in 1921, it remained immune from the penalties applied to male homosexuals. Radclyffe Hall's novel, *The Well of Loneliness* (1928), drew heavily on Ellis's notions of "congenital inversion" and had for many women as great an impact as had the Wilde trials for men. For many years it offered the best available, and most often cited, defense of lesbianism.

During the 1930s and 1940s a cautious sex-reform movement emerged. Under the leadership of liberals like Norman Haire, it pressed for legal change in the status of male homosexuals. After the Second World War the number of men indicted for homosexual offences grew rapidly, further fueling the demand for a change in the laws. This led the government to appoint a committee to examine those laws, chaired by Sir John Wolfenden. In the *WOLFENDEN REPORT* (1957), the committee called for the decriminalization of homosexuality. Although the Homosexual Law Reform Society was created in 1958 to press for the implementation of the Report's recommendations, law reform only came about in the changed moral climate of the 1960s with the passage of the Sexual Offences Act in 1967, which decriminalized private homosexual acts between men over the age of twenty-one in England and Wales. (Parliament lowered the legal limit to eighteen in 1994 and to sixteen from 2001.) Lobbying by the Scottish Minorities Group, founded in 1969, in part led to the exten-

sion of the Act to Scotland in 1980. The Act was extended to Northern Ireland in 1982.

Many support groups for homosexuals emerged in the 1960s, including the Minorities Research Group (1963) for lesbians. The Campaign for Homosexual Equality (CHE) was established later by those who believed that education and reform were still necessary following the passage of the 1967 Act. By the early 1970s, a period in which the values of consumer culture penetrated an increasingly vibrant gay subculture, it was the largest gay organization in Britain. While women were initially active in the organization, the rapid growth of the Women's Liberation Movement attracted women who believed that the CHE was not an adequate vehicle for the promotion of lesbian issues.

The 1970s marked a turning point in the evolution of homosexual consciousness in Britain. When the Gay Liberation Front was established in 1970, it spearheaded a much larger movement that stressed "coming out", openness, pride, and self-assertion. Arguing that homosexuals needed to play a more active role in their own liberation, radical lesbians, inspired by the Women's Liberation Movement, along with members of the new gay movement, called for profound changes in hegemonic sex roles and a rejection of prevailing images of homosexuality. By the early 1980s many of the newer gay groups, including those established by members of ethnic minorities, were funded by local LABOUR councils. This led to a CONSERVATIVE backlash, evident in Section 28 of the Local Government Bill (1988) which prohibited the "promotion" of homosexuality as an acceptable lifestyle by the councils. The 1980s also witnessed the emergence of new organizations to deal with the devastating consequences of the AIDS crisis, most notably the Terrence Higgins Trust, named after the first Briton known to have died of AIDS.

Throughout the twentieth century gay men fought to change the laws that made them criminals. Lesbians and gay men have also worked to create supportive communities and struggle against prevailing homophobic attitudes. But it has only been since the 1960s that those struggles have led to significant changes in the status of homosexuality in British society.

Chris Waters

Bibliography

Cant, Bob, and Susan Hemmings, eds. *Radical Records: Thirty Years of Lesbian and Gay History, 1957–1987.* 1988.

Jeffery-Poulter, Stephen. *Peers, Queers, and Commoners: The Struggle for Gay Law Reform from 1950 to the Present.* 1991.

Lesbian History Group, ed. *Not a Passing Phase: Reclaiming Lesbians in History 1840–1985.* 1989.

Weeks, Jeffrey. *Coming Out: Homosexual Politics in Britain from the Nineteenth Century to the Present*. rev. ed. 1990.

Horse Racing

Horse racing, a sport that has traditionally brought together the aristocratic and plebeian elements of British society, is composed of two main branches: flat racing (under Jockey Club rules), and jumping (governed by National Hunt rules). The latter is further sub-divided into steeplechasing and hurdling. Races are arranged according to the ages of horses, which are officially "handicapped" by weight on the basis of their performances. A complex range of races therefore operates. The best known are the "classics"—flat racing events for three-year-olds at Newmarket (1,000 and 2,000 Guineas), Epsom (the Derby and the Oaks) and Doncaster (St. Ledger); and the premier steeplechasing event, the Grand National, first run in 1839, held in the spring at the Aintree course (Liverpool), notorious for its difficult fences.

Race crowds have always been socially mixed, and in the nineteenth century at holiday times often had a festive atmosphere. The attraction of certain meetings—notably Royal Ascot—for the upper classes is a reminder that racing also fulfils a purpose in the social hierarchy. To be seen in the Royal Enclosure at Ascot is an important mark of status.

Since the eighteenth century horse racing has been a highly organized and scientific business of rearing and racing thoroughbreds. Vast amounts of capital have been required to participate, hence the sport's association with the landed classes and royalty. More recently, the costs involved have prompted the emergence of syndicates of owners, frequently non-British. For the general public, however, interest in racing is, and always has been, largely confined to betting. It was betting that accounted for the popularity of racing as a spectator sport from the late nineteenth century to the 1950s. During this period most racecourses were enclosed, admission fees charged and the more disreputable elements associated with race-going controlled. The immense popularity of betting drew large crowds to the racecourses, though the proceeds of their transactions benefited racing itself hardly at all. This parasitic feature did not escape the attention of the sport's organizers. After several efforts to rectify the problem, a solution was tried in 1929 in the form of the Totalisator ("Tote"), a system of centralized on-course betting in which a proportion of the total pool of bets placed was redirected into the further development of the sport itself. The principle was sound, though early practice marred its effectiveness, and in the

1930s the amounts of money accruing to racing were small. Subsequent modifications to the Tote system, together with legislation to channel some of the proceeds of private bookmakers into racing through the Horse Race Betting Levy Board, have ensured a healthier return. The flow of funds into racing has been further enhanced by extensive television coverage since the 1960s, which has induced companies to sponsor events. By the mid 1980s some 20 percent of all prize money derived from this source.

Television, however, has been a factor in reducing the crowds at racecourses, as has the legalization in 1961 of ready money betting. The opening of betting shops meant that people could place their bets and watch a televised race without having to journey to the nearest racecourse. In this new climate of falling attendances some courses found it hard to meet the cost of upkeep and were forced to close. Nevertheless there are still many courses operating up and down the country and the race-goer is assured of a rich variety of meetings on most days of the week.

Jeffrey Hill

Bibliography
Arlott, John ed., *The Oxford Companion to Sports and Games*. 1975.
Vamplew, Wray. *The Turf: A Social and Economic History of Horse Racing*. 1976.

Hospitals

During the twentieth century the role of hospitals within the Britsh medical care system changed substantially. In 1900 hospitals constituted one of several treatment alternatives for the sick; by the 1990s they had become the central focus of the national medical system. This development was associated with the gradual transition from a private to a publicly funded medical service; with the expansion of medical technology, medical teaching, and MEDICAL RESEARCH, which were located in hospitals; and with the professional ambitions of the hospital consultants, whose status and influence were increasingly enhanced by the expansion of the biomedical sciences. By the 1990s all major cities and country towns contained at least one district hospital, offering accident, emergency, and maternity services, as well as a range of more specialized treatments. These hospitals are mostly funded and administered within the NATIONAL HEALTH SERVICE. Admissions, except for accident and emergency cases, are by referral from the family doctor (general practitioner). The general hospitals are complemented by special hospitals treating selected types of cases, such as the Hospital for Sick Children and the Brompton Hospital for Diseases of the Chest. Except in the relatively small number of private hospitals, treatment is gratuitous under the National Health Service provision.

In the early twentieth century there were three major types of hospitals in Britain: the old established voluntary hospitals, dating mainly from the eighteenth century and financed by endowments and voluntary contributions, where patient admission was an act of charity; some of these were the specialist hospitals, nineteenth-century foundations, which delivered care to selected categories of patients, most of whom paid for their treatment; the Poor Law infirmaries, financed by local taxation and providing care for the poor and needy; and municipal hospitals including locally funded isolation hospitals for infectious disease cases. There were also cottage hospitals run by provincial general practioners for their own patients.

Each of these types of hospital performed a somewhat different function. The voluntary hospitals were the largest sector and the closest to modern general hospitals. Their staffing was important to the career structure of the medical profession, and it was in them that the elite consultant physicians and surgeons had their hospital practice. Many, notably the LONDON foundations, had associated medical schools, and they increasingly became centers of medical research. The great London hospitals dominated this sector, but voluntary hospitals were also found in the major provincial cities.

In the early nineteenth century hospitals in general had been resorted to reluctantly by ordinary people, who considered them to be tainted by the stigma of charity. This perception, changing by 1900, had disappeared completely by 1950. In the second half of the twentieth century hospital treatment has come to be considered as a rightful benefit by the British people.

The National Insurance Act of 1911 was a major step in this progression. Although the hospitals were not directly involved in this legislation, it had profound consequences for the hospital system. Hitherto out-patient departments had functioned as alternative doctors' surgeries, but under the act free medical benefits could be obtained only through general practitioners. Fears of financial insolvency led the hospitals to introduce pay-beds, and to revise their admissions policies. Out-patient services were increasingly restricted and came to provide a specialist consultative service, complementing that of the general practitioner. The referral system, in which patients are passed on to hospitals for surgery, or specialist diagnosis or treatment by general practitioners, became an established feature of this new order.

Following the First World War the financial position of the voluntary hospitals became increasingly acute, and the policy of charging patients more widespread. Between 1891 and 1938 hospital revenue derived from gifts and investments fell from 88 percent to 33 percent, while that derived from patient charges rose from 11 to 59 percent of total revenue. Changing social and political circumstances also brought change to other parts of the hospital sector. Under the Local Government Act of 1929 hospitals administered by the Poor Law authorities (the infirmaries and the infectious disease hospitals) were transferred to local authority responsibility. The lingering deterrent effect of Poor Law application was thus finally removed from this sector.

During the SECOND WORLD WAR some of the hospitals were placed under government control for the first time. At the outbreak of war the government set up the Emergency Medical Services (EMS), to deal with expected heavy civilian air raid casualties. The Ministry of Health took charge, at the national level, of part of the voluntary and municipal hospital sector, which was regionally and locally administrated. A regional blood transfusion service, and national pathology and public health laboratory services, were established. This wartime experience encouraged a positive attitude towards the reorganization of the hospital services among the medical profession and demonstrated also that such reorganization was possible.

The foundation of the National Health Service (NHS) in 1948 saw the complete transformation of hospital administration in Britain. Most of the hospitals were nationalized, although hospital consultants retained the right to treat private patients in NHS hospitals (pay-beds). The nationalized hospitals came under the overall control of the Ministry of Health (later the Department of Health and Social Security). England and Wales were divided into thirteen regions, on the principle that each region should contain a university with a medical school. Regional Hospital Boards were to plan for the hospital and specialist services, while day-to-day management was in the hands of 388 Hospital Management Councils, each responsible for one large hospital or a group of hospitals. The thirty-six teaching hospitals (ten in Scotland, twenty-six in England and Wales) were independently administered. They retained their own boards of governors, and had separate funding; thus they continued to have a privileged status within the NHS.

From the beginning the hospital sector took the major share of NHS spending. In 1950 hospitals accounted for 54.9 percent of the total NHS budget; by 1987–8 this had risen (with some fluctuations) to 66.2 percent.

Although the British government quickly realized that NHS expenditure would have to be carefully regulated, there was little attempt to plan or rationalize the hospital system during the 1950s. In this decade hospitals competed to acquire specialist consultants and new medical technology. Government constraints meant that there was little capital expenditure, however. Further, the NHS had left the old unequal distribution of hospital facilities between the different regions of the country unchanged. While London and the southeast generally were almost overprovided with hospitals, large areas of the north and northeast were relatively poorly served.

In 1962 the government responded to this situation by introducing a Hospitals Programme, which aimed to secure a better distribution of hospital beds by building new hospitals, and to improve efficiency and cut costs by reducing the average length of stay in a hospital. The plan proposed ninety new hospitals, and the modernization of others. It was believed that larger hospitals would mean significant economies of scale, and the plan promoted a movement towards district general hospitals with 600–800 beds serving a population of 100,000–150,000, and providing treatment and diagnostic facilities for both in-patients and out-patients in all the common specialties, including geriatrics and mental illness.

The 1960s were a decade of expansion; the 1970s brought economic uncertainty, and the rising price of fuel brought a new dimension of crisis into the funding and management of the hospital service. The continuing rapid expansion of expensive medical technology and the realities of an ageing population both contributed to ever-increasing pressure on the hospital service. From the early 1970s British governments were engaged in a continuous search for improved management and reduced, or at least controlled, spending in the hospital sector. This trend resulted in a series of crises within the service, including repeated major industrial action by doctors, nurses, and ancillary staff in the later 1970s and 1980s. Until 1989, however, government policy was remarkable for its continuity, focusing on issues of management and the reallocation of resources, despite much publicized arguments about minor issues such as the abolition of pay-beds in hospitals.

In 1989 the Conservative government introduced proposals that marked a radical departure from established policy in the NHS. The White Paper *Working for Patients* proposed changes in the organization of the delivery of services, rather than changes in the level or sources of finance. Since April 1991 hospitals may choose to opt out of local authority control and to establish their own self-governing hospital trusts. A number of big hospitals, including Guy's Hospital in London, have already chosen to manage their own resources in this way, and many others have indicated that they intend to follow suit. Under this new system, district health authorities are obliged to contract with the independent hospital for services and may also contract with other health authorities for services unavailable (or unsatisfactory) within their own districts.

Since 1950 financial constraints and scientific and professional developments have combined to change the role of the British hospital. Whereas at mid-century hospitals were essentially treatment centers for in-patient care, they now function increasingly as diagnostic centers, with a large out-patient constituency seen after referral. Length of stay for in-patients has been substantially reduced, while the number of in-patients treated has greatly increased. The care of the elderly and of the mentally ill is increasingly short-term and directed towards rehabilitation and community care. Since the 1990s British hospitals provide a technical support service within a framework of community care, but they supply the latest technology and specialist medical treatment, continue to train medical students and pursue medical research, and provide a recognized professional career structure for large numbers of medically-qualified persons.

Anne Hardy

Bibliography

Abel-Smith, Brian. *The Hospitals 1800–1948: A Study in Social Administration in England and Wales.* 1964.

Allsop, Judith. *Health Policy and the National Health Service.* 1984.

Rivett, Geoffrey. *The Development of the London Hospital System, 1823–1982.* 1986.

Watkin, Brian. *The National Health Service: The First Phase 1948–1974 and After.* 1978.

Webster, Charles. *The Health Services Since the War: vol. 1: Problems of Health Care: The National Health Service before 1957.* 1988.

Hotels

LONDON before the First World War saw the heyday of the grand hotel, many recently built during the speculative building boom encouraged by the two Jubilees of 1887 and 1897. The most opulent were Claridge's in Brook Street, favored by visiting royalty, the huge Savoy in the Strand, built by Richard D'Oyly Carte, and the Carlton in Piccadilly, built by César Ritz, who came to England to manage the Savoy but decided to build his own hotel, taking for it the Savoy's great chef, Auguste Escoffier, whose organizational genius made possible the à la carte menu. There were numerous other large hotels, including the Victoria near Trafalgar Square, owned by the Gordon Hotels chain, the world's largest, founded by the forgotten Victorian entrepreneur Frederick Gordon. With 500 rooms, the Victoria had only four bathrooms, no running water in the rooms, no elevators and no central heating. Chamberpots and shallow tin baths kept under the bed were still the order of the day here and in most hotels. Hotels were largely managed and staffed by Continental IMMIGRANTS and REFUGEES, though the myth that only a foreign male could be a great chef and hotelier was punctured at Rosa Lewis's small, ultra-exclusive Cavendish Hotel, patronized by EDWARD VII. Two hotels particularly favored by American visitors were the large and bustling Langham in Portland Place, and the small, discreet Brown's in Dover Street, where Franklin and Eleanor Roosevelt honeymooned in 1905.

In major provincial cities the main hotels were usually owned by RAILWAY companies. These generally had excellent restaurants, as indeed at least until 1939 it was a point of pride for a major hotel to have a top class restaurant and wine cellar. A significant development outside London was the growth of the Trust House chain, founded by Earl Grey, to take over small rural inns and wean them from excessive dependence on the drink trade by providing reasonably priced accommodation and meals to travelers, especially touring cyclists, and later motorists. The seaside hotel trade continued to expand with the new development of the all-inclusive holiday camp and hotel offering constant programmed activities, an idea pioneered by the Canadian Billy Butlin.

London saw some inter-war hotel building, particularly on the former sites of the great ducal town houses, the Dorchester in Park Lane being the best known. But the stock of hotel accommodation suffered heavily from requisition, neglect, and bombing during the SECOND WORLD WAR. This created opportunities for post-war property speculation: men like Max Joseph, Charles Forte, and Charles Clore made great fortunes in the hotel business, which boomed as overseas tourists created great demand for hotel rooms. New hotels were built with government grants to encourage tourism, some of them assaulting the London skyline, like the high-rise Hilton in Park Lane. Meanwhile the practice of converting private housing to hotel use, common since the mid-Victorian era in Bloomsbury, extended outward to Pimlico, Kensington and beyond.

Christopher A. Kent

Bibliography

Borer, Mary C. *The British Hotel Through the Ages.* 1972.

Fielding, Daphne, *The Duchess of Jermyn Street: The Life and Good Times of Rosa Lewis of the Cavendish Hotel.* 1964.

Taylor, Derek. *Fortune, Fame and Folly: British Hotels and Catering from 1878 to 1978.* 1977.

Hours of Work

In 1900 the normal working week for male manual workers in Britain was fifty-four hours, a figure which had fallen to thirty-nine hours by the mid-1980s. This significant shortening of the working week has been matched by a shortening of the working year as holidays with pay have been introduced, and with a shortening of the working life-span as more education has delayed entry into the labour force for the young and increased retirement provision has accelerated withdrawal from the workforce at older ages. Within these overall trends, white collar workers have consistently enjoyed shorter working hours than blue collar workers, and WOMEN have worked for fewer hours per week than men.

At the beginning of the century most British men worked a nine-hour day and a six-day week. Average hours of work tended to be higher in agriculture and the service sector and marginally lower in the heavily-unionized construction, COAL MINING, and printing trades. Trade unions had campaigned vigorously for an eight-hour day (forty-eight-hour week) since the 1890s, but success in achieving this goal was patchy and often temporary. In 1919 and 1920, however, most employers, with the encouragement of the government, adopted the forty-seven or forty-eight-hour week. This was partly to recompense the workforce for the sacrifices of the war years, partly to mollify the trade unions and aid post-war industrial recovery. There was little change to this normal working week until the end of the Second World War when, between 1945 and 1947, a forty-four-hour working week became established as the norm. This new norm survived for fifteen years, but fell to forty hours between 1960 and 1966 and has edged down further to thirty-nine hours in the early 1980s. Since the Second World War the actual hours worked by male manual workers have been three to four hours per week above the contractual norm because of regular overtime working. Full-time female manual workers have worked about four hours per week less than men, and white-collar workers have typically worked one hour a week less than manual workers.

Holidays with pay were exceptional before the First World War, but by 1938 unions had negotiated a week's paid leave for over 4 million manual workers. Holiday entitlements have grown considerably since 1945, and by the mid 1980s stood at an average of thirty-three days per year, eight of which were public holidays. In consequence the average annual working time of a fully-employed British male manual worker has fallen from around 2760 hours in 1900 to 1770 hours by the mid 1980s. The average number of years worked by men has also fallen as the minimum school leaving age has risen to sixteen, and as average retirement ages have fallen. For women, however, the trend in years worked is upwards, because of the pronounced rise in married women's labor force participation since the Second World War.

Paul Johnson

Bibliography

Bienefeld, M.A. Working Hours in British Industry. 1972.
Cross, Gary. A Quest for Time: The Reduction of Work in Britain and France, 1840–1940. 1989.

House of Lords

In 1900 the House of Lords was a legislative body of just under 600 members, all of whom (except for half-a-dozen judges, appointed to enable the House to continue in its ancient role as a supreme court of appeal in judicial matters decorously and without any claims to intervene by the lay majority, and 26 CHURCH OF ENGLAND bishops) held hereditary titles. Nobody could be exactly sure how many people could sit as peers, because titles might be in abeyance because they had descended to women or to foreigners, and it was always possible that legitimate heirs might be able to prove their claim to titles thought to be extinct. The peers stood at the head of a wider aristocracy of titled men, some who held noble titles that did not entitle them to sit in the Lords, some hereditary holders of the title of knighthood (baronets) and a larger number of men who had won the honour of knighthood, with the title Sir before their names, but had not gained the right to pass it down to their sons. While its membership was mainly English, it contained 16 of the old (pre-1707) Scottish peers and 28 of the old (pre-1810) Irish peers chosen from among themselves by those who had not yet gained United Kingdom titles. This titled aristocracy was itself only the most visible part of a landowning elite of several thousand people who lived mainly or entirely on their rental incomes and—at least in the countryside—enjoyed considerable political influence as a direct consequence of owning land.

The families of the landowning elite dominated the upper ranks of politics—in 1900 members of the House of Lords had held the Premiership for 17 of the past 25 years and the Foreign Secretaryship for 43 of the past 50 years—and of activities like the Church of England and the ARMY that were closely linked to politics. There was a constitutional convention that the House of Lords did not intervene in financial issues, but its capacity to affect other legislative matters had been shown by its destruction of the LIBERALS' Home Rule Bill in 1893.

The power of the landowning elite had been declining for some time, directly because of the agricultural depression of the last quarter of the 19th century, and less directly because the owners of the commercial and industrial wealth that had grown up in the 19th century and, to a far lesser extent, the industrial working class wanted more political power. The most publicly visible step in the reduction of the position of the House of Lords was the Parliament Act of 1911 but it continued to resist Liberal legislation in the years before 1914.

Its prestige suffered considerably from the activities of LLOYD GEORGE, who increased the membership, which had risen to about 650 by 1916, by over a hundred peers in the six years of his Premiership; some of these creations were the traditional recognition for services in the FIRST WORLD WAR and some of them were an acknowledgement of the role of industrialists in the economy and the war effort, but some of them were given to newspaper owners for their support, or to less easily defined allies for services which clearly included cash contributions to Lloyd George's political machine. The diminished position of the House of Lords was symbolised by the decision not to give the Premiership to the distinguished Conservative peer, LORD CURZON, in 1923; Curzon had other shortcomings but it was widely believed that the decisive point was that parliamentary business would now be mainly a matter for the House of Commons, partly on general democratic grounds and partly because the LABOUR PARTY, by this stage the official Opposition, had virtually no supporters in the Lords.

The respectability of the Lords was rebuilt between the wars, and its membership increased very little in the second quarter of the century. The post-war Labour government further diminished its powers by reducing its right to reject legislation from two sessions to one, and at the same time the Lords accepted a convention that they had no right to interfere with legislation if it had been discussed at the previous general election. This left the House of Lords as a revising body for the details of legislation passed in the Commons which could gain greater respect for this role by moving from acceptance of legislation produced by Conservative governments and guarded hostility to Labour legislation to a more detached attitude.

Two substantial changes were made in the Premiership of HAROLD MACMILLAN. In 1958 he brought forward legislation that provided for men and women to be made life peers and this change allowed governments to offer, and recipients to accept, membership in the House of Lords without having to worry about the social and financial difficulties that might face heirs to the title. The official opposition, and later on the Liberals, were allowed to select some life peers of their own for the Lords; it was understood that these peers would be chosen because they would take an active role in the work of the House, and new creations came to be announced as titles for past services or as "working peers".

In 1963, the Hon. ANTHONY WEDGWOOD BENN, who was determined not to leave the House of Commons on the death of his father, Lord Stansgate, stood in the by-election in his Bristol constituency caused because he had legally become a peer. When he was re-elected Macmillan's government brought forward a Peerage Act that allowed heirs to renounce titles upon succeeding to them: the immediate effect, apart from allowing Benn to stay in the House of Commons, was to let LORD HOME and Lord Hailsham leave the House of Lords to stand for the leadership of the Conservative party when Macmillan retired. About a dozen people renounced peerages early in the life of this Act, but the right of renunciation was used very little since 1975. This Act allowed all remaining Scottish peers to sit in the Lords—no new Irish peers had been selected for the Lords after 1922, and none benefitted in 1963—and it also allowed 'peeresses in their own right' (heiresses to peerages whose grant allowed women to call themselves by the title) to sit in the Lords, which had not previously been permitted.

By 1997, when a Labour government led by TONY BLAIR was elected on a platform that included abolition of any hereditary right to sit in the House of Lords, its membership had increased to 1200. Slightly over a third were life peers under the 1958 Act and just under two-thirds were the surviving peers by hereditary succession. As only seven hereditary titles were created after 1964, four of them for members of the Royal Family, the hereditary membership would presumably have died away very slowly by the failure of heirs. The Labour proposals spoke of the future of the House of Lords after the hereditary peers had been removed in terms vague enough to remind people that the 1911 Parliament Act had been accompanied by similar assurances that proposals for further change would soon be introduced. The CONSERVATIVE leadership in the Commons began arguing that all the members of the House of Lords should be elected, although on a system of voting which avoided the oversimplification of a first-past-the post system. Before anything could come of this the Conservative leadership in the Lords (led by the heir to the Marquis of Salisbury, Lord Cranbourne, who had been promoted to the Lords before his father's death) worked out an arrangement with the government which passed into law in 1999 that allowed 92 of the hereditary peers to remain full members of the House. The government may

have believed that there should be as much interparty agreement on the issue as possible or it may have reflected that, if the hereditary peers felt they had nothing to lose and chose to express their personal feelings without regard for constitutional convention, they could destroy the work of one parliamentary session and greatly complicate the work of the next session before being driven out.

The hereditary peers then proceeded to elect in party caucuses those who were going to survive, after those who eager to survive had sent out statements of their claims to be among the 92. Most of the hereditary aristocracy then passed into the social world of titles unconnected with political power known to readers of Proust, though the provision for party caucuses to reassemble to choose new representatives when death caused vacancies among the 92 did indicate that the hereditary peerage would not lose all its power in the immediate future. At the same time Blair appointed life peers at the rate of 40 a year with so marked an attention to the claims of friendship and generous support for the Labour party that the opposition dubbed them "Tony's cronies". The cry of the peers against the people will not be heard again, but the House may be useful in future reorganization of the four countries in the United Kingdom, or in handling relations with the EUROPEAN UNION.

Trevor Lloyd

Bibliography

Bromhead, Peter A. *The House of Lords and Contemporary Politics, 1911–1957.* 1958.

Cannadine, David. *The Decline and Fall of the British Aristocracy.* 1990.

Housing

During the twentieth century the provision and built form of British housing has been transformed. In aggregate terms the overall housing stock has tripled since 1900, and the spatial implications of such quantitative additions on the formerly compact nineteenth-century cities have been considerable. Of greater significance has been a transition in housing tenure. Owner occupancy has replaced rented accommodation as the predominant form of tenure. Before the FIRST WORLD WAR approximately 10–20 percent of occupants owned their own home; by 1938 this figure had risen to 32 percent and by 1983 to 62 percent. The decline in privately rented accommodation was also accompanied by a growth in COUNCIL (or public) HOUSING, rising from approximately 1 percent of the housing stock in 1914 to 10 percent in 1938 and to 32 percent in 1980. As public authorities and mortgage companies replaced private landlords in the finance and management of the housing market, so social relationships, community organizations, and landlord-tenant relations have altered. Though both quantitatively and qualitatively British housing experienced significant changes during the twentieth century, this has taken place against a background of considerable geographical variations, as in Scotland where council housing represents about 70 percent of the housing stock. Also, dwellings built before the twentieth century still constitute locally up to 20 percent of the national housing stock, thus providing a measure of visual and residential continuity to the urban landscape.

The simultaneous development of council housing and owner occupancy, both at the expense of private sector rented accommodation, gathered pace after the First World War. Historians have sought to interpret these developments with reference to the pre-1914 housing market, and four explanations are customarily advanced. One interpretive strand emphasizes the emerging intervention by municipal authorities in the late nineteenth and early twentieth centuries to regulate construction standards, TOWN PLANNING, and insanitary housing. Council housing after 1919 is explained as a logical consequence of the failures of unregulated private enterprise, specifically the activities of the building industry, and the limited achievements of philanthropic housing associations; twentieth-century housing policy is analyzed in terms of the gradual and inevitable acceptance of state intervention as the replacement for market-based housing provisions. A second interpretive framework has been offered by Marxist historians, who explain the provision of council housing as a response to the long run decline of landlords', builders', and investors' profits, though this does not accord with the buoyancy of owner occupancy after 1920. A third explanation is also ideologically based. Historians have viewed the CONSERVATIVE PARTY's encouragement to home ownership as a tactic to counter the sustained early twentieth-century LIBERAL attack on landowners' and property interests. Whether this "ramparts strategy" was a consciously manipulative policy remains unclear, however, though tax advantages to private homeowners, introduced between the wars, remain a totem of the Conservative Party.

A fourth approach claims not that the crisis in the housing market prompted state intervention, but that state intervention prompted a crisis in the housing sector from which council housing resulted. More specifically, a virtual ban on wartime building and a restriction on rental increases in response to intense political pressure to contain wartime inflation so distorted the market that it could not return to normal after the war.

The rents of 85 percent of the housing stock of 8 million homes were restricted under government legislation passed in 1915, and since the shortage of houses was estimated at almost 1 million in 1919, rising to 2.8 million in 1931, this disequilibrium between housing supply and demand could not be addressed by abandoning rent controls and using the price mechanism. Rent restrictions continued to apply to 70 percent of accommodation throughout the 1920s, and this restraint on builders' and landlords' profits caused housing finance to be re-routed through building societies. The decline of landlordism was initiated; the rise of mortgage finance for owner occupancy assured.

The transformation in the housing sector was accentuated by broader national trends. For those in work, disposable incomes rose significantly; real earnings, though largely unchanged in the early and mid-1920s, rose by about 20 percent during the inter-war years, with real net national income rising by almost 40 percent. Savings mirrored these trends, with a sevenfold increase in the value of building society deposits. As a result, and with the single exception of 1932, mortgage advances were higher in each successive year from 1921 until the threat of war reined in private investment from 1937. Between 1928 and 1938 the number of private individuals who turned to mortgage companies for housing finance increased from 500,000 to 1.5 million, largely because the cost of borrowing to homeowners declined sharply from its 6 percent interest rate level in the 1920s to 4.5 percent in the mid-1930s once Britain abandoned the GOLD STANDARD in 1931, and because the amount of housing finance required fell as building costs lurched downwards between 1921 and 1937. Many national economic indicators reinforced characteristics within the housing sector so as to produce a strong trend towards both a rising owner occupancy and a consequential structural shift away from privately rented accommodation.

The spatial implications of inter-war housing developments have had long-standing effects for British society. Since council housing was undertaken on green field sites, in projects involving the simultaneous construction of hundreds of dwelling units, and planned, financed, and administered by an emerging bureaucracy of experts in housing and town planning departments, homogeneity remains its most striking and durable feature. Designs and costings were submitted to a central government department in London for approval where prevailing GARDEN CITY principles were strongly influenced by Raymond Unwin (1863–1940). As the leading architect of the Garden City movement before the First World War, Unwin had been heavily involved in projects at Letchworth (1903) and Hampstead Garden Suburb (begun in 1906). It was Unwin's contribution to the Tudor Walters Report (1918), a pathbreaking treatise on housing standards and designs for the working class, which determined street layout, internal designs, and building materials to be incorporated in council housing projects. The initial standards were generous in land, materials, and internal space, but in a period of financial austerity the proposals were successively scaled down to produce the architectural monotony of council housing still apparent in most British cities and rural areas today.

Private housing developments were also undertaken mainly on the periphery of British cities. Together with the financial considerations noted earlier and inner city housing demolition programs, a halving in the average price of automobiles between 1924 and 1936, and a proliferation of new household goods combined to encourage an exodus to semi-detached villas (duplexes) in new suburbs and commuting zones. This was most marked in LONDON, the southeast counties, and in the Midlands during the 1930s, where the service sector and the emergence of new manufacturing industries provided more stable employment for an expanding middle class and the upper strata of the working class.

Two distinctive housing types—the council house and the private semi-detached villa—developed in the inter-war years. These replaced the geometrically laid out streets of terraced houses for those with low incomes, and the Victorian villas organized on the presumption of cheap servant labor. Minimum standards of space, decency, and amenity governed both new forms of housing, though the 2/3 bedrooms, 1/2 public rooms, kitchen, WC and bathroom, and small garden plot of council housing developments was both meaner in dimensions and detailing than for private housing. The most important long term consequence was to perpetuate the class dimension of British housing. Crudely, residential segregation in the form of SLUMS and suburbs characterized social segregation in the nineteenth-century city; council housing and "3 bedroom semis" reproduced this separation of the working and middle classes in the twentieth century.

Wartime enemy action accounted for the loss of about 500,000 houses, or about 4 percent of the housing stock, and together with the suspension to housebuilding during the Second World War, the combined housing shortage in 1945 was estimated at 1.25 million houses. Because of new household formation in the intervening period before such housing could be completed, the real shortage of housing was estimated at around 3 million houses—equivalent to about 24 percent of the pre-war housing stock. An annual programme of 300,000 houses—not far short of the record 366,000 built in 1936—was planned in 1946 by the LABOUR administration. In six years, 1945-51, housebuilding for private owners never approached the levels achieved in a single year from 1933-9. Rent restrictions froze private rentals at 1939 levels. Faced with such shortages, the political consensus accorded council housing the highest priority, yet despite the construction of 1.2 million houses between 1945-51, the shortage, still estimated at between 1-2 million houses in 1951, dominated housing policy for the ensuing two decades.

Housing in the 1950s was dominated by "general needs", that is, by the urgency of adding significant numbers to the housing stock. This was achieved by continuing provision of central government finance to local councils, and in the course of the 1950s, 2.45 million new houses were built, two-thirds of them by councils. To a considerable degree this was a replication of the approach adopted in the 1920s, and, as in the inter-war years, a subsequent, developing strand of housing policy was based on slum clearances. This gathered pace in the 1950s and continued throughout the 1960s and 1970s, so that councils demolished 1.4 million older houses, displacing more than 3 million individuals in the process, often to new multi-story block flats on the periphery of cities. The social dislocation which resulted, together with media coverage hostile to the provision of high rise housing for family dwelling, proved instrumental in restricting the extent of tower block housebuilding.

As private-sector housing provision resumed its quantitative ascendancy in the 1960s, public priorities, though never abandoning the general provision of housing for low income families, increasingly recognized the aged, disabled, single-parent, and problem families as having discrete housing requirements. By the 1970s public housing provision was more carefully targeted, an approach also adopted in respect of a program of housing renovation, undertaken partly as a reaction to the soulless image of council housing estates and the dilapidation of private rented housing, but also in response to central government funding in the wake of urban riots. A system of improvement grants was expanded in the 1970s to provide many households with exclusive rather than shared access to baths, WCs, kitchens and sinks, as well as providing for electrical re-wiring, insulation, and structural repairs. The combined effect of post-war new building and improvement programs has meant that whereas in 1950 approximately half the British population shared either washing or cooking facilities, only 5 percent did so in the 1980s.

While local and central government officials grappled with the quantity and quality of the post-war housing stock, simultaneously, private builders responded to new supply opportunities. The framework of integrated town and regional planning which developed after 1947 identified areas for housing expansion. This, the consolidation of firms within the building industry, and other factors such as the mushrooming of mortgage finance, contributed to significant inflation in land values, which was translated into increased house prices. Aside from the tax advantages available to mortgage holders, the rising capital value of houses penalized those who did not participate in home ownership. Again, housing became an agent of social polarization, particularly in the house price booms of 1972, 1979, and the late 1980s.

A different housing phase developed with the election of the Conservatives in 1979. Based on an ideological critique of council housing, the THATCHER administration presented the housing problem as the very existence of municipal landlordism. Two overlapping phases of policy resulted. One, from 1979–86, pursued a policy of reluctant collectivism, with the public sector providing only for special needs housing where private enterprise was unable to meet it. Consequently, central government restrictions on local authority capital expenditure greatly reduced the volume of new council housebuilding. Coupled with it was a "right to buy", a tenant's right to acquire, at heavily discounted prices, the council house which he or she occupied. With sales exceeding completions in 1982, the council housing stock began to decrease for the first time in its history. The second phase, announced in 1987, and given legislative force in 1988–9, signalled another anti-collectivist approach to housing provision. Though the promotion of home ownership remained a priority, Conservative attention was aimed at extending privatization to the rented housing sector. Diverse strategies were employed: investment and tax incentives for privately rented accommodation, de-regulation of new lettings, and the creation of umbrella organizations such as Housing Action Trusts and Tenants' Choice schemes, designed to demunicipalize the housing stock by enabling tenants to opt for private housing association status to address their housing concerns. Such initiatives are designed to break down the social and residential segregation which has become more pronounced in British society in almost every decade of the twentieth century.

Richard Rodger

Bibliography

Ball, Michael. *Housing Policy and Economic Power: The Political Economy of Owner Occupation.* 1983.

Bowley, Marian. *Housing and the State 1919–1944.* 1945.

Burnett, John. *A Social History of Housing 1815–1985.* 2nd ed. 1986.

Daunton, Martin J. *A Property Owning Democracy? Housing in Britain.* 1987.

Dunleavy, Patrick. *The Politics of Mass Housing in Britain 1945–1975.* 1981.

Rodger, Richard. *Scottish Housing in the Twentieth Century.* 1989.

Huxley, Aldous Leonard (1894–1963)

Aldous Huxley, novelist, essayist, poet, biographer, and mystic, is most famed for three of his novels: *Point Counter Point* (1928), an innovatively-structured account of upper-class and bohemian London life on the eve of Fascism's rise; *Brave New World* (1932), a dystopian forecast of life in the year A.F. (after Ford) 600; and *Island* (1962), a utopian account of a present-day paradise in which persons achieve individual integrity, freedom from the fear of death, and fine attunement to reality by means of mysticism and discriminating use of drugs.

Huxley was the grandson of the Victorian scientist and proponent of Darwinism, T.H. Huxley, and the great-nephew of the Victorian literary critic and poet Matthew Arnold. Three intense encounters with mortality marked Huxley's early years: his beloved mother's death in 1908; a disease of the cornea in 1910, which blinded him for more than a year; and the suicide of his elder brother in the opening days of the First World War. In spite of these troubles, Huxley achieved distinction as an OXFORD undergraduate and published his first book of poems in 1917. He participated in the brilliant circle of writers, thinkers, and politicians at Lady Ottoline Morrell's Garsington Manor, where he befriended the novelist D.H. LAWRENCE and met Maria Nys, a Belgian refugee, whom he married in 1919.

Huxley's first novels, *Crome Yellow* (1921), *Antic Hay* (1923), and *Those Barren Leaves* (1925), are influenced by Thomas Love Peacock's novels from a century earlier, as well as by *South Wind* (1917) by Norman Douglas (1868–1952). The novels represent clever young men adrift in the post-war world who are surprised to discover that amorality in general, and sexual promiscuity in particular, do not free them from unhappiness and self-division. Personal self-division becomes in *Point Counter Point* a "human fugue" of social fragmentation and incoherence, which is replicated in the fragmented, counter-pointed structure of the novel's narrative. But a pair of redeemers from incompleteness also appears in the novel in the figures of Mark and Mary Rampion, characters based on D.H. Lawrence and his wife. Huxley's adherence to Lawrence (he edited the first posthumous edition of Lawrence's letters in 1932), combined with the impact on Huxley of Buddhism and Gandhian pacifism during a Far Eastern tour in 1925, intensified his already strong didactic bent.

This didacticism dominates *Brave New World,* and shapes the rest of Huxley's career, in an impressively unabated manner, even during the moments of Huxley's further aesthetic experiments with narrative form (after *Point Counter Point*) in *Eyeless in Gaza* (1936) and *Time Must Have A Stop* (1944). The primary tenets of Huxley's teaching are a non-dogmatic belief in personal immediate experiences of eternity, which transcend time and the world, yet nevertheless enlighten and guide mundane actions; and a quasi-anarchist advocacy of international PACIFISM, urging non-attachment to politics (albeit not detachment from them altogether). These tenets, however much they seemed sensible to the young of the post-war generation, appealed less to the young men and women of the 1930s, whose anti-fascist leftism and whose sympathy with the republicans of Spain prided itself on political engagement. Fighting a losing battle on behalf of pacifism, Huxley migrated in 1937–8, with his wife and a fellow mystic Gerald Heard (1889–1971)—who also influenced the novelist CHRISTOPHER ISHERWOOD—to Los Angeles. He undertook film work, writing scripts for MGM, Fox, Disney, and Universal; his novels *After Many A Summer Dies the Swan* (1939) and *Ape and Essence* (1948) are in part satiric visions of Hollywood.

Huxley undertook to become an American citizen in 1954. His application was rejected because he could not claim that his pacifist objection to the right to bear arms was a religious conviction rather than a purely philosophical one. But this disclaimer of religious inspiration did not mean a lessening of the mysticism which Huxley had summed up at the end of the Second World War in *The Perennial Philosophy* (1945). As an experiment in mysticism, in 1954 Huxley asked Humphrey Osmond, an English psychiatrist researching the effect of the mescaline on schizophrenia, to supervise Huxley's taking of the drug in order for him to explore the possibilities of expanded consciousness. The blissful results are described in Huxley's *The Doors of Perception* (1954) and are elaborated in *Island,* which presents a program for averting both the dystopia of *Brave New World* and the post-nuclear age horror of *Ape and Essence.*

It now appears that Huxley's work includes a forecast of literary criticism's recent castigations of modernist art for its alleged irresponsibly disinterested relation to the world's political state. Although the modernist artistic forms of Huxley's work are at one with those of JAMES JOYCE, VIRGINIA WOOLF, and WYNDHAM LEWIS (and are more like theirs than like Lawrence's), Huxley appears more up-to-date than they in his didactic contention that art and aesthetics, no matter how avant garde, are of secondary importance in comparison with clear-eyed historical consciousness and with historical well-being. Equally up-to-date, Huxley's mixture of novelistic and documentary modes in his two remarkable biographies of seventeenth-century French clergy, *Grey Eminence* (1941) and *The Devils of Loudon* (1952), instance the mixed modes of the academy's current "new historicism." Nevertheless the contemporary interest of Huxley is probably mitigated by his contention, especially in the biographies, that politics damnably betrays mysticism; and mitigated too by both the datedness (however full of charm) and the irony (however produced by chance) of *Island*'s embodiment of the ways of living and the values of California's 1960s "counter-culture."

Robert L. Caserio

Bibliography
Bedford, Sybille. *Aldous Huxley: A Biography.* 1974.
Nance, Guinevera A. *Aldous Huxley.* 1988.
Woodcock, George. *Dawn and the Darkest Hour: A Study of Aldous Huxley.* 1972.

Huxley, Julian Sorell (1887–1975)

Although by profession a biologist, publishing his most significant work, *Evolution, the Modern Synthesis* in 1942, it is perhaps as a popularizer and statesman of science that Huxley made his greatest impact. He was elected a Fellow of the Royal Society in 1938 and knighted in 1958. His grandfather was T.H. Huxley, the scientist and evolutionist, and his brother was ALDOUS HUXLEY, the novelist. After Eton and a first class degree in natural science (zoology) from OXFORD (1909), his career was characterized by a large number of comparatively short appointments, including chairs in biology at Rice Institute, Texas (1913) and zoology at King's College, London (1925). He was Secretary of the Zoological Society of London (1935–42) and first Director General of UNESCO (1946–8).

His scientific work was equally varied. His 1914 paper on the ritualization of behavior in the courtship of the great crested grebe is considered a landmark in the scientific study of animal behavior. His early laboratory research into ontogeny (the study of the development of individual organisms) included work on the metamorphosis of amphibians on an experimental diet of ox thyroid gland (1920). His *Problems of Relative Growth* (1932) investigated the relative development of different parts of animals, challenging some of the assumptions of animal taxonomists. From 1935 he took a close interest in evolution, publishing on "clines," the "gradations in measurable characteristics" within species.

Evolution, the Modern Synthesis combined some of his own findings with those of other scientists in field studies, genetics, and mathematical studies of inheritance. Together with Ernst Mayr's synthetic account published in the same year, this book was an important landmark in evolutionary studies. Huxley continued to theorize about the nature of evolutionary change, publishing further editions of his book in 1963 and 1974.

Huxley extended science into the public sphere in two main ways. He published widely in magazines essays that were later collected in volumes such as *Essays of a Biologist* (1923) and *On Living in a Revolution* (1944). Several themes, including his notion of "scientific humanism" and man's place in evolution recur in these works. *The Science of Life*, with G.P. and H.G. WELLS (1929–30), is an influential textbook aimed at the general reader. Huxley was awarded the Kalinga Prize for popularization of science in 1953. As a public advocate of science, and believer in rational, scientistic solutions to human problems, he personified the socially concerned scientist. He was an important reforming influence within the British Eugenics Society and was active in several 1930s "middle opinion" organizations such as Political and Economic Planning. Similarly, he appeared in socially reforming documentary films, including *Enough to Eat?* (1936), where he presented the arguments of scientists and doctors on working class malnutrition. Later, he was a regular panel member for BBC radio's *Brains Trust*. His term at UNESCO provided the opportunity for him to develop on a global scale his views of the importance of science.

It has been said that Huxley was one of the best-known figures of his day. It is perhaps, therefore, as a communicator of science, both to specialist academic audiences, and to the general public, that he may best be remembered.

T.M. Boon

Bibliography

Baker, J.R. *Julian Huxley: Scientist and World Citizen: A Biographical Memoir*. 1978.

Huxley, Julian. *Memories*. 2 vols., 1970–2.

I

Immigration

During the twentieth century Britain has been a net exporter of people, and at all times immigrant groups have represented a small percentage of the total population. Even so, immigration has been a persistent phenomenon. Although emphasis has been placed on the immigration since 1945 of BLACK PEOPLE (Afro-Caribbean peoples) and Asians (groups originating on the Indian sub-continent), the earlier arrival of these groups has captured less interest. Furthermore, the immigration of Europeans and other groups, whether before or after 1945, has usually been largely ignored.

Blacks and Asians were present in Britain before 1914, but the arrival of military personnel and workers increased their numbers during the FIRST WORLD WAR. The inter-war Depression inhibited migration but not the arrival of Black and Asian students, many of whom were later to become prominent in their own countries. The SECOND WORLD WAR, like the earlier world conflict, increased the demand for labor, bringing a number of Black workers to Britain from the Caribbean. The cumulative effect of such developments was that by 1945 small Black and Asian populations, spatially concentrated in LONDON, a few ports, and university towns, were already in evidence.

The immigration of Afro-Caribbean and Asian groups has increased since the end of the Second World War. The shakiness of immigration records and a number of lacunae in census returns make it difficult to be precise about the quantitative flow of immigration during this period. However, recent Labour Force Survey figures, which update the 1981 census data, suggest an Afro-Caribbean immigrant population of 318,000; the size of Asian immigrant groups is estimated at 739,000, the majority of whom would have arrived after 1945.

This immigration produced a concentration of Black and Asian groups in the conurbations of Britain. Brixton, in South London, an old haunt of music hall artists, witnessed the growth of a Black population. Bradford, in the north of England, attracted various communities whose origins can be traced to the Indian sub-continent. Many of the immigrants, whether Black or Asian, found public sector employment, on the

buses, on the London underground, with British Rail, and also in the NATIONAL HEALTH SERVICE. Mixed in with these immigrants were a number of middle-class professionals (some of whom became "de-skilled" in Britain). In general, Black and Asian groups have remained predominantly working class.

It has, however, been the Irish who have constituted the largest single immigrant minority in Britain. In 1981 the number of Irish from the Republic were estimated at 606,851. Since 1922 there has been a continual flow of immigrants into Britain from the southern counties, a process that continued even during the Second World War when Eire was a neutral country. In the late 1940s and 1950s Irish immigration reached levels last attained in the nineteenth century. These workers figured prominently in the building trade, helping Britain to overcome the shattering impact of the war and to modernize its infrastructure. In the post-war years an increasing number of middle class professional Irish people also crossed the water to Britain. Still, the Irish immigrant community remained essentially working class. Moreover, although less visible spatially than some other immigrant groups, in certain cities it possessed notable geographical concentration, especially London, a traditional magnet for all immigrants, Birmingham, and Lancashire, where Liverpool remains the most Irish of English cities.

In the early part of the twentieth century the arrival of Russian Polish Jews fleeing westwards provoked heated debate. An indeterminate number, estimated at approximately 100,000, came to Britain. The East End of London, particularly Whitechapel and Stepney, drew in a large number of the newcomers, as did Leeds and Manchester. In Scotland Russian Poles settled in Glasgow, especially in the Gorbals area of the city. This immigration from Russian Poland was effectively halted by the outbreak of the First World War, although restrictions had been effective since the aliens legislation of 1905. The next important phase of Jewish immigration occurred in the 1930s when approximately 50,000 Jewish REFUGEES arrived from Austria and Germany. Following the Second World War much smaller Jewish immigrations have occurred. The granting of independence to India led to the arrival of a small number of the so-called Baghdadi Jews. The SUEZ CRISIS in 1956 and the resulting expulsion of Jews from Egypt resulted in a further small influx. Finally, although immigration from Eastern Europe since 1945 has so far been slight, there were a number of Jews among the 21,000 Hungarians who came in 1956–7 in response to the Soviet invasion.

Blacks, Asians, Irish, and JEWS have attracted the most attention, but there are other immigrants and refugees who have remained largely invisible. In the early twentieth century a number of Germans settled in England and Wales where, according to the 1911 Census, they numbered 53,324. They were a mixed community which included German-Jewish financiers at the social apex. In the middle were German clerks who worked in the business houses of Manchester and London. Below these groups were German workers, such as those who toiled in the Cheshire saltworks, and women who served as governesses. In the years leading up to the First World War Germans came increasingly under hostile scrutiny; after the outbreak of war in 1914 they were subjected to violence in a number of British cities. The strength of public hostility led to the internment or deportation of Germans remaining in Britain. In effect, therefore, the First World War helped to destroy an important immigrant community. It took the arrival of refugees in the 1930s to reconstitute the German community, but whereas the pre-war community were religiously diverse, the refugees of the 1930s were primarily of Jewish origin.

Among other immigrant groups who have added to the texture of British life are the Italians. During the Second World War they, along with people of Austrian and German nationality, were interned and deported as enemy aliens. Following the war, however, the British government actively recruited workers from Europe to help rebuild the nation, and Italian workers featured among these recruits. In addition, Latvians, Estonians, and Poles were brought to Britain from Displaced Persons camps in Europe. In the case of Poles, these newcomers added to a Polish population already living in Britain, consisting of ex-military personnel and their dependents who had resisted a return to Poland. Mainly as a result of such developments the 1951 Census counted 161,020 residents in Britain born in Poland. In the early post-war years the government also recruited approximately 8,000 Ukrainians from a POW camp at Rimini rather than allow them to be returned against their will to the Soviet Union.

However important it is to recognize this European dimension to immigration, it should not result in the neglect of those groups who, in common with Blacks and the various peoples from the Indian sub-continent, came to Britain from "beyond the oceans". A small Chinese presence can be detected before the First World War, but since 1945 the Chinese population has undergone a substantial increase, principally as a consequence of immigration from Hong Kong. Whereas before 1914 the small Chinese population congregated in a specific part of London (the Pennyfields area), as well as in Liverpool and Cardiff, there is today scarcely a town in Britain which does not have a small Chinese population. Furthermore, in contrast to their role earlier in the century when they worked mainly in merchant shipping and laundries, the Chinese since 1945 have become heavily involved in the food trade, especially as owners of take-away restaurants. When to this mosaic of immigration is added other groups that have come to Britain, for example from West Africa, East Africa, Cyprus, and indeed the United States, it can be readily understood why perceptive observers have described the British as "among the most ethnically composite of the Europeans".

Immigration into Britain has not proceeded without legislative controls. Until the 1905 Aliens Act no restrictions were imposed on the entry of aliens, but agitation over immigration from Russian Poland produced the first serious breach in the long-standing open door policy. Further legislation in 1914, 1919, and 1971 guaranteed that the Home Office maintained strict control over the entry of alien immigrants and refugees.

For much of the twentieth century the entry of COMMONWEALTH subjects remained unhindered. The Commonwealth Immigrants Act of 1962 marked the onset of a more restrictive process. Further controls were imposed in 1965 and 1968. Then in 1971 the Immigration Act tidied up the entire legislative apparatus of immigration controls affecting both aliens and Commonwealth subjects. Henceforth anyone who could not establish a patrial link with the United Kingdom through having parents or grandparents born in the U.K. was denied automatic entry as an immigrant. Additional controls since 1971 have re-affirmed that principle, making it more difficult for immigrants and refugees to enter Britain in the 1990s than at the beginning of the century.

Colin Holmes

Bibliography

Colpi, Terri. *The Italian Factor. The Italian Community in Great Britain.* 1991.

Fryer, Peter. *Staying Power. The History of Black People in Britain.* 1984.

Hansen, Randall. *Citizenship and Immigration in Post-War Britain.* 2000.

Holmes, Colin. *John Bull's Island. Immigration and British Society 1871–1971.* 1988.

Spencer, Ian R.G. *British Immigration Policy Since 1939: The Making of Multi-Racial Britain*. 1997.

Visram, Rozina. *Ayahs, Lascars, and Princes: Indians in Britain 1700–1947*. 1986.

Walvin, James. *Passage to Britain*. 1984.

Imperial Preference

Schemes of imperial preference were first advocated in the late nineteenth century by British and Dominion advocates of federation of the Empire. In the late 1840s as Britain moved into the heyday of free trade, the colonies lost all tariff privileges in the mother country's market with the abolition of the Corn Laws in 1846 and then by the Navigation Acts in 1849. All late Victorian advocates of preference believed its revival would bring two benefits. They agreed with the resolution of the Ottawa conference of 1894 which stated that a customs agreement between Britain and the self-governing colonies would place trade within the Empire on a more favorable basis than that carried out with foreign countries; and, secondly, they were confident that such economic links would strengthen imperial sentiment in the face of growing challenges from rising powers, notably Germany and the United States.

Joseph Chamberlain gave imperial preference its most powerful impetus when in 1895 he became Colonial Secretary in Lord Salisbury's Unionist coalition. Passionately committed to the ideal of closer imperial ties and concerned about Britain's relative decline in the face of new empires, Chamberlain envisaged a grand scheme of imperial federation modeled on the earlier German Zollverein. He was encouraged to proceed with his large vision because, just before the 1897 Diamond Jubilee, Canada, the senior Dominion upon which his main hopes hinged, had granted a preference on British goods of 25 percent which was raised to 33 1/3 percent in 1900. Indeed, virtually the entire debate over the question revolved around the self-governing Dominions, with the other British colonies excluded.

During the meetings with the Dominion Premiers, both in 1897 and at the Colonial Conference of 1902, Chamberlain's hopes for imperial federation through a combination of political union, shared imperial defense, and commercial union had foundered on the rock of increasing Dominion nationalism, especially in Canada. His vaulting aim failed even though the Canadian Premier, Sir Wilfrid Laurier, had urged Britain to implement the policy of reciprocal preference. By 1902 Chamberlain was prompted to advance boldly on preference because of what he perceived as the heightening of imperial sentiment by the Dominion military contributions during the BOER WAR. In addition, Britain now had something to offer the Dominions, since in 1902 the Chancellor of the Exchequer revived an old Corn Duty on grain and flour to help defray costs from the war. Chamberlain then visited South Africa in the late winter of 1903 convinced that the CABINET had agreed to an abatement of the duty in favour of the colonies. Upon his return, however, Chamberlain found that the Cabinet had caved in to free traders within their ranks and withdrawn the preference.

In a dramatic speech, Chamberlain on 15 May 1903 at Birmingham appealed over the heads of the Cabinet for a reappraisal of the country's fiscal system, including the introduction of imperial preference. Since free trade sentiment was so strong in Britain and so many industries were prospering under the system, Chamberlain's call split his own coalition, alienated the new Prime Minister, ARTHUR BALFOUR, helped reunite the LIBERAL PARTY, and antagonized much of the electorate, fearful that preference would mean "dear food".

At a stroke, Chamberlain had catapulted fiscal issues into the center of British political debate. But so strong were free trade beliefs that tariff reform, as Chamberlain's program was called, led the Unionists to three successive electoral defeats—1906 and twice in 1910. In 1913 ANDREW BONAR LAW dropped preference from the Unionist platform. Although preference remained a strong element in the Unionist party thereafter, nothing was done until after the First World War. In 1919 Britain, which had imposed tariffs during the conflict, lowered duties by one-third for goods of imperial origin only. It was not until the advent of the Great Depression and the formation of the National government late in 1931 that widespread preferences became feasible. At the Imperial Economic Conference in Ottawa in the summer of 1932, NEVILLE CHAMBERLAIN, the Chancellor of the Exchequer, negotiated a wide range of preferential agreements between the Dominions and Britain.

In the wake of Britain's severe economic difficulties following the end of the SECOND WORLD WAR, especially the cessation of American LEND-LEASE in late August 1945, the new Labour government was forced to seek a large loan from the Truman administration. This loan of $3,750,000,000 was only approved on the condition that Great Britain accept policies of increasing multilateral trade through adhering to the General Agreement on Tariffs and Trade (GATT) whereby the United States sought to dominate the world economy. Thereafter, although Britain retained imperial perference and while for some years after 1945 the Commonwealth remained Britain's major export market, United Kingdom entrepreneurs became increasingly focused on multi-national enterprises outside the area of the former empire. In 1973 Britain was finally admitted to the EUROPEAN COMMUNITY on terms whereby she disavowed imperial perference, much to the chagrin of a number of old-fashioned Tories and Commonwealth countries such as New Zealand and Canada, which lost important economic benefits. In retrospect, the aspirations of Chamberlain and his followers to develop imperial preference to reassert British power appear chimerical.

Richard A. Rempel

Bibliography

Garvin, J.L., and Julian Amery. *The Life of Joseph Chamberlain.* Vols. 3–6, 1934–69.

Hancock, W.K. *Survey of Commonwealth Affairs.* vol. 2. 1942.

Porter, A.N., and A.J. Stockwell. *British Imperial Policy and Decolonization, 1938–64.* Vol. 2. 1989.

Sykes, Alan. *Tariff Reform in British Politics, 1903–1913.* 1979.

Independent Labour Party
Formed at a conference held in Bradford in January 1893, the ILP played a major part in the creation of the alliance between socialists and trade unionists that became the LABOUR PARTY. About 120 delegates representing a variety of local socialist and labour groups created a national organization with a Labour title and a socialist objective. The inaugural meeting was chaired by KEIR HARDIE, an Independent Labour MP who came to symbolise the style of the ILP.

The new party faced some fundamental strategic problems. Several of its leading figures, advocated an ethical approach to politics, sometimes characterized as the "religion of socialism", although this ethical commitment gradually became more a matter of style and rhetoric. Its prospects were measured increasingly in electoral terms, despite an often disappointing performance. In the 1895 election none of its twenty-eight candidates was successful. The only compensation came with the establishment of a small bridgehead in municipal authorities.

Electoral and financial weaknesses forced the ILP to consider a wider alliance. A small but significant section of the British working class was organized industrially often in trade unions with Liberal leaderships. The initial ILP position was critical of such leaders, but by the late 1890s the ILP's position had become much more accommodating. In part this reflected the emergence of a party leadership known as "the Big Four"— Hardie, RAMSAY MACDONALD, PHILIP SNOWDEN, and Bruce Glasier—who played a vital role in defeating moves for a combination between the ILP and the Marxist Social Democratic Federation. Instead the ILP leaders worked for an alliance between socialist groups and trade unions.

Backed by ILP members and sympathizers in some major unions, the result in February 1900 was the creation of the LABOUR REPRESENTATION COMMITTEE, renamed six years later the Labour Party. Although the unions had the voting strength within this alliance and provided much of the money, the ILP was well represented in the leadership. MacDonald became the LRC's secretary, and in the election of 1900 Hardie was one of the LRC's two successful candidates.

Hardie's victory was surprising since the election was held when popular support for the BOER WAR was at its peak. The ILP's position was strongly anti-war, and in 1901 its membership reached a low of just over 5,000. Yet the war helped to open up a new strategic option for the party. Shared sentiments and common experience of hostility from jingoistic crowds brought ILPers and some anti-war Liberals together. Many ideological continuities remained, and some ILPers believed that a splintering of the LIBERAL PARTY could perhaps produce a realignment on the Left. It was in this context that MacDonald in 1903 negotiated a secret electoral deal with the Liberals to give a small number of LRC candidates (including ILPers) a free run against the CONSERVATIVES.

The result was that in the 1906 general election twenty-nine LRC candidates were successful together with one other who joined the Labour group. Most of these had had no Liberal opponent, several were ILP members, and seven were financed by the ILP, including Hardie, MacDonald, and Snowden. The ILP strategy of accommodation publicly with the unions and privately with the Liberals had been successful.

Yet within the ILP there were soon recriminations. Critics began to show impatience about the cautious implications of the alliance with the unions and to complain that the post-1906 Liberal dominance of the Commons made Labour's cautious parliamentary style an irrelevance. One symbol was provided by a 1907 by-election gain by the young and flamboyant Victor Grayson, a critic of parliamentary conventions. Volatile and unstable, he was a member of the ILP whose candidacy had not been endorsed by the Labour Party. He served as a focus for growing discontent with the ILP's strategy. Grayson's defeat in the January 1910 election marginalized one focus for critics, but hostilities did not really decline until many dissidents quit the ILP in 1911 to join the new British Socialist Party.

In 1914 the ILP reacted critically to British support for the war. Its opposition incorporated a variety of sentiments—PACIFISM, socialist internationalism, often a broad opposition to militarism and secret diplomacy. MacDonald's own position was characteristically tortuous, but he became the symbol of the ILP's resistance to militarism. Links developed with anti-war Liberals especially through co-operation in the UNION OF DEMOCRATIC CONTROL. Many ILPers resisted CONSCRIPTION and went to prison. This anti-war stance strained the ILPs relationship with the patriotic trade unions. When the Labour Party was reconstructed in 1917–18, the trade unions strengthened their control over the organization, and the reforms threatened the ILP's position. Hitherto the Labour Party had had no national scheme of individual membership. Any attachment had to be through a constituent body, normally the ILP. The 1918 reforms included a scheme for individual Labour Party membership that challenged the ILP's *raison d'etre*.

The election of 1918 removed all critics of the war from the Commons, but in 1922 they made a triumphant return. MacDonald became Leader, and some of the ex-Liberals who had joined the ILP became Labour MPs. The ILP presence in Parliament also included a new element. On Clydeside during the war the local ILP had played a leading role in housing agitations and gained a dominant position in the local labor movement. In 1922 Labour made substantial gains in Glasgow; some of the new men, most notably JAMES MAXTON and JOHN WHEATLEY stood on the Left.

The ILPs parliamentary revival was paralleled by apparent success in discovering a new role. Under the chairmanship of CLIFFORD ALLEN, a wartime CONSCIENTIOUS OBJECTOR, the party seemed set to become a "think tank" for the labor movement. Study groups were established, one of which produced in 1926, as an alternative to fiscal orthodoxy, the celebrated "Living Wage" doctrine. The party paper, renamed the *New Leader* became, under H.N. BRAILSFORD's editorship, perhaps the best journal ever produced by the British Left. But in 1925 Allen resigned, weary of attacks from the Left, and in 1926 Brailsford's editorship ended. The Clydesiders, effectively Maxton and Wheatley, became the ILP leadership.

Their attempt to use the ILP as an instrument for Left policies failed. ILP strength in the unions was limited: most trade union leaders had a general hostility to the Left which they saw as Communist-dominated. In fact from 1928 Communists in their "Class Against Class" phase were bitterly hostile to the ILP. Squeezed from Left and Right, the ILP leadership could not count on committed support from the party's rank and file or from several of the ILP MPs. Even with the disappointing record of the 1929 Labour government, only a few MPs backed the radical criticisms of the ILP.

The sight of a small group of parliamentary critics legitimizing their behavior by reference to ILP policy produced a crisis. ARTHUR HENDERSON indicted the ILP rebels as a "party within a party". The collapse of the second Labour government in August 1931 did not resolve the conflict. Eleven months later a special ILP Conference voted to break away from the Labour Party. The decision proved disastrous. Many erstwhile ILPers stayed with Labour, while the ILP under Maxton's leadership found itself overshadowed on the Left by a COMMUNIST PARTY entering into its POPULAR FRONT phase. Yet even in its declining years its anti-Stalinist position on the SPANISH CIVIL WAR inspired GEORGE ORWELL briefly to become a member. During the Second World War the party was marginalized by its anti-war stance, and its parliamentary presence effectively ended with Maxton's death in 1946. A dwindling membership lingered on until 1975 when the party reformed as Independent Labour Publications and rejoined the Labour Party.

The ILP's trajectory illuminates much about the character of the socialist movement in Britain—the strategic debates, the compromises with pragmatic trade unionists, the attempts to build a socialist constituency that was neither orthodox Communist nor cautiously reformist.

David Howell

Bibliography

Dowse, Robert E. *Left in the Centre: the Independent Labour Party 1893–1940*. 1966.

Howell, David. *British Workers and the Independent Labour Party 1888–1906*. 1983.

James, David, Tony Jowitt and Keith Laybourn, eds. *The Centennial History of the Independent Labour Party*. 1992.

Mackinlay, Alan, and R.J. Morris, ed. *The Independent Labour Party on Clydeside: 1893–1932: From Foundation to Disintegration*. 1990.

Morgan, Kenneth O. *Keir Hardie: Radical and Socialist*. 1975.

India, Partition of

The Second World War changed the Indian situation very dramatically. With a LABOUR government under CLEMENT ATTLEE in power in England in 1945, it was not a question of whether India would be granted independence but when and to whom power would be handed. The situation had also changed dramatically regarding the relative power of the Indian National Congress, led by Mahatma Gandhi and Jawaharlal Nehru, and the All-Indian Muslim League, headed by Muhammad Ali Jinnah. Before the war the Congress was the dominant party in the country. During the war the leaders of the Congress party languished in prison and the organization was left without dynamic leadership or an effective organization. The League, however, was free to organize and it flourished, gaining strength as never before. On 23 March 1940 it passed its "Pakistan Resolution", whereby the League's official demand was for a separate homeland for the Muslims of India. League leaders believed that only in a homeland of their own could Muslims protect their interests and way of life; they could not do this as a Muslim minority in a Hindu-dominated nation.

The Viceroy of India, Lord Wavell, tried through a series of meetings and conferences to reach an agreement between the Congress and the League on a constitution for an independent India but was ultimately unsuccessful. On 19 February 1946 Prime Minister Attlee informed the House of Commons that a three-man CABINET mission, composed of Lord Pethick-Lawrence, SIR STAFFORD CRIPPS, and A.V. Alexander, would be sent out to India to meet with Indian politicians in another attempt to solve the constitutional problem. By the end of April they had come up with a plan for a three-tier federal structure of province, group, and union that would give the League a measure of the power it was demanding. This plan would be discussed at the second Simla conference that followed.

The Cabinet mission agreed that the Muslims should be given the power to ensure the well-being of their religious, cultural, and economic interests, but rejected League demands for control of the six provinces that would comprise Pakistan. It also rejected the idea of partitioning Bengal and the Punjab since non-Muslims would be left on the Muslim side. Furthermore, the mission argued, the new Pakistan would not be a viable sovereign state. What the mission proposed was a union with the powers of the central government limited to defense, communication, finances, and foreign affairs. An executive and legislature would govern the center, and any major communal issue would require the approval of both the Muslims and the Hindus. All other issues would be decided by the provinces, which would form groups A, B, and C. Group B was in the western part of India (Baluchistan, the Northwest Frontier Province, the Punjab, and Sind); group C in the east (Assam and Bengal), and group A the center (the rest of India). A constituent assembly would be formed to work out the exact details of the plan, but in the meantime an interim government made up of Indians would be created to carry on the business of governing the country. The League accepted the plan as it might lead to the creation of Pakistan. The Congress met and on 6 July reluctantly approved the plan. After so many years of discussions, maneuvers, and disagreements, it looked as if the two parties might cooperate. Then, at a press conference on 9 July, Nehru stated that the Congress was in no way bound by the agreements reached at Simla. He also said that the groups might never occur and that, even if they did, the powers of the central government were sure to grow. This was a startling statement that negated all of the understandings that had come about as a result of years of informal discussions and the result of hundreds of hours of formal negotiations.

For the League it was the last straw, demonstrating conclusively that Muslim interests would not be respected if the Congress came to power in an independent India. When Wavell appointed the members of his interim Executive Council, he appointed six Congress members rather than the agreed-upon five. The League felt betrayed all around. On 27 July Jinnah denounced both the acts of the government and the attitude of the Congress. He called for 16 August to be declared Direct Action Day, a day when the League would demonstrate its strength in the streets. These demonstrations turned violent, especially in Calcutta where after a week of violence several thousand lay dead, more than 20,000 were injured, and more than 100,000 became homeless. The violence then spread across India.

The government went ahead with its plan for an interim government on 2 September. At first the League refused to appoint members to the new Cabinet headed by Nehru. This decision gave the advantage to the Congress, and by October Jinnah changed his mind, allowing Liaquat Ali Khan and four other League members to join the Cabinet while remaining aloof himself. As Finance Minister, Liaquat was able to block all Congress proposals and plans. Amidst acrimony and accusations on both sides, the League demonstrated that a united government was impossible. With the League in a stronger position, the British made one more attempt to reach an agreement by inviting the leaders of the Congress and the League to London in December for more discussions, but these negotiations proved futile.

Following the failure of the negotiations, Attlee announced on 20 February 1947 that the British were going to transfer power by June 1948 to a government capable of maintaining peace. In addition, Lord Wavell would be replaced by LORD LOUIS MOUNTBATTEN. Arriving on 22 March, Mountbatten decided within two weeks that India would be partitioned. Gandhi, however, never accepted what he believed to be the vivisection of India, but, while he was widely revered, he had been effectively supplanted by the politicians. The British government announced that India would be granted independence on 14 August 1947. In July Mountbatten informed the princes that upon independence they should accede to either India or Pakistan as British paramountcy would cease and sovereignty would be assumed by India and Pakistan only. By 14 August most of them had done so except for the large states of Hyderabad and Kashmir and the tiny state of Junagadh. Kashmir acceded to India on 26 October amidst a great deal of fighting and bloodshed between Hindus and Muslims, but Junagadh and Hyderabad were invaded by India, thus becoming part of India as well. All three states had a majority population of Muslims.

The newly created Pakistan included West Pakistan, comprising the states of the Punjab, the Northwest Frontier Province, Sind, Baluchistan, and parts of Kashmir, and East Pakistan comprising Bengal. Both the Punjab and Bengal were partitioned. The rest of the country became India. Mountbatten remained as the Governor-General of India with Jawaharlal Nehru as Prime Minister, but Muhammad Ali Jinnah became Governor-General of Pakistan and appointed Liaquat Ali Khan as Prime Minister. Independence was accompanied by large numbers of Hindus migrating to India and Muslims to Pakistan. In the Punjab this led to widespread violence between Muslims, and Hindus and Sikhs to the extent that law and order had broken down completely in large areas of the state. Independence had come about amidst the violence and anarchy that the British had feared. Gandhi remained aloof from the independence celebrations, touring Bengal in a successful attempt to keep the peace.

The virtual civil war between the communities caused Gandhi a great deal of anguish. He blamed the Congress leaders for the Hindu persecution of Muslims in Delhi and also for withholding funds that should have been given to Pakistan. On 12 January he announced a fast to quicken people's conscience. Fearful of his death, Congress leaders quickly agreed to transfer Pakistan's funds, and Gandhi's fast lasted just a week. He earned the gratitude of Muslims in Delhi but antagonized members of the paramilitary Hindu communal group, the Rashtriya Svayamsevak Sangh, who accused him of being too partial to Muslims. It was a member of this group who assassinated him on 30 January. Gandhi's death achieved what his life could not, and peace was gradually restored throughout India.

Pakistan also faced the task of dealing with millions of refugees, a task that absorbed all the resources and time of the government, especially the Prime Minister Liaquat Ali Khan. Jinnah, amidst an enormous workload of his own, was slowly succumbing to the cancer he had been battling for a decade and died on 1 September 1948.

The last British troops, those of the Somerset Light Infantry, left India on 28 February. Mountbatten continued as Governor-General of India until 21 June 1948. British rule in India ended in a way they had tried so hard to avoid: partition.

Roger D. Long

Bibliography
Brown, Judith M. *Gandhi: Prisoner of Hope.* 1989.
Gopal, Sarvepalli. *Jawaharlal Nehru: A Biography,* vol. I, 1889–1947. 1976.
Menon, V.P. *The Transfer of Power in India.* 1957.
Wolpert, Stanley. *Jinnah of Pakistan.* 1984.
Ziegler, Philip. *Mountbatten.* 1985.

Indian Nationalism

The nationalist movement in India underwent radical changes in the twentieth century. Although it was dominated at first by those who shared the political ideals of British liberals, more radical voices soon came to the fore. Respect for British political institutions was replaced by demands for a political system reflecting Indian traditions, and the desire for greater participation in the imperial system was overtaken by the cry for independence. The two world wars were crucial, greatly altering the political situation in India. Complicating matters was the growth of a separate Muslim nationalism, which culminated in the PARTITION OF INDIA in 1947.

In 1900 Indian nationalism was dominated by the Indian National Congress, led by moderates, such as G.K. Gokhale (1866–1915), who wished to use constitutional means to persuade the imperial government to open up greater political opportunities for Indians. A stiff challenge to this method emerged among extremists, such as B.G. Tilak (1856–1920), who appealed to the Hindu masses with politicized religious revivals and who condoned the growing violence directed at British officials. This split intensified after 1905, when the British partitioned Bengal despite strong dissent from all leading Indian nationalists. Intense political unrest resulted, as extremists engineered a noisy, popular campaign to overturn the partition decision. The imperial government responded with harsh repression, thereby further weakening the moderate position, which depended on the good will of British liberals. The moderates managed to remain in control of the Congress, but only by expelling the extremists in a bitter contest in 1907. Liberal measures, such as the Morley-Minto reforms of 1909 and the reunification of Bengal in 1911, were insufficient to repair the damage done to the moderates.

The FIRST WORLD WAR significantly changed the nationalist movement. Most Indian politicians initially supported the war effort, believing that the reward for loyalty would be greater self-determination. Some radicals argued otherwise and in the Punjab revolutionaries, prodded by

German promises of aid, plotted an abortive up-rising in 1915. About the same time Home Rule leagues were founded in Madras by Annie Besant (1847–1933), and in Pune by Tilak, and both organizations were instrumental in revitalizing the nationalist movement. Muslim political consciousness rose dramatically during the war too, since India was now at war with the Ottoman Empire, home of the Caliphate. By 1916 a pact had been reached between the Congress and the Muslim League (founded in 1906) regarding a unified list of demands for greater political participation by Indians in both the central and provincial governments. The next year EDWIN MONTAGU, Secretary of State for India, announced in Parliament that the British goal for India was eventual self-government within the Empire.

But Montagu's promise proved to be a hollow one. Once the war was over, British officialdom dragged its feet on the matter of constitutional reforms. Furthermore, the Rowlatt Acts were passed in 1919, extending some of the government's wartime emergency powers to meet the threat of sedition in the Punjab and elsewhere. Indian nationalists were outraged at this reward for their loyalty, and violent protests erupted throughout the land. Mohandas Gandhi (1869–1948) organized his first national demonstration, a successful general strike. In the Punjab matters came to a head in 1919 when British-commanded troops opened fire on a crowd of peaceful demonstrators in Amritsar, killing over four hundred. Indian nationalists were additionally appalled when the imperial government treated the officials in charge with leniency.

Gandhi emerged from the war as the dominant figure in Indian nationalist politics. He forged an alliance with Muslims, by joining the Khilifat movement, which was protesting the lack of imperial attention to Muslim interests, especially the perceived threat to Islam in the treaty ending the war with the Ottomans. Gandhi also gained control of the Congress leadership in 1920, fundamentally altering the style and content of Indian nationalism. A new constitution for the Congress was established, creating an effective grass-roots organization capable of reaching out to nearly every village in India. Furthermore, swaraj, or self-government, was now the proclaimed goal of the Congress, and a campaign of non-cooperation was planned, involving resignations from governmental and educational posts, surrender of honorary titles and lucrative legal practices, non-payment of taxes, and other measures directed against the imperial government. Gandhi's message, with its emphasis on Indian self-reliance, fired the imagination of a rising generation of young nationalists, led by S.C. Bose (1897–1945) and Jawaharlal Nehru (1889–1964). But Gandhi disappointed his fiery disciples in 1922, when he called off the non-cooperation campaign because of an isolated incident of violence by protesters.

The 1920s was a relatively quiet period for Indian nationalism. The Khilifat movement collapsed in 1924, after the Turkish government abolished the Caliphate. The abrupt end to non-cooperation left the Congress listless, with debate confined to the question of participation in the moderate reform measures implemented in 1923–4. Gandhi was arrested for political agitation, spent two years in prison and afterwards retreated to his ashram, concentrating on village improvement. Radicalism languished until 1927, when the CONSERVATIVE government sent a commission to India to investigate the matter of further constitutional reforms. Angry at the lack of Indian representation on the commission, both the Congress and the Muslim League, now headed by M.A. Jinnah (c.1875–1948), boycotted its proceedings and appointed their own bodies, which made separate recommendations for a new Indian constitution. Nehru and Bose, meanwhile, began a socialist league in 1928, and made purna swaraj, or complete independence, their demand. In 1929 Congress, with Nehru presiding, adopted the purna swaraj resolution, unfurled the flag of India, and proclaimed 26 January 1930 as independence day.

Gandhi reemerged in 1930 to lead a new campaign of civil disobedience. A dramatic march to the sea was organized, drawing world-wide attention to Gandhi's unique tactics and Indian nationalism. Soon most of the Congress leadership was in prison, and in the coming year many thousands more would join them as the campaign of civil disobedience gained momentum. The British government responded with a series of Round Table conferences, designed to gain Indian cooperation in fashioning a new constitution for India. The talks failed, and the British government created a constitution on its own, in the form of the 1935 GOVERNMENT OF INDIA ACT. Gandhi and other nationalists were re-arrested during this period, as Indian opposition to British measures remained steadfast. When elections to provincial assemblies were held in 1937, Congress won an overwhelming victory and proceeded to implement its nationalist agenda in those provinces where it controlled the majority of seats. Muslim fears of persecution at the hands of the Hindu majority escalated after 1937, and Jinnah successfully exploited the issue, rejuvenating the Muslim League with the charge of Hindu tyranny in those provinces governed by Congress administrations.

In 1939 the British government unilaterally declared India to be at war with Germany. The Congress provincial ministries resigned in protest, but the Muslim League seized the moment to declare their loyalty to the British, thereby gaining the support of the imperial government for most Muslim political demands, which after 1940 centered on a separate Muslim state. In the fall of 1940 Gandhi initiated a new protest campaign, involving individual acts of civil disobedience. In 1942, after rapid Japanese advances in Asia, the British government dispatched STAFFORD CRIPPS to India, in a vain effort to gain Congress's cooperation for the duration of the war. Congress rejected Cripps's offer of dominion status after the war, Gandhi deriding it as a post-dated check on a failing bank. Soon Gandhi launched the Quit India campaign, which involved mass civil disobedience, large protests, violent acts of sabotage and assassination, and other measures, planned and unplanned. Gandhi and the bulk of the Congress leadership were arrested and spent most of the remaining war years in prison. Meanwhile, Bose, who was in exile, organized an army composed of Indians captured by the Japanese in Singapore, and invaded India in 1944. His forces were quickly in retreat, and Bose himself died on a plane flight to Japan in 1945.

In June 1945 Congress and Muslim League officials were invited to Simla for talks on effecting a transition to self-government. Attempts to create a unified, independent India failed, largely because the Congress and Muslim League leaders could not agree on a formula for creating a central government with safeguards for Muslim minority rights. Escalating communal violence in 1946 exacerbated the situation, and by early 1947 the Viceroy, LORD MOUNTBATTEN, decided to grant independence in August 1947 and to create two nations, India and Pakistan. Congress leaders, such as Nehru and Gandhi, agreed to partition with the greatest of reluctance, while Jinnah and the Muslim League were pleased at the decision, but not at the proposed boundaries. The decision to divide the subcontinent unleashed a fury of communal violence, which neither Indian nor Pakistani officials, let alone the British, could control.

Lynn Zastoupil

Bibliography
Brecher, Michael. Nehru: A Political Biography. 1959.
Brown, Judith M. Gandhi's Rise to Power: Indian Politics, 1915–1922. 1972.
Hardy, P. The Muslims of British India. 1972.
Hutchins, Francis. India's Revolution: Gandhi and the Quit India Movement. 1973.
Wolpert, Stanley. Tilak and Gokhale: Revolution and Reform in the Making of Modern India. 1962.

International Brigade

Since it ended over sixty years ago, one of most enduring legacies of the Spanish Civil War (1936–9) has been the dramatic story of the approximately 59,380 international volunteers from fifty-three countries who went to Spain to serve in the International Brigades of the Republican army. During the course of the war between 2,000 and 4,000 British men and women joined this "anti-Fascist" crusade, primarily because they were convinced that, if Franco, Hitler and Mussolini were defeated in Spain, democracy would emerge triumphant and another world war could be averted.

The idea of using organized groups of foreign volunteers to fight for the republican side first materialized in late July 1936 in Paris. With the backing of the Soviet Union, the Comintern launched in September a formal campaign to recruit an international corps of volunteers. In the following weeks thousands of prospective candidates were interviewed by Communist Party officials, and those selected were funneled through the Comintern's international network.

For many years the true composition of the volunteer units was obscured by the publicity surrounding the famous artists, poets, and writers identified with the conflict. This was especially true in Great Britain, where events in Spain attracted the attention of a number of eminent public figures. Even though only a handful of these celebrities actually went to Spain, their reputations overshadowed the fact that they constituted only a fraction of the overall number of individuals who took a stand on the war. Apart from a handful of middle-class professionals (mostly clerks and ARMY veterans), the vast majority of British volunteers serving in the IBs were of working-class extraction. A large number of them were sailors, shipyard workers, industrial laborers, and miners.

There is insufficient evidence to establish a precise profile of the political affiliations of most English volunteers, but it is reasonable to assume that well over half of the volunteers were either communist or sympathetic to the official COMMUNIST PARTY line. A small number of British participants on the republican side, such as the novelist GEORGE ORWELL, regarded themselves as left wing but anti-communist.

In any event, it became immediately apparent to the newly inducted volunteers that their individual political beliefs were of secondary importance. This is because the communists played a central role in determining the fate of all those serving in the International Brigades. Not only was the party in charge of recruitment but, through its network of advisers and military strategists, it exercised considerable control over the operations of the Brigade units. For example, the greater part of the Political Commissariat system—the organizational framework of the International Brigades—was dominated by communists like the Englishman Bill Alexander, who served as Political Commissar of the Anti-Tank Battery and, later in the war, as Commander of the British Battalion.

Since the war, scholars and IB veterans alike have debated the the communists' commanding role in the International Brigades. Some have argued that the strict discipline and military strategy imposed by the communists was a necessary "evil" in the context of war. Others have condemned communist practices, pointing to the fact that there were men and women who left Spain disillusioned by their experiences in the International Brigades.

Although a few English volunteers were among the first IB units serving in Spain—the Cambridge student and poet, John Cornford, and the artist Felicia Browne had been there since August—most British recruits arrived after October 1936. On arriving at Albacete, the base camp for the International Brigades, the British and other recruits underwent an intensive period of military induction and political indoctrination. The British troops were then sent to Madrigueras, where a training depot had been established. From this point, they were dispatched to the front lines.

Not everyone in the brigades was sent into battle: a small but significant number of men and women served in non-combative roles, mostly as medical assistants (nurses), cooks, and as ambulance and truck drivers. Fresh recruits were assigned to a unit in one of the five permanent International Brigades (XI–XV), which were themselves divided along linguistic lines. Nearly all of the English-speaking volunteers belonged to the XV Brigade, which was formed on 8 February 1937. This was composed of the 600-man British Battalion as well as members of the Dimitrov Battalion (mostly Czech, Polish and Slavic volunteers). The XV Brigade later included Commonwealth and North American volunteers.

British volunteers saw some of the heaviest fighting of the war: they were used as shock troops at the battle of Jarama (February 1937) and the battle of Brunete (July 1937). Because the XV Brigade suffered heavy casualties in these engagements, it was reorganized to incorporate other groups. Thus, following Jarama, the British Battalion was restructured, comprising the CLEMENT ATTLEE company as well as a battalion of Spanish regulars.

Like most of the foreigners who participated in the war, the English volunteers enjoyed good relations with the Spanish soldiers and civilians.

This was amply demonstrated in November 1938, when the greatly reduced number of International Brigaders were asked to withdraw from Spain. They departed with the well wishes of thousands of Spaniards whose cheers made it clear that they would never forget the International Brigaders' contribution to the Republican war effort.

George Esenwein

Bibliography

Alexander, Bill. *British Volunteers for Liberty*. 1982.
Gurney, Jason. *Crusade in Spain*. 1974.
Johnston, Verle B. *Legions of Babel: The International Brigades in the Spanish Civil War*. 1967.
Richardson, R. Dan. *Comintern Army: The International Brigades and the Spanish Civil War*. 1982.

Internment of Enemy Aliens

Though lacking in precedent, the internment of enemy aliens—those nationals of enemy states either residing or traveling in Britain when war broke out—became a controversial feature of British security policy in both world wars. In each case a growing fear that enemy aliens were engaging in espionage or sabotage was the motive for internment schemes.

Already primed by a spate of pre-war novels and plays dealing with the prospect of a German invasion made possible by agents carefully disguised as waiters and other innocuous figures, the PRESS and the public, as soon as the war broke out in August 1914, began to call for the pre-emptive rounding up of German and Austrian nationals. Known spies were at once arrested, but internment was at first very limited in nature. In the autumn of 1914, however, growing public outrage over largely fictitious stories of German atrocities in Belgium, coupled with a widespread belief that military and naval reverses in the early weeks of fighting were the work of enemy spies, led to a progressive widening in the scope of internment. By the end of October 1914 the Home Office, responding to public and War Office pressure, had issued orders for the arrest of all male enemy aliens of military age. By November 1914 over 10,000 aliens were incarcerated in a variety of temporary locations, their final destination a makeshift camp on the Isle of Man.

The internment camps hurriedly set up often lacked adequate facilities, and living conditions for for the internees on the Isle of Man were so sub-standard that a revolt occurred in which five internees were killed. This led to the release of 2,700 internees in December 1914. Hatred for the "Huns", however, continued to mount, public hysteria reaching a new peak after the sinking of the *Lusitania*. Aware of the popular mood of retribution and spy mania, Prime Minister HERBERT ASQUITH announced on 13 May 1915 that "all enemy aliens of fighting age" were to be placed behind barbed wire. In all, nearly 30,000 German, Austrian, and other male aliens of lesser Central Powers were interned for the duration under less than ideal conditions on the Isle of Man and elsewhere.

On the outbreak of the SECOND WORLD WAR, the Home Office, under Sir John Anderson, adopted a more discerning internment policy. Enemy aliens were examined by special tribunals and divided into three categories. Class "C" were judged harmless and were allowed to go free; class "B" consisted of those Germans whom it was considered safe to leave at large for the time being; and class "A" were those enemy aliens who were considered a security threat and were interned. As most German nationals living in Britain in 1939 were JEWS and other anti-Nazi REFUGEES, it is not surprising that of 73,800 cases reviewed, 64,200 were judged class "C" and only 600 men were interned.

In the spring of 1940, however, a new wave of hysteria over the "threat from within" arose as German forces struck at Norway and then the Low Countries. The success of the German assaults was widely, though erroneously, believed to be the work of traitors, and fears grew that Britain too had its Fifth Column—not least among German refugees. Spurred on by the new Prime Minister, WINSTON CHURCHILL, the civil and military authorities, with the help of MI5, progressively extended the scope of internment. By June 1940 over 27,000 men and women, most of them hostile to Hitler, were confined under armed guard.

Again problems arose. Living conditions in the hastily prepared internment camps were often bad, and a plan advocated by Churchill to ship enemy aliens to Canada and Australia began to unravel after the ocean liner *Arandora Star*, carrying a mixed bag of internees and POWs to Canada, was sunk by a U-Boat at the cost of over 650 lives. In July 1940 the internment process was halted and shipment overseas abandoned. As the invasion panic ebbed and public sympathy for the refugees increased, the Home Office began to release class "C" internees (by early 1941 at the rate of 1,000 a month). The same applied to those already transported to Canada and Australia, and by the end of 1942 virtually all but the class "A" internees had been released. Most of those who remained were repatriated in exchanges arranged by the International Red Cross in 1943 and 1944.

S.P. MacKenzie

Bibliography

Gillman, Peter & Leni. *"Collar the Lot!": How Britain Interned and Expelled its Wartime Refugees*. 1980.
Lafitte, Francois. *The Internment of Aliens*. rev. ed. 1990.
Speed, Richard B. *Prisoners, Diplomats, and the Great War: A Study in the Diplomacy of Captivity*. 1990.

Irish Land Purchase Act (1903)

Between 1885 and 1903 Conservative governments enacted a succession of Irish Land Acts directed at "killing home rule with kindness." This policy assumed that the agitation for home rule derived mainly from rural discontent, and that if tenant farmers became owners, discontent would fade away. Although the land policy failed in its political objective, it succeeded in creating a large class of small land owners. In 1885 fewer than 5 percent of Irish farmers owned their land, but by 1921 about 70 percent did.

The various Land Acts, beginning with Ashbourne's Act in 1885, enabled tenants wanting to purchase their holdings to borrow the full amount from a government fund on generous terms. Until 1891, however, the loan fund was small, and between 1891 and 1903—although the fund was substantially increased—procedures were so complex that prospective purchasers were discouraged. Moreover, many landlords were reluctant to dismantle their estates.

A breakthrough came in 1903 with the passage of the bill that became known as Wyndham's Act, after Chief Secretary George Wyndham who introduced it. The 1903 Act implemented recommendations of the Irish Land Conference of 1902 chaired by the Earl of Dunraven. The main differences from previous Land Acts were bonuses to landlords to sell their entire estates, and assurances to tenants that repayment rates would not exceed their rents. The repayment period was also extended from forty-nine years to 68.5.

The Wyndham Act was attacked by leaders of the Irish Nationalist party—many of whom demanded compulsory sale by landlords—but it accelerated the breaking up of the great estates into family-owned farms. Between 1903 and 1910 about 270,000 of the remaining 500,000 Irish tenants became owners.

Don M. Cregier

Bibliography

Pomfret, John E. *The Struggle for Land in Ireland, 1800–1923*. 1930.
Winstanley, Michael J. *Ireland and the Land Question, 1800–1922*. 1984.

Irish Literature

The twentieth century has been marked by the establishment of Irish literature as a fully separate body of writing aimed at Irish publishers and theatres and enjoyed by an expanding readership within the most literate country in the world. However, this occurred only after centuries during which Irish writing in English seemed largely controlled by the need to appeal to English publishers, readers, and theatres. The radically different nature of the Irish past is underscored by remembering that early writing in English about Ireland tended to be dominated by imperialist English accounts and Irish reactions to them—such as the work of Jonathan Swift, the first major Irish writer in English.

While writing in Irish Gaelic enjoyed an impressive tradition of its own since the time of the ancient epic the *Táin Bó Cuailnge* (Cattle raid of Cooley), most of the best known pre-twentieth-century Irish writers in English achieved what they did by living and writing in England or by writing works aimed largely at English audiences—in drama (Congreve, Sheridan), poetry (Goldsmith), and fiction (Sterne, Edgeworth). At the end of the nineteenth century two Dubliners, Oscar Wilde (1854–1900) and GEORGE BERNARD SHAW, capitalized on their perspectives as outsiders in writing their extremely successful London satiric comedies. While Wilde was tragically destroyed by English society because of his HOMOSEXUALITY, Shaw fulfilled his stated ambition, since "England had conquered Ireland," to "come over and conquer England." Shaw always turned English rationalism an extra twist or two in his plays, thus "beating the English at their own game" and becoming the most successful and persistent dramatist of the twentieth century. Shaw's only play set in Ireland, *John Bull's Other Island* (1904), was staged in London after it was rejected by the Abbey Theatre in Dublin. His English satire *The Shewing-Up of Blanco Posnet* (1909) was suppressed in England and staged at the Abbey.

The nineteenth century saw the creation of Irish periodicals such as the *Nation* and the *Dublin University Magazine,* but the establishment of Irish literature as independent came only at the beginning of the twentieth century in the form of the Irish theatre movement founded by WILLIAM BUTLER YEATS and his colleagues. Yet it is worth noting that Yeats spent formative years in London as well as Dublin and Sligo, that he was much influenced by English writers, and that several of the key early events of his Irish movement occurred in London: the foundation of the Irish Literary Society in 1891, for example, and the staging of his play *The Land of Heart's Desire* on a double bill with Shaw's sharply different *Arms and the Man* in 1894. This production was funded by Annie Horniman, a rich Englishwoman who was opposed to IRISH NATIONALISM but interested in DRAMA and in Yeats personally. Ironically, the pioneering Irish nationalist theatre, the Abbey, was housed in a building bought by Horniman in 1904. This curious relationship continued until 1910, when Lady Augusta Gregory (1859–1932) and Lennox Robinson (1886–1958) failed to close the theatre on the occasion of KING EDWARD VII's death; as

a result, Horniman withdrew her support, and Yeats and his colleagues were obliged to turn to Irish sources for funds.

Beginning his movement in London, depending on an English patron, illiterate in the Irish language and much better schooled in Blake and Shelley, Yeats nonetheless gave the impression that he and his movement came straight out of the Irish tradition of bards and rebels. He was championed by the Fenian rebel John O'Leary (1830–1907), and Yeats' nationalist heroines in *The Countess Cathleen* (1892) and *Cathleen ni Hoolihan* (1902) were played by Maud Gonne (1866–1953), a leader in the Irish nationalist movement and the woman who inspired many of his poems and plays. Less often remarked but very crucial were Yeats's critical activities in creating an Irish literary canon, including his editing of the anthology *Representative Irish Tales* (1891), his promulgation of lists of the "Best Irish Writers," and his many essays on Irish literature, which have colored critical views of Irish literature ever since. More than anyone else, Yeats succeeded in creating an audience for a distinctively new Irish literature, not only in Ireland and England, but internationally.

Interrelated with Yeats and his movement was the revolution in Irish politics and society. Indeed, future Irish rebels such as Pádraic Pearse (1879–1916), the leader of the 1916 Easter Rising, were inspired by Yeats's Poor Old Woman, who convinces a young man to lay down his life for Ireland. Pearse was driven by a messianic sense of mission that culminated in the Rising, which he led even though he knew it would fail in the short term. Of course, more than provoking historical events, Yeats and his movement reacted to them. While nineteenth-century Irish leaders and writers were largely Protestant and upper class, the Catholic middle class came to dominate the Republic of Ireland, as reflected in its leaders and writers. Yeats's movement was as much the romanticized swan song of the Ascendancy as it was the provocateur of the revolution.

The great works of Yeats and his close colleagues included his poetry volumes *The Rose* (1893), *The Wind among the Reeds* (1899), *The Green Helmet* (1910), *The Wild Swans at Coole* (1919), *The Tower* (1928), and others; his plays such as *On Baile's Strand* (1904), *The Only Jealousy of Emer* (1919), *The Words upon the Window-Pane* (1930), and *The Death of Cuchulain* (1939); John Millington Synge's (1871–1909) "peasant" plays, including *Riders to the Sea* (1904) and *The Playboy of the Western World* (1907); Lady Gregory's *Spreading the News* (1904), *The Rising of the Moon* (1907), and other plays; and Sean O'Casey's (1880–1964) Dublin trilogy of plays, *The Shadow* of the *Gunman* (1923), *Juno and the Paycock* (1924), and *The Plough and the Stars* (1926). Inspired by the translations of Douglas Hyde (1860–1947), Gregory and Synge invented a new Irish-English rural idiom that captured the distinctive features of English spoken in Ireland (influenced by its two major sources, the Irish language and archaic forms of English preserved in Ireland). Their works were more Irish than writing in English had ever been before, while resisting nineteenth-century stereotypes and futile attempts to capture Irish pronunciations in deliberate misspellings. O'Casey wrote similarly artful Dublin dialogue. Yet Yeats rejected O'Casey's experimental play set in London, *The Silver Tassie* (1928). Thereafter, the Abbey Theatre and Irish society in general began a conservative phase marked by censorship and less risk-taking.

The greatest master of Dublin writing, of course, was JAMES JOYCE. From the time of his 1901 pamphlet attacking Yeats's movement, *The Day of the Rabblement*, Joyce initiated a countermovement in Irish literature that was critical of Irish society and determined to become fully European, not just Irish. His four books of fiction are masterpieces of modernism and postmodernism: *Dubliners* (1914), *A Portrait of the Artist as a Young Man* (1916), *Ulysses* (1922), and *Finnegans Wake* (1939). Perhaps the most representative and influential writer after Yeats was Sean O'Faoláin (1900–91), who grew up with the century, reacting to and helping to shape many of its major events. He fought in the Irish Republican Army in the 1920s but became disillusioned by the conservative Irish state, establishing himself as one of its major critics in his prolific fictional and nonfictional prose. Especially as editor of the journal *The Bell* during 1940–6, O'Faoláin was a crucial conscience and the mentor of many younger Irish writers. Perhaps his closest successors today are the writers of the Field Day movement: the playwright Brian Friel (1929 –), author of *Translations* (1980) and *Dancing at Lughnasa* (1990); Seamus Heaney (1939 –), the leading contemporary poet, influenced by Yeats but not overcome by him as were other twentieth-century Irish poets; and Seamus Deane (1940 –), the most influential critic writing in Ireland today and editor of the ambitious (and controversial) *Field Day Anthology of Irish Writing* (1991).

The riches of Irish literature can be suggested by listing other great writers: SAMUEL BECKETT, Austin Clarke (1896–1974), Patrick Kavanagh (1904–1967), George Moore (1852–1933), Flann O'Brien (1911–1966), Kate O'Brien (1907–1974), Máirtín O Cadhain (1907–1970), Pádraic O Conaire (1883–1928), Frank O'Connor (1903–1966), Liam O'Flaherty (1896–1984), Æ (George Russell, 1879–1916), Somerville and Ross (Edith So-

merville [1858–1949] and Violet Martin [1862–1915]), and James Stephens (1882–1950).

James M. Cahalan

Bibliography

Cahalan, James M. *The Irish Novel: A Critical History.* 1988.

———. *Modern Irish Literature and Culture: A Chronology.* 1993.

Deane, Seamus, ed. *The Field Day Anthology of Irish Writing.* 3 vols. 1991.

Maxwell, D.E.S. *A Critical History of Modern Irish Drama, 1891–1980.* 1984.

Welch, Robert, ed. *The Oxford Companion to Irish Literature.* 1993.

Irish Nationalism

The phrase "Irish nationalism" was not used before the 1840s. However, the goal of an independent Irish nation-state dates to the 1770s, when Henry Grattan and others tried to establish an Irish parliament free of British control. The Rising of 1798, influenced by the French Revolution and aiming toward an Irish republic, was another important milestone. From these two sources derived the competing forces of constitutional and revolutionary nationalism, both active throughout the nineteenth century. Constitutional nationalism, associated with Daniel O'Connell, Isaac Butt, and Charles Stewart Parnell, sought Irish political autonomy within a British imperial framework. Revolutionary nationalism, associated with the United Irishmen, Young Ireland, the Fenians, and the Irish Republican Brotherhood, wanted an independent republic wholly separated from Great Britain. The former worked openly through political parties represented in the British Parliament, the latter secretively through conspiratorial networks.

Irish constitutional nationalism reached its apex between 1910 and 1916. The Irish Nationalist Party, led by John Redmond, acquired great political weight in the two 1910 parliamentary elections, for without the support of its more than seventy MPs Prime Minister ASQUITH's Liberal government would have fallen. Under Irish Nationalist pressure the Liberals, after ending the legislative veto of the HOUSE OF LORDS, proceeded to enact an Irish Home Rule Bill. This bill—decreeing an autonomous legislature in Dublin—became law in 1914, but was suspended for the duration of the FIRST WORLD WAR. The resistance of the ULSTER Unionists to home rule had threatened to nullify the new legislation and might have precipitated an Irish civil war.

At the turn of the century the principal Irish separatist movement was the Irish Republican Brotherhood (IRB), descended from—and still popularly known as—the Fenians. Less important was the semi-legal party calling itself Sinn

Fein (Gaelic for "Ourselves Alone"), led by journalist Arthur Griffith. Both organizations condemned the Nationalist party for subservience to the British, a charge strengthened by John Redmond's outspoken support for the British cause in the First World War. In April 1916 the IRB launched the militarily hopeless Easter Rising against British rule. Although at first unpopular in Ireland, the Easter Rising gained widespread public sympathy due to the execution of its leaders—Padraic Pearse, Thomas J. Clarke, James Connolly, and others—following military trials. An abrupt decline in the Nationalist Party's reputation was shown in parliamentary by-elections won by separatists in 1917 and 1918.

In 1917 the IRB took control of Griffith's Sinn Fein Party, and thereafter used it as its political front. Sinn Fein elected 73 MPs in the 1918 British parliamentary election, eclipsing the Nationalists who won only six seats. The Sinn Fein MPs boycotted the House of Commons, instead constituting themselves as Dail Eireann, the constituent assembly of the Irish Republic. The Dublin-based Dail in turn established a de facto government and the Irish Republican Army (IRA), which successfully fought the Irish War of Independence against Great Britain between 1919 and 1921.

The IRB, IRA, and Sinn Fein split over approval of the IRISH TREATY of 1922 with Britain, with the majority of each body supporting the treaty giving the Irish Free State—excluding six northern counties—dominion status within the Empire. Two years before, the six Unionist-majority counties had acquired the very "home rule" the Unionists had rejected for all Ireland before the war. Irish nationalist politics was now recast. Most former constitutional nationalists in the south threw in their lot with William T. Cosgrave's pro-treaty Cumann na Gaedhael party, a breakaway from Sinn Fein. (In the north, the Nationalists remained a significant party through the 1960s.) The anti-treaty forces—appropriating the Sinn Fein and IRA labels—under Eamon de Valera continued the revolutionary, separatist tradition by fighting—and losing—the Civil War of 1922–3 against the Free State.

Following the Civil War, de Valera broke with the hard-line separatists and organized the Fianna Fail Party, committed to achieving Irish independence through constitutional means. Defeating Cosgrave in elections in 1932, de Valera gradually—and peacefully—enlarged the Free State's powers. During the SECOND WORLD WAR, the Free State (now known as Eire) remained neutral, and in 1949 it officially became the independent Republic of Ireland. The goals of the republican separatists were thus achieved for southern Ireland, after 1922 using methods which constitutional nationalists could approve.

Nevertheless Ireland remained partitioned, the six northern counties still under British sovereignty. Ending partition perpetuated a mission for revolutionary nationalism. Sinn Fein and the IRA, after de Valera's departure, rejected first the Free State, then Eire, and in 1949 the Republic because they did not include all Irseland. The IRA went underground in the 1930s after de Valera outlawed it, initiating decades of resistance to British rule in the north. Its tactics embarrassed successive Free State and Republic governments whose nationalism was hardening into official patriotism. After 1970, the Northern Ireland ("Provisional") wing of the IRA raised the level of violence to the point where London in 1972 had to replace home rule with direct rule. Revolutionary Irish nationalism, represented mainly by the Provisional IRA, enjoyed a resurgence and attracted financial support or sympathy from Irish expatriates overseas—although remarkably little in the Irish Republic. It also became integrated into the transnational complex of nationalistic, revolutionary, and terrorist movements active from the 1970s onward.

Don M. Cregier

Bibliography

Boyce, D. George. *Nationalism in Ireland.* 1982.

Cronin, Sean. *Irish Nationalism: A History of Its Roots and Ideology.* 1981.

Garvin, Tom. *Nationalist Revolutionaries in Ireland, 1858–1928.* 1987.

Rumpf, Erhard, and Anthony C. Hepburn. *Nationalism and Socialism in Twentieth-Century Ireland.* 1977.

Isherwood, Christopher William Bradshaw (1904–1986)

Christopher Isherwood's reputation as a novelist was established with the publication of his third novel, *The Last of Mr. Norris* (1935). His fourth, *Goodbye to Berlin* (1939), later the subject of two movies, *I Am A Camera* and *Cabaret*, became his best known work. Praised by E.M. FORSTER and closely associated with W.H. AUDEN, STEPHEN SPENDER, and John Lehmann, Isherwood and his finely written prose won world wide attention. His late works include several distinguished autobiographies as well as critically acclaimed novels.

Isherwood, born in Cheshire, England on 26 August 1904, was a descendant of Judge John Bradshaw who had signed King Charles I's death warrant. His his first and strongly autobiographical novel, *All the Conspirators* was published in 1928. *The Memorial*, which received more favorable critical reviews, followed in 1932 and featured a strong-willed female character similar to his mother Kathleen. From 1930–3, having dropped out of history studies at CAMBRIDGE and quit medical studies at King's College, London, Isherwood moved to Berlin where he wrote and worked as a tutor. His third novel, *The Last of Mr. Norris* was first published by the Hogarth Press and titled *Mr. Norris Changes Trains*. This work and his next, *Goodbye to Berlin*, drew heavily from his pre-war experience in Germany. Both novels have an open-eyed narrator whose involvement with the world around him brings the reader swiftly into the manners and morals of the times, revealing many dimensions of the Nazi threat.

In 1939 Isherwood and Auden, having had three plays produced in London (*The Dog Beneath the Skin*, 1936; *The Ascent of F6*, 1937; *On the Frontier*, 1938) moved to New York. Isherwood subsequently relocated to Los Angeles, where he wrote filmscripts and joined an active intellectual community that included ALDOUS HUXLEY, Thomas Mann, and Igor Stravinsky. Isherwood converted to Vedanta and began to edit and translate works with Swami Prabhavananda. His next novel was *Prater Violet* (1945), one of his wittiest and most popular. The book drew on experiences Isherwood had in London in 1933 when he wrote the screenplay for *Little Friend*, directed by Berthold Viertel. After a lapse of nine years, many of which were devoted to Vedanta and to writing screenplays, Isherwood published his least successful novel, *The World in the Evening*. Meanwhile, in 1959 Isherwood began to teach in college, first at California State College, Los Angeles, an experience that would be valuable to his writing later.

Down There on a Visit, his seventh novel, is an episodic book narrated by Isherwood the author in 1962 and describes Isherwood the person as he was during certain periods of his past, beginning in 1928. *A Single Man* (1964) was considered by Isherwood to be his finest novel. Tracing the events of a single day in the life of George, a British expatriate and homosexual professor living in Los Angeles, the novel reveals George's alienation from the world around him. Isherwood's last novel, *A Meeting by the River* (1967) draws heavily on his Vedanta beliefs and his visit to the Ramakrishna Institute in Calcutta. This novel, about two brothers, one of whom decides to become a Hindu monk, was adapted into an unsuccessful Broadway play (1979).

Isherwood's accomplishment as a prose stylist is characteristic of his writing and the reason that SOMERSET MAUGHAM said "that young man holds the future of the English novel in his hands." Typically witty, Isherwood's style possesses an immediate clarity and vivid psychological detail. His books frequently have an articulate narrator occasionally called Christopher Isherwood. His grand subject and theme, however, has often been ignored. Almost everything Isherwood wrote from his first novel *All the Conspirators* (1928) is autobiographical—nine novels, four non-fiction memoirs and the journal, thousands of pages in length, part of it published by his estate.

Isherwood's reputation has had to overcome the unpopularity of his personal convictions. After he and Auden emigrated to the United States, both refused to return to England during the Second World War. Many British intellectuals reacted in print with hostility. Meanwhile, critics in the United States generally have continued to consider Ishwerwood a British writer, despite his American citizenship. His conversion to Vedanta and his early espousal of HOMOSEXUAL causes adversely affected the critical attention he has received in the United States.

In 1965 Isherwood published *Ramakrishna and His Disciples*, a biography. *My Guru and His Disciple* (1980), his last and one of Isherwood's most powerful works, describes his spiritual development and gives remarkable insight into the author and his convictions, as does the earlier memoir, *Christopher and His Kind* (1976).

Miscellaneous works by Isherwood include two travel books. *Journey to a War* (1936), written with Auden and reporting on the Sino-Japanese War, is structured by alternating sections of Isherwood's diary entries and Auden's poetry. The book gives the reporters' reactions to an unorganized, dangerous situation. *The Condor and the Cows* (1949), composed during a trip to South America, contains some of Isherwood's most entertaining prose.

Isherwood's reputation as one of the leaders of the 1930s intellectual movement in England and as a writer of successful autobiographical novels and memoirs will be re-evaluated upon the publication of his long private journal. His books generally should be considered as a continuous narrative about his life.

James White

Bibliography

Finney, Brian. *Christopher Isherwood: A Critical Biography*. 1979.

Fryer, Jonathan. *Eye of the Camera: A Life of Christopher Isherwood*. 1977.

Funk, Robert W. *Christopher Isherwood: A Reference Guide*. 1979.

Isherwood, Christopher. *Diaries*. 1996.

Summers, Claude J. *Christopher Isherwood*. 1980.

Jarrow

The name Jarrow is synonymous with the horrendous levels of UNEMPLOYMENT of the 1930s. It was made famous by the Jarrow March, or Crusade, of 1936, which symbolized to a generation the failures of the British economy during the inter-war years.

Jarrow was a relatively prosperous shipbuilding town in the northeast of England until the end of the First World War. From the mid-nineteenth century it had been dominated by Palmer's shipyard and was often referred to as "Palmerstown." However, shipbuilding began to decline after the First World War in the face of increasing overseas competition. As a result the large shipbuilding interests came together in 1930s to form the National Shipbuilders' Security Ltd. The main purpose of the NSS was to reduce the capacity within the industry by buying up redundant or obsolete yards, and in this process Palmer's yard was bought up and closed in early 1934. At that time about three-quarters of the workers who paid into the state insurance scheme were unemployed. Indeed, the recorded percentage of unemployment in Jarrow was 72.9 percent in September 1935.

Out of this grim situation emerged the demand for work for Jarrow. Towards the end of 1934 it had seemed that there was the possibility of the Palmer site being used by a new steel syndicate and the "Jarrow scheme" for an integrated steelworks was even discussed in the House of Commons in December 1935. But the Iron and Steel Federation objected, and the scheme was strangled at birth in July 1936. At this point it was decided that the Jarrow March would be organized. The inspiration came from "Red Ellen", Ellen Wilkinson, who had become the LABOUR MP for Jarrow in 1935. She, and many others, had for some time come to believe in the need to petition Parliament for a new steelworks, but it was not until July 1936, with all-party support, that a March Committee was formed to organized 200 men to march to London. Its purpose was to present to Parliament a petition from the citizens for Jarrow demanding work and to draw the attention of the British public to the plight of Jarrow and depressed areas. The march, which began on Sunday, 4 October 1936, was joined on many occasions by Ellen Wilkinson and was greeted in London, at Hyde Park and Memorial Hall on 31 October, coinciding with the opening of Parliament. The marchers presented two petitions to the House of Commons, one from 12,000 people in Jarrow and the other from about 70,000 citizens on Tyneside, and then returned home by train to a hero's welcome. Although the Jarrow March did not bear immediate fruits, by 1939 the Jarrow steelworks, much smaller than the integrated steelworks which had been projected, was built on the site of Palmer's shipyard. The "Crusade" had been partly successful; the image of Jarrow haunted many wartime and post-war economists, and politicians worked to avoid mass unemployment in the future.

Keith Laybourn

Bibliography
Kingsford, Peter. *The Hunger Marchers in Britain, 1920–1939*. 1982.
Vernon, Betty D. *Ellen Wilkinson*. 1982.
Wilkinson, Ellen. *The Town that was Murdered*. 1939.

Jenkins, Roy Harris (1920–)

A politician, intellectual, and historical biographer, Roy Jenkins was a CABINET minister in the WILSON governments of the 1960s and 1970s, but in 1981 led a group of breakaway Labour MPs to create the SOCIAL DEMOCRATIC PARTY (SDP). Ironically, the SDP's attempt dramatically to smash the settled structure of British politics was associated with a man who was temperamentally opposed to visionary conceptions of politics and whose cool rationality, Olympian detachment, and apparent indolence recalled the stolid classicism of his hero HERBERT HENRY ASQUITH, as opposed to the romantic radicalism of those figures who had been responsible for the previous major realignments in British politics, Joseph Chamberlain and DAVID LLOYD GEORGE.

Roy Harris Jenkins was born on 11 November 1920 into the very heart of the labor movement. His father, Arthur Jenkins, was a former South Wales miner and trade union official who became Labour MP for Pontypool in 1935 and CLEMENT ATTLEE's Parliamentary Private Secretary. However, Roy's formative years in Wales were largely erased by his time at Balliol College, OXFORD, where he readily adopted the combination of public service and effortless superiority for which the college was notorious. In the late

1940s and 1950s Jenkins, together with ANTHONY CROSLAND and Denis Healey, was part of a circle of young socialists, self-consciously revisionist in outlook, who became increasingly influential in the LABOUR PARTY after the election of HUGH GAITSKELL as leader in 1955. Jenkins, while the first of the group to enter Parliament (becoming MP for Central Southwark in 1948, before moving on to Birmingham Stechford in 1950) seemed to lack the focused ambition of his peer group. In the late 1950s his reputation was something of a dilettante, a man who preferred foreign travel, writing political biography, and fine cuisine to debates in the Commons and whose almost Edwardian "grand manner" was hardly likely to endear him to genuine (and spurious) proletarians in the Labour Party. He also became estranged from Gaitskell after the latter's emphatically anti-European speech at Brighton in September 1962.

After a brief spell as Minister of Aviation in 1964–65, Jenkins was appointed by HAROLD WILSON as Home Secretary in December 1965. Here he gave official support to a cluster of liberalizing measures—"civilized" to their supporters, "permissive" to their critics—initiated by backbench MPs relating to censorship, abolition of the death penalty, decriminalization of ABORTION and HOMOSEXUALITY, and DIVORCE LAW REFORM. In the aftermath of the devaluation crisis in November 1967 Jenkins became Chancellor of the Exchequer, and his success in restoring the balance of payments and securing the pound enhanced his reputation with PRESS and public and ensured his election as Labour's Deputy Leader in 1970. However, he resigned the Deputy Leadership in 1972 out of frustration over Wilson's equivocation over entry into the EUROPEAN COMMUNITY. Indeed, Europe, supplemented by the growing power of the party's left wing, played a central role in Jenkins' alienation from the party, and while he served as Home Secretary again in 1974–76, growing disillusion with Labour sectarianism and his loss to JAMES CALLAGHAN in the 1976 leadership election encouraged him to quit British politics entirely and to assume the Presidency of the EEC Commission from 1977 to 1980. In the winter of 1979–80 he made several speeches in favor of electoral reform and coalition politics, condemning what he saw as the negative partisanship and "pendulum" politics of both Labour and CONSERVATIVES. In January 1981, together with other former Labour ministers (Shirley Williams, William Rodgers, and David Owen) who comprised the "Gang of Four," Jenkins launched the Social Democratic Party. In the first by-election the SDP contested, the safe Labour seat of Warrington in July 1981, Jenkins came a close second, and he re-entered Parliament as MP for Glasgow Hillhead in March 1982.

In July 1982 he defeated Owen to become the SDP's first sole (as opposed to the joint arrangement which had existed since 1981) leader. While differences between the two men largely involved style rather than policy, Jenkins' success ensured the SDP fully committed itself to an electoral alliance with the Liberals during the 1983 general election. While the Alliance's performance was the best for a third party in the postwar era, they (narrowly) failed to push Labour into third place, and, the SDP's high tide having clearly passed, a disappointed Jenkins resigned as party leader. In 1987 he was elevated to the peerage as Baron Jenkins of Hillhead and elected Chancellor of the UNIVERSITY OF OXFORD, and in 1991 published a highly acclaimed autobiography in which he chose to identify himself as a flexible radical, while conceding that he could perfectly understand why many observers had chosen instead to portray him as the last Whig grandee.

Martin Francis

Bibliography

Campbell, John. *Roy Jenkins: A Biography.* 1983.

Crewe, Ivor, and Anthony King. *SDP: The Birth, Life and Death of the Social Democratic Party.* 1995.

Jenkins, Roy. *The Labour Case.* 1959.

———. *A Life at the Centre.* 1991.

———. *Partnership of Principle.* 1985.

Jennings, Humphrey (1907–1950)

Humphrey Jennings may be the most important British documentary filmmaker of the twentieth century. John Grierson (1898–1972) was the founder of the movement, and there were others who were extremely important and made more films than Jennings. But his may have the most lasting value.

Jennings came to making films in his late twenties, but their quality was much enriched by his previous experiences. He was born in Suffolk of middle-class parentage and went to the Perse School in Cambridge. He remained in CAMBRIDGE as an undergraduate at Pembroke College and spent some years as a research student, studying Thomas Gray, but did not go on into academic life. Instead, he devoted some time to discovering his true metier. He was fascinated by the industrial revolution as both a creative and destructive force, and was continually amassing quotations about it. A much abbreviated version of this collection, *Pandemonium*, was finally published in 1985. He was a painter and a poet and regarded himself as a surrealist. He was also centrally involved in organizing—and exhibiting in—the famous surrealist exhibition in London in 1936. The following year he was one of the founders of MASS OBSERVATION, dedicated to using anthropological techniques to find out about the natives of the British Isles.

Under Grierson's supervision, he started making films in 1934 with the General Post Office group. With the outbreak of the SECOND WORLD WAR, the group began to work for the Ministry of Information as the Crown Film Unit. It was not until 1940 that Jennings came into his own, with a group of masterly films that were artistically strong as well as effective propaganda. In a characteristically understated way, British virtues and strengths were put forward while the enemy was not directly attacked. The first of his major films was the ten minute *London Can Take It,* made for the United States, in 1940. Similarly effective short films, *Heart of Britain* and *Words for Battle* were made in 1941, and the longer (twenty minutes) *Listen to Britain* in 1942. These plotless films were presentations of images (and his surrealist and Mass Observation experiences helped shape his instinct for the telling image) that conveyed the essence of Britain. His masterpiece, *Fires Were Started,* was made in 1943. It was a "docudrama," recreating the BLITZ of two years before but using real firemen in order to recount twenty-four hours in their lives: training a new member of the group, fighting a fire at a warehouse and hence protecting a freighter, and the death of one of the firemen. In its unobstrusive way, it is a film about heroism and civilized values. He made seven more films before his early death, his most notable being *A Diary for Timothy* of 1944–5, in which the commentary, written by E.M. FORSTER and read by Michael Redgrave, suggested the new world that would emerge for the infant Timothy in Britain after the war. Film is very much a co-operative venture, but in these films Jennings was the controlling intelligence. His tough-minded lyricism raised the documentary film to new heights.

Peter Stansky

Bibliography

Hodgkinson, Anthony W., and Rodney E. Sheratsky. *Humphrey Jennings: More than a Maker of Films.* 1982.

Jennings, Mary-Lou, ed. *Humphrey Jennings: Film-Maker, Painter, Poet.* 1982.

Stansky, Peter, and William Abrahams. *London's Burning: Life, Death, and Art in the Second World War.* 1994.

Sussex, Elizabeth. *The Rise and Fall of British Documentary.* 1975.

Swann, Paul. *The British Documentary Film Movement 1926–1946.* 1989.

Jews

The Jewish community in Britain, never more than 1 percent of the total population, has played a disproportionately prominent role in the political, cultural, and economic life of the nation in this century. Over the period British Jews have become highly integrated into the nation and progressively assimilated to the general culture and society.

Until the 1880s a small Jewish community, numbering no more than 60,000, consisted primarily of descendants of immigrants from Holland and Germany. Three new waves of IMMIGRATION after 1881 created the contemporary community. The first and largest, between 1881 and 1914, consisted mainly of REFUGEES from economic hardship and ANTI-SEMITIC persecution in Russia. This wave increased the size of the community to about 250,000 by 1914. The second, composed of refugees from Nazism, arrived from Germany, Austria, and Czechoslovakia between 1933 and 1939 and numbered at least 50,000. The third and smallest wave entered after 1945 and included survivors of European Jewry as well as a trickle of Jews from former British-ruled territories such as Iraq, Egypt, Aden, and South Africa.

The Jewish population of Britain probably reached its highest point in the 1950s when it numbered at most 450,000. At that time some 280,000 Jews lived in LONDON, 30,000 in Manchester, 25,000 in Leeds, and 15,000 in Glasgow. Since then a number of demographic factors have produced a decline: EMIGRATION (including a small but significant flow to Israel) has exceeded immigration; Jewish outmarriage has greatly increased; many persons of Jewish origin have chosen not to identify with the community; Jewish marriages have occurred at a later age; and families have grown smaller. By the 1970s the number of Jewish deaths each year greatly exceeded the number of births. The estimated Jewish population in 1992 was barely 300,000. The decline has been most striking in the provincial communities (other than Manchester). For example, by 1992 Glasgow had only about 7,000 Jews.

Before 1914 immigrant Jews concentrated in the East End of London, the Gorbals in Glasgow, the Leylands in Leeds, and Cheetham Hill in Manchester. In these so-called "ghettos" Yiddish-speaking Jews developed a distinctive sub-culture with their own synagogues, newspapers, trade unions, and friendly societies. The immigrants worked long hours in small workshops, especially in the clothing industry. Housing conditions were abominable, working conditions primitive, and over-crowding acute.

In the inter-war period the social composition of the community changed. The immigrants of the 1930s tended to be from the professional and business classes, while many of the second generation of Russian-origin Jews too made their way in the business world or acquired educational qualifications that facilitated entry to the professions. Accompanying this upward social mobility was a change in residential patterns. The old

Jewish East End declined as London Jews moved to areas in the north-west such as Golders Green. In Leeds Jews moved to Chapeltown. There were similar movements elsewhere.

These trends accelerated after 1945. London Jews moved further out to districts such as Ilford, Finchley, Edgware, and Stanmore, in Glasgow to Giffnock, in Leeds to Moortown. By the 1990s yet further dispersion had occurred, taking substantial Jewish populations to the fringes of the great metropolitan areas.

The Jewish community had become overwhelmingly middle and upper middle class. Old wealth in the great banking patriciate of the nineteenth century, the so-called "Cousinhood" (Rothschilds, Montagus, Samuels, Cohens, and other interrelated families), had now been overtaken by the new plutocracy of commercial and real estate millionaires represented by figures such as Sir Isaac Wolfson (creator of Great Universal Stores), the Marks, Sacher, and Sieff families (of MARKS AND SPENCER), Jack Cotton and Charles Clore (both real-estate tycoons). By the 1990s self-made men such as the tycoon David Young (later Lord Young), the bookmaker Cyril Stein, or the hairdresser Vidal Sassoon (who, however, moved to the United States) or self-made women such as the television personality Esther Rantzen were more characteristic of the community than the worthies of old.

British Jewry was unique in the diaspora in enjoying exceptionally strong centralized communal institutions. The most important religious figure was the Chief Rabbi. J.H. Hertz, Chief Rabbi from 1913 to 1946, was the most significant holder of the office. His religious authority extended over the United Synagogue. This umbrella group of orthodox congregations in London and associated synagogues in the provinces (and elsewhere in the Empire/Commonwealth), commanded the loyalty of the majority of practicing Jews.

The President of the main representative body, the Board of Deputies of British Jews, was recognized by the government as chief spokesman for the community in secular matters. The Jewish Board of Guardians (later known as the Jewish Welfare Board) was the foremost charitable body. And the Joint Palestine Appeal (later Joint Israel Appeal) raised large sums each year for Zionist causes. The *Jewish Chronicle*, with a circulation in the post-war decades of around 50,000, dominated the Jewish PRESS and drove out most competitors.

A general movement towards secularization and weakening of religious orthodoxy gathered pace after the 1950s. The number of kosher butchers declined and in most smaller provincial communities disappeared altogether. Synagogue attendance, other than on the High Holy Days (the New Year and the Day of Atonement) diminished. The proportion of Jews married in civil ceremonies increased. Sabbath observance deteriorated: many orthodox synagogues could be found with large numbers of cars parked nearby on the sabbath—denoting sabbath-breaking even by congregants attending services.

Membership of Reform and Liberal congregations grew steadily. Overall these sections grew from around 10 percent to nearly a quarter of the community between 1950 and 1990. Over the same period the strict ultra-orthodox, living particularly in the Stamford Hill area of London, grew significantly, mainly because of their high rate of natural increase.

Pressure from right and left tended to diminish the authority of the "centrist" orthodox United Synagogue. It was further weakened in the early 1960s by a controversy between the Chief Rabbi, Sir Israel Brodie, and Rabbi Louis Jacobs. The latter questioned some "fundamentalist" beliefs, such as the literal truth of the biblical description of the revelation. Jacobs led his congregation out of the United Synagogue. Although no other congregation seceded, by the early 1990s several other "masorti" (traditionalist) congregations were established. Their outlook was similar to that of American Conservative Judaism. There was never any real "Jewish question" in British politics, although Jewish issues occasionally bubbled to the surface of public debate. In the early years of the century resentment of Jewish immigration led to the Aliens Acts of 1905 and 1913 which limited the influx. The Marconi scandal in 1912–13 brought anti-Semitic sentiment into political discourse. During the FIRST WORLD WAR Jews were often the victims of anti-German feeling and later of anti-Bolshevik agitation. In the 1930s the British Union of FASCISTS, headed by SIR OSWALD MOSLEY, conducted provocative marches through Jewish areas, leading to violence.

In the period 1945–8 Zionist terrorism in PALESTINE provided the pretext for anti-Semitic incidents in Liverpool and elsewhere in England and led to accusations of "double loyalty". But in recent decades, perhaps because xenophobia has focused on Black and Asian immigrants from the Commonwealth, Jews encountered little hostility save from fringe elements.

Jews have played a significant role, as individuals rather than as a group, in British political life. A number of Jews rose to prominence in the LIBERAL PARTY in the first third of the century, notably HERBERT SAMUEL, EDWIN MONTAGU, and Lord Reading, all of whom held CABINET office. The LABOUR landslide at the 1945 election brought a large cohort of Jews into the House of

Commons. By 1969 there were thirty-nine Jewish MPs, of whom all but two were Labour members. Subsequently the number of Jewish CONSERVATIVE MPs increased. In 1986 there were five Jews in MARGARET THATCHER's twenty-two member Cabinet.

Only rarely did a "Jewish vote" manifest itself. In the early years of the century Jews voted heavily for the Liberals; between 1918 and the 1960s most voted Labour; thereafter the Conservatives and Liberals appeared to gain Jewish support. Jewish voters were heavily concentrated in only a few constituencies but they rarely voted as a bloc and were seldom swayed primarily by Jewish issues. In Whitechapel in the early decades of the century and later in districts such as Hendon and Finchley (Mrs Thatcher's constituency) they may have made an electoral difference. But such cases were the exception, not the rule.

By the early 1990s British Jewry was affluent, demographically declining, heavily concentrated in the outer suburbs of London and Manchester, inclining towards secularization (save on the ultra-orthodox fringe), and worried about its collective future. Major efforts in Jewish education, notably the expansion of Jewish day schools, offered one of the few signs of vitality in what was otherwise a community that, in spite of the successes of its individual members, appeared to be in danger of gradually dwindling away.

Bernard Wasserstein

Bibliography

Alderman, Geoffrey. *Modern British Jewry*. 1992.

Bermant, Chaim. *Troubled Eden: An Anatomy of British Jewry*. 1969.

Freedman, Maurice, ed. *A Minority in Britain: Social Studies of the Anglo-Jewish Community*. 1955.

Krausz, Ernest. *Leeds Jewry: Its History and Social Structure*. 1963.

Lipman, V.D. *A History of the Jews in Britain since 1858*. 1990.

London, Louise. *Whitehall and the Jews 1933–1948*. 2000.

Wasserstein, Bernard. *Vanishing Diaspora*. 1996.

John, Augustus Edwin (1878–1961)

Most accounts of Augustus John, even when sympathetic, dwell on his relative failure as an artist. He began spectacularly and on graduation in 1898 won first prize for the Summer Composition at the Slade School with "Moses and the Brazen Serpent." In 1904 ROGER FRY recognized him as the most remarkable member of the mildly anti-establishment New English Art Club, and in 1907 W.B. YEATS wrote: "The students consider him the greatest living draughtsman, the only modern who draws like an old master." Yet in 1952 when John Rothenstein summed up his career in *Modern English Painters* it was that of "a forgotten man," an artist who

had lacked "all those qualities that go to make a great organizer."

He did undertake some major projects, the first of which was the large "Lyric Fantasy" (Tate Gallery) which was begun in 1911 and abandoned in 1915 unfinished. In 1916 the Arts and Crafts Society commissioned him to undertake a large study of folk life in Galway, but that too was not completed. Nor was the huge frieze, "Canadians at Lievin Castle," which he proposed in 1918 when employed as a war artist with the Canadian forces. The problem was that, although an old master born out of his time, his gifts were for draughtsmanship and, more importantly, for publicity.

Rothenstein's judgment in 1952 was premature, for in 1974–5 he was the subject of an engrossing two-volume biography by Michael Holroyd which dealt largely with John the personality, the King of Bohemia. The legend transcended the artist, and it is as a legend that he is primarily remembered. He seemed to touch the imagination of all who met him. He accrued fables, the earliest of which was that his genius stemmed from a diving accident in the sea near to Tenby, his hometown, in 1897. Clearly handsome, as his photographs show, he was also charismatic and was rumored, by the end of his days, to have fathered more than 100 children. He epitomized the idea of a life lived to the prompting of the instincts. In 1906 WYNDHAM LEWIS, a friend, wrote that John would "end by building a city and being worshipped as sole man therein,—the deity of masculinity." That was apropos of John's Parisian *ménage à trois* with Ida Nettleship and Dorelia (Dorothy McNeil), to which the painter hoped shortly to add Alick Schepeler and Frieda Bloch. These women, and their children, appear in many of his idylls of that period, and it was a picture of Dorelia as a gipsy Gioconda, "The Smiling Woman," which finally made his name in 1909. The gipsy element entered John's art in 1901 when he was employed at the Liverpool Art School, where he was influenced by John Sampson, a librarian and Romany specialist.

John's relative failure as a painter, despite his genius, may have been due to the number of influences to which he was exposed as a gifted student. He was an early devotee of El Greco, well before the El Greco craze of 1902, and he was an admirer of Rembrandt, Daumier, and Puvis de Chavannes. He was impressed by Gauguin and by Picasso, whom he met in 1907—although he thought Fry's Manet and the Post-Impressionists of 1910 "a bloody show." Then in 1907 he returned to London from Paris and came into close contact with the painter Dickson Innes, who lived in Fitzroy Street but painted mainly in Merionethshire in North Wales. John worked intermittently with Innes in the Mt. Arenig area until Innes's death from consumption in 1914, and in his company produced his finest work. In 1908 John had met Lady Ottoline Morrell, who introduced him to high society, within which he found a new milieu and source of energy. He became a portraitist to the talented and well-placed, painting Lord Leverhulme, "His Margarine Majesty," in 1920 and Thomas Hardy in 1923. After the gipsy caravanning which had preoccupied him during the first decade of the century, he began to feature prominently in the café life of London, at Madame Strindberg's Cave of the Golden Calf in Soho, at the Crab-tree in Greek Street, the Cavendish Hotel in Jermyn Street, and at The Eiffel Tower in Percy Street. His café friends included the poet DYLAN THOMAS, to whom he introduced Caitlin McNamara in 1936. Although he painted King Feisal of Iraq in 1919 and Tallulah Bankhead in 1930, his portrait years are best remembered for drawings of T.E. LAWRENCE in 1919 and JAMES JOYCE in 1930. Elected an Associate of the Royal Academy in 1921, he became a Royal Academician in 1928. In 1952 *Chiaroscuro: Fragments of an Autobiography: First Series* was published.

Ian Jeffrey

Bibliography

Easton, Malcolm, and Michael Holroyd. *The Art of Augustus John.* 1974.

Holroyd, Michael. *Augustus John: A Biography.* 2 vols. 1974–5.

Joyce, James Augustine Aloysius (1882–1941)

On the strength of a book of short stories (*Dubliners,* 1914) and three longer works of fiction that perplex what we mean by the word "novel" (*A Portrait of the Artist as a Young Man,* 1916; *Ulysses,* 1922; *Finnegans Wake,* 1939), Irish-born James Joyce stands as one of the most inventive and influential novelists to write in English in the twentieth century. To call him a "British" writer, however, would be a politically fraught misnomer. He spent most of his working life on the Continent, drew his inspiration mainly from European models, and had undiluted scorn for both English and IRISH NATIONALISM. But his subject was invariably "Dear Dirty Dublin" and the powerful influence of that "gallant, venal city" on its inhabitants. Ireland, where his books were banned for decades, now claims him as her own.

Most of the fifteen *Dubliners* stories were written in Trieste around 1905 but only published after a decade of struggle with skittish publishers and printers. These uneventful slices of Dublin life reveal a general paralysis of will, an inherited inability on the part of the central characters to free themselves from a moribund Catholic Church, as well as stifling family traditions, an ossified politics of nostalgia, ubiquitous alcoholism, empty routines of work, repressed sexuality, and the tyranny of the dead over the living. In "Eveline" a young woman offered an escape from the purgatory of life with her widowed father goes catatonic at dockside, unable to board the ship that will take her to a new life in Argentina. In "Counterparts" a man humiliated then sacked at work, comes home drunk and beats his son, passing on that gift for impotent violence that Joyce saw as a central curse of Irish life. In "The Dead" a man realizes that his wife is more in love with the memory of a young man, now dead, who had loved her years ago, than she is with her husband here and now. It was in composing these stories that Joyce borrowed from the Church the term "epiphany," which has entered common parlance as a synonym for "any revelation," but which in Joyce's hands means some fragment of speech, thought, or gesture that momentarily lifts the veil to reveal (most typically) a character's spiritual deficiency.

A Portrait of the Artist as a Young Man is Joyce's semi-autobiographical *Kunstlerroman*—a saga of the artist's early education. Stephen Dedalus, like Joyce, is shaped by a rigorous, sometimes violent, Jesuit pedagogy. As he moves from childhood to young manhood, Stephen grows into knowledge of himself, his five wayward senses, his family, Ireland, the Church, and the mysteries of Woman. He undergoes a series of archetypal experiences that awaken within him permanent appetites and ineradicable revulsions. Unjustly punished by a patriarchal Church that requires submission and the subordination of self to group, he is drawn toward the verbally rich and sensuous balm of Mariolatry. Even when Stephen begins to frequent brothels, the Virgin Mary does not "humiliate the sinner who approached her." When asked if he wishes to become a priest himself, he is tempted; but a deep-rooted instinct of rebellion makes him refuse. His spirit begins to distance itself from the Church, yet despite his apparent apostasy, the forms and language of worship he learned in Mary's Church stick with him. He does not avoid a sense of vocation and devotion; he only shifts its focus from the ecclesiastical to the secular world. He will become "a priest of the eternal imagination." His enemies will be whatever would hamper the soul from its free expression: repressive parochialisms of language, nationality, religion, family. The book ends with his triumphant self-exile from the island prison of Ireland.

Ulysses breaks new ground both structurally and stylistically. The episodes of this Day in the Life of a City (16 June 1904) roughly parallel the episodes of Homer's *Odyssey.* But Leopold Bloom is no Ulysses: he is a wandering Jew in

Christian Dublin, a pacifist, a sensual, compassionate cuckold, a humble servant of his languid wife Molly, a man in search of a son to fill the void left by the death of his own son, Rudy. The surrogate son Joyce offers is none other than Stephen Dedalus, back in town after his Parisian exile is aborted by the terminal illness of his mother. Bloom and Stephen keep crossing paths during the day; late that night, after both visit the same brothel, Bloom takes bruised and drunken Stephen home for a tenuous communion over cocoa and biscuits.

What makes this comic epic so formidable to the average reader is the richness and variety of stylistic devices Joyce deploys, from highly allusive banter and parody, to "stream of consciousness" in which the unedited flow of a character's thoughts either complements or usurps the traditional third-person voice of the narrator, to Molly's great "interior monologue" that ends the book, forty-odd pages of unpunctuated (and uncensored) thoughts. *Finnegans Wake* (which began as a series of modernist exercises under the title *Work in Progress*) builds on the more hallucinatory experiments in *Ulysses*. The book is written in a hybrid, pan-European dream-language rich in "verbivocovisual" effects that left Joyce's admirers scratching their heads. The nuclear family here—H.C. Earwigger ("Hear Comes Everybody"), his wife, the alluvial Anna Livia Plurabelle, their twins, Shem the "Gracehopper" artist and Shaun the bourgeois "Ondt," and loony daughter Isobel—is in fact all families, and their story is All Our Stories. The book is a densely textured challenge, but it can appeal to the mumbling dreamer we all have buried in our collective unconscious.

Minor works include a play, *Exiles* (1918) and *Collected Poems* (1936).

David Gullette

Bibliography
Ellmann, Richard. *James Joyce*. 1959.
Henke, Suzette. *James Joyce and the Politics of Desire*. 1990.
Kenner, Hugh. *Dublin's Joyce*. 1956.
Levin, Harry. *James Joyce*. 1941.

Judicial System

As a result of reforms undertaken in the late nineteenth century the British judicial system has enjoyed a period of unparalleled respect in the twentieth century. Rapidity of procedure, access to the courts, and efficient administration, as well as essential fairness, have made British courts an object of admiration by many other legal systems. No judicial system escapes criticism completely and debates about British justice, usually with respect to the Diplock courts (non-jury trials) in Irish affairs, have called into question the reputation that British courts have otherwise earned.

The judicial system in the twentieth century has changed repeatedly as the courts have attempted to make themselves responsive to the complex demands of modern society. The most important principles for reform have relied upon simplified procedure and a timely appeals process. Any legal system represents an impenetrable maze to the layperson, but the British system has built upon the advantages of unitary jurisdiction.

The High Court of Justice has been the central institution of the judicial system since 1873. It is divided into three divisions, with the Queen's Bench Division exercising the jurisdiction formerly held by the historic common law courts of King's Bench, Common Pleas, and Exchequer. The Queen's Bench Division possesses the basic civil and criminal authority in the country. The second division is that of Chancery, replacing the old Court of Chancery that had originated in the middle ages as a court of equity. Most actions in the Chancery Division deal with property, and the principles of equity prevail when in direct conflict with those of the common law. Since 1971 the third division has been called the Family Division because it handles legal matters with respect to matrimony, DIVORCE, and adoption. Appeals from decisions in these courts go to the Court of Appeal, civil or criminal division as appropriate. The final court of appeal in each case is the Judicial Committee of the HOUSE OF LORDS.

Most citizens in Britain never become involved with this part of the judicial system. For ordinary purposes the courts are either the county courts, crown courts, or magistrates' courts. Most minor civil litigation is heard in a county court, and appeals go to the Court of Appeal and then to the House of Lords. Appeals in the British legal system are relatively rare, and appeals to the House of Lords are permitted only when a substantial point of law is at issue. Major criminal cases are heard in the Crown Court with a jury and presided over by a High Court judge. Minor criminal offenses are tried before a panel of justices of the peace. These justices are ordinary citizens without specific legal training who have a solicitor in court to instruct them on points of law that might arise. Justices of the peace may imprison for up to six months or levy a fine of up to £2000. This latter court represents the sinews of the judicial system.

Another fundamental aspect of the judicial structure is the judges themselves. For the most part the upper echelon of the judiciary has sought anonymity. Public opinion throughout the century has generally held the judiciary in high regard. Criticism of the judiciary, when it occurs, usually focuses on two points: class bias and judicial legislation. The first complaint is based partly on the procedure by which judges are chosen from the ranks of practicing barristers. Surveys of the social backgrounds of the judiciary have shown a strong similarity based on public school education, attendance at OXFORD or CAMBRIDGE, and middle-class social origins. The English bar itself represent an elite even within the LEGAL PROFESSION. Such a class of judges, unconsciously or otherwise, could hardly fail to reflect the experiences of a lifetime. Yet, in many instances, judges have earned a reputation as "liberal" or "conservative" where the social background is almost identical. Throughout the twentieth century a debate has ensued about the extent to which a judge should, if ever, allow personal policy preferences to affect the process of rendering a decision. In theory judges do not make the law but rather take the extant law and apply the appropriate set of facts to arrive at a correct decision. This mechanical model fails on historical grounds because the common law until the nineteenth century was essentially a judge-made body of law. If taken literally, it would mean that judges posessed no discretion to alter the course of law in response to changing social circumstances. A decision not to change the law represents a policy preference just as clear as an attempt to create new law. The judge, beyond semantic quibbling, always engages in policy decisions of one sort or the other.

This enduring dilemma has become more important in the latter part of the twentieth century because the courts have had to address issues that reflect the changing nature of British society. On RACE RELATIONS, for example, the courts have had to interpret various statutes, including the first Race Relations Act (1965). The attempt to remove color discrimination has tested the limits of judicial ability to modify basic social attitudes. Additional legislation has tried to close the loopholes left by various statutes but the power of the judiciary is limited. Within the constitutional framework of Great Britain, for example, there are restraints on the doctrine of judicial review. No court has the authority to rule an act of Parliament unconstitutional; a court may only decide whether actions taken under the language of the statute have exceeded the parliamentary grant of those powers. It is to Parliament, not the courts, that the British citizen looks for redress of grievances.

Finally, some important practical elements of the law now exist outside the formal judicial structure. The most obvious example in this regard is plea bargaining, by which an accused person negotiates a lesser charge rather than face a trial that might entail more severe punishment in return for which the prosecution does not bear the expense and hazards of a trial. Mediation arrangements for conflict resolution outside the purview of the courts is another example of a non-legal part of the judicial system. Despite some infamous examples of judicial complacency (the Birmingham Six, 1974–91), the judicial system of Great Britain has on the whole continued to serve the country well.

Richard A. Cosgrove

Bibliography

Lee, Simon. *Judging Judges*. 1988.
Paterson, Alan. *The Law Lords*. 1982.
Roshier, Bob, and Harvey Teff. *Law and Society in England*. 1980.
Stevens, Robert B. *Law and Politics: The House of Lords as a Judicial Body, 1800–1976*. 1978.

Juvenile Delinquency

The law provides one way of defining juvenile delinquency: in England and Wales criminal responsibility begins at the age of ten. (Before 1964 it was eight.) A child of this age is considered to be capable of deliberate criminal intent, and liable to legal punishment. Up to the age of eighteen, however, he or she is dealt with by special "youth courts." (Before the 1991 Criminal Justice Act, the cut-off point for juveniles was the seventeenth birthday, and they were tried in "juvenile courts.") The first point of substance is that juveniles contribute substantially to the official statistics of crime. In 1984, for example, juvenile males aged ten to sixteen accounted for only 12 percent of the male population of England and Wales but for well over one-third of all males cautioned or successfully prosecuted for burglaries, thefts, and criminal damage ("vandalism"). There is a similar over-representation of juveniles among women who are detected in offenses. The year-groups most prone to delinquency are those aged fifteen and sixteen, who have left school or are close to doing so. Only the young adult age-group (aged seventeen to twenty) makes a more disproportionate contribution, especially to the graver offences: it accounted for eight percent of the male population in 1984, but for one-third of all males cautioned or successfully prosecuted for robberies, and close to a third of those likewise dealt with for personal violence.

To this catalogue of juvenile delinquency, however, four telling annotations should be appended. The first is that self-report studies indicate that the great majority of young people commit delinquent acts at some time, but only a minority of these acts result in a court appearance. The second annotation is that the increase in recorded juvenile crime is due, in part, to the massive increase since the 1960s in the use of police caution (administered to both parents and juvenile at the police station). Intended as a way of diverting children from the juvenile courts, the caution has had the effect of bringing into the legal net a wider range of delinquent behavior. The police have cautioned youngsters whom previously they would have treated informally. Thirdly, despite the belief that delinquents are destined to a life of CRIME, delinquency constitutes a "passing phase." Most delinquents cease to appear in court once they enter their twenties, due perhaps to the influence of MARRIAGE and parenthood, or of involvement in lawful occupations and recreations. And, finally, the latest official statistics suggest that offending by juveniles, in relation to their numbers, is currently decreasing, due possibly to an even greater incidence of cautions relative to prosecutions (and thus greater diversion from the juvenile court), and to more diversion from custody in young offender institutions.

It is a staple of contemporary political discourse that delinquency is the product of moral decline brought about by the permissive society. The historian is hard pressed, however, to discover a time when delinquency was not a cause of public anxiety. Today's soccer hooligans were anticipated by "Mods" and "Rockers" disturbing the Bank Holiday calm at seaside resorts in the mid-1960s; or by "Teddy Boys" destroying cinema seats to the sound of "Rock around the Clock" in the early 1950s. Between the wars chief constables and magistrates laid the blame for an increase in recorded delinquency on parental neglect, "Americanized" entertainment, and over-lenient juvenile courts. In the Edwardian years it was gangs of "hooligans," city-bred youth employed in "dead-end" jobs, which aroused public anxiety. Thus, crime fears or "moral panics" have frequently punctuated the history of delinquency, created by different anxieties, from fear over national decline in the Edwardian era to the financial and cultural independence of post-war youth.

Proportional to the anxiety delinquents have caused is the volume of literature attempting to explain the rise in delinquency, especially since the mid-1950s. Leslie Wilkins, one of the first to explore the phenomenon of rising crime in

Delinquent Generations (1960), argued that the generation of children growing up during the Second World War, when fathers were abroad, mothers working, and the school system disrupted, had a greater tendency to commit offenses. The main flaw in the argument is that the cohorts of children born after the war were even more delinquent. The most dominant explanation of delinquency, however, has been that of the so-called "reformists" (sociologists, psychologists, and makers of social policy), who claim that youngsters who live in areas of urban decay or on vast housing estates, victims of poverty, broken homes and bad HOUSING, will almost invariably become involved in delinquent activities. This interpretation of delinquency, moreover, inspired the legislation of 1933 and 1969, which made the young offender's welfare the prime consideration of juvenile justice.

A more down-to-earth explanation of the rise in delinquency has been advanced in recent years, one which links it to increased opportunities: a huge increase in the number of motor vehicles; an enormous expansion of self-service shops. In the past twenty-five years, however, the criminologists' focus has shifted from the origins of delinquency to the social and legal processes by which some individuals get "labeled" as delinquent. Their argument is that the reactions of the police and the juvenile courts, at times exacerbated by PRESS and public fears, confirm and amplify an offender's deviance. As such, delinquency is not an inherent property of an individual, but a property conferred by society.

Victor Bailey

Bibliography

Bailey, Victor. *Delinquency and Citizenship: Reclaiming the Young Offender, 1914–1948.* 1987.

Burt, Cyril. *The Young Delinquent.* 1925.

Cohen, Stanley. *Moral Panics and Folk Devils: The Creation of the Mods and Rockers.* 1972.

Pearson, Geoffrey. *Hooligan: A History of Respectable Fears.* 1983.

Rutter, Michael, and Henri Giller. *Juvenile Delinquency. Trends and Perspectives.* 1983.

Keynes, John Maynard (1883–1946)

The importance of the career of John Maynard Keynes lay on three levels. First, as a publicist, he presented the classic critique of the Versailles peace settlement and later emerged as a spokesman for radical changes in British economic policy between the wars. Secondly, as a public servant, he exercised influence on British government policy from the time of his attachment to the Treasury during the First World War, and during the Second World War had an official responsibility for restructuring international financial relations. He was created Baron Keynes of Tilton in 1942. Thirdly, as an academic economist, he wrote *The General Theory of Employment, Interest and Money* (1936), which challenged the theoretical assumption that the economy was in principle self-correcting. All three roles helped establish "Keynesianism" as a doctrine of demand management by the state, aimed at maintaining full employment.

Keynes was born into an intellectual aristocracy clustered around the UNIVERSITY OF CAMBRIDGE. At King's College, Cambridge, he gained a first class degree in mathematics in 1905—twelfth in the rank order of his class—a good but not brilliant result. As an undergraduate he was president of both the Liberal club and the students' debating society (the Cambridge Union Society), with a well-formed aptitude for political controversy, especially on the side of free trade. He was also a member of the select society, known as the Apostles, several of whom became the core of the BLOOMSBURY GROUP. Keynes's close friendship with such figures as the writer LYTTON STRACHEY and the painter DUNCAN GRANT was reinforced by their HOMOSEXUALITY.

It was as a protégé of Alfred Marshall that Keynes became an economist. His strictly academic research was initially in the field of probability. The full significance of his work here has only recently been appreciated, not least in providing a ground for knowledge which fell short of certainty yet was still rational. Such concepts resurfaced in the economic theories of his mature years. Keynes's attitude towards economics was somewhat ambivalent. He never held a university chair of economics, and no one was less content to leave economics to the economists.

With Marshall's backing, Keynes became editor of the prestigious *Economic Journal* in 1911 as a young university teacher still under thirty. This was to be an important thread of professional continuity in an otherwise extraordinarily diverse career. Keynes had started work as a civil servant in the India Office in 1906 but returned to Cambridge two years later to teach economics. Already in 1913 he was combining his academic expertise with his administrative experience in sitting as a member of the Royal Commission on Indian Finance and Currency.

During the FIRST WORLD WAR he entered the Treasury and was soon entrusted with wide responsibility for the external finance of the war. His ability to handle these problems prepared him to assume a later role as an expert adviser, an insider who really understood the system. The paradox was that he provided the sinews of a war in which he did not fully believe and, in denouncing its aftermath, made an even bigger name for himself as an outsider and a critic.

Sent to the Versailles peace conference as the official representative of the Treasury, Keynes resigned in June 1919, dismayed by the heavy scale of reparations demanded from Germany. He was determined to expose the treaty's shortcomings. In *The Economic Consequences of the Peace* (1919), Keynes fused high moral passion with hard economic analysis, and revealed, moreover, his striking distinction as a writer. The nub of his case was that reparations implied a transfer of wealth from poverty-stricken Germany in the form of real resources, which Germany could only generate by establishing an economic domination over the rest of Europe for which no one was prepared. The fulsome reception accorded to the book, which made its author a household name in educated circles on both sides of the Atlantic, gave Keynes a platform of which he made full use thereafter.

Though keeping his fellowship at King's, Keynes did not revert to full-time academic teaching and research after the war but divided his time between Cambridge and his house in Bloomsbury, where the cultural and business life of London, as well as politics, were open to him. He became a rich man through speculation, worth half a million pounds at the peak in 1936. He married the ballerina Lydia Lopokova in 1925, and they appear to have had a happy if childless marriage, sustained by a common interest in the arts, of which Keynes was a great patron. Indeed he was later to play a vital role in enlisting government support for the arts through the formation of the ARTS COUNCIL OF GREAT BRITAIN.

Although he was called on periodically by government for expert advice over economic policy, Keynes found his view overruled·in 1925 when he argued against an imminent return to the GOLD STANDARD at the traditional parity of $4.86. The Chancellor of the Exchequer, WINSTON CHURCHILL, bore the brunt of Keynes's public criticisms for doing "such a silly thing". Keynes maintained that, with an inappropriately high parity for sterling, the monetary mechanism would not in fact work smoothly to deflate domestic prices but would provoke UNEMPLOYMENT. At this stage, however, Keynes did not doubt the (Marshallian) postulate that a market-clearing equilibrium would be established in the long run.

Keynes's most famous dictum—"In the long run we are all dead"—is customarily cited to show his irresponsibility. What Keynes meant when he proclaimed this in the 1920s, of course, was not that the future could be treated with feckless disregard, but that it was irresponsible for policy-makers to close their eyes to the immediate impact of their actions. He wanted them to appreciate the consequences of big decisions, not to ignore them.

Keynes had already become actively involved in LIBERAL PARTY politics. From 1923 he was chairman of the weekly paper the *Nation* (later amalgamated with the *New Statesman*) which, under the editorship of Cambridge economist Hubert Henderson, pressed for a more radical policy stance. This brought Keynes into close cooperation with LLOYD GEORGE—a man of dynamic and optimistic temperament like himself. Little wonder that he later endorsed the New Deal policies of Franklin Roosevelt, with his message to the American people that they had nothing to fear but fear itself. Keynes was the quintessential exponent of "can-do" economics.

When the Liberal Party entered the the 1929 general election with a pledge to cut the high level of unemployment to "normal" proportions, Keynes was thus identified as a prominent partisan opponent of BALDWIN's CONSERVATIVE government and of the "Treasury view" which it espoused. There were certainly other arguments against public works on the grounds of feasibility, but in 1929 the Treasury view that public expenditure necessarily diverted resources from more productive uses by private enterprise was crucial. To counter it, Keynes and Henderson produced their famous pamphlet *Can Lloyd George Do It?*.

Public works, it suggested, notably a loan-financed scheme of road-building, could stimulate a cumulative process of economic recovery. Essentially this was a plea for a bold state-led initiative, in the confident hope that, with spare capacity available, such a program would succeed in mobilizing idle resources.

The inconclusive election results, however, suggested that Keynes had failed to persuade "outside opinion" of the merits of the Liberal proposals, and a minority LABOUR government took office from 1929 to 1931. Keynes was now given a chance to influence "inside opinion" through his concurrent membership of the (Macmillan) Committee on Finance and Industry and the newly-instituted Economic Advisory Council (especially its committee of economists, of which Keynes was chairman). There is a well-known jibe, in circulation from as early as 1931, that among five economists you would find six opinions, two of them held by Keynes. His interventions in policy debates over the previous couple of years may have fostered this impression of inconsistency. After all, he had advocated public works in 1929 in his pamphlet *Can Lloyd George Do It?*. Yet he published an academic book, *A Treatise on Money* (1930), which stated that cheap money was the real solution. Then again, he outlined no less than seven remedies for unemployment, including both public works and cheap money, in testimony to the Macmillan Committee at the beginning of 1930. And later that year he moved towards the option of tariffs. But all these different remedies were congruent, and in fact were based upon a common analysis of the *Treatise*.

The novelty of the *Treatise on Money* was to repudiate the identity of investment and saving. Instead it talked of enterprise and thrift as different processes controlled by different people—albeit in theory brought into equilibrium by the adjusting mechanism of interest rate. With cheap money, enterprise could be relied upon to do the trick. But, he contended, cheap money was not on offer so long as the bank rate had to be kept up in order to protect the high parity of sterling fixed under the gold standard. Thus, given these rigidities in the real world, Keynes was ready to outline the case for a number of unorthodox policy expedients and joined forces with others who were prepared to consider appropriate action.

He supported the proposals put forward by SIR OSWALD MOSLEY, then a minister in the Labour government, for state development programs. By 1931, however, such proposals were marginalized, as the government became caught in a mounting financial and political crisis which threatened the pound sterling on the foreign exchanges. Only when the position seemed untenable did Keynes himself opt for devaluation, though he was relieved when the new National government found itself forced off gold in September 1931.

After 1931 Keynes severed many of his direct political connections and, with an unaccustomed single-mindedness, devoted his energies to economic theory. Within a surprisingly short time he had stepped outside the analytical framework of the *Treatise* and was arguing his new theory of effective demand. He was crucially stimulated at this point by the "Circus" of younger economists at Cambridge, especially the ideas of R.F. Kahn and J.E. Meade, suggesting a fresh approach to the problem of saving and investment. Instead of investment depending upon prior saving—the orthodox assumption—savings were seen as being generated by an initial act of investment through a process which multiplied income, output, and employment.

Thus saving and investment were brought into equality by the equilibrating mechanism of changes in income or output. It followed that equilibrium might be reached while output was still below full capacity or full employment. It followed, too, that changes in output were now assigned the equilibrating task which was fulfilled under orthodox theory (including the *Treatise*) by changes in interest rate. What role, then, did interest play? Keynes proceeded to explain interest in terms of "liquidity preference"—the premium which wealth-holders exacted for tying up their resources in ways which sacrificed the liquid advantages of holding cash.

The *General Theory* thus gave a wholly new account of how the economy worked—or failed to work. No longer did Keynes point to particular rigidities in the real world as the crucial reason why prices were prevented from making efficacious adjustments which would clear the market. He argued now that reductions in wages or interest rates, even if forthcoming, might simply be incapable of restoring full employment, which was a function of effective demand (that is, of prospective consumption plus investment).

Keynes claimed that his theory would "revolutionise the way the world thinks about economic problems"; but he acknowledged that it would necessarily be infused with political considerations in the process. The *General Theory* itself was largely silent on policy. Keynes, moreover, was fairly tentative in his subsequent practical recommendations, well aware that bottlenecks in production constrained the full use of resources, and reluctant to advance a practicable target for "full employment" above a level of 95 per cent.

It was only with the Second World War that Keynes's ideas gained widespread acceptance. In 1940 he was invited back into the Treasury, where he served as a top-level adviser for the rest of his life. A macro-economic approach—designed to contain inflation by restraining demand for finite resources rather than simply to raise revenue—became the basis of the 1941 budget in Britain. Conversely, the feasibility of maintaining full employment after the war was proclaimed in the government's White Paper of 1944. But Keynes's own attention was increasingly consumed by planning for the post-war international economy, seeking new means of discharging the functions of the historic gold standard.

Keynes played a large part at the Bretton Woods conference (1944) which helped to set up the International Monetary Fund and the World Bank. In contrast to his advocacy of tariffs in the conditions of the 1930s, he now reverted to fundamentally liberal trade policies. His abilities as a negotiator were put to a supreme test at the end of the war when American support for Britain under the LEND-LEASE agreement was abruptly terminated. Keynes was largely responsible for securing a large dollar loan from the U.S.A. and Canada to tide Britain over the transition to peace. It was an arrangement which he recognized as at once imperfect and necessitous—a case which he made with telling effect in the HOUSE OF LORDS in December 1945. There can be little doubt that these wearisome transatlantic negotiations taxed Keynes's strength—he had suffered a major heart attack in 1937—and he died suddenly at Easter 1946, just before the Order of Merit, Britain's highest honor, could be conferred.

The thirty-year boom in the world economy after his death boosted Keynes's own stock to dizzy heights; conversely, the rise of THATCHERISM in Britain and of "Reaganomics" in the United States were subsequently to see the explicit repudiation of a Keynesian approach to economic problems. Yet his own theoretical insights, which continue to fascinate scholars around the world, can hardly be dismissed as ephemeral. The *General Theory* may not offer an infallible way to conquer unemployment, still less inflation, but it remains the central pillar of Keynes's reputation as the most influential economist of the twentieth century.

Peter Clarke

Bibliography
Clarke, Peter. *The Keynesian Revolution in the Making, 1924–36.* 1988.
Harrod, R.F. *The Life of John Maynard Keynes.* 1951.
Moggridge, D.E. *Maynard Keynes: An Economist's Biography.* 1992.
Skidelsky, Robert. *John Maynard Keynes: Hopes Betrayed, 1883–1920.* 1983.
———. *John Maynard Keynes: The Economist as Saviour, 1920–1937.* 1992.
———. *John Maynard Keynes: Fighting for Britain, 1937–1946.* 2000.

Kinnock, Neil Gordon (1942–)
Born into a working-class family in the largely pro-Labour community of Tredegar, South Wales, Neil Kinnock was Leader of the LABOUR PARTY and of the Opposition from 1983 to 1992. Educated at University College Cardiff, his academic record was undistiguished, his political passion and ambition evident. There he met his future wife, Glenys Parry, who held strong left-wing views and became a substantial, sustaining influence. His career has been entirely within the Labour movement; he was elected Member of Parliament for Bedwellty and has held the seat until 1995. A vigorous, combative but often popular figure, Kinnock rebelled against the party leadership on many occasions but disassociated himself from the "hard Left." He was elected to the party's National Executive Committee in 1978 and became Education spokesman in 1979. His rapid rise to the party leadership owed something to the patronage of MICHAEL FOOT, its leader from 1980, and much to the agility with which he picked his way through the minefield of bitter party conflicts at a time when Labour was both polarized and dispirited.

Kinnock succeeded Foot after Labour's disastrous 1983 election campaign. The party was at a very low ebb: institutionally archaic and cumbersome, it was challenged from within by a growing left wing which alarmed many voters, from without by the rise of the SOCIAL DEMO-CRATIC PARTY/LIBERAL alliance, and by the need to adapt to demographic, economic, and social changes which had eroded its traditional working-class base. Its savage internal struggles at times suggested the death throes of a party committing political suicide. Kinnock attempted to unify and modernize the party, with energy, nerve, and some degree of skill and success. Before the 1987 election he launched a strong attack on the Trotskyist Militant group which was burrowing into the party. Organizational reforms proceeded, if unevenly, and the 1987 election campaign saw greatly improved logistics and use of the media. It did not, however, bring victory. Kinnock launched a comprehensive policy review: while critics accused him of excessive flexibility, supporters admired his determination to rehabilitate Labour as a convincing alternative party of government. Under his leadership the party abandoned earlier unpopular positions, preferring managed market capitalism to extensive public ownership, stressing growth more than redistribution, accepting membership of the EUROPEAN COM-MUNITY, rejecting unilateral nuclear disarmament, and attempting to see voters as citizens and consumers rather than as foot-soldiers in a class struggle.

Although Kinnock dragged the party back from the precipice of 1983, he was unable to overcome popular distrust of his own capacities. Hampered by his inexperience of government, he also suffered from a largely hostile PRESS; most of the tabloid newspapers caricatured him as a verbose lightweight who had disguised rather than adapted his socialist views. After the 1992 election returned a fourth consecutive CONSERVATIVE government, Kinnock resigned the Labour leadership. It is ironic that while his handling of the party's flaws and divisions was vital to its survival, he was too clearly associated with its most troubled times to escape their shadow. Kinnock resigned his parliamentary seat in 1995 to accept an appointment as a member of the European Commission.

Steven Reilly

Bibliography
Harris, Robert. *The Making of Neil Kinnock.* 1984.
Hughes, Colin, and Patrick Wintour. *Labour Rebuilt: The New Model Party.* 1990.
Morgan, Kenneth O. *Labour People: Leaders and Lieutenants.* 1987.

Kipling, (Joseph) Rudyard (1865–1936)
Rudyard Kipling, British poet, short-story writer, and novelist, born in India, is still known primarily as the poet of the British Empire, the author of "The White Man's Burden" (1899), as well as of *The Jungle Book* (1894), *Stalky & Company* (1899), *Kim* (1901), and *Departmental Ditties and Barrack Room Ballads* (1890). Kipling is also identified with a nostalgia for the Anglo-India of his young manhood, brought to the screen through Hollywood film adaptations of *Gunga Din* (1939), *Wee Willie Winkie* (1937), *Kim* (1950), and, more recently, *The Man Who Would Be King* (1975). In addition to his literary significance, acknowledged in the award of the Nobel Prize for Literature in 1907, Kipling's vigorous imperialism and anti-democratic propaganda made him an important figure in twentieth-century British social and political history.

As with many British children born in India, he was sent to England to attend boarding school, where bullying and brutality, vividly described in *Stalky & Co,* made his childhood one of unhappy memories. Returning to India in 1882, Kipling became a journalist for the *Civil and Military Gazette,* a Lahore newspaper, and later for the more prestigious *Allahabad Pioneer,* where he could indulge his passion for short-story writing. In *Plain Tales from the Hills* (1888) Kipling combined insights into Anglo-Indian society with fascinated appreciation for the cultured diversity of Indian life. Kipling's light, vernacular, and slangy verses from this period describe and celebrate the pathos of the ordinary

British soldier doing his duty for Queen, country, and British civilization. *Gunga Din, Fuzzy-Wuzzy, Tommy, Danny Deever,* and *Mandalay* are all poems in this celebratory mode from *Ballads and Barrack Room Ballads* (1890). Kipling became increasingly popular after 1890, notwithstanding personal travails. The novel *The Light That Failed* (1890) was regarded as a failure, partly because readers objected to its English setting and to its pessimism about the success of empire. While on honeymoon with his new American wife, the former Caroline Balestier, in Japan, a bank collapse ruined Kipling financially. He then decided to live in his wife's home at Brattleboro, Vermont until he could recoup his losses. While in Vermont Kipling produced the two popular *Jungle Books* (1894–5) which have made him famous with children to this day. Kipling continued to produce copious distinguished stories after 1900, but he increasingly became identified with an aggressive, muscular brand of imperialism. He also developed close relationships with Cecil Rhodes, South African diamond tycoon and advocate of British expansion, and Theodore Roosevelt, the energetic champion of the "strenuous life" and of American expansion overseas. The poem "The White Man's Burden" was written to encourage the United States to assume a colonizing destiny in the Philippines. The United States finally disillusioned Kipling, who viewed Americans as strangers to the British imperial ethos.

Just before the First World War, Kipling's extreme imperialist and conservative views marginalized him as a British man of letters. During the war, as before, Kipling was virulently anti-German, spurred on by the loss of his son in combat. Thereafter he remained an unreconstructed believer in the British Empire, incapable of adjusting to commonwealth notions that had begun to emerge. But Kipling from the start of his writing career had always mixed criticism of British society and imperialism alongside of his advocacy. His later stories, such as *Debits and Credits* (1926), show considerable ideological and political complexity. Moreover, the mature Kipling's artistry does not falter. His stories brilliantly experiment with forms of ambiguity, ellipsis, and condensation in a way characteristic of modernist literary art—irrespective of the political persuasions of the artist.

Richard A. Voeltz

Bibliography

Carrington, Charles E. *Rudyard Kipling.* 1955.

Mason, Philip. *Kipling: The Glass, The Shadow, and The Fire.* 1975.

Moore-Gilbert, B.J. *Kipling and "Orientalism".* 1986.

Wilson, Angus. *The Strange Ride of Rudyard Kipling.* 1977.

Kitchener, Horatio Herbert (1850–1916)

Promoted to Field Marshal in 1909 and given an earldom in 1914 after serving as Commander-in-Chief in South Africa (1900–2) and India (1902–9), Horatio Herbert Kitchener was Secretary of State for War from 5 August 1914 until his death on 5 June 1916. In this capacity he expanded the existing military forces into a mass citizen ARMY—the biggest in the country's history—enabling Britain to play an increasingly weighty part in the land campaigns of the FIRST WORLD WAR, particularly on the Western Front.

Born near Listowel in County Kerry on 24 January 1850, Kitchener passed out of the Royal Military Academy, Woolwich, in December 1870. He was then commissioned into the Royal Engineers, spending much of his early service in the Middle East and taking up a post in the Egyptian army in 1882. Apart from a period as Governor General of the Eastern Sudan (1886–8), he remained with the Egyptian army for most of the next sixteen years, being appointed its Adjutant General in 1888 and Sirdar, or commander-in-chief, in 1892. This phase of his military career reached its peak in the reconquest of the Sudan and the victory at Omdurman in 1898, achievements which established Kitchener as a national hero.

In December 1899, following British reverses at the hands of the BOERS, Kitchener was sent to South Africa as chief of staff to Lord Roberts (1832–1914), succeeding the latter as Commander-in-Chief in November 1900. His reply to Boer guerilla tactics was to set up lines of blockhouses from which drives by mounted troops were launched, and if, as in the Sudan, his success owed more to his organizational ability than battlefield flair, Kitchener's attrition policy eventually wore down Boer resistance. He provoked considerable outrage by introducing civilian concentration camps, but he adopted a conciliatory stance in the peace settlement of May 1902. From 1902 to 1909 Kitchener held the coveted post of Commander-in-Chief, India. He was soon involved in a prolonged dispute with the Viceroy, LORD CURZON, over the system of dual control whereby the military member of the Viceroy's Council exerted an influence which rivalled that of the Commander-in-Chief. Curzon's resignation in 1905 both reaffirmed the authority of the Commander-in-Chief and further enhanced Kitchener's personal prestige. Kitchener also began to reform the Indian army in several other respects, modernizing training, founding a staff college, improving mobilization machinery and instituting standardized corps and divisions to deal mainly with external threats rather than internal security problems. On his departure from India, Kitchener toured the Far East, Australasia, and the United States, advising the Australian and New Zealand governments on defense matters, before returning to Egypt, in 1911, as British Agent and Consul General. His benevolent yet autocratic rule there in the ensuing three years stifled political progress, but he developed Egypt's economic infrastructure and pushed through various social reforms protecting peasants against vested interest groups.

Home on leave at the outbreak of the First World War, a reluctant Kitchener was persuaded by the Prime Minister, HERBERT ASQUITH, to accept the post of Secretary of State for War. Despite his ignorance of domestic conditions, Kitchener, like DOUGLAS HAIG, was one of the few leading British soldiers or statesmen to foresee that the war would be long and costly. Aiming to build an army large enough for Britain to assume a major role at the decisive stage of the war, he raised nearly 2.5 million recruits by voluntary methods in under seventeen months, making it possible for Britain to place more than seventy divisions in the field during the conflict. In the absence of a government plan for the corresponding mobilization of manufacturing resources, Kitchener's achievements in expanding munitions output in the early months were also impressive. However, indiscriminate recruiting removed many skilled workers from the factories, and this, coupled with Kitchener's hostility to outside inference in War Office affairs, hindered the efforts of industry to respond quickly and fully to the new demands. Thus, while he undoubtedly laid the foundations for the spectacular production figures of later years, he was savagely attacked in May 1915 for the shell shortages afflicting the British Expeditionary Force in France. With the creation of the MINISTRY OF MUNITIONS under DAVID LLOYD GEORGE, the War Office, by the end of 1915, was shorn of most of its powers in this sphere save those of fixing the army's needs in munitions and overseeing their distribution, since control of the Royal Ord-

nance Factories and of research and development had been transferred to the new ministry.

As Secretary of State for War Kitchener did not pioneer alternative strategic policies, retaining his belief in the primacy of the Western Front. He also understood the realities of coalition warfare, stressing the importance of arms supplies to Russia. Though he generally supported the idea of operations in the Dardanelles, he displayed irresolution throughout the actual campaign on GALLIPOLI in 1915. Similarly, as voluntary recruiting steadily declined in 1915, he failed to give a clear lead on the CONSCRIPTION issue, making it harder for the government to prepare adequate machinery for the systematic use of available manpower. Inarticulate and uncomfortable in CABINET and political debate, Kitchener saw his influence in government circles wane further after military setbacks in France and the Dardanelles in the second half of 1915. In December that year Lieutenant General Sir William Robertson (1860–1933) took office as Chief of the Imperial General Staff on condition that the CIGS would henceforth be the principal source of advice to the Cabinet on military operations. Kitchener remained popular with the public but, by 1916, his authority was effectively limited to areas of War Office administration, supply, and recruiting. He drowned on 5 June 1916 when HMS *Hampshire*, taking him on a mission to Russia, struck a mine off the Orkneys and sank. Nevertheless, the mass army which Kitchener bequeathed to the nation contributed significantly to the ultimate Allied victory.

Peter Simkins

Bibliography
Arthur, George. *Life of Lord Kitchener*. 3 vols. 1920.
Cassar, George H. *Kitchener: Architect of Victory*. 1977.
Magnus, Philip. *Kitchener: Portrait of an Imperialist*. 1958.
Royle, Trevor. *The Kitchener Enigma*. 1985.
Simkins, Peter. *Kitchener's Army: The Raising of the New Armies, 1914–16*. 1988.

Labour Party

The Labour Party has experienced a rapid, if troubled political ascendancy in the twentieth century. In 1924, after only eighteen years of formal existence, Labour formed its first minority government, replacing the LIBERAL PARTY as the main rival to the CONSERVATIVES. Labour has formed governments in 1924, 1929–31, 1945–51, 1964–70, 1974–9, and 1997– . The third Labour government, which took power under CLEMENT ATTLEE after the SECOND WORLD WAR, is regarded as the single most important reforming ministry of the twentieth century, laying down the foundations of the post-war WELFARE STATE and the "mixed" economy. Despite these achievements, Labour has been plagued by internal tension throughout the century, which undermined its claim to power.

After the election of 1906 the LABOUR REPRESENTATION COMMITTEE formally adopted the name Labour Party, electing KEIR HARDIE as its parliamentary chairman. Initially, Labour proved an effective pressure group, but after 1907, the party seemed content to follow Liberal initiatives. By-elections between 1910 and 1914 do not show that Labour was gaining substantial ground against the Liberals among working-class voters. Trade unions were, however, affiliating in increasing numbers, lending the party financial security.

Though the party was divided over support for Britain's war effort in 1914, the FIRST WORLD WAR strengthened Labour's position. In May 1915 the party leader, ARTHUR HENDERSON joined the CABINET as President of the Board of Education, giving Labour its first taste of office. When DAVID LLOYD GEORGE became Prime Minister in 1916, he confirmed Labour's place in government by including Henderson in a smaller War Cabinet and giving two other MPs ministerial posts. Henderson left the government in 1917 and, out of office, turned his energies toward the framing of a new constitution for Labour in close consultation with the major unions and with SIDNEY WEBB. The new constitution—adopted formally in 1918—replaced a loose federal structure with a more centralized framework. The annual conference became the sole determinant of National Executive Committee (NEC) membership, a development which effectively shifted power to the unions. This was offset somewhat by the adoption of a socialist imperative in Clause IV of the party's objects, which committed the party to realise the "common ownership of the means of production." The socialist commitment was underlined by the adoption of Webb's *Labour and the New Social Order* (1918), a statement which laid down the future avenues of policy, including the establishment of a national minimum, the control of industry, educational reform, and the redistribution of wealth through taxation. Equality and collective economic action became pillars of Labour ideology until the 1990s.

The 1918 constitution was Labour's declaration of independence from the Liberal Party, ideologically and structurally. Fighting the 1918 "Coupon Election"—the first under complete manhood suffrage—without any electoral pacts, the party saw limited gains in the number of seats won, but real growth of almost 2 million votes. In the election of 1922 Labour increased its parliamentary strength markedly to 142 and improved its total poll to 4.2 million votes. The new party leader was RAMSAY MACDONALD, a charismatic figure intent upon broadening Labour's appeal to all classes. This search for respectability paid off in the election of December 1923, which left Labour with the second highest number of seats in the Commons. When the Conservatives were defeated over the question of TARIFF REFORM in January 1924, Labour formed its first minority government. Its aim was simply to cope, having neither the power in Parliament, nor a developed vision of a socialist program. There were modest successes in foreign policy and in HOUSING, but otherwise, Labour concentrated upon governing without undue humiliation. Though it lost the election of 1924, it had, by its experience of government, further discredited the Liberal Party as a viable political alternative.

The election of May 1929 saw Labour returned to power, again with a minority government. It won 288 seats and 8.3 million votes, 39.3 percent of the voting public. The major problem for the new government was its lack of an alternative economic policy in the face of deepening crisis in capitalism. Labour was as committed to financial orthodoxy as its Conservative rival, relying upon balanced budgets, the GOLD STANDARD, and laissez-faire. Within the party, there was much disquiet at the lack of socialist direction. The Depression of 1931 forced the question in a dramatic fashion. At the prompting of American banks and the all-party May committee of enquiry, MacDonald and his Chancellor of the Exchequer, PHILIP SNOWDEN, recommended a reduction in government expenditure in the summer of 1931, including a 10 percent decrease in the rate of UNEMPLOYMENT benefits. The unions and many of the Cabinet balked at supporting such proposals. Faced with irreconcilable divisions, MacDonald formed a National government with the Conservatives and Liberals in August 1931. Snowden, J.H. THOMAS, and a handful of lesser Labour politicians joined MacDonald as the National Labour contingent in the government. Criticized by both their former leaders, and facing a powerful cry for national unity in the midst of economic crisis, Labour suffered a catastrophic defeat in the election of October 1931, with its parliamentary strength reduced to 52 seats and its more prominent leaders losing their seats. Henderson returned to the leadership briefly, succeeded by GEORGE LANSBURY in 1932.

Ironically, this defeat did much to clarify Labour's identity. Following the 1931 debacle much closer cooperation between the party and the trade union movement was established, formalized in a reinvigorated National Council of Labour. There was also greater emphasis upon devising a distinctive socialist approach to the economy. Under the aegis of HUGH DALTON and HERBERT MORRISON, proponents of planning put together a credible program of economic action based upon centralized economic planning and NATIONALIZATION, an approach best expressed in the statements *For Socialism and Peace* (1934) and *Labour's Immediate Programme* (1937). Socialist planning became Labour's main weapon against unemployment. The 1930s also saw a major shift in Labour's international policy, which moved from PACIFIST internationalism to support for rearmament by the late 1930s. The 1935 election marked a slight improvement in Labour's fortunes: it increased its parliamentary ranks to 154. With the retirement of George Lansbury, Clement Attlee became party leader.

The SECOND WORLD WAR proved to be a turning-point for Labour. The party, which played a major role in the downfall of NEVILLE CHAMBERLAIN in May 1940, joined the coalition of WINSTON CHURCHILL. Despite its relatively small numbers in the Commons, Labour was given a disproportionate number of places in the government. Attlee, Arthur Greenwood (1880–1954), Morrison, and the trade unionist ERNEST BEVIN were Cabinet members for all or part of the war.

War also encouraged a movement of the Left in public opinion. By 1943, opinion polls were pointing towards a substantial Labour lead over the Conservatives. The election of 26 July 1945 was, until 1997, the zenith of Labour's electoral fortunes. It captured 393 seats, a majority of 146 over all other parties, on a total poll of 11.9 million votes.

The 1945–50 Labour government was certainly one of the strongest of the century, including Attlee as Prime Minister, Bevin at the Foreign Office, Morrison as Lord President, STAFFORD CRIPPS at the Board of Trade, Dalton as Chancellor of the Exchequer, and ANEURIN BEVAN at the Ministry of Health. The problems facing the new government were enormous, both at home and abroad. Almost immediately after the war, for example, it had to negotiate a large American loan to sustain Britain's economy. Despite these constraints, Attlee and his ministers enjoyed much initial success, particularly in domestic policy. Between 1945 and 1948 the foundations of the welfare state and the mixed economy were laid. The National Insurance, National Assistance, and NATIONAL HEALTH SERVICE (NHS) Acts were passed in 1946, the first two realizing many of the aims of the BEVERIDGE Report, the last promising free and universal health care. In addition a substantial program of nationalization was enacted: the Bank of England (1946), COAL (1946), civil aviation (1946), cable and wireless (1946), inland transport (1948), and gas (1948), iron and STEEL (1949). By the end of the decade fully 20 percent of the economy was in the public sector. Full employment was also maintained throughout the life of the government.

The government stumbled in 1947 into a series of economic crises, beginning with a coal shortage which contributed to export and currency crises just at the time sterling was scheduled to become convertible according to the terms of American loan of 1946. The economic crises undermined government confidence and deepened domestic austerity. On the international front, Bevin's effort to involve the United States in the defense of Western European democracy and British strategic interests bore fruit with the establishment of the North Atlantic Treaty Organization in 1949. Britain's atomic relationship with America was less successful, prompting the Labour government to proceed on its own with the manufacture of a British bomb at great cost. Within the Empire, significant strides were made towards DECOLONIZATION, beginning with the concession of independence to India in August 1947. By the end of the decade Pakistan (1947), Sri Lanka (1948), and Burma (1948) had also become independent.

Despite these achievements, in February 1950 Labour was returned with a majority of only 6 seats in the general election. By this time Attlee, Cripps, and Bevin were all in failing health. The government was also sapped by internal divisions within the leadership and the Parliamentary Labour Party. The most serious split was between the new Chancellor of the Exchequer, HUGH GAITSKELL, and Bevan over budget proposals to impose charges in the NHS, in part to cover rising defense expenditure as a result of the Korean War. In January 1951 Bevan, HAROLD WILSON, and John Freeman resigned over this issue. In the October election Labour polled the highest total vote in political history (13.9 million votes), but the Tories were returned with a majority of 16 seats.

The party's spell in opposition was to last thirteen years. In the 1950s Labour was plagued by further divisions over strategy, foreign policy, ideology, and leadership. The first splits emerged in the Parliamentary Labour Party, where the "Bevanite" wing became increasingly fractious, especially over foreign policy issues. Bevanism gained considerable influence on the National Executive Committee and in the constituencies, while at the same time the right wing of the party was beginning to coalesce around the parliamentary leadership of Attlee, Gaitskell, and Morrison, and around such new thinkers as ANTHONY CROSLAND. Party disunity did not help Labour's electoral fortunes. In May 1955 an election was called, at which Labour's parliamentary strength fell from 295 to 277. After Attlee retired in December 1955, Gaitskell scored an easy victory over Bevan and Morrison to become leader.

Despite a rapprochement between Gaitskell and Bevan, lack of political success persisted into the late 1950s. The question of nuclear weapons opened up further divisions between a pronuclear leadership and a large activist movement within the party centred on the CAMPAIGN FOR NUCLEAR DISARMAMENT. There was also a growing breach between the Left and Right over the future of socialist planning and nationalization in an increasingly affluent society. The 1959 election was another blow: the party lost further ground to the Conservatives, generating discussion about decline in Labour support not only among middle-class supporters, but also in its traditional working-class base. Desperate to modernize the party's image and reinvigorate its popular appeal, Gaitskell attempted to eliminate the commitment to public ownership from the constitution, an initiative that was defeated at the 1959 party conference. A year later, the leader was defeated again, this time over nuclear weapons, when the conference endorsed unilateral disarmament. By 1961 Gaitskell was, however, able to secure the reversal of the unilateralist decision at the party conference.

Success for Labour came only as the British economy faltered in the early 1960s. In January 1963 Gaitskell died suddenly of a rare viral infection and was succeeded as leader by Harold Wilson. The election of October 1964 gave Labour a slim majority of 4 seats over the Conservatives and the Liberals. The Labour Cabinet of 1964 started out with determination, abolishing prescription charges in the National Health Service, moving towards industrial reform with the National Board for Prices and Incomes, and shoring up Britain's economic health with a five-year plan committed to 25 percent growth in the GNP by the end of the decade. Wilson's call for an election for March 1966 resulted in a resounding personal triumph. Labour won 363 seats with 48.7 percent of the vote.

Despite its substantial parliamentary majority, the 1966–70 government faced disunity and declining popularity, largely as a result of economic problems. Wilson's ministry dithered over the balance of payments problems, abandoning any pretense of long-term planning. Confronted with inflationary wage pressures and growing union militancy, it failed to find a credible industrial policy, yielding instead to union demands. In the foreign sphere, it was unable to prevent the accession to power of a racist white-minority government in Rhodesia in 1966 and muted its criticism of American policy in Viet Nam. Yet, Britain became a more liberal society through the reforms of Home Secretary, ROY JENKINS such as the decriminalization of ABORTION and HOMOSEXUALITY; education and the arts were vastly expanded with the advent of new universities and the expansion of comprehensive schools; and housing was increased significantly. By 1969–70 the government was regaining popularity. With favorable opinion polls, Wilson called an election in June 1970, but the Conservatives were elected with a 30 seat majority.

During the period of opposition between 1970 and 1974 there was some rebuilding of links within the party, such as the establishment of the TUC-Labour Party Liaison Committee and its promised "social contract" between any future Labour government and the unions. Other issues were more difficult. Britain's entry into the EUROPEAN COMMUNITY proved divisive: the NEC, the Left, and the unions opposed entry, while a significant proportion of the parliamentary party, mostly center and right wingers, were in favor. Splits between Left and Right hardened over questions of party structure. Within the party there was a burgeoning movement for constituency control over the election manifesto, the election of the leader, and the re-selection of local

MPs, organized by the Campaign for Labour Party Democracy.

The two elections of 1974 returned Labour to power, first with a minority government, then, in October, with a small majority. The impression was again one of division. The Cabinet was generally drawn from the Right, while the party outside Westminster was dominated by the Left. Even within the parliamentary party, there were organized factions, the Tribune group of the Left and the Manifesto group of the Right, which were divided over foreign and domestic issues. In March 1976 Wilson resigned unexpectedly and was succeeded by JAMES CALLAGHAN. Through 1976 and 1977 the party was further weakened in power. The $3 billion International Monetary Fund loan of 1976 raised the specter of 1931 and provoked much opposition within the party. By 1977 the party had declined in parliamentary strength and was forced to adopt the expedient of a more formal Lib-Lab pact, based on a Liberal-Labour Consultative Committee. The "winter of discontent", characterized by wide-ranging public sector strikes, brought the government down in March 1979. Labour lost the May 1979 election to the Conservatives under MARGARET THATCHER.

In opposition Labour's long-simmering tensions boiled over. TONY BENN became the unofficial leader of the Left within the party, which in October 1979 succeeded in vesting control of the manifesto with the National Executive Committee and in making re-selection of sitting MPs mandatory. The following year the annual conference overturned the decision on the manifesto, but decided that the election for the leadership would be made the responsibility of the party conference, not simply the Parliamentary Party, a shift which favored the Left. Callaghan resigned as leader following the conference and was succeeded by the veteran left winger MICHAEL FOOT. In January 1981 a special conference set out the details of a new "electoral college" to choose the party leader. The unions would get 40 percent of the vote, the constituencies and Parliamentary Party 30 percent each. This was the last straw for some right-wing MPs, provoking the most serious split in the party since 1931. A group of prominent right wingers broke from Labour and, later in the year, established the SOCIAL DEMOCRATIC PARTY. In June 1983 Labour fought a disastrous general election, gaining only 28 percent of the vote with 209 MPs.

Between 1979 and 1992 Labour lost four straight elections. This forced the party to respond to the new political landscape created by Thatcherite reforms and Conservative electoral success. This engagement resulted in the most profound revision of the party's outlook and identity since 1918.

After the 1983 election, Foot was replaced by NEIL KINNOCK. Under Kinnock's leadership between 1983 and 1992, Labour slowly, and often painfully healed many of its wounds. Relations with the unions improved, despite the divisiveness of the miners strike of 1984–5. Kinnock also succeeded in reducing the power of the Left within the party, most notably in a showdown with the far left Militant Tendency faction. But most striking was the revision of policy in the late 1980s and early 1990s. This process was driven in part by electoral frustration. In 1987 Labour lost a third campaign to Margaret Thatcher and her Conservative party, while making back some of the lost ground of four years before. After the election Kinnock launched a policy review which lasted until 1991. The policy review resulted in a major shift in Labour policy. The most obvious change was the party's acceptance of the centrality of the market as the foundation of economic life. Labour espoused low inflation and low taxation, preaching economic restraint rather than government activity. From equality of outcome, Labour turned to equality of opportunity, stressing individual rather than communal endeavor and responsibility. In its emphasis upon the market and the individual, the policy review reflected the influence of the rightward turn in British politics since 1979. Changes in policy for Labour in the 1980s and 1990s were also accompanied by a shift in authority within the party. The power of the trade unions waned, as did that of the Left-dominated National Executive Committee and the annual conference. After 1987 more authority was centralized with the leader and his advisers, marking the ascendancy of the Right. This change facilitated what was increasingly known as the "modernization" of the Labour Party in the 1990s.

Modernization was not immediately successful with voters. Despite an effective campaign, Kinnock lost the April 1992 election to JOHN MAJOR. He resigned immediately afterward, and the leadership was assumed by John Smith (1938–94). Smith, more cautious about modernization, slowed the pace of party revision. Nonetheless, during his tenure there was a significant constitutional reform in 1993, "one member, one vote," which reduced the power of the trade union bloc vote within the party. Smith also stressed the party's new commitment to economic prudence. In 1994 Smith died of a heart attack. He was succeeded by TONY BLAIR. Though much of the actual work of changing the Labour party had already been set in place, Blair and his allies, including Gordon Brown (1951-)and Peter Mandelson (1953-), loudly proclaimed their transformation of Labour to "New Labour" through the project of modernization.

The most spectacular example of this came in 1995 with the abandonment of Clause IV, the long-standing commitment to public ownership. Blair also distanced himself and the party from the trade unions and other traditional foci of democratic socialism in Britain, courting instead disaffected Conservatives and voters who had prospered under Thatcherite reforms with talk of a "third way," eschewing reference to either social democracy or democratic socialism. A tough stand on law and order and a commitment to respect existing public spending limits outflanked the Conservatives on the right. After leading in the polls for several years, the party won a stunning victory in the May 1997 election, gaining a 179 seat majority, the largest in the party's history, and 44.4% of the popular vote.

Between 1997 and 2002 the Blair government's record was uneven. Unlike its Labour predecessors, it enjoyed economic stability. It also showed some constitutional innovation by setting up national assemblies in Scotland and Wales. In 2000 the government set in motion reforms of the health and welfare system with a new spending plan. It was much less successful in resolving the critical question in current British politics, European integration. Nor did power help clarify the ambiguities of Labour's own identity and direction after the changes of the 1980s and 1990s. With the demise of the Liberals in the 1920s, Labour became the progressive alternative in British politics. In the 1940s and 1950s it etched out a distinctive democratic socialist path. As a new century began, Labour was poised uncertainly between taking up this inheritance and claiming the mantle of Thatcherite Conservatism.

Stephen Brooke

Bibliography

Fielding, Steven, Peter Thompson, and Nick Tiratsoo. *"England Arise": The Labour Party and Popular Politics in 1940s Britain*. 1995.

McKibbin, Ross. *The Evolution of the Labour Party 1910–1924*. 1974.

Morgan, Kenneth O. *Labour People: Leaders and Lieutenants*. 1987.

Pelling, Henry. *A Short History of the Labour Party*. 10th ed. 1993.

Tanner, Duncan. *Political Change and the Labour Party 1900–1918*. 1990.

——, Pat Thane, and Nick Tiratsoo, eds. *Labour's First Century*. 2000.

Thorne, Andrew. *A History of the British Labour Party*. 2nd ed. 2001.

Labour Representation Committee (1900–1906)

Established in London in February 1900 by conference of trade unions, cooperative societies, and socialist groups, the Labour Representation Committee resolved to work for a distinct labor group in Parliament with its own whips and policy, but ready to cooperate with any other party to promote legislation in the direct interests of labor. It was thus a triumph for the principle of independent labor representation in Parliament.

For some years endorsement of this principle had been urged on the TRADE UNION CONGRESS (TUC) by socialists, notably those in the INDEPENDENT LABOUR PARTY (ILP). In general the trade union leaders were LIBERAL in their political sympathies, and often anti-socialist, but by 1899 there was widespread concern among trade unionists about the threat to their legal rights. Thus at the 1899 Congress a resolution was passed that paved the way for the conference at which the LRC was born; representatives of about one quarter of the total trade union membership attended. Of those which affiliated to the LRC most were of the "New Unionism" variety; many of the older craft unions, and the large mining, engineering, and cotton workers' unions, remained aloof.

The LRC was formed as an exercise in policial pragmatism. Its stated aims were designed not to alienate "Lib-Lab" trade union opinion. This implied no commitment to socialism; the Marxist Social Democratic Federation (SDF) failed to get its "class-war" message endorsed at the conference. The role of the ILP, by contrast, has been viewed as decisive by labor historians. The ILP leader, KEIR HARDIE, dominated the founding conference and was the main parliamentary spokesman after the general election of 1900; Hardie was returned with one other LRC candidate. RAMSAY MACDONALD, LRC secretary and ILPer, envisaged the LRC as a progressive development from radical liberalism which bolstered the cause of social reconstruction, not as a mere pressure group.

In the LRC's short history before it was renamed the LABOUR PARTY in 1906, two developments were of particular historic significance. The first was the TAFF VALE JUDGMENT of 1901, which rendered trade unions financially liable for damages caused through strike action, a decision that resulted in waves of union affiliations to the LRC. By 1905 the MINERS' FEDERATION was the only significant body still outside it. In 1903 MacDonald entered into talks with the Liberal Chief Whip Herbert Gladstone about an electoral arrangement between the parties. This produced a "pact" that operated with remarkable success in the general election of 1906: in the Liberal landslide, 29 LRC candidates were returned.

The LRC has to be placed in the context of the debate on the emergence of class as the main determinant of political allegiance in British politics. It was an important manifestation of this development, although those historians who caution against the notion of an inevitable eclipse of the Liberals by Labour as the progressive class-based party would stress that its significance was limited.

Graham Walker

Bibliography

Bealey, Frank, and Henry Pelling. *Labour and Politics 1900–1906: A History of the Labour Representation Committee.* 1958.

Poirier, Philip P. *The Advent of the Labour Party.* 1958.

Labour Revisionism

Labour revisionism was an ideological tendency within the LABOUR PARTY which prevailed during the 1950s and early 1960s. Its principal aim was to reformulate socialist principles and to revise Labour policies through a new analysis of the changed social and economic conditions of post-1945 British society. First outlined in *New Fabian Essays* (1952), Labour revisionism was most thoroughly and coherently expressed in ANTHONY CROSLAND's major work, *The Future of Socialism* (1956). The period from 1956 onwards, following HUGH GAITSKELL's accession to the party leadership, witnessed its increasing prominence as a major ideological influence within the Labour Party. During those years revisionist ideas—particularly on public ownership and economic strategy—were widely propagated and incorporated into official party policy statements such as *Industry and Society* (1957).

Labour revisionism can be examined most clearly in the ideas and writings of two distinct but connected groups—first, the parliamentary friends and supporters of Hugh Gaitskell (who included Crosland, Douglas Jay and ROY JENKINS) and second, the organization Socialist Union and its related periodical *Socialist Commentary*. Revisionism conspicuously became a "Gaitskellite" position from 1956 to 1963, since the party leader was strongly committed to revisionist ideas. It was, however, Crosland rather than Gaitskell who provided the main intellectual thrust behind this new political movement.

The emergence of Labour revisionism in the early 1950s was an intellectual response to the completion of the ATTLEE-led Labour government's program in 1951 and to the party's subsequent election defeat. The body of ideas that gradually took shape during the 1950s involved two major deviations from accepted Labour orthodoxies. First, revisionism repudiated the traditional view that socialism could be adequately defined as, or at least identified with, the public ownership of the means of production. It thereby questioned the established Labour commitment to extensive public ownership as a precondition for achieving all major socialist objectives. Second, revisionism presented a distinctive ethical restatement of socialism—in terms of such values as personal liberty, social welfare, and equality. Particular emphasis was placed on the pursuit of equality which, revisionists argued, would involve a variety of fiscal and social policy measures—including redistributive taxation, educational reform, and expanded social services (to be financed through economic growth). Public ownership and NATIONALIZATION were to be regarded merely as useful means for promoting socialist ends. Moreover, revisionists challenged traditional Labour opinion by insisting that such ends could be attained within the framework of a market-oriented mixed economy.

The intellectual justification for this demotion of public ownership was provided by Crosland's analysis, refined in *The Future of Socialism*, of changes within post-1945 capitalism. Crosland maintained that during that period capitalism had been transformed as a result of a threefold transfer of economic power—towards the State, organized labor, and salaried managers in private industry. In the post-capitalist society that had emerged from this process the public ownership had become, in Crosland's view, a matter of declining importance.

Revisionists sharpened differences within the party over its identity, direction, and purpose. Ultimately, they even appeared to threaten the foundations of party unity—most perilously during Gaitskell's ill-fated attempt to amend Clause IV of the party constitution in 1959–60. Its effect was to provoke a confrontation with both the fundamentalists of the Party's Left and the traditionalists of its Right and Center. The damaging consequences of this were contained only by a subtle compromise that involved, from the early 1960s, a partial reinstatement of public ownership in party policy and rhetoric.

By the time of Gaitskell's death in January 1963 revisionist positions—a more instrumental view of public ownership, support for egalitarian fiscal and social policies, acceptance of the mixed economy—were firmly entrenched. But Labour revisionism continued to be embraced by a relatively small group of Gaitskellite MPs and trade union leaders and London-based party intellectuals. The movement never really captured the hearts and minds of the bulk of Labour activists.

HAROLD WILSON's succession to the leadership in 1963 combined traditional socialist rhetoric with pragmatic policy-making. Yet in reality it was an unsatisfactory settlement, concealing deep differences over the nature and purpose of public ownership and over the future direction of democratic socialism—differences which Labour revisionism had never sought to evade.

Tudor Jones

Bibliography
Bogdanor, Vernon. "The Labour Party in Opposition, 1951–1964" in Vernon Bogdanor and Robert Skidelsky, eds. *The Age of Affluence*. 1970.
Crosland, C.A.R. *The Future of Socialism*. rev. ed. 1964.
Crossman, R.H.S. ed. *New Fabian Essays*. 1952.
Haseler, Stephen. *The Gaitskellites*. 1969.
Jay, Douglas. *Socialism in the New Society*. 1962.

Lang, Cosmo Gordon (1864–1945)

Cosmo Gordon Lang was a major leader of the CHURCH OF ENGLAND throughout the first part of the twentieth century, beginning with his appointment as Bishop of Stepney in 1901. He was promoted successively to the archbishoprics of York in 1908 and of Canterbury in 1928, remaining as Primate until his retirement in 1942. He died in 1945.

Lang played an important role both within the Church of England and outside. He helped develop the Church of England's Mens Society (from 1901) and was active in the National Mission of Repentance and Hope during the First World War. He also was involved in forming a Commission on Church and State (1913) which led to the creation of a Church Assembly. In 1929 he had a brief role in the ill-fated revision of the *Book of Common Prayer*.

Within the Anglican Communion he was involved in the Lambeth Conference of 1920, and chaired its successor in 1930. He also made an important contribution to ecumenical relations, for example in the 1920 Lambeth Conference's Appeal to all Christian People. This led to improved relations with the Orthodox and Swedish Lutheran Churches, and, in 1932, to intercommunion with the Old Catholics.

He also played a significant, if not central, part in affairs of state. He entered the HOUSE OF LORDS in 1909, contributing to debates surrounding the constitutional crisis of 1911. He remained a member until his death, having been made a peer as Baron Lang of Lambeth in 1942. Outside Parliament he served as a member of the Royal Commission on DIVORCE and Matrimonial Causes (1909) and the Joint Committee upon the Indian Constitution (1933).

He also achieved prominence through his extensive relations with the royal family, including, most notably, the period of the abdication crisis. As Archbishop of Canterbury at the time of GEORGE V's death, he became embroiled in the controversy surrounding EDWARD VIII's intention to marry an American divorcee. Given the Church's MARRIAGE laws, Lang saw grave difficulties in participating in the coronation planned for 1937. When the crisis came to a head in November–December 1936, Edward abdicated, but mainly because of political rather than ecclesiastical pressures.

Lang's career represented a shift towards recruitment from professional rather than aristocratic groups (his father having been a senior clergyman in the Church of Scotland and Principal of Aberdeen University). But he followed the traditional leadership path of an Oxbridge education, attending Balliol College, OXFORD, and becoming a Fellow of All Souls College.

His lasting significance is questionable. He was immensely industrious, an exceptional administrator, and was well-connected to leading politicians and aristocrats. But his accomplishments as Archbishop of Canterbury were modest.

George Moyser

Bibliography
Lockhart, J.G. *Cosmo Gordon Lang*. 1949.

Lansbury, George (1859–1940)

Born on 22 February 1859, George Lansbury became active in LIBERAL politics in East London during the mid-1880s and converted to socialism by 1892. A prominent figure in East End politics thereafter, he finally entered Parliament in December 1910, as Labour Member for Bow and Bromley, but relinquished his seat in 1912 to force a by-election over WOMEN'S SUFFRAGE, which he lost. The previous year, however, he had helped to found and had become principal editor of the *Daily Herald*, which developed into the liveliest newspaper the British Left possessed, so that, even outside Parliament, he retained a significant voice. He opposed the FIRST WORLD WAR on grounds of PACIFISM, and by 1918 his popularity among Labour supporters was unrivalled. Returned to Parliament in 1922, again for Bow and Bromley, he held the seat until he died. In 1924 he refused a minor position in the first Labour government but in 1929 accepted appointment as First Commissioner of Works. He alone of RAMSAY MACDONALD's CABINET survived the debacle of 1931, becoming leader of the much reduced parliamentary party. He resigned this position in 1935 and thereafter devoted himself to the peace movement, meeting with Hitler, Mussolini, Roosevelt, and Leon Blum in a vain attempt to avert the coming war. He died on 7 May 1940.

Lansbury's achievements were many. Early on, as a socialist member of the Poplar Board of Guardians, he led the campaign to humanize treatment of indigents under the old Poor Law. He helped establish the Laindon and Hollesley Bay farm colonies where Poplar's unemployed might be sent to work. In 1921, as Poplar's mayor, he led the borough council in passive resistance to taxes called "precepts", payable to the London County Council, until poor rates were equalized. Lansbury maintained that the current policy unfairly penalized boroughs, like his own, where

UNEMPLOYMENT was high. The government imprisoned Poplar's councillors for contempt, Lansbury among them, but they all held firm. Eventually Prime Minister LLOYD GEORGE relented. The rates were equalized; the councillors were freed, although they refused to purge their contempt.

This may have been Lansbury's greatest triumph. He suffered two grave defeats during his lifetime. The first occurred in 1912 when he resigned his parliamentary seat to compel a by-election on the issue of women's suffrage. He wanted the LABOUR PARTY to refuse to support ASQUITH's LIBERAL government until it had enfranchised women, even if this brought the CONSERVATIVES to power. Lansbury sought to force the hands of the Labour hierarchy by this strategy, but KEIR HARDIE was the only party leader who agreed. Other "rebels", some of whom were associated with the *Daily Herald* also rallied to the cause, as did the FEMINIST movement, including, most prominently, the PANKHURSTS.

Lansbury was a great resigner. He never hesitated to face the political wilderness, and he was too much of an individualist to acquiesce in policies with which he disagreed. He quit the Liberals in 1892 and the Marxist Socialist Democratic Party early in the twentieth century. He quit the Labour Party in 1912, although rejoining shortly after the First World War. In 1935 he resigned the leadership of the Labour Party when it would not support his pacifist program in a world menaced by Fascism. This resignation represents his greatest political defeat.

He had inherited the leadership almost by default. After MacDonald's apostasy in 1931, there were no other senior Labour figures left. Lansbury led the 46 Labour MPs with verve and skill, but everything was overshadowed by the terrible denouement. Always opposed to war, he had become an out-and-out pacifist during the First World War. Repelled by crass materialism, he had returned, early in the century, to Christianity (which he had briefly abandoned during his Marxist phase). Now as leader of the Labour Party and also as a Christian socialist, he wanted a world conference to appease the "have not" powers, especially Germany. At the conference Britain and other wealthy nations would divest themselves of colonies and other material advantages and disarm to the level permitted Germany by the Versailles settlement. In fact, Lansbury believed that only if Britain disarmed completely and unilaterally would it be possible to avert another war.

This plan combined Labour's traditional anti-imperialist, internationalist, and pacifist aims and rhetoric, but, after 1933, unilateral renunciation of any British advantage over Germany seemed foolish to most people, including most of the Labour Party. For two years the Party Leader held views unacceptable to the vast majority of party members and supporters. In 1935 ERNEST BEVIN, leader of the Transport and General Workers' Union, made a brutal and somewhat unfair speech at the Party Conference attacking Lansbury. Although Bevin was nearly shouted down for his unkindness, he secured a majority of the votes. Lansbury resigned as Leader in order to campaign unequivocally for the world conference and pacifism. At the age of seventy six, he now accepted the presidency of the PEACE PLEDGE UNION. He had audiences with all the major world leaders except Stalin, spending his energy in a vain effort to head off the conflagration which he could see coming. He welcomed the MUNICH settlement and CHAMBERLAIN's own last-ditch efforts to save Britain from war with Germany.

Lansbury was a talented politician, speaker, and organizer. What made him remarkable was the stubbornness with which he clung to his principles. This explains why he quit so many organizations and positions and why he must have been a difficult colleague, but paradoxically it also helps explain why he became one of the best-loved and most-respected figures in the labor movement.

Lansbury's legacy has been the adamantine insistence among an element within the Labour Party that Britain must stand for moral principle, must set the world a moral example. Concretely this has meant demanding the total abolition of capitalism and unilateral disarmament, policies which Labour's leaders have usually thought utopian or worse.

Jonathan Schneer

Bibliography

Holman, Bob. *Good Old George: the Life of George Lansbury.* 1990.

Postgate, Raymond. *The Life of George Lansbury.* 1951.

Schneer, Jonathan. *George Lansbury.* 1990.

Larkin, Philip Arthur (1922–1985)

Philip Larkin, one of the best-loved poets of his generation, is known for his wryly ironic verse, which by-passes modernist literary experimentation and returns to more traditional poetic structure, modes of scansion, and rhyme. Writing about England, solitude, and mortality in a way that mixes traditional forms with colloquial language, Larkin's work is lucid, clear, and accessible to a wide range of readers, even as its apparent simplicity—and the ordinary and even meager life it pictures—is matched with complex art and emotional intensity. His poetic subjects range from celebrations of provincial English mores to expressions of impatience with middle-class domesticity. At times the poetry embraces solitude to the point of bitter reclusiveness, thereby conveying the tones of a nineteenth-century moralist who has lived on alone in the increasingly chaotic twentieth century. The poignant expression of this sense of alienation, mixed with yearning for alternatives, has won him his wide audience.

Born in Coventry on 9 August 1922, Larkin attended Henry VIII Grammar School and went up to OXFORD in 1940 to attend St. John's College. There he became acquainted with fellow writers and jazz enthusiasts Kingsley Amis and Bruce Montgomery (writer of detective novels under the name of Edmund Crispin). While Larkin was at Oxford, some of his verse was chosen to be included in the anthology *Poetry from Oxford in Wartime* (1944). In 1943 he was awarded a first class honors in English Language and Literature, and later the same year he took up the post of librarian at a small library in Wellington, Shropshire. He published two novels in succession, *Jill* (1946), and *A Girl in Winter* (1947). His failed attempt to write a third novel led eventually to his turning exclusively to POETRY, though he claimed never to have relinquished his disappointment at abandoning the dream of writing novels full-time. Larkin's first book of poems *The North Ship* (1945) was heavily influenced by WILLIAM BUTLER YEATS. He had little luck in publishing until *The Less Deceived* (1955), the volume of poetry that established his reputation.

Larkin's career as a librarian continued through moves to the University College of Leicester, then to Queen's University, Belfast, and finally to the University of Hull in 1955, where he remained until his death in 1985. During his tenure the university underwent a rapid expansion, and Larkin personally oversaw the construction of the new Brynmor Jones Library.

Larkin's volume of poetry *The Whitsun Weddings* (1964) garnered him the Queen's Gold Medal for Poetry and was followed a decade later by *High Windows* (1974). During 1970–1 Larkin was a Visiting Fellow at All Souls College, Oxford, in connection with which he edited *The Oxford Book of Twentieth-Century English Verse* (1973).

Larkin expressed his keen interest in jazz by writing record reviews for the *Daily Telegraph*, subsequently collected under the title *All What Jazz* (1970; revised edition 1985). The expressiveness of jazz provided a counterpoint to the tight control and reserve of his poetry, although his reviews also contain a sense of alienated disappointment: he loathed the development of jazz after the 1930s and 1940s, and he supplements his contempt for Pablo Picasso and Ezra Pound with denunciations of Charlie Parker in his introduction to the volume.

Larkin vaunted himself as a self-proclaimed philistine, adopting the pose of the common man who does not know art but knows what he likes. At the same time his literary judgments are sophisticated as well as shrewd. Though he seldom wrote book reviews, their acute insights and vivid style reveal him to be a formidable critic. Several of these essays were issued in the volume *Required Writing: Miscellaneous Pieces 1955–1982* (1983).

Larkin's attempt to align his art with common persons and experiences is not as straightforward as it appears to be. Dissociating himself from modernism—for example, he claimed to have disowned Yeats's influence in favor of Thomas Hardy's—Larkin nevertheless courted for himself the elite authority he criticized in the modernist masters. And in taking sides with ordinary, even mediocre, democratic life, he seemed to become an apologist (especially in *High Windows*) for anti-democratic political conservatism and reaction.

Janice Rossen

Bibliography

Bloomfield, Barry Cambray. *Philip Larkin: A Bibliography, 1933–1976.* 1979.

Booth, James. *Philip Larkin: Writer.* 1992.

Motion, Andrew. *Philip Larkin: A Writer's Life.* 1993.

Rossen, Janice. *Philip Larkin: His Life's Work.* 1989.

Thwaite, Anthony, ed. *Selected Letters of Philip Larkin, 1940–1985.* 1993.

Whalen, Terry. *Philip Larkin and English Poetry.* 1986.

Laski, Harold Joseph (1893–1950)

During his life Harold Laski was a major influence as a theorist and political activist in socialist and progressive circles both in Britain and the outside world. He was elected to the Constituency Section of the National Executive Committee of the LABOUR PARTY (NEC) every year from 1937 to 1949—an unprecedented achievement for someone who was never an MP. He was almost equally well-known in the United States, and he secured a substantial following in India as a prominent supporter of INDIAN NATIONALISM. However, he was always a controversial figure and was discredited in the West during the Cold War era.

His earliest major writings—*Studies in the Problem of Sovereignty* (1917) and *Authority in the Modern State* (1919)—were completed during a six year period as a lecturer in North America (he was at Harvard Law School from 1916–20) and quickly established his reputation as a major pluralist critic of the sovereign state. However, his scholarly tone masked a burning political commitment, and Laski soon upset the Boston elite by supporting the 1919 police strike. This effectively ended his academic career in the United States, and he returned to Britain as a lecturer at the LONDON SCHOOL OF ECONOMICS (subsequently promoted to a professorship at the age of thirty-three), where he was to remain as an inspiring teacher for generations of political science students.

During the early 1920s his pluralist belief in decentralized participation was tempered by a growing conviction that firm state action was necessary to bring about radical change, and he became active in the Labour Party and FABIAN SOCIETY. He tried to attain a synthesis between the pluralist and Fabian outlooks in *A Grammar of Politics* (1925)—an encyclopedic work, which outlined a socialist approach to political theory, constitutional practice, economic organization, and national sovereignty. However, in the latter part of the decade he began to fear that socialism would not be established by peaceful means, a feeling reinforced by the failure of the Labour government of 1929–31 to deal with the economic crisis. The establishment of a Conservative-dominated National government by RAMSAY MACDONALD, followed by the rise of Fascism in Europe, led Laski to despair about the continuation of democratic government in capitalist societies. *Democracy in Crisis* (1933) was a passionate critique of the contemporary situation that urged political leaders to make progressive reforms to save constitutional government. However, the triumph of Hitler in Germany seemed to undermine any remaining optimism that he had felt about the resilience of parliamentary democracy. He now turned to a personal form of Marxism, which he used analytically in *The State in Theory and Practice* (1935) and historically in *The Rise of European Liberalism* (1936). However, he retained a deep commitment to liberal values and hated the thought of violence. His position was therefore never Marxist in any conventional sense: his real message was that it was imperative for capitalism to accept socialist reform so that liberal civilization could be preserved. *Parliamentary Government in England* (1938) epitomized these contradictions, for the book simultaneously revered constitutional democracy and argued that it was impossible to implement in practice in an unequal society.

Because he was searching for a viable theoretical stance that would combine potentially incompatible goals, his political activity was often also tortuous. His pessimism about the West now led him to perceive virtues in Stalinist Russia, and in 1936 he became one of the founders of the LEFT BOOK CLUB, which often promoted pro-Soviet propaganda in an attempt to bring about a POPULAR FRONT against Fascism. However, his continuing commitment to liberalism meant that he could never fully accept any dictatorship. His real enthusiasm in this period was therefore for the New Deal, and he hoped that Roosevelt's reinvigoration of capitalist democracy would triumph and be emulated in Europe.

In September 1939 he had no doubt that the war against Nazi Germany was justified and, until Hitler's attack on the Soviet Union in June 1941, he played a major role in countering Communist propaganda within the Labour Party. But he remained convinced that both Fascism and war stemmed from capitalism, and that it was vital to use the emergency situation to begin the process of a "revolution by consent." Now at the height of his influence with the Labour rank-and-file, he constantly urged the leaders of his own party and the American administration to institute fundamental domestic reform and to maintain unity with the Soviet Union. Such arguments alienated the political establishment on both sides of the Atlantic, including CLEMENT ATTLEE, the Labour Leader.

In June 1945, as chairman of the Labour Party NEC, Laski publicly announced that Attlee should not be bound by any agreements made by CHURCHILL at Potsdam, and should attend the conference only as an "observer." Attlee immediately rejected this demand, and Laski served as the *bete-noire* for the Conservatives throughout the election campaign. Although he continued to be prominent after the Labour victory, his position was now substantially weakened, and his isolation was reinforced when he lost a notorious libel case at the end of 1946. In this case his writings were used to sustain a claim that he had advocated violent revolution—a bitter blow for a man whose life's work had been to bring about peaceful change. In his last years he was thus a rather tragic figure whose influence had waned. He became increasingly disillusioned with both the United States and the Soviet Union, while condemning the Labour Party for its pro-American stance and for its anti-Zionist policy.

Convinced that the problems of his time were too urgent for leisurely academic reflection, Laski wrote too much, over-estimated his influence, and sometimes failed to distinguish between analysis and polemic. But he was a serious thinker and a charismatic personality whose views have been distorted because he refused to accept Cold War orthodoxies. His contribution to socialist thought and practice deserves far greater recognition than it has received in recent years.

Michael Newman

Bibliography

Deane, Herbert A. *The Political Ideas of Harold J. Laski.* 1955.

Kramnick, Isaac, and Barry Sheerman. *Harold Laski: A Life on the Left.* 1993.

Martin, Kingsley. *Harold Laski (1893–1950): A Biographical Memoir.* 1953.

Newman, Michael. *Harold Laski: A Political Biography.*
1993.
Zylstra, Bernard. *From Pluralism to Collectivism: The Development of Harold Laski's Political Thought.* 1968.

Lawrence, D(avid) H(erbert) (1885–1930)

D.H. Lawrence, best known as the author of *Sons and Lovers* (1913), *The Rainbow* (1915), *Women in Love* (1920), and *Lady Chatterley's Lover* (1928), is ranked by many, along with JAMES JOYCE and VIRGINIA WOOLF, as one of the greatest British novelists of the twentieth century.

Born in Eastwood, a small Nottinghamshire town, Lawrence had humble beginnings. His mother, the former Lydia Beardsall, was a cultured, ambitious ex-schoolteacher whose family had declined socially; his father, Arthur John Lawrence, was an illiterate collier who worked underground for more than fifty years. Lawrence attended Nottingham High School between 1898 until 1901 and, in 1906, enrolled at University College, Nottingham to study for a teacher's certificate. Disillusioned with university life, Lawrence wrote the first draft of a novel, "Laetitia" and in 1908 took a job at the Davidson Road School in Croydon where he excelled as an art teacher. Teaching discouraged him, however, so he left Croydon in 1912 and, for the rest of his life, concentrated on writing.

Lawrence first appeared in print after Jessie Chambers, his childhood sweetheart and the model for Miriam in *Sons and Lovers*, sent four of his poems to the editor of the prestigious *English Review*, Ford Madox Hueffer (later FORD MADOX FORD). Ford published the poems in 1909 and in 1911 published the short story, "Odor of the Chrysanthemums." Meanwhile, Lawrence revised "Laetitia," which was published as *The White Peacock* (1911) and was dedicated to his mother, who had died of cancer in December 1910.

Lydia Lawrence was a dominant force in her son's life. He claimed that she breathed him "like an atmosphere" and had his soul. He loved her, however, and was so badly shaken by her death that he was ill during much of what he called "the sick year" (1911). But he continued to write. Setting aside the manuscript of *Sons and Lovers* (begun in 1910 as "Paul Morel"), he wrote *The Trespasser* (1912), based on an episode in the life of his friend Helen Corke and her music teacher, who killed himself. Then, in a conscious effort to purge himself of his mother's influence, Lawrence completed *Sons and Lovers,* his novel about a young man inordinately attracted to his mother and hostile toward his father.

Long before *Sons and Lovers* was published, Lawrence broke his six-year engagement to Jessie Chambers. In 1912 he met Frieda Weekley, the wife of his French professor and a member of the illustrious German von Richthofen family. They married in 1914 after an elopement to Germany and began a nomadic existence, which continued for much of their life together, tempestuous, passionate, and marked by lack of money. During the tumultuous period that preceded the marriage, Lawrence worked energetically on a novel called *The Sisters,* the story of three generations of Brangwens. Focusing on Ursula Brangwen, a young woman who decides to go to college, to have a career, and to remain unmarried, *The Sisters* was divided, late in 1914, into two volumes, *The Rainbow* and *Women in Love.* When *The Rainbow* was published just weeks after Great Britain declared war on Germany, critics and general readers alike were hostile. They objected to the novel's frank accounts of passion and were offended by the opposition of Lawrence's heroine to war and nationalism. Bowing to pressure, the publisher, Methuen, suppressed the novel.

Lawrence completed *Women in Love* in 1916; this novel, which many critics regard as his best, did not appear in print until 1920 in America and 1921 in Great Britain, because of the reaction to *The Rainbow.* In fact, Lawrence published no novels between 1915 and 1920. He did, however, publish four volumes of poetry and a travel book, *Twilight in Italy* (1916). He also completed *The Lost Girl* (1920); wrote his novella about lesbianism, *The Fox* (1922); and published *Studies in Classic American Literature* (1923). In addition, he began *Aaron's Rod* (1922), the first of three "leadership" novels which explore the connection between politics and personal relationships.

Partly because of the treatment of *The Rainbow,* Lawrence left England in 1919 and returned only for brief visits. Continuing the series of "leadership novels," he wrote *Kangaroo* (1923) in Australia and *The Plumed Serpent* (1926), the novel he regarded as his most important, in Mexico. He also produced two more travel books, *The Sea and Sardinia* (1921) and *Mornings in Mexico* (1927), and the novella *St. Mawr* (1925), which records his response to the American Southwest.

Lawrence's last years, like his first, were clouded by illness. Living in Italy, he wrote *Lady Chatterley's Lover* (two earlier versions of which have been published posthumously). More infamous than *The Rainbow,* the story of a love affair between Lady Chatterley and a gamekeeper was widely condemned for its sexual frankness and violation of social mores, and had to be smuggled into Great Britain. Exulting this time over the furor his fiction produced, Lawrence continued to write even as he was dying. He produced more short stories, a number of essays, a travel book called *Etruscan Places* (1932), and *The Man Who Died* (1929), a novella about Jesus' sexuality originally called *The Escaped Cock.*

During his lifetime Lawrence received only one literary award, the James Tait Black Memorial Award for *The Lost Girl*. His stories about male-female relationships, his criticism of abstractions and idealisms, his insistence that sex is an all-formative mystery, his advocacy of amoral intuitive life "blood-knowledge," and at the same time of civilized order and values, his experiments with traditional novelistic narrative, continue to attract controversy.

Duane Edwards

Bibliography
Leavis, F.R. *D.H. Lawrence, Novelist.* 1955.
Moore, Harry T. *The Priest of Love: A Life of D.H. Lawrence.* 1974.
Schneider, Daniel J. *The Consciousness of D.H. Lawrence: An Intellectual Biography.* 1986.
Worthen, John, Mark Kinkead-Weekes, and David Ellis. *D.H. Lawrence 1885–1930.* 3 vols. 1991.

Lawrence, T(homas) E(dward) (1888–1935)

Lawrence of Arabia was a young Oxford archaeologist who became during the FIRST WORLD WAR an intelligence officer in Cairo and a liaison officer with the Arabs revolting against the Turks. His post-war notoriety was partly the result of publicity from the slide lectures presented in London by Lowell Thomas, an American journalist. Fame helped Lawrence influence aspects of the Middle East settlement, but he soon sought to evade media attention through anonymity in the ranks of the ROYAL AIR FORCE and the ARMY while pursuing literary interests. His death on a motor cycle in 1935 added to the romance surrounding the man who remains a popular historical figure, especially after David Lean's 1962 film, *Lawrence of Arabia*.

Lawrence's father, who came from an Anglo-Irish landowning family, married and had four daughters but separated from his wife when the family's Scottish governess became pregnant. He and the former governess never married but had five sons, of whom T.E., born in 1888, was the second. His illegitimacy affected him personally, but his childhood, lived mostly in France and Oxford, was economically secure and otherwise conventional. He studied languages and history at OXFORD, receiving first class honors in 1910. His Oxford mentor, David George Hogarth, introduced Lawrence to excavations in Syria and surveys in Sinai and, after the British declared war on the Ottoman Empire in 1914, secured his appointment to the Arab Bureau in Cairo.

Lawrence's pre-war exposure to Arabic language, people, and lands and familiarity with British Intelligence were helpful in 1916, when he was posted to the Hejaz, along the Arabian coast of the Red Sea. While Cairo subsidized and supplied Sharif Husayn, who unilaterally declared an Arab Revolt against the Turks, Lawrence worked more closely with Husayn's sons, Abdullah and Faisal, and their largely Bedouin followers to defeat Turkish garrisons in the northwestern Arabian peninsula and to blow up the Turkish-operated Hejaz Railway. Further operations led by Lawrence complemented the successful British liberation of PALESTINE in 1917 and of Syria in 1918 by General Edmund Allenby. While the military role of the Arab forces led by Lawrence was not decisive, the value to the British of Husayn and his sons was important as a counterweight to French territorial claims in Lebanon and Syria. Lawrence's partisanship on behalf of Faisal and his Arab following in Syria would not have been as significant had Thomas not publicized Lawrence's feats extensively to a London public hungry for colorful exploits after the horrors of the Western Front.

In 1919 Lawrence dramatically accompanied Faisal to the Versailles conference, where both were disabused of their illusion that the Allies might gratify the demands of Arab nationalism, especially if it meant the sacrifice of continued British influence in the region. In 1920, when Syrians ousted Faisal and the French occupied Lebanon and Syria, Lawrence wrote letters of protest to London daily newspapers. Then, in 1921, WINSTON CHURCHILL took over the Colonial Office and called on Lawrence to help him organize a new Middle East Department to reduce the huge costs of maintaining the British position in Egypt, Palestine, and Iraq after the war. Lawrence supported Churchill's handling of the Cairo Conference and worked to secure Abdullah's position in Trans-Jordan and Faisal's in Iraq. Tired of public life, particularly his relentless pursuit by the media, Lawrence turned to revising his account of the Arab revolt written immediately after the war as a Fellow of All Souls College. An aesthete and bibliophile, he published an expensive edition limited to subscribers, entitled *Seven Pillars of Wisdom* (1926), and an abridgement called *Revolt in the Desert* (1926). Joining the military ranks gave him enough anonymity and security to translate Homer's *Odyssey* and a French novel, as well as to write his account of the Royal Air Force, *The Mint* (1929).

Roger Adelson

Bibliography
Knightley, Philip, and Colin Simpson. *The Secret Lives of Lawrence of Arabia.* 1969.
Mack, John E. *A Prince of Our Disorder: The Life of T.E. Lawrence.* 1976.
Wilson, Jeremy. *Lawrence of Arabia: The Authorized Biography of T.E. Lawrence.* 1989.

League of Nations

Britain played a major role in the creation and operation of the League of Nations. No other country left so great an imprint on this organization; certainly no other gave the League so much public support. Its appeal went across party lines, but the League still became an issue in British politics.

In Britain, as in the United States and elsewhere, the outbreak of the FIRST WORLD WAR led to discussions among intellectuals and politicians as to why the war had erupted and what could be done to prevent future wars. The suggestions of a CAMBRIDGE scholar, G. Lowes Dickinson, sparked the creation of one such group and had great influence on planning for the post-war world. Dickinson explained the war as the product of an anarchic world system and urged the creation of a "peace league" to end this anarchy.

As the war progressed, many other suggestions emerged, and two groups were established to promote post-war planning for an international organization: the League of Nations Society and the League of Free Nations Association. Lord Robert Cecil, a minister in the Foreign Office, drafted a memorandum in September 1916 which was placed before the CABINET and helped shape official British attitudes to the creation of collective machinery to insure peace. Cecil played a principal role in drafting the final version of the Covenant at the Paris Peace Conference.

Cecil also accepted the chairmanship of the League of Nations Union, which had unified the two rival groups of League supporters. Under his leadership, the LNU became the chief bulwark of the international League movement and a force in British politics. It attracted over 1 million members over the course of inter-war period and helped shape support for the League.

The appeal of the League ideal in Britain was based on the widespread sentiment that the sacrifices of the war must be justified by the emergence of a better world. The League became for many the symbol of that better world and they desperately wanted it to succeed. It was assigned the tasks of settling international disputes, of furthering disarmament, and a range of other functions. Some hoped that it would also pave the way for a future world government. All of the optimism about the League's future could not conceal its obvious shortcomings. Its members were sovereign states who could not be transformed overnight into dedicated world citizens.

It became commonplace in Britain in the 1920s for politicians of all parties to heap praise on the League. In fact, few were anxious to have the League assume greater responsibility in world affairs, as Cecil, GILBERT MURRAY, and other leaders of the LNU wished. LABOUR PARTY leaders were suspicious of the way the Covenant had been grafted onto the peace treaty. They often

said that the peace settlement would have to be revised and the new world body made over so that it was less of a "League of Victors" before they could give it their full support. CONSERVATIVE leaders had their own objections to the League, which many perceived as a threat to national sovereignty. They generally favored it as an extension of conventional diplomacy but objected to its more far-reaching objectives.

In the 1920s, when no clear challenge to the peace arose, support for the League was a high-minded but rather abstract goal, based on the hope that any future dispute could be resolved by peaceful means. League supporters and politicians rarely mentioned publicly that peaceful restraints might fail, and that aggression might again provoke war.

When challenges to the League began to emerge in the 1930s, the difficulties of this limited view of collective security became apparent. Japanese action in Manchuria in 1931 was not regarded in Britain as a clear case of aggression. No one in Britain was sure of what was happening or what the rights and wrongs of it all were. When the League sent a COMMISSION headed by a British Conservative, LORD LYTTON, to investigate the situation, its inconclusive report neither labelled Japan an aggressor, nor raised the issue of sanctions against her.

Only when Italy invaded Abyssinia did League supporters face a challenge they could not ignore. The PEACE BALLOT, which the LNU supervised in 1934–5, provided an impressive demonstration of how widespread public suport for the League was in Britain. With responses from about half the electorate, more than 11 million participants, the ballot demonstrated support for sanctions, even military sanctions against an aggressor.

The National government went along with a limited policy of sanctions, which the League imposed, but these sanctions failed to deter Italy. Cecil and other LNU leaders tried to lead British opinion into accepting rearmament, so that the League would be able to back up its sanctions policy. They even joined forces with old rivals like WINSTON CHURCHILL in an "Arms and the Covenant" campaign to meet the challenge of Fascism. The League had to be given a real trial, so that other potential aggressors would see that aggression did not pay. Instead the League backed off from a reliance on sanctions, and public confidence in the League waned after 1936. The League of Nations Union lost many of its members, some to dynamic new PACIFIST groups such as the PEACE PLEDGE UNION. The central beliefs of British League supporters were hard to maintain in the late 1930s. They had hoped that public opinion was capable of creating a new world order by influencing the British government, which in turn could lead the League of Nations and the world. But the illusion was dispelled when the government—despite the encouragement of the Peace Ballot—refused to pursue a full sanctions policy against Italy.

Internationalists continued to oppose the APPEASEMENT policies of the CHAMBERLAIN government and to press for collective security in the last years before the outbreak of the Second World War. However the League was no longer viable and their struggle had been lost. Their hope had been to support the League in order to put foreign policy on a new basis, to build a world regulated by law and not force.

Donald S. Birn

Bibliography
Birn, Donald. *The League of Nations Union.* 1981.
Cecil, Viscount. *A Great Experiment.* 1941.
Walters, F.P. *A History of the League of Nations.* 1952.
Winkler, Henry R. *The League of Nations Movement in Britain 1914–1918.* 1952.

Leavis, F(rank) R(aymond) (1895–1978)

An influential and controversial figure, F.R. Leavis helped establish LITERARY CRITICISM as a major force in British culture. His method of analyzing texts deeply influenced a generation of intellectuals that included RAYMOND WILLIAMS and Richard Hoggart. Leavis's critique of modern culture, which daringly encompassed the privileged literary elites of London, attracted disciples from across the political spectrum and reinforced the academic standing of literary studies in the major universities.

Leavis was born in Cambridge in 1895, the son of a shopowner who sold musical instruments. Educated at the Perse School, he served in the FIRST WORLD WAR with a medical unit on the Western Front. After the armistice he gained a scholarship to Emmanuel College, CAMBRIDGE, where he graduated with first class honors in English in 1921. Three years later he received his Ph.D. from Cambridge for a dissertation on "The Relationship of Journalism to Literature", a topic that, like the field of English literature itself, was not in high repute. Leavis then embarked on his long, frustrating struggle for a permanent academic position at Cambridge, a quest that deeply embittered him. In 1929 he married Queenie Dorothy Roth, whose *Fiction and the Reading Public,* published in 1932, became a central text in his pessimistic critique of modernity. Borrowing heavily from contemporary figures such as I. A. RICHARDS and WYNDHAM LEWIS, as well as the crowd psychologists of the late nineteenth century, Leavis argued that the organic community of pre-industrial England had gradually succumbed to a debilitating commercialism, most obvious in advertising and other forms of Americanized culture, but infecting influential novelists and reviewers as well. Only an intense program of education in English literature, involving the close, discriminating reading of texts, might preserve an authentic culture among a new, revitalized minority. Literary criticism would help re-create the "common reader" that industrialism destroyed.

In 1932, Leavis launched *Scrutiny,* a journal of literary and cultural criticism that, until its last issue in 1953, became the major medium of exchange for Leavis and his disciples. Many of his most influential books consisted of articles written for *Scrutiny,* including *The Great Tradition* (1948), about George Eliot, Henry James, and JOSEPH CONRAD. An impassioned defender of "critical standards", Leavis evaluated the relative merits of the central figures of English literature. Among modernists, Conrad, James, T.S. ELIOT, and W.B. YEATS stood high in his literary canon, but it was Dickens and especially D.H. LAWRENCE whom Leavis most vigorously championed. In a series of penetrating essays, he argued that Lawrence remained "our last great writer". Critics complained that Leavis never really defined his "standards" and that his "revaluations" too often consisted of arbitrary judgments.

Leavis' influence as a teacher at Cambridge reached its peak in the decade following the Second World War. Many students found it easy to identify sympathetically with a social and cultural rebel whose opinions defied the intellectual elitism and privilege of BLOOMSBURY intellectuals and whose literary criticism involved a deep seriousness of purpose not always evident in academic study. Cambridge finally made him a University Reader in 1959. Leavis reaffirmed his controversial status in 1962 in a stinging, often *ad hominem* polemic against C.P. Snow and his ideas about the cultural superiority of science. After retirement from Cambridge, Leavis accepted a number of visiting appointments and honorary degrees. He continued to publish extensively during his last years, but his influence waned considerably as other schools of criticism—Marxist and deconstructionist, especially—gained favor.

D.L. LeMahieu

Bibliography
Bell, Michael. *F.R. Leavis.* 1988.
Billan, R.P. *The Literary Criticism of F.R. Leavis.* 1979.
Hayman, Ronald. *Leavis.* 1976.
Samson, Anne. *F.R. Leavis.* 1992.

Left Book Club

Established by the publisher VICTOR GOLLANCZ in May 1936, the Left Book Club (LBC) was to become a highly influential force. At its peak in

April 1939 it had 57,000 members, who received a book and the journal *Left News* every month. However, the aim of the LBC was always political, for it was designed to create an anti-Fascist POPULAR FRONT movement. It was based on local study groups, of which there were 1,500 in 1939, and these were buttressed by social and cultural activities. It campaigned for such causes as the Spanish Republic, Chinese resistance to Japan, and the establishment of an alliance with the U.S.S.R., and its rallies were often far larger than those of the LABOUR PARTY. However, the LBC was deeply divided by the Nazi-Soviet Pact and the war. It continued until October 1948, but never regained its vitality, and had dwindled to 7,000 members when Gollancz finally closed it down.

The LBC was created soon after the COMMUNIST PARTY had adopted its United Front policy against Fascism, and its success owed much to this fact. The CP now wanted to create a broad alliance and Gollancz was prepared to collaborate with them to this end. He had two major associates: JOHN STRACHEY, who was effectively a Communist at the time, and HAROLD LASKI, who was on the left wing of the Labour Party. Gollancz and Strachey ensured that the overwhelming majority of the Club's books were acceptable to the CP, and Communists played the leading role in its central organization. Laski was not informed of the extent of the collaboration between the CP and the LBC and, although he occasionally took an independent line, he generally played a less active role in its affairs than his co-selectors.

By 1938 the LBC had published many of the most influential left-wing works of the era—above all, those by Strachey himself. However, by the autumn of that year, Gollancz was becoming increasingly worried by Communist domination of the LBC and began to assert a greater degree of independence. Laski was now highly critical of the CP, and in August 1939 he threatened to resign from the Club unless it distanced itself from the Nazi-Soviet Pact. Gollancz managed to maintain unity when the CP appeared to support the war the next month, but the division in the LBC became evident when the Communists changed their stance. In the December 1939 issue of *Left News* Strachey argued that the war should be opposed, while Laski urged total support for it. Gollancz agreed with Laski and, in April 1940, Strachey also endorsed their position. Communists were now purged from the LBC's headquarters and Gollancz used the Club to rally support for the war.

Between 1936 and 1939 the LBC had provided hope for thousands of people who were seeking a solution to the burning moral issues of the era.

Despite its pro-Communist line, the Club's socialist propaganda and education probably ultimately strengthened the Labour Party and contributed to its victory in the post-war election.

Michael Newman

Bibliography

Dudley Edwards, Ruth. *Victor Gollancz: A Biography.* 1987.

Lewis, John. *The Left Book Club.* 1970.

Legal Profession

After centuries of public disdain and criticism the greatest change in the legal profession in twentieth-century Britain has been the extraordinary increase in prestige and status by both barristers and solicitors. The historic differences between the two branches of the profession have narrowed considerably. The prominence of the barrister has given way to a new respect earned by solicitors. The sharp demarcation between the two groups has blurred because legal responsibilities are now discharged more in common, and the financial rewards of legal practice are more evenly distributed. The traditional distinction, that only barristers may plead in court while solicitors handle other legal affairs no longer holds. Solicitors may now act as advocates in county courts, magistrates' courts, and in certain actions in Crown Court; barristers still hold a monopoly on appearances in the High Court, the Court of Appeal, and before the Judicial Committee of the House of Lords. In 1990 the number of barristers in England was approximately 3600 and the number of solicitors was about 40,000. Despite some demands for fusion into one legal profession as in the United States, this prospect does not seem likely in the near future.

Both segments of the legal profession have completed the process of professionalization in the twentieth century, whereby educational requirements have been strengthened and internal disciplinary control have won greater confidence from the public. Education for the bar remains vested in the four Inns of Court in LONDON: Inner Temple, Middle Temple, Lincoln's Inn, and Gray's Inn. Where once qualification for the bar depended upon attendance at a set number of dinners, competitive examinations have replaced the earlier system. With respect to solicitors the older system of vocational education through apprenticeship has given way to a more sophisticated process that combines UNIVERSITY EDUCATION with clinical practice. This has reduced greatly the public perception of the profession as unethical and self-seeking.

Barristers have retained some of their customary privileges. In Britain, for example, judges are chosen only from the ranks of barristers, and, more particularly, from the elite group of Queen's

Counsels (QCs). A barrister remains an independent contractor who shares chambers (offices) with others, with whom they may sometimes find themselves on opposite sides in a particular case. The barrister may not deal directly with a client nor solicit litigation. The barrister instead takes instructions through the services of a solicitor. Success at the bar still depends to some extent on the ability of the barrister to win the attention of solicitors who provide briefs (cases). The barrister is entitled to a specific fee win or lose and does not render services on a contingency basis. The limited number of barristers hones the advocacy skills of practitioners, so trials are usually legal battles between qualified adversaries.

In terms of public esteem the solicitors have made even greater advances. In 1900 the work of solicitors was restricted primarily to the conveyancing (drawing of deeds, or, more simply, doing the paperwork) of landed property. The increased complexity of business transactions made the role of the solicitor more crucial. Another source of greater public contact came in the business caused by the Legal Aid and Advice Act (1949). Although some provision for legal services for those who could not afford them had existed previously, the scope of this aid was narrow. This statute not only brought access to the legal system for many who otherwise could not have afforded it, but it also gave both an increase and stability to solicitors' incomes. Where too many lawyers had been a constant refrain, by the 1960s more solicitors were required to handle legal matters effectively. By the 1990s an equilibrium had been reached after a dramatic increase in numbers between 1960 and 1985.

Additional evidence for the improvement in the image of the legal profession occurred in its fictional portrayal. Where the attorney had previously served as an object of ridicule or contempt, the profession now gained a more favorable depiction. Perhaps the most famous barrister in this genre was the irascible Horace Rumpole, who was all too human and yet usually got it right in the end. Rumpole was the creation of Sir John Mortimer (1923–), himself a practicing barrister before turning to literature as a career. If nothing else, the Rumpole sagas dispelled the myth of the barrister as removed from problems of daily life.

As public confidence in the legal profession grew, its place as confidant and advisor grew proportionately. Both branches have opened their ranks to women, making them somewhat more representative of society at large. Female membership in the profession hovers at about 10 percent, so the process of full integration is certainly not complete. The growing intellectual demands of the law have helped recruit individuals of wider outlook, and even greater specialization has

not prevented this trend. The legal profession has prospered because its role in litigation and its alternatives has demonstrated the broad range of benefits that competent counsel might provide.

Richard A. Cosgrove

Bibliography

Abel, Richard L. *The Legal Profession in England and Wales.* 1988.

Abel-Smith, Brian, and Robert B. Stevens. *Lawyers and the Courts: A Sociological Study of the English Legal System.* 1968.

Kirk, Harry. *Portrait of a Profession.* 1976.

Leisure

Over the century as a whole there has been an increase of about twelve hours a week in leisure time for most of the employed population. The first major reduction in hours of work came in 1919–20 when the normal working week for manual workers in the better organized trades was reduced from fifty-four to forty-eight hours. There was a further substantial reduction in 1946–9 with normal weekly hours falling to 44.6 by 1950. In the second half of the century there has been further reduction of normal hours to under forty by the 1980s. Already at the beginning of the century the Saturday half-holiday was well-established, but it was only after the Second World War that large groups of workers began to achieve a whole holiday on Saturdays.

A select group of workers had negotiated annual paid holidays before the beginning of the century, but the numbers only became significant in a series of staged advances from the end of the FIRST WORLD WAR. By 1945 10 million workers were covered by paid holiday agreements, most of them for two weeks. Since then the time available for holidays has increased to the point where, in 1988, 99 percent of full-time manual employees were entitled to four or more weeks. In addition there were Bank Holidays, the most famous of them being the Monday August Bank Holiday, and established holidays at Christmas or New Year and at Easter and Whitsuntide.

Over the life cycle, constrained as it was by family commitments, the early working years tended, throughout the century, to provide most opportunities for leisure; youth culture can be discerned in more than embryo from its beginning. MARRIAGE reduced, for both men and women but particularly for the latter, the time and opportunity for leisure, and it was not until the second half of the century that consistent patterns of retirement (at age sixty for women and sixty-five for men) and increasing longevity produced a new age of leisure for those who came to be called "senior citizens". Throughout the century, and particularly in the inter-war period and from the late 1970s onwards, UNEMPLOYMENT gave many people unwelcome periods of non-working time which it would be paradoxical to describe as leisure time.

In terms of leisure activities the century in many ways may be described as a spectator society. The chief forms of spectating have been two: cinema in the first half of the century (annual admissions peaked at 1,635,000,000 in 1946), and television thereafter. Whereas in 1955 every resident in the United Kingdom made on average twenty-three visits to the cinema, in 1988 the equivalent figure was only 1.5; but by the latter date people were on average watching television for twenty-five hours each week. Watching sport live came a poor second to these two dominant forms of spectating.

Spectating, however, has not prevented more active participation in leisure activities; indeed it may have encouraged it, with the stars of sport, for example, offering role models for others less talented. Some sports, like golf, middle class in its origins, have grown from small beginnings to become major participant leisure activities. Others, like fishing, may be seen as part of the growth of hobbies in the twentieth century.

Spectating has also not prevented the continuation of leisure activities more deeply rooted in the past. Of these the most important are those associated with drink and the pub, the location for the biggest expenditure of money in leisure time over most of the century. Only in 1987 did expenditure on holidays, at 7.17 percent of total expenditure, take the lead from alcohol consumed away from home. The pub has had an ability to adapt to social changes and has facilitated a culture of participant competitiveness, in darts for example, which has been sustained throughout the century.

But if the sociability of the pub has been one theme of leisure, the privacy of leisure within home and family has been another. Technology has facilitated this: the home has become more comfortable, and first radio (effectively universal by the late 1940s) and then television have provided forms of leisure enjoyable within the home. The automobile has similarly, outside the home, tended to make the family the organizing unit for leisure time; in the "family saloon" families could visit the seaside or parts of the national heritage of architectural and natural beauty.

The universality of spectating has helped create a national leisure calendar, dominated by sporting events (the Grand National, the Derby, the Cup Final, Wimbledon), but including also the celebration of Guy Fawkes night and Christmas. This national pattern can suggest that in leisure distinctions of class, nation, gender, and race dissolve; everyone can place a bet on the Grand National and take an interest in its outcome. Un-

doubtedly over the century the more extreme forms of exclusiveness in leisure, represented by LONDON society or by sporting and other clubs barring certain types of people, have diminished, but leisure activities tend to reflect rather than break down the divisions in society; perhaps the most important of these is gender, for WOMEN, and particularly mothers, have rarely established for themselves any clearly demarcated time for leisure. Even those women in full-time employment enjoyed in 1991 ten hours less free time per week than men.

Leisure has often seemed to individuals to be properly free time, free not only from work, but from other constraints. Governments have not taken so relaxed a view. For them, leisure is potentially a problem; it can lead to the disorder of FOOTBALL crowds, or to drunkenness, or to damage to the environment, or simply to indulgence in entertainment perceived to be of low quality. Governments have therefore been concerned to control leisure activities, through licensing of pubs and of all places of public entertainment, through censorship, and through establishing a partially independent agency such as the BRITISH BROADCASTING CORPORATION (1927) to provide a particular service. Governments have also been a major supplier of leisure of kinds of which they approve: libraries, parks, museums, swimming pools. And they have, particularly in the period after the Second World War, subsidized cultural activity through the ARTS COUNCIL (1946).

Until the latter part of the century governments have often seen themselves in opposition, as suppliers of leisure, to the leisure industries. The commercial supply of leisure was well-established and large-scale at the beginning of the century, for example in music hall or HORSE RACING, but it has grown in scale at both national and international level. Most leisure throughout the century, it is probably true to say, has been supplied through the market, but despite some striking examples of commercial supply and near monopolization of forms of leisure activity, for example in the production of literature, there are also many ways in which leisure is organized without direct reference to the market. Voluntary organizations remain key suppliers: the churches were leaders in this in the first half of the century, and their role remains important; for young people, organized child and youth movements, most of them, like the Boy Scouts (1908) and the Girl Guides (1910), recruit large numbers of young people; community organizations, increasingly subsidized by the state, are also major suppliers, as are national ones such as the Youth Hostels' Association (1930).

There is some evidence that, just as the supply of leisure has become of increasing importance in the economy, so also leisure over the century has become a more important part of people's lives. The inadequate figures that exist suggest that they have spent on it a fairly constant proportion of their disposable income, somewhere between 17 percent and 20 percent. It is in fact very difficult to allocate expenditure to leisure; in the late twentieth century it should, for example, almost certainly include much expenditure on CLOTH-ING, but the statistical series which are available do not do this, and there is therefore almost certainly an underestimate of expenditure on leisure for more recent years. Certainly leisure has come to occupy a greater proportion of people's time; that in turn may mean that it has begun to become more important than work in the formation of individual identities, as a basis for sociability, and as the means by which people relate to their locality, nation, age group, class, race, and gender.

Hugh Cunningham

Bibliography

Clarke, John, and Charles Critcher. *The Devil Makes Work: Leisure in Capitalist Britain.* 1985.
Cunningham, Hugh. "Leisure and Culture" in F.M.L.Thompson, ed. *The Cambridge Social History of Britain 1750–1950.* vol 2. 1990. pp. 279 –339.
Halsey, A.H., ed. *Trends in British Society Since 1900: A Guide to the Changing Social Structure of Britain.* 1972.
Jones, Stephen G. *Workers at Play: A Social and Economic History of Leisure, 1918–1939.* 1986.

Lend-Lease
American military assistance to countries that fought Germany in the SECOND WORLD WAR, Lend-Lease helped Britain defeat Axis forces and committed the United States to enter the war as Britain's ally.

Franklin D. Roosevelt conceived of Lend-Lease to assist Britain, whose resources for purchasing military supplies became depleted soon after Germany occupied Paris. "The moment approaches," WINSTON CHURCHILL warned Roosevelt in December 1940, "when we shall no longer be able to pay cash for shipping and other supplies" needed to defeat Berlin. Roosevelt realized the strategic necessity of supplying Britain, but his hands were tied by the 1934 Johnson Act, banning government loans to foreign states, and the 1939 Neutrality Act, preventing foreign sale of war materials on any terms but cash.

In late 1940 Roosevelt publicly declared that the United States would become "the great arsenal of democracy" and proposed Lend-Lease legislation. He used his famous analogy of loaning a garden hose to a neighbor whose house was on fire to justify Lend-Lease as a measure to defend the United States by enabling Britain to douse the conflagration in Europe.

Congress approved the first Lend-Lease law in March 1941, authorizing the president to "sell, transfer title to, exchange, lease, lend, or otherwise dispose of . . . any defense article . . . [to] any country whose defense the President deems vital to the defense of the United States." By 1945 the United States provided some $50 billion in assistance to its allies, including $27 billion to Britain. Lend-Lease supplies were vital to the defeat of the Axis in all theaters.

Lend-Lease also proved significant in the United States's entry into war as Britain's ally. To protect Lend-Lease supply lines, Roosevelt in 1941 authorized repair of British ships in American yards, declared a protectorate over Greenland and the Azores, occupied Iceland, authorized navy convoys to sail midway to Britain and track German submarines, and convinced Congress to allow merchant ships to deploy deck guns and sail into war zones. By November 1941 three American navy ships had been damaged and more than 100 sailors killed safeguarding Lend-Lease material. A virtual Anglo-American naval alliance existed months before the attack on Pearl Harbor.

Lend-Lease encompassed the best and worst of the Anglo-American wartime partnership. Churchill praised Roosevelt's "most unsordid act", and Roosevelt allowed British officials to participate in planning deliveries to European powers. On the other hand, many American officials saw Lend-Lease as a lever to reduce British trade barriers. At the second Quebec Conference (1944), Roosevelt committed Lend-Lease funds to restore Britain's industrial capacity after the war, but Harry S. Truman reneged on Roosevelt's pledge, terminated Lend-Lease when the war against Japan suddenly ended, and used the British loan of November 1945 to elicit free trade pledges from London. Though grateful for Lend-Lease assistance, British officials chafed at Truman's policy.

Peter L. Hahn

Bibliography

Dobson, Alan P. *US Wartime Aid to Britain, 1940–1946.* 1986.
Kimball, Warren F. *The Most Unsordid Act: Lend-Lease, 1939–1941.* 1969.
Stettinius, Edward R. *Lend-Lease: Weapons for Victory.* 1944.

Lessing, Doris May Tayler (1919–)
As a chronicler of our century, the writer Doris Lessing sits securely at the center of twentieth-century British literature, her fiction having documented directly the experience of living in postwar Britain from the shabby 1940s to the ethic of greed in the 1990s. With over thirty-five books, among them twenty novels, a parade of short stories, plays, poetry, essays, memoirs, fables, Less-

ing provides a glimpse into a particular historical period by way of her intelligent depiction of that time. Hers has been a long-standing narrative critique of nation responding to cultural, economic, political, psychological, sexual, and intellectual change, having set for herself the task of giving fictional shape to large social questions and the individual's experience of them as new and unpredictable.

A prolix, and sometimes ponderous writer, Lessing has nevertheless drawn from her readers passionate commitment to those contemporary subjects she has been excavating. Feminism and sexual imbroglios are as much themes in her work as religious zealotry, schizophrenia, racial animosity, left-wing politics, terrorism, the death of planets and parents. Thus her most important novel, *The Golden Notebook* (1962)—where the conjoining of a particular historical and political moment permitted the creation of a remarkable tract for the times—stands as the paradigmatic example of Lessing's ability to reward the common reader, the feminist scholar, and the informed intellectual. (Since its publication, over 900,000 hardback copies alone of the book have been sold.) In the novel's protagonist, Anna Freeman Wulf, Lessing comes close to realizing her vision of creating a twentieth-century Anna Karenina and of becoming herself an English Tolstoy.

Born in Persia to British parents, she was raised on a farm in Southern Rhodesia, where her father had settled in the 1920s on subsidized land offered to British citizens willing to farm in then colonial Africa. Lessing's first interrogations—sexual as well as racial—thus were from early on percolated through the marginality of a colony that still perceived itself to be central to the British Empire. Married twice and involved in radical politics, she moved to England in 1949 with the manuscript of her first published novel, *The Grass is Singing* (1950). Questions about long-standing assumptions among British colonialists in Africa regarding the certainty of their imperial role inform many of Lessing's African stories as well as the first four of her five volume series, *Children of Violence* (1952–69), a quintet whose *Bildungsroman* form traces Martha Quest from childhood in Rhodesia through post-war Britain to an apocalyptic ending, the year 2000 marking both the century's and the series's end.

Her transition from the realistic to the fabular found itself modulated through three works: *Briefing for a Descent into Hell* (1971), *The Summer Before the Dark* (1973), and *The Memoirs of a Survivor* (1974). Forming a kind of secular triptych, each novel concerns itself with its protagonist's mid-life crisis, a symptomatic fragmentation expressive of personal, gender, and societal malaise. While *The Summer Before the Dark* represents the

novel most connected to Lessing's earlier concerns, its forty-five-year-old heroine being so typical of woman's estate as to seem almost a flattened Anna Wulf, *The Memoirs of a Survivor* becomes the work most connected to Lessing's later concerns. Its landscape—a London without name in the death throes of scavenging survival—prefigures those wastelands imagined in such novels as *The Good Terrorist* (1985) and *The Fifth Child* (1988) while its austere voice forecasts that of the Chronicler in the series, *Canopus in Argos* (1979–83).

The speculative fantasy and mysticism of Lessing's second series, *Canopus in Argos*, marks remarkable invention; in five volumes a set of galactic empires are engaged in rivalries and battles while a mythical and benevolent force manipulates, relocates, eradicates, and massages other empires in service of notions of commonweal and commonwealth. In retrospect, Lessing's aesthetic and political aversion to the England she had adopted in coming to London is evident here. Then and for some years it was a place where she could join others in the political debates represented by THE NEW STATESMAN, *The Reasoner*, the CAMPAIGN FOR NUCLEAR DISARMAMENT (CND), and the COMMUNIST PARTY, from which she resigned in 1956 following the invasion of Hungary and revelations about Stalinism. By the 1980s she proclaimed that political dogma was neither more nor less than religious bigotry. In *Prisons We Choose to Live Inside* (1987), for example, she describes her short-lived commitment to communism as a sudden, total conversion to both a system of faith and a structure of belief, while *Shikasta* (*Canopus in Argos*'s first volume, 1979) has a chronicle section devoted to the fictive biographical mappings of individuals inspired by late twentieth-century secular and national fanaticisms to systematic acts of terrorism.

Fictionalizations of the violent partisan passions inculcated by political orthodoxies may have propelled Lessing away from galactic fables and back to realism. Three novels, *The Diaries of Jane Somers* (1984), *The Good Terrorist*, and *The Fifth Child*, as well as a collection of short stories about and sketches of London in the 1990s titled *The Real Thing* (1992), describe a country in perilous social malaise. Its ironic title underscoring the matter, *The Good Terrorist* asks whether Britain in the last decades of the twentieth century be piloted forward through storms of class division, civil disaffection, vandalism, racial discord, UNEMPLOYMENT, the intransigence of government and trade unions alike, the fanaticism of both secular and religious orthodoxies. Panoramic in sweep and civilizing in intent, Doris Lessing chronicles the moral climate of late twentieth-century Britain, remaining true to the goal announced so early on in "The Small Personal Voice" (1957): in registering the intellectual and moral climate it is imperative for the writer to create dispassionately a world fed by social and philosophic urgencies.

Lessing was named a Companion of Honour in 1999.

Virginia Tiger

Bibliography

Draine, Betsy. *Substance under Pressure: Artistic Coherence and Evolving Form in the Novels of Doris Lessing.* 1983.

Knapp, Mona. *Doris Lessing.* 1984.

Seligman, Dee. *Doris Lessing: An Annotated Bibliography of Criticism.* 1981.

Sprague, Claire, ed. *In Pursuit of Doris Lessing: Nine Nations Reading.* 1990.

Thorpe, Michael. *Doris Lessing.* 1973.

Lewis, (Percy) Wyndham (1882–1957)
Artist, writer and critic, Wyndham Lewis was the founder of the only indigenous British avant-garde movements of the century, VORTICISM. Acknowledged by T.S. ELIOT as "the most fascinating personality of our time" and as "one of the few men of letters in my generation whom I should call, without qualification, men of genius," Lewis was a catalyst for the ideas of European cultural modernism in Britain. Though best known for his work as a painter, Lewis was also a prolific writer and the author of more than fifty books (including novels and works of philosophy or cultural criticism) and 360 essays and pamphlets.

Lewis was born off Nova Scotia of Canadian and American parentage. Unlike both Ezra Pound and Eliot, however—the other North American cultural expatriates with whom he associated—Lewis was raised and educated in Britain and Europe. Travelling extensively in pre-First World War Europe, he was exposed not only to the work of the European avant-garde, but also to the philosophical writings of Bergson, Nietzsche, and Sorel. Though Lewis constantly reinvented himself by casting off all previous influences, the elitist and anti-democratic strain of these early aesthetic, philosophical, and political influences were to remain important throughout his career, imbuing him with a dislike of compromised liberal democracy.

Lewis's irascible nature as well as his abstract and energetic aesthetic program alienated him from the clannish circle of early British modernists represented by ROGER FRY, and his feud with this circle stood in the way of any substantial commercial success in either his literary or his artistic endeavors. For Lewis, Fry and the BLOOMSBURY GROUP—with their subtle cultural influence-peddling—epitomized the hopelessly anachronistic embroilment of British cultural life in the established privileges of wealth and status.

As a platform for his own theories, Lewis founded the short-lived Rebel Art Centre (1914) from which Vorticism developed as a movement in literature and the plastic arts. The major Vorticist exhibition was held at the Doré Galleries in June 1915. Though the literary monuments to this movement—*Blast I* (June 1914) and *Blast II* (July 1915)—marked a collaboration with the leading avant-garde figures such as Pound, Lewis would claim at the end of his life—and not without reason—that "Vorticism, in fact, was what I, personally, did, and said, at a certain period."

Lewis published his first great novel, *Tarr,* in 1918 and mounted his first one-man show in 1919, but his lack of popular success in publishing and exhibiting subsequently served to spur his eccentric movement outside the cultural mainstream. This movement took a more decidedly political turn in the 1920s, when Lewis turned his attention to the task of cultural criticism. His aesthetic estrangement from the British mainstream was compounded by his interest in right-wing and reactionary politics, which he expressed in a series of books such as *The Art of Being Ruled* (1926), *Paleface* (1929) and *Left Wings Over Europe* (1936). Certainly, Lewis was not alone in this interest, but for him it was central to the inspirational impetus of his work.

In 1931 he published a work which was to prove disastrous to his career, and which has marred his critical reception ever since. This work—*Hitler*—stands as one of the most important texts for the understanding of the interaction of Fascism and the avant-garde in the inter-war years, and though subsequently (and belatedly) recanted in two works of 1939 (*The Jews, Are They Human?* and *The Hitler Cult*), the mixture of casual ANTI-SEMITISM and authoritarianism in all three works has stood in the way of an adequate assessment of Lewis' role in European modernism.

In the war years Lewis was practically obliged to exile himself to Canada and the United States, and the experience of those years is distilled in what some consider his greatest work, *Self Condemned* (1954). If the period of exile in the Second World War fed Lewis's literary work, however, it was less productive for the visual artist. Painting portraits for money, Lewis also began to notice a deterioration in his vision, and in 1951 he became completely blind and ceased painting. On his return to Britain, he turned his last years of darkness to profit by concentrating on his writing. In these prolific last years he completed *Rotting Hill* (1951)—a satirical work on the decay of contemporary Britain—as well as *Self Condemned.* Most notably, he completed the monumental metaphysical trilogy *The Human Age*—begun in 1928 with the publication of *The Childermass*—publishing two volumes—*Monstre Gai* and *Malign Fiesta*—in 1955.

The enigma of Lewis's biography consists in his apparent lack of any lasting influence on the subsequent development of British arts and letters. Of the "men of 1914"—Pound, Eliot, JOYCE, and Lewis—he is the only one not to have established an unassailable place in the critical canon. His implacable opposition to any and every other strain of British modernism and his political views go some way to explaining this anomaly, but it is also necessary to take note—as Lewis himself did in works such as *Time and Western Man* (1927), *The Apes of God* (1930), and *Men Without Art* (1934)—of his idiosyncratic notion of aesthetic modernism. Eschewing the modernist fragmentation of individual experience, Lewis consistently favored an aesthetics of individualism in which the possibility for historically decisive action has not been lost.

Andrew Hewitt

Bibliography
Bridson, D.G. *The Filibuster: A Study of the Political Ideas of Wyndham Lewis*. 1972.
Jameson, Fredric. *Fables of Aggression: Wyndham Lewis, the Modernist as Fascist*. 1979.
Lewis, Wyndham. *Rude Assignment: An Intellectual Autobiography*. 1984.
Meyers, Jeffrey. *The Enemy: A Biography of Wyndham Lewis*. 1980.
Normand, Tom. *Wyndham Lewis the Artist: Holding the Mirror Up to Politics*. 1993.

Liberal Party
The Liberal Party was one of two alternative British parties of national government between 1832 and 1924, vying with the CONSERVATIVE PARTY. During this period, it governed the country for forty-five years, participated in governing coalitions for thirteen, and was in opposition for thirty-four. It was also within this period a major force in local governnment. Between 1924 and 1945, the Liberals—having lost their party of government status to LABOUR—nevertheless remained an important national political party, taking office in governing coalitions or keeping a minority government in office during nine of the twenty-one years. Their significance in local government, however, faded rapidly during these years. After experiencing near-extinction between 1945 and 1958, the Liberal Party—known from 1988 as the Liberal Democratic Party—achieved a modest revival. Although it has an insignificant parliamentary representation and only modest success on the local scene, the party draws millions of votes in parliamentary elections and holds the balance of power in scores of constituencies.

After its mid-Victorian electoral triumphs Liberal party fortunes declined after 1886, when a large section of Liberal Unionists—including a radical reformist group led by Joseph Chamberlain—seceded in reaction to Gladstone's suppport for Irish self-government. The Liberals were also weakened in the 1880s and 1890s by dissension over foreign affairs between "Little Englanders" and "Liberal Imperialists," a tepid interest in social reform, unpopular policies such as temperance, and—after Gladstone's long-postponed retirement—a destructive leadership struggle.

The new century found the Liberal party debilitated and—as shown in the 1895 and 1900 general elections—losing ground within the electorate. The BOER WAR dangerously sharpened the imperialist-isolationist division, threatening another party split. At this juncture the Conservative government came to their opponents' aid by enacting the controversial Education Bill of 1902, which infuriated Nonconformists by providing tax support for ANGLICAN and ROMAN CATHOLIC schools. In 1903 Joseph Chamberlain—who had split the Liberals in 1886—almost did the same for the Conservatives with his protectionist schemes. Although only a few Conservatives (including young WINSTON CHURCHILL) abandoned their party to fight with the Liberals for free trade, a good many Liberal Unionists returned to their old party over the education issue.

Education and free trade, the main issues in the 1906 general election, enabled the reunited, resurgent Liberals to elect 400 out of 670 MPs, and garner almost 53 percent of the contested vote. Under its successive Prime Ministers, SIR HENRY CAMPBELL-BANNERMAN (1905–8) and HERBERT H. ASQUITH (1908–15), the Liberal Party veered leftward. Inspired by the collectivist ideas of the NEW LIBERALISM, progressive ministers like Churchill, Charles Masterman, HERBERT SAMUEL, and especially DAVID LLOYD GEORGE sponsored welfare reforms—including OLD-AGE PENSIONS, health insurance, and school meals—abhorrent to Gladstonians. The Parliament Act of 1911 stripped the Conservative-controlled HOUSE OF LORDS of its veto, and only the coming of the FIRST WORLD WAR prevented the Liberal government from implementing Gladstone's goal of Irish home rule. Although the Liberals lost their absolute majority in the two parliamentary elections of 1910, they were able to continue in office with the backing of Labour and Irish Nationalist MPs. Shaken by the Marconi scandal of 1912–13, which implicated several ministers, and by labor, feminist, and Irish agitation from 1911 onward, the Liberals were searching for a winning election issue when the war burst upon them in August 1914.

The Liberal Party reluctantly supported the government's decision to fight Germany, except for a few pacifists who gravitated to the anti-war UNION OF DEMOCRATIC CONTROL and eventually into the Labour camp. But the war soon inflicted shocks upon the Liberals from which they never recovered. While Liberal Imperialists like Asquith, SIR EDWARD GREY, and R.B. HALDANE, as well as pragmatists like Lloyd George, took the conflict in stride, many party members were alienated by its devastating effect upon liberal principles.

For several months the Asquith government advocated a business-as-usual policy, although a faction within the parliamentary party—later called the Liberal War Committee—stood behind Lloyd George's efforts to mobilize the country for all-out war. In May 1915 Asquith bowed to pressures within and outside the party and became head of a multi-party coalition. Lloyd George, as Minister of Munitions, acquired unprecedented power to regiment industry and labor in the national interest. The War Committee mobilized backbench Liberal votes for compulsory military service in January 1916, but CONSCRIPTION was a deadly blow to the party's voluntarist tradition. Many disillusioned Liberals thereafter became critical of government policies or apathetic.

The heaviest blow to the Liberal Party was the schism caused by Lloyd George's resignation from the Asquith government in December 1916 and his formation of a new Coalition administration. As many as 175 Liberal MPs stood behind him, but the Asquith Liberals went into opposition and most of Lloyd George's ministers were Conservatives. The Liberal Party, in Parliament and outside, was now in disarray, with the organizational machinery still in Asquithian hands but most Liberals supporting Lloyd George's more vigorous war leadership. In May 1918 the Asquithians' failure to defeat Lloyd George in a confidence vote resulted in their proscription when the Prime Minister went to the country in the first postwar election the following December. Only thirty-six "Free Liberal" MPs were returned, while 127 Liberal recipients of Lloyd George's "coupon" were successful.

Lloyd George's attempts to transform his coalition into a progressive center party was rejected by his Conservative allies, who dumped him as Prime Minister in October 1922. Asquith and Lloyd George agreed to reunite their Liberal factions in 1923 in order to fight Conservative Prime Minister STANLEY BALDWIN's call for protectionism. In the crucial general election of 1923 the Liberals and Labour each won about 30 percent of the vote, but Labour elected more MPs and was asked to form a minority government when

Baldwin resigned. The decision of the Liberal leaders to admit Labour to office unconditionally was criticized, then and later, as politically suicidal. No longer seen as a party of government and weakened by internal bickering, the Liberals elected a mere forty MPs in the October 1924 election.

More ominous, perhaps, than electoral defeats was the Liberals' steady decline in municipal council seats throughout Britain in the 1920s. This trend, which had begun before the war, reached disastrous proportions by the end of the decade and resulted in the almost total collapse of the party's local leadership cadres. The endless feuding of the chiefs over money, policies, and personalities incurred public contempt and ridicule. By the time Lloyd George succeeded to the party leadership in 1926, the Liberals were probably beyond salvation as a governing party. Lloyd George made a valiant effort in the 1929 general election to revive the party on a platform of "conquering UNEMPLOYMENT," but only fifty-nine Liberal MPs were returned.

During the second Labour government Lloyd George attempted with little success to promote constructive economic policies. He failed to persuade Labour to enact proportional representation or the alternative vote in order to give the Liberals a chance to elect MPs proportionate to their share of the electorate. Bad luck dogged the Liberal leader. Early in 1931 SIR JOHN SIMON and about a third of the parliamentary party rejected his whip, and in July he fell seriously ill. Hospitalized when the August 1931 economic crisis occurred, Lloyd George watched helplessly as his deputy, Sir Herbert Samuel, took the party into RAMSAY MACDONALD's National government, and—against his advice—agreed to its fighting an election against Labour.

Although seventy-four Liberals were returned in the October 1931 election, as a party they were divided ineffectually among "Simonites," "Samuelites," and Lloyd George's tiny family group. These factions never reunited. The Simonites or Liberal Nationals, in existence organizationally as late as 1966, like the Liberal Unionists before them gradually were absorbed into the Conservative Party. The Samuelites retained the official Liberal machine but not access to the National Liberal Fund that Lloyd George had acquired during his coalition days. Lloyd George took a conspicuous part in the 1935 election, distinct from the official Liberals, but afterward was semi-retired. All three Liberal factions contributed ministers to the successive National and coalition governments of the 1930s and 1940s, and included many articulate backbenchers and peers, but electorally the Liberals were insignificant until the 1960s. The number of official Liberal

MPs fell from thirty-three in 1931 to six in 1951, while its share of the parliamentary vote dropped to a low of 3 percent in 1951 and 1955.

As the Conservatives and Labour had, over the years, appropriated so many of its ideological positions, the shrunken party had difficulty proving its right to life. Had Clement Davies, the Liberal Leader in 1951, accepted Churchill's offer of a ministry in the new Conservative government, the party might well have gone the way of the Liberal Nationals. The decision to soldier on independently bore fruit in 1958, when the Liberals won their first by-election since 1929. By then, a new Leader, Jo Grimond, had begun to restate Liberal principles of human rights and freedoms in contemporary terms. As British enthusiasm for collectivism waned, the Liberals' "middle way" became attractive to educated, middle-class, suburbanites. Grimond's public image as a trendy television performer did his party no harm with its new constituency. In 1962 a Liberal won a spectacular by-election victory at Orpington, a commuter suburb, leaving the Labour candidate with a forfeited deposit. At about the same time, the Liberals fleetingly led the other two parties in popularity in a national opinion poll. The 1964 general election increased the Liberal MPs only to nine, but their share of the total vote rose to over 11 percent.

During the 1970s the Liberals enjoyed a degree of rejuvenation on the local level, elected hundreds of councillors, and in a number of communities rebuilt the leadership cadres that had disappeared forty or fifty years earlier. Reconstruction of local parties and identification with grass root causes was encouraged by Grimond's successor as leader, Jeremy Thorpe (1967–76). Thorpe's strategy paid off in the February 1974 general election, in which the Liberal vote exceeded 6 million—the largest in the party's history, and close to 20 percent of the total vote—although electing only a disappointing fourteen MPs. Thorpe was criticized for turning down a coalition offer by Conservative Prime Minister EDWARD HEATH, which would have brought Liberals into a government for the first time in a generation.

The next Liberal Leader, David Steel (1976–88), was more Machiavellian, first negotiating a pact to keep a minority Labour government in office (1977–9), then contracting an electoral Alliance (1981) with the SOCIAL DEMOCRATIC PARTY, a breakaway from Labour. The Alliance drew an impressive 25 percent of the vote in the 1983 general election, and 23 percent in 1987, but managed to elect only twenty-three and twenty-two MPs respectively—seventeen of them Liberals. In 1988 Steel used what many Liberals and Social Democrats viewed as strong-arm tactics to effect a merger of the Alliance parties. Known now as the Liberal Democrats, and with Liberal Paddy Ashdown as Leader following Steel's retirement (1988–1999), the enlarged party performed impressively in several by-elections, reaping the benefits of disillusionment with Tory rule. The Liberal Democrats made substantial gains in the 1997 election and found a new party leader in Charles Kennedy, but their efforts to promote proportional representation and to make a significant political impact proved no more successful at the century's close.

Don M. Cregier

Bibliography

Cregier, Don M. *Chiefs Without Indians: The British Liberals 1918–1935.* 1982.

Cyr, Arthur. *Liberal Party Politics in Britain.* 1977.

Douglas, Roy. *The History of the Liberal Party 1895–1970.* 1971.

Morgan, Kenneth O. *The Age of Lloyd George: The Liberal Party and British Politics, 1890–1929.* 1971.

Searle, G.R. *The Liberal Party: Triumph and Disintegration 1886–1929.* 1992.

Wilson, Trevor. *The Downfall of the Liberal Party, 1914–1935.* 1966.

Literary Criticism

Reflecting its epoch, twentieth-century criticism in Great Britain is best characterized by its radical diversity. If it has embraced an ideological militancy from time to time, it has also shown a fertility of invention, a willingness to combine with other fields, and a capacity to renew itself.

Around 1900 the university study of literature was dominated by philology and historical criticism, both strongly indebted to German and French models and evolutionism. While historical criticism had professionalized the discipline, it tended to lose the work of art in a background of origins and causes. Philology waned by the 1930s; historical criticism, which includes literary biography, remained the road most traveled by twentieth-century scholars.

The attempt to wrest the work of art from the control of other disciplines began towards the end of the Victorian period with a revolt against historicism, part of the larger idealist reaction to science and materialism. In Britain this was initiated by aestheticism, then taken up and carried much further by the early modernists. Aestheticism, which had proponents both in and beyond the academy, and which often ran under such names as impressionism, symbolism or decadence, had its roots in the Pre-Raphaelites, A.C. Swinburne, and Walter Pater, reached its zeneth in the 1890s, and lingered well into the Edwardian period. Its themes and values included skepticism and relativism; a subjectivizing tendency; aesthetic autonomy and the divorce between nature (or science) and art; formalism and craftsmanship; flight from the drab and an emphasis on novelty, the remote, and the irrational; a blurring of the line between criticism and creation; the spurning of social concerns and defiance of bourgeois morality and taste; faith in art; and hedonism.

The greatest single movement in twentieth-century criticism is modernism, which in the form given it by Ezra Pound and T.S. ELIOT maintained its supremacy in Anglo-American high culture from the First World War to the early 1940s. Even afterwards, movements were often refinements, narrowings, or reactions to modernism, to the point where some could divide the century between two broad periods, modernism and postmodernism. In a series of articles dating from 1910, T.E. Hulme protested the naturalism, subjectivism, and sentimental emotionality of Victorian writing and demanded a type of poetry that was concrete, accurate, and sophisticated.

An American, Pound arrived in London in 1908, was the motive force behind Imagism, edited the anthology *Des Imagistes* (1914), and supported WYNDHAM LEWIS' VORTICISM (a vortex was a symbol of patterned energy and concentration). Arguing that poetry should be as well-written as prose, Pound urged the "direct treatment of *the thing*" as the basis of his objectivist aesthetics. The work of art should result from conscientious craftsmanship rather than from spontaneous expression of private feeling.

An American who was trained in philosophy at Harvard, Eliot, like Pound, wrote criticism in partial justification of his poetics. *The Sacred Wood* (1920), which contains "Tradition and the Individual Talent," his essays on the Metaphysical Poets and Elizabethan dramatists, and his journal *Criterion* (1922–39), re-established the canon of literature and articulated modernist principles. These principles include linguistic precision; complexity; irony and ambiguity; self-referentiality; impersonality by means of the creation of a narrator and masks; oblique as opposed to direct statements; and myth as a structural principle. Three of Eliot's main themes are his idea of tradition, the "dissociation of sensibility," and the "objective correlative." By tradition Eliot did not mean history per se, but the knowledge of the truly significant works, each of which altered the entire previous tradition. By dissociation of sensibility, Eliot called attention to the fragmentation of the self in modernity and pointed to a time when thought and feeling were integrated and mutually informing, that is, before the mid-seventeenth century and the rise of science and modernity. The objective correlative, a distancing strategy that derived ultimately from romantic aesthetics, means the events, symbols, or situations that are the objective equivalent for the poet's emotions.

Modernism entered the academy in the 1920s and 1930s through the pioneering effort of I.A. RICHARDS whose *Principles of Literary Criticism* (1924) set forth concepts of psychological value, communication, attitude and belief, internal equilibrium, and irony. His *Practical Criticism* (1929) came at the end of the decade in which many of the high modernist masterpieces appeared and was designed to enable readers to come to terms with some of the most difficult and experimental literature ever written in the West. In this book Richards commented on students' misreadings of thirteen poems, categorized them by type of errors, and outlined a corrective method of "close reading," also known as contextualism. The method became part of the first-level teaching of literature in the English-speaking classroom (and eventually elsewhere) for half a century.

In Britain Richards exerted a potent influence on William Empson (who was his student at Cambridge) and F.R. LEAVIS, two of the principal critics of their generation. Empson's *Seven Types of Ambiguity* (1930) gave close reading its first "practical" masterpiece; its kernel idea combines contextualism with the notion that ambiguities of poetic language can be plotted in "stages of advancing logical disorder." *The Structure of Complex Words* (1950) carried the theme of ambiguity and lexical analysis to the micrological level. His later criticism takes up history and biography in an often polemical mode. Leavis' *Mass Civilization and Minority Culture* (1930) engages such themes as the neutralization of nature, cultural leveling, and the commercialization of taste through the power of the media. The cultured minority was a saving remnant in the machine age. He was the major force behind the journal *Scrutiny* (1932–53) to which D.W. Harding, L.C. Knights, and Derek Traversi contributed.

New Criticism, so named from a book by the American John Crowe Ransom (1941), occupied the theoretical high ground in the academic study and teaching of literature from the 1940s to the 1960s. High modernist aesthetics furnished its poetic canon and main premises, while Richards, who is the acknowledged father of New Criticism, and Empson provided central components of its method: the poem as object, self-reflexivity, polysemousness, complexity, anti-didacticism, impersonality, craft and technique, anti-historicism. New Critics proposed a highly formalistic approach to the work of art and rejected history and biography; their readings are characterized by a focus on irony, ambiguity, a tension of opposites, and equilibrium or closure. While the New Critics produced brilliant readings of texts, by the mid-1950s the movement was in decline, and readings became frequently repetitive and monotonous. Moreover, works were found to be so ambiguous that the value of formal closure was being seriously undermined. New Criticism had its principal success in America, but it was influential in Great Britain as well. While no New Critic, Christopher Ricks shows its influence in his close readings.

In the 1950s and 1960s myth-and-symbol criticism flourished, living in part on New Critical premises (anti-historicism, objectivism, formalism, tension of opposites, and a quasi-religious quest for totality). The chief representative of this school is the Canadian Northrop Frye, whose *Anatomy of Criticism* appeared in 1957. What autonomy the New Critics invested in the poem, Frye extended to the entire world of literature, which operates along lines capable of being interpreted by a gigantic seasonal myth, a system mapped and managed by the genres.

Unlike the New Critics and myth-and-symbol critics, the Welsh Marxist RAYMOND WILLIAMS refused to exclude history. His analysis of cultural context embraces sociology, economics, and politics, but his application of Marxist and other theories shows that he is neither controlled nor captured by them. His works include *Culture and Society, 1780–1950* (1958), *The Long Revolution* (1961), and *The Country and the City* (1973). At CAMBRIDGE Williams's influence (along with allied inspirations from Richard Hoggart and the Institute for Contemporary Cultural Studies at the University of Birmingham) replaced Leavis's. Williams's students include the OXFORD Marxist cultural critic, Terry Eagleton.

Although existentialism had made some inroads into Anglo-American criticism, it was not until the 1960s that European, mainly French and German, schools began to have a larger impact with (among others) T.W. Adorno, Michel Foucault, and Jacques Derrida. Inspired by Derrida, deconstruction takes linguistic ambiguity to the furthest limits into a radical undecidability of the text. The boundary of closure is dissolved, and the author, even as a fiction, is effaced. Where New Criticism values formal closure and the beautiful, deconstruction prefers the infinity of significations and the sublime. Deconstructive or postmodernist criticism (a label which includes deconstruction but also a number of other movements) valorizes plurality, indeterminacy, chance, novelty, anti-rationality, parody, rewriting, mixing genres, open form, multiple models, and *pietas* (a reverence for the local scene and private life—which relates to the increasing privatization of life).

During the 1980s the response to deconstruction has come from many quarters: New Historicism, feminist criticism, and cultural studies. Late twentieth-century criticism attempts to historicize the work of art, though the limits of the historical context vary considerably with individual critics. By returning to history, however, criticism has come full circle. At the outset of the century the work of art was lost among its causes; it was rescued, defended from external disciplines, and explored internally until its meanings were shown to be so superabundant that closure gave way to undecidability. Finally, in order to explain this semantic richness, history returned, and the work of art is again in danger of being lost in its backgrounds. One notes even a repetition of the aesthetic practice of dissolving the border between art and criticism in the so-called absence of textual boundaries (between life and art, from text to text) as well as in the tendency of postmodern critical readings to be performances. This is not to say that the end merely repeats the beginning, because in its century-long journey criticism has been informed by intense study and refinement of its theory and practice.

John Paul Russo

Bibliography

Fekete, John. *The Critical Twilight: Explorations in the Ideology of Anglo-American Literary Theory from Eliot to McLuhan.* 1977.

Mulhern, Francis. *The Moment of 'Scrutiny'.* 1981.

Norris, Christopher. *Deconstruction: Theory and Practice.* 1982.

Robinson, Alan. *Symbol to Vortex: Poetry, Painting and Ideas, 1885–1914.* 1985.

Wellek, René. *History of Modern Criticism.* vols. V–VI. 1986.

Lloyd George, David (1863–1945)

David Lloyd George, the most prominent Welsh politician of the century, was born in Manchester on 17 January 1863. He was a Liberal Member of Parliament (1890–1945), Cabinet minister (1905–16), Prime Minister (1916–22), and Leader of the LIBERAL PARTY (1926–31). Admitted to the peerage as the first Earl Lloyd-George of Dwyfor in January 1945, he died of cancer in Llanystumdwy, North Wales, on 26 March 1945.

Although born in England, Lloyd George was of Welsh parentage and bilingual. When his father, a teacher named William George, died in 1864, David was adopted by his uncle, Richard Lloyd, a master shoemaker and Baptist lay preacher. Raised as a son by "Uncle Lloyd," David always used the double surname. In later life, Lloyd George recalled an impoverished childhood, but by contemporary local standards his family was middle class.

Richard Lloyd's family—including David's mother, sister, and younger brother—moved to the nearby, larger town of Criccieth in 1880. Meanwhile, Lloyd George attended an Anglican elementary school and was apprenticed as clerk to a law firm in neighboring Portmadoc. After experience in free-lance journalism and Liberal Party electioneering, Lloyd George was licensed as a solicitor in 1884.

Concealing his lack of religious commitment, Lloyd George exploited—both professionally and politically—the acrimony between North Wales's Nonconformist Welsh peasantry and its Anglican gentry. Married in 1888 to the wealthy Margaret Owen of Criccieth, in 1890 Lloyd George was elected Liberal MP for the Carnarvon Boroughs—a seat he held for fifty-five years. An intelligent woman with considerable political acumen, Margaret Lloyd George disliked London and chose to raise her family in Criccieth—living apart from her husband much of the time. His notoriety as the most philandering politician of his day, as well as Margaret's Nonconformist piety, explain why the couple's fondness increased with distance. Nevertheless, their marriage ended only with Margaret's death in 1941. Two of their five children—Gwilym and Megan Lloyd George—followed their father into politics, the former becoming a Cabinet minister.

While his sober brother, William George, managed their North Wales law practice, the youthful MP lost no time establishing a colorful political reputation—based largely on boldness and rhetoric. Parliamentary fights on behalf of Welsh (Anglican) Church disestablishment, local option drink prohibition, and Welsh home rule produced newspaper stories (some written by Lloyd George) in London as well as North Wales. Outside Parliament Lloyd George was in demand as a platform orator and stump speaker before Nonconformist and temperance audiences—who were not informed of his occasional tippling.

Although gradually abandoning purely Welsh issues, Lloyd George was slow to become known as more than a backbench gadfly. He sat in Parliament for almost a decade before his unpopular opposition to the BOER WAR brought him nationwide publicity—at some risk to his personal safety. Lloyd George was drawn into an influential circle of radical Liberals—including the party leader, Sir HENRY CAMPBELL-BANNERMAN—who deplored the war as imperialistic and costly.

Lloyd George strengthened his Liberal Party credentials after the war by his leadership of the turbulent struggle against the CONSERVATIVE government's Education Act of 1902—which favored ANGLICAN and ROMAN CATHOLIC schools. Detested by Nonconformists, this law contributed to the Liberal electoral landslide of 1906. By then Lloyd George had become President of the Board of Trade in the CABINET formed by Campbell-Bannerman late in 1905. At the trade ministry, Lloyd George modified his radical image by promoting legislation useful to British business. He also achieved success as a labor negotiator, and—in conjunction with his friend and Cabinet colleague, WINSTON CHURCHILL—began to develop an interest in social reforms.

The accession as Prime Minister of HERBERT ASQUITH in 1908 resulted in Lloyd George's promotion to Chancellor of the Exchequer. He drastically changed the thrust of this office, usually occupied by fiscal moderates. In the celebrated "People's Budget" of 1909, Lloyd George not only appropriated funds for greatly enhanced defense spending—in response to German naval competition—and for the expensive new OLD AGE PENSION Act of 1908, but for an ongoing "war on poverty." The use of a money bill to initiate policies—including a development fund to improve roads and agriculture—as well as to levy heavy new taxes brought about a showdown with the Conservative-dominated HOUSE OF LORDS. The year 1911 featured both a Parliament Act stripping the Lords of their legislative veto and a pioneering National Insurance Act in which Lloyd George introduced contributory health and UNEMPLOYMENT benefits.

His anxiety to minimize defense costs to save funds for social programs gave the misleading impression that Lloyd George was a pacifist. He was, on the contrary, becoming ever more worried by German aggressiveness. During the dangerous Agadir crisis of 1911, he acted as the Cabinet's spokesman to warn Germany of the risk of war. Henceforth Lloyd George paid close attention to foreign affairs, simultaneously urging peaceful accommodation with Germany and defense preparedness. As early as 1910, in suggesting an all-party coalition to solve national problems, he had recommended compulsory military training.

Lloyd George's political career was nearly terminated in 1912–13 by the Marconi scandal, in which he was accused of speculation and corruption and forced to apologize publicly. An ambitious rural land reform campaign, which Lloyd George launched in 1913 to revive flagging Liberal popularity, proved of marginal interest to the heavily-urbanized electorate.

After helping Asquith carry a largely united Liberal Party into the FIRST WORLD WAR, Lloyd George quickly emerged as one of the most bellicose ministers. His sharp criticisms of the Liberal government's "business as usual" policy led to its fall in May 1915 and replacement by a coalition, still headed by Asquith. Appointed to a new MINISTRY OF MUNITIONS, Lloyd George ruthlessly thrust aside obstacles to increased production, especially restrictive trade union practices and pressed successfully for military conscription. His complaints against the ARMY's static Western Front policy were unavailing, and the GALLIPOLI and Salonika campaigns of 1915—which he endorsed—were fiascos.

The rift between Lloyd George and Asquith widened as the latter failed to master such crises as the war's battle casualties and the ominous loss of British ships to German submarines. A movement for a negotiated peace, following the costly battle of the SOMME in 1916, elicited from Lloyd George a demand for a "knock-out blow" against the enemy. He joined Conservatives, dissident Liberals, and powerful newspaper publishers in a conspiracy that toppled Asquith in December 1916—also splitting the Liberal Party.

Innovations such as a small War Cabinet, an Imperial War Conference, a Cabinet Secretariat, and the appointment of "push-and-go" businessmen to critical jobs were among Lloyd George's contributions to an invigorated war effort. He also used the convoy system in 1917 to reduce shipping wastage, and in 1918 forced unity of Allied command upon distrustful British generals—but ultimately it was American entry on the Allied side that brought victory over Germany. Skillful manipulation of Parliament, the PRESS, and public opinion enabled Lloyd George to ride out numerous attacks on his wartime leadership. As "the man who won the war," he led his coalition to a stunning electoral victory after the November 1918 armistice. But as a renegade Liberal, whose old party had been decimated by the voters, Lloyd George was a prisoner of the Conservative parliamentary majority.

Although Lloyd George had electioneered for tough peace terms for Germany, at the Paris Peace Conference of 1919 he took a moderate, constructive middle stance between American idealism and French vengefulness. More concerned now to stop the spread of Russian Bolshevism than to punish Germany, Lloyd George wanted to restore prewar economic normality as far as possible. While acceding to severe arms limitations for the former enemy, the Prime Minister fought successfully to minimize Germany's war reparations and preserve its territory and industrial base. He accepted Wilson's peacekeeping LEAGUE OF NATIONS, although preferring to trust British diplomacy and seapower.

As the Versailles Treaty left much undone, Lloyd George during 1920–2 shuttled between London and various European cities to attend a succession of international conferences on European recovery. He failed to restore Germany and Russia to full European community membership, but succeeded in ending military intervention against Moscow's communist regime and in reestablishing Anglo-Russian trade. Lloyd George's

government also integrated several former Arab provinces of Turkey (a wartime enemy) into Britain's sphere of influence, and established a Jewish "national home" in PALESTINE.

At home, one of Lloyd George's earliest endeavors, Welsh Church disestablishment, was finally accomplished (1920), but another pre-war bugbear—Irish self-government—still defied easy solutions. Two years of guerrilla war (1919–21) by Irish republicans forced the coalition government to concede dominion status to Catholic southern Ireland, while according Protestant-majority Northern Ireland more limited home rule. The IRISH TREATY of 1921 alienated many Conservatives. Others were infuriated by the touting of peerages and other honors by Lloyd George's whips to raise money for his National Liberal party. The Prime Minister's ambitious plans to allay the post-war economic slump, restructure the failing COAL industry, construct "homes fit for heroes," and extend social services foundered on Conservative demands for fiscal restraint. After failing to organize a new, progressive center party, Lloyd George tried various expedients to keep the coalition alive—and himself in power. The end came suddenly in October 1922, following a revolt of junior ministers fearful that the Prime Minister's bellicosity toward the new Turkish Republic might ignite a new war.

The 1920s were frustrating to the still-dynamic Lloyd George. Liberal Party reunion (1923) was halfhearted. Many followers of ex-Prime Minister Asquith still accused Lloyd George of apostasy and disloyalty. One source of intra-party discord was the the huge National Liberal Fund garnered during the coalition, which Lloyd George employed to run a London newspaper, the *Daily Chronicle*, and to finance policy studies of the coal industry, agriculture, and industrial reconstruction. Succession to the de facto Liberal leadership, following Asquith's retirement in 1926, came too late for Lloyd George. He made a final, failing effort to revivify the Liberal Party in the 1929 general election by a dramatic pledge to "conquer unemployment". In the midst of a serious illness in 1931, he abandoned the Liberal leadership.

Partially retired during the 1930s, the famous Welshman kept busy writing his memoirs, managing a model farm in Surrey (celebrated for its raspberries), and making occasional histrionic forays into politics. In 1935 he launched a "new deal" program inspired by the American example, and organized a Council of Action to fight for it—with little success—in that year's general election. In high-paid articles for British and American newspapers, he stumped for rearmament, cooperation with the Soviet Union, and jettisoning of the Conservative government's APPEASEMENT policy. Lloyd George's curious admiration for Adolf Hitler, whom he visited in 1936, was balanced by outspoken support for the republic during the SPANISH CIVIL WAR.

When the Second World War began in September 1939, he viewed British preparation as hopelessly inadequate and recommended a negotiated peace with Germany. Mainly to nullify Lloyd George's defeatism, Churchill in 1940 offered him first a Cabinet seat and then the Washington embassy. Possibly expecting a recall to power, he declined these posts but kept in close touch with the war and politics until poor health slowed him down in 1943. In that year Lloyd George married as his second wife Frances Stevenson (1888–1972), his longtime secretary—and mistress. In 1945 he was created Earl Lloyd-George of Dwyfor.

David Lloyd George has been controversial since death as in life. His commanding, charismatic personality attracted dedicated followers, some of whom were dropped unceremoniously after serving their purpose. His caustic repartee made bitter enemies, some of whom he later brought round to his side. The consensus of biographers and historians is that Lloyd George was a constructive politician, despite such personality flaws as egocentrism, amorality, and opportunism. His prewar public career, with its contributions to the British WELFARE STATE, is rated more favorably than what followed. Lloyd George's achievements during the First World War, while important, were exaggerated by contemporaries to the detriment of less spectacular figures. The post-war years brought him more failures than successes, but his peacemaking efforts in 1919–22 deserve marks for effort if not accomplishment. Bad luck dogged him after 1922. With a few thousand more Liberal votes in the right constituencies in the critical 1923 election, and good health during the 1931 political crisis, he might have returned to the corridors of power—where he was needed. Although Lloyd George has been portrayed as the consummate politician, his political skills were inferior to those of less imaginative and enterprising rivals. His private life, scandalous enough in the early twentieth century, raises few eyebrows today.

Don M. Cregier

Bibliography
Cregier, Don M. Bounder from Wales: Lloyd George's Career Before the First World War. 1976.
Gilbert, Bentley Brinkerhoff. David Lloyd George, A Political Life: The Architect of Change 1863–1912. 1987.
———. David Lloyd George, A Political Life: Organizer of Victory 1912–1916. 1992.
Grigg, John. The Young Lloyd George. 1973.
———. Lloyd George: The People's Champion, 1902–1911. 1978.
———. Lloyd George: From Peace to War, 1912–1916. 1985.
Rowland, Peter. David Lloyd George: A Biography. 1975.

London

London in 1900 was the world's largest and most prosperous city. The Metropolis accounted for a fifth of the population and a third of the income tax receipts of England and Wales. The financial institutions of the ancient CITY OF LONDON serviced the international economy, and the West End remained the metropolitan home of Britain's aristocratic elite. Yet late-Victorian Londoners were as fascinated by the city's poverty as by its wealth. Charles Booth's social survey, published between 1889 and 1902, described a Metropolis in which one in three lived in poverty, one in eleven in "chronic want." Residential densities of up to 180 persons per acre existed in parts of the East End, where 1 million people crowded into five of London's poorest boroughs, tied to casual or sweated labor, particularly in the London docks. A city wealthy enough to support Britain's earliest department stores—Whiteley's in 1872, the more socially exclusive Harrods in 1884, Selfridges in 1909—and ninety cinemas even before 1914 was also, for the only time in its history, the UNEMPLOYMENT capital of Great Britain, struggling to cope with waves of REFUGEES from agrarian depression in the English shires and ANTI-SEMITIC persecution in Russia and Poland. The 2,000 men sleeping rough on the Thames Embankment and the 500 successful and 700 attempted suicides per annum in the early 1900s provide grim indices of urban anomie.

The service sector had been the most dynamic component of the economy of late-Victorian London; heavy industry had been deterred by the capital's high rents and labor costs. The growth of services accounted for much of London's wealth, the absence of large-scale industry for its failure to dispel mass poverty. The FIRST WORLD WAR began the process of resolving this paradox. The war touched London only lightly, though bombs dropped by German Zeppelins from May 1915 killed 670 and injured 2,000. Many of London's buses disappeared from her streets, conscripted to carry troops on the Western Front, but, overall, total war inflicted few of its horrors upon the capital and brought a substantial benefit in the establishment of government munitions factories in the western suburbs. In peacetime these became the basis of London's inter-war industrial renaissance, resting largely upon new industries, particularly AUTOMOBILES and electronics. London now benefited from its limited role in the first wave of British industrialization, largely escaping the problems of obsolescence and failing markets afflicting the older industrial areas in the Depression years. With the development of the national electricity grid in the 1920s, industry was free to gravitate to Britain's most buoyant market, and London became an attractive location for new consumer goods industries. Industry of all kinds was drawn by the proximity of the financial services of the City and of central government, and by London's position at the center of national and international transport networks. After Britain's adoption of IMPERIAL PREFERENCE in 1932, American firms were particularly tempted by the chance to operate from within the imperial tariff wall: Hoover and Gillette came to London in 1933 and 1937. More than half the new firms founded in inter-war Britain were established in London and the southeast.

The *New Survey of London,* the sequel to Booth's work, though published at the height of the British Depression in the early 1930s, conveys an optimism contrasting strongly with the earlier survey. Booth's central problem of structural poverty had greatly diminished over the intervening years: the real wages of the unskilled worker had improved by 30 percent and casual labor had virtually disappeared. Indeed the London of these years emerges generally as a less nightmarish place than Booth's city. A drop of 40 percent in per capita beer consumption, and the substitution of light for heavy ales had dispelled much of the drunkenness endemic in Victorian London and the violent crime that had accompanied it. The Londoner was now at greater risk of injury from the automobile than from his fellow man. A fall in levels of squalor and overcrowding had matched the drop in poverty levels, facilitated by the suburban extensions of the underground railway system and the electrification of the Southern Railway's suburban network in the 1920s. "Metroland"—the suburban hinterland of the Metropolitan Railway, sprawling into Buckinghamshire—epitomized the middle-class residential development of the period, unplanned and often architecturally unimaginative, but comfortable and well built. Private working-class house-building never recovered from the First World War, but municipal building filled much of the gap, accounting for more than a third of all new houses built during the 1920s. Much of the old inner city remained visibly poor in the 1930s, but by all measurable indices of income, overcrowding, and NUTRITION, the problem of poverty in London had improved substantially since Booth's day. The unemployment rate, nearly twice the national average in 1913, had fallen to half the national figure by 1929. Inter-war London was, by and large, and optimistic city.

This optimism was threatened during the 1930s less by the fear of internal decline than by the deterioration of the international position and the knowledge of London's vulnerability to aerial bombing. The Committee of Imperial Defense estimated in 1938 that 175,000 Londoners would die in the first twenty-four hours of war. Air raid precautions began at the time of the MUNICH crisis, with the digging of trench shelters in London's parks and squares and the free issue of one and a half million metal "Anderson" shelters, but at the same time public swimming baths were being covertly requisitioned for the mass storage of papier-mache coffins. To protect London's next generation nearly 1 million schoolchildren and 200,000 mothers were evacuated into the shires, an operation conducted with exemplary efficiency by the local authorities but nullified almost from the outbreak of war as homesick evacuees drifted back. In the event the BLITZ failed to justify more pessimistic predictions. Inevitably London suffered far more severely than in 1914–18: 30,000 civilians were killed and 50,000 seriously injured by enemy action between 1939 and 1945 (around half of them in the Blitz proper between September 1940 and May 1941) and only one building in ten in the entire administrative county escaped damage, but London did not suffer as Hamburg, Dresden, Hiroshima, or Nagasaki suffered. Civilian morale fluctuated but never collapsed. Londoners endured some very low moments, notably in 1944 with the resumption of aerial bombing in the "little Blitz" of January, the arrival of the V2 rockets in the autumn, and the passing of the year without victory, but the traditional image of Cockney resilience was not baseless. Communal shelter in the deep-level tube stations—Piccadilly Circus accommodated 4,000 people—generated its own camaraderie, while the "blackout" and other air raid precautions produced their own consoling rituals.

The return of peace saw the resumption of many of the pre-war trends in London's development. The capital's economy became still more strongly focused upon the Commonwealth, the up-river docks and their ancillary industries enjoying an Indian summer of properity as, by 1950, a third of all Commonwealth trade passed through the Port of London. Once again war stimulated peacetime industrial growth, as outer London became a center of aircraft production in the 1950s.

The pressure of population in the inner city diminished further as the drift to the suburbs continued. The planning vogue of wartime had instilled the urge to control this centrifugal movement: Patrick Abercrombie's County of London Plan of 1944 envisaged the regulated movement of 1 million people from the central area in ten years, with around half of them to be accommodated in ten projected satellite new towns. Stevenage in Hertfordshire was designated the first new town of November 1946, and after the failure of its residents' legal challenge to the proposal to swamp their village with metropolitan refugees, another six new towns were created within thirty miles of London. The ordered decentralization policy of the post-war years succeeded in curbing London's inter-war sprawl and in protecting the "green belt" around the built-up area, at the cost of advancing the emaciation of much of the inner city.

The growing distinction between core and periphery was emphasized further, in many areas, by the arrival of new Commonwealth immigrants in the 1950s, drawn by labor shortages in the booming London economy, and by the relaxation of IMMIGRATION controls in the 1948 British Nationality Act. By the end of the decade 20,000 West Indians were settling in London annually, a figure that rose to 66,000 in 1961, along with 48,000 Asians, in anticipation of the controls introduced in the following year. By 1981 a sixth of London's population would be West Indian or Asian by birth or descent. For BLACK PEOPLE in London, the price of a relative prosperity, compared to home circumstances, was prejudice, "ghettoization", and social tension, first manifested on a large scale in the Notting Hill race riots of 1958. For many, moreover, the transformation of the London economy in the 1960s would limit even their relative prosperity.

Britain's rapid retreat from Empire in the early 1960s destroyed the Commonwealth-oriented economy of the up-river docks and precipitated their closure from 1967. Riverside industry declined with them, and the collapse of other London industries followed. The 45 percent fall in manufacturing employment in Lambeth in the 1970s was mirrored in other inner London boroughs: by the mid-1980s only one in seven of the London workforce worked in manufacturing industry. For the metropolitan economy as a whole these were symptoms of structural transformation rather than collapse, as Britain changed its economic orientation from Empire to Europe. The period from the mid-1950s saw an explosion of the business sector that led central government to control new office building in central London from 1964. With occasional exceptions such as Seifert's Centre Point (1967), office building brought aesthetic disaster to much of the central business district, but it generated 100,000 jobs in ten years. The commercial office boom was followed by the expansion of financial services, as the overseas earnings of the City of London climbed from £200 million in 1965 to a peak of £9.3 billion in 1986. In the meantime London had prospered as a tourist center, receiving 8.4 million visitors a year by the mid-1980s.

These developments compensated the Metropolis as a whole for the decline of her manufacturing sector, but did not provide new jobs for the displaced manufacturing workforce. London's unemployed numbered nearly 1 million, from a total population of 7.6 million, in the recession of 1980–1, and still stood at around 500,000 in the mid-1980s. Worst affected were London's young Blacks, with a 40 percent unemployment rate, a statistic that exacerbated endemic tension between host and immigrant communities. This tension exploded into rioting in Brixton, Southall, Battersea, and elsewhere as part of the national wave of urban riots in the summer of 1981. These events provided the most conspicuous symptoms of the steady erosion of social cohesion in the inner city. Other symptoms included, by the early 1980s, the 25 percent of schoolchildren under the Inner London Education Authority coming from single-parent families, the 50,000 ILEA children who did not speak English as their mother tongue, and, above all, the increase in inner-city CRIME rates (the number of robberies in Brixton rose by 138 percent between 1976 and 1980). This loss of social cohesion was matched by the physical decay of the inner-city, with 31 percent of inner London dwellings classified as unsatisfactory by the Greater London Council in 1981. A new manifestation of metropolitan poverty appeared in 1988 with the abolition of housing benefit for those under eighteen, creating "cardboard cities" of youths sleeping rough on the South Bank, in Covent Garden, and elsewhere in the West End. A century of metropolitan development has changed much of Charles Booth's London, but the reemerging juxtaposition of wealth and deep poverty has produced a pattern with which Booth would have been familiar.

John Davis

Bibliography

Humphries, Steve, and John Taylor. *The Making of Modern London, 1945–1985*. 1986.

Jackson, Alan Arthur. *Semi-Detached London: Suburban Development, Life and Transport*. 1973.

Mack, Joanna, and Steve Humphries. *London at War: The Making of Modern London, 1939–1945*. 1985.

Porter, Roy. *London: A Social History*. 1994.

Schneer, Jonathan. *London 1900: The Imperial Metropolis*. 1999.

Sheppard, Francis. *London: A History*. 1998.

Weightman, Gavin, and Steve Humphries. *The Making of Modern London, 1914–1939*. 1984.

London Government Since 1900

Victorian London had struggled to solve the problems of governing a conurbation too large for unitary government, a city whose government needed to reflect both the metropolitan and the parochial allegiances of its inhabitants. The model completed by the 1900 London Government Act comprised two tiers, with a central London County Council, created in 1888, handling metropolitan functions, and twenty-nine Metropolitan Boroughs exercising local powers. The apparent simplicity of this arrangement was marred, however, by various anomalies reflecting earlier ad hoc treatment of London's municipal needs. In London's central business district the City Corporation was a wealthy and powerful relic, exercising municipal authority—including police control—within the square mile of London's original medieval settlement. The boundaries of the administrative county of London, first defined in the 1850s, now failed to reflect the extent of the built-up area: by 1901 more than 30 percent of Londoners lived outside the county. Several standard municipal powers were denied London's authorities: water, gas and electricity supply, and the docks remained in private hands, while the Metropolitan Police force had been controlled by central government since its creation in 1829.

The scope for a "municipal revolution" in London akin to that in Victorian provincial towns was therefore limited. The LCC, with its superior resources and its ability to promote metropolitan rather than parochial policies, possessed the greater potential, and it was this potential that the Progressive Party, mostly radical LIBERALS with a LABOUR fringe, sought to realize during their control of the council down to 1907. They promoted London's first large scale HOUSING schemes, purchased and operated her tramway network, and attempted to alleviate the capital's poverty, but their ambitious policies aroused local opposition in a city where metropolitan identity remained limited. They were defeated by the reaction to high spending municipal government in an inflationary period, emanating from the highly assessed West End and from the Conservative suburbs. Between 1907 and 1934 control of the council passed to the CONSERVATIVES or "Municipal Reformers."

Municipal Reform did not imply municipal nihilism. Progressive totems such as the direct labor Works Department and the loss-making Thames steamboat services were sacrificed, and the council failed to support proposals to extend the administrative county put before Viscount Ullswater's Royal Commission on London Government of 1921–3, but circumstances ensured that the LCC remained active. In 1904 it had inherited 500 schools on the demise of the London School Board; by the 1930s it was responsible for the education of 750,000 children. After the First World War it became the principal agent in London of central government's housing drive;

the inter-war period saw the building of both "cottage" estates and block dwellings on a far greater scale than before 1914, and the council was landlord to almost 100,000 households by 1939. With the reform of the Poor Law in 1929, it inherited responsibility for public assistance and for poor law medical services, including 140 HOSPITALS and the London ambulance service. As education authority, housing authority, health authority and, before 1933, tramways authority, the inter-war council approached the ideal of the omnicompetent metropolitan body. Though the SECOND WORLD WAR curtailed the council's normal activity, it increased its prominence as it supervised evacuation, civil defense, and the Rescue Service, which saved 25,000 lives during the conflict.

The council reached its zenith in the 1930s and 1940s; the subsequent development of the WELFARE STATE limited the scope for municipal enterprise. In 1948 the LCC's health services passed to the new NATIONAL HEALTH SERVICE. Following the loss of the council's tramways to the nationalized London Passenger Transport Board in 1933, Whitehall was emerging as the top tier of London's administrative system. With local powers already in the hands of the boroughs and London's water supply, docks and electricity managed (from 1902, 1908, and 1925 respectively) by joint boards on which the LCC had only minority representation, the council's future role became doubtful. Political friction between the LCC, under Labour control since 1934, and Conservative central government reinforced these doubts in the 1950s. In 1957 another Royal Commission on metropolitan government was appointed under Sir Edwin Herbert. It prompted legislation in 1963 creating an enlarged Greater London Council governing almost the entire built-up area, but at the same time reshaping the second tier with the creation of thirty-two enlarged London Boroughs, envisaged as principal authorities in the new system. The GLC, at its inception in 1965, was assigned a "strategic" London-wide role, and given control of London's buses and underground railways in the only significant devolution of power from central government in the entire period, but it was not entrusted with the education services already run by the outer boroughs, and it saw its own education service transferred to a new Inner London Education Authority on which its representatives shared power with those of the inner-London boroughs. From the start the Greater London Council was therefore a body with a large budget but a limited raison d'etre, making it vulnerable to politically inspired dismemberment in the 1980s. The election of a Labour Council in 1981, under the controversial

Ken Livingstone, brought conflict with the THATCHER government over the Council's proposals for industrial regeneration, aid to voluntary groups, and cheap public transport. Thatcher's reelection in 1983 led to the end of a century of democratic metropolitan government with the Council's abolition in 1986. Its replacements included the unimaginatively titled London Residuary Body, charged with winding up its affairs and obligations, a number of ad hoc metropolitan agencies such as London Regional Transport and the London Fire and Civil Defence Authority, and various joint committees of the boroughs. Some powers devolved to the boroughs and the City Corporation, while substantial reserve powers passed to central government. In 2000 democratic self-government in London was restored in line with the Labour government's plans for DEVOLUTION, and Ken Livingstone, MP, former G.L.C. leader and maverick socialist, was elected as London's first mayor.

John H. Davis

Bibliography

Davis, John. *Reforming London: The London Government Problem, 1855–1900.* 1988.

Gibbon, Gwilym, and Reginald W. Bell. *History of the London County Council 1889–1939.* 1939.

Hebbert, Michael, and Tony Travers, eds. *The London Government Handbook.* 1988.

Saint, Andrew, ed. *Politics and the People of London: The London County Council, 1889–1965.* 1989.

Young, Ken, and Patricia Garside. *Metropolitan London.* 1982.

London School of Economics and Political Science

The London School of Economics and Political Science was founded in 1895, when SIDNEY AND BEATRICE WEBB used a FABIAN SOCIETY bequest to found a college devoted to the social sciences. The LSE was intended to demonstrate their belief that the objective study of social facts would ineluctably establish the case for state control of social and economic life.

The socialist reputation of the School was later reinforced by the presence of such future LABOUR PARTY leaders as CLEMENT ATTLEE and HUGH DALTON. In the inter-war years the main symbol of LSE socialism was the Government Department under HAROLD LASKI, whose transition by the 1930s to a sort of Marxism attracted an international-nationalist audience. During and after the Second World War, RICHARD TITMUSS and Brian Abel-Smith identified the Social Administration Department with the Labour government-led WELFARE STATE.

However, the Webbs were collectivists in general before they were socialists in particular: state regulation was to become the creed of all parties, not just Labour. It was appropriate therefore that the School's first Director, W.A.S. Hewins, was a Conservative protectionist imperialist, and that another director, WILLIAM BEVERIDGE, was a Liberal who in 1942 founded a welfare state whose aim was to make socialism unnecessary.

The open nature of the Webbs' legacy licensed other developments which made the School something very different from "a school for socialists." The emphasis on objective enquiry (the School's motto is *Rerum Cognescere Causas*) could easily generate research inconsistent with or irrelevant to collectivism. The School's title—"Economics and Political Science"—was clearly intended to be heuristic rather than mandatory: its subjects came to include anthropology, history, geography, sociology, psychology, linguistics, and philosophy (a department which, revived by Karl Popper, was as interested in natural as in social science). There is, oddly, no department of political science: politics is taught in the Department of Government.

In the Economics Department of the 1930s, following the earlier example of Edwin Cannan, Lionel Robbins, Arnold Plant, and Friedrich von Hayek were combatting not only socialism and collectivism, but also J.M. KEYNES—and this at a time when the trend of public policy in Britain was moving in the opposite direction. Anthropologists such as Bronislaw Malinowski, Raymond Firth, and Maurice Friedman, historians such as William Medlicott, and sociologists such as Morris Ginsberg were not primarily (or at all) exercised by questions of the practical relevance of their work. Robbins, an economist always deeply involved in public life, never lost his philosophical interest in questions of methodology, and this latter concern led him to emphasize the importance of mathematics to economics. His efforts here helped to create an Economics Department whose "pure" mathematical and econometric character came to replace its earlier "applied" concerns.

Most revealing of all was the succession, in 1951, of Michael Oakeshott to Laski's chair of political science. Oakeshott established himself as a "conservative" thinker of international repute, and his controversial inaugural (*On Political Education*) argued for the utter irrelevance of academic enquiry to practical politics and announced his view of the university as concerned solely with the former. Oakeshott's arrival exemplifies two important aspects of the School. First, it confirms that indifference to "practical relevance" is as strong an element in its tradition as is "engagement." Second, its shows that, nonetheless, the question of the relationship between theory and practice has been a perennial theme in the School's academic life. Oake-shott himself was best known, before his arrival, for his published hostility to post-war British socialism.

What the Webbs had bequeathed was not a school for socialists or collectivists, still less a school where uncommitted scholarship had a subordinate place. The inheritance was, rather, a school solely concerned with social science (and the intellectual implications of that concern) and therefore with the relationship between academic enquiry and "practical" public policy. This core concern explains both the status of its library as the pre-eminent social science collection in Europe, and the attractions of its Graduate School, which has now come to constitute more than half of its 5,000 students. These students come from almost every country: more than half of the student body comes from outside Britain.

But the collective identity of the LSE does not reside only in this intellectual core; there is, in addition, the underlying question of how the School is governed. In the formal, teaching sense, the collective social science focus was given concrete form in the B.Sc.(Econ.) degree. This (the School's major degree) sought to expose undergraduates both to the variety and scope of the social sciences and to later specialized study in one particular field: it attempted to avoid the incommensurate and atomistic world of university institutions based on a variety of single-subject degrees. Academic specialization has inevitably imposed strains on these inter-departmental/-inter-disciplinary collaborations, but there have always been compensating pressures. There has been a productive tension between successive directors (and the bureaucracy of which they are in nominal charge) and the academics. The autocratic ambitions of Beveridge were an important stimulus to this process, but the participatory values of the School probably owe more to the nature of social science enquiry itself—another unintended legacy of the Webbs. Since the 1970s, the strength of this collective identity has enabled the School to face numerous external pressures with a significant degree of self-confidence. It has so far weathered public expenditure cuts by moving rapidly to a self-financing position, attempts by successive British governments to dictate its future, and the oscillations of British educational policy in general.

Alan Beattie

Bibliography
Beveridge, Janet. *An Epic of Clare Market.* 1960.
Caine, Sir Sydney. *The History of the Foundation of the London School of Economics and Political Science.* 1963.
Dahrendorf, Ralf. *LSE: A History of the London School of Economics and Political Science.* 1995.
Robbins, Lord. *Autobiography of an Economist.* 1971.

Lutyens, Edwin Landseer (1869–1944)

The ARCHITECTURE of Edwin Lutyens was grounded in the venerable associations of the English village, sustained by an Arts and Crafts sensitivity to materials and traditional building techniques, and invigorated by a spatial ingenuity which contributed to the creation of some of the most accomplished work of his generation in England. During an era of "pioneer modernism" it was the traditionalist Lutyens who established a position of preeminence in twentieth-century British architectural history unmatched since Christopher Wren.

Lutyens was born in the Surrey village of Thursley, and it was here amidst rambling country lanes, dense woodland copses, and hoary village structures that he formed his earliest architectural aesthetic. His first major work to embody this Lutyenesque domestic style was Crooksbury (1889–91), a rambling Surrey house whose added east brick wing of 1898 (since altered) would also introduce his restrained classical aesthetic wittily dubbed "Wrenaissance." It was also here that Lutyens met Gertrude Jekyll, whose plantings would join Lutyens house designs and garden layouts to create an Edwardian tradition of comfortable cottages and old-fashioned gardens.

Lutyens' country houses of the 1890s and early twentieth century especially give evidence of this traditionalism. Munstead Wood (1894), Jekyll's home and garden laboratory, was a small estate of huts, cottages, and seasonal gardens. Munstead Wood house itself was a stone cottage, accented by oak casement windows, tall brick chimneys, and sheltering expanses of plain tile roofs which nestled the domestic forms close to the land and Jekyll's plantings. High Hascombe (1896), Fulbrook (1897), Orchards (1898), and Tigbourne Court (1899)—all in Surrey—continued to establish Lutyens's reputation, advanced significantly by the frequent publication of his houses in *Country Life*. Indeed, in 1904 Lutyens designed for *Country Life* its London headquarters, the architect's first office building and another exercise in the "Wrenaissance style." Moreover, it was for *Country Life* editor, Edward Hudson, that Lutyens built his most published house, the Deanery Garden (1901), and that he made habitable the ruined Lindisfarne Castle on Holy Island, Northumberland (1903), and altered Plumpton Place, Sussex (1928). These varied yet related architectural manipulations of history, traditional form, and contextualism help define the essential ingredients of Lutyens's vernacular aesthetic.

Deanery Garden lies unobtrusively behind ancient garden walls in the heart of the village of Sonning, Berkshire, the house less than 100 years old yet capturing the timeless spirit of the village setting. Folly Farm (also 1901 and in Berkshire) joins an existing aged farmhouse to a classical "seventeenth-century Dutch" wing by Lutyens (1906) and further to a 1912 vernacular wing, whose southwest corner suggests forms approaching the American Henry Hobson Richardson in his translations of the English Queen Anne traditions of Richard Norman Shaw. Little Thakeham (1902) in West Sussex offers ironic declarations and denials of axis and symmetry in its garden elevation and Elizabethan hall-plan. Tigbourne Court is also remarkable in its architectural contradictions, juxtaposing a picturesque garden front, traditional building techniques, and unexpected classical references.

Homewood (1901) in Hertfordshire provides Lutyens's ultimate synthesis of these vernacular and classical themes; on Homewood's garden elevation a classical villa sprouts forth from the flanking and nestling farmhouse roof. Almost metaphorically, Lutyens declared here the birth of his classical persuasions from the womb of native vernacular traditions; as his twentieth-century work evolved, classicism for individual projects would become dominant and explicit.

Nashdom (1905–9) monumentalized eighteenth-century Georgian facades, defined wholly by fenestration, axis, and projecting bays. His compact Georgian house in Kent, The Salutation (1911), with its red brick construction in two main stories and five bays with quoins, its central door, and its hipped roof with tall chimneys and three dormers created the model for the twentieth-century neo-Georgian suburban detached house. At Marsh Court (1901) Artisan Mannerist details provide classical detail within a Haddon Hall-inspired Tudor shell. And in Yorkshire Lutyens produced his most playful exercise in the "high game of architecture." Heathcote (which Lutyens called Sanmichele), was a Mannerist pile of transmogrified classicism which more than vaguely referenced the Mannerist decorative overlays of sixteenth-century Italy, the sculptural richness and scale manipulations of Nicholas Hawksmoor, and the composition of such Anglo-Palladians as Colen Campbell.

It is certainly at New Delhi (1912–29) that Lutyens both rationalizes and monumentalizes British classicism in the most "elemental" and memorable way. While his orderly layout at Hampstead Garden Suburb (1908–9), balancing The Institute with his Free Church and St. Jude's Church, looks forward to his classical planning at the Indian capital, the monumentality of his city plan of New Delhi and the masterful handling of climax, scale, and detail at his domed Viceroy's House is unsurpassed in his oeuvre. Only his Thiepval Memorial Arch (1924) and Liverpool Cathedral project (1929–43) would

approach this classical grandeur and monumentality in their free composition of triumphal arch motifs. The elemental, abstract simplicity of Lutyens's Cenotaph in Whitehall (1919) distilled and conveyed the essential message of war's desolation. In a similar way at New Delhi, Lutyens masterfully embodied the final glories of imperial Britain; the focal climax of his plan, the Viceroy's House, is architecturally localized by Moghul details in a subtle and comfortable symbiosis with classical motifs, and humanized, especially by its gardens, by retaining the scale and spirit of an English country house. From his roots in the English vernacular, Lutyens crowned his career in India with a demonstration that he was a master of western architecture's oldest established language: classicism.

Among his other major commissions were the Midland Bank in the City and the British Embassy in Washington. Lutyens was knighted in 1918, served as President of the Royal Academy, 1938–44, and received the Order of Merit in 1942.

Robert M. Craig

Bibliography

Brown, Jane. *Gardens of a Golden Afternoon: The Story of a Partnership, Edwin Lutyens and Gertrude Jekyll.* 1982.

Butler, A.S.G., with George Stewart and Christopher Hussey. *The Architecture of Sir Edwin Lutyens.* 1950.

Gradidge, Roderick. *Edwin Lutyens: Architect Laureate.* 1981.

Inskip, Peter. *Lutyens.* 1979.

O'Neill, Daniel. *Sir Edwin Lutyens: Country Houses.* 1980.

Lytton Commission (1931–1932)

Named after its British chairman, Victor, Second Earl of Lytton (1876–1947), the commission was set up in December 1931 by the LEAGUE OF NATIONS in response to an appeal by China concerning the violation of its sovereignty by Japan. The Lytton Commission was to study and report on the circumstances surrounding Japanese military action following the Mukden incident of September 1931. Japanese troops of the Kwantung army had staged a mock bandit attack on the Japanese-controlled South Manchuria Railway near Mukden, and were using this as a pretext to take over Manchuria. The final report of the commission and how it was perceived highlighted the extent to which Great Britain and the other European powers were anxious to avoid a confrontation with Japan in the early 1930s.

The Foreign Office, under SIR JOHN SIMON, saw no vital interest at stake in Manchuria, an attitude shared by the other powers. It was accepted that Japan had acted with an unnecessary measure of force, but with the partial exception of the United States (which, at the instigation of Henry Stimson, adopted a policy of non-recognition toward the new puppet state of Manchukuo), there was a fair degree of sympathy and understanding among the powers concerning the need to intervene in order to protect economic interests when the local Chinese authorities appeared unable to maintain order.

Given that its members were mostly representatives of the European powers, the Lytton Commission tended to reflect this mentality. A sympathetic point of view, however, was counter-balanced by the undeniable evidence that all control over Manchurian affairs had been forcibly taken out of Chinese hands. In drafting the commission's final report after many months of travel, Lord Lytton felt compelled to state that while no clear-cut violation of sovereignty had taken place in view of the inability of the Chinese government to keep the peace in Manchuria (and the right of the Japanese to defend their lives and property), the new status quo was unacceptable. He proposed that limited Chinese sovereignty be reestablished, with adequate safeguards for Japanese interests in the region and strict limitations on the number of Japanese and Chinese troops in the region.

The British government hoped that the even-handedness of the final report would allow room to negotiate a face-saving formula that would avert a confrontation between the leading members of the League of Nations and Japan. Overt action by the League, it was feared, would drive Japan towards further aggression and might even provoke military action against the naval base at Singapore at a time when Britain was fully occupied with the political and economic consequences of the Depression. However, despite lack of action by Britain and the other powers in response to the report—the possibility of an arms embargo was raised and swiftly abandoned in CABINET—when the League Assembly voted overwhelmingly in favor of the solution proposed by Lytton on 24 February 1933, the Japanese delegation walked out and announced that Japan would be leaving the League the following month.

S.P. MacKenzie

Bibliography

Bassett, R. *Democracy and Foreign Policy.* 1952.

Louis, Wm. Roger. *British Strategy in the Far East, 1919–1939.* 1971.

Northedge, F.S. *The League of Nations: Its Life and Times.* 1986.

Thorne, Christopher. *The Limits of Foreign Policy: The West, the League and the Far Eastern Crisis of 1931–1933.* 1972.

MacDiarmid, Hugh [Christopher Murray Grieve] (1892–1978)

Hugh MacDiarmid—poet, critic, nationalist, Marxist, polemicist—was the key figure in the literary and cultural movement called the Scottish Renaissance. As an editor, publisher, and essayist he defined and promoted it; as a poet he produced its finest work. Throughout his life, moreover, he sustained a public commitment to SCOTTISH NATIONALISM and the Scots language that has profoundly influenced the development of twentieth-century Scottish literature and language. His early poetry, written in Scots, appeared in *Sangschaw* (1925), *Penny Wheep* (1926), his book length masterpiece, *A Drunk Man Looks at the Thistle* (1926), and *To Circumjack Cencrastus* (1930). Both an activist and a writer, MacDiarmid founded the Scottish Centre of PEN, helped found the National Party of Scotland and was active in the COMMUNIST PARTY OF GREAT BRITAIN. Both his Marxism and his nationalism were part of a life-long resistance to English cultural, political, and literary dominance in Great Britain.

In the 1920s MacDiarmid launched the Scottish Renaissance by publishing a three-volume series, *Northern Numbers*, to introduce new Scottish poets. In 1922 he started *The Scottish Chapbook,* a journal of Scottish literature and cultural criticism aimed at redefining the national scene. His own Scots lyrics first appeared there, along with regular editorials on Scots as a literary medium that could be recuperated as a distinctive national language; his motto was "Not Burns, Dunbar." *The Scottish Chapbook* (August 1922–November/December 1923) was succeeded by *The Scottish Nation* (May 1923–December 1923) and *The Northern Review* (May 1924–August 1924). In 1926 he wrote a series of articles in *The Scottish Educational Journal*. In every venue he argued for Scotland's culture, literature, and distinctive languages (Scots and Gaelic).

MacDiarmid's early lyrics were, in part, linguistic experimentation. Written in "Synthetic Scots"—a composite of words from any region or historic period—they were intended to assimilate the full range of Scottish life into literature and to demonstrate that modern intellectual poetry could be written in the Scots vernacular. His poetry was intended to instance a new, modern aesthetic as well as a vehicle for transforming Scottish national culture.

In *A Drunk Man Looks at the Thistle* (1926) MacDiarmid moved from lyrics to the long poem, a form he increasingly championed as a way of "opening out" and incorporating the complexity of modern life. Also written in Scots, it includes translations of poems from Russian and European writers as well as references to a wide range of literatures. Using quotation and allusion, MacDiarmid draws on alternative traditions to create a highly complex modernist text deliberately countering the canonized European tradition. *To Circumjack Cencrastus,* MacDiarmid's last long poem in Scots, reflects his increasing interest in Gaelic literature and history as Scotland's most distinctive tradition.

In the 1930s MacDiarmid shifted from writing lyrics in Scots, strongly based in the sounds and rhythms of the vernacular, to long poems in "Synthetic English" that experimented with both technique and theme. Several poems, notably "On a Raised Beach," use obscure, technical English vocabulary or minute examinations of physical detail in stones, plants, water, or landscapes to create a poetry that joins "aesthetic effects" with what MacDiarmid called "the work of prose." He wished to push English to express more complex possibilities of meaning and, in the process, to continue to challenge the English-based tradition. Many of his later poems explore Gaelic values and cultural forms such as bagpipe music and the Celtic myth. His most radical break with poetic tradition was the late "poetry of fact," including *The Kind of Poetry I Want* (1961) and *In Memoriam James Joyce* (1955), both containing extensive quotations, long lists of obscure words and references, commentaries on world language, and extended images. Little understood at the time, this poetry is postmodern in its move towards multiculturalism, linguistic play, and the dissolving of genre boundaries.

In his poetry, prose, political activity, and cultural analysis, Hugh MacDiarmid challenged the dominance of English language, values, and ideas in Britain. He called instead for a mutually complementary interchange of distinctive contributions from all the countries that make up

Britain. His major importance is as a leading proponent of Scots as a distinct language and as the foremost Scottish poet in the twentieth century.

Nancy K. Gish

Bibliography

Gish, Nancy, ed. *Hugh MacDiarmid: Man and Poet.* 1992.

MacDiarmid, Hugh. *The Letters of Hugh MacDiarmid.* 1984.

———. *Lucky Poet: a Self-Study in Literature and Political Ideas, Being the Autobiography of Hugh MacDiarmid (Christopher Murray Grieve)* 1943.

MacDonald, [James] Ramsay (1866–1937)

No twentieth-century British political leader has been more reviled than Ramsay MacDonald, Britain's first Labour Prime Minister in 1924 and 1929–31. His decision to offer the resignation of the second Labour government and to accept the King's commission to form a National government during the financial crisis of August 1931 provoked much animus among his supporters and sustained the view that he had planned to ditch the Labour government. It has long been an axiom of the LABOUR PARTY that his actions in 1931 marked him out as a traitor, and William Lawther remarked that MacDonald was "bereft of any public decency." To many of his former supporters, the man who had created the Labour Party had also helped to undermine it in the 1930s.

MacDonald was born at Lossiemouth in Scotland on 12 October 1866, the illegitimate son of Anne Ramsay and, possibly, John MacDonald, a ploughman. Despite his social disadvantage he was a bright child, became a pupil teacher, and appeared destined for a career in teaching. However, in the summer of 1885 he took up an administrative post in Bristol and in 1886 went to London where he took up a number of clerical positions, until he became private secretary in 1888 to Thomas Lough, a Liberal Radical politician. He left Lough's employment in 1892 to pursue a career in politics and journalism.

MacDonald acquired wide political experience between 1885 and 1892. He joined the Social Democratic Federation, a quasi-Marxist organization, while in Bristol. His employment with Lough also put him in contact with many leading Liberal Radicals. Indeed, he continued to move within Liberal, Radical, and socialist circles throughout the 1890s. Initially he had ambitions of becoming a Liberal MP and was selected as the Liberal candidate for the Dover constituency shortly after the 1892 general election, but he was thwarted in his attempt to become a Liberal candidate for Southampton in 1894. Thereafter, he cultivated his socialist connections more assiduously, campaigning for the INDEPENDENT LA-BOUR PARTY (ILP) candidate in the Sheffield Attercliffe parliamentary by-election in June 1894, joining the ILP in July 1894, and becoming the ILP and Labour Electoral Association candidate for Southampton in 1894, on whose behalf he was thoroughly trounced in the 1895 general election.

During the early 1890s MacDonald was introduced to SIDNEY WEBB, joined the FABIAN SOCIETY, and acted as a Fabian lecturer in 1892, touring South Wales, the Midlands and the northeast, speaking on topics such as "Why are the many poor?" In 1896 and 1897 he was also a member of the Rainbow Circle, which first met in the Rainbow Tavern in Fleet Street and brought together some collectivist Liberals, such as HERBERT SAMUEL, who felt that the old LIBERAL PARTY was about to disintegrate. This group published papers and, briefly, *The Progressive Review*, in the hope of encouraging the formation of a new center party in British politics. This desire, as well as an interest in foreign policy, were to be two of the abiding passions which MacDonald pursued throughout the rest of his political career.

Marriage to Margaret Gladstone in November 1896 provided MacDonald with the financial security which enabled him to develop his political career. The marriage settlement provided the MacDonalds with £160 rising to £300 per year, a considerable income for the time, in addition to his own earnings. The couple moved to 3 Lincoln Inn Fields, London, which was later to be the base for the LABOUR REPRESENTATION COMMITTEE in its formative years. Margaret died on 8 September 1911, but in their brief marriage they had six children; Alister, born 1898; Malcolm in 1901; Ishbel in 1903; David in 1904; Joan in 1908; and Sheila in 1910. Margaret played an active part in Ramsay's early political career and was a partner whose loss he never overcame. MacDonald's political career had begun to blossom in the mid-1890s. He was elected to the executive of the Fabian Society in the spring of 1894, although various conflicts within the body led him to move his energies to the ILP. He had joined the party in 1894, its National Administrative Council in 1896, and remained a leading figure in it, often acting as either its Chairman or Secretary, until the FIRST WORLD WAR. Thereafter he drifted away from the ILP and formally resigned from it in May 1930. MacDonald's work for the ILP alone would fill most lifetimes, but his real claim to fame arose from the fact that he, more than others, was responsible for the formation and early development of the British Labour Party.

The Labour Representation Committee (LRC) was formed in February 1900, and changed its name to the Labour Party in 1906. MacDonald was its leader, acting as Secretary, until he resigned over the decision of the Labour Party to support the British war effort in 1914. From the start he attempted to obtain trade union support, an endeavor which was greatly helped by the attack upon trade union funds which was leveled by the TAFF VALE dispute in 1901. Although trade union support did flow into the LRC, MacDonald quickly realized that the infant organization needed to improve its parliamentary position in the short term. Only two of its candidates had been returned in the autumn 1900 general election, and MacDonald had been badly defeated in his Leicester contest. As a result, he held at least eight secret meetings with Jesse Herbert, confidential secretary to Herbert Gladstone, the chief Liberal Whip, to arrange the infamous "Lib-Lab" pact of 1903 whereby the Labour Party would be allowed a straight run against the CONSERVATIVES in about thirty seats in return for a similar arrangement for the Liberals. Despite denying that the pact existed, MacDonald operated it in the general election of December 1905 and January 1906. The LRC put fifty candidates into the field, had twenty-nine returned, of whom only five had faced Liberal opposition.

The 1906 general election was something of a personal triumph for MacDonald for he had built up the organization of the party, an enormous task in its own right but even more so when set against his ILP and other political activities. From the start, the LRC was an alliance of socialists and trade unionists rather than a socialist organization as such. Its main purpose was to attract trade union support. This exigent need qualified MacDonald's own ambition to create a party which would attract support from all the political classes, an ambition which was always thwarted by the increasing trade union domination of the LRC/Labour Party. Nevertheless, he helped to shape the new party in its gradualist approach to social change through his creation of the Socialist Library, to which he contributed his own books, including *Socialism and Society* (1905), *Socialism and Government* (1909), and *The Socialist Movement* (1911). The dominating theme of his work was that a form of social Darwinism ensured that private organizations would get bigger, that the state would need to intervene, and that socialism would emerge from the success, not the failure, of capitalism. Because of the influence of MacDonald and of the Webbs during the First World War, these essentially Fabian views became the defining factor in the socialism which the Labour Party eventually espoused in 1918.

Following his successes in 1906, MacDonald dominated the Labour Party, rising to be Leader of the Parliamentary Labour Party. He was also considered to be an effective MP for Leicester,

the two-member constituency which he represented from 1906–18. But the price of his success was support for the Liberal governments of the pre-war years to such an extent that he was strongly criticized for creating a Labour "tail to the Liberal party." But his reputation for radicalism was restored, briefly, by his opposition to the First World War, which ultimately lost him his seat for Leicester in the 1918 general election and earned him the appellation "traitor."

In the immediate post-war years, relieved of his parliamentary duties, he concentrated his efforts upon building up the propaganda machine of the Labour Party. However, in 1922 he was returned to Parliament for Aberavon, and shortly afterwards became Leader of the Parliamentary Labour Party. When the Conservatives failed to win a majority for their protectionist policies in December 1923 MacDonald, at the beginning of 1924, was asked to form a minority Labour government, with Liberal support. It lasted less than ten months, achieved little, and was replaced by the Conservatives after the 1924 general election. For the next five years, he led a Labour Party to which, according to PHILIP SNOWDEN, he was becoming a stranger. He was criticized for his inactivity in the GENERAL STRIKE and retreated into his concern for peace in international relations. Yet his fortunes improved greatly when he was returned for Seaham, a safer seat than Aberavon, and when the Labour Party won the general election of May 1929, although once again it was a minority government propped up by Liberal support.

The fortunes of the Labour government rose as the economy prospered and improved throughout 1929, but the Wall Street crash in the autumn of 1929 changed all that. As a result of the world recession, UNEMPLOYMENT in Britain rose from about 1 million to 3 million in two years, the Labour government grossly overspent its budget and precipitated the financial crisis of August 1931, in which the CABINET attempted to find the spending cuts demanded by the opposition parties, the May Committee, and the international community. The Cabinet split on the decision to cut unemployment benefits by 10 per cent. MacDonald offered the resignation of his government to the King but returned with a mandate to form a National government, which would include Conservative and Liberal parties as well as any Labour support which he could muster. These events led many within Labour ranks to suggest that MacDonald had schemed to ditch the second Labour government, although the recent work of David Marquand has refuted such an idea.

During the years 1931–5 MacDonald was Prime Minister of a National government, which won an overwhelming victory in the 1931 general election. During this period his power depended upon the Conservatives, who encouraged a move towards protectionism. MacDonald indulged himself in foreign policy and was very much involved in two conferences in 1932—the Geneva disarmament conference and the Lausanne conference, which was concerned with German reparations. Thereafter, his political career declined. He found himself attacked by former colleagues, most notably Snowden, went into physical and mental decline and was forced to resign as Prime Minister on 7 June 1935. He stayed on in government but had lost any real power. Indeed, his political decline was further evident when, in the general election of November 1935, he lost his seat at Seaham to Emanuel Shinwell, the man who had put him forward as Parliamentary Labour Party Leader in 1922. MacDonald subsequently found a seat for Scottish Universities but thereafter played a diminishing part in the activities of the National government. He died of heart failure on 9 November 1937 whilst cruising in the Caribbean on the *Reina del Pacifico*. His body was returned to Britain and cremated on 26 November 1937, and his ashes were interred in the Spynie graveyard, near Lossiemouth, next to those of his wife.

Keith Laybourn

Bibliography

Barker, Bernard, ed. *Ramsay MacDonald's Political Writings*. 1972.

Laybourn, Keith. *The Rise of Labour*. 1988.

Marquand, David. *Ramsay MacDonald*. 1977.

Ward, Stephen R. *James Ramsay MacDonald: Low Born Among the High Brows*. 1990.

Weir, L. MacNeill. *The Tragedy of Ramsay MacDonald*. 1938.

Macleod, Iain Norman (1913–1970)

Of Conservative leaders between WINSTON CHURCHILL and MARGARET THATCHER, Iain Macleod was one of the most distinctive. He set the British tropical Empire on the road to swift DECOLONIZATION, purveyed a soundly progressive form of Conservatism, and by his example showed that middle class men could succeed in a socially exclusive party. To many in the 1960s he was the best proof that the CONSERVATIVE PARTY was neither stupid nor illiberal.

Macleod was born on 11 November 1913 at Skipton, Yorkshire, where his father, a Liberal, practiced medicine. Both his parents were from the Hebrides, and Macleod went to a Scottish school, Fettes, before reading history at CAMBRIDGE. Between graduation in 1935 and 1945, his ambitions centred on bridge, a major source of income until 1952, and on which he wrote extensively. Until 1945, when he was thirty-two, he ap-

pears to have been non-political, although in that year he unsuccessfully contested his home constituency of the Western Isles.

After ARMY service during the Second World War, he joined a brilliant group of future ministers in the Conservative Research Department, where his mentor was R.A. BUTLER, and concentrated on the modernization of Conservative social policy. In 1950 he became MP for the London suburban seat of Enfield, which he held until his death.

In Parliament he specialized in health, making his reputation by demolishing ANEURIN BEVAN (27 March 1952), founder of the NATIONAL HEALTH SERVICE, and becoming, at thirty-eight, Minister of Health (1952–5) under Churchill, a post then outside the CABINET. As Minister of Labour (1955–9) under EDEN and MACMILLAN, he handled the trade unions tactfully but on occasion firmly. Neither post gave him much scope.

As Macmillan's Colonial Secretary (1959–61), Macleod, in contrast to his predecessor, was an enthusiastic decolonizer. His achievement was that, without bloodshed, Britain left Africa, its tropical Empire becoming a COMMONWEALTH of independent states. Though Macleod did not complete his task, his policies were never reversed. He treated the interests of white settlers as secondary, released imprisoned African leaders, and stood for a "deliberate speeding-up" of independence. Any other policies, he said,"would have led to terrible bloodshed in Africa."

The episode did him irreparable damage, and Lord Salisbury branded him "too clever by half," a phrase that stuck. An unsuccessful period as Party Chairman and Leader of the House (1961–3) did not help matters, and Macleod was unable to contest the leadership in 1963 or 1965, when he supported Butler and EDWARD HEATH respectively.

He retired from office in 1963, disagreeing with the choice of LORD HOME as Leader, and became editor of the *Spectator*, rejoining the shadow Cabinet after the 1964 defeat. He became Chancellor of the Exchequer (20 June–20 July 1970) under Heath and died in office.

Convivial, an effective speaker, endowed with photographic memory, debating skills and courage, he had the talents and ambition to lead his party, though not the health; in the last twenty years of his life, he was in constant pain from severe arthritis and war wounds. Often called the "wordsmith" of his party, he was not original, but vividly expressed the ideas of his time, and as such was the least dull "Tory" (as he always called himself) of his era.

John Vincent

Bibliography

Darwin, John. *The End of the British Empire*. 1991.

Fisher, Nigel. *Iain Macleod*. 1973.

Goldsworthy, David. *Colonial Issues in British Politics, 1945–1961*. 1971.

Shepherd, Robert. *Iain Macleod*. 1994.

Macmillan, (Maurice) Harold (1894–1986)

As Prime Minister from January 1957 to October 1963, Harold Macmillan was the most prominent representative among CONSERVATIVE Prime Ministers of the British post-war consensus. Like HAROLD WILSON, he was the first Prime Minister of his party to recognize, while failing to halt, British decline. The remarkable success of the first part of his premiership was followed by a second half marked by exceptional setbacks and scandals. Economically, he set Britain on a mildly inflationary path. Externally, he will be remembered for initiating, if not completing, the final DECOLONIZATION of the British Empire, chiefly in Africa.

Harold Macmillan was the son of an American-born mother, Helen Hill, *née* Belles, by Maurice Macmillan, the son of the Scottish founder of Macmillan & Co., booksellers and publishers. He retained a lifelong connection with the firm, becoming chairman on retirement from politics in 1964. Despite the relatively recent arrival of his family on the scene, Macmillan took readily to the part of aristocrat.

Intellectually as well as socially, Macmillan from youth was part of the British intellectual and social elite. At Eton, he was one of that select intellectual minority, the scholars; at Balliol College, Oxford, then the leading academic college, he won an exhibition or minor award, and a first class degree in classics in 1919, despite having been wounded three times, once severely, in the First World War. At Oxford, he moved in a brilliant circle around Monsignor Ronald Knox, the Catholic wit and scholar, and indeed perhaps nearly became a Catholic.

Instead, he became aide-de-camp (1919–20) to the ninth Duke of Devonshire, then Governor-General of Canada, marrying in 1920 his daughter, Lady Dorothy Cavendish (d. 1966). Despite final reconciliation, the marriage was unhappy, and for most of his public career Macmillan, not through his own fault, was separated, a fact of which the general public was then unaware.

He was MP for the marginal seat of Stockton in 1924–9, and again in 1929–45, despite defeats in 1923, 1929 and in the 1945 landslide. His constituency perhaps shaped his outlook, as he always claimed. As a northern industrial town in an area of high UNEMPLOYMENT, it focused Macmillan's mind on the need to defeat LABOUR on its own terms.

In the 1930s Macmillan was seen as distinctly on the left wing of his party and as an ineffectual figure unlikely to hold office. For a time in the mid-1930s he renounced the party whip, and in 1938–9 opposed CHAMBERLAIN's foreign policy. As a very minor member of the CHURCHILL group, he voted against Chamberlain (May 1940), thus helping to put Churchill in power. His numerous books on social topics made little impact except as marking his dissatisfaction with pre-war Conservatism.

Under Churchill, however, he became, none too quickly, one of the premier's rising stars, holding very junior office in 1940–2 and minor office, briefly, in 1942. The fortunes of war then led him to be Minister Resident at Allied H.Q. in North-West Africa (1942–5). There, under a succession of changing titles, he was the British minister immediately responsible for the whole Mediterranean theater. In this post he showed infinite sagacity, but in his old age his achievement was blurred by controversy over the British repatriation of Soviet nationals and others to death at the hands of the Soviet Union and Yugoslavia. His undoubted success established him as a serious political figure, and he was briefly Air Minister in Churchill's "caretaker" government of May–July 1945.

Despite defeat in the 1945 general election, Macmillan soon (November 1945) won a safe London suburban seat, holding it easily until retirement (October 1964). He took a vigorous part in the conduct of the Conservative opposition in 1945–51. When his party regained power in 1951, his appointment as Minister of Housing and Local Government (1951–4) placed him in the limelight.

Faced with an acute HOUSING shortage, the Conservatives had rashly pledged themselves to build 300,000 dwellings annually, a seemingly impossible target. Using business advisers and methods, and reducing quality somewhat, Macmillan achieved an increase, taking public and private dwellings together, from 172,400 in Labour's last full year, to 309,000 in 1954, taking figures for England and Wales alone. This fact reflected real ability as well as a general rise in prosperity, and was Macmillan's most unqualified personal achievement. Since this was a quiet period in education and health, Macmillan's success in housing was the most prominent element in Conservative social policy in the 1950s.

Macmillan was the only Prime Minister to reach sixty without having held one of the great offices of state. Even after that age, he had scant experience of senior posts, serving as EDEN's Foreign Secretary in 1955 for only eight months, and as his Chancellor of the Exchequer for thirteen months (December 1955–January 1957), in neither case making any particular mark. His one budget attracted attention only by introducing premium bonds, a form of state lottery.

It was the SUEZ CRISIS rather than ministerial achievement which made Macmillan Prime Minister, an office which at sixty-two he could hardly have expected. It was Suez, too, which destroyed R.A. BUTLER, Macmillan's main rival, and a consistent skeptic about the Suez invasion. Macmillan initially was all for war, not just to regain international control of the Suez Canal, but to conquer Egypt and overthrow Colonel Nasser. He ignored Treasury warnings that sterling would collapse; when it did so, because of American displeasure, he more than anyone insisted on stopping the campaign when victory seemed in sight. As Harold Wilson said, "he was first in and first out." When an ill and discredited Eden resigned (9 January 1957), Macmillan was the inevitable successor, having overwhelming CABINET backing, and probably general party approval despite the absence of any formal election.

As Prime Minister, Macmillan achieved much. He reunited a divided party. In his only general election (8 October 1959) as Prime Minister, his party won for a third time and with an increased majority. He restored Anglo-American relations, at a low ebb because of Suez, and supposedly achieved an almost paternal relationship with President Kennedy. He initiated, and partly carried through, a second and final phase of decolonization in Africa. Unlike Labour's decolonization of India, this was bloodless.

In defense he abolished CONSCRIPTION, placing his reliance on a professional ARMY and the British independent nuclear deterrent, a footing that successive governments have followed. In foreign affairs he announced the nuclear Test Ban Treaty and gradually persuaded his party to apply to join the EUROPEAN COMMUNITY (July 1961). These policies can be seen as an attempt to restore British fortunes after the loss of empire.

After a subdued year in 1957, Macmillan in 1958 set about adapting the ideas of J.M. KEYNES to a mildly inflationary environment and to his electoral needs. The result was the boom of 1958–60, a surge not seen since the war, with the stock market doubling. The loss of his entire Treasury team in January 1958 over what they considered excessive expenditure, though dismissed by Macmillan as "a little local difficulty," and ostensibly involving only a modest sum, marked deep differences over his connivance at mild inflation.

Macmillan's phrase, "You've never had it so good," though taken out of context and meant as a warning, was widely held to embody his outlook. Similarly, the use of the epithet "Supermac" by the cartoonist Vicky reflected the confidence Macmillan inspired in 1959. In the 1959 general election, helped by the poor electioneering of HUGH GAITSKELL, Macmillan swept home on a tide of prosperity.

An African tour in January–February 1960 revealed attitudes not evident before the general election. Speaking in South Africa, he said "a wind of change is blowing through the continent," and his appointment of the liberal IAIN MACLEOD as Colonial Secretary confirmed his new-found commitment to decolonization. Thereafter Macmillan's star waned. The economy required deflation, including a wage freeze, which caused not only resentment, but much debate about Britain's "stop-go" economy. Only the policy of entry into Europe heralded a new departure.

When President de Gaulle finally vetoed British entry (14 January 1963), he denied Macmillan greatness and left him without a policy. Macmillan paid a heavy price for his good relations with the United States, one of his main claims to fame, but also the main obstacle to his European ambitions.

At home, a newly volatile public opinion temporarily made the hitherto insignificant LIBERALS the leading party. A sensational Liberal by-election gain at Orpington (14 March 1962), followed by the Vassall spy case (September 1962), a severe winter in 1962–3 with unemployment rising to the then supposedly unacceptable level of 4 percent, did not improve matters. Against this background, the Profumo scandal (June 1963), though essentially unimportant, brought to light much seediness, raised lurid expectations, and generated an obsessive excitement very damaging to the government. Nothing like it had occurred since the war.

Macmillan's main reaction was to move towards "liberal conservatism," chiefly by dismissing seven Cabinet ministers in the "night of the long knives" (13 July 1963), bringing in able new men, returning to inflationary policies, and laying the foundations of the fairly successful progressive politics of 1963–4.

After some hesitation, Macmillan finally decided in the summer of 1963 to continue as premier. He then fell victim to prostate trouble, resigning on 9 October 1963, though playing a large, and controversial, part while still in hospital in the choice of his successor. He then tactfully disappeared from active politics. Macmillan succumbed to a poor economic climate, to a chapter of newsworthy accidents, to an overserious estimate of his medical condition, to a shift in public mood associated both with loss of deference towards public figures, and a new sense that Britain was the "Sick Man of Europe."

Macmillan, after 1984 Earl of Stockton, died at age 92, the longest-lived of British Prime Ministers, and was buried beside his wife at Horsted Keynes, West Sussex. In his later years, spent in conditions of frugality bordering on hardship, he made much of his role as Chancellor of the UNI-VERSITY OF OXFORD, both in its ceremonial capacity, and informally, talking late into the night to students, who were often startled by his radical views. Politically, he made known his disquiet over aspects of THATCHERISM, such as privatization ("selling off the family silver"), the handling of the 1984 MINERS' STRIKE, and over the social background of the Cabinet ("more Estonians than Etonians").

He presented himself as a patrician, as the last Edwardian, as a Whig (in the tradition of his wife's family), as a romantic Tory, as an intellectual, as a man shaped by the comradeship of the trenches and by the slump of the 1930s, as a shrewd man of business of bourgeois Scottish stock, and as a venerable elder statesman at home with modern youth. There was something in all these views, which he did little to discourage, and which commanded public respect into the early 1960s. Whether he was ever a mainstream Conservative, rather than a skillful exponent of the post-war consensus, is more doubtful.

During his lifetime Macmillan wrote copiously. Of his social and economic books *Reconstruction: A Plea for a National Policy* (1933) and *The Middle Way* (1938) were the best known, but he also wrote his memoirs in six volumes published 1966–73, as well as war diaries which appeared in 1984. His own writings form the main primary source for his life.

John Vincent

Bibliography

Evans, Harold. *Downing Street Diary: The Macmillan Years 1957–1963.* 1981.

Fisher, Nigel. *Harold Macmillan.* 1982.

Hutchinson, George. *The Last Edwardian at No. 10: An Impression of Harold Macmillan.* 1980.

Horne, Alistair. *Macmillan: The Official Biography.* 2 vols. 1988–9.

Turner, John. *Macmillan.* 1994.

MacMillan, Kenneth (1929–1992)

The first and greatest choreographer to emerge from the ranks of the Sadler's Wells Ballet (the Royal Ballet after 1956), Kenneth MacMillan decisively redefined the language of classical BAL-LET in Britain by applying it to contemporary subjects and probing studies of emotion and psychology. In contrast to FREDERICK ASHTON, who provided British ballet with sunny, romantic works and serene visions of pure classicism, MacMillan created narratives of profound dramatic intensity and abstract works that echoed the texts and textures of their scores with remarkable sensitivity.

Born in Scotland and trained as a dancer, MacMillan choreographed several apprentice pieces while still a member of the Sadler's Wells Theatre Ballet; following the premiere of his first professional work, the astringent *Danses Concertantes* (1955), he abandoned dancing entirely and became the company's resident choreographer. Equally at ease working on a grand or intimate scale, he began exploring the themes of isolation, despair, and sexual fervor that would frequently engage him over the years. He also discovered his most important and inspiring interpreter, Lynn Seymour, who became for him the lonely adolescent in *The Burrow* (1958), the blithe young maiden in *Le Baiser de la Fée* (1960) and the shattered victim of a graphically portrayed rape in *The Invitation* (1960). MacMillan drew his most passionate and memorable dance portraits for Seymour, including the title roles of his full-evening *Romeo and Juliet* (1965)—now a staple of repertories around the world—and of the one-act (1967) and three-act (1971) versions of *Anastasia*.

By reshaping the classical vocabulary in striking, expressionistic terms, MacMillan invested his plotless ballets with a sharply dramatic focus. From the primitive barbarism of *The Rite of Spring* (1962) to the haunting austerity of *Song of the Earth* (1965), *Requiem* (1976), and *Gloria* (1980), they depicted both personal and universal emotion through visual imagery that distilled the subtlest nuances of text and music.

As director of the Berlin Opera Ballet (1966–9) and of the Royal Ballet (1970–7), MacMillan used the full resources of his companies to express his devotion to the nineteenth-century classics, mounting new productions of *The Sleeping Beauty* and *Swan Lake.* While leading the Royal Ballet, he expanded its repertory with the work of George Balanchine, Jerome Robbins and Glen Tetley.

At the same time, he continued to adapt the classical steps and conventions to startling dramatic purposes, choreographing three-act narrative works in which *pas de deux* of exceptional intricacy and sensuality alternated with sweeping crowd scenes and solos fashioned as perceptive character sketches. These massive epics included *Manon* (1974); *Mayerling* (1978), the story of a doomed love affair between Crown Prince Rudolf of Austria and Maria Vetsera; *Isadora* (1981), a lavish rendering of the tragic life of Isadora Duncan; and the fairy-tale *The Prince of the Pagodas* (1989), set to music by BENJAMIN BRITTEN.

In 1979 MacMillan received the Queen Elizabeth II Coronation Award from the Royal Academy of Dancing, and he was awarded a knighthood for his services to British ballet in 1983. He died suddenly backstage of a heart attack during a revival of his most ambitious ballet, *Mayerling*.

Barbara Newman

Bibliography

Thorpe, Edward. *Kenneth MacMillan: The Man and the Ballets.* 1985.

MacNeice, Louis (1907–1963)

Louis MacNeice, a poet and junior member of the W.H. AUDEN-CHRISTOPHER ISHERWOOD-STEPHEN SPENDER "literary axis" was born 12 September 1907 in Belfast of Irish parents. His father, John Frederick MacNeice, was the Anglican Bishop of Down, Connor and Dromore, Ireland. After attending Sherbourne Preparatory School for Boys, Dorset (described in his poems "The Kingdom" and *Autumn Sequel*, XXII), he removed to Marlborough College (described in his *Autumn Journal*, XIII), where his close friends included Bernard Spencer, John Betjeman, Graham Shepard, John Hilton, and Anthony Blunt. During 1926–30 he studied at Merton College, OXFORD, reading classics and philosophy, taking a "double first" in Honour Moderations and "Greats." While still an undergraduate, he edited *Oxford Poetry: 1929* with Stephen Spender. He published his first collection of personal poetry, *Blind Fireworks* in 1929; was appointed lecturer in classics at the University of Birmingham in 1930; and published *Poems* in 1935, during which year he visited both Spain and Iceland. In 1936 he was appointed lecturer in Greek at Bedford College, University of London. His translation of Aeschylus' *Agamemnon*, with music by BENJAMIN BRITTEN, was produced in November 1936 at the Westminster Theatre, London. He returned to Iceland with Auden in 1937; their joint travel diary in prose and poetry was subsequently published as *Letters from Iceland*. In December 1937 his two-act play, *Out of the Picture*, was produced by the Group Theatre.

MacNeice's visit to Barcelona in December 1938–January 1939 blossomed into *Autumn Journal: A Poem*, a poetic commentary on national and international affairs. The collection is the last expression of his identification with left-wing politics and with the discussion of momentous political issues in verse inspired by music hall rhymes and rhythms. The Non-Aggression Pact between Germany and the Soviet Union shattered MacNeice's poetic group, which had pledged allegiance to Soviet Communism as the only political force disciplined enough to counter the menace of Nazism. MacNeice's next collection, *Plant and Phantom* (1941) abandoned politics and returned to the philosophic and moral interests he had exhibited as an Oxford undergraduate, although he continued to be hostile to capitalism.

When war came, MacNeice volunteered for the ROYAL NAVY but was rejected because of poor eyesight. As a patriotic alternative, he served as a London firewatcher in the HOME GUARD. The impact of war also led him to join the BBC as scriptwriter and producer, where he remained until 1954, aside from an eighteen-month stint as Director of the British Institute in Athens (1950–1). His second critical study, *The Poetry of W.B. Yeats* appeared in 1941.

In 1942 he memorialized his school friend Graham Shepard, drowned in action on the Atlantic, in "The Kingdom", "The Casualty (in memoriam G.H.S.)", and *Autumn Sequel*, II. His poetry continued its more philosophic mood in *Springboards: Poems, 1941–1944* and *Holes in the Sky: Poems, 1944–1947*. A visit to India in 1947 was reflected in "The Crash Landing" and "Mahabalipuram."

MacNeice published a translation of *Faust* in 1951. What some critics and the poet himself considered his best work, *Ten Burnt Offerings*, appeared in 1952. In 1954 MacNeice received the Premio Italiano Award, in 1957 a D. Litt. degree from the University of Belfast, and in 1958 a C.B.E. His last three poetic works were *Visitations: Poems* (1957); *Solstices: Poems* (1959); and *The Burning Perch: Poems* (1963). He died of pneumonia in London, 3 September 1963.

Elton Edward Smith

Bibliography

Coulton, Barbara. *Louis MacNeice in the BBC*. 1980.

Heberer, Adolphe. *Louis MacNeice, 1907–1963: L'homme et la poésie*. 1986.

MacNeice, Louis. *The Strings Are False: An Unfinished Autobiography*. 1966.

Smith, Elton Edward. *Louis MacNeice*. 1970.

Major, John (1943–)

Prime Minister and Leader of the CONSERVATIVE PARTY from 1990 to 1997, Major rose rapidly from relative obscurity to succeed MARGARET THATCHER in 1990 and was one of the longest-serving of twentieth-century premiers. However, his term was fraught with difficulties and is regarded as one of the least successful premierships, ending in the Conservative defeat of May 1997.

Major had the most ordinary background of all the leaders of the Conservative Party, and this played a part in his selection as leader in 1990 and his popularity between then and the 1992 general election. His upbringing was unusual, affording a contrast with his image as the "gray man" of British politics. Born on 29 March 1943, Major was the younger son of Thomas Ball. His father spent much of his life as a performer in circuses and the theatre, and Major was a stage name which he adopted for general use. He then ran a small business producing garden ornaments, but this ran into difficulties. The family's living standards were much reduced, and John was aged 12 when they moved from a middle-class LONDON suburb to Brixton, a poor and multicultural district nearer the city centre. John attended grammar school but was more interested in sport (and especially CRICKET, a life-long interest) than academic subjects. He had an undistinguished school career and left at the minimum legal age of 16; unlike previous Conservative leaders from lower-middle-class backgrounds, he did not attend university.

His early career included periods of laboring and casual work, and of unemployment. He then secured a job with the Standard Bank, and during a posting in Nigeria was injured in a car accident; although his leg was saved from amputation, damage to his kneecap permanently affected his ability to walk long distances. After returning to England he rose steadily within the bank, and from 1965 became active in Conservative local politics in Brixton. He contested a safe LABOUR inner-city constituency in the 1974 general elections, and took a crucial step forward by securing the candidacy for Huntingdon in 1978. This rural area was one of the safest Conservative seats in the country, and Major entered the House of Commons in 1979.

In 1970 he married Norma Johnson, a dressmaker, and they had two children; their relationship was a focal point of calm during his years as Prime Minister, although Norma preferred to live in their Huntingdon home rather than the official residence of 10 Downing Street.

Major's advancement through the junior ranks of the Thatcher administration was rapid but attracted little notice—it was always others who were singled out as possible future leaders. It was typical of Major that his undemonstrative competence was appreciated by his superiors and that he made no enemies, both factors which were crucial in 1990. From 1981 to 1983 he occupied the lowest rung of the ladder, as a Parliamentary Private Secretary to middle-ranking Home Office ministers. He then served from 1983 to 1985 as a whip, and was then Under-Secretary (1985–6) and Minister of State (1986–7) for Social Security. After Thatcher's third victory in 1987 he entered the CABINET as Chief Secretary to the Treasury. The position was junior to the Chancellor of the Exchequer and concerned mainly with limiting the spending of other departments. Major's unconfrontational success in this was noticed by Thatcher, and she unexpectedly made him Foreign Secretary in July 1989. Three months later the resignation of Nigel Lawson resulted in his move to more familiar ground as Chancellor of the Exchequer. These elevations catapulted him into the front rank and a year later made him a serious contender when Thatcher resigned after the first ballot of the leadership contest. Major's comfortable victory in the second round of voting on 27 November 1990 was the result of his undefined position and the drawbacks of his opponents—Michael Heseltine could not unite the

party after bringing Thatcher down, whilst Douglas Hurd was too patrician and identified with the discredited left-wing. However Major was in the mainstream, and so appeared to be a sound but undogmatic Thatcherite. In fact, his social views were more liberal and his outlook more pragmatic than Thatcher's supporters had expected; after 1992 many of them regretted having supported him for the leadership, and some turned openly and contemptuously against him.

Major became Prime Minister on the day after the second ballot, and the period up to the election of April 1992 was relatively successful. His "ordinary man" image, talk of a classless society (in his first conference speech as leader, October 1991) and less abrasive style of leadership were popular and boosted the Conservatives' low poll ratings. His pragmatic approach was acceptable to most Conservative MPs, and he replaced the disastrous "poll tax" with a much less controversial Council Tax. His abilities as a negotiator were put to effective use at the Maastricht conference of EUROPEAN UNION leaders in 1991, where he secured "opt-outs" for Britain in sensitive areas of social and economic affairs. Europe had become the most divisive issue within the Conservative Party, but Major's careful course secured the support of almost all his MPs for the Maastricht Treaty. The Gulf War had begun before Thatcher's fall, but Major's calm yet firm temperament was shown to good effect during the military operations in early 1991. Even so, and despite a long and expensive pre-election campaign of negative attacks on Labour, most commentators expected a narrow Labour victory or a "hung parliament" to be the outcome of the election which Major finally called in April 1992. Major fought the election in energetic and populist style, using an old-fashioned soap box to address the public, and he was given the credit for the narrow Conservative majority of 20 seats.

The period immediately after the election was the high point of Major's career, but within a few months his government was beset by problems. The election had been won despite the economic recession which had been in progress since 1990. However, unlike previous downturns, this was hitting the Conservative heartlands of southern England. The continuation of the recession after the election, despite promises of recovery, led to a fall in party membership and a series of unprecedented by-election defeats. The worst moment came on "Black Wednesday", 16 September 1992, when a sterling crisis forced a humiliating withdrawal from the European Exchange-Rate Mechanism (ERM). The government's standing and popularity never recovered from this debacle, which was linked to the two sensitive areas of the economy and European integration. In May 1993 Major sacked his Chancellor of the Exchequer, Norman Lamont, and replaced him with the capable but pro-European Kenneth Clarke. The economic position improved considerably from 1995, but by then it was overshadowed by the government's other difficulties.

The most serious of these was the bitter hostility of the "Euro-sceptic" right of the Conservative Party to anything which hinted of closer integration with Europe. This situation resulted in barely concealed rifts within the Cabinet, further highlighted by Major's unguarded reference to the "bastards" who were thwarting his efforts. It also led to the revolt of a small group of backbench MPs, but with the government's slender majority this was enough to turn the parliamentary ratification of the Maastricht Treaty into a lengthy struggle marked by setbacks and votes of confidence. The other long-running and damaging element was the series of personal scandals about the conduct of Conservative MPs and ministers. This undermined Major's appeal in October 1993 for a return to traditional values— "back to basics"—and tarred the party with an image of "sleaze" and arrogance. Another problem was the agricultural crisis resulting from BSE, the "mad cow" disease, which led to European bans on British beef exports. Major's pragmatic style of leadership made it seem as if the government was tossed from side to side by these storms, lacking principles or a sense of direction. The Prime Minister's capacity and style were attacked even by normally loyal newspapers; he was derided as dull and nondescript, the "gray man". There was mounting talk of a leadership challenge, but in June 1995 Major seized the initiative and called a leadership election himself. He won this by 218 votes to 89, and his boldness and the winning margin were enough to secure his position until the next general election. There was only one area where Major was credited with having made a positive and significant impact—NORTHERN IRELAND. Working with the government of Eire, the joint Downing Street Declaration of December 1993 led after patient effort to a cease-fire, political progress and a normalisation of life in the troubled province. Elsewhere, the government's problems continued or even worsened, and by early 1997 by-election losses and defections had eroded its majority in the House of Commons. Major delayed as long as possible, but it was only the scale of the Conservative defeat on 1 May 1997 which caused any surprise. He resigned as Conservative leader the next day, and later announced that he would leave the Commons at the end of that Parliament.

Stuart Ball

Bibliography

Jones, P., and J. Hudson. "The Quality of Political Leadership: A Case Study of John Major," *British Journal of Political Science,* vol. 26 (1996), pp. 229–44.

Kavanagh, Dennis, and Anthony Seldon, eds. *The Major Effect.* 1994.

Major, John. *John Major: The Autobiography.* 1999.

Seldon, Anthony. *Major: A Political Life.* 1997.

[Manchester] Guardian

Since its founding in 1821, the *Manchester Guardian* has evolved from a regional newspaper to a national one. Launched shortly after the 1819 Peterloo massacre, the paper has maintained a liberal stance down to the present time, though it has always been too determinedly independent to be in any sense a party newspaper.

C. P. SCOTT, its editor from 1872 to 1929, came out firmly against British conduct and policy in the BOER WAR. This criticism was so unpopular that police protection was required for his home, and *Guardian* reporters at times had to sneak into the building to avoid attack. But although the incident temporarily hurt the paper's circulation, in the longer term it confirmed Scott's and his paper's integrity and increased his influence. He worked behind the scenes for the Zionist cause and was influential in urging the Balfour Declaration of British support for the idea of a Jewish homeland in PALESTINE. *The Guardian* under Scott also strongly disputed the official pronouncements about the Irish uprisings of 1916 and 1919. Telling unpopular truths at the risk of being perceived as unpatriotic became something of a *Guardian* trademark, further enchancing its reputation for journalistic integrity. Contributors to the paper during the first few decades of the century included such distinguished journalists as J.B. Atkins, H.N. BRAILSFORD, J.L. HAMMMOND, H.W. MASSINGHAM, KINGSLEY MARTIN, C.E. Montague, Malcolm Muggeridge, and Arthur Ransome.

American President Woodrow Wilson sought *Guardian* support for his policies, as did British leaders. Critical of Allied treatment of the defeated Germany, the paper was widely read in the Weimar Republic. But it was from the start wary of Hitler and as early as 1932 warned its readers of Nazi ANTI-SEMITISM, its respected foreign correspondents, F. A. Voight and Alexander Werth, reporting the situation more accurately than most other papers of the 1930s. Its wartime editor, W.P. Crozier, met frequently with WINSTON CHURCHILL, and staunchly supported his policies. The paper shortages of the 1940s reduced the *Guardian* to about one third its pre-war length, but its circulation increased, and it emerged from the war even less regional both in scope and readership.

The post-war decades saw the paper expand and improve its international coverage. Among its best-known correspondents during that era were Alistair Cooke from America, Darsie Gillie from France, and Sylvia Sprigge from Italy. The paper went national in the 1950s, finally removing the regional advertisements that had for so long covered its front page and replacing them with news stories—and, in 1959, removing the work "Manchester" from the title. In 1960, it began publishing in London.

Even though the *Guardian* supported the CONSERVATIVE PARTY in 1950s elections, it continued to adhere to Liberal philosophy and to maintain its independence from the official government line on the news. It firmly opposed the SUEZ campaign in 1956, and again was called unpatriotic during the FALKLANDS WAR, when, unlike most papers, it steadfastly referred to "the British" rather than to "us". It was strongly critical of government policies during the THATCHER years and has leaned towards LABOUR in recent general elections unlike the other "quality" papers. In 1986 its editor, Peter Preston, led a reform movement to print attributions for information handed out in Downing Street briefings, an attempt to break up the comfortable anonymity the PRESS corps had for so long allowed the government.

After some hard financial times in the recession of the 1960s, the *Guardian* strengthened its circulation and advertising revenue base while maintaining its journalistic reputation for quality reporting and perceptive analysis by commentators like Norman Shrapnel, Ian Aitken, Peter Jenkins (who later defected to the *Independent*), and Hugo Young. In the mid-1980s it launched a number of successful initiatives to appeal to younger readers, and in 1993 it acquired control of the Sunday OBSERVER.

Raymond N. MacKenzie

Bibliography

Ayerst, David. *Guardian: Biography of a Newspaper.* 1971.

Hennessy, Peter, and David Walker. "The Lobby" in Jean Seaton and Ben Pimlott, eds. *The Media and British Politics.* 1987. pp. 110–30.

Koss, Stephen. *The Rise and Fall of the Political Press in Britain: vol. 2: The Twentieth Century.* 1984.

Mills, William Haslam. *The Manchester Guardian: A Century of History.* 1921.

Marks and Spencer

"Goods and services once regarded as luxuries have become conventional comforts and are now almost decreed necessities. A fundamental change in people's habits has been brought about." Thus Simon Marks explained how Marks and Spencer contributed to improving the national STANDARD OF LIVING. This was all the more impressive because what became Britain's largest and most successful retail firm had a beginning so modest as to seem mythical. In 1884 Michael Marks, a Russian Jewish immigrant who came to England to escape persecution, opened a stall in Leeds market. Soon after, the poor peddler hit upon a clever way to compensate for his inability to speak English while also drawing attention to his varied wares. "Don't ask the price, it's a penny," was the slogan he used to attract working men and women. His simple, straightforward approach was sufficiently successful that when he formed a partnership with Yorkshireman Tom Spencer, a Gentile cashier in a local business, there were "original penny bazaars" in a number of towns, notably Manchester, which became his center of operations.

It was Simon Marks, Michael's son, and Israel Sieff, a close friend since Manchester Grammar School days, who reshaped the business during the inter-war years. They were responsible for establishing Marks and Spencer branches throughout English high streets and expanding turnover from £550,000 in 1919 to £23.4 million in 1939. Long after Marks and Spencer became a public company in 1924, it retained some of the character of a family business, not least because of the continuing presence of the Sieff clan. Fundamental to its success was the joint pursuit of business efficiency and worker welfare, a humane, intelligent approach also shared by Cadburys. During the 1930s M and S focused on foods and textiles; in so doing, it helped break down the social barriers dividing class and the masses by offering appealing garments at affordable prices. Determined to adapt advanced business methods that he saw at work during visits to America, Simon Marks used attractive premises, stock control, product testing, and rational administration methods to provide the highest quality at the lowest price under St. Michael's label. M and S pioneered cooperative relations with suppliers, turning competitors into allies by helping them improve production methods and ensuring a long-term association. "Close, personal, and friendly relations" was an ideal that applied not only to suppliers. In 1934 Flora Solomon, a Russian Jewish refugee, became the head of the newly formed Personnel Department of M and S. Under her direction, it pursued a policy of "management without tears," adopting welfare schemes to improve the well-being of workers and instituting training schemes to improve individual opportunity while strengthening teamwork.

The story of Marks and Spencer suggests that the work ethic did not die at the end of the nineteenth century, that the entrepreneurial failure all too common in heavy industry did not apply to retailing, and that social reform and competitive success are not adversaries.

Charles Dellheim

Bibliography

Briggs, Asa. *Marks and Spencer, 1884–1984.* 1984.

Rees, Goronwy. *St Michael: A History of Marks and Spencer.* 1969.

Sieff, Israel. *Memoirs of Israel Sieff.* 1970.

Marriage

Marriage is often given serious consideration only when it breaks down, which means that anxiety about its stability as an institution has increased in the late twentieth century and that unfavorable comparisons have been drawn with the apparently more settled relationships of the early 1900s. As with so many aspects of human behavior, the reality is more complicated and contradictory.

Marriage has always been part of the typical experience of adult men and women throughout the century, but the proportion of women reaching their late forties who were (or had been) married fell during the first three decades of the century (from 87 percent in 1891 to 83 percent in 1931). Many women never married, in large part because of the imbalance in the sex ratio, which increased steadily from 1871 to 1911 and dramatically as a result of the FIRST WORLD WAR. But, since the Second World War marriage has become more and more popular. Indeed, contrary to the popular view of the 1960s as a decade of sexual licence, the marriage rate peaked, rising to a high of 357,000 in 1971 (compared to 307,000 in 1931 and 254,000 in 1986). The proportion of marriages that were remarriages for one or both partners rose steadily from 11 percent in 1931 to 20 percent in 1971 and 35 percent in 1986, being in large part a product of the even more dramatic rise in the DIVORCE rate. In addition, the age at marriage for previously unmarried men and women dropped substantially from 26.8 for men and 24.6 for women in 1951 to 24.6 for men and 22.6 for women in 1971. From the late 1970s it began to climb again (to 25.1 for men and 23.1 for women in 1986). Thus, despite the publicity accorded the political activities of both the student movement and FEMINISTS, there was no rebellion by young people against the institution of marriage in the 1960s.

For WOMEN, to remain unmarried continued to carry the idea of failure until well after the Second World War. Marriage was also the main hope of financial well-being. Job opportunities remained very limited for women in the early part of the century, and it did not become common for middle-class women to work outside the home, even before marriage, until after the First World War. The professions (including teaching) imposed a "marriage bar" on women during the inter-war years. During the early part of the century marriage was, as Cicely Hamilton, a prominent feminist, put it grimly in 1909, the main "trade" for women.

The married couple was considered by most early twentieth century social commentators to be the fundamental unit of society and the key to social order. The dominant model of marriage was based on the assumption of the male breadwinner and dependent wife and children, which was believed by social investigators, PHILANTHROPISTS, and policymakers to provide the best hope of ensuring work discipline on the part of working-class men. The reality was somewhat different. While middle-class married women did not go out to work, large numbers of working-class women engaged in part-time or casual work to make ends meet. Working men and women broadly agreed that a "good" husband meant one who brought home a regular wage and showed some regard for women's anxiety regarding the possibility of frequent PREGNANCY AND CHILDBIRTH. A "good" wife was above all a good household manager.

As Ellen Ross has convincingly demonstrated, the meaning of marriage for working men and women rested less on romantic love or verbal and sexual intimacy and more on an understanding of financial obligations, services, and activities that were gender specific. However, if either partner failed to keep his or her side of the bargain, separation was considered reasonable. This departed from the injunctions of middle-class commentators who insisted on the importance of marital stability as well as on gendered responsibilities within marriage. The 1912 Royal Commission on Divorce recommended relaxation of the strict laws on divorce, not so much out of a commitment to liberalization as a desire to make it possible for the large numbers of working people living "in sin" to remarry. Its recommendations were not followed. Views such as those of Mary (Mrs. Humphry) Ward, philanthropist and novelist, who wrote a passionate denunciation of divorce in 1909, prevailed. Ward saw marriage as a discipline and an order. The institution imposed rational bonds on irrational (sexual) urges, something many late Victorians and Edwardians regarded as a threat to civilized codes of behavior. In addition, if differences could not be worked out between husband and wife, then there was felt to be little hope for the wider society. The fact remained that in the early decades of the century separation followed by cohabitation was most common among working people. In contrast, by the third quarter of the twentieth century it was more likely that working people would indulge in all the rituals of the white wedding and that the middle class would engage in at least a period of cohabitation before or between marriages.

Prescriptive ideas regarding marriage underwent considerable change during the century. By the inter-war years members of the legal profession and policymakers were beginning to conceptualize marriage as "companionate." WILLIAM BEVERIDGE, for example, whose 1942 blueprint laid the foundations for post-war social policy, insisted on the equal-but-different contributions of men and women within marriage. This changed little regarding assumptions as to the proper division of labor within marriage (Beveridge himself believed that women's most important job in the post-war world would be to ensure "the adequate continuance of the British race"), or the extent to which social policies such as national insurance assumed married women to be completely financially dependent on their husbands. Nevertheless, it promoted a view of marriage as a partnership rather than the patriarchal relationship beloved of the Victorian paterfamilias.

In addition, beginning in the 1920s, a growing body of opinion among moral philosophers, churchmen, and professionals had come to question the restrictive divorce laws that were designed to preserve the stability of marriage as an institution. Attention began to focus more on marriage as a relationship and the morality keeping "dead shell" marriages in being was increasingly questioned. Truly moral behavior, it was suggested, first by people like Herbert Gray, a Methodist minister and a founder of the marriage guidance movement, and later in the 1960s by a growing number of the ANGLICAN establishment, could only come from within the individual and could not be imposed by external regulation. This new-found emphasis on the importance of a privately grounded sexual morality was an important influence promoting the relaxation of the divorce law in 1969. However, once the priority accorded marital stability was abandoned in favor of securing better personal relationships, there was little left by way of defense against sexual relationships outside marriage as long as they were based on love and mutual respect.

In the 1968 House of Commons debates on divorce law reform, as in the recommendations of the 1912 Royal Commission, easier divorce was justified in terms of strengthening the institution of marriage. Divorce rates increased fourfold after 1969, but remarriage rates also doubled. In addition, the British Social Attitude Survey continues to show a surprising conservatism regarding expectations of marriage, moral values, and social roles within marriage; for example, while the idea of a "working mother" is now accepted by men and women, the vast majority of domestic labor continues to be performed by women. But behav-

ior indicates that marriage is no longer regarded as the only acceptable place for sexual activity. Premarital cohabitation became virtually a majority practice in the 1980s. The extra-marital birth rate doubled in the 1980s from 12 to 25 percent, although more and more children born outside marriage are being registered by two parents.

Thus marriage in the sense of a lifelong, legally constituted relationship is no longer as common as it was in the early part of the century, but the reasons for this are far from clear. Post-war income maintenance systems and increased job opportunities have made it possible for women to support children independently of men, albeit with extreme difficulty. But the shift in values informing personal life has probably been more significant and is certainly more complicated. There is no slackening in the search for a meaningful personal relationship, but both the prescriptions regarding its form and the social reality are much more fluid now than in 1900.

Jane Lewis

Bibliography

Gillis, John. *For Better, For Worse. British Marriages, 1600 to the Present.* 1985.

Kiernan, Kathleen, and M. Wicks. *Family Change and Future Policy.* 1990.

Lewis, Jane. *Women in England, 1870–1950.* 1984.

——. *Women in Britain Since 1945.* 1991.

Ross, Ellen. *Love and Toil: Motherhood in Outcast London, 1870–1918.* 1993.

Martin (Basil) Kingsley (1897–1969)

Between January 1931 and 1960 Kingsley Martin established the *NEW STATESMAN AND NATION* as a widely-read and internationally respected outlet for all shades of progressive thought. A scholar who never entirely turned his back on his academic roots, Martin's first newspaper experience came at the *MANCHESTER GUARDIAN* in the late 1920s. In the same period he was to help establish, and then briefly to edit, the *Political Quarterly.* An inveterate dissenter and a relentless polemicist, Martin was both writer and activist, witness his commitment to the CAMPAIGN FOR NUCLEAR DISARMAMENT in the 1950s, the National Council for Civil Liberties a generation earlier, and as a young man, THE UNION FOR DEMOCRATIC CONTROL. His views rarely reflected those of the LABOUR PARTY leadership, but he was without doubt a pivotal figure on the Left in mid-century Britain.

Martin's radicalism was the legacy of his Nonconformist upbringing, and in particular the family values of tolerance, non-violence, and cooperation. A pacifist, like his father, Martin registered as a CONSCIENTIOUS OBJECTOR on leaving school, and served as an orderly in the Friends' Ambulance Unit during the final two years of the FIRST WORLD WAR. The Western Front served only to strengthen his PACIFISM, and, like so many socialists in the late 1930s, accepting the necessity of fighting Fascism was to prove a painful emotional experience. In the early 1920s Martin enjoyed academic success at both CAMBRIDGE and Princeton, culminating in tenure at the LONDON SCHOOL OF ECONOMICS.

At the LSE HAROLD LASKI quickly became a close friend and influence, introducing Martin to leading figures in the FABIAN SOCIETY and the Labour Party. In 1927, following a series of clashes with the LSE's director, WILLIAM (later Lord) BEVERIDGE, Martin left to become a leader-writer at the *Manchester Guardian*. Martin enjoyed a stormy relationship with his editor, the legendary C.P. SCOTT. Editorials espousing the need for democratic socialism were unlikely to meet with Scott's approval, and by 1930 Martin was lobbying hard to secure a new post: as editor of the sickly Fabian weekly, the *New Statesman*, about to merge with its Liberal counterpart, the *Nation*. ARNOLD BENNETT and JOHN MAYNARD (later Lord) KEYNES, chairmen of the respective boards, gambled on a virtual unknown to make their new venture a commercial and critical success. The gamble more than paid off, as Martin took a circulation of 14,000 and added another 100,000 subscribers in the course of the next thirty years. Leaving a succession of outstanding literary editors, most notably Raymond Mortimer and V.S. Pritchett, to establish a stylish and influential review in the back half, Martin promoted undiluted English radicalism in the front half. For the editor, if not always his directors, the "Staggers and Naggers" was the socialist conscience of the British labor movement, an assumption unlikely to endear Martin to trade unionists such as ERNEST BEVIN. Despite the presence of Keynes—a Liberal—as chairman, sales figures ensured editorial integrity.

In the 1930s and 1940s the *New Statesman and Nation* voiced first the concerns and then the aspirations of progressive middle-class opinion in Britain. Succeeding years saw the paper extending its influence to leaders of African and Asian independence movements, most notably in India where Martin was a regular and welcome guest in his later years. Admirers such as Nehru recognized that Martin could on occasion be guilty of appalling misjudgments, most evidently over the 1938 MUNICH agreement, and more contentiously, over his refusal to publish GEORGE ORWELL's despatches from Spain; but that the generosity, the idealism, and the sheer brilliance of his journalism more than counter-balanced a naivete and inconsistency that would have destroyed any lesser editor.

Adrian Smith

Bibliography

Howe, Stephen, ed. *Lines of Dissent: Writing from the New Statesman 1913 to 1988*. 1988.

Hyams, Edward. *The New Statesman: The History of the First Fifty Years*. 1963.

Martin, Kingsley. *Father Figures*. 1966.

———. *Editor*. 1968.

Rolph, C.H. *Kingsley: The Life, Letters & Diaries of Kingsley Martin*. 1973.

Masefield, John Edward (1878–1967)

John Masefield, Poet Laureate from 1930 to his death, was a versatile writer: lyric poet, narrative poet, playwright, novelist, autobiographer (four books), essayist, historian, children's writer, and critic. He was trained as an officer in the British Merchant Marine but jumped ship in New York City and worked in a carpet factory in Yonkers before illness and depression brought him back to England. After his return, for four years in London he struggled to put his nautical experiences into verse. In 1900 his work was discovered by WILLIAM BUTLER YEATS. He was first successful with *Salt Water Ballads* (1902) and is still considered Britain's greatest sea poet despite the fact that he spent only two years at sea.

Masefield adopted and rejuvenated the British narrative verse tradition that goes back to Chaucer. Five long verse narratives led to the Laureateship. The first, *The Everlasting Mercy* (1911), the tale of a reformed drunkard, shocked the reading public with its explicit street language and its raw energy. *The Widow in the Bye Street* (1912), *Dauber* (1913), *The Daffodil Fields* (1913), and *Reynard the Fox* (1919) sustained his popularity, but subsequent narratives seemed strained, and critics and the public lost interest in the form. Unfortunately, the loss of interest especially obscures the distinction of *Dauber*, a story about a failed sailor-artist, and of *Reynard the Fox*, a story that evokes the community of sensations between animal and human life during a hunt.

Since Masefield always considered himself a storyteller, it was natural for him to gravitate toward the novel. Of his sixteen adult novels, two continue to be read, both tales of the sea: *The Bird of Dawning* (1933) and *Victorious Troy* (1935). One novel for young people *Jim Davis* (1911), a tale of a boy caught up with smugglers during the Napoleonic Wars, and reminiscent of Robert Louis Stevenson, remains popular and in print.

During the FIRST WORLD WAR, Masefield served with the British Red Cross in France. He commanded an evacuation boat for the wounded of the battle for the Dardanelles, leading to his writing one of the finest campaign histories to come out of the conflict: *Gallipoli* (1916).

From 1904 to 1914 Masefield strove for success as a playwright but failed in his attempt to create an audience for the kind of poetic folk dramas that his friends Yeats and John Millington Synge had introduced in Ireland. Masefield married an Anglo-Irish woman, Constance de la Cherois-Crommelin in 1903, with whom he lived happily until her death in 1960.

Masefield was awarded the Order of Merit in 1935 but outlived his literary reputation. He was buried in Westminster Abbey, ignored by contemporary critics; nevertheless, MURIEL SPARK's distinguished study of him in 1953 shows Masefield's ability to influence contemporary writing.

Sanford Sternlicht

Bibliography

Drew, Fraser B. *John Masefield's England: A Study of National Themes in His Work.* 1973.

Smith, Constance Babington. *John Masefield: A Life.* 1978.

Spark, Muriel. *John Masefield.* 1953.

Sternlicht, Sanford. *John Masefield.* 1978.

Massingham, H(enry) W(illiam) (1860–1924)

Editor of the *Nation* (1907–23), Massingham was born on 25 May 1860, near Norwich. Following an education at the King Edward VI School, he was employed as a reporter by the *Eastern Daily Press*. In London, after a few years' work as a writer and editor for the national Press Agency, Massingham joined T.P. O'Connor's sensationalist paper, the *Star*, in 1888, serving briefly as assistant editor during 1889–90. He moved from the *Star* to the editorial chair of the *Labour World* during 1891 and a year later to the *Daily Chronicle*, where he worked as leader-writer, literary editor, parliamentary correspondent, and assistant editor until his appointment as managing editor in 1895. Massingham was also an active member of the FABIAN SOCIETY and, until his resignation from the Society in 1894, assisted in the publication of the *Fabian News* and the *Fabian Tracts*.

As managing editor of the *Daily Chronicle*, Massingham made the paper a major voice of advanced Liberalism and a highly respected medium of literary criticism. But in November 1899 he was compelled to resign as editor because of his uncompromising condemnation of the BOER WAR. During the following eight years he worked as a free-lance writer contributing special articles and reports to the MANCHESTER GUARDIAN and the *Daily News*.

In early 1907 the Rowntree Social Service Trust employed Massingham to establish the weekly *NATION*, of which he became editor in March 1907. Under Massingham, the *Nation* became one of the most significant weeklies and, although not an uncritical mouthpiece of the LIBERALS and Labourites, was welcomed by both parties. With an innovative staff, Massingham increased the circulation of the *Nation* and made it a "jewel in the crown" of the journals owned by

the Rowntree Trust. As his friend and colleague, H.W. Nevinson, later wrote, Massingham's journalism was "an expression of his ardent and impatient spirit" and reflected his "eager appreciation of literature, drama, and the pictorial arts." Indeed, he made the *Nation* a cultural as well as a political force in the British PRESS firmament.

In his politics Massingham was basically an independent radical and something of a "troublemaker." Hence, in his criticism of the ASQUITH government, Massingham opposed large armament expenditures, supported the demands of the trade union movement, and was especially vocal in his advocacy of peace, WOMEN'S SUFFRAGE, social reform, and Irish home rule and in his condemnation of jingoism, anti-German prejudice, and the *entente* with Tsarist Russia. Above all, Massingham championed freedom of the press and its right of "fair criticism" and objective reporting during wartime.

Massingham opposed Britain's entry into the war in 1914, the establishment of an authoritarian wartime coalition government, and CONSCRIPTION, and turned against his pre-war heroes DAVID LLOYD GEORGE and WINSTON CHURCHILL. As the war became a bloody stalemate by 1916, Massingham urged a negotiated peace, so irritating the new Prime Minister, Lloyd George, that he requested the Rowntree Trust to restrain their "unpatriotic" editor. Unable to sway Massingham's employers, Lloyd George interdicted the overseas circulation of the *Nation*, but even this punitive device failed to silence Massingham's criticism. Throughout 1917 and 1918 Massingham continued to insist that Lloyd George must be forced out of office. Despairing of ousting the wily Prime Minister, following his victory in the "coupon" election of 1918, Massingham offered to resign as editor but was dissuaded by the Rowntree Trust. However his hopes for a sensible lasting peace were buoyed by President Wilson's Fourteen Points and the prospects of a LEAGUE OF NATIONS. But, as his animus against Lloyd George and the continuation of the coalition government intensified, Massingham turned to the LABOUR PARTY and its "pragmatic socialism" as the only hope for the nation. Here, too, he was soon disappointed as the Labour Party leadership seemed to compromise its principles for short-term gains.

After the war Massingham assailed the postwar policies of the Lloyd George administration and Allied intervention in Russia and urged diplomatic recognition of the Soviet regime and the establishment of "responsible" government in Ireland, India, and Egypt. But his health declined, often necessitating long absences from the *Nation*'s office. This situation and disagreements with the Rowntree Trust over the weekly's parlous financial situation constrained Massingham to resign as editor in April 1923. A year and a half later he died, on 23 August 1924.

J.O. Baylen

Bibliography

Havighurst, Alfred F. *Radical Journalist: H.W. Massingham, 1860–1924.* 1974.

Mass-Observation (1937–1949)

Mass-Observation was an organization founded in 1937 by Tom Harrisson, an anthropologist, Charles Madge, a journalist (later a sociologist), and HUMPHREY JENNINGS, a DOCUMENTARY FILM-maker. Their purpose was political as well as academic. They believed that ordinary people's consciousness was stifled or distorted in the 1930s by those with political, commercial, and media power, and that establishing "a democratic social science" devoted to revealing what ordinary people did and said would lead to social change. Ironically in 1949 the organization was handed over to market research and became a limited company. In the meantime the enterprise amassed a huge amount of data, and the deposits of M-O material at the University of Sussex represent a major archive for the study of British social history in the period 1937–49.

M-O began with a study of everyday life of "Worktown" in Lancashire from 1937 to 1940. A group led by Harrisson investigated Bolton's social and political life using the method they called "scientific observation". The Mass-Observers recorded people's conversations and behavior in places like pubs, churches, and on holiday in Blackpool, usually without the subjects knowing they were being observed.

The methods used remained central to M-O's research. Meanwhile Madge developed another technique, the "day survey". He recruited volunteers to write a personal diary on the 12th of each month. The project lasted from February 1937 to February 1938, by which time over 500 volunteers had participated. The dates included the day of the coronation of GEORGE VI, and M-O's first publication was based on the May 12th day surveys. Subsequently Mass-Observation used its panel of volunteers to describe other special days, like Armistice Day, and to report on particular topics such as reading, drinking habits, and the political crisis of 1938.

From January 1939 to 1949 Mass-Observation sent out short questionnaires ("directives") to panelists each month to which detailed, candid, personal answers were expected. After the outbreak of the SECOND WORLD WAR the directives became concerned with the way civilians were adapting to the war. The panel was asked about things like RATIONING, evacuation, air raids, CONSCRIPTION, war work, reactions to the politi-

cal situation, and post-war aspirations. In addition panelists were asked to send in diaries covering not just one day, but the entire month.

During the period 1937 to 1945 a total of 2,847 individuals replied to at least one directive, though in any one month the number of replies received never exceeded 500. About the same number kept wartime diaries, though they did not all contribute every month. The panelists were mainly in lower middle-class occupations such as clerk and schoolteacher. A minority of the men were industrial manual workers. Many of the women classified themselves as housewives, though few were mothers with small children. Most felt under-educated, and many were politically left-wing. Approximately equal numbers of men and women kept M-O diaries, though women's contributions were more sustained. Mass-Observation may have appealed particularly to WOMEN because it gave them a sense of being listened to at a time when they were still largely deprived of a voice in politics, trade unions, and the media.

Mass-Observation's work was commissioned by various agencies. For example, from early 1940 to the end of 1941 the Home Intelligence department of the Ministry of Information paid for regular Mass-Observation reports on civilian morale. In 1942–3 M-O undertook on behalf of the management an investigation of attitudes towards work in a factory producing RADAR equipment. The Advertising Service Guild, an association of eight advertising agents, funded at least seven M-O studies. In addition the organization's own small team of observers investigated topics such as reactions to the BEVERIDGE Report and family planning, which formed the substance of newspaper articles and broadcasts, the income from which helped fund other M-O activities. Mass-Observation material was disseminated in over twenty books between 1937 and 1950.

Since 1949 there have been three attempts to re-use M-O's original techniques. In 1959 Harrisson returned to Bolton to assess the changes since the Worktown study. In 1977 a new survey of attitudes to royalty was undertaken. And in the 1980s a panel of volunteers was recruited to send in directive replies and diaries in a direct revival of the original project.

Penny Summerfield

Bibliography

Calder, Angus. "Mass-Observation 1937–1949" in *Essays on the History of British Sociological Research.* Martin Bulmer, ed. 1985. pp. 121–36.

———, and Dorothy Sheridan. *Speak for Yourself: A Mass-Observation Anthology 1937–49.* 1984.

Summerfield, Penny. "Mass-Observation: Social Research or Social Movement?" *Journal of Contemporary History,* vol. 20 (1985), pp. 439–52.

Maugham (William) Somerset (1874–1965)
Maugham was the most popular literary entertainer of the first half of the twentieth century, but when he died his realism and naturalism were no longer appreciated, and his direct, unadorned, subtle, ironic style no longer fashionable. A skilled observer and chronicler of the British character at home and abroad, he is now regarded as Britain's first short story writer, while his novels and plays are generally given short shrift.

Maugham's father was a lawyer attached to the British Embassy in Paris in 1874, and Maugham was born in the Embassy to insure his British citizenship. His mother was an Englishwoman brought up in France. Orphaned at ten, he was taken to England for the first time to live with a clergyman uncle. But he remained an outside observer, spending much of his life abroad. After education at the King's School, Canterbury, he studied in Germany and then qualified as a physician at St. Thomas' medical school in 1897. He used his medical experiences in his early writing about the SLUMS of London, as in his first novel *Liza of Lambeth* (1897). Its success encouraged him to abandon medicine for a literary career.

The work that made Maugham famous is the autobiographical *Of Human Bondage* (1915), the story of a young, club-footed, artist-physician enslaved by his love for an unworthy woman. It is generally believed, today, that the protagonist's handicap is code for Maugham's HOMOSEXUALITY. His other major works of fiction include *The Moon and Sixpence* (1919), a sardonic representation of the life and career of the French painter, Gauguin; *Cakes and Ale* (1930), a satire on London literary life; *Ashenden: or, the British Agent* (1928), detective stories based on Maugham's own First World War experience as a secret agent; and *The Razor's Edge* (1944), the story of an American protagonist who tries to escape his war experiences by seeking serenity in Indian philosophy.

Maugham was an extremely successful playwright in the inter-war period because of his gift for dialogue and his ability to portray the social scene in dramatic form. His most popular drama, still frequently performed, *The Circle* (1921), illustrates the author's cynical view of marriage. Other plays include *Our Betters* (1917), *The Constant Wife* (1926), and *For Services Rendered* (1932).

Maugham's First World War service included driving ambulances on the Western Front. In 1915 he married Syrie Barnardo Wellcome, a marriage of convenience that produced one child and divorce in 1927. In 1926 Maugham bought a villa on Cape Ferrat in the south of France and lived there for the rest of his life except for a Second World War exile in the United States. In 1954 Maugham was made a Companion of Honour. Maugham's themes in fiction and drama include the difficulty young men face in trying to find purpose and place in life; the impermanence of love and the frailty of marriage; the hypocrisy implicit in conventional morals, especially those rooted in Victorian values and practices; and the pomposity and pretentiousness of many, if not most, writers and other artists. Most importantly, perhaps, Maugham's stories retain interest for their depiction of British colonialists during the decay of Empire. Whereas in CONRAD's stories the agents of empire retain close ties with home, in Maugham's stories the imperialists themselves are adrift, seeming not to know whose interests they serve. They are outsiders both to England and to the native cultures surrounding them. All Maugham's themes are conveyed for the most part through conventional, and often slackly managed, narrative forms; but the Ashenden stories are an exception, and make metafictional play out of the similarities between novelists and spies.

Sanford Sternlicht

Bibliography
Barnes, R.E. *The Dramatic Comedy of Somerset Maugham.* 1968.
Cordell, Richard Albert. *Somerset Maugham: A Writer for All Seasons.* 2nd ed. 1969.
Calder, Robert L. *Willie: The Life of W. Somerset Maugham.* 1989.
Curtis, Anthony. *Somerset Maugham.* 1977.
Morgan, Ted. *Somerset Maugham.* 1980.

Maxton, James (1885–1946)
James Maxton was one of the most charismatic Labour politicians in British public life. His parliamentary career spanned the years from 1922 until his death. Essentially a Scottish radical, and often portrayed as a revolutionary wildman, he nonetheless became a highly respected and popular figure at Westminster among politicans of all parties. He never attained a position of ministerial power, and his parliamentary achievements were limited to backbench influence on pieces of social legislation. However, his impact on the public as an orator, a propagandist, and a protester have ensured scholarly attention to his career and the celebration of his memory in left-wing circles.

Maxton was born into a comfortable middle-class home near Glasgow and took advantage of educational opportunities to become a schoolteacher. In 1904 he joined the INDEPENDENT LABOUR PARTY (ILP), having cast off a youthful allegiance to Conservatism. His political motivation sprang practically from his experience working in school in working-class areas of Glasgow. He was outraged by both the poverty of many of the children and the repressiveness of aspects of the educational system.

Maxton took a high-profile stance against the FIRST WORLD WAR and endured a prison sentence for sedition. His reputation as an agitator and a rebel was never to fade. In the 1922 general election he was returned as Labour MP for Bridgeton, a Glasgow constituency that was a byword for social deprivation. More than anyone else, with his declamatory oratory and his long-haired bohemian physical appearance, he typified what the English press were disposed to find alarming about the new Scottish Labour intake to Parliament.

In the House of Commons Maxton did create a stir: in 1923 he labelled as "murderers" CONSERVATIVES who supported a government motion to cut health grants to local authorities. This resulted in suspension from the House, but it was not long before Maxton won the affection of political foes as well as friends. WINSTON CHURCHILL became perhaps his greatest admirer. Maxton's humanitarianism disarmed potential critics.

The folksy legend that surrounded him has led many historians to dismiss him as a political thinker and strategist. Certainly, Maxton's strengths lay in popularizing ideas rather than patenting them. On the other hand he knew clearly where he wanted Labour politics to go; in the 1920s, along with his ideological mentor and fellow Scot JOHN WHEATLEY, he set out to supplant the gradualism of LABOUR PARTY policy. He pursued this goal through the medium of the affiliated ILP, which had developed into a rallying point for left-wing critics of the Labour Party under RAMSAY MACDONALD. In 1926 Maxton, now Chairman of the ILP, led a campaign for the party program "Socialism in Our Time," a critical analysis of UNEMPLOYMENT and poverty much influenced by the underconsumptionist economics of J.A. HOBSON. The gulf between Maxton and the moderate Labour leadership widened in 1928 with the publication of the Cook-Maxton Manifesto, a declaration of class war which took the ILP closer to the COMMUNIST politics of A.J. Cook (1883–1931), the miners' leader. During the minority Labour government's tenure in 1929–31 Maxton was one of its fiercest critics, and his behavior raised questions about relations between the Labour Party and the ILP which came to a head after the fall of the government. In 1932 the ILP and Maxton opted for disaffiliation. Most historians, in the light of the ILP's subsequent decline, have viewed this as a calamitous error of judgment; some left-wing commentators, including Maxton's most recent biographer, have applauded it as principled opposition to gradualism.

After disaffiliation, Maxton drifted into the world of the marginalized extreme Left, although his command of his Bridgeton constituency never weakened. He remained a PACIFIST despite the worsening international situation, and when war finally came in 1939, he opposed it.

Maxton was essentially a figure of propagandist significance: he inspired, uplifted and evangelized. He was the legend of "Red Clydeside" personified.

Graham Walker

Bibliography
Brown, Gordon. *Maxton*. 1986.
Knox, William. *James Maxton*. 1987.
McKinlay, Alan, and R.J. Morris, eds. *The ILP on Clydeside 1893–1932: From Foundation to Disintegration*. 1991.

Means Test

The Means Test achieved notoriety in the early 1930s following the budgetary and financial crisis of 1930–1. Having witnessed the mounting insolvency of the Unemployment Insurance Fund, the National government decided in 1931 to divide those out of work into two distinct groups, imposing upon the long term unemployed a means test as a qualification for state assistance. Henceforth there was to be no agreed schedule of payments to those who had exhausted their legal entitlement to UNEMPLOYMENT insurance. Such persons were now to receive payments according to need. The exercise was initially carried out by local government officials, but widespread variations arose in the severity with which the test was administered. Some authorities regarded such payments as an extension of insurance and therefore a matter of right; others adopted very different standards as to what constituted an individual's available resources.

The political and financial wrangling to which this gave rise prompted the National government in 1934 to bring the determination of means-tested unemployment payments under the aegis of a national body called the Unemployment Assistance Board. Insurance was now a matter of rights and assistance a matter of needs as efforts continued to secure greater financial solvency.

W.R. Garside

Bibliography
Garside, W.R. *British Unemployment, 1919–1939: A Study in Public Policy*. 1990.
Deacon, Alan, and Jonathan Bradshaw. *Reserved for the Poor: The Means Test in British Social Policy*. 1983.

Medical Profession

Medicine in twentieth-century Britain, as in most Western nations, has seen the growth of specialization. This has been the basis of an increasing gap between general practitioners (GPs) and HOSPITAL-based practitioners or consultants, a division which extends an older distinction which was founded to some degree on social class. Repeated state intervention in the provision of care has helped preserve the world's largest body of GPs but also encouraged a referral system that ensured a non-competitive flow of patients between GPs and consultants. To some extent it was the maneuvering of consultants which led to GPs being excluded from the hospital world where consultants developed "firms" of aspiring young specialists.

As the century opened, the profession was beset with problems. Most medical men worked in general practice. Some had full- or part-time appointments at Poor Law or municipal hospitals. A very few had prestigious positions at voluntary hospitals. Most of the men who held them were general physicians or surgeons, not specialists; they were unpaid and gave their services for a few hours each week. Such men, most of whom were Fellows of the Royal Colleges, usually had large, lucrative private practices. In England two colleges existed: the oldest, covering physicians, was probably more elitist than the one embracing surgeons. There were similar colleges in Edinburgh, Glasgow, and Dublin. Surgeons were referred to as "Mr" rather than "Dr", usages that still apply. Some members of these colleges practiced in specialized fields, but there were no specialist qualifications. Not until 1929 was a third college formed—for obstetricians and gynaecologists—and the qualifications it awarded were not formally recognized until 1950. Since then, other royal colleges have been created for psychiatrists, pathologists, radiologists, as well as one for GPs.

Around 1900 most of the profession, numbering over 20,000, served mainly as GPs. Many of these practitioners would treat complex conditions in the provincial towns and smaller hospitals of the nation. All doctors owed their right to call themselves members of a medical profession to the 1858 Medical Act, which established a General Medical Council to register and oversee them, but neither it nor the qualifications offered by the royal colleges and universities provided unique rights to practice. GPs were free to offer specialist care, and many unqualified people practiced healing. Aside from public appointments as medical officers of health, the only field reserved for medical men under the 1858 Act was so-called club practice. This had been started in the 1820s by groups of workers who had formed self-help organizations called "friendly societies," and it was there that many of the profession's troubles began.

Club work undertaken by GPs was always poorly paid, but doctors accepted it as a way of securing income until they could attract a sufficient number of individual fee-paying patients. By the end of the nineteenth century club practice covered one-third of the workforce—five out of fifteen million wage-earners (non-working women and children generally being excluded). Half the GPs were thought to be involved and for a quarter—4,000 to 5,000 doctors—the work bulked so large as to be crucial for their existence.

Between 1895 and 1910, in a conflict called the "battle of the clubs," the doctors formed trade unions in an attempts to improve their conditions but were frustrated by divisions within their own ranks. The profession was overcrowded, and whenever local doctors boycotted a club post, the friendly societies found a practitioner elsewhere to fill it. Consultants also failed to cooperate since the narrow sphere of club work tended to protect them from GP competition, the holding of club posts being enough to bar a doctor from hospital appointments. Between 1902 and 1910 consultants and others holding leading offices in the British Medical Association resisted the efforts of club doctors to transform that organization into one capable of reforming club practice.

State intervention broke friendly society control in the form of the National Insurance Act (1911), which provided medical care for insured workers. Doctors were free to build up a "panel" of such patients. Though the doctors resisted the act at first, they soon found the panel system led to a stable income. The system of GPs referring patients to consultants, grew out of the 1911 act and was steadily strengthened as more and more patients and practitioners were drawn into panel practice. By 1938 40 percent of the population in England and Wales was covered by National Health Insurance, and 90 percent of GPs participated, drawing over one-third of their income from the work.

Still, the panel did not cover non-working wives, children, the self-employed, or those earning above a certain income. Nor did the system offer hospital or specialist care. As time-honored charities offering free or low-cost care to the working class, voluntary hospitals expected consultants to give their services free, only small payments occasionally being offered. Municipal and Poor Law hospitals employed doctors on a salaried basis. The main source of consultant income came from private referrals, with nursing homes used for in-patient care. As the Depression deepened, many fee-paying clients disappeared. Young doctors found it easier to join the panel and use the income it provided to build a viable general practice. If they wanted to specialize, they could find places in the provincial and cottage hospitals. By the 1920s it was claimed that GPs formed the majority of voluntary hospital staffs, despite the fact that such hospitals operated on the closed staff principle.

By the time the Second World War began, consultant leaders were determined to act; specialization seemed rampant but there were no specialty boards to certify or restrict practice. Two-and-a-half million operations were performed by GPs in 1938–9, and too much of the paid work was thought to be going to GP-specialists. Led by Lord Moran, President of the Royal College of Physicians, consultants made use of the new NATIONAL HEALTH SERVICE to replace "consultoids" (as the GP-specialists were called) with fully-qualified men. By 1991 there were 18,000 consultants as compared with 5,300 in 1949, with 40,000 juniors to aid them.

Still, in 1948, more than 20,000 GPs remained, and their number in 1991 exceeded 30,000. Like hospital doctors, they were spread more evenly throughout the country owing to the administration of the Health Service. By removing the last vestige of friendly society control in 1948, state intervention also gave the profession more freedom than it had enjoyed since club practice began in the 1820s. But a sharp division had been created in British medicine: consultants and their juniors worked almost entirely in hospitals, while GPs worked in the community, and only rarely did they meet.

In the aftermath of 1948 many GPs were demoralized by the split, and to raise their status, a College of General Practitioners was formed in 1952, securing the title of Royal College in 1967. It strove to make an independent speciality of work in the community, focusing GP interest on the social and psychological aspects of treatment rather than on the more heroic forms of clinical care.

Not until 1990 did a different movement begin, stimulated by a government determined to make doctors more accountable for services performed. Through the introduction of an internal market, cost consciousness in the Health Service has forced hospitals and consultants to forge closer ties with GPs to attract the patients they need. GPs, on their part, find it profitable to widen the care they offer, extending even to minor surgery. Though the internal market may falter for other reasons, it promises to narrow the division within the profession, producing a partnership that may promote the integration of British medicine.

Frank Hongisbaum

Bibliography
Digby. Anne. *The Evolution of British General Practice 1850–1948*. 1999.
Honigsbaum, Frank. *The Division in British Medicine: A History of the Separation of General Practice from Hospital Care 1911–1968*. 1979.
———. *Health, Happiness and Security: The Creation of the National Health Service*. 1989.
Stevens, Rosemary. *Medical Practice in Modern England: The Impact of Specialization and State Medicine*. 1966.

Medical Research

Medical research, in the sense of an organized and institutionally-based program of inquiry into the phenomena of health and illness, is almost exclusively a twentieth-century enterprise in Britain. That is not to ignore the important developments in medical science that occurred during the nineteenth century. Statistical and occasional experimental investigations, for instance, were employed in various nineteenth-century enquiries into public health. Likewise, research was encouraged by the expansion of the university system, where medical professionalization intersected with a new middle-class culture of technical expertise. But such developments were very modest when compared with the enormous expansion of research that has occurred since the start of the twentieth century as a result of the growing interest in health care of state and industry alike.

In the industrial sector British pharmaceutical companies began to establish their own research laboratories in the closing years of the nineteenth century, emulating recent developments in the research-intensive German fine chemicals industry and in American marketing techniques. Research played a dual role in the development of the British pharmaceutical industry. In the first place, the publication of scientific data on chemical composition and pharmacological activity provided a way for companies to distinguish their products, including a variety of new vaccines and anti-toxins, from the unstandardized herbal preparations and secret remedies that had previously made up the bulk of the market. This strategy, aimed primarily at doctors rather than the lay public, enabled such companies to corner the growing market in prescribed drugs. Secondly, research supported a strategy of product innovation and especially of patenting, which introduced a new kind of competition into the industry. As a result, the British industry has been increasingly dominated by research-based companies like Burroughs Wellcome, Glaxo, Boots, and ICI. Such companies now fund an enormous range of medical research in their efforts to maintain a footing in this highly competitive market.

Government support for medical research in Britain developed at much the same time as pharmaceutical research, though initially inspired by rather different interests. Growing concern at the poor HEALTH OF THE working POPULATION in the early decades of the twentieth century prompted considerable expansion of state involvement in PUBLIC HEALTH administration. As nineteenth-century efforts to promote sanitary reform and other forms of environmental control were augmented, with the establishment of National Health Insurance in 1911 and the NA-TIONAL HEALTH SERVICE in 1948, by state-sponsored schemes intended to provide improved medical care for all sectors of the population, so medical research gained support as a means of promoting efficiency and economy in the development and implementation of policy. Statistical research into the incidence of various forms of environmental causes and biological processes implicated in such illness, offered a way of identifying the least costly and most appropriate means of prevention and treatment. At the same time, the evident success of the science-based pharmaceutical companies, particularly in standardizing doctor's prescribing habits, encouraged government to undertake its own research into experimental therapeutics and allied sciences. These preventive and therapeutic interests came together into the establishment, in 1913, of the Medical Research Committee (reconstituted in 1920 as the Medical Research Council), which remains the main channel through which the government funds medical research in Britain.

The same concern with efficient welfare provision lay behind the growth of medical research charities. Through the nineteenth century medical philanthropy had aimed primarily at providing general medical care, chiefly through voluntary HOSPITALS and dispensaries. By the late nineteenth century, however, benefactors had begun to take a growing interest in the development of new medical knowledge, and medical research increasingly displaced hospitals as the favored object of private and public PHILANTHROPY. Single-disease organizations like the Imperial Cancer Research Fund (established 1902), the British Empire Cancer Campaign (1923), the Asthma Research Council (1928), and the Empire Rheumatism Council (1936) proved particularly successful in attracting private gifts. More diversified programs of funding, closer to the program pursued by the MRC, were adopted by industry-based research foundations, notably the Rockefeller Foundation, which spent copiously on medical research in British universities and research institutes between the wars; the Wellcome Trust, established in 1936 with profits from the Wellcome drug company; and the Nuffield Foundation, which funded both bio-medical research and policy research into hospital provision.

Funding in each of these three sectors has shown roughly the same pattern of increase since 1900. From around £50,000 p.a. during the First World War, MRC funding increased slowly to £195,000 in 1937-8, but grew with increasing speed in the post-war years to reach £97 million in 1981-2 and £146 million in 1988-9. Total charity funding for medical research reached £128 million in 1987-8. But both of these are consider-ably outweighed by the British pharmaceutical industry's spending on research and development, which came to £871 million in 1989.

These diverse sources of funding have fostered a variety of approaches to medical research. At one extreme lies much of the in-house research conducted by drug companies, which routinely test large numbers of natural and synthetic chemicals for possible biological or chemical effects. At the other extreme lie the more speculative programs of research into what are taken to be the fundamental phenomena of life. Several British scientists have received the Nobel Prize for Medicine for their work on such projects: A.V. Hill (1922) for his studies of the chemistry of muscle activity; C.S. Sherrington and E.D. Adrian (1932) for their work on the nervous coordination of muscular function; Hans Krebs (1953) for his research into the chemistry of cell metabolism; and J.C. Eccles, A.L. Hodgkin, and Andrew Huxley (1963) for their investigations into the mechanism of nerve conduction.

Most research has fallen between these extremes, however, and reveals a continuing dialogue between the pursuit of fundamental biological principles and their search for specific medical applications. This combination of interests is apparent in several other Nobel Prize-winning research projects. For instance, Henry Dale's fundamental study of the chemical mechanism of communication between nerve cells (1936) grew out of a long-standing program of research into the pharmacological properties of various naturally occurring chemicals. The work of Frederick Gowland Hopkins on vitamins (1929) combined an interest in the basic chemistry of nutrition with an immediate concern to address problems of public health. The development of penicillin, for which ALEXANDER FLEMING, Howard Florey, and Ernst Chain were awarded the Nobel Prize in 1945, likewise straddled the divide between purely academic work on the chemistry of immunity and the commercial exploitation of new drugs, while the work of F. MacFarlane Burnet and Peter Medawar on the nature of the immune response (1960) was stimulated by developments in organ and tissue transplant techniques. Perhaps most spectacularly, the program of research into the chemical structure of the genetic code, which earned the Nobel Prize for FRANCIS CRICK, James Watson, and Maurice Wilkins in 1962, has since grown into the burgeoning biotechnology industry.

This tendency to combine fundamental and applied research, often within the same program of investigation, has been actively supported by all three sectors—industry, state, and charity. Indeed, though different organizations have frequently disagreed over the details of research policy, and notably over the issue of medical versus scientific or bureaucratic control of research, there has nevertheless been a remarkable degree of collaboration in promoting what has become in many respects a common enterprise. This is particularly clear in the case of university science, which has attracted support from the whole spectrum of funding agencies, at least in part because of the perceived independence of academic and especially fundamental research from particular sectional interests.

Such collaboration indicates basic agreement on the aims of medical research. In particular, the persistently close collaboration between the MRC and the large industrial foundations has resulted from a shared commitment to medical research as a means of promoting industrial and national efficiency: much twentieth-century medical research, in this respect, has been motivated by a corporate philosophy of welfare, which identifies a healthy population as an important ingredient of a healthy industrial economy. Whether sponsored by industry, charity, or the state, medical research has been dominated by a search for new technology and especially pharmaceutical solutions to the problems of ill health, while politically contentious environmental and low-technology responses have been relegated to second place. This link between medical and industrial policy is particularly clear in the increasingly close collaboration between the MRC and the pharmaceutical industry during the inter-war years, which it was hoped would not only yield new forms of treatment, but would also help to boost British trade figures.

Overall, then, this research agenda reflects the dominance of industrial priorities in British medical science. It also reveals the important service role that university-based research has played in providing the scientific raw materials for commercial developments, and more generally in maintaining links between government, industry, and charity-funded research.

Steven W. Sturdy

Bibliography

Austoker, Joan. *A History of the Imperial Cancer Research Fund, 1902–1986.* 1988.

——, and Linda Bryder, eds. *Historical perspectives on the role of the MRC.* 1989.

Hall, A. Rupert, and B.A. Bembridge. *Physic and Philanthropy: A History of the Wellcome Trust 1936–1986.* 1986.

Tweedale, Geoffrey. *At the Sign of the Plough: Allen and Hanbury's and the Pharmaceutical Industry 1715–1990.* 1990.

Merchant Banks

The merchants banks, also known as Accepting Houses, owe their name to their early role of financing international trade by accepting bills of exchange, which reached its peak in the period 1880–1914. The merchant banks, however, were able to survive the decline in the use of the bill of exchange, particularly after the Second World War, by specializing in new financial activities, such as corporate finance or funds management. The most succesful merchant banks have enjoyed exceptional longevity, from the early nineteenth century to the present day, and include some of the most famous names in the CITY OF LONDON, such as Rothschild, Baring, Morgan Grenfell, Warburg, Schroeder, Kleinwort, or Hambro.

Identifying a merchant bank before 1914 remains a problem. Their two main activities consisted in accepting bills of exchange and issuing foreign loans and securities. It should be added that most merchants banks, in any case those established in the City before 1860, started as merchants before gradually abandoning trade and concentrating on its finance. Since 1914, however, merchant banks can be identified through the membership of the Accepting Houses Committee, which was formed on the outbreak of the First World War. Of the twenty-one firms which joined the Accepting Houses Committee on its foundation, ten were still members in the 1980s.

With the exception of Baring Brothers & Co., founded in 1763, the oldest merchant banks were established during the Napoleonic Wars: N.M. Rothschild & Sons and J.H. Schroeder in 1804, Wm Brandt in 1805, Fredk. Huth in 1808, Frühling & Goschen in 1814, all of German origin; while Brown Shipley, established in 1810, came from America; only Antony Gibbs & Sons, dating from 1810, was of English origins. Two major merchant banks appeared a generation later: Morgan Grenfell, founded in 1838 by American George Peabody & Co.; and C.J. Hambro, who came from Denmark and opened a London house in 1840. A third wave of foundations took place some twenty years later, with Kleinwort, Sons & Co. in 1858, who came from Hamburg via Cuba, Seligman Brothers in 1864, and Lazard Brothers in 1870, respectively of German and French origins with American connections. Very few firms founded after that date were to play a major role in merchant banking; they started in the issuing rather than in the acceptance business. One is Philip Hill, who began as an estate agent and established the issuing house Philip Hill & partners in 1932, which merged in 1965 with the old City firm M. Samuel & Co. (the founder of Shell) under the name Hill Samuel & Co. Another is S.G. Warburg, founded in 1946 by Siegmund Warburg, scion of an old Hamburg banking dynasty who had emigrated to Britain in 1934. Warburg was to prove the most innovative bank of the post 1945 era by organizing the first hostile takeover bid and launching the first Euro-bond issue.

The merchant banks have been able to survive because the specialization of the English banking system allowed them to concentrate on what would today be called "niches". The clearing banks did not really compete with the merchant banks for the accepting and issuing businesses; despite some competition from the foreign banks based in London, over 70 per cent of the £140 million acceptances in 1913 were taken by the merchant banks, and between 1860 and 1904, Barings and Rothschilds issued some 250 loans worth £1.9 billion. Both the volume of acceptances and of new issues fell after the First World War. The decline in world trade in the 1930s hit the merchant banks' accepting business by reducing the demand for trade finance; even in the 1920s the volume of acceptances never went beyond 80 percent of its pre-war level. Foreign issues in London also fell in the 1920s as a result of a series of embargoes in order to protect the pound and of competition from New York and Paris, and further declined in the 1930s. Some old established firms such as Fredk Huth or Goschen & Cunliffe had to be liquidated during the 1930s, but on the whole the major merchant banks were able to survive. They were able to compensate for the decline of foreign issues by arranging domestic issues, as more companies were formed in the 1920s, in particular large companies which could use the services of a merchant bank. Morgan Grenfell and Lazards arranged issues for a number of electrical companies, Barings and Rothschilds were involved in several of MONTAGU NORMAN's schemes to rationalize declining sectors of the British industry, while new investment banks such as Charterhouse Investment Trust or Philip Hill handled smaller issues. After the Second World War merchant banks continued to raise funds for British industry and local authorities, but they increasingly tended to specialize in the more lucrative business of advising on take-over bids. In 1986 Morgan Grenfell's mergers and acquisitions department handled 111 deals worth £15.2 billion and generating 32 percent of the firm's revenues. They also took up funds management on behalf of pension funds and other investment institutions such as unit trusts as well as for individual customers. However, in the Eurocurrencies business, which has been at the heart of the rebirth of the City of London as a major international financial centre, the merchant banks had to abandon the lion's share to foreign banks, especially American banks, based in London.

Despite being dwarfed by the clearing banks, the merchant banks have retained a kind of mystique in the English banking system. The scale of their operations, the persistence well into the twentieth century—and for some of them up to this day—of family ownership, the wealth of their partners, unequalled in any other segment of the business community, their massive representation on the Court of Directors of the Bank of England as well as on the boards of innumerable City companies, their early integration into the upper classes, all these reasons have contributed to the position of merchant bankers at the heart of the City aristocracy.

Youssef Cassis

Bibliography
Burk, Kathleen. *Morgan Grenfell 1838–1988: The Biography of a Merchant Bank.* 1989.
Chapman, Stanley D. *The Rise of Merchant Banking.* 1984.
Hobson, Dominic. *The Pride of Lucifer.* 1990.
Kellett, Richard. *The Merchant Banking Arena.* 1967.

Methodism

John Wesley saw the Methodist societies as a movement within the Church of England whose vocation was to spread scriptural holiness throughout Britain. By his death in 1791 there were 70,000 Methodists. Separation from the Church of England followed soon after his demise. The next hundred years saw rapid growth, despite schism and the formation of a number of separate Methodist churches. By 1900 Methodism was the largest strand of Nonconformity, its churches full and its spiritual earnestness and concern for the social welfare of the people were impressive. Much of this vitality has been maintained throughout the twentieth century, and the Methodist Church remains the biggest of the Free Churches. Nevertheless the numerical decline has been severe, and Methodist influence in an increasingly secularized society has diminished.

The Wesleyan Methodist Church was marked by liberal evangelicalism, a social witness basically individualist though claiming to be collectivist, and the encouragement of cultural interests around the church. It had stronger emphasis on church, sacraments, and ministry than other branches of Methodism and appealed principally to the business and professional middle and aspiring lower middle classes.

Nearer to the proletarian groups was the Primitive Methodist Church. Its success was greatest in the larger villages of the Midlands and north of England. The laity had a greater role in this church, which was not without a hint of anticlericalism. Worship was free in style, and a Free Church orientation was more noticeable than in Wesleyanism.

The first steps toward the reuniting of the Methodist people were taken in 1907 with the union of the Methodist New Connexion, the Bible

Christians, and the United Methodist Free Churches to form the United Methodist Church. Churchmanship here was similar to that of Primitive Methodism.

All three branches declined in membership before and after the First World War, despite some revival in Wesleyan Methodism during the 1920s. Union among all three had been mooted as early as 1913, and strong leadership in this direction was exercised by Arthur Samuel Peake (1865–1929) and John Scott Lidgett (1854–1953), the most able and influential Methodist of the century. It eventually came about in 1932 when the Methodist Church was formed. The Wesleyans at this stage had 517,551 members, the Primitive Methodists 222,021 and the United Methodists 179,527. Wesleyan influence was strongest in the new church. The other two united churches granted a major concession with the establishment of a Pastoral Session of Conference consisting solely of ordained ministers, hardly compensated for by the setting up of the office of lay Vice-President.

Methodism after the Second World War was marked by energetic evangelism in Christian Commando campaigns, a World Methodism Year of Evangelism (1953), and special calls to evangelism (1971 and 1976) but without significant success. More impressive were progressive youth activity in the Methodist Association of Youth Clubs and university Methodist Societies, liturgical reform with the publication of the *Methodist Service Book* (1975), and greater social awareness. Longstanding concern over temperance and gambling had given the church's social witness a too negative and individualistic flavor, but the imbalance was corrected by greater stress on such issues as RACE RELATIONS, world development, peace and war, and matters related to MARRIAGE, the family, and human sexuality.

In 1946 the Archbishop of Canterbury called upon the Free Churches to establish intercommunion with the CHURCH OF ENGLAND by "taking episcopacy into their system." The only church to respond was the Methodist Church, and in 1955 the two churches appointed teams to begin conversations to that end. Intercommunion was quickly seen as insufficient, and the report produced in 1963 proposed a two-stage process leading to organic union. The first stage was to include a service of reconciliation by which the ministries of both churches would be mutually accepted, the consecration of some Methodist ministers as bishops, and agreement that all future Methodist ordinations would be episcopal. The second stage would be organic union. Protracted discussion and voting was not completed until 1972 when the Methodist Conference agreed to go forward, but the General Synod of

the Church of England failed to achieve the 75 percent majority required. A later attempt to bring the mainstream churches in England into a covenant giving recognition to each others' members and ministries and full intercommunion together with a commitment to seeking futher ways of expressing visible unity also came to nothing. Failure to achieve union at this level did not dampen enthusiasm for local action, and many Methodist churches became involved in local ecumenical ventures.

A significant step was taken in 1974 when the first women were ordained to the Methodist ministry. The Conference of 1939 had declared that there were no theological objections to such a move, but the practical difficulties and fear that it would delay union with the Church of England hindered progress.

Signs of renewal marked the late 1980s and early 1990s in increased numbers of candidates for the ministry and for local preaching, a new awareness of the variety of ministry with the development of ministers in sectors and in local appointment and of lay workers, and the renewal of the Methodist Diaconal Order. Concern for streamlining the organization of the church to enable greater effectiveness in policy making was evident. In 1989 there were 431,549 members. Nevertheless continuing numerical decline did not lead to introvertedness or defensiveness, and the Methodist Church remains a vital part of the British scene.

T. Mervyn Willshaw

Bibliography

Brake, George Thompson. *Policy and Politics in British Methodism, 1932–1982*. 1984.

Davies, Rupert. *Methodism*. 1976.

———, ed. *The Testing of the Churches 1932–1982: A Symposium*. 1982.

———, A. Raymond George and E. Gordon Rupp eds. *A History of the Methodist Church in Great Britain*. vol. 3. 1983.

Milner, Alfred (1854–1925)

Alfred Milner was a statesman and diplomat whose career straddled the nineteenth and twentieth centuries, known especially for his imperial activities in South Africa during the BOER WAR (1899–1902). He served as a member of LLOYD GEORGE's War Cabinet (without Portfolio) (1916–18), as Secretary of State for War (1918–19), and as Colonial Secretary (1919–21). Knighted in 1895 and elevated to the peerage in 1901, he became Viscount Milner in 1902 and a Knight of the Garter in 1921.

The son of a British physician, he was born and lived for several childhood years in Germany. After three years at a Tübingen gymnasium, he received a traditional British education at King's

College, London, and Balliol College, Oxford. Although called to the bar by the Inner Temple in 1881, he was drawn to a life of public usefulness. For several years he attempted a journalist's career, working under John Morley and W.T. Stead on the *Pall Mall Gazette,* ultimately becoming disenchanted with what he considered the crassness of the profession.

In 1884 Milner launched his public career as personal secretary to Viscount Goschen, a Liberal Unionist politician, who was able, in 1890, to procure for Milner the director-generalship of accounts in Egypt, where he served under imperial consul Sir Evelyn Baring. From this experience Milner was able to derive some notoriety with his publication in 1892 of *England in Egypt.* The turning point in his career, however, was his appointment in 1897 as high commissioner for South Africa, after he had come to the attention of Colonial Secretary Joseph Chamberlain.

When Milner arrived in South Africa, tensions over rights in the Boer gold and diamond mines were already high between Britain and the Boer republics of the Orange Free State and the Transvaal. Although he arrived with an open mind as to the dispute between the British and the Boers, he eventually concluded that the political problems could only be resolved by reform in Transvaal or by war. Scholars have concluded that Milner's intransigence at negotiations with the Boers may have made war inevitable. During the war Milner was made administrator of the Orange Free State and the Transvaal, and at its conclusion he was a British signatory to the treaty of Vereeniging (1902).

After 1902 Milner (by now a Viscount) set about the repatriation of Boer farmers and organized a system of education which established English as the language of instruction. He encouraged settlement by British farmers and was partially responsible for the importation of Chinese laborers into the Rand, a policy which aroused a storm of opposition in England and helped to defeat the CONSERVATIVE government in the 1906 general election. Milner also cultivated what became known as his "kindergarten", a group of young men, including L.S. Amery, Philip Kerr (Lord Lothian), and Lionel Curtis, whose involvement in imperial affairs was to continue beyond the Second World War. Milner's efforts, however, were directed, ultimately, toward the unification of all South African colonies. By the time of his departure, steps had been taken leading toward the eventual creation of the Union of South Africa.

On his return to Britain Milner received a mixed response. His arrival coincided with a change in government and in attitudes toward jingoistic imperial adventures. The Liberal CAMPBELL-BANNERMAN ministry was cool toward Milner's South African endeavors, one MP going so far as to introduce a motion of censure against him. Although unsuccessful, it did cause Milner to withdraw from the political limelight, devoting himself instead to the movements for national service and TARIFF REFORM, to the Rhodes Trust, and to discussions with his "kindergarten" which evolved into the political review *The Roundtable.* Milner opposed Lloyd George's "People's Budget" of 1909, the subsequent Parliament Act of 1911, and the prospect of Irish Home Rule. In 1913 he published a volume of his speeches entitled *The Nation and the Empire* and planned to collaborate with Amery on a biography of Joseph Chamberlain, a project sidetracked by the outbreak of the First World War.

Despite their earlier disagreements, Lloyd George appointed Milner to his War Cabinet in 1916, with responsibility for such matters as the allocation of shipping tonnage between competing government departments. He also worked to strengthen the imperial relationship between the CABINET and the Dominion Prime Ministers. In April 1918 he accepted the position of Secretary of State for War, assuming responsibility for the decision to enforce unity of Allied command. A hard-liner in his attitudes toward the German army and General Staff, he was moderate in statements regarding the treatment of the defeated German nation.

At the time the peace conference convened, he changed portfolios from the War Office to the Colonial Office. At Versailles his was not one of the more influential voices, and his tenure at the Colonial Office was relatively brief. In February 1921 he retired from public service and, at this advanced age, married for the first time, a widowed daughter of his old friend Admiral Frederick Maxse. Another volume of essays appeared in 1923, and in the fall of 1924 he and Lady Milner visited South Africa. After viewing some of the fruits of his labor he returned home, having contracted sleeping sickness, and he died on 13 May 1925. An influential public servant for three decades, Milner was a visionary exponent of imperial unity at a time when imperialism was beginning to be called into question. His reputation exceeded his achievements: office and honors were heaped upon him despite his lack of identification with either major political party. At the time of his death he had been chosen Chancellor-elect of the UNIVERSITY OF OXFORD.

Newell D. Boyd

Bibliography

Crankshaw, Edward. *The Forsaken Idea: A Study of Viscount Milner.* 1952.

Gollin, A.M. *Proconsul in Politics: A Study of Lord Milner in Opposition and Power.* 1964.

Marlowe, John. *Milner: Apostle of Empire.* 1976.
Wrench, John Evelyn. *Alfred Lord Milner: The Man of No Illusions, 1854–1925.* 1958.

Miners Federation of Great Britain

The Federation was founded at a Conference held in Newport, Monmouthshire in November 1889. Its constituents were existing district unions in the coalfields, and much power remained at the district level. The original members came from coalfields producing primarily for the domestic market, most significantly Yorkshire, Lancashire, Derbyshire, Nottinghamshire, and other Midlands districts. The Scottish Miners joined in 1894, and South Wales in 1899. By 1900 the MFGB claimed a membership of 363,000. The Federation's coverage was completed in 1908 with the entry of the Durham and Northumberland Miners organizations. At the outbreak of the First World War the membership had climbed to 761,000, a testimony to the prime place of COAL MINING in the British economy and to the Federation's credibility.

Diverse conditions of production and contrasting market situations meant that there were always potential conflicts of interest within the Federation. Its leaders were conscious of the difficulty in constructing any cohesive national strategy. Nevertheless, the MFGB made a successful defence of existing wage levels in a fifteen week lockout in 1893 and moved towards a more aggressive strategy in the years before 1914. Conflicts in South Wales centered around the desire of employers to cut costs by attacking traditional practices, not least the financial compensation often paid to faceworkers who worked in difficult conditions. The pressures became generalized in the MFGB demand for a national minimum wage leading to the first national coal STRIKE in March 1912, a stoppage lasting six weeks. The LIBERAL government responded with legislation which acknowledged the principle of the minimum wage, but left its level to be settled by district negotiation.

Initially, the MFGB's politics were predominantly Liberal. The Federation's first President Ben Pickard was a Yorkshire Liberal MP from 1885 until his death in 1904. In some constituencies miners dominated the electorate and could ensure that the Liberal nominee was a miner. Nevertheless most Scottish Miners leaders were socialists, and in 1903 the Lancashire Miners joined the LABOUR REPRESENTATION COMMITTEE. Within the wider MFGB the political balance shifted. Respected Liberal officials died; Liberal Associations showed reluctance to endorse more miners' candidates; some coalfields experienced intensified demands by coalowners. From 1906 the LABOUR PARTY with its 30 MPs,

including three Miners, seemed a viable option. The MFGB held ballots on political allegiance in 1906 and in 1908. At the second attempt the supporters of the Labour Party won the vote by 213,000 to 168,000. After the January 1910 Election almost all Miners Members sat as Labour Party supporters. In July 1912, the Scotsman Robert Smillie became the Federation's first socialist President. The miners moved relatively slowly to Labour politics but once made, the attachment, cemented by work experience, community ethos, and union solidarity proved durable. By the 1920s the coalfields were Labour citadels and also included most of the communities where the COMMUNIST PARTY had a credible presence.

Miners' officials and many miners were strong supporters of British involvement in the FIRST WORLD WAR, Smillie with his thorough ILP background an exception to the rule. He maintained a sharp demarcation between his industrial and his political work, presiding over a union that made significant wartime gains. Gradually the industry became state controlled, a shift that had a buoyant effect on the aspirations of miners. The MFGB achieved a longstanding objective, wage increases on a national rather than a district basis, and had some slight involvement in the management of the industry. Experience of state control strengthened demands for public ownership, but initial post-war militancy was blunted in 1919 by the appointment of the SANKEY COMMISSION. In the autumn of 1920 the Miners staged a brief wages strike, but within months any ground for optimism had been destroyed.

The winter of 1920–1 saw the collapse of many export markets for British coal. The LLOYD GEORGE coalition decided on a precipitate return of the industry to uncontrolled private ownership. Predictably, coalowners in several coalfields demanded major wage cuts as from 1 April 1921. The MFGB's resistance was undermined by the refusal of its "Triple Alliance" partners—the Railwaymen and the TRANSPORT WORKERS—to engage in sympathetic strike action. The date of this climb-down, 15 April 1921, became known as "Black Friday" and marked the virtual end of post-war labor militancy.

The MFGB resisted for three months but were defeated. The Federation for the next two decades had to operate in an industry where lack of international competitiveness and depressed domestic demand meant surplus capacity and downward pressure on wages. The French occupation of the Ruhr meant a transitory revival in British coal exports, but by 1925 the coalowners were demanding more wage cuts. The MFGB were now led by Herbert Smith, the President, a brusque Yorkshireman and A.J. Cook, the Secretary, strongly identified with the Left, a passionate yet pragmatic advocate. Initially the BALDWIN government retreated before the Miners resistance, backed by threats of sympathetic action. The crisis was simply delayed. At the end of April 1926 a seven months' lockout began backed for just nine days by a GENERAL STRIKE. It ended in disaster for the Miners with heavy wage cuts, mass UNEMPLOYMENT and short-time working, victimization and non-unionism. In Nottinghamshire a breakaway, the so-called "Spencer Union", achieved recognition from the employers. Members of the Federation had peaked at 945,000 in 1920; at the start of the 1926 lockout it was 783,000, but in some years in the early thirties it fell below half a million.

The beleaguered MFGB sought help from the 1929 Labour government, but little was achieved due to the government's minority status and its thorough economic orthodoxy. The Federation spent the thirties patiently rebuilding its organization. Leadership had passed to two Labour pragmatists, Joseph Jones and Ebby Edwards, while in South Wales and later in Scotland Communists played significant roles. Progress was slow, but in 1935 the MFGB felt strong enough to run a forceful wages campaign, while drawing back from any general stoppage. Similarly, in 1937 breakaway unionism was virtually eliminated, although on terms that involved the negotiated reabsorption rather than the destruction of the Spencer Union.

With the outbreak of the SECOND WORLD WAR the MFGB's position was transformed. The industry ceased to be dominated by the question of excess capacity and became preoccupied with the maximization of output. The legacy of decades of decline became apparent as miners battled to meet production targets in pits that were often obsolescent. Predictably the coalfields were the scene of much unofficial strike action. The political complexities of the CHURCHILL coalition meant that the development of state control stopped decisively short of public ownership for the industry. Nevertheless the MFGB achieved significant objectives, a national minimum wage in 1942 and a national conciliation system a year later. Such developments helped to encourage the Federation's transformation into the NATIONAL UNION OF MINEWORKERS.

The MFGB acquired heroic status in the labor movement. Its pitched political battles and the physically demanding character of much mining work ensured pre-eminence. Yet the real achievements often came at local level where the presence of mining unionism was a testimonial to working-class creativity, a vital resource in the battle to make mining communities islands of decency amongst the rigors of coalfield capitalism.

David Howell

Bibliography

Arnot, R. Page. *The Miners*. 3 vols. 1949–61.
Francis, Hywel, and David Smith. *The Fed: A History of the South Wales Miners in the Twentieth Century*. 1980.
Gregory, Roy. *The Miners in British Politics 1906–14*. 1968.
Kirby, Maurice W. *The British Coalmining Industry 1870–1946: A Political and Economic History*. 1977.
Supple, Barry. *The History of the British Coal Industry 1913–46: The Political Economy of Decline*. 1987.

Ministry of Munitions

In May 1915, in the midst of the FIRST WORLD WAR, the government created a new CABINET-level department, the Ministry of Munitions, to improve the inadequate supply of military stores to the ARMY. In charge was DAVID LLOYD GEORGE, previously Chancellor of the Exchequer, who created a ministry which in power and scope was unlike any other seen in modern history.

Lloyd George had taken up the pursuit of the war with customary enthusiasm, and reports of an insufficient supply of munitions at the Front inspired him to make that his cause. He pressed for the appointment of several government committees to hasten armaments deliveries, but the War Secretary, LORD KITCHENER, who distrusted Lloyd George and his proposed innovations, proved uncooperative.

In May 1915, in response to evidence that the war was not being won as expected—the PRESS reporting insufficient supplies of munitions at the front—the Prime Minister, HERBERT HENRY ASQUITH, striking a bargain with the frustrated and rebellious Lloyd George and the Tory Leader, ANDREW BONAR LAW, agreed to a coalition government. Part of the cost of political peace was the creation of a Ministry of Munitions with full responsibility for the supply of war materiel. The passage soon after of a Munitions of War Act gave the new department almost total control over workers, management, and capital in order to improve munitions supply. It was an unprecedented gamble on the philosophy of state control by a liberal democracy.

Lloyd George's hostility to the War Office had made him an enemy of established CIVIL SERVICE practice in wartime. He assembled at the ministry a senior staff made up of civil servants and politicians, but also of businessmen, academics, and other "outsiders", dubbed by the press "the men of push and go". Their sole qualification was their ability to get things done.

By the time the department was disbanded after the war, they had built hundreds of state-owned factories and exercised authority over hundreds more of privately-owned contractors. In each factory were posted rules of factory discipline which workers were required to obey. Trade union rules were suspended. The ministry controlled the supply of skilled labor and limited the rights of workers to leave the employ of a government contractor. Equally remarkable was the introduction onto the shop floor of thousands of young women workers ("dilutees") to replace the increasingly scarce men of military age who were called into uniform.

The ministry also controlled profits of contractors: manufacturers were permitted to make only goods required by the ministry, and prices were set by the ministry on a "cost plus" basis. Factories were compelled to provide canteens, hot meals, sanitary facilities, and other amenities far beyond what had been typical practice.

The Ministry of Munitions was a success in transforming Britain's woefully inadequate facilities to develop and manufacture military stores. By the end of the conflict her industrial capacity was better organized for the purpose than any other country. Lloyd George and the Ministry of Munitions—and the thousands of men and women who worked so untiringly under their leadership—proved that Britain achieved victory because of effective organization rather than military success.

R.J.Q. Adams

Bibliography

Adams, R.J.Q. Arms and the Wizard: Lloyd George and the Ministry of Munitions. 1978.

Bourne, J.M. Britain and the Great War, 1914–1918. 1989.

Gilbert, Bentley Brinkerhoff. David Lloyd George, A Political Life: Organizer of Victory 1912–1916. 1992.

Grigg, John. Lloyd George: From Peace to War, 1912–1916. 1985.

The History of the Ministry of Munitions. 1922.

Monarchy

The best description of the early twentieth-century British monarchy was provided by Walter Bagehot, who, in 1867, in The English Constitution stated that the institution had become primarily a "dignified" rather than an "efficient" aspect of government. The monarch served as a focus of obedience, as the formal head of society and of the CHURCH OF ENGLAND, as an exemplar of morality, and as a symbol of historic continuity. The monarch served as head of state, but it was the Prime Minister who served as head of government. With their CABINET colleagues, successive Prime Ministers bound the legislative portion of the realm (in which they served as members of the House of Commons or the HOUSE OF LORDS) to the executive (in that they administered both domestic and foreign policy in the name of the monarch). Admittedly, that monarch might still nominate a Prime Minister if no single political party held an overall majority

in the House of Commons or if that party lacked an agreed leader, but once a ministry had been duly appointed, the monarch's "efficient" functions were limited to three: "the right to be consulted, the right to encourage, and the right to warn".

Queen Victoria's powers in her final decades were greater than Bagehot surmised. She helped determine the appointment of a number of Cabinet members, diplomats, and churchmen, and as late as 1894 she initiated the selection of Lord Rosebery as William Ewart Gladstone's successor as LIBERAL Prime Minister. By the time of her Diamond Jubilee in 1897, she had also acquired two additional "dignified" responsibilites that Bagehot had wholly ignored. She was the personal link that, as Empress of India and as Queen, served as focus of unity for the still expanding but increasingly heterogeneous British Empire. At the same time the Queen had helped transform the royal family into the prime catalyst of that growing web of PHILANTHROPY that caused Victorians to take enormous pride in a gigantic complex of voluntary, civic-minded benevolence designed to aid the poor, the sick, and the unemployed.

To an understandable degree the personalities of successive monarchs and their spouses helped mold the public conception of the twentieth-century monarchy. The succession of Victoria's eldest son as EDWARD VII in 1901 meant that in the eyes of most Britons a remote, formidable, and moralistic grandmother was being replaced by a genial, if somewhat rakish uncle, a man who was known to enjoy himself and who wanted his subjects to enjoy themselves as well. Unlike his mother, he was also happy to be seen by his people and encouraged the notion of monarchy as spectacle. He resumed the pageantry of the annual State Opening of Parliament and of reading the Speech from the Throne in person, traditions that his mother had largely abandoned during her long decades of widowhood. The King's coronation in 1902 had to be postponed because of an emergency appendectomy that saved Edward's life. His publicly expressed reluctance to disappoint the people who had gathered for the ceremonies won him new popularity that grew with the passing years. In private the King could be a short-tempered and difficult taskmaster, but in public he possessed an enviable gift for combining great dignity with the ability to put at ease people of all social classes.

Members of the older aristocracy may have been made uncomfortable by Edward's willingness to associate with and to distribute honors to parvenus (as well as to poorer, if meritorious, commoners), but the King in turn encouraged his wealthy friends to make large contributions to many of the 250 charities that he patronized. Chief among them was the King's Fund to support the voluntary HOSPITALS of LONDON and to transform them and their research facilities into a medical center for the entire British Empire. The monarch's greater visibility did not, however, reflect greater involvement in the details of domestic politics. Edward had less influence on Cabinet, episcopal, and diplomatic appointments than his mother had had, but he did play a vital public role in encouraging and in publicizing the diplomatic *entente* with France (and to a lesser degree with Russia) that resolved long standing imperial rivalries. The widespread sense of personal loss felt by his subjects at the time of his death in May 1910 suggests that, far from weakening the popular repuation of the monarchy, Edward had strengthened it. In due course the inhabitants of the imperial metropolis were to erect nine statues in his honor, two more than were erected in honor of his mother (who had reigned for a period six times as long).

Although less charismatic than his father, GEORGE V, who succeeded his father in 1910, was deeply conscious of the need to be seen by his people and to interact with members of all social classes during an era of political democratization at home and of revolution abroad. Like his grandmother, Queen Victoria, George V believed that the monarch should serve as an exemplar of personal morality, and he sought to become a dignified head of state and benevolent father-figure (though not a particularly benevolent father). He and his consort, Queen Mary, added a tone of neo-Victorian propriety to the image of monarchy during the next generation.

His success was far from certain during the years immediately before the First World War, when Conservatives urged the King to oppose the Liberal government's attempts to curb the powers of the House of Lords and to enact Home Rule for Ireland. After the King had tried, but failed to persuade the major political parties to seek a compromise on both issues, he ultimately decided that he had no alternative but to support the program of the Liberal Prime Minister (as long as the latter retained a majority in the Commons), even if that meant a threat by the King to create new peers *en masse*. The Parliament Act of 1911, which severely curbed the legislative power of the House of Lords, therefore became law. Although the provision of Irish Home Rule was delayed by the onset of war, George V was ultimately persuaded that even substantive independence for most of Ireland (as established by the 1921 IRISH TREATY) was preferable to intermittent civil war.

Although the monarch had no significant influence on the day-to-day conduct of the FIRST WORLD WAR, he and Queen Mary played a central role in maintaining public morale in the face of more than 700,000 deaths on the battlefield and on the high seas and a yet larger number of wounded troops. Both inspected munitions factories and food distribution centers, and he toured naval bases and visited British soldiers in France. On at least 300 occasions he toured military hospitals. In the course of the war he also bestowed 50,000 awards including the new OBE (Order of the British Empire), designed as "the order of chivalry of British democracy". The role of fount of honor remained central in the lives of all twentieth-century monarchs; most of the awards they bestowed were recommended by their Prime Ministers, but they retained a measure of personal discretion.

George V successfully held in check republican tendencies in the socialist LABOUR PARTY as, during the 1920s, it replaced the Liberals as one of the two major political parties. In 1931, at a time of economic depression, he persuaded RAMSAY MACDONALD, the leader of a minority Labour government who had resigned his office, to head an all-party National government instead. MacDonald was soon disowned by a majority of Labour MPs, but later that year the electorate gave the National government the most one-sided triumph in British history. The popularity of the royal couple was confirmed by the Silver Jubilee celebrations of 1935 and by the outpouring of grief on the occasion of the death of George V in January 1936.

The popularity of the monarchy was soon threatened. As Prince of Wales, Edward VIII had been an effective good-will ambassador throughout the British COMMONWEALTH, and an ever larger public had avidly followed the Prince's doings on the radio and in the cinema. As King, Edward wished to abandon much of the pomp, pageantry, and protocol of the monarchy, and to speak out on subjects such as UNEMPLOYMENT and Anglo-German friendship without first consulting his ministers. What led to his abdication in December 1936, however, was not his attitude toward policy or pageantry, but his insistence on marrying Wallis Warfield Simpson, a twice-divorced American who impressed the Church of England, the ministries of the day—and the broader public—not only in Britain, but in Canada and Australia—as a person altogether unsuitable to become Queen.

The abdication crisis undermined the British monarchy, but Edward's younger brother GEORGE VI succeeded with remarkable speed in restoring a sense of duty, dignity, and domesticity to Britain's royal family. The new King resembled his father more than his elder brother had done, and, although afflicted with painful shyness and a stammer, the new King's sense of duty won out. His path was much eased by his wife, a member of an Anglo-Scottish noble family who, first as Duchess of York, then as Queen Elizabeth, and, after 1952, as "the Queen Mum" established herself as a model of charm, grace, tact, and good sense in the innumerable public appearances that became part of her routine during a life that was to last for more than a century. The King was aided also by his two daughters, Elizabeth and Margaret, in reestablishing the notion of the royal family as a model family. During the SECOND WORLD WAR the royal couple became both victims—when Buckingham Palace was bombed—and symbols of Britain's war effort, and hundreds of thousands of Londoners streamed to the Palace on V-E Day in 1945 to hail the victors waving from the balcony—the King, the Queen, and Prime Minister WINSTON CHURCHILL.

It was George VI who, in the years immediately after 1945, was compelled to come to terms with a majority Labour government that NATIONALIZED INDUSTRIES, instituted the WELFARE STATE, and embarked on the dissolution of the British empire. His influence on domestic politics was minimal, but the nationalization of Britain's voluntary hospitals seemed initially to undermine completely the long-term pattern of philanthropy. Networks of local voluntary contributors were deliberately replaced by a national tax-supported bureaucracy. It soon turned out, however, that the ever-expanding demand for medical as well as other social services required private philanthropy as well as CIVIL SERVANTS, and that members of the royal family were as much in demand as ever as patrons of good causes. By the 1980s, when there was a reaction against collectivism, members of the royal family had become patrons of some 3,500 charities in Britain and abroad. At the same time, even as George VI ceased to be Emperor of India, he remained the "Head of the Commonwealth", a collection of independent states, many of them now formally republics, whose leaders continued to meet at regular intervals and to maintain cultural and athletic ties.

When Elizabeth II succeeded her father as Queen in February 1952, she emulated him both in her dignity and her sense of duty, and the monarchy won new popularity in 1953 with the most spectacular coronation ceremony of the century. Representatives from all over the British Empire and Commonwealth were in attendance to celebrate the continuity of Britain as a world power. For the first time a major royal occasion was televised, and some 27 million people were believed to have watched it. In the course of the following decades the Queen took seriously her obligations as Head of the Commonwealth and as British emissary to foreign countries. At the same time she continued to confer on a weekly basis with successive Prime Ministers. Both in 1957 and 1963 the Queen chose a new Prime Minister (after consultations) when an old Prime Minister resigned while his CONSERVATIVE PARTY retained a majority in the House of Commons. As of 1965, however, the Conservatives, like Labour before them, arranged for a process of party election—should such an eventuality recur.

The "permissive society" of the 1960s was marked by a general rebellion against formality and authority, and Britons became accustomed to seeing members of the royal family in informal as well as formal settings on their television screens. Public opinion polls revealed that 60 per cent of the public retained an "entirely favorable" attitude toward the monarchy, and 30 per cent believed that Elizabeth II had been "especially chosen by God". Only 13 per cent of the public professed a "largely or entirely unfavorable" point of view. Women tended to view the monarchy more favorably than men, the old more than the young, and members of the upper and middle classes marginally more favorably than did members of the skilled and unskilled working classes.

By the 1980s Britain and Japan had survived as the only populous countries to retain a hereditary monarch as head of state, and in 1981 and again in 1986 the British monarchy received an enormous boost as the elaborate weddings of Queen Elizabeth's eldest son, Prince Charles, and her second son, Prince Andrew, were shown on television screens in more than 750 million homes throughout the world.

Both fairy-tale marriages collapsed in the course of the 1990s, and the private lives of Diana, Princess of Wales, and of her husband, Prince Charles, became the subject not only of intense scrutiny by "the paparazzi" but also part of a media duel. The remarkably charismatic and photogenic princess complained about the manner in which the rest of the royal family had treated her and publicly pronounced her ex-husband unsuitable to become King. The death of Princess Diana and a male companion in an automobile accident in Paris in August 1997 and the subsequent funeral in London evoked a mass outpouring of grief in Britain that—along with the avowedly republican stands taken by several major British newspapers—seemed to herald the approaching end of Britain's monarchy. Yet, as the century ended, such controversy had died down, and the public remained as interested in the doings of Charles's eldest son, Prince William, as he entered adulthood, as it had early found fascination in the lives of his parents, grandparents, and great-grandparents. In the year 2000 most hereditary members of the House of Lords were deprived of their right to participate in the activities of that chamber, but—as Queen Elizabeth approached her Golden Jubilee in 2002—the hereditary monarchy seemed likely to persist. Its precise role had changed over time, but the monarch remained—as she had for Bagehot—a focus of national loyalty and obedience and a personal symbol of historic continuity.

Walter L. Arnstein

Bibliography

Bogdanor, Vernon. *The Monarchy and the Constitution.* 1995.

Hardie, Frank. *The Political Influence of the British Monarchy 1868–1952.* 1970.

Nairn, Tom. *The Enchanted Glass: Britain and Its Monarchy.* 1988.

Pimlott, Ben. *The Queen: A Biography of Elizabeth II.* 1996.

Prochaska, Frank. *Royal Bounty: The Making of a Welfare Monarchy.* 1995.

Mond, Alfred Moritz (1868–1930)

Alfred Mond was a prominent politician, businessman, and industrial statesman. The son of Ludwig Mond (1839–1909), co-founder of Brunner, Mond, Britain's principal alkali manufacturer and one of its largest enterprises, Mond took up law in preparation for a political career. His legal expertise, however, brought him into the chemicals business before he could secure a parliamentary seat. By the time he was elevated to the peerage as the 1st Lord Melchett of Landford in 1928, Mond had left his mark on the political and on the industrial life of his country.

Elected to the Commons for Chester as a LIBERAL in 1906, Mond gained a safe seat at Swansea in 1910 and was made a baronet. In 1913 he was made a privy councillor. An ardent proponent of an all-out war effort, Mond actively backed LLOYD GEORGE to replace ASQUITH as Prime Minister, and in 1916 he was rewarded with the First Commissionership of Works. In 1921 he moved to head the Ministry of Health. Lloyd George's fall ended Mond's ministerial career, though he retained his Swansea seat until 1923 and represented Carmarthen from 1924 to 1928.

Following his exit from office, Mond emerged as a forceful advocate of business reorganization and the reformulation of British economic policy. He was particularly active in the movement to rationalize industry, the attempt to establish cooperation as the governing principle of industrial relations, and the campaign to strengthen imperial economic ties. In each sphere Mond's political activity in the private sector sustained his statemanship on the national stage.

As an entrepreneur and manager, Mond endeavored to build businesses that would be large enough to reap economies of scale and to affect the organization of their industries internationally. In 1923 he presided over the formation of the Amalgamated Anthracite Collieries, a combine that would in five years control 85 percent of the Welsh anthracite industry. He also merged Mond Nickel with the International Nickel Company of New Jersey and was instrumental in the creation of the Finance Corporation of Great Britain & America Ltd. The crowning glory of Mond's rationalizing efforts was the creation, with Sir Harry McGowan (1874–1961), of the Imperial Chemical Industries Ltd. (ICI) in 1926. Formed from Britain's four largest chemical companies, Brunner, Mond, Nobel Industries, British Dyestuffs, and United Alkali, ICI was the largest manufacturing merger in inter-war Britain, and the company has remained one of the country's leading industrial enterprises. Mond also championed amalgamation and concentration as general principles of economic development, and in 1928 he won the agreement of the TRADES UNION CONGRESS to a resolution recommending the further reorganization of British industry.

Mond recognized that industrial restructuring threatened workers and that its success required their support. At ICI he tried to conciliate the labor force by establishing works councils, a profit-sharing plan, a workers' shareholding scheme, and a staff grade system. At the national level Mond organized an unofficial delegation of businessmen to meet with representatives of the TUC in the late 1920s after the Federation of British Industries and the National Confederation of Employers' Organisations had responded coolly to TUC overtures. Their talks (the Mond-Turner talks, 1927–8) produced a series of resolutions that included, in addition to their joint endorsement of rationalization, the industrialists' recognition of the TUC and its constituent unions, the employers' renunciation of the victimization of trade union activists, a plan for a standing National Industrial Council and conciliation machinery for the resolution of industrial disputes, and a joint statement of concern about Britain's adherence to the GOLD STANDARD.

The First World War converted Mond from a Liberal free-trader to a proponent of imperial economic unity. He supported BALDWIN's protectionist proposals, took part in BEAVERBROOK's Empire Free Trade campaign, chaired the Empire Economic Union, and toured South Africa on behalf of the cause. The same impulse animated Mond's stewardship of ICI, from the deliberate inclusion of "Imperial" in the company's title to the support the firm gave to the development of chemical industries in Australia, Canada, and South Africa.

Mond was the pre-eminent business spokesman for industrial and economic change in inter-war Britain. He was an early champion of corporate capitalism, and he established a singular example of the enduring benefits of integration, consolidation, and centralization in ICI. Mond also helped to turn the business community toward protection and to define a consensual alternative in industrial relations after the GENERAL STRIKE.

Michael Dintenfass

Bibliography
Goodman, Jean. *The Mond Legacy: A Family Saga.* 1982.
McDonald, G.W., and Howard F. Gospel. "The Mond-Turner Talks, 1927–1933: A Study in Industrial Co-Operation," *Historical Journal,* vol. 16 (1973), pp. 807–29.
Reader, W.J. *Imperial Chemical Industries: A History,* 2 vols. 1970–5.

Montagu, Edwin Samuel (1879–1924)

Edwin Montagu was a Liberal politician and statesman. The second son of the banker Samuel Montagu, Lord Swaythling, he was educated at Clifton School, the City of London School, and Trinity College, CAMBRIDGE. After graduation in 1902, he soon translated the promise he had shown as President of the Union into the Liberal candidacy for West Cambridgeshire. He was elected to Parliament from that constituency in the Liberal landslide of 1906 and held the seat until defeated in the general election of 1922. He served in the last Liberal government and the wartime and post-war coalition governments. In 1915 Montagu married H.H. ASQUITH's beloved correspondent, Venetia Stanley, daughter of Lord Sheffield. Montagu was one of the talented politicians who made their mark in the Edwardian LIBERAL PARTY but whose careers were subsequently damaged or wasted after the party's split in 1916.

With his cousin HERBERT SAMUEL, Montagu was one of several Jewish Liberals who gained ministerial posts under Asquith. After serving as Asquith's private secretary, Montagu was a junior minister at the India Office (1910–14) and the Treasury (1914–15), the Chancellor of the Duchy of Lancaster (1915–16), the second Minister of Munitions (1916), and Secretary of State for India (1917–22). The target of ANTI-SEMITIC attacks, he was particularly embarrassed in 1912 by completely unfounded charges of corruption when the Indian government commissioned Samuel Montagu and Company, his family's financial house, to purchase silver for Indian currency.

In 1916 he resigned rather than remain in office after DAVID LLOYD GEORGE's overthrow of Asquith. In 1917, however, he returned to the CABINET as Indian Secretary and soon declared Britain's intention of eventually permitting re-

sponsible government in India. An opponent of Zionism, he fought a losing battle against adoption of the Balfour Declaration (1917) on the formation of a Jewish state in PALESTINE. Montagu's main efforts were devoted, of course, to the cause of Indian reform. On the basis of the Montagu-Chelmsford Report (1918), he introduced legislation that established a degree of representative and responsible government at the provincial level but reserved certain key powers and functions for the British authorities. In the eyes of many Indians, the Government of India Act 1919 fell far short of meeting the demands for home rule or independence. It was Montagu's misfortune, moreover, that such bloody events as the Amritsar Massacre (1919) occurred during his tenure.

In 1922 Montagu was forced to resign when he permitted the publication of the Indian Government's protest against the policy of Lloyd George's coalition government towards Turkey. Defeated in the general election of 1922, Montagu spent the last two years of his life as a political outsider. His premature death occurred soon after the general election of 1924, which confirmed the succession of LABOUR as the natural party of opposition during the CONSERVATIVE-dominated inter-war decades.

Ian Christopher Fletcher

Bibliography
Levine, Naomi B. *Politics, Religion and Love: The Story of H.H. Asquith, Venetia Stanley and Edwin Montagu.* 1991.
Waley, David. *Edwin Montagu.* 1964.

Montgomery, Bernard Law (1887–1976)

Montgomery was the most famous—and most controversial—British general of the SECOND WORLD WAR, noted especially for his victory at EL ALAMEIN, Egypt. He became a Field Marshal in 1944 and was named Viscount Montgomery of Alamein in 1946.

Son of an ANGLICAN bishop, Montgomery was commissioned in 1908 from Sandhurst and fought in France during the FIRST WORLD WAR. In the peacetime ARMY he became known for his dedication to professional excellence, yet he often rubbed people the wrong way. His marriage to Mrs. Betty Hobart Carver in 1927 was a happy one, but her death in 1937 caused his personality to turn inward again.

Montgomery served with distinction as a division commander in France in 1940 and then in England until August 1942, when he went to North Africa to lead the Eighth Army against General Erwin Rommel's forces. His task was to turn stalemate into victory; this he accomplished in the Battle of El Alamein (23 October–4 November 1942) by virtue of a growing superiority in manpower and materiel and his own genius at organization and training. It had been an expensive victory, and his pursuit of Rommel afterwards was uninspired; yet Montgomery became an instant hero, achieving a knighthood as well.

After campaigns in Italy, Montgomery took command of Allied ground forces during the invasion of Normandy in June–July 1944. This campaign caused friction between Montgomery and Supreme Commander Dwight D. Eisenhower, who regarded him as promising much but delivering too slowly. When Eisenhower assumed personal control of the ground forces, Montgomery resented being relegated to commanding only the northern wing of the line. He demanded the lion's share of supplies and troops, including many Americans, for a "narrow" thrust into Germany, but Eisenhower refused, preferring a "broad" front better suited to logistical realities—and to American pride. Montgomery's failed attempt to cross the Rhine in September 1944, along with his arrogant disregard of American sensibilities during the Battle of the Bulge (December 1944–January 1945) exacerbated tensions between the generals.

In 1946 Montgomery became Chief of the Imperial General Staff. From 1948–51 he served as Chairman of the Commanders-in-Chief Committee of the Brussels Treaty Powers, and in 1951 he became Deputy Supreme Commander of the North Atlantic Treaty Organization—ironically, under Eisenhower again from 1951–2, retiring in 1958.

Montgomery was certainly egotistical and cantankerous, and that may have colored some of the criticism he has received; slow he may have been, yet no one doubted his basic competence.

Karl G. Larew

Bibliography

Hamilton, Nigel. *Monty*. 3 vols. 1981–6.

Lewin, Ronald. *Montgomery as Military Commander*. 1971.

Montgomery, Bernard Law. *The Memoirs of Field Marshal the Viscount Montgomery of Alamein, K.G.* 1958.

Moore, G(eorge) E(dward) (1873–1958)

Of English-speaking philosophers in the twentieth century none enjoyed greater esteem and affection than did G.E. Moore. An almost stereotypical CAMBRIDGE don, Moore lived a busy and happy life of great moment within the English intellectual community but of little notice outside that narrow universe. His enduring reputation rests on the originality of his work on epistemology and ethics, on the memory of his remarkable personality, on the appropriation of some of his ideas by the BLOOMSBURY GROUP, and on his role—in conjunction with BERTRAND RUSSELL—in redirecting the course of contemporary British philosophy from idealism to realism.

G.E. Moore was born in the London suburb of Upper Norwood on 4 November 1873 and was a younger brother of the distinguished poet Thomas Sturge Moore. Educated at Dulwich College and precociously adept in classical languages and literature, Moore went up to Trinity College, Cambridge in October 1892 intending a career teaching in a public school. At Cambridge Moore excelled both intellectually and socially. Not merely did he place in the first class in Part I of the Classical Tripos in 1894 and win the Craven Scholarship in 1895, but he was elected to the celebrated undergraduate discussion society, the Apostles, in 1894. It was in the company of the latter—younger dons and fellow undergraduates such as ALFRED NORTH WHITEHEAD, J.M.E. McTaggart, and Bertrand Russell—that Moore's interest in philosophy was first piqued and then nurtured. Encouraged by his apostolic brethren, Moore devoted his fourth year to reading for the second part of the Moral Science Tripos, in which he placed first in 1896. In 1898 he was elected to a prestigious Prize Fellowship at Trinity College where, but for a brief interruption, he remained for the rest of his life—as Lecturer in Moral Science 1911–25, as Professor of Philosophy 1925–39, and as editor of the pre-eminent British philosophy journal, *Mind* 1921–47.

Moore came to the study of philosophy, as he repeatedly confessed, not from a passion to understand "the world or the sciences" but from a bewilderment at the "things which other philosophers have said about the world or the sciences." In particular, it was the curious statements which his Cambridge teachers and friends—McTaggart, Russell, James Ward, G.F. Stout, and Henry Sidgwick—made about the world which provoked his interest. Denying the ultimate reality of time and space, affirming the transcendental existence of good and immortality, and urging the study of Kant, Hegel, and their contemporary continental interpreters, the British neo-Hegelians at once redirected British philosophy off its traditional empiricist tracks, convinced their students of the transcendent importance of philosophical study, and produced arguments—such as McTaggart's celebrated "view that Time is unreal"—which Moore at least judged to be "perfectly monstrous."

This brief neo-Hegelian novitiate provided Moore with both his characteristic intellectual method and his abiding philosophical legacy: a revulsion against idealism and a defense of common sense, an insistence on clarity of expression, and a preoccupation with questions of epistemology and ethics. Beginning with early papers on "The Nature of Judgment" (1899), "Necessity" (1900), and "The Refutation of Idealism" (1903) and culminating in "The Defence of

Common Sense" (1925), Moore, complemented by Russell, offered a critique of the prevailing idealist orthodoxy so compelling as to reorient the course of twentieth-century Anglo-Saxon philosophy back towards its traditional realist ambitions.

Nearly all of Moore's finest papers were directly prompted by the writings—and by what he judged to be the errors—of other thinkers, and he soon developed an argumentative strategy that at once clarified problems, fit his own temperament, and served as a model for others. Most striking and insistent was Moore's preoccupation with precision of meaning and argumentation. Fully two generations of British philosophers heard—in seminars, conferences, lectures, and conversations—Moore's incessant plea: "What *precisely* do you mean ?", and this relentless quest for clarity helped in its turn to promote the development of linguistic philosophy in the two decades before and after the First World War. So too did Moore's own writings. Never a fluent writer or winning stylist, Moore wrote relatively little and always slowly, although he did produce one masterpiece, *Principia Ethica* (1903), one pot-boiler, *Ethics* (1912), and two sober volumes of papers and lectures, *Philosophical Studies* (1922) and *Some Main Problems of Philosophy* (1953).

Moore's life was quintessentially academic—rooted in the Cambridge routine of lectures, supervisions, committee meetings, editing, and writing to which he devoted himself single-mindedly from 1898 until his retirement in 1939. Blessedly for him, his family, and his friends, Moore seemed to possess a self-renewing source of youth and happiness which made him a splendid teacher and delightful friend. Above all else, Moore was a good man—of transparent and genuine simplicity, modesty, integrity, and kindliness. Never known to have spoken a cross word or to have stood upon his dignity, Moore was that rarity in academic life—a scholar wholly lacking in self-importance. And it was this beauty and sweetness of character, combined as it was with his earnestness of style and quality of work, which won him the affection and admiration of his many friends and colleagues.

Kirk Willis

Bibliography

Ayer, A.J. *Russell and Moore: The Analytical Heritage.* 1971.

Baldwin, Thomas. *G.E. Moore.* 1990.

Levy, Paul. *Moore: G.E. Moore and the Cambridge Apostles.* 1979.

Schilpp, Paul Arthur. *The Philosophy of G.E. Moore.* 2nd ed. 1952.

Regan, Tom. *Bloomsbury's Prophet: G.E. Moore and the Development of His Moral Philosophy.* 1986.

Moore, Henry Spencer (1898–1986)

Henry Moore is widely regarded as Britain's foremost visual artist of the twentieth century and as a major force in modern sculpture. His work is dominated by two themes: the mother-child relationship and the reclining female figure. An innovative and radical artist, closely allied with the modern movement in British art, Moore took liberties with form but never completely abandoned its human, figurative inspiration. Instead, his work actively synthesizes forms from different periods of art and various sources in nature. Much of the psychological power of his work and the popular response it elicits is believed to derive from this binding together of influences and associations.

Moore was born to a family of coal miners in the northern industrial town of Castleford. Like his great advocate, the critic and poet Herbert Read, and his fellow sculptor BARBARA HEPWORTH, he was a Yorkshireman. After active military service in the FIRST WORLD WAR, where he was gassed at Cambrai, Moore studied at Leeds, where a sculpture department was set up especially to accomodate him, its only student. Afterwards he won a scholarship to the Royal College of Art, London, where he subsequently taught for several years. As a student he already sensed a conflict between the conventional tuition he received and a burgeoning interest in avant-garde experiments. He was particularly drawn to the non-Western traditions in sculpture he was able to study at the British Museum; his interest in African carving dated back to Leeds where he was influenced by ROGER FRY's recently published *Vision and Design.* JACOB EPSTEIN was an early mentor and patron of Moore's, encouraging the Warren Gallery to give the young sculptor his first solo exhibition. Moore infused his work with the look of primitive art and carved "directly" from the block, in the spirit of a "truth to materials" advocated by Epstein and others. His *Reclining Figure* (1929; Leeds City Art Gallery) was inspired by a Mexican Chac Mool river deity encountered in reproduction in a magazine. It was also one of his first reclining female figures, which was to prove his most distinctive sculptural form. Such avant garde attitudes met with disapproval in some quarters of the Royal College, and Moore was encouraged to move to the Chelsea School of Art in 1932, becoming its first head of sculpture.

In the 1930s Moore forged relations with other experimental artists when he and his Russian emigré wife, Irina Radetsky, acquired a studio in Hampstead, where his neighbors included Read, Hepworth, BEN NICHOLSON, PAUL NASH, Roland Penrose, and Adrian Stokes. During this period Moore was involved in various group activities, such as Unit One, the short-lived alliance in 1934 of leading figures in the future abstract and Surrealist camps, and the anti-Fascist Artists International Association. Moore was unable to accept the doctrinaire opposition between the Surrealists (he sat on the organizing committee of the International Surrealist Exhibition held in London in 1936) and abstract artists such as Nicholson, whose group of constructivist artists and architects, Circle, he also joined. Typically for an artist who believed in synthesis and creative oppositions, Moore argued that "all good art has contained both abstract and surrealist elements, just as it has contained both classical and romantic elements." The synthesis at which he arrived attracted the label "biomorphism" to denote the general sense of growth and metamorphosis, a term which was soon used in relation to other artists. Despite his continued protestation that "vitalism" was the motivating force in his work, Moore's output of the 1930s represents the most cerebral and refined work of his career, as the primitive-looking and robust carvings of his early period gave way to more extreme experiments in abstraction. The most momentous "breakthrough" of the 1930s was quite literally that, his pierced forms, in which he carved his legendary holes through the block to achieve a heightened sense of three-dimensionality—or "sculpture in the round" as he like to call it—and to extend the metaphor of woman as landscape implicit in all his reclining figures. *Recumbent Figure* (1938; Tate Gallery), the first stone figure in which he pierced a hole right through, was commissioned for the terrace of modernist architect Serge Chermayeff's home on the Sussex Downs. Moore described it as mediating between the stark horizontals of the modern architecture and the undulating hills in the background. The idea of sculpture in the open air, with nature and the sky as ideal background, was crucial to Moore's aesthetic.

A desire to experiment more liberally with pierced forms led him to work in metals for the first time, as a way of avoiding the risks involved in using stone or even wood. Besides bronzes, he worked in lead which complemented his sense of biomorphic fluidity. The outbreak of war in 1939 also had an impact on his methods. Restrictions in materials and an unwillingness to embark on long term projects in such uncertain times led him to store ideas in plaster maquettes for later realization. When the time came, the growing demand for his work made it necessary to produce works more rapidly and in editions. Thus, bronze casting took over from direct carving as the principal means of expression for an artist who had insisted—and continued to insist—that he was a carver not a modeler. However, his technique of creating hard plaster finishes which had to be chiseled back, or later of taking the mold from polystyrene cut-outs, were indeed more oriented towards carving than modeling.

Moore's response to the SECOND WORLD WAR laid the foundation of his post-war popularity, transforming him into a "public artist" and an institution. He was commissioned by his friend and patron KENNETH CLARK as an official war artist and, as such, recorded the experience of BLITZ victims sleeping in the Underground stations and bomb shelters in his series of Shelter Drawings. These were exhibited in the National Gallery, its treasures removed for safe keeping. Moore then attempted to repeat his success with a series of drawings of "Britain's underground army," the coal miners of his native Yorkshire. In 1942 he was commissioned to carve a Madonna and Child for the Church of St. Matthew's, Northampton by its rector, Walter Hussey, a major ecclesiastical patron of the arts. This consoling, almost neo-classical image, although greeted with bafflement by local people, represented a new degree of accessibility and humanism on Moore's part, a reflection of his sense of the needs of the times.

Moore's post-war sculpture represents a sometimes uneasy combination of civic humanism and the continuation of the experimentation of the 1930s. *Family Group* (1948–9; Moore Foundation) was made by a school and could almost serve as an icon of the emergent WELFARE STATE. By the time of the FESTIVAL OF BRITAIN in 1951, however, Moore was evidently more confident in reconciling public work with freedom of sculptural expression. His *Festival Reclining Figure* is a skeletal, completely opened-out, angular figure with a bold use of incised lines recalling the jigsaw-like marks on his drawings.

By the 1960s Moore enjoyed a phenomenal international reputation and was frequently called upon to produce monumental sculptures for prestigious architectural projects. His mammoth two- and three-piece bronze reclining figures extended the metaphor of woman as landscape by actually depicting limbs as eroded cliffs and craggy rock formations (even borrowing from paintings such as Monet's *Cliffs at Etretat* or Seurat's *Le Bec du Hoc* to reinforce the point). One of these bronzes was destined for the Lincoln Center in New York. Other commissions included city squares, the forecourts of skyscapers, parliament buildings, and museum wings around the world, to the point where Moore sculpture in a city center became almost ubiquitous. Certainly among younger artists Moore's reputation suffered as a result of his popularity and success. A crowning moment for him, however, was the retrospective organized by the City of Florence at the Belvedere Fort where his sculptures vied with Brunelleschi's Duomo and his achievements were, implicitly, compared with Michelangelo, his artistic hero.

David Cohen

Bibliography

Berthoud, Roger. *The Life of Henry Moore*. 1987.

Moore, Henry, and John Hedgecoe. *Henry Moore*. 1986.

Read, Herbert. *Henry Moore: A Study of His Life and Work*. 1965.

————, and Alan Bowness, eds. *Henry Moore: Sculpture and Drawings*. 6 vols. 1944–88.

Russell, John. *Henry Moore*. 1968.

Stansky, Peter, and William Abrahams. *London's Burning: Life, Death, and Art in the Second World War*. 1994.

Morel, E(dmund) D(ene) (1873–1924)

Born Georges Edmund Morel de Ville in Paris, the son of a minor French official and his English Quaker wife, Morel was educated in English schools until the age of fifteen. Settling permanently in England at the age of seventeen, he began his career as a clerk in a Liverpool shipping firm. He soon became a journalist specializing in West African affairs and adopted his pen name "E.D. Morel" for use in private life as well. Utilizing his expertise in African affairs, he wrote numerous exposés of the harsh system of exploitation imposed on Congo natives by King Leopold of Belgium. He became the organizer, leader, and chief propagandist first of the Congo Reform Association and subsequently, during the FIRST WORLD WAR, of the UNION OF DEMOCRATIC CONTROL (UDC), a group critical of Britain's pre-war diplomacy. Alienated from his previous Liberalism, he entered the INDEPENDENT LABOUR PARTY (ILP) in 1919, served as a Labour MP from 1922 to 1924, and became a crucial influence in formulating the LABOUR PARTY's post-war foreign policy.

Most of Morel's career was devoted to fomenting and organizing public pressure to bring about changes in British foreign policy. His Congo campaign, undertaken with Roger Casement, then a consular official, as silent partner, was a successful effort to force the British government to use its diplomatic weight to insist that Belgium eliminate the system of forced labor in the Congo. In the course of that crusade he became distrustful of Foreign Office officials and an opponent of the Anglo-French *entente* which he felt had posed as an obstacle to Congo reform. These anti-Foreign Office and anti-French views were fully developed before the outbreak of the FIRST WORLD WAR, and they account for his opposition to Britain's entrance into the war on the side of France. Concluding that the cause of the war had been the system of secret diplomacy,

rather than Germany's perfidy, he joined with like-minded Liberals and Labourites in the UDC to agitate for parliamentary control of foreign policy as well as the establishment of an international organization to replace the system of alliances based on the balance of power.

Morel paid a heavy price for his unpopular war-time dissent. He lost his position as a prospective LIBERAL parliamentary candidate for Birkenhead. In a politically inspired trial he was convicted and sentenced to six months imprisonment for a minor breach of war-time regulations in sending a copy of his widely-read *Truth and the War* (1916) to a neutral country.

Emerging from prison in 1918, Morel discovered that the Labour Party, having recaptured much of its pre-war internationalism, had embraced much of his program for the post-war world. Though supremely indifferent to its domestic program, he entered the socialist ILP, judging that the working class would be the group most receptive to his foreign policy views. In the election of 1922 he stood successfully as a Labour candidate for Dundee, handily defeating WINSTON CHURCHILL in a lively contest.

Morel's final crusade was his effort to gain revision of the Treaty of Versailles. While initially a supporter of Wilsonian views on the post-war world, he became convinced that the American president had betrayed his own principles in acquiescing in a settlement which was undeservedly harsh in its treatment of defeated Germany. The reparations imposed on that nation, the war guilt clause, and the transfer of her colonies to the victors were all the constant objects of Morel's denunciations in *Foreign Affairs*, the journal he edited, and elsewhere. Other critics of the Treaty, such as JOHN MAYNARD KEYNES, may have been more influential on public opinion in general, but Morel, who targeted his writings on the Labour Party, played an important role in creating sympathy for Germany on the Left. By the time of his death in 1924 the Labour Party had been fully persuaded of the iniquity of the Treaty of Versailles.

As an organizer of public protest on matters of foreign policy Morel was a transitional figure linking nineteenth-century humanitarian crusades such as the anti-slave trade movement and the campaign against Bulgarian atrocities with more broadly-based mid-twentieth-century phenomena such as the CAMPAIGN FOR NUCLEAR DISARMAMENT. While he, like his predecessors, relied heavily on the churches and the middle class for support during the Congo campaign, the UDC recruited members from women's groups and working-class organizations newly arrived on the political scene. The legacy of these efforts was mixed. The elimination of the infamous rubber system in the Congo can only be judged an un-qualified benefit to African natives. His depiction of Germany as a nation cruelly treated by the peacemakers in 1919 helped, however, to under-mine support for the peace settlement and thus to pave the way for the APPEASEMENT policy of the 1930s.

Catherine Ann Cline

Bibliography

Cline, Catherine Ann. *E.D. Morel (1873–1924): The Strategies of Protest.* 1981.

Louis, Wm. Roger, and Jean Stengers, eds. *E.D. Morel's History of the Congo Reform Movement.* 1968.

Swartz, Marvin. *The Union of Democratic Control in British Politics during the First World War.* 1971.

Taylor, A.J.P. *The Troublemakers.* 1958.

Morris, William (1877–1963)

William Morris, founder of Morris Motors Ltd., an important British motor vehicle firm, and benefactor of numerous organizations in-cluding the Nuffield Foundation, was a major figure in twentieth-century British economic history. Born in 1877, Morris began his business career selling, repairing, and later manufacturing bicycles in Oxford. In 1913 he manufactured his first motor vehicle, and by 1929 he was the lead-ing British producer supplying nearly half of the British market. Unlike most of his competitors in the British motor vehicle industry, Morris en-tered the industry with the intention of mass producing an affordable vehicle and competing head on with Henry Ford and the Model T. Adopting a strategy of buying major compo-nents from external parts supplier, Morris was essentially an assembler at first. During the 1920s he was forced to increase the level of manufac-ture, usually through the purchase of major sup-pliers, such as Hotchkiss, who supplied engines but was reluctant to produce the volume of com-ponents needed.

Morris's early success was due mainly to effec-tive product design, such as the famous Morris Cowley (1915), which was suited to the special needs of the British market. Major break-throughs in manufacturing techniques were less significant. Morris was slow to move towards mechanized assembly, although he did experi-ment, albeit unsuccessfully, with automation in his Coventry engine shops in the 1920s. Morris ruled his workforce as a benevolent autocrat, firmly anti-union but willing to grant higher wages and, for the period, progressive benefits such as holidays with pay. He was also influential as a critic of state intervention in the economy, preferring a more laissez faire environment. He was one of the major financiers of OSWALD MOSLEY's New Party in the early 1930s and be-came the president of the League of Industry in

1932, set up by the National Council of Industry and Commerce to advocate a free enterprise economy.

Morris's domination of the British AUTOMO-BILE INDUSTRY was relatively short lived. Increas-ing competition after 1945 from the American firms Ford and General Motors and questionable reinvestment policies led to a merger between Morris and the other leading British firm, Aus-tin, in 1952. The newly formed British Motor Corporation was unable to rationalize the British sector of the industry and American, European, and eventually Japanese firms continued to ab-sorb market share. Further mergers brought nearly all the major British vehicle manufacturers under the control of British Leyland Ltd. This move was no more successful and, in an ironic twist of fate, the state was forced to bail-out BL in the early 1970s as British market share contin-ued to fall to less than 20 percent. In July 1988 the firm was returned to private hands through a controversial purchase by British Aerospace, but then sold to the German firm BMW in 1994.

Morris was well known as a philanthropist, giving over £30 million to various charities. He used his wealth to promote his own vision of so-ciety, one in which a voluntary welfare system would replace state organized relief. Major dona-tions included the endowment of a number of chairs at Oxford and the creation of the Nuffield Foundation in 1943.

Wayne Lewchuk

Bibliography

Adeney, Martin. *Nuffield: A Biography.* 1993.

Andrews, P.W.S., and Elizabeth Brunner, *The Life of Lord Nuffield: A Study in Enterprise and Benevolence.* 1955.

Overy, R.J. *William Morris, Viscount Nuffield.* 1976.

Whiting, R.C. *The View From Cowley: The Impact of In-dustrialisation upon Oxford, 1918–1939.* 1983.

Morrison, Herbert Stanley (1888–1965)

Alongside ATTLEE and BEVIN, Morrison was one of the three most powerful political figures in the Labour governments of 1945 to 1951. His real im-portance to Labour was as the organizer of the victory of 1945 and of the WELFARE STATE that emerged. He was also Attlee's deputy and is con-sidered to be the finest administrator that the LABOUR PARTY has ever produced.

Morrison was born in London on 3 January 1888 into a middling working-class family. He received an elementary education and then held a variety of shop assistant jobs. Deeply interested in politics, he joined the Westminster branch of the quasi–Marxist Social Democratic Federation in 1907. That was not to be his brand of social-ism, and, in 1910, he switched to the Brixton branch of the INDEPENDENT LABOUR PARTY, quickly becoming its chairman and developing contacts with many socialist leaders. Indeed, by the end of 1910 Morrison was appointed the Secretary of the South-West London Federation of the ILP and stood, unsuccessfully, as ILP candidate for the Vauxhall ward of the London County Council in 1912. Between 1910 and 1913 he was active as chairman of the Brixton branch of the National Union of Clerks. His involvement in Labour politics led him to be appointed as circulation traveler for the *Daily Citizen*, the new Labour daily paper. During these years he developed a clear socialist perspective, advocating public works to deal with UNEMPLOYMENT, and supported the WOMEN'S SUFFRAGE movement.

During the FIRST WORLD WAR he assumed an anti-war stance and became even more closely involved with the ILP and the Labour movement, becoming part-time secretary to W.C. Anderson, the ILP MP, a part-time traveller for the National Labour Press, and Secretary of the London Labour Party. He received his call-up papers in 1916, and though his blind right eye exempted him from military service, he attended the Military Service Tribunal and agreed to work on the land.

From 1920 onwards Morrison rose quickly in Labour circles. He became a member of Hackney Borough Council, acting as Mayor in 1920 and 1921, and was member of the London County Council from 1922 to 1945, becoming its leader 1939–40. At the same time he was also prominent in the Labour Party, joined the National Executive in 1920, was MP for South Hackney from 1923–4, 1929–31 and 1935–45, for East Lewisham from 1945–50 and South Lewisham 1950–9. He was also Minister of Transport in the Labour government of 1929–31 and was Minister of Supply for a few months in 1940 before becoming Home Secretary and Minister for Home Security from 1940 until 1945 and a member of the War CABINET from 1942. Yet Morrison's finest hour came when he became the Lord President of the Council, Leader of the House of Commons, and Deputy Prime Minister in Attlee's Labour governments of 1945–51. In 1951 he became Foreign Secretary and, following Labour's defeat, continued to act as deputy leader of the Labour Party from 1951 to 1955.

By any standards, Morrison's political career was impressive. There is no doubt that he was a supreme organizer and administrator, whether organizing the London Passenger Transport Board in the early 1930s, imposing air-raid precautions during the SECOND WORLD WAR, or promoting the FESTIVAL OF BRITAIN in 1951. A skillful parliamentarian, he pushed through more than 70 bills in the first session of Attlee's post-war Labour government as Leader of the House, including NATIONALIZATION of the COAL MINES,

the RAILWAYS, and other industries. He was largely responsible for the formulation of Labour's nationalization program, and his book *Socialization and Transport* (1933) committed Labour to the idea of a corporate public body as the model for state control. He was, above all, the supreme party organizer keeping the Labour backbenchers happy by creating subject committee groups among them. In the end, his epitaph must be that he gave cohesion to the Labour Party and Attlee's post-war Labour governments.

Nevertheless, there were many personal and political failures in his life. His first marriage was never happy, and he appears to have had several flirtations, including one with ELLEN WILKINSON. Margaret, his first wife, died of cancer in 1953, and he married Edith Meadowcroft in 1955. Politically, his main setbacks occurred at the hands of Attlee, who defeated him for the Labour Party leadership in 1935, thwarted him in an attempt to assume the party leadership in 1939 and 1945, and delayed his retirement sufficiently long enough to enable HUGH GAITSKELL to become Leader in 1955. Morrison's other major political failing was at the Foreign Office in 1951, where he was considered to be out of his depth.

He stood down as MP in 1959 and was raised to the House of Lords as Lord Morrison of Lambeth. In 1960 he became President of the Board of Film Censors, holding the post until shortly before his death on 6 March 1965.

Keith Laybourn

Bibliography

Donoughue, Bernard, and G.W. Jones. *Herbert Morrison: Portrait of a Politician*. 1973.
Morgan, Kenneth O. *Labour People*. 1987.
Morrison, Herbert. *An Autobiography*. 1960.

Mosley, Oswald Ernald (1896–1980)

Sir Oswald Mosley is best remembered as the founder and leader of the British Union of Fascists, an organisation which he formed in 1932. Before that development Mosley had been a Member of Parliament, affiliated initially with the CONSERVATIVE PARTY and, following his alienation, with the LABOUR PARTY. He also formed the short-lived New Party in 1931. Fierce in his ambitions, even to the point of recklessness, Mosley failed to break the mold of British politics. A political exile for many years, he died in France in 1980.

Mosley was born in London on 16 November 1896, the eldest of three sons of Sir Oswald Mosley (who succeeded to the baronetcy in 1915) and Katherine Maud Mosley (*née* Edwards-Heathcote). When Oswald Mosley was five years of age, his mother separated from his father and took her young children to live in Shropshire, near her father's house.

In 1909 Mosley entered Winchester College where he developed proficiency in both boxing and fencing. He left Winchester in 1912 for Sandhurst in January 1914 but was expelled after some months. In October 1914, shortly after the outbreak of war, Mosley was commissioned in the 16th Lancers. He applied subsequently to join the Royal Flying Corps, serving as an observer between December 1914 and April 1915. While attempting to secure his pilot's licence, he crashed his plane and broke his ankle, later returning to the front with the 16th Lancers. However, the condition of his ankle deteriorated, and in March 1916 he was invalided out of the armed forces. By then he had gained sufficient wartime experience to savor the camaraderie of the trenches, a feeling which remained with him and later assumed a political significance.

Mosley spent the remainder of the war in the MINISTRY OF MUNITIONS and the Foreign Office but nurtured political ambitions. His first political step came in December 1918, when he won the Harrow division of Middlesex for the Tories with a majority of 10,943 out of a total vote of 16,957. Then, in May 1920 he married Cynthia Blanche, the second daughter of LORD CURZON of Kedleston, former Viceroy of India and Foreign Secretary in LLOYD GEORGE's Cabinet, a marriage which could do no harm to his political ambitions. The Mosleys' personal wealth and social connections provided them with a glittering base from which to operate. But his discontent surfaced in public late in 1920 when he crossed the floor in protest against the government's policy on Ireland. At first Mosley retained the confidence of his local Conservative organization, but in 1922 he stood at Harrow as an Independent and retained the seat.

In the 1923 election Mosley held Harrow with a reduced majority, and in March 1924, two months after RAMSAY MACDONALD had formed the first Labour government, Mosley joined the INDEPENDENT LABOUR PARTY. In the 1924 election he stood against NEVILLE CHAMBERLAIN at Birmingham Ladywood and went down to a narrow defeat by 77 votes. However, in December 1926 he was returned to Parliament after winning a by-election at Smethwick with a large majority. The period between 1924 and 1926 was not wasted. In collaboration with JOHN STRACHEY, he devised a program influenced by the economic theory of JOHN MAYNARD KEYNES. Furthermore, Mosley's active support of the miners in the GENERAL STRIKE created a fund of goodwill in the Labour ranks. Indeed at this juncture Mosley was regarded in some quarters as a potential leader of the Labour Party.

In the 1929 election Mosley (who had succeeded to the baronetcy in 1928) was returned for Smethwick. Cynthia, his wife, entered Parliament as Labour MP for Stoke-on-Trent. With the Labour election victory in 1929 Mosley assumed the office of Chancellor of the Duchy of Lancaster outside the CABINET. But the rebellious, impatient streak in his personality became evident as friction developed between Mosley and J.H. THOMAS, the Lord Privy Seal, over how to cure the increasing UNEMPLOYMENT problem. In making his stand Mosley also challenged PHILIP SNOWDEN, the Chancellor of the Exchequer, who shared the orthodox economic views which Thomas represented. Things came to a head with the Mosley memorandum of 1930 which made radical recommendations for economic recovery, involving state intervention and a public works program. When it was rejected by the Cabinet, Mosley resigned on 20 May 1930.

When his proposals were defeated at the Labour Party Conference in October 1930, he began to plan the foundation of the New Party, launched on 28 February 1931. During its brief life the Party attracted such figures as ANEURIN BEVAN, HAROLD NICOLSON, the philosopher Cyril Joad, and JOHN STRACHEY. The New Party's results in the election of 1931 can only be described as disastrous: all twenty-four candidates suffered defeat.

In 1932 Mosley visited Italy to observe the Fascist experiment of Mussolini, the visit spurring the formation of a British FASCIST MOVEMENT. Impatient with the slow grinding wheels of parliamentary democracy, Mosley envisioned a decisive role for himself in a dictatorial system which, he believed, could solve pressing problems. On 1 October 1932 Mosley launched his new political movement, the British Union of Fascists.

The first two years of the BUF were successful and, according to some commentators, comparatively respectable. This image changed after the fiery, violent meeting at Olympia in London on 7 June 1934. Mosley's organization became increasingly associated with political violence and extremism, and public opinion began to harden against the movement.

Once the BUF began to espouse ANTI-SEMITISM more openly, a good deal of energy was devoted to street politics in East London. The BUF itself was increasingly influenced by developments in Germany and in 1936 changed its name to the British Union of Fascists and National Socialists. Mosley's Keynesian economic policies were abandoned in favor of a mixture of corporatism, totalitarianism, patriotism, and racism. The initially sympathetic Rothermere press withdrew its support. The government, disturbed by the increasing para-military style of the BUF, passed the Public Order Act in 1936 which forbade the wearing of political uniforms. The Act did not prevent disorder or stop Fascist political activity, but it did exercise a degree of control over the movement, limiting the BUF's provocative marches through the East End.

In the midst of this political change Lady Cynthia, who had always shared Mosley's political ambitions, died of peritonitis. It was three years before Mosley re-married, this time to the Hon. Diana Mitford Guinness, the third daughter of the second Baron Redesdale and one of the celebrated Mitford sisters.

Increasingly in the late 1930s the BUF argued that if hostilities were to break out between the England and Germany, it would result from a conspiracy organized by Jewish interests. When hostilities began in the autumn of 1939, some members of the BUF entered the ranks of the armed services. But in May 1940 Mosley and his wife were arrested and detained under Regulation 18B. The Mosleys were released from prison in November 1943 on humanitarian grounds, Mosley suffering at this time from phlebitis.

After the war Mosley attempted to justify his pre-war attitudes in such publications as *My Answer* (1946) and *My Life* (1968). He channeled his political energies between 1944 and 1966 into the Union Movement with an emphasis on European unity based on racial criteria. Much of Mosley's activity was conducted in exile from his home at Orsay, just outside Paris, but he did fight parliamentary contests on two occasions, at North Kensington in 1959 and Shoreditch in 1966. The former occurred in the aftermath of racial violence in Notting Hill in 1958, from which he hoped to derive political benefit. In both elections he lost his deposit. Nevertheless, to the end Mosley nurtured the belief that he had a European role to play when the great social crisis finally broke. The anticipated role never materialized. Mosley died at Orsay on 3 December 1980.

Colin Holmes

Bibliography

Lewis, D.S. *Illusions of Grandeur: Mosley, Fascism and British Society 1931–1981.* 1987.

Mosley, Nicholas. *Rules of the Game: Sir Oswald and Lady Cynthia Mosley 1896–1933.* 1982.

———. *Beyond the Pale: Sir Oswald Mosley 1933–80.* 1983.

Skidelsky, Robert. *Oswald Mosley.* 2nd ed. 1981.

Thurlow, Richard. *Fascism in Britain: A History 1918–1985.* 1987.

Mountbatten, Louis Francis Albert Victor Nicholas (1900–1979)

Lord Mountbatten was the last Viceroy of India. He also commanded Allied forces in Southeast Asia during and after the SECOND WORLD WAR. In these two positions he had an important influence over the withdrawal of Britain from its empire in Asia.

Born on 24 June 1900 as Prince Louis of Battenberg, Mountbatten was the son of Prince Louis Alexander of Battenberg (later Louis Mountbatten, Marquess of Milford Haven) and Princess Victoria Alberta Elizabeth Irene, the daughter of Louis IV of Hesse-Darmstadt. Mountbatten's father was the brother-in-law of Princess Beatrice (Princess Henry of Battenberg), and his mother was the granddaughter of Queen Victoria. Mountbatten was, therefore, closely related to several branches of European royalty, and he spent much of his childhood visiting them in Britain, Germany, and Russia. He attended Locker's Park School in Hertfordshire and the naval colleges at Osborne, Dartmouth, and Devonport. Mountbatten graduated in 1916 at the height of the FIRST WORLD WAR and soon saw action as a midshipman aboard the *HMS Lion*. His family's ties to Germany, however, overshadowed much of his war service. Anti-German hysteria forced his father to resign his position as First Sea Lord in 1914 and to change the family's name from Battenberg to Mountbatten in 1917. Nevertheless, these crises did not sever the young Mountbatten's connections to the rich and powerful. In 1921 he married Edwina Cynthia Annette Ashley, heiress to three sizeable estates and to £2.3 million. He also befriended his cousin, the Prince of Wales, and accompanied him on his tours of the globe. Between the wars Mountbatten acquired the reputation of a playboy, but his service from 1925 to 1932 as a signals officer earned him the respect of the ROYAL NAVY top brass.

Mountbatten's connections, courage, and inventiveness all accounted for a remarkably rapid series of promotions during the Second World War. He served courageously as captain of the destroyer *Kelly*. In March 1940 he returned the *Kelly* to port under tow during three days of almost constant enemy bombardment. He survived the sinking of his ship in May 1941 only by swimming out from under it after it capsized. Mountbatten's exploits caught the attention of the British public and became the subject of NOEL COWARD's war film, *In Which We Serve* (1942). His daring also won the attention of Prime Minister WINSTON CHURCHILL, who supported his promotion to command the aircraft carrier *Illustrious*. In April 1942, however, before the *Illustrious* was ready, Mountbatten was reassigned to Combined Operations in London, promoted simultaneously to the ranks of vice-admiral, lieutenant-general and air marshal, with a de facto membership of the Chiefs of Staff Committee. In this new position Mountbatten shared responsibility for the controversial and costly landing at Dieppe in August 1942 and the early preparations for the invasion of Normandy.

In autumn 1943 Mountbatten received the rank of admiral and the supreme command of Allied forces in Southeast Asia. He presided over the successful reconquest of Burma and prepared for an arduous campaign through the rest of Malaya and Indochina, but the atom bomb transformed this invasion into a series of unopposed landings.

After the war Mountbatten became directly involved with the most important result of Japan's brief dominion over Southeast Asia, the rise of nationalism. As Supreme Commander of Allied forces in the region, he faced the onerous task of restoring British, French, and Dutch colonial governments to territories that had recently been under the local administration of indigenous leaders. Mountbatten's liberal leanings went back at least as far as a brief period of study at CAMBRIDGE during 1919–20. He put these convictions into practice through efforts to accommodate the nationalist aspirations of Southeast Asian leaders. Given the demands of the European governments involved, however, he could do little to prevent rebellion in the East Indies and decades of war in Indochina. He resigned his command in the summer of 1946, was created Viscount Mountbatten of Burma in December, and Earl Mountbatten of Burma in 1947.

Mountbatten's experience in the Far East, his liberal political leanings, and his sympathy toward Asian national movements made him an obvious choice to supervise the LABOUR government's transfer of power in India. The government's previous failures to reconcile the differences between the Indian National Congress and the Muslim League made the task so daunting that he agreed to serve as India's last Viceroy only on the condition that the CABINET would set June 1948 as the deadline for Britain's withdrawal. He arrived in Delhi in March 1947 determined to transfer power to a united India that would remain a member of the Commonwealth. Congress, however, rejected his proposal for a loose federation of Hindu and Muslim states, and the Muslim League's refusal to accept a more powerful central government forced him to agree to a partition of the subcontinent between India and Pakistan.

The most controversial aspect of the agreement, which Mountbatten announced on 3 June 1947, was that independence would arrive on 15 August 1947 rather than in June 1948. The advanced date was the result of Mountbatten's hasty compromise with Congress that ensured India's membership in the Commonwealth until it drafted a new constitution. He hoped that this membership would keep India and Pakistan at peace with each other and allied to Britain. But the speed of Britain's withdrawal left much of the partition incomplete by the appointed day and did not adequately account for the status of the princely states after the end of British rule. The failure to resolve these issues brought India and Pakistan to the brink of a general war during the months immediately following independence. As India's first post-independence governor-general, Mountbatten contended with communal massacres and war in Kashmir. Even after his departure from the post in June 1948, he influenced the Commonwealth's decision to maintain India's membership once it became a republic.

Mountbatten returned to the navy in 1948 as a rear-admiral, and in 1953 he became Second Sea Lord and commander of NATO's fleets in the Mediterranean. The following year he became First Sea Lord. In spite of his opposition to Britain's role in the SUEZ CRISIS, Mountbatten became Admiral of the Fleet in 1956 and Chief of the Defense Staff in 1959. Even after he retired in 1965, he continued to serve the government, first, in its attempt to forestall Rhodesia's declaration of independence the same year, then in its inquiry into prison reform in 1966. But his continued public activities and his connection with the royal family made him a target for the Irish Republican Army, which assassinated him on 27 August 1979 in a bomb explosion while he was fishing in Mullaghmoor Harbor in Ireland. The manner of his death aroused great public indignation, and he received a funeral in Westminster Abbey.

Lord Mountbatten embodied many contradictions. He was an aristocrat and relative of the royal family. Yet he supported many of the policies of the Labour government. He often appeared egotistical. Yet he tolerated and even welcomed criticism. He devoted much of his career to preserving the Commonwealth as the British Empire disappeared. Yet some of his most significant decisions may have made the Commonwealth less effective than he intended. Nevertheless, he was perfectly suited for his most important role as India's last Viceroy. His combination of courage, imagination, and charm allowed Britain to part with India on surprisingly cordial terms.

A. Martin Wainwright

Bibliography

Mountbatten of Burma, Louis, Earl. *From Shore to Shore: The Tour Diaries of Earl Mountbatten of Burma, 1953–1979.* Philip Ziegler, ed. 1989.

———. *Reflections on the Transfer of Power and Jawaharlal Nehru.* 1968.

Ziegler, Philip. *Mountbatten.* 1985.

Multinational Corporations

Twentieth-century Britain has been one of the world's most important sources of multinational investment. Before the Second World War

British-owned multinational enterprise was more extensive than that of any other country. Subsequently, and up to the present day, it has remained the second most important source of foreign direct investment. At the beginning of the 1990s British multinationals were the largest foreign investors in the United States, with investments almost twice as large as those of Japanese corporations. Multinational corporations have been, therefore, highly significant for the British economy.

By the first decade of the twentieth century many British enterprises had extensive international operations. Britain has long been known to have been the world's largest capital-exporting nation before the First World War, but this has been traditionally regarded as mostly portfolio in nature—that is, not involving managerial control. Recent research has dramatically altered such a view. On the most reliable estimates, Britain owned 45 per cent of the world's stock of foreign direct investment in 1914, which amounted to some $14,302 million.

British corporations were active abroad in virtually all economic sectors. There was extensive investment, for example, in extractive and natural resource industries in search of precious minerals, ores, and petroleum. The Shell Group, which since 1907 has been Anglo-Dutch, originated in part as a British company shipping oil from Russia to Asia in the late nineteenth century, and then found oil fields in Indonesia. British Petroleum originated as a British company which discovered oil in Iran in 1908, marking the birth of the Middle Eastern oil industry. British companies were equally active in tin and copper mining and in tea plantations.

British companies were also active abroad in the service sector. Before 1914 British accounting, engineering, and construction firms had extensive foreign operations, as did insurance companies. In 1913 over 40 British insurance companies were active in the United States alone, and they played a significant role in meeting the costs of the San Francisco earthquake in 1906. Britain was also the world's leading multinational banker. From the 1830s British banks had established overseas branches, first in colonial settlements in Australia and Canada, and later in Asia, Latin America, and Africa. By 1914 approximately 30 British banks owned and operated almost 1,400 branches outside the United Kingdom.

In terms of overall value, British multinational corporations had fewer investments in foreign manufacturing before the First World War, although Britain, together with the United States and Germany, was an active participant in this first stage of multinational manufacturing. Pioneer British companies included Dunlop, which

owned tire factories in France, Germany, and Japan, and Lever Brothers and J.& P. Coats, manufacturers of soap and cotton thread respectively, with factories in the United States, Canada, South Africa, Australia, Russia, Switzerland, France, and Germany by 1914.

A number of factors prompted these British manufacturers to erect factories abroad. The spread of protectionism gave British companies the stark choice of losing their markets or surmounting tariff barriers by erecting factories behind them. The early British multinationals also found that they could service the needs of foreign markets better by producing in them. Different markets often had different requirements and tastes, and a local factory could help a British firm to respond more effectively.

Although the First World War interrupted the growth of multinational enterprise, and led to British companies being stripped of their factories in enemy territory, the 1920s saw further foreign expansion by British multinational corporations. A new generation of manufacturing firms invested abroad in the inter-war years. The Quaker chocolate firms of Cadbury and Rowntree, for example, established factories in Australia, Canada, New Zealand, Ireland, and South Africa in these years. It was not war, but depression that slowed the foreign growth of multinational enterprise. In the 1930s, as economic nationalism and exchange controls proliferated, and as political extremism and instability spread from country to country, many British firms preferred to participate in international market-sharing agreements, or cartels, rather than run the risks of owning assets abroad.

The Second World War seems to have inflicted more damage on British multinational enterprise than its predecessor. There were spectacular losses, such as the forced sale of Courtaulds' American subsidiary to the Americans in return for assistance during the war. In the late 1940s and 1950s the granting of independence to former colonies in Asia and Africa was often followed by reductions in British direct investment, especially in the extractive and agricultural-related sectors. By 1960 Britain accounted for only 16 per cent of the total stock of world foreign direct investment, while the United States accounted for 48 per cent.

British multinational corporations showed some signs of stagnation, or at least lack of dynamism, in the post-war period. Between 1945 and 1960 about 80 per cent of new British direct investment went to the Commonwealth, especially Australia, Canada, and South Africa. British firms were locked into small, slow-growing economies and invested comparatively little in the dynamic markets of Western Europe, the United

States, and Japan. British multinationals were clustered in such traditional sectors as food, drink, and tobacco, and weak in more technologically intensive sectors. British multinational banking remained prolific—with almost 4,000 overseas owned in the 1960s—but branches and assets were concentrated in Asia and the Southern Hemisphere, with practically no presence in the United States or Continental Europe.

From the 1960s there was an accelerating change in the structure of British multinational investment. By 1981 food, drink, and tobacco was no longer the dominant sector of British multinationals, its place assumed by chemicals. There was also a geographical re-orientation to Western Europe and the United States. From the late 1970s British multinational investment grew very rapidly, increasing five-fold between 1979 and 1986. For the 1980–9 period the United Kingdom was the world's largest home economy for outflows of foreign direct investment, with average annual outflows of $17 billion, or 20 per cent of world outflows. Around three-fifths of this investment went to the United States. By the mid-1980s the value of British-owned assets in the United States exceeded those of American corporations in the United Kingdom.

Much of the huge flow of British direct investment abroad over the last fifteen years, especially in the United States, has taken the form of acquisitions of existing foreign firms. Unlike Japanese or Continental European firms, British corporations, used to mergers, acquisitions, and hostile takeovers at home, found it easy to finance foreign acquisitions on the well-developed British capital markets. Finally, few British corporations had the kind of technological or managerial advantage which they could exploit by new "greenfield" investment. They were, in fact, seeking to escape from their own small and slow-growth market into a more dynamic one.

This strategy was by no means always successful. During the late 1970s and early 1980s, for example, British banks made a series of major acquisitions of Californian banks, but most of these ventures proved unsuccessful, and by the end of the 1980s the British banks had all divested from California. The most spectacular failure was that of the Midland Bank, whose ill-fated purchase of Crocker National in 1980 led to losses of around £1 billion in the following six years before Midland withdrew from California. Many British manufacturing companies also experienced difficulties with their American acquisitions.

The only systematic attempt to study the costs and benefits of British foreign direct investment has been the Reddaway Report on British direct investment abroad, published in 1968, which suggested a favorable impact on the balance of payments, though on the basis of certain questionable assumptions. The gains from inward investment into Britain by foreign firms can be more readily gauged than those from outward investment. In the first half of the century American firms, and since the 1970s Japanese firms, have created employment, introduced and improved managerial practices, and transferred technologies into Britain. But it is certainly evident that Britain's ownership of some of the world's largest multinational corporations has failed to prevent its relative economic decline throughout the century.

Geoffrey Jones

Bibliography

Jones, Geoffrey. *British Multinational Banking 1830–1990*. 1993.

——. *Merchants to Multinationals: British Trading Companies in the 19th and 20th Centuries*. 2000.

Stopford, John M., and Louis Turner. *Britain and the Multinationals* (1985).

Munich Conference

On 29 September 1938 the British Prime Minister, NEVILLE CHAMBERLAIN, met with the French, German, and Italian premiers in Munich to resolve the dispute between Germany and Czechoslovakia over the Czech western border region, the so-called Sudetenland, which contained three million ethnic Germans. The leaders agreed to transfer the territory to the German Reich, and war was averted.

The Munich conference was a by-product of the foreign policy of APPEASEMENT of the pre-war Chamberlain government (1937–40). British CABINETS, since the end of the First World War, had generally followed a policy of accommodation among the European powers. Chamberlain, however, took a more pro-active approach and strove to seek out what he deemed were the reasonable grievances of the dissatisfied nations and resolve them through generous compromise. British opinion seemed to agree. Many wished, at all costs, to avoid another war; others thought that Germany had been treated too harshly by the Treaty of Versailles. Some felt that accommodation with the admittedly unappealing FASCIST powers was the only alternative to a war which would leave Europe at the mercy of the Soviet Union.

The Sudetenland, formerly part of the Austro-Hungarian Empire, had been incorporated into the succession state of Czechoslovakia after the First World War. Leadership of much of the Sudeten German minority had come by the mid-1930s into the hands of Konrad Henlein and his Sudeten German Party, who, under the guise of seeking autonomy, were secretly working under German orders for unification with the

Reich. By March 1938, in the hope of causing a crisis, Hitler instructed Henlein to press for demands that the Czech state could never grant.

Britain did not want war with Germany over distant Czechoslovakia; neither, despite their protestations, did France or the Soviet Union (both of whom had mutual defense treaties with Prague). In May 1938 rumors spread throughout the capitals of Europe that Hitler had lost his patience with the Czechs and meant to invade the Sudetenland. The British, to Hitler's surprise, warned him off, and there was no invasion. In fact, Hitler held his hand not because of the British warning but because he was not ready. Since 1937 German military commanders had been preparing their plans ("Operation Green"), but the army would not be prepared until October 1938. Hitler was certain that under no circumstances would the British and French fight to keep the Sudetenlanders within Czechoslovakia.

By the end of August German-Czech violence flared in the Sudetenland, and German propaganda filled the airwaves and the press with further threats. Chamberlain's attempt to negotiate a settlement to the quarrel through an independent British mediator, Lord Runciman, had also failed. Fearing that war was imminent, he took matters into his own hands and conceived his "Plan Z": to fly unannounced to Germany and confront Hitler directly to save the peace. It was quixotic, typical of the abrupt style of the Prime Minister; he had faith, ultimately, in no one but himself and believed only he could prevent war. Though the Czech government had agreed to Sudeten autonomy by this point, this was rejected by Henlein and his Nazi masters. By mid- September the British and French governments had decided that the Czechs must yield the Sudetenland to the Reich if the worst were to be prevented.

Chamberlain obtained an invitation to Hitler's Berchtesgaden retreat (a seven hour airplane flight followed by a three hour railway journey for the sixty-nine year old Prime Minister). They met on 15 September, and he came away feeling that he and Hitler were in agreement that the areas of 80 percent German population in the Sudetenland would be peacefully transferred to Germany. A second meeting followed in Bad Godesberg one week later, but this time Hitler raised the stakes: the transfer of the entire Sudetenland must be completed by 1 October, and the issue of Polish and Hungarian minorities in eastern Czechoslovakia must be dealt with at the same time. The two met the following day and remained deadlocked; as the Czech army was mobilized, even the optimistic Chamberlain felt war could not be avoided.

Chamberlain appealed to Mussolini to use his influence with Hitler to break the deadlock; the Duce—fearful of war himself—did so, convincing Hitler that he would have his way without war. Hitler then invited the leaders to Munich—the Czechs were allowed to come, but were kept under house arrest in their hotel while the conference was in session—and the result was essentially as Hitler had planned. The Reich received the whole Sudetenland, and Chamberlain dared to believe that he had gained "peace for our time." Czechoslovakia was dismembered as Hitler affirmed that he had no more territorial demands in Europe. Privately he was annoyed that he was denied his war to crush the Czechs.

The following March Hitler violated the Munich agreement by seizing the rest of Czechoslovakia and turned his attention to Poland. The democracies, shocked to reality, abandoned appeasement and reluctantly prepared to stop Hitler. Guarantees were issued by Britain to Poland and the Balkan states, but Hitler refused to believe that Britain and France might actually fight to prevent his plans. He was wrong, as September 1939 proved, but it is understandable why he felt as he did, given the tragedy of Munich.

R.J.Q. Adams

Bibliography

Adams, R.J.Q. *British Politics and Foreign Policy in the Age of Appeasement 1935–39*. 1992.

Charmley, John, *Chamberlain and the Lost Peace*. 1989.

Gilbert, Martin, and Richard Gott. *The Appeasers*. 1963.

Wheeler-Bennett, John W., *Munich: Prologue to Tragedy*. 1948.

Murdoch, Iris (1919–1999)

Iris Murdoch, prolific novelist, was born in Dublin of Anglo-Irish parents in 1919. After graduating from the Badminton School in Bristol, she read classics at Somerville College, OXFORD. During the Second World War she was an Assistant Principal at the Treasury; immediately afterward she did relief work for the UN in London, Belgium, and Austria. In Brussels, she read Sartre and the French existentialists, and when she returned to England in 1947 she studied philosophy at CAMBRIDGE. The following year she became a Fellow of St. Anne's College, Oxford, where she remained until 1963. Though Murdoch is best known as a novelist, she has published five philosophical books, ranging from *Sartre: Romantic Rationalist* (1953) to *Metaphysics as a Guide to Morals* (1993). Between 1954 and 1993 she published twenty-five novels; *The Sea, The Sea* won the Booker Prize in 1978; she was awarded the C.B.E. in 1976 and made a D.B.E. in 1987.

The popularity of Murdoch's novels is remarkable because she is a twentieth-century rarity, a philosophical novelist. Although Murdoch says that bad art collaborates with our fantasy mechanisms, offering consolation instead of truth, she sees good art as a model for selfless contemplation of the actual world (*The Fire and the Sun: Why Plato Banished the Artists*, 1977). Her novels reflect the view that the study of literature is "an education in how to picture and understand human situations" (*The Sovereignty of Good*, 1970). They raise issues familiar to moral philosophy—the nature of justice, love, evil, social responsibility; the place of suffering; the possibility of believing in God; the question of how one decides to risk one's life, or sacrifice one's pleasures, for the Good. Indeed, a Platonic vision of the Good as the necessarily fundamental philosophical category dominates her later works. Murdoch's fiction shows us the practical consequences, the human significance, of ideas. Her characters frequently embody a philosophical stance or more loosely conceived set of attitudes; thus Palmer Anderson in *A Severed Head* (1961) not only is a psychoanalyst but shockingly acts out the implications of an uninhibited belief in psychoanalysis. Although Murdoch sometimes illustrates her own beliefs in her fiction, she also tests and even modifies them. In *The Sacred and Profane Love Machine* (1974), for example, she demonstrates the psychological truth of the idea that suffering will not make us virtuous, but she also shows that people who lead happy comfortable lives can remain children.

In "Against Dryness" (1961) Murdoch praises the nineteenth-century novel, with its broad social scope, its multiple plots and detailed descriptions, partly because it shows the world as offering resistance to the ego, replicating the financial arrangements, emotional entanglements, and sheer accidents that pressure the lives of real people. In contrast, she argued, many twentieth-century novels appear "crystalline," depicting a hero agonizing over radical decisions, apparently free to control his destiny. As she went on to develop the argument elsewhere, the moral life ought not to consist of such moments of decision, but of attention: by attending to other people, and to the Good, we become humbler, we learn that other people are real, we discover that many choices no longer need to be made, for we are "compelled almost automatically by what we can see".

Murdoch's preference for some of the features of the nineteenth-century novel—though reflected in her own multiple plots, her occasional didacticism, even in her detailed evocations of, say, a marvelous *cassoulet* in *A Fairly Honourable Defeat* (1970) or the squalid bedroom in which the eponymous hero of *Bruno's Dream* (1969) lies dying—should not blind us to the experimental side of her fiction. Her plots are really parodies of plots, playing with the marriage plot (*A Severed Head*), the Gothic (*The Unicorn*, 1963), the mystery (*The Black Prince*, 1973). In the early books

the parody of plot is connected with the way Murdoch's characters engage in a bewildering number of sexual liaisons, both heterosexual and homosexual and occasionally incestuous: in *A Severed Head* Antonia, a married woman, sleeps with a psychoanalyst who sleeps with his sister, who ends up with Antonia's husband after she has eloped with his brother, the psychiatrist having eloped with Antonia's husband's mistress. Such relationships, and the innumerable accidents and coincidences that always characterize Murdoch's plots, make her realism not a matter of reproducing what is statistically probable, but of reproducing the variety, the unexpectedness, of human experience.

Since the late 1970s Murdoch's novels have grown longer, even less firmly anchored in social reality. Reviewers have complained that they need more editing, center too much on the painful love affairs of the upper classes, are too allegorical, and even (surprisingly, since Murdoch continues to reject such traditional religious conceptions as belief in a personal God) too Christian; many women object to her avoidance of female protagonists and narrators who, in Murdoch's view, mark a book as a "woman's novel." Yet many of the characteristic themes and devices remain. In *The Message to the Planet* (1989), as in her first novel, the plot is driven by the protagonist's intense, quasi-romantic admiration for a philosopher whose ideas he pursues even as their author abandons them. Her heroes still share her embattled faith in words and ideas, still look for answers and messages. In the later books, however, the quest is more distinctly metaphysical. Although both *Nuns and Soldiers* (1980) and *The Message to the Planet* offer the familiar Murdoch picture of the contemporary sensualist, comfortably wreaking havoc in other private lives, they also meditate at length on the Holocaust as it is experienced, after the fact and in England, by the son of a Polish emigrant and a contemporary Jewish intellectual. Throughout her work Murdoch continued to present readers with an austere morality and a vision of the human personality so bleak as to recall Original Sin. Readers who want to observe how a brilliant mind, contemplating objects as diverse as Plato's cave and the suitcases at Auschwitz, deployed the conventions of the English novel can find no better writer.

Her final years were clouded by the onset of Alzheimer's disease, which her husband, the literary scholar John Bayley, movingly depicted in his memoir, *Elegy for Iris*.

Margaret Scanlan

Bibliography
Bayley, John, *Elegy for Iris*. 1999.
Bove, Cheryl K. *Understanding Iris Murdoch*. 1993.

Byatt, A.S. *Degrees of Freedom: The Novels of Iris Murdoch*. 1965.
Conradi, Peter J. *Iris Murdoch: A Life*. 2001.
Dipple, Elizabeth. *Iris Murdoch: Work for the Spirit*. 1982.
Ramanathan, Suguna. *Iris Murdoch: Figures of Good*. 1990.
Todd, Richard. *Iris Murdoch*. 1984.

Murray, (George) Gilbert (Aimé) (1866–1957)
Gilbert Murray was an eminent scholar and leader of the British internationalist movement. The best-known classicist of his generation, Murray won renown for verse translations from Greek which were popular on the stage and in books. From the time of the First World War he became deeply committed to the cause of peace and began another highly public career which eventually made him leader of the League of Nations Union and Chairman of the Committee of Intellectual Cooperation of the LEAGUE OF NATIONS.

Born in Australia, the son of a Catholic landowner who died when Murray was seven, he was brought to England at the age of eleven. He distinguished himself as a student at OXFORD for his command of the classics and was appointed Professor of Greek at the University of Glasgow at the age of twenty-three. Murray married Lady Mary Howard, the daughter of the Earl of Carlisle, in 1889 and went on to become the Regius Professor of Greek at Oxford (1908–36). A celebrity who tried his hand at writing for the stage, he was close to other celebrated figures, including BERNARD SHAW, who based characters in *Major Barbara* on Murray and his wife, Mary.

A supporter of British involvement in in the FIRST WORLD WAR, he still pressed for reform of the international system to reduce armaments and secure the peace once the war ended. The creation of the League of Nations was warmly welcomed by Murray, and he served on two League commissions, one on minorities and the other intellectual cooperation. He represented South Africa as a delegate to the Assembly in Geneva, 1921–3. When the League established the Committee of Intellectual Cooperation in 1922 to provide books and periodicals to libraries, Murray became involved. In 1928 he was elected Chairman of this body, a position he held for eight years.

Murray's other contribution to the internationalist cause was his leadership of the League of Nations Union (as Chairman of the executive committee 1923–38 and joint President 1939–45). The LNU attracted over 1 million members during the inter-war period and exerted influence on foreign policy. It was the main sponsor of the PEACE BALLOT in 1934–5, which polled some 11,640,066 people on disarmament and resistance to aggression and provided impressive evidence of British public support for the League of Nations.

The outbreak of war in 1939 did not cause Murray to lose faith in internationalism, and he became a President of the United Nations Association in 1945, a position he held until his death in 1957.

Donald S. Birn

Bibliography
Smith, Jean, and Arnold Toynbee, eds. *Gilbert Murray: An Unfinished Autobiography*. 1960.
Wilson, Duncan. *Gilbert Murray O.M. 1866–1957*. 1987.

Namier, Lewis Bernstein (1888–1960)

Lewis Namier was one of Britain's most renowned historians—a highly creative scholar who gave his name to a school of historians, to a unique research methodology (Namierism), and whose contributions to historical studies have been of lasting consequence.

Born into a JEWISH family in Polish Russia, Namier was educated privately and, after brief stints at Lvov and Lausanne universities, came to England in 1908 where he spent a year at the LONDON SCHOOL OF ECONOMICS and subsequently entered Balliol College, OXFORD. He achieved first class honors in modern history and was co-winner of the Beit Prize in 1913. Offered an appointment by one of his father's business associates, Namier went to the United States in 1913. During the FIRST WORLD WAR Namier served briefly in the 20th Royal Fusiliers and was then transferred to the Foreign Office where he worked from 1915 to 1920, first in the PROPAGANDA, then the political intelligence sectors.

After the war Namier sought financial and professional security in various occupations, ranging from a temporary lectureship at Balliol (1920–1) and work for a Manchester cotton firm to a brief period as a correspondent for the *MANCHESTER GUARDIAN*. Supported ultimately by earnings from journalism, the generosity of friends, and several grants, Namier devoted himself from 1924 to 1929 to full-time historical research, the results of which appeared in two distinguished works, *The Structure of Politics at the Accession of George III* (1929) and its sequel, *England in the Age of the American Revolution* (1930). Immediately establishing him in the forefront of British historians, these works marked a new stage in the study of eighteenth-century politics, Namier demolishing the long fashionable Whig interpretation of George III as would-be tyrant, denying the reality of two party conflict by mid-century, playing down the extent of political corruption at the time, and emphasizing the importance of personal ambitions and vested interests in determining men's political actions. Even more influential than his conclusions was Namier's particular historical method: the procedure of structural analysis, a detailed investigation of the inner workings of eighteenth-century government, supported in turn by the technique of prosopography or collective biography. By collecting evidence about life, career, connections, and behavior of each parliamentary figure, Namier was able to identify and test empirically the factors motivating the political actions of an individual or group. Although not as insensitive to the role of principles and ideas as some critics have implied—Namier was well aware of the complex forces influencing men's actions—his reliance on Freudian psychology, combined with a cynical view of human nature, caused him to regard all professions of principle as mere rationalizations of self-interest, thus oversimplifying the complex problem of political motivation.

Although rejecting Judaism early in life, Namier had always been a Jewish nationalist, and his commitment to Zionism intensified during the post-war decade. In 1929 he became political secretary to the Jewish Agency for Palestine, a post he quit in 1931 to take up the Chair of Modern History at the University of Manchester. He held this position until his retirement in 1953. As a professor, Namier was popular and successful, though much of his attention was absorbed during the 1930s in assisting Jewish REFUGEES from Germany fleeing Nazi oppression. In 1939 he was selected as adviser to Chaim Weizmann at the PALESTINE conference, and from 1940–5 he was involved once again with the Jewish Agency. The wartime years intensified his interest in European history, and in 1946, he published *1848: The Revolution of the Intellectuals,* a modified version of his Raleigh Lecture delivered to the British Academy in 1944, the year he was elected a Fellow. It was followed by other writings dealing with the recent world conflict: *Diplomatic Prelude* (1948), based on the notes and recollections of contemporary statesmen, and two volumes of essays on pre-war diplomatic developments—*Europe in Decay* (1950) and *In the Nazi Era* (1952). Like so much of his work, these books were intended as preliminary to a larger enterprise—a full scale History of Modern Europe—which was never completed. In 1951 Namier returned to his primary field of interest—British parliamentary history—devoting the last ten years of his life to editing, with other scholars, three volumes in *The History of Parliament* series, a massive compendium of parliamentary biographies to which he personally contributed hundreds of entries. He also began a life of Charles Townshend, a work completed by a collaborator and published posthumously in 1964. Namier was knighted in 1952 and became an honorary D.Litt. of Durham (1952), Oxford (1955), Rome (1956), honorary Litt.D. of Cambridge (1957), and honorary D.C.L. of Oxford (1960).

Few historians have been as influential as Namier in making the historical discipline what it is today. In no case is a knowledge of the historian's life more essential to the understanding of his work as it is in Namier's. The paradoxes of the man parallel a life that began with a childhood ordeal and never strayed far from the brink of mental disorder. Registered at birth as a Jew only to be shielded from any knowledge of his cultural background until the age of ten, the future historian became an Anglican. The scholar who, denying the role of abstract ideas in history, removed mind from the historical universe, himself reflected many of the intellectual tendencies of his time. A convinced skeptic, he routinely leaned on the dubious science of graphology to analyze the handwriting of long-dead Members of Parliament. Often perceived as idolizing the leisured gentry, he had become a FABIAN socialist as early as 1916. Often deplored as a practitioner of the narrowest kind of history, he anticipated econometric historiography, as well as later interest in such topics as patronage. Neurotic and abrasive, plagued by insomnia and recurrent ill-health, Namier inspired more respect than affection, and his scholarly reputation, which peaked during his lifetime, has not survived the vagaries of historical fashion untarnished.

Karl W. Schweizer
C. Krantz

Bibliography

Colley, Linda. *Namier.* 1989.
Namier, Julia. *Lewis Namier: A Biography.* 1971.
Rose, Norman. *Lewis Namier and Zionism.* 1980.

Nash, Paul (1889–1946)

As one of the outstanding landscape painters in twentieth-century Britain, Paul Nash fulfilled a pivotal role in the history of English art during the 1930s and 1940s. His work embodies a characteristic "Englishness" in its almost exclusive insistence on depicting favorite sites in the southern counties, while at the same time it assimilated influences from the contemporary avant-garde from across the Channel.

Nash's earliest sketches established a set of fundamental themes and strategies which were to nourish his output for the rest of his career. His drawings of childhood haunts already typify an approach in which crisp, dry strokes delineate wooded settings that seem to secrete an unnamed emotionality, and create an effect of preternatural clarity.

Nash came to public notice with the startling pictures produced during his brief assignment as an official war artist at the Western Front in 1917. While the large oil-painting *The Menin Road* (1918–19)—completed after the Armistice and housed in the Imperial War Museum in London—shows infantrymen stumbling across a landscape of dead trees, mud, and shell-craters, the bulk of Nash's war scenes are empty of human presence, the spectacle of nature grotesquely ravaged serving as a sufficient metaphor for the dehumanizing horror of modern warfare.

Back in England, Nash suffered a collapse in part due to the strains of his front-line experience, and spent months recuperating at Dymchurch in Kent. Here he developed a most austere style, expelling all allusion to human figures and accentuating the symmetries of sea-wall, breakwaters, and skyline. One masterpiece from this period (begun in 1925 though completed only in 1937) is *Winter Sea,* the all but monochrome depiction of stylized waves folding within an icy darkness onto a frozen shore. The bleakness of the image is redolent of psychic trauma, but also reflects Nash's conscious interest in the geometric or non-organic aspects of the Constructivist style which his friends BEN NICHOLSON, the painter, and BARBARA HEPWORTH, the sculptor, had already adopted. Nash's affinity with this clean-cut and essentially abstract aesthetic inspired him to set up an artistic circle called Unit One, which lasted just long enough to give rise to a group show and a collective album edited by Herbert Read in 1934.

Using a camera his wife had given him just before they left on a 1931 trip to the United States, Nash had begun experimenting with photography, characteristically avoiding his shipboard companions in favor of carefully framed shots of masts, rails, and life-belts, elements congruent with the orderly aesthetic of Constructivism. In subsequent years Nash would use his photos both as blueprints for paintings and as a documentary resource—for instance, the *Dorset Shell Guide* (1936), Nash's act of homage to a beloved county, is illustrated with several photos of his favorite places.

Just when Nash's style was veering towards abstraction, he was intrigued and seduced by a very different impulse in continental art, that of Surrealism. Though reluctant to voice whole-hearted allegiance, Nash was an impressive participant at the International Surrealist Exhibition which Read and Roland Penrose mounted in London in 1936; that such canvases as *Harbour and Room* (1936) held their own alongside the provocative imagery of continental practitioners like Giorgio de Chirico and René Magritte explains Nash's international standing within Surrealism— though this did not prevent him sharing a show in 1943 with Hepworth, an unashamed partisan of pure form. Essentially, Nash's style arose from the confluence of two major currents of avant-garde innovation during the inter-war years.

Yet if Nash enjoyed toying with abstractions and dreams of foreign derivation, he could never finally bring himself to abandon explicit reference to the natural shapes of the places he loved. What makes his paintings so memorable is the controlled disposition across the canvas of such motifs as fences, hills, and copses, seemingly commonplace features of the actual countryside which, through poetic suggestion, become compelling emblems of the visionary and pointers to a kind of metaphysical order. A major instance of Nash's deepening interest in the invisible resonances of landscape is the oil *Landscape from a Dream* (1936–8), which persuades us that an identifiable tract of the Dorset coast might quite reasonably become the site of a magical ritual wherein a dark, brooding hawk—arguably a symbol of the artist as one who seeks to possess the earth from an aerial vantage-point—contemplates its own image in a mirror in whose unreal depths we discern the reflections of a soaring bird and a sinking scarlet sun—allusions which bring together intimations of death and transcendence.

In 1940 Nash was able once again to negotiate an appointment as official war artist and this time visited airfields and a wreckage dump near Oxford with camera and sketch-pad; his tabulations of flying bombers and monstrous wrecks led to such masterpieces as the huge *Battle of Britain* (1941), which celebrates the victory of the ROYAL AIR FORCE over the Luftwaffe in a breathtaking skyscape full of convoluted trails of white smoke, and the horrifying *Totes Meer (Dead Sea)* (1940–1), in which crashed aircraft lie inert beneath a spectral moon, as in some otherworldly graveyard for slaughtered birds.

Some of Nash's most hypnotic images emerged in the last few years of his life when, as an invalid slowly succumbing to chronic asthma, he spent hours sketching from inside a motor-car at favorite sites like the Avebury Circles or from a hotel balcony with a view to the Malvern Hills. The majestic climax of his career is a cycle of late oil-paintings based on the view from a friend's garden near Oxford from which he could just make out the distant Wittenham Clumps, those wooded hilltops which had been almost his first outdoor subject. Steeped in cultural and personal associations as both the site of archaic burial rites and in a sense the locale of Nash's own artistic birth, the Clumps, as evoked in such

a late and poignant oil as *Landscape of the Vernal Equinox* (1944), became a magnetic focal point for the viewer, whose eye grazes across the surfaces of woodland forms transmuted by the soft hues and graceful lighting of a master of atmospheric effect. These panoramas set the seal on Nash's achievement as an illustrator and transformer of the English landscape, being images both of an actual view and of a transfigured or surreal version thereof, one which secretes a lifetime's fund of meditations upon the poetry of places.

Roger Cardinal

Bibliography
Bertram, Anthony. *Paul Nash. The Portrait of an Artist.* 1955.
Cardinal, Roger. *The Landscape Vision of Paul Nash.* 1989.
Causey, Andrew. *Paul Nash.* 1980.
Colvin, Clare. *Paul Nash. Places.* 1989.
Nash, Paul. *Outline: An Autobiography and Other Writings.* 1949.

Nation (1907–1931)

After purchasing the faltering *Speaker* in 1906, the Rowntree Social Service Trust employed the advanced Liberal journalist, H.W. MASSINGHAM, as editor to transform the weekly into the *Nation*, which was launched on 1 March 1907. Comprehensive, innovative, and lively, the *Nation* was produced by Massingham and a small brilliant staff which included J.L. HAMMOND, L.T. Hobhouse, F.W. Hirst, LYTTON STRACHEY, Desmond MacCarthy, Holbrook Jackson, H. N. BRAILSFORD, H.W. Nevinson, ARNOLD BENNETT, and BERNARD SHAW. Indeed, under Massingham, the *Nation* became an important medium for many British men of letters during the first third of the twentieth century. Nevertheless, although the circulation of the paper rose to 5,000 by 1909, its financial condition remained precarious, and it was kept afloat only by subsidies from the Rowntree Trust. Massingham's independence, advanced views, and role as an impartial critic of the major political parties (especially on foreign policy and naval expansion before 1914) merited great respect but prejudiced the *Nation's* circulation and revenues. The paper also extolled peace initiatives, condemned jingoism, opposed large armament expenditures, supported WOMEN'S SUFFRAGE, and urged social reform on the LIBERAL PARTY.

During the FIRST WORLD WAR, the *Nation* advocated the right of the press to "fair criticism" of the government and endeavored to provide objective reporting of the news. Inevitably, the paper ran foul of the government by opposing CONSCRIPTION and by criticizing the authoritarianism of LLOYD GEORGE and the War CABINET.

And, as the war became a bloody stalemate, the *Nation* called for a negotiated peace. After failing to persuade the Rowntree Trust to restrain the paper, Lloyd George attempted to silence the *Nation* in March 1917 by prohibiting its foreign circulation on the grounds that it was providing PROPAGANDA for the enemy. But the ban provoked an uproar in Parliament which constrained Lloyd George to rescind it in mid–October. A major result of the *Nation*'s uncompromising independence, role as a forum of dissent, and demands for ending the war was a temporary surge in its circulation to approximately 11,000. What also increased the popularity of the paper was its enthusiastic advocacy of President Wilson's Fourteen Points and a League of Nations as "the future safeguard of civilisation". However, after the war, the *Nation* continued its vendetta against Lloyd George and the coalition government and, despairing of the fractured Liberal Party, shifted its loyalties to the rising LABOUR PARTY.

During the immediate post-war years, the quality of the *Nation*'s staff was enchanced by the work of such able assistant editors as H.M. Tomlinson, Gertrude M. Cross, and LEONARD WOOLF, and the paper was enriched by the literary talents of Edmund Blunden, J. Middleton Murry, Frank Swinnerton, ALDOUS HUXLEY, Osbert Sitwell, BERTRAND RUSSELL, HAROLD LASKI, and G.D.H. COLE. In early 1922 the Rowntree Trust merged the venerable *Atheneum* with the *Nation* and supported the paper's unrelenting criticism of British intervention in Russia and its advocacy of recognition of the Soviet regime, Irish independence, home rule for India, and the NATIONALIZATION of the COAL INDUSTRY.

Worn out by hard work and the persistent financial troubles plaguing the paper, as a result of its declining circulation and advertising revenues and mounting costs of production, Massingham resigned as editor in April 1923. He had implemented the Rowntree Trust's drastic economies, but the paper continued to lose ground and, when the Trust rejected his proposals to increase the *Nation*'s popular appeal, Massingham gave up, most of the staff leaving with him. He continued to contribute articles to the paper until his death in August 1924.

Massingham's successor, H.D. Henderson, ably edited the *Nation and Atheneum* from 1923 to 1930, when he was succeeded by its last editor, the less able Harold Wright. Neither Henderson nor Wright could resuscitate the paper which continued to decline until it was merged with the *NEW STATESMAN* in 1931. It was the demise of an outstanding weekly journal that had outlived its usefulness.

J.O. Baylen

Bibliography

Havighurst, Alfred F. *Radical Journalist: H.W. Massingham, 1860–1924*. 1974.

Koss, Stephen. *The Rise and Fall of the Political Press in Britain: vol. II: The Twentieth Century.* 1984.

National Front

Dating from before the SECOND WORLD WAR, there have been two principal traditions within the British extreme Right, identified by continuities both in ideology and also of some personnel. One tradition derives from the Imperial Fascist League (IFL) of Arnold Leese (1878–1956) and the other from the British Union of Fascists (BUF) of SIR OSWALD MOSLEY (1896–1980). Although the latter was the more important during the 1930s, the former tradition has dominated extreme Right politics in Great Britain during most of the period since 1945. The National Front (NF), brought together in late 1966 and early 1967 as an amalgamation of several earlier extreme Right and racist organizations, was a political party in the tradition of the IFL, especially when later in 1967 John Tyndall (1934–) and Martin Webster (1943–) managed to insinuate themselves into the leadership after moving from a self-avowedly neo-Nazi group, despite the intentions of the NF's original founders to exclude them. By 1972, as the NF entered its most significant period, Tyndall was its chairman and Webster, as National Activities Organizer, his deputy.

The NF was able to take advantage of the increasing public hostility during the 1960s to the presence of Afro-Caribbean and Asian immigrant settlers from the former British Empire, hostility that was also articulated by mainstream politicians such as the Conservative MP ENOCH POWELL. The NF's halcyon period, however, was from 1972 to 1977. Because of the first-past-the-post electoral system, it never came close to winning a seat in the House of Commons, but it was seen as a significant force especially in parts of London (most noticeably the East End, where there has been an intermittent tradition of extreme Right support throughout the twentieth century), the West Midlands, the city of Leicester and its environs, some of the northern textile towns in Lancashire and Yorkshire (such as Preston, Blackburn, and Bradford), and some of the New Towns around London inhabited largely by former Londoners. Again, although the NF made no electoral gains, it was securing sufficient votes in local elections in these places during the mid-1970s to trouble the major political parties.

It retained among its politicized and activist elite the conventional ANTI-SEMITISM of the extreme Right, but its more populist appeal was based on hostility to immigrants and on a demand for the repatriation of them and their descendants to their country of origin. Its emphasis on IMMI-GRATION set a political agenda that the CONSERVATIVE PARTY was able to accept, albeit in a less extreme form.

In the mid-1970s the party survived a major split that produced the short-lived National Party, which did manage briefly to have two councillors on the District Council of Blackburn in Lancashire. By 1978 the NF's unexpectedly poor performance in that year's local elections, especially those for the London borough councils (for which it had extended candidate-coverage, especially in the east and north-east London boroughs) showed that support had declined from a peak in 1976 and early 1977. Harassed by critical publicity about its leadership, increasingly the object of the attentions of an active anti-Fascist movement from late 1977, and with its principal policy issue taken over (albeit in a muted version) by the Conservative Party, the NF's decline accelerated. In the May 1979 general election it managed to run 303 candidates, but they averaged only 1.3 percent of votes cast in their contests.

After this major setback the NF experienced considerable internal turmoil. Several splinter groups broke away but in most cases were short-lived. Principal figures in the 1970s leadership, notably Webster and Tyndall, were marginalized or felt obliged to resign. Tyndall left the party in June 1980 and in April 1982 founded a British National Party (BNP), the fourth extreme Right party to bear this name. For several years it survived only in the political wilderness but has seen some slight local revivals since 1990, partly in the light of the extreme Right resurgence across much of Western Europe. It should be said that, throughout the late 1970s and 1980s, the NF has been symbolically attractive to certain sections of urban white working-class male youth; for example, the party particularly focused upon mobilized support among selected groups of FOOT-BALL supporters and certain clubs became notorious for the racist chanting at Black players by some of their supporters.

In the 1983 general election the NF had managed only 1.0 percent of votes cast in sixty seats fought. This setback was the occasion for a further split. One group to emerge from this became increasingly exclusive, rejected electoral participation and flirted with ideological positions borrowed from Italian neo-Fascist terrorism; in 1991 it disbanded as a claimant to the NF name and formed a self-consciously exclusive grouping from a small number of dedicated activists. The other product of the mid-1980s split has had a checkered existence since then. It was able to offer only a single candidate in the 1987 election; in 1992 it fought fourteen constituencies, averaging merely 0.7 percent of votes cast.

The NF has been the most important component of post-war extreme Right politics in Great Britain. However, by the 1990s, associated with individuals having no public credibility or recognition, it seems most unlikely to be able to participate in any revival of the extreme Right, despite the political resonance on its name. The vanguard role in the extreme Right movement, such as it is, has passed to other groupings, especially the BNP.

Christopher T. Husbands

Bibliography
Husbands, Christopher T. *Racial Exclusionism and the City: The Urban Support of the National Front.* 1983.
———. "Extreme Right-wing Politics in Great Britain: The Recent Marginalisation of the National Front," *West European Politics,* vol. 11 (1988), pp. 65–79.
Taylor, Stan. *The National Front in English Politics.* 1982.
Thurlow, Richard. *Fascism in Britain: A History 1918–1985.* 1987.

National Health Service

The National Health Service, established on 5 July 1948, made available to the entire population a comprehensive system of health care, free at time of use and funded overwhelmingly out of taxation.

Prior to the NHS, health care in Britain had been provided by a rather confused patchwork of services that had grown up in a piecemeal and unco-ordinated fashion. Public health legislation had been put in place over the course of the nineteenth century, with the 1875 Public Health Act the zenith of the "environmental sanitation" movement. At the beginning of the twentieth century there were three major kinds of hospital: the voluntary (supported by a combination of public donations, income from endowments and charges to patients), those run by the Poor Law (which were generally lower in quality), and municipal hospitals run by local authorities. Doctors tended to be either general practitioners (GPs), or consultants. The former served local communities and worked in Poor Law hospitals and received their income from fees to patients; the latter worked part of their time in the teaching hospitals, and earned large incomes from treating wealthy patients in their private practices.

The British health care system of the early twentieth century was thus a highly market-oriented one. Collectivist provision only existed in the Poor Law medical service (for the destitute), in trade union medical benefit societies, friendly societies (which covered only the skilled minority of workers), and in a few company medical schemes. Two problems were particularly evident: the geographical maldistribution of doctors and HOSPITALS (both of which tended to gravitate towards wealthy areas); and marked differentials in health status between social classes. Wide extremes existed within the medical profession: even in the 1930s, a low-paid doctor might earn £600 per annum, while a Harley Street specialist could charge 100 guineas for one operation. These differences in income symbolized marked differences in quality of care offered.

In the early 1900s there were increasingly clamorous demands from socialists for a state medical service. Some interest was also shown by the British Medical Association, in its *Report on Contract Practice* (1905). An important early milestone was the 1911 National Insurance Act, which introduced National Health Insurance (NHI) coverage for 14 million men and women wage-earners aged between sixteen and seventy. In return for small weekly contributions from employee, employer, and the state, those earning less than £160 per annum (raised to £250 per annum in 1920) were provided with the free services of a GP, sickness benefit (followed, if necessary, by disability benefit), treatment for tuberculosis, and maternity benefit. The scheme was very limited, and indeed was seen by its originator, LLOYD GEORGE, as no more than an "ambulance wagon". It had two major defects: the lack of coverage for the dependents of an insured person (which left outside the scheme working-class wives and children; and failure to provide access to specialist treatment (thus leaving many life-threatening diseases untreated). Nonetheless, the 1911 health insurance scheme was a very significant incursion by the state into the provision of health care.

In the 1920s and 1930s there was a steadily-developing consensus on the need for some sort of state medical service, to which many sections of the political spectrum subscribed. In 1919 the Ministry of Health was established. The 1926 Report of the Royal Commission on National Health Insurance suggested that the ultimate solution should be a health care system funded principally out of taxation rather than by extensions of NHI. In 1930 the British Medical Association published its Report on *A General Medical Service For the Nation,* which suggested a service based on the extension of NHI coverage to wives and dependents and others of similar income status (such as the self-employed). However, within this apparent consensus, there were marked divisions over precisely what *form* a state medical service should take. A few radicals (represented, for example, by the Socialist Medical Association) wished to see the total abolition of private medicine, with complete hospital nationalization and all doctors employed by the state; at the other end of the political spectrum, conservative opinion favored as large a private sector as possible, and any future state service limited in coverage. The GPs wanted a service based upon the extension of NHI, and some access to specialist treatment; above all, they feared the prospect of becoming a "salaried service" in which they would have to work under the direction of central planners. The Poor Law hospitals had been taken over by the local authorities in 1929, and were thus vulnerable to NATIONALIZATION; but, being of inferior status, they would have provided an inadequate basis for a fully comprehensive health service. The voluntary hospitals were in a stronger bargaining position, but their financial basis was weak. Lastly, no state health service would have been able to operate effectively without the full participation of the consultants. The irony was, therefore, that this most conservative group within the MEDICAL PROFESSION knew that they possessed considerable bargaining power in any negotiations and thus were less afraid of state medicine than were many GPs. Substantial differences of viewpoint existed over such key questions as the role of private medicine, the extent of hospital nationalization, the degree of state control over doctors' clinical freedom, and the basis upon which any new service would be funded.

In effect, the logjam of disagreement in the late 1930s was broken by the SECOND WORLD WAR. First, the Emergency Medical Service, set up in 1938 and implemented at the start of the war, achieved at a stroke the nationalization of hospitals, and the co-ordination of other sectors. Second, the temporary radicalism of the early war years led to demands for a post-war WELFARE STATE, the centerpiece of which would be a National Health Service. Third, the peculiar political circumstances of wartime produced a landslide victory for the LABOUR PARTY in the 1945 general election. While it is likely that a post-war Conservative government would have introduced some kind of NHS, Labour's victory (and the appointment of ANEURIN BEVAN as Minister of Health) made it certain that the Service would be universal, comprehensive, and tax-funded. These principles were embodied in the 1946 National Health Service Act, and—after some rather tortuous negotiations with the doctors—the Service was launched two years later.

The new NHS was based on a tripartite administrative structure: hospitals; primary health care (for example, GPs and dentists); and the local authority services (such as the school medical service). Private medicine continued for those who wished to pay for it: this was part of Bevan's "deal" to win the support of the consultants, and was seen by many as a right. In no way did planners of the new Service imagine that its introduction would usher in a revolution in medicine. Essentially, its aims were threefold: to remove the barrier of cost at time of treatment; to open up access to comprehensive and specialist treatment for those hitherto excluded (notably, working class women and children); and to enable rational planning under democratic control.

The progress of the NHS in its first twenty years was relatively tranquil. The main area of controversy was over the funding of the Service. Very soon after its establishment, there was concern that the overall cost was rising too rapidly; from certain quarters came the argument that a "free-at-time-of-use" health care system encouraged consumer irresponsibility. It was in partial response to these concerns, plus overall budgetary constraints, that the Labour government introduced the first round of NHS charges in 1951. These concerns also led to the appointment of the Guillebaud Committee on the cost of the NHS which reported in 1956 and showed that, firstly, expenditure on the NHS was not rising as a proportion of GNP, and, secondly, that abuse by the public was not a major problem: instead, the NHS was having to deal with wage and salary claims, the rising cost of goods and services, and increased demands consequent upon the AGEING of the population.

Nevertheless, the question of how demands should be fairly and efficiently rationed in a state service like the NHS was one that came under considerable scrutiny in the 1970s. Health economists began to examine all the economic and behavioral variables that could affect clinical judgements: the decision whether or not to treat a patient in hospital was the most important factor determining the level of health expenditure. Through rationing devices at micro-level, such as "clinical budgeting", attempts were made to improve the prioritizing of scarce resources.

Another related problem discussed in the 1970s was the geographical maldistribution of health care resources. This had been a feature of the pre-NHS system, and by the 1970s little seemed to have changed: regions which had been poorly endowed with hospital resources in the late 1930s were in an identical relative position in the 1970s. In order to address this problem, a Resource Allocation Working Party was set up, and reported in 1976. It recommended a slow reallocation of hospital resources from rich to poor regions, and this was implemented.

The election of a Conservative government in 1979 seemed to portend a large-scale privatization of the NHS, but this did not happen. Health expenditure was constrained, as part of tight controls on overall public spending, but the NHS survived intact, although private medicine continued to grow steadily. In 1955 a mere 585,000 people had been covered by private medical insurance; by 1984 this figure had risen to 5.1 million. By the 1990s, however, major changes in health policy were underway. The 1990 National Health Service and Community Care Act introduced three major reforms. First, NHS hospitals were to be allowed to "opt out" of direct NHS control and enjoy quasi-autonomous status as "trust hospitals"; they were to take on a new role as providers of health care, negotiating competitive contracts for patient treatment with health authorities. By introducing an "internal market" discipline into the NHS and infusing health care providers with more of a business ethos, the government hoped to improve efficiency. Second, GPs were to manage their budgets more independently, becoming "fund-holding" practices. The third was perhaps the least controversial change, since it represented the culmination of a series of efforts in this direction since the 1970s: clinical audit was to applied to more areas of health care provision, in order to monitor the unit cost of such services. These reforms were controversial: their supporters argued that they would, at long last, bring the discipline of the market into a state monopoly; their critics argued that they were designed to achieve the eventual privatization of the NHS. As the century drew to a close, the NHS remained the center of controversy as the Labour government sought to shore up its foundations and remedy its deficiencies.

John Macnicol

Bibliography

Allsop, Judith. *Health Policy and the National Health Service.* 1984.

Klein, Rudolf. *The Politics of the National Health Service.* 2nd ed. 1989.

Navarro, Vincente. *Class Struggle, the State and Medicine.* 1978.

Pater, John E. *The Making of the National Health Service.* 1981.

Webster, Charles. *The Health Services Since the War: vol. I: Problems of Health Care: The National Health Service Before 1957.* 1988.

National Trust

The National Trust for Places of Historic Interest or Natural Beauty is a private charity dedicated to the preservation of buildings and landscape of special aesthetic or historic interest. Its ambit covers England and Wales only; there is a separate, much smaller Trust for Scotland. Though not a branch of government, the National Trust was from its early days recognized as the principal repository for land that government was not able or willing to acquire for itself. For this reason, Parliament endowed the Trust with tax exemptions, statutory powers, and special responsibilities which helped it to grow over the course of the century into the largest nongovernmental landowner and the largest membership organization in the country.

The Trust was founded in 1895 by a quartet of liberal philanthropists: the great landowning first Duke of Westminster, the social reformer Octavia Hill, Sir Robert Hunter, a lawyer with a long-standing interest in the preservation of open spaces, and Canon H.D. Rawnsley, a crusading Lake District clergyman. All had long histories of concern for the deteriorating spiritual as well as material condition of the urban masses and a conviction that exposure to natural beauty could serve as an antidote to both. The respectability of its founders and the careful distance it kept from party politics earned the Trust many bequests of land and money. By 1924 it had acquired over a hundred properties, especially in the Lake District and parts of Surrey threatened by London's expansion.

Though historic buildings figured in the Trust's founding charter, only a few were acquired in these early years, mostly medieval relics recommended by the associated Society for the Protection of Ancient Buildings. But in the 1930s the more aristocratic section of the Trust's membership began to look to the Trust to take over some of the great COUNTRY HOUSES whose survival was threatened by agricultural decline after the First World War. Lords Zetland, Esher, and Lothian masterminded the establishment of a Country Houses Scheme in 1936. With the way smoothed by Parliamentary legislation in 1937 and 1939, the Trust was able to acquire many of the greatest houses, especially after the Second World War when owners were under financial pressure. Many of these acquisitions were secured by James Lees-Milne, the Scheme's Secretary until 1951.

Although the Trust's holdings of open space continued to grow unabated, the Country Houses Scheme wrought considerable changes. The Trust acquired with its houses much agricultural land meant to be worked commercially: 85,000 acres by 1958. It sought to become a model landlord as well as a nature conserver and countryside advocate. Its leadership became more aristocratic. Somewhat paradoxically, its membership also began to grow more quickly, as country-house tourism took off in the 1950s and the Trust subscription (giving free entrance to all properties) looked a bargain. Before the war the Trust had been the property of a small handful; by 1960 it had 100,000 members. This growth, coupled with the enhanced environmental consciousness of the decade, stirred up division over the Trust's identity in the 1960s. Agriculture, conservation, and tourism made uneasy bedfellows. The Trust's properties had also expanded to include everything from palaces to canals, gardens to working mills. A major appeal was made from 1963 to fund purchases of unspoilt coastline threatened by development ("Enterprise Neptune"). A feeling that the Trust's oligarchic leadership was not well-suited to managing this diverse national collection in a modern, accessible way culminated in an Extraordinary General Meeting in 1967. The leadership resisted this challenge, but gradually reformed itself and paved the way for a rapid professionalization of the Trust's publicity and management. The new corporate style ushered in a period of spectacular membership growth, from 250,000 in 1971 to 2 million in 1990. Commercial activities swelled the Trust's coffers further: center-city boutiques sold crafts and interior decorations, publishing ventures catered to the country-house craze. Properties amounted to over half a million acres, including one-third of the coastline designated of "heritage" value by the government. Visitors to houses and gardens alone topped 10 million a year. Schoolchildren and community groups were offered educational and cultural services. Having fended off the charge of snobbery and exclusiveness in the 1960s, the Trust found itself in the 1980s still considered too "heritage"-minded by critics of the Left, but now also too socialist and bureaucratic by critics of the Right.

Peter Mandler

Bibliography

Gaze, John. *Figures in a Landscape: A History of the National Trust.* 1988.

Hewison, Robert. *The Heritage Industry: Britain in a Climate of Decline.* 1987.

Mandler, Peter. *The Fall and Rise of the Stately Home.* 1997.

National Union of Mineworkers

The NUM dates from January 1945, succeeding the earlier MINERS FEDERATION OF GREAT BRITAIN, formed in 1889. At its peak the MFGB had organized over a million miners, but the subsequent decline of the industry combined with shattering defeats in 1921 and 1926 to reduce membership substantially.

The federal structure of the older organization left its mark on the NUM. The new union represented a compromise between advocates of a genuinely national union and those who felt the need to protect local interests. The constituent unions of the Federation became Areas of the NUM, but retained much of their old power. Most of the NUM's full time officials were employed in the Areas; often their bureaucracies and financial resources were extensive. The NUM had just two full time national officials—a President and a General Secretary.

For several years this potentially divisive structure maintained its cohesion. The NUM was controlled by a right-wing LABOUR faction based on the coalfields of North Eastern England,

Yorkshire, Nottinghamshire, and Lancashire. A left-wing, frequently COMMUNIST minority was centered in Scotland and South Wales. The majority faction's control was strengthened by the miners' post-war experiences. The Labour government brought the mines into public ownership as from 1 January 1947. The long standing hostilities between union and coalowners ended; the NUM's status was enhanced and buoyant demand for coal protected employment.

This security began to disintegrate in the late 1950s, when cheap oil supplies and changed energy demand meant widespread pit closures especially in Scotland, South Wales, the North East, and Lancashire. Miners' wages showed a relative decline, and the hope that a Labour government would reverse the trend proved illusory after 1964. The old NUM leadership became discredited, and a more militant response began to develop.

Even at the height of the Cold War, the Left had had some strength in the NUM. Successive Communists had been elected to the General Secretaryship in 1946 and in 1959 and had worked harmoniously with the dominant faction. In the late sixties and early seventies the Left expanded its influence, eventually gaining control of the large Yorkshire coalfield. In 1972 the Union embarked on its first national stoppage since 1926. A mid-winter strike revealed the vulnerability of the electricity industry to any witholding of coal supplies. A heavy blow was inflicted on the credibility of the HEATH government. Two years later the battle was repeated; this time the Conservative government called an election but lost very narrowly. The myth that the NUM had brought down a government was born.

The stoppages were over wages. Mechanization had led in 1966 to the negotiation of the National Power Loading Agreement (N.P.L.A.). This aimed to gradually equalize wages for face workers whose earnings had hitherto varied between coalfields. The result was to generalize discontent and to provide a solid basis for national STRIKES. These industrial victories were claimed by the Left as demonstrating the value of a more militant strategy. Yet from 1971 the NUM President was Joe Gormley, a man of the Right who successfully rode the tide of militancy.

From 1974 Gormley used his machiavellian skills to avoid embarrassing a Labour government, tenuously clinging to office and facing economic difficulties. His efforts culminated late in 1977 in the destruction of the NPLA; its replacement by local productivity schemes ended one basis for national action. Relationships between Left and Right became increasingly bitter with accusations of procedural malpractice.

The ballot for Gormley's successor late in 1981 produced an easy victory for the Left's standard-bearer Arthur Scargill. The central figure in the Left's advance in Yorkshire, he secured over 70 percent of the vote. With the once-dominant Right faction thoroughly demoralised, the Left effectively controlled the Union. But the THATCHER government was unsympathetic to the public sector and hostile to the unions; more symbolically there was perhaps a need to reverse 1972 and 1974. A sizeable contraction of the industry was signposted by the appointment of Ian Mac-Gregor as its Chairman in the summer of 1983.

NUM members in the early 1980s proved repeatedly unwilling to vote for strike action on either wages or closures. There were clear divergences of interest between more and less profitable Areas. Eventually the Left leadership endorsed the so-called domino strategy to avoid the holding of a national strike ballot. Each Area would call a strike and cumulatively there would be a stoppage. The tactic was employed in March 1984 and met with mixed success. Coalfields with fears of redundancies or strong Left leaderships struck; a minority of miners, especially in the Midlands, were reluctant or hostile. Among strikers, there was principled, solid, often moving commitment to the NUM. The government and the police responded with authoritarian measures; much of the media were hostile to NUM and especially to Scargill. Some unions gave sympathetic support; other proved unable or unwilling.

The strikers' resistance was heroic but eventually unavailing. From November 1984 increasing numbers returned to work, and in March 1985, after almost a year, the stoppage ended without an agreement. The consequences for the NUM have been disastrous. A breakaway Union of Democratic Mineworkers emerged based largely in Nottinghamshire, the stronghold of the anti-strikers. The industry has seen mass closures; prior to the dispute the industry had around 200,000 employees; by 1991 the number was fewer than 60,000. The Conservative victory in the 1992 General Election led to further pit closures in anticipation of legislation to privatize the coal industry.

Debate about this decline has often been conducted in terms of a personalised argument over Scargill's industrial strategy. The President has become a highly controversial figure even within the NUM Left. Yet such a diagnosis can all too easily ignore the wider context. The vicissitudes of the NUM must be located within the changing fortunes of the post-war labor movement of the coal industry.

David Howell

Bibliography
Adeney, Martin, and John Lloyd. *The Miners Strike of 1984–85: Loss Without Limit. 1986.*

Arnot, R. Page. *The Miners in Crisis and War.* 1961.
Howell, David. *The Politics of the N.U.M.* 1989.
Taylor, Andrew J. *The National Union of Mineworkers and British Politics 1944–1995.* 2000.

Nationalization and Nationalized Industries
The story of the nationalized industries provides one of the more curious episodes in Britain's contemporary history. Between the late 1940s and the late 1970s a considerable part of British business was nationalized and taken into state ownership. In 1979 the nationalized industries employed almost 2 million people and accounted for 10 per cent of British output. However, the following decade saw the return of much of this industry to the private sector in the privatization program of Prime Minister MARGARET THATCHER. By the early 1990s only a few economic activities remained in state ownership. Both nationalization in the 1940s and privatization in the 1980s were politically popular at the time, both sought in part to address the intractable problems of the British economy, and both achieved ambiguous results.

The era of nationalization is conventionally dated to the Labour government of 1945–51, but there was a pre-history of state investment in business, even though British governments had traditionally been strong advocates of *laissez-faire* policies. In 1914 the British government subscribed £2 million of capital, or over half the equity, to the Anglo-Persian Oil Company (later known as British Petroleum) in an attempt to secure an adequate supply of fuel oil for the ROYAL NAVY. During the inter-war years a number of public corporations were established as a solution to market failure. These corporations were designed to ensure that the industries concerned were freed from day to day political interference in their affairs. The most important public corporations were the Central Electricity Board, established in 1926 to supervise the generation of electricity and to construct a national grid, the BRITISH BROADCASTING CORPORATION, and the London Passenger Transport Board. The public corporation became the standard administrative model for the real wave of nationalization after 1945.

The Labour government that came to power in 1945 implemented an extensive nationalization program. The principal nationalizations measures, in chronological order, were the Bank of England (1946); civil AVIATION (1946); COAL (1947); inland transport, notably the RAILWAYS (1947); electricity (1948); gas (1948); and iron and STEEL (1949).

There was no single motivation in this sweeping legislation. The LABOUR PARTY had been committed, at least since its 1918 constitution, to take the basic activities of the economy under state control, and the aim of widespread nationalization was the basis of the policy manifesto, *Let Us Face the Future,* on which Labour fought the 1945 election. Labour believed that publicly-owned industry could serve the public interest better than the private sector, and that the nationalized sector could assist in the implementation of government policies. It also argued that the private ownership of industries had involved wasteful competition, which had led in turn to failures to invest in modern equipment.

There was very little change to the structure of the nationalized industries in the 1950s and 1960s, despite the return of a Conservative government in 1951. The new government privatized the iron and steel industry and the goods side of road transport, but otherwise left the nationalized sector in place. There were some minor extensions of state ownership under the Labour governments of 1964–70. In 1968, for example, the National Bus Company combined the already state-owned bus sector with most of the remaining private sector to create a large passenger transport corporation. However, a new wave of nationalization occurred in the 1970s. The continuing decay of British industry, rather than socialist ideology, was the driving force. The Conservative government of 1970–4 nationalized the aero-engine business of Rolls-Royce after the firm went bankrupt. In 1975 British Leyland, the last British-owned volume car manufacturer, was nationalized after a financial crisis following a long period of declining market share. In 1977 shipbuilding and ship repairing industry, which had long been in a financially disastrous condition, was taken under state control, and in the same year Britain's aircraft manufacturing industry was nationalized to form British Aerospace.

The performance of the nationalized industries has aroused considerable controversy, in part because it is so difficult to judge. An initial point is that many of the nationalized industries began their public sector lives as industries with considerable and longstanding problems. The new National Coal Board created in 1947 acquired 800 firms which ran 1,470 collieries, with a notorious reputation for underinvestment and bad industrial relations. The Gas Council created in 1948 took over 1,000 separate gas undertakings of all shapes and sizes, the largest of which made one eighth of all British gas output, and the smallest of which had just 132 customers. The shipbuilding and vehicle companies nationalized in the 1970s had been brought to the brink of disaster by incompetent private sector management.

The performance of the sector after nationalization was mixed. Between the late 1940s and the late 1950s financial performance was generally poor. Between 1959 and 1967 the rates of return were generally much higher and compared well with the private sector. Between the late 1960s and the late 1970s the financial performance of the sector deteriorated again. There were, however, considerable differences between industries in their financial performances, and the figures are hard to interpret because of industry differences. The financial performance of the coal industry, for example, was poor, but it faced a contracting market, and its performance was in some respects superior to other Western European coal industries. There was also a great diversity in terms of productivity growth, both in different industries and in different time periods. The growth of labor productivity in the nationalized airlines, which were eventually merged into British Airways, was much higher than for manufacturing as a whole throughout the period 1948–85, while labor productivity growth in the National Bus Company was always much lower.

Critics claimed that the mere fact of public ownership produced inefficient managements, which contributed to the poor productivity of some industries, but the historical evidence would qualify such an image. The 1960s saw a form of managerial revolution in the public sector, which in some ways out-paced the private sector in developing investment appraisal techniques and new methods of corporate planning. These innovations were often associated with particular strong chairmen, such as Alfred Robens in coal, WALTER CITRINE in electricity, and Richard Beeching in rail. It remains unclear whether the poor productivity performances in industries such as coal, rail, and steel can be ascribed to management failings, or to more general problems in securing productivity increases in capital-intensive industries in difficult economic conditions.

Many of the difficulties of the nationalized industries stemmed not from managerial performance or motivation, but from the behavior of their single shareholder—the British government. The government did not, especially in the first decades of nationalization, specify what it wanted the nationalized industries to do. Each was told to provide an efficient, reliable, and economical service, and expected to be financially self-supporting, "taking one year with another", a vague phase which offered little guidance to managers. There was no effective instruction as to how prices were to be set or the rates of return which were expected until 1967, when the government ruled that prices should reflect long-run marginal costs. Later still, in 1978, a required rate of return was set for each industry's investment program. Governments regularly interfered with the investment, pricing, and employment strategies of the nationalized industries.

During the 1970s there was growing disatisfaction with the nationalized industries. In 1974–5 the government had to supply £2.75 billion of financial assistance to them, although much of this money was spent on keeping prices low at the government's request, or keeping uneconomic railway lines in operating, again at the government's request. The nationalization of failed companies in the 1970s reinforced the sector's association with failure. The stage was set for the complete reversal of policy following the return of the CONSERVATIVE PARTY to power in 1979.

The Thatcher government's program included a commitment both to reduce the public sector and to improve the efficiency of what remained in it. Privatization began slowly in 1981, when Cable and Wireless and part of British Aerospace were sold. After 1983 the programme accelerated. British Airways, British Gas, British Leyland, British Shipbuilders, British Steel, British Telecom, the National Bus Company, and the water and electricity industries had been privatized by 1990, with British Rail to follow. A nationalized sector continued into the 1990s, but as a shrunken residual of its former self, comprised of industries such as coal and nuclear power for which it was exceptionally hard to find buyers in the private sector.

The initial attraction of privatization was as an *ad hoc* means of raising funds. Asset sales were written off against public spending, and this cut the public sector borrowing requirement of the government. As time passed, the Thatcher government developed broader justifications. It was argued that wider share ownership in general was economically beneficial, and the government encouraged individual investors to buy shares in privatization issues, often by under-pricing assets so as to provide a give-away element in the flotation price. The government also argued that private sector ownership would enhance economic efficiency as market forces exercised discipline on managers.

The performance of several firms, such as British Airways, appeared to improve dramatically with privatization, though often the most remarkable gains were made in the period immediately before privatization as managers prepared for the upheaval. In retrospect, however, the privatization program has been judged as a rather unsatisfactory exercise. Few efficiency gains have been identified, and studies have indicated that the principal gainers were the senior managers of the privatized companies, who awarded themselves large salary increases as they caught up with the level of the private sector.

A particular problem was that large corporations such as British Telecom were privatized as large and weakly regulated near-monopolies, reflecting the greater priority awarded to raising money from asset sales than to promoting competition. The subsequent predatory behavior of British Telecom, British Gas, and other privatized monopolies caused considerable concern and pressure for more satisfactory regulatory regimes. Passenger transport was one of the few sectors where competition was vigorously promoted. The National Bus Company was split and privatized in 1988 as over fifty separate companies. However, new entrants were not attracted to the industry, fares rose, and Britain's bus manufacturing industry collapsed because of a lack of orders. In addition, bus passengers continued to fall as many rural services were abandoned. Within a few years most of the privatized companies had been acquired by a few large groups.

Nationalization and, later, privatization were both attempts to deal with the problems of low competitiveness and poor productivity which beset so much of twentieth-century British industry. The British largely placed their faith in private ownership before 1945, in public ownership between the 1940s and the 1970s, and then in private ownership again in the 1980s. The results were in all cases ambiguous.

Geoffrey Jones

Bibliography

Ashworth, William, *The History of the British Coal Industry, vol. 5, 1946–1982: The Nationalized Industry* (1986).

———. *The State in Business, 1945 to the mid-1980s.* 1991.

Chester, D.N. *Nationalization of British Industry.* 1975.

Gourvish, Terry. *British Railways 1948–73.* 1986.

Kay, John, Colin Mayer, and David Thompson, eds. *Privatisation and Regulation: the UK Experience.* 1986.

Pryke, Richard. *The Nationalised Industries: Policies and Performance since 1968* 1981.

Navy, Royal

British imperial, naval, and maritime dominance, was a fact of global life during the nineteenth century. Such hegemony was maintained by the Royal Navy, the largest naval fleet in the world during the century after 1815. It provided security for the largest merchant marine force and for the financial, banking, insurance, and shipping services controlled from London. At this time the Royal Navy was the "senior service" of the British armed forces in addition to being the premier international naval force. It was overseen by the Board of the Admiralty, whose responsibilities encompassed the operating fleets, dozens of supporting bases, and several major dockyards at home and abroad.

The fleets consisted of a wide variety of warships. Most important during the early decades were the battleships, the replacements for the sailing Ships-of-the-Line which had dominated naval warfare earlier. Important modifications in battleship features, many initiated by the British, resulted in the *Dreadnought* revolution and in an innovative design called the battlecruiser, both introduced about 1905. The supporting warships of the early decades were cruisers and destroyers, the fast scouting and security forces responsible for maintaining international lines of communication and trade routes. Improvements in torpedo design and capabilities caused corresponding changes in destroyer tactics and use. The submarine as a viable and lethal warship originated during this early part of the century.

The American naval writer A.T. Mahan's influential "blue water" paradigm, touted as the strategic model which determined the British emphasis on imperial and maritime rather than continental land factors, called for a major confrontation between opposing battle fleets. More perceptive maritime and naval observers abandoned Mahanian concepts and recognized Sir Julian Corbett (1854–1922) as the most influential articulator of British maritime strategy. Corbett stressed continuous control of routes of communication and alternative uses of naval forces.

The occasion providing the most potential for a Trafalgar-type naval confrontation was the FIRST WORLD WAR Battle of Jutland fought in the North Sea on 31 May—1 June 1916, when the Grand Fleet under Admiral Sir John Jellicoe challenged the High Seas Fleet under Admiral Reinhard Scheer: the British-German figures were, respectively 37 capital ships vs. 27; 149 warships vs. 99. Losses amounted to 14 British ships and 6100 killed; 11 German ships and 2550 killed. The Germans immediately declared a victory, but the battle was indecisive; nothing changed and the Germans remained blockaded for the duration of the war. Perhaps the most telling result was that the Grand Fleet was prepared for action immediately upon returning to its bases while the High Seas Fleet was not ready for several months.

During the inter-war period economic, political, and strategic commitments stretched British resources. This precipitated internal budgetary competition whereby the government was forced to set priorities among demands from the ROYAL AIR FORCE, now an independent agency, the Royal Navy, once deemed dominant, and the ARMY. Naval air forces remained dangerously deficient resulting in serious gaps in reconnaissance capabilities against German use of U-boats.

Significant combat action during the SECOND WORLD WAR included a British naval aviation attack against the Italian naval base at Taranto, immobilizing major units of the Italian fleet; a British squadron defeating an Italian squadron in the Mediterranean at Matapan; the contest between the British battleship *Prince of Wales* and battle-cruiser *Hood* and the German battleship *Bismarck* and cruiser *Prinz Eugen*, in which *Hood* was lost and hundreds of British warships converged in the North Atlantic to sink the *Bismarck;* and the later loss of *Prince of Wales* and *Repulse* off Indochina, victims of Japanese land-based aircraft. All of these occurred between September 1939 and December 1941.

The critical aspects of naval warfare for the British during both world wars were the German U-boat campaigns against merchant shipping. In the First World War Germany immediately declared unrestricted submarine warfare, later cancelled it, but resumed it on 1 February 1917. The critical stage of sinkings of allied shipping was in the spring of 1917 following American entry into the war. Implementation of a convoy system, the influx of American warships, and improved detection and weapons of anti-submarine warfare slowly tipped the balance in favor of the Allies. Similarly in the Second World War sinkings were spectacular up to the spring of 1943 when various countermeasures, use of small aircraft carriers for reconnaissance to protect convoys, and an increasing ability to read German secret codes contributed to the final defeat.

The fall of Singapore in 1942 signaled the end of British hegemony as a Pacific power; the SUEZ CRISIS of 1956 meant the virtual demise of influence in the Middle East; and the FALKLANDS WAR demonstrated only a temporary military revival. The Falklands campaign in the spring of 1982 when British forces, mostly naval, expelled about 12,000 Argentine invaders from the South Atlantic islands of South Georgia and the Falklands, was the primary operation of British naval and marine forces after Suez. The volunteer basis of the British forces, the highly professional manner with which the campaign was conducted, and the capability to overcome complicated logistical problems with no British base within thousands of miles were factors repeatedly praised. The naval forces were supplemented by "STUFT," Ships-taken-up-from-trade, a total of fifty commercial ships including two major liners, *Queen Elizabeth II* and *Canberra,* tankers, a superferry, and specialized cargo ships. The British lost six warships, some to Exocet missiles.

Personnel of the naval forces consisted of officers, enlisted members including men and women, the shore establishment, and the Royal Marines, officers and enlisted. During wartime the merchant marine came under naval control. Naval officers were symbolically placed on the quarterdeck, enlisted persons on the lower deck. During the first two decades of the century Lionel Yexley (real name James Woods, 1862–1933), an advocate and journalist, led an important re-form and representation movement. During the 1920s pay, morale, and conditions on the lower deck deteriorated, culminating in a serious disturbance aboard a dozen battleships at Invergordon in northern Scotland in September 1931. The government conceded most of the demands and refrained from punitive measures. After the Second World War the volunteer character of the navy necessitated the improvement of conditions and pay and the associated professional status.

The leaders most identified with the Royal Navy during the twentieth century have been WINSTON CHURCHILL, First Lord of the Admiralty, the civilian head, during the early years of both world wars; Admiral Sir John Fisher, First Sea Lord, the professional head, 1904–10 and 1914–15; Admiral Sir Andrew Cunningham (1883–1963), a fleet commander and First Sea Lord during the Second World War; and Admiral EARL MOUNTBATTEN, First Sea Lord after the Second World War. Fisher was instrumental in the Dreadnought and battlecruiser innovations and other lower deck and strategic reforms. Cunningham came closest to the "Nelson touch" of aggressive offensive operations. Mountbatten guided the Royal Navy through the post-war transition.

In 1964 the armed forces of Great Britain were consolidated and unified under the Ministry of Defence, with Lord Mountbatten as the first unified chief of staff. An important strategic role, first for the RAF, and later for the Royal Navy, has been the independent nuclear capability for Great Britain. The naval vehicles for deployment of intercontinental ballistic missiles have been: first Polaris missile submarines and subsequently, Trident missile submarines. In each case a submarine carried sixteen missiles, later ones containing multiple nuclear warheads. The plan for the 1990s was four ballistic missile submarines. The program is closely tied to and dependent upon American strategic weapons systems.

Consistent reductions in the size of the forces of the Royal Navy have been achieved through a series of defense White Papers and retrenchment plans in 1957, 1968, 1981, and 1985. In 1968 the British naval forces shifted from an independent to a dependent status linked to NATO.

Eugene L. Rasor

Bibliography

Carew, Anthony. *The Lower Deck of the Royal Navy, 1900–1939: The Invergordon Mutiny in Perspective.* 1981.

Kennedy, Paul M. *The Rise and Fall of British Naval Mastery.* 4th ed. 1991.

Marder, Arthur J. *From Dreadnought to Scapa Flow: The Royal Navy in the Fisher Era, 1904–19.* 5 vols. 1961–70.

Roskill, Stephen W. *Naval Policy between the Wars, 1919–1939.* 2 vols. 1969–76.

Nevinson, C(hristopher) R(ichard) W(ynne) (1889–1946)

The son of the noted journalist and author Henry W. Nevinson, C.R. W. Nevinson was educated at Uppingham and the Slade School, which he attended from 1908 and 1912. He then moved to Paris for a year, where he worked at the Cercle Russe and the Academie Julian, mixing with the Italian Futurists who had just exhibited in Paris and with the French avant-garde and sharing a studio with Modigliani. Returning to London in 1913, he altered the character of his painting from atmospheric Post-Impressionism to Futurism and was included in the 1913 exhibition of Post-Impressionists and Futurists at the Dore Gallery in London. There he showed *The Departure of the Train de Luxe from the Gare St. Lazare* (1913, present whereabouts unknown), which displayed a mixture of Cubist and Futurist technique. For the exhibition Nevinson arranged for Marinetti to lecture in London, and a banquet organized by Nevinson and WYNDHAM LEWIS was held in his honor.

Although Nevinson participated in Wyndham Lewis's Rebel Art Centre, which saw the birth of VORTICISM, his allegiances were with Marinetti and the Futurists. In 1914 this was stressed unequivocally when he co-signed and published with Marinetti *Vital English Art: Futurist Manifesto*. By this time Wyndham Lewis, defining the Vorticist aesthetic as being in opposition to Futurism, was doubly annoyed to find his name and those of his colleagues at the Rebel Art Centre appended without their knowledge to the Manifesto.

By 1914 Nevinson' manipulation of Futurist imagery—which always owed a lot to the work of Gino Severini—was becoming more accomplished. However, with the outbreak of the FIRST WORLD WAR he joined the Royal Army Medical Corps as an ambulance driver. He was quickly horrified by the impersonally-wrought carnage of modern warfare, which the Italian Futurists in 1915 declared to be "the only hygiene of the world". Despite exhibiting as a Futurist at the 1915 Vorticist exhibition at the Dore Gallery, and contributing to the second issue of *Blast*, Nevinson's painting was becoming increasingly figurative, less indebted to Futurist preoccupations and their pictorial conventions.

Discharged from the ARMY on health grounds, Nevinson held a successful exhibition of his war paintings at the Leicester Galleries in 1916 and the following year was appointed as an official war artist. His paintings and prints of this period such as *The Road from Arras to Bapaume* (1917, Imperial War Museum, London), *The Cursed Wood* (1918) and *After a Push* (1917, Imperial War Museum, London) highlight the way in which he allied their structured compositions to a strongly evocative expression of the horror and alienation of war. Critically, these works were among the most successful British war paintings.

In 1919 and 1920 Nevinson visited New York, whose architecture he was inspired to portray as symbolic of an optimistic New Age in prints such as *Metropolis* (1920–2) and *The Temples of New York* (1920). These were exhibited at the Leicester Galleries in 1921. Through the 1920s and 1930s he executed many contemplative landscape paintings, turning his back on his past. The 1930s also saw him conceive a number of ambitious and large-scale contemporary history paintings of urban life, such as *Amongst the Nerves of the World* (1928–30, The Museum of London) and *The Twentieth Century* (1932–5, Laing Art Gallery, Newcastle-upon-Tyne). In the public's eye he was understood to be an epitome of the modern artist as a result of his skill at manipulating the press to report his activities as an artist, all of which contributed to making his art more accessible and making a celebrity out of himself. Like his more famous contemporary, PAUL NASH, he was one of the few to serve as an official artist in both World Wars.

Andrew Wilson

Bibliography
Knowles, Elizabeth, ed. *C.R. W. Nevinson*. 1988.
Konody, P.G. *Modern War: Paintings by C.R. W. Nevinson*. 1917.
Nevinson, C.R.W. *Paint and Prejudice*. 1937.

New Liberalism

The term New Liberalism describes the change both in Liberal ideology and in the LIBERAL PARTY that occurred in the two decades before the FIRST WORLD WAR. In general, it marked a shift toward acceptance in both theory and practice of collectivism, the use of the state to overcome the shortcomings of an unregulated market economy.

Liberalism as an ideology had developed in the nineteenth century as a defense of the individual against both the state and society. Seeing the individual as rational, able to develop his personality and talents if freed of political and social restraints, Liberalism embraced *laissez-faire*, the idea that government should interfere as little as possible with the economy and with private property. It optimistically assumed that if individuals were free to follow their own self interest, society would be self-regulating. The outcome would be progress—a gradual enrichment of the entire community and eradication of remaining social problems. In the last quarter of the nineteenth century Liberal assumptions and Liberal politics were subjected to severe strain. The long downturn in the economy that began in the early 1870s called into question the belief that the capitalist market economy, if freed of restraints, would result in continuous economic progress.

After the 1884 franchise reform act the Liberal Party had to concern itself more with attracting support from the large number of new working-class voters who were now being courted by the CONSERVATIVE PARTY and, after 1900, by the new LABOUR PARTY. Disappointed by the 1892 Gladstone government, which had focused on such traditional Liberal causes as Irish home rule and disestablishment of the Anglican Church in Wales, and convinced that the Conservative electoral victory of 1895 demonstrated the need for an updated Liberalism, the new Liberals worked in the late 1890s to revise traditional political and social theory to justify a more active social reformism, one that might also make the Liberal Party more electorally attractive. The active propagators of a New Liberalism, as it was called at the time, were never a coherent group; they consisted of disparate journalists, academics, politicians, and Liberal activists. Most new Liberals rejected imperialism and saw their support for national self-determination and opposition to militarism as an important link to the Gladstonian insistence that the same moral principles applied abroad as at home.

At the beginning of the twentieth century men like the sociologist L.T. Hobhouse, the economist J.A. HOBSON, and the journalist H.W. MASSINGHAM worked out a new version of Liberalism that justified collectivism, though understood in terms derived from an individualist Liberalism. Recognizing that an unregulated market economy failed to provide the means for many people to take care of themselves, they advocated reforms that addressed such problems while preserving the market economy on the grounds that state action actually made possible the fulfillment of a traditional Liberal ideal of freedom. Most radically, on the grounds that wealth was socially created, they extended the distinction between earned and unearned income from land to all forms of wealth. Claiming that all high incomes had unearned elements, they defended progressive taxation as an attack on unearned income, not a deterrent to enterprise or initiative. They thereby provided theoretical justification for the taxes necessary to support a more socially reformist state.

Responding to the growth of the new Labour Party and to the perception that it had to develop a new reformist program to retain working-class support, the new Liberal government introduced the first OLD AGE PENSIONS in 1908. Although recognizing that many aged working people had never earned enough money to be able to save for their old age, the pensions act reflected older Liberal concerns for character. It disqualified anyone who had previously applied for poor relief and provided a pension that was too small to live on in order to encourage thrift. In the next years, however, led by LLOYD GEORGE and WINSTON CHURCHILL, the Liberal government passed a budget in 1909 that applied the idea of taxing unearned income more highly than earned income and a National Insurance Act in 1911 that for the first time acknowledged officially that an unregulated market economy made it impossible for many workers to provide for themselves no matter how diligent they were.

Although still partially informed by older Liberal concerns for character, self-reliance, and the capitalist market, this legislation nevertheless marked a significant shift in Liberal approaches to the state and social reform, approaches that later governments would slowly expand and that would grow into the WELFARE STATE after the SECOND WORLD WAR. What was new in these reforms was the underlying assumption that the state could be a positive force, that the measure of individual freedom, as T. H. Green, the Oxford philosopher whose work inspired many new Liberals, had said, was not how much the state left people alone but whether it gave them the capacity to fulfill themselves as individuals. Implicit in the reforms as well, and in the theoretical justification of them, was an expanded notion of community. The New Liberalism recognized that Gladstonian Liberalism had proven inadequate because its ideal of the public good was based on a narrow individualism that failed to recognize human interdependence.

Certainly, New Liberalism had serious shortcomings. Its view of human nature was simplistic, with no allowance for the irrational. It was naively optimistic about the possibility of overcoming all social problems. It failed to understand the rootedness of social and class conflict. And it overestimated the ability of the Liberal Party to represent, not just the middle class, but the public good. It was not responsible, however, for the collapse of Liberalism as an organized political force. The reasons for that have to be sought in the growth of class consciousness among the enlarged post-war electorate, in the changing allegiances of the growing trade union movement, and in the parochialism of the Liberal Party at a local level, not in the ability of Liberalism to respond to the problems of an urban, industrial society.

Peter Weiler

Bibliography

Allett, John. *New Liberalism: The Political Economy of J. A. Hobson.* 1981.

Clarke, Peter. *Lancashire and the New Liberalism.* 1971.

———. *Liberals and Social Democrats.* 1978.

Collini, Stefan. *Liberalism and Sociology: L. T. Hobhouse and Political Argument in England, 1880–1914*. 1979.

Freeden, Michael. *The New Liberalism: An Ideology of Social Reform*. 1978.

Weiler, Peter. *The New Liberalism: Liberal Social Theory in Great Britain, 1889–1914*. 1982.

New Statesman (1913–)

Since April 1913 the *New Statesman* has been the weekly voice of progressive opinion in the United Kingdom. Having absorbed the social science review *New Society* in 1989, it is presently entitled *New Statesman & Society*. However, in its most influential period, the three decades following merger with the Liberal *NATION* in 1931, it was the *New Statesman and Nation*, affectionately nicknamed the "Staggers and Naggers."

Inadequate capital and poor sales thwarted the early ambitions of the magazine's Fabian founders, SIDNEY AND BEATRICE WEBB, and their chief asset, GEORGE BERNARD SHAW. That their journal survived and thrived is attributable to the professionalism of Clifford Sharp and his deputy, J.C. (Jack, later Sir John) Squire. Although after wartime service its editor became a slave to both alcohol, and, more puzzlingly, ASQUITH, the *New Stateman*'s early success reflected that of RAMSAY MACDONALD's Labour Party; modest circulation belied accumulative influence in the corridors of power. The boorish Sharp, although burnt out by the late 1920s, had laid the foundations for the internationally renowned voice of the British Left edited between 1931 and 1961 by KINGSLEY MARTIN.

The mid-century golden age of the *New Statesman* has been eclipsed by the magazine's mixed fortunes since the disastrous editorial appointment in 1970 of ex-Cabinet minister and one-time deputy, Richard Crossman. The ailing and inadequate Crossman, and the competent but uninspiring Anthony Howard, failed to stem a decline in sales initiated a decade earlier when the Sunday broadsheets usurped the weeklies' predominance in opinion and review. The 1970s and 1980s saw the problems of high overheads and low circulation exacerbated by declining advertising revenue. Financial instability fuelled disharmony between directors and their editorial and administrative staff.

The absence of a firm commercial footing, and the succession of policy U-turns, mirrored LABOUR PARTY fortunes in the 1980s. Bruce Page brought headline-grabbing but costly investigative journalism from the *Sunday Times*. Hugh Stephenson, another highly-regarded Fleet Street newsman, failed to adapt to weekly journalism. For veteran readers the *New Statesman*, however worthy the exposés, was now dull and too often poorly written—an insistence on political correctness maintained at the expense of stylish contributors and mainstream Labour supporters. A painful process of recovery, initiated by John Lloyd prior to an early return to the *Financial Times*, was maintained in the face of boardroom upheaval by Stuart Weir, and following his stormy departure, Steve Platt. While Labour after 1987 reconstructed itself as a credible alternative party of government, the *New Statesman* also edged towards the center as a qualified supporter of the "Kinnockite" social democracy.

Defeat in April 1992 saw the paper provide an important forum for debate on Labour's future strategy. Although the preceding thirty years had seen sales slump from around 100,000 to nearer 20,000, *New Statesman & Society* in the early 1990s seemed to have weathered the storm. Spurred on by the success of Charter 88, the magazine's high-profile campaign for constitutional reform, it faced the new millenium with qualified optimism under the editorship of Peter Wilby.

Adrian Smith

Bibliography

Howe, Stephen, ed. *Lines of Dissent: Writing from the New Statesman 1913 to 1988*. 1988.

Hyams, Edward. *The New Statesman: The History of the First Fifty Years*. 1963.

Rolph, C.H. *Kingsley: The Life, Letters & Diaries of Kingsley Martin*. 1973.

Nicholson, Ben (1894–1982)

Ben Nicholson grew up in an artistic home where the urbanity of his artist father, Sir William Nicholson, and the down-to-earth nature of his mother, Mabel Pryde, are reflected in both the elegance and the uncompromising and primitive nature of his contribution to modernist painting in Britain. His sister Nancy married the poet ROBERT GRAVES. Despite a short period spent at the Slade School in 1910–11, where be became friendly with PAUL NASH, he was not formally trained, and traveled abroad a great deal in Europe and America between 1912 and 1918.

It was only following his marriage in 1920 to the painter Winifred Dacre that he threw himself into his painting and specifically into the English avant-garde, partly as a reaction against the reputation that his father held both as a painter and, in collaboration with his uncle James Pryde (as the Beggarstaff Brothers), as a poster artist and illustrator. During this period he spent much time in Paris where he came into direct contact with Cubism and saw works by Picasso and Braque. Following this experience he painted his first abstract paintings in 1924.

These were however an isolated experiment. Through the 1920s he painted landscape or still-life subject-matter in a primitive and naive manner. This approach was taken up by other painters in England, especially those belonging to the Seven and Five Society, an exhibiting group of which Nicholson had been a member since 1924 and its dominating force from 1926 until its last, all abstract, exhibition in 1935. Although Nicholson found that this primitive approach was confirmed in 1928 when he and Christopher Wood discovered the naive artist Alfred Wallis during a visit to St. Ives, many of the other painters in the Society painted in a naive style, while Nicholson adopted a Cubist concern with flatness, an application in paint of the sculptor's tenets of truth to materials.

It is not then surprising that Nicholson should gradually move towards non-objective abstraction in the 1930s. In 1932 he visited Paris with his second wife, the sculptor BARBARA HEPWORTH, where they met Picasso, Braque, Arp, and Brancusi. They participated with the group Abstraction-Creation as well as the short-lived Unit 1 in London, and by 1934 he was making his first all-white abstract relief carvings and rectilinear abstract paintings. In the same year he visited Piet Mondrian in Paris—who between 1938 and 1940 lived in London close to Nicholson and a like-minded group of artists that included Cecil Stephenson and HENRY MOORE, writers such as Herbert Read, and émigres such as Naum Gabo, Marcel Breuer and Moholy-Nagy—all of which led to a number of exhibitions of modernist art in Britain which included Nicholson as the major British contributor. In 1937 he and Naum Gabo co-edited the book *Circle*, a statement of faith for these Hampstead Modernists.

In 1940 Nicholson and Hepworth moved to St. Ives which shortly became the center for continued modernist activity in Britain. During this time and after the war Nicholson moved between abstraction and figuration, predominantly through the carved and painted shallow relief. His international reputation grew as he won prizes at the Carnegie International in 1952 and the Sao Paulo Bienal in 1957; in 1954 he had a retrospective mounted at the 1954 Venice Biennale. In 1958 he left England to live in Switzerland, returning in 1972. In 1968 he had been awarded the Order of Merit, the same year in which he had a major retrospective at the Tate Gallery.

Andrew Wilson

Bibliography

Checkland, Sarah Jane. *Ben Nicholson: The Vicious Circles of His Life and Art.* 2000.

Harrison, Charles. *Ben Nicholson.* 1969.

Lewison, Jeremy. *Ben Nicholson: The Years of Experiment 1919–1939.* 1982.

———. *Ben Nicholson.* 1991.

Read, Herbert. *Ben Nicholson: Paintings, Reliefs, Drawings.* 1948.

Russell, John. *Ben Nicholson: Drawings, Paintings and Reliefs 1911–1968.* 1968.

Nicolson, Harold George (1886–1968)

Diplomat, novelist, biographer, broadcaster, critic, journalist, garden designer, MP, and ubiquitous committee man, Harold Nicolson (Sir Harold from 1952) will unfortunately be remembered by posterity for his marriage to writer Vita Sackville-West, an unusual early example of an "open" marriage punctuated regularly by HOMOSEXUAL affairs on both sides. This relationship has been endlessly celebrated first in the memoirs of friends and relations, later by feminist and gay writers seeking precursors, and finally fossilized by the immense academic output relating to the BLOOMSBURY GROUP (to which Nicolson and Sackville-West were only peripheral).

Socially and politically, Nicolson was far closer to the mainstream of the British establishment than to the self-conscious bohemians of Bloomsbury. Son of a Scottish baronet of ancient (but now landless) family, he followed his father into the diplomatic service and enjoyed there a successful twenty-year career. His aesthetic sensibilities were not in the end compatible with a top-flight Foreign Office post, and he left the service in 1929. The catalyst was publication of his best-known book, *Some People* (1927), nine pen sketches of thinly-fictionalized characters in Nicolson's life that were too frank and penetrating for certain Foreign Office higher-ups.

At first uncertain about his place in the modern world, he suffered through two unhappy episodes, as a popular journalist writing a gossip column for LORD BEAVERBROOK's *Evening Standard* and as a political journalist editing the paper of OSWALD MOSLEY's short-lived New Party (breaking with Mosley over the latter's FASCISM). By the mid-1930s, however, he had established himself as one of the leading and most prolific critics and essayists of his day. He wrote the official, best-selling biography of GEORGE V (1952), for which he received his knighthood, novels of no great importance, influential tracts on diplomatic theory, a highbrow column for the *Spectator* and middlebrow reviews for the *Daily Telegraph* and *OBSERVER*. He also served as a National Labour MP for West Leicester (1935–45), was a governor of the BBC and for many years Vice-Chairman of the NATIONAL TRUST, and still found time to spend with Sackville-West at their Kent retreat of Sissinghurst Castle, where he designed the initial layout for her famous garden. His biographer has estimated that in a sample year (1938–9) Nicolson wrote 4,000 letters, 101 articles (including 52 book reviews), and one book, gave 120 talks (mostly on radio) and delivered 23 lectures, served on 27 committees, and travelled 77,281 miles (including 25 visits to his constituency).

Nicolson's style is charming and confiding, but his ideas are rarely profound. He was an essentially Edwardian character who found it hard to compete with the more arresting style of younger contemporaries like EVELYN WAUGH or Cyril Connolly. He was too literary for the Foreign Office, but too Foreign Office for the literary set. Nicolson's lasting importance must be as a communicator between the highbrow world and the general public, a task for which his respectability served him well. His incessant lecturing and broadcasting, including on television as early as 1937, made him a familiar voice and face in millions of households. His old-fashioned public service ethic persuaded him of the importance of diffusing "civilization" downward to the masses, to whom he tried (perhaps unsuccessfully) not to condescend, and he got into trouble with the BBC's LORD REITH for lecturing on JAMES JOYCE's *Ulysses*. Like a kind of upper-class J.B. PRIESTLEY, he undoubtedly contributed to the better understanding between the classes that prevailed after the SECOND WORLD WAR. In the 1950s he came to seem increasingly like a leftover from a bygone age, but his fame revived in quite a different context after his death in 1968, with the publication of his candid diaries.

Peter Mandler

Bibliography
Lees-Milne, James. *Harold Nicolson: A Biography*. 2 vols. 1980–1.
Nicolson, Nigel, ed. *Harold Nicolson: Diaries and Letters, 1930–1962*. 3 vols. 1966–8.
———. *Portrait of a Marriage*. 1973.
———. *Vita and Harold: The Letters of Vita Sackville-West and Harold Nicolson*. 1992.

1922 Committee
The 1922 Committee of CONSERVATIVE backbenchers in the House of Commons, reputed to possess decisive power within the party, has become the best known parliamentary organization in British politics. It was not created for this purpose, however, and has only become important since 1945. The Committee evolved from a group of MPs who first entered Parliament in the general election of November 1922. The date in the name derives from this fact, and not from any connection with the fall of DAVID LLOYD GEORGE in October 1922: by definition, none of its founders played any part in those events. The 1922 Committee was formed on 18 April 1923 with the simple aim of helping these new MPs to find their parliamentary feet. For most of the inter-war period it functioned more as a lecture club than as a pressure group. Unlike other similar unofficial groups, the 1922 Committee did not fade away. This was due to two factors. First, the Committee resolved in December 1925 to open its doors to all Conservative backbenchers, thus continually renewing the membership. The 1922 had no factional purpose and was loyal to the leadership: the party whips found it useful and took it under their wing. Although originally unofficial, since the mid-1920s the Committee has become closely integrated into the formal party structures. Since 1965 the 1922 Committee has acquired administrative functions in leadership elections due to the fact that the leader has always been chosen by the parliamentary party. The influence of the Committee grew during the CHURCHILL coalition ministry of 1940–5 and was further extended during the thirty years after 1945. It provides a unique sounding board of opinion within the party. The leadership can be swiftly and often sharply alerted to matters causing concern among both MPs and the constituency rank and file. However, the belief that it ensures that unpopular policies are not adopted requires reassessment after the poll tax fiasco of 1987–90.

Stuart Ball

Bibliography
Ball, Stuart. "The '1922' Committee: the formative years 1922–1945," *Parliamentary History*. vol. 9 (1990), pp. 129–57.
Goodhart, Philip. *The 1922*. 1973.
Norton, Philip. "The Parliamentary Party and Party Committees" in Anthony Seldon and Stuart Ball, eds. *Conservative Century: The Conservative Party Since 1900*. 1994. pp. 97–144.

No-Conscription Fellowship (1914–1919)
The No-Conscription Fellowship (NCF) was formed late in 1914 by young socialist/PACIFISTS, including Fenner Brockway, editor of the ILP's *Labour Leader,* and CLIFFORD ALLEN, a CAMBRIDGE graduate active in socialist politics and journalism. Initially founded with the modest aim of providing a focus for the anti-war sentiments of men of military age who had vowed to resist the imposition of enforced military service during the FIRST WORLD WAR, the NCF eventually became the largest and most effective anti-war movement in modern British history, providing its 15,000 members with aid, comfort, and camaraderie while simultaneously testing the limits of dissent in a modern liberal society at war.

Until January 1916 the NCF, in conjunction with allied Christian pacifist bodies, especially the SOCIETY OF FRIENDS, developed an elaborate and efficient national organization while conducting a broad-based PROPAGANDA campaign against the threatened imposition of CONSCRIPTION. After compulsory military service was imposed, the NCF announced its intention to resist the implementation of conscription and, even though the Military Service Act included provisions for CONSCIENTIOUS OBJECTION, to accept only absolute exemption from all forms of enforced wartime service. The Fellowship's determination not to cooperate with any designs of the warrior state, adopted in April 1916 at an emotionally charged national convention, not only brought on a confrontation with the government but also threatened to alienate the majority of its members who were willing to accept something less than absolute exemption as an alternative to combatant military service. Faced with the possible dissolution of their organization, NCF leaders subsequently reversed their position and resolved to support all members whatever the level of their resistance. This decision reflects the moderating influence of older men and women, who took control of the Fellowship after most of its younger "absolutist" leaders, including Allen and Brockway, had been imprisoned. Most important in this respect were Catherine E. Marshall, who interrupted her work in the National Union of Women's Suffrage Societies and the Women International League to take responsibility for the day-to-day operation of the NCF, BERTRAND RUSSELL, who spoke, wrote, acted as chairman of the Fellowship until he was imprisoned in early 1918, and Edward Grubb, an elderly Quaker who, as NCF treasurer, raised the money the Fellowship needed to carry on its activities on behalf of imprisoned COs and against continuation of the war.

Throughout the last two years of the war the NCF remained a minor but troublesome irritant to the authorities, using its surprisingly resilent propaganda machinery to expose brutal or illegal treatment of conscientious objectors as well as to agitate, especially among the industrial working classes, for an end to the conflict. The government struck back, raiding NCF headquarters, prosecuting its leaders and attempting, unsuccessfully, to halt the publication of its weekly paper, *The Tribunal*. But if the NCF managed to survive official persecution, it could claim no great victories, either in helping to shorten the war or even in securing the release of its imprisoned members.

For the individual war resister, its justification was perhaps that the Fellowship made it easier for a small minority to follow the dicates of their consciences; for posterity, there was the fact that the injustices and abuses exposed by the NCF in its relentless pursuit of liberty of conscience had a significant impact upon the more humane and rational treatment of COs during the SECOND WORLD WAR. Thus, the great achievement of the No-Conscription Fellowship was that in seeking to ensure freedom of conscience for one tiny and despised minority, it helped to establish an important precedent for protecting the civil liberties of all individuals in British society.

Thomas C. Kennedy

Bibliography

Kennedy, Thomas C. *The Hound of Conscience: A History of the No-Conscription Fellowship, 1914–1919.* 1981.

———. "Fighting About Peace: The No-Conscription Fellowship and the British Friends' Service Committee, 1915–1919," *Quaker History*, vol. 69 (1980), pp. 3–22.

Vellacott, Jo. *Bertrand Russell and the Pacifists in the First World War.* 1980.

Norman, Montagu Collet (1871–1950)

Montagu Norman, Governor of the Bank of England from 1920–44, was the most influential financial figure of the inter-war period. His reign at the Bank of England proved controversial, contentious, and critical to the events of the 1920s and 1930s.

Norman inherited a strong connection with the Bank of England as his maternal grandfather had been a governor. After a stint at his grandfather's firm of investment bankers, Brown, Shipley & Co., Norman joined the Bank in a full-time capacity in 1915. The FIRST WORLD WAR was as much a turning point for the "Old Lady of Threadneedle Street", as the Bank was called, as it was for Britain as a whole. The unprecedented financial demands of the conflict placed new demands on the Bank and on Norman, who became Deputy Governor in 1918 and Governor in 1920. While remaining a private institution answerable to its shareholders, the Bank's efforts on behalf of the government intensified as Britain became increasingly reliant on American financing, both public and private, to meet the rising costs of the war.

The armistice left Norman in charge of an institution uneasily facing a brave new world. Virtually every European economy was in shambles while the destruction of the Austro-Hungarian and Turkish Empires together with the German and Russian Revolutions devastated the manufacturing and trading links upon which European prosperity depended. Most currencies had radically lost value during the war; all had been removed from the GOLD STANDARD, which in the pre-war world had reigned supreme.

Against this backdrop Norman developed his principles of central banking. Central banks, he believed, should be independent entities entrusted with financial and fiscal questions, while governments could take care of budgetary and political issues. Central to Norman's position was the notion that all currencies must first be stabilized and then returned to the gold standard. Together with his counterparts, Benjamin Strong and George

Harrison, the first two governors of the Federal Reserve Bank of New York and Hjalmer Schacht, Governor of the Reichsbank, Norman set out to make his goals into reality. British governments appreciated Norman's efforts while resenting his highhandedness and lack of accountability.

During the late 1920s it seemed that Norman's program would be a success. Together with his counterparts he presided over currency stabilizations in France, Belgium, and Germany after first restoring the British gold standard at the pre-war level of £1 = $4.86. However, the American stock market boom and crash, followed by the Great Depression, ended the chimerical recovery. By the summer of 1931 Norman knew he faced the prospect of world financial chaos. The failure of the Austrian Credit Anstalt triggered banking catastrophes across Central Europe. With the collapse on 14 July of the Darmstadter und Nationalbank, one of Germany's largest banks, and the subsequent freezing of German banking assets, came a massive British credit exposure and a run on the pound. Suddenly at the beginning of August the survival of British financial stability seemed in question.

Norman, who had long suffered from intermittent nervous exhaustion, found himself unable to cope with the stress of this crisis. However, instead of retreating to South Africa, a frequent choice in such cases, Norman journeyed to Canada. While there, he remained in steady contact with Harrison, advising the American central banker as to the efficacy of the newly-formed National government's attempt to rescue the gold standard.

When this effort failed, on 20 September, Norman was en route to Britain. On his arrival he found a changed economic world. He no longer sought to tie British finance to the gold standard; the establishment and nurturing of the Sterling Area became an acceptable substitute. As the 1931 financial crisis had exposed the defects in Norman's control over major financial decisions, he lost autonomy, the Treasury increasing its control over international financial transactions.

At the beginning of the SECOND WORLD WAR Norman, who had already served longer in his position than any other governor, postponed his retirement. An illness in 1944 forced his departure with a peerage as a reward; thereafter, until his death in 1950, he remained completely isolated from public affairs.

Diane B. Kunz

Bibliography

Boyle, Andrew. *Montagu Norman: A Biography.* 1967.

Clay, Sir Henry. *Lord Norman.* 1957.

Kunz, Diane B. *The Battle for Britain's Gold Standard in 1931.* 1987.

Sayers, R.S. *The Bank of England: 1891–1944.* 1976.

Harmsworth, Alfred Charles William, Lord Northcliffe (1865–1922)

Lord Northcliffe, the great newspaper proprietor, born Alfred Harmsworth, was the son of an unsuccessful barrister who soon moved the family from his birthplace near Dublin to England. Northcliffe's younger siblings included Harold, who became Northcliffe's business partner and the future Lord Rothermere. The premature death of their father forced Northcliffe to leave school and seek work in 1880. Over the next four decades he created a press empire and became one of the most powerful figures in the overlapping worlds of British journalism and politics. In due course he received a baronetcy (1903), a barony (1905) and a viscountcy (1917).

After freelancing as a boy journalist and working for a Coventry publisher, Northcliffe launched a weekly, *Answers to Correspondents* (1888). This successful venture was followed by other weeklies, including *Comic Cuts*, which were both entertaining and informative. They addressed a popular rather than a gentlemanly readership, composed of schoolboys and girls, housewives, and men employed in lower middle-class and even working-class occupations. The expanding circulation of these publications enabled the Harmsworth brothers to amass the necessary financial resources to enter the competitive field of daily evening and morning newspapers. They first purchased the *Evening News* (1894) and then founded the *Daily Mail* (1896). The *Daily Mail* broke the mold of mass journalism by offering readers a very inexpensive and atttractive morning newspaper. Its circulation soared during the BOER WAR. The steady success of Northcliffe's weekly and daily publications created and sustained the impression that he understood the mind and mood of the masses, primarily the lower middle classes.

Historians have cut Northcliffe's larger than life figure down to size, but his commercial and political achievement remains extraordinary. Atlhough not the only innovator on Fleet Street, he was able to divine which stories, advertisements, contests, and other features would hold the attention of his readers. Sometimes, however, he came close to overreaching himself. The *Daily Mirror* (1903), launched as a woman's newspaper, had to be salvaged by the introduction of photographic illustrations. Less than a decade later, however, it had reached a circulation of 1 million. Northcliffe was not satisfied with his commanding lead over his competitors in the realm of "cheap" or popular mass journalism. With the acquisition of the Sunday OBSERVER (1905), he entered the realm of "quality" or elite journalism. Many in the PRESS and political worlds shuddered when he became the proprietor

of *The Times* (1908), but he maintained its special position as a fairly moderate voice of the national and imperial interest. Both the journalistic
and financial sides of *The Times* improved under
Northcliffe, even if the price for these changes
was increased management from the top, directly
from the proprietor or indirectly through his new
editor, GEOFFREY DAWSON (1912).

In politics Northcliffe was a relatively straightforward imperialist and patriot. After standing
unsuccessfully as a Conservative candidate for
Portsmouth (1895), he never entered the fray
again. Although sometimes seen as the epitome
of a press baron whose newspapers forwarded his
own party-political views, Northcliffe served the
CONSERVATIVE PARTY without becoming bound
to them. Indeed, for a time around the turn of the
century he inclined towards the Liberal Imperialist Lord Rosebery. Northcliffe was prepared to
abandon unpopular Conservative causes like
TARIFF REFORM and to cultivate some Liberal
politicians. His newspapers, for example, gave
the benefit of the doubt to the accused Liberal
ministers during the pre-war Marconi scandal
(1913). In any case, his business interests took
precedence over his party loyalties. His un-
abashed imperialism probably flowed from the
fact that the newsworthiness of the empire benefited his newspapers.

If Northcliffe deserved his reputation for partisanship, it was due to the pressure he applied to
governments during the FIRST WORLD WAR. His
newspapers campaigned against the alleged pro-
Germanism of LORD HALDANE and the alleged
incompetence of LORD KITCHENER, and for the
creation of an all-party government of national
defense. That government emerged in stages, beginning with H.H. ASQUITH's first coalition government (1915), and then, upon the resignations of
Asquith and his friends from the CABINET, with
LLOYD GEORGE's second coalition government
(1916). Although he never forfeited the right of his
newspapers to criticize the government, Northcliffe cooperated with Lloyd George during the
remainder of the war. He served as Minister Plen-
ipotentiary in charge of the British war mission to
the United States (1917) and then as Director of
Propaganda in Enemy Countries (1918). Northcliffe's fall from political grace was as rapid as his
rise. Resigning his directorship when the Armistice was agreed, Northcliffe argued with Lloyd
George about the composition of the post-war
government. Consequently, Lloyd George refused
to include him in the British delegation to the
Peace Conference and publicly denounced him
(1919). Northcliffe expended what little political
capital he retained on promoting an Irish settlement (1921). Increasingly mentally unstable, he
died soon after completing a world tour.

Northcliffe's drive for success and respectability found its main outlet in the commercial world
of journalism, not the political world of parties
and parliaments. Perhaps his greatest accomplishment, underlying the relentless acquisition
of newspapers and perfection of their "copy", was
the simple incorporation of millions of readers
into his press empire.

Ian Christopher Fletcher

Bibliography
Koss, Stephen E. *The Rise and Fall of the Political Press
    in Britain*. 2 vols. 1981–4.
Pound, Reginald, and Geoffrey Harmsworth. *North-
    cliffe*. 1959.
Thompson, J. Lee. *Northcliffe: Press Baron in Politics
    1865–1922*. 2000.

Northern Ireland

Britain's solutions to its "Irish question" have
never fared well, partly because of naivete regarding the divergent political, religious, and cultural
elements ingrained through Irish and especially
Ulster history. The anomaly of Northern Ireland—six counties incorporating most of ancient
Ulster—created in 1920 was an expedient rather
than a viable settlement. Thus, Ulster's history
predicted its reappearance on the British political
scene in the 1960s.

Ulster Unionism, born with the 1886 home
rule effort, was formalized by the creation of the
Ulster Unionist Council in 1904, led by Sir ED-
WARD CARSON. Militant Protestants opposed to
home rule launched the Ulster Volunteer Force
in 1912, the first of many Ulster paramilitary organizations which relied upon the threat of
force to obtain political objectives. Protestant
fears of becoming a persecuted minority in a
CATHOLIC Irish state have shaped Protestant
politics in Northern Ireland throughout the twentieth century.

The threat of an Irish civil war during the
1912–14 home rule debates caused the LIBERAL
government to consider dividing the predominantly Protestant north from the Catholic south.
Partition satisfied Ulster Unionists and was popular with British public opinion. ASQUITH in 1914
and LLOYD GEORGE in 1916 pledged to Unionist
leaders that the government would not coerce
Ulster into a unified Ireland. As a result, Carson,
anxious for Protestant majority rule in a northern
state, agreed to renounce three Catholic majority
counties in Ulster.

Since the Irish conflict was the dominant political issue in Britain after the First World War,
the Lloyd George government sought to end the
crisis in December 1920 through passage of the
Government of Ireland Act. The measure implemented the principles of partition and devolution
with separate Parliaments in the north and south,

while both divisions retained a limited number of MPs at Westminster. Ulster Protestants opposed the inclusion of a Council of Ireland representing both Irish governments, intended by the British to facilitate Irish unity. Although the republican south rejected the proposal and signed a 1921 treaty which created the Irish Free State as a Dominion, Ulster Unionists accepted the 1920 Act as the basis of their new state.

Sir James Craig (1871–1940) succeeded Carson in 1921 as leader of the Ulster Unionist Council. Unionists won forty seats in the first Commons, while nationalists and Sinn Fein each elected six members. All twenty-four Senate seats were filled by Unionists. Craig (later Lord Craigavon) became the first Prime Minister of Northern Ireland. The 1920 Act, however, retained important links with Westminster, including a Lord Lieutenant with veto power over the Northern Ireland Parliament, headquartered at Stormont outside Belfast. Britain anticipated that its "excepted" or reserved powers—foreign policy, the military, foreign trade, currency, postal service, and certain taxes—would later be transferred to a unified Irish government. Also, the Stormont Parliament shared governance with local councils. Hence, it was caught in a vise between British and local authorities with no constitutional autonomy.

The egregious structural problems of Northern Ireland's government compounded rule by a Protestant majority, representing about 60 percent of the population, over a Catholic minority. Convinced of Catholic disloyalty to the United Kingdom and support for Sinn Fein, Unionists rationalized the suspension of proportional representation in local government (1922) and Parliament (1929) which contravened the 1920 legislation. The British Home Secretary, overseer of civil and religious protections, ignored discrimination against Catholics in political representation, employment, and housing. Unionists used the IRA violence in 1922 as an excuse to employ *carte blanche* police authority permitted by the Special Powers Act (1922). Repression of Catholics resulted from instruments such as the "B" Specials auxiliary police, an exclusively Protestant body used to assist the integrated Royal Ulster Constabulary (RUC).

Ulster Unionists were also backed by Britain during the Boundary Commission's 1925 deliberations. The Commission, created by the 1921 Anglo-Irish Treaty to redraw the Northern Ireland border, encouraged nationalist hopes for unification. Yet, when the Commission's proposals proved anathema to the Free State, STANLEY BALDWIN's CONSERVATIVE government pressured the Free State leader, William T. Cosgrave, to accept the 1920 boundary. In return, Britain agreed to rescind certain Irish financial obliga-

tions, and Craig promised to release political prisoners and relax the repression against Ulster Catholics. Also, the Council of Ireland was terminated, which pleased Protestants but disappointed Britain.

In addition to Britain's reluctance to moderate Unionist policies, the British taxpayer heavily subsidized Northern Ireland's economy and unemployed workers. Economic depression in farming and in the linen and shipbuilding industries between the wars was offset only partially by a spurt of economic activity during the Second World War. Catholic and Protestant workers alike suffered as residents of the United Kingdom's poorest region. British subsidies not only made Northern Ireland dependent upon the imperial government, but also frustrated economic and hence political unity with the Irish Free State.

When Eamon de Valera (1882–1975) succeeded Cosgrave in 1932 as head of the Free State, he quickly pressed for changes in the imperial connection which included an end to partition. During British negotiations with de Valera in 1937–8, Lord Craigavon refused to allow Northern Ireland's status to enter the discussion. Notwithstanding British PRESS criticism and a fainthearted investigation by the Home Office into anti-Catholic discrimination charges, the Ulster Unionist government again emerged from the episode with virtually no British interference.

The stagnant economy, religious divisions, and political inequities ultimately forced the British as well as Stormont governments to face the consequences of unattended issues. In the mid-1950s, the long quiescent Irish Republican Army launched a new campaign of violence along the divided Irish border. When IRA appeals to Catholic nationalists failed to energize support, the strategy ended in 1962. Yet, the door for possible reform was opened with the accession in 1963 of the moderately liberal Unionist Prime Minister Terence O'Neill (1914–90).

O'Neill's government drafted a new economic policy, a six-year plan to stimulate new industry and modernize the economic infrastructure. O'Neill also opened a dialogue with Catholic communities regarding education and civil service reform as well as jobs. Full of symbolism but lacking substance, O'Neill's policy at least modified the historic mold. The economic plan generated only 5,000 of the 65,000 jobs O'Neill predicted, and Northern Ireland continued to have the highest UNEMPLOYMENT rate in the United Kingdom. Virtually no progress was made in dismantling the religiously segregated schools. In fact, the Education Act of 1968 actually increased funding for private schools. Public HOUSING remained under the control of gerrymandered local councils. Thus, O'Neill's program failed to satisfy Catholics. Instead, it encouraged them to launch a new campaign patterned after the civil rights movement in the United States.

A unique organization, the Northern Ireland Civil Rights Association, founded in February 1967, de-emphasized Catholic nationalist goals and disavowed violence. The Association sought equal opportunity for Catholics under the existing Northern Ireland government in education, housing, jobs, and voting rights as well as the end of the Special Powers Act and the "B" Specials. When the Association resorted to public marches in Ulster communities in the summer of 1968, demonstrators clashed with Protestant mobs and the RUC. HAROLD WILSON's Labour government, less sympathetic toward Unionism, favored a reconciliation between northern and southern Ireland and urged Stormont to institute reforms. O'Neill responded to the pressure with a five-point reform program which undercut the authority of local councils.

Extremists on both sides sabotaged potential negotiations. Catholic civil rights advocates split, some wanting further pressure upon the government. Stirred by the Presbyterian Reverend Ian Paisley (1926–), radical Unionists portrayed reform as a prelude to the Republic's annexation of Ulster. Such fears were rampant especially in Protestant working-class neighborhoods. The 1969 elections to the Northern Ireland Parliament revealed an electorate more polarized than ever.

Circumstances overwhelmed O'Neill's government and he resigned in April 1969. The new Prime Minister, ex-army officer James Chichester-Clark (1923–2002), pursued the single-minded objective of law and order. Even so, Britain was compelled increasingly to direct Northern Ireland's affairs. In August Wilson proposed various reforms but assuaged Protestant fears by insisting that any changes must receive majority support.

Hard core violence exploded during 1970, beginning with the creation of the "Provisional" Irish Republican Army committed to the use of force and largely funded by American sympathizers. Although British troops separated Catholic and Protestant mobs, put the RUC under British authority, and disbanded the infamous "B" Specials, chaos continued. The new policy produced little success in the early 1970s under Conservative Prime Minister EDWARD HEATH and Northern Ireland Prime Minister Brian Faulkner (1921–77), an experienced civil servant. Britain instituted its controversial "internment" policy in August 1971, which allowed the military to arrest and detain suspects without bringing them to trial.

Two new parliamentary parties made their appearance in 1970: the Catholic Social Democratic and Labour Party (SDLP) favored a socialist economic program and a peaceful union with the Republic, while the Alliance Party appealed to liberals among Catholics and Protestants, a scarce commodity in Northern Ireland. Protesting the lack of progress, the SDLP members withdrew from Parliament in July 1971. When violence peaked in 1972 with 467 deaths, Heath prorogued the Northern Ireland Parliament, and Britain began "direct rule" with William Whitelaw as Secretary of State for Northern Ireland. Britain intended direct rule to be temporary with restoration of a devolved, proportionally represented government to follow in due course.

A March 1973 White Paper proposed a "power sharing" assembly and executive based upon proportional representation. Although extremists on both sides condemned the idea, Parliament created a seventy-eight seat assembly and a plural executive. At the 1973 Sunningdale Conference in England, Heath obtained the Republic's concurrence in majority determination of Northern Ireland's future and established another Council of Ireland to foster an Anglo-Irish exchange.

In May 1974 the Protestant Ulster Workers' Council's successful strike combined with Paisley's anti-power sharing Democratic Unionist Party to undermine Faulkner's power sharing government. The assembly was prorogued and direct British rule reasserted. Parliament's Northern Ireland Act in July sanctioned a constitutional convention based on proportional representation which met from May 1975 to March 1976, but it could not agree upon the type of government. Yet another power sharing attempt in 1982 by MARGARET THATCHER's Conservative government launched a proportional assembly. The SDLP refused to take their seats, leaving only Unionists participating. To break the impasse, Mrs. Thatcher held face-to-face meetings in 1986 with Unionist leaders James Molyneaux (1920–) and Paisley as well as SDLP leader John Hume (1937–). When Hume appeared flexible, clashes with police followed another Unionist strike and led to the dissolution of the assembly in June 1986.

The Thatcher government resumed attempts at cooperation with the Republic of Ireland, both to quell violence and to initiate a dialogue between north and south. The Anglo-Irish Agreement of 1985, signed at Hillsborough Castle by Mrs. Thatcher and Republic Taoiseach Dr. Garret Fitzgerald reiterated that the majority must approve changes in Northern Ireland's status. An Anglo-Irish Intergovernmental Conference co-chaired by the British Secretary of State for Northern Ireland and the Irish Foreign

Secretary discussed regularly matters such as border security, protecting Catholic rights, and stimulating the Irish economy. Formal discussions between Britain and the Republic concerning Ulster caused Protestants considerable uneasiness. Unionist MPs at Westminster resigned en masse to protest the Anglo-Irish Agreement, but the SDLP supported the pact and undercut Sinn Fein's Catholic support.

British nonpolitical measures have been instituted with modest success in Ulster. Labour's Fair Employment Act (1976) aimed at elimination of job discrimination, but loopholes prevented adequate enforcement. Thatcher's government enacted a new fair employment law in 1989 to eliminate "indirect or unintentional discrimination" against Catholics through a Fair Employment Commission which monitored hiring practices. The Thatcher government also concentrated upon job creation. The 1986 joint Anglo-Irish International Fund solicited investment funds for an all-Ireland economic development. Still, Northern Ireland's unemployment rate at more than 17 percent in 1987 was much higher than Britain's.

Since the 1970s, Britain has learned difficult lessons about law enforcement in Northern Ireland, e.g., that simple repression could not end either violence or hatred. Even though the infamous Special Powers Act was repealed in 1973, the Emergency Provisions Act replaced it with controversial Diplock courts which tried terrorists without a jury. Catholics criticized the denial of constitutional protections and the treatment of republican prisoners. Several deaths resulting from a 1981 hunger strike at the infamous Maze Prison refocused world opinion on Northern Ireland and sensitized Britain to human rights issues in their police and prison policies, as reflected in the Prevention of Terrorism Act (1984).

Britain's role in Northern Ireland has frustrated many well-meaning people. Presently, Britain's commitments seem certain: a devolved government with proportional representation and majority bipartisan support, no changes in Northern Ireland's status without a clear majority, and a formal dialogue between the governments of the Republic and Britain for an acceptable solution to Northern Ireland's future. Among trends in Northern Ireland, the growing strength of the SDLP in elections reflected greater disenchantment among Catholics with IRA terrorist acts. Unionists were not sanguine about cooperation with the Republic, but internal divisions skewed an accurate reading of Protestant opinion. Finally, the changing tone of nationalist rhetoric in the Republic now favored a peaceful, broadly backed settlement in Northern Ireland. As a result of the Anglo-Irish Agreement (1985) the status of Northern Ireland was no longer a matter to be determined solely by the United Kingdom. The Republic's voice continued to play a significant role as it altered its claims for Northern Ireland.

The December 1993 Downing Street Declaration by Conservative Prime Minister JOHN MAJOR and Republic Taoiseach Albert Reynolds proposed yet another devolved government for Northern Ireland based on proportional representation and contingent upon a cease fire by paramilitaries. The Provisional IRA announced a cease fire in August 1994 followed by a similar pledge by Protestant paramilitaries in October. Yet, intense negotiations led by the British and Irish governments failed to reach a consensus and the PIRA resorted to bombings again in February 1996. Nonetheless, moderate elements on all sides pressed forward toward the multiparty Good Friday agreement of April 1998. Ulster Unionist Party leader David Trimble and SDLP head John Hume received the 1998 Nobel Peace Prize for their efforts in achieving the accord. The roles played behind the scenes by President Bill Clinton, his emissary, former Senator George Mitchell, Prime Minister TONY BLAIR, and Northern Ireland Secretary Mo Mowlam, were instrumental in bringing negotiations to a successful conclusion.

The plan called for an elected assembly based on proportional representation, and an executive council of ten ministers made up of the four main political parties: Ulster Unionist, Democratic Unionist, SDLP, and Sinn Fein. Implementation of the peace agreement depended upon a disarmament plan supervised by an international commission headed by General John de Chastelain. In late 1999 the PIRA finally pledged to begin disarming within two months, but failed to fulfill its timetable. Thereupon, Mowlam's successor, Peter Mandelson, suspended the devolved government in February 2000 and authorized direct British rule again. The move was applauded by unionists and opposed by nationalists.

Prime Minister Blair and Taoiseach Bertie Ahern sought to uncouple the militia dissolution from the restoration of devolved government. The Ulster Unionist Party narrowly approved a return to power-sharing with the other parties based only on a PIRA promise to allow the de Chastelain commission to inspect arms caches by early summer 2000. When the first inspections took place on schedule, the Northern Ireland executive returned to power in June without participation by the two DUP ministers, although they did not resign their posts. Following the recommendation of the Patten Commission on police reform, Parliament passed a police bill changing the name of the Royal Ulster Constabulary to the

Police Service of Northern Ireland and requiring recruitment of police on a 50/50 Protestant-Catholic ratio.

Daniel W. Hollis, III

Bibliography

Buckland, Patrick. *A History of Northern Ireland.* 1981.

Caterall, Peter, and Sean McDougall, eds. *The Northern Ireland Question in British Politics.* 1996.

Darby, John, ed. *Northern Ireland: The Background to the Conflict.* 1983.

Miller, David W. *The Queen's Rebels: Ulster Loyalism in Historical Perspective.* 1979.

Moody, T.W. *The Ulster Question, 1603–1973.* 1974.

Wilson, Tom. *Ulster: Conflict and Consent.* 1989.

Novel, English, 1900–1945

The prestige of British fiction from the early part of the century is associated with innovative artistic aims, which are commonly referred to under the term *modernism.* The meaning of the term is vexed by enduring controversy. Usually *modernism* in literary criticism designates the antagonism of artists flourishing between 1900 and 1930 to most or to all conventions—not just aesthetic, but social, religious, political and ethical as well—which they identify with a superseded past. In literary production, modernism thus means a break with formerly customary form and content in art—e.g. a break with linear, continuous, and unified storytelling, with consistent "life-like" characters, with art's intention to mime or represent history or reality, and with meaning itself. Abstraction of artistic form and of life from ordinary appearances and significances, and a heightening of artistic form for its own sake, are modernist hallmarks.

Simultaneously, in a way that makes palpable the controversial complexity and indeed the self-contradiction of the term and of its reference points, modernism may also stand not for the rejection of the past but for a radical transformative use of past traditions: a way, sometimes, of invoking the importance of history, even if only to announce history's end; a way, at other times, of claiming for modern art a hitherto unprecedented fidelity to history and to history's problematic nature. Modernism may also claim an unprecedented fidelity to reality or to the phenomenology of experience or to Being itself. Perhaps the one unifying thread amidst such manifold characteristics is the constant intention to produce what is unprecedented.

The literary art resulting from modernism's complex of aims is, not surprisingly, highly various. The experimental techniques that compose the celebrated novels *Ulysses* (1922) by JAMES JOYCE or *The Waves* (1931) by VIRGINIA WOOLF can be read as the product of the modernist emphasis on form for the sake of form. The momen-

tariness and immediacy of authentic experience that are evoked in *Nostromo* (1904) or *Chance* (1913) by JOSEPH CONRAD or in *Pilgrimage* (1913–67) by Dorothy Richardson (1873–1957) can be read as the product of the modernist emphasis on unexampled fidelity to history and being. But such ways of reading would be more limited in nature than the works themselves. The various characteristics of modernism typically are in play, no matter how self-contradictorily, in any one modernist text. In works by Joyce, Woolf, Conrad, and Richardson one finds equal traces of the intentions to heighten the artifice of art, to heighten the fidelity of art to historical life, and to doubt (no less than to celebrate) the reality or the intelligibility of art, history, and life together.

For a typical example of modernist impulses in fiction one might refer to *Howards End* (1910) by E.M. FORSTER, albeit this work lacks the glamor and obvious experimentation of Joyce and Woolf. Forster's two heroines, upper middle-class orphans, inherit the estate called Howards End in a way that represents the victorious undermining by feminist impulses of male patriarchy and of British imperialism. In the fact that one sister becomes an unashamedly unwed mother, whose child's father has working-class origins and has lost his life to class conflict, Forster suggests the interconnected political ascendancy of women and workers. The forging of hitherto repressed political and social alliances and connections becomes the novel's motto: "Only connect . . ." Nevertheless *Howards End,* in spite of its motto, exhibits ironic self-consciousness about the real possibilities of novel connections. The story about creating newly liberating collective interests is pervaded by abrupt discontinuities. Indeed without the latter, no new connections or collectives can come into being. The life-line of the narrative itself is gaps in sequence, a constant pressure exerted upon unity and coherence. In the more celebrated modernist classics, *Ulysses,* Forster's own later *A Passage to India* (1924), and Woolf's *To the Lighthouse* (1927), a similar pressure is writ large.

A baffled political search for new forms of collective life might account for the constant perplexing of formal unity and continuity in modernist works. One basis for the bafflement is a persistent (if unfulfilled) attempt to theorize a place in nineteenth-century political theories and practices for new twentieth-century responses to gender and sexuality. *The New Machiavelli* (1911) by H.G. WELLS illustrates the problem. The novel's protagonist searches for a theory of politics that intends to surmount the factitiousness of current ideological distinctions. As he cobbles together features of conservative, anarchist, and socialist thought, the protagonist also turns against the nation-state, in favor of accepting the global interdependencies that are an irreversible inheritance of global imperialism. Yet the obstacle to the political search is the current insufficiently thought-out place of eros in the world order. Traditional heterosexual norms, including monogamous MARRIAGE, are identified by Wells with a destructive order of jealousy, a stumbling block in all modern political ideologies. But in *The New Machiavelli* the attempt to theorize sex and gender anew, in a way that will politicize them without at the same time victimizing either conventional or unconventional erotic desires, fails. To come to terms with the failure, or to reverse it, becomes the thematic as well as the formal basis of some of the era's most distinguished novelistic careers.

In Richardson and Woolf FEMINISM mediates the opposing claims of eros and politics. Richardson suggests that both political theory and sexual psychology need to revise themselves, by taking as a starting-point for change the experience of a unique, transcendental female selfhood. Woolf's polemic *Three Guineas* (1938) solicits feminism's critique of compulsory gender-division to urge her readers to opt out of gender and political business-as-usual, and to insist on international PACIFISM as the key to a new collectivity. In Woolf's *Orlando* (1928), and in novels by Ronald Firbank (1886–1926) and Sylvia Townsend Warner (1893–1978), as well as in suppressed work by Forster, transexualism, transvestism, and HOMOSEXUALITY are enlisted as forms of liberation from political and imperialist oppressions. Meanwhile, Wells's criticism of the jealous god that is heterosexuality is shared by Joyce and, more complexly, by D.H. LAWRENCE. Lawrence's novels and stories, highly sensitive to the role played by class and race differences and conflicts in the construction of sexuality, try to formulate a radically original ethos for heterosexual conduct. But although Lawrence newly locates in bodily eros the sources of tenderness, of personal autonomy, and of a passion for justice, he laments his inability to attach his sexual ethos to a satisfyingly collective political purpose. Similarly, FORD MADOX FORD, surveying in *Parade's End* (1924–8) the murder of modern democracy by callous national and international interests, represents the ironic history of a pair of lovers whose public-minded virtues have no public political sphere on which to operate and are driven in upon a purely private domain. In all these novelists, the engagement with the politics and anti-politics of eros (arising, not surprisingly, alongside the ascent of Freud's thought) remains an open tradition of puzzled inquiry, handed on to the century's latter half.

The novels of Ivy COMPTON-BURNETT, ELIZABETH BOWEN, and Henry Green (1905–73) typ-

ify most powerfully the second generation of modernism, and modernism's extension into mid-century. Compton-Burnett's dramas erode the boundary between realism and anti-realism, even as her novels play up their high, pure artifice. Their artificiality inheres in their unspecified historical time and in their exactingly subtle dialogue (spoken with equal facility by bourgeois families and their servants). Yet the emotional medium of the novels is real enough: the familiar atmosphere of "family values". *Parents and Children* (1941) typically exhibits Compton-Burnett's picture of these values, which amount to a horrible self-perpetuating selfishness, promulgated in the father's name, constraining even when the patriarch is withdrawn by absence or death. The horror is registered coldly, however, as if the writer wants partly to concede that an artistic representation is not to be strictly identified with any social or historical reality.

Similar contradictory oscillations of attitude towards art's relation to reality inform Bowen and Green. On the one hand Bowen's work is minutely realistic, both in its concentration on the daily domestic life of women and children and in its attention to world history. In *The Heat of the Day* (1949) the personal lives of two women of different classes are inescapably caught up in the conflict with fascism. The story of one of them, who finds out that her English lover is a Nazi spy, symbolically discovers a disturbing political possibility: that fascism is the inveterate double, and not the opposite, of modern democracy. But the novelist's aim to make fiction serve the investigation of real history goes hand in hand with her production of tales in which she portrays history itself as merely a ghost story. Spectral, both real and unreal, the ghostly nature of history in Bowen results partly from the SECOND WORLD WAR's uncanny revival of the experiences of the First. In Henry Green's work the multiple characteristics of modernism (of what might be more accurately called various modernisms) are even more strikingly on show than in the other "second-generation" modernists. Green's *Living* (1929), one of the best modern fictions about urban industrial employers and workers, protests economic inequity, in terms of searching sociological realism. However, Green's career also encompasses, in marked contrast to realism, the fantastic narrative *Concluding* (1948), set in a girls' school in a welfare-state future. *Concluding* plays an elaborate puzzle-like game with the reader (some of the game's pieces are deliberately left out), in a manner predicting the experimental novels, beginning with SAMUEL BECKETT's *Molloy*. But written in a style midway between the aesthetic polarities of *Living* and *Concluding* is Green's *Party-Going* (1939), in which fog-bound passengers in a major London railway station figure the communal and erotic liberation that comes from the ruin of everyday routines. Not incidentally, "party-going" in Green repeats a narrative event and a motif that turns up repeatedly in modernist fiction, most prominently in Woolf and in WYNDHAM LEWIS, because of its apparent convenience for dramatizing collective partisan movements, no less than social partying.

Clearly, English experiments with the forms of fiction remain the order of the day in the century's first half. At times the experiments change the genre beyond recognition. The narrative form of novels and histories dissolves into an illogic of fantasies and puns in Joyce's *Finnegans Wake* (1922–39), which represents novel-writing and history-writing alike as opaque lyric dreamwork. Wells's novels about sex and politics eschew the novel's traditional ambition to show life rather than tell it: Wells insists that novels become *essays* about the need for social change. The work of ALDOUS HUXLEY is similarly anti-novelistic. It derides the novel form for stimulating the reader's sense of subjectivity, at the expense of personal and social change, and complains of "the wearisomeness . . . of all those merely descriptive plays and novels, which critics expected one to admire" (*After Many a Summer Dies the Swan*, 1939).

Anti-novel novels in the period are complemented by an equally anti-novelistic resurgence of romance and fantasy writing, which burgeons alongside the growth of science fiction. Principal among the romance-writers is John Cowper Powys (1872–1963). *Weymouth Sands* (1934), a typical Powys work, shows how the previous century's realism and naturalism can shade into romance. Its cultural landscape is rooted in the elemental sea-side meeting of earth and water, but its story is also about persons who oppose nature by means of intellectual and artistic aims, utopian political aspirations, struggles against the Oedipal structure that has become our second nature, and mysticism. In Powys both nature and culture are the grotesque masks of underlying mysterious cosmic forces, which Powys labors to house in narratives that strain the limits of literary form.

Nowadays it is a critical commonplace that modernism and what follows it—postmodernism—are radically different in character. Yet postmodernism is associated with precisely the mixing of realist and historical aims alongside anti-realist and anti-historical ones (and in the same self-conscious, questioning way) exhibited by both generations of modernist novelists. Nowadays it is also claimed that postmodernist writing is acutely conscious, in a way modernism is not, of the political bearings of art. If the latter claim is true, present-day critics may yet have something to learn from the way modernist practices demonstrate that no aesthetic form carries the guarantee of one sort of politics rather than another, and vice versa.

The political antitype of most of the modernist figures mentioned here is RUDYARD KIPLING, whose name remains a byword for the British Empire at its most bloated. Yet Kipling's political conservatism is not matched by aesthetic conservatism, and Kipling's innovative storytelling form issues sometimes in conservative political morals—and sometimes not. Kipling's art exploits foreshortened and elliptical means of narration in order to produce the startling ambiguities that are characteristic of modernism. In "Little Foxes" (1909) these techniques flatter imperialism; in "The Church That Was at Antioch" (1929) these techniques condemn all imperialism (Christianity's especially) for not respecting the multiplicity of human cultures. Frequently Kipling's aesthetic is the ally of promiscuous or illicit sexual passion: "The Wish House" (1924) turns away as much as do the anti-imperialists Joyce and Wells from what Joyce's heroine Molly Bloom calls "stupid husbands jealousy". Of course, the restless play of myriad forms of art that structures Joyce's work makes us expect an alliance of such play with liberal or radical politics, if only because they appear in the work of an Irish rebel against religious and political tyrannies. Yet one finds similarly restless formal novelties structuring Wyndham Lewis's *The Apes of God* (1930) and *The Revenge of Love* (1937), where aesthetic innovation provides—in contrast to Joyce—a conservative rather than liberal perspective on the allegedly bottomless political factitiousness of the GENERAL STRIKE of 1926 and the SPANISH CIVIL WAR.

Thus, given the way modernist aesthetic innovation guarantees no fixed accompanying (or even fully legible) political position, it is not surprising that traditional modes of fiction in the early twentieth century also resist easy translation into political terms. The art and politics of writers who were contemporaries of modernism but were not touched by its prestige has been unfairly obscured in literary history. Woolf attacked her senior contemporaries, the popular novelists ARNOLD BENNETT and JOHN GALSWORTHY for their old-fashioned realism and their putative conservatism. But Bennett's *Clayhanger* trilogy (1910–15) uses a conservative aesthetic means to portray the abrupt discontinuities that constitute history, no less than Woolf uses a radical means to portray the same in *The Years* (1937). And Galsworthy's study of a domestic rapist, the "hero" of *A Man of Property* (1906), uses a narrative form reminiscent of Thackeray's to express a feminism that is in line with *Three Guineas*.

Robert L. Caserio

Bibliography
Caserio, Robert L. *The English Novel 1900–1950: Theory and History.* 1999.
Eysteinsson, Astradur. *The Concept of Modernism.* 1990.
Gilbert, Sandra, and Susan Gubar. *No Man's Land: The Place of the Woman Writer in the Twentieth Century.* 1988.
Green, Martin. *The English Novel in the Twentieth Century.* 1984.
Levenson, Michael. *A Genealogy of Modernism.* 1984.
Nash, Christopher. *World Postmodern Fiction.* 1991.

Novel, English, since 1945

During the strife-torn 1940s British publishers averaged 1,419 new novels a year; during the 1980s, this figure had risen to 3,183, approximately one work for each of the estimated 3,400 active novelists in Great Britain. These figures, however, disguise the fact that post-war British fiction has had to struggle as never before to find and to maintain its audience and its dominance in the publishing world. In 1939, 12.5 percent of all books published were fiction; by 1989, this number had declined to 6 percent. Other forms—film, television, music video, compact discs, "audio-tape books"—have appropriated large portions of the audience. Moreover, the very notion of a literate culture has often been aggressively devalued during the last thirty years. As a result, a number of schemes have been evolved to publicize and to support fiction, among them the 1979 Public Lending Right Act, which distributed more than £3 million to 14,149 authors in 1990, and literary prizes, with the prestigious Booker [McConnell] Prize becoming a media event almost eclipsing the Whitbread, W.H. Smith, Somerset Maugham, and other awards.

Throughout the upheavals in the market, novelists have struggled to reinvent their genre, to adopt traditional forms to contemporary culture, and to give a uniquely British shape to the forces of postmodernism. Each decade has given the world an indisputably major work of fiction: L.P. Hartley's *The Go-Between* (1953), John Fowles's *The French Lieutenant's Woman* (1969), Margaret Drabble's *The Realms of Gold* (1975), D.M. Thomas's *The White Hotel* (1981), and Graham Swift's *Waterland* (1983). While it is perhaps still too early to discern the cultural dominant of the post-war years, one can see a new and intriguing interaction among high, mass, and emerging cultures.

The moralists and social activists who came to prominence in the 1930s at first dominated the serious fiction market in the decade following Allied victory. EVELYN WAUGH and GRAHAM GREENE explored religious dimensions they felt had been missing from British fiction: Waugh's *Brideshead Revisited* (1945) and Greene's *The Heart of the Matter* (1948) and *The End of the Affair* (1951) depicted numinous worlds transformed by miracles and characterized by the paradoxes of love. Greene's pursuits put him on the cover of *Time* magazine and brought censure from the Vatican. The representation of political nightmares, from which the reader was to infer the necessity of maintaining the best in British humanist thought and action, was epitomized in GEORGE ORWELL's *Nineteen Eighty-Four* (1949), whose title immediately became synonymous with the essence of the totalitarian state. It remains the most frequently read and taught novel from this period. Similar political inferences can be drawn from ALDOUS HUXLEY's *Ape and Essence* (1948), a protest against the arrival of the Atomic Age. Meanwhile, Hartley (1895–1972) completed his *Eustace and Hilda* trilogy (1947) and *The Go-Between* (1953), both of which rigorously argued that Freudian and Marxist explanations of guilt and evil should be displaced by a renewal of concepts of individual responsibility. In offering their religious, political, and humanistic perspectives, this generation of novelists continued and reaffirmed the directions they had taken in the 1930s. Greene remained an active voice in British fiction until his death in 1991.

The mid-1950s and early 1960s brought new sociological voices in those novelists often labeled the Angry Young Men. The novels of William Cooper (1910–), John Wain (1925–1994), Kingsley Amis (1922–95), John Braine (1922–86), and Alan Sillitoe (1928–) addressed the LABOUR government's failures to reshape British society to benefit all its citizens, the persistence of class struggles, the alienation of the worker in the workplace, the psychological helplessness felt by individuals during the Cold War. The novelists' charges constituted a global anger directed, often misdirected, toward the Establishment. In Cooper's *Scenes from Provincial Life* (1950), Wain's *Hurry on Down* (1953), Amis's *Lucky Jim* (1954), Braine's *Room at the Top* (1957), and Sillitoe's *Saturday Night and Sunday Morning* (1958), virile, aggressive, often amoral protagonists use cunning and sexuality as survival skills necessary to wage their picaresque adventures against the post-war world. The characters show a comic sensibility often overlooked by readers more intent on the sociological and political implications of their authors' works. That these novels were often brilliantly adapted by the revitalized British FILM INDUSTRY helped earn them wide recognition. By the early 1960s, however, new winds were sweeping fiction in other directions. The "Angries" continued to publish on into the 1980s, but they never achieved the dominance they enjoyed for a few years in the 1950s and 1960s. Such later writers as Barry Hines and David Storey (1933–), who emphasized the dignity of craftsmanship and talent on the playing field and the workshop, tempered the earlier anger, even as they maintained the class focus of fiction.

Sociological and historical ambitions for fiction are represented also in popular *roman fleuves* such as Anthony Powell's *A Dance to the Music of Time* (1951–75) and Lawrence Durrell's *The Alexandria Quartet* (1957–60). But telling blows against the sociological focus came from Anthony Burgess's *A Clockwork Orange* (1962), Fowles's *The Collector* (1963) and *The Magus* (1965), and B.S. Johnson's *Albert Angelo* (1964). These works savaged especially the moralist's and the activist's fiction and spoke urgently of reinstating the modernist projects of JAMES JOYCE, VIRGINIA WOOLF, and others. Burgess's fifteen-year-old Alex, Fowles' almost neurasthenic Ferdinand Clegg, and Johnson's Mr. Albert quickly unmasked the anger of the earlier novels by exhibiting the antisocial thug, the anarchistic kidnapper incapable of intellectual growth, and the reforming teacher overwhelmed by the social forces unleashed by the late 1950s in ways that neither the fashions of Carnaby Street, the music of THE BEATLES, nor a plethora of consumer goods could contain. By foregrounding language directly descended from Joyce's *Finnegans Wake* (1939), existential thought directly imported from Jean-Paul Sartre, and rebellion against the traditional look of the written page, Burgess (1917–93), Fowles (1926–), and Johnson (1933–73) announced that postmodernism had arrived in British fiction. The announcement would be completed by Michael Moorcock's *Breakfast in the Ruins* (1971), which deconstructed the very form of the novel by unraveling its historical, subjective, mythic, and thematic tendencies, and Johnson's *Christie Malry's Own Double Entry* (1973, but planned in 1964), a hilarious send-up of the angry young hero.

Postmodernism has taken many forms in British fiction since the 1960s, some of them topical, some formal, some thematic. Experimental, iconoclastic engagement with the past and with ideas of history, or with fantasies of the future, have shaped the works of such novelists as Drabble (1939–), Swift (1949–), Fowles (1926–), Peter Ackroyd (1949–), Alasdair Gray (1934–), Brigid Brophy (1929–95), MURIEL SPARK, J.G. Ballard (1930–), and even WILLIAM GOLDING. Between the publication of *Lord of the Flies* (1954) and the awarding of the Nobel Prize in 1983— Great Britain's first such award since 1953— Golding seemed ambiguously independent of literary fashions, yet his "counterbooks"—Jorge Luis Borges's term for a book that invades, escapes from, or replies to an earlier book—mark one of the major tendencies in postmodern British fiction, seen in such works as David Lodge's

The British Museum is Falling Down (1965), Jean Rhys's *Wide Sargasso Sea* (1966), ANGUS WILSON's *No Laughing Matter* (1967), Brian Aldiss's *Frankenstein Unbound* (1973), George MacDonald Fraser's *Flashman Papers* (1969–90), and Drabble's *The Gates of Ivory* (1992). The best-known representative work, though, remains Fowles's *The French Lieutenant's Woman* (1969), which folds an existential parable and concerns with the "death of the author" and the "death of the subject" around a loving simultaneous recreation and interrogatation of every aspect of the Victorian realistic novel. Fascination with works, figures, and fashions of earlier centuries, without turning to historical fiction, remains strong in Ackroyd's *Hawksmoor* (1985) and Antonia S. Byatt's extremely popular *Possession* (1990). The pasts of individuals have been brilliantly explored by DORIS LESSING's *The Golden Notebook* (1962), Drabble's *The Realms of Gold* (1975), and Swift's *Waterland* (1983), whose narrators' quest for meaning, purpose, and shape in their lives (within the issues raised by FEMINISM in the cases of Lessing and Drabble). The experimentalism of Johnson, Fowles, Brophy, and Spark has been fruitfully extended by Thomas's *The White Hotel* (1981), an extraordinarily powerful novel that both uses and abuses Freud, and by Julian Barnes's *Flaubert's Parrot* (1984) and *A History of the World in 10 1/2 Chapters* (1989), both of which test the very boundaries of narrative, moving, as they do, toward the spatial rather than the more usual temporal and historical features of narrative. A "French connection" has been nurtured by Christine Brooke-Rose (1926–), who lives and teaches in France and who has written some of the most challenging postmodernist works from *Such* (1966) to *Textermination* (1991).

One need only look at the names of a number of recently published authors to realize the importance of postcolonialist COMMONWEALTH LITERATURE in contemporary British fiction: J.M. Coetzee, Kazuo Ishiguro, Hanif Kureishi, Timothy Mo, V.S. Naipaul, and Salman Rushdie. While these authors bring issues of pluralism in race, religion, family, even diet to British fiction, lesbian and gay authors such as Neil Bartlett, Patrick Gale, Alan Hollingshurst, and Jeanette Winterson have placed the sexually marginalized worlds before the readers in *Ready to Catch Him Should He Fall* (1990), *The Aerodynamics of Pork* (1986), *The Swimming Pool Library* (1988), and *Oranges Are Not the Only Fruit* (1985).

Of course, the postmoderns also keep company with a number of authors more traditional in matters of forms and topics: IRIS MURDOCH, Anita Brookner (1928–), Penelope Lively (1933–), and Ian McEwan (1948–). Also, contemporary British fiction continues the earlier traditions of fantasy, DETECTIVE FICTION, and science fiction in authors such as Richard Adams, P.D. James, and Ballard.

David Leon Higdon

Bibliography
Higdon, David Leon. *Shadows of the Past in Contemporary British Fiction*. 1985.
Massie, Allan. *The Novel Today: A Critical Guide to the British Novel, 1970–1989*. 1990.
McEwan, Neil. *The Survival of the Novel: British Fiction in the Later Twentieth Century*. 1981.
Scanlan, Margaret. *Traces of Another Time: History and Politics in Postwar British Fiction*. 1990.
Stevenson, Randall. *The British Novel since the Thirties*. 1986.

Nuclear Weapons

After the United States and the Soviet Union, Britain became the world's third nuclear weapon state. Britain's weapon program draws attention to the specific problems confronted by a medium power in trying to sustain a military capability at the leading edge of technology: while policy has been driven by both political and military needs for independence, practically Britain's program has been characterized by high levels of reliance on American weapon systems.

British interest in the military potential of the atom was sparked during the SECOND WORLD WAR by the fear that Germany might be working on such a project. A study by two scientists working in Britain (Frisch-Peierls memorandum) led to the establishment in 1940 of the official Maud Committee which recommended, in July 1941, the development of an atomic bomb. By secret war-time agreements between Prime Minister WINSTON CHURCHILL and President Roosevelt, signed at Quebec in August 1943 and at Hyde Park in September 1944, Britain joined in a collaborative program of research with the United States.

British expectations that a joint British-American atomic venture would be continued in the post-war period were dashed by the McMahon Act of 1946, which prohibited sharing of sensitive nuclear information with foreign countries. In any case, there was a widespread assumption at the highest levels of British government that a British atomic bomb should be manufactured and, after decisions in 1945 and 1946 to establish a research establishment and a nuclear reactor, a CABINET sub-committee formally decided on 8 January 1947 to proceed to develop a British weapon. Simultaneously, work was commenced on design of a new generation of strategic bombers (V-bombers—Valiant, Victor, and Vulcan).

The first British device was tested on the Monte Bello Islands off North-West Australia in October 1952. This success was marred by the fact that the United States and Soviet Union were already embarking on tests of the much more powerful hydrogen bomb, and in mid-1954 the Cabinet decided that Britain too must have the most-up-to-date weapons possible. A British thermonuclear device was tested at Christmas Island in 1957.

Britain began to acquire an operational atomic capability from 1956 but discovered that the technological competition of the two super-powers was already pressing into the missile age. The fear was that Britain's V-bombers would become progressively vulnerable either to attack by Soviet missiles before they could leave the ground or to new surface-to-air missiles which would defend Soviet territory. Accordingly, Britain had also begun to develop its own medium-range ballistic missile, known as Blue Streak and, as an interim measure, had also decided in March 1957 to deploy American Thor missiles at bases in Britain. Both of these missiles were liquid-fueled, which would mean a fueling delay before they could be launched, and fears grew that this would render them vulnerable to attack on the ground.

Increasingly, the British government felt itself seeking assistance from the United States. Despite an official statement on defense in 1957 which emphasized Britain's need for an independent deterrent, efforts were redoubled to secure information from the United States about warhead design which would permit Britain to produce a lighter weapon that made more efficient use of scarce fissile material. This objective was achieved in July 1958 with the signing of a bilateral agreement on atomic energy which made Britain a privileged partner of the United States as far as nuclear information was concerned. In 1960 the Cabinet decided to cancel the Blue Streak program but, before doing so, Prime Minister HAROLD MACMILLAN secured initial American agreement to sell to Britain the Skybolt missile that was then under development for the US Air Force. This missile could be launched from the V-bombers and, having a range of some 1000 miles, would avoid the need for the bombers to enter into heavily defended air space.

A crisis was created for the British nuclear deterrent when, in December 1962, the Kennedy administration announced cancellation of the Skybolt program. At an emotional and difficult meeting between Macmillan and President Kennedy at Nassau in the Bahamas in December 1962, the President agreed, against the wishes of many senior State Department advisers, to sell to Britain the Polaris missile which would be launched from a submarine. Under the terms of the agreement, Britain would build its own submarines and design its own warheads, but much of the technical information for this effort was supplied by the Americans.

The fleet of four submarines carrying Polaris submarine-launched ballistic missiles has been the mainstay of the British strategic deterrent since 1969 to the present day. In the 1970s the government undertook a secret program, known as Chevaline, to enhance the ability of Polaris to evade the anti-ballistic missile system which the Soviet Union was deploying around Moscow. It was believed that a combination of three warheads, and various decoys, would penetrate Soviet defenses, but the cost of Chevaline, estimated at £1 billion, was very high. Accordingly, when planning commenced for the eventual replacement of the Polaris fleet, there was financial pressure to buy from the United States rather than develop a purely British weapon. In 1980 the United States agreed to sell to Britain the C4 Trident I missile, and in 1982 this was changed to allow Britain to acquire the more advanced D5 Trident II version. It was expected that the first of the four projected submarines equipped with Trident would become operational from around the mid-1990s.

British determination to acquire nuclear weapons was driven by a combination of military and political considerations each of which changed over time. During the Second World War the fear of facing an atomic-armed Germany was the determining factor but, even then, it was recognized that an atomic weapon would be vital in the post-war period. Early British strategic thinking was very much obsessed with the potential vulnerability to Soviet atomic attack of the small British Isles, with dense population, and hence with the need to have a deterrent against such attack. By the first half of the 1950s the military case for an independent British deterrent was being expressed primarily in terms of having the capacity to destroy targets in the Soviet Union which directly, and much more immediately, threatened Britain and which might not be given such high priority in American war plans. However, the endeavor to target Soviet air bases and atomic installations became increasingly unrealistic by the late 1950s with the growth of Soviet nuclear power, and henceforth British doctrine rested largely on being able to mount an effective threat against Soviet population and industrial centers.

Underlying British policy statements has undoubtedly been the concern not to be wholly dependent upon the nuclear guarantee offered by the United States through NATO. Absolute confidence in the willingness of the United States to put itself at nuclear risk for the sake of its European allies was questioned once the USSR developed intercontinental missiles capable of reaching the continental United States and since the attainment of broad strategic parity between the Soviet Union and the United States. Independent deterrents have therefore been argued to contribute to British security and, in recent years, the official doctrine justifying maintenance of a British nuclear force has been that of the "second center of decision".

Politically, the British program has reflected both specific and general motivations. Much of this has been associated with the special relationship with the United States. Early post-war British concerns were a somewhat contradictory determination to avoid undue dependence upon the United States, coupled with an intensive effort to prove to the United States that Britain was a worthwhile nuclear partner and thereby hasten the reestablishment of wartime collaboration. Additionally, in the first half of the 1950s British leaders felt that a deterrent would give Britain influence over American policy at a time when there was much anxiety over American policy in Korea and Indochina. In the late 1950s there was also some political incentive to emphasize the nuclear aspects of Britain's defense policy as a less costly alternative to conventional defenses, thus permitting some reduction in the overall costs of British defense which had touched 10 per cent of GNP during the Korean War. Finally, at a time when Britain was in relative political and economic decline, some saw political value in a British deterrent as a symbol of international status.

British nuclear policy became controversial in the late 1950s as people became concerned about the effects of atmospheric testing, and during this period the CAMPAIGN FOR NUCLEAR DISARMAMENT became a vocal champion of opposition to the country's policy. Renewed disquiet about the British deterrent emerged in the early 1980s with large-scale demonstrations. Despite this, and despite the LABOUR PARTY having periodically favored unilateral nuclear disarmament, the British deterrent has been maintained by both Labour and Conservative governments when in power.

Ian Clark

Bibliography
Clark, Ian, and Nicholas J. Wheeler. *The British Origins of Nuclear Strategy, 1945–1955.* 1989.
Freedman, Lawrence. *Britain and Nuclear Weapons.* 1980.
Gowing, Margaret. *Britain and Atomic Energy, 1939–1945.* 1964.
———. *Independence and Deterrence: Britain and Atomic Energy, 1945–1952.* 2 vols. 1974.
Navias, Martin S. *Nuclear Weapons and British Strategic Planning 1955–1958.* 1991.

Nutrition: see Diet and Nutrition

Observer, The

The *Observer*, launched in 1791, is Britain's oldest Sunday newspaper. Under a succession of editors and proprietors it has enjoyed periods of considerable influence during the twentieth century, particularly under its two most celebrated editors, JAMES LOUIS GARVIN and David Astor.

Founded by W.S. Bourne, the *Observer* had an undistinguished Victorian history, and by the end of the nineteenth century the paper was under the uninspired direction of the Beer family, with a net sale of between only 2,000 and 4,000 copies a week. By the early 1900s the Beers were looking for a buyer to relieve them of a property that was losing £15,000 a year. In 1905 they sold the paper for £4,000 to LORD NORTH-CLIFFE, a journalist of genius, if at times an overpowering and interfering proprietor, who was determined to, as he put it, rescue the *Observer* from the "Fleet (Street) ditch". To this end, he appointed J.L. Garvin as editor in 1908. Garvin, probably the most gifted journalist of his generation, was born in 1868 in humble circumstances in Birkenhead and largely self-educated. In politics, Garvin's early political hero was Parnell, but he transferred his allegiance to Joseph Chamberlain in 1903 when he helped to campaign for Chamberlain's program of TARIFF REFORM and imperial unity. He remained attached to Chamberlain's brand of Liberal Imperialism, within the Unionist Party, for the rest of his life.

Under Garvin the fortunes of the *Observer* improved rapidly, both in journalistic and financial terms. Garvin can be credited with the invention of modern Sunday journalism on the *Observer*, and as the Victorian sabbath was giving way to the Edwardian weekend, so the middle classes responded to a paper that sought, in Garvin's own words, to be "half a newspaper; half a magazine or serial." His trenchant weekly signed column on the editorial pages soon became required reading for the political classes and became the most famous feature of the paper until he left the *Observer* in 1942. Garvin established the *Observer*'s reputation for informed and independent political comment with a series of campaigns such as his warnings of the German danger and the need for naval rearmament in 1908–11 and his principled defense of the HOUSE OF LORDS during the 1911 constitutional crisis.

So independent a writer as Garvin, however, could not have been expected to survive too long in harmony with a proprietor such as North-cliffe, a man of equally strong view, and the inevitable irreconcilable disagreement came in 1911. Northcliffe generously allowed Garvin three weeks to find an alternative buyer for the paper before he would buy Garvin's share in the paper and own it outright. Garvin, however, found William Waldorf Astor, who bought the *Observer* for £45,000 in 1911, beginning the paper's connection with the Astor family that would last until 1976. The moving spirit behind William Waldorf Astor's purchase of the paper was, in fact, his son Waldorf Astor, who, from the start, was the *de jure* proprietor, becoming the *de facto* proprietor on his father's death in 1919. It was during the early years of the Astor proprietorship that Garvin's *Observer* reached the peak of its influence and commercial success—the paper was selling 200,000 copies a week by the early 1920s.

During the 1930s, however, Garvin's powers began to wane, and the reputation of the *Observer* began to suffer. The paper also attracted criticism for its support of the NEVILLE CHAMBERLAIN government's APPEASEMENT of Nazi Germany during the late 1930s. Garvin and Astor began to disagree seriously on this issue after the MUNICH conference and on the support that the paper gave to Chamberlain from 1939 to 1940 and to Churchill from 1940 to 1942. Garvin's enthusiasm for, and Astor's reservations about, Churchill's competence as a war leader led to Garvin's enforced resignation amidst considerable bitterness in February 1942.

Garvin's peremptory departure plunged the paper into crisis, and a series of temporary editors brought the paper out for the rest of the war, most notably the paper's drama critic, Ivor Brown, from 1942 to 1948. However, the most important figure in the history of the post-Garvin era was David Astor, Waldorf's second son. Astor was, politically, a liberal strongly interested in foreign affairs, and through his recruitment of a number of new, often émigre, writers, he had transformed the *Observer* from the largely Conservative paper that it had become under Garvin to the leader of liberal opinion in Britain from the late 1940s through to the

1960s. Astor attracted a high caliber of writer, like GEORGE ORWELL, Sebastian Haffner, Isaac Deutscher, and Anthony Sampson, who gave the paper an intellectual distinction greater than any of its rivals. In 1945 a trust was created to run the paper, and in 1948 David Astor was appointed editor, although he had been effectively determining policy since 1942.

Under Astor the *Observer* enjoyed a period of influence that surpassed Garvin's "golden age" during the First World War. The paper became widely known for its principled progressive campaigns, most notably against the continuation of white minority rule in Africa (and particularly in South Africa) and against CAPITAL PUNISHMENT in Britain. The paper was involved in the founding of such organizations as Amnesty International. Its most important political intervention under Astor was its attack on ANTHONY EDEN's government during the SUEZ CRISIS in 1956; the *Observer's* leader of 4 November did much to undermine confidence in Eden's handling of the crisis.

However, from the early 1960s onwards, with increasing competition from the *Sunday Telegraph* and a revitalized *Sunday Times*, the *Observer* experienced increasing financial difficulties, which, in 1976, led to its sale to the American oil company, Atlantic Richfield, controlled by Robert Anderson. Astor retired as editor in 1975 and was replaced by his deputy Donald Trelford, who was still editor in the 1990s. After investing a lot of money in the paper for little return, Anderson, a patron of liberal causes throughout the world, sold the paper to "Tiny" Rowland's Lonrho corporation in 1981. The sale to Lonrho aroused considerable controversy, as it was feared that Lonrho's extensive commercial interests in Africa would compromise the *Observer's* capacity to speak out independently on African affairs. In 1993 the *Observer* was taken over by the *Guardian*, the one quality daily lacking a Sunday publication, which helped to revive its flagging liberal reputation.

Richard Cockett

Bibliography

Ayerst, David. *Garvin and the Observer.* 1985.

Cockett, Richard. *David Astor and the Observer.* 1991.

Gollin, Alfred M. *J.L. Garvin and the Observer 1908 to 1914: A Study in a Great Editorship.* 1960.

Official Secrets Act

Dating from 1889, the Official Secrets Act, amended several times in the course of the twentieth century, has been the British government's legal weapon against espionage. It has been used successfully to prosecute dozens of British subjects caught spying for a foreign power. Portions of the act dealing with the disclosure of official information, however, have given rise to considerable controversy. Issues such as freedom of the press, government accountability, and the rights of the citizen have been used by critics in arguing that the act is anachronistic and open to abuse by the state.

The Official Secrets Act of 1889 was drawn up after it became clear that existing laws were inadequate in dealing with suspected spies and CIVIL SERVANTS who leaked confidential documents to the PRESS. Section I of the act dealt with espionage, while Section II made it an offense for any Crown servant or contractor, "corruptly or contrary to his official duty," to reveal anything learned at work to someone to whom "it ought not, in the interests of State or otherwise in the public interest, to be communicated at that time."

In 1911, amid a growing fear of German spies, the government amended the act to increase its scope and make it more effective. The 1911 Official Secrets Act made it an offense not only to communicate official information but also knowingly to receive it. In 1920 further amendments were introduced, chief among them a shifting of the burden of proof from the prosecution to the accused: the defendant, rather than the Crown, now had to demonstrate that no "guilty intent" was involved. A new Section VI, furthermore, made it a crime to withhold any information concerning a suspected offense under the act. Amendments in 1939, however, strengthened the rights of the individual and the freedom of the press in relation to Section VI.

Controversy continually dogged Section II of the act, especially when questionable cases came to public attention. Among these were the 1938 Duncan Sandys affair, in which the protagonist, an MP and Territorial Army officer, publicly disclosed sensitive information on the state of Britain's anti-aircraft defenses; the 1971 *Sunday Telegraph* affair, in which secret information on arms sales to Nigeria was printed; and the 1978 "ABC" trial, held in the wake of investigation by journalists into the actions of British ARMY intelligence. The mid-1980s witnessed several high-profile cases of unauthorized disclosure by servants of the Crown resulting in further attempts—some successful, others not—at prosecution under the act: Sarah Tisdall leaking information on the introduction of cruise missiles to Greenham Common, Clive Ponting making public the true story of the sinking of the Argentine cruiser *Belgrano* in the FALKLANDS WAR, and Peter Wright exposing the inner workings and operations of MI5 in his controversial memoir, *Spycatcher*.

Such cases highlighted either the inequities or the inadequacies of the act, depending on one's view of state restrictions on public access to sensitive information. Various attempts were made to overhaul the act after a government-appointed departmental committee under Lord Franks confirmed in 1972 that serious problems existed. It was only at the end of the 1980s, however, that the law was further amended under the CONSERVATIVE government of MARGARET THATCHER. A new Section II in the 1989 Official Secrets Act generated its own share of controversy, being regarded by critics as a move designed to muzzle civil servants once and for all, irrespective of the nature of the material they might leak and regardless of whether or not the disclosure might be in the public interest.

A novel Freedom of Information Bill, introduced by the LABOUR government of TONY BLAIR at the end of the twentieth century, sought to set limits to what could be labeled "secret". At the same time, speculation arose concerning whether or not the more draconian features of the Official Secrets Act would come into conflict with the European Convention of Human Rights. As of 2000, however, the act was still being used against current or former government servants such as David Shayler, the ex-MI5 agent, who went public with secret information.

S. P. MacKenzie

Bibliography

Hooper, David. *Official Secrets: The Use and Abuse of the Act.* 1987.

Rogers, Ann. *Secrecy and Power in the British State: A History of the Official Secrets Act.* 1987.

Thomas, Rosamund S. *Espionage and Secrecy: The Official Secrets Acts 1911–1989 of the United Kingdom.* 1991.

Vincent, David. *The Culture of Secrecy: Britain, 1832–1998.* 1998.

Old Age Pensions

A system of state old age pensions was first introduced in Britain by the 1908 Old Age Pensions Act. Prior to this, most old people had supported themselves by working—in the early 1900s two-thirds of males aged over sixty-five were gainfully occupied—or by reliance on the Poor Law; a small and fortunate minority lived off savings or the few company pension schemes that had developed in the nineteenth century.

The campaign for old age pensions between 1878 and 1908 aroused the interest of both Conservatives and socialists, but for different reasons. For the former, pensions (if funded from contributions) would remove old people from the Poor Law. For the latter, a tax-funded, non-contributory pension scheme would fund an honorable retirement for working people, redistributing wealth to the elderly poor. Thus by the early 1900s the labor movement was spearheading the campaign through organizations such as the National Committee of Organised Labour for the Promotion of Old Age Pensions.

In eventual response to these pressures the 1908 Act, sponsored by DAVID LLOYD GEORGE as Chancellor of the Exchequer, was passed by the LIBERAL government. The scheme set up was very limited in both generosity and coverage. The pension was only five shillings per week (about one-quarter of the average unskilled urban wage), paid at the age of seventy, and subject to strict eligibility criteria relating to means, character, and nationality. However, in some ways the scheme was quite radical: it primarily benefited WOMEN (who comprised 63 percent of pensioners); it targeted the poor; it carried no retirement condition (thus acting as a wage-subsidy); and, being tax-funded, it was highly redistributive. When old age pensions were first paid in 1909, they covered 490,000 pensioners. By 1912 this number had risen to 642,500, largely because of increased take-up and a relaxation of some of the eligibility criteria.

For the next fifteen years old age pensions were a source of political controversy. Sections of the labor movement envisaged a universal, tax-funded state pension of £1 per week, paid to all from the age of sixty, unfettered by any means tests. Pensioners were beginning to add their voice to these demands, and in 1916 an important pressure group, the National Conference on Old Age Pensions, was formed. Conservative opinion—especially within the Treasury—viewed such a prospect with alarm, since it would have cost (in 1919) an estimated £214 million in contrast to the existing scheme's £17.7 million. Discussion of this and other policy disagreements dominated the deliberations of the 1919 Ryland Adkins Committee. The immediate outcome was a doubling of the pension level to ten shillings per week.

The issue of pension funding was resolved by the CONSERVATIVE government in its 1925 Widows', Orphans' and Old Age Contributory Pensions Act. This introduced a new contributory scheme for those aged 65–70; it was a supplement to the 1908 plan, designed eventually to replace it. By this Act (for which NEVILLE CHAMBERLAIN as Minister of Health must be given credit) the labor movement's challenge was deflected and pension funding made less directly redistributive.

Demographic pressures inexorably increased the proportion of old people: those age sixty-five or over rose from 5.3 percent of the population in 1911 to 10.9 percent in 1951. By the mid-1930s there was much discussion of the fiscal burden of future pension costs, and even a belief in certain quarters that the presence of older workers in the heavy industries was a factor hindering economic recovery. To this pessimistic view was added the support of trade union leaders (such as ERNEST BEVIN) for the introduction of a new, improved pension which, by carrying a retirement condition, would encourage older workers to leave the labor market and hence reduce UNEMPLOYMENT.

By the late 1930s pressure for pension reform was mounting again: for example, a campaign by the National Spinsters' Pensions Association succeeded in lowering the woman's pension age to sixty in 1940, and the newly-formed National Federation of Old Age Pensions Associations demanded that the basic pension be doubled (to £1 per week) and made universal without a MEANS TEST. Essentially, the 1942 Beveridge Report recommended the amalgamation of the 1908 and 1925 schemes into a new universal, contributory scheme, with pensions conditional upon retirement from work. The levels proposed by BEVERIDGE were relatively ungenerous: full "subsistence" pensions were attainable only after twenty years of gradual increments. However, these low rates were unacceptable to both the wartime coalition and the post-war LABOUR government and the new scheme, introduced in 1946, paid pensions of twenty-six shillings (single pensioner) and forty-two shillings (pensioner couple). The attachment of a retirement condition, though having little measurable effect on the steady, labor market-driven spread of retirement, marked the end of pensions paid solely by virtue of old age and financial need. From 1946, therefore, there began a new system of state retirement pensions.

John Macnicol

Bibliography

Blaikie, Andrew. "The Emerging Political Power of the Elderly in Britain, 1908–1948," *Ageing and Society,* vol. 10 (1990), pp. 17–39.

Macnicol, John. *The Politics of Retirement in Britain 1878–1948.* 1998.

Thane, Pat. "Non-Contributory versus Insurance Pensions, 1878–1908" in Pat Thane, ed. *The Origins of British Social Policy.* 1978. pp. 84–106.

Wilson, Sir Arnold, and G.S. Mackay. *Old Age Pensions: An Historical and Critical Study* (1941).

Olivier, Laurence Kerr (1907–1989)

The most celebrated English actor of the century, Laurence Olivier performed on the stage and in films during the course of a career that lasted nearly sixty years and served as the first Artistic Director of the National Theatre from 1963 to 1973. Knighted in 1947 for his achievements as an actor, he was created a life peer (the first actor ever so honored) in 1970 and received the Order of Merit in 1981.

The son of a clergyman, Olivier was born on 22 May 1907 in Dorking, Surrey, and enrolled in the Central School of Speech and Drama in London at the age of seventeen. His earliest professional roles were with the Birmingham Repertory Company and at the Royal Court Theatre. In the late 1920s he made frequent appearances in commercial West End theatres, where he hoped to achieve popularity as a matinee idol. In 1930 Olivier married the actress Jill Esmond, the same year that he appeared with NOEL COWARD and Gertrude Lawrence in Coward's *Private Lives* and made his film debut in *Too Many Crooks.* His first successful film was Samuel Goldwyn's production of *Wuthering Heights* in 1939 in which he portrayed Heathcliff. Olivier next worked with ALFRED HITCHCOCK, playing Maxim de Winter in the adaptation of Daphne du Maurier's *Rebecca* (1940), and with MICHAEL POWELL in *The 49th Parallel* (1941).

These film triumphs paralleled forays into more serious stage drama. His first major Shakespearean roles were Mercutio amd Romeo (alternating the parts with John Gielgud) in 1935, and, after joining the Old Vic in 1937–8, he undertook a range of parts which established his pre-war reputation as a Shakespearean actor: Sir Toby Belch in *Twelfth Night,* Henry V, Macbeth, Hamlet, and Iago (to Ralph Richardson's Othello).

During the SECOND WORLD WAR Olivier served in the naval air force but was released in 1943 to direct a film production of *Henry V,* in which he reprised his title role performance, deliberately evoking strong patriotic sentiments in wartime. From 1944 to 1949 Olivier co-directed the Old Vic company, initially at the New Theatre, essaying such varied parts as Richard III, Lear, Astrov in *Uncle Vanya,* Hotspur in *Henry IV,* Part I, and Oedipus. Films of Hamlet (1947) and Richard III (1954) brought him further international acclaim.

During the 1940s and 1950s Olivier frequently acted with his second wife, Vivien Leigh, including alternating productions of *Antony and Cleopatra* and SHAW's *Caesar and Cleopatra* in London during the FESTIVAL OF BRITAIN in 1951 and *Macbeth, Twelfth Night,* and *Titus Andronicus* at Stratford in 1954–5. Earlier, in 1941 they had also made a film adaptation of the life of Lord Nelson entitled *That Hamilton Woman,* which like his *Henry V,* was designed to boost national morale during the war years.

Olivier's distinctive acting style, which relied heavily on physical mannerisms, worked effectively in the modern idiom, and he achieved notable success as the down-and-out music hall performer Archie Rice in JOHN OSBORNE's *The Entertainer* (1957), playing opposite Joan Plowright, who became his third wife in 1961. Other modern plays in which he starred were Ionesco's

Rhinoceros (1960) and Anouilh's *Becket* (1960–1). In 1961 he became the first Director of the Chichester Festival Theatre and in 1963 was appointed the Artistic Director of the newly formed National Theatre at the Old Vic. As an actor and director at the Old Vic, Olivier gave landmark and sometimes controversial performances as Astrov in *Uncle Vanya* (1963), Brazen in *The Recruiting Officer* (1963), Othello (1964), Edgar in Strindberg's *Dance of Death* (1967), Shylock (1970), James Tyrone in *Long Day's Journey into Night* (1971), and John Tagg in Trevor Griffiths' *The Party* (1973).

After worsening health compelled him to relinquish the artistic directorship of the National Theatre in 1973, he ceased to perform on the stage but continued to act in films and on television. Among his last films were *Sleuth* (1972), *Marathon Man* (1976), and *The Boys from Brazil* (1978), but he also made memorable appearances in *Brideshead Revisited* (1981) and in John Mortimer's *A Voyage Round My Father* (1982). He died in 1989, hailed as the pre-eminent actor of his generation and one of the last great actor-managers in the British theatre.

Martha A. Schütz

Bibliography
Cottrell, John. *Laurence Olivier.* 1975.
Gourlay, Logan, ed. *Olivier.* 1973.
Holder, Anthony. *Olivier.* 1988.
Lewis, Roger. *The Real Life of Laurence Olivier.* 1996.
Olivier, Laurence. *Confessions of an Actor.* 1982.

Open University

The Open University was founded in 1969 to serve the needs of British men and women who had missed the chance of a university education. It offers professional, academic, and self-enrichment courses to students in their homes via a combination of correspondence, group tutorial meetings at local study centers, residential summer schools, radio, and televised lectures broadcast by the BBC. By the early 1990s the Open University had 9 percent of all British students enrolled in higher education. It has justly attained public recognition for the high quality of its multi-media courses, but its real historical significance may prove to be its ability to provide mass access to UNIVERSITY EDUCATION at a very modest cost to state and students alike.

Between 1964 and 1970 HAROLD WILSON's LABOUR government increased access to higher education, creating the polytechnics and expanding the university system according to the recommendations of the ROBBINS REPORT. It was Wilson's idea to use television to create a truly democratic university serving older men and women without formal educational qualifications, whose work and family obligations forced

them to study intermittently at home. Academics were originally critical of an idea that violated cherished assumptions about the nature of higher education: universities were expected to be small-scale, academically selective, personalized, residential, and socially elite institutions, such as OXFORD and CAMBRIDGE. Under the leadership of its first Vice-Chancellor, Sir Walter Perry, the Open University attempted to ensure its acceptance as a university by recruiting an outstanding academic staff and by an extensive publicity campaign. It allowed for variations in students' preparation and ability by designing its curriculum to progress from the basic elementary "foundation courses" to more specialized and demanding advanced courses, the successful completion of which indicated a high level of achievement. Unlike the other British universities, it employed a system of credits which enabled students to take time out from the course and to combine courses in ways designed to reflect their individual needs and interests.

By the early 1990s the Open University had become a respected institution and a model for the provision of adult university education. It has not, however, proved to be an avenue to higher education for the most poorly-trained student. Instead, it has been an avenue for professional retraining, in particular for teachers to improve their qualifications and WOMEN to study while raising families. Although it has retained its policy of access without admissions requirements, it has established a selective graduate program. In the climate of economic privation of the 1980s, the Open University reluctantly made some places available to eighteen-year-olds, and will almost certainly continue to do so, functioning increasingly as a conventional university, but retaining its character as the first British university fully to utilize the media to promote study for older men and women working at home.

Elizabeth Morse

Bibliography
Ferguson, John. *The Open University from Within.* 1975.
Perry, Walter. *The Open University.* 1977.
McIntosh, Naomi E. *A Degree of Difference: The Open University of the United Kingdom.* 1977.
Tunstall, Jeremy, ed. *The Open University Opens.* 1974.

Opera and Opera Companies

Before 1914 efforts to promote opera in English at the Royal Opera House, Covent Garden ended in failure. Even such a successful plan as that launched by the conductors Hans Richter and Percy Pitt, and that culminated in the first performance of Wagner's *Ring* in English (1908), did not lead to the establishment of a national opera. Nonetheless, this period was noteworthy for the London debuts of Caruso and Tetrazzini, as well as the first performances in England of Puccini's *Tosca* (1900) and *Madama Butterfly* (1905), Debussy's *Pélleas et Mélisande* (1909), and Wagner's *Parsifal* (1914). THOMAS BEECHAM introduced Strauss's *Salome* and *Elektra* in 1910, succeeded by Diaghilev's Ballets Russes the following year, but his 1920 season of international opera ended in liquidation, although he was tempted to return to Covent Garden from 1932 to 1939, conducting Concita Supervia in Rossini, Tauber in Mozart, and Flagstad and Melchior in Wagner. Meanwhile German opera had been flourishing under Bruno Walter (1924–31) with such singers as Lehmann, Elisabeth Schumann, and Schorr.

After the Second World War plans were adopted to establish Covent Garden as a permanent national home for opera and BALLET and to place its running on a firm financial footing. Sir David Webster became general administrator (1945–70) with Karl Rankl, musical director (1945–51), and an annual grant from the newly-formed ARTS COUNCIL OF GREAT BRITAIN was forthcoming. At first, opera in English was preferred, although by the mid-1950s the original language was often used. During the 1960s Sir Georg Solti confirmed its international status; among the highlights of his period as music director was the British premiere of Schoenberg's *Moses und Aron* (1965). Before succeeding Solti in 1971, Sir Colin Davis directed new productions of Berlioz's *Les Troyens* (1969) and of MICHAEL TIPPETT's *The Midsummer Marriage* (1970), together with the premiere of Tippett's *The Knot Garden* (1970), one of the ten British operas that had their first performances at Covent Garden between 1945 and 1977. Others included RALPH VAUGHAN WILLIAMS's *Pilgrim's Progress* (1951), BENJAMIN BRITTEN's *Billy Budd* (1951), Peter Maxwell Davies's *Taverner* (1972), and Tippett's *The Ice Break* (1977).

In contrast to the sporadic attempts to stage opera in English at Covent Garden, other companies such as the Carl Rosa Opera Company (1875–1960) and the Moody-Manners Company (1897–1916) specialized in its promotion, providing London seasons as well as provincial tours. Both also acted as a training ground for British artists. The Carl Rosa Company gave the first performances in English of Wagner's *Siegfried* (1901) and Verdi's *La forza del destino* (1909), and by the 1930s was providing most of the opera heard outside London. Opera in English was also staged for two nights a week at the Old Vic by LILIAN BAYLIS, who, in 1931, moved her company to the Sadler's Wells Theatre, subsequently renaming it Sadler's Wells Opera. Her repertory of almost thirty operas was gradually expanded and the company enlarged, so that by 1939 its reputation as the leading provider of opera in English in

London was assured. Deprived of a permanent home during the SECOND WORLD WAR, the company, under the direction of Joan Cross (1900–93) was forced to spend most of its time on tour, but it continued to extend its repertoire. Its reputation was further enhanced when Sadler's Wells was reopened after the war with the first performance of Britten's *Peter Grimes* (1945), with Peter Pears and Cross in the leading roles. A particularly adventurous period followed as several operas of Janáček were introduced—Davis, musical director 1961–4, conducted the first British performance of *The Cunning Little Vixen* (1961). In 1968 the problems associated with the move to the Coliseum, which possesses the largest stage in London, were surmounted, and major triumphs followed with the production of Wagner's *Ring* conducted by Reginald Goodall (completed in 1973) and the first British stage production of Prokofiev's *War and Peace* (1972). Mark Elder, during his first ten years as musical director (1979–89), conducted many new productions including Tchaikovsky's *Mazepa* (British premiere, 1984) and Busoni's *Doktor Faust* (British stage premiere, 1986), and first British performances also included Philip Glass's *Akhnaten* (1985) and Harrison Birtwistle's *The Mask of Orpheus* (1986). In 1974 the company was renamed the English National Opera.

Outside London, John Christie (1882–1962) established an opera house at Glyndebourne, near Lewes, Sussex, in 1934, with the intention of mounting operas by both Mozart and Wagner, although under the guidance of his wife, he adopted the sensible plan of concentrating on the former. With Fritz Busch as musical director and Carl Ebert as producer, new standards of performance and production of Mozart's operas were established and have been pursued ever since. To mark the reopening of Glyndebourne following the Second World War, the English Opera Group gave the first performances of Britten's *The Rape of Lucretia* (1946) and *Albert Herring* (1947), and the repertoire was further expanded to include Rossini under the musical directorship of Vittorio Gui (1951–64). By the mid-1950s a policy of including a new work each year was implemented—the first French opera to be performed was Debussy's *Pélleas et Mélisande* in 1962—and subsequently Strauss's operas became a specialty, particularly those on a smaller scale. Among first performances of British operas, Glyndebourne has recently staged Nicholas Maw's *The Rising of the Moon* (1970), Nigel Osborne's *The Electrification of the Soviet Union* (1988), and Tippett's *New Year* (1990).

The demand for opera in the regions led to the formation of two national companies, Welsh National Opera at Cardiff in 1946 and Scottish

Opera at Glasgow, formed by Sir Alexander Gibson in 1962. The reputation of the former was originally built on its fine chorus and Verdi productions, although more recently such successes as the first British performance of Berg's *Lulu* (1971) and a new production of Tippett's *The Midsummer Marriage* have broadened its repertoire considerably. Both companies have been keen to commission operas by native composers, the WNO, Alun Hoddinott's *The Beach of Falesá* (1974), and the SNO, Thea Musgrave's *Mary, Queen of Scots* (1977), for instance.

Other regions have also benefited from having their own company. For example, Kent Opera was formed in 1969 by Norman Platt (artistic director) and Roger Norrington (musical director until 1984) as an example of a regionally-based English opera company funded by the Arts Council. Playing principally in theaters at Canterbury and Tunbridge Wells, but also touring throughout the southern counties, Kent Opera built up a repertoire with a broad appeal but enlivened with less well-known works and some commissions. Unfortunately, the withdrawal of its grant in 1989 led to its demise. Opera North, formed in 1977 and centered on Leeds, provides a similar service for the north of England and, more recently, Opera East for East Anglia. The regions have also benefited from the touring companies of the major opera houses, together with Phoenix Opera (1965–80), Birmingham Touring Opera, which uses reduced forces and community venues, and Travelling Opera, founded in 1986 by Peter Knapp, possibly the most active of the smaller groups. Opera for All, formed by the Arts Council in 1949, was the first of these small companies created specifically to take opera in English to towns and villages unlikely to experience the art form live, and although it originally consisted of a group of four singers, a pianist, and a stage manager-cum-compère, had expanded to three groups of twelve members by 1966. Its role was subsequently taken over by similar groups run by the main houses and by Opera 80, founded by the Arts Council in 1980 with similar aims, but with its own orchestra.

Increasingly historical awareness produced a whole series of revivals of previously unknown pre-nineteenth-century operas, the Intimate Opera Company, formed in 1930 by Frederick Woodhouse, specializing in this field and being launched with Thomas Arne's *Thomas and Sally*. Subsequently, early English opera has been the specialty of the touring company, Opera Restor'd, founded in 1985. The Handel Opera Society (1955, and since 1977, Handel Opera), inspired by E.J. Dent, began its productions with *Deidamia* (in Dent's translation), and during its first twenty years of existence staged revivals of nearly the same number of Handel's operas, including *Ariodante, Orlando,* and *Theodora*. Some university opera societies, too, have been enthusiastic to explore not only the byways of earlier opera but also of the nineteenth- and twentieth-century repertoire. Cambridge University Opera Society, for instance, staged within a few years such different operas as Smetana's *The Kiss* (1969, a revival), Dessau's *The Trial of Lukullus* (1970) and Philidor's *Tom Jones* (1971), both British premieres.

Finally, dissatisfaction with the lack of enthusiasm shown by the main houses for promoting new British operas led to the formation of both the English Opera Group (1947) and the New Opera Company (1957). The former commissioned five operas from Britten, Lennox Berkeley's *Ruth,* WILLIAM WALTON's *The Bear,* and Birtwistle's *Punch and Judy,* among others; the latter, Arthur Benjamin's *Tartuffe,* Gordon Crosse's *Purgatory,* Musgrave's *The Decision,* and Elisabeth Lutyens's *Time Off? Not a Ghost of a Chance!* By 1975, the New Opera Company had also staged fifteen British premieres of operas from abroad, including Schoenberg's *Erwartung,* Henze's *Boulevard Solitude,* Shostakovich's *The Nose,* and Szymanowski's *King Roger.* In both companies, leading British singers took most of the roles, Janet Baker, Heather Harper, Owen Brannigan, Peter Pears, John Shirley-Quirk, and Robert Tear regularly appearing with the English Opera Group. Indeed, since the Second World War a considerable number of British singers have pursued distinguished careers in opera, some, like Geraint Evans, Gwyneth Jones, and Bryn Terfel elevated to international stardom.

Trevor Bray

Bibliography

Donaldson, Frances. *The Royal Opera House in the Twentieth Century.* 1982.

Higgins, John, ed. *Glyndebourne: A Celebration.* 1984.

Northouse, Cameron. *Twentieth Century Opera in England and the United States.* 1976.

White, Eric Walter. *A History of English Opera.* 1983.

Orchestras

The founding of the Queen's Hall Orchestra in 1895 marked a new departure in London's musical life. Hitherto, orchestras, including those for the many theatres, had been drawn on an ad hoc basis from a pool of professional musicians who lived and taught in the capital. However, although the QHO was not originally constituted on a permanent basis, it became so, benefiting from a corporate identity and a stable management (initially Robert Newman). In 1904, a dispute with Henry Wood, its conductor, over a long-standing right to send a deputy if a player had a prior engagement, led around fifty players to break away and form the London Symphony Orchestra, which from the outset was self-governing. Hans Richter became the orchestra's first principal conductor, succeeded more recently by Pierre Monteux (1961), André Previn (1969), and Claudio Abbado (1979). A tour of the United States and Canada in 1912 was the first by a British orchestra, as was the world tour of 1964.

In 1927 the BBC took over the QHO (since 1915, New QHO), and its players became the nucleus of the BBC Symphony Orchestra, formed in 1930 and conducted by Adrian Boult, who rapidly brought it to the front rank. Players were salaried on a year-round contract, thereby gaining greater security, although this new arrangement was never adopted on a permanent basis by other orchestras (except those at the Royal Opera House, Covent Garden and the English National Opera), players usually being paid a fee for each engagement. Soon after the BBCSO's inception, guest conductors included Richard Strauss, Felix Weingartner, and Bruno Walter, and it was the first British orchestra to be conducted by Arturo Toscanini (in 1935). Other BBC orchestras were formed in the regions, the three most important being the BBC Northern Orchestra at Manchester in 1934 (renamed the BBCN Symphony Orchestra in 1967), and, in the following year, the BBC Scottish Orchestra at Glasgow (the BBCS Symphony Orchestra, 1967) and the BBC Welsh Orchestra at Cardiff (the BBCW Symphony Orchestra, 1974).

Both the London Philharmonic Orchestra (1932) and Royal Philharmonic Orchestra (1946) were founded by SIR THOMAS BEECHAM, testifying to his great entrepreneurial flair. The LPO soon rose to preeminence among London orchestras, and, despite financial troubles in the 1950s, regained its corporate identity during the 1960s and 1970s under such principal conductors as John Pritchard (from 1962), Bernard Haitinck (1967) and Georg Solti (1979). Finance for the RPO's launching was generated from substantial recording contracts, a similar arrangement funding the formation of the Philharmonia Orchestra (New PO, 1964–77) in 1945, by Walter Legge. Its considerable reputation, created through recordings, was consolidated in the 1960s when Otto Klemperer became its principal conductor.

Two orchestras had already been formed in the provinces before 1900—the Hallé at Manchester (1857) and the Bournemouth Municipal Orchestra (1897, renamed Bournemouth Symphony Orchestra, 1954)—and these were joined by the City of Birmingham Orchestra (1920, City of Birmingham Symphony Orchestra, 1948), the Royal Liverpool Philharmonic Orchestra (which became a full-time body in 1943), and orchestras for

Scotland, the Scottish National Orchestra (1951) at Glasgow, and for Northern Ireland, the Ulster Orchestra (1966) at Belfast. All these orchestras have gained considerable reputations, particularly when directed by such visionary conductors as John Barbirolli (Hallé, from 1943), Simon Rattle (CBSO, 1979), Charles Groves (Liverpool PO, 1963),and Alexander Gibson, the first Scotsman to conduct the SNO (1959).

In response to the growing awareness of how music written before 1800 was performed, a significant number of chamber orchestras were established, an early example being the London Chamber Orchestra (1921), founded by Anthony Bernard to specialize in seventeenth- and eighteenth-century repertoires. Both the Boyd Neel Orchestra (1932) and the Jacques Orchestra (1936) concentrated on Baroque and twentieth-century works, and the Goldsbrough Orchestra (1948), originally focusing on the eighteenth century, broadened its scope in 1960 when it was renamed the English Chamber Orchestra, becoming associated in particular with the English Opera Group, the Aldeburgh Festival, and BEN-JAMIN BRITTEN's music. The high standards of discipline and musicianship evident in the performances and recordings of the Academy of St. Martin-in-the-Fields (1959), formed and directed by the violinist Neville Marriner, set new standards, as did those of the London Sinfonietta (1968), conducted by David Atherton, an ensemble specializing in contemporary music, and capable, because of the flexibility of its consitution, of coping with almost any instrumental combination. The regions could also support new chamber ensembles, most notably the Northern Sinfonia (1961) at Newcastle-upon-Tyne and the Scottish Chamber Orchestra (1974) at Edinburgh. During the 1970s and 1980s, the quest for authenticity led to the formation of yet further specialist ensembles, but using period instruments (and some of the same players), most significantly the Academy of Ancient Music (conducted by Christopher Hogwood), the English Baroque Soloists (John Eliot Gardiner), the English Players (Trevor Pinnock), the Hanover Band (Roy Goodman), the London Classical Players (Roger Norrington), and the Taverner Players (Andrew Parrott), testifying to the continued richness and diversity of British musical life and confirming London's position as one of the most important musical capitals of the world.

Trevor Bray

Bibliography

Kennedy, Michael. *The Hallé 1858–1983: A History of the Orchestra*. 1983.

Kenyon, Nicholas. *The BBC Symphony Orchestra: The First Fifty Years, 1930–1980*. 1980.

Pearton, Maurice. *The LSO at 70: A History of the Orchestra*. 1974.

Pettitt, Stephen J. *Philharmonia Orchestra: A Record of Achievement, 1945–1985*. 1985.

Orwell, George (1903–1950)

George Orwell was the wintry conscience not only for England, but for much of the world through his two most influential books, *Animal Farm* (1945) and *Nineteen Eighty Four* (1949). He was born Eric Arthur Blair in India where his father was a civil servant engaged in supervising the opium trade. In 1907 Eric, his older sister Marjorie, and his mother returned to Henley in England, where his younger sister Avril was born. Orwell characterized himself, with that exactness of observation that would become his hallmark, as a member of the lower upper middle class. By that he meant that his father was a member by descent of the "established" classes, justifying the "upper" in his class designation, but that the family was not well off, justifying the term "lower". The family was determined that their son would have as many advantages as possible, and at the age of eight, he was sent away to St. Cyprian's, a "prep" school in Eastbourne. This was a traumatic experience as he felt, whether rightly or wrongly, that he was scorned by the formidable headmistress and his fellow students because of his comparative poverty. The years at St. Cyprian's were also important in shaping his attitude towards his country, as he was swept up in the intense patriotism of the First World War. The value of his education was that in his writings at the time of the Second World War he was able both to be a patriot and to call for a radical transformation of British society.

St. Cyprian's served its purpose and gave him the sort of education that won for him a position as a King's Scholar at Eton. There he would mix with the rich and the grand, as well as the extremely intelligent who were his fellow members of College, the home of the Scholars. He was at Eton from 1917 to 1921, but, rather unusually for a member of College, he did not go to university or into a prominent profession. Rather he became a police officer in Burma; in a sense going into his father's business. The beginning of his career was rather conventional, although less distinguished than one might have expected considering his education. What was unusual was that when he returned to England on leave in 1927, he decided to abandon his secure position in order to be a writer.

The first five years of this attempt were extremely difficult, but he used his partially self-inflicted experience of poverty to provide the material for his first book, *Down and Out in Paris and London*, published in 1933. Partially not to embarrass his family, and partially because he felt

a need to distance himself from his past, he chose to write under a pseudonym, choosing that most English of first names, George, and as a last name, the name of the river Orwell in Suffolk, near where his parents were now living in Southwold. Orwell was developing an extremely effective plain style that convinced the reader of the truthfulness of his account. During the 1930s he became a fairly well-known minor novelist. His first novel, *Burmese Days* (1934), drew upon his police experience. What was unusual in the book, as well as one of the most famous essays in the language, "Shooting an Elephant" (1936), was that he pointed out the illegitimacy of imperialism without feeling sentimental about those who were "oppressed". In 1935 he published *A Clergyman's Daughter* and in 1936 *Keep the Aspidistra Flying*. Both of these novels, of which later he was not particularly proud, dealt with the effects of poverty on members of the middle class. He himself was barely surviving financially, although he was doing an increasing amount of journalism. He came to the attention of VICTOR GOLLANCZ, the publisher and proprietor of the LEFT BOOK CLUB, and was commissioned to write an account of poverty in England. The result, *The Road to Wigan Pier* (1937), was a powerful account of the ravages of the Depression. Contrary to wishes of the Club, it was also an idiosyncratic autobiographical essay combining a critique of the pretensions of middle-class socialists whose crankiness would keep them at a distance from the working class with an attractive, but also a romantic, vision of the warmth and positive values of working-class life.

As a reporter, he went to Spain shortly after the outbreak of the SPANISH CIVIL WAR. The new socialist world that he found in Barcelona was one that he felt he must fight for, and he joined the militia of the POUM, a dissident semi-Trotskyite group. He was almost killed at the front by a bullet through his throat, and on his return to Barcelona he was caught up in the betrayal of the revolution by the Communists. Through his experience in Spain he became a committed socialist, but he also discovered that the socialist dream was as likely to be betrayed by those who claimed to be on the Left as by those who were on the Right of the political spectrum. He wrote a magnificent account of his Spanish experience, *Homage to Catalonia* (1938), which received scant attention when it was originally published and did not become well known until it was reissued in 1952. Upon his return to England he published one further traditional novel, *Coming Up for Air* (1939), which contrasted the false values of contemporary English society with what Orwell considered the greater genuineness of life before the First World War.

The Spanish experience, and his marriage to Eileen O'Shaughnessy in 1936, made him better able to come to terms with himself and his ideas. He now had become George Orwell, and thus he was known to those whom he met for the rest of his short life. He became much more prolific as a writer with innumerable essays and reviews. He was a founder of a new sort of approach to society, a combination of literary and sociological values that provided new insights, such as his famous essay on Charles Dickens (1940), and his non-patronizing and insightful approach to popular culture in his essays on Boy's Weeklies (1940) and on the significance of the slightly smutty postcards that were sold at seaside resorts, "The Art of Donald McGill" (1941). With great effectiveness, he drew attention to the ways in which language can be used to manipulate thought and hide truths in his essay "Politics and the English Language" (1946). With the outbreak of the SECOND WORLD WAR, he wanted to help the war effort, but his age and health meant that he could only be active in the HOME GUARD. He worked at the BBC, organizing broadcasts to India, and he wrote regular columns for the socialist weekly, *Tribune*. In *The Lion and the Unicorn* (1941) he put forward his analysis of England as a family but "with the wrong members in control". It was a family that needed to be both preserved in its respect for individualism and liberty and transformed into a more egalitarian society.

In Spain he had observed the Communists' betrayal of the socialist dream. The idea of the betrayal of the revolution crystallized in his brilliant fable, *Animal Farm* (1945), which he had difficulty getting published while the Soviet Union was still an ally. The book was a powerful indictment in its accuracy of what had happened in Russia but also fitted into the development of the Cold War in the aftermath of the Second World War. It made Orwell an internationally famous author. That was even more true four years later when he published *Nineteen Eighty-Four* (1949), his account of what has happened to England, now called Airstrip One, an outpost of the West, now known as Oceania, which is in constant battle with the East, although sides change easily, and the past is constantly rewritten to conform with the party line, the job of the very minor official, Winston Smith, who is the central figure in the novel. Orwell made permanent contributions in his conceptions of Big Brother, the Thought Police, Newspeak, "two plus two equals five." He remained his own special sort of socialist and saw the book as a warning of what might happen. Those on the Right chose to see it as a prophecy of what was the inevitable result of socialism. The book has had a continual influence and was much remarked upon around the world when the actual year, 1984, came and went.

Orwell died of tuberculosis in 1950, at the very beginning of his greatest fame. It was not until the years after his death that many of his essays were generally made available. He and his wife had adopted a son, but shortly thereafter she died unexpectedly in 1945 after a minor operation. He married Sonia Brownell in 1949.

For such a short life, particularly considering that he did not start writing until 1927 and did not publish his first book until 1933, he was amazingly prolific. Of his traditional novels, *Burmese Days*, which had the longest period of gestation, was his best. All of his books of reportage are excellent, with *The Road to Wigan Pier* being written with the most sense of personality and *Homage to Catalonia* with the greatest moral authority. *Animal Farm* is a gem, and *Nineteen Eighty-Four*, although crude at times (having been written by a dying man), has tremendous and memorable power. He was a great artist who created what at the same time was a plain prose in the great English tradition but also reflected the personality he wished to project, a teller of truth.

Peter Stansky

Bibliography

Crick, Bernard. *George Orwell*. 1980.

Meyers, Jeffrey and Valerie. *Orwell: An Annotated Bibliography of Criticism*. 1977.

Shelden, Michael. *Orwell: The Authorized Biography*. 1991.

Slater, Ian. *Orwell: The Road to Airstrip One*. 1985.

Stansky, Peter, and William Abrahams. *The Unknown Orwell*. 1972.

———. *Orwell: The Transformation*. 1979.

Woodcock, George. *The Crystal Spirit*. 1967.

Osborne, John James (1929–1994)

Born in Fulham, the son of a barmaid and a commercial artist, John Osborne came from the impoverished lower middle-class background he depicted in his plays. He worked as a journalist, stage manager, and actor before achieving fame with the production of his play *Look Back in Anger* by the English Stage Company at the Royal Court Theatre in 1956, which ushered in a new wave of playwrights and theatre practitioners. They sought to create a theatrical vocabulary to replace the conventions which had prevented mainstream theatre from reflecting the current social and political realities of twentieth-century history. Jimmy Porter, the play's famous protagonist, gave voice to the discontent of Osborne's generation: the play's title was used to label a group of young writers, including Osborne himself, as "angry young men".

Set in a shabby Midlands bedsitting room, the play exposes Jimmy's merciless attempts to undermine his wife Alison's upper middle-class complacency, a Strindbergian battle witnessed by Jimmy's peace-loving university chum, Cliff. The power of *Look Back in Anger* resides in its rhetoric, which integrates Osborne's naturalistic portrait of marital discord with an expressionistic attack on inertia and moral bankruptcy in the post-war British Establishment.

This stylistic tension became a fundamental principle of structure in Osborne's next successful stage play, *The Entertainer* (1957), in which the death of the British music hall symbolizes the decline of post-war Britain. The pathetic philanderings of the failed comedian Archie Rice are revealed in a series of short naturalistic scenes, while the the music hall routines express the "state of Britain" theme, performers and audience alike revealed as "dead behind the eyes". The play provided a vehicle for LAURENCE OLIVIER, whose seedy and tragic portrayal of Archie Rice was one of the highlights of the London theatre in the 1950s and a successful film as well.

Osborne's next successful ventures turned away from the contemporary world. *Luther* (1961) emphasizes Osborne's identification with heroes who are temperamentally unable to compromise their faith. In 1963 he wrote the screenplay for the highly succesful film, *Tom Jones*.

In 1964 the Royal Court staged *Inadmissible Evidence* with Nicol Williamson in the role of Maitland, a divorce lawyer who might be Jimmy Porter at forty. Many critics regard this as his finest play, pointing out that Osborne has here provided a more balanced perspective on the protagonist's rage against the world. By presenting the action of the play as a series of cinematic flashbacks framed by Maitland's tirade against a world of compromise and double standards, Osborne allows his audience to question the validity of Maitland's views without sacrificing its sympathy for his situation. The strategy reveals the play's overt theme to be the tragic failure of individuals to connect with the passion and suffering of others. The play was revived by the National Theatre to mixed reviews in 1993.

A Patriot for Me (1965), *Time Present* and *The Hotel in Amsterdam* (1968), and *West of Suez* (1971) all enjoyed successful runs and a measure of critical acclaim, but Osborne lost touch with the left-wing audiences who had thrilled to the rhetoric of Jimmy Porter. By the early 1970s his plays had begun to seem both dated and reactionary. But his first two volumes of autobiography, *A Better Class of Person* (1981) and *Almost a Gentleman* (1991), achieved critical and popular success.

Robert Gordon

Bibliography

Carter, Alan. *John Osborne*. 2nd ed. 1973.

Goldstone, Herbert. *Coping with Vulnerability: The Achievement of John Osborne*. 1982.

Hayman, Ronald. *John Osborne*. 2nd ed. 1970.

Hinchliffe, Arnold P. *John Osborne*. 1984.

Northouse, Cameron, and Thomas P. Walsh. *John Osborne: A Reference Guide*. 1974.

Trussler, Simon. *The Plays of John Osborne*. 1969.

Owen, Wilfred Edward Salter (1893–1918)

Wilfred Owen is the youngest of the War Poets whose writing inspired the protest of trench conditions and slaughter on the Western Front of the FIRST WORLD WAR, and whose death in the final week of the war became (like RUPERT BROOKE's) a symbol of the fate of a generation of "doomed youth".

Born in Oswestry, Shropshire, of Welsh descent, Owen failed to win a university scholarship and, after some months as an unpaid church worker in Berkshire, went to Bordeaux as a language tutor, remaining in France until autumn 1915 when he enlisted. He arrived on the SOMME as a platoon commander in January 1917. After three months in the front line he was sent home due to hysterical "neurasthenia" or shell shock. He said that it was not the fighting that caused his collapse but having to hold a position for several days alongside a dead fellow officer whose body "lay in various places around and about." He was treated at Craiglockhart War Hospital, Edinburgh, under the holistic regime of Dr. A.J. Brock, a disciple of Patrick Geddes. Owen returned to the Western Front in September 1918 and was awarded a Military Cross in October. He was killed in action 4 November, and the news of his death reached the family as church bells announced the Armistice.

Owen's early verse was influenced by Keats, Swinburne, Decadence, and French Symbolism, and it is strongly flavored by narcissistic homoeroticism, encouraged in Owen by Laurent Tailhade (1854–1919), the Decadent poet and anarchist poseur. When Owen met SIEGFRIED SASSOON at Craiglockhart, where Owen edited the hospital magazine, Sassoon inspired him to merge his poetic sensibilities with response to the horrors of trench warfare and with angry protest (shared by ROBERT GRAVES as well as Sassoon) at civilian failure to understand what front-line soldiers were enduring. This gave purpose and sinew to Owen's poetry. His return to the front was for the sake of both leadership and witness. Blending the purple diction of Decadence with the realism and homely language adopted by the pre-war Georgian Poets, he produced some of the most striking literature of the First World War, in tragic satires like "Strange

Meeting, "Spring Offensive," "Mental Cases," "Futility," "Disabled," "Smile, Smile, Smile," and "Dulce et Decorum Est".

Owen's reputation began posthumously with the publication in 1920 of *Poems*, edited by Sassoon. Unlike Sassoon and Graves, who survived, Owen came to represent the young men sacrificed in the cause of absolute but futile "Victory" and the gulf between old and young.

The blend of disgusting detail and tender feeling in Owen's verse resonated with the mood of ELIOT'S *The Waste Land* (1922) and influenced inter-war writers like AUDEN, MACNIECE, and SPENDER. Technically, Owen's experimental use of heavily stressed lines and pararhyme (e.g. silent/salient) remain accessible to the general reader whom modernism's more rigorous experiments deter.

Increasingly, the younger generation saw the First World War through the eyes of Owen. His life and work had renewed impact in the 1960s, with the publication of *Collected Poems*, edited by C. DAY LEWIS (1963), and of his complete family letters and his brother Harold Owen's memoir, *Journey from Obscurity* (1963–5). Through inclusion in War Poetry anthologies studied in schools and colleges Owen's writing contributed to the widespread "anti-war" culture in Britain at the time of the Vietnam conflict.

Most recently, his idealizing response to the male body (previously unmentioned at the family's behest) has been recovered and integrated into the long British tradition of homoerotic literature. Owen remains the most powerful and best known War Poet of the century, still able to rouse horror and pity in new readers.

Jan Marsh

Bibliography

Bergonzi, Bernard. *Heroes' Twilight*. 1965
Fussell, Paul. *The Great War and Modern Memory*. 1975.
Hibberd, Dominic. *Owen the Poet*. 1986.
Owen, Harold, *Journey from Obscurity*. 3 vols. 1963–5.
———, and John Bell, eds. *Wilfred Owen: Collected Letters*. 1967.
Stallworthy, Jon. *Wilfred Owen*. 1974.

Oxford, University of

In 1900 Oxford was one of the two principal seats of learning in England. This dominant position was maintained in the late twentieth century despite changes in the structure of English education following the creation of new universities and a considerable expansion of student numbers. State intervention in the Victorian period had created in Oxford an essentially self-governing university. The age of state funding, which began in 1919 and which by 1950 accounted for more than half of the university's income,

barely altered this picture. A royal commission appointed in 1919 under the chairmanship of H.H. ASQUITH took an evolutionary approach to university reform. A later internal commission of inquiry chaired by Lord Franks, set up in response to a growing body of criticism levelled at Oxford's traditional structures, represented one of the most extensive exercises in self-scrutiny undertaken by a university in modern times. But its report, published in 1966, and its aftermath, while leading to significant modernization of the university's administrative machinery, left Oxford essentially a collegiate university.

In 1900 there were twenty fully-fledged colleges; new colleges, notably St. Catherine's (1960), the foundation of graduate colleges, and the full recognition of the existing women's halls had raised the total to thirty-five by 1990. The majority were primarily concerned with undergraduate education. The colleges' strongly pedagogic emphasis was associated with the tutorial system, a method of individual tuition developed in Oxford and CAMBRIDGE in the previous century.

Undergraduate studies continued to be dominated by the demands of the honor schools (as the various courses of studies leading to the examinations for the B.A. degree were called). In 1900 the range comprised *Literae Humaniores* ("Greats") comprising Greek and Latin literature, philosophy, and ancient history (established in 1800); Mathematics (1807); Natural Sciences (1850); Jurisprudence (1850); Modern History (1850); Theology (1869); Oriental Studies (1886); English (1894). To these were added Modern Languages (1903); Philosophy, Politics, and Economics (1920); Geography (1932); Psychology, Philosophy and Physiology (1947); and Music (1950). The Natural Sciences, envisaged by the Victorians as a totality, divided into the various disciplines comprising the physical and biological sciences. Combinations of honor schools were introduced in the 1960s and following decades.

The Oxford curriculum had some markedly conservative tendencies. A knowledge of Greek remained compulsory until 1920, and Latin until 1960, while an examination in Divinity, a vestige of Oxford's earlier character as an exclusively CHURCH OF ENGLAND institution, remained obligatory for Anglicans until 1932. *Literae Humaniores* remained the most prestigious of the arts diciplines until the second half of the century, despite the numerical predominance of Modern History. But the modern course of Philosophy, Politics, and Economics (PPE) rapidly established itself both in standing and numbers. In their formative years both English and Modern Languages were hindered by tensions between the competing claims of philology and literature.

The growth of science, while perhaps the most siginficant change in curricular patterns in twentieth-century Oxford, was slow to take effect, and well into the second half of the century sixth-formers considering university entrance were advised, "Oxford for Arts, Cambridge for Science". In 1923 80 percent of students were reading arts and social sciences, and only 20 percent science and medicine; in 1958 scientists remained heavily in a minority (27 percent). The most rapid growth in science came in the following thirty years (42 percent of Oxford students were studying science disciplines in 1990).

The weakness of Oxford science in the early part of the century, though often exaggerated, was undeniable. The revival of the Clarendon laboratory through research in the field of low temperature PHYSICS took place between the wars, and was strengthened by the arrival of academic REFUGEES from Nazism. CHEMISTRY had traditionally been the strongest area of Oxford science; for most of the period it had the largest number of students among the science disciplines, and its reputation was confirmed by Nobel Prize-winning research. But the most celebrated achievement of Oxford science was the development of penicillin in the Pathology laboratory, for which a Nobel Prize was awarded in 1945.

Oxford scholarship in the arts was sustained by the Bodleian Library, which by 1987 had some 5 million books, and disseminated by the Oxford University Press, which became a model for other university presses. A New York branch opened in 1896. Its publications—notably the *Oxford English Dictionary* (1933)—became standard throughout the English-speaking world. Dictionaries came to replace bibles as the flagship publications of the press.

Although the scholarly output of Oxford's dons was often considerable, the local academic style in the first half of the century, particularly in the arts disciplines, was resistant to what was regarded as the teutonic pedantry of organized research. Research degrees (the B.Sc. and B.Litt.) were first introduced in 1895, but a doctoral-level credential (the D.Phil.) was not created until 1917. This was done mainly to attract overseas students, especially Americans, who had traditionally sought research training in Germany. Numbers of research students rose slowly: there were only 200 in 1939. By 1970 this figure reached 3,000; and in 1990, 3,700 (27 percent of the student population). Six new colleges were established to cater for graduate students: Green (1979), Linacre (1962), Nuffield (1937), St. Antony's (1948), St. Cross (1965), and Wolfson (1964).

Women's education at Oxford dated from the creation in the late nineteenth century of residential single-sex colleges, of which the earliest were Lady Margaret Hall and Somerville (both founded in 1879). Although permitted to enter university examinations, women were not admitted as full members of the unversity until 1920. Thereafter assimilation seemed to be the dominant theme, culminating in the constitutional changes which brought the five women's colleges into line with the men's colleges in 1959. Numerically, however, Oxford was still predominantly a male university: women represented 16 percent of students in 1965. Five of the men's colleges began to admit women in 1974; the remainder soon followed, while three of the women's colleges started to admit men. By 1986 only St. Hilda's and Somerville survived as single-sex colleges. The results of this sudden transformation to coeducation were much debated. Meanwhile the proportion of women students at Oxford doubled from 19 percent in 1968 to 38 percent in 1988.

Oxford continued to be nursery for future politicians: it educated nearly half of the Prime Ministers who held office between 1900 and 1987, a third of CABINET ministers, and a fifth of MPs. Institutions such as the Oxford Union Society (a student debating society) had traditionally acted as a preparation for political life. New developments, such as the university's extra-mural work, and the establishment in 1899 of Ruskin College for working-class students, provided the basis for links with the LABOUR PARTY.

For much of the century the university was best known to the British public for its sporting activities: annual fixtures with Cambridge, especially the boat race and rugby match, and individual feats, such as the breaking of the four minute mile record by Roger Bannister in 1954, commanded national attention. The essence of Oxford sport, however, was participation; university clubs were self-financing and run by the students themselves, while professionalism had been eschewed at an early date.

Oxford's position as an international university of the Anglophone world was reinforced by the scholarships founded by Cecil Rhodes to bring students from the Empire and the United States. These came into effect in 1903. By 1964 overseas students at Oxford were still predominantly drawn from the Commonwealth and the United States. DECOLONIZATION and Britain's entry into the EUROPEAN COMMUNITY suggested a change in the pattern, though in 1990 students from other EC countries still represented only 3 percent of the 13,948 students at Oxford (the total from overseas being over 18 percent). The creation, in 1992, of European Rhodes scholarships raised the possibility that in the next century Oxford might more fully reclaim its medieval inheritance as one of the original network of European universities.

M.C. Curthoys

Bibliography

Harrison, Brian H., ed. *History of the University of Oxford: The Twentieth Century.* vol viii. 1994.

———. "Oxford and the Labour Movement," *Twentieth Century British History,* vol. 2 (1991), pp. 226–71.

Halsey, A.H. *Decline of Donnish Dominion: The British Academic Professions in the Twentieth Century.* 1992.

Hibbert, Christopher, ed. *The Encyclopaedia of Oxford.* 1988.

Soares, Joseph. *The Decline of Privilege: The Modernization of Oxford University.* 1999.

Pacifism

While pacifism was certainly extant as a distinctive ideology in British society prior to the twentieth century, the Society of Friends being a prime example, scholars tend to see its modern manifestation beginning with the First World War. It was the issue of conscription that galvanized pacifists into action, leading to the formation of the No-Conscription Fellowship in late 1914 under the leadership of Fenner Brockway and Clifford Allen. The Fellowship of Reconciliation was also founded that same year by an energetic group of Christian pacifists, including Henry T. Hodgkin, the Rev. Richard Roberts, and Lucy Gardner, most of whom emerged out of a Free Church or Quaker tradition. While the number of young men who defied the state and went to prison rather than fight was relatively small, their courage, suffering, and dignified witness became important in the developing mythology of the peace movement.

After the war the No-Conscription Fellowship was abolished and the F.O.R. experienced a decline in membership, the latter's problems no doubt due in part due to the founding of two new organizations, the War Resisters' International and the No More War Movement, both of which tended to attract pacifists who believed that socialism was a necessary prerequisite to achieving peace. By far the most successful peace organization during the 1920s was the League of Nations Union, which was not strictly pacifist. Headed by Lord Robert Cecil and Gilbert Murray, it eventually claimed over 400,000 members devoted to the concept of international order and collective security. Its popularity was probably due to the fact that the favorable state of international relations during the 1920s led people to believe that the League of Nations was the organization best positioned to secure disarmament and international security, and that its authority to impose economic, financial, and even military sanctions would deter potential aggressors.

Ironically, as the international scene deteriorated in the early 1930s, interest in peace quickened. Pacifist books and plays enjoyed immense popularity; peace rallies could attract large crowds; famous personalities announced their conversion to pacifism; and anti-war resolutions were adopted by universities, trade unions, women's groups, and even major political parties. Not surprisingly the 1930s has sometimes been referred to as the hey-day of British pacifism. However, this peace sentiment was the product of an uneasy coalition of several disparate groups, and its unity was put to the test by the rise of the Fascist dictators. An important turning point occurred in 1935 when Fascist Italy invaded Abyssinia. A number of peace advocates rallied to the League of Nations, calling for economic sanctions to be imposed upon Italy, even at the risk of war. Then in the following year, the Spanish Civil War broke out, and many British socialists, previously committed to peace, rallied to the cause of Spanish republicanism, calling for arms and volunteers in the struggle against Fascism. The fragility of the peace coalition stood starkly exposed.

But those peace societies that resisted the call for economic sanctions or military assistance experienced much growth. For them pacifism had always implied unconditional opposition to all wars and taking of human life, regardless of the issues involved. The Fellowship of Reconciliation saw membership almost triple to 9,800 between 1934 and 1939, and the Council of Christian Pacifist Groups was founded to coordinate the ever increasing activity of pacifists within the various Christian denominations. But the real success story of the 1930s was the phenomenal growth of the Peace Pledge Union, founded by the Rev. Dick Sheppard in 1936. Its members signed a pledge to renounce war and never support another one, and within a short time the PPU claimed over 100,000 members, a figure that would eventually rise to 136,000. Another important development was the creation of the Embassies of Reconciliation in 1936, which pioneered in the field of personal diplomacy by sending noted pacifists abroad to meet with heads of state and present to them the Christian call for peace and a Christian program of peacemaking. George Lansbury, a former leader of the Labour Party, visited a number of European leaders, including Hitler and Mussolini, and secured publicity for the pacifist cause in the process.

When war broke out in 1939, many pacifists defected and supported the war effort, including such names as Maude Royden, Bertrand

Russell, Storm Jameson, Cyril Joad, Rose Macaulay, and A.A. Milne. Significantly, many of these ex-pacifists belonged to the Peace Pledge Union, while the Fellowship of Reconciliation, on the other hand, experienced few defections. None of the existing peace societies attempted seriously to obstruct the war effort; instead, these societies offered dignified witness to their belief and engaged in a variety of religious, humanitarian, and service projects, and some individuals even participated in civil defence schemes. It should also be emphasized that Christian pacifists from many denominations established close ties with one another during the war, and this cooperation and goodwill contributed substantially to the success of the world ecumenical movement in the post-war period.

After the war some societies ceased to exist while others went into a period of swift and noticeable decline. Occasionally, certain issues could galvanize large segments of the British public into action, notably the CAMPAIGN FOR NUCLEAR DISARMAMENT, opposition to America's involvement in Vietnam, and the attempt during the 1980s to install and maintain American cruise missiles on British soil. Admittedly, these issues were not always strictly pacifist in nature, but the younger generation found it difficult to separate pacifism from other causes, such as imperialism, sexism, racism, social injustice, gay liberation, and ecological concerns.

David C. Lukowitz

Bibliography

Ceadel, Martin. *Pacifism in Britain, 1914–1945: The Defining of a Faith.* 1980.

———. *Thinking About Peace and War.* 1987.

Moorehead, Caroline. *Troublesome People: The Warriors of Pacifism.* 1986.

Robbins, Keith. *The Abolition of War: The Peace Movement in Britain, 1914–1919.* 1976.

Wallis, Jill. *Valiant for Peace: A History of the Fellowship of Reconciliation, 1914 to 1989.* 1991.

Palestine

The three decades of British rule in Palestine after 1917 crucially changed the demographic and political shape of the country, paving the way for the establishment of the State of Israel upon the British departure in 1948.

The British administration in Palestine was inaugurated in December 1917 when General Sir Edmund Allenby entered Jerusalem after ousting the Ottoman Turks from southern Palestine. The remainder of the country was occupied by the British in the autumn of 1918. Until 30 June 1920 a British military administration ruled Palestine under the military law of occupation which called for the maintenance, so far as practicable, of the *status quo ante bellum.*

Even before the British occupation the question of the post-war disposition of Palestine had been the subject of dispute among the Allied governments as well as the Zionists and the Sherifian Arab regime in the Hejaz. In 1915 the British-Arab exchange of letters known as the McMahon-Hussein correspondence provided an ambiguous basis for later Arab claims that Palestine was within the area promised by the British for a future pan-Arab state. In 1916 secret Anglo-French discussions resulted in the Sykes-Picot agreement which provided for the partition of the central Middle East into zones of British and French dominance; central Palestine, under this scheme, was assigned to a vaguely defined international regime. In November 1917 the British government, after lengthy discussions with the Zionists, issued the Balfour Declaration, which promised to facilitate the establishment of a Jewish National Home in Palestine. Later statements by the Allied governments promised that the liberated peoples of the Ottoman Empire would be granted the right to self-determination.

At the Paris Peace Conference in 1919 both Zionist and Arab delegations appeared. On 3 January 1919 a tentative agreement was signed by the Zionist leader, Dr Chaim Weizmann, with the Emir Faisal, leader of the Hejazi delegation which seemed to indicate Hejazi acquiescence in the establishment of a Jewish National Home in Palestine. But it was later repudiated by Faisal and rejected by Arab nationalists in Palestine itself.

The British, convinced that they were the only suitable rulers for Palestine, persuaded the French and other powers to grant Britain a "mandate" under the authority of the LEAGUE OF NATIONS to rule Palestine until it was fit for independence. Sophisticated lobbying by the Zionists secured the insertion into the mandate of several clauses which furnished guarantees in international law for the establishment and development of the Jewish National Home.

Meanwhile, anti-Jewish riots in Jerusalem in April 1920 led the British government to replace the military by a civil administration prior to finalizing the mandate. On 30 June 1920 SIR HERBERT SAMUEL, a former LIBERAL minister, took office as first High Commissioner. The first of seven holders of the post and the only one who was a Jew, Samuel embarked on efforts to persuade the Arab nationalist leadership, drawn mainly from the notable class, to acquiesce in the establishment of the Jewish National Home. Further anti-Jewish riots in Jaffa and elsewhere in May 1921 led him to issue a reformulation of British policy in 1922 in a white paper. This sought to balance support for the Jewish National Home with assurances of safeguards for the Arab majority. Samuel also tried to establish an elected legislative council, but the elections were boycotted by the Arabs. Subsequent attempts to set up an unelected Advisory Council and an Arab Agency on a par with the recognized Jewish Agency (at that time identical with the Zionist Organization) also failed. As a result, from 1917 to 1948 Palestine was, in effect, an unfettered British colonial autocracy.

Under Samuel's rule, which continued until 1925, immigration, mainly from eastern Europe, gradually increased the Jewish proportion of the population. Large tracts of cultivable land, particularly in the Valley of Jezreel, were purchased for Jewish settlement, mainly from absentee Arab landlords. Jewish institutions, such as *Vaad Leumi* (National Council), the *Histadrut*, the Zionist labor union, and the underground *Haganah* (Zionist defence force) created the embryo of the national institutions of the Jewish state.

In an effort to provide some institutional counterweight for the Arab majority, Samuel established the Supreme Muslim Council, which was given charge of all Muslim *awkaf* (religious trusts), mosques, and other Muslim bodies in Palestine. He selected Haj Amin al-Husseini to serve as President of the council and in early 1921 engineered his appointment as Mufti of Jerusalem. Husseini's additional office as head of the Supreme Muslim Council endowed him with unparalleled authority, and by the end of the 1920s he had emerged as the leading figure of Arab Palestine. His prestige was enhanced by a controversy between Arabs and Jews in 1928–9 over religious rights on the Temple Mount *(Haram al-Sharif)* and the Western ("Wailing") Wall in Jerusalem, culminating in severe riots in Jerusalem in August 1929.

In the early 1930s Jewish immigration, mainly from Poland and Nazi Germany, reached unprecedented levels. By 1935 the 355,000 Jews in Palestine constituted 27 percent of the total population. The Arabs now feared that, if the influx continued unchecked, they might soon become a minority in their own country. In 1936 an Arab general strike in protest against Jewish immigration developed into a nationwide revolt against British rule and against the Jewish National Home. When efforts of the High Commissioner, Sir Arthur Wauchope, to conciliate the Arabs failed, the British turned instead to repression. Military forces, eventually amounting to some 40 percent of the entire field strength of the British ARMY, were deployed to put down the rebels. Over a hundred captured Arab rebels were hanged before the revolt collapsed in early 1939.

Meanwhile the Mufti, whose Arab Higher Committee was regarded as the chief inspiration of the revolt, had evaded arrest and fled the country. In 1937 a Royal Commission, headed by Earl Peel, reported in favor of partition of Palestine into separate Jewish and Arab states, with a residual British mandatory area. The government at first accepted the report but, in the face of Arab opposition to partition, eventually backed away from the idea. In February–March 1939 a conference in London failed to produce agreement. The government felt an overriding need, given the dangerous international situation, to reduce its military commitment in Palestine. The policy announced in May 1939 limited Jewish immigration to no more than 75,000 over the next five years and sought to restrict land transfers from Arab to Jews.

This policy was maintained throughout the war, the British authorities resorting to extreme measures, including force, to prevent boatloads of Jewish refugees from Nazi Europe from landing in Palestine. Jewish resentment led to the rise of terrorist organizations such as the Irgun Zvai Leumi, headed by Menahem Begin, and the Stern Gang. In 1944 members of the Stern Gang assassinated the British Minister in the Middle East, Lord Moyne, in Cairo. Thereafter an escalating conflict between the Jewish terrorist organizations and the British army inflamed the politics of Palestine.

When the LABOUR government assumed office in Britain in 1945, British policy did not change. In spite of earlier pro-Zionist party policy statements, Labour in power, and particularly the Foreign Secretary, ERNEST BEVIN, resisted pressure to admit large numbers of Jewish immigrants to Palestine or to permit the establishment of a Jewish state. The government found itself caught between conflicting pressures: in Palestine the mainstream Zionist underground, the Haganah, joined forces with the terrorist groups in order to try to compel the British to admit Jewish immigrants; in the United States, on which Britain was now heavily dependent for economic aid, the Zionists mobilized effectively as a political lobby; but the newly formed League of Arab States demanded that Britain concede the Palestinian Arab demand for an independent Arab state in Palestine; the government feared that the entire British position in the Middle East, including vital assets such as the Suez Canal and the oil fields of Iraq, might be endangered if it acceded to Zionist demands; it feared the consequences for ANGLO-AMERICAN RELATIONS if it yielded to the Arabs.

The result was a long period of irresolution and drift. In the autumn of 1945 the British and American governments agreed on the appointment of a joint Anglo-American Committee of Inquiry to look into the problems of Palestine and of the Jewish "displaced persons", as the survivors of Hitler's death camps in Europe were called. The committee reported in April 1946, but its major immediate recommendation, to admit 100,000 Jewish refugees to Palestine, was rejected by the British government. Prime Minister CLEMENT ATTLEE, announced that an essential pre-condition would be the disarming of all illegal forces in Palestine, a proposal the Zionists rejected.

Meanwhile the military situation on the ground deteriorated in spite of the deployment of huge British forces. Terrorist incidents such as the massive bomb explosion in 1946 at the King David Hotel, the British military headquarters in Jerusalem, which killed ninety British, Jewish, and Arab victims, led to a partial breakdown of morale in the British army in Palestine and counter-terrorism against Jewish targets. At the same time Arab-Jewish violence also increased.

After further efforts to obtain a settlement by agreement failed, the government announced in 1947 that it would return the mandate to the United Nations and withdraw from Palestine. The United Nations sent a committee to Palestine to investigate the position, and on the basis of its proposals the UN General Assembly, on 29 November 1947, voted by the necessary two-thirds majority in favor of the partition of Palestine into separate Jewish and Arab states.

The remaining five and a half months of British rule were a descent into chaos. British authority collapsed as the rivals for the succession attempted to take over power on a local level in advance of the British withdrawal. By early 1948 the British army made no pretense of doing more than protecting British installations and personnel. By April full-scale civil war was in progress between Jewish armed forces and Arab irregulars supported by the armies of surrounding Arab states. A massive flight began of the Palestinian Arab population, in some areas forced to leave by the Zionists.

On 14 May the Zionist leader, David Ben Gurion, declared the establishment of the State of Israel. At midnight on the same day British rule ended when the last High Commissioner, Sir Alan Cunningham, embarked on a British warship at Haifa. Thirty years of British rule collapsed in ignominy and historic recriminations of which echoes resound to the present day.

Bernard Wasserstein

Bibliography

Morris, Benny. *The Birth of the Palestinian Refugee Problem 1947–1949.* 1987.

Stein, Leonard. *The Balfour Declaration.* 1961.

Segev, Tom. *One Palestine, Complete: Jews and Arabs Under the British Mandate.* 2000.

Sykes, Christopher. *Crossroads to Israel: Palestine from Balfour to Bevin.* 1965.

Wasserstein, Bernard. *The British in Palestine: The Mandatory Government and the Arab-Jewish Conflict 1917–1929.* 1978.

Pankhurst, Emmeline (1858–1928), Christabel (Harriette) (1880–1958), (Estelle) Sylvia (1882–1960)

Known primarily for their instigation of militancy on behalf of WOMEN'S SUFFRAGE, the Pankhursts injected vitality and imagination into the politics of the early twentieth century. Emmeline (née Goulden) and her daughters Christabel and Sylvia contributed their considerable energies to progressive causes, though only Sylvia would remain constant to the beliefs instilled in her from childhood by her parents.

Emmeline Pankhurst, hailing from a Radical family in Manchester and marrying at the age of twenty a prominent Radical lawyer, Richard Marsden Pankhurst (1835–98), became involved in suffrage and feminist politics at an early age. The birth of her children, Christabel, Sylvia, Frank, Adela, and Harry, did not deter her from an active political life, which included organizing for suffrage and for married women's property rights, membership in the socialist INDEPENDENT LABOUR PARTY (ILP), and a stint as a Poor Law Guardian in the 1890s. When the ILP refused to espouse votes for women, Emmeline formed the WOMEN'S SOCIAL AND POLITICAL UNION (WSPU) in 1903 to mobilize working-class women on behalf of suffrage.

Christabel Pankhurst, while still a law student at Owens College, first initiated WSPU acts of militancy in 1905, when she and Annie Kenney (1879–1953) were ejected from Free Trade Hall in Manchester for heckling SIR EDWARD GREY. Christabel spat at a policeman in an effort to force her arrest; she was fined and, upon refusing to pay, put in prison. The ensuing publicity brought the cause of women's suffrage into the public eye as never before. The WSPU moved to London where it pursued a policy of spectacular public protest. In 1907 the WSPU organized a "Mud March," in which 3,000 women carrying banners and stepping to the beat of brass bands, proceeded from Hyde Park to Exeter Hall demanding votes for women. Such activities succeeded beyond all expectations in focusing the public spotlight upon the women's cause and in increasing the ranks of suffragists, but much of that success depended upon the willingness of suffragettes, as WSPU members were called, to follow the Pankhursts without question. Many were unable to do so. In 1907 Teresa Billington-Greig (1877–1964), Charlotte Despard (1844–1939), and others, disillusioned by Christabel and Emmeline Pankhurst's anti-democratic ways and their abandonment of the ILP and of socialism, broke away and formed the Women's Freedom League. Sylvia Pankhurst, who had interrupted her art studies to work for the WSPU, shared their disillusionment but remained loyal to her mother and sister until 1912.

Until the summer of 1909 the Pankhursts eschewed violence. Suffragettes heckled CABINET ministers and obstructed political meetings; they marched on Parliament to demand meetings with MPs. Often they were met with violence at the hands of the police and civilian bystanders before being arrested. In the summer of 1909 the militants turned to stone-throwing to protest against politicians who refused their demands. Their symbolic protests also served to cut short the sometimes brutal struggles with police before they were arrested. Also during the summer of 1909 militant suffragists began to hunger strike in prison, demanding that their sentences be reduced to reflect more accurately the nature of their crimes and that they be treated as political prisoners rather than as criminals. The authorities responded with forced feedings, whose violence led both sympathizers and opponents of women's suffrage to decry the government's actions.

By 1910, with a large measure of support for women's suffrage within Parliament, it appeared that a bill enfranchising women had a good chance of passing, and the WSPU ceased its militancy. When, however, Prime Minister AsQUITH torpedoed a Conciliation Bill designed to appeal to all parties, the WSPU abandoned its truce. On November 18, a day that became known as "Black Friday" in the annals of suffrage history, Emmeline Pankhurst led suffragettes on a march from Caxton Hall to Parliament Square, where they were attacked and sexually molested by police and civilian bystanders in a confrontation that lasted six hours. While the Pankhursts did not court these assaults, such vivid demonstrations of sexual violence against women acted as powerful recruiting agents.

In 1911 the Conciliation Bill was revived, and again the Pankhursts halted their militant activities. But when the government appeared to sink the bill for a second time, the WSPU erupted in acts of intentional law-breaking. In March 1912 Mrs. Pankhurst joined in smashing windows at 10 Downing Street, while coordinated attacks left countless windows shattered elsewhere in London. Arrested were 217 suffragettes, including Emmeline Pankhurst and Emmeline (1867–1954) and Frederick (1871–1961) Pethick Lawrence, who were charged with inciting to riot and sentenced to nine months in prison. Embarking upon a hunger strike, they became so ill that officials were forced to release them. Mrs. Pankhurst announced her intention of continuing violent acts and of expanding them to include arson. The Pethick Lawrences, who had financed the activities of the WSPU since its earliest days, resigned in protest, taking their newspaper, *Votes for Women,* with them. Christabel, meanwhile, had fled to Paris, and began to edit the *Suffragette* in its stead. In it she published a series of articles on venereal disease, later compiled in a volume entitled *The Great Scourge and How To End It* (1913), that reflected on the direct connections between women's political powerlessness and their vulnerability to the sexual depredations of men. Sylvia, who could no longer countenance the behavior of her mother and sister, broke with them and devoted all her energies to the East London Federation of Suffragettes, a working-class women's organization that retained its affiliation with the ILP. She also began a newspaper called *The Woman's Dreadnought,* which featured the concerns of working-class women.

In 1913 the WSPU embarked upon another round of law-breaking, again in response to the government's betrayal of a promise to bring in a women's suffrage provision. DAVID LLOYD GEORGE's country house was set afire, prompting authorities to arrest Emmeline Pankhurst for inciting to commit a felony. She received three years imprisonment. In anticipation of her cutting short her prison term by embarking on a hunger strike, the government passed the "Cat and Mouse Act" (1913), which enabled it to release a hunger-striking prisoner and reincarcerate her after she had recovered from her ordeal. Under the Cat and Mouse Act, Mrs. Pankhurst was released and re-imprisoned numerous times, so that she had served only thirty days of her sentence between April 1913 and April 1914.

The split between Sylvia and her mother and sister worsened during the FIRST WORLD WAR. While Emmeline and Christabel devoted their energies to the war effort, Sylvia, denouncing war, concentrated on socialist rather than on feminist issues, changing the name of her newspaper to *The Worker's Dreadnought,* and welcoming wholeheartedly the Russian Revolution. In 1920 she helped to form the COMMUNIST PARTY in Britain and was tried and sentenced to a five month term for sedition for an article she published in the *Dreadnought.* Her refusal to marry the father of her son, Richard Pankhurst (1927–), an Italian exile by the name of Sylvio Corio, completed the estrangement of her mother. With Corio, Sylvia Pankhurst continued to pursue radical causes, engaging in anti-Fascist activity in the 1920s and 1930s and devoting her life after 1936 to the cause of Ethiopia.

Emmeline and Christabel Pankhurst, by contrast, abandoned their FEMINIST activity, although they did help to organize a demonstration demanding "women's right to serve" in munitions factories and other jobs that would support the war effort in 1915. In 1917 they transformed the WSPU into the Women's Party but did not involve themselves in the negotiations that resulted in a measure of women's suffrage in 1918. Christabel's failure to win election to Parliament in 1918 and 1919 resulted in the demise of the Women's Party. She joined the Second Adventist movement, seeing in the second coming of Christ the solution to the ills she had hoped suffrage would alleviate. Withdrawing from politics, she spent most of her later years in the United States, where she died in 1958.

Emmeline, in 1918, embarked for Canada, where she lectured on behalf of the National Council for Combating Venereal Disease for seven years. In 1925 she returned to England, joined the CONSERVATIVE PARTY, and was adopted as a parliamentary candidate for Whitechapel, much to the distress of Sylvia, but did not live long enough to contest the seat.

Although the women's suffrage campaign had existed for almost forty years before the WSPU burst upon the scene, and the victory won in 1918 owed at least as much to the efforts of the constitutional suffragists within the National Union of Women's Suffrage Societies, there can be no doubt that the provocative tactics of the Pankhursts brought to the cause of votes for women an energy and visibility that transformed the movement and helped to challenge the whole gender system of the early twentieth century.

Susan Kingsley Kent

Bibliography

Mitchell, David. *Queen Christabel.* 1977.

Pankhurst, Emmeline. *My Own Story.* 1914.

Pankhurst, E. Sylvia. *The Suffragette Movement.* new ed. 1977.

Raeburn, Antonia. *The Militant Suffragettes.* 1973.

Romero, Patricia W. *E. Sylvia Pankhurst: Portrait of a Radical.* 1987.

Sarah, Elizabeth. "Christabel Pankhurst: Reclaiming Her Power (1880–1958)" in Dale Spender, ed., *Feminist Theorists.* 1983. pp. 256–84.

Passchendaele [Third Battle of Ypres]

The British Commander-in-Chief, SIR DOUGLAS HAIG, had planned an attack from the Ypres Salient as early as 1916. However, the SOMME operation in that year and the British role in the Nivelle offensive the following spring delayed the plan until the summer of 1917. The operation called for an attack by fifteen British divisions from the Salient. They would first capture the Passchendaele Ridge and then advance on Roulers and Thourout. Finally, in conjunction with a force attacking from Nieuport, the Belgian coast would be cleared, their U-boat bases captured,

and German lateral communications to the south cut, ensuring a general German withdrawal from the entire northern section of the Western Front.

The operation was misconceived from the outset. Haig had to capture the Messines Ridge to deny the Germans observation over the section of the Salient from which his main operation was to be launched. In an action brilliantly planned by General Sir Herbert Plumer, this was achieved on 7 June. But Haig had never intended launching his main strike until the end of July. Thus the Germans were given seven weeks to prepare their defenses for the coming battle. By the time the main attack began 31 July 1917, they had created a checkerboard defense to a depth of 10,000 yards.

Nevertheless, after a sixteen-day artillery bombardment of unprecedented ferocity, the first day of battle was a partial success for the British. General Sir Hubert Gough's Fifth Army, aided by a French Corps, gained good ground in the northern section of the Salient, penetrating almost halfway to the Passchendaele Ridge. Little ground was gained however on the Gheluvelt Plateau from which the Germans overlooked the remainder of the British front. During August hardly any progress was made by the British. Operations were much hampered by the rain but were in any case ill-thought out, hastily conceived affairs that would have stood little change whatever the weather.

In September Haig turned the battle over to Plumer who determined that no further progress was possible until the Gheluvelt Plateau was captured. In three successful battles conducted in fine conditions on 20, 26 September and 4 October, he managed to capture most of the Gheluvelt Plateau and advance within striking distance of the Passchendaele Ridge. Poor weather then set in again, and the time for further operations seemed over. Haig was undeterred. During the next six weeks British troops were driven by the Commander-in-Chief, with Plumer's approval, through some of the worst conditions ever experienced by the British army on the Western Front. This period (the Battles of Passchendaele) with the armies struggling through the bog came in the popular mind the characterize the whole battle. With the capture of the ruins of Passchendaele village and part of the ridge on 17 November the operation was finally called off. For a cost of more than 200,000 casualties the British had not even taken their first objective. Given the strength of the German defense, a grand advance on the Belgian coast was always chimerical, and in any case the small coastal U-boats operating from its ports were of little consequence. All that was possible at this stage was more cautious step-by-step advances as achieved by Plumer in September. Haig never accepted these tactics, and the Third Battle of Ypres was just one of a series of costly campaigns whence in striving for grandiose objectives he achieved little but the attrition of his own army.

Robin Prior
Trevor Wilson

Bibliography
Terraine, John. *The Road to Passchendaele*. 1977.
Wilson, Trevor. *The Myriad Faces of War: Britain and the Great War 1914–1918*. 1986.

Peace Ballot

The Peace Ballot of 1934–5 marked a high point of British popular support for the LEAGUE OF NATIONS and played a key role in the response to the challenge to the League and world order posed by Fascist Italy in Abyssinia.

In April 1934 the League of Nations Union under the leadership of Lord Robert Cecil and GILBERT MURRAY had organized a National Declaration Committee to muster support for the League cause. It proposed to poll the public on whether it supported British membership in the League, the reduction of armaments, the abolition of military aircraft by international agreement, and the end to the private manufacture of arms. The critical fifth question it posed was: "Do you consider that, if a nation insists on attacking another, the other nations should combine to compel it to stop by (a) Economic and non-military measures? (b) If necessary, military measures?"

These questions were framed to elicit positive answers, and as the 11.5 million answers came in, it was clear that they would. More than 90 percent of the answers were in the affirmative, except for 5(b), and even this got a majority of positive replies, with only 20 per cent voting against military measures. When the final results were announced on 27 June 1935, it provided an impressive display of public opinion to Prime Minister STANLEY BALDWIN. From denouncing a collective peace system as "perfectly impracticable", he reversed himself and now proclaimed the League of Nations "the sheet anchor of British policy".

There was still opposition to a policy of sanctions imposed through the League from CONSERVATIVES as well as from PACIFISTS and the extreme Left, and other polls were soon conducted to counter the Peace Ballot. They attracted little attention, however, and the British government took the lead in mustering League support for imposing sanctions against Italy in October, 1935, when she invaded Abyssinia. Economic sanctions were incompletely applied and failed to stop the Italian conquest. The episode confirmed peace ballot supporters in their view that an historic opportunity to make collective security work had

been wasted. The National government, meanwhile, concluded that a sanctions policy was risky and ineffective.

Donald S. Birn

Bibliography
Birn, Donald S. *The League of Nations Union*. 1981.
Livingstone, Adelaide, and Marjorie Scott Johnston. *The Peace Ballot: The Official History*. 1935.
Waley, Daniel. *British Public Opinion and the Abyssinian War*. 1975.

Peace Pledge Union

The Peace Pledge Union was the largest PACIFIST society in modern British history. It was formed under dramatic circumstances by the Rev. Dick Sheppard, a popular and well-known Anglican priest who was one of the few truly charismatic personalities to be produced by the pacifist movement. Alarmed by the deteriorating international situation, Sheppard sent off his famous letter to several newspapers in October, 1934, requesting those who agreed with his pacifist position to send him a postcard stating their willingness to support the following resolution: "We renounce war and never again, directly or indirectly, will we support or sanction another." The response was overwhelming. Within weeks thousands of postcards poured in, and by December, 1935 he had received 100,000. In May 1936 he proceeded to organize this powerful expression of peace sentiment into a new body, the Peace Pledge Union.

During its early years a number of famous novelists, scientists, poets, philosophers, clergy, and politicians joined its ranks, including such names as ALDOUS HUXLEY, BERTRAND RUSSELL, VERA BRITTAIN, Rose Macaulay, SIEGFRIED SASSOON, Storm Jameson, GEORGE LANSBURY, and Lord Ponsonby. The PPU acquired its own weekly paper, *Peace News,* formed over 1,100 local and regional groups, held mass rallies, distributed pamphlets, and organized demonstrations and street corner speeches. The society suffered a grievous setback when Sheppard died suddenly on 31 October 1937, but membership, which was subsequently opened to women, continued to climb and peaked at 136,000 in early 1940.

When hostilities broke out in 1939, the PPU decided not to oppose war efforts, but rather to offer dignified witness to its pacifist beliefs. Still, the society did provide assistance to CONSCIENTIOUS OBJECTORS, engage in relief work to alleviate suffering, explore new forms of communal living, encourage any initiatives to secure an armistice or negotiated peace, and offer fellowship and solace to pacifists who felt isolated and demoralized.

After the war the PPU entered a period of swift and noticeable decline. By 1947 the society claimed only 16,000 members; the connection

with *Peace News* was severed; and the organization no longer commanded the public attention
and respect it once did. The society was debilitated by internal wrangling, disagreement over
both tactics and policy, and the tendency of the
younger generation to broaden their interests
from simply war resistance to more fashionable
causes, such as racial justice, anti-colonialism, ecological concerns, and unilateral nuclear disarmament. Lacking funds, members, and a distinctive ideology, the PPU, while still in existence in
the early 1990s, had become weak and ineffective.
David C. Lukowitz

Bibliography

Ceadel, Martin. *Pacifism in Britain 1914–1945: The Defining of a Faith.* 1980.

Lukowitz, David C. "British Pacifists and Appeasement: The Peace Pledge Union," *Journal of Contemporary History,* vol. 9 (1974), pp. 115–27.

Morrison, Sybil. *I Renounce War: The Story of the Peace
Pledge Union.* 1962.

Roberts, R. Ellis. *H.R.L. Sheppard: Life and Letters.*
1942.

Scott, Carolyn. *Dick Sheppard: A Biography.* 1977.

Periodicals

British periodicals in the twentieth century have
gradually shifted from expressing the ideas of a
relatively unified elite culture to addressing the
interests of a much wider, but more fragmented
popular culture. As a result, they have lost something of the prestige they inherited from the Victorian period, while gaining in circulation and
profitability. Moreover, the story of periodicals in
this century is intertwined with the story of advertising, and the success of a British magazine
came to depend on its value as a marketing tool.

A number of nineteenth-century magazines
and reviews survived well into the twentieth. *The
Cornhill Magazine* (1860–1975), for example,
whose distinguished early editors included Anthony Trollope, William Makepeace Thackeray,
and Leslie Stephen, continued to attract prominent writers through the 1940s. But in the 1950s
its circulation was cut in half, a victim of the rise
of television and cheap mass-market competitors, and the magazine's prestige waned along
with its circulation. Similar fate awaited other
great Victorian periodicals like *Quarterly Review*
(1809–1967) and *Blackwood's Edinburgh Magazine* (1817–1980), which slowly lost their vitality
and traditional audience.

Though many older magazines stagnated, the
periodical as such became increasingly important
with the rise of modernism after the FIRST
WORLD WAR. A new generation of writers and
intellectuals first exploded upon the scene in the
pages of WYNDHAM LEWIS' ground-breaking but
short-lived *Blast* (1914–15). T.S. ELIOT, Ezra

Pound, and JAMES JOYCE were among those who
found a home in Richard Aldington's *Egoist*
(1914–19). Perhaps the most influential of modernist periodicals was *The Criterion* (1922–39), edited by Eliot himself, which attracted not only
major British and American writers, but also European contributors, such as Hermann Hesse,
Marcel Proust, Benedetto Croce, and Andre Mal-
raux. Next to *The Criterion* in importance as a
showcase for modernist writing was *The Calendar
of Modern Letters* (1925–7). The BLOOMSBURY
sensibility found its expression in *Life and Letters*
(1928–50), which featured the work of VIRGINIA
WOOLF, E.M. FORSTER, and BERTRAND RUSSELL.

There were also important periodicals that expressed the views of the anti-modernist opposition. J.C. Squire's *London Mercury* (1919–39) saw
its duty as combatting the pernicious influence of
literary "abnormalities"—that is, writers like Eliot
and Pound. Squire attracted the work of many of
the Georgian, traditionalist writers, including
Thomas Hardy and Hilaire Belloc. Other magazines proliferated to defend tradition, one of the
most notable being the regionalist *Decachord*
(1924–46). But Squire's *London Mercury* remained
the periodical the new generation loved to hate;
several new magazines were founded solely in
order to satirize or attack it, notably Jack
Lindsay's *London Aphrodite* (1928–9).

The 1930s saw periodicals founded or adapted
to articulate the opinions of the new Left. John
Middleton Murry's *The Adelphi* (1923–55) reveals
the temper of the changing times, as it adapted
itself from a purely literary publication (with an
emphasis on Murry's version of the ideas of
D. H. LAWRENCE) to a primarily political one of
Marxist orientation. The *Left Review* (1934–8)
devoted itself to the proposition that all good art
must serve the purposes of revolution; it also
argued vigorously against war with Germany and
for supporting the Soviet Union. And the once-
conservative *London Mercury* shifted gears in 1934
with a new editor who emphasized politics, publishing left-wing writers like STEPHEN SPENDER
and W.H. AUDEN. One of the more unusual of
the many leftist periodicals was *The Bermondsey
Book* (1923–30), whose pages mingled work by
both middle-class intellectuals and ordinary
workers. John Lehmann's important *New Writing*
(1936–46) likewise opened its doors to proletarian writers but avoided dogmatism in its political
orientation, publishing not only Spender and
Auden, but Woolf and Forster.

With the coming of the war in 1939, a new era
also began in periodicals. As if to signal this, the
two antagonists, *The Criterion* and *The London
Mercury,* both ceased publication in that year. In
1940 the government instituted a ban on new
publications due to the paper shortages; the

shortages and wartime crisis in the economy forced the closing of dozens of other magazines in the early 1940s. In spite of these obstacles, some important new publications were founded, notably Cyril Connolly's *Horizon* (1939–50). At the beginning of the war the indefatigable editor and publisher John Lehmann approached Allen Lane, founder of Penguin Books, and their collaborative effort resulted in *Penguin New Writing* (1940–50), a literary anthology with phenomenal sales, the circulation of nearly every issue hovering between 75,000 and 100,000.

The post-war period in Britain saw dramatic changes in the content and orientation of periodicals. Alongside well-established weeklies like the *Economist,* the *Spectator,* and the NEW STATESMAN, new magazines tried to reach an audience of intellectuals and common people with a mixture of literary and political opinion, but such periodicals became fewer and less vital in the second half of the century. One important example is *Encounter,* founded in 1953 by Spender and Irving Kristol as a voice of anti-communist and pro-American thought. It achieved initial success and influence, with contributions from celebrated writers on literature, politics, and economics. But when in 1967 it was revealed to have been secretly funded by the CIA from its inception, Spender resigned, most of *Encounter*'s array of contributors abandoned it, and the magazine lost its standing as an influential forum.

A more specialized, but equally significant periodical, *Scrutiny,* was published at CAMBRIDGE by F.R. LEAVIS from 1932 to 1953. Leavis argued for the centrality of literature and LITERARY CRITICISM in modern culture, but *Scrutiny* appealed mainly to the academic community in Britain and the United States. An exception to the trend toward greater specialization in intellectually-oriented periodicals is the *Times Literary Supplement,* published on its own since 1914 and still providing a forum for intellectual debate across the various academic disciplines.

The periodicals that try to reach a wide audience are the slick magazines featuring a great deal of color and less challenging content. Because serious discussions of issues are largely confined to academic journals of limited readership, the field has been left to magazines emphasizing primarily entertainment, and these have been shaped by market forces. Advertising revenue supports most such magazines, so that success is defined in terms of sales figures. One of the more profitable magazines of recent years has been the glossy *Harpers & Queen,* formed in 1970 by the merger of *Harper's Bazaar* and *Queen.*

Magazine consumption per capita has generally risen in recent decades, but more and more titles compete for the buying public. One large category that has blossomed in recent years is the woman's magazine (although magazines aimed specifically at women have enjoyed popularity in Britain since the early nineteenth century). In 1981 nine of the top ten magazines in Britain were women's magazines; *Woman's Weekly* alone reported a circulation of nearly 1.5 million. In 1986 there were over 120 different women's magazines being published, and new titles continue to be launched.

The recessions of the early 1980s and early 1990s claimed many casualties among magazines. In 1991 over 130 titles ceased publication, with some 1000 writers and editors losing their jobs, a clear indication that the economics of the marketplace now dominates British periodical publishing. For the immediate future, there seems little reason to foresee a revival of periodicals that either reflect or help create a coherent and homogeneous culture.

Raymond N. MacKenzie

Bibliography

Hewison, Robert. *Under Siege: Literary Life in London, 1939–1945.* 1977.

Mulhearn, Francis. *The Moment of "Scrutiny".* 1979.

Sullivan, Alvin, ed. *British Literary Magazines: vol. 4: The Modern Age, 1914–1984.* 1986.

White, Cynthia L. *The Women's Periodical Press in Britain 1946–76.* 1977.

Philanthropy

No nation on earth can lay claim to a richer charitable past than Great Britain. And philanthropy in twentieth-century Britain has shown itself to be remarkably resilient in the face of the vast expansion in state health and welfare provision. Although the WELFARE STATE has overshadowed the voluntary sector since the Second World War, it has not altered many of its traditions or undermined its flow of funds. Indeed, in recent years British charities have shown a steady increase of financial support, which in 1991 reached an estimated £17 billion. Innovation and cost effectiveness are thought to be among the principal virtues of contemporary charity, and these have become increasingly apparent against the background of government economies and the spiraling costs and bureaucratic inefficiencies of the state welfare services. The virtues of democratic action inherent in voluntarism have also become increasingly apparent. In the first half of the century philanthropists did their best to limit the expansion of state power; in the second half of the century, many campaigning charities, from Friends of the Earth to Save the Children, have turned their attention to government deceits and limitations.

The Victorian years were the heyday of British philanthropy, but by the end of the nineteenth century the consensus in favor of voluntary social action came under increasing attack. Given the philanthropic world's love of local autonomy and ad hoc remedies, and its tendency to sectarian rivalry, muddle and confusion proliferated. Across the spectrum of charitable activity, competition and imbalances in provision were rife. In the Edwardian years the criticism of charity mounted, fuelled by the social investigations of Charles Booth, Seebohm Rowntree, and the evidence of the Royal Commission on the Poor Laws (1905–9). To many social reformers, such as BEATRICE AND SIDNEY WEBB, those age-old charitable remedies of self-help and personal service looked rather threadbare. What was needed, they argued, was a radical overhaul of the social services and greater state intervention.

From the late nineteenth century onwards philanthropists responded to the criticism by a variety of means, including the introduction of social casework and better charitable coordination. Among the leaders in the field were the Charity Organisation Society (1869), which prided itself on its "scientific" outlook, and the King Edward's Hospital Fund for London (1897), a pioneering foundation in hospital provision. Such institutions sought to put charity's house in order before further government action sapped erstwhile philanthropic campaigns. But the social reforms of the LIBERAL administration in the years 1905–11, albeit piecemeal, further challenged charitable predominance and altered the relationship between voluntary and state welfare provision. Perhaps greater government involvement was inevitable as the focus of social policy shifted from what could be done to help "the poor" to what could be done to abolish "poverty."

The FIRST WORLD WAR further unsettled the philanthropic movement, for it undermined religious faith and fractured those pillars of charitable activity, family and parish life. Nor were the charities assisted by the record tax levels at the end of the war, which reduced the amount of disposable wealth available for philanthropic purposes. But while the First World War exposed the shortcomings of voluntarism and pointed to the need for greater state involvement, it also offered the voluntary movement fresh opportunities. Over 10,000 new societies were set up before its close, including the National Federation of Women's Institutes (1915) and King George's Fund for Sailors (1917). The government, reluctant to expand state welfare projects at the end of the war, welcomed their activities. In the inter-war years some in the welfare field looked to a "new philanthropy", in which charities would work in closer partnership with government departments. In practice, partnership worked most effectively in causes such as family planning and infant welfare. In the hospital world, with its longstanding rivalries between voluntary and state-aided institutions, it failed to live up to expectations.

While small, parish societies continued to typify the charitable world, they were joined in the early decades of the century by a host of large trusts and foundations, whose commissions allowed them to deal with a wide range of issues. The model for them came from America, as did much of the money. Among the premier British foundations were the Carnegie United Kingdom Trust (1913), the Wellcome Foundation (1924), the Pilgrim Trust (1930), the King George's Jubilee Trust (1935), and the Nuffield Foundation (1943). Most of them saw themselves as pioneering experimental projects. They would provide the "venture capital", but once a scheme had passed through its pilot stage, the expectation was that other voluntary bodies or government agencies would take it over. The Carnegie United Kingdom Trust, for example, established libraries throughout the country, but in 1935 it concluded that public bodies were sufficiently committed to library provision and moved into other fields. Foundations were unique institutions in having sizeable capital reserves and freedom of operation. Without being accountable to the electorate or to annual subscribers, they were able to take risks in a way that was impossible for public agencies of unendowed charities.

The trend to bigger institutions in the twentieth century was in part shaped by the criticism that charities in the past were too small in scale to be effective and too unstable and understaffed to provide adequate care. But the larger the institution the more likely it was to distance individual philanthropists from beneficiaries. This posed a threat to charity's much heralded quality of personal service, which was all the more evident in those organizations which worked with government agencies where utility and cost-efficiency were at a premium. Still, in a relatively informal and secular society, charities continued to play a crucial role as repositories of moral and ethical values.

The impact of the SECOND WORLD WAR on philanthropy has been obscured by the attention given to state social policy. As in 1914, the crisis both threatened and challenged voluntarists, and it accelerated the process of cooperation with state officials. While the number of CIVIL SERVANTS rose dramatically, a problem for charities was how to cope with the continual calling-up of their personnel for the forces. The answer was for WOMEN to fill many of the places formerly held by men, which further strengthened their already powerful position within the voluntary world. Some of the charities came and went with the war. The "Bundles for Britain" campaign, for example, provided American money and supplies for voluntary hospitals during the BLITZ. Other projects had more enduring responsibilites, such as the Women's Voluntary Service and the Association of Jewish Refugees in Great Britain. The emergency also gave important work to established charities: the British Red Cross and the Order of St. John of Jerusalem ran the auxiliary hospitals on behalf of the Ministry of Health. In short, the war disrupted the work of most charities, killed off some, and promoted a host of others.

In the atmosphere of "total war", with the government making inroads on every front, the philanthropic world was bound to look diminished even where it thrived. In creating and exposing scarcity and deprivation, the war made traditional charitable remedies look inadequate. Compared to the prospect of universal state provision offered by the BEVERIDGE Report, published in 1942, the charitable emphasis on local initiative did not appear very compelling, nor were appeals to self-help after all the sacrifice the war itself demanded. With the vast expansion of the post-war social services, voluntarists had to take stock. Government absorbed many of philanthropy's health and welfare functions and nationalized many charities, most notably the voluntary hospitals. But other societies soldiered on. Many had a welfare role peripheral to government concerns. Others transformed into new institutions with a stronger social element in their makeup. Some shifted their priorities and changed their names. The Charity Organisation Society became the Family Welfare Association in 1946 and concentrated on social casework. Others still started up to fill the gaps in state social provision. MIND (1946), War on Want (1951), the Samaritans (1953), and Help the Aged (1963) are just a few prominent examples.

Despite signs that the philanthropic establishment could respond successfully to the new social environment, it was unsettled by the creation of the welfare state and uncertain about its future in a semi-collectivist society. To some extent it was the victim of changed public expectations. It was not obvious at the time that government could never fully satisfy them. The years 1960 to the mid-1970s were the heyday of state-directed health and social services in Britain. Few people doubted that central government had a primary responsiblity for welfare provision, and most commentators assumed that it was well-equipped to administer the system devised by Parliament. The consensus did little to enhance the status of philanthropists, whose impulses were to decentralize, to break a problem down into pieces. As they settled into a decent anonymity, they had the consolation that charity was its own reward.

The strategic planning in state welfare provision which characterized the 1960s and 1970s ended in doubts and recrimination. The drift of opinion away from statutory provision in the 1980s widened the public's awareness of philanthropic influences and stimulated voluntary campaigns. With collectivism in retreat, voluntarism began to be taken much more seriously by politicians. But while charities welcomed the publicity, they had to cope with greater pressure on their services. In the HOSPITAL sector, for example, they had long provided amenities and thousands of volunteer workers; now they were being asked to fund capital projects, including the building of new NATIONAL HEALTH SERVICE hospitals. Just what privatization meant for welfare provision was unclear, but it suggested a primary role for philanthropy that it had largely abdicated. After decades of state supremacy in welfare it was doubtful whether there was a cultural basis for a dramatic expansion of charity, or that charity was a suitable way of providing basic services according to need.

There has been a transformation in philanthropic attitudes since the nineteenth century. The change is perhaps most remarkable in regard to perceptions of the role of the state. Though they remain chary of state power, most philanthropists now look to government for greater expenditure on health and welfare and for leadership in tackling the causes of social deprivation. For its part, the government, aware that voluntary bodies are an effective way of delivering a range of health and social service, increasingly contributes to charitable campaigns. In its various guises, government increased its payments in the 1980s to such an extent that it is now the single largest contributor to charitable causes. Britain has reached a stage in the evolution of social policy in which the philanthropic sector wants the state to do more and the state wants the philanthropic sector to do more. There are signs that the long-standing battle between philanthropists and collectivists, which many assumed to have been won by the latter, now appears to be heading for the ropes, with the combatants holding each other up.

Frank Prochaska

Bibliography

Owen, David. *English Philanthropy, 1660–1960.* 1964.
Prochaska, Frank. *The Voluntary Impulse: Philanthropy in Modern Britain.* 1988.
———. "Philanthropy" in F.M.L. Thompson, ed. *The Cambridge Social History of Britain, 1750–1950.* vol. 3. 1990. pp. 357–93.

Physics

Physics could be used as an indicator of Britain's international standing generally throughout the twentieth century. In 1900 Germany and France rivaled Britain in numbers of physicists and support for physics research. By the 1930s the United States overtook European nations, a lead dramatically emphasized by the events of the Second World War and the development of RADAR and atomic weapons, which owed much to the work of American physicists. While physicists from Britain still contribute to such fields as high energy physics, they now participate internationally through CERN, near Geneva, one of the many such collaborations that have developed since 1945.

At the beginning of the twentieth century only a few hundred of those trained in physics were involved in some aspect of the field, the main center being the Cavendish Laboratory in CAMBRIDGE, where some fifty physicists worked under J.J. Thomson (1856–1940). Cambridge connections dominated British physics until the Second World War. Growing numbers and professional sensitivities, particularly in relation to chemists, led to the founding of the Institute of Physics in 1919. By the end of the century its membership approached 20,000, the majority working in industrial or government-funded laboratories. The National Physical Laboratory, established in 1900 with R.T. Glazebrook (1854–1935) as its first Director, undertook work on standards, which was particularly important for industry.

Early in the century the most significant work was on the structure of matter. In 1911 ERNEST RUTHERFORD, then in Manchester, proposed that the atom had a nucleus or core. His collaborator H.G.J. Moseley (1887–1915) helped to determine the electrical charge on the nucleus. In 1912, during a stay in Britain working in Rutherford's laboratory, Niels Bohr developed these ideas into a model of atoms in which he assumed that the electrons moved round the nucleus in orbits with fixed energies. This model became one of the foundations of quantum mechanics. However, the main development of quantum mechanics took place on the Continent, with the exception of P.A.M. Dirac, who made fundamental contributions at Cambridge in the late 1920s to quantum mechanics, notably a theory of emission and absorption of radiation, a prediction of the positron and antimatter, and by his development of the relativistic wave equation for the electron.

During the FIRST WORLD WAR Rutherford and others, on behalf of the Admiralty Board of Invention and Research, used sonar to detect submarines. The wartime experience, which demonstrated the technical inferiority of British industry, led to the setting up of the Department of Scientific and Industrial Research (DSIR) in 1917, the forerunner of the present day Science and Engineering Research Council (SERC), to support research.

During the 1920s and 1930s physicists at the Cavendish Laboratory played a remarkable role in the development of nuclear physics. Shortly before he moved to the Cavendish in 1920, Rutherford had observed disintegrations of nuclei. At the same time, F.W. Aston (1877–1945), also at Cambridge, showed that chemical elements had isotopes; while all atoms of an element had the same chemical properties they did not all have the same masses. Such evidence suggested that the nuclei of atoms were made from a small number of components. Aston won the Nobel Prize in 1922. Further clues came from the work of C.T.R. Wilson, another Cambridge physicist, who developed the cloud-chamber which allowed fragments of nuclear reactions to be observed. Wilson shared a Nobel Prize in 1927.

In 1932, the pinnacle of Cavendish achievement in nuclear physics, J. Chadwick discovered the neutron, a component of the nucleus long predicted by Rutherford. J.D. Cockcroft and E.T.S. Walton carried out the first successful experiments using a particle accelerator, and P.M.S. Blackett and G.P. Occialini extended work on the positron, a positive counterpart to the electron. New electrical methods of counting particles were also developed. In the case of the new accelerators, the Cavendish physicists had relied on the assistance of the Metropolitan-Vickers industrial laboratory in Manchester, where the problems of high voltages had been investigated, work encouraged by the development of the national grid for distributing electricity.

In the early 1930s N.F. Mott, another Cambridge product, moved to Bristol, where one of the first groups to study the problems of solid-state physics came into being. W.H. and L. Bragg, the only father and son pair to share a Nobel Prize, variously working in Leeds, London, and Cambridge, developed X-ray diffraction which could be used for investigating the structure of crystals and later organic molecules. In 1927 G.P. Thomson, Professor of Natural Philosophy at Aberdeen, demonstrated the wave-nature of the electron which could be used to probe even finer details of atomic structures. Thomson shared a Nobel Prize in 1937.

During the Second World War two important areas of research were radar and atomic weapons. The development in 1940 of the cavity magnetron by J.T. Randall and H.A.H. Randall at Birmingham was important for radar. After the discovery of nuclear fission in the winter of 1938–9, the early experiments had suggested that it was not practicable to build a weapon using the energy released in this process. However, early in

1940 O. Frisch and R. Peierls, REFUGEE physicists in Britain, recognized that by using one rare isotope of uranium, a weapon might be practicable. On this basis the Tube Alloys project was set up to investigate the matter further. Though they made progress, it became clear the only option in wartime conditions was to join in with the Manhattan project in the United States.

After the war there was more generous funding for physics. The decision to build NUCLEAR WEAPONS in Britain led to new government laboratories at Harwell and Aldermaston where nuclear reactors were designed, initially for the production of weapons plutonium, and later for the production of electricity.

Research on nuclear fusion was undertaken, although since the late 1980s this has been carried out at Culham as part of a European project, JET, the Joint European Torus.

During the post-war years many university physicists returned to the problems of the structure of matter. The techniques developed for radar during the war could be adapted to make more powerful accelerators. In the few years this took to happen, studies of cosmic rays came to the fore. Government funding allowed the development of new photographic emulsions for detecting cosmic rays. In 1947 C.F. Powell and his group in Bristol discovered the pion in this way. Later that year G.D. Rochester and C.C. Butler discovered the K meson.

However, physicists working new larger accelerators soon displaced cosmic ray research. The largest accelerator in Britain, Nimrod, a proton synchrotron, operated from 1964 to 1978, when it was closed to allow support for CERN.

Alan Q. Morton

Bibliography

Crowther, James G. *The Cavendish Laboratory 1874–1974.* 1974.

Forman, P., J.L. Heilbron, and S. Weart. *Physics c.1900: Historical Studies in the Physical Sciences,* vol. 5. 1975.

Gowing, Margaret. *Britain and Atomic Energy 1939–1945.* 1964.

Hendry, John, ed. *Cambridge Physics in the Thirties,* 1984.

Pick, Frank (1878–1941)

Frank Pick brought the worlds of business and art together through his roles as a ranking official of the London Underground (1906–33), as Vice-Chairman and chief executive officer of the London Passenger Transport Board (1933–40), as Chairman of the government's Council for Art and Industry (1934–9), and as a long-time member and President (1932–4) of the Design and Industries Association. Pick admired the aesthetic and social goals of William Morris, and believed that the transport system could shape London into an artistic and integrated civic community

uniting art and industry, creativity, and commerce. To further this goal Pick hired modern artists and architects to fashion a unified corporate design for the Underground, encompassing everything from trash bins to tube stations; he also commissioned advertising posters designed in post-impressionist styles, in order to increase revenues and to introduce the public to visual modernism. Under Pick's supervision the Underground became known as "the people's picture galleries," and Pick himself was hailed widely as one of the greatest art patrons of the age.

Pick was born on 23 November 1878 at Spalding, Lincolnshire to a lower middle-class family; his father was a draper who moved the family to York in 1883. Pick was raised as a Nonconformist, and although he abandoned any formal adherence to religion later in life he continued to be devout, calling himself a "Christian agnostic" and associating art with spirituality. He received a scholarship to St. Peter's School in York, and upon graduation worked for a solicitor. In 1902 he went to work for the North Eastern Railway Company and in 1906 moved to London to work for the London Underground, rising to the position of Managing Director by 1928.

Pick was such an effective administrator that the General Manager of the Underground, Albert Stanley (Lord Ashfield, 1920), gave him wide latitude to pursue his aesthetic projects, especially since Pick argued persuasively that a beautiful transport system would be a lucrative transport system. He also believed that if the public were exposed to modern art they would become more aesthetically discerning and demand better designed consumer goods; industries and the government would have to respond to the public's demand, thereby leading to the gradual transformation of England into an Earthly Paradise.

Pick shared this philosophy with fellow members of the Design and Industries Association, which had been formed in 1915. He hired an architect from the DIA, Charles Holden, to design many of the new stations in the International Style, and he commissioned Edward Johnston to design a special typeface to be used throughout the transport system in 1913. Pick also commissioned modern artists, such as E. McKnight Kauffer, to design posters and fixtures for the system. Controversial modern sculptors like JACOB EPSTEIN and HENRY MOORE were given prominent exposure when Pick commissioned them to carve figures directly onto the new Underground headquarters designed by Holden, which opened in 1929 to a heated debate in the press over the merits of modernism.

Pick continued to play a commanding role within the transport system when the Underground became part of the London Passenger

Transport Board in 1933. He resigned from the LPTB in 1940, briefly became Director of the Ministry of Information, and later worked for the Ministry of Transport before his death of a cerebral hemorrhage on 7 November 1941. Through his patronage, Pick introduced a generation to modern art and ARCHITECTURE, and turned the London Underground into the culminating project of the arts and crafts movement: a union of the arts created for the service and pleasure of the common person.

Michael Saler

Bibliography

Barman, Christian. *The Man Who Built London Transport.* 1979.

Pevsner, Nikolaus. "Frank Pick" in *Studies in Art, Architecture and Design.* vol. 2. 1968. pp. 190–209.

Saler, Michael. *The Avant-Garde in Interwar England: Medieval Modernism and the London Underground.* 1999.

Pinter, Harold (1930—)

Since the mid-1960s Pinter has been regarded as a pre-eminent British playwright. Although employing a typically British form of theatrical naturalism, his art derives equally from the traditions of Continental modernism as exemplified in Kafka and Beckett.

Growing up as a Jew in London's East End, Pinter's experience of ANTI-SEMITISM during the Second World War may lie behind the powerful images of intimidation and violence in early plays like *The Room* (1957), *The Dumb Waiter* (1957), and his first full-length play, *The Birthday Party* (1957). Although *The Birthday Party* failed in its first London production, it was favorably reviewed by Harold Hobson in *The Sunday Times,* and Pinter was accordingly commissioned by BBC radio to write *A Slight Ache,* broadcast in 1959.

The television production of *A Night Out* and the success of the West End production of *The Caretaker* in 1960 brought him recognition as a major new dramatist. *The Caretaker* received numerous productions around the world over the next few years, acquiring the status of a modern classic.

The influence of BECKETT may be discerned in Pinter's redefinition of plot: instead of employing conventional exposition to give the audience a privileged perspective on the action, the dramatic situation is presented as a series of unresolved—and possibly unresolvable—mysteries. Denied a straightforward explanation of the contradictions and indeterminacies of character, an audience comes to realize that objective truth in human relationships collapses into a drama of conflicting subjectivities, a power struggle which is the basis of all human behavior.

His savage anatomy of the terms of English social behavior satirizes the tradition of comedy of manners inherited from NOEL COWARD. The adjective "Pinteresque" was coined in recognition of his theatrical style, which relies on pregnant pauses and silences.

Although more naturalistic than the preceding plays, *The Caretaker* is typical of Pinter's "comedies of menace." Its presentation of the struggle of a tramp (Davies) to secure possession of a squalid room in a house which is owned by Mick and looked after by his brother Aston becomes a darkly comic emblem of the problem of authenticating one's identity.

The battle for living space gives way to an exploration of the dynamics of sex as power in *The Collection* (1962), *The Lover* (1963) and *The Homecoming* (1964). The deconstructed naturalism of these plays is replaced in *Landscape* (1968), *Silence* (1969), *Night* (1969), and *Old Times* (1971) by a looser, more expressionistic structure in which the static image of a group of characters motivates interwoven interior monologues through which men and women battle to establish the truth of their memories as a way of validating their identities. In these plays Pinter for the first time makes women the subject of the drama.

A new phase of his work began with the production of *One for the Road* in 1984. From this point his drama has begun to reflect his liberal left-wing engagement with world politics. It employs the Pinteresque language of menace and ambiguity to explore the banal terrors created by the abusers of political power.

Pinter's many screenplays have received acclaim, as has his handling of scripts for radio and television. He has also pursued a successful career as a director and occasional actor.

Robert Gordon

Bibliography

Dukore, Bernard Frank. *Harold Pinter.* 1982.

Esslin, Martin. *Pinter: the Playwright.* 4th ed. 1982.

Gale, Steven H. *Harold Pinter: An Annotated Bibliography.* 1987.

Hayman, Ronald. *Harold Pinter.* 4th ed. 1980.

Thompson, David T. *Pinter: The Player's Playwright.* 1985.

Poetry, English

The moribundity of English poetry at the turn of the century might be inferred from the number of groups committed to its reform—the Georgians and the Imagists being the most prominent. Despite strong individual efforts, like RUDYARD KIPLING's *Barrack Room Ballads* (1892), Thomas Hardy's *Wessex Poems* (1989), A.E. Housman's *A Shropshire Lad,* and W.B. YEATS' *The Wind Among the Reeds* (1899), English poetry in the 1890s seemed to have lost historical relevance, craftsmanly rigor, and intellectual purpose. Aestheticism had given rise to a highbrow poetics of impressionistic sensualism and decadence, as in poetry by Arthur Symons and Ernest Dowson. On the other hand, the poetry familiar to most readers reasserted Victorian moral certainties. Stephen Phillips, Alfred Austin, Henry Newbolt, and Alfred Noyes delivered in didactic fashion generalizations about a moral universe that Darwinism and agnosticism had already thrown into doubt.

The term "Georgian poetry" refers to the anthologies edited by Edward Marsh and published by Harold Monro between 1912 and 1922, which represented a prevailing dissatisfaction with both moralism and precious artificiality. Contributors included RUPERT BROOKE, Walter de la Mare (1873–1956), Edmund Blunden (1896–1974), ROBERT GRAVES, D.H. LAWRENCE, Edward Thomas (1878–1917), and WILFRED OWEN.

Though the anthologies included poets representing different techniques and sensibilities, Georgian poetry has recognizable characteristics: a return to the sounds of English song and speech, and to love of the English countryside. The principal boast of its supporters was the realism of Georgian poetry, its insistence upon narrating experience without referring to abstract categories (like the beautiful and the lofty), and without overt intellectual biases (like supernaturalism or socialism). Georgians wrote in traditional poetic forms and created an air of dreamlike unreality, a good example of which is "Adlestrop" by Edward Thomas. Based on such a general definition, Hardy (1840–1928), Housman (1859–1936), and the American Robert Frost—who lived in England 1912–15 and published his first two volumes there—might be thought the best of the Georgian poets. Hardy's poetry, with its rugged metrical irregularities and guttural phonetic conglomerations, its blend of deeply-felt emotion and philosophically-principled irony, has had a continuing influence on British poetry greater than that of any other poet of the period except Yeats, whose influence stems mostly from the poetry he wrote after 1914.

After the success of the Georgian experiment, publishing poetry in London became, to a significant extent, a group activity. This marketing device has hardened into an academic habit of lumping poets into schools that obscure their crucial individualities. No one took better advantage of this new way of presenting poetry than the Imagists, who used small, exclusively avant-garde publications to promote their movement.

Georgians and Imagists alike insisted that the poet should keep his eye upon the object itself and maintain direct contact with experience. The differences between the two movements concerned subject matter, attitude toward the world, and verse form. The Imagists described the concrete details of circumscribed objects (natural and rural, or urban and technological). They wrote in free verse (like some French symbolists) and imported other foreign verse forms such as Japanese *tanka* and *haiku*.

Imagism was begun in 1909 by T.E. Hulme (1883–1917) and F.S. Flint (1885–1960), along with the American Ezra Pound, who arrived in London that year. The group published yearly anthologies between 1914 and 1917. More stridently experimental, revolutionary, modern, and intellectual than the Georgians, the Imagists published essays and manifestos explaining the substance and importance of their work. Flint wrote the most definitive statement of Imagist principles for *Poetry* (March 1913): "1. Direct treatment of the 'thing' whether subjective or objective. 2. To use absolutely no word that did not contribute to presentation. 3. As regarding rhythm: to compose in sequence of the musical phrase not in sequence of a metronome." Pound, Flint, and Hulme published their own poems alongside contributions from JAMES JOYCE, FORD MADOX FORD, D.H. Lawrence, as well as American poets William Carlos Williams and H.D. (Hilda Doolittle).

The principal claim of Hulme and of Imagism under his influence was that the late romantic poets had over-refined the expression of emotion and lost touch with living speech. Imagism attempted to restore immediacy to poetry by turning from the clichés of sentimental late romanticism to sharper perceptions of reality.

Imagism was a contained movement, of interest mainly to people professionally writing, reviewing, and publishing poetry. Not so the poetry of the FIRST WORLD WAR that described events affecting the nation as a whole. The war's history is reflected in the shifting moods of English poetry about the conflict. In 1914 and 1915 the most popular poetry was still nationalistic and militaristic. Housman's *A Shropshire Lad* became more popular at this time, along with more shoddy nationalistic stuff, such as the anthology called *For England's Sake* (1900), from which Henley's lines are typical: "What if the best of our wages be/ An empty sleeve, a stiff-set knee,/ A crutch for the rest of life—who cares,/ So long as the One Flag floats and dares?" Henley's poem exemplifies what First World War poets reacted against.

The first stage of war poetry written by participants was marked by Brooke's hugely popular five sonnets, which stress the pathos of homesickness, fear of death, and hope of personal redemption. The second phase of war poetry was written by the men who endured the prolonged horrors of trench war in Belgium and France.

The anti-war poetry of Owen, SIEGFRIED SAS-SOON, and Isaac Rosenberg (1890–1918) tells how far the actualities of gas attacks and filthy trenches were from heroic notions of soldiering. The poems of Owen and Sassoon are sometimes elegiac, sometimes satiric, and sometimes polemical demystifications of war. Their poems are deliberately choked with pathetically realistic descriptions of the battlefield, intended to educate civilians about the ugliness and moral stupidity of the war. Rosenberg's poems, written from the point of view of the common soldier, express the gallows-humor of the trenches. His address to a rat in "Break of Day in the Trenches" anticipates the renewed taste for the grotesque tropings of Donne and Marvell that T.S. ELIOT would valorize after the war. Rosenberg's use of rapidly juxtaposed images and staccato syntax to depict the mechanization of bodies in "Marching" also anticipates high modernist descriptions of mechanized bodies and depersonalized human beings in urban life, as in Eliot's "Preludes".

Interest has been greatest in war poetry by men who witnessed the events first-hand. Catherine Reilly's anthology *Scars upon my Heart* (1981) has brought to light war poems by women that have unfortunately been neglected. Nosheen Khan's *Women's Poetry of the First World War* (1988) is dedicated to examining the politics and emotions of women poets who experienced the war from the homefront. Such studies have created new interest in the work of Charlotte Mew (1869–1928), Alice Meynell (1846–1922), Frances Cornford (1886–1960), Sylvia Townshend Warner (1893–1978), and Valentine Ackland (1906–69).

The main drama in English poetry after the war was the conflict between modernist and traditional modes, a conflict incipient in the differences between Imagist and Georgian approaches to realism. At the end of the war Yeats, Hardy, de la Mare, and Robert Bridges (1844–1930), all writing in traditional forms, were the central British poets for most critics and readers. But the postwar era, which seemed to usher in a new age of international, mechanized, and dehumanized urban life, brought with it the perception that a new kind of poetry was needed to address the modern age relevantly. Eliot argued in "Tradition and the Individual Talent" that the unparalleled complexity of the age required unparalleled complexity of poetic form. Whether or not one believes in such historical necessity, the high modernist mode produced brilliant and innovative books in the 1920s and 1930s such as Pound's *Hugh Selwyn Mauberly* (1920), Lawrence's *Birds, Beasts and Flowers* (1921), Eliot's *The Waste Land* (1922), and *Facade* (1922) by Edith Sitwell (1887–1964).

The high modernist mode which dominated English and American poetry from the early 1920s to the early 1950s incorporated *vers libre*, French symbolism, Imagistic detail, realistic dramatic speech, jazz syncopations, and Freudian free-association of words and images. Eliot's *Prufrock and Other Observations* (1917) created a sensation with its witty clichés. Sitwell's *Facade* uses many of these techniques to experiment with synesthesia and cadence. Pound, Eliot, and Yeats emerged as the central figures of high modernism when they used these techniques to develop a prophetic overview of their culture.

The expatriate Americans in particular, Eliot and Pound, wrote fragmented, montage-like poems that attempt to embody the confusion into which these poets felt European culture had fallen. Pound in *Hugh Selwyn Mauberly* and Eliot in *The Waste Land* give the impression that the poem is not a description of the world from a personal perspective, but a collection of shards dug up by the objective poet-archeologist who, on the strength of his erudition and understanding, can begin the process of reforming cultural coherence. Like all avant-garde movements, modernism was largely an attack on "bourgeois complacency" and upon its own bourgeois roots.

Yeats's relationship to modernism was more complicated. His poetry of the 1890s, combining the delicate effects of late Victorian verse and French symbolism with Irish folklore, creates a dreamy alternative to worldly interests. But with *Responsibilities* (1914) and *The Wild Swans at Coole* (1919) Yeats showed an ability to engage the world of contemporary reality, especially Irish politics, using sharper idiom and imagery. Yet Yeats was from beginning to end a mystical rather than a modernist poet. He wrote always in traditional forms and eschewed the metrical experimentations of other modernists. His greatest gift was that he could be at once a shrewdly modern, politically engaged poet, yet write of life as a drama of supernatural, mythical, and spiritual forces.

Lawrence's departure from his own Georgian beginnings was as radical and revolutionary as Eliot's or Pound's departure from late romanticism. But where Pound and Eliot advocated a "modern" poetry of craftsmanship, tradition, and "impersonality", Lawrence strove for an intensely personal union of poetic form and feeling. If Lawrence felt as much as Eliot or Pound that modern culture was painfully fragmented, he saw the relief from fragmentation not in artistic or intellectual control, nor in political discipline, but in recovery of a primally libidinal self.

The most important development of English poetry between the wars was the emergence of the Auden group at Oxford: W.H. AUDEN, STEPHEN SPENDER, LOUIS MacNEICE, and C. DAY LEWIS. Their poetry is as conventional in verse forms as the Georgians had been, but as unconventional in its ideas as the most innovative modernists. Politically, the group was openly leftist whereas Yeats, Pound, and Eliot had been conservative. They combined a Georgian love of England with a modernist awareness of the international scene. From the modernists they learned to describe urban and technological subjects, from the Georgians how to place those subjects in and against the English landscape.

In contrast to the prophetic and high-pitched literary voices of modernism, Auden develops the tone of a sophisticated conversationalist and invents a poetry in which he can discuss Marx, Freud, and Kierkegaard equally with labor strikes, cricket, lunch counters, and traffic jams. He is a brilliant parodist of sermons, ballads, public announcements, and popular songs, and uses these forms to expose the alienation of the proletariat. He is unsurpassed in English as a poet of public address; his "Letter to Lord Byron", which uses the device of a letter to the dead poet as an excuse for a survey of modern culture, is an amalgam of serious poetry and light verse.

Auden's match of radical inspirations with traditional form and with the decorum of Hardy and the Georgians has become central to English verse in the latter half of the century.

While the Auden group was emerging, modernism in Britain changed from being the practice of foreigners—Pound, Eliot, and Yeats—to the practice of natives. In the 1930s David Jones (1895–1974), HUGH MACDIARMID, Basil Bunting, and William Empson (1906–84) emerged as native practitioners of modernism. To Bunting's modernist eye for images and ear for language both colloquial and literary, is added a Wordsworthian feeling for the Northumbrian countryside. Empson's greatest contributions may have been his literary criticism, especially *Seven Types of Ambiguity* (1930), which shows how the investigatory eye of science can be brought to bear upon the complex structures of poetic language. Empson's poetry itself uses image, syntax, and sound effects to produce arguments rather than impressions. Like early Donne, whom Empson imitates, his meanings are convoluted, his subject matter psychological, his rhythms bumpy.

During the 1940s Pound, Eliot, and Auden shared the limelight. In *Four Quartets* (1943) Eliot developed from his satiric, theatrical, modernist style an incantatorily liturgical and philosophical one. Although Pound discredited himself by broadcasting Fascist propaganda during the Second World War, his *Pisan Cantos* (1948) is a distinguished heir to *The Waste Land*. Auden, having abandoned his Marxist stance of the 1930s, reinterpreted *The Tempest* in a lyric *ars poetica*, *The Mirror and the Sea* (1945).

Many of the new poets of the 1940s belonged to a "neo-romantic" reaction against modernism in a way that included even Auden among its modernist targets. The reluctant guru behind this movement was the Welshman DYLAN THOMAS, who, during his short career, evinced a knack for profuse imagery and for hurling words together in a weirdly suggestive eldritch keen of sexual symbols and earthly magic.

The poets of the 1940s who followed Thomas's lead included a group that called itself "The New Apocalypse", made up of J.F. Hendry, Norman MacCaig, Henry Treece, and G.S. Fraser. Their use of myth as a means of personal reintegration characterizes what some have called the introspective turn of neo-romanticism away from the more public poetries of modernism and the Auden group. Hendry and Treece later explained their movement as a reconciliation between the tyrannies of modernist subjection of the personality to objects, and surrealist subjection of personality to dream images. They proposed rather that poetry should allow conscious intelligence to shape the spontaneous images of dream into narrative and organic unity.

Somewhat more enduring poets of mystical or introspective turn during the 1930s and 1940s are David Gascoyne (1916–2001) and Kathleen Raine (1908–). Surrealist Gascoyne attempted to follow Breton's method of allowing images from the unconscious to cluster about a subject by free association. In the introduction to her collected poems Raine, much influenced by Yeats and neo-platonism, explains why poetry must turn away from social history: "The ever-recurring forms of nature mirror eternal reality; the never-recurring productions of history reflect only fallen men, and are therefore not suitable to become a symbolic vocabulary for the kind of poetry I have attempted to write." Other neo-romantics were Thomas' friend Vernon Watkins, George Barker, and Lawrence Durrell (1912–90).

Some poets whose work was largely unaffected by modernism, Audenism, or neo-romanticism succeeded in writing in traditional modes between 1930 and 1950, among them Graves and Edwin Muir (1887–1959). Graves's mature style tends toward the Augustan: neat and carefully witty, lucid despite syntax that withholds a noun or verb through several subordinate clauses. The drama of many other of his poems is of critical intelligence examining the passions of emotional man. Muir's early poems express nostalgia for the Orkney farm life his parents were forced to abandon in 1900. His verse, syntactically straightforward but allegorically complex, fuses his lost childhood home and the decline of agrarian life in Britain with biblical myths of Eden and the great flood. He wrote his two most famous poems after the Second World War, "One Foot in Eden", about divine redress of evil by a great, post-historical harvest; and "Horses", a narrative of nuclear holocaust fitted to the pattern of the seven-day biblical creation.

Spender began by imitating Auden's confidently ironic, intellectual style, but in the 1940s he discovered his own dreamier, emotionally liquid persona. Where Auden ridiculed the absurdities of his culture, Spender seemed to suffer its wounds. John Betjeman (1906–84) was also of Auden's generation, but his popular, unintellectual social satire, seen from the point-of-view of the amiable, hypochondriacal everyman, was quite unlike Auden's Marxist-Freudian outlook. He became very popular in the 1950s alongside poets of the Movement who also cultivated self-mocking, anxiety-ridden, man-in-the-street personae. Stevie Smith [Florence Margaret Smith] (1902–71) was also of Auden's generation but belonged to no school or movement. Like Betjeman, she gained a large readership, especially in the 1950s, among people unaccustomed to reading poetry. Idiosyncratic and bitterly sardonic, Smith used the voice and viewpoint of a child in order to sharpen the satirical edge of her poems.

The experience of the SECOND WORLD WAR, so different from the Great War, was reflected in the character of the poetry. This time Britons were disillusioned with war before it broke out, and there was no pompous nationalistic rhetoric to be answered. Some felt that mechanized weaponry made fighting more impersonal, a matter of technological competence or sheer victimization. Moreover, much of the war, endured on British soil, affected the civilian population directly. There was no longer a naive populace needing to be made aware, by some new Wilfred Owen, of the actualities of war. Eliot portrayed bombing raids in *Four Quartets,* Day Lewis responded to the war with Virgilian contemplations of England, and Sitwell used Christian symbolism to write about Hiroshima. Several single poems about the war have become celebrated anthology pieces, such as F.T. Prince's "Soldiers Bathing", Gavin Ewart's "Officer's Mess", and Henry Reed's "Lessons of War".

Keith Douglas (1920–44) and Alun Lewis (1915–44) are recognized as the most important of the poets who described the war and died during it. They do not remark the shocking, cataclysmic tragedy of the conflict, but its depressing dullness, its idiotic repetition of horror. Both poets, but particularly Douglas, feel the futility of writing war poetry in the shadow of Owen and Rosenberg. In Lewis's poetry, written from the Indian sub-continent—he died in Burma—the destructiveness of the war serves as background for lamentation over the diminished role of the

soldier-hero and moral-objector, and over the fate of moral choice in a world where choices have become ineffectual. The neo-romantic poet Sidney Keyes (1922–43) deserves mention as another war poet complaining of the boredom of war. In contrast, poems by Roy Fuller (1912–91) are bitter in tone but light in form; they express the assumption that "verse in our time must try to comprise the experience of the majority, despite working in minority terms."

In the post-war period skeptical, humorous, deflatingly anti-romantic poets were gathered together in what came to be called "The Movement", celebrated in Robert Conquest's 1956 anthology *New Lines.* Its character was not based on any distinct program of technical inovation or ideological statement, reflecting instead a pervasive dispiritedness and self-ironizing post-war humor. The nine poets chiefly identified with the Movement are PHILIP LARKIN, Kingsley Amis, Donald Davie, Elizabeth Jennings, D.J. Enright, John Holloway, Robert Conquest, Thom Gunn, and John Wain. Beyond a shared disdain for the romantic afflatus of the 1940s and its rhetorical excesses, these are poets of strongly different characters.

Larkin, who never claimed membership in the Movement, is nevertheless its poetic exemplar. The persona of his most popular poems is an affably self-critical defeatist, not entirely unlike Larkin himself, whose awkwardness, ineffectualness, and anxiety are consonant with a national mood of post-imperial letdown. Yet because the poems are deft, sure-footed performances, a complex tension between poet and persona emerges. "Church Going" is a fine example of Larkin's ambivalence towards English customs and institutions, which he both yearns for and rejects. His range of tones is wide and dynmaic. Larkin can begin a poem with "he's fucking her and she's on the pill," yet rise to the guarded apotheosis of "High Windows".

Davie (1922–95) has been the most willing of the Movement poets to acknowledge its existence and to claim membership. For him the Movement is a return from neo-romanticism to controlled craftsmanship, moral responsibility, and civilized intelligence. Like Graves, his style can be Augustan, and his subject matter intense self-scrutiny. Davie's poetry is assertive yet also alertly self-conscious and self-questioning.

Gunn (1929–), the youngest poet included in the *New Lines* anthology, is rarely associated with that group now. His career since the 1950s has been a process of artistic growth that has followed the course of pop culture from writing about leather-jacketed "rockers", motorcycle toughs, and Elvis Presley in the 1950s to tripping on LSD in the 1960s, to watching friends in San

Francisco die of AIDS in his latest book *The Man with Night Sweats* (1992).

Since the 1960s Gunn's name is more often linked with that of the controversial Ted Hughes (1930–98), a tough-minded realist with romantic inclinations. In poems about animals Hughes confronts the brutality of life and seems to admire animal vitality for its unalterable violence. His blunt syntax and diction are well-suited to his subject. His imagery is concrete, but the poems are philosophical considerations of general categories of the primal and the natural.

Charles Tomlinson (1929–), like Gunn and Davie, is one of the English poets who has praised the Americans William Carlos Williams, Edward Dorn, and Charles Olson, recommending them as models for British poets. (All three British poets have taught in America, although only Gunn has made it his permanent residence.) Tomlinson's poems are descriptions of landscapes viewed with an analytic, compositional eye. Unlike the emotional, "free-spirited" poets he praises, Tomlinson's persona is coldly aesthetic, like that of another American poet, Wallace Stevens. Like Stevens, he has a gift for making small matters of description into deep questions of human perception.

Since the popular thrust of the Movement, no poet has been as antithetically unconcerned about public taste, or as impenetrably difficult, as Geoffrey Hill (1932–). His fierce contemplations of spiritual and political power are placed in remote and obscure historical frameworks such as King Offa's Mercia, or in invented historical ones like that of the poet "Sebastian Arrurruz". Even when Hill writes of actual historical figures such as Hitler, Stalin, or Idi Amin, his dense punning and allegorical conflations are uncompromisingly opaque. Nevertheless, his authoritative voice is in the line of Yeats, and his weaving together of historical moments with mythological symbols recalls Eliot and David Jones.

Seamus Heaney (1939–) is the most recent of Irish poets to play a central role in English poetry, and his impact has been greater than that of Austin Clarke or Patrick Kavanagh. A Catholic from Northern Ireland, Heaney has had to reconcile his gift for writing a universal poetry with his feelings of political allegiance to his countrymen. In *Death of a Naturalist* (1965) and *Door into the Dark* (1969) Heaney writes the best narratives of physical, country work since Frost. His descriptions of physical labor are parables of sexual and moral initiations. Since the 1970s Heaney's poetry has become more political, but not shallowly or propagandistically so.

Lewis Klausner

Bibliography
Corcoran, Neil. *English Poetry Since 1940.* 1993.
Davie, Donald. *Under Briggflatts: A History of Poetry in Great Britain 1960–1988.* 1989.
Morrison, Blake. *The Movement: English Poetry of the 1950s.* 1980.
O'Neill, Michael. *Auden, MacNeice, Spender: The Thirties Poetry.* 1992.
Parfitt, George A.E. *English Poetry of the First World War.* 1990.
Press, John. *A Map of Modern English Verse.* 1969.
Ross, Robert H. *The Georgian Revolt 1910–1922: Rise and Fall of a Poetic Ideal.* 1965.
Shires, Linda. *British Poetry of the Second World War.* 1985.

Political and Economic Planning (PEP)

The Political and Economic Planning group is best remembered for having pioneered the modern think-tank in the 1930s and 1940s. Indeed, the group was long upheld as an example of the growing influence in modern society of professional and expert opinion, whose disinterested and technocratic outlook was thought to have fostered the progressive intellectual climate in the 1930s that helped pave the way for the erection of the WELFARE STATE and the Keynesian revolution after the Second World War. More recent research, however, suggests that the story of PEP is far more complex. Certainly, though the group came to proclaim itself as a non-political and strictly fact-finding research institute, its mission was neither politically disinterested nor, at first, ideologically progressive.

The founding of PEP was inspired by the publication, as a supplement to the *Week-end Review* of 14 February 1931, of a radical call for economic and institutional reconstruction, entitled *A National Plan for Great Britain*. Issued at the height of the economic and political crisis in 1931, the plan attracted the interest of reformers from all walks of life, including the banker Sir Basil Blackett, the economist Sir Arthur Salter, the biologist JULIAN HUXLEY, Max Nicholson, the journalist who had drafted the original plan, and Israel Sieff of MARKS & SPENCER. From its inception, the new group's purpose was explicitly ideological. Inspired as much by their alarm over the apparent collapse of the free market economy as by their fear of the possibility of a socialist solution to the crisis, its founders set out to design an explicitly capitalist blueprint for a planned economy in Britain as an alternative both to laissez-faire and state collectivism. To this end, PEP came to fashion a new doctrine of "capitalist planning", which envisioned a quasi-corporatist economy run by autonomous associations of private industry, set up as self-governing industrial councils in all sectors of the economy.

In the form of its campaign for a "Self-Government for Industry Bill", this definition of

planning became the central theme of PEP propaganda in the mid-1930s, attracting the support of
Tory planners around HAROLD MACMILLAN and
prominent businessmen in Lord Melchett's Industrial Reorganization League. The bill was
strongly resisted by the LABOUR PARTY, the TUC,
and more orthodox critics, who all noted the dangerous constitutional and economic implications
of what the *Economist* described as a "new economic feudalism". In the event, the bill was rejected by the National government in 1935 mainly
because of divisions within the business community itself, where many opposed the initiative as
an attempt to give monopolistic powers over their
enterprises to their larger business rivals.

It was this failure of its original campaign for
"capitalist planning" that forced PEP to re-think
its role and purpose. Growing dissatisfaction with
its early ideological direction had prompted some
members to leave the group; others called for its
dissolution. In the end, the group decided to
carry on with its research work and even retain its
original name, but it quietly dropped its commitment to "capitalist planning" or any other single
policy-cause. Instead, PEP began to reinvent itself as an organization of public-spirited experts
and professionals, dedicated to disseminating
specialist knowledge and fostering the growth of
"informed opinion". Priority came to be given to
in-depth studies of diverse aspects of national
life, from the ailing export industries and the national PRESS, to administration of Britain's health
services. The research was published in articles in
the monthly broadsheet *Planning* and in more
detailed special reports.

Thus transformed, PEP began to build its reputation as an independent research institute, attracting to its staff researchers from all parties,
including Michael Young, the head of the Labour Party Research Department after the war,
Angus Maude, founder of the CONSERVATIVE
One Nation group, and Jo Grimond, leader of
the LIBERAL PARTY in the 1950s. The group's success in the 1940s rested partly on the high quality
of its work and the relative absence of serious
competition. At a time when the collection of information was in its infancy in both the public
and private sectors, PEP filled the gap by offering
detailed research about many of the important
policy issues of the day.

Yet it would be difficult to ascribe the group's
success to an apolitical or strictly technocratic
stance. On the contrary, its growing influence was
due in large measure to its fortuitous move towards the progressive centre at a time when British politics were undergoing a convergent shift.
During the SECOND WORLD WAR the group
emerged at the forefront of the debate on social
and economic reconstruction, setting the tone

with its influential evidence to the BEVERIDGE
Committee. PEP's 1943 report on the economics
of full employment anticipated similar statements by the Labour Party, Beveridge, and the
government itself by more than a year, and firmly
established its reputation as one of the authors of
the new progressive consensus.

PEP was thus well-positioned to benefit from
the dramatic transformation in political culture
after the war. Though its stance was manifested
more in its selection of topics than explicit advocacy of policies, its support for the postwar consensus was unmistakable. After 1945 the group
undertook research in areas such as social services, government-industry relations, and trade
unionism. In the 1950s PEP led the way with
studies of closer links with Europe and research
into strategies for economic growth. The 1960s
saw PEP return to the again-fashionable concept
of economic planning. Its 1967 report on racial
discrimination is thought to have been decisive in
persuading the Labour government to pass the
second Race Relations Act. PEP's work in the
1970s targeted issues menacing the postwar consensus: inflation, labour relations, and incomes
policy.

If PEP's views came to be regarded as impartial
and disinterested, it is in large measure because
they fit so neatly into the postwar ideological climate. Revealingly, PEP fell upon hard times once
this climate began to change in the mid-1970s.
In 1978 the group merged with the Centre for
Studies in Social Policy to form the Policy Studies
Institute.

Daniel Ritschel

Bibliography
Denham, Andrew, and Mark Garnett, *British Think-
   tanks and the Climate of Opinion*. 1998.
Marwick, Arthur. "Middle Opinion in the Thirties",
   English Historical Review. vol. 79 (1964). pp. 285–98.
Pinder, John, ed. *Fifty Years of Political and Economic
   Planning*. 1981.
Ritschel, Daniel. *The Politics of Planning: The Debate on
   Economic Planning in Britain in the 1930s*. 1997.

Popular Culture

If, as many historians argue, the first decades of
the nineteenth century in Britain witnessed the
development of a radical popular culture by self-
taught artisans, the twentieth century has seen
the demise of that culture and the triumph of a
commercial culture that has as much to do with
business as with pleasure or politics. The commercialization of popular culture has led to many
laments for a declining, yet more "authentic," culture of "the people." Nevertheless, although the
leisure industries have transformed popular culture in the twentieth century, their products have
often been creatively appropriated by individuals

eager to maintain those very forms of popular creativity that critics argue have been lost.

In urban communities in Victorian Britain workers developed a rich associational life that flourished well into the twentieth century. Centered around communal activities like choral singing, club membership, betting, brass band competitions, drinking, FOOTBALL games, pigeon-racing, and going to fairs, the culture of the home, the street, and the neighborhood offered a crucial sense of belonging to many workers. Although activities were often segregated along gender lines, they served to bind members of the working class together in a cohesive community. Captured in Kathleen Woodward's *Jipping Street* (1928) and Robert Roberts's *The Classic Slum* (1971), this culture has more recently become central to televised representations of traditional working-class life in programs like "Coronation Street."

In the late nineteenth and early twentieth centuries this culture was penetrated by newer forms of commercial entertainment. A significant rise in real wages, coupled with a gradual decline in working hours, solidified the division between work and LEISURE and afforded many workers the opportunity to purchase hitherto unavailable pleasures. The advent of the cheap excursion train led to the rapid growth of working-class resorts like Blackpool, which attracted 1 million visitors in 1883, 4 million in 1914, and 7 million in 1939. Major investment in football teams, music halls, and the popular PRESS also transformed popular culture. While music halls emerged in the 1850s, it was only after the 1880s that they became highly-capitalized ventures, attracting a mass audience. Likewise, readership of the popular press expanded rapidly, particularly with the advent of new papers like the *Daily Express* and the *Daily Mail* around the turn of the new century. While one adult in five or six read a daily newspaper in 1900, that number had climbed to one in two by 1920.

While working-class culture was largely an urban phenomenon, rural communities were also subject to commercial penetration. The increasing erosion of traditional rural culture led turn-of-the-century folksong collectors like Cecil Sharp to preserve the musical artifacts of a decaying way of life. This fueled the idealization of the popular culture of a once "Merrie England," which intensified as the last vestiges of traditional rural life were marginalized by newer forms of mass entertainment. By the 1940s the decline of traditional rural popular culture was almost complete, occasioning many elegiac laments for a lost way of life, of which Flora Thompson's trilogy, *Lark Rise to Candleford* (1945), is perhaps the best.

The inter-war years were marked by the development of new forms of popular culture. Although the cinema expanded rapidly after 1906—there were some 400 million tickets sold in 1914—it only came to dominate popular culture after the First World War. In 1936 there were 903 million cinema admissions, a number that climbed to a peak of 1,635 million in 1946. Most popular films were made in the United States, leading the government to establish a quota system in 1927 that called for 20 percent of all films exhibited in British cinemas to be made in Britain by 1936. Although this led to the production of inexpensive "quota quickies", it also aided the development of a highly successful British FILM INDUSTRY in the 1930s and 1940s.

During the 1920s and 1930s the influence of the United States on popular culture in Britain was enormous. Not only were American films ubiquitous, but dance halls were dominated by American jazz, and American consumer goods were in great demand. These trends alarmed many intellectuals, who bemoaned the loss of national identity brought about by Americanization. They argued that popular culture should be more British, that it should be grounded in the concerns and traditions of local communities. Although this was often at odds with the cosmopolitan modernism of contemporary popular tastes, it led to the encouragement of indigenous forms of popular culture. Music hall entertainment, which had been attacked in the late nineteenth century, was now championed as an "authentic" voice of the British people, while in the 1930s a DOCUMENTARY FILM movement emerged that attempted to capture the uniqueness of those voices. MASS OBSERVATION also began to study the popular culture of local communities, culminating in such publications as *The Pub and the People* (1943) and *The Press and its Readers* (1949).

Between the wars popular culture was increasingly organized around the home and family, a tendency that was intensified by the growth of radio listening. By 1928 radios existed in a quarter of all British homes and by the 1940s few homes were without one. Established early in the 1920s, the BRITISH BROADCASTING CORPORATION (BBC) enjoyed a monopoly over the airwaves until commercial television was licensed in 1956. Under the direction of JOHN REITH, who viewed radio as a source of cultural enlightenment in the battle against the dark forces of mass culture, the BBC was devoted to moral and cultural improvement. Classical music dominated the BBC's offerings in the 1930s, although the Corporation began to capitulate to its listeners' preferences, particularly during the SECOND WORLD WAR with the advent of the Forces Programme, which entertained British troops. After the War, the

BBC played a greater role in reflecting the nation's popular taste, especially through its new Light Programme.

Although working-class culture was traditionally male-centered, many activities like radio listening were shared by men and women alike. A separate female world of popular culture also developed between the wars, in part due to the influence of Women's Institutes (established in 1915) and the continuing strength of the Women's Cooperative Guild. In addition—and despite the increasingly commercial nature of popular culture—a number of new voluntary organizations attracted both men and women in their pursuit of recreation, including the Holiday Fellowship (established in 1913), the Workers' Travel Association (1921), and the Youth Hostels Association (1930). Following the passage of the Holidays With Pay Act in 1938, more workers began to enjoy annual holidays. While this encouraged the growth of traditional resorts, it also led to the advent of the new holiday camp, which, under the entrepreneurial initiatives of Billy Butlin, flourished, especially in the later 1940s and 1950s.

During the twentieth century the state has come to play a major role in the regulation and provision of popular culture. Local authorities had always been responsible for licensing places of entertainment and providing amenities like parks and swimming pools; before the First World War the London County Council was particularly well-known for its active, municipal culture. By the 1940s, however, the national government had also become a major purveyor of popular culture, especially through the Entertainments National Service Association (ENSA), which provided entertainment for the armed forces and in war-production factories, and the COUNCIL FOR THE ENCOURAGEMENT OF MUSIC AND THE ARTS (CEMA), which promoted amateur music, drama, and painting in Britain. Although the latter organization inspired the establishment of the ARTS COUNCIL in 1946, which turned increasingly to the funding of artistic excellence, the state has continued to promote popular culture, largely through the National Film Finance Corporation (created in 1949), and the Sports Council (1964).

The late 1940s witnessed a surge in the number of people who enjoyed the cinema and football matches, although traditional working-class culture declined rapidly in the 1950s. By the end of the decade a number of writers lamented that decline, most notably Richard Hoggart, whose *The Uses of Literacy* (1957) evoked a whole way of life that was in the process of disintegrating. The rapid advance in ownership of cars and television sets hastened the decline of the cinema and drove much popular culture into the home. In addition,

traditional working-class neighborhoods, with their rich associational life that revolved around the street, the corner shop, the pub, and the club, were the target of urban redevelopment schemes in the 1950s and 1960s, leading to the destruction of the built environment in which much popular culture had once flourished.

Real disposable income in Britain doubled between 1951 and 1972, unleashing an unprecedented consumer boom that transformed popular culture, especially for the young. By the end of the 1950s, critics were noting the existence of the new "teenage consumer" who rebelled against traditional forms of working-class culture and engaged in the consumption of fashionable clothes, records, and entertainment in night clubs. With the advent of the teenager came the development of new youth cultures—the Teddy Boys in the 1950s, the Mods and the Rockers in the 1960s, and the more ominous Skinheads in the 1970s. They rejected traditional forms of popular culture, along with the homogeneity increasingly associated with highly commercialized forms of mass culture. In the "swinging London" of the 1960s, the style of the new youth culture pervaded society, especially after the BEATLES were catapulted to fame and Britain began to make a major contribution to an increasingly global popular culture.

The post-war emphasis on personal choice in the uses of leisure undermined communal forms of popular culture, as did the emergence of ethnic cultures. IMMIGRATION to Britain from nations of the Commonwealth grew rapidly from the 1950s, each group bringing its own cultural baggage with it. On the one hand, this enriched dominant forms of popular culture: Jamaican reggae soon entered the British musical mainstream, while eating out, an increasingly popular pastime, often included the patronage of ethnic establishments. On the other hand, cultural diversity has been viewed by many as a threat to native forms of popular culture and to established idioms of national identity. Although Skinhead violence against immigrants peaked in the late 1970s and early 1980s, many white Britons have become increasingly nostalgic for traditional forms of British popular culture, fueling the growth of the heritage industry in the 1980s.

Present-day popular culture in Britain cannot be understood without taking note of the importance of shopping and video arcades, of television and travel, and of the rapid emergence of a global entertainment market. By the 1980s leisure consumed more than 25 per cent of consumer spending in Britain, much of it devoted to personal consumption and home-centered leisure activities. But other activities have also become popular, including overseas package holidays to places like the Spanish Costa Brava, which has led to the demise of Blackpool and other traditional British resorts. Although Blackpool has often tried to regain its reputation, largely through skillful advertising ("Costa Notta Lotta" was the mid-1980s rallying cry), traditional forms of popular culture in Britain have been transformed beyond recognition since the 1950s. Once defined by the communities that often made—and always enjoyed—it, popular culture has become a more complex and more fragmented phenomenon, increasing the opportunities for individual expression while undermining the social cohesiveness with which earlier forms of popular culture were often associated.

Chris Waters

Bibliography

Chambers, Iain. *Popular Culture: The Metropolitan Experience.* 1986.

Clarke, John, and Charles Critcher. *The Devil Makes Work: Leisure in Capitalist Britain.* 1985.

Davies, Andrew. *Leisure, Gender, and Poverty: Working-Class Culture in Salford and Manchester, 1900–1939.* 1992.

Jones, Stephen G. *Workers At Play: A Social and Economic History of Leisure 1918–1939.* 1986.

Walvin, James. *Leisure and Society, 1830–1950.* 1978.

Popular Fiction

Throughout the century reading has been one of the most popular and accessible leisure activities among all ages and classes. The preferred choice has been popular or "light" fiction—romances, thrillers, Westerns—in book and magazine form. The desire to "escape" with a good story has rarely waned and during wartime has intensified. Because popular fiction is a commercial venture, it is susceptible to changing tastes and to external influences, particularly from the cinema.

At the turn of the century publishing was expanding along with the reading public, one result of the spread of education and the rise in literacy. By 1900 publishers responded to increasing demand by giving readers what they apparently wanted—weekly magazines filled with tales of romance and adventure, and inexpensive editions of best-selling novels. In 1900 there were two acknowledged best-selling authors of popular fiction: Marie Corelli and Hall Caine. Corelli wrote lush romances laden with religion and morality, Caine romantic adventures set in exotic locales. Each author had average annual sales of 100,000 copies at a time when 5,000 qualified as a runaway bestseller. They inspired many, including Florence J. Barclay, whose purpose in writing was "the joy of helping people along the road to heaven." An estimated 20 million people read Barclay's *The Rosary* (1909), her biggest success. Charles Garvice and Nat Gould were also popu-

lar, but more secular, romantic novelists than Barclay, as was the Baroness Orczy (1865–1947), author of the swashbuckler, *The Scarlet Pimpernel* (1905). The more daring Ethel M. Dell's erotic, violent love stories were in the tradition of the Gothic novel, while E.M. Hull's *The Sheik* (1919) inspired legions of harem romances. Elinor Glyn's 1907 novel, *Three Weeks,* the story of an affair between a Balkan princess and her younger English lover, sold over 2 million copies.

The magazine leader was the Amalgamated Press, founded by Alfred Harmsworth, Lord Northcliffe, who built an empire of ninety titles targeted at working women, housewives, and children. *Woman's Weekly* (1911) is still one of Britain's best-selling magazines. Two titles for boys, the *Gem* (1907) and the *Magnet* (1908), set the standard for school stories, featuring the adventures of Tom Merry and Billy Bunter. Several prolific children's authors got their start in the serial world, including the adventure writer Percy Westerman and Angela Brazil, the mistress of the girls' school story.

Surveys showed the broad popularity of murder mysteries as well. The leader by far was Edgar Wallace, nicknamed "The Fiction Factory," who wrote 170 books, including *The Four Just Men* (1905). By 1939 one in four of books bought in Britain were written by him. During the First World War soldiers and housewives alike read E. Phillips Oppenheim's detective novels, escapist fantasies often set in the French Riviera.

In the 1920s and 1930s publishing expanded and was commercialized, with advertising used as never before to promote new books. Radio and the cinema did not detract from reading; adaptations were common, and Hollywood glamor, "cops and robbers," and the Wild West inspired new writers. The new leader in popular weekly magazines was the Scottish firm D.C. Thomson. Its "Big Five" boys' papers *(Adventure, Wizard, Rover, Skipper, Hotspur)* took boys out of the classroom for thrilling international adventures. The firm also cornered the expanding comics market *(The Beano* and *The Dandy),* and dominated magazines for middle- and working-class women, with romance papers (including current bestsellers *The People's Friend* and *My Weekly),* and the so-called "erotic bloods" *(Red Letter, Red Star,* and *Secrets),* which contained graphic morality tales with good, clean violence.

The three most popular children's authors of the 1920s and 1930s are still read: Enid Blyton, Richmal Crompton, and Captain W.E. Johns. Blyton's success with the "Famous Five" and "Secret Seven" adventure series preceded her hit "Toyland" books, featuring Little Noddy and Big Ears, in the 1950s. Crompton's William Brown series was launched in 1922 with *Just William.*

Johns's *Biggles* and *Worrals of the W.A.A.F.* series taught boys and girls lessons in sportsmanship and loyalty to both monarchy and parents.

Given the Depression, and the frequency of novel reading, borrowing books was preferred over buying. The commercial or "tuppenny" libraries were the popular alternative to the public libraries, which tended not to stock lighter fare. Several firms, including the romantic fiction publishers Mills & Boon, became library houses, targeting novels to specific readers. Collins's enormously successful "Crime Club" detective series, featuring AGATHA CHRISTIE, and Hodder and Stoughton's "Yellow Jackets" popular novels, are other examples of commercial publishing ventures.

Popular inter-war detective writers included DOROTHY SAYERS, Peter Cheyney, John Creasey, Dornford Yates, and Nicholas Blake (C. DAY LEWIS). "Sapper" (Herman Cyril McNeile) launched his "Bulldog Drummond" series in 1920, and Leslie Charteris's "Saint" made his first appearance in 1928. Ruby M. Ayres and Denise Robins penned romances; P.G. WODEHOUSE dominated comedy with 120 novels, and the American author Zane Grey's Westerns were sell-outs. Daphne du Maurier's novels, including *Jamaica Inn* (1936) and *Rebecca* (1938), have never been out of print.

During the SECOND WORLD WAR reading choice was restricted by paper rationing, but blackout hours increased the demand. The bestsellers of the war years were both thrillers: James Hadley Chase's *No Orchids for Miss Blandish* (1939), and *Who Killed Oliver Cromwell?* (1937) by Leonard Gribble. Since 1945 the influence of cinema and television has been profound. Magazines, for example, became more visual and less text-intensive. Color and photography were used extensively. Fiction also broadened; romances reflected the improved status of women with more independent heroines and familiar situations. Mass market weeklies, launched before the war, were redesigned in the 1950s and still dominate the market, with circulations near the million mark: *Woman* (1937), *Woman's Own* (1938), *Woman's Weekly*, and *My Weekly*. Children's magazines also evolved into "picture-story papers." One of the first, the *Eagle* (1950), was an instant success, selling over a million copies per week. Its companion paper, *Girl,* started in 1951, followed by D.C. Thomson's girls' publications *Bunty* (1958) and *Judy* (1960). D.C. Thomson also launched a Second World War nostalgia craze with its popular *Commando* and *Warlord* library novelettes (1974).

The decline of the commercial libraries inspired innovative schemes, including book clubs, to get people to buy books. Mills & Boon, for ex-

ample, launched a successful direct-market subscription service in the 1960s. But it was the introduction of the mass market paperback which would have the greatest impact. Penguin Books (1935), the first paperback venture, was joined after the war by the Pan, Corgi, Panther, Sphere, and Fontana paperback imprints, publishers of romance, crime, and war stories. At sixpence or less, books were now accessible, inexpensive, and as disposable as a weekly magazine.

Overall, it is striking to note how little reading tastes have changed since the Second World War, with the exception of Westerns, which declined in popularity both in print and on the screen. School stories, for example, continue to be popular among girls. Old favorites like Dorita Fairlie Bruce's "Dimsie" books and Elinor Brent-Dyer's "Chalet School" series endured, alongside novels spun off from the popular television series "Grange Hill" in the 1970s. Romantic fiction is still dominated by Mills & Boon. Behind the firm's longevity lies aggressive market research and a willingness to change with the times. The once-chaste Mills & Boon romance, for example, now includes pre-marital sex scenes. Barbara Cartland (1901–2000), the most visible British symbol of romance, may hold the world's record for the most novels written (over 600), but her dated tales of virginal heroines are no longer popular. More respectable—and marketable—romantic fiction is written by Catherine Cookson and Barbara Taylor Bradford.

The reading public still enjoys crime fiction and adventure thrillers. Novelists like Ian Fleming *(Casino Royale)*, Frederick Forsyth *(The Day of the Jackal)*, and Jeffrey Archer *(Kane and Abel)* have achieved celebrity status at home and abroad and sell in the millions. Ruth Rendell, P.D. James, and Elizabeth Ferrars are among those who have followed in Agatha Christie's footsteps.

Joseph McAleer

Bibliography

Cadogan, Mary, and Patricia Craig. *You're a Brick, Angela! The Girls' Story 1839–1985.* 1976.

Hoggart, Richard. *The Uses of Literacy.* 1958.

McAleer, Joseph. *Popular Reading and Publishing in Britain 1914–1950.* 1992.

Symons, Julian. *Bloody Murder: From the Detective Story to the Crime Novel.* 1985.

Turner, E.S. *Boys Will Be Boys.* 1975.

Popular Front

The Popular Front campaign aimed to unite all political forces opposed to the government's policy of appeasing the Fascist dictatorships. It was first advocated by the COMMUNIST PARTY OF GREAT BRITAIN in 1935 and was endorsed by many leading Liberals. Despite official opposition from the LABOUR PARTY, which nursed a profound distrust of the Liberals and Communists and discounted the claim that a united effort would help defeat the government, the Popular Front slowly gathered support among Labour leftists. In April 1938 SIR STAFFORD CRIPPS, ANEURIN BEVAN, and other left-wing leaders launched a campaign to change Labour's position. They failed but continued the campaign publicly. Cripps was consequently expelled from the Labour Party in January 1939; Bevan and four others followed in March. Thus denied the essential objective of Labour Party participation, the campaign rapidly fizzled out.

The immediate inspiration for the Popular Front campaign in Britain was the election of Popular Front governments in France and Spain in 1936. In line with Soviet foreign policy, which aimed to form alliances with the democracies in order to contain Germany, the Communist International endorsed the strategy in 1935 following the formation of the French Popular Front in the previous year. This led the CPGB to broaden its earlier aim of forming a United Front consisting only of socialist organizations. As a first step the CPGB applied for affiliation to the Labour Party in 1936. The application was resoundingly defeated at the Labour Party conference in October despite the support of the SOCIALIST LEAGUE (the official organization of the Labour Left), which at that stage supported socialist unity, but opposed the Popular Front on the grounds that non-socialists could not be reliable allies.

In June the Socialist League's secretary, J.T. Murphy, left the League to form the People's Front Propaganda Committee, which gained support from individuals of all parties and sponsored some well-attended public meetings, but made little real political headway. The outbreak of the SPANISH CIVIL WAR in July 1936 lent the Popular Front further support, but it took Germany's annexation of Austria in March 1938 to bring wholehearted endorsement from the Labour Left.

In October and November 1938 the Labour Party refrained from nominating candidates against "Independent Progressive" candidates in two by-elections. The first, A.D. Lindsay—a member of the Labour Party—considerably reduced the Conservative majority in Oxford; Vernon Bartlett, a Liberal, won at Bridgwater. Such passivity was as near as the Labour leadership ever came to accepting Popular Front forms of action.

Although the Popular Front is often seen simply as a Communist ruse, it struck deep chords among some Liberals and socialists, many of whom had advocated and practised cross-party collaboration intermittently for decades, particularly in times of international political crisis.

David Blaazer

Bibliography
Blaazer, David. *The Popular Front and the Progressive Tradition: Socialists, Liberals and the Quest for Unity 1884–1939.* 1992.
Cole, G.D.H. *The People's Front.* 1937.
Jupp, James. *The Radical Left in Britain 1931–1941.* 1982.
Pimlott, Ben. *Labour and the Left in the 1930s.* 1977.

Popular Music

Britain's most lasting exports in its long years of decline as a manufacturing power since the Second World War have been the commodities associated with the popular music industry. Various "British waves" have hit the shores of other countries since Beatlemania led the first pop invasion of the United States in the early to mid-1960s which included Herman's Hermits, The Rolling Stones, The Kinks, and many more. New Pop (in the form of Boy George and the Culture Club, Spandau Ballet, Duran Duran) repeated the exercise in the early 1980s, while the madcap imagery of "Madchester", the global media name for music supposedly associated with the region around Manchester in the late 1980s, made the cover of *Newsweek* without guaranteeing automatic Stateside success for bands like Happy Mondays, Stone Roses, and 808 State. However, it is arguable that the British recording industry has never really regained its position after the economic crisis in the industry immediately after punk in the late 1970s.

In 1976–7 punk ideology managed, fleetingly, to discredit the rock myths which were manifestly decaying in Britain by the mid-1970s. It did so by laying bare the business techniques and tactics involved in its own production. One of the many contradictory effects of punk on the pop music industry was that it better prepared subsequent pop stars for the task of attempting to control their own destinies to a greater degree than before.

Alongside the musical form of punk itself came a resuscitation of rock meanings: what the music stood for, what, and whom, it represented. Politicization of pop in Britain in the period from the mid-1970s to the mid-1980s depended, mainly, on the notion of pop as an art form, rather than, as in pre-punk days, rock as a folk form. Whether, as consumers of the music press mythologies have claimed, it was indeed U2, or Simple Minds, or The Smiths, or Stone Roses that constituted the last great rock monument in pop culture remained, largely, besides the point. The influence of rock culture lies beyond any simple analysis of its political economy—in other words it involves analysis of more than just its market potential, its part in patterns of profitability. Music industry corporate strategies have shifted significantly since the late 1970s, necessitating the creation and targeting of multiple new consumer categories, as well as the exploitation of rights in intellectual property (copyright in songs, for instance) rather than merely the orthodox reliance on selling as many units as possible.

Rock's late 1960s myths, amalgamating counterculture with a certain melange of musical styles, have provided the raw material for a host of young bands and performers to reference pop (and youth culture) pasts even though they were not personally present in the making of such popular memory. They also sustain older musicians and singers who first built their styles and reputations in those years and could not realistically have expected a prosperous, life-long career in an industry which had institutionalized the notion of "permanent teenage". Recycling the 1970s for the compact disc 1980s frequently demanded a rather partisan reconstruction of the pop signs of that decade: this view tends to play down glamrock's androgyny and punk's garage and pub rock roots. There is, though, always ample scope for rewriting the narrative for different audiences at different times to meet various consumer markets. The sight of a cluster of ageing rock stars rattling their jewellery for royalty on Prince's Trust concert stages and records not only recalls the BEATLES' moral dilemmas of the 1960s, but emphasizes the historical development of the formularization of rock as "rebellion" and underscores the respectable face of rock and pop which has constantly been present. The sheer healthiness of the popular music industry was what stood out for the casual pop consumer in the mid to late 1980s, just as it did in the mid-1970s prior to punk's emergence in 1976–7. In the shop window were the familiar selling points: the quality of digital production, the vitality of the speed and energetic movement on stage or video, and the super-efficiency of much of the playing, however simulated. It was this context which prompted a younger generation to develop what has become labeled as rave culture in the 1990s, promoting the role of the DJ, mixer, and engineer, and dance culture as more radical than mere pop or rock.

Steve Redhead

Bibliography

Chambers, Iain. *Urban Rhythms: Pop Music and Popular Culture.* 1985.

Clarke, Donald. *The Rise and Fall of Popular Music.* 1995.

Lee, Edward. *Music of the People: A Study of Popular Music in Great Britain.* 1970.

Taylor, Paul. *Popular Music Since 1955: A Critical Guide to the Literature.* 1985.

Population

In contrast to the nineteenth century when the population of Great Britain increased by more than 350 percent, the twentieth century has been characterized by diminishing fertility and a much slower rate of population growth. The 1901 Census counted some 38 million people in the country compared to 10.5 million a hundred years earlier. These figures reflected an increase of nearly 14 percent every ten years. They were closely associated with a higher incidence of MARRIAGE than in most other Western countries and an unprecedentedly high crude birthrate of nearly 35 births per 1000 of the population.

Although the closing years of the century were marked by the beginning of a protracted decline in the birthrate and steady diminution in the number of children born per marriage, the increase in population remained high (10.9 percent) in the pre-First World War decade before it began to fall precipitously after 1911. Indeed the population grew by less than 5 percent in the next ten years, a diminished rate of increase compounded to some extent by the disruptions and losses of the FIRST WORLD WAR, but which despite minor fluctuations continued in subsequent decades. An influx of IMMIGRANTS from the Commonwealth in the 1950s and 1960s resulted in a modest surge in the decennial rate of growth to about 5.5 percent before plummeting at times to a nearly static 0.83 percent in the 1970s and 1980s. Instead of rising to the 76 million that planners predicted in the comparatively fertile post-Second World War decade when the population stood at approximately 50 million, the figure as Great Britain entered the last decade of the century was closer to 57 million. If current trends continue, it is not likely to reach even 60 million until the year 2025.

The much slower rate of population growth in the twentieth century as compared to the nineteenth was closely correlated with the at first gradual and then precipitous decline in fertility that began in the 1880s. It has, despite temporary surges after the First and Second World Wars, more or less continued to the present day. At its peak in the 1870s the crude birthrate of 35 per 1000 when corrected translated into nearly 290 offspring per 1000 women between the child-bearing ages of fifteen to forty-four. By the First World War the birthrate had fallen some 33 percent, to 24 per 1000 and the corrected rate stood at 191 per 1000. The large Victorian family of five or six children per marriage was fast being replaced by its more modern counterpart of three or four.

Contemporaries were often puzzled and distressed by this rapid reversal of demographic patterns that had persisted for more than a century, and they began a process of prognostication and inquiry that continued off and on throughout the remainder of the century. Their anxieties focused upon the inverse correlation between family size and social status as middle- and upper-class birthrates fell much more rapidly than those of the unskilled laboring poor—a phenomenon that allegedly threatened the "quality of the race". Others fearful of "race suicide" warned of the possibility of an absolute decline in population that would imperil Great Britain's economic and imperial position in the world.

The First World War only compounded these worries as casualties soared while fertility fell another 30 percent. Despite a brief recovery after the war stimulated by a temporary surge in marriages, the birthrate started down again in 1922, reaching a low of around 15 per 1000 in the 1930s. Women who married in the postwar decade gave birth to an average of 2.2 children well below the 3.5 produced by their parents in the first decade of the century.

Although the mean age at which women married has increased steadily throughout the century from around 25 to nearly 28 today, the overall rate of marriage in Great Britain, despite numerous fluctuations, remains, as it has been since the nineteenth century, the highest in Europe. If in the past decade the number of marriages per thousand people has fallen from around 15 to 14, the figures are not remarkably different from those that prevailed at various times in the preceding decades. What has changed dramatically is the number of these marriages that end in DIVORCE, up from only 7,000 before the Second World War to nearly 150,000 a year during the past decade, the second highest rate in Europe. Whatever the marital problems of the twentieth century, it is clear that couples, however long they were together, increasingly determined for a variety of economic, social, and cultural reasons to limit the number of children they were willing to have and families grew smaller with each succeeding generation.

Initially there were heated disputes about the causes of the falling birthrate; to resolve them the government authorized the taking of a unique *Fertility of Marriage Census* in 1911 that was not made public until after the war. It confirmed what by then was obvious—whatever their reasons British couples were rapidly adopting BIRTH CONTROL as an important facet of domestic culture. The first voluntary birth control facility, MARIE STOPES's Mother's Clinic, was opened in 1921; by 1939 their number had expanded to seventy, most of them allied with the newly-established Family Planning Association. In addition, with the grudging acquiescence of the Ministry of Health, contraceptive advice was being provided in more than 280 local welfare centers. Most of the clinics were established to assist the working classes whose greater fertility was a source of numerous concerns and complaints as well as an explanation for the persistence of poverty. In reality the clinics and welfare centers were visited by a very small proportion of the population between the wars while birth control practices were increasingly adopted by people at every level of society, a pattern that has continued to the present day.

By the mid-1930s the birthrate had fallen so far that there were serious fears that the current generation was no longer even replacing itself and that at some point in the not-too-distant future the population of Great Britain would begin to decline precipitously. This so-called "depopulation panic" preoccupied social reformers and demographic planners throughout the remainder of the decade and on into the Second World War. It stimulated numerous pronatalist schemes to encourage larger families and led to the appointment in 1943 of a Royal Commission on Population, which, when it finally reported in 1949, provided the most comprehensive survey of demographic patterns since the *Fertility of Marriage Census* of 1911.

As if to demonstrate the unpredictability of determining the domestic strategies of married couples, by the time the Commission's findings began to appear the birthrate was already on the rise again from a record low of around 14 per 1000 in 1941. During the post-war "baby boom" fertility hovered around 20 per 1000 into the mid-1960s before it began a steady decline towards what some described as a "birth dearth". By the mid-1970s birthrates approached 12.5 per 1000 before gradually creeping back up to around 13.5 per 1000, a rate that has persisted more or less to the present day. As a result the general fertility of women fifteen to forty-four remains at near 62 per 1000, while the average number of children born has fallen from 2.4 to 1.8 since the boom ended in 1971, a figure that remains below the replacement level of 2.1 estimated as necessary to sustain the population at its current level.

The effects of diminishing fertility on population size have been moderated by parallel century-long declines in mortality and improvements in longevity. Fueled by striking advances in the reduction of infant and childhood mortality overall deathrates fell from 17 to 18 deaths per 1000 of the population at the end of the Victorian era to approximately 11.5 in recent years. The result has been an increase in life-expectancy from fifty-five years to seventy-eight years for women and from fifty-one to seventy-two years for men. When coupled to the low fertility of modern marriages, these trends have resulted in an ageing population in which the percentage of people under fifteen has declined by 3 percent since before the Second World War while the percentage of those over sixty-five has nearly doubled.

The integration of birth control instruction into the family welfare system and the NATIONAL HEALTH SERVICE since the Second World War, coupled to the remarkable technological and biological developments in contraception such as the ubiquitous "pill" have greatly facilitated recent trends in reproduction. But in the broader context of twentieth-century developments the evidence seems to confirm that the post-war baby boom was but a temporary reversal in the decline of family size that began a hundred years ago as part of a social-demographic revolution characteristic today of all Western industrialized countries.

Richard A. Soloway

Bibliography

Coleman, David, and John Salt. *The British Population* 1992.

Mitchison, Rosalind. *British Population Change Since 1860.* 1977.

Soloway, Richard Allen. *Birth Control and the Population Question in England, 1877–1930.* 1982.

———. *Demography and Degeneration: Eugenics and the Declining Birthrate in Twentieth-Century Britain.* 1990.

Teitelbaum, Michael S. *The British Fertility Decline: Demographic Transition in the Crucible of the Industrial Revolution.* 1984.

Tranter, Neil. *Population Since the Industrial Revolution: The Case of England and Wales.* 1973.

Post-Modernism in Architecture

ARCHITECTURE in the last quarter of the twentieth century has manifested two trends both of which emerged in the 1960s: a modern technological and structural expression, principally in steel and glass, embodied in High Tech design, and a return to pre-Modern historicism, especially evidenced in a Post-Modern Classicism and the Neo-Vernacular.

Work in the 1960s by James Stirling demonstrated the transition to an industrial aesthetic which consciously expressed the structural and techtonic elements of a building. Stirling and (James) Gowan's Leicester Engineering Laboratories (1959–63) borrowed forms from a factory vernacular including traditional brick construction and industrial windows. The closed forms of the brick lecture theaters jutted dramatically from either side of the entrance and contrasted with the glass-enriched towers in a composition reminiscent of Constructivist projects. Stirling's History Faculty Library, CAMBRIDGE (with Michael Wilford, 1964–9) and his Foley Building, Queen's College, OXFORD (1968) presented greenhouse walls of steel and glass as expressive declarations of the aesthetic potential of the materials of Modernism.

Such displays of steel and glass would characterize two phases of Late Modern design: a High

Modern Miesian Aesthetic, as evidenced by American architects' 1960s work in England and by the early work of Norman Foster, and a High Tech structural expressionism promoted initially by popular images of the Archigram Group and evidenced in executed work in Britain from the 1970s on. Eero Saarinen's 1964 Chrysler-Cummins factory at Darlington continued the late High Modernism of Mies Van der Rohe. Kevin Roche and John Dinkaloo's 1965 companion Cummins Factory was a classical steel and glass temple with columns and full entablature in cor-ten steel (its first use in Britain) on a steel sylobate. Norman and Wendy Foster (with Richard Rogers) directly expressed the frame and cross-shaped wind bracing at the Reliance Controls factory, Swindon (1967), a work with corrugated steel cladding in a building which was fast and cheap to erect and American in appearance. In 1974, however, Foster built a highly expressive Late Modern steel and glass curtain wall which he wrapped around the curved face of the Willis Faber and Dumas Insurance Building in Ipswich.

While the structural histrionics of the Archigram Group envisioned such fanciful mechanistic images as Peter Cook's Plug-In City (1964) or Ron Herron's Walking City (1964), few built works immediately brought to fruition such cartoon-inspired futuristic images of High Technology. At the London Zoo, Cedric Price and Lord Snowdon had built an Aviary (1962) constructed of steel tubes and glass, with pedestrian paths penetrating the volumes; the resulting experiences in the birds' environment recalled Price's Fun Palace project (1961) with its changeable stage sets for High Technology "happenings". The closest approximation to Archigram's High Tech imagery in a constructed work in London during the 1960s was the Ministry of Public Buildings and Works' Post Office Radio Tower of 1965. However, a dozen years later, a Post-Modern High Tech presence on the British urban landscape, comparable to Rogers and Renzo Piano's Pompidou Centre in Paris (1974–6), was evidenced in London at Rogers's Lloyd's Bank Building (1978–86).

In Britain, the shift from the Late Modern Miesian Aesthetic to a High Tech display of a building's constructional and service elements was especially evidenced in the work of Norman Foster and is prefigured in his IBM Head Office, Hampsire (1971). Foster's Warehouse and Showroom for Modern Glass Ltd., Thamesmead (1973) more expressively displayed blue stove enameled corrugated steel skin enclosing steel portal frames and served as a prototype for the architect's more famous 1978 addition of the Sainsbury Center at the University of East Anglia. Subsequent High Tech works of note include Rogers's Inmos Microprocessor Factory in Gwent, Wales (1982), Foster's Renault Building, Swindon (1982), and Rogers and Michael Hopkins's Schlumberger Research Institute, Cambridge (1984).

The Post-Modern era also ushered in a return to a history-based aesthetic, finding inspiraton in vernacular forms, classical traditions, and pre-Modern British Free Style design. The pastiche dimensions of Post-Modern historicism were evidenced by the dream-world traditionalism of Clough Williams-Ellis who at Portmeirion built a Mediterranean resort town in North Wales, or the "dress up" history (cladding modern office buildings with classical garb) of the Richmond Development, London (1989) by Quinlin Terry. An accomplished exercise in Post-Modern Classicism is Robert Venturi's Sainsbury Wing of the National Gallery of Art (1990) whose colossal pilastered facade and staircase succeed as more monumental gestures than William Wilkins's weak dome, the classical focus of the original National Gallery building of 1832–8. A second Post-Modern Classical work of note is Stirling and Wilford's One Poultry (1989), which employs the same V-windows which Stirling introduced at his Clore Gallery (1987). Both works are remarkable in scale, relating a large but well-proportioned building mass to neighboring classical structures.

On the enlarged urban scale, the pluralism of Post-Modernism is seen at Broadgate (1986–92), a redevelopment project larger than anything seen in London since the days of Christopher Wren's rebuilding after the Great Fire. At Broadgate (Phases 1–4 by Arup Associates, remaining phases by Skidmore, Owings, & Merrill), various architectural styles cluster around pedestrian squares and maintain a more human scale through what has been called "groundscrapers", skyscrapers turned horizontally. Canary Wharf (Phase I, 1992), with master planning also by SOM and designs by I.M. Pei, Cesar Pelli, and Kohn Pederson Fox, brings to London an American urbanism of unprecedented scale.

When the more traditional and Free Style languages of recent British architectural history are revived—the Queen Anne, Arts and Crafts, and Edwardian forms—then the High Tech/Late Modern finds a more humanistic and urbane aesthetic. Contemporary Post-Modern work by John Melvin broadens the historicist references beyond Neo-Classicism and Palladianism to Artisan Mannerism and the English Baroque, and British architecture in the 1990s looks once again to Richard Norman Shaw, or even earlier to Wren and John Vanbrugh for inspiration.

Robert M. Craig

Bibliography

Jencks, Charles. *The Language of Post-Modern Architecture*. 1977.
———. *AD Profile 91: Post-Modern Triumphs in London*. 1991.
Sudjic, Deyan. *Norman Foster, Richard Rogers, James Stirling: New Directions in British Architecture*. 1986.

Powell, (John) Enoch (1912–1998)

Enoch Powell was one of the most controversial figures who shaped British politics from the middle of the twentieth century until his death. His view on the undesirability of non-white IMMIGRATION into the United Kingdom, on which he delivered his famous "rivers of blood" speech in April 1968, was to influence the subsequent course of British RACE RELATIONS. His hostility to UK membership of the EUROPEAN COMMUNITY, his early monetarism, and his free market beliefs suggest that he was a precursor of THATCHERISM.

Powell was born in 1912 in Birmingham, and his intellectual brilliance was apparent from an early age. He won a scholarship to study classics at Trinity College, Cambridge. Soon after completing his studies, he was appointed at the age of twenty-five to a professorship of Greek Studies at the University of Sydney. Following the outbreak of the SECOND WORLD WAR Powell returned to Britain to join the ARMY, and by the end of the war he was the youngest man to have attained the rank of brigadier.

He joined the CONSERVATIVE PARTY's Research Department in 1946 and was one of the team of young men under the tutelage of R.A. BUTLER, who sought to give intellectual definition to post-war Conservatism. In 1950 he entered Parliament as Conservative MP for Wolverhampton South-West, a seat which he retained for the next twenty-four years. In 1958 he resigned his post as Financial Secretary of the Treasury out of sympathy with the determination of the Chancellor of the Exechquer Peter Thorneycroft to cut government spending in opposition to the rest of the Conservative administration. HAROLD MACMILLAN brought Powell back into his government as Minister of Health in 1960. He proved to be a diligent and effective minister, but he resigned this office in 1963 to protest, for reasons which remain unclear, Sir ALEC DOUGLAS-HOME's succession to the Prime Ministership.

Following the 1964 election defeat, Powell contested the leadership of the Conservative Party, but he was unable to win support and lost to EDWARD HEATH. He served on the opposition front benches as Conservative spokesman on defense. However, interests outside his portfolio began to concern him. Since the later 1950s non-white immigration from the COMMONWEALTH had been on the increase. In April 1968, without informing his Conservative Party colleagues, who at the time were attempting to devise party policy on this issue, Powell delivered a speech in Birmingham which painted an apocalyptic picture if non-white immigration were to continue: the situation as he foresaw it would be, in the words of Virgil, like "the river Tiber flowing with much blood". The language of this speech was deemed by Conservative colleagues to have been "racialist" and inflammatory, and Heath dismissed him from the party's front benches. However, in consequence of this speech Powell achieved considerable popular support in the country. Perhaps as many as 100,000 London dockworkers marched to express their approval of Powell's views. Even so, from this point onwards Powell was marginalized from the mainstream of politics.

Although he had supported British entry into the European Community in the 1960s, he violently opposed it in the 1970s, urging Tory voters not to vote for Heath during the 1974 general election. At the same time, he resigned from the party and stood for—and won—the Ulster Unionist seat for South Down, because he believed that NORTHERN IRELAND should remain inextricably and forever a part of the United Kingdom. However, he remained outside the inner circle of Northern Irish politics because he was unable to construct proper working relations with Ulster Unionist politicians. He disagreed with MARGARET THATCHER's support for the Anglo-Irish Agreement, which allowed the Republic of Ireland a say in the affairs of Northern Ireland. He resigned his seat in protest but was subsequently re-elected, only to face defeat in the 1987 general election.

Throughout his life a belief in and vision of the integrity of Britain as a nation guided him. From this concept flowed his opposition to Europe, his support of Northern Ireland's continued union with the UK, and his extreme attitude towards immigration. Although he knew that his views were frequently unpopular, he held fast to them. As such, he was to remain a controversial figure, respected by many, despised by others, even after his death in 1998. His body was allowed to lie in Westminster Abbey principally because he had been an active member of the Abbey's community, but the authorities refused him the privilege of lying "in state".

Michael David Kandiah

Bibliography

Heffer, Simon. *Like the Roman: The Life of Enoch Powell.* 1998.

Shepherd, Rob. *Enoch Powell.* 1996.

Powell, Michael (1905–1990)
As a filmmaker, Michael Powell rose to fame during the Second World War after making a se-

ries of "quota quickies" during the 1930s. Rejecting the dominant realist mode of British cinema, he maintained that film is a medium more suited to fantasy, and distrusted the claims of contemporary DOCUMENTARY FILMMAKERS that film could mirror life. As such, his films explore surreality, superreality, and the practice of filmmaking itself.

His career started in Rex Ingram's (1893–1950) film unit near Nice. Moving to Britain, he worked as a stills photographer on ALFRED HITCHCOCK's *Champagne* (1928) and as screenwriter on Hitchcock's first talkie *Blackmail* (1929). Powell's first major film was *On the Edge of the World* (1937). Set on a Scottish island, it already contained elements of the mystic relationship of people and nature that emerged in his later films. During 1939 he was introduced to Emeric Pressburger (1902–88) by Alexander Korda (1893–1956), for whom he was then working, in order that Pressburger could tighten up the script of *The Spy in Black* (1939). The partnership with Pressburger, lasting until 1956, produced a series of films that achieved prominence during the war, including *49th Parallel* (1941) and *One of Our Aircraft Is Missing* (1942).

Their most significant achievements were *A Matter of Life and Death* (1946), chosen as the first Royal Command film; *The Red Shoes* (1948); and the wartime epic *The Life and Death of Colonel Blimp* (1943), their most controversial film, which WINSTON CHURCHILL tried to have banned.

Films like *A Canterbury Tale* (1944) and *I Know Where I'm Going* (1945) explored the interconnectedness of history, tradition, nature, and human nature, which also helped keep *Gone to Earth* (1950) from being a conventional melodrama. Powell's films seemed to cross traditional genre boundaries, none of them fitting comfortably within precise categories. The sublimation of the erotic into the *mise-en-scène* of *Black Narcissus* created an intensely powerful film, equally notable for its recreation of the Himalayas in a studio by photographing landscapes painted onto glass.

Powell and Pressburger, releasing their movies under the Archers' signature, made one film each year during the war, but seemed to lose touch with popular taste in the post-war years. *The Red Shoes*, their last success, earned an Oscar for art director Hein Heckroth, who deserves credit for the visually stunning effects of several Archers' films. It followed the fortunes of a ballerina torn between a career and marriage, symbolically playing out the dilemma of many other women during that period; the ballet dancer also reflected the prominence that British BALLET had achieved during the war. The morbidity of the fairy tale story was reassessed and reviled in 1960 when

Powell released his first major film without Pressburger for twenty years. *Peeping Tom* is self-consciously about film-making and film-viewing. A powerful study of voyeurism in its plot of a young photographer/filmmaker who uses a camera with a spike to stab young women so that he may film them as they die, it has been taken up as the subject of feminist debate about the gendered psychological processes of cinema viewing.

After the shocked reception of *Peeping Tom* (made at the same time as Hitchcock's *Psycho*), Powell found it increasingly difficult to secure financial backing, although he did make two films in Australia, one of which was written by Pressburger under the pseudonym Richard Imrie. However, during the 1970s a number of British critics and film theorists helped to revive Powell's reputation, which eventually led to the reprinting of some films for the National Film Archive, a season at the National Film Theater, and a series on BBC television.

Initially Powell was rediscovered within auteur theories of the cinema, but later the uniquely shared roles were acknowledged. In their films between 1943 and 1956, the credits read: written, directed and produced by Michael Powell and Emeric Pressburger. A number of American filmmakers of the 1980s acknowledged the significant impact of the Archers' films on their own craft. Francis Ford Coppola made *One from the Heart* (1982) as a homage to Powell, who was then working in his Hollywood studio, and Martin Scorsese has consistently cited Powell's influence on his work. Powell died in February 1990 while completing the second volume of his autobiography *A Life in Movies*.

Nannette Aldred

Bibliography

Aldred, Nannette. "A Canterbury Tale: Powell and Pressburger's Film Fantasies of Britain" in David Mellor, ed. *A Paradise Lost*. 1987. pp. 117–25.

Christie, Ian. *Arrows of Desire: The Films of Michael Powell and Emeric Pressburger*. 1985.

Durgnat, Raymond. *A Mirror for England*. 1970.

Powell, Michael. *A Life in the Movies*. 1986.

——. *Million Dollar Movie*. 1990.

Pregnancy and Childbirth

Women's experience of pregnancy and childbirth in Britain at the end of the twentieth century is associated with a high degree of medical and HOSPITAL involvement. In 1985 99 percent of all women in England and Wales gave birth in hospital. This contrasts the pattern at the beginning of the twentieth century. In 1900 the majority of women gave birth at home. By 1927, however, 15 percent of all births took place in an institution. This had risen to 53.7 percent in 1946. While the number of hospital births remained constant at

approximately 65 percent during the 1950s, they increased substantially in the 1960s and 1970s. The shifts that have taken place in the location of birth also reflect the wider changes that have occurred in women's experience of pregnancy and childbirth in the twentieth century.

At the beginning of the century childbirth was primarily a private domestic affair between mothers and those they chose to attend them. During succeeding decades, however, childbirth has increasingly become a public event which no longer relies solely on the decisions of a mother and her birth attendant, but involves a range of medical and lay experts, municipal and hospital bodies, as well as charitable and government authorities. This has had far-reaching implications for the social and cultural perceptions surrounding pregnancy and childbirth. Indeed pregnancy and childbirth, formerly viewed as a natural physiological phenomenon has increasingly become regarded as a hazardous and dangerous event, necessitating expert medical attention and intervention.

Much of this change was linked to anxiety over the persistently high rates of maternal mortality. Unlike other forms of mortality which began to diminish from the 1870s, and infant mortality which had begun to fall after 1906, maternal mortality remained high, and even rose in the 1920s and 1930s. Before the late 1930s, after tuberculosis, deaths in childbed were the most common cause of death among women of childbearing age. Between 1855 and 1934 the maternal death rate in England and Wales averaged around 4.6 per 1,000 live births, amounting to some 3,000 to 4,000 deaths a year. The major cause of these deaths was puerperal sepsis, followed by haemorrhages and toxaemia. There has been extensive debate by historians about the determinants of high maternal mortality in these years, but most agree that before the late 1930s the quality of obstetric care was probably more important than social and economic factors.

While maternal mortality was the subject of a number of medical reports in the 1870s, it became a national concern for many statesmen and medical experts in the years following the First World War. What was particularly worrying was that, unlike infant mortality, maternal mortality had not declined, despite measures taken to train and regulate midwives (through the Midwives' Act of 1902), the provision of a range of maternal and infant welfare services, as well as the introduction of maternity benefit in 1913. Their concern was reinforced by a massive public outcry over the sharp rise in maternal mortality in the 1920s and 1930s.

The debate during these years centered on the influence on maternal mortality of social and economic factors, such as poor NUTRITION and bad HOUSING, or clinical practice. The need for more preventive action, including better antenatal care, hospital provision, more clinics, and improved training of midwives and doctors, were stressed. This was a policy not only promoted by many medical professionals, but also requested by women campaigners, who called for improved social and economic conditions alongside greater hospital provision and pain relief.

The 1936 Midwives Act answered some of these demands, making it obligatory for every local authority to provide an adequate salaried domiciliary service. Together with the introduction of sulphonamides, this played a vital part in reducing maternal mortality. Maternity services were extended during the Second World War, when consultant services were made more widely available, and blood transfusion and penicillin were introduced. After 1948 the NATIONAL HEALTH SERVICE also provided a well-coordinated and high standard of obstetric care free to all mothers.

Yet despite these advances and the fall in maternal mortality, disputes have continued over jurisdiction in the management of childbirth. While much of the earlier tension was between the midwife and the obstetrician, recently many women, particularly those involved in the National Childbirth Trust, have also begun to argue for greater control over their own bodies, control that they see as having been diminished by increased medical intervention and hospital care since the 1960s.

Lara Marks

Bibliography

Campbell, R., and A. Macfarlane. *Where to be Born? The Debate and the Evidence*. 1987.

Garcia, Jo, Robert Kilpatrick, and Martin Richards, eds. *The Politics of Maternity Care: Services for Childbearing Women in Twentieth Century Britain*. 1990.

Loudon, Irvine. *Death in Childbirth: An International Study of Maternal Care and Maternal Mortality, 1800–1950*. 1992.

Oakley, Ann. *The Captured Womb: A History of the Medical Care of Pregnant Women*. 1984.

Tew, M. *Safer Childbirth?: A Critical History of Maternity Care*. 1990.

Press, British

The United Kingdom in the 1990s could still boast twelve daily and nine Sunday newspapers available nationwide. In addition, Scotland, Northern Ireland, and to a lesser degree Wales, retain their own titles and traditions. Regular and substantial advertising revenue supports an extensive regional press; local evening newspapers are complemented by a few surviving morning editions in the Midlands, the north, and the west

of England. A century earlier, local daily and weekly newspapers were a common phenomenon, but improved distribution methods during and after the First World War facilitated easier access to the metropolitan press. The same period witnessed the demise of the "newspapers of opinion": London-based daily and evening forums of Liberal debate, their readers scarcely evident beyond the clubland of St. James. The disappearance of titles such as the *Westminster Gazette* reflected not only the rise of LABOUR at the expense of the LIBERAL PARTY, but also the emergence of heavily-subscribed, genuinely national newspapers, each tailored to a mass audience happy to accept less copy, larger headlines, more photographs, and maximum advertising.

Throughout this century the British press has played a uniquely central role in the political process. Prominent and powerful proprietors have not been averse to assuming office, particularly during the two world wars, while in peacetime Conservative CABINETS have invariably included ministers whose wealth is based upon extensive media interests. No less than three Labour leaders—MACDONALD, LANSBURY, and FOOT—have edited newspapers, their parliamentary party since the 1920s boasting a disproportionate number of journalists. Governments, particularly if CONSERVATIVE, liaise regularly with the owners and editors of sympathetic newspapers, relying on the honors system to reward loyalty and obeisance. During and after the First World War, LLOYD GEORGE proved that neither was the Liberal Party averse to cultivating Fleet Street, even to the extent of his purchasing the *Daily News*.

In no other liberal democracy does the impact of editorial bias upon public opinion, and in particular voting behavior, generate such intensity of debate, most recently in the aftermath of the 1992 general election. Similarly, the tension between what government judges the public "needs to know," and what the media assumes people are "entitled to know," highlights an historic concern over the control and management of information. Uniquely British institutions survive, battered but intact, most notably the Lobby: Westminster and Whitehall's elite of authorized correspondents, heavily dependent upon unattributable leaks and briefings delivered "off the record" by ministers, opposition leaders, or their spokespersons.

Three facets of the modern British press are already evident: the unusual degree of partisanship, the consolidation of newspaper ownership, and the continuing importance of personality. Countless correspondents, columnists, and cartoonists have become celebrities in their own right, respective examples being the *News Chronicle*'s James Cameron, the *Daily Mirror*'s

"Cassandra" and the *Evening Standard*'s David Low. Yet, the dominant personalities since 1900 have been proprietors, and, to a much lesser degree, their editors. The golden age for editors was between the wars: the THE TIMES's GEOFFREY DAWSON and the OBSERVER's J.L. GARVIN were nearly as famous as their newspapers. Yet inter-war contemporaries such as Express Newspaper's LORD BEAVERBROOK or Associated Newspapers' Lord Rothermere were, rightly or wrongly, seen as the power-brokers of high politics. Newspaper groups were under the de facto control of individuals or families that held majority shareholdings. These companies in a few cases became trusts, of which the MANCHESTER GUARDIAN was the best-known example (transfer to London in 1959 saw "Manchester" dropped from the masthead). More often they became absorbed into large holding companies with diverse interests, witness the *Observer*'s sale to Atlantic Richfield, and then to Lonrho, but then to the *Guardian*.

Nevertheless, the chief executive or chairman still wielded extensive management and editorial powers, enjoying the high profile secured by running a famous title. Thus, the original "press barons" made way for "multi-media" tycoons, some of whom were themselves ennobled. Those who were not, notably Rupert Murdoch and Robert Maxwell, reveled in their influence and notoriety across at least three continents. Just as the Harmsworth brothers—the future Lords NORTHCLIFFE and Rothermere—had exploited late Victorian technology to pioneer a mass-circulation popular press via the *Daily Mail*, so a century later Murdoch harnessed a favorable political climate, and a revolution in telecommunications and printing/publishing, to pursue equally aggressive marketing methods.

The Boer War and then the First World War had fuelled the British public's hunger for news, albeit massaged by a largely voluntary system of censorship, and Fleet Street's enthusiasm for xenophobic PROPAGANDA. The popular press consolidated the advances made during the "Northcliffe Revolution" of the 1890s, and in the inter-war years the *Daily Express, Daily Mail,* and initially Labour-controlled *Daily Herald,* relied on ever-more outrageous promotions to maintain individual circulations in the millions. The Second World War and after saw the tabloid *Daily Mirror* secure its position as the principal working-class newspaper for the next twenty-five years. Merger and closure resulted in the *Daily Mirror* after 1970 being Labour's only guaranteed supporter in Fleet Street, the *Daily Herald* ultimately metamorphosizing into Murdoch's stridently pro-Tory *Sun*. With the *Daily Express* and *Daily Mail* striving to widen their primarily lower middle-class readership with only modest suc-

cess, efforts to secure and retain average sales of 4 million focused upon the two major tabloids (and Express Newspapers' 1980s attempt to go downmarket, the *Daily Star*).

The *Daily Mirror* boasted a laudable record of campaigning and hard news reporting, but the challenge of the *Sun* forced it to move away from reportage to personality features and show business gossip. News International's repackaging of the *News of the World* as a de facto sister tabloid to the *Sun* had a similar impact upon the *Sunday Mirror*. By the 1990s the priority given to soap opera stars or royalty, and the total lack of balance in reporting in domestic politics, led to hefty libel awards against allegedly intrusive tabloids, and the establishment of the popularly perceived "independent" BBC and ITN as the principal sources of hard news. The general public's continuing respect for the integrity of terrestrial public-service broadcasting antagonized Murdoch and the present Lord Rothermere, major shareholders in the BSkyB satellite television service. Relentless promotion of News International's non-print interests is most evident in its tabloids, the aforementioned *Sun* and *News of the World,* and *Today* (bought from the original pioneer of IT-based national newspaper production in the UK, Eddie Shah); but mass advertising and "loaded" copy extends to its upmarket "quality" newspapers, *The Times* and the *Sunday Times*.

Internationally if perhaps no longer at home, *The Times* retains its "Establishment" image, while the *Sunday Times* remains the market leader, despite having moving sharply to the Right since Murdoch's purchase in 1981. Previously, under the editorship of Harold Evans, the *Sunday Times* was the first weekend broadsheet to promote in-depth investigative journalism, multi-sections, and color supplements. Ironically, Evans's equally professional and innovative successor, Andrew Neill, became more widely known as a maverick figure of the Right unconcerned by accusations of having sullied his newspaper's reputation in its unashamed promotion of Sky and then BSkyB TV. The *Sunday Times*'s traditional rival is the *Observer*, but further competition comes from the all-week *Independent* and the *Daily/Sunday Telegraph*. The recent emergence of cost-conscious seven-days publishing parallels a move to Saturday as the main focus of multi-sectioned reading, witness the *Guardian*'s larger weekend format and continued absence on Sundays. As in the 1960s the volume of review and opinion available on Sundays heralded a dramatic decline in sales of major weeklies such as the *Spectator* and NEW STATESMAN, so thirty years later the *Observer et al* struggle to retain sale and advertising at a time when even Saturday's *Financial Times* boasts saturation sports and arts coverage. Bucking the trend is the tabloid *Mail On Sunday*, which in the early 1990s initiated a modest move upmarket and in so doing nearly doubled its circulation. Skillful editing ensured the retention of older lower middle-class readers, and the recruitment of a younger, well-educated audience with a level of disposable income such as to generate substantial advertising revenue.

The *Mail On Sunday*'s success in not alienating readers shared with its sister paper demonstrates that title loyalty (if not necessarily identification with the opinions and values espoused by the particular title) remains a distinct feature of the British newspaper industry. It also highlights the potential for recruiting fresh readers, and not simply at the expense of rival's circulations. The unique variety of newspapers in the United Kingdom notwithstanding, there still exists a large pool of potential new readers. Despite exaggerated fears of a future semi-literate society, courtesy of multiple television channels, video films and computer games, the future for the British press looks by no means bleak. A decade of industrial upheaval in the 1980s ended with a reasonably efficient and cost-effective industry ready to embrace the next generation of media-related IT. The price of such stability had been hundreds of print workers' jobs, journalists who placed a high premium on integrity, independence, and individuality, and, above all, Fleet Street itself. Within high-tech plants scattered around or even beyond central London are cost-conscious managers and editors, their computer monitors revealing up-to-the-minute stories and up-to-the-minute spread sheets. For most enterprises new technology and new methods brought the holy grail of sustained profitabiliy. The price was—if it ever existed in the first place—romance.

Adrian Smith

Bibliography

Boyce, George, James Curran, and Pauline Wingate, eds. *Newspaper History from the Seventeenth Century to the Present Day*. 1978.

Curran, James, and Jean Seaton. *Power Without Responsibility: the Press and Broadcasting in Britain*. 4th ed. 1991.

Koss, Stephen. *The Rise and Fall of the Political Press in Britain*. 2 vols. 1981–4.

Seaton, Jean, and Ben Pimlott, eds. *The Media in British Politics*. 1987.

Seymour-Ure, Colin. *The British Press and Broadcasting Since 1945*. 1991.

Priestley, John Boynton (1894–1984)
In the 1930s and 1940s few writers were as widely-read and well-loved in Britain as J.B. Priestley. The publication of *The Good Companions* (1929) catapulted him to fame, the book selling over 1 million copies. In the following decades he became a prolific broadcaster, essayist, novelist, playwright, screenwriter, and social critic, his voluminous output totaling more than 100 books. In the early 1940s he was second only to WINSTON CHURCHILL as the public voice of the nation at war. A populist, a self-proclaimed socialist, and a fierce critic of mass culture and state regimentation, Priestley was a keen observer of social change and an avid story-teller of the lives of ordinary people who attempted heroically to keep their heads above water in an increasingly complex world.

Born in Bradford ("Bruddersfield" in his novels), Priestley grew up in a Nonconformist lower middle-class household and immersed himself in the world of Edwardian, provincial POPULAR CULTURE. He wrote frequently for the socialist *Bradford Pioneer*, championing a whole way of life that he later claimed ended abruptly in the trenches of the FIRST WORLD WAR. After a brief career in the ARMY, Priestley studied English literature at CAMBRIDGE and moved to London, where he became a free-lance writer. While he was praised for his topical essays, and while his first novel, *Adam in Moonshine* (1927), was a modest success, it was *The Good Companions* (1929), a novel about the fortunes of a third-rate traveling concert troupe, that placed his name on the literary map. Equally successful was his next major novel, *Angel Pavement* (1930), a brilliant fictional portrait of lower middle-class life in London.

In the 1930s success followed success for Priestley. He spent much time in the United States, where he wrote screenplays for Hollywood while developing an intense dislike of American mass culture. His criticism of mass culture surfaced in many of his works, particularly *Journey Down a Rainbow* (1955), written with his third wife, Jacquetta Hawkes. In Britain his reputation as a dramatist in the 1930s was established through a number of plays, ranging from conventional comedies to experimental plays that dealt with the philosophy of time. His most notable plays in this decade were *Dangerous Corner* (1932), *Laburnum Grove* (1934), *Eden End* (1934), *Time and the Conways* (1937), *I Have Been Here Before* (1937), *When We Are Married* (1938), and *Johnson Over Jordan* (1939). In addition to writing two screenplays for the popular working-class comedienne, Gracie Fields, along with a comic novel dealing with similar themes, *Let the People Sing* (1939), Priestley wrote two serious, documentary novels in the 1930s, *Wonder Hero* (1933) and *They Walk in the City* (1936). He also became an outspoken social critic during the Depression, vividly describing the state of the nation in *English Journey* (1934). His attack on the class system, plutocrats, media moguls, and the policies of NEVILLE

CHAMBERLAIN won him a sympathetic following, although he remained suspicious of the LABOUR PARTY and championed a sentimental and populist brand of socialism that harked back to the patriotic radicalism of William Cobbett and ROBERT BLATCHFORD.

During the SECOND WORLD WAR Priestley became famous for his "Postscripts," broadcast on the radio on Sunday evenings following the nine o'clock news. In attempting to define the enduring qualities of Englishness for his many listeners, Priestley both looked back to the golden age of his remembered Edwardian childhood and forward to a more egalitarian future. Both themes later resurfaced in one of his most successful novels, *Bright Day* (1946). After a brief period of infatuation with Richard Acland's Forward March movement and the independent Common Wealth party, Priestley campaigned tirelessly for the cultural, political, and spiritual renewal of British society. In the polemical tracts he wrote, in plays like *They Came to a City* (1944), and in his demobilization novel, *Three Men in New Suits* (1945), Priestley imagined a bold new order in which all the virtues he identified with the English people at their best would flourish.

After the war Priestley became a disillusioned critic of the post-war settlement, attacking the materialism, mass culture, and conformity of the age. Although he was one of the most enthusiastic supporters of the FESTIVAL OF BRITAIN, and wrote *Festival at Farbridge* (1951), a comic novel about a town in the Midlands attempting to stage its own festival, Priestley's reputation began to fade. Following his brief involvement in the early days of the CAMPAIGN FOR NUCLEAR DISARMAMENT, Priestley turned once again to fiction to dramatize his discontent with the post-war world, culminating in perhaps his best novel, *The Image Men* (1968), a satirical romp through the world of public relations, advertising, THE PRESS, and government. More and more, however, he retreated into a world of nostalgia for the past, captured poignantly in his novel of Edwardian music-hall life, *Lost Empires* (1965), in his illustrated social history, *The Edwardians* (1970), and in various essays, published in *The English* (1973) and *Lost and Found: The English Way of Life* (1976).

Despite his widespread appeal in the 1930s and 1940s, Priestley's literary reputation has declined significantly. Although some of his plays are still performed, virtually all of his novels are now out of print. An immensely popular novelist with the middle-brow reading public, Priestley fared less well with the critics. F.R. LEAVIS, for example, championed modernist writers and often belittled Priestley's work; likewise, GEORGE ORWELL viewed him as a blatantly second-rate novelist.

And yet for many decades Priestley both entertained the nation and became one of its foremost social critics. *English Journey* still offers an evocative portrait of England during the Depression, while his better novels vividly capture the trials and tribulations of ordinary people in their attempts to make sense of the world around them and their roles in it.

Chris Waters

Bibliography

Brome, Vincent. *J.B. Priestley.* 1988.

Day, Alan Edwin. *J.B. Priestley: An Annotated Bibliography.* 1980.

Nicholas, Sian. "'Sly Demagogues' and Wartime Radio: J.B. Priestley and the BBC," *Twentieth Century British History,* vol. 6 (1995), pp. 247–66.

Priestley, J.B. *Margin Released: A Writer's Reminiscences and Reflections.* 1962.

———. *Instead of Trees: A Final Chapter of Autobiography.* 1977.

Waters, Chris. "J.B. Priestley, 1894–1984: Englishness and the Politics of Nostalgia" in Susan Pedersen and Peter Mandler, eds. *After the Victorians: Private Conscience and Public Duty in Modern Britain.* 1994. pp. 209–26.

Primary Education

Before the First World War education for children between ages three and ten was provided free in elementary schools, run by a mixture of church and local authority bodies, after the 1902 Education Act. In these schools children were taught in large groups by teachers who had begun to be qualified, under a formal regimented system. They sat on long benches, facing the teacher, and learned to read and write on slates by a process of verbal repetition. All days began with some formal religious assembly. Terms ran from September to July with breaks at Easter and Christmas. Teachers could and did use physical punishment to discipline their charges. All schools kept a record of the day's proceedings in log-books, which have provided a valuable source for historical work on child life before 1918. Schools were mostly local, with one provided in almost every village.

Most reforms in schooling after the 1918 Fisher Act were in SECONDARY EDUCATION. Primary schooling was first changed by legislation by eradicating child labor, which was allowed by license in individual cases provided children were attending some schooling, or collectively through the half-time system for those over ten. Reform without legislation was achieved by improving the training of teachers and relaxing some of the more formal aspects of instruction that were ineffective in eliminating illiteracy and in educating for work and adult life. Nature study and history became subjects in which children were encouraged to use imaginative skills. The Inspectorate of schools, an independent body responsible to the Crown, helped to spread good practice by encouraging it in their reports. However, the interests of higher goals also imposed some contraints upon teachers in the elementary system: the increasing significance of eleven-plus examinations meant that resources were often concentrated on children who might get scholarships and go on to special free places in secondary school. This exam concentrated on English, arithmetic, and verbal reasoning/intelligence tests, so schools were dominated by testing for ten-year-olds and nearly all schools were streamed by ability.

The biggest inequality between children of this age was the rural-urban divide. In cities elementary schools were improving educational quality by separating children into junior and senior sections and providing a differentiated, progressive curriculum. Rural schools tended to place children of all ages together with one teacher and a common program of teaching across the ages, sometimes with low levels of teacher expectation.

The Consultative Committee on Education, chaired by Sir Henry Hadow, published *The Primary School* in 1931, which suggested differentiation of children beyond that warranted by secondary education selection through "streaming" within the junior school. It recommended that large schools should follow a "triple-track system" of organization. City children were then described according to their level of intelligence, usually as measured by tests. On the other hand the same report argued for "activity and experience" rather than "facts" and "knowledge". Inspectors and teachers could interpret this statement either as a call for more attention to the highest achievers among children in primary education or a demand for a liberalized curriculum. War-time arrangements were equally ambiguous in leaving teachers to get on with their task with limited central scrutiny or support.

In the post-war reorganization of education the primary system was ended at eleven, although some authorities were to develop middle schools which took nine to thirteen year olds. Much of the new school building was in the primary sector since the rising birth-rate fed an expanded population into the infant and junior schools from 1951 on. Architects developed open plan classrooms where work was undertaken on tables rather than desks, and homework was reduced except for "scholarship" pupils. Art and craft teaching reflected increased concern for visual edcuation, with Marion Richardson-style writing becoming the norm.

Sociologists have contributed much on the procedures and effects of primary schooling. In J.W.B. Douglas' *The Home and the School* (1964), based on a longitudinal study of a large group of children, educational success or failure was attributed to a large extent to the influence of the home. The Plowden Committee of 1967 investigated reading and encouraged mixed ability teaching and learning as a means of encouraging higher levels of achievement for the lower ends of the ability range. Disadvantage was attacked by introducing "educational priority areas" which were given extra staff and resources to iron out inequalities. Migration from the New Commonwealth was thus dealt with successfully, although rich migrant cultures tended to be treated as problems in educational administration reactions. Class rather than race remained the main theoretical concept explaining inequalities in outcome.

Educational standards became a political issue again in the 1980s when a new CONSERVATIVE administration sought a change in education, the largest component of local government expenditure. They also moved against increasingly militant teaching unions, which were strongest in the primary school and had been organizing STRIKES to reduce pay differentials. Governors were given increased power over their schools, and local financial management, introduced in the 1990s, detached them further from local government. The national curriculum tried to standardize practice, while nationally administered tests for all seven and eleven year olds ensured that educational performance was publicly accountable. However all the careful understanding of educational experts was undermined by the government's disdain for expertise; scores were to be used without any contextual material which explained whether high performance was in fact attributable to well-prepared and resourced intake. Concern for the underachievement of some groups in society was not reflected in any action. Schools were again assumed to be largely responsible for the educational success or failure of their charges. Classroom experience predominated in the training of teachers, just as it had in 1900.

Deborah Thom

Bibliography

Dent, Harold Collett. *Education in England and Wales.* 1982.

Gordon, Peter. *Education Since the Second World War.* 1983.

Lowe, Roy, ed. *The Changing Primary School.* 1987.

Lowndes, G.A.N. *The Silent Social Revolution: An Account of the Expansion of Public Education in England and Wales 1895–1965.* 2nd ed. 1969.

Propaganda

Propaganda played a major role in Britain's effort at sustaining morale at home, encouraging defeatism among its enemies, and appealing to neutral sympathies during both world wars of the twentieth century. Britain entered the FIRST WORLD WAR with no propaganda department at all, but ended it with the most sophisticated such organization among the belligerents. Between 1914–18 the need to mobilize mass opinion in war time became apparent, not just in Britain, but also in enemy countries, where propaganda could be deployed to undermine morale, and among Britain's allies, who must be assured of Britain's resolve. Neutrals were included as well, for their benevolence was needed in order to maintain supply lines.

Organization of British propaganda was haphazard, operating for several years without central coordination. A number of agencies were set up to deal with censorship, news management, military recruitment, appeals to allies, neutrals, and Dominions, and subversion of enemy morale: the Parliamentary Recruiting Committee (PRC), formed to coordinate War Secretary LORD KITCHENER's appeal for volunteers, the Censorship and Press Bureau, the Neutral Press Committee, the Foreign Office News Department, and—from the War Office—MI7, all agencies responsible for managing the news as the government wanted. Reorganization in 1916 resulted in the Department of Information, the National War Aims Committee, whose duty it was to keep the public committed to the British cause, Crewe House, devoted to propaganda in enemy countries, and an overall coordinating body, the Ministry of Information.

These organizations employed a multitude of channels for dissemination. The PRC liked mass rallies and posters to get its message across, and others agencies deployed postcards, stamps, pamphlets, news items strategically placed in both domestic and foreign newspapers (Reuters News Agency was the primary overseas channel in this regard), and film. Newsreels and war-film grew in importance as the war progressed. The War Office released *Britain Prepared* in 1915, which was shown as far away as Imperial Russia. For the enemy, Crewe House deployed clandestine tactics including smuggled newspapers, pamphlets, and leaflets. The content varied, but the themes were generally the same: heroic British soldiers contrasted with cowardly CONSCIENTIOUS OBJECTORS, supportive British wives and mothers, resolute leaders, and a display of German atrocities.

When the war ended, the anti-war reaction fostered repudiation of propaganda. It was only in the 1930s that the COMMITTEE OF IMPERIAL DEFENSE (CID), albeit reluctantly, undertook to make provision for the dissemination of propaganda in the event of an emergency. A propa-

ganda planning committee for war time was established in 1936, its terms of reference being to prepare for a Ministry of Information (MOI) which would spring into action should war come. In the meantime, it was to remain secret and avoid upsetting either Mussolini or Hitler.

In 1937 Parliament demanded a response to Italian anti-British broadcasts aimed at the Middle East, and the Foreign Office began to organize broadcasts in retaliation. A year later German success in Austria and Czechoslovakia convinced some officials that war was no longer avoidable, but the status of propaganda planning scarcely changed, a fact that became painfully clear the following September when war began.

In September 1939 the MOI was put into operation, but for the next year it achieved little if anything, the propagandists because they were trying to figure out how the machinery of the new organization was supposed to work, the military because, short of the RAF dropping propaganda leaflets, they had no real way to engage the enemy, save at sea. The MOI was reorganized in October 1939, and again in 1940, and then again in 1943, after which it remained more or less intact, though never efficient. After 1943 the MOI consisted principally of offices for censorship, relations with the PRESS, supervising propaganda at home, in the Empire, and among neutrals and allies, and planning and executing this propaganda through broadcasting, film, and print media. Propaganda to enemy countries was under the Political Warfare Executive, administered jointly by the MOI, Foreign Office, and the Ministry of Economic Warfare.

Compared to 1914, the objectives were clear: victory in a just cause over an evil adversary. With the advent of the bombing war of English cities, the home audience was assured that they could take it, a perception the government also imparted to the Empire and to neutral and friendly countries. After the Soviet Union, Japan, and the United States entered the war, and Britain won its first major victories, the new message was that Britain would win the war, and become again a European, if not a world, leader.

Propaganda channels were similar, but more extensive than those of the First World War. They included press, broadcasting, posters, postcards, pamphlets, newsreels, film, talks by prominent figures, "whispering" campaigns, and leaflets dropped over enemy lines. "Black propaganda" was reserved for enemy and enemy-occupied countries: this was propaganda of dis- and misinformation, designed to disrupt military operations and undercut civilian and troop morale.

The content of propaganda was at least as varied as in the First World War. Posters warned soldiers and sailors against venereal disease, and civilians to mind the blackout and to avoid spreading rumors or disclosing information. "Careless talk costs live" was the theme of hundreds of posters. Pamphlets described the importance of RATIONING and gave directions for air raid protection. Newsreels displayed and newspapers reported whatever good news about the war was available and, in order to avoid D notices, kept quiet about the rest, especially about the extent of bomb damage, casualties, and tons of shipping lost to submarines in the Atlantic. Newsreels also provided reassurance about the courage and resourcefulness of the people at home. Much of this kind of propaganda was aimed at the United States or transmitted to neutral countries, who were encouraged either to join in the struggle against Fascism, or at least to remain benevolently neutral towards Britain.

Robert Cole

Bibliography

Cole, Robert. *Britain and the War of Words in Neutral Europe, 1939–1945.* 1990.

Crofts, William. *Coercion or Persuasion? Propaganda in Britain After 1945.* 1989.

Grant, Mariel. *Propaganda and the Role of the State in Inter-war Britain.* 1994.

McLaine, Ian. *Ministry of Morale: Home Front Morale and the Ministry of Information in World War II.* 1979.

Messinger, Gary S. *British Propaganda and the State in the First World War.* 1992.

Sanders, Michael, and Philip M. Taylor. *British Propaganda During the First World War.* 1982.

Taylor, Philip M. *The Projection of Britain.* 1981.

———. *British Propaganda in the Twentieth Century.* 1999.

Public Health

Public health as a form of state regulation has a long history. In Britain in the nineteenth century state intervention was more extensive in the area of health than in any other largely because of the threat of disease to the whole population. Environment and health were seen as interconnected; questions of HOUSING and of sanitation were normally included within the public health remit.

C.E.A Winslow, the early twentieth century American authority on public health, identified three phases in its development. The first, from 1840, was characterized by environmental sanitation; the second from 1890 to 1910, by developments in bacteriology and germ theory, resulting in an emphasis on isolation and disinfection; and the third, beginning around 1910, by an emphasis on education and personal hygiene, referred to as personal prevention. This chronology is broadly applicable to developments in Britain. Germ theory brought a realization that it was not dirt as such which caused infectious disease; the broad mandate of public health to deal with housing and sanitation disappeared. During the years of

LIBERAL welfare reforms before the First World War the health and welfare aspects of policy were more firmly separated than previously. The focus of public health work shifted to personal hygiene and health education. There was increasing concern about the apparent deterioration of the race and the high infant mortality rate. The revelations of the Select Committee on Physical Deterioration (1904) about the poor physical condition of Britain's recruits in the BOER WAR resulted in the establishment of a school medical service. A variety of infant welfare clinics were established, and local authorities were given statutory authority for services for mothers and infants by the Maternity and Child Welfare Act of 1918. Medical Officers of Health focused on improving the quality of maternal care to the virtual exclusion of factors such as low incomes, poor housing and sanitation, and contaminated milk.

In the years from 1929 to 1948 public health departments in local authorities delivered a wide range of health services. Chief among these was responsibility for municipal hospitals, transferred to public health departments by the Local Government Act of 1929. Medical Officers of Health in local authorities could also provide maternity and child welfare services, the school medical service, dentistry, school meals and milk, tuberculosis schemes, infectious disease, ear, nose and throat, and venereal disease services; and health centres. Some commentators have seen these years as the "golden age" of public health. But an opposing point of view has criticized this expansion of functions for its lack of a clear vision of what was distinctive about public health. There has been further criticism of inter-war Medical Officers of Health for failing (with some exceptions) to address the relationship between UNEMPLOYMENT, poverty, and ill-health.

The coming of the NATIONAL HEALTH SERVICE in 1948 represented a considerable setback for public health. ANEURIN BEVAN, as Minister of Health, achieved consultant support for the new service through the nationalization of the HOSPITALS, a victory for the voluntary hospitals and a clear defeat for the idea of a state medical service based on local authorities and public health. Public health doctors in local authorities lost their hospital empires and were left with a substantially reduced range of responsibilities. Attempts were made in the 1940s to reorient public health practice round a new academic discipline of "social medicine", an attempt to link the planning of health and social services to the needs of the population. It was remote from the practice of public health and failed to have much impact on medical education.

From the 1950s to the 1970s public health was increasingly fragmented, at both organizational and conceptual levels. Parts of the public health sphere in the local authorities began to break away, first sanitary inspectors in the 1950s, then social workers, transferred to separate social work departments after the Seebohm committee report of 1968. "Community medicine" replaced what was seen as the outdated concept of public health. The 1974 reorganization of the National Health Service transferred public health (as community medicine) into the health service with a twin function of epidemiology and medical administration. The community physician became preoccupied more with administration than with the health of the population and its determinants.

A new focus on the prevention of ill-health became government policy in Britain in the 1970s and 1980s. But the emphasis was again on individual responsibility for health, and the focus was on single-issue campaigns (smoking, alcohol, heart disease) rather than an analysis of structural determinants of public health. The Black Report on Inequalities in Health (1979) and the subsequent Whitehead Report (1987), which drew attention to questions of class and poverty in relation to health, were not popular with the CONSERVATIVE government.

The 1980s saw a revival of public health concerns. The desire to integrate personal prevention and environmental perspectives became associated with the WHO's *Health for All by the Year 2000* strategy (1981) and the "new public health". In Britain the revival of infectious disease (legionella, salmonella, AIDS) led to a determined effort in the 1988 Acheson Report to upgrade the status of public health medicine. The future of public health in Britain remained uncertain even after this Report, not least because of its primary focus on public health as a *medical* speciality. This has been a distinctive feature of British public health by contrast with the multi-disciplinary American approach; but by the 1990s a broader range of disciplines were also laying claim to expertise in public health.

Virginia Berridge

Bibliography

Draper, Peter, ed. *Health Through Public Policy: The Greening of Public Health.* 1991.

Fee, Elizabeth, and Roy Acheson, eds. *A History of Education in Public Health.* 1991.

Lewis, Jane. *What Price Community Medicine? The Philosophy, Practice and Politics of Public Health Since 1919.* 1986.

Punch

Punch, an illustrated humorous weekly, appeared in 1841 and ceased publication in April 1992. By the 1890s it had shed its original radicalism and become a national institution—a complacent re-

pository in prose, verse, and cartoons of late Victorian middle- and upper-class values and views. It blended wry and whimsical commentary with illustrated reviews of the media. Many of the finest comic artists, caricaturists, and illustrators of this century enlivened its pages. Circulation in 1905 was 105,000, topping out at 175,000 in 1948. Advertisers used it from 1908 on to reach its affluent readers. Once the austere 1940s were over, color-filled advertisments flanked genteel, eccentric humor and satire in prose and cartoons. *Punch* is a primary source of the vagaries of fashion, mores, and moods of the Home Counties upper and middle classes in the twentieth century.

Punch's Edwardian tone was slight and safe; it rarely, if ever, gave offense. What Owen Seaman (editor, 1906 –32) wanted was lucidity, intelligibility, and "soundness," i.e., conservative political reliability. What he got was a self-satisfied, stodgy, increasingly right-wing, often unfunny weekly. Light stories, even lighter verse and social cartoons, mostly of middle- and upper-class activities, interspersed with *Charivari*—a page of "humorous" clippings—two full-page political cartoons, usually by Bernard Partridge from 1910 to 1945, reviews of stage plays, some concerts, and "the Essence of Parliament," kept an ageing readership reassured. Aside from the contributions of P.G. WODEHOUSE and A.A. Milne, most *Punch* prose and verse before and during the First World War is unmemorable. During the war *Punch* sought to sustain morale, while it trivialized the trenches and demonized the enemy.

In the 1920s *Punch* contributors groused about flappers, jazz, cocktails, the Charleston, upstart Americans, and the servant problem, hoping somehow that the pre-war certainties would return. The exception to the prevailing mediocrity were such gems as A.P. Herbert's witty *Misleading Causes* and singable verses, Milne's whimsical rhymes, *When We Were Very Young*, and Seller and Yeatman's burlesque history text, *1066 and All That*. Seaman's last years were redeemed by H.M. Bateman's irate colonels, Fougasse's comic abstrations, Lewis Baumer's lissom flappers, George Belcher's cockneys, Bert Thomas's caricatures, and Arthur Watts's slightly crazed panoramas. Under the formidable Marion Jean Lyon, *Punch* became a "shop window" for the advertising industry, and increased in size, with some color, especially in the annual almanack.

EVOE [E.V. Knox] (editor 1932–49) and Fougasse [Kenneth Bird] (art editor, 1937–49, editor, 1949 –52) gradually modernized the magazine. New contributors such as Richard Mallett, Eric Keown, Basil Boothroyd, and R.G.G. Price, brought it topicality and wit. Verbal and visual humor about tennis, ski holidays, broken plumbing, bridge playing, the BBC, domestic and foreign FASCISTS remain informative and amusing. In the late 1930s *Punch* became a showcase for sophisticated comic art and illustration. Thomas Derrick's modernistic energy, E.H. Shepard's decorative illustrations, Rowland Emmet's eccentric trains, Paul Crum's (Roger Pettiward) pensive hippos, David Langdon's lively, linear gags, and Anton's (Antonia Yeoman) elegant spivs can still be appreciated. Pont's (Graham Laidler, 1908–40) series "The British Character" and "Popular Misconceptions" aptly captured the bemused English in decline, muddling through the Depression, the looming war, and the BLITZ. Leslie Illingworth's post-war political cartoons were moderately Tory, gently critical of LABOUR and the WELFARE STATE. In the late 1940s *Punch* reached its highest circulation.

In 1953 Bradbury Agnew brought in the iconoclastic outsider Malcolm Muggeridge. To give *Punch* topicality and style Muggeridge enlisted, among others, Claude Cockburn, John Betjeman, Anthony Powell, and coaxed P.G. Wodehouse to contribute again. Russell Brockbank, art editor in the 1950s, enhanced what was already a showcase for cartooning. Ronald Searle's zany line, exclusively in *Punch* for several years, influenced a generation of artist-caricaturists, especially Ralph Steadman and Gerald Scarfe. Robert Sheriffs' caricatures, Osbert Lancaster, and Mark Boxer's pocket cartoons, the exuberant Giovanetti, Andre François, and Gerard Hoffnung's zaniness added to the comic spirit of the *Punch* regulars.

Between 1957 and 1988 the editors, Bernard Hollowood, William Davis, Alan Coren, and David Taylor struggled with mixed results to find a role for *Punch*. Aimed at an educated, middle-class, mature audience, *Punch* sought to be literate and witty. Cartoonists of the last thirty years such as Trog (Wally Fawkes), Bill Hewison, Quentin Blake (Michael) ffoukes, Larry (Terry Parkes), Bill Tidy, John Jensen, Steadman and Scarfe, Norman Thelwell, Ken Mahood, Michael Heath, Ed Mclachlan, Mike Williams, among others, sustained it as an arena for satirical commentary and eccentric comic art.

Despite its considerable efforts, *Punch* never redefined itself effectively in the increasingly competitive media environment of the last thirty years. When readership and revenues fell in the late 1980s, United Newspapers ordered the youthful William Thomas to "reposition" *Punch* downmarket. This change and an infusion of money to celebrate its 150th year, however, could not staunch *Punch*'s losses, as advertising revenues and circulation dropped dramatically. United Newspapers closed *Punch* on 8 April 1992 and put it up for sale. Mr. Punch died of circulation failure, it was said, brought on by trying to be youthful and vulgar, something it never was.

Peter Mellini

Bibliography
Prager, Arthur. *The Mahogany Tree: An Informal History of Punch*. 1979.
Price, R.G.G. *A History of Punch*. 1957.

Quakers: see Friends, Society of

Race Relations

Although it is impossible to comprehend the contemporary shape of race relations in Britain without reference to the legacy of the slave trade and the experience of British imperialism, it is nevertheless clear that the era of a racial "question" in British society and politics commenced no earlier than the late 1940s. With the arrival of some 800 Jamaican immigrant workers between December 1947 and October 1948 and the eventual settlement of tens of thousands of others from the West Indies and the Indian subcontinent over the next decade and a half, a race relations "problem" and, hence, the foundations for "politics of race" in Britain became firmly established.

Since the late 1950s race-related conflict and state policies that regulate the IMMIGRATION of non-whites into Britain have persisted as socially divisive and politically charged issues that have challenged the capacity of Britain's political system to respond. Since the arrival of the initial wave of New Commonwealth immigrants, racial disturbances have flared periodically, a racist, neo-Fascist political movment, the NATIONAL FRONT, has surged and declined, and successive British governments, in responding to illiberal public attitudes, have radically altered the country's immigration and nationality statutes. An unseen mover of votes, race is believed to have influenced the outcome of at least two general elections during the 1970s and contributed to eroding the long-held attachments of many voters to the CONSERVATIVE and LABOUR parties. Moreover, pervasive conditions of racism and economic disadvantage among non-whites are almost universally recognized as partial causes of a series of urban riots that rocked several English cities during the 1980s.

The main response of Britain's political elites to the evolution of a multi-racial society has been to extricate race-related subjects from the political arena. Particularly between 1964 and 1975 the principal parties forged an implicit consensus to depoliticize race. The simplest and least effective strategy the parties pursued to de-politicize race-related issues was to deny their political relevance. During the 1964 general election campaign, for example, only eight Conservative, fourteen Labour, and three LIBERAL candidates for Parliament cited the subjects of immigration or race relations in their campaign addresses despite the acute concern of the British public about the overall number of immigrants entering Britain and the difficulties that even long-settled immigrants were experiencing in assimilating into British society. This trend continued: immigration was cited in the election addresses of only 6 percent of all parliamentary candidates in 1966 and 14 percent in 1970. Although the national manifestos of the parties cited this area of public policy more frequently, such discussions were often purposely vague.

The second strategy pursued to depoliticize race was to enact cosmetic anti-discrimination legislation in conjunction with the implementaion of even tighter immigration controls. For every piece of restrictive immigration legislation adopted between 1965 and 1976, an accompanying race relations act either preceded or shortly followed its passage. Labour was especially adept at this game of political football; in 1965 and again in 1968 a Labour government successfully introduced both restrictive legislation and an anti-discrimination statute. The genesis of the 1965 Race Relations Act can be traced to the fear that racial issues were then beginning to influence the outcome of parliamentary contests in a number of local constituencies.

The third strategy adopted by the parties to depoliticize race-related issues was to create "racial buffers", quasi-governmental, bureaucratic bodies designed to assume the primary responsibility of addressing race-related problems. By establishing the National Committee for Commonwealth Immigrants (1965–8), the Race Relations Board (1965–76), the Community Relations Commission (1968–76), and the Commission for Racial Equality (1977–), the parties shielded politicians from the political hazards of addressing race-related issues squarely and also inhibited non-whites from participating in conventional interest group and party politics. By bureaucratizing race-related issues, buffer institutions, at least until the late 1970s, acted as political road-blocks for BLACK PEOPLE rather than as bridges between the non-white community and government.

Buffeted over time by the pressures of public opinion dissatisfied with the approach of the parties to race-related issues and of party-affiliated pressure groups clamoring for change, the Conservative Party, and then Labour, eventually disengaged from the racial consensus. Since the mid-1970s race-related subjects have become more frequent topics of intra-party discussion, inter-party differences on race have visibly widened, and the race relations and immigration policies of the post-1979 Conservative governments have been challenged by the Opposition.

Throughout the 1960s and 1970s public opinion polls revealed that a substantial percentage of citizens felt that too many immigrants had been admitted into Britain and that immigration constituted one of the most urgent problems confronting the country; even into the early 1980s, more than 80 percent of the electorate expressed the view that controlling immigration was very important and, despite a series of immigration measures passed by successive governments, almost half of all voters felt that the political parties were not addressing the immigration issue adequately. Although issues of race relations appear less salient at the beginning of the 1990s than a decade before, such issues have far from disappeared from the consciousness of the British public. Heated debates in British society and politics persist over the political representation of Black people—there were only nine non-whites among the 650 members of the House of Commons in 1997, despite the fact that non-whites account for more than four percent of the total population—as well as over the necessity for affirmative action laws, the alleged decline of law and order in inner-city areas where there are large concentrations of immigrants, and other issues.

In the 1990s, some forty-five years after the initial wave of new Commonwealth immigration, Britain's new ethnic and racial minorities, most of whom are full citizens, are still not fully integrated into the mainstream of British politics, racial discrimination persists at all levels of society, and racial violence perpetrated against non-whites is a recurrent feature of the British urban experience.

Anthony M. Messina

Bibliography

Goulbourne, Harry. *Race Relations in Britain Since 1945.* 1998.

Katznelson, Ira. *Black Men, White Cities: Race, Politics, and Migration in the United States, 1900–30, and Britain, 1948–68.* 1973.

Messina, Anthony M. *Race and Party Competition in Britain.* 1989.

Panay, Panikos. *Racial Violence in Britain, 1882–1958.* 1993.

Paul, Kathleen. *Whitewashing Britain: Race and Citizenship in the Postwar Era.* 1997.

Rich, Paul B. *Race and Empire in British Politics.* 1986.

Radar

The term radar—an acronym for *ra*dio *d*etection *a*nd *ra*nging—refers to the means of locating distant objects by radio. Although several countries were investigating the use of radio waves to locate obstacles at sea, it was Britain which decided to develop radar for defense purposes in 1935. One of its strongest advocates, Robert Watson-Watt (1892–1973), staged a trial in February 1935 in which the progress of a bomber, flying through the beam of a short-wave radio transmitter, was successfully plotted by detecting the small amounts of energy reflected from it. This, and the government's concern over the worsening situation in Europe, prompted the decision to equip Britain with an early warning system against aerial attack.

A development program of unprecedented urgency and secrecy was initiated. By 1939 many "Chain Home" radar stations were in service on the eastern fringes of Britain, and by 1941 most of the coastline had radar coverage. With their large antennas supported by 300-foot high towers, the radar stations were conspicuous, illuminating the sky with high-power pulses of radio energy. Radar operators observed echoes on the screens of cathode-ray tubes and determined the position and height of intruding aircraft by adjusting the line of sight of the directional receiving aerials. Since their screens did not provide any sort of map, operators could only guess the numbers of the attackers from the nature of the echoes.

This system played a crucial role in the BATTLE OF BRITAIN in September 1940, when outnumbered defenders took to the skies and repulsed waves of German attackers. Despite the excellence of the British aircraft and the skill of the RAF, the battle would have been lost without the warnings provided by radar, fed in to the fighter squadrons by a highly-developed communication and control network. Daytime raids diminished in frequency and intensity, and the threatened invasion of Britain was halted. The emphasis turned to night raids and the war in the Atlantic, calling for smaller, more mobile radar systems which could be fitted to aircraft and ships.

By this time the Chain-Home system was already out of date. All radar engineers knew that more accurate, sensitive and, above all, transportable radar sets would have to operate at centimetric, rather than metric wavelengths. Crude mobile radars for gunnery and for airborne interception had already been constructed, operating at wavelengths of around a meter. A University of Birmingham group commissioned by the Admiralty undertook a program to develop components for centimetric radar. The result was a thermionic tube called the cavity magnetron, which could give pulses of tens of kilowatts at wavelengths of a few centimeters. Manufacturing this device in quantity proved problematical until a British mission under SIR HENRY TIZARD secured an agreement for the American Bell Telecommunication Laboratories to produce improved copies of the magnetron.

By early 1942 warships defending North Atlantic convoys were beginning to moderate the losses suffered by merchant ships carrying war material to Europe, thanks to the improved performance of radar using the magnetron. At the same time, centimetric radars for aircraft were being designed with two main functions in mind. Forward-looking radars for airborne interception were urgently needed to replace the earlier metric sets. This would improve the interception of attacking aircraft in cloud and at night, following their earlier detection by ground radar. Their other function was to look downwards from the aircraft. For maritime reconnaissance aircraft, the ASV (air-to-surface vessel) radars were so successful that they finally rendered the North Atlantic uninhabitable for the U-boats. Over land a radar using similar technology gave bomber crews a picture of the ground at night and through cloud, allowing them to bomb specific targets accurately, assisted by navigation systems based hundreds of miles behind them in the United Kingdom.

A less glamorous role for radar was in directing anti-aircraft guns. In this field, the United States had an enviable lead, and supplies of the now-celebrated SCR-584 radar, which could track fast-flying targets and aim guns at them automatically, were supplied to Britain and proved themselves in the fight against the V1 flying bombs.

Fighter control in the form of Ground Controlled Interception (or GCI) followed from the 1940 success of the Chain Home system. One of the weaknesses of that system had been its inability to plot individual aircraft in detail, especially if they were flying at low altitudes. Smaller rotating-antenna radars, known as Chain Home Low (CHL) were installed at many sites to overcome the deficiency. More compact radars, eventually adopting centimetric techniques, evolved from these and were installed separately from the main Chain Home stations for fighter direction. GCI radars, compact enough to be transportable, proved invaluable in the theaters of war beyond the British coastlines.

The techniques developed, both electronic and operational, presaged the peacetime role of radar and air navigation. Modern air traffic control now relies upon the methods that were effective in combat during the Second World War. Ground-based radars, airborne "weather" radar, short- and long-range radio navigation systems, and ways of identifying individual aircraft all had their origins in the frantic battle for electronic superiority in 1939–45.

Eryl Davies

Bibliography

Bowen, E.G. *Radar Days*. 1987.

Brown, R. Hanbury. *Boffin: A Personal Story of the Early Days of Radar and Radio Astronomy*. 1991.

Lovell, Bernard. *Echoes of War: The Story of H2S Radar*. 1991.

Pritchard, David. *The Radar War; Germany's Pioneering Achievement 1904–45*. 1989.

Railways

Britain inherited from the nineteenth century a densely built, efficiently-operated, and privately-owned railway network, which, in the days before substantial development of the automobile and modern highways, provided through some 9,000 stations the country's primary transport system for both passengers and freight. In mid-century every spot in England was still within eighteen miles of railway line. By the closing decade of the twentieth century the system, drastically pruned, offered on its remaining routes a modernized service arguably no longer an economic necessity because of the dominance of road transport.

In 1910 about 150 railway companies operated within Britain; the most important included the Great Western, running westward from Paddington Station, London, to destinations arching from Cornwall to Chester, the London and North Western from London's Euston Station through Lancashire, connecting with the Caledonian into Scotland, and the Great Northern, from London's King Cross to Yorkshire, connecting with Scotland via the North Eastern and the North British. Passenger service was frequent and often competitive. Between London and Manchester there were sixteen trains daily on the London and North Western, twelve on the Midland, and six on the Great Central. During the FIRST WORLD WAR the government assumed temporary ownership of the railways. The Railways Act of 1921 forced a major consolidation. Most of the railways south of London were grouped into the new Southern. The London, Midland and Scottish was created from the former London and North Western, Midland, Lancashire and Yorkshire, Caledonian, and other smaller lines. The London and North Eastern included the former Great Northern, Great Central, Great Eastern, North Eastern, and North British. The fourth of the post-grouping lines was the original Great Western, augmented by acquisition of previously independent lines in

South Wales. Grouping was intended to help the railways cope with increasing highway competition, which between the wars began to erode receipts and forced closure of some rural lines. Of the new companies only the Southern, which undertook extensive electrification in its commuter territory south of London, made major changes in its physical plant, while the London and North Eastern attracted public attention by developing, under the direction of Sir Nigel Gresley (1876–1941), a series of handsome express locomotives for non-stop London-Edinburgh service. One achieved a speed of 126 miles per hour in 1938.

Railways were again temporarily nationalized during the SECOND WORLD WAR, when freight traffic rose 50 percent and passenger traffic 68 percent over pre-war levels. Definitive and permanent governmental purchase came from the Transport Act of 1947, which created in theory a unified national transportation system, including not only railways, but also air, canal, and highway freight and passenger services. In 1962, when the attempt to coordinate all transport under single management was abandoned, British Rail began to function as a distinct entity. For operational purposes it was divided into six semi-autonomous regions, Southern, Western, Eastern, London Midland, North Eastern, and Scottish. True integration of the railway network was achieved hesitantly: ten years after NATIONALIZATION there continued to be London to Manchester service on three separate routes. Modernization came only slowly. In the late 1950s the majority of freight cars were still not equipped with air-brakes, and horse-drawn British Rail vans still plodded the streets of London bearing the slogan "British Rail—Safe, Fast, Efficient." It was hoped that eventually the railway might operate profitably, but soon governmental subsidies, to supplement inadequate revenues, became a continuing reality, justified as the cost of maintaining socially necessary but inherently unremunerative lines.

The Beeching Report (1963), by British Railways chairman Richard Beeching (1913–85), resulted in a major cutback of lines and service, as the Victorian ideal, with a nearby station for almost everyone, was abandoned, to be replaced by a relatively sparse network offering frequent service between major points, but conceding rural services to local bus lines. About one-third of all stations along with 5,000 miles of route were to be eliminated. The Beeching cuts allowed abandonment of steam, only five years after construction of British Rail's last steam engine in 1960. In the 1960s the west coast line from London through Lancashire toward Scotland was rebuilt and electrified, with a consequent speed-up of service, and in the 1980s new equipment brought similarly fast service to the old Great Western and the east coast line from London to Scotland, electrified in 1991.

At the beginning of the 1990s the railway network constituted 10,307 route miles, of which 2,825 were electrified, with 2,483 passenger stations and a staff of approximately 130,000. Passenger service dominated, freight traffic accounting for less than 13 percent of total train-miles. But less than 7 percent of British passenger-miles were rail-generated, the same percentage as that produced by long-distance buses, whereas 84 percent of passenger-miles come from private automobiles. Statistics such as these fueled the tendency of MARGARET THATCHER's administration to regard the railway as an expensive and unnecessary luxury and accounted for the government's reluctance to finance construction of a projected high-speed line from London to connect with the new Channel tunnel. LABOUR politicians continued to be more sympathetic to the railways than the CONSERVATIVES, in part a reflection of an ideological bias toward the collectivity of mass transport rather than the individuality of the private automobile, and in part to assure the maintenance of jobs for the dwindling number of railway workers. Supporters of railways resented public concentration on rail deficits, unbalanced by similar attention to far greater highway costs. In 1971, for example, while British Rail was spending only £26 million on maintenance or construction of roadbed, £687 million was spent on maintaining or building highways. During the 1990s the Conservative government privatized the railways once again, separating passenger and freight service from rolling stock, but the ending of nationalization merely compounded problems of obsolescence and insufficient investment. While a rise in accidents stirred public attention, the Labour government after 1997 struggled to find remedies in a transportation system that was no longer publicly managed.

John Ranlett

Bibliography
Aldcroft, Derek H. *British Railways in Transition*. 1968.
Bagwell, Philip S. *The Transport Revolution, 1770–1985*. 1988.
Ellis, C.H. *British Railway History*. vol. II. 1959.
Freeman, Michael, and Derek H. Aldcroft. *The Atlas of British Railway History*. 1985.
Howell, David. *Respectable Radicals*. 1999.
Gourvish, T.R. *British Railways, 1948–73: A Business History*. 1986.
Ottley, George. *A Bibliography of British Railway History*. 2nd ed. 1983.

Rathbone, Eleanor Florence (1872–1946)

Eleanor Rathbone is remembered today as the leader of the thirty-year campaign for FAMILY

ALLOWANCES and as the most important feminist politician of her generation. In her own day, however, she also had a formidable reputation as a social thinker. Her classic work, *The Disinherited Family* (1924), remains the most lucid critique of a distributive system organized around a male family wage, and an eloquent plea for a comprehensive family policy.

Rathbone was born into a Liverpool shipbuilding family with a distinguished record of public service. Her father, William Rathbone IV (1829–1902), was a Member of Parliament, prominent in philanthropic and reforming circles; his daughter would write his biography and succeed to his positions. In 1893 Rathbone entered Somerville College, OXFORD, where she was remembered as serious and as a "fierce feminist". She returned to Liverpool after taking a second class degree in 1896, and over the next twenty-five years built up a career in local politics and social work. Her work as a charitable visitor, settlement worker, and social investigator gave her an intimate knowledge of the social problems of the city, and she published studies of dock workers (1909), women's wages (1912), and the condition of widows under the poor law (1913). She was elected the first woman member of the City Council in 1909, a position she held until 1935.

Through her pioneering social investigations Rathbone became aware of the devastation wrought in working-class families by the cyclical nature and occasional failure of wages; even before 1914 she was developing a critique of a distributive system which left the support of women and children to the vagaries of the male wage. After helping to organize a comprehensive system of state aid to soldiers' wives and children during the FIRST WORLD WAR, she became convinced that only similar peacetime policies could improve the status of mothers and children. By destroying men's claim to a "family wage," she argued, direct state support for dependents could also make the EQUAL PAY of men and women possible. In 1917 she formed a Family Endowment Committee, and over the next thirty years devoted much of her time, energy, and private resources to the campaign for family allowances.

Rathbone also came to hold an important place within feminist politics in the inter-war years. Initially involved in the WOMEN'S SUFFRAGE movement in Liverpool, she supported the "pro-war" wing of the National Union of Women's Suffrage Societies and in 1919 succeeded MILLICENT GARRETT FAWCETT as President of the renamed National Union of Societies for Equal Citizenship. NUSEC suffered a sharp decline in its membership and fortunes after 1919, no doubt largely because of the war and the par-

tial achievement of the vote, but some adherents also disagreed with Rathbone's leadership, and especially with her espousal of a "new FEMINISM" aimed less at the achievement of strict equality than at the improvement of conditions for wives and mothers. In 1929 Rathbone was elected to the Commons as an Independent for the Combined English Universities, a seat she held until her death. Although she continued to argue for social supports for mothers and children, she devoted much of the 1930s to a series of campaigns aimed at raising the status of women in the British colonies. Her interventions were sometimes tactless and not always welcomed by their purported beneficiaries, but in some cases she was able to force the Colonial Office to consider women's issues and to establish contacts between women across national lines.

If a single thread united Rathbone's many writings and interests, it was her concern to mitigate women's subordination to men—whether legal, customary, or economic—within the family. Convinced of the dignity and worth of "women's work" of childbearing and childrearing, she tended to attribute all opposition to her campaigns simply to the desire of men of all classes and races to preserve their domestic and sexual privileges—a predilection she notoriously labeled the "Turk Complex" in *The Disinherited Family*. This belief in men's universal disposition towards familial tyranny is intriguing, particularly in light of her close relations with her own father and her strong identification with the Rathbone heritage. Perhaps the key to this puzzle, and the source of her ability to imagine that marriage need not entail economic dependence, is to be sought in her lifelong relationship with Elizabeth Macadam, a feminist and social worker with whom she lived until her death. Eleanor Rathbone died on 1 January 1946, barely six months after the passage of the Family Allowances Act.

Susan Pedersen

Bibliography

Land, Hilary. "Eleanor Rathbone and the Economy of the Family" in Harold L. Smith, ed. *British Feminism in the Twentieth Century*. 1990. pp. 104–23.

Pedersen, Susan. "Eleanor Rathbone, 1872–1946: The Victorian Family Under the Daughter's Eye" in Susan Pedersen and Peter Mandler, eds. *After the Victorians: Private Conscience and Public Duty in Modern Britain*. 1994. pp. 105–25.

Stocks, Mary D. *Eleanor Rathbone: A Biography*. 1949.

Rationing

Rationing, the sharing of food and other necessities among the population through controls imposed by the government during the FIRST WORLD WAR and the SECOND WORLD WAR, was an essential element in homefront war policy.

At the onset of both wars the country produced only about one-third of its food, measured in calories. The rest was imported by ship. This put the nation at risk of starvation in wartime, when merchant vessels came under attack by the enemy and when more cargo space was needed for munitions and other war materiel. Rationing reduced pressure on shipping by compulsorily lowering demand for imported foodstuffs and by limiting imports to the most economical in terms of NUTRITION and shipping space. It also prevented one region or social group going short while others had plenty by distributing available supplies fairly.

At the start of the First World War there were no plans to ration civilians. Despite German submarine attacks, shipments of most foods remained adequate for the first two years of the war. By mid-1916, however, dwindling imports necessitated control of distribution. The British public got its first taste of rationing in July 1916 when "datum period rationing" went into effect for sugar. Shopkeepers were allotted amounts equal to 65 percent of their 1915 sales. It was their responsibility to share supplies among customers. In February 1917 other shortages forced the government to announce "voluntary rationing". The public was asked to eat no more than four pounds of breadstuffs, two and one-half pounds of meat, and three-quarters of a pound of sugar each a week. Since most working people ate much more bread and less meat than this and could not afford to substitute other foods for bread, the cheapest staple of the day, there was much resistance to voluntary rationing as unfair pressure on those least able to economize. In June the government acknowledged the importance of safeguarding the diet of industrial workers by promising that, whatever other foods might have to be rationed, bread would not. Moreover, the price of bread would be subsidized.

The public reacted positively when compulsory rationing began in January 1918. It was first intended to use a complex five-tier scheme based on calorie needs according to sex, age, and occupation. Instead, because of the need to move quickly, coupons were issued that provided equal rations to all adults, with extra supplies for men on heavy industrial work. To start with, weekly rations were one-half pound of sugar; four ounces of butter or margarine; two ounces of lard; and varying amounts of tea, cheese, jam, and other items depending on supplies. In a popular move, meat was rationed by price, not weight, which left working-class consumption virtually unchanged. Milk was not rationed, but expectant and nursing mothers and children under five received priority tickets that gave them first call on supplies. Vegetables, like bread, remained unrationed. Those who could afford it were free to buy whatever unrationed items remained in the stores and restaurants.

Rationing satisfied public demands for equality of treatment and maintained the DIET of most people at a caloric level similar to pre-war while reducing consumption of wealthier people to a level closer to the norm.

With the lessons of the past and inter-war nutritional research to draw on, rationing in the Second World War was more efficient and scientifically designed. Plans formulated before the war went into effect in January 1940. The key policy that distinguished British rationing from that of other countries was, again, that of leaving cereals and vegetables unrationed and subsidizing the price of bread. Individuals thus determined their own calorie intake by eating more or less of these items in addition to their rations. This made possible the division of the population into just three groups for ration books: "normal consumers" eighteen and over, children aged six to seventeen, and children under six. Only about 50 percent of the average person's calories were controlled by coupons. These allowed each person fixed quantities of protective foods needed in similar amounts by all adults, such as meat, cheese, milk, fats, and eggs, with extra milk for children. Sugar, jam, tea, and coffee were also shared equally. In 1943 weekly basic rations provided eight ounces of sugar, four ounces of fats, three ounces of cheese, two ounces of tea, and one and a half dried eggs. Meat was again rationed by price. In 1943 the coupon bought about eight ounces of bacon and a pound of other meat. In addition, each person was allotted a monthly number of "points" which could be "spent" on such foods as canned fish or biscuits, as the consumer wished. Extra food for people engaged in heavy labor was provided through communal feeding. About 12 million people a day ate a coupon-free meal in canteens at large industrial plants or in "British restaurants" (public, government-run cafés) near smaller factories. Children were served additional food and milk at school, free if the family could not afford to pay. Pre-school children and expectant and nursing mothers benefited from priority tickets for highly nutritious foods in short supply, such as milk, fresh eggs, fruit, and juice. The milk was free, if necessary. Rationing continued after the war, with bread added to the coupon book from mid-1946 to mid-1948. Starting with milk in 1950, controls were gradually dismantled and ended in 1954.

Britain's wartime experience with rationing was probably the most successful in Europe. Average calorie intake remained close to pre-war levels and for the lowest income groups rose. Health improved due to the increased consumption of milk and vegetables and the special care paid to the diet of children and pregnant women. Rationing thus not only contributed to national survival in wartime but to narrowing the socioeconomic gap between classes.

L. Margaret Barnett

Bibliography
Barnett, L. Margaret. *British Food Policy During the First World War*. 1985.
Beveridge, William H. *British Food Control*. 1928.
Hammond, R.J. *Food*. 3 vols. 1951-62.
Zweiniger-Bargielowska, Ina. *Austerity in Britain: Rationing, Controls and Consumption, 1939-1955*. 2000.

Rattigan, Terence Mervyn (1911-1977)

Between 1936 and 1956 Terence Rattigan was the one West End playwright who achieved both critical acclaim as a serious writer and huge commercial success. The son of a diplomat, educated at Harrow and Trinity College, OXFORD, he became a celebrated playwright at the age of twenty-five. The light comedy *French Without Tears* (1936) was his first hit, running for 1,030 performances. *Flare Path* (1942), his drama about an RAF bomber squadron during the SECOND WORLD WAR, ran for 679 performances, and *While the Sun Shines* (1943), a comedy, ran for 1,154 performances.

Beneath the light-hearted surface of *French Without Tears,* an awareness of the pain and humiliation of unrequited love is interwoven with well-observed if exaggerated social comedy. Throughout his career, Rattigan's output alternated between light comedies and dramas of pathos. His critical reputation rests on the darker side of his output: the studies of individuals or groups of characters whose heroism consists in courgeously facing a world in which injustice, intolerance, and unreciprocated sexual infatuations are the norm, moral integrity and fullfilment of romantic passion mere ideals. Rattigan's identification as a writer with the outsider or the underdog may have been a consequence of the tension he experienced as a pillar of the upper middle-class theatrical Establishment forced to keep his own HOMOSEXUALITY a secret until the partial decriminalisation in 1967 of homosexual relations among men.

All of his critical successes from *The Winslow Boy* (1946) to *Cause Celebre* (1977) were written as variations on the formulaic well-made play which constituted the dominant tradition of British drama from 1890 to 1956 (the year of *Look Back in Anger* by JOHN OSBORNE). His persistent themes are the suffering endured by principled but reticent individuals in conflict with a dishonest and repressive society, and the inequalities which characterize sexual relationships as a consequence

of class or gender differences. However limited in their treatment of social and intellectual issues, plays such as *The Browning Version* (1948) and *The Deep Blue Sea* (1952) are characterized by a Strindbergian relentlessness in plumbing the depths of human misery.

The Deep Blue Sea is a harshly realistic study of a middle-class woman's struggle to come to terms with living alone after realizing that circumstances condemn her to a comfortable but passionless marriage or a relationship with a lover who is incapable of reciprocating her intensity. At the beginning of the play she has attempted suicide; the end of the play makes it clear that she is facing up to life with no illusions.

Although Rattigan was criticized in the 1950s and 1960s for the middle-brow quality of his plays, *The Winslow Boy, The Browning Version, The Deep Blue Sea,* and *Separate Tables* (1954) have become classics of the British theatre, and his reputation, having waned, now seems to be undergoing a revival. Most of Rattigan's popular plays were made into films, and he himself wrote a number of successful screenplays. He was knighted in 1971 for his contribution to the theatre.

Robert Gordon

Bibliography
Darlow, Michael, and Gillian Hodson. *Terence Rattigan: The Man and His Work*. 1979.
Wansell, Geoffrey. *Terence Rattigan*. 1995.
Young, B.A. *The Rattigan Version: Sir Terence Rattigan and the Theatre of Character*. 1986.

Reed, Carol (1906-1976)

Described in 1949 as "probably the most brilliant craftsman of the modern cinema" after his worldwide success, *The Third Man*, Carol Reed was never one of those autocratic directors who impose themselves forcefully and wilfully on the course of production. "I don't think the director should stand out," Reed maintained in 1971. "The audience should be unconscious that the damned thing's been directed at all." His avowedly expressed ambition was to become "technically impeccable" and always alert to the contributions made on both sides of the lens, thereby earning the affectionate title, "an actor's director". Reed's best films showed all the signs of fruitful collaboration with actors, cinematographers, writers, and others alike.

Working as a jobbing actor in the 1920s, Reed was taken under the wing of the prolific playwright and thriller novelist, Edgar Wallace, and soon joined him at British Lion. After Wallace's death, Reed embarked on an eclectic series of films—*Midshipman Easy* (1935), *Laburnum Grove* (1936), *Bank Holiday* (1938), and *Penny Paradise* (1938)—which cemented his national repuation as a director of note, not least in the eyes of the *Spectator* critic, GRAHAM GREENE. Moreover, the pronounced realism that informed his 1939 adaptation of A.J. Cronin's mining novel, *The Stars Look Down,* proved especially well-suited to the dire circumstances of wartime Britain. Reed's subsequent propagandist features—*The Young Mr. Pitt* (1942), starring Robert Donat, and *The Way Ahead* (1944) with David Niven—culminated in the Oscar winning Anglo-American documentary, *The True Glory* (1945), co-directed with Garson Kanin, charting the war's progress from D-Day to V-E Day.

By the war's end Reed was acknowledged as Britain's leading director and at the peak of his creative powers. The four films that followed won international acclaim and classic status. Based on F.L. Green's novel, *Odd Man Out* (1947) was a sensitively rendered story about a dying Irish gunman. James Mason's acting and Robert Krasker's cinematography admirably enhanced the film's sombre message. However, it was the collaboration with Graham Greene as scriptwriter on both *The Fallen Idol* (1948) and *The Third Man* (1949) that produced the very best of quality British cinema in the 1940s. The inspired casting of Orson Welles for the latter, along with Joseph Cotton, Alida Valli, and Trevor Howard, as well as the haunting musical score provided by Anton Karas on the zither and some atmospheric photography from Krasker, once again, all combined to wonderful effect in a film of lasting appeal. If *Outcast of the Islands* (1952), based upon JOSEPH CONRAD's novel, was greeted coldly by the critics, it still displayed moments of considerable cinematic acumen.

Thereafter, however, Reed's reputation fell into decline. *The Man Between* (1953) was thought, albeit unfairly, no more than an inferior and pale imitation of *The Third Man,* while *A Kid for Two Farthings* (1955) turned out a sentimental tale of London East End life. *Trapeze* (1956) was Reed's first excursion into the grand arena of Hollywood filmmaking. Despite its evocative use of Cinemascope to convey the excitement of the big ring and circus life, little could redeem its essentially trite and melodramatic plot line. A short-lived stint as the initial director on the 1962 remake of *Mutiny on the Bounty,* where he encountered problems in dealing with an intransigent Marlon Brando, led to Reed's replacement by Lewis Milestone. Undeterred, however, he returned for another Hollywood epic, *The Agony and the Ecstacy* (1965), a sorry story about the painting of the Sistine Chapel.

Ironically, Reed's biggest Hollywood success came in the form of an Academy Award for Best Director on *Oliver* (1968), which also won several other awards, including Best Picture. A lavish,

spectacular musical, the film is too easily dismissed by critics as mindless, escapist trivia. The film has much to recommend it and certainly merits substantial revision. It hints at least of a once great director's hallmarks and, if nothing else, it is surely appropriate that Reed received his Oscar along with many members of his production crew. Ever a believer in team talent, Carol Reed must have been especially pleased that due recognition was afforded their joint efforts.

Tony Aldgate

Bibliography

Moss, Robert F. *The Films of Carol Reed.* 1987.
Wapshott, Nicholas. *The Man Between: A Biography of Carol Reed.* 1990

Refugees

There is a tradition of IMMIGRATION into Britain, despite the fact that in the recent past the country has been a net exporter of population. Within this wider process of immigration can be found a constant flow of refugees. In the nineteenth century Britain became a haven for many fleeing from persecution, although eventual reluctance to admit more refugees manifested itself in restrictive legislation. The 1905 Aliens Act, together with the acts of 1914 and 1919, allowed the government to exercise tight control over the entry, movement, and deportation of all aliens. In spite of such controls, imposed by whichever party was in power and reinforced by subsequent restrictions, refugees continued to come to Britain throughout the century. A small number of émigrés arrived from Russia after 1917, while the advent of Mussolini's Fascist regime brought Italian exiles to Britain from the 1920s onwards.

The decisive period for the arrival of refugees, however, was the 1930s when a significant number came from Germany and, following the *Anschluss* in 1938, from Austria. After the MUNICH agreement and the continued penetration of Czechoslovakia, refugees also arrived from that part of Central Europe. The advent of Hitler in 1933 did not initially result in a large scale exodus from Germany, but emigration grew as the nature of Nazism became clearer. A significant increase in Jewish emigration followed *Kristallnacht* in November 1938. With restrictive immigration controls already in place, refugees encountered little official encouragement and widespread public opposition to their entry. Between 1933 and 1939 an estimated 56,000 refugees from the German Reich entered Britain, of whom 90 per cent were Jewish. Such figures suggest that Britain was generous in its welcome, but official policy remained cautious.

Many refugees from the Greater Germany found it difficult to make a new beginning. The

British government required that Jewish refugees would not become a public charge: the JEWISH community had to provide guarantees on this score. Moreover, refugees in general encountered opposition to their employment: architects, doctors, and university teachers were among those occupational groups who reacted with antipathy. As a result, some refugees departed to the United States which they perceived as a more open, less selective society. Some refugees who remained in Britain gradually made a significant impact, notably in business and the academic world. But other refugees, often invisible to historians, never fully adjusted to life in exile.

Apart from German refugees, the 1930s witnessed the arrival of groups fleeing from the impact of the SPANISH CIVIL WAR, including a number of Basque children whose entry was assisted by the National Joint Committee for Spanish Relief.

Since the 1930s other refugees have come to Britain, such as Poles and Hungarians fleeing from repressive Communist regimes. Increasingly, however, refugee problems have become world-wide; the arrival in Britain of groups from Chile in the 1970s and from Vietnam in the 1980s revealed merely the tip of an international problem. At the time of writing, the issue of asylum for refugees and government proposals to tighten entry laws are the subjects of impassioned debate.

Colin Holmes

Bibliography

Holmes, Colin. *John Bull's Island: Immigration and British Society 1871–1971*. 1988.

Kushner, Tony. *The Persistence of Prejudice: Anti-Semitism in British Society during the Second World War*. 1989.

Sword, K., with Norman Davies and Jan Ciechanowski. *The Formation of the Polish Community in Great Britain 1939–1950*. 1989.

Tannahill, John Allan. *European Volunteer Workers in Britain*. 1958.

Reith, John Charles Walsham (1889–1971)
The first Director-General of the BRITISH BROADCASTING CORPORATION, John Reith was a seminal figure in the development of twentieth-century mass communication. A figure of enormous energy and ambition, Reith helped shape the structure of broadcasting in Great Britain. His notion of public service, most forcefully enunciated in the 1920s, provided the BBC with an institutional identity and national purpose which it never wholly abandoned.

Reith was born in Scotland in July 1889, the seventh and youngest child of George and Adah Reith. A minister in the Free Church of Scotland, George Reith had served the College Church in Glasgow since 1866. Educated at Glasgow Academy and Gresham's School in Norfolk, John Reith was withdrawn from school under mysterious circumstances at age seventeen and apprenticed as an engineer to the North British Locomotive Company. From 1906 to 1914 he studied and worked as an engineer, first in Glasgow and then for a brief period in London. Long interested in the military, Reith served with valor in the FIRST WORLD WAR, where in 1915 a sniper's wound left his face scarred. Prohibited from returning the the front, Reith was sent to the United States in 1916 to help organize the manufacture and supply of rifles for the British ARMY. His managerial skills and deep moral seriousness greatly impressed American and British authorities. Three years after the war ended, while manager of a factory, Reith married Muriel Odhams, the daughter of a wealthy publisher.

In 1922 Reith was offered the leadership of the newly-formed BBC, a tiny company of limited resources and no fixed identity. Distressed by the commercialism of American broadcasting and mass communication generally, Reith struggled hard for the ideals of public service broadcasting. Demanding and receiving monopoly powers for the BBC in 1923 and then again in two subsequent renewals of the charter (1926, 1936), Reith argued that high culture need only be made available for most people to embrace it. With its emphasis on classical music, instructional talks, and Sunday religious programs, the BBC became the embodiment of cultural respectability during the inter-war period and gained wide support across the political spectrum as a successful experiment in public ownership and control.

A prominent national figure in the 1930s, Reith longed for greater authority and responsibility in national affairs. In 1938 he resigned from the BBC to become head of Imperial Airways, an audacious gesture that proved a mistake for his career and a disaster for him personally. Never again would he occupy an office of such power, prestige, and access. During the Second World War he served in a variety of posts, including Minister of Information, but his authoritarian manner, self-absorption, and personal bitterness, especially towards CHURCHILL, soured the considerable achievements of this period. From 1950 to 1959 Reith led the Colonial Development Corporation, retiring at age seventy with many honors, not least the peerage granted in 1942, but with also an abiding sense of personal failure that haunted his later career and bewildered his admirers. His monument remained the BBC, which despite enormous changes after his departure retained the sense of mission bequeathed by its first Director-General.

D.L. Le Mahieu

Bibliography
Le Mahieu, D.L. "John Reith, 1889–1971: Entrepreneur of Collectivism" in Susan Pedersen and Peter Mandler, eds. *After the Victorians: Private Conscience and Public Duty in Modern Britain.* 1994. pp. 189–206.
Reith, John (Lord). *Into the Wind.* 1949.
Stuart, Charles, ed. *The Reith Diaries.* 1975.

Richards, Ivor Armstrong (1893–1979)

In a career spanning sixty years I.A. Richards made major contributions to semantics, literary theory and practice, linguistics, and education. *Practical Criticism* (1929) revolutionized the academic study of literature and dominated classrooms in the English-speaking world from the 1940s to the 1960s. Its method of "close reading" remains a continuing influence. His programs in beginning reading and second language training embraced the use of modern media, from slide, recording, and film-strip to television, video, and cassette.

Richards was born in Sandbach, Cheshire and was educated at Clifton and Magdalene College, CAMBRIDGE, where he read moral sciences under G.E. MOORE and received first-class honors in 1915. Shortly thereafter he suffered a serious attack of tuberculosis and recuperated by climbing mountains in North Wales. There he met his future wife Dorothea Elinor Pilley, a journalist and mountaineer. In 1919 the new English School at Cambridge invited him to teach courses on contemporary literature and the theory of criticism. His first book was *The Foundations of Aesthetics* (1922, co-authored by C.K. Odgen and James Wood) in which he outlines sixteen aesthetic theories with a preference for psychological "synaesthesis," a harmonious state of thought and feeling together with an equilibrium which prevents any immediate tendency to action. In *The Meaning of Meaning* (1923, with C.K. Ogden) he presents a contextual theory of meaning where context is given a psychological and physical definition; though the authors are rooted in British philosophical psychology, they borrow elements of behaviorism in constructing a model of interpretation. They postulate two broad uses of language, the emotive and the referential (or symbolic), as well as five separate functions, each more or less present in a given speech-act. In later books Richards raises the number to seven: indicating, charactering, realizing, valuing, influencing, controlling, and purposing.

The nature of the literary text and the reader's response are the subjects of his next books. *Principles of Literary Criticism* (1924) elaborates theories of communication and value, defined in terms of the enrichment of the mental personality. The treatment of poetic texts places a strong emphasis on balance and attitudinal equilibrium

in which irony is seen as a literary device for bringing in opposed or complementary attitudes to ensure complexity and wholeness. In *Practical Criticism* (1929), his masterpiece and one of the most famous experiments in the history of criticism, he examines hundreds of undergraduate reports on poems of varying quality, categorizes the types of misreading, and proposes a corrective method of textual "close reading" (sense, irony, ambiguity, metaphor, feeling, tone, intention, etc.). *The Philosophy of Rhetoric* (1936) advances a revolutionary theory of metaphor, defined as a "transaction between contexts." *Interpretation in Teaching* (1938) rounds out his theory of criticism, applying his method to the study of critical or expository prose.

The influence of these books has been deep and lasting. One of his pupils was William Empson, whose *Seven Types of Ambiguity* (1930) had its origins in tutorial. Richards is often acknowledged as the "father" of American New Criticism, an academic movement stressing the objectivity of the work of art, contextualism, and "close reading."

During the 1930s Richards turned his attention from higher education to problems in beginning reading and language training. He spent several years in China promoting Ogden's "Basic English," a normal version of English based on an initial knowledge of 850 key words and grammatical patterns. Of the books that emerged from his experience in China *Mencius on the Mind* (1931) and *A First Book of English for Chinese Learners* (1938) are particularly noteworthy. In 1939, after twenty years at Cambridge, he accepted a post at Harvard where he became a University Professor (1944–63). He pioneered the use of audio-visual media in the teaching of reading and second language learning. *English through Pictures* (1945, with Christine M. Gibson) was the first of a series of *Language through Pictures* in seven languages. He also translated Homer, Plato, and the Book of Job into simplified English so that students could have major works among their first literary experiences in the language.

In 1974 Richards published *Beyond*, which examines the dialogues with deities in Homer, Plato, Job, Dante, and Shelley. In the same year he returned to Cambridge, England. At the age of sixty he had begun writing poetry, eventually bringing out four collections and three verse-plays. In his eighty-seventh year he undertook a tour of China lecturing on the teaching of English. He fell seriously ill and was brought back to England where he died on 7 September 1979.

John Paul Russo

Bibliography
Hotopf, W.H.N. *Language, Thought and Comprehension: A Case Study of the Writings of I.A. Richards.* 1965.

Needham, John. *The Completest Mode: I.A. Richards and the Continuity of English Literary Criticism.* 1982.

Russo, John Paul. *I.A. Richards: His Life and Work.* 1989.

———. "A Bibliography" in Reuben Brower, Helen Vendler, and John Hollander. *I.A. Richards: Essays in His Honor.* 1973, pp. 319–65.

Schiller, Jerome P. *I.A. Richards' Theory of Literature.* 1969.

Robbins Report (1963)

In the first half of the twentieth century higher education in Britain consisted of three distinct segments: universities, teacher training colleges, and institutions of further education, which included technical, commercial, and art colleges. After 1945 the priority of economic recovery and an unprecedented number of university-qualified secondary school graduates signaled the need for a coordinated system of higher education in Britain. In 1961 a sub-committee of the University Grants Committee was established to analyze the current state of higher education and provide recommendations for its future. Lionel Robbins, a leading academic economist at the LONDON SCHOOL OF ECONOMICS, known for his interest in liberal education, was invited to be chairman.

As no comprehensive picture of the status of higher education yet existed, the committee undertook a thorough stock-taking of the nation's educational system. Four hundred written submissions of evidence were solicited from individuals and organizations and a series of statistical surveys were commissioned. Surveys of full-time undergraduates, postgraduates, students in teacher training programs, members of academic staff, and twenty-one-year-olds formed the bulk of the research. The surveys revealed a sizeable scholastic potential and untapped ability in students aged above sixteen, particularly among girls. It was apparent that Britain, like the Continent in general, lagged behind the United States in student enrollment and would benefit by providing more opportunities for higher education.

The Committee on Higher Education published their findings in 1963. The Robbins Report focused criticism on the uncoordinated state of British higher education, concluding that without systematic reform there was little chance of "maintaining an adequate position in the fiercely competitive world of the future." With reform, the committee predicted an increase in the number of postgraduates from 9,500 in 1961 to 32,000 by 1980–1.

The seven-volume Report offered both general strategies and specific proposals for educational reform. In all, it set forth 178 recommendations touching on every aspect of university organization: staffing, student life, research, teaching, finance, academic coverage, and governance. Four principal objectives for higher education were cited. First, educational institutions should help prepare students for the marketplace by providing the means to specialization. Second, there should be no sacrifice of liberal learning and cultivation of the mind. Third, a new emphasis should be placed on teaching and research. Fourth, common citizenship values should be inculcated in higher education.

The Robbins Report provided guidelines for the fledgling new universities of the 1960s and came to be associated with the method for selecting university students. The concept that all young Britons qualified by ability and achievement (based on sixth form Advanced level exams) were entitled to a full-time course of higher education if they chose became known as the Robbins principle.

Martha A. Schütz

Bibliography

Anderson, Sir David. *Robbins Report on Higher Education.* 1964.

Carswell, John. *Government and the Universities in Britain: Programme and Performance 1960–1980.* 1985.

Report of the Committee on Higher Education, 1961–3 (Robbins Committee) 1963 Cmnd. 2154.

Stewart, W.A.C. *Higher Education in Postwar Britain.* 1989.

Roman Catholicism

Numerical growth, institutional development, social and intellectual advance, and national acceptance have been the principal characteristics of Roman Catholicism in Britain throughout much of the twentieth century. It was only in 1850 that a Catholic hierarchy was restored in England and Wales, with Cardinal Nicholas Patrick Wiseman (1802–65) appointed to head the Archdiocese of Westminster and its twelve suffragan sees. The restoration resulted in an outburst of anti-Catholic criticism and even rioting. Wiseman and his immediate successors, Henry Edward Manning (1808–92) and Herbert Vaughan (1832–1903), were successful, however, in winning increased acceptance of the growing Catholic community. The twentieth century has been a period of further development, growth, and consolidation to the point where Roman Catholics are found in virtually every walk of life.

Within two decades after the turn of the century, there were over 2 million Catholics in England and Wales, almost three times the number assessed at the time of the hierarchy's restoration. They were served by 4,000 priests, double the number recorded just thirty years earlier. Catholic schools educated 400,000 students, significant in accounting for the cohesion of the Catholic body. By 1951 there were 2,837,000 Catholics, served by nearly 7,000 priests. At the turn of the century

Catholic landed families still played a dominant role in church life as they had in the nineteenth century. They were overwhelmingly outnumbered, however, by Irish IMMIGRANTS and their descendants, most of whom belonged to the working class in cities such as Liverpool and, to a lesser extent, Birmingham, and LONDON. This explains the fact that in 1911 the Holy See divided the Archdiocese into three ecclesiastical provinces—Birmingham, Liverpool, and Westminster. In 1916 the Diocese of Newport was raised to archiepiscopal rank as well, under the title of Cardiff. It should be noted that Scotland's hierarchy was restored in 1878 and today consists of two provinces, St. Andrews and Edinburgh and that of Glasgow.

As their educational opportunities increased at every level, Catholics became increasingly affluent, with a large proportion soon numbered among the middle class. The growing diversity within the Catholic population meant that increasing numbers were no longer confined to the large industrial cities. In 1915, for example, 58.4 percent of the Catholic population lived in the Archdiocese of Liverpool, while 26.2 percent lived in the Archdiocese of Westminster and the Diocese of Southwark, the two sees which divided London. By 1951 Liverpool's share of the Catholic population was down to 37.8 percent, while Westminster and Southwark claimed 51 percent. In recognition of the population shift, the Holy See, in 1965, raised Southwark to the status of an archdiocese.

In spite of the creation of new provinces, the archbishops of Westminster have retained a unique status, especially in dealing with the Holy See. For the most part they have been recognized primarily for their pastoral and administrative skills rather than their erudition or social presence. Francis Bourne (1861–1935), who succeeded Cardinal Vaughan in 1903, quietly presided over the Westminster Archdiocese until his death. These were years of steady progress for Catholics, with landmarks such as an International Eucharistic Congress (1908); the opening of Oxford theological degrees to non-Anglicans (1920); the beatification of the English martyrs (1929); and the restoration of the shrine of Our Lady of Walsingham (1935). Bourne was succeeded by Arthur Hinsley (1865–1945), who thoroughly endeared himself not only to the Catholic community, but to the British public at large for his promotion of social reform and his leadership in support of the war effort. He also had the honor of welcoming the first apostolic delegate for Britain since the Reformation, William Godfrey (1888–1963), who later succeeded William Griffin (1899–1956) as Archbishop of Westminster. Godfrey's successor was John Carmel Heenan

(1905–75), an able communicator and a man already recognized for his commitment to Catholic social teaching. It was his responsibility to implement the liturgical reforms after the Second Vatican Council. Heenan's popular successor, George Basil Hume (1923–99), an Oxford graduate and Ampleforth Benedictine, in many respects, followed the policies of his predecessor, especially in matters of social justice and a commitment to ecumenism.

While the English and Welsh bishops have not encouraged specific political positions in Britain, they have struggled consistently to obtain and retain government funding for the support of Catholic schools. There has not been a Catholic political constituency, as such, so that in the last Parliament prior to the independence of southern Ireland in 1918, there were ten Catholic Members from England and seventy-eight from Ireland. The *Catholic Directory* for 1990 listed forty-three Catholic MPs and seventy-eight peers.

Catholics have been allowed by their hierarchy to attend OXFORD and CAMBRIDGE since 1895. This has certainly been a factor in their intellectual as well as their social advance. No discussion of Catholicism in twentieth-century Britain would be complete without reference to some of the more famous authors and scholars who have either converted to or been born into the church. Among them have been G.K. CHESTERTON, Hilaire Belloc (1870–1953), Ronald Knox (1888–1957), EVELYN WAUGH, Martin D'Arcy (1888–1976), J.R.R. Tolkien (1892–1973), and GRAHAM GREENE. The similar listing could be made of Catholics identified with other professions.

Following the Second Vatican Council there has been some controversy and unrest among Catholics, particularly with regard to liturgical reform and the introduction of the vernacular. Certainly Britain has shared the religious problems that have been commonplace in the West. Yet a National Pastoral Congress in Liverpool (1980) urged even further liturgical reform. A decline in the number of vocations to the priesthood and religious congregations of both men and women is a serious setback, especially for Catholic education. Yet Catholics can no longer be accused of nursing a "fortress mentality," as is commonly alleged to have been the case in the past. Cooperation with and acceptance by other churches has been one of the more noteworthy characteristics of Roman Catholicism in recent years.

R.J. Schiefen, CSB

Bibliography

Beck, George Andrew, ed. *The English Catholics, 1850–1950.* 1950.

Hastings, Adrian. *A History of English Christianity, 1920–1990.* 3rd ed. 1991.

Hornsby-Smith, Michael P. *Roman Catholics in England: Studies in Social Structure since the Second World War.* 1987.

Riddell, Neil. "The Catholic Church and the Labour Party, 1918–1931," *Twentieth Century British History,* vol. 8 (1997), pp. 165–93.

Royal Air Force

The Royal Air Force (RAF) was the world's first independent air force, not merely separate from the ARMY and the ROYAL NAVY, but on an equal footing with them in the councils of government and represented by its own Secretary of State and the Air Ministry. Established in April 1918, the RAF was preceded as a fighting service in Britain by the Royal Flying Corps (RFC), which was formed in May 1912 and included both Military and Naval Wings. In 1914, when Britain entered the FIRST WORLD WAR, the Naval Wing became separate as the Royal Naval Air Service.

In these early days the airplane's role in warfare was undeveloped, and it was regarded merely as an adjunct to military and naval operations, a machine to be used in support of an army in the field or a fleet at sea. Air power, in any strategic aspect, did not play a decisive role in the conflict of 1914–18. Nevertheless there were already those who realized that the aircraft had the potential to wage an entirely new "independent" warfare in its own element. But the views of the existing services dominated military and strategic thinking, and the ideas of the visionaries were not welcome.

This situation changed profoundly in 1917, when German Gotha four-engined aircraft bombed London. Up to that time there had been only a few scattered raids by Zeppelin airships, causing negligible damage. In the Gotha raids nearly 500 people were killed. This was the advent of war in a new dimension, both spatially and conceptually. It ignored frontiers and battle lines, the division between land and sea, and the distinction between the fighting servicemen and the non-combatant civilian. In response to public outcry a Cabinet committee was formed under General Jan Christian Smuts (1870–1950) to examine defense arrangements and the organization of the air services. The Committee quickly saw that the existing organization had two serious limitations. First, if air power was tied to the needs of armies and navies, its potential to operate independently, whether in offense or defense, was unlikely to receive the attention it demanded. Second, the air itself was a single entity covering both land and sea; the separation of the air services was an anomaly. The Committee recommended the formation of a third service, to be responsible for all the military applications of air power. And so the Royal Air Force was created, on 1 April 1918, absorbing both the RFC and RNAS.

The early years of the RAF were precarious. At the end of the war there was strong sentiment, backed by the Royal Navy and the army, in favor of disbanding the third service. It was suggested that the Air Ministry be disestablished and the component parts of the RAF returned to the Admiralty and the War Office. The lobby reckoned without the enigmatic Sir Hugh Trenchard (1873–1956), the Chief of the Air Staff. His early military career was undistinguished, but he had a vision of a new service and managed to carry it to reality.

There was nothing Trenchard could do to increase the size of the RAF, but he saw to the establishment of Boy Entrants and Apprentice Schemes, the Royal Air Force College at Cranwell for Officer entrants, and the Royal Air Force Staff College. If the numbers at his disposal were few, he wished to ensure that they were highly trained and imbued with distinctive *esprit de corps*. He also created University Air Squadrons, Reserves, Auxiliary squadrons, and Short Service Commissions—all schemes which would foster air-mindedness in the population at large, provide a cadre of skilled people on whom any sudden expansion of the RAF could be based, should that ever become necessary.

But without a role for it, the case for the continued existence of an independent air force would have been hard to sustain. Opportunely such a role emerged very quickly, one quite unlike anything which had been envisaged. It came to be called "Air Control" and entailed the policing of immense areas of Britain's colonial and mandated territories in Africa, the Near and Middle East, and India. It was WINSTON CHURCHILL, Air Minister in 1919, who decided that it would be the first duty of the RAF to garrison the British Empire.

This would previously have been a role for the army, but the cost of covering this vast commitment by stationing troops on the ground would have been crippling and unsustainable. In 1921 Churchill, by then Colonial Secretary, convened a conference in Cairo to settle the regional affairs and insisted that Trenchard be there, confirming Air Control as a major role for the RAF. In parts of the world where hostilities had been endemic Air Control fostered greater peace and stability. This was done with a considerable saving in lives and money, and in a way which tended to win respect from the local populations. It may also have been instrumental in ensuring the survival of the RAF as an independent service.

It was not until the latter half of the decade of the 1930s that the threat from Germany came to be recognized. It was at this time that the RAF placed orders for the Hurricane, the Spitfire, and the Lancaster bomber. Various schemes to enlarge the service were initiated but foundered or were delayed through lack of money. The build-up did not gain real momentum until almost the last moment. During the years from 1920 to 1935 the RAF rarely numbered above 30,000. By 1939 it was over 100,000, and by 1943 over 1 million.

The RAF's first real test came early in the SECOND WORLD WAR, with the BATTLE OF BRITAIN in the summer of 1940. Since Hitler could not launch his invasion fleet while it was vulnerable to air attack during the Channel crossing, the first stage of his plan was the neutralization of the RAF. But RAF Fighter Command, under Sir Hugh Dowding (1882–1970), fought back doggedly, while aircraft of Bomber Command and Coastal Command attacked the German invasion fleets gathering in the French ports. Hitler had to delay his decision to launch the invasion, and on 17 September 1940 he was forced to postpone it indefinitely.

The Battle of Britain has historical significance not only as one of the turning points of the Second World War, but because it was the first—and probably the last—major battle to be fought exclusively in the air. As the war progressed, the RAF played a key part in all the major campaigns: the Battle of the Atlantic, which was the long campaign against the German U-Boats to keep open the vital sea lines of supply with the North American continent; North Africa, where the principles of land/air warfare were thoroughly consolidated; the Strategic Bombing Offensive against Germany, which claimed more RAF lives than all other campaigns put together; in the Far East where air transport was essential to supply the forces fighting in the jungles; and in the final campaign in Northern Europe which led to the defeat of Germany.

For about twenty-five years after the end of the Second World War the RAF maintained a major presence in the Far East, the Middle East, and in Germany. It participated in the long Malayan Campaign (1948–60) leading to the defeat of communist insurgency, in "confrontation" with Indonesia (1962–6), in most of the recurring crises in the Middle Eastern region, in the FALKLANDS WAR in 1982, and in the Gulf War of 1991. For a large part of the period of the Cold War it also covered Britain's contribution to the strategic nuclear deterrent until this role was assumed by the Royal Navy with Polaris submarines.

The RAF now numbers about 75,000 men and women. It is based mainly in Britain, with a few squadrons in Germany. With the exception of long-range bombers, it covers all the roles of air power: offensive, defensive, maritime, transport and reconnaissance, and operates world-wide. The three services in Britain no longer have their separate Departments of State; since 1964 all now come under a single Ministry of Defence.

Ian Madelin

Bibliography

Armitage, Michael. *The Royal Air Force: An Illustrated History.* 1993.

Boyle, Andrew. *Trenchard.* 1962.

Dean, Maurice. *The Royal Air Force and Two World Wars.* 1979.

Richards, Denis, and Hilary St.G. Saunders. *The Royal Air Force 1939–1945.* 3 vols. new ed. 1993.

Terraine, John. *A Time for Courage: The RAF in the European War 1939–1945.* 1985.

Trevenen, James. *The Royal Air Force: The Past Thirty Years.* 1976.

Russell, Bertrand (1872–1970)

No British intellectual in the twentieth century spanned as many decades, filled as many pages, provoked as many arguments, enraged as many worthies, launched as many crusades, inspired as many disciples, or served as much jail time as did Bertrand Russell. Born into one of the proudest families of the Whig aristocracy, Russell died a social renegade; accepted into the highest reaches of the British intellectual elite by virtue of his astonishing philosophical creativity, he ended his days outside the academy and at war with dominant philosophical fashions; championed by conventional PACIFISTS and unorthodox dissenters, he died at the head of a bitterly divided and divisive protest movement. From the BOER WAR to Vietnam, from neo-Hegelianism to linguistic philosophy, from nuclear disarmament to BIRTH CONTROL, there was no public issue, scholarly fashion, intellectual preoccupation, or political question on which he flinched from offering an heretical opinion.

Russell was born on 18 May 1872 to John and Kate Stanley Russell, Lord and Lady Amberley. Members of the radical wing of the late-Victorian Whig aristocracy, the Amberleys both died tragically young—she in 1874, he in 1876—and the young Russell was left in the care of his paternal grandparents, the Earl and Countess Russell. The only child in a world of adults, Russell was carefully inculcated with the hereditary aristocratic Whiggism embodied by his grandfather and prepared for an inevitable political career devoted to continuing those principles into the twentieth century. Educated by private tutors, Russell gave early evidence of both a formidable intelligence and a consuming passion for mathematics, and in October 1890 went up to Trinity College, CAMBRIDGE intending to study mathematics. Almost immediately Russell blossomed both intellectually and socially. Not merely did he place in the first class in Part I of the Mathematical Tripos in 1893 and in Part II of the Moral Sci-

ence Tripos in 1894, but he was elected to the celebrated undergraduate discussion society the
APOSTLES, where he made intimate friends
among the brethren, such as J.M.E. McTaggart,
G.E. MOORE, Robert Trevelyan, and ALFRED
NORTH WHITEHEAD. In their company Russell—lonely and friendless upon his arrival—
flourished, and under their encouragement and
guidance turned his interests to questions of the
logical foundations of mathematics, to the study
of which he was elected to a prestigious Trinity
College Prize Fellowship in 1895.

In even his earliest writings Russell demonstrated those traits which would come to characterize his entire intellectual life: an enviable lucidity, an astonishing fertility, a brave iconoclasm,
an irrepressible wit, and limitless energy. His initial work, such as *An Essay on the Foundations of
Geometry* (1897), was well within the confines of
the dominant neo-Hegelian orthodoxy in which
he had been schooled. By the turn of the century,
however, Russell had joined Moore in launching
an ultimately fatal challenge to that orthodoxy. In
a mood of exhilaration and liberation Russell entered the most creative period of his career, writing a dazzling series of papers (e.g. "On Denoting" (1904) and books (e.g. *The Principles of
Mathematics* [1903]) culminating in the three collaborative volumes of *Principia Mathematica*
(1910–13). His technical mastery of logic, unparalleled command of mathematics, sparkling virtuosity of style, and incomparably wide reading
in contemporary continental thought all combined to enable him to achieve a commanding intellectual ascendancy. Elected to the Royal Society in 1907 and to a Trinity College lectureship in
logic and the philosophy of mathematics created
especially for him in 1910, Russell was by the
summer of 1914 at the peak of his scholarly reputation and intellectual prestige.

The outbreak of the FIRST WORLD WAR
transformed Russell's life. Although never an ar-
chetypically cloistered Cambridge don—he had
been active in the TARIFF REFORM campaign of
1903 and the WOMEN'S SUFFRAGE movement from
1907—Russell had nonetheless not been a public
man in the sense his grandfather would have approved. But as Britain lurched towards war in the
summer of 1914, Russell threw himself first into
the pro-neutrality and then into the anti-war
movement—speaking, writing, organizing, and
counseling. No pacifist, Russell passionately believed that this particular war—not all war—was
a mistake; indeed, it offended his every political
instinct and principle. And as the war lengthened
and Britain's commitment extended, Russell's
opposition sharpened—to mistreatment of CON-
SCIENTIOUS OBJECTORS, to the suppression of
civil liberties, and to the arrogant wastefulness of

British commanders. This opposition—strident,
unrelenting, and deeply unpopular—was the defining experience of Russell's life; not merely did
emotions run so high on all sides that he alienated friends, exasperated allies, and nettled enemies, but his opposition cost him his Trinity College lectureship and a six-months' spell in prison.

In the years after 1918 Russell was at once intellectually unwilling and emotionally unable to
return to his former life. Satisfied with his work
in philosophy, prepared to allow his former pupils
(especially Ludwig Wittgenstein) to make the
running for the next philosophical generation,
and determined to do all he could to reconstruct
society and to regenerate individuals so as to
eliminate war, Russell turned his attention in the
1920s and 1930s to lecturing, writing, teaching,
and traveling (to Russia in 1920 and China in
1920–1). Although much of his writing proved
evanescent, it nonetheless reached a wide audience and served to heighten his notoriety; indeed,
for all that his liberal views on religion, science,
and sexuality attracted the young, independent,
and free-thinking, they also offended the comfortable, conforming, and established.

The outbreak of the Second World War found
Russell teaching in America. Eager to return to
Britain, he was prohibited from doing so by a
British government willing to remember his earlier anti-war activities but not to believe his current—and genuine—support for this conflict. He
therefore remained in America until 1944—writing, lecturing, teaching, and preparing the manuscript for what would become his most widely-
known book, *A History of Western Philosophy*
(1945). Russell returned to considerable acclaim
and, in the 1940s and 1950s, unaccustomed respectability. Reconciled to Trinity College, he was
a popular teacher and lecturer at Cambridge and,
indeed, to all of Britain as a BBC broadcaster and
pundit. The award of the Order of Merit in 1949
and the Nobel Prize for Literature in 1950 were
further evidence of the healing of old wounds.

In the end, this quiet proved only temporary,
for by the late 1950s Russell had entered a new
period of even greater controversy that would
continue until the end of his life. Convinced of
the irresistible threat of nuclear annihilation and
of the absolute necessity of Britain's unilateral renunciation of its nuclear deterrent, Russell was
one of the founders of the CAMPAIGN FOR NU-
CLEAR DISARMAMENT in 1958 and, beginning in
1960, of the more radical Committee of 100.
With an astounding robustness for a man now in
his mid-eighties, Russell once again threw himself headlong into a contentious and divisive public campaign—writing, marching, lecturing, and
getting arrested—a course of action he repeated,
in his nineties, in the late 1960s in opposition to

American and British involvement in the war in Vietnam.

Russell died, on 2 February 1970, in the midst of bitter recrimination. Convinced of the criminality of the war in Vietnam, of the irresistible slide towards nuclear holocaust, of the wrongheadedness of contemporary philosophy, and of the incapacity of any of Britain's political leaders to arrest his beloved nation's apparently inexorable decline, Russell died railing like Lear against the storms about him. To many contemporaries, he appeared to have been a man who squandered his gifts and betrayed his position in a series of unnecessarily offensive and wholly quixotic ventures. But to Russell himself, his life had been if not a success then at least a worthy effort—to help mankind to save itself from its own extinction, to speak directly to the deepest sources of human spirituality, to search for the truth of philosophy and mathematics, and to appeal to wellsprings of humanity and generosity.

Kirk Willis

Bibliography

Clark, Ronald W. *The Life of Bertrand Russell*. 1975.

Monk, Ray. *Bertrand Russell*. 2 vols. 1996, 2000.

Russell, Bertrand. *The Autobiography of Bertrand Russell*. 3 vols. 1967–9.

———. *My Philosophical Development*. 1959.

Ryan, Alan. *Bertrand Russell: A Political Life*. 1988.

Rutherford, Ernest (1871–1937)

Ernest Rutherford became the most prominent physicist in Britain, known for his work on radioactivity and the structure of the atomic nucleus. He received the Nobel Prize for Chemistry in 1908 for showing that radioactivity involved the change of an atom of one chemical element into an atom of another. In 1911 he proposed that atoms had a central core or nucleus, and in 1919 he reported he had disintegrated the nucleus. He built up successful schools of research in both Manchester and later CAMBRIDGE. He was President of the Royal Society, 1925–30. In 1931 he became Lord Rutherford of Nelson.

Rutherford was born in New Zealand to a family of Scottish extraction. After graduating from Canterbury College, Christchurch, he became a research student at the Cavendish Laboratory, Cambridge under J.J.Thomson in 1895. There Rutherford worked on the electrical conductivity of gases and radioactivity. He identified and named two types of radioactive decay, alpha and beta. It was an exciting time, for X-rays and the electron were also discovered in the last few years of the 19th century.

Leaving Cambridge, Rutherford became Professor of Physics at McGill University, Montreal in 1898, where he continued to work on radioactivity. There Rutherford, in collaboration with Frederick Soddy, showed that radioactive change involved the transmuting of an atom of one chemical element into an atom of another, quite unlike the more familiar chemical changes.

In 1907 he moved to Manchester, entering a fruitful period of collaboration with James Chadwick, Hans Geiger, Niels Bohr, and Henry Moseley. Rutherford, investigating the internal structure of the atom, argued in 1911 that an atom had a central nucleus, containing most of its mass and with a positive electrical charge. These ideas were extended by Niels Bohr to account for the properties of simple atoms, such as hydrogen. The Rutherford-Bohr model of the atom became one of the foundations of quantum mechanics, the modern theory of atomic behavior.

In 1919 he published the results of the first experiments on nuclear disintegration. He had caused nitrogen nuclei to emit particles with a single positive electrical charge which he took to be a constituent of all nuclei to which he later gave the name proton. That year he succeeded J.J. Thomson as Cavendish Professor of Physics at Cambridge. Here he assembled a group of researchers, including Chadwick, P.M.S. Blackett, and John Cockcroft who profoundly influenced the course of nuclear research, and Peter Kapitsa who worked on magnetic research until he returned to Russia. Chadwick discovered the neutron, Cockcroft and Walton built the first particle accelerator, and electronic methods of counting particles were built, advances which owed much to the vision of Rutherford.

From 1930 until his death Rutherford was chairman of the Advisory Council of the Department of Scientific and Industrial Research (DSIR). He was head of the Academic Assistance Council which provided assistance to refugee scholars from Germany between 1933 and 1936.

Alan Q. Morton

Bibliography

Eve, A.S. *Rutherford*. 1939.

Chadwick, James. *The Collected Papers of Lord Rutherford of Nelson*. 1962–5.

Wilson, David. *Rutherford, Simple Genius*. 1983.

Samuel, Herbert (1870–1963)

Herbert Samuel (1st Viscount Samuel, cr. 1937), statesman, philosopher, and leading figure in the JEWISH community, served as a government minister (1905–16), as High Commissioner in PALESTINE (1920–5), and as Leader of the LIBERAL PARTY (1931–5).

Samuel was born in Liverpool, the son of a wealthy Jewish banker, but lived most of his life in London. He was educated at University College School, London, and Balliol College, OXFORD, where he gained a first class degree in modern history. Even as a student he was active on the radical wing of the Liberal Party. His book, *Liberalism* (1902), foreshadowed many of the social reforms enacted by Liberal governments after 1905.

Samuel entered Parliament in 1902 as Liberal MP for Cleveland, retaining the seat until 1918. He made his name as a debater in 1903 by denouncing the "barbarism" of the autocracy of King Leopold of the Belgians in the Congo. In 1904–5 Samuel was among those who attacked the CONSERVATIVE government's scheme for the importation of Chinese labor to work in gold mines in South Africa. The controversy helped bring down the Conservative government of A.J. BALFOUR in December 1905.

As Under-Secretary at the Home Office in the CAMPBELL-BANNERMAN and ASQUITH governments between 1905 and 1909, Samuel helped devise, draft, and defend social reform legislation. He was particularly identified with the Probation Act (1907) which established a national system of probation officers, and the Children Act (1909), which extended state responsibility for the welfare of children. With his appointment in 1909 as Chancellor of the Duchy of Lancaster, Samuel became the first unconverted Jew to hold CABINET office. As Postmaster General (1910–14 and May 1915 to January 1916) he presided over the NATIONALIZATION of the telephone service. But his plans for social reform as President of the Local Government Board (February 1914 to May 1915) were cut short by the outbreak of the First World War. His brief tenure as Home Secretary (January to December 1916) brought him into conflict with former radical allies over such civil liberties issues as CONSCIENTIOUS OBJECTION.

When LLOYD GEORGE formed his coalition government in December 1916, Samuel refused a post, remaining with Asquith on the opposition front bench. His main preoccupation now was Zionism. In early 1915 he had been the first to propose to the Cabinet the creation of a British-sponsored Jewish home in Palestine and played an essential behind-the-scenes role in the discussions that led to the pro-Zionist Balfour Declaration in 1917. He was therefore a natural choice in 1920 to serve as first High Commissioner in Palestine under the LEAGUE OF NATIONS mandate. His five years there laid the groundwork for the Jewish National Home, although Arab anti-Zionist riots in 1921 led him to restrict Jewish immigration according to the principle of "economic absorptive capacity".

Samuel had hoped to spend the rest of his life writing philosophy, but he was called back to public life to head a Royal Commission on Coal which reported in March 1926. The report failed to end strife in the COAL INDUSTRY that led to the GENERAL STRIKE of May 1926. Samuel, acting as an unofficial mediator, helped persuade the TRADES UNION CONGRESS to call off the strike on 12 May.

As Liberal organization chief before the 1929 election, Samuel reinvigorated the party in its last serious bid for power. He himself triumphed at Darwen, but the party's 5.3 million votes earned it only fifty-nine seats. In 1931, deputizing for an ailing Lloyd George, Samuel led the Liberals into the National government in which he became Home Secretary. But in the October 1931 election the Liberals suffered further setbacks. Cabinet disagreements over the return to protection were papered over in January 1932 by the "agreement to differ". In September, however, Samuel and his supporters (but not those Liberals who followed SIR JOHN SIMON) withdrew from the government. In 1933 he carried thirty Liberals with him to the opposition benches. But in the 1935 election the Liberal Party was reduced to only nineteen seats, and Samuel himself was defeated. Samuel never held office again. In retirement he wrote extensively on philosophy, broadcast on the BBC, and after 1937 spoke frequently in the HOUSE OF LORDS.

The Liberal Party probably owed to Samuel, more than to any other person, its survival as a distinctive, albeit attenuated element in British politics: he lived just long enough to witness the revival of party fortunes under in the early 1960s. His most lasting historic achievement must be reckoned his contribution to the advancement of Zionism and to the laying of the foundations for the State of Israel.

Bernard Wasserstein

Bibliography

Wasserstein, Bernard. *Herbert Samuel: A Political Life*. 1992.

Samuel, Viscount. *Memoirs*. 1945.

Sankey Commission (1919)

The Sankey Commission was constituted in February 1919 to deal with a crisis in the COAL INDUSTRY. Its origins lay in the war-time experiences and consequent expectations of miners. Their industry had been taken under state control with generally positive results for them. The MINERS FEDERATION OF GREAT BRITAIN's post-war program demanded a 30 percent wage increase, the reduction of the underground working day from eight hours to six, and public ownership.

Although the LLOYD GEORGE coalition had won an overwhelming election victory in December 1918, ministers felt nervous about the destabilizing consequences of any large-scale industrial conflict. On 10 February 1919 a government offer of one shilling a day increase and a committee of inquiry was rejected by the miners; a subsequent strike ballot favored a stoppage by a margin of almost six to one. Lloyd George anticipated this result by offering a Royal Commission with miners' participation. Initially a Miners' Conference seemed hostile to the proposition, but pressure from their President Robert Smillie and other advocates of involvement eventually won the day.

The composition of the Commission was three Miners' officials, three intellectuals sympathetic to the Union (including R.H. TAWNEY and SIDNEY WEBB), three coal owners and three other industrialists. The Chairman was Sir John Sankey, a cautious, formerly Conservative lawyer. The appointment of the Commission was a device to lessen the risk of industrial confrontation at what was for the government a worrying time. Proceedings began on 3 March 1919, with a commitment that the questions of wages and hours should be the subject of an interim report by 20 March. The hearings, held in the Robing Room of the House of Lords, soon acquired the trappings of political theater as the pro-miner members of the Commission, seizing the initiative, subjected their adversaries to vigorous cross-examination.

The Commission's membership guaranteed conflicting conclusions. In the middle, Sankey and the industrialists argued for a two shilling a shift increase, the reduction of the working day to seven hours with a further cut to six hours in July 1921 if warranted by the industry's situation. These proposals became the effective offer and were strongly endorsed in a Miners' ballot on 5 April.

The public ownership question remained. Further hearings of the Commission were held for almost two months beginning 23 April. Once again conflicting reports emerged. The pro-miners section backed public ownership; the coal owners and two industrialists were adamantly against. The other industrialist, Sir Arthur Duckham, backed a scheme for unification under private ownership. Sankey's decision to support public ownership, albeit with minor differences from his pro-NATIONALIZATION colleagues, gave a majority of seven to six.

For two months the government made no public pronouncement. Then, on 19 August Lloyd George rejected any possibility of public ownership. There had never been any prospect of a unanimous report, and there were few within the CABINET who would accept public ownership. There was certainly no Commons majority for the appropriate legislation. The Miners' Federation, already with a wages and hours settlement, found it impossible to mobilise sufficient support for any industrial action on public ownership. If the Miners had a moment of opportunity, it had been in the spring when they chose an inquiry rather than a strike. Yet the Sankey Commission left one major legacy: the organization of the industry became a political question that required responses by successive governments.

David Howell

Bibliography

Arnot, R. Page. *The Miners: Years of Struggle*. 1953.

Cole, G.D.H. *Labour in the Coal-Mining Industry 1914–1921*. 1923.

Heuston, R.F.V. *Lives of the Lord Chancellors 1885–1940*. 1964.

Supple, Barry. *The History of the British Coal Industry 1913–1946: The Political Economy of Decline*. 1987.

Wrigley, Chris. *Lloyd George and the Challenge of Labour: The Post-War Coalition 1918–1922*. 1990.

Sassoon, Siegfried (1886–1967)

Siegfried Sassoon's career as a poet spanned almost six decades (1903–60), but he is best known for his bitter anti-war poetry which first appeared in the pacifist *Cambridge Magazine* and later in two collected editions, *The Old Huntsman* (1917) and *Counter-Attack* (1918). In the early stages of the FIRST WORLD WAR Sassoon, serving with distinction as an officer in the Royal Welch Fusiliers, was awarded the Military Cross for valor and recommended for a D.S.O. But in July of 1917 he openly allied himself with PACIFISTS and CONSCIENTIOUS OBJECTORS in a reckless statement of "willful defiance of military authority," which invited a court martial and imprisonment. The War Office wisely decided not to press the issue as a disciplinary case. Sassoon was examined by a medical board, declared unfit for active duty, and transferred to the convalescent home for neurasthenics at Craiglockhart in Scotland, where he was a patient of W.H.R. Rivers. Sassoon's poetry and defiant, if futile gesture against the war made him a national symbol of disillusionment. His name was soon linked with two other "war poets", ROBERT GRAVES and WILFRED OWEN.

In spite of his instant fame Sassoon was temperamentally ill-suited for the brave new postwar world. He initially took up the cause of socialism and launched a poetic assault on capitalist exploitation, the press lords, mob patriotism, and the injustice of privilege in general, but his attack was vague and fragmented. He hated violence, distrusted revolutionary change, and was more than half in love with the world that the socialists sought to reform or destroy. Despite his pacifism, in 1940 he published a poem, entitled "The English Spirit," which might have come from the pen of RUDYARD KIPLING, whom he had satirized as late as 1935. The post-war "political" Sassoon is usually confused, illogical, and inconsistent. After his brief period of notoriety, he wisely withdrew from public debate. The major theme of the poetry of Sassoon's mature years is a tortuous search for religious belief, which culminated in his formal conversion to ROMAN CATHOLICISM in 1957. Beyond his opposition to the First World War, Sassoon was never a rebel. He was in many ways a tragic figure, a living survivor of a lost generation and a lost way of life.

Sassoon's poetry, like his temperament, seems old-fashioned and out of step with the major events and intellectual currents of the turbulent times in which he lived. He was oblivious to Freud and, in spite of his initial rebelliousness, ignored Marx, the Russian Revolution, and the SPANISH CIVIL WAR. Sassoon was one of the last of the "Georgian Poets," a Wordsworthian nature poet in the era of ELIOT and AUDEN. In an age of analysis, social criticism, and political commitment, he chose to celebrate the beauty of nature and the tragic mysteries of life.

Ironically, a deepening sense of alienation from the present and ever-growing nostalgia for the past led logically to Sassoon's major literary achievement, his memoirs: *The Sherston Trilogy* [*Memoirs of a Fox-hunting Man* (1928), *Memoirs of an Infantry Officer* (1930), and *Sherston's Progress* (1936)], which was followed by *The Old Cen-*

tury (1938), *The Weald of Youth* (1942), and *Siegfried's Journey* (1945). Sassoon's fictionalized memoirs are likely to be read long after his poetry is forgotten. His war volumes, *Memoirs of an Infantry Officer* and *Sherston's Progress*, compare favorably with the accounts of Robert Graves and C.E. Montague. But Sassoon is at his best when he takes us back to the innocent, rustic, lost world of his youth, although his sentimental account of the years "before the war" cannot be read as history. Foreign affairs, Ireland, industrial strife, and the angry suffragettes do not intrude upon the seasonal rituals of these contented fox-hunting provincials. Sassoon himself recognized that they were blissfully unaware the "the next twenty-five years would be a cemetery for the civilized delusions of the nineteenth century." Perhaps because his autobiography is so long and intimate, there is as yet no full-length biography of Siegfried Sassoon.

Gordon B. Beadle

Bibliography

Keynes, Geoffrey. *A Bibliography of Siegfried Sassoon.* 1962.

Moeyes, Paul. *Siegfried Sassoon, Scorched Glory.* 1997.

Roberts, John Stuart. *Siegfried Sassoon.* 1999.

Thorpe, Michael. *Siegfried Sassoon: A Critical Study.* 1967.

Wilson, Jean Moorcroft. *Siegfried Sassoon: The Making of a War Poet.* 1998.

Sayers, Dorothy Leigh (1893–1957)

Dorothy L. Sayers, the creator of the fictional detective characters Lord Peter Wimsey and Harriet Vane, is regarded as one of the most important writers of modern British DETECTIVE FICTION. Although Sayers was not as prolific as AGATHA CHRISTIE, the twelve detective novels she published between 1923 and 1937, extremely successful at the time, remain popular in the late twentieth century. Recent televised serializations of her books have brought Sayers a new audience.

Sayers was born in Oxford, to upper middle-class parents—her father was a Church of England clergyman—and she was educated at the Godolphin School and Somerville College, OXFORD, where she completed her studies in medieval French literature in 1915 with first class honors. When Oxford finally admitted women to degrees in 1920, Sayers took part in the first degree-granting ceremony in which women participated.

After leaving Oxford, she taught school but soon abandoned an occupation unsuited to her temperament. By 1917 she was employed as an editor for the young Oxford publishing firm Basil Blackwell's, and by 1922 she was working in London for Benson's, one of the country's largest advertising agencies, a connection which lasted until

1931. A talented copywriter, she was responsible for several celebrated advertising campaigns.

Meanwhile, as early as 1920 she was attempting to write detective fiction. Her first Lord Peter Wimsey novel, *Whose Body?*, completed in 1921, did not find a publisher at first, but once it was published in Britain and the United States in 1923, it was immediately successful, and from then until the publication of the final Wimsey-Vane novel, *Busman's Holiday* in 1937, Sayers' detective fiction brought its author popular fame and financial success.

About her difficult personal life, she was intensely private. In 1923 Sayers and a man whose identity is not generally known—the authorized biography refers to him only as "Bill"—became lovers. Sayers never publicly acknowledged John Anthony, born in 1924, as her natural son, and while she supported him financially, he was reared by her cousin Ivy Shrimpton. In 1934 she did, however, informally "adopt" Anthony, who took the surname of Oswald Atherton "Mac" Fleming, the ex-army Captain she had married in 1926.

Sayers always regarded her detective fiction as entertainment, and from the late 1930s until her death she concentrated on what she believed to be literary work of a more serious nature. She wrote plays and essays reflecting her deep religious faith—for example *The Man Born to Be King* (1941)—and published works of literary translation and criticism, the most important being her work on Dante. (Her translation of the *Inferno* was published in 1949). But her lasting literary reputation rests on the charm and wit of the Wimsey novels, with their debonair, insouciant hero Lord Peter and their independent, "strong-minded" heroine, detective novelist Harriet Vane. In the late twentieth century the best of them—for example, *Gaudy Night* (1937)—survive not only as first-rate detective fiction, but as evocative expressions of the mores of the inter-war period.

Deborah Gorham

Bibliography
Brabazon, James. *Dorothy L. Sayers: A Biography.* 1981.
Brunsdale, Mitzi. *Dorothy L. Sayers: Solving the Mystery of Wickedness.* 1990.
Reynolds, Barbara. *Dorothy L. Sayers: Her Life and Soul.* 1993.
Tuschler, Nancy M. *Dorothy L. Sayers: A Pilgrim Soul.* 1980.

Scott, C(harles) P(restwich) (1846–1932)

C.P. Scott acquired an unusual eminence in the opening decades of the twentieth century. He was not a politician (apart from an undistinguished spell as a backbench MP) and the newspaper that he edited and subsequently owned was not a London-based or mass-circulation journal. Yet he enjoyed ready access to leading political figures (and kept an illuminating account of some of his interviews with them). And the journal over which he presided evolved into a newspaper of international reputation.

Scott came from a commercial, dissenting background. Graduating from OXFORD, he was appointed in 1872—aged only twenty-five—editor of the *Manchester Guardian*, then owned by his cousin. Scott ran the paper with a firm hand, skimped on salaries to himself and others, and brought in a succession of literate, perceptive writers.

Under his direction the *Manchester Guardian* soon became distinguished for its cogent and principled views on political and international affairs, often maintained in defiance of prevailing tastes and at cost to circulation and revenue. In the 1880s, coincident with Gladstone's conversion to Irish home rule, Scott's formerly whiggish views moved decisively to the Liberal Left. Thereafter the paper espoused a succession of radical causes, at least some of which reached fulfilment: WOMEN'S SUFFRAGE, IRISH NATIONALISM, protection of trade unions, free trade, amelioration of the lot of the needy, hostility to aggressive imperialism, retrenchment on naval expenditure.

In Parliament from 1895 to 1905 Scott had formed associations with up and coming Liberals that persisted thereafter. They sought his endorsement and respected his opinions—even when failing to act on them. Longest-lasting, if often brought near breaking point, was his relationship with DAVID LLOYD GEORGE, which went back to mutual opposition to the BOER WAR.

Until the last moment, Scott seemed prepared to oppose another war: that of 1914–18. Under the myopic guidance of Lord Loreburn (another one-time associate in Parliament), he attributed the deteriorating international relations to "imperialist" elements in the Liberal government rather than to external challenge. But with the outbreak of war he espoused its vigorous and devoted prosecution—if not such draconian measures as military CONSCRIPTION. On grounds of energy as against lethary, he campaigned for the ousting of ASQUITH by Lloyd George in 1916—but in 1918 utterly condemned Lloyd George's jingoist campaign and disruption of the LIBERAL PARTY in the notorious "coupon" election.

In the 1920s the disintegration of the Liberals, LABOUR's rejection of the pre-war radical alliance, and the bleak CONSERVATIVE dominance diminished Scott's influence. His stature as a great moral force, identified with social reform and international reconciliation, received wide recognition.

Robin Prior
Trevor Wilson

Bibliography

Ayerst, David. *Guardian: Biography of a Newspaper*. 1971.

Hammond, J.L. *C.P. Scott of the Manchester Guardian*. 1934.

Wilson, Trevor ed. *The Political Diaries of C.P. Scott 1911–1928*. 1970.

Scottish Literature

In 1919 T.S. Eliot asked "Was there a Scottish Literature?" The implication here that there is no identifiable or readable literature from Scotland points to the necessity of marking Scotland's vexed national history in any consideration of its literary traditions.

One might begin dating the modern period in Scottish literature in the 1920s with what is now referred to as the Scottish Literary Renaissance. The movement, dubbed, it is said, in 1924 by Denis Saurat, Professor of English at the University of Bordeaux, is most closely associated with HUGH MACDIARMID [Christopher Murray Grieve]. He is counted along with Ezra Pound, T.S. ELIOT, and JAMES JOYCE as one of the premiere English modernists. It is, of course, revealing of the problematics of the category of modernism and of the differences among the writers that of these so-called English literary innovators, two were American, one Irish, and the other Scottish—all former or approximate British colonials.

The thing that perhaps most distinguishes and at the same time obscures MacDiarmid is his self-conscious revival of Scots in his work. Though Gaelic is identified as Scotland's native language, akin to Irish Gaelic, Scots, often referred to as a dialect of English, was dominant in the fourteenth century in almost all areas east and south of the Highlands and has prevailed as the local vernacular since the seventh century. MacDiarmid did not see his revival of Scots as a nostalgic act, in line with W.B. YEATS's reconstruction of Irish mythology for the "Celtic Twilight"; he saw the revival, rather, as an effort to bring modern Scottish literature into the realm of linguistic experimentation associated with modernist writers in Europe and the United States. MacDiarmid's work is also associated with the resurgence of SCOTTISH NATIONALISM and with the rise of the National Party of Scotland (1928), later to become the SNP (Scottish National Party). These two readings would suggest a link between modernism and a nationalist impulse, in the sense that cultural and linguistic dispossession underwrites linguistic innovation. MacDiarmid believed that the Scottish spirit was repressed through English cultural and political domination and that the way to restore the Scottish psyche was through the use of the vernacular. His most famous expression of this is *The*

Drunk Man Looks at the Thistle (1926), identified as a nationalist poem and written very much in the modern epic form of Joyce's *Ulysses*. In "In Memoriam James Joyce" (1955) MacDiarmid makes this tribute clear. And like Joyce's work, MacDiarmid's problematizes rather than romanticizes national identity.

The immediate contemporaries of MacDiarmid are Violet Jacob, Marion Angus, Helen Burness Cruikshank, William Soutar, and Lewis Spence. Successive decades claim poets such as Robert Garioch Sutherland and Maurice Lindsay, and eventually novelists Neil M. Gunn and Eric Linklater, Naomi Mitchison (also a poet), and James Leslie Mitchell (1901–1935), author under the pen name Lewis Grassic Gibbon of the trilogy, *A Scots Quair* (*Sunset Song*, 1923; *Cloud Howe*, 1933; *Grey Granite*, 1934). The trilogy, like some of MacDiarmid's work, proffers socialism as a remedy for the oppressive system identified with the British state.

The Scottish Renaissance writers—in particular Gibbon—are also credited with the reaction against the "kailyard" school of Scottish literature (kailyard means cabbage patch), representative of rural sentimentality and of conformity to the romantic stereotypes of Scotland (i.e. the gentle highlander, with kilt and spade, lumbering in the croft). The kailyard period precedes the Renaissance, beginning in the late nineteenth century and including, however arguably, writers like J.M. Barrie. Some prefer to link Barrie with Robert Louis Stevenson, the nineteenth-century writer who is certainly better known for his horror story *Dr. Jekyll and Mr. Hyde* (1886) than for his Scottishness, and whose adventure novels (e.g. *Treasure Island,* 1883) line up with Barrie's fantasy works for and/or about children. Like Gibbon, George Douglas Brown has written a classic anti-kailyard novel, *The House with Green Shutters* (1901).

A Scottish writer with one of the more international reputations who does not fall neatly into any category is Edwin Muir (1887–1959). His best-known works, *We Moderns* (1918), a collection of aphorisms, *The Labyrinth* (1949), a collection of poetry, and with his novelist wife, Willa Muir, his many translations of Kafka and other writing in German, have given him modernist standing in European letters; at the same time, his conclusion that "Scotland can only create a national literature by writing in English" alienated him from fellow Scottish writers like MacDiarmid. Another maverick figure, considered within Scottish letters to be one of its greatest living poets, is Norman MacCaig (*Collected Poems* 1985, 1990). MacCaig takes up where both MacDiarmid and Muir leave off by using English in a way that, however formal the semantic and structural elements, however pastoral the setting, represents the inflections of a Scots cultural vernacular.

Since the time of Muir's death there has been an explosion of writing in Scotland in English, Scots, and Gaelic. Poets like Tom Leonard and Edwin Morgan, in keeping with immediate literary ancestors, have made language the metaphorical subjects of their investigations into national (literary) identity. Morgan, recently one of Scotland's few self-acknowledged gay writers, writes a poem like "The First Men on Mercury" (*From Glasgow to Saturn*, 1973) to underscore the linguistics of imperialism. In Leonard's "Jist Ti Let Yi No", from his collection *Bunnit Husslin* (1975), he pays linguistic tribute to the American modernist William Carlos Williams by rewriting an imagist poem "This is Just to Say" (1934) from a Glaswegian cultural and phonetic point of view.

Leonard has been identified as part of the movement dubbed the Glasgow school of artists, although this label was conceived to designate the fine art emerging from Glasgow alongside the recent revivification of the city. The renaissance of painting has spread to the other arts, especially to poetry and theatre. The writer Liz Lochhead bridges the genres, though more recently she has become identified almost exclusively with drama. Lochhead has vocalized what has been true of Scottish writing, that the literary establishment has excluded women. Having begun as a painter, Lochhead moved on to producing poetry whose cadences and themes redress and retell the gendering of fairytales and myth (*Dreaming Frankenstein and Collected Poems*, 1984). She has produced performance poetry in which she provides what she calls "new cliches" (*True Confessions & New Cliches*, 1985); and she has written and performed in more than ten plays and several revues since 1985. Her play *Mary Queen of Scots Got Her Head Chopped Off* (first performed in 1987 in Edinburgh) creates a dialogue between country and gender, and between past and present, in a Scottish historical and literary context. The play also takes up the clash of religions, whose political import is not confined to the Irish conflict. Lochhead has remarked on her work's journey from "my country of gender" to a recognition of the necessity for dialogue between nationality and sexuality, such as the one between Mary and Elizabeth in her play, and the one implicitly between herself and a male writer like MacDiarmid. In fact, several women writers, Jessie Kesson (*The White Bird Passes*, 1987) and Agnes Owens (*Gentlemen of the West*, 1984), as did their female Renaissance predecessors, have, like Lochhead, turned to Scots, perhaps in an effort to reverse the belief that country and language are "malecentred" domains. Lochhead has also been engaged in translating "classic" texts of other languages into Scots, such as Moliere's *Tartuffe* (1985). Other women writers who contribute to the dialogue are poets Carol Ann Duffy, Kathleen Raine, Kathleen Jamie, and Jackie Kay, and fiction writers Dylis Rose (who also writes poetry), Janice Galloway (author of *The Trick is to Keep Breathing*, 1990 and *Blood*, 1991). Even the more established writer MURIEL SPARK is lately being considered within a Scottish and feminist literary context. If the women writers are not in every case confronting the issues of gender and nationality as directly as Lochhead, they are fortifying the dialogue by being visible and readable.

Two fiction writers and sometime poets identified with the Glasgow school whose work has traveled to the United States are James Kelman and Alasdair Gray. Such travel is not only difficult, but uncharacteristic of Scottish writing not undertaken under the auspices of the British/English publishing industry. The use of the Scots vernacular that is associated with the Glasgow school cannot be separated out for the most part from attention to class and urban life in most of this work, attention for which both these writers are particularly noted. Gray is perhaps the first writer since MacDiarmid to be compared specifically with Joyce. In his case the comparison is most justified by virtue of the narrative innovations of Gray's texts, which are a cross between Joyce, Laurence Sterne and Thomas Pynchon—the characters are (Leopold) Bloomian, the tone and graphics are (Tristram) Shandyish, and the atmosphere is surreal. Kelman's work, on the other hand, is relentlessly "real" in subject and style (*Greyhound for Breakfast*, 1987; *A Dissaffection*, 1989).

It has been as true of Scotland as of Ireland that the nation harbors a small but enduring Gaelic speaking and writing population. And it is true of both places that the literature has experienced a kind of revival in the last fifteen years among the younger generation. In Scotland this is more remarkable since there is no national policy, as in Ireland, requiring students to learn Gaelic in school. Today, approximately 80,000 of the 5 million inhabitants of Scotland are Gaelic speaking. The name most often associated with Gaelic writing in a bardic tradition is Somhairle MacGilleain/Sorley Maclean; he is grouped with MacDiarmid in terms of the magnitude of contribution to Scottish letters in this century. As is true of many of the island populations of Scotland, MacLean's community of Osgaig on the Isle of Raasay is Gaelic speaking. His poems are like lyrical histories. They recall in Scotland's first language its cultural monuments. A poem like "Hallaig" (*Selected Poems 1945–1972*) commemorates and laments the Highland clearances of the eighteenth century. This event, in which thousands of inhabitants were displaced to make way for grazing sheep, has become a tragic marker of English domination. But Maclean is also affected by the socialist vision of MacDiarmid and the circumstances of national communities in the world around Scotland. In his poem "The Cry of Europe" he places himself as artist in a national tradition in relation to writers who died in the SPANISH CIVIL WAR. Maclean studied English literature at the University of Edinburgh, which until recently included almost no writing by Scots in its curriculum (this was reserved for the School of Scottish Studies); he does his own translations. Iain Crichton Smith, another writer of Gaelic poetry, is one of the most versatile of Scottish writers, in all genres, in each of three British languages; he is praised for his deftness in all. He also has contributed to the critical literature and has helped to bring Gaelic writing to international attention. Among the younger writers in Gaelic are Roderick Watson, Christopher Whyte, and Meg Bateman.

Marilyn Reizbaum

Bibliography
Cairns, Craig, ed. *The History of Scottish Literature: vol. 4: Twentieth Century*. 1987.
Dunn, Douglas, ed. *The Faber Book of Twentieth Century Scottish Poetry*. 1992.
Kerrigan, Catherine. "The Ugsome Thistle: Hugh MacDiarmid and the Nationalism of the Modern Literary Revival" in Horst W. Drescher and Hermann Volkel, eds. *Nationalism in Literature-Literarischer Nationalismus: Literature, Language and National Identity*. 1989. pp. 181–9.
Royle, Trevor. *The Macmillan Companion to Scottish Literature*. 1983.
Smith, Iain Crichton. "The Internationalism of Twentieth Century Gaelic Poetry," *Scottish Literary Journal*. vol. 18 (1991), pp. 82–6.

Scottish Nationalism

Broadly defined, Scottish nationalism has been a movement geared to the political and cultural expression of Scotland's national identity. It has made a significant, if episodic, impact on twentieth-century British politics, and can be given credit for the re-emergence of DEVOLUTION and constitutional change as an important issue of political debate since the late 1960s.

The demand for self-government for Scotland within the United Kingdom was a central feature of the wider constitutional debate in British politics before 1914. Then, ideas of "Home Rule All Round"—separate Parliaments for Scotland, England, Ireland, and Wales along with an Imperial Assembly—were current. However, the particular problems of Ireland took precedence, and a combination after the FIRST WORLD WAR,

of their resolution and changed political circumstances, notably the decline of the LIBERAL PARTY, thwarted the federalist-style devolution schemes. Between 1919 and 1928 successive bills allowing for varying measures of self-government for Scotland failed to make headway in Parliament.

In the belief that a separate party was required to fight for self government, the National Party of Scotland (NPS) was formed in 1928. The NPS absorbed, among other groups, the Scottish National League (SNL), which had been in existence since 1920. The SNL promoted Gaelic cultural concerns and was the first organization to advocate complete independence and separation from England. The 1920s, moreover, saw the flowering of a literary "renaissance" in Scotland in which leading figures such as the poet HUGH MACDIARMID [Christopher Murray Grieve] came to prominence and robustly enforced the SNL line. However, the NPS included people of differing views on the national question: from those in favor of a mild degree of devolution to outright separatists, with federalists and supporters of dominion status in between. In 1934 it merged with the moderate Scottish Party (a CONSERVATIVE breakaway group set up in 1933) to form the Scottish National Party (SNP), and the balance of the new organization shifted decidedly away from the extremists. The SNP pursued a policy of self-government within the Empire, and cultural nationalists like MacDiarmid were ousted. The tone of the new party was pragmatic rather than romantic.

The apparent popularity among Scots of at least some measure of administrative devolution saw the transfer of the Scottish departments of state from London to Edinburgh in 1939; the office of Secretary of State for Scotland had been established in 1885. These governmental arrangements buttressed the enduring sense of distinctive national identity enshrined in the separate Scottish educational, legal, and Church establishments.

The SNP split during the SECOND WORLD WAR and a secessionist movement made the political running into the 1950s with a national covenant campaign for home rule. When this ran out of steam, the SNP gradually reasserted its claim to represent the only realistic way forward: through the ballot box. In 1967 this strategy finally paid off when the SNP won a by-election in the Labour seat of Hamilton. In the views of most commentators this was a protest vote against Labour's failure to rebuild the Scottish economy. In the 1970s the SNP held out the hope of a prosperous future if, through independence, Scotland took advantage of the recently discovered North Sea oil. Unprecedented success followed in the second general election of 1974, which saw the SNP win eleven seats.

The revived constitutional debate eventually produced a commitment by the Labour government to devolution, conditional on the endorsement of at least 40 percent of the Scottish electorate in a referendum to be held in March 1979. The required threshold was not reached, although a majority did vote in favor. Amid anticlimax and disillusionment the SNP, which viewed devolution as a first step to ultimate independence, suffered electoral decline. The 1980s were a period of in-fighting and rebuilding.

The THATCHER era saw increasing political divergence between Scotland and England. The arousal of social resentments in Scotland benefited the LABOUR PARTY; class loyalties remained stubborn. However, the anti-government mood was also increasingly nationalistic; cultural nationalism revived in a fusion of literary, artistic, and popular music developments. By the 1990s the Scottish question was pivotal to a new decentralist movement for constitutional modernization, and the SNP's policy of "Independence in Europe" signaled the salience to this debate of the European community.

Nevertheless, the general election of 1992 saw the SNP win only three seats. A nationalist mood did not necessarily imply votes for the party of independence. In addition, the SNP was severely criticized by the Scottish PRESS for snubbing the cross-party Scottish Constitutional Convention which had been set up in 1989. The Convention produced a blueprint for devolution and tied Labour more highly to its commitment to deliver it. Thus, in the wake of the Labour landslide in the general election of 1997, a referendum was held on the matter. The Scottish people voted resoundingly—74.3 per cent in favour—for their Parliament, with 63.5 per cent also endorsing tax-varying powers.

Devolution created dilemmas for the SNP, led since 1990 by the astute and pragmatic Alex Salmond. If it helped the new structures to work effectively, then support for independence might be likely to wane. Conversely, the employment of wrecking tactics would result in the party appearing irresponsible and unfit to govern. The SNP chose to campaign for devolution and to play their part as the main opposition to the Labour-Liberal Democrat coalition, which emerged as the first government.

In 2000 Salmond stood down as SNP leader and handed over to his protégé, John Swinney. The SNP thus chose to marginalize further the fundamentalist body of opinion in the party and adhere to the gradualist route it had adopted under Salmond.

Scottish nationalism in the twentieth century has encompassed a variety of positions on the constitutional issue, a range of ideological tendencies, and a broad, if insufficiently concentrated social base of support. It has largely been free of any association with physical force to achieve its aims.

It has grown as a political and cultural force in Scotland since the 1960s, yet has also witnessed the decline of the traditional nineteenth-century model of the nation state. As thinking about the meaningfulness of concepts such as "independence" and "sovereignty" has become increasingly skeptical in an age of global capitalism and a powerful EUROPEAN UNION, the challenges facing Scottish nationalism also lie beyond Labour's electoral grip on Scotland.

Graham Walker

Bibliography
Brand, Jack. *The National Movement in Scotland.* 1978.
Finlay, Richard J. *Independent and Free: Scottish Politics and the Origins of the Scottish National Party.* 1994.
Gallagher, Tom, ed. *Nationalism in the Nineties.* 1991.
Hanham, H.J. *Scottish Nationalism.* 1969.
Harvie, Christopher. *Scotland and Nationalism.* 1977.
Mitchell, James. *Strategies for Self-Government.* 1996.

Second World War: Homefront

Historians formerly viewed the Second World War's effect on Britain as an example of how "total war" permanently altered a society. But recent studies have undermined this "war and social change" model by drawing attention to the pre-war origins of reforms attributed to the war, by challenging the belief that the post-war WELFARE STATE was the result of a wartime consensus on social policy innovations, and by demonstrating that few of the wartime changes in class, gender and demographic structures continued beyond the end of the war.

Public support for greater state intervention to promote social welfare increased during the war. The evacuation of British troops from DUNKIRK and the subsequent BATTLE OF BRITAIN contributed to a heightened sense of social solidarity that strengthened public pressure for social reform, although the degree and duration of this sentiment should not be exaggerated. This benefited the LABOUR PARTY, perceived as more committed to reform than the Conservatives, and contributed to the Labour victory in the 1945 general election.

Although the December 1942 Beveridge Report became a watershed in the history of social policy, this was not the government's intent in appointing WILLIAM BEVERIDGE to chair what was considered a minor committee reviewing the social insurance system. Beveridge seized the opportunity to produce proposals that went far beyond what the goverment desired. He recommended a comprehensive social insurance scheme providing a subsistence level income to protect members of all classes from poverty, and insisted the scheme would be effective only if accompanied by FAMILY ALLOWANCES, full employment, and a free NATIONAL HEALTH SERVICE. The social insurance proposal was an extension of the pre-war system rather than a radical departure; it also continued the insurance principle, financing the scheme by regressive flat-rate contributions from employers and employees rather than from general taxation as socialists preferred. It was novel in being comprehensive, universal, and, as there was no means test, in providing benefits as a right of citizenship.

Beveridge's report embarrassed the government because it drew attention to the disagreement between the major parties on social reform. Conservative backbenchers privately informed WINSTON CHURCHILL of their opposition to the proposals, reinforcing the Prime Minister's preference for avoiding a commitment to reform. But confronted with strong public support for Beveridge's report and a Labour backbench revolt, the government reluctantly issued a White Paper on social insurance in September 1944 that accepted the main features of Beveridge's scheme.

The 1944 White Paper, *Employment Policy*, has been viewed as implying government responsibility for maintaining full employment and for using Keynesian economic policies to achieve it. In fact, the government issued the White Paper because it knew Beveridge was planning to publish employment proposals more radical than it could endorse and hoped that by publishing first it could deflect the public support for his recommendations that followed his report on social insurance. Whereas Beveridge sought a government commitment to maintain full employment, i.e. that unemployment would not be allowed to rise above three percent, the White Paper only proposed maintaining a high level of employment, defined as limiting unemployment to no more than eight percent. While the White Paper did imply a greater degree of government responsibility for sustaining high employment than pre-war governments had accepted, it did so in order to avoid endorsing full employment and Keynesian economic policies.

There was wide agreement before 1939 on the need to reform the health services. The Labour Party had been committed since 1934 to establishing a national health service financed by the central government; even the British Medical Association was urging during the 1930s that the health insurance system be expanded to include nearly all adults and their dependents. At the onset of war the government set up the Emergency Medical Service to care for civilians injured by enemy action. But it was not until Beveridge included a national health service as part of his report that the government addressed the issue. In February 1944 it issued a White Paper outlining its proposals for a reformed health service. While there was agreement on the need for change, the two major parties differed as to its form. Under pressure from the BMA the Tory Minister of Health, Henry Willink, abandoned several key features in the White Paper scheme, including the proposal for a salaried service. At the time the coalition government ended in 1945, he was preparing a new White Paper with proposals significantly different from the system Labour instituted after the war.

ELEANOR RATHBONE had been campaigning for family allowances for nearly two decades prior to the Second World War, but it was not until Beveridge included this reform in his report that implementation seemed likely. Athough the government preferred to postpone the matter until after the war, it reluctantly agreed to proceed with reform because of strong public support. It delayed two years before introducing a bill strikingly different from what Rathbone and Beveridge desired. Whereas Beveridge intended the allowance to provide subsistence level maintainence for a child, and calculated it must be no less than eight shillings weekly to achieve this end, the government viewed the allowances as a means of avoiding demands for higher wages. Since the government considered the benefit to be a general subvention toward family needs rather than subsistence for a child, the 1945 Family Allowances Act provided only five shillings weekly for each child beginning with the second one.

The 1938 Spens Report recommended free secondary education be provided up to age fifteen through three different types of schools: secondary modern, technical, and grammar. They were incorporated into the 1944 EDUCATION ACT after R.A. BUTLER, President of the Board of Education, overcame Churchill's initial resistance to introducing an Education Bill. Treasury officials viewed the legislation as a less expensive alternative to Beveridge's proposals and hoped it would satisfy the public pressure for reform. It was the most important social legislation enacted during the war; the percentage of fourteen-year-olds in school rose from 38 in 1938 to nearly 100 after 1947 when the school leaving age was raised to fifteen.

Due primarily to a steady decline in the birth rate, population growth during the inter-war period slowed to less than one-half the pre-First World War rate. The war strengthened concern over this trend and encouraged a revival of pronatalism. Beveridge's report included proposals intended to encourage a higher birth rate by making the roles of housewife and mother more attractive to women. Parliamentary concern led to the appointment of a Royal Commission on Population in 1944. Although policy-makers feared the high level of wartime WOMEN'S EMPLOYMENT would further reduce the birth rate, the war had the opposite effect. In 1941 the birth rate fell to the lowest level since official records had been kept (13.9 per 1,000 population), but it then rose steadily until it peaked in 1947 (at 20.6 per 1,000). This wartime change proved temporary, however; in the 1950s the birth rate resumed its pre-war decline.

The wartime rise in the MARRIAGE rate was partially responsible for the increase in the birth rate. This trend was well-established by 1939 rather than being initiated by the war. The change in the marital status of young women was especially striking: 42 percent of all women aged twenty-five to twenty-nine were single in 1931, but by 1951 only 22 percent of this age cohort were unmarried. Although some historians have suggested the war emancipated women, the changes in birth and marriage rates suggest that it reinforced traditional roles.

The wartime labor shortage became in important pressure for change by forcing Britain to make greater use of female workers. The December 1941 National Service (No. 2) Act granted the government the power to conscript women into industry or military service. Britain's use of womanpower far exceeded that of other belligerent nations; by September 1943, 46 percent of all women between the ages of fourteen and fifty-nine were engaged in some form of national service. But this trend did not undermine the sex segregation of jobs; women who undertook wartime jobs were considered temporary workers and at the end of the war were usually either dismissed or transferred to traditional women's work.

During the war's first year backbench women MPs from all parties joined with the leaders of influential women's organizations to form the Woman Power Committee. The committee pressed the government to establish equal employment opportunities and to eliminate sex-differentiated policies. Although they succeeded in forcing the government to grant sex equality in the rates of compensation paid civilians injured by enemy action (women originally received two-thirds the rate paid men), in other areas women's reform effects were usually unsuccessful. An attempt to secure EQUAL PAY for women teachers was defeated when the government threatened to resign rather than accept reform; it then prevented further action on the matter by appointing a Royal Commission to study the issue.

The belief that the post-war welfare state should be attributed to a wartime consensus on reform pays insufficient attention to Conservative concern with the nation's financial position. During the war Churchill had privately expressed doubts that Britain would emerge from the war in a position to finance costly social reforms. Since Britain was virtually bankrupt by 1945, the election of a Conservative government in that year would likely have meant the subordination of social legislation to the improvement of the nation's financial position. The 1945 general election thus seems more directly responsible for the post-war welfare state than wartime developments; the shock of overwhelming defeat in that election should not be underestimated in explaining the CONSERVATIVE PARTY's subsequent acceptance of the main features of the welfare state.

Harold L. Smith

Bibliography

Addison, Paul. *The Road to 1945: British Politics and the Second World War.* 1975.

Calder, Angus. *The People's War: Britain 1939–45.* 1969.

Harris, Jose. "War and Social History: Britain and the Home Front during the Second World War," *Contemporary European History.* vol. I (1992), pp. 17–35.

Jefferys, Kevin. *The Churchill Coalition and Wartime Politics, 1940–1945.* 1991.

Smith, Harold L., ed. *War and Social Change: British Society in the Second World War.* 1986.

Titmuss, Richard M. *Problems of Social Policy.* 1950.

Second World War: Military

Britain was a belligerent throughout the Second World War as she struggled to prevent Germany, Italy, and Japan from dominating Europe, Africa, and Asia. The principal theaters of war were the Atlantic, the English Channel, the skies over Europe, North Africa, northwest Europe and Burma. Although suffering initial defeat on the continent, submarine blockade, bombing, and economic strain, Britain ended the war victorious through a combination of her own exertions, Russian efforts and sacrifices, and military and economic aid from the Commonwealth and the United States.

Britain went to war on 3 September 1939 in order to prevent German domination of Eastern Europe and the consequent threat to Anglo-French security. The specific cause of war was Germany's invasion of Poland on 1 September. The Allies could not save Poland from quick defeat and, in fact, made little effort to do so. They did impose a blockade on Germany, but the latter could still obtain supplies from neutral Sweden, Russia, and other continental areas. Meanwhile, the First Lord of the Admiralty, WINSTON CHURCHILL, proposed to interrupt Germany's iron ore imports from Sweden by mining Norwegian waters, a violation of Norway's neutrality— which, to be sure, had been violated by both sides before. Hitler, however, beat Churchill to the punch by an audacious invasion of Denmark and Norway in April 1940; a subsequent Anglo-French expedition to Norway had to be withdrawn some weeks later.

The Germans' next move was a "blitzkrieg" attack on the Lowlands and France beginning on 10 May 1940. Allied forces, unaccustomed to modern tank warfare, were quickly outmaneuvered. As France fell, the British Expeditionary Force had to be evacuated from DUNKIRK and elsewhere in May and June. This left Britain alone, her ARMY shattered. Fortunately an immediate German invasion was impracticable since the enemy had first to secure control of the Channel skies in order to have any hope of neutralizing the ROYAL NAVY. Churchill, as Prime Minister, refused Hitler's offer to negotiate; therefore the Germans began an aerial bombing campaign, soon to be called the BATTLE OF BRITAIN (July–October 1940). ROYAL AIR FORCE fighter planes, assisted by a well-developed RADAR system, blunted the German air attack, thereby frustrating Germany's plans for a landing on England's southern coast in September. Subsequent German night bombing of Britain from that month until May 1941—the BLITZ—did not cause the British to yield.

However, Britain was still in grave danger. German submarines, and to a lesser extent surface raiders, seriously threatened the economy from 1940 until mid-1943. In this phase of the war the British employed a code and cipher breaking system nicknamed ULTRA for the reading of German radio messages. The British, Canadian, and—after 1941—the United States navies eventually defeated the German submarines with the help of ULTRA, increased long-range aerial patrols, aircraft-carrier protection of convoys, advanced anti-submarine radar, American mass production of cargo ships, and an increased supply of escort vessels.

At the same time Britain had to deal with Italy, which had entered the war just before the fall of France. During 1940–1 British forces trounced the Italians in Ethiopia, Libya, and the Mediterranean only to face German air attacks against the British base on Malta and an expeditionary force in North Africa under General Erwin Rommel. Although Africa was always of secondary interest to Hitler—gearing up for his campaign against the Soviet Union—to the British it was a vital area of the world where important bases in Gibraltar, Malta, Cyprus, PALESTINE, Alexandria, and Suez were endangered. In June 1941 Hitler invaded Russia, thereby draining German resources away from both Africa and the Atlantic.

Meanwhile, President Roosevelt was leading the United States in a policy of helping Britain with measures just short of co-belligerency. In 1940 the Americans sold guns and ammunition to Britain and traded fifty old United States destroyers for the right to build bases on British islands in the western Atlantic. In 1941 LEND-LEASE began, and the American navy waged a quiet, undeclared, quasi-war against German submarines in support of Lend-Lease convoys. When the Japanese attacked Pearl Harbor on 7 December 1941, Hitler declared war on the United States; American factories henceforth poured even more of their output into the hands of the British, the Russians, and the other Allied powers.

The Japanese, questing for riches in southeast Asia, attacked the British Empire and Commonwealth immediately after going to war with the United States. Britain now had to pay for her previous support of American opposition to Japanese imperialism. Hong Kong, Malaya, most of Burma, and other British holdings were soon lost. Worst of all in terms of strategy and prestige was the ignominious fall of the great naval base at Singapore in February 1942. Preoccupied with Europe and North Africa, the British thereafter could do little more than guard India from a possible Japanese invasion, or an Indian uprising, or both, leaving the United States to carry on most of the war against Japan.

Yet, by late 1942 and early 1943 the tide of war was turning all over the world. In addition to the great Russian victory at Stalingrad and American victories in the Pacific, there were accomplishments more closely related to Britain's war effort. Although Rommel had driven the British back into Egypt in the summer of 1942, that proved to be the worst he could do at the end of his overstretched supply line. British naval and air forces now gained the upper hand, mangling Italian convoys carrying such supplies to Rommel as Hitler could spare. The British Eighth Army in Egypt grew stronger, and by September 1942, a new commander, GENERAL SIR BERNARD L. MONTGOMERY, had checked a fresh German offensive at EL ALAMEIN; on 23 October he attacked in the same area, grinding down the Axis by weight of men and materiel until Rommel had to retreat. In November Anglo-American forces landed in western North Africa, violating the neutrality of French Morocco and Algeria; these landings threatened the Axis from the west while Eighth Army threatened them from the east. By May 1943 all of North Africa was free of the enemy.

The Americans had at first resisted an African campaign, believing that side-shows in the Mediterranean area would only prolong the war. They had wanted a cross-Channel invasion of France as soon as possible. The British, on the other hand, argued that the Allies should postpone the risky and difficult task of invading France until better prepared. Thus the British urged Africa upon the Americans, and with reason: the French and Italians could easily be defeated, thus knocking the props out from under Rommel's forces; inversely, for the Allies to do nothing against Hitler except stockpiling for an eventual invasion of France would damage public morale as well as anger the hard-pressed Russians.

Roosevelt had been convinced by such arguments, but when he and Churchill met in Casablanca in January 1943, the President's staff renewed its demand for an early invasion of France. They were disappointed to find the British staff again recommending a possible postponement of the harder task, using many of the same kinds of arguments as before. Now the British wanted to attack Italy, another relatively easy target, thereby gaining control of both the Italian peninsula and the central Mediterranean. Among other reasons for such a strategy, it was crucial to open the route from Gibraltar to Suez so that Allied shipping, always scarce, would not have to go all the way around southern Africa. Since the British were still carrying most of the burden of the war against Hitler, they got their way yet again—and many historians believe rightly so. The result was an Anglo-American invasion of Sicily in July 1943 and of the Italian mainland in September, leading to Italy's surrender; German troops, however, prevented an Allied conquest of the entire peninsula until the end of the war.

Another decision made at Casablanca involved British acceptance of Roosevelt's unconditional surrender policy, placing the war more than ever on the level of a crusade against Fascism. This suited the psychological needs of the Allied peoples and made it possible for the American, British, and Russian governments to postpone serious arguments among themselves as to the ultimate fate of Europe.

The conferees also agreed to continue the strategic bombing of Europe, America by day, the British by night. The Royal Air Force had turned to night bombing early in the war as a way of reducing bomber losses, but with an inevitable cost in accuracy. By 1943–4 Britain had inflicted serious damage on German cities, as witness, for example, the destruction of Hamburg (July–August 1943). Although the Allied bombing program did not fulfil the expectations of bomber enthusiasts, it did force the Germans to expend resources on counter-measures such as night fighters—the latter costing Britain's bomber fleet tremendous losses despite the cover of darkness.

Churchill had wanted to reinforce the bogged-down Italian campaign and even open up new theaters in the eastern Mediterranean; he was willing to postpone the landing in France until Mediterranean operations, the Russians, and the strategic bombers could do so much damage to Germany as to guarantee an easy conquest of northwest Europe. The United States and Russia, however, insisted on a cross-Channel attack in 1944, and Churchill acquiesced at the Teheran Conference in Iran in November and December of 1943. By that time Britain's role was diminishing, her resources becoming over-strained, while the United states and Russia were just then achieving full mobilization. General Dwight D. Eisenhower was chosen as Supreme Commander for Operation Overlord, the Anglo-American landing at Normandy in northern France which began on 6 June 1944. Even so, British and Canadian troops were responsible for three out of five of the beaches, and British officers commanded all of Eisenhower's air, sea, and land invasion forces. After the breakout from the beachheads in August 1944, however, Eisenhower assumed direct management of the land war in France.

The British and Canadian armies, led by Montgomery, held the north end of the line facing Germany, while the Americans, with the help of pro-Allies French forces, held the rest. Montgomery's idea was to annex most of the supplies and ground forces—even the Americans among them—to his command for a concentrated thrust into northern Germany. The Americans, however, regarded Montgomery as arrogant, quarrelsome, and too slow-moving for such a daring, "narrow" thrust; moreover, he seemed to Eisenhower to be oblivious to logistical imperatives. Eisenhower maintained a more or less "broad front", while giving Montgomery only some of what he wanted. The American view of Montgomery seemed to be vindicated when he failed to secure a bridgehead over the Rhine in September 1944, while Montgomery's frustrated claims to overall direction of the land war seemed to be justified when American troops got into serious trouble during the Battle of the Bulge (December 1944). At that point Eisenhower gave Montgomery temporary command over yet more American troops; but the Supreme Commander secured from Montgomery what amounted to an apology for the latter's arrogance.

The war in Europe ended on 8 May 1945 with British forces in control of northwestern Germany. Britain's contribution to the Asian war had increased somewhat by then: in 1944 General William J. Slim had led Empire and Commonwealth forces in the successful defense of India; in spring 1945 he carried out a brilliant reconquest of southern Burma. On 2 September Japan surrendered to the United States and the other Allied powers, Britain among them.

Karl G. Larew

Bibliography
Barnett, Correlli. *Engage the Enemy More Closely.* 1990.
Calvocoressi, Peter, and Guy Wint. *Total War.* 1972.
Churchill, Winston S. *The Second World War,* 6 vols.
    1948 –53.
Lewin, Ronald. *Ultra Goes to War.* 1978.
Liddell Hart, Basil H. *History of the Second World War.*
    1970.
Parker, R.A.C. *Struggle for Survival: The History of the
    Second World War.* 1989.

Secondary Education

Secondary schooling debates have been the mainstay of the perennial English enthusiasm for discussions of class and social change, and its history has followed the same pattern, concentrating on organization rather than curriculum, legislation rather than practice. In 1900 grammar school pupils received a secondary education, and those in elementary schools received what later became primary schooling. Thus the pattern of secondary education was organized in the interests of the few for an academic education for professional middle-class or white collar employment. About 10 percent of children received such schooling. Its curriculum, reflecting the practice of the great public schools, emphasized classical languages and arts, which ensured that the educated product of such schooling was eloquent in speech and on paper but not well versed in science or technology. Girls were included in secondary education but in smaller numbers. In the universities had established their dominance over the content and structure of secondary education, and the higher education offered to girls precluded much emphasis on their academic development. Secondary education was constructed in the interests of academic excellence of young men. Secondary schools were administered locally through the structure of government set up by the 1902 Education Act and the interpretative regulations of 1904.

The central government regulated, inspected, and funded secondary education through the Education Committee of the local council which constituted the local education authority. Children of respectable artisans were encouraged to enter secondary schools with government help under the special places regulations of 1907, providing those children who could demonstrate ability the education for which the rest of secondary school population paid fees. Social mobility was to be promoted by this "ladder of opportunity", to be promoted through a mixture of national regulation and local initiative, with secondary schools partly funded through the rates as well as from central government. They had some autonomy over their curriculum despite regulations that insisted on three hours of English, an-

other language (usually Latin), some mathematics and science, and housewifery for girls. Teaching had to reflect the demands of a standardized assessment of school leavers through the system of matriculation by examination—the schools certificate.

The post-war (Fisher) Education Act of 1918 compelled local authorities to develop a national system of secondary as well as elementary education. Fisher attacked the idea of the "half-timer" who attended school while working and advocated compulsory part-time education from fourteen to eighteen. The proportion of twelve to fourteen year olds who could be in either type of school was roughly 10 percent in secondary schools rising to 20 percent by 1938. The content of secondary education changed little until the late 1930s, although its organization and funding were subject to frequent change. The "Geddes axe" on expenditure cut salaries and meant few new buildings for secondary schools. Yet education was a subject of intense, vigorous debate in the inter-war years. The association of curricular change with social reform took a back seat, except over questions of gender, and the dominant argument became one about access to education rather than about its content. Yet commercial or technical education expanded slightly in day continuation schools for apprentices in which engineering, printing or building trades were taught in classes rather than on the job, as well as a few central or technical high schools for clerical or artisan trades.

Public debate on education in the 1930s concentrated on the physical state of schools. The Board of Education listed inadequate schools in the so-called "black book," including even some of the elite secondary schools. The building stock was decayed, investment insufficient, and interest too slight for the purpose. Selection for secondary schools was increasingly based on standardized examinations sat at eleven by all potential secondary students, or sometimes, by all the age groups. Some local authorities were making all their secondary school entrants behave as if they were applying for a "scholarship" that is a free place, which became "special" (means-tested) places in 1932, subject to entry by examination. In other words, although pupils still paid for their secondary education, they were also all academically selected and assessed. Assessment increasingly followed a standardized pattern of English, arithmetic, and verbal reasoning or "intelligence" test, the so-called eleven-plus examination.

In 1936 the school leaving age was ostensibly raised to fifteen, but implementation of this provision was deferred, initially to 1939. Once again an educational principle was accepted but not enacted because of financial constraints. The outbreak of war in 1939 both encouraged and inhibited further change. The development of a free secondary education system for all did not include the expansion of building programs, and most of the additional school population was housed in huts known by their acronym of HORSA. In 1947 the leaving age was finally raised to fifteen.

Historical debate has focused around the question of parity of esteem between schools, enjoined by the 1944 EDUCATION ACT, in relation to their tripartite structure. The Norwood committee report in 1943 described three types of child—the academic, the technically minded, and the rest, for whom there should be three types of education, which Ministry of Education officials interpreted as three types of school. Of the senior children of the elementary school, about 70 percent of eleven-year-olds were to go to secondary modern schools, 25 percent to grammar schools, and 5 percent to technical schools. It was not until the late 1950s that London was able to build new comprehensive schools and educate all under the same roof. Education in schools after the Act was highly stratified, particularly for the most academic children in the grammar schools where they were "streamed" by ability.

The other historical debate has been about equality of opportunity and Britain's industrial decline. Education absorbed a large part of governmental welfare expenditure and pursued egalitarian aims, it was argued, at the expense of efficiency, accelerating the relative failure of the technical schools to compete with the grammar and secondary modern schools. The technology of selection which used standardized test batteries to place children in rank order allowed for a single scale of merit, seeing technical ability as inseparable from the general. Technical schools took second place to the education offered by the grammar schools. They did not then generate a large group of technically accomplished engineers or craftsmen with high public esteem.

In the 1950s the selective system was challenged, and local authorities began to move towards comprehensive systems of secondary education. In 1965 the LABOUR government insisted that local authorities reorganize along comprehensive lines. The number of students sitting the GCE "O" and "A" levels rose slowly over the 1965 period onward, so comprehensive education appears to have widened access to secondary qualifications. Many grant maintained schools went independent at this period rather than lose the power of selection.

After 1987 the CONSERVATIVE government made it possible for schools to be centrally funded, thereby diminishing the local authority contribution to governing schools. Tests were to be used to establish schools' success or failure, administered to cover the topics of the new national curriculum. Centralization thus replaced local autonomy and the content of secondary education re-entered debate.

Deborah Thom

Bibliography
Fenwick, I.G. Keith. *The Comprehensive School 1944–1970.* 1976.
Halsey, A.H., A.F. Heath, and J.M. Ridge. *Origins and Destinations: Family, Class and Education in Modern Britain.* 1980.
Judge, Harry. *A Generation of Schooling: English Secondary Schools Since 1944.* 1984.
Simon, Brian. *Education and the Social Order, 1940–1990.* 1991.
———. *The Politics of Educational Reform, 1920–1940.* 1974.
Sutherland, Gillian. *Ability, Merit and Measurement.* 1984.

Shaw, George Bernard (1856–1950)

The playwright Bernard Shaw (the name by which he preferred to be known) was born into a lower middle-class Protestant family in Dublin in 1856. When his parents separated in 1876, the young Shaw came with his mother to London where, as he put it, he did not throw himself into the battle of life but threw his mother in instead. He was determined to write and made his way into journalism. He wrote five novels which remained unpublished for many years, but, by the end of the century, he had established a reputation as a critic of music, painting, drama, and all forms of literature and had become known as a formidable political publicist, debater, and controversialist. An energetic campaigner for socialism, he was active in politics, becoming an elected member of the St. Pancras Vestry in London.

The twentieth century brought two great changes in Shaw's life. In 1898 he had married Charlotte Payne-Townshend, whom he called "a green-eyed Irish millionairess". This union, although childless, was one of lasting affection, which gave stability to a personal life that was previously unsettled. The other great change was the beginning of his career as a dramatist. In the early 1890s Shaw had started to write plays and had written ten by the end of the century, but none of them had met with success. Shaw then met a young dramatist and producer, Harley Granville Barker, who co-operated with J.E. Vedrenne, the manager of the Court Theatre in the west of London, to present seasons of new plays. The new and exciting repertory attracted large audiences; of the 988 separate performances presented by Barker and Vedrenne between October 1904 and June 1907, 701 were of plays by Shaw. Several of the earlier plays were produced but, in addition, in a most fertile period, Shaw wrote new plays for the new enterprise. *Man and Superman* (1903), the first play that Shaw wrote in the twentieth century, was given the description, "A Comedy and a Philosophy." The comedy consisted in Shaw's taking the theme of Don Juan, the great seducer, and turning it upside down. In the play it is woman, the embodiment of the "life force," who pursues and man who is "the marked-down victim, the destined prey." Underlying the comedy is Shaw's enunciation of his own theory of "creative evolution," in which he attempted to improve on Charles Darwin. The Don Juan theme is linked with Mozart's *Don Giovanni,* and, in an act which the author did not originally intend for stage performance, characters in the comedy are translated in a dream into the figures of Mozart's opera.

Other plays had more contemporary political subjects. The problems of Shaw's native country were the theme of *John Bull's Other Island* (1907). *Major Barbara* (1907) showed the conflict in society between religious vision and the hard facts of material power in terms of the personal relations between the Salvationist Barbara and her father, the munitions manufacturer, Undershaft. In *The Doctor's Dilemma* (1911), the "tragedy" of the death of a gifted but unprincipled artist, Shaw made a persuasive plea for the establishment of a national health service. The plays, while undoubtedly polemic, were never crudely propagandist. Shaw, indeed, often showed a readiness to present a stronger case for those characters with whom he himself was less in sympathy. Some audiences found the plays excessively wordy, but this potential fault was offset by Shaw's humor. On the eve of the war in 1914 he had one of his greatest successes in *Pygmalion* (published 1916), which combined an original treatment of the Galatea story with commentary on the effect of English speech on the class system.

Shaw's political activities had been subordinated to his work in the theatre, but he had continued to be active in the FABIAN SOCIETY, in close collaboration with SIDNEY AND BEATRICE WEBB and others. With them he had co-operated in founding the weekly journal the *NEW STATESMAN,* which first appeared in April 1913. The outbreak of war in 1914 provoked him into powerful attacks on the mentality and policies that had made the conflict inevitable and, while convinced that once the war had come it had to be fought, he had contempt for those who had blundered into the war and were now blundering through it. This attitude, expressed in precisely marshaled arguments and with an attitude of lofty superiority to his opponents, lost him friends.

After the war he returned to the stage with three important plays, all of which were presented first in New York. *Heartbreak House* (1919) was an attempt to combine his own style with that of Chekhov, of whom he had become a great admirer. In this "fantasia in the Russian manner on English themes," Shaw purported to show the ineffectiveness of the upper classes in England when confronted with the problems of a declining civilization. The play combines farce and apocalyptic vision with, at the centre, a strange enigmatic figure, Captain Shotover, described by the critic James Agate as "Ibsen and Shaw, Whitman and General Booth rolled into one." This was followed by an even stranger and more controversial creation, *Back to Methuselah* (1921). With the descriptive subtitle, "A Metabiological Pentateuch," this was five plays in one and traced the course of human history from the Garden of Eden to "As Far as Thought Can Reach," in the year AD 31920. In this work Shaw returned to his doctrine of creative evolution, but here he was concerned to warn that, if human beings did not learn to live longer and more wisely, life itself would tire of them and look elsewhere for a new experiment. The next play brought unanimously favorable responses from critics and playgoers. This was *Saint Joan* (1924), a chronicle of the life, death and canonization of Joan of Arc, called by Shaw, "the most notable warrior saint in the Christian calendar and the queerest fish among the eccentric worthies of the Middle Ages." Shaw was awarded the Nobel Prize for literature for 1925, which he accepted despite previous refusals to receive any kind of award or title.

Shaw continued to write plays up to the time of his death at the age of ninety-four, but few of his later works have been considered among his best. Nevertheless, *The Apple Cart* (1930) contains sharp observations on the political scene in the United Kingdom, and *In Good King Charles's Golden Days* (1939) is an elegant presentation of King Charles II and his entourage, in which the "merry monarch" is shown as a kind of Shavian version of a Platonic philosopher-king. Some of the plays of the 1930s such as *Too True to Be Good* (1934), which Shaw described as "a political extravaganza", have been seen as forerunners of the so-called "theater of the absurd" of such writers as BECKETT and Ionesco.

Although Shaw wrote over fifty plays, he was prolific in other fields. He was a voluminous correspondent. He threw himself into every public campaign: the opposition to the censorship of plays (several of his own works had suffered); the campaign for a National Theatre; all the problems of Ireland; international politics and the issues of peace and war (his writings during the First World War were collected in a volume called *What I Really Wrote about the War,* 1930); feminist causes; electoral reform; and his lifelong championing of socialism, explaining his own idiosyncratic interpretation of that creed in a long treatise, *The Intelligent Woman's Guide to Socialism and Capitalism* (1928). Shaw insisted on the improvement of society as a whole rather than on individual satisfaction. *Everybody's Political What's What?* (1944), written as he approached the age of ninety, remains remarkably stimulating. In addition to these more public causes, Shaw was always calling for reform in a multitude of directions: religion, the marriage laws, the education of children, standards of dress, food and drink, the language and the alphabet itself. Between the wars Shaw's continuing admiration for Stalin caused many of his admirers to question the soundness of his political judgment.

Shaw had no time for "fine writing" and declared that "effectiveness of assertion" was the basis of style. Even such an unsympathetic critic as T.S. Eliot considered Shaw one of the greatest of English prose stylists. Humor was an essential part of his method of writing. Shaw maintained that humor strengthened his arguments and called laughter "my sword, my shield and spear".

T.F. Evans

Bibliography

Holroyd, Michael. *Bernard Shaw.* 3 vols. 1988–91.

Sickert, W(alter) R(ichard) (1860–1942)

W.R. Sickert, born in Munich of a Danish father and an Anglo-Irish mother, is admired both as a British successor to Degas and as a precursor of Andy Warhol. During the 1930s he painted from photographs and on a large scale. This practice had begun in 1906 with a portrait of a *Lady in Red: Mrs. Swinton*, now in the Fitzwilliam Museum, Cambridge.

He was for a time the most modern of British artists, in that his work was consistently topical, determined by artistic developments in France and by British life and times. Although his father was a painter and illustrator, the young W.R. Sickert began in 1879 as an actor and maintained an interest in theatrical subjects through his career. He was introduced to painting by Whistler in 1879, entered the Slade School in 1881, becoming Whistler's assistant in 1882. The next year Whistler introduced him to Degas, a decisive turn in his career. He remained a follower of Degas all his life, using the same beige palette and reporting on similar subjects: theaters, entertainments, sequestered models. Summers were mainly spent in Dieppe, and between 1898 and early 1905 he settled in Dieppe, with visits to Paris and Venice.

A Degasian modernist, he enjoyed a heyday in the first decade of the century, before being sidelined by the great Post-Impressionist exhibitions

of 1910 and 1912. Having learned in one school, he was unable to adapt and entered on a course of eccentricity which resulted in the photographically-based work of his later years. However, on his return to London from Dieppe in 1905 he confidently pursued a role as innovator both as a painter and as a reviewer. His subjects were the music hall and intimate domestic scenes, sometimes with a topical slant, as in the so-called *Camden Town Murder* pictures of 1908 and 1909. These pictures, of reclining female nudes and seated clothed men, were studies of the quotidian, of boredom and of post-coital *tristesse,* culminating in his celebrated renderings of *Ennui* in 1914. Always a publicist and teacher, he gathered young artists around him, including Spencer Gore (1878–1914) and Harold Gilman (1876–1919). In 1907 these artists formed the Fitzroy Street Group, which in 1911 became the Camden Town Group. By 1914 that group had expanded to become The London Group and to include JACOB EPSTEIN, WYNDHAM LEWIS, and Frederick Etchells (1886–1973). Sickert resigned on the grounds of Epstein's pornography.

In 1914 he parted company with convention in a way which anticipated his "topical" work of the 1930s. He painted two patriotic Belgian subjects, *The Soldiers of King Albert the Ready* and *The Integrity of Belgium.* After the vanguard, *intimiste* years they represent an abrupt accomodation with the status quo.

Immediately after the First World War he moved back to Dieppe where he remained until 1922. He was, through the 1920s, a prolific etcher, and in 1925 was elected an Associate of the Royal Society of Painters, Etchers and Engravers. His painting practice as outlined in letters to CHURCHILL, to whom he gave lessons in 1927, and to other students involved transfers from photographs and the use of very deliberated, even automated, painting practices. In 1927 he began a series of self-portraits in which he appeared variously as Lazarus and as *The Servant of Abraham* (1929). In the same year he also appeared on a large scale as Christ in *The Raising of Lazarus.*

By 1929 Sickert was entering the most inexplicable, post-modern phase of his career, characterized by his "English Echoes" series, based on Victorian illustrations and designs. These later pictures, including several theater and news images, represent Sickert over-collaborating with the status quo, putting himself almost entirely in the hands of the media and of popular taste. Having pledged himself to the accurate rendering of real life in his Camden Town years, he now committed himself whole-heartedly to mediated topicality. In 1932, for example, he celebrated the arrival of the American aviatrix Amelia Earhart in London after a transatlantic flight. An equally celebrated picture of *King George V and his Racing Manager: A Conversation Piece at Aintree* (1929–30) also derived from the newspaper. Another picture, of a miner being embraced by his wife owed a lot to the attention in the mid-1930s to the plight of miners in Wales and in the North. In fact, Sickert appeared to nominate himself as a kind of national laureate, responsible for rendering such major subjects as *Sir Thomas Beecham Conducting* (1938). In this respect he was merely putting into effect another implication of the automated procedures which he had consistently applied to the act of painting, almost from the beginning, or from the moment when he exchanged Whistler's *alla prima* manner for the planning of Degas (1885). The final results, in his old age, are paintings which stand as uncanny prefigurations of the *pittura buffa* of the international art scene in the 1980s and 1990s.

Ian Jeffrey

Bibliography
Baron, Wendy. *Sickert.* (1973).
———, and Richard Shone. *Sickert: Paintings.* 1992.
Emmons, Robert. *The Life and Opinions of Walter Richard Sickert.* 1941.
Sitwell, Osbert. *A Free House. or, the Artist as Craftsman: The Writings of Walter Richard Sickert.* 1947.

Simon, John Allsebrook (1873–1954)

John Simon was born of Welsh parents in Manchester on 28 February 1873. Leaving Fettes College in 1892, he went up to Wadham College, Oxford, as a classics scholar. After being elected President of the Oxford Union, he took a first class degree in 1896 and was elected a Fellow of All Souls. Called to the Bar two years later, he advanced rapidly, becoming a King's Counsel after only nine years. Enormously successful in his practice, he was soon one of the most sought after barristers in London and, in 1909, standing counsel to the UNIVERSITY OF OXFORD.

Simon's true ambition was for a political career. He was elected in the landslide election of 1906 as Liberal MP for the Walthamstow Division of Essex. In 1910 he first held office when Prime Minister HERBERT HENRY ASQUITH appointed him Solicitor-General, accompanied by a knighthood. In 1912 he became a Privy Counselor and the following year joined the CABINET as Attorney-General.

Simon, uneasy about British participation in the FIRST WORLD WAR, considered resignation but was convinced to remain in office. After the formation of Asquith's multi-party government in May 1915, he refused the offer of the Lord Chancellorship and became Home Secretary instead. The decision to introduce a CONSCRIPTION bill in January 1916 offended Simon's classical liberal values, and he resigned office, serving for the remainder of the war with the Royal Flying Corps in France.

Simon opposed the LLOYD GEORGE coalition and lost his seat in the Coupon Election of 1918. He returned to Parliament four years later representing the Spen Valley. The failure of the second Labour ministry of RAMSAY MACDONALD and the creation of the National Government in 1931 provided Simon the opportunity for a second term in office. By this time he led a faction of the splintered LIBERAL PARTY and accepted the Foreign Secretaryship in this CONSERVATIVE-dominated coalition.

Simon's foreign policy, oriented toward disarmament and non-interventionism, entirely suited MacDonald. He took no steps to impede the aggressiveness of the Fascist dictators and can be considered one of the architects of the policy of APPEASEMENT. In 1935, when the Conservative STANLEY BALDWIN replaced MacDonald, Simon returned to the Home Office. When NEVILLE CHAMBERLAIN replaced Baldwin in 1937, he recognized a kindred spirit and appointed Simon Chancellor of the Exchequer. For the remaining years of peace, Simon enjoyed Chamberlain's full confidence and was one of the small number of ministers who made up the inner Cabinet. Only after Hitler struck the first blow against Poland did Simon accept the need to resist the Nazis and led a delegation of ministers to Chamberlain demanding a war declaration.

Simon took little part in the direction of the war. With the advent of WINSTON CHURCHILL's coalition in May 1940, he was appointed Lord Chancellor, with the title Viscount Simon of Stackpole Elidor. He retired from office in 1945 and died in 1954.

R.J.Q. Adams

Bibliography
Adams, R.J.Q. *British Politics and Foreign Policy in the Age of Appeasement, 1935–39.* 1992.
Dutton, David. *Simon: A Political Biography of Sir John Simon.* 1992.
Heuston, R.F.V. *Lives of the Lord Chancellors, 1940–1970.* 1987.
Simon, Viscount. *Retrospect: The Memoirs of the Rt. Hon. Viscount Simon.* 1952.

Slums

Slums are poor urban districts characterized by extreme overcrowding, badly maintained residential properties, and unsanitary living conditions which have been represented by non-residents as socially dangerous and unacceptable. "Slum" signified not only a physical space, but also a set of attitudes defining that space and its inhabitants as problems demanding intervention. Once reformers and politicians labeled an area a "slum," they were able to justify a range of often coercive interventions into heretofore private landlord-tenant relations. The history of "slums" and "slumming"—casual, often voyeuristic visits to slum districts by the well-to-do—were closely intertwined with elite ideas and policies toward the poor, criminality, PUBLIC HEALTH, HOUSING and property ownership, RACE RELATIONS, and sexual morality. Debates about the nature and meaning of slums and attempts to respond to their problems lie at the heart of modern British social policy, and help to demarcate the economic, social, and ideological contours of party politics in the twentieth century.

The word "slum" acquired its modern usage by the mid-nineteenth century; however, it was popularized in the 1880s by sensational journalistic exposés depicting the slums of East and South London as haunts of criminality, deviant or immoral sexuality, and extreme poverty. While earlier social investigators like Thomas Chalmers and J.P. Kay publicized the squalor of Glasgow and Manchester, from the 1880s onwards the slums of LONDON disproportionately dominated national discussions about how the poor lived. The London slums were the destination for large numbers of Irish and Jewish IMMIGRANTS in the nineteenth century followed by immigrants from Britain's former colonies in the Caribbean, Africa, and the Indian sub-continent. Throughout the twentieth century slums have been touchstones for anxieties about Britain's declining imperial fortunes (Mafeking riots, May 1900) as well as scenes of racist conflict (OSWALD MOSLEY's British Union of Fascists demonstrations in Bethnal Green in the 1936; Brixton and Toxteth race riots, spring/summer, 1981).

Twentieth-century reformers, bureaucrats, and politicians inherited a rich legacy of Victorian philanthropic and legislative approaches to slums which influenced their own policy choices. Victorian philanthropic ventures such as the settlement movement, the Salvation Army, and slum missions, for example, survived and sometimes even flourished well into the new century; however, their initial aspirations to transform society were often tempered by their limited achievements.

Whereas nineteenth century discussion of slums were usually couched in terms of disease and sanitary reform, on the one hand, and cultural and moral elevation, on the other, in the late nineteenth and twentieth centuries, public and private remedies favored transforming the physical environment of slums. Twentieth-century slum policy emphasized population densities and the character of housing for the poor. Clearance, renovation, and redevelopment debates revolved around several concrete issues reflecting the interests of landlords and tenants and the pressures of municipal and national politics: financing (level of compensation for landlords, public and private funding); location (central urban, suburban, GARDEN CITY or new town); physical layout (vertical multi-story flats, cottages); and qualitative amenities (lifts, wc's, balconies, sculleries). These housing concerns became increasingly important electoral issues in inter-war politics after the enfranchisement of women, usually to the benefit of the LABOUR PARTY.

Slum clearance and redevelopment schemes in the twentieth century drew on a variety of models, each deriving in part from earlier initiatives. Following the lead of the Victorian housing reformer and charity organizer, Octavia Hill, NEVILLE CHAMBERLAIN in the 1920s advocated reconditioning existing dwellings along with personal supervision of tenants by lady property managers. Such programs combined attention to the physical condition of buildings with concern for the behavior and use of them by occupants. Others, drawing on Ebenezer Howard's late-Victorian vision of the garden city, called for dispersing slum populations and integrating them into cross-class garden suburbs and cities (Bournville, Hampstead Garden Suburb). Still others called for municipal purchase and demolition of large blocks of derelict properties. Most proponents of slum clearance in the twentieth century, unlike their nineteenth-century predecessors, insisted that new housing specifically be set aside for displaced tenants.

While "slums" continue to carry many negative late-Victorian connotations, an alternative tradition of social commentary emerged after the First World War celebrating slums as sites of tightly knit, indigenous working-class communities threatened by rationalizing urban planners. This "counter-tradition" was fueled in part by commentaries written by "slum dwellers" themselves as well as by critics of large scale COUNCIL HOUSING for the poor. In the early twentieth century, reformers condemned as soulless and degrading model housing erected by PHILANTHROPIES such as the Peabody Trust. Similarly, the sprawling, multi-storied council estates erected before and after the Second World War are today often blamed for reproducing a demoralized, permanent underclass. Ironically, solutions to the problems of slum life implemented by one generation have often been identified as problems by the next.

Seth Koven

Bibliography

Chapman, Stanley D., ed. *The History of Working-Class Housing.* 1971.

Roberts, Robert. *The Classic Slum: Salford Life in the First Quarter of the Century.* 1971.

Gaskell, S. Martin, ed. *Slums.* 1990.

White, Jerry. *Rothschild Buildings: Life in an East End Tenement Block, 1887–1920.* 1980.

———.*The Worst Street in North London: Campbell Bunk, Islington, Between the Wars.* 1986.

Yelling, J.A. *Slums and Redevelopment: Policy and Practice in England, 1918–1945.* 1993.

Young, Michael, and Peter Willmott. *Family and Kinship in East London.* 1957.

Snowden, Philip (1864–1937)

Philip Snowden was a profoundly controversial figure in the early years of the British labor movement. His name is closely associated with that of RAMSAY MACDONALD in the "betrayal" of 1931 which saw the collapse of the second Labour government, an event which many contemporaries saw as having arisen from his policies as Labour's first Chancellor of the Exchequer. Between 1906 and 1931 Snowden was certainly a prominent Labour leader, comparable to MacDonald and KEIR HARDIE in political importance.

Snowden was born on 18 July 1864 in the remote Pennine moorland parish of Cowling, near Keighley, in the West Riding of Yorkshire. He was raised in a small textile community where Nonconformity, particularly Wesleyan METHODISM, shaped the life of the community. He received a basic elementary education but, as a bright boy, was destined to become a schoolmaster. Changed family circumstances led him to become a clerk and, eventually, to join the civil service. An accident and illness in the early 1890s forced him out of employment, and while he was recuperating, he became involved in LIBERAL and then socialist politics, joining the INDEPENDENT LABOUR PARTY (ILP), which was active in the West Riding, in January 1895.

At the local level, Snowden became prominent in Keighley politics, being returned to Cowling School Board in 1895, acting as editor of the *Keighley Labour Journal* between 1898 and 1902, and winning seats on both the Keighley School Board and the Keighley Town Council in 1899. He was also involved in the Labour Church movement, soon becoming recognized as a fine orator on ethical socialism. It was evident that Snowden was a rising man in the independent Labour movement, and it surprised few when he became a member of the National Administrative Council of the ILP in 1898.

Parliamentary politics was to be Snowden's real forte. He stood, unsuccessfully, for Blackburn in 1900 and Wakefield in 1902 before being returned as MP for Blackburn in 1906 and twice in 1910. Snowden represented Blackburn from 1906 to 1918 when, due to his opposition to the First World War, he lost his seat. Subsequently, he was MP for Colne Valley from 1922 until 1931,

being returned at four general elections, before being raised to the HOUSE OF LORDS as Viscount Snowden of Ickornshaw in November 1931. During his time in the Commons, he was Chancellor of the Exchequer of the first and second Labour governments in 1924 and between 1929 and 1931. As Viscount Snowden he was briefly a member of MacDonald's National government, acting as Lord Privy Seal until his resignation on 28 September 1932.

Throughout his life Snowden adhered to Liberal radical sentiments and was particularly concerned to oppose war, to support free trade, and to discourage borrowing. Indeed, he was a good old-fashioned Gladstonian Liberal in his economic policies. His wife, Ethel Annakin, whom he married in 1905, also directed him towards the need to press for WOMEN'S SUFFRAGE. It was these policies and forces which shaped his political career. They helped him rise within the ILP, of which he was Chairman 1903–6 and 1917–20 and Treasurer 1920–1. His staunch Liberal Radical ideas also led him to attack Britain's involvement in the First World War and to mount the ILP's Peace Campaign in 1917. From 1916 onwards he attacked the use and abuse of military tribunals against CONSCIENTIOUS OBJECTORS and by the end of the war was demanding that the LLOYD GEORGE government declare its war aims in order to secure the peace more speedily. He also attended the Workmen's and Soldier's Council Convention held at Leeds in June 1917, where a mixture of Marxists and socialists sought to force international peace in the wake of the first Russian Revolution of 1917. Not surprisingly, he was vilified for his actions and opposition to the war.

Snowden's commitment to Liberal Radicalism helped to move him out of the ILP in the early 1920s, when it became committed to left-wing socialism. From 1922 onwards, having been returned as MP for Colne Valley, he made the LABOUR PARTY his political home. He was frustrated by the return of MacDonald as Labour's parliamentary leader but served under him as Chancellor of the Exchequer and Shadow Chancellor. In the former role he gave full vent to his notions of balancing the budget, reducing the National Debt and, if necessary, deflating the economy. Although his tenacity brought him some personal success, and Britain some economic saving at The Hague conference on reparations in 1929, it is clear that his policies were inappropriate in the economic climate of 1929–31, which saw UNEMPLOYMENT and government expenditure rise, the pound sink under pressure from the money markets, and the Labour government split on the issue of cutting unemployment benefits by 10 percent. The Labour split was a result of MacDonald's support for Snowden's economic policies and the reluctance of a substantial minority of the CABINET to accept such views. Thus it was not surprising that Snowden was obliged to support MacDonald's National government and to ditch Labour, claiming two months later in the October 1931 General Election that Labour's economic policies, which he himself had forged, were "Bolshevism run mad".

After less then a year in the National government Snowden resigned because he could not accept its abandonment of free trade. Subsequently, although a spent force in British politics, he engaged in making personal attacks on MacDonald. He died of a heart attack, following a long illness, on 15 May 1937.

Keith Laybourn

Bibliography
Cross, Colin. *Philip Snowden*. 1966.
Laybourn, Keith. *Philip Snowden: A Biography 1864–1937*. 1988.
——, and David James, eds. *Philip Snowden*. 1987.
Snowden, Philip. *An Autobiography*. 1934.

Social Democratic Party

The Social Democratic Party was founded in 1981, largely as a breakaway from the LABOUR PARTY at a time when it had fallen under the influence of a left-wing and trade-union compact. The SDP, as it was generally known, enjoyed a remarkable surge of initial popularity, reaching a peak in the winter of 1981–2. Its first leader, ROY JENKINS, was instrumental in forming the Alliance with the LIBERAL PARTY, and together the Alliance parties polled over 25 percent of the vote in the 1983 general election. Thereafter its fortunes fluctuated under the leadership of Dr. David Owen, and tensions with the Liberals became more apparent in the run-up to the 1987 general election. After it, the party voted for a merger with the Liberals and became a constituent part of the new Social and Liberal Democrats (though Owen for a time led his own faction which continued to use the name SDP).

For most of the twentieth century the term social democrat had continental European rather than British connotations. Only in the 1970s did the revisionist right wing of the Labour Party become generally known as social democrats. One reason was because of their own strong European credentials. As deputy leader, Jenkins had led sixty-nine Labour MPs into the lobby to vote for British accession to the EUROPEAN COMMUNITY in 1971, in defiance of the party line. A further reason for the adoption of the social democratic terminology was to draw a distinction between the essentially liberal, parliamentary, and moderate outlook of this section of the Labour Party and the strident, purist, militant socialism proclaimed by an increasing number on the Left.

It was not so much the rise of the Left which produced the friction, however, as its new-found support from the trade unions, on whom the right wing had been able to rely in the days of former leaders like CLEMENT ATTLEE and HUGH GAITSKELL. This highlighted trade-union control of the Labour Party through the "block vote" system (whereby trade unions had historically affiliated their millions of members to the party and cast their blocks of proxy votes at the party conference accordingly). It was on the issue of "one member, one vote" that the SDP finally split from the Labour Party at the beginning of 1981, after its special conference at Wembley (January 1981) had granted the trade unions the major say in electing the parliamentary leadership.

In another sense, however, the SDP could trace its origin to the Dimbleby Lecture which Jenkins gave on television in 1979. Jenkins spoke now as an exile from British politics, having served since 1976 as President of the European Commission. His message was that the Labour Party no longer offered a relevant vehicle for reformist politcs in Britain. This was an unashamed plea for the strengthening of the political centre. As such it cut no ice with the leaders of the social democratic faction within the Labour Party. Here the key figures were Jenkins's old lieutenant, William Rodgers, and two ex-CABINET ministers, Shirley Williams and David Owen.

Williams had become one of the representatives of the women's section on Labour's National Executive Committee from 1970; Owen had had a brilliant career as a Labour MP, rising to become Foreign Secretary in 1977 at the age of thirty-eight. Following Labour's swing to the left after losing the 1979 General Election, Williams's decision to work in concert with Owen and Rodgers—the "Gang of Three"—was indispensable in rallying solid support from within Labour ranks for what became the SDP; but their initial rebuff to Jenkins's initiative showed the strategic gap between them. It was only the inexorable slide of the Labour Party under trade-union control during the course of 1980 which brought all these forces together. In a move which Owen subsequently regretted, the Limehouse Declaration (January 1981) signaled full cooperation with Jenkins. Initially pledged only to a campaign for social democracy, the "Gang of Four" quickly moved during the next few weeks to set up a new party.

Many saw Williams as its natural leader, but she could not or would not press this claim. It was Jenkins who meanwhile consolidated his position by taking on the first by-election challenge in the northern industrial borough of Warrington, which he almost won from Labour in July 1981.

No longer could the SDP be dismissed as a manoeuvre by the parliamentary elite; its burgeoning popular support now made the running and
the headlines. The Alliance with the Liberals was
forged at this stage, and opinion polls showed it
having more support than either the Labour or
CONSERVATIVE parties. The zenith came in the
sensational by-election victory which Williams
achieved over the Conservatives at Crosby in November 1981. In the House of Commons she
joined twenty-six MPs who had now defected
from Labour, plus one ex-Conservative MP.

Jenkins too resumed his parliamentary career
when, in March 1982, he won the Glasgow constituency of Hillhead for the SDP. But the tide
was now on the turn, and the invasion of the
Falkland Islands (April 1982) created a new situation. What made—and left—an impression was
Owen's firm support for the government in
mounting a military expedition. When he stood
for the leadership of the SDP shortly afterwards,
he ran Jenkins a fairly close second. Indeed the
new leader not only failed to command the
House of Commons from his backbench seat but
also lagged behind Owen's popular ratings.

Parliamentary constituencies were to be divided between the Liberals and the SDP as part
of the Alliance strategy. Naturally the Liberals
took the most immediately promising prospects,
as a result of their previous strength on the
ground; what the SDP needed was a broad-based
breakthrough to surmount the crucial threshold
imposed by the electoral system. But no longer
was the Alliance ahead in the opinion polls, now
that THATCHER had established her post-
FALKLANDS WAR ascendancy, and could point,
moreover, to increasing signs of economic recovery. The 1983 General Election saw an impressive
vote for the Alliance, which polled 25.4 percent of
the national vote as compared with Labour's 27.6
percent. But this gave the Alliance only 23 MPs
to Labour's 209. It was worst of all for the SDP,
which won only six seats.

On Jenkins's resignation at this point, Owen
was unanimously elected to the leadership. He
succeeded in making the SDP presence felt at
Westminster; if it was, as critics alleged, a one-
man band, it was still a virtuoso performance,
against all numerical odds. But the Alliance with
the Liberals in the country entered a more traumatic phase. Owen resisted moves towards closer
affiliation. He wanted the SDP to maintain a distinctive image, notably upon issues like defense,
where he took a hard line in favor of Britain's independent nuclear deterrent. Owen's talk of a
"social market" also suggested to some that his
economic views were disconcertingly close to
THATCHERISM.

Owen's relations with David Steel as Liberal
leader were civil but not as close as they had been
in Jenkins's day. In the 1987 general election the
double leadership of the Alliance was widely seen
as a disadvantage, especially when Steel seemed
to incline towards the Left, Owen towards the
Right. The Alliance poll slipped (though not as
badly as it had feared) to 22.6 percent, electing
twenty-two MPs. In the aftermath, Steel's
prompt initiative for merger was met by Owen's
dismissive rejection. Williams worked effectively
for closer cooperation with the Liberals and now
voiced the wish of most SDP members for a full
merger. Repudiated by the bulk of SDP members
voting in a national ballot, Owen resigned the
leadership in August 1987. There was no reconciliation; and in 1988 Owen rallied his own followers in a tightly-organized movement of uncertain
size, which perpetuated the old SDP name for a
couple of years.

Constitutionally the SDP had now become
merged into a new party, the Social and Liberal
Democrats, which a majority of its old members
joined. Their efforts to break the mold had come
up against the bias in the electoral system, the
stubborn resilience of traditional Labour support
(especially in Scotland), and the impact of events
(notably the Falklands factor). Electorally, the
SDP missed the boat; but ideologically it caught
the tide. Its stance in favor of the European
Community and electoral reform, and against
unilateral disarmament and large-scale NA-
TIONALIZATION posed fundamental differences
with Labour during the early 1980s.

Peter Clarke

Bibliography
Bradley, Ian. *Breaking the Mould? The Birth and Prospects
    of the SDP.* 1981.
Crewe, Ivor, and Anthony King. *SDP: The Birth, Life
    and Death of the Social Democratic Party.* 1995.
Harris, Kenneth. *David Owen.* 1987.
Jenkins, Roy. *A Life at the Centre.* 1991.
Stephenson, Hugh. *Claret and Chips: The Rise of the
    SDP.* 1982.

Socialist League (1932–1937)

The Socialist League was founded in 1932 as an
affiliate organization of the LABOUR PARTY and
dissolved itself in 1937 under pressure from the
Labour leadership. The League was the chief organization of Labour's intellectual Left, a role
which brought it into frequent conflict with the
party's moderate mainstream. The League was
closely identified with the views and policies of
SIR STAFFORD CRIPPS, who led it from the death
of its founding chairman, E.F. Wise, in Nove-
menber 1933. Its membership included virtually
every prominent intellectual in the Labour Left.

The immediate trigger for the foundation of
the Socialist League was the INDEPENDENT

LABOUR PARTY's decision to disaffiliate itself from the Labour Party in 1932. A substantial minority of ILP members believed that the ILP would lose all influence as a result and accordingly formed a "National ILP Affiliation Committee" led by Wise and H.N. BRAILSFORD. This group soon entered into negotiations with G.D.H. COLE to amalgamate with the Socialist Society for Inquiry and Propaganda, a recently formed Labour discussion circle. Despite the disquiet of some members of the SSIP, who feared that any new body would repeat the ILP's history of perpetual conflict with the Labour Party leadership, the amalgamation was concluded and the League launched in October 1932. Some members of the SSIP, notably ERNEST BEVIN, never joined the Socialist League. Others, such as CLEMENT ATTLEE, J.A. HOBSON, and Cole, left it within twelve months.

The Socialist League enjoyed its greatest success in its early days, while the Labour Party, still recovering from the shock of RAMSAY MACDONALD's "betrayal" of 1931, sought to repudiate the gradualist tradition which MacDonald represented. League speakers were well-received at Labour's 1932 conference which passed a number of the League's radical motions, including one for the NATIONALIZATION of banking. It was somewhat less successful at the 1933 conference, and not a single League-sponsored motion was accepted by the Labour Party thereafter.

The pattern of estrangement between the League and the Labour Party became obvious during 1933, when Cripps and other prominent League spokesmen advocated the use by the next Labour government of an Emergency Powers Act in order to counter capitalist resistance to socialist measures. The proposals caused outrage in the press, and an embarrassed Labour leadership publicly condemned the League.

The final crisis in the Socialist League's life was precipitated by its involvement in the Unity Campaign of 1937. In January the League published a "Unity Manifesto" jointly with the COMMUNIST PARTY and the ILP. The Labour Party, which at its 1936 conference had banned collaboration with Communists, disaffiliated the League within the month, and shortly after declared that the League would be proscribed after 1 June. In May, in order to avoid its members' explusion from the Labour Party, the League dissolved itself at a poorly organized and sparsely attended meeting. A few dissentients immediately attempted to resurrect the League as the Socialist Left Foundation, but with no success.

David Blaazer

Bibliography
Jupp, James. *The Radical Left in Britain 1931–1941.* 1982.
Pimlott, Ben. *Labour and the Left in the 1930s.* 1977.
Seyd, Patrick. "Factionalism within the Labour Party: The Socialist League, 1932–1937" in Asa Briggs and John Saville, eds. *Essays in Labour History 1918–1939.* 1977. pp. 204–31.

Society of Friends: see Friends, Society of (Quakers)

Somme, Battle of the

The Battle of the Somme was devised late in 1915 as part of an Allied offensive on all fronts intended for mid-1916. The French were seen as the senior partners in this Anglo-French battle, contributing forty-one divisions to the British twenty-five. Nevertheless, this would be Britain's largest military undertaking so far, employing the men who had volunteered in the opening phase of the war.

There were good reasons for attacking in the Somme region. The Anglo-French armies met there. They would not be confronting imposing high ground. And, as long as the weather held, the clay soil would constitute good campaigning territory. Certainly the district had disadvantages. As was true all along the Western Front, the Germans occupied what raised ground was available. They had enjoyed ample time to prepare their defenses. And the firm soil had enabled them to construct a complex system well below the surface. Nevertheless, the notion that the Somme was manifestly a silly region at which to attack is unfounded. It ignores the advantages of the district and the painful lack of a better alternative.

The Somme campaign was not launched as planned. It did coincide, roughly, with a Russian offensive on the Eastern Front. But from February 1916 the French had been subjected to a murderous blood-letting at Verdun (which also took heavy toll of the Germans). Hence the twenty-five British divisions became the major contributor to an attack whose first purpose had become relief of the pressure on Verdun.

Yet the wider purpose remained, despite the reduced Allied force. SIR DOUGLAS HAIG, the British Commander-in-Chief, hoped to rupture the enemy line with guns and infantry and pour his cavalry into open country. Whether he possessed sufficient ammunition to crush the German defenses nobody seemed to be calculating.

The ensuing campaign, of 141 days, falls into six pieces. The attack of 1 July 1916 was a bloody failure. The preliminary bombardment had been too meager and was spread too wide to achieve its purpose. Of the 120,000 Britons who went forward, 57,000 became casualties, including 19,000 killed. No ground was gained except on the right, which was not the main objective.

Phase two occupied 2–13 July. It consisted of sporadic attacks by small units. Then on 14 July (phase three) a considerable attack was launched at night, after an appropriately heavy bombardment. It enjoyed initial success, until the cavalry—called in for exploitation—outran their artillery and were cut down.

Phase four was the longest and most confused episode of the campaign. From 15 July to 14 September small sections of Haig's army were thrown into uncoordinated attacks for limited objectives. They attracted disproportionately heavy artillery resistance. The casualties suffered and the negligible ground gained were equivalent to the disastrous opening day.

More dramatic, and even somewhat rewarding, were the operations of phase five (15–25 September). On 15 September the British employed tanks for the first time. Regrettably, to facilitate the new weapon they restricted the role assigned to artillery. Hence not very much was gained. More profitable was an operation ten days later, making highly effective use of artillery—not least in the form of a creeping barrage moving just ahead of the attacking infantry.

After this, meaningful campaigning became impossible, as bucketing rain turned the clay soil into a quagmire. Haig, nonetheless, persisted in attacking. Apart from a minor closing success at Beaumont Hamel, this sixth phase (October–November) is the sorriest episode of all.

For the British, the Somme campaign was not entirely barren. It ended the pressure on Verdun, killed many Germans, saw the birth of a new weapon, and witnessed noteworthy developments in artillery techniques. But overall it was a failure. It did not break the German line, or capture strategically-important territory, or destroy the German will to persevere. Most of all, it did not inflict on the enemy casualties as great as those sustained by the Allies. (British casualties numbered 420,000 and French 200,000; those of Germany, 500,000.)

The Somme casualties reduced whole towns in Britain to mourning, ended the political authority of the ASQUITH coalition, and raised doubts about the wisdom of Britain's military command.

Robin Prior
Trevor Wilson

Bibliography
Farrar-Hockley, A.H. *The Somme.* 1964.
Keegan, John. *The Face of Battle.* 1976.
Prior, Robin, and Trevor Wilson. *Command on the Western Front: The Military Career of Sir Henry Rawlinson 1914–1918.* 1992.

Spanish Civil War (1936–1939)

The outbreak of civil war and revolution in Spain in the summer of 1936 coincided with the sharpening of tensions in the international arena. In March German troops brazenly violated the Treaty of Versailles and Locarno agreement of 1925 by reoccupying the Rhineland, and, in May, the Italians marched into Addis Ababa, thereby demonstrating the impotence of the LEAGUE OF NATIONS as an instrument of diplomacy. Notwithstanding these developments, the prevailing view at the time was that another European war could be averted. So potent was this belief that from 1936 until the war ended in April 1939 it conditioned British reaction to events in Spain.

British public opinion was deeply divided. Many saw Spain as the stage on which the major political and ideological struggles of the period were being played out. Those who sided with the republican cause—a group that embraced middle-class professionals, intellectuals, and rank-and-file trade unionists—tended to be sympathetic to the left-wing coalition of Popular Front parties resisting the rebels. On the other hand, the predominantly middle- and upper-class supporters of Francisco Franco and his Nationalist forces regarded the rebellion as a struggle against Bolshevism and were inclined to see Fascism in a positive light. Among those who favored Franco were some of Britain's most prominent businessmen, diplomats, army and naval officers, conservative politicians, as well as the relatively small community of British ROMAN CATHOLICS.

To members of the British government the idea of a "Red" Spain was anathema, but all were highly alarmed at the possibility that the Spanish conflict might ignite another European conflagration. Immediately following the outbreak of the Spanish Civil War the BALDWIN government adopted a "wait and see" policy. If at all possible, Britain wanted to maintain Spain's territorial integrity and secure the benevolent neutrality of whichever side emerged victorious. How the government was to pursue these goals remained unclear until the end of July, when it became clear that both Germany and Italy were openly assisting the insurgent cause. Britain then joined the French in promoting the idea of a multilateral non-intervention agreement.

In August 1936 a Non-Intervention Agreement (NIA) was signed by some twenty-seven countries, and, one month later, a non-intervention committee, the NIC—officially known as the International Committee for the Application of Nonintervention in Spain—was set-up to monitor outside interference in Spanish internal affairs. Based in London, the NIC was convened under the auspices of the British Foreign Office and chaired by Lord Plymouth, the Parliamentary Under-Secretary. From its inception until its formal disbandment in April 1939, the Committee's effectiveness was diminished by its lack of powers to stop or control even the most obvious forms of intervention. Flagrant violations of the NIA, especially by Germany, Italy, and the Soviet Union, further undermined the credibility of the Committee. Ironically, what the NIC did succeed in doing was to obstruct the legitimate Republican government from securing desperately needed materiel from countries that might otherwise have come to its aid.

One particularly pressing problem facing the British was how to respond to the naval blockades imposed by the Nationalists. Unwilling to compromise its neutrality and fearing an overwhelmingly negative public reaction to the use of force, the government initially opted for a policy of restraint. Then, following a series of submarine attacks on neutral commercial shipping vessels in the summer of 1937, some high ranking officials, including Foreign Secretary ANTHONY EDEN, felt compelled to take a firmer stand. To stop the unidentified submarines, generally known to be Italian, France and Great Britain recommended the use of multinational naval patrols. At the Nyon Conference convened in September 1937, their plan was formally adopted and, for a brief while, the sinkings stopped.

Meanwhile, on the domestic front in Britain, the Spanish Civil War deepened existing political and class divisions. Like no other event of the period, the war mobilized the forces of the Left and, to a lesser extent, of the Right. Spain's troubles inspired countless public rallies and street demonstrations, and debates over the nature and significance of the war filled newspaper columns, books, and pamphlets. An informal survey taken by *Left Review* during 1937 revealed that nearly every major British artist, writer, and intellectual held strong convictions about the war. The vast majority, like W.H. AUDEN, STEPHEN SPENDER, and GEORGE ORWELL, favored the Republicans, whereas EVELYN WAUGH and a handful of lesser-known authors sided with the Nationalists.

The Spanish Civil War not only served to polarize national politics, it also divided parties among themselves. Most CONSERVATIVES instinctively supported the Nationalists, but a few, like WINSTON CHURCHILL and other "anti-appeasers", came to believe that a pro-Axis Spain would threaten British interests in the Mediterranean. For different reasons the leadership of the labor movement was divided over the question of intervention. In the early stages of the war, union leaders like WALTER CITRINE and ERNEST BEVIN advocated a cautious approach towards Spain, a position at first overwhelmingly endorsed by the rank-and-file of the TRADE UNION CONGRESS (TUC). What guided their thinking was the belief that direct British involvement would most likely split the labor movement and thereby destabilize trade unionism. One of their

greatest fears was that the Communists, spearheading a United Front campaign to provide active aid to Spain, might gain control of organized labor. But clearly the main preoccupation of the leadership was the threat of another war: both Citrine and Bevin rightly sensed that few workers were prepared to sacrifice the fragile European peace for the sake of the Spanish Republic.

As it became increasingly apparent that non-intervention was working in the interests of the Nationalists, the pro-Republican passions of the labor movement became more difficult to restrain. In the autumn of 1937 both the TUC and Labour Party, though still opposed to directly intervening in Spain, began pressuring the British government to lift its embargo on arms to the Republican forces. For its part, the National Council of Labour expressed its disapproval of non-intervention by providing humanitarian aid. Food, clothing, medical supplies, and other forms of assistance were generously provided by such groups as the Socialist Medical Association as well as many other organizations affiliated with the labor movement. Perhaps the most successful relief programs were those aimed at helping children displaced by the war: mineworkers contributed over £55,000 to orphaned children of Asturian miners, and a publicly-supported adoption scheme brought some 4,000 Basque orphans to England by the time the war had ended.

The COMMUNIST PARTY OF GREAT BRITAIN launched an even stronger initiative aimed at supporting Republican Spain. Obeying the Communist International's (Comintern) call for the formation of an international contingent to be sent to Spain, British communists actively recruited volunteers. Thanks to their efforts between 1936 and 1939 over 2,000 men and women served in the INTERNATIONAL BRIGADES of the Republican army. Though they came from different social backgrounds and represented a variety of left-wing opinions, these mostly young and idealistic volunteers went primarily because they were convinced that if Hitler and Mussolini could be stopped in Spain another general war could be averted.

On arriving in Spain, the volunteers underwent an intensive, if extremely brief, military training program. Most were then assigned to combat units, although some served in non-combative roles as ambulance and truck drivers and as medical assistants. Despite their lack of military training and limited wartime experience, the British volunteers displayed considerable valor and courage. The 600 members of the British Battalion attached to the XV International Brigade were used as shock troops in some of the bloodiest engagements of the war, such as the Battles of Jarama and Brunete. By the time the International Brigades were obliged to with-draw from Spain late in 1938, the casualty figures for the British contingent was staggeringly high: of the approximately 2,000 combatants who served over 500 had been killed and 1,200 had been wounded.

Public interest in the fate of Spain remained high throughout 1937 and 1938, not least because the tragedy of the Spanish war was kept alive in the printed media. The vicious destruction of the small Basque town of Guernica in 1937, for exam-ple, commanded the headlines of the British press for several weeks. No less disturbing—at least for those on the Left—were the eye-witness reports from George Orwell, Fenner Brockway, and other representatives of the INDEPENDENT LABOR PARTY (ILP), which disclosed that deep-seated animosities between the left-wing parties were seriously undermining Republican unity.

In any case, by the autumn of 1938 Spain's problems were almost completely overshadowed by events taking place elsewhere in Europe. As far as Spain was concerned, it was now clear that the European powers were not prepared to go to war over her domestic crisis. By the winter of 1938 the Republicans were all but defeated, although, for the next few months, the Negrín government clung to the slender hope that the war would be absorbed into a general one. On 27 February 1939 the British and French governments recognized Franco, thus hastening the conclusion of the war which came on 1 April 1939.

George Esenwein

Bibliography
Buchanan, Tom. *Britain and the Spanish Civil War.* 1997.
———. "'A Far Away Country of Which We Know Nothing'? Perceptions of Spain and its Civil War in Britain, 1931–1939," *Twentieth Century British History.* vol. 4 (1993), pp. 1–24.
Edwards, Jill. *The British Government and the Spanish Civil War, 1936–1939.* 1979.
Fyrth, Jim. *The Signal Was Spain: The Spanish Aid Movement in Britain, 1936–1939.* 1986.
Hopkins, James K. *Into the Heart of the Fire: The British in the Spanish Civil War.* 1998.
Watkins, K.W. *Britain Divided: The Effect of the Spanish Civil War on British Public Opinion.* 1963.

Spark, Muriel Camberg (1918–)

Ever since the publication of *The Comforters* in 1957, Muriel Spark has been one of the most highly regarded novelists writing in English. Al-though she has published critical and biographi-cal works on the Brontes, JOHN MASEFIELD, and Mary Shelley in addition to two collections of poetry, numerous short stories, a play, and a children's book, Spark is primarily recognized for the nearly twenty novels she has written over the past four decades. Scottish by birth, Spark

achieved her greatest recognition with the film, stage, and television adaptations of the novel based upon her years at James Gillespie's High School for Girls in Edinburgh, *The Prime of Miss Jean Brodie* (1961). She was awarded the James Tait Black Memorial Prize for her novel *The Mandelbaum Gate* (1965). *Curriculum Vitae* (1993) traces her autobiography to the moment of her conversion to ROMAN CATHOLICISM in 1954.

Born Muriel Camberg in 1918, Spark is the daughter of Jewish-English parents. She was married briefly to Sydney Oswald Spark, with whom she traveled to Southern Rhodesia, the setting of many of her short stories. During the Second World War Spark worked with the secret intelligence service. She has spent most of her life as an expatriate and currently lives in Tuscany. In 1993 she was awarded a DBE for her contribution to literature.

According to Spark, the world of fiction is a lie, but it is also a reference, however parodic, to the world outside the fiction. Both the real world and fictions are alike for Spark, because they are equally mysterious realms of fabrication and ma-nipulation. In Spark's novels, as in the world out-side them, what happens is often more apparent than why.

Such elusiveness has led critics to interpret Spark's work in a variety of ways. Her fiction has been labeled postmodern, metafictional, satiric, metaphysical, and, at the very least, paradoxical. Her deadpan tone and use of present tense are unsettling, leaving it up to readers to discriminate between the trivial and the essential in her narra-tives, between the artistic lie and the anagogical truth in them, and to determine for themselves Spark's intention and stance.

Jennifer L. Randisi

Bibliography
Bold, Alan. *Muriel Spark.* 1986.
Massie, Allan. *Muriel Spark.* 1979.
Randisi, Jennifer Lynn. *On Her Way Rejoicing: The Fic-tion of Muriel Spark.* 1991.
Spark, Muriel. *Curriculum Vitae: Autobiography.* 1993.
Whittaker, Ruth. *The Faith and Fiction of Muriel Spark.* 1982.

Spencer, Stanley (1891–1959)

Stanley Spencer belonged to the last generation in Britain which believed in the possibility of a great art continuous with tradition. His own style harks back to that of Giotto, whom he admired during his time at the Slade School (1909–12). His other major debt was to Post-Impressionism, which he saw at the first exhibition organized in 1910 by ROGER FRY for the Grafton Gallery. In 1912, at the second of these exhibitions, Spencer himself was included with a picture of *John Donne Arriving in Heaven*.

Like William Blake—another influence—Spender was a visionary capable of redeeming local life, of which he was also a scrupulous observer. Commonplace sites, especially the village of Cookham in Berkshire where he was brought up, became settings for miracles and for religious events. In 1937, for example, he represented Cookham Moor with its war memorial as a stage for *A Celebration of Love in Heaven*. The war memorial is as priapic as it is commemorative, and points to a pantheistic and unorthodox element in Spencer's quasi-religious art.

The FIRST WORLD WAR was formative. After service in the Royal Army Medical Corps he went to Macedonia as an orderly, before joining a front-line unit in 1917. Although briefly appointed an official war artist in 1918 his true war work came later. Engrossed by memories of the front, he sought patrons and a space, and in 1923 entered into negotiations to decorate the Sandham Memorial Chapel at Burghclere in Hampshire, a work finally completed in 1932. Painted on canvas, it is a comprehensive record of the practicalities of soldiering life, and it established Spencer as the artist of British laboring vernacular. On its east wall is a scene of *The Resurrection of the Soldiers*, characteristic of an artist who visualized the present in biblical terms.

Spencer's other great project, *Shipbuilding on the Clyde*, was the result of an official commission awarded in January 1940 which took him to the shipyards of Port Glasgow in May of that year. The first image, *Burners*, was completed in 1940 and was successful when shown at the National Gallery. He continued to work on such other scenes as *Plumbers*, *Riveters*, and *Bending the Keel Plate* until 1943. The pictures, now in the Imperial War Museum, London, recall the murals of Diego Rivera painted in the United States in the early 1930s.

Spencer's tendency was to think, in the medieval manner, in terms of cycles and series, and at Burghclere and in the Lithgow shipyard commission and inclination coincided. Otherwise he was obliged to imagine an overall scheme which might give sense to his production. After Burghclere he envisaged a notional chapel: "The Village Street of Cookham was to be the nave and the river which runs behind the street was a side aisle." The idea of the chapel was more suggestive than programmatic; it helped him envisage Cookham as a sacred site. Spencer's thinking at this time anticipates *arte povera* aesthetics of the 1960s to a quite surprising degree. After the Port Glasgow commission he imagined another project based on the Resurrection. Between 1945 and 1950 he painted four triptychs and the vast *Resurrection: Port Glasgow* now in the Tate Gallery, London.

Although known as an appreciative documentarist of British folk life, Spencer is famous for his unsparing portraits of 1936 and 1937 of himself and his second wife, Patricia Preece. He was, for a while, a practitioner of a kind of pitiless New Objectivity. He either acceded to or denied time. The self-portraits dwell on human ageing. The many resurrection scenes reiterate moments of joyful return. Intent on confronting and on denying time he, for instance, maintained a correspondence with his first wife, Hilda Carline, long after her death in 1950. His visualizations of Cookham as a paradise on earth, and of suburban cemeteries as sites of the resurrection also helped to dissolve strictly quotidian concepts of time, involving the present in a mythic past.

He earned his living mainly as a landscape painter, where his manner was strict and objective. His preference was for quite unspectacular park landscapes and suburban scenes, notable for an orderliness which was at odds with his often turbulent married lives. Despite controversy, however, he was established in the 1950s as Britain's senior painter, marked by the award of a knighthood in 1958.

He can be compared to the sculptor ERIC GILL, with whom he shared a pantheistic and carnal view of religion and an affinity for Indian art. On the other hand, he can also be compared to his contemporary, the photographer Bill Brandt, who also envisaged Britain in near-mythic terms, as an apocalyptic space newly cleared for the business of the Last Judgement.

Ian Jeffrey

Bibliography

Bell, Keith. *Stanley Spencer: A Complete Catalogue of the Paintings.* 1992.

Carline, Richard. *Stanley Spencer at War.* 1978.

Pople, Kenneth. *Stanley Spencer: A Biography.* 1991.

Robinson, Duncan. *Stanley Spencer.* 1990.

Rothenstein, John. *Stanley Spencer The Man: Correspondence and Reminiscences.* 1979.

Spender, Stephen (1909–1995)

Stephen Spender, poet, critic, and essayist, was born into a Liberal family of comfortable means. His father was a journalist and an unsuccessful candidate for Parliament; his uncle was the legendary J.A. Spender, editor of the *Westminster Gazette*. Both of Spender's parents died while he was a troubled and sickly adolescent. The most important figure in his early intellectual development was his maternal grandmother, an affluent second generation German Jewish immigrant of advanced opinions and artistic tastes.

The shy Spender was an indifferent student at University College School, a London day school, Gresham's School, Holt, the Lycée Clemenceau in Nantes, and finally OXFORD. Withdrawn and initially unpopular, Spender declared himself to be unpatriotic, "a pacifist and a socialist, a genius." He later believed that his Oxford years were a waste of time because he simply wanted to write. But at Oxford Spender first met W.H. AUDEN, a major force behind his subsequent literary and political views. At the age of twenty, Auden was already the center of an emerging literary movement, which included CHRISTOPHER ISHERWOOD, C. DAY LEWIS, and LOUIS MAC-NEICE. Auden introduced Spender to Isherwood, who convinced him to go to Germany.

Spender arrived in Hamburg in July 1929, determined to leave Oxford and fulfill his literary aspirations. He was initially enchanted by the freedom and hedonism of the young Germans, but the misery of Weimar Germany in its last years aroused profound feelings of guilt. Spender saw himself as a member of the exploiting class that had brought on the economic disaster that it was unable or unwilling to alleviate. Democracy had failed, Fascism was on the rise, and the only hope seemed to lie in the east, where a new egalitarian society was emerging. Spender was by nature an outsider, a contemplative observer of life, a poet. But Hitler and the nature of the times drove him inexorably in the direction of Communism as the only answer to "The Waste Land." The turning point for Spender and many others was the SPANISH CIVIL WAR.

By 1936 Spender had become a man dedicated to the cause. In *Forward From Liberalism* (1937), a LEFT BOOK CLUB selection, he argued that "Liberals must reconcile Communist social justice with their liberal regard for social freedom, and that they must accept the methods which it might be necessary to use in order to defeat Fascism." Spender toured the Spanish Front, wrote for the *Daily Worker*, and attended the Writers' Congress in Madrid in the summer of 1937. But Spender was always more of a liberal than a dogmatic Marxist; his Communism was "a matter of conscience, not of belief." The comrades bitterly criticized his work, even when he attempted to write Communist propaganda as in the case of *Trial of a Judge* (1938). He soon drifted away from the COMMUNIST PARTY.

Spender's political soul-searching did not inhibit the rise of his literary reputation. By the end of the 1930s he was part of *New Writing* and a recognized member of the "Auden Generation". When the Second World War began, he joined Cyril Connolly to edit *Horizon*, the most influential English periodical of the war years. After the war, Spender continued to write poetry and criticism, but his literary reputation went into a long period of decline. He is still most often thought of as a young writer of the 1930s. Spender's memoirs—*World Within World* (1951), *The Thirties*

and After (1978), and *Journals 1939–1983* (1986)—are likely to be read by critics and historians after his poetry is out of print. Nevertheless, Spender's poems—like Auden's—movingly commit themselves to the "invention of the human city" ("Explorations"); in other words, to civic poetry and to the renewal of public life. One aspect of the project is an attempt to re-define personal subjectivity (as in "Subject: Object: Sentence"); another is to wed private erotic experiences to public order.

Gordon B. Beadle

Bibliography

Hynes, Samuel. *The Auden Generation.* 1976.

Kulkarni, H.B. *Stephen Spender: Poet in Crisis.* 1970.

———. *Stephen Spender, Works and Criticism: An Annotated Bibliography.* 1976.

Leeming, David. *Stephen Spender: A Life in Modernism.* 1999.

Pandey, Surya Nath. *Stephen Spender: A Study of Poetic Growth.* 1982.

Spender, Stephen. *Journals 1939–1983.* 1986.

Sport

Sport is a singular noun in Britain, but under its large umbrella many different activities shelter. Like the British climate, sport had its seasons. The year began with winter and FOOTBALL (soccer), two versions of rugby, union and league, cross-country running, boxing, and HORSE-RACING over the jumps. Spring signaled the start of the flat-racing season and the summer sports of track and field athletics, bowls, CRICKET, golf, TENNIS, and rowing. Angling had its own particular seasons. These were the sports that most players played, that most spectators watched, and that took up most of the space in the newspapers and later on the air time of radio and television. There may have been some slight shifts in popularity and support between the major sports, and badminton, squash, snooker and swimming have all enjoyed popularity since the 1970s. The transport and communications revolution may have distorted the idea of the sporting season, but what sports are played and watched in Britain in the 1990s show a stubborn similarity to the 1890s.

If sport is not a single thing, Britain is not a single place. England, Northern Ireland, Scotland, and Wales all have particular sporting preferences. Curling remains a largely Scottish game. Golf remains strongly associated with Scotland, some districts having four or five times the British average per capita number of golf clubs. Professional rugby league called itself the Northern Union until 1922, and its strength remains in the northern counties of Lancashire and Yorkshire, though it has been played for fun more widely in the last twenty years. Cricket is most popular in the southeastern counties of

Kent, Surrey, Oxfordshire, Cambridgeshire, Sussex, and Essex and in the north, in Yorkshire. Sport in twentieth-century Britain has contributed to and reflected local, regional, and national identities. Many sports had separate national organizations, English, Irish, Scottish and Welsh. The England-Scotland football match, one of the first international sporting events, was played almost every year from 1872 until 1989. It increasingly became an opportunity to celebrate Scottishness and to express dislike of the economically, numerically, politically, and socially dominant English. The same opportunity was provided by Rugby Union in Wales.

Sport also played an important role in the British Empire, both cementing ties with the mother country and fuelling local national feeling. Cricket test matches began with Australia in 1876–7, South Africa 1888–9, West Indies 1928, New Zealand 1929–30, India 1932, and Pakistan in 1954. In track and field the British Empire Games was founded in 1930. As the British Empire and Commonwealth Games, from 1952, and since 1970, the Commonwealth Games, it takes place every four years in a different Commonwealth country. Sport became an important British export and an ideological package. Fair play and sportsmanship were regarded as making sports worthwhile. These ideas were accompanied by an amateur tradition which is in decline but still capable of occasional vigor.

At the beginning of the twentieth century it was only a slight exaggeration to say that sport was played, run, and written about by gentlemen. It had long been important in public schools where sport was thought to shape character by stressing the sacrifice of self-interest for the good of the team in a context of competition. Fair play meant not only sticking to the letter of the rules but their spirit as well. It involved self-control and accepting winning or losing with equal modesty. Sporting clubs could exclude all those who had not been to the right schools and did not know how to play the game.

There were many working-class amateurs, but they rarely mixed with their better off colleagues off the field or the track. And gentlemen did not need to play for money. The man who did found himself either totally excluded or rigorously controlled. Before the 1960s hired hands were never allowed anywhere near the Jockey Club, the MCC (Marylebone Cricket Club), the National Sporting Club, and rarely the Football Association. English rowing was split into two organizations largely because the Amateur Rowing Association adhered to a draconian definition of amateurism which excluded working men. The two bodies did not merge until 1956. In track and field athletics the professional was outlawed and

marginalized. In English football he was confined by a maximum wage and his freedom to change employers severely restricted. In county cricket most of the hard work—the bowling—was done by professionals. Many batsmen and all captains before 1945 were amateurs. The amateur gentlemen were called Mr. and often had a separate dressing room. The professionals had inferior accommodation and were known by their family names. A professional did not captain the English cricket team until 1952. The categories amateur and professional or Gentlemen and Players, were not abolished until 1962.

Such class distinctions seemed somewhat anachronistic after the Second World War and the ideas of a fairer society which had generated the welfare state. Fewer gentlemen could afford the time to practice and train in order to play at the highest level. Some took generous expense allowances, yet still maintained their amateur status. "Shamateurism" provoked much criticism which gradually had its effect. The year 1968 saw the first open Wimbledon. The FA amateur cup, which started in 1894, was competed for for the last time in 1974. In 1982 track and field athletes were allowed trust funds to store appearance money, sponsorship, and advertising fees. By 1992 even the elite of the aggressively amateur Rugby Union were being allowed to exploit their fame and prowess for money. The amateur tradition at its best stood for a more balanced approach to sport and a better way of playing it. But at its worst it promoted snobbery and hypocrisy. In Britain it also held back the tide of commercialization of sport until the last twenty-five years.

Sport was and has remained a voluntary activity. But several factors combined to attract the attention of the state. Local governments were able to spend taxpayers' money on public parks, but playing sport in them was not usually allowed. It was not until the Public Health Act of 1907 that facilities for cricket and football specifically and "any other games or recreation" were mentioned as worthy items on which local authorities might spend their money. In the next half century or so many did so. But there was never enough supply of playing fields to meet the demand.

By the 1930s sport was becoming more international. The Fascist governments in Germany and Italy made it clear that sport was the business of the state and deliberately sought the prestige which success in international sport could bring. Anxieties about the condition of the nation during the Great Depression also contributed to the first tentative action by the British Parliament, the Physical Training Act of 1937. Money released under this Act paid for some of the first

generation of post-war athletic coaches. Perhaps
more significant was that the 1944 EDUCATION
ACT made it compulsory for state schools to include sport in the curriculum.

Sport itself also began to clamor for a greater
share of state resources. For much of the twentieth century there was no organization that represented British sport as a whole. The British
Olympic Assocation was founded in 1905, but its
sole concern was to liaise with the bodies which
ran individual sports in order to select Olympic
teams. In 1935 a number of these organizations
joined together in the Central Council of Recrea-
tive Physical Training—later renamed the Central Council of Physical Recreation. It was the
CCPR that set up its own inquiry into the state
and future of British sport in 1957. It followed
twelve post-war years of under-achievement on
the field and the erosion of facilities off it. The
Wolfenden Report suggested a Sports Development Council, and the reforming Labour government set up the Sports Council in 1965. By
1971 it had received a Royal Charter and was trying both to encourage participation in sport and
improve the standards of British elite performers. It dispensed taxpayers' money to individual
sports and presided over a considerable increase
in facilities with, for example, the twenty-seven
Sports Centres of 1972 becoming 770 in 1981.
MARGARET THATCHER's governments showed
that there was a price to be paid for state aid
when she asked the leaders of the various sports
to support her government's protest at the Soviet
invasion of Afghanistan by boycotting the Moscow Olympics in 1980. Most competitors defied
her, as did some Sports Council officials who
later lost their jobs.

By the end of the twentieth century more men,
and especially women, were enjoying sport than
ever before. Although it is unlikely that crowds at
sporting events will return to the heights of 1945–
9, only outdoor pop concerts attract more people
and on many fewer occasions. Color television has
altered the relationship between sport and the
public especially by its encouragement of commercial sponsorship, only £2.5 million in 1971 but
more than £200 million in 1992. Gambling also
makes a large financial contribution, notably to
horse-racing and football. Sport is an industry, the
making of sports goods big business. But it is also
a passion among a significant minority of the
British population and remains an important part
of the British way of life.

Tony Mason

Bibliography
Holt, Richard. *Sport and the British.* 1989.
———, and Tony Mason. *Sport in Britain 1945–2000.*
2000.
Mason, Tony, ed. *Sport in Britain: A Social History.* 1989.

Spy Novel, British

The origins of the modern British spy novel,
which has enjoyed bestseller status since 1900,
can be traced to a confluence of developments:
the rise of mass literacy in nineteenth-century
Britain; the emergence of new forms of popular
literature, epecially serialized stories in mass circulation newspapers and journals; and a climate
of fear surrounding Britain's global security and
future as a great power. The subject matter of the
spy novel was uniquely a product of the political
climate in Britain at the turn of the century. That
climate was a compound of anxieties about the
societal implications of fast-paced economic and
political change at home and about the destabilizing effects of the rise of foreign powers such as
Germany. The spy hero emerged as a fictional device that built on the existing genres of adventure
and DETECTIVE FICTION, but operated as a new
kind of hero with a political mission: nothing less
than the rescue of British civilization from the
destruction of war and from foreign barbarisms.
Obviously functioning as a form of political escapism as well as a form of political anxiety, the
spy genre has been the product of British writers
primarily.

The first generation of spy fiction writers,
most notably Erskine Childers (1870–1922), William le Queux (1864–1927), E. Phillips Oppenheim (1866–1946), and John Buchan (1875–1940),
established some of the genre's trademark features in the decade before the outbreak of the
First World War. They wrote male adventure
stories with a strongly patriotic and moralizing
bent. Their heroes belonged to imagined intelligence communities whose scope and power far
surpassed the historical reality. The fiction preceded the reality and began that process which
saw the intertwining of popular culture images of
espionage with revolutionary changes in the nature of intelligence services themselves. The
bridge between the fiction and the reality has
subsequently been sustained by the intermingling
of careers in writing and espionage, first seen in
the case of John Buchan.

But even before writers like Buchan could
bring a degree of earned verisimilitude to their
fiction, pioneers like William le Queux, with his
prodigious output, had established one of the enduring features of British spy fiction—namely
the deliberate blurring of fiction and fact, using
some of the standard devices of the historical
novel, but more blatantly foregrounding the hero,
and often the author, as narrator of a thinly disguised reality. Le Queux loudly proclaimed himself as a master spy and had his characters, in
novels such as the dramatic *Spies of the Kaiser*
(1909), narrate tales supposedly freshly gathered
from the secret chancelleries of Europe.

Fantasies of espionage as a symbol of darker fears of societal survival were displaced in the years after the First World War by a literature that fed on both sensationalized memoir accounts of spy missions during the conflict and on more personally grounded experience. John Buchan contributed the Hannay series of four novels *(The Thirty-Nine Steps, Greenmantle, Mr. Standfast, and The Three Hostages)*, the writing of which spanned the years 1915 to 1924, and which allowed him to build on his experience of imperial politics, on personalities such as Aubrey Herbert and General Ironside (models for Hannay), and on Buchan's wartime involvement with British intelligence. Writers such as Compton Mackenzie and SOMERSET MAUGHAM drew even more directly than Buchan on an insider's knowledge of British espionage—Mackenzie served with the wartime British secret service in Greece, while Maugham was engaged on an improbable mission to spy out the nature of the new Bolshevik leadership in Russia in 1918.

It was Maugham who first established higher literary credentials for the spy novel in his set of linked stories, *Ashenden* (1927). Arguably, Maugham's effort to undermine the device of "faction" (the overlaying of fact and fiction) had little impact on the development of the genre as a whole; the double act of the espionage agent and the spy writer remained potent. Of more significance was the way in which Maugham introduced a new element to the spy narrative, namely a concern with the ethics of spying. His depiction of a world of spy master Machiavellis, and their oppressed and sometimes innocent victims, established a troubling discourse with which spy writers since Maugham's day have struggled, often unsuccessfully. Indirectly, *Ashenden* also helped lay the foundation for the most significant development in inter-war spy fiction.

The 1930s novels of Eric Ambler (1909–98) and GRAHAM GREENE transformed the political landscape against which previous British spy fiction had been written. Moving beyond Maugham's Machiavellian world, Ambler and Greene fashioned a new kind of spy novel out of political struggle between the forces of Left and extreme Right, often fought out on the home front (as in Greene's *The Confidential Agent* (1939). The heroes in Ambler and Greene were figures on the political Left, acting out the drama of the Popular Front strategy of the 1930s. Political oppression at home, creeping totalitarianism, and fear of war gave the new spy novel of the 1930s a darker tone, with radically altered definitions of what constituted global threats and political decency, as compared with the spy novel of pre-1914 days.

A post-war reaction to Ambler and Greene was heralded by the popular success of the Ian

Fleming (1908–64) series of James Bond novels. Fleming's writing was untroubled by moral concerns; his political backdrop a hearty and patriotic caricature of the Cold War. The Bond novels attempted, very succesfully, to return the genre to its roots in simple political adventure and civilization-saving. The Bond novels also featured large dollops of exotic travel, sex, and brand-name consumerism.

Fleming's monopoly on the spy fiction market was destined to be brief, not least because the genre already contained a historical reminder of alternative narratives. The 1960s saw the takeover bids of Len Deighton (1929–), starting with *The Ipcress File* (1962) and John le Carré (1931–), with *The Spy Who Came in from the Cold* (1963), both rooted in echoes of Ambler and Greene of the 1930s. Deighton and Le Carré reintroduced morality, left-wing politics, and angst into the spy novel, while retaining the sure foundations of adventure, cautionary tale, and heroic endeavor by individuals who prove to be historic forces in their own right. Le Carré's most enduring fictional hero, George Smiley, battles on the literal front lines of the Cold War while growing ever more reflective about the role of human agency, morality, and political purpose, a trend which culminates in *The Secret Pilgrim* (1991). Le Carré remains the standard by which contemporary spy fiction writing is judged; he has also proclaimed fiercely that spy fiction has a future in the post-Cold War world. The proof he offers is *The Night Manager* (1993), which targets the arms traders and the Thatcherite *nouveau riche* as the new villains and the new conspirators against order and good.

Wesley K. Wark

Bibliography

Bennett, Tony, and Janet Woollacott. *Bond and Beyond: The Political Career of a Popular Hero.* 1987.

Cawelti, John G., and Bruce A. Rosenberg. *The Spy Story.* 1987.

Denning, Michael. *Cover Stories: Narrative and Ideology in the British Spy Thriller.* 1987.

Stafford, David. *The Silent Game. The Real World of Imaginary Spies.* 1988.

Wark, Wesley K., ed. *Spy Fiction, Spy Films and Real Intelligence.* 1991

Standard of Living

Sustained and almost continuous economic growth in Britain since 1900 has led to a great increase in average real incomes. These higher incomes have allowed people to buy more and better food, HOUSING, LEISURE, and good HEALTH, all of which have contributed to an overall rise in living standards. This improvement in living standards has led to the virtual disappearance from Britain of diseases associated with malnutrition, such as rickets, but there remain great differences between the living standards of the richest and poorest groups in society.

Direct measures of changes in living standards over time are problematic because many goods and services that contribute to today's overall standard of living, such as television or air travel, have no direct equivalents in the early years of the century. One common way to circumvent this problem is to compare the monetary value of national income per capita, adjusted for changes in the price level over time. Using constant 1990 prices, national income per capita has risen from around £2000 in 1900 to £2500 in 1930, £4000 in 1960 and £9000 in 1990. By this measure, the average Briton was over four times better off in 1990 than in 1900.

This improvement has not meant that spending power has increased at the same rate. The average weekly earnings of an adult male manual worker in 1900 were £1 8s. (£1.40), which equals £63 in 1990 prices, whereas the average male manual worker in 1990 actually earned £214 per week. Up to 1940, however, manual workers paid no direct (income) tax, but since then virtually all earners have had to pay tax on their income which has reduced their spending power. The post-tax income of the representative manual worker in 1990 was about £160, or two and a half times greater than in 1900. Some economic growth appears to have been "lost" from the worker's earnings, but this has mainly been paid in taxes and used by governments to extend the range of services provided by the state, services which have played a major role in increasing living standards. Better and more extensive education and health care, together with comprehensive income support for the sick, the old, and the unemployed are the most obvious manifestations of this public provision, but tax revenue has also been used to extend the road network, construct the electricity supply system, and so on.

Higher incomes have allowed people much more choice over spending, and so have provided the necessary economic foundation for a modern consumer society. Yet this consumer society is not simply a consequence of economic growth; it has also been encouraged by a profound demographic change which has seen average family size (fertility) fall from 3.4 children per woman in 1900 to 2.0 children in 1940 and 1.8 in 1990. In 1900 over a quarter of married women under forty-five had five or more children, but by 1940 fewer than one in ten had very large families. Since largeness of family was found by Seebohm Rowntree in his social study of York in 1900 to be the second most important cause of poverty (after low wages), it is clear that the decline in fertility has contributed to the overall improvement of family living standards. Smaller families have also allowed more

married women to engage in paid employment and so contribute to family income; up to 1940 about 10 percent of married women were in work, but this figure increased sharply during the war and stood at 26 percent in 1951, rising to 62 percent by 1981. Higher family incomes have resulted, but this may have been at the cost of other, less easily measurable, welfare criteria; by the mid-1970s most mothers with dependent children were in paid (usually part-time) employment, and an increasing amount of child care was being carried out by paid helpers.

Smaller families and higher incomes together have led to a substantial improvement in housing conditions. Overcrowding—defined as more than 1.5 persons per room—affected one in six households in England and Wales in 1911 but by 1966 was a problem for only one in eighty. The quantitative increase in living space has been matched by a qualitative improvement in housing amenities, which itself reflects both higher incomes and technical change. In 1951 over a third of households possessed neither a bath or shower, but thirty-five years later these fittings were practically universal. Such changes have had a significant impact on the way people live their lives; homes are now more comfortable, and allow more privacy for all family members, than ever before. Homes are also more likely to be owned by their occupiers; before the First World War the great majority of all households, whatever their income level and social class, rented their homes, and even in 1961 it was still more normal to rent than to own. By 1990, however, two-thirds of houses were owner-occupied, and real estate had become the most valuable of all personal assets.

The improvement in housing conditions has been permitted in part by a reduction in the proportion of income that has had to be spent on food. In the late nineteenth century it seems that working-class households spent over half their weekly income on food, compared with 30 percent in 1957 and less than 20 percent by 1990. At the same time diets have become more varied, not only because of higher income but also because of new food technology, new sources of overseas supply and new tastes. More extensive foreign travel since the 1960s, particularly for Mediterranean holidays, has introduced many people to a less bland cuisine than was the norm in post-war Britain, and the simultaneous development of local Indian, Chinese, and Italian restaurants has made exotic flavors available on almost every high street. High streets themselves have changed as rising incomes have transformed shopping from being a necessary subsistence chore into a major leisure activity focused on the purchase of fashion clothes, consumer durables, cars, and holidays.

Not everyone has benefited to the same degree in this overall improvement in living standards. There are still very large differences in the economic resources and living standards of different groups in Britain, and although welfare provision has prevented the old, the sick, and the unemployed from becoming even poorer, it has certainly not made them rich. The poorer half of the population in 1949 received about one quarter of total after-tax income, and after forty years of comprehensive welfare provision and redistributive taxation they still receive almost exactly the same proportion. There have, however, been some changes within this poorer group. Until the early 1970s, to be old in Britain meant to be poor, with the elderly dominating poverty statistics; in 1990 it was young families headed by unemployed males or by single parents who were the worst off. Although these groups have living standards much higher than the poorest people in 1900, nevertheless their income is not sufficient to allow them to engage in the modern consumerist activities of dining out, traveling abroad, buying a home, or accumulating durable goods.

The substantial increase in real incomes in twentieth-century Britain has not necessarily made people more satisfied with life. At an individual level the rising ownership rates of consumer durables such as video recorders or washing machines may have reduced the relative contentment of that diminishing proportion of the population whose poverty precludes purchase. At the national level the relatively poor performance of the British economy since the Second World War compared with those of France and Germany may have created a more general dissatisfaction with living standards. Since there is no necessary or direct relationship between affluence and happiness, it is not appropriate to draw conclusions about living standards simply from quantitative evaluations of income or spending patterns. There is, however, one indicator which is unambiguous—life expectancy. In 1900 154 of every 1000 infants died within a year of their birth. By 1939 better nutrition, housing conditions, and medical care had reduced this number to fifty-one, and by the mid-1980s it had fallen to only ten. Over this same period life expectancy at birth has risen from an average of forty-eight to seventy-five years. Whether people in 1990 were happier than people in 1900 we cannot say, but they were certainly better clothed, better housed, better fed and longer-lived.

Paul Johnson

Bibliography

Burnett, John. *A Social History of Housing 1815–1985.* 2nd ed. 1986.

———. *Plenty and Want.* 3rd ed. 1989.

Steel Industry

In 1900 Britain ranked third among the world's steel producers, having been surpassed in turn during the previous decade by the United States and Germany; her own and their respective shares of world tonnage were 36 percent, 23 percent and 18 percent. By 1990 Britain ranked tenth the world with 2.3 percent of the output; the United States produced 11.6 percent and Germany 5.4 percent. Throughout the century the industry has struggled to reshape its inheritance of too many, too small, and sometimes inadequately equipped works operating in locations better suited to nineteenth-century conditions. Although steel continued to be regarded as one of the "commanding heights" of the national economy, its leaders lacked opportunity, capital, or sometimes resolution to change all these adverse conditions at the same time or sufficiently. Even so, by the end of the 1980s, the British steel industry was again one of the most technically efficient in the world.

Since the Industrial Revolution the steel industry had benefited from abundant, easily accessible mineral resources. Home ore and fuel supported iron production in distinct districts from mid-Scotland to South Wales. In wrought iron and later in steel there was strong regional product specialization. Northeast England, Scotland, and Lincolnshire concentrated on heavy products, notably plate, angles, and structurals. South Wales made rails for world markets throughout the Victorian age, but then gradually concentrated on its old specialty of tinplate, to which was added sheet and strip. The northwest coast district of Cumbria, always prominent in steel rails, now contains the only rail mill in Britain. South Lancashire and West Yorkshire had major portions of the wire trade. Tubular products came mainly from the Black Country of the West Midlands and from central Scotland. Sheffield has always been exceptional, not so much for the forms of its finished products as for their quality. It has had a quite disproportionate share of special and alloy steel production. Since 1900 it has normally turned out only 11 to 14 percent of national output by tonnage, but about half by value. During the present century some of these regional specializations have been modified. In the 1930s for instance, the search for lower cost material brought much of the bulk tube trade to the orefields of Northamptonshire where the Basic Bessemer process was reintroduced: thirty years later the development focus for tubes shifted to Teeside in Northeast England. In the late 1950s, as shipbuilding declined, and in the hope of encouraging new, consumer durable industries, the traditionally heavy emphasis of Scottish steel was lightened by the construction of a hot strip mill.

Throughout the first third of the twentieth century, with the exception of the First World War, a persistent problem was foreign competition. This was not confined to traditional outlets overseas, but involved large imports to home markets. In 1932 the free trade principles under which the industry had always operated were abandoned, and an *ad valorem* import duty of 33.33 percent was imposed. In return for protection, the industry committed itself to create a new, stronger, central organization, the British Iron and Steel Federation (BISF), and to a rationalization program. To maximize efficiency it was intended that reconstruction, though financed by private companies, should be coordinated. Mergers, concentration of production, plant closures and a good deal of new construction were carried through before the outbreak of the Second World War. However most old companies survived, and the limited nature of their cooperation as well as the large number of plants sub-optimal in location, size, and equipment limited the achievement. Those who, usually from the outside, had advocated massive demolition and a new start proved to have been far too simplistic. By 1939 some twenty-two integrated steelworks, and many more not linked with iron making, were involved in that year's record production of 13.4 million tons.

Well before the war ended active planning for more far-reaching and fully coordinated reconstruction was underway. A series of development plans were carried through between 1945 and the mid-1960s. The first fifteen years of this period were in some ways uniquely favorable; demand was rising, and indeed apparently insatiable, and for a time the industry was operating in world markets from which some leading competitors had been removed by war and its aftermath. Production rose rapidly, though still largely within the old constraints of companies and locations. In 1955 20.1 million tons of steel were produced. The industry still had twenty-two integrated works as well as at least twenty-seven other plants each making more than 100,000 tons of steel. In these post-war programs there were a number of major "brownfield" developments, essentially new works grafted onto existing complexes of plants, though sometimes far exceeding in size what was there before—Port Talbot, Ravenscraig, Lackenby and redevelopment at Scunthorpe. There was only one wholly new, "greenfield" development, the works at Newport, South Wales, built between 1959 and 1962.

At the end of the 1950s trade recession and revived competition from old rivals brought the first serious check to increasing output. Matters then improved, so that by 1964, at 26.6 million metric tons Britain was producing twice as much steel as in any pre-war year and over five times the

output of 1900. Shortly after, the industry's organization was dramatically changed. Long a subject of keen political dispute, it was first nationalized in 1951; there was a speedy return to private ownership under the incoming CONSERVATIVE administration. In the summer of 1967 the fourteen major companies—defined as those producing over 500,000 tons of steel annually—were again nationalized under the title of the British Steel Corporation. The remaining firms, producing over 2 million tons of steel, but in a multitude of generally small works, remained privately owned. This sector contained much of the Sheffield special steel industry. Over the next few years, the independent industry grew more rapidly than British Steel with which it collaborated in a few joint ventures.

BSC began operations with thirty-nine works making steel, of which twenty-two were integrated with blast furnaces. In a world that already contained works of 12 million tons annual capacity or more, British Steel was recognized as needing still more concentration. For its first seven or eight years it was believed that progress towards a planned system of fewer, bigger, better located works would be eased by an overall large-scale expansion of capacity. Instead, deep recession led to abandonment of these plans, to reductions of national capacity and to plant and other closure programs more radical than any that had gone before. The twenty-two integrated works with which BSC had begun work were reduced to five by the mid-1980s. By the end of 1992 there were only four of them. Home production of iron ore, which reached a twentieth century peacetime peak of 17.4 million metric tons in 1960 shrank rapidly after the mid-1960s and has practically ceased. Coking coal came wholly from British mines until 1970; now it is procured mainly from overseas. The British Steel workforce fell from 257,000 at the time of NATIONALIZATION to 47,000 by the first half of 1991. Production has fallen much less, from 23.3 million metric tons in 1967 to 17 million in 1990.

Despite its traumatic twentieth-century career, the industry's heritage is still important. Only one of the five sites for integrated works with which it entered the 1990s had been developed from a green field since 1900. Steelmaking began around Ravenscraig in the 1870s, Scunthorpe derives from an iron making site of the mid-1860s, Teesside from 1851, and there has been iron making and later a steel industry in the neighborhood of Port Talbot since the mid-nineteenth century. The ideal location for today's bulk steel plants is at a deepwater ore dock, but of the present five plants only Port Talbot and Redcar have ore docks next to their furnace stockyards. Scunthorpe and Ravenscraig must haul their ore from ore terminals respectively twenty-two and forty-seven miles from the iron works. Newport is at tidewater, but has no terminal of its own, instead drawing its ore through the Port Talbot docks forty-five miles away.

As a result of the draconian changes of the last fifteen years, Britain's steel industry has become one of the most efficient in the western world. BSC was returned to private ownership in 1988. Having suffered heavy losses in the late 1970s and early 1980s, for a time in the late 1980s it made large profits, but then, in the sharp recession of the early 1990s, it again fell into the red. Study of its longer term development shows that it is difficult but not impossible to modernize an old industrial structure. When the task is carried through, the result may be a revitalized, even a world-competitive industry. However its economic history and past geography cannot be wholly erased.

Kenneth Warren

Bibliography

Burn, Duncan L. *The Economic History of Steelmaking, 1867–1939.* 1961.

Carr, James C., and Walter Taplin. *History of the British Steel Industry.* 1962.

McCloskey, Donald N. *Economic Maturity and Entrepreneurial Decline: British Iron and Steel, 1870–1913.* 1973.

Tolliday, Steven. *Business, Banking and Politics: The Case of British Steel, 1918–1939.* 1987.

Vaizey, John. *The History of British Steel.* 1974.

Stopes, Marie Charlotte Carmichael (1880–1958)

The preeminence of Marie Stopes in shaping a new cultural consensus about sex and reproduction in the 1920s can hardly be overestimated, as she herself would have been quick to agree. Her flair for public controversy and her numerous books on BIRTH CONTROL, sexuality, and motherhood made her the best-known British champion of women's right to birth control and marital satisfaction. Her works include *Married Love* (1918), *Wise Parenthood* (1918), *A Letter to Working Mothers* (1919), and *Radiant Motherhood* (1920).

Stopes was born in Edinburgh into a middle-class family dedicated to learning. Her father, Henry Stopes (1851–1902), was an enthusiastic amateur archaeologist whose work failed to find approval in the academy. Her mother, Charlotte Carmichael Stopes (1840–1929), a passionate suffragist, attained considerable distinction as a Shakespeare scholar, writer, and literary lecturer. Stopes's own career as a palaeobotanist and attainment of doctoral degrees from both London and Munich were perhaps undertaken to win the academic laurels denied her parents. She quickly gained a reputation as an able scientist, in 1904 becoming the first woman appointed lecturer in botany at the University of Manchester.

Convinced by her unconsummated first marriage that the majority of men and women were ignorant of the endless possibilities for conjugal bliss—as she had been before reading up on the subject in the British Museum—Stopes published *Married Love* in 1918. This paean to marital sexuality included little information on contraception, but it evoked so many inquiries that she wrote and published *Wise Parenthood* later the same year. The latter, besides supplying practical birth control information, argued that contraception was an essential component of Christian marriage, social harmony, and progress for the British "race."

Both books were sensationally successful. Almost overnight Stopes became Britain's foremost arbiter of sexual knowledge. During the next four decades she received, and answered, thousands of letters asking for advice on sexual matters, published the *Birth Control News,* and wrote about a dozen books on related subjects. In 1921, with her prosperous second husband, aviation pioneer H.V. Roe (1879–1949), she opened the Mother's Clinic in North London to provide birth control to poor women. She also launched the Society for Constructive Birth Control and Racial Progress to pressure the Ministry of Health to give contraceptive services at maternal and infant welfare centers.

Stopes and her organization ceased to be a political force by the 1930s, but her cultural influence persisted through book sales and her knack for self-publicity. Although most of her ideas were not new, she combined disparate elements in original ways. Erotic rapture was expressed in religious images of spiritual bonding, while advice on sex technique was proffered in the frank (and, at the time, shocking) vocabulary of scientific discourse. Moreover, Stopes's message of the "radiant motherhood" that would result from women's freedom to determine when to bear children was conventional enough to fit within the inter-war renewal of a domestic ideology; it also included a strong element of pronatalism to assuage fears of population decline.

Stopes's idiosyncratic and sometimes confused social philosophy enabled her to represent a number of contradictory strands. Her vision appealed not only to women seeking reproductive freedom and enhanced health but to physicians, eugenists, clergymen, population scientists, and "respectable" people on all sides of the political spectrum. She saw no reason to doubt that all these constituencies would follow her once they understood the scientific, social, and religious bases of her "new gospel." Yet, in the end, Stopes was more successful at changing private attitudes toward women's sexuality than she was at influencing public policy.

Roberta A. Clark

Bibliography
Hall, Ruth. *Marie Stopes: A Biography*. 1977.
Leathard, Audrey. *The Fight for Family Planning: The Development of Family Planning Services in Britain, 1921–74*. 1980.
Rose, June. *Marie Stopes and the Sexual Revolution*. 1992.
Soloway, Richard Allen. *Birth Control and the Population Question in England, 1877–1930*. 1982.
Weeks, Jeffrey. *Sex, Politics and Society: The Regulation of Sexuality Since 1800*. 2nd ed., 1989.

Stoppard, Tom (1937–)

The playwright Tom Stoppard, born Tomas Straussler in Zlin, Czechoslovakia, is the author of *Rosencrantz and Guildenstern Are Dead* (1967), *Jumpers* (1972), *Travesties* (1974), *Night and Day* (1978), *The Real Thing* (1982), *Arcadia* (1993), and *The Invention of Love* (1997). His plays have earned commercial and critical success and have won Tony and New York Drama Critics Circle awards in the United States, the Shakespeare Award, Laurence Olivier and *Plays and Players* awards in Britain, and the Prix Italia. Stoppard has also won an Oscar nomination as co-author of the original screenplay of *Brazil* (1990). He has written numerous radio and television plays and several other screenplays, including the adaptations of Vladimir Nabokov's *Despair* (1978), J.G. Ballard's *Empire of the Sun* (1987), John le Carre's *The Russia House* (1989), and E.L. Doctorow's *Billy Bathgate* (1991); he has also freely adapted several stage plays: Ferenc Molnar's *Rough Crossing* (1984) and Arthur Schnitzler's *Undiscovered Country* (1984) and *Dalliance* (1986). Stoppard's attempt at film direction, his adaptation of *Rosencrantz and Guildenstern* (1991), won the Grand Prize at the Venice Film Festival. Since 1989 he has served on the Royal National Theatre Board.

In 1939 Eugene Straussler, Stoppard's father, moved the family from his native Czechoslovakia to Singapore where, in 1942, he was killed. His wife and sons were evacuated to India. In India, Stoppard's English mother, Martha, met and married a major with the British ARMY, Kenneth Stoppard. The family moved to Nottinghamshire after the war and later to Bristol. After leaving school, Stoppard worked as a newspaper reporter and reviewer, experience that likely figured in his writing of *Night and Day* (1978) which deals with journalistic responsibility. He did not attend university.

Stoppard's youthful career as a theatre reviewer left him with an encyclopedic knowledge of theatre and stagecraft. Influenced equally by Oscar Wilde and SAMUEL BECKETT, he offers the unlikely combination of entertainment and intellectuality in his works, which are characterized by pyrotechnic wordplay and a highly allusive, self-referential exploitation of dramatic traditions. His early plays interpolate dialogue and characters from the canon of great drama: *Rosencrantz and Guildenstern* draws directly upon *Hamlet*; *Travesties* upon Wilde's *The Importance of Being Earnest*. His later plays are comedies of ideas: philosophy is the subject of *Jumpers*; aesthetics, of *Travesties*; physics, of *Hapgood* (1988); mathematics and literary sleuthing, of *Arcadia*; classics and the Victorian academic world, of *The Invention of Love*.

Unlike mainstream post-war British writers and dramatists, Stoppard does not chronicle the decline and despair of Britain, but affirms what he identifies as the traditions of "Western liberal democracy, favouring an intellectual elite and a progressive middle class and based on a moral order derived from Christian absolutes." Stoppard has actively campaigned for human rights in Eastern Europe, a commitment that appears in *Cahoot's Macbeth* (1979), the television play *Professional Foul* (1977), and *Every Good Boy Deserves Favour* (1977). He received a knighthood in 1997.

Joan FitzPatrick Dean

Bibliography
Corballis, Richard. *Stoppard: The Mystery and the Clockwork*. 1984.
Dean, Joan FitzPatrick. *Tom Stoppard: Comedy as a Moral Matrix*. 1981.
Tynan, Kenneth. *Show People*. 1979.
Whitaker, Thomas R. *Tom Stoppard*. 1983.

Strachey, John (1901–1963)

In the 1930s John Strachey was preeminent as a pro-Communist propagandist and theorist. He was the most widely-read Marxist writing in English, almost as well-known in the United States as in Britain. However, he had already changed his political affiliations several times, and subsequently shifted again. He rejoined the LABOUR PARTY in 1942 and became Under-Secretary of State for Air, and then Minister for Food, finally Secretary of State for War, in the ATTLEE governments of 1945–51. During the 1950s he gradually moved towards the REVISIONIST right-wing of the party and, had he not died prematurely, he would certainly have achieved high office in the WILSON government.

Educated at Eton and OXFORD, and the son of the editor and owner of the *Spectator*, Strachey was brought up in a conventional "Establishment" environment. However, he joined the Labour Party in 1923 and was adopted a candidate for a Birmingham constituency the next year. He was unsuccessful in the election, but observed, with dismay, the failure of the short-lived Labour government to make any real impact on the stagnating economy. He collaborated closely with OSWALD MOSLEY in campaigning for a more radical, expansionist approach, and his first book, *Revolution by Reason* (1925), provided a theoretical rationale for such ideas. In this book he argued that, by combining increases in the money supply with economic redistribution and the establishment of a state planning body, it was possible both to provide an incentive to manufacturers and to help the working classes. The book revealed Strachey's unusual qualities as a popularizer of complex theories and established him as a thinker who was attempting to find a new strategy for democratic socialism.

The 1926 GENERAL STRIKE affected him deeply, and he immersed himself in the workers' cause, becoming the editor of both the ILP's *Socialist Review* and the *Miner*. He was elected to Parliament when the second Labour government assumed office in 1929, and acted as Parliamentary Private Secretary for Mosley who now had special responsibility for UNEMPLOYMENT policy. Both of them resigned in May 1930, when the CABINET rejected Mosley's expansionist program in favor of economic orthodoxy, and early the next year they left the Labour Party to form the New Party. However, Strachey wanted to establish a left-wing movement, and he abandoned the New Party in July 1931 when he discerned Mosley's growing sympathy for FASCISM. This episode, and the subsequent collapse of the Labour government, led him to reject reformist ideas. He had been attracted to Marxism since the latter half of the 1920s and now embraced it as the solution to the problems of the era. His application to join the COMMUNIST PARTY (CPGB) in the summer of 1932 was rejected—because he was regarded as an unreliable intellectual—but for the rest of the decade he effectively wrote and worked as a Communist.

The essential factor in Strachey's outstanding success as a propagandist in these years was his extraordinary ability as a writer. He was able to mount a compelling argument on a theme that addressed the most fundamental problems of the times. For example, in *The Coming Struggle for Power* (1932) he conveyed one urgent message across a vast range of subject matter: that capitalism would lead to barbarism, while Communism was the hope for the world. In 1936 he secured a still wider audience when he joined VICTOR GOLLANCZ and HAROLD LASKI in forming the LEFT BOOK CLUB and became its most popular author. *The Theory and Practice of Socialism* (1936) was the most influential book ever produced by the Club, and *Why You Should be a Socialist* (1938) sold more than 250,000 copies within two months of its publication.

Yet by 1938 Strachey was beginning to change course again, for Keynesian economic theory and the experience of the New Deal led him to believe that capitalism might be reformed. He expressed this view in *A Programme for Progress* (1940)—a book that was criticized by the CPGB hierarchy. When he thought that the Communists were prepared to see Britain defeated by Nazism, he could stand it no longer, and in April 1940 he broke with the party. Shortly afterwards, he joined the RAF and spent the latter part of the war as a propagandist for the Air Ministry.

As Minister of Food from 1946 Strachey was unlucky to bear the brunt of the criticism for the abortive attempt to grow groundnuts in East Africa. He returned to writing after the CONSERVATIVES were returned to power in 1951, and his *Contemporary Capitalism* (1956) was a major work of democratic socialist theory that combined KEYNES and Marx to explore the current situation. He concluded that the inherent conflict between capitalism and democracy could be contained and controlled by a purposeful government that understood the dynamics of the economic system. This text was complemented by *The End of Empire* (1959), a timely book that sought to demonstrate that imperialism was unjust to its victims and unnecessary for the economies of its beneficiaries. However, in his final years Strachey became more conventional in his political outlook. A supporter of Anglo-American NUCLEAR WEAPONS policy, he was a bitter opponent of CND and his last book, *On the Prevention of War* (1962), was influenced by current deterrence theories.

Strachey's reputation has suffered because of his volatility, and because his work did not fit neatly into the reformist or Marxist traditions. However, he was consistently preoccupied with the problem of UNEMPLOYMENT, and in each of his phases he explained his current thinking to his contemporaries with brilliant clarity. His writing was at its most powerful during his Communist years, but the works in which he tried to find a synthesis between differing theories were more original. In particular, *Contemporary Capitalism* remains an important text of "revisionist" socialism that still deserves to be read alongside C.A.R. CROSLAND's *The Future of Socialism* (1956).

Michael Newman

Bibliography

Newman, Michael. *John Strachey*. 1989.

Thomas, Hugh. *John Strachey*. 1973.

Thompson, Noel. *John Strachey: An Intellectual Biography*. 1993.

Strachey, (Giles) Lytton (1880–1932)

Lytton Strachey, biographer, critic, and member of the BLOOMSBURY GROUP, is best known for his iconoclastic *Eminent Victorians* (1918) in which he questioned the reputations of the Victorian worthies Cardinal Manning, Florence Nightingale, Dr. Thomas Arnold, and General Gordon. In writing these lives he pioneered a form of "new biography", challenging the standard Victorian two-volume life and letters with a more psychologically penetrating approach. His *Queen Victoria*, more fully researched and more sympathetic, followed in 1921. The notably psychologically oriented *Elizabeth and Essex* (1928) was influenced by his brother James's interest in Freud, who Strachey heard speak in Berlin in 1922 and who praised the book for being "steeped in the spirit of psychoanalysis".

Strachey was born in Clapham, London, on 1 March 1880. In 1884 his family (retired colonial administrators) moved to Lancaster Gate, London, the family home until 1907. After attending schools at Poole, Abbotsholme, and Leamington, Strachey entered Liverpool University College in 1897, and then transferred to Trinity College, Cambridge in 1899. In 1902 he was elected 239th Apostle of the elite Cambridge Conversazione Society. The same year he received the Chancellor's Medal for his "Ely: An Ode". Strachey's Cambridge friends included J.M. KEYNES, G.E. MOORE, and LEONARD WOOLF. Failing twice to be elected a fellow of Trinity, Strachey joined the staff of his cousin St. Loe Strachey's *The Spectator* as drama critic in 1907.

On 17 February 1909 Strachey proposed marriage to VIRGINIA Stephen (later WOOLF) and on the same day withdrew his proposal. Ensuing relationships with painters DUNCAN GRANT and Henry Lamb both ended unhappily. *Landmarks in French Literature* (1912) was Strachey's first book. The same year he conceived the idea of *Victorian Silhouettes* (later *Eminent Victorians*). He worked on the four historical portraits during the FIRST WORLD WAR, and they can be read as an expression of Strachey's antipathy for the war and the shrill patriotism associated with it. In 1916 he requested exemption from military service on grounds of CONSCIENTIOUS OBJECTION. Though his request was rejected, he was exempted following a medical examination. In 1915 Strachey began a friendship with the painter [Dora] Carrington. They lived together at The Mill House, Tidmarsh where they were joined by Ralph Partridge in a *ménage à trois*. It was at The Mill House until 1924 that Strachey enjoyed the happiest years of his life and achieved his greatest success. In 1923 Carrington and Partridge, who had married two years earlier, separated, and Strachey and Carrington moved to Ham Spray House, Hungerford in 1924.

A prominent man of letters, Strachey received numerous honors. He delivered the Leslie Stephen lecture on Pope at Cambridge in 1925 and the next year received an honorary doctorate from the University of Edinburgh. Strachey began *Elizabeth and Essex* in 1925 and a final, and ultimately unhappy relationship with Roger Senhouse in 1926. Strachey became ill in January, 1930. Though specialists diagnosed typhoid, colitis and ulcer, he died of stomach cancer on 21 January 1932. His friend Carrington committed suicide within two months of Strachey's death.

Strachey's historical essays show the irony of personal and social impulses that have created "modern" life. In *Eminent Victorians*, for example, Thomas Arnold's and Florence Nightingale's passions aimed at modernization are shown to be rooted in their wilful and unavowed intellectual and spiritual muddles; the realizing of their passions creates a modern order at once improved and worsened, free and yet more oppressively disciplined than what precedes it. Moreover, in a way characteristic of the paradoxes of literary modernism, Strachey's histories pair their distrust of the eminent authors of modernity with Strachey's self-reflexive doubts about the possibility of writing reliable stories and interpretations about history.

John Ferns

Bibliography
Edmonds, Michael. *Lytton Strachey: A Bibliography.* 1981.

Ferns, John. *Lytton Strachey.* 1988.

Holroyd, Michael. *Lytton Strachey: A Biography.* 1971.

Strikes

Elections, petitions, and mass mobilizations give Western publics numerous means of voicing their objections and demands, and they provide at least the hope of change and redress. Many ordinary people, particularly manual workers, add another method to this repertoire—the strike—and have seen fit to make repeated use of it. In no country has this been more true than in Britain, where workers seem to have been proficient at putting together effective unions, normally the prerequisite for sustained strike activity. Just as unions have been key to strikes, however, so the history of strikes has provided many of the turning points in the history of trade unionism.

Sporadic use of the strike can be found back in the eighteenth century, and the infamous Combination Act of 1799 was testimony to its increased frequency in the era of the Napoleonic Wars. From the 1850s, however, workers could make use of the financial and organization backing of the so-called "new model" unions that were established by skilled workers, especially in large cities. Gradually, unions became adept at choosing when and against whom to strike, and when their efforts were underpinned by a buoyant labor market, they could be extremely effective. During the prosperous years 1871–3, for example, there was a large explosion of highly successful strikes which had the effect of enrolling quite large numbers of previously unorganized workers into unions. The Depression of 1873–96 quickly tipped the balance of power back towards the employers, and workers suffered bitter defeats, particularly in COAL MINING and in textiles.

The late 1880s witnessed yet another outburst of strikes and union organization. This "new unionism" emerged in 1889, with major strikes in London on the part of matchgirls, dockers, and gas workers. Advocates of the "new unionism" were particularly concerned to bring the unskilled within the orbit of trade unionism. To do that required the creation of more inclusive unions with lower qualifications and appropriately lower dues, inevitably providing fewer benefits as well. It was further held that to be effective these broader unions would have to adopt a more aggressive approach towards employers and also make demands upon the state.

The period of the FIRST WORLD WAR was the most strike-prone in British history. A number of very large strikes broke out before the war, as the effort to bring unionization to the less skilled revived with great intensity. The miners engaged in bitter strikes aimed at securing a national minimum wage, railway men and port workers sought recognition from employers, and many other groups sought redress for declining real wages. The pre-war battles witnessed increasing involvement by the state, either as conciliator or—more controversially—as policeman, and also more effective organization on the part of workers. Particularly impressive, at least on paper, was the Triple Alliance of miners, dockers, and railwaymen that threatened to strike in concert over issues of mutual interest.

The war postponed confrontation but served also to change the terms on which employers and workers contended. Union membership jumped massively from just over 4 million in 1914 to 8.3 million by 1920, and government became even more implicated in setting wages, controlling prices, and fixing working conditions, and hence more easily drawn into conflict. Employers also became more organized during the war and by its end were firmly resolved to resist the encroachments of unions and of the state. After the war, therefore, there was a series of bitter strikes that swept up workers in one industry after another. For about two years workers succeeded in winning recognition, higher wages, and shorter hours in a number of industries. By mid-1920 the post-war boom had ended, and UNEMPLOYMENT had begun to spread into the staple industries, e.g. coal, shipbuilding, and textiles. From 1921,

therefore, employers began to take back many of the concessions granted during and just after the war. The Triple Alliance was revealed as a "paper tiger" on Black Friday (23 April 1921) when the TRANSPORT WORKERS and railwaymen refused to back up the miners. The worst defeat, of course, came in 1926, when the GENERAL STRIKE was called off after nine days and the miners left to carry on their ultimately unsuccessful strike alone.

The losses of the 1920s had a sobering effect on the unions and the workers they represented. To begin, the Trade Disputes Act of 1927 narrowed the political rights that the unions thought they had secured in 1906. While the framework of laws governing industrial conflict remained much the same after 1926, so, too, did the depressed state of the labor market, which discouraged strikes throughout the inter-war years. The SECOND WORLD WAR shifted the balance of advantage in the labor market back to the workers, but the war also brought political changes whose effect was to convince many workers to refrain from striking. Unions used their leverage within the state to press for economic policies more favorable to working-class interests, and the unions themselves grew rapidly. By the end of the war the membership losses incurred during the inter-war decades had been made up, and a LABOUR government, pledged to a major program of reform, was in power. Thus strikes remained infrequent throughout the 1940s, as workers gained through politics much of what they had previously sought through industrial action.

What the organizational gains of the 1940s did, however, was to give workers the shopfloor strength with which to wage a different sort of strike later on. This new pattern did not emerge immediately, but as prices began to climb and growth to falter in the late 1950s, workers began to employ small, "unofficial" strikes aimed at local management. The coming of mass production in the AUTOMOBILE INDUSTRY gave greater clout to small groups of workers and to shop stewards who used this leverage to press for improvements in wages and conditions. Prolonged full employment increased the bargaining power of other workers as well, and from the late 1950s strikes began to spread across a wide range of industries. Miners, dockers, and car workers invoked the strike most often and effectively, but by the mid-1960s the habit had caught on much more broadly. Successive governments during the 1960s became fixated on strikes, seeing them as responsible for inflation and lagging productivity, and the Labour government moved to impose statutory control over "unofficial action" with the publication of In Place of Strife in 1969.

The effort to reshape the legal framework for

strikes was a sign that the question of industrial conflict and trade union rights had taken center stage in British political debate. The issues would be kept there throughout the 1970s and into the 1980s by continued high levels of strike activity, worsening inflation, and the nation's deepening economic malaise. Despite government efforts to discourage disputes, workers found them to be the most effective means of improving their STANDARD OF LIVING. The Labour government backed off from its plan to legislate a new order in industrial relations, but the CONSERVATIVES under EDWARD HEATH were less cautious. The Industrial Relations Act of 1971, however, met with sustained resistance from the unions and was made inoperative before being repealed by the WILSON government in 1974. In the meantime, strikes became more frequent and massive: between 1970 and 1975 there were on average more than 3,000 strikes per year, involving approximately 1.3 million workers and costing over 12.5 million working days annually. These disputes also were waged with novel tactics that met with considerable success: sympathy strikes and boycotts, flying pickets—pioneered by the miners in 1972—and factory occupations, as at Upper Clyde Shipbuilders. The climax came with the miners' strike of 1973–4, which led the government to impose a three-day week on industry and to call an election that, they hoped, would provide popular backing for their stance against the unions. The Tories lost, however, and Labour was returned to office with a narrow majority, pledged to restore, and even increase, the legal rights of workers and of unions.

Labour was unable, however, to cope with the enormous economic problems of the 1970s. The oil price increases of 1973–4 and 1979 fueled inflation while slowing growth, and workers were almost forced to demand compensating wage increases. Labour was able to use its influence with union leaders to moderate wage claims and to avert a major wave of strikes until the fall of 1978, when a dispute broke out at Ford. That proved the signal for what came to be known as the "winter of discontent," when truck drivers and a number of public sector workers went out on strike. Labour paid dearly for its failure in the election of May 1979, when MARGARET THATCHER led the Conservatives to a major victory. Thatcher came into office resolved to avoid the industrial relations failures of previous governments, to tame the unions, and to restrict strikes. Overall, the Conservatives were remarkably successful, though the price was very high. Aided no doubt by the sharp recession of 1981–2—from which the older industries in the north never truly recovered—the Tories inflicted a series of defeats upon the unions. The national

steel strike of 1980 was a bitter loss for the unions and confirmed the long-term decline of the STEEL INDUSTRY and its workforce; CIVIL SERVANTS lost a long-running dispute in 1981, NATIONAL HEALTH SERVICE staff and railway workers in 1982; workers in the public utilities were beaten in 1983; and the miners were brutally crushed in a dispute over pit closures that began in March 1984 and dragged on for more than a year.

The Conservatives also transformed the legal framework of trade unionism through a series of Employment Acts that restricted secondary picketing, made unions liable to civil actions by employers over strikes, mandated secret ballots prior to official strike action and for union elections, and weakened the closed shop. In this increasingly inhospitable environment, union membership declined from nearly 13.3 million in 1979 to less than 10.5 million in 1985, or from 54.4 percent to 43.3 percent of the workforce. Inevitably, strike activity languished as well. Between 1979–80 and 1989–90 strike activity declined by more than half, and neither the legal framework, the economic climate, nor the recent evolution of union/management relations suggests that an early revival is imminent.

Strikes thus remain an important means by which workers can make their grievances and demands heard, but they are unlikely in the near future to play so prominent a role in the nation's social and economic life as they did earlier in the last century.

James E. Cronin

Bibliography

Church, R., and Q. Outram. *Strikes and Solidarity: Coalfield Conflict, 1880–1966.* 1998.

Cronin, James E. *Industrial Conflict in Modern Britain.* 1979.

———. "Strikes and Power in Britain, 1870–1920" in L. Haimson & C. Tilly, eds. *Strikes, Wars, and Revolutions in an International Perspective: Waves in the Late Nineteenth and Early Twentieth Centuries.* 1989. pp. 79–100.

Durcan, J.W., W.E.J. McCarthy, and G.P. Redman. *Strikes in Post-War Britain.* 1983.

Price, Richard. *Labour in British Society.* 1986.

Also see: GENERAL STRIKE (1926)

Suez Crisis (1956)

From the British perspective the Suez crisis began in July 1956 when the Egyptian government nationalized the Paris-based Suez Canal Company. The British government, led by SIR ANTHONY EDEN, feared that this move would sooner or later be followed by an Egyptian refusal to allow passage to vessels headed for Great Britain with catastrophic implications for British industry in an era when most of the country's oil was imported from the Middle East via the Suez Canal. But the CABINET did not feel able to respond with any immediate military action and hence, against their better judgment, found themselves drawn into international negotiations aiming at a compromise diplomatic solution. By mid–October this began to look as if it would be the ultimate outcome, but in a surprising development Eden and a few senior colleagues decided to join with France in "arranging" for a second crisis to occur. This took the form of an Israeli attack on Egypt, thereby giving the British and the French the pretext to send forces to occupy the Canal, not ostensibly to reverse the nationalization decree but simply to separate the combatants. But the operation had to be aborted in the face of overwhelming pressure from many quarters. The upshot was that the Suez Canal remained nationalized, and the British government was widely perceived to have been humiliated.

When Egypt, led by Gamal Nasser, announced that the Canal Company would be nationalized, the British Cabinet's initial reaction was to resolve that "while our ultimate purpose was to place the Canal under international control, our immediate objective was to bring about the downfall of the present Egyptian Government." But the view of the Chiefs of Staff was that the immediate objective could not be achieved rapidly, since many weeks would be needed to assemble an expeditionary force in Malta capable of landing in strength at Alexandria. Orders were accordingly given to make the necessary preparations for what was code named "Operation Musketeer". And agreements were made to enable France to take part in an essentially subordinate role.

Meanwhile, however, the Americans had concluded that Egypt's action, however unfriendly, did not constitute a sufficient provocation to justify the use of armed force. They accordingly sought to draw the British and the French into diplomatic negotiations aimed at securing a compromise solution. Eden and his colleagues reluctantly recognized that they had no practical alternative to going through the motions of seeking a peaceful outcome while preparations proceeded for use of force as "a last resort." The upshot was many weeks of essentially unwelcome discussion at two successive international conferences held in London and then under the auspices of the United Nations in New York. Gradually it became clear even to most members of the Cabinet, including Eden himself, that the planned assault on Alexandria ("Musketeer") or even just the Suez Canal itself ("Musketeer Revise" as it had become known) had ceased to be practical politics unless and until Egypt actually proved itself unwilling or unable to permit British shipping to use the Canal. For diplomacy had revealed that too many countries (including both superpowers and several members of the Commonwealth) were otherwise in favor of a solution involving vague international "guarantees" of the Canal's future status. Moreover, the opposition LABOUR PARTY, after an initial outburst of hostility towards Egypt, had now moved decisively into a position where it would oppose the use of force in the absence of the approval of the United Nations.

By mid-October, therefore, Eden appeared to be reconciled to accepting a compromise formula (known as the "Six Points") in the process of being made final in discussion between British Foreign Secretary Selwyn Lloyd and his Egyptian counterpart, Mohammed Fawzi. But the Prime Minister had been left in no doubt by the CONSERVATIVE PARTY conference, held in Llandudno in early October, that he would be widely condemned by party activists as an "appeaser" if he consented to any compromise deal. And his Chancellor of the Exchequer, HAROLD MACMILLAN, indicated that he might resign and attempt to play Winston Churchill to Eden's Neville Chamberlain. In these circumstances Eden proved unwisely receptive to a plan presented to him by French representatives on 14 October at Chequers.

The French proposed that the Israelis should be secretly induced to attack Egypt, thereby enabling the British and French, pretending lack of foreknowledge, to send forces to occupy the Canal in order to protect it by separating the combatants. Once Eden had expressed an interest in this approach the French invited the Israeli leaders to Sèvres on the outskirts of Paris. The upshot was that Lloyd met David Ben-Gurion, the Israeli Prime Minister, on 22 October, and in the ensuing days the three countries negotiated what amounted to a collusive bargain as to how each would play its hand after Israel had invaded Egypt on 29 October.

Several leading Cabinet ministers were informed about every aspect of the plan, and even the entire Cabinet was given a broad hint as to what was afoot. Some of Eden's colleagues were undoubtedly uneasy either on practical or moral grounds, but none resigned. It does not seem therefore that the Prime Minister can be accused of acting alone or even "unconstitutionally"; on the other hand, few civil servants or diplomats were in the picture, and ministers undoubtedly deceived the House of Commons and the country when the scenario unfolded.

Perhaps more important was that the Americans were not consulted about the devious plan. For in the event President Eisenhower simply did not believe the rather threadbare public justification offered by London and Paris. With great alacrity, therefore, he set out to wreck the operation. American delegates at the United Nations helped to mobilize an overwhelming vote of condemnation—forcing the use of British and French vetoes on the Security Council. U.S. diplomats ruthlessly exploited the British need for oil supplies that became acute when the Egyptians blocked the Canal with sunken vessels, as well as refusing to allow the British to draw on the resources of the International Monetary Fund when sterling came under acute selling pressure.

The decisive day was 6 November when the Cabinet met to review the position. The military aspect was satisfactory: by now Anglo-French forces were ashore in Egypt and were in control of about one-third of the Canal; and bombing of airfields on the edge of Cairo was proceeding— necessitated by the vulnerability of Israeli cities to possible Egyptian bombing. The political-diplomatic outlook, however, was grim. Macmillan reported on the vulnerability of sterling; concern was expressed lest conventional Soviet forces intervene in the Middle East—something apparently taken more seriously than Soviet threats to use nuclear weapons on London; the position at the United Nations was deeply disturbing; several members of the COMMONWEALTH were expressing opposition—with threats of resignation being mooted; the Labour Party had reflected passionate divisions in the country—even leading to a Commons sitting having to be suspended owing to disorder; and, above all, Eisenhower had spoken on the telephone to Eden in unmistakably vigorous terms: the operation must be halted. Facing a Cabinet that had earlier revealed potential splits, Eden took the initiative in proposing a ceasefire. By midnight, Anglo-French forces were accordingly halted in their progress down the Canal.

In the ensuing weeks the British government strove desperately to persuade the United Nations (and the United States in particular) that the Anglo-French force should be allowed to form the nucleus of a UN peacekeeping operation. But the Americans remorselessly used economic pressure (and secret dealings with several treacherous British Cabinet ministers willing to go behind Eden's back) to enforce an unconditional and humiliating withdrawal—which was duly announced on 30 November.

From that day onwards London tacitly accepted that the Egyptian nationalization of the Suez Canal Company could not be reversed. And Eden, after brazenly lying to the House of Commons on 20 December ("There was not foreknowledge that Israel would attack Egypt"), resigned on 9 January 1957 citing ill-health. The whole affair had indeed been "no end of a lesson" not only for him but for the entire British nation.

David Carlton

Bibliography
Carlton, David. Britain and the Suez Crisis. 1988.
Kelly, Saul, and A. Gorst, eds. Whitehall and the Suez Crisis. 2000.
Kunz, Diane B. The Economic Diplomacy of the Suez Crisis. 1991.
Kyle, Keith. Suez. 1991.
Lucas, W. Scott. Divided We Stand: Britain, the US and the Suez Crisis. 1991.
Thomas, Hugh. The Suez Affair. 3rd ed. 1986.

Sutherland, Graham Vivian (1903–1980)

Although at the height of his career Graham Sutherland was feted as one of Britain's great modern artists, his reputation began to dwindle before the end of his life, and it no longer seems as credible as it once was to speak of him in the same breath as HENRY MOORE and FRANCIS BACON. In the last decades critical attention was stronger on the Continent than in Britain, although interest in the artist has revived more recently along with the neo-romantic movement with which his name is now closely associated. It is a fascination with transformations in nature and a tendency towards spiritual subjects which made him an exemplary member of this school, drawing as it does on insular British concerns. Peers included PAUL NASH and John Piper, as well as younger artists such as Michael Ayrton and Keith Vaughan.

Sutherland staked his affiliation with the British romantic tradition at the very outset of his career which began as an engraver heavily indebted to Blake's follower, Samuel Palmer. A student at Goldsmiths' School of Art (1921–6), he adopted a pastoral image in his intaglio prints of the 1920s, with an abundance of churchyards and thatched cottages, although technically they were innovative with their deep creative use of over-biting. The 1929 Wall Street crash brought the post-war print boom to an abrupt halt, forcing a change of direction upon Sutherland.

He turned to oils and watercolors, but it needed the shock of nature to launch his painting career in earnest. In 1934 he visited Pembrokeshire: his experience of the landscape there was, according to his own testimony, an epiphany of Wordsworthian proportions. Significantly, however, he chose to live in Kent, where the landscape of the surrounding North Downs were not allowed to influence his painting in the same way. He needed his inspiration to be in some remote place, or to be discovered in chance encounters. A painter of nature, rather than landscape, he was disposed to incorporate geographically disparate elements in single pictures.

Eager to bridge the gap between romanticism and avant garde art, Sutherland briefly associated with the English Surrealists, taking part in their 1936 exhibition at the Burlington Galleries. The boldly imaginative commercial posters he was designing at the time were surreal fantasies, but what attracted him to Surrealism was the idea of the "objet trouvé", a commonplace object rendered exotic and marvelous by its chance discovery. Like Nash and Moore, but unlike continental Surrealists, his inspiration lay in nature, not manmade objects. His vision of nature was neither benign nor lyrical, and he always sought exotic and disturbing phenomena. What excited him were hybrids, anthropomorphic characteristics in stones and plants, threatening conglomerations of tree roots, upturned trunks, and unruly vegetal growths.

In common with other artists of the 1930s Sutherland's brooding, apocalyptic canvases reflected the mood of impending conflict. He was among the first to be enlisted by KENNETH CLARK as an official war artist with the outbreak of hostilities. Sutherland's experiences as a war artist were almost as significant as his epiphany in the Welsh landscape. Recording bomb damage in Wales and sketching among the ruins of the London BLITZ stimulated his fascination with the violence of growth and change, as twisted girders and shattered walls began to assume the mysterious life hitherto detected in plants and rocks.

Toward the end of the war Sutherland undertook his first religious commission, a "Crucifixion" for St. Matthew's Parish Church, Northampton, whose vicar, Walter Hussey, had already commissioned Moore's "Madonna and Child" and a cantata by BENJAMIN BRITTEN. Sutherland had never attempted such a large work before, but his poignant interpretation of the theme, which combines the influence of Grunwald and the recently published photographs of concentration camp victims, marked a major departure in his career. For most of the 1950s he was engaged in designing the tapestry "Christ in Glory in the Teramorph" which was unveiled in 1962 in the rebuilt Coventry Cathedral. A convert to CATHOLICISM, Sutherland used his religious paintings to express his personal artistic preoccupations. Arising from the Northampton commission was

a series exploring thorns both as a Christian symbol of the passion of Christ and as a metaphor of threatening nature.

A visit to the Picasso Museum in Antibes in 1947 encouraged the introduction of totemic figures, a development also indebted to Moore and Bacon, although rooted in his own practice. It was as though the upturned trees and bombed houses, imbued with a life of their own, had given birth to ambiguous amalgams of animal, human, and vegetal elements. His mural for the FESTIVAL OF BRITAIN, "The Origins of the Land", 1951, populated by such threatening beings, and his series of standing forms in garden settings can be related to contemporary expressions of neo-romantic angst like the Quatermass films and John Wyndham's novel *The Day of the Triffids*. The climax of Sutherland's international career was marked with a retrospective exhibition at the Venice Biennale, which then transferred to the Musée National d'Art Moderne in Paris.

After SOMERSET MAUGHAM invited him to paint his portrait in 1949, commissions came from many celebrated personalities of the day, including Kenneth Clark, Konard Adenauer, Helena Rubinstein, and WINSTON CHURCHILL, whose portrait was a gift from Parliament. Churchill never hid his dislike of the painting, which like all Sutherland's best portraits, focuses on psychological strain in the face of the sitter. Some critics argue that the conventional, naturalistic portraits detract from Sutherland's reputation as an original artist. Others attribute a decline in the quality of his work to his move to the south of France, where he was cut off from the English landscape. In 1967 he renewed contact with Pembrokeshire when he returned to make a documentary film. He later bequeathed much of his work to the gallery that bears his name at Picton Castle in Pembrokeshire.

David Cohen

Bibliography

Berthoud, Roger. *Sutherland: A Biography*. 1982.

Cooper, Douglas. *The Work of Sutherland*. 1961.

Sackville-West, Edward. *Sutherland*. 1943.

Sutherland in Wales: A Catalogue of the Collection at the Graham Sutherland Gallery, Picton Castle, Haverfordwest, Dyfed. 1976.

Tassi, Roberto. *Sutherland: Complete Graphic Work*. 1978.

Taff Vale Judgment (July 1901)

The Taff Vale Judgment undercut trade unions' immunity from legal action to secure financial compensation for losses arising from STRIKES, an immunity that had hitherto been presumed to have been conferred by trade union legislation in 1871. This had major political effects, for many more trade unions turned to the newly-formed LABOUR REPRESENTATION COMMITTEE (LRC) to secure through Parliament legal changes to reverse this judgement by the Law Lords.

The legal case arose from a railway strike in South Wales in August 1900. It began as an unofficial action by workers on the Taff Vale Railway to gain union recognition at a propitious time, there being high demand for the local coal and less labor in the area because of the BOER WAR. The executive of the Amalgamated Society of Railway Servants (ASRS) made it an official dispute. Throughout the dispute the general manager of the railway company repeatedly used the law against the strikers, and after its settlement he moved against the ASRS. Legal opinion was surprised when the HOUSE OF LORDS overturned a Court of Appeal verdict that would have prevented the Taff Vale Company taking action for damages against the union. By December 1902 the ASRS had incurred a total of £42,000 in settlement with the company and in legal costs.

In the year following the Taff Vale judgment the numbers of trade unionists affiliating to the LRC roughly doubled. This proved to be an important point in the move of British trade unionism away from Liberal politics. The case was also one of several factors that contributed to relative industrial peace between 1899 and 1907.

C.J. Wrigley

Bibliography

Bagwell, Philip S. *The Railwaymen: The History of the National Union of Railwaymen.* 1963.

Brown, Kenneth D. "Trade Unions and the Law" in C.J. Wrigley, ed. *A History of British Industrial Relations 1875–1914.* 1982. pp. 116–34.

Clegg, H.A., Alan Fox, and A.F. Thompson. *A History of British Trade Unions Since 1889: vol. 1: 1889–1910.* 1964.

McCord, Norman. "Taff Vale Revisited," *History,* vol. 78 (1993), pp. 243–60.

Tariff Reform

Often dismissed as a mere euphemism for protection, tariff reform amounted to much more than a revival of the agitation for fair trade that had characterized the 1880s. Its emergence is conventionally dated to May 1903 when Joseph Chamberlain (1836–1914), the Unionist Colonial Secretary, called for the re-evaluation of Britain's existing tariff policy, even if this meant challenging the prevailing dogma of free trade to which, it was widely believed, national prosperity was due. For the next decade, and again in the early 1920s, no issue in domestic politics would prove more controversial. Manufacturers, especially in the iron and STEEL INDUSTRY, had longed for protective tariffs against foreign competition, and to their voices were added many from the agricultural interest which had suffered from the depressed prices and cheap imports of the preceeding three decades. Ranged against them in defense of free trade were those sectors which relied on the freest exchange of raw materials or services (such as banking or the textile trades) and those individuals who feared either an unprecedented tariff war with heightened international tensions, an unwarranted extension of state interference, or an unpopular rise in the cost of living.

Yet tariff reform's controversial nature lay not just in the conflicting economic interests it galvanized, but also in its centrality as the touchstone of CONSERVATIVE PARTY commitment. Chamberlain himself regarded tariff reform not as a protectionist end in itself, but as a means to reinvigorate the British polity. Accordingly, he stressed the fundamental importance of binding the Empire together through a preferential remission of duties for the colonies, conceding that to do so would elevate the price of agricultural imports (thus leading his critics to label tariffs as "food taxes"), but insisting that such transient sacrifices were essential to a constructive policy that would secure fuller employment, raise additional revenue to fund social reforms, and prompt greater Anglo-Saxon imperial solidarity in commercial and military matters. But the Prime Minister, ARTHUR BALFOUR, resisted Chamberlain's policies, because he feared that food duties would be electorally disastrous and that Chamberlain's avowed intention to convert the party to tariffs would shatter it, much as Peel's repeal of agricultural protection had done during the 1840s. Initially, Balfour's fears were justified. A number of prominent Unionist free traders defected to the LIBERALS (including WINSTON CHURCHILL), while even more chose to retire from politics. The party entered the 1906 election divided, with Balfour attempting to steer a middle course, endorsing only the idea of enacting tariffs as a means of retaliation designed to elicit more equitable treatment from Britain's protectionist trading partners. Not surprisingly, this compromise satisfied nobody, and undoubtedly magnified the party's crushing defeat in the 1906 election.

Over the next four years, however, tariff reform grew more attractive to the Conservatives as a form of indirect taxation they could propose as an alternative to the Liberal government's measures of direct, redistributive taxation aimed directly at affluent, propertied Tory supporters. Defensive and domestic-centered, tariff reform was now shorn of the more radical, constructive, and imperial agenda that Chamberlain had originally envisioned. By 1913 Balfour's successor, ANDREW BONAR LAW, judged that other issues, such as strident opposition to Irish Home Rule, would better serve his party's defensive posture, and tariff reform was shifted to the back burner.

Backbench sentiment in favor of tariffs persisted, however, and the issue resurfaced in the Conservative Party's program for the election of 1923. It would not be until 1932 though, in the very different climate of economic depression, that the British government finally committed itself to a full policy of tariffs.

Frans Coetzee

Bibliography

Coetzee, Frans. *For Party or Country: Nationalism and the Dilemmas of Popular Conservatism in Edwardian England.* 1990.

Semmel, Bernard. *Imperialism and Social Reform: English Social-Imperial Thought 1895–1914.* 1960.

Sykes, Alan. *Tariff Reform in British Politics, 1903–1913.* 1979.

Tawney, Richard Henry (1880–1962)

He may have been christened Richard Henry Tawney, but to the world he became simply "Tawney" (sometimes also "Harry" to a few intimates). He was a major social philosopher of the British Left, perhaps *the* major social philosopher, for much of the first half of the twentieth century. His writings, especially *The Acquisitive Society* (1921) and *Equality* (1931), came to exercise a profound and enduring influence, continuing long after his death.

He was born, as many others of his class and generation were, in India, but was soon returned to England for a conventionally classical education (at Rugby and Balliol). At Oxford, his own deep religious faith—he was to become a leading apostle of a social ANGLICANISM—combined with a prevailing ethic of social service to point him in the direction of both social action and social reflection. There followed a period at Toynbee Hall, the Oxford settlement in London's East End; a spell running a charity to provide country holidays for poor city children; a short bout of economics lecturing at the University of Glasgow; and (in 1908) an adult education tutorship under the joint scheme between the UNIVERSITY OF OXFORD and the Workers' Educational Association (WEA) which was the origin of university extramural education.

This last experience was an important moment both for Tawney and for the working class ADULT EDUCATION movement. His classes (in the Staffordshire Potteries and the North) were landmarks in the history of this movement. They also turned Tawney into an economic historian, his professional discipline thereafter (his first book, *The Agrarian Problem in the Sixteenth Century* (1912), was a product of this period), but an economic historian with a clear and contemporary social purpose. It only needed a final experience, of the FIRST WORLD WAR trenches (he was badly, nearly fatally, wounded on the SOMME) to give the rest of his life and work a clear pattern and direction.

There were three books, all essentially the products of the first post-First World War decade, which expressed his social philosophy and established his reputation. *The Acquisitive Society* (1921) excoriated the growth of an atomistic, possessive individualism and embraced a new communalism of social purpose and responsibility. In *Religion and the Rise of Capitalism* (1926) the economic historian and Christian moralist sought to demonstrate how the loss of a moral reference for social and economic affairs had come about, combined with a passionate argument on the need for the retrieval of such a reference. Most influential of all, his *Equality* (1931) marshaled an elegantly ruthless assault on the English "religion of inequality" and its baneful consequences for social life. In its place, Tawney advanced a social philosophy of equal worth (in which equality of treatment was not to be confused with identity of treatment), which he presented as the precondition of a "common culture" of social unity and shared participation.

These books had a vast influence, not just on British socialists but on the wider currents of thought and opinion. For a generation of British socialists, those who grew up in the inter-war period and inhabited the post-1945 world, Tawney's work was the predominant philosophical influence. It represented the authentic and distinctive voice of English ethical socialism.

His influence and activity was evident in more specific and practical directions too. Within Anglicanism it was his voice (along with that of his friend WILLIAM TEMPLE) which constantly sought to confront the church with its social mission. He remained a leading spokesman for the adult education movement in general and for the Workers' Educational Assocation in particular. He was a prolific writer on educational issues, especially for the MANCHESTER GUARDIAN, and his prospectus for the LABOUR PARTY on *Secondary Education for All* (1922) decisively shaped the party's education policy. In 1919 he had represented the trade union side on the SANKEY COMMISSION on the COAL INDUSTRY, to wide acclaim; and he had a hand in many of Labour's policy statements, including a decisive hand in *Labour and the Nation* (1928).

This document is a reminder that Tawney was a resolutely party man, sometimes critical but always a loyalist as far as Labour was concerned. His political loyalties, and activities on their behalf, coexisted with his professional work as an economic historian who did pioneering studies of the sixteenth and seventeenth centuries. A chair at the LONDON SCHOOL OF ECONOMICS in 1931 might have come sooner but for his other engagements. There was a remarkable unity to all his work, whether as economic historian, adult educator, churchman, social theorist, or party intellectual; and he remains a central reference point for the British socialist tradition.

Anthony Wright, MP

Bibliography

Blackburn, Sheila C. "A Very Moderate Socialst Indeed? R. H. Tawney and Minimum Wages," *Twentieth Century British History*, vol. 10 (1999), pp. 107–136.

Terrill, Ross. *R.H. Tawney and his Times.* 1973.

Wright, Anthony. *R.H. Tawney.* 1987.

Taylor, Alan John Percivale (1906–1990)

A.J.P. Taylor was a historian, political commentator, and radical dissenter over five decades. A gifted journalist, he wrote for the "popular" and the "quality" press, appeared regularly on television, challenged orthodoxy, and became the "traitor within the gates". Taylor was the most controversial and widely read English historian of his time, perhaps the only one, with the possible exception of G.M. TREVELYAN, whose name was universally recognized.

Born in Lancashire into a family of well-to-do cotton manufacturers, Taylor was educated at Quaker schools and at Oriel College, OXFORD, where he took a first class degree and joined the COMMUNIST PARTY. After Oxford he learned research in diplomatic history from A.F. Pribram in Vienna, and in 1930 was appointed as a lecturer at the University of Manchester, where he was strongly influenced by LEWIS NAMIER. He published his first studies in European diplomatic history, *The Italian Problem in European Diplomacy, 1847–1849* (1934) and *Germany's First Bid for Colonies* (1938) and began to work as a reviewer and leader-writer on the *MANCHESTER GUARDIAN*. Meanwhile, he left the Communist Party and became an "out-of-hand radical".

In 1938 Taylor was appointed a Fellow of Magdalen College, Oxford. It was the year of the MUNICH agreement, and he was soon speaking out against APPEASEMENT. Although he remained at Oxford throughout the Second World War, Taylor broadcast frequently and was employed to lecture for the Ministry of Information. However, his talks challenged government policy in the Mediterranean, for which he was criticized in the House of Commons, and MOI soon found they could do without him.

In that period, Taylor addressed himself to issues involving the war, in part as a result of his association with Slav refugees in Oxford. These included ethnic issues in Central Europe, the subject of various articles and of *The Habsburg Monarchy, 1815–1918*, published in 1941, and German aggression, treated in *The Course of German History* in 1946, the latter earning him a reputation as an anti-German. After the war Taylor expanded his research in diplomatic history and in 1954 published *The Struggle for Mastery in Europe, 1848–1918*, a masterpiece of synthetic scholarship which enhanced his reputation as a serious historian. He followed this *magnum opus* with an impressively succinct study of *Bismarck* (1955).

Never satisfied with being respectable, Taylor turned from European to English diplomacy with an eye towards exploring its relationship to populist dissent. This began with his 1956 Ford Lectures at Oxford, published as *The Troublemakers: Dissent Over Foreign Policy, 1792–1939* (1958), always his "favorite brainchild". In the same year, when England became embroiled in the SUEZ CRISIS, Taylor took to the stump in protest, remaining there after Suez to agitate for the CAMPAIGN FOR NUCLEAR DISARMAMENT. In 1956 the politically heterodox Taylor was passed over for appointment as Regius Professor of Modern History, a slight by his own university which continued to rankle, although Oxford remained his academic base until 1976, when he retired as an honorary fellow of Magdalen.

The year 1956 began Taylor's "English Period". He started writing for the populist *Daily Express* and *Sunday Express* radical pieces usually on British political or social subjects, and in the process became close friends with the proprietor, LORD BEAVERBROOK, who became Taylor's mentor and patron. In 1961 Taylor published *The Origins of the Second World War,* his most controversial work. In it he argued that no one and everyone was responsible for the outbreak of war in 1939, and that Hitler was "no more wicked than any other statesman." For questioning the most sacred of modern historiographical sacred cows, Taylor was soon accused of everything from mere perversity to neo-fascism. Though it threatened his reputation, the book did not destroy it, and he was asked to write the twentieth-century volume in the Oxford History of England. *English History, 1914–1945* was published in 1965; an idiosyncratic account of his own time, its theme was the "rise of the people". It was his last major work of serious scholarship, enthralling but hardly judicious, his passionate involvement with his own history coupled with skepticism about the motives of politicians.

In 1967 Taylor was named director of the Beaverbrook Library and began his biography of Beaverbrook, which appeared in 1972 to a cool critical reception. *Beaverbrook* was overly long, and its shameless hero-worship did little to enhance Taylor's scholarly reputation. Thereafter, until the debilitating illness began that presaged his death, he wrote, lectured, and published collections of his essays, remaining actively engaged with both history and political commentary. In addition he became something of a television celebrity, dazzling audiences with his lucid exposition of the international history of the twentieth century.

Robert Cole

Bibliography
Burk, Kathleen. *Troublemaker: The Life and History of A.J.P. Taylor.* 2000.
Cole, Robert. *A.J.P. Taylor: The Traitor Within the Gates.* 1993.
Sisman, Adam. *A.J.P. Taylor: A Biography.* 1994.
Taylor, A.J.P. *A Personal History.* 1983.
Wrigley, Chris. *A.J.P. Taylor: A Complete Annotated Bibliography.* 1980.

Temple, William (1881–1944)

William Temple is widely regarded as Britain's greatest religious leader of the twentieth century. Rising rapidly in the CHURCH OF ENGLAND, he was appointed a Canon of Westminster Abbey in 1919 and Bishop of Manchester in 1921. He became Archbishop of York in 1928 and of Canterbury in 1942. In these two decades he established an international reputation as a philosopher-theologian, reformer, churchman, and ecumenical leader. He was widely mourned when he died in office in 1944.

Temple was born the second son of Frederick Temple, at the time Bishop of Exeter and later also Archbishop of Canterbury (1897–1902). The paternal influence was a strong one, Temple attending Rugby School where Frederick had been headmaster (1857–69). William then attended OXFORD where he received a first class degree and was elected President of the Oxford Union. While at Oxford, he became an avowed socialist which, with his Anglican commitments, established the intellectual basis for his future contribution. This was first expressed through his membership (1904) and then presidency (1908–24) of the Workers' Educational Association (WEA). To Temple, education was the means of individual cultural and spiritual emancipation. Initially, he followed an academic career, first at Queen's College, Oxford (1904–10) and then, after ordination, as Headmaster of Repton School (1910–14).

His growing ecclesiastical stature was signalled by his appointment in 1914 as Rector of St. James's Piccadilly, London and also, in 1915, as Honorary Chaplain to KING GEORGE V. He established lasting fame when he became full-time chairman in 1917 of the newly-formed Life and Liberty Movement. Dedicated to internal church reform, it was one of the pressures which led to the creation of the Church Assembly in 1919.

After Temple served briefly as a canon of Westminster Abbey, his growing reputation was confirmed by appointment to the Bishopric of Manchester in 1921. Here he emerged as a church leader of the first rank. Notable among his many activities was his chairmanship of a Conference on Christian Politics, Economics and Citizenship (COPEC) in 1924 which established influential principles for the Church's social and ecumenical engagement. In the latter area he became a major figure, acting as a leader for the 1927 Lausanne World Conference on Faith and Order. He also led the Committee on Unity of the 1930 Lambeth Conference and in 1938 chaired a committee which laid the basis for the World Council of Churches. In 1942 Temple helped form the British Council of Churches and supported the unity scheme for the Church of South India finally approved just after his death.

He continued to emphasize the social relevance of Christianity. Following his work for the WEA and COPEC, he chaired the influential Pilgrim Trust enquiry on UNEMPLOYMENT (*Men without Work,* 1938). His legacy for the post-war period was assured through his chairmanship of the 1940 Malvern Conference on reconstruction and his help in passing the 1944 EDUCATION ACT to reform secondary education.

Among his many publications are *Mens Creatrix* (1917), *Christus Veritas* (1924), and *Christianity and Social Order* (1942). It is difficult to underestimate his contribution as teacher, prophet, thinker, church leader and man of God.

George Moyser

Bibliography
Iremonger, F.A. *William Temple, Archbishop of Canterbury.* 1948.
Kent, John. *William Temple.* 1992.

Tennis, Lawn

The exploits of Fred Perry apart, British tennis has little international success of which to boast. As in the case of soccer, Britain invented and developed a sport only to find it taken over and perfected by more skillful opponents in other countries. Though tennis has a long history, stretching back to the late middle ages, the version played today originated in England in the 1870s. A retired army officer, Major Wingfield, patented a game called "Sphairistike" in 1874, and from this tennis quickly emerged. In 1875 the Marylebone Cricket Club drafted rules, while in the same year tennis was included in the program of the All England Croquet Club at Wimbledon. Two years later the first Wimbledon championships were held, using the rectangular court and scoring system known today. In 1888 the Lawn Tennis Association was formed to oversee the activities of tennis clubs, which at this time were to be found almost entirely in an upper-class milieu.

Of the major British sports, tennis is the one that has remained the most socially restricted. By the early twentieth century it had become virtually synonymous with middle-class status—the popular saying "Anyone for tennis?" instantly denoting social privilege and a leisured lifestyle. This image, together with a series of financial constraints—the cost of equipment, the high ratio of land to participant, the preference for expensive grass courts—which also account for the absence of tennis in the educational curriculum outside a small group of private schools, ensured the sport's continuing exclusivity. Municipal authorities did begin making tennis courts available to the general public in the inter-war years, and since the Second World War there have been several attempts to promote it more widely, especially among the young. In spite of this, tennis is still far short of being a "national game".

Nevertheless, Britain has made one outstanding contribution to world tennis—Wimbledon. As the senior event of the international tennis calendar, Wimbledon is familiar, through press and television, to millions of people who otherwise know little of the sport. Following the first competition of 1877 (and the introduction in 1884 of one for women) Wimbledon gradually established its eminence, still under the control of the All England Club. It was not until the 1920s that the dominance of overseas players became apparent, the French star Suzanne Lenglen being the first of many. But the marginalization of British players (Perry's triumphs of 1934–6 being the outstanding exception) did nothing to affect Wimbledon's popularity. To accommodate a massive increase in interest immediately following the First World War the present stadium was opened in 1922, incorporating the famous Centre Court (15,000 spectators) and the No. 1 court (5,000). Other innovations have been relatively few. Seeding (to prevent the meeting of star players in early stages of the tournament) was introduced in 1924. The "tie break" to curtail excessively long matches, arrived in the 1970s. The principal change, however, has been the recognition of professionals, a move in which the Wimbledon authorities took the lead. The first "open" Wimbledon came in 1968. By thus attracting the world's leading players the event's future as an international sporting occasion was secured, and continuing fees for television coverage have helped to ensure appropriate prize money. Maria Bueno received £20 for winning the Ladies' title in 1960; almost a quarter of a century later Martina Navratilova earned £90,000 for the same achievement. Wimbledon's awareness of the need to move with the times is as keen as ever.

Jeffrey Hill

Bibliography
Barrett, John. *100 Wimbledon Championships: A Celebration.* 1986.
Robertson, Max. *The Encyclopedia of Tennis.* 1974.
Walker, Helen. "Lawn Tennis" in Tony Mason, ed., *Sport in Britain: A Social History.* 1989. pp. 245–75.

Thatcher, Margaret Hilda Roberts (1925–)

During her eleven year tenure as Prime Minister, from May 1979 to November 1990, Margaret Thatcher was the most controversial, most discussed, and perhaps most effective of Britain's post-war leaders. She was the first woman in European history to be Prime Minister, the longest continuously serving Prime Minister since 1827, and the first since then to win three successive elections without intervening loss of office.

She rejected the post-war consensus, sold most NATIONALIZED INDUSTRIES to the public, showed that direct taxation could be sharply reduced, abolished incomes policy, encouraged economic liberalism, and reduced the power of the unions. Yet in defense, social security, health, and education, she left matters largely as she found them; and public attitudes to social questions changed little during her premiership.

In foreign policy she maintained close relations with the United States, and especially with President Reagan. As the Cold War ended, she developed good relations with the Soviet Union. In the FALKLANDS WAR (1982), caused by Argentine invasion, she exhibited resolve not only over a local issue, but in the wider context of the final phase of the Cold War. She presided over perhaps the last war to be fought by the U.K. on its own, the last to evoke intense patriotism, and the first television war. Her greatest failure lay in her relations with the EUROPEAN COMMUNITY, where gradual erosion of national sovereignty occurred against her will.

Thatcher was the daughter of an ex-Liberal Methodist lay preacher, a grocer who was mayor of the small Midlands town of Grantham. Ambitious as a schoolgirl, she went from local day school to OXFORD, where she studied CHEMISTRY. Excluded from speaking in the all-male Oxford Union debates, she went unnoticed at university, becoming a research chemist (1947–51) until she married fellow-Methodist Denis Thatcher, by whom she had twins (1954).

After qualifying as a lawyer, she was elected in 1959 as CONSERVATIVE MP for the North London constituency of Finchley, which she never lost. Soon promoted to a minor post (October 1961), she was successively a party spokesman on pensions, housing, energy, transport, education, and environment (1961–70), entering the Shadow Cabinet in 1967. However, when appointed Education Minister (1970–4) in EDWARD HEATH's Cabinet, she was almost unknown to the public. On resigning in 1990, she had had twenty-nine years of continuous official responsibility, twenty-three of them at CABINET level.

As Education Minister, her policies on higher public spending and the creation of comprehensive schools reflected the progressive orthodoxy of the day. A minor transfer of funds from school milk to science created a furor about "Thatcher the milk-snatcher", so that when Heath's government fell, Thatcher appeared unpopular as well as unimportant. A second Conservative election defeat in 1974 caused a leadership election in which she stood, for want of anyone else, as the nominee of a bankbenchers' revolt. Her victory (1975) by 130 to 119, was less a vote for her, than a vote for removing Heath. Of the Shadow Cabinet, all but one opposed her.

Thus, as opposition leader (1975–9) Thatcher saw herself as leader on sufferance. At first, she had no definite following or policies. She did not reconstruct the front bench with her own supporters. Nevertheless, by 1979 she had marginalized Heath, prevented Scottish devolution, imbued an intellectual "New Right", whose role is highly controversial, with a sense of her leadership as a mission, and defeated the Labour government of JAMES CALLAGHAN first in Parliament, then at the polls.

The 1979 election saw the largest swing between one major party and another since the Second World War, and the highest Conservative lead in votes cast since 1935. Yet the Conservative share of the vote was the lowest of any winner since 1922, and Thatcher was personally less popular than Callaghan. This showed how much THATCHERISM depended on a divided opposition.

Thatcher's first year lacked sureness of touch, with the economy not under control, until monetarism, involving hitherto unthinkable levels of UNEMPLOYMENT, became a central issue in 1980. Politically, this was the first episode to publicize Thatcher's will to succeed at all costs. The most conspicuous single episode was the 1981 budget which, contrary to Keynesian orthodoxy, raised taxes during a recession, and was denounced by 364 economists in a letter to THE TIMES. In fact a tighter tax policy was accompanied by an easier monetary policy, the two together producing a sharp fall in inflation (from 21.8 percent in April 1980 to 3.7 percent in June 1983, the lowest for fifteen years) and a mild economic recovery prior to the 1983 election.

In 1980–1 the picture was grim, with anti-police urban riots, hunger strikes by IRA prisoners (March–August 1981), and unemployment reaching 3 million. Yet Thatcher gained some ground politically, winning control of the Cabinet by dropping five dissenting colleagues.

In the FALKLANDS WAR, Thatcher gained greatly in stature, her popularity briefly rising to 80 percent. She succeeded in ensuring a national consensus, unlike over SUEZ in 1956. Within the small war Cabinet, she is thought to have provided the necessary political backing for the aims of the armed forces and to have recognized that a compromise with Argentina was unattainable. The extent to which the "Falklands factor" affected the 1983 election is highly disputed, the poor state of Labour, the improving economy, and the division between the opposition parties, being also important.

Thatcher's second parliament (1983–7) lacked a legislative program. Instead, privatization became an unexpected success, decisively changing the balance between the public and private sectors. Dominating all else, however, were two political dramas: the coal strike (10 March 1984–5 March 1985), and the unrelated Westland affair.

The coal strike changed the structure of British politics. Faced with a militant leader, Arthur Scargill, who had already done much to destroy one Conservative government, Thatcher had little choice but to resist. Preparations were good; there were no power cuts. Neither the long struggle, nor the final victory, brought electoral advantage, for the middle class did not rally in defense of stability. As with the Falklands, Thatcher was extremely lucky to win, and win unconditionally;

only Scargill's intransigence saved her from a disconcerting compromise.

In the midst of this episode, an IRA bomb exploded (12 October 1984) at the Grand Hotel, Brighton, during the Conservative conference, with five killed and thirty-two injured. Thatcher escaped narrowly and by chance, but carried on undeterred next day at the conference.

The other critical event of Thatcher's second Parliament was the resignation (9 January 1986) of Defense Secretary Michael Heseltine, following prolonged dispute over the future of the Westland helicopter firm. The resignation itself was not damaging; it was the subsequent escalation over secondary points which made the question of her allegedly presidential style of government a central issue.

Not until late summer 1986 did it become clear that Westland had changed nothing. Thereafter, with good economic news, falling unemployment, and a cut in income tax, Thatcher was unassailable, as the June 1987 general election indicated. The Conservative share of the vote, at 42.3 percent, was almost exactly the same as in 1983. In other ways, the election was traumatic, as that of 1983 had not been. It showed the Conservatives virtually eliminated in the major cities, and Labour virtually eliminated in the South.

The "British economic miracle" of 1987–8 appeared at the time to be Thatcher's crowning glory and a matter for national pride. The budget of spring 1988 reflected this, with higher rate income tax cut dramatically to 40 percent, the lowest top rate in Europe, combined with increased public spending and a public sector surplus. Yet within two years this winner of three elections had gone, for four reasons: the unpopularity of the poll tax, the inevitable downturn in the economic cycle, her resistance to closer links with the EUROPEAN COMMUNITY, and less support from senior colleagues.

Nothing has aroused bitterer opposition in post-war Britain than the poll tax, a direct result of Thatcher's personal commitment to abolishing property-based rates. The principle of the poll tax, that each adult should pay the same for the same local services, was widely seen as unjust. In addition, local authorities used the change as a smokescreen for an exceptional spurt in spending, and the Conservative Party conference insisted on the poll tax being implemented in one year instead of being phased in gradually over four years as planned.

The European issue concerned fewer people but in higher places. Since 1985, the EC had regained momentum. In a famous speech at Bruges (20 September 1988) Thatcher declared her whole-hearted opposition to any diminution of U.K. sovereignty, thus placing herself in conflict with a tacit coalition of business, Labour, the media, much of her party and Cabinet and the general trend of articulate public opinion. After Bruges, Europeanism was a particularly effective form of anti-Thatcherism.

Despite all this, Thatcher's policies showed continuing confidence; indeed, it was perhaps only in her third Parliament that one could truly speak of a coherent Thatcherism not confined to narrowly economic issues. Thus the 1988 Education Reform Act, introducing a national curriculum, and changes in the NATIONAL HEALTH SERVICE in 1989, led to difficulties with the teachers and doctors.

In 1989, and still more in 1990, inflation reappeared, and with it high interest rates. The year 1990 saw Thatcher an isolated figure, facing a newly credible LABOUR PARTY, at issue with a pro-European consensus, associated with high mortgages, and without a natural constituency, even her claim to be the leader who kept inflation down no longer holding good. In London, the anti-poll tax riots (31 March 1990) were the worst since 1886, with 339 arrests.

Thatcher's downfall was dramatic. Under party rules, the leadership may be contested annually. Thatcher was unchallenged until 1989, when a backbench candidate lost 314–33. In November 1990, after a sensational attack on Thatcher by her closest former colleague, Geoffrey Howe, Michael Heseltine stood, but lost in the first ballot by 204 to 152. Under party rules, this meant that Thatcher was four votes short of the majority required for outright victory on the first round.

Thatcher, then in Paris, announced her intention to fight on, but on returning to London and meeting Cabinet ministers individually, decided under some pressure to resign once a new leader was elected. JOHN MAJOR, the candidate hailed by Mrs. Thatcher as her natural heir, won the second round (with 185 votes, against Thatcher's 204 in the first round). Her departure was followed by a temporary sharp rise in Conservative support, thus seeming to justify her opponents. In 1992 Margaret Thatcher accepted a life peerage and took her seat in the HOUSE OF LORDS as Baroness Thatcher of Kesteven.

Her impact on British life remains a matter of controversy. Some would argue that she changed the way the country was run; others, that she changed the way people thought. Both views stress her achievement. Another, more skeptical school asserts that the U.K. remained a typical West European state in its pattern of social security, health, education, and taxation. Skeptics would also cite poll evidence showing that Thatcher had not changed social attitudes, as proof of the persistence of the post-war consensus.

In some areas, she redrew the map. The removal of trade unionism from its place at the heart of government was not only her greatest feat, but the greatest change in the structure of politics since 1940. It cannot be said that it would have occurred anyway. Privatization folded back the frontiers of the state to a quite unexpected extent, while introducing, again unexpectedly, a much higher degree of regulation in the public interest. Her liberalization of the economy and rejection of incomes policy decisively rejected the policy consensus of the 1970s and 1980s. Thatcher demonstrated that mass unemployment did not spell political disaster. She also showed, perhaps for the first time since Gladstone, that highly visible cuts in direct taxation were possible. In both cases, she overthrew central assumptions of post-war politics.

Thatcher rose to the top despite being a woman, being of modest social origin, being a scientist, and not being good with words. In power, she was rarely popular with the public or much of her party. She owed her two greatest successes, the Falklands War and the coal strike, to the folly of her opponents. Her most serious opponents were extra-parliamentary: the trade unions, the media, the churches, the arts world, the intelligentsia and the educational establishment, the public sector payroll vote, parts of the CIVIL SERVICE (after 1983), the MEDICAL AND LEGAL PROFESSIONS (intermittently), the pro-European consensus of the later eighties, a pervasive sense of social guilt among the gently bred, and simple inertia. No previous Conservative leader had encountered such strong middle class opposition.

John Vincent

Bibliography

Campbell, John. *Margaret Thatcher: vol. 1: The Grocer's Daughter.* 2000.

Jenkins, Peter. *Mrs. Thatcher's Revolution.* 1987.

Young, Hugo. *The Iron Lady: A Biography of Margaret Thatcher.* 1989.

———, and Anne Sloman. *The Thatcher Phenomenon.* 1986.

Thatcherism

British politics in the 1980s were dominated by the CONSERVATIVE PARTY and by its leader MARGARET THATCHER, Prime Minister from 1979 to 1990. She established a rare personal ascendancy over her party and in some ways over the nation—although it should be remembered that in an era in which Britain's two-party system fragmented, her governments never rested on as much as 50 percent of votes cast. Thatcher combined a forceful style of leadership with an eclectic set of values hard to locate within any one of Britain's main political traditions: hence the use of "Thatcherism" to denote the ideas and approach to government which she represented.

It is true that in the 1980s many other liberal democracies shifted rightwards as governments tried to defeat inflation, control public spending, and promote economic growth, and as disillusionment with state power was matched by a resurgent faith in markets. Within that context however, Thatcherism was a distinctive blend of ideas and policies. It is variously seen as a break with the pragmatism of modern British conservatism; as a radical rejection of the bipartisan foundations of post-1945 politics; and as an approach to politics founded on Thatcher's confrontational, assertive temperament.

By the usually undoctrinaire standards of British conservatism, Thatcherism was an intensely ideological movement. It was founded upon a belief in the virtues of economic markets and a distrust of managed economies, public ownership, and the WELFARE STATE. Few British institutions were to escape its reformist ambitions, while Thatcher and her supporters envisaged a change in cultural values, hoping to create a more self-reliant, entrepreneurial spirit. Thatcherism rejected basic elements of the bipartisan and elite consensus which had, since 1945, sustained a commitment to a mixed economy of private and public ownership, the maintenance of full employment, and the comprehensive provision of welfare services as a matter of right. Government was regarded as a positive force, able effectively to intervene in the economy and to reconcile competing social interests without compromising its own authority.

By the late 1970s this consensus was in tatters. A mediocre long-term economic performance had further degenerated. Industry seemed sluggish and uncompetitive, labor relations disastrous, demands on government greater than could be met. Thatcherism claimed to offer an alternative. Thatcher's rise to power was not initially seen as an ideological crusade; her election as party leader in 1975 was more a rejection of her predecessor, EDWARD HEATH, than an endorsement of radical change. She had, however, given some signs of her distinctive outlook, and by 1979 the main outlines were in place. Although described by many commentators as "instinctive", her beliefs, which sometimes seemed at odds with one another, and sometimes gave way in the face of party or popular resistance, were nonetheless an animating force. Some were bolstered by the arguments of neoclassical economists such as F.A. Hayek or of monetarists such as Milton Friedman. These and other intellectual strands were woven together in the institutions of a British "New Right"—a network of policy institutes in which long-term dissenters from the old consensus were joined by zealous converts.

Thatcher had little sympathy with traditional

conservative views of society as an organic, inter-dependent (if also hierarchical) entity. Her indi-vidualist stress on personal freedom and choice sustained her faith in markets, hostility to labor unions, and distrust of government as an instru-ment of economic planning or social engineering. Her belief in the "Victorian values" of self-help, thrift, and hard work underpinned her critique of the welfare state, which she saw as not only im-possibly costly and inefficient but as encouraging dependence and passivity. She was, perhaps, an economic liberal and social conservative, whose individualism co-existed with a conventional Tory stress on law and order and traditional moral values, and certainly did not extend to tol-erance for such causes as FEMINISM or gay rights.

Thatcherism's economic strategy began with a strong commitment to monetarist policy, enthu-siastically inherited from the preceding Labour government, as the main weapon against infla-tion—at a price of UNEMPLOYMENT levels not seen since the 1930s. The monetarist experiment fell by the wayside in the early 1980s, although the tolerance for high unemployment did not. Much of inherited economic policy was swept aside. The Thatcher governments abandoned exchange controls, prices and incomes policies, subsidies for weak companies, large state invest-ment programs and regional development pro-jects. A tough stance on public-sector strikes (notably the Miners' Strike of 1984–5) was com-bined with a careful, incremental legislative ap-proach to shifting the balance of power between unions and management, and with a dismantling of machinery which had previously given union leaders a voice in many policy areas. The return of NATIONALIZED INDUSTRIES to the private sec-tor redrew the boundaries of the economy and was increasingly seen to have an electoral by-product. The sale of shares linked with the sale of COUNCIL HOUSING to occupiers enlarged the social groups which, Thatcherites assumed, would adopt a more thoroughly middle-class aversion to socialism.

In social policy areas Thatcherism did not achieve the aims of its most devoted advocates, yet attracted great hostility from the other politi-cal parties. The welfare state was not subject to wholesale demolition, but underwent numerous changes which were widely—but not univer-sally—seen as diminishing its scope, reducing its standards of provision, and in such areas as health care and education as widening the gap between public and private services.

Thatcherism arguably included a distinctive approach to foreign affairs, although given Thatcher's strength of will and her supporters' primarily domestic concerns, this aspect is per-haps best seen in personal terms. It is question-able whether another Prime Minister would have undertaken the FALKLANDS WAR, or displayed the same mixture of aggression and skepticism towards the EUROPEAN COMMUNITY. Thatcher was deeply attached to British sovereignty—al-though this did not prevent her from signing the Single European Act in 1987, which propelled Britain further along the path to a more inte-grated Europe. She was more at home sustaining Britain's relationship with the United States, not least because she was more ideologically in step with President Reagan than with the social democrats whom she saw as dominating the EC.

The effects of Thatcherism are hotly disputed. In at least two main areas it cannot be judged a success on its own terms. Government expendi-ture as a proportion of the national product was not significantly reduced, although the burden of taxation was redistributed by a greater reliance on indirect taxation and less progressive direct taxes. The state of the British economy in the early 1990s does not suggest an economic miracle: many commentators believe that the Thatcher governments allowed the nation's manufacturing base to decline, showing an excessive faith in "post-industrial" sources of wealth while under-investing in education and training. The sugges-tion that society became more materialist and selfish during the 1980s must be balanced against the failure of Thatcherism to attract a majority of votes, in an electoral system producing exagger-ated Parliament majorities, and against a striking consistency of opinion poll evidence on such is-sues as public health care.

Although her own party turned against her in-creasingly idiosyncratic leadership in 1990 and the government led by JOHN MAJOR often pro-voked her private anger and public criticism, it continued to operate largely within the parame-ters of Thatcherism. In sum, it may be said that whatever its particular successes and failures, Thatcherism profoundly altered the direction of contemporary British politics.

Steven Reilly

Bibliography
Dellheim, Charles. *The Disenchanted Isle: Mrs. Thatcher's Capitalist Revolution*. 1995.
Evans, Brendan. *Thatcherism and British Politics 1975–1999*. 1999.
Kavanagh, Dennis. *Thatcherism and British Politics: The Age of Consensus?* 1987.
Jenkins, Peter. *Mrs Thatcher's Revolution*. 1987.
Riddell, Peter. *The Thatcher Decade: How Britain Has Changed During the 1980s*. 1989.

Thomas, Dylan Marlais (1914–1953)

A writer whose work ranged from obscure quasi-religious poetry to comic essays, plays, and short stories, Thomas was born and brought up in

Swansea, in Wales, and was educated at the Swansea Grammar School. He was an inattentive student, but his literary talent appeared early as he took part in school publications and dramatic performances. After leaving school in 1931, Thomas worked as a reporter on a local newspaper for about a year and a half, and moved to London toward the end of 1934.

He had begun writing poetry when he was fifteen, preserving his poems in a series of notebooks. His first publications were a version of "And death shall have no dominion," which appeared in the London magazine, *New English Weekly*, in May 1933 and some poems in the Poet's Corner column of the *Sunday Referee*. But his poetic career had its real start in 1934 when the *Sunday Referee* awarded Thomas its semi-annual book prize, which meant the publication of a book of verse. Despite the obscurity of this first volume, *18 Poems*, it was favorably received. Apparently, the reviewers could not miss the poetic authority the poems projected, even if their meanings were not clear. Many of the poems came from Thomas's notebooks, and for some years afterward, Thomas would continue to draw material for his books from poems he had written between the ages of fifteen and nineteen.

In 1933 he began to exchange letters with Pamela Hansford Johnson, herself a young poet, who had written to him after reading one of his poems. The two met, became lovers and spoke of marriage, but Thomas's drunkenness, poverty, and Bohemian life made it impossible. He moved to London toward the end of 1934, and survived there on very little money, bedding down with any friend who would take him in, spending much time in bars, and incidentally meeting London literary figures.

Thomas continued to publish poems and book reviews in periodicals, and in September 1936 a second collection, *Twenty-five Poems*, appeared. He had gained the influential poet Edith Sitwell as an advocate, and her enthusiastic review of this volume made it a great success. By this time, Thomas' poetry had made a strong impression on the literary community, in spite of its obscurity and unfashionable romanticism.

In July 1937 Thomas married Caitlin Macnamara, and the couple, after living with others for a time, took a cottage in Laugharne, the Welsh village that was eventually to be their permanent home. In the first years of his marriage Thomas had no regular source of income and no settled home, and struggled to live on the poems, short stories, and book reviews he published, and on what he could borrow from friends and relatives.

The two books Thomas produced during this period earned little because the outbreak of the Second World War interfered with their sales.

The Map of Love (1939), a collection of material that had been appearing in periodicals, contained some of his best-known poems, including "After the Funeral," and seven fantastic short stories with surrealistic overtones. The stories of *Portrait of the Artist as a Young Dog* (1940), on the other hand, are well-controlled, realistic narratives set in Swansea and the nearby countryside. Thomas next attempted, but never finished a full-length comic novel, *Adventures in the Skin Trade*, published posthumously in 1955.

He was rejected for military service on medical grounds, and he and Caitlin continued to move about in the turmoil of wartime England and Wales, partly in order to avoid creditors. In 1941, however, he obtained employment as a scriptwriter for a cinema company and in the following years wrote a number of dramatic and DOCUMENTARY FILMS. The best of the dramatic films, *The Doctor and the Devils*, was the only one actually produced, but not until 1985, long after Thomas' death. Thomas had occasionally spoken on the Third Programme of the BBC since 1937, and during the war began to work regularly as a broadcaster and to write his own scripts. Sketches and essays on poetry from these broadcasts were published posthumously in 1954 under the title *Quite Early One Morning*. The radio and cinema work produced a comfortable income, but Thomas, unable to keep up with his expenses, was invariably in debt.

The war years were a productive time for Thomas. In spite of the hack work he had to do and the confusion of the times, he published two books which contain the bulk of his mature poetry, *New Verse* (1943) and *Deaths and Entrances* (1946). In 1949, after a friend bought him the Boat House on the bank of the river Towy that has since become a Thomas memorial, he moved back to Laugharne with his family, which now included two children, with a third soon expected. By this time Thomas had become well known in America as well as in Britain and in 1950 was invited to come to the United States to do a well-paid reading tour. In the following years, he undertook four of these American tours, giving dozens of performances, usually at colleges, and impressing his audiences with his sonorous reading style. But he also became drunk, misbehaved on social occasions, had affairs with several women, and gained a reputation as an amusingly disreputable figure.

These tours were intended to earn money, but Thomas, as usual, spent what he earned and was still in debt, and his relations with Caitlin, always difficult, deteriorated. He was still writing, but America tempted him as an escape from both work and home life in Wales as well as a way of earning money.

During these last years Thomas was in poor health and his drinking increased. But in spite of these handicaps and his strenuous tours, his radio play, *Under Milk Wood*, gradually came into shape and had a first reading with a full cast, and Thomas as one of its voices, in New York in the spring of 1953. When he came back to New York later in the year, he began to drink and to exhibit signs of mental disturbance. He fulfilled a few engagements, and saw friends, but then, after drinking heavily, collapsed, fell into a coma and died on 9 November 1953.

Thomas's most popular and accessible work is *Under Milk Wood*. However, he is best represented by the body of verse in his *Collected Poems 1934–1952* (1952). These poems, densely packed with verbal ingenuities and personal mysticism, anticipated a brief mid-century neo-Romantic revival in English poetry, and are among the most important lyric poems of the century.

Jacob Korg

Bibliography

Ferris, Paul. *Dylan Thomas: A Biography*. 1977.

Fitzgibbon, Constantine. *The Life of Dylan Thomas*. 1965.

Maud, Ralph N. *Entrances to Dylan Thomas' Poetry*. 1963.

Moynihan, William T. *The Craft and Art of Dylan Thomas*. 1966.

Rolph, J. Alexander. *Dylan Thomas: A Bibliography*. 1956.

Thomas, James Henry (1874–1949)

Jimmy Thomas was for long a very bright star in Labour's firmament. He was the dominant figure in the National Union of Railwaymen (NUR) when General Secretary (1916–31), a major moderate member of the General Council of the TRADES UNION CONGRESS (TUC) in the 1920s, and at the forefront of the Parliamentary LABOUR PARTY from 1914 until 1930, holding major office in the 1924 and 1929–31 Labour governments and subsequently in 1931–6 in the National governments.

Thomas had a hard unbringing in Newport. The illegitimate son of a domestic servant, he was raised by his widowed grandmother, a washerwoman. Leaving school at twelve, he was employed in a series of unskilled jobs, culminating, at fifteen, in being an engine cleaner for the Great Western Railway. From this he graduated to engine driver, only leaving shunting in the freight years on becoming a full-time trade union official in early 1906.

Thomas's political impact stemmed from his being the leader of a major trade union. He had risen fast, being elected a delegate to its 1898 congress, president in 1904–6, organizing secretary 1906–10, assistant general secretary 1910–16 before winning the post of general secretary by a 3:1

majority. The NUR grew rapidly during the FIRST WORLD WAR, its membership rising by 80 percent and its funds by 150 percent between 1913 and 1919. From 1914 the NUR's potential industrial strength had been enhanced by an alliance with the MINERS and TRANSPORT WORKERS. In the turbulent post-war years this Triple Industrial Alliance posed a challenge to the government, with clashes threatened or occurring over these unions' various demands, which ranged from wage increases to NATIONALIZATION. Though Thomas and the NUR took on the government in the national rail strike in the fall of 1919, he was generally seen as a figure urging compromise and moderation. He was vilified by the Left when the NUR and the Transport Workers declined to provide sympathy strikes for locked-out miners in 1921 and when TUC leadership called off the 1926 GENERAL STRIKE.

Thomas was a Labour councillor in Swindon (1901–6) and MP for Derby (1910–36), both railway towns. In 1916 he declined office under LLOYD GEORGE. In MACDONALD's Labour governments he was Colonial Secretary (1924), Lord Privy Seal (1929–30) and Dominions Secretary (1930–1). His unsuccessful attempts to grapple with mass UNEMPLOYMENT in 1929–30 undermined his reputation and ended talk of him as a likely successor to MacDonald. His links with the labor movement ended when he joined MacDonald in the National governments, holding office again in the Colonial and Dominion Offices. His career ended ignominiously after an inquiry into a budget leak in 1936.

Thomas was a colorful personality who often outraged the Left by his willingness to make secret deals and to fraternize with opponents. Yet as a union leader he took great pains to represent individual union members at tribunals, and he frequently emerged from collective bargaining with substantial gains. Politically, he was often astute and as a speaker frequently won over hostile audiences by his personality, rhetoric, and considerable wit.

C.J. Wrigley

Bibliography

Bagwell, Philip S. *The Railwaymen: The History of the National Union of Railwaymen*. 1963.

Blaxland, Gregory. *J.H. Thomas: A Life for Unity*. 1964.

Thomas, James H. *My Story*. 1937.

Thompson, E(dward) P(almer) (1924–1993)

E.P. Thompson, English historian and radical, ranks as one of the great historians of our time, and his book, *The Making of the English Working Class* (1963), is arguably the most influential work of social history ever written. It has informed and inspired the labors of a generation and more of social historians not only in Britain, but around the world, perhaps most especially in the United States. Thompson provided a poetic manifesto for radical historians to pursue the recovery of the lives and agencies of the laboring classes and the oppressed.

Thompson was born 3 February 1924, the second son of Edward John and Theodosia Jessup Thompson, who had been METHODIST education missionaries in India. Raised near Oxford, the younger Edward went to CAMBRIDGE to study literature but eventually switched to history. At this time he also joined the British COMMUNIST PARTY. Like most of his generation, Thompson's studies were interrupted by the SECOND WORLD WAR. Commissioned an officer, he was given command of a tank unit and served in Italy.

Following the war, Thompson returned to Cambridge where he met his wife and fellow historian-to-be, Dorothy Sale. Completing their B.A. degrees in 1946, they went with other young volunteers to Yugoslavia to work on the building of a railway. Returning to England, Thompson was appointed an ADULT EDUCATION lecturer in the Leeds University Extra-Mural Department. He and Dorothy remained active in both the Communist Party and the Communist Party Historians' Group, which included Christopher Hill, Eric Hobsbawm, John Saville, Victor Kiernan, and George Rudé, who, with Thompson, were the founding figures of the British Marxist historical tradition and the approach to the past known as "history from the bottom up." An important project of the group was the creation of the journal, *Past & Present*, on whose editorial board Thompson later served for many years. His own writings of the time include his first book, *William Morris: Romantic to Revolutionary* (1955).

In 1956 Thompson left the party—as did many of his historian comrades—in protest against the Soviet invasion of Hungary. Still, he remained a committed and engaged democratic socialist and a founding figure of the early British New Left and the journals, *New Reasoner* and *New Left Review*. Also, he became energetically involved with the CAMPAIGN FOR NUCLEAR DISARMAMENT (CND).

The publication of *The Making of the English Working Class* led to Thompson joining the faculty of the newly established University of Warwick as Reader in the Center for Social History in 1968. His scholarly investigations turned to eighteenth century English class relations and struggles, especially aspects of popular culture, crime, and the law. These studies significantly revised our historical understanding of modes of power and authority and rebellion and resistance and resulted in the publication in 1975 of *Whigs and Hunters* and, with his students (British and North American) *Albion's Fatal Tree*—

plus a remarkable set of articles only just recently published as *Customs in Common* (1992). Also, Thompson continued to be engaged as a public intellectual, as such works as *May Day Manifesto 1968* (1968) and *Warwick University Ltd* (1970) demonstrated.

Thompson left Warwick in the mid-1970s to write full time; however, during the next fifteen years he took up visiting professorships at Brown University and Rutgers University, and at Queen's University in Canada. Among his writings of the late 1970s was a powerful defense of the historical discipline and of human agency in the making of history against the claims of French structuralist philosophers published in *The Poverty of Theory* (1978).

Increasingly, Thompson's historical imagination and commitments propelled him into full-time political labors. Concerned about what he recognized to be threats to the rights and liberties of "free-born Britons", he directed his broadsides and public speeches at the power and abuses of the British state and establishment in *Writing by Candlelight* (1980) and *Beyond the Cold War* (1982). And, in the face of the "Second Cold War" of the 1980s, Thompson penned the pamphlet *Protest and Survive*, which mobilized hundreds of thousands to the cause of nuclear disarmament, and joined with other peace activists to establish END (European Nuclear Disarmament). To the lament of many academics, he put aside his historical scholarship for almost a decade, though he did find time to write a satirical work of science fiction, *The Sykaos Papers* (1988).

With the end of the Cold War, Thompson was able to return to historical study. Unfortunately, he suffered a series of debilitating illnesses. Yet, despite his declining health, his scholarly output continued. In addition to putting in order the eighteenth century collection, *Customs in Common*, and writing *Alien Homage: Edward Thompson and Rabindranath Tagore* (1993) about his father, Thompson completed his long-promised book on the Romantic poets, *Witness against the Beast: William Blake and the Moral Law* (1993), and prepared another collection of historical essays, *Making History* (1994), which he delivered to the publishers just weeks before his death. He died on 28 August 1993 at his home Wick Episcopi, for many years a gathering place for historians and writers from around the globe.

Harvey J. Kaye

Bibliography

Bess, Michael D. *Realism, Utopia, and the Mushroom Cloud: Four Activist Intellectuals and their Strategies for Peace, 1945–1989.* 1993

Kaye, Harvey J. *The British Marxist Historians.* 1984.

——, and Keith McClelland. *E.P Thompson: Critical Perspectives.* 1989.

Palmer, Bryan D. *The Making of E.P. Thompson: Marxism, Humanism, and History.* 1981.

The Times

The Times is Britain's oldest surviving daily newspaper and, certainly from the Victorian period to the 1970s, remained the country's primary journal of record. It also attained a reputation for independent, intelligent, and informed opinion, expressed through its famous editorials or "leaders", that has probably never been rivaled.

John Walter founded the *Daily Universal Register* in 1785, changing the name of the paper to *The Times* three years later. However, the prosperity and reputation of the paper were only secured by his son, John Walter II. It was he who appointed Thomas Barnes as editor in 1817, and Barnes and Walter succeeded in establishing *The Times* as a paper of "independent" conviction, not beholden unto any party or government. Barnes was succeeded by the other great Victorian editor of *The Times*, John Delane, in 1841. Under Delane, who served as editor until 1877, the influence and prestige of the paper reached its zenith.

After the death of Delane in 1877, a series of editors maintained the paper's reputation, although increasing competition from a new generation of alternative newspapers meant that *The Times* lost its unchallenged position in the marketplace. Increasing financial losses forced the Walter family to sell the paper to LORD NORTHCLIFFE in 1908 (although the Walter family retained a minority shareholding in the paper until the 1960s). Northcliffe, founder of the *Daily Mail* in 1896, brought a somewhat unsavory reputation as the creator of the "yellow press" to *The Times*, which provoked a certain amount of anxiety among some of the staff. However, the character of the paper survived Northcliffe and contributed significantly to the course of British politics during the FIRST WORLD WAR, playing an important role in the political process that led to ASQUITH being replaced by LLOYD GEORGE as Prime Minister in 1916. On Northcliffe's death in 1922, *The Times* was bought by J.J. Astor, and it remained in the Astor family until 1966.

The most important editor of *The Times* during the first half of the twentieth century was GEOFFREY DAWSON, editor 1912–19 and 1922–41. He dominated the paper in the tradition of Barnes and Delane but, unlike his Victorian predecessors, he failed to keep *The Times* independent of government. Through his frequent and close contacts with members of successive British governments during the inter-war years, he may have enhanced the level of intelligence that *The Times* was able to call on when the leader-writers

sat down to pen their editorials, but by the same token he was at least in part responsible for making *The Times* too dependent on the government of the day for its views and, indeed, often its news as well. The process reached its peak with the close collusion between Dawson and NEVILLE CHAMBERLAIN's government over the policy of APPEASEMENT towards Germany in the late 1930s, an episode that damaged the reputation of *The Times* for honest and informed independence. Indeed, the close links that *The Times* had sought to cultivate with the government, just as all governments had sought to gain the support and cooperation of *The Times*, led to the charge that *The Times* was the official mouthpiece of the British government; under Dawson there was some truth in this allegation. *The Times'*s close relationship to the government was only really broken with the SUEZ CRISIS in 1956, when the editor, Sir William Haley, refused to support Prime Minister ANTHONY EDEN's military action against Egypt despite being one of the very few people privy to Eden's secret plan of military collusion between Britain, France and Israel for the attack on Egypt.

The most important editors of the post-war era were Sir William Haley (1952–66) and Sir William Rees-Mogg (1967–81). Rees-Mogg, in particular, did much to maintain the intellectual distinction of *The Times*, as the paper was, for instance, very important in introducing the economic doctrine of monetarism to a wider audience during the early 1970s. However the cost of producing *The Times*, which always had a relatively small, if affluent, readership, grew dramatically in the 1960s and 1970s. These rising costs led to the sale of the paper by the Astor family to Lord Thomson in 1966, who combined the paper with the *Sunday Times* (previously a quite separate title) in one newspaper group. However, after a series of protracted union disputes in the later 1970s, the Thomson group was obliged to sell both papers to Rupert Murdoch's News International company in 1981.

The position of *The Times* as Britain's preeminent newspaper was threatened by several factors during the 1980s. Under Murdoch's management, *The Times* sought to appeal to a wider readership in order to make the paper financially viable, which inevitably led to a deterioration of its standards, both as a journal of record and as a leader of intellectual opinion. Furthermore, in 1986 *The Independent* was launched to try to capitalize on this by utilizing the old journalistic strengths of *The Times* to replace the latter paper as Britain's most important daily newspaper. In 1985–6 *The Times* was also at the center of a bitter industrial dispute arising out of the move of all of Murdoch's papers to a new, central location in Wapping, East London. The close identification of *The Times* with the rest of Murdoch's newspaper empire meant that the paper lost, in some people's eyes, its reputation for intellectual and political independence that other proprietors, such as the Astors, had struggled to maintain.

Today, no paper in Britain plays the role that *The Times* once played in public life during its heyday, and the place of *The Times* as Britain's primary journal of record and opinion is now in doubt. However, given the paper's checkered financial history during the twentieth century it may also be considered a small miracle that the paper still exists at all, let alone continues to play an important, if diminished, role in the public life of contemporary Britain.

Richard Cockett

Bibliography
Evans, Harold. *Good Times, Bad Times*. 1984.
McLachlan, Donald. *In the Chair: Barrington-Ward of The Times, 1927–1948*. 1971.
The Official History of The Times. 5 vols. 1935–84.
Woods, Oliver, and James Bishop. *The Story of The Times*. 1983.
Wrench, John Evelyn. *Geoffrey Dawson and Our Times*. 1955.

Tippett, Michael Kemp (1905–1998)
The output of English composer and conductor Michael Tippett reveals in retrospect a majestic progression of five OPERAS interspersed with five string quartets, and four each of piano sonatas, concertos and symphonies. Although a late-developer musically, he has created a highly individual neoclassical style, drawing on rhythmic techniques found in English Renaissance music and Stravinsky, and strongly influenced by his admiration for Beethoven's music and for jazz, particularly the blues. His initial visit to the United States in 1965, a liberating experience, led to his first American commission, the Fourth Symphony, which was given its world premiere in Chicago in 1977. Subsequent American world premieres have included the first performances of *The Mask of Time* (Boston), the Fourth Piano Sonata (Los Angeles), and the opera, *New Year* (Houston). Among official honors Tippett has been the recipient of several doctorates as well as a knighthood (1966) and the Order of Merit (1981).

Born in London, the son of an entrepreneur of Cornish stock, Tippett had little formal musical tuition while at school except piano lessons, but by the time he left, he had made up his mind to become a composer. Following a period of study at the Royal College of Music, London (1923–8) with Charles Wood and then Charles Kitson as composition teachers (the latter uncongenial) as well as help with conducting from Adrian Boult and Malcolm Sargent, Tippett settled in Oxted,

Surrey, teaching French part-time. There he gained much useful practical experience from local music-making, conducting a choir and staging operas, but a concert of his own music in 1930 demonstrated the need for further tuition, which he received from R.O. Morris (1930–2). In 1933 he was invited to conduct the South London (Morley College) Orchestra for professional unemployed musicians, and he became the Director of Music at Morley College from 1940–51. His PACIFIST convictions were put to the test during the Second World War when, as a registered CONSCIENTIOUS OBJECTOR, he was sentenced to three months' imprisonment. Following the war he could devote himself more fully to composition, although he acted as the Musical Director of the Bath Festival for a five-year period (1969–74). In 1951 he left Oxted, subsequently settling in the West Country, where he lived until his death.

With the completion of the First String Quartet (1935) and First Piano Sonata (1938), Tippett withdrew or destroyed all his earlier compositions thereby marking the emergence of his mature style. Indeed the finale of the quartet contains the first example of his highly individual use of assymetrical rhythms, more fully explored in the virile counterpoint of the exultant Concerto for Double String Orchestra (1939) and the presto scherzo of the Second String Quartet (1942). In contrast to Tippett's self-confessed preoccupation with form in these works, the oratorio, *A Child of Our Time* (Tippett: 1941), reveals his commitment to expressing fundamental truths about the contemporary human condition, in this case, man's inhumanity to man, inviting our understanding and compassion. Although the subject-matter of the opera, *The Midsummer Marriage* (Tippett: 1952), is different—two lovers can be united only after having attained self-knowledge—the *raison d'etre* is the same. The opera's "images of abounding, generous, exuberant beauty" are conveyed in a luminous opulence that also pervades the subsequent Fantasia Concertante on a Theme of Corelli for strings (1953) with its rich profusion of arabesques, and the glittering textures of the Piano Concerto (1955).

A move, already evident in the Second Symphony (1957), towards greater concentration, with the music evolving as the statement of many contrasting ideas in different juxtapositions rather than the lengthy development of a few, gains fuller expression in the mosaic-like structures of the Second Piano Sonata (1962) and the more sophisticated "collage" treatment in the Concerto for Orchestra (1963). The complex multi-layered textures of *The Vision of St. Augustine* (1965) for baritone, chorus, and orchestra, Tippett's most radical work, form the climax of this development. The opera, *King Priam* (Tippett: 1961), gains its starkness from the accumulation of often brutally juxtaposed gestures, but in his next opera, *The Knot Garden* (Tippett: 1969), a contemporary comedy of forgiveness influenced by Shakespeare's *The Tempest,* Tippett draws on a synthesis of his earlier styles to portray the characters' separations and reconciliations. Tippett's inclusion of blues at the end of Act I, together with the blues sequence in the second part of the Third Symphony (1972), point to his renewed enthusiasm for the United States, which forms the implied setting for his fourth opera, *The Ice Break* (Tippett: 1976), although the plot's themes of racial conflict (including mob violence), the generation gap, and the polarity of Communist and capitalist political systems have resonances worldwide. Tippett's preoccupation with the New World led him to reassess his attitude to the Old World, symbolized by the music of Beethoven, quoting the "Ode to Joy" in the Third Symphony, both to assert values and to criticize them. A similar process can be heard in the Fourth String Quartet (1978), with the rhythmic allusions to Beethoven's *Grosse Fuge.*

Tippett's later works, while continuing to explore new sound worlds, also relate back to earlier developments. The warm lyricism of the radiant Triple Concerto (1979) echoes to a certain extent that of the Fantasia Concertante on a Theme of Corelli; in the opera, *New Year* (Tippett: 1988), the portrayal of the tension that exists between our dream worlds and their inevitable conflict with reality reminds us of the personal problems confronting Jenifer and Mark in *The Midsummer Marriage. The Mask of Time* (1982) for four soloists, chorus and orchestra, "fragments or scenes from from a possible 'epiphany' for today," is a rich musical metaphor of the multi-faceted nature of contemporary humanity that celebrates reconciliation.

Trevor Bray

Bibliography
Kemp, Ian. *Tippet: The Composer and His Music.* 1984.
Tippett, Michael. *Moving into Aquarius.* 1974.
———. *Those Twentieth Century Blues: An Autobiography.* 1991.
Whittall, Arnold. *The Music of Britten and Tippett.* 1982.

Titmuss, Richard Morris (1907–1973)

Richard Titmuss occupies a deservedly important place in the study of social policy in Britain. Many of his contemporaries would share Margaret Gowing's verdict that, by the time he died, Titmuss had "created a new discipline and was one of the few truly original social scientists of his generation." Given all the obstacles he had to overcome, his rise to academic eminence was remarkable. Born in 1907, he was forced by the pressure of family finances to leave school at

fourteen and take an office job, eventually becoming a clerk in an insurance firm. The work was unremittingly dull, but it taught Titmuss actuarial skills and developed in him a fascination for the vital statistics of demography. Possessed of a lively and enquiring mind, Titmuss became interested in politics and gradually in the 1930s began to cultivate an ever-widening circle of important friends who later were to act as useful patrons.

It was these *autodidact* leanings that impelled him to write his first important book, *Poverty and Population* (1938). It made skillful use of mortality statistics to argue trenchantly against the government's apparent lack of concern over differential mortality rates by social class and region. Two more part-academic, part-polemical works followed in quick succession: *Birth, Poverty and Wealth* (1943), and (with his wife, Kay) *Parents Revolt* (1943). He also joined the Eugenics Society, editing the *Eugenics Review* for a time, and advised the government on a variety of health and demographic matters during the Second World War.

Such activities attracted public attention and led to Titmuss's appointment as one of the official historians of the SECOND WORLD WAR. The resultant volume, *Problems of Social Policy* (1950), was an exploration of how the social services had coped with the human consequences of bombing, evacuation, homelessness, and other social disruptions of wartime. A central tenet of the book was the belief that universal, state-provided welfare was not only efficient but socially integrative. The plaudits earned led to Titmuss's appointment as Professor of Social Administration at the LONDON SCHOOL OF ECONOMICS in 1950—a remarkable achievement for one who had left school with no formal academic qualifications.

For the next two decades Titmuss established himself as the personification of social policy studies in Britain. In a number of important publications, such as *Essays on "The Welfare State"* (1958) and *Commitment to Welfare* (1968), he argued the case for a social democratic, universal WELFARE STATE which would protect its weakest citizens and bestow equality of rights. One of his most imaginative books, *The Gift Relationship* (1970), was a study, using criteria taken from both economics and moral philosophy, of the superiority of an unpaid, state-run system of blood donating over one organized on free market principles. Indeed, one of his strengths was the combination of a strong moral commitment to greater equality with a mastery of statistical detail—as in his study of inequality, *Income Distribution and Social Change* (1962).

Since his death in 1973 Titmuss's work has been subject to the criticism that it was often dilettantish or that it failed to explore the realities of political power. Nevertheless, his status as a modern "founding father" of social policy remains unchallenged.

John Macnicol

Bibliography
Gowing, Margaret. "Richard Morris Titmuss," *Proceedings of the British Academy*. vol. LXI (1975), pp.401–28.
Reisman, David A. *Richard Titmuss: Welfare and Society* (1977)
Wilding, Paul. "Richard Titmuss and Social Welfare," *Social and Economic Administration*. vol. 10 (1976), pp. 147–66.

Tizard, Henry Thomas (1885–1959)

Henry Tizard was a senior civil servant, scientific adviser, and academic administrator, concerned above all with the application of science to war, especially with AVIATION. He was the son of a naval officer and Fellow of the Royal Society, and was educated at public school and Magdalen College, OXFORD. In 1911 he was elected a Fellow of Oriel College, where he taught CHEMISTRY. He volunteered for the ARMY in 1914 and transferred to the Royal Flying Corps in 1915, where he developed testing procedures for a new aircraft. He ended the war as a Lt. Colonel and second in command of the new Air Ministry's scientific and technical branch. After a very brief interlude in Oxford he returned to government as a senior civil servant at the new Department of Scientific and Industrial Research in 1920, at first with responsibility for coordinating research for the services. In 1927 he became the permanant secretary of the Department. He left the civil service in 1929 to become Rector of Imperial College, London; in 1942 he became President of Magdalen College, Oxford. He returned full time to the civil service in 1946 as Chairman of the Defence Research Policy Committee and the Advisory Council on Scientific Policy and retired in 1952.

While outside the civil service he undertook many important advisory roles in military aviation, operating at the very highest official and political levels. He was from the early 1930s to the middle of the SECOND WORLD WAR the most senior scientific adviser to the ROYAL AIR FORCE and to the Ministry of Aircraft Production. As such he was closely involved with advising on the development of RADAR, jet engines, atomic weapons, and much else. Tizard's associations were primarily with the air war, not with the naval or land wars. He did not have the ear of Prime Minister WINSTON CHURCHILL, who relied on Lord Cherwell as his scientific adviser. However, Tizard did chair an inter-service committee of scientific advisers on weapons of the future in 1944–5, which was in effect a prelude to becoming scientific adviser to the Ministry of Defence after the war. For all his wide-ranging responsibilities Tizard did not have responsibility for atomic weapons.

Tizard became known to a wider public soon after his death largely through C.P. Snow's misleading picture of him as an opponent of strategic bombing. That analysis has been thoroughly rebutted by evidence that Tizard did not object in principle to strategic bombing, only to what he saw as a diversion of bombers away from where they were most needed in 1942. It would indeed have been extraordinary if the RAF had had as its adviser an opponent of its primary strategy since 1918. Tizard was at the center of Britain's military-scientific complex for decades, in peace and in war. But unlike other scientist-civil servants and advisers like Lord Cherwell, Lord Hankey, Sir John Anderson, or Sir John Grigg, he achieved neither ministerial office, nor a peerage, although he received a knighthood in 1937.

David E.H. Edgerton

Bibliography
Clark, Ronald W. *Tizard*. 1965.

Town and Country Planning

The most urbanized country in the world in 1900, Britain was also a world leader in thinking about the rational planning of cities, but its strong political traditions respecting the sanctity of private property meant that theory remained well ahead of practice until mid-century. A comprehensive planning system embracing both town and country was erected in the late 1940s and was widely envied and imitated abroad. The system was most successful in protecting the countryside from creeping suburbanization, but it was only halfheartedly implemented in the towns. Planners were blamed for the soulless building boom of the 1950s and 1960s, and towards the end of the century physical planning was just as politically unpopular as it had been at the beginning.

Limited elements of town planning, such as regulation of the layout and density of private housing, had in the nineteenth century been justified on public health grounds. The first modern town planning acts derived from this tradition but also pointed the way towards a more deliberate and comprehensive system. An Act of 1909 encouraged local authorities to link their disparate powers to regulate land use, density, road-building, and sanitary and amenity provision in the drawing up of local plans. A few did, and town planning departments emerged in some cities, notably Birmingham. A professional association, the Town Planning Institute, was in place by 1914. But at this stage the practice of statutory planning was rudimentary by the standards being set by theorists like Ebenezer Howard or Patrick

Geddes, by philanthropic efforts such as the Cadbury family's Bournville or William Lever's Port Sunlight. Even the First World War, a catalyst for government growth in so many other areas, had relatively little impact. The post-war Housing and Town Planning Act of 1919 contributed more to the former than the latter. It did, however, make compulsory the development plans for towns permitted by the 1909 Act. The 1932 Town and Country Planning Act extended these plans to all local authorities, rural as well as urban, and to all kinds of land (whether or not ripe for development), but in other respects was looser and more permissive.

Planning between the wars therefore proceeded on a piecemeal and local basis. A few central government officers—Raymond Unwin, a veteran of Howard's GARDEN CITY movement who became chief planner at the Local Government Board, George Pepler at the Ministry of Health—provided encouragement and pooled expertise, but had little funding to provide and no powers of compulsion. Ambitious local authorities such as the London County Council achieved much under this regime (e.g., regional coordination, open-space reservation, transport schemes), but little pressure was applied to laggards. In consequence, the face of Britain changed dramatically in this period without much conscious direction: countryside was eaten up by suburban extension and disfigured by ribbon development and the mushrooming road and electricity supply networks, cities sprawled yet remained congested, industry and employment became increasingly maldistributed.

Probably this chaos would have triggered an environmental planning revolution even if the SECOND WORLD WAR had not popularized planning in all spheres. During the war environmental planning came to be seen as a national task, linked to other forms of planning, taking into account social, economic, and cultural needs as well as PUBLIC HEALTH and HOUSING. The Barlow, Scott, and Uthwatt Reports on planning matters had an effect on public opinion parallel to that of the BEVERIDGE Report on social security. Their principal fruit was the 1947 Town and Country Planning Act, supplemented by legislation facilitating the creation of new towns and national parks. Planning powers were concentrated in the larger local authorities (counties and county boroughs) and coordinated by a central Ministry of Town and Country Planning (Housing and Local Government from 1951; Department of the Environment from 1970). A complicated "compensation and betterment" mechanism was established which enabled local authorities to direct land use without having to pay ruinous compensation to private owners: development rights had essen-

tially been nationalized. A land-use map for the whole nation could gradually be compiled and lightly guided from the center. Historic buildings were protected, cities were ringed by "green belts" of undeveloped land to prevent sprawl, the road network and the distribution of industry and population were now matters of national policy.

Under this regime, physical planning improved on the national and regional level but probably deteriorated locally, especially in cities. City planning departments were overwhelmed both by their new powers and by pressure from developers and politicians not to use them lest they dampen housing and commercial growth, booming in the 1950s and 1960s. CONSERVATIVE governments responded to these pressures by de-nationalizing development rights, which put a question mark over local authorities' ability to plan land use compulsorily. "Planning blight"—non-development for fear that planning powers *might* be applied in future—resulted regardless. Thus planners tended to be blamed for developments they had not controlled and for non-development they had not planned, against which credit for their positive achievements paled.

In the 1970s the momentum given by the 1947 Act ran out. By this time the building boom had ended anyway. Local planning ground to a halt, and central planning had largely attained its stated goals. The election of an anti-planning Conservative government in 1979 only capped this process. The 1947 machinery largely remained in place, but its public profile and popularity had melted away: no change was preferred to planned change. Just as before the First World War, urban renewal was largely the work of the private sector; London's Docklands and other riparian schemes were deliberately exempted from normal planning controls.

Peter Mandler

Bibliography

Cherry, Gordon E. *Cities and Plans: The Shaping of Urban Britain in the Nineteenth and Twentieth Centuries*. 1988.

Cullingworth, J.B. *Town and Country Planning in Britain*. 10th ed. 1988.

Hall, Peter et al. *The Containment of Urban England*. 2 vols. 1973.

Mandler, Peter. "New Towns for Old: The Fate of the Town Center," in Becky Conekin, Frank Mort, and Chris Waters, eds. *Moments of Modernity: Reconstructing Britain 1945–64*. 1999, pp. 208–27.

Sheail, John. *Rural Conservation in Inter-War Britain*. 1981.

Trade Union Legislation

For more than two centuries the exercise of trade union power has been a matter of political controversy in Britain. During the nineteenth century many of the legal restrictions were removed which had been placed on the trade unions by the Combination Acts of 1799 and 1800 and by earlier legislation. However, from the 1890s there was a series of legal decisions hostile to the unions, most famously the TAFF VALE JUDGMENT (1901), which fueled trade union demands for legislative action to restore what they saw as their rights under 1871 and 1875 legislation.

Such legislation came soon after the LIBERAL PARTY's landslide victory in the 1906 general election. Prime Minister Sir HENRY CAMPBELL-BANNERMAN went further than many of his ministerial colleagues wished when he supported the giving of unlimited legal immunity to trade unions for damages incurred during the course of trade disputes rather than simply providing limited protection for union funds as his CABINET initially had agreed. The Trades Disputes Act (1906) enabled unions to organize STRIKES without fear of bankruptcy, and thereby restored to them their most important card in collective bargaining.

The Liberals redressed another trade union grievance in 1912. The Osborne Judgment (1910) had banned trade unions from funding political activity, a decision which was very damaging to the young LABOUR PARTY. The Trade Union Act (1913) permitted trade unions to use their funds for political purposes providing that a majority of members agreed and that those who did not wish to support such expenditure were entitled to contract out.

During both world wars trade union action, along with most economic activity, was restricted. In the FIRST WORLD WAR the most important measure was the Munitions of War Act (1915). This substituted arbitration for strikes and lockouts, controlled war industries, and set up special courts (munitions tribunals) to enforce good working practices within them, suspended trade union restrictive practices, and indirectly controlled labor mobility. The definition of "munitions" was wide—and was later extended by the Munitions of War (Amendment) Act (1916) and by the courts so that compulsory arbitration was also applied to groups such as textile workers and dockers. During the SECOND WORLD WAR the government again took a range of exceptional powers. The most important in regard to labor were Defence Regulation 58A and Order 1305, the latter banning strikes and lock-outs and establishing a National Arbitration Tribunal.

After the First World War the number and nature of strikes led many in governing circles to feel that the wartime extraordinary powers under the DEFENCE OF THE REALM ACTS should be continued to enable governments to deal with any future labor unrest which threatened to undermine the political system. Hence LLOYD GEORGE's government put on the statute book the Emergency Powers Act (1920), which gave governments virtually unlimited powers should they declare there to be a national emergency. This Act has been used by several governments, most notably EDWARD HEATH's (1970–4).

The labor unrest of 1910–20 brought the issue of trade union power to the forefront of British politics. During 1910–14 the Conservative leadership considered proposing legislative curbs. After the First World War the party's right wing became increasingly restless. In early 1925 STANLEY BALDWIN persuaded Tory backbenchers to withdraw a bill to reinstate the Osborne Judgment. In the aftermath of the 1926 GENERAL STRIKE he found that Conservative pressure for trade union legislation was irresistible. The Trade Disputes and Trade Unions Act (1927) banned general strikes and strikes by local government workers, made picketing more difficult, forbade central and local government employees from joining unions which could affiliate to the TUC and charged the onus of effort in the trade union political levy to the Labour Party from contracting out to contracting in (which immediately cut the Labour Party's funds from this source by a third). The ATTLEE government repealed this legislation with the Trade Disputes and Trade Unions Act (1946).

In the 1960s higher levels of inflation, declining competitiveness of much of British industry, and growing concern about strikes in export industries brought trade union legislation back as a major issue in British politics. With the Rookes v. Barnard case (1964) the courts threw doubt on the legal immunity of trade union officials which had hitherto been believed to have been given by the Trade Disputes Act (1906). Following the election in 1964 of HAROLD WILSON's Labour government, the Royal Commission on Trade Unions and Employers' Associations (1965–8) under Lord Donovan was set up to investigate British industrial relations. The resulting Report argued against major legislation. However, with the CONSERVATIVE PARTY demanding legislation and public opinion being critical of many strikes, Wilson and Barbara Castle, the Employment Secretary, produced the White Paper "In Place of Strife", which proposed legislation that exceeded the Royal Commission's suggestions. However the trade union movement reacted strongly against the proposals that the minister should have the power to impose a twenty-eight day cooling-off period before a strike occurred, to settle inter-union disputes, and to order strike ballots. The Wilson government was humiliated when its Industrial Relations Bill, which included the first two of these proposals, had to be withdrawn because of a revolt by Labour backbench MPs.

In the 1970 general election the Conservatives were returned to power with a commitment to trade union legislation. Heath's Industrial Relations Act (1971) went further than "In Place of Strife". While it gave a special court, the National Industrial Relations Court, the power to order cooling-off periods and to require a strike ballot, this legislation also gave this court the power to fine unions for "unfair industrial practices," to award compensation to workers unfairly sacked, and to require union recognition. The Act also dealt with the closed shop, gave workers the right to belong or not to belong to a union, and made collective agreements legally binding (unless specified in the agreements that they were not). Under the Act a new Registrar of Trade Unions and Employee Associations was appointed, who had some powers of regulation over such unions as registered with him. The passage of this legislation was marked by large hostile demonstrations, organized by the TUC and the Labour Party. Well before the miners' strike that led to the early general election of February 1974 which the Conservatives lost, much of the Act's provisions were becoming ineffective. Organized labor was hostile, the imprisonment of five dockers under the Act gave its opponents martyrs, employers often were unwilling to risk worsening industrial relations by taking their workers to court, and Heath's own government came to see trade union legislation as secondary to securing union cooperation for its prices and incomes policy.

With the return of Labour under Wilson (1974–6) and JAMES CALLAGHAN (1976–9), Heath's trade union legislation was repealed by the Trade Union and Labour Relations Acts (1974, 1976). These Acts did take up what the unions regarded as the more positive aspects of the 1971 legislation, notably on unfair dismissals. Working people were given further safeguards with the Health and Safety at Work Act (1974) and by the Employment Protection Acts (1975, 1978).

MARGARET THATCHER's victory in the 1979 general election began an era of trade union legislation that aimed to weaken the unions. Unlike 1971, this was carried out in a step-by-step manner which did not arouse the united opposition that Heath's legislation had done. Moreover in the 1979, 1983 and 1987 general elections many trade unionists voted Conservative, probably more than voted Labour. The Conservative attack on the trade unions was also buttressed by monetarist economic thinking in which unions could be seen as a restriction on an ideal free market where wages go down as unemployed people compete to do for lower wages the work currently being done by those still employed. Between 1980 and 1992 the Conservatives made parliamentary time available for nine trade union bills, which became the Employment Acts (1980, 1982, 1988, 1989, 1990), the Trade Union Act (1984), and the Trade Union and Labour Relations (Consolidation) Act (1992).

The main feature of the 1980–92 legislation was to take trade union law back to before 1906. Trade unions, not just individual trade unionists, were again liable for damages arising from collective action. Unions lost their immunity from legal action if they called strikes without first holding a secret ballot or if a dispute involved secondary action. Picketing was limited to those directly involved and to their workplace. The closed shop was banned except where a ballot showed 85 percent of those voting supported it. The legislation helped union members who disregarded majority verdicts in their union: unions could not discipline members who crossed picket lines or refused to strike. It also provided advice and funds to members who took legal action against their own union. There were also public funds for union secret ballots. There had to be ballots for union officers and executive committee members and, every ten years, for unions to maintain political funds. All in all the 1980–92 legislation shifted the legal balance in industrial relations to the benefit of employers and to the detriment of the unions.

C.J. Wrigley

Bibliography

Brown, Kenneth D. "Trade Unions and the Law" in C.J. Wrigley, ed. *A History of British Industrial Relations 1875–1914.* 1982. pp. 116–34.

Ewing, K.D. *Trade Unions, the Labour Party and the Law.* 1982.

Kessler, Sidney, and Fred Bayliss. *Contemporary British Industrial Relations.* 1992.

McCarthy, W., ed. *Legal Intervention in Industrial Relations.* 1992.

McIlroy, J. *The Permanent Revolution? Conservative Law and the Trade Unions.* 1991.

Wedderburn, K.W. *The Worker and the Law.* 3rd ed. 1986.

Trades Union Congress (TUC)

By 1900 the TUC was well established as the collective voice of much of the British trade union movement. Some 70 percent of trade unionists were members of unions which were affiliated to the TUC. Set up in 1868, the TUC provided a national forum for the unions and acted as a pressure group on central government. Through its Parliamentary Committee, which was made up of the main trade union leaders of the day, the TUC lobbied ministers and MPs. Up until the

1890s the TUC leadership, like most trade unionists had been predominantly LIBERAL or Lib-Lab
in politics. This changed in the twentieth century.

Indeed the 1899 Congress passed a resolution
calling on the Parliamentary Committee to arrange a conference which would ensure more Labour Members of Parliament. The resulting conference of February 1900 marked the
establishment of a separate LABOUR PARTY, initially the LABOUR REPRESENTATION COMMIT-
TEE (LRC). A major reason for this action by the
TUC was dismay at the adverse decisions on
trade union law that were being made in the law
courts. The TAFF VALE JUDGMENT (1901) turned
a slow flow of unions affiliating to the LRC to a
flood. Between 1901 and 1906 the proportion of
the TUC membership affiliated to the LRC doubled from 29 to 58 percent. In the 1906 general
election nine members of the thirteen-strong
Parliamentary Committee of the TUC were
elected to Parliament, three still as Lib-Labs but
six through the LRC. By the early stages of the
First World War the TUC and Labour Party
were very close, a situation helped by the latter
then being led by such prominent trade unionists
as ARTHUR HENDERSON, J.R. Clynes, and William Adamson.

The FIRST WORLD WAR greatly strengthened
British trade unionism and thereby the TUC.
During the course of the war, 5,670,000 men
joined the armed forces from a male labor force
at the war's outbreak of some 15 million. Thus
labor generally, and skilled labor in particular,
was in a potentially very powerful position in "a
war of production." The TUC and the leaderships of most unions backed the war and did not
try to exploit fully their much enhanced position
in the labor market. Indeed the TUC was a
major party to the declaration on 28 August 1914
of an industrial truce for the duration of the war
and to the Treasury Agreement of March 1915, a
voluntary agreement which included the suspension of trade union restrictive practices as well as
various schemes to move labor to war priority
work and to curtail labor benefiting from free
market forces.

However while the TUC did not take advantage of the wartime labor market, it nevertheless
emerged stronger from the war and the post-war
economic boom. For one thing it benefited from
the doubling of trade union membership from
4,145,000 in 1914 to 8,348,000 in 1920 (with the
proportion affiliated to the TUC rising from 65
to 77 percent). For another, it gained in prestige as
the wartime governments had needed to pay attention to its views on a wide range of industrial
and social matters.

The TUC became a more efficient pressure organization after the First World War. It moved

into a bigger building, began appointing full-time
officials, and providing its affiliates with information on industrial relations. Most important of all,
in 1921 it replaced its Parliamentary Committee
with the General Council. This was elected on a
more representative basis than its predecessor,
taking into account industrial groupings and
union size. Within the limits that individual trade
union autonomy would permit, the General
Council had much potential for giving direction
to the whole trade union movement.

The TUC also took on an international role
from the later stages of the First World War
when it felt the need to be involved in discussing
the post-war world. In 1920 the TUC elbowed
aside the General Federation of Trade Unions
(GFTU) which until the middle of the war had
been allowed to be the sole collective voice overseas of British trade unionism.

In 1924 the General Council was given powers
to intervene to try to achieve settlements in industrial disputes and, where such mediation
failed, to organize the whole resources of the
movement to support the trade union involved.
In 1925 the TUC became embroiled in the affairs
of a large, militant union when the MINERS were
faced with wage cuts, longer working hours, and
an end to national collective agreements. This led
in May 1926 to the General Council calling a
GENERAL STRIKE in support of the miners, intended to affect government policy, not to overthrow constitutional government. After nine days
the General Council called off their action, leaving the miners to their fate. The bitter experience
of the 1926 General Strike reinforced most trade
union leaders in their hostility to "direct action."
Thereafter, until the Second World War, the
TUC was willing to work with moderate employers (as shown in the MOND-Turner talks of 1928 –
9) and with governments, regardless of their political complexion. In this WALTER CITRINE, its
General Secretary (1926 – 45), and the General
Council were following a strong tendency which
had alway been present in the TUC, even during
the tumultuous years of 1917 – 26.

The TUC was fully behind Britain's war effort
during the SECOND WORLD WAR. When WINS-
TON CHURCHILL formed a coalition government
in May 1940 he appointed ERNEST BEVIN, a
major figure in the TUC for nearly the whole
inter-war period, as Minister of Labour. Bevin
saw that the TUC and the unions were actively
involved in the organization of the war. Nevertheless controls in the labor market and in industrial relations were as rigorous as during the First
World War. As in the earlier conflict the TUC
benefited not only from its enhanced status but
also from increased trade union membership,
which rose from 6,298,000 in 1939 to 8,875,000 in

1946 (with the proportion affiliated to the TUC rising from 77 to 86 percent).

After 1945 the TUC continued to be much consulted by government when their management of the economy involved incomes policies. The relative success of CLEMENT ATTLEE's government in holding wage levels down in 1948–50 owed a great deal to the support of the General Council. Economists have suggested that as a result weekly wage rates were 2 percent lower than they would have been. When HAROLD MACMILLAN's government brought in a pay freeze in 1961 followed by a pay norm in 1962, the TUC refused to cooperate with these policies, complaining in particular of lack of prior consultation, its effect on collective bargaining, and the failure to deal similarly with prices and profits. With the return to office of Labour under HAROLD WILSON, the General Council reluctantly agreed to support a national economic plan and to cooperate in a voluntary prices and incomes policy. At the annual Congresses, however, the trade union representatives made clear their opposition both to voluntary or statutory policies. Hence subsequently the General Council refused to support either a voluntary or a statutory policy on wages, prices, and incomes when EDWARD HEATH's government (1970–4) pursued them. It did, however, support Labour's wider mix of measures (covering not only wages, prices, and profits but also rent freezes, increased pensions, and tax benefits) in the "Social Contract" of 1975–7, brought in to deal with soaring inflation. Again the General Council found, as in the late 1940s and mid-1960s, that it could only deliver support for a limited period. Trade union unrest over JAMES CALLAGHAN's government's (1976–9) 5 percent pay policy was an important element in Labour's 1979 electoral defeat.

The TUC continued to play a major public role on other trade union matters. It campaigned vigorously against proposals for trade union legislation under Wilson in 1969, Heath in 1971–2, MARGARET THATCHER and JOHN MAJOR in 1979–92. It also took a lead in many major industrial disputes, including over cuts in NATIONAL HEALTH SERVICE expenditure in 1983 and closing coal mines in 1992.

During the post-1945 period until 1979 the TUC was frequently consulted by governments and sent representatives to government-appointed committees. Even during the premiership of Margaret Thatcher (1979–90) Chancellors of the Exchequer discussed economic policy with both sides of industry on the National Economic Development Committee (set up in 1962, abolished in 1991). However, outside the world wars few historians have found that the TUC had a major and sustained influence over central government policy. Nevertheless on occasions the TUC, as the voice of the British trade union movement, has had a marked impact on British politics since 1914.

C.J. Wrigley

Bibliography
Lovell, John, and B.C. Roberts. *A Short History of the TUC.* 1968.
Martin, Ross M. *TUC: The Growth of a Pressure Group, 1868–1976.* 1980.
Middlemas, Keith. *Politics In Industrial Society.* 1979.
Nicholson, Marjorie. *The TUC Overseas: The Roots of Policy.* 1986.
Pelling, Henry. *A History of British Trade Unionism.* 4th edition, 1987.
Roberts, B.C. *The Trades Union Congress, 1868–1921.* 1958.

Transport and General Workers' Union

Britain's largest trade union represents inland transport workers, other than railways, and has manual worker membership in engineering, motors, aircraft, oil refining, chemicals, wool textile, food processing, drink and tobacco, national and local government, and milling industries. It has a semi-autonomous section for non-manual workers.

The TGWU was founded in 1922 by an amalgamation of eighteen sectional unions of dockers, carters, tram and busmen, and general laborers. Their origins lay in the "new unionism" of the 1880s, which created permanent organization in the poorest layers of society neglected by the craft-dominated Victorian unions. The TGWU's forerunners also turned the trade union movement away from its adherence to the LIBERAL PARTY and played a role in the creation of the LABOUR PARTY and its adoption of socialist objectives.

Between 1911 and 1921 they won recognition from the employers, leading to national bargaining over wages and conditions, and from the state, for conciliation and arbitration services. In this process, they used both the mass STRIKE, associated with syndicalist advocacy, and political pressure for legislative reforms deriving from GUILD SOCIALIST doctrine.

In the inter-war years the TGWU was led by its first General Secretary, ERNEST BEVIN. The formative influence on its founding structure, he was driven by a large vision of the role of trade unions in a democratic socialist society. He created a strong executive authority but also a system of internal Trade Group Committees to manage the union's diverse industrial interests. Yet there were sectional revolts against central authority in the Docks' Group and among London busmen, which were often supported by the British COMMUNIST PARTY.

After the defeat of the 1926 GENERAL STRIKE Bevin took the leading role in discussions between the TRADES UNION CONGRESS and prominent industrialists on trade union functions and industrial rationalization (the MOND-Turner talks). After the fall of the Labour government of 1929–31 he worked to strengthen trade union influence in the Labour Party from his powerful position in the TUC. He advocated Keynesian economics and greater authority for the International Labour Office.

Following its merger with the Workers' Union in 1929, the TGWU recruited widely, both men and women, in assembly-line factories. Its numbers grew from 300,000 in 1922 to 750,000 in 1940, and to 1.5 million in 1966. Bevin used his powers, conferred when CHURCHILL appointed him Minister of Labour in the war-time coalition government, to achieve a greater degree of mobilization of the civilian work force than either the United States or Nazi Germany, by combining state manpower planning with the promotion of trade union influence in industry.

On Bevin's departure to the Foreign Office in 1945, the union confirmed the acting General Secretary, Arthur Deakin, in office. He used his authority to provide loyal support for the Labour government of 1945–51. Its wage-restraint policies, intended to fight inflation and the balance of payments crisis (the dollar shortage), collided with workers whose bargaining power was enhanced by full employment. As the Cold War intensified, Deakin came to interpret industrial militancy as Communist-inspired. In 1949, he persuaded the union's Delegate Conference to ban members of the Communist Party from holding union office.

These tensions continued until the election of Frank Cousins to the general secretaryship (1956–69). Cousins provided a more militant, left-wing leadership, and placed the TGWU in the vanguard of the CAMPAIGN FOR NUCLEAR DISARMAMENT. He joined the Labour CABINET of 1964 as Minister for Technology but resigned in 1965 in opposition to its policies of wage restraint.

His successor as General Secretary, Jack Jones (1969–78), restructured the union and extended the role of the shop steward, whom he saw as "the instrument of industrial democracy." He lifted the ban on Communists. Bargaining was decentralized to plant level, and the union became the principal opponent of state regulation of wages and legal constraints on strike action. Yet Jones, in the tradition of TGWU leadership, was the architect of the voluntary "Social Contract," designed to harmonize relations between the unions and the Labour government of 1974–9. He negotiated many mergers with other unions, and in 1977 membership reached 2 million,

one in six of all trade unions, as overall trade union density surpassed 50 percent of the working population.

During the 1980s Moss Evans (1978–85) and Ron Todd (1985–92) led the TGWU in more conflicts with the THATCHER government's trade union laws than any union other than the miners and the printworkers. High UNEMPLOYMENT and the collapse of manufacturing industries combined with the hostile political and social climate to drive membership down to 1.2 million 1991. In 1992 Bill Morris was elected, the first black general secretary of any British union.

Tony Topham

Bibliography

Allen, V.L. *Trade Union Leadership: Based on a Study of Arthur Deakin.* 1957.

Bullock. Alan. *The Life and Times of Ernest Bevin.* vols. 1–2. 1960, 1967.

Coates, Ken, and Tony Topham. *The Making of the Transport and General Workers' Union: The Emergence of the Labour Movement.* 1991.

Goodman, Geoffrey. *The Awkward Warrior: Frank Cousins: His Life and Times.* 1979.

Minkin, Lewis. *The Contentious Alliance: Trade Unions and the Labour Party.* 1991.

Trevelyan, George Macaulay (1876–1962)

An historian of immense fame during his lifetime, G.M. Trevelyan wrote some of the most popular works of this century; many titles are still in print and have sold hundreds of thousands of copies. Many professional historians, however, questioned his approach to evidence and decided that he was not asking the right questions, while a devoted minority followed his example. Although Trevelyan acknowledged scientific elements in research, he devoutly believed in the artistic nature of historical writing and argued that style is as integral as substance in accomplishing the historian's primary task, the presentation of the past to the public.

Born the third son of the historian and LIBERAL politician, Sir George Otto Trevelyan and his wife Caroline, a grandniece of Thomas Babington Macaulay, Trevelyan was educated at Harrow and Trinity College, CAMBRIDGE. After achieving first class honors in history (1896), he wrote a dissertation on Lollardy and was awarded Trinity's first history fellowship in 1898. The dissertation was published the next year as *England in the Age of Wycliffe* (1899).

Trevelyan left Cambridge in 1903, having decided that London was a more congenial place to write "literary" history and to continue his interest in social reform and the Working Men's College. The next year he married Janet Penrose, younger daughter of Humphry and Mary Ward (the novelist), and published *England Under the*

Stuarts (1904), a textbook that has had twenty-one editions and is still in print.

A wedding present inspired Trevelyan to write a trilogy on Garibaldi (1907, 1909, 1911) that made him famous. As preparation Trevelyan retraced the steps of his hero and talked with survivors of Garibaldi's campaigns. The result was a romantic narrative full of excitement and beautifully written. A biography of Victorian Radical statesman John Bright followed in 1913; that same year *Clio: a Muse* (1913), a defense of literary history established Trevelyan as a principal opponent of the dominant "scientific" approach to writing history.

Declared unfit for combat at the outset of the FIRST WORLD WAR, Trevelyan accepted the command of a British ambulance unit in Italy and served with distinction. In 1920 he was awarded a CBE and published *Lord Grey of the Reform Bill* (1920). Ten years later he received the Order of Merit.

During the 1920s Trevelyan increased his popularity with the public with *British History in the Nineteenth Century* (1922) and the *History of England* (1926), though his return to Italian history, *Manin and the Venetian Revolution of 1848* (1923) was not a success. The Lowell lectures at Harvard University (1924) were followed by the Romanes lectures at Oxford (1926) and a happy return to Cambridge as Regius Professor of Modern History (1927). The final years of the decade were occupied with another trilogy, entitled *England Under Queen Anne* (1930, 1932, 1934), which he considered his best work along with the Garibaldi trilogy. A laudatory biography of his friend and former Foreign Secretary SIR EDWARD GREY was published in 1937.

Even as the Queen Anne trilogy was coming out, many professional historians saw Trevelyan's approach as irrelevant. The principal attack came from LEWIS NAMIER who denied Trevelyan's belief in the continuity of party history and from Herbert Butterfield who chastised historians who take sides in history.

In 1940 Trevelyan was named Master of Trinity College, Cambridge, where he remained until 1951. During the Second World War he published *English Social History* (1944)—a continuation of Macaulay's famous third chapter—which became his most popular work, though denigrated by many professional historians. At the end of the decade he offered a short autobiography in *An Autobiography and Other Essays* (1949) in which he proclaimed himself to be "not an original but a traditional kind of historian" with a passion for poetry in history. He died in Cambridge on 21 July 1962.

There are still historians who denounce Trevelyan's "simplistic" optimism, views on morality, and liberal humanist outlook, but most professionals at least acknowledge the need to write well, even if they disagree on "why" they should care about writing at all. Trevelyan ardently believed that these attributes were not shortcomings but virtues and were the basis for his popularity with the public.

Michael Douglas Smith

Bibliography

Cannadine, David. *G.M. Trevelyan: A Life in History.* 1992.

Moorman, Mary. *George Macaulay Trevelyan: A Memoir.* 1980.

Plumb, J.H. *Trevelyan.* 1951.

U

Ulster: see Northern Ireland

Unemployment

Unemployment, in the general sense of being without work, has been with us for much of human history, but it was not until the turn of the twentieth century that the term was widely used. It was only in the 1920s in Britain and in the 1940s in the United States that governments began to collect statistics of unemployment on any regular basis. It had been clearly recognized throughout the nineteenth century that fluctuations in the business cycle threw people out of work, but one reason for the lack of recognition of unemployment as a major problem was because its existence was ascribed to a defect in character. Industrialization, it was believed, had generated work for all those who needed it. Idleness or want of employment therefore had to be the result of the moral failure of the individual.

This view of unemployment was challenged by Marx, who regarded unemployment as the result of the capitalist need for a reserve army of labor to keep wages low relative to profits. Other investigators produced evidence of large scale involuntary unemployment, the result of fluctuations in the business cycle over which individuals had little control whatever their moral qualities. The title of one of the most influential investigations, WILLIAM BEVERIDGE's *Unemployment: A Problem of Industry*, published in 1909, recognized that imperfections in the demand for and supply of labor were the result of market forces and the business cycle. By the end of the first decade of the century unemployment was seen both as an industrial as well as a social problem.

The word unemployment was not introduced into the language of political economists until 1888, and its first formal definition, in terms of involuntary idleness of the able bodied, was advanced by J.A. HOBSON in 1895. The term unemployment is generally subdivided into frictional unemployment (temporary unemployment inevitably suffered by those moving from one job to another); cyclical unemployment (the loss of jobs caused by the downswing of the trade cycle); seasonal unemployment (displaying regular and fairly predictable fluctuations); and structural unemployment (the result of longer-term changes in demand or technology and frequently affecting particular groups of workers or industrial regions). From 1910–40 neo-classical theory produced a view of unemployment as an inevitable product of the business cycle. The overriding perception therefore was that there was little that governments could or should do about it. It was recognized that some unemployment was necessary for economic growth, normally presumed to be about 2 percent in the skilled trades, but if it persisted at higher levels, as it did in Britain in the 1930s in particular, it was believed to be the result of interferences with the free working of the market, either from monopolistic employers, trade unions, or government legislation. There was a profound conviction that if the free market were left to its own devices, it would push the economy towards equilibrium at the level of full employment. All that social policy could do was to reduce the pain that the business cycle caused to the unemployed. Employers and workers, meanwhile, would strive to contact each other through the operation of labor exchanges, while government would ease the financial hardships of short-term unemployment through the implementation of insurance schemes.

From 1940 to the late 1970s this neo-classical view was replaced by the Keynesian message that unemployment was caused by deficiencies of aggregate demand and therefore subject to manipulation and control by the activities of the state. While consumption might be fairly stable in the short run, investment was liable to erratic fluctuations. In a cyclical downturn business confidence recedes and less investment takes place as businessmen's expectations of future profits become depressed. KEYNES saw no reason why, when employment failed in a recession, it should be followed by a fall in wages to create a demand for more labour. At a time of rising unemployment Keynes deemed it essential to maintain or increase the level of investment in order to increase the demand for labor. With careful management by the state, high levels of unemployment could be eliminated.

The concept of Keynesian full employment was able to gain hold on both sides of the Atlantic for a number of reasons. The SECOND WORLD WAR demonstrated the possibility of running the economy effectively with virtually no unemployment and pushing political leaders towards an acceptance of full employment as a policy goal. The 1945 election, giving power to the LABOUR PARTY, helped to strengthen the commitment to full employment. Governments were able to sustain this commitment through most of the 1950s and 1960s because of the growth of international trade and the rising levels of investment.

Circumstances changed dramatically in the late 1970s when the Keynesian view was replaced by the concept of monetarism which again saw unemployment as a product of market forces over which the state had little direct control. Against a background of continued relative economic decline, financial instability, and a dramatic increase in inflation which started in the early 1970s following a substantial rise in commodity, and particularly oil, prices, Britain embarked on a policy of deflation. Unemployment started to rise substantially above the levels to which the country had become accustomed in the post-war period. The rate of unemployment, which had generally stayed below 2 percent between 1948 and 1966, rose from 5.6 percent (1.3 million) in the United Kingdom in 1979 to 13.2 percent (over 3.1 million) at its peak in the third quarter of 1983. The combination of rising inflation and rising unemployment led to a questioning of Keynesian employment policies. For decades past the prevailing view had been that higher unemployment meant lower inflation and lower unemployment meant higher inflation. As unemployment decreased, the argument ran, the bargaining power of trade unions increased enabling them to obtain higher wages. In a buoyant market employers could easily pass on these increased costs as higher prices. However, in the 1970s inflation accelerated independently of the level of unemployment which was previously thought to have determined it. As a consequence the control of the accelerating rate of inflation became a policy priority. Under the THATCHER administration particular emphasis was placed upon controlling the money supply. If there was no control over the money supply, then inflation would follow as more money expenditure would be chasing a given amount of goods and services. Such expenditure could be contained by keeping a tight reign over the medium term on the growth of the money supply. Although it was recognized that this might cause unemployment in the short run, monetarists believed that employment would gravitate to its natural level if the market was left to operate with minimum interference by the state.

With unemployment in the 1980s reaching levels reminiscent of the 1930s (even though its occupational, industrial, and spatial characteristics were often quite different from the inter-war

years), the problem became a major political issue. Debate raged over whether high unemployment benefit rates and the actions of the trade unions were more responsible for the prevailing state of affairs than the monetarist doctrine allowed for, with its emphasis on the power of government to influence only the inflation rather than the unemployment rate. There were those who argued that a determined attack on the power and legal status of trade unions and on particular features of the social security system would be an effective response to the persistent unemployment that had come to characterize the mid- to late 1980s.

The unemployment rate in 1990 was only half the measured rate of 1982, but there were serious doubts as to the comparability of official statistics over time. The basis of the figures were subjected to numerous changes over the decade after 1979, most of which are judged to have understated the real rate of unemployment. The restriction of the category of the unemployed to those receiving relief, at a time when the regulations for receipt of such relief were tightened, is said to have reduced the official count substantially.

                                                                    W.R. Garside

Bibliography
Constantine, Stephen. *Unemployment in Britain Between the Wars.* 1980.
Garside, W.R. *British Unemployment, 1919–1939.* 1990.
Gordon, Alan. *The Crisis of Unemployment.* 1988.
Harris, Jose. *Unemployment and Politics: A Study in English Social Policy, 1886–1914.* 1972.
Layard, Richard, R. Jackman, and Stephen Nickell. *Unemployment, Macroeconomic Performance and the Labour Market.* 1991.
Whiteside, Noel. *Bad Times: Unemployment in British Social and Political History.* 1991.

Union of Democratic Control

The Union of Democratic Control (UDC) was a peace organization whose principal aim was to replace "secret diplomacy" with a foreign policy controlled by Parliament. It was formed in 1914, at the beginning of the FIRST WORLD WAR, by Charles Trevelyan, E.D. MOREL (its secretary and driving force), RAMSAY MACDONALD, Arthur Ponsonby, and NORMAN ANGELL. Although some of its members were absolute pacifists, the UDC's mainstream advocated a negotiated peace without annexations or indemnities. As the most important single vehicle of criticism of the government's war policy, the UDC was extremely unpopular, but its ideas came to exert considerable influence on inter-war thinking, particularly within the LABOUR PARTY. It is also significant because it acted as a conduit for disaffected LIBERALS who joined the INDEPENDENT LABOUR PARTY during or shortly after the war. Although the UDC survived until the 1960s as a discussion group and occasional publisher, it lost its momentum and importance after 1924.

The UDC in its early years was frequently condemned as "anti-war" or even "pro-German." It was neither. Its members differed over who was to blame for the war and whether an Allied victory was desirable. It published a wide range of opinions on these questions in its signed pamphlets and its monthly journal, *UDC* (1915–19; continued until 1924 as *Foreign Affairs*). The UDC propounded four cardinal points: there should be no annexations of territory without indigenous popular consent; the British government should make no agreements with foreign powers without parliamentary approval; the balance of power should be abandoned in favor of a council to resolve international disputes; and armaments production should be both nationalized and severely curtailed.

All the leaders of the UDC, except Angell, had criticized the conduct of British foreign policy along these lines in their pre-war writings. Angell, who did not regard armaments manufacturers as blameworthy and was skeptical about the benefits of open diplomacy, argued that wars were caused by irrational beliefs which were at least as widespread among the population at large as among the ruling classes. He therefore took little active part in the UDC's affairs, since its propaganda placed heaviest emphasis upon the evils of secret diplomacy—Morel's consuming passion.

Although some of the UDC's members had previously collaborated in political campaigns, they began the First World War with diverse opinions and political affiliations. Ponsonby and Trevelyan were Liberals, the latter a junior minister until he resigned upon Britain's entry into the war. Morel and Angell were non-party liberals; the former had made his name campaigning against Belgian atrocities in the Congo before turning his attention to secret diplomacy. MacDonald was secretary of the ILP and chairman of the parliamentary Labour Party. Among other leaders, H.N. BRAILSFORD and J.A. HOBSON had developed the influential thesis that imperialism and international rivalry were the results of capitalism's search for outlets for surplus capital; Helena Swanwick was a moderate leader of the WOMEN'S SUFFRAGE movement; and LEONARD WOOLF was a prominent member of the FABIAN SOCIETY. By 1924, however, all of the leaders of the UDC had joined the ILP, the only party officially to oppose not only the war, but also the punitive peace terms.

The UDC's fortunes began to improve in 1917 when the United States entered the war. President Woodrow Wilson's peace proposals resembled those of the UDC, thus making the latter respectable. In the same year the revolutionary Soviet government published the "secret treaties," a series of pre-war agreements between the Allied powers, which appeared to validate UDC allegations that the war was an imperialist venture. Finally, the post-war economic slump lent credence to UDC arguments against war reparations.

Between the wars the UDC dominated the Labour Party's Advisory Committee on International Questions. While this increased its influence, it greatly reduced the necessity for separate activity, which virtually ended with the advent of MacDonald's first Labour government. Although Morel criticized its foreign policy, most other UDC members were reluctant to campaign against a government whose Cabinet included nine of their own members. Morel's death in 1924 effectively finished the UDC as a significant, independent pressure group.

David Blaazer

Bibliography
Cline, Catherine Ann. *E.D. Morel, 1873–1924: The Strategies of Protest.* 1980.
Swanwick, H.M. *Builders of Peace.* 1924.
Swartz, Marvin. *The Union of Democratic Control in British Politics during the First World War.* 1971.

University Education

University education in Britain at the beginning of the twentieth century was an elite affair and has remained so for much of the century, although provision began to expand and to change significantly from the end of the 1950s.

There were eighteen institutions and clusters of institutions using the name "university" in 1900. The four Scottish universities, Edinburgh, Glasgow, St. Andrews and Aberdeen, cherished lineages nearly as long as those of OXFORD and CAMBRIDGE. But all the remainder, the constituent colleges of the University of London, and of the University of Wales, the universities of Durham, Manchester, Leeds, Newcastle, Birmingham, Bristol, Sheffield, and Reading, and the university colleges of Nottingham and Southampton, were nineteenth century creations.

Their funds came from three sources: student fees, endowments, and the state. The Scottish universities had received some government funding throughout the nineteenth century; and in 1889 the Treasury finally conceded the principle of grant aid to English and Welsh institutions outside Oxford and Cambridge, few of whom had anything substantial in the way of endowments. By 1906 this had been pushed up to £100,000 per annum.

In 1900–1 full-time students at all British universities, including the medical schools, totaled 20,249, just under 1 percent of the appropriate age group. Although London had pioneered the external, part-time degree and nineteenth century Scottish universities had contained students of widely varying ages, the dominant model for the composition of the student body was one derived from Oxford and Cambridge, or "Oxbridge" as the composite was known: resident, full-time, and largely between the ages of eighteen and twenty-two.

There were some scholarships, but fees and full-time residence meant that this elite was as much a social as an intellectual one. No child born to an unskilled or semi-skilled father before 1910 could expect to get to university. The children of the professional middle classes were the dominant group. However, the children of the lower middle classes and of skilled workers were beginning to appear in student bodies outside Oxford and Cambridge, in particular those in Scotland. The elite was also largely male: only 3,284 of those students of 1900 were women.

Despite grand statements by politicians about the importance of investment in education during the last years of the First World War, the university sector grew only slowly in the inter-war period. The loss of fee income during the war hit all universities badly. In 1919 Oxford and Cambridge joined those seeking government funding, followed in the 1920s by four more new university colleges, Exeter, Swansea, Hull, and Leicester. From 1919 the Treasury was advised by the University Grants Committee (UGC), which endeavored to make its allocations on a quinquennial cycle. Yet even by the mid-1930s, government grants to the universities were running at only £2 million per annum, representing about one-third of their income.

Their student populations remained small and exclusive. In 1938–9 there were just under 50,000 full-time students, one-quarter of whom were women. Almost all came from upper middle and middle-class backgrounds. Of children born to an unskilled or semi-skilled father between 1920 and 1929, 0.5 percent could expect to find their way to university. With social exclusiveness went intellectual traditionalism. At Oxford and Cambridge the vast majority of students—80 percent and 70 percent respectively—were in the arts faculties. Science dominated only in London, Manchester, Leeds, and Edinburgh. The first research degrees had been developed in the 1890s, in an effort to challenge the German universities. But the numbers of research students grew only very slowly.

The SECOND WORLD WAR finally pushed universities into financial dependence upon the state. It also brought manpower planning on an unprecedented scale, preparing the ground for a radical review of the nature and extent of higher education as a whole. However, the pressures of this, coupled with the demand represented by the post-war "baby boom," were slow to make themselves felt. Although in the four years after the end of the war numbers were swelled by returning servicemen, they fell back again. In 1954 only 3.2 percent of the relevant age group were going to university, 3.8 percent of boys and 1.5 percent of girls.

The first clear sign of growth came at the end of the 1950s, with the foundation of the first of the new universities, Sussex, in 1958. In 1960, the recommendation of the Anderson Committee, that everyone who could secure a place at a university should, subject to a parental means test, get a grant to attend, was accepted. Expansion and wider access were then both signaled and legitimated by the ROBBINS COMMITTEE on Higher Education, which reported in 1963. They recommended that all students who wished to attend university and could achieve the requisite standard should be found a place, envisaging a student population in 1980 two-and-a-half times the size of that in 1962. The lion's share of the extra places were to be provided in science and technology. By 1967 already 6.3 percent of the age group were entering university. Simultaneously the development of the "binary system," the expansion and upgrading of polytechnics, offering degree-earning courses of far greater variety, including the vocational, to a far more varied student population, including mature part-time adults, sometimes with very few formal qualifications, began the redefinition of notions and expectations of higher education as a whole.

The pace of expansion was checked, however, in the 1970s. In part this was a consequence of the deteriorating national and international economic situation; in part it was a function of the spiraling cost element to which the Robbins Committee had paid little attention, that of the system of mandatory student support recommended by the Anderson Committee. By the end of the decade quinquennial planning had collapsed. The full-time university student population in 1980 was 45,000 short of that envisaged by Robbins.

The end of the 1980s saw a reconstruction of university funding and government more concentrated and thorough-going than any which had preceded it. Student grants were phased out and replaced by loans. The Education Reform Act of 1988 replaced the UGC by the Universities Funding Council (UFC) and created a parallel Polytechnics and Colleges Funding Council (PCFC). The Education Act of 1992 then replaced both with a single Higher Education Funding Council (HEFC), and 44 polytechnics were designated universities.

The increase of demand for places generated by the post-war demographic surge and the rapidity of the financial see-saw meant that the Robbins-led expansion altered the composition and activities of the student population less than might have been expected. The expansion of numbers in science and technology was far less than the Robbins Committee had hoped. Between 1962 and 1980 they envisaged the numbers of students working in these fields in universities and other institutions of higher education increasing over three-fold. In the event they barely doubled.

By 1990 women students made up more than 40 percent of the full-time students population of universities, but very few of these were working-class girls. The chances of access to university education for all social classes improved, but the middle and upper classes preserved, indeed even enhanced, their position of advantage. In 1962 4 percent of the sons of skilled manual workers could expect to get to university; the sons of unskilled manual workers statistically did not figure at all. By 1992 4 percent of them could expect to do so, while the daughters of unskilled manual workers still did not feature in the statistics. By contrast, while in 1962 15 percent of the daughters and 29 percent of the sons of professional fathers could expect to go to university, in 1992 the respective percentages were 22 and 33 percent.

By 1991 just over 20 percent of eighteen-year-olds were entering some form of higher education, roughly half of them going to universities. The elite was larger than that of 1900, but still recognizably its descendant.

Gillian Sutherland

Bibliography

Berdahl, Robert O. *British Universities and the State.* 1959.

Carswell, John. *Government and the Universities in Britain: Programme and Performance, 1960–1980.* 1985.

Halsey, A.H., A.F Heath, and J.M. Ridge. *Origins and Destinations: Family, Class and Education in Modern Britain.* 1980.

Layard, Richard, John King, and Claus Moser. *The Impact of Robbins.* 1969.

Report of the Committee on Higher Education, 1961–3 (Robbins Committee) 1963 Cmnd. 2154.

Urban Transport

In 1900 an unusually high proportion (80 percent) of Britain's population already lived in towns; but only in LONDON, by far the largest of them all, where the world's first steam underground had been started in 1863 and the world's first deep electric tube added in 1890, did RAILWAYS play a significant part in passenger movements within any British town. And even in London the 400 million passengers carried per year in the underground or by suburban surface railway were considerably fewer than the total who traveled by road: 300 million by bus and 280 million by tramcar. Of Britain's four other main cities, only Glasgow had opened a small, cable-hauled underground (1896), and, as they covered a much more limited surface area, they relied much less than London on suburban trains. Most journeys were made either on foot—some remarkably long walks to work were recorded—or in horse-drawn vehicles, usually double deckers because of a mid-nineteenth century change in the method of vehicle taxation. The growing number of slow-moving passenger (and even slower freight) vehicles struggling to get along the often narrow streets created more congestion, street filth, and atmospheric pollution.

Relief was at hand in the form of the electric motor and the internal combustion engine. The first commercially viable electric tramway system, benefiting from earlier U.S. experience and with American equipment, was introduced in Bristol in 1895. By 1902 782 route miles of electrified track had already been laid in a total route mileage of 1,321, most of it within or, to encourage building, just outside towns. A peak of 2,599 route miles was reached in 1923, most of it municipally owned and operated, the London County Council (LCC) being the main operator in the capital. There, but not elsewhere, electric trams were kept out of the central streets but offered faster services from the suburbs. They were cheaper, too, for horses were costly to feed and maintain, and a stud of eleven or twelve were needed to keep each vehicle on the road throughout the day. The number of passengers carried by tram throughout the country grew from just under 1 billion per year in 1899–1900 when electric systems were augmenting the horse hauled, to a peak of just over 4.7 billion in 1927–8. Motor buses also started to appear early in the century, but it was not until the advent of the London General Omnibus Company's (LGOC's) X-type in 1908 and more particularly its B-type in 1910, that these vehicles were capable of constantly starting and stopping in traffic without shaking themselves to pieces. Hackney carriages and cabs were motorized at about the same time. By 1913 few horse-drawn passenger vehicles were to be seen in Britain's towns, though many carts, each pulled throughout the day by the same horse and often with much standing and waiting while freight was loaded and unloaded, were in evidence in the 1920s and some even survived the 1930s. Private companies played a more notable part than municipalities in the spread of motor buses: they required less fixed capital than the tramways, were more flexible in operation, could make money on more lightly-trafficked routes, and were generally more profitable.

In London, unlike most other towns, private capital played a larger role, despite the tramway activities of the LCC, mainly because of the more heavily capitalized tube railways which came into use in, and soon after, 1900. The Central London Railway (now known as the Central Line), running under the main east-west thoroughfare between Shepherd's Bush and the City and originally charging a flat fare of 2d, was an immediate financial success (unlike its predecessor, the City & South London in 1890) and encouraged the well-known American urban transport speculator Charles Tyson Yerkes to raise the finance (mainly from American sources) to electrify part of the existing steam underground and to build three more electric tubes: from Baker Street to Waterloo and the Elephant & Castle; from Charing Cross to Hampstead with a branch to the foot of Highgate Hill (Archway); and from South Kensington via Piccadilly Circus to Finsbury Park. These lines, together with the other part of the steam underground, electrified by its owner, the Metropolitan Railway, all opened for traffic between 1905 and 1907, adding greatly to London's passenger carrying capacity just as an effective motor bus was also to become available. Too greatly, in fact, for the new Underground Electric Railways of London (UERL) had to struggle hard to win enough passengers to avoid liquidation. Albert Henry Stanley (1874–1948), then Superintendent of the Public Service Corporation of New Jersey, was sent over by the American shareholders in 1907 to save their investment. This he gradually did and then, at the beginning of 1912, he made to the LGOC, with large profits from their new motor bus, an offer they could not refuse. The Combine so created became profitable overall, the motor buses supporting the less profitable—but, for London and Londoners enormously important—underground system. The new electric railways and the faster motor buses and trams eased the urban road congestion despite the survival of the slower moving freight vehicles, still horse drawn. The Combine remained in private shareholders' hands, with Stanley (created Lord Ashfield in 1920) in charge. In the early 1930s he turned to advantage political experiences gained during the war as President of the Board of Trade by coming to terms with the London County Council, other local tramway authorities outside central London and the Metropolitan Railway to form the London Passenger Transport Board, a public corporation which from 1 July 1933 ran all the capital's underground and tramways and almost all its buses. Only the taxicabs, many still privately owned by their drivers, and the suburban services of the main-line railways remained independent, the latter pooling their receipts with the LPTB.

As the profitable petrol bus, and its oil engine successor, was allowed by the authorities to run on pneumatic, instead of solid, tires, received a covered top deck, and became altogether larger, more comfortable and efficient, it began to win more traffic from the electric tramways which reached peak carryings in 1927–8. By 1937 London's road services were responsible for 2 billion journeys by bus and a further 203 million journeys by trolley bus, the capital having taken to these hybrids in a big way after 1930. LPTB railways were responsible for 480 million journeys. Between the wars much more spacious subsurface central stations had been opened on the underground. More lines had been extended to the suburbs and beyond, FRANK PICK, the managing director, earning a well deserved reputation for his encouragement of modern, functional design in these new stations.

The spread of private cars, from 2 million licensed in 1950 (roughly the same number as in 1938) to 19,750,000 in 1990, has caused a great decline in the excellent urban public transport system, used by people in all walks of life, which had been developed earlier in the century. In the 1930s even the middle-class minority who could afford cars used them mainly for "pleasure motoring" and not for traveling by day to and from work. It was then more of the wage earners, not the salaried, who went to work by private vehicle: the pedal cycle, still a popular mode of travel until the early 1950s has since then been used less and less, especially in congested, fume-laden city centers. Motor bicycles, too, often with sidecars attached, were popular among some better-off wage earners in the 1930s, 462,000 being registered in Britain in 1938. With the advent of mopeds after the war, this form of transport was even more widely supported by younger people, peaking at 1.7 million in 1962. By 1990, however, only half this total was registered.

When electric tramways were finally phased out—the last of them ran in Manchester in 1949, London in 1952 and everywhere else apart from the seaside promenade in Blackpool, Lancashire, by 1960—soon to be followed by trolley buses, urban passenger transport by road came to depend wholly upon the motor bus. But bus traffic fell as more people stayed at home in the evening to watch television, went to work five, instead of six, days a week, and increasingly used their own cars. Bus operators cut services, which encouraged more use of private transport and increased congestion. Urban bus services became unreliable for users and unprofitable for operators who became increasingly reliant upon tax concessions and public subsidies. In London, two new tube railways (the Victoria and Jubilee lines) were opened (1968–72 and 1979), and refugees from the unreliable buses took to the underground even for shorter journeys. Its traffic grew remarkably, from 498 million to 815 million journeys a year between 1982 and 1989, encouraged by the introduction of daily and weekly contract tickets. The elderly underground became seriously overloaded, and a disastrous escalator fire at King's Cross tube station in 1987 drew national attention to the urgent need for renovation. Tyneside linked its suburban railways by a new underground line, Glasgow modernized its old subway, and Manchester brought back a street tramway along which small suburban trains passed through the city center. Elsewhere, however, all cities relied entirely for their public transport upon the bus, once again struggling hard to make its way along roads becoming increasingly congested. Many towns had been diverting through traffic with by-pass roads since the inter-war years and more recently by ring roads. Other attempts to encourage the bus by discouraging the car were parking meters, first introduced into British towns in 1958, bus lanes, the setting up of passenger transport authorities in the main conurbations outside London (1969) and, in 1986, the freeing of buses outside London of certain aspects of public regulation to which they had been subjected since 1930. But as in 1900, the true solution is likely to be found in new technology: sophisticated forms of road pricing whereby private cars and commercial traffic can be charged for using urban roads at busy times, the sums involved being directly related to the extent of congestion. With urban road once again sufficiently clear for them to operate a fast service, buses of various sizes, from small runabouts to large double deckers capable of carrying up to seventy passangers at a time, would dispel public transport's tarnished image and allow people to move about in urban centers more freely once again—and at fares subsidized by the income from the road pricing of cars and commercial vehicles.

T.C. Barker

Bibliography

Barker, T.C. *Moving Millions: A Pictoral History of London Transport.* 1990.

———, and C.I. Savage. *An Economic History of Transport in Britain.* 1974.

Collins, Michael F., and Timothy M. Pharoah. *Transport Organisation in a Great City: The Case of London.* 1974.

Munby, Denys Lawrence. *Inland Transport Statistics: Great Britain 1900–1970.* 1978.

Vaughan Williams, Ralph (1872–1958)
An English composer, conductor, writer and
folksong collector, Ralph Vaughan Williams succeeded ELGAR as the leading British composer of
his generation. Of central importance to his output is a series of nine highly individual symphonies, interspersed with large-scale choral and orchestral works, OPERAS, concertos, and some
chamber music. His melodic writing, when influenced by his enthusiasm for folksong, imparts
a nationalist flavor to several of his works, although others are more cosmopolitan in nature,
sharing to a certain extent in the development of
modernism. No type of music-making, however
humble, was shunned by Vaughan Williams; he
was equally at home composing for local musicians as for the *cognoscenti*. His involvement with
the community found expression in his conduc-
torship of the Leith Hall Festival (Dorking)
from 1905–53. Following the award of an honorary doctorate from the UNIVERSITY OF OX-
FORD (1919), he received many other official honors including the Order of Merit (1935), although
he declined a knighthood.
Born in Down Ampney, Gloucestershire,
Vaughan Williams, a vicar's son with distinguished forebears on both sides of his family,
lived for most of life in or near Dorking, Surrey
and in London. He was slow to develop musically, and two years at the Royal College of
Music, London (1890–2) led to three at Trinity
College, CAMBRIDGE (1892–5), before he returned to the Royal College—his composition
teachers were Parry, Charles Wood and Stanford. At the Royal College, in 1895, he met and
befriended GUSTAV HOLST, and on "field-days",
which were held regularly until Holst's death,
they would discuss the progress of each other's
compositions. Further encouragement was provided by lessons with Max Bruch in Berlin (during 1897, on his honeymoon with his first wife,
Adeline Fisher), but more significant for the development of his style was a deepening interest
in folksong, culminating in the collection of
more than 800 examples beginning with "Bushes
and Briars" in 1903. The adaptation of folksongs
as hymns was an important part of his task as
music editor of the *English Hymnal* (1904–6), as
well as writing new tunes himself, for instance
Sine nomine ("For all the saints") and *Down*

Ampney ("Come down, O Love Divine"), and
subsequently he made many folksong arrangements. The first works to include folksongs were
the three *Norfolk Rhapsodies* (1905–6), but a more
integrated use comes in three pieces dating from
1908–9, the String Quartet in G minor, the song
cycle, *On Wenlock Edge*, for tenor and piano quintet, and the incidental music to *The Wasps* (Aris-
tophanes). All three also exhibit evidence of
Vaughan Williams' lessons in instrumentation
with Ravel (1908). Bestriding this early period
and crowning it is Vaughan Williams' first symphony, *A Sea Symphony* (Whitman: 1903–9) for
soloists, chorus, and orchestra, a visionary exploration of humanity's place in the universe.
Vaughan Williams's interest in the contemporary revival of Elizabethan and Jacobean music
can be heard in his first masterpiece, the *Fantasia
on a Theme by Thomas Tallis* (1910) for double
string orchestra, where passages of mystical tenderness contrast with others of spiritual ardor
and exaltation. Similar feelings pervade the *Five
Mystical Songs* (Herbert: 1911) for baritone,
chorus, and orchestra, but in *A London Symphony*
(1913), the more down-to-earth existence of city
life is portrayed in some of the most colorful or-
chestration Vaughan Williams ever wrote. An
attempt in *Hugh the Drover* (H. Child: 1914) to
compose an opera, "written to *real* English
words, with a certain amount of *real* English
music and also a *real* English subject" was equally
colorful if not as successful because of its inadequate libretto, whereas the romance for violin
and orchestra, *The Lark Ascending* (1914), a medi-
tative, unclouded idyll, is a gem.
Because Vaughan Williams felt duty-bound
to enroll for military service during the First
World War, seven years separate *The Lark Ascending* from his next important work, the *Pastoral Symphony* (1921). This is a bleaker portrait of
nature, at time forbidding and austere, characteristics further explored in the oratorio, *Sancta ci-
vitas* (Revelation: 1925) and the suite, *Flos campi*
(1925) for viola, small (wordless) chorus and
small orchestra, which opens bitonally. Turning
to the stage, Vaughan Williams drew on the expanded harmonic and melodic resources contained in these works to produce spiritually
numbing portrayals of a woman almost defeated
by nature in the opera, *Riders to the Sea* (Vaughan

Williams, after Synge: 1932), and of Job almost defeated by Satan in the "masque for dancing," *Job* (1930). Despite the noble strains of the triumphant Galliard of the Sons of the Morning in the latter, it is Satan's music, brutal and angular, which is most memorable, a type fully developed in the harshly discordant and violent Fourth Symphony (1934).

With the death of Holst in 1934, the warmth of Vaughan Williams' earlier style returned. The opera, *Sir John in Love* (Vaughan Williams, after Shakespeare: 1928), from which Ralph Greaves arranged the *Fantasia on Greensleeves*, had kept this quality alive during the 1920s, and in the next decade it was amply demonstrated in the sensuously ravishing *Serenade to Music* (Shakespeare: 1938) for sixteen soloists, chorus, and orchestra and the rich, glowing textures of the *Five Variants of "Dives and Lazarus"* (1939) for string orchestra and harp(s). This development culminated in the splendor and spiritual security of the Fifth Symphony (1943). That Vaughan Williams, now in his seventies, could follow this symphony with another, the Sixth (1947), which from its opening minor/major clash to its desolate, anti-human epilogue, negates the message of the *Fifth*, is evidence of a remarkable range of expression.

Although bitterly disappointed by the failure of the morality opera, *The Pilgrim's Progress* (Vaughan Williams, after Bunyan: 1949) at its premiere at Covent Garden in 1951, Vaughan Williams found new reserves of energy to marry a second time (Ursula Wood in 1953), to undertake a lecture tour in the United States in 1954, as well as to continue composing. His involvement with film music, which had begun in 1940 with *49th Parallel* (1941) and *Coastal Command* (1942), now impinged on his symphonic writing when he transformed his score for *Scott of the Antarctic* (1948) into his seventh symphony, *Sinfonia antarctica* (1952), characterized by a renewed interest in unusual sounds, particularly those of the tuned percussion. This feature he explored further in the light-hearted and exuberant Eighth Symphony (1955). Finally, conflicts similar to those in the Sixth Symphony can be heard in the sombre, tough Ninth Symphony (1957), but here they find a hard-won resolution of qualified hope.

Trevor Bray

Bibliography

Kennedy, Michael. *The Works of Ralph Vaughan Williams*. 1964.

Mellors, Wilfrid. *Vaughan Williams and the Vision of Albion*. 1989.

Vaughan Williams, Ralph. *National Music and Other Essays*. 1963.

Vaughan Williams, Ursula. *R.V.W.: a Biography of Ralph Vaughan Williams*. 1964.

Vorticism

Despite WYNDHAM LEWIS's retrospective assertion that "Vorticism, in fact, was what I personally, did, and said, at a certain period," and given that Lewis was the animating force behind Vorticism, there is no doubt that it constituted a recognizable movement which, however shortlived, can probably claim to have been the first coherently modernist group of artists in Britain.

Initially impressed by the work of the Italian Futurists, who had first exhibited in London in 1912, and their celebration of the machine in the flowering of the industrial age, by 1914 these artists were unhappy about becoming coopted into the Italian movement. Ultimately Vorticism and their publication *Blast* (which ran to two issues published in 1914 and 1915) was formed as a statement of independence from the Italians and what was perceived as their misguided, romanticized view of the machine. Although differences between Lewis and the Italian Futurists had been visible for some time, the catalyst had been the publication of C.R.W. NEVINSON's *Vital English Art: Futurist Manifesto* in June 1914, to which he penned the signatures of Lawrence Atkinson, David Bomberg, JACOB EPSTEIN, Frederick Etchells, Cuthbert Hamilton, William Roberts, Edward Wadsworth, and Wyndham Lewis, not only without their permission, but also as if they were under the direction of Nevinson and Marinetti.

The address used without authorization by Nevinson for his manifesto had been the Rebel Art Center, founded in March 1914 as a rival to the Omega Workshops for which Lewis had worked. Four months earlier that group's (Lewis, Nevinson, Wadsworth, Epstein, Etchells, Hamilton, and Bomberg) independence from the Impressionism of SICKERT's Camden Town Group, the BLOOMSBURY GROUP, as well as the Futurists had been declared by exhibiting in a separate "Cubist" room at "The Camden Town and Others" exhibition.

Although Nevinson claims to have invented the title of their magazine, *Blast,* before joining the Futurist camp, the theorist of Vorticism was initially the poet Ezra Pound. He built on the philosophy of T.E. Hulme, whose belief in the rebirth of a geometric art was a formative influence on the nascent Vorticists, and especially on Epstein and Bomberg, whom he particularly championed. For Pound, Vorticism's birth was to be found in Imagism—a literary movement that might be akin to non-representational painting. In the first issue of *Blast* Pound held that "the vortex is the point of maximum energy. It represents in mechanics the greatest efficiency." Lewis explained this "point of maximum energy" by recourse to the metaphor of the whirlpool, "At the heart of the whirlpool is a great silent place where all the energy is concentrated. And there, at the point of concentration, is the Vorticist."

This belief sought an art that could be identified with the new machine age in which technology and rationality ruled, an art that echoed the characteristics of the machine through its formal simplification and coherence of vision. The paintings produced by the Vorticists, although often severely abstract, operate on a number of levels, as reflection, vision, and criticism of a predominantly urban life of present and future. This vision was unable to survive the First World War in whose mechanized slaughter Vorticism was seen to be implicated. The two Vorticist exhibitions, in 1915 at London's Dore Galleries and at New York's Penguin Club in 1917 (organized by Pound and the American collector John Quinn), were both unsuccessful. The sculptor Henri Gaudier-Brzeska had been killed at the Front, and many of the others were psychologically affected by military service or aesthetically by the demands placed on them through the commissions they received as war artists, and so welcomed the post-war aesthetic "Call to Order". Lewis's ultimately unfruitful attempts with McKnight Kauffer to regroup some of the artists under the banner of Group X were symptomatic of this changed situation. Nevertheless, the rolecall of those who signed the Vorticist manifesto—Richard Aldington, Malcolm Arbuthnot, Lawrence Atkinson, Jessica Dismorr, Henri Gaudier-Brzeska, Cuthbert Hamilton, Wyndham Lewis, Ezra Pound, William Roberts, Helen Saunders, and Edward Wadsworth—testify to a moment which set the Modernist agenda and through its ambitious energy and dynamic experimentation changed the history of British art.

Andrew Wilson

Bibliography

Cork, Richard. *Vorticism and Abstract Art in the First Machine Age*. 2 vols. 1976.

Wees, William. *Vorticism and the English Avant-Garde*. 1974.

Wilson, Andrew, ed. *Vorticism*. 1988.

Wallas, Graham (1858–1932)

Overshadowed by the reputation of Shaw and the Webbs, Graham Wallas remains the forgotten man of the early FABIAN SOCIETY. Not only did he play a leading part in forming it, he retained a lifelong connection with its offshoot, the LONDON SCHOOL OF ECONOMICS, where he served as Professor of Political Science (1914–23). His academic interests produced a seminal book, *Human Nature in Politics* (1908), which was widely influential in bringing the insights of social psychology to bear upon the study of politics.

Wallas was the son of an Evangelical clergymen of the CHURCH OF ENGLAND and, after a conventional education at public school (Shrewsbury) and OXFORD, took a post himself as a classics teacher at a London public school. In 1885 the break came: he rejected Christianity on rationalist grounds, resigned accordingly from his teaching post, and threw himself into the study of socialism. Like his friends Sydney Olivier, BERNARD SHAW, and SIDNEY WEBB, Wallas found in the Fabian Society the sort of intellectual milieu where he felt at home. With them he elaborated the theory of evolutionary collectivism which *Essays in Fabian Socialism* (1889), edited by Shaw, proclaimed to a wider public. Critical of Marxism, Wallas remained a LIBERAL in party politics, committed to a strategy of permeation rather than an independent socialist or workers' party.

Wallas worked for years on *The Life of Francis Place* (1898), analyzing the activities of an early nineteenth century radical who played a notable part in changing the labor legislation of his day. This readiness to take "a great deal of trouble to find out how things were really done before we began trying to do them" won high praise from Shaw. It was this practical, dispassionate, empirical aspect of Fabianism which really appealed to Wallas. In 1895 he was strongly in favor of the scheme for using a bequest to the Fabian Society, not for political propaganda, but for academic research and teaching—the origin of the London School of Econmics, of which he was appointed the first Director. He declined to serve in this post but remained associated with the LSE for the rest of his life.

In the process his Fabian commitment waned. One influence upon him came through his years of service in local government, first on the London School Board and subsequently on the education committee of the London County Council. He thus knew local politics from the inside and was thrown, moreover, into opposition to the CONSERVATIVES' Education Act of 1902, which Webb supported on administrative grounds. Wallas finally resigned from the Fabian Society in 1904 because of Shaw's attempt to associate it with protectionism, another Conservative policy. The root cause was a divergence between the manipulative and authoritarian temper which Shaw and the Webbs increasingly displayed and Wallas's Liberal outlook. Beatrice Webb adjudged Wallas less "democratic" than themselves; Wallas had another concept of democracy altogether.

The political thinking of Wallas's mature years was associated with NEW LIBERALISM, as propagated by his friends and colleagues L.T. Hobhouse and J.A. HOBSON. Like them he argued for a democratic collectivism in social policy to be implemented through a progressive alliance between the Liberal and LABOUR parties. Yet in *Human Nature in Politics* (1908) he sought to inject some worldly skepticism into idealistic notions of how a democratic political system actually worked. The critical impact of the book is admittedly more powerful than its constructive suggestions. Wallas sought to remedy this deficiency in later works like *The Great Society* (1914) and *Our Social Heritage* (1921), but they lack the cutting edge of his masterpiece. For all that his insights into irrationalist trends had made him fearful of war, the events of August 1914 came as a shock to Wallas. He worked with Hobson in organizing a British Neutrality Committee, but the German invasion of Belgium doomed their efforts. By 1915 he was telling American readers that "I intensely desire victory for the Allies" and, like many other Liberals, his hopes were now pinned upon the prospects of post-war international cooperation.

It was the attempt to rethink democratic theory in the light of modern findings in social psychology which became Wallas's lifework. He pointed to the strong irrational—or, at any rate, non-rational—forces which influenced political attitudes and to the role of party in mediating electoral opinion. Yet he manifested a strong faith in democracy. Wallas's point was that progressives needed a clear-eyed understanding of the frailties of the democratic process. The influence of his ideas was felt particularly in the Unites States, which he frequently visited.

Peter Clarke

Bibliography

Clarke, Peter. *Liberals and Social Democrats*. 1978.

Qualter, Terence H. *Graham Wallas and the Great Society*. 1980.

Wiener, Martin J. *Between Two Worlds: The Political Thought of Graham Wallas*. 1971.

Walton, William Turner (1902–1983)

Largely self-taught, William Walton was an English composer who, despite a relatively small output, produced at least one major work in almost every genre. Although at first considered something of an *enfant terrible*, Walton's fundamental traditionalism soon became apparent, his style, characterized by its unique lyricism and the use of traditional structures invigorated by modernistic harmonies, forming a parallel with Prokofiev's later idiom. Among official honors he received seven doctorates, a knighthood (1951) and the Order of Merit (1967).

Born in Oldham, Lancashire, the son of a local choirmaster and singing teacher, Walton won a place as a chorister at Christ Church Cathedral, Oxford in 1912. He began to compose two years later, and such was his promise that he was accepted as an undergraduate at Christ Church at the early age of sixteen, although he left OXFORD in 1920 without completing his degree. At Oxford he met Osbert and Sacheverell Sitwell and for many years lived under their protection. By the age of twenty Walton had already completed a piano quartet (1919), which received a Carnegie Award, a string quartet (1922), according to the composer "full of undigested Bartok and Schoenberg", and *Façade* (Edith Sitwell: 1922), for reciter and chamber ensemble. The langorous Southern melancholy and witty use of parody (including the (mis-) quotation of popular song), provide *Façade* with a Gallic sensibility, at once knowing and fresh, that was virtually unique in English music of the time. Having drawn on and developed characteristics of *Façade* in the robust, jazz-inspired rhythms of the overture, *Portsmouth Point* (1925) and in the lassitude of *Siesta* for small orchestra (1926), Walton finally felt prepared to tackle a full-scale instrumental work in the *Sinfonia Concertante* for orchestra with obbligato piano (1927), themes from its three movements, which are portraits of the Sitwells, exhibiting a suitable family likeness. Stylistic maturity came with the richly poetic Viola Concerto (1929) and the ultra-virtuosic Violin Concerto (1939), between which Walton wrote two other masterpieces, the oratorio, *Belshazzar's Feast* (Osbert Sitwell, after Bible: 1931), pagan in tone, violent and savage, and the First Symphony (1935). In both works, Walton revitalized traditional genres, and in the latter, provided a twentieth-century counterpart to the Beethovenian symphonic model of initial conflict finally resolved in triumph.

The Second World War marks a watershed in Walton's output, because, although he gained in fluency through being involved in film music—he completed six film scores between *Major Barbara* (1941) and *Henry V* (1944)—there is a loss of conviction, and the quality of the masterpieces of the 1930s is attained only in such works as the String Quartet in A minor (1947), the Cello Concerto (1956), and the Variations on a Theme of Hindemith (1963). Other works, like the Improvisations on an Impromptu of BENJAMIN BRITTEN, for orchestra (1969), where manner takes precedence over matter, are less inspired. Even the opera, *Troilus and Cressida* (C. Hassell: 1954), grand and sumptuous, betrays a lack of depth.

Trevor Bray

Bibliography

Howes, Frank. *The Music of William Walton*. 2nd ed. 1974.

Kennedy, Michael. *Portrait of Walton*. 1989.

Tierney, Neil. *William Walton: His Life and Music*. 1984.

Walton, Susana. *William Walton: Behind the Façade*. 1988.

Waugh, Evelyn Arthur St. John (1903–1966)

Evelyn Waugh, satiric novelist, was the son of Arthur Waugh, managing director of the publishing firm, Chapman and Hall, and Catherine Raban Waugh. After attending Lancing, he went to OXFORD, where he led a life he described as "idle, dissolute and extravagant," and left in 1924 without taking a degree. Within a few years, however, he began to establish a literary reputation. In 1928 he published two books: a critical and biographical study of Rossetti and his first novel, *Decline and Fall*. In the same year, he married Evelyn Gardner. The marriage lasted barely a year; his wife left him, in August 1929, to live with a mutual friend.

After the shock of this marital break-up, Waugh embarked on a series of travels, all of which provided material for his books. In 1930 he went as a *TIMES* correspondent to Emperor Haile Selassie's coronation in Abyssinia; out of this came a travel book, *Remote People* (1931), and a novel about the clash of cultures, *Black Mischief* (1932). An assignment to cover the Italo-Abyssinian War in 1935 for the *Daily Mail* yielded another travel book, *Waugh in Abyssinia*, and a satire of the newspaper world, *Scoop* (1938).

Following a period of instruction by Jesuit

priest and author Martin D'Arcy, Waugh was received into the ROMAN CATHOLIC CHURCH in 1930. One effect of his conversion was his biography of an Elizabethan Jesuit martyr, Edmund Campion, in 1935. In 1936 the Church annulled his first marriage, enabling him to marry a Catholic, Laura Herbert, the following year. In time they had five children, one of whom, Auberon, became a journalist—as acerbic a commentator on the contemporary scene as his father before him.

When the war began, Waugh received a commission in the Royal Marines. He joined the Commandos and underwent parachute training even though he was approaching forty, but his military career was anything but distinguished. He was assigned to the British military mission for Marshal Tito's partisans in Yugoslavia, where he attempted unsuccessfully to save a large number of Jewish refugees from deportation and certain death.

One further journey took him to Hollywood to prepare a film script for his novel *Brideshead Revisited* (1945); the film was never made, but the experience led to a satire on Californian burial customs, *The Loved One* (1948). As he grew older, he assumed the guise of a crotchety country gentleman who had abandoned the modern world. But the *Sword of Honour* trilogy (1952–61) mingles comic inventiveness with its theme of moral decency adrift in the Second World War.

In his early novels Waugh creates an Alice-in-Wonderland type of world, in which outrageous actions are performed by characters with names like Tantamount and Pastmaster. Yet the title *Decline and Fall* creates the suspicion that the fantasy is anchored in reality, that he is writing of a civilization in decline. His second novel, *Vile Bodies* (1930), describes the amusing social whirl of the Bright Young People in London, of which Waugh was very much a part; yet, by ending on the biggest battlefield so far in world history, the story stresses the price of the fun.

His best novel of the 1930s, *A Handful of Dust* (1934), contains a farcical account of divorce proceedings such as he himself had gone through but reflected his conversion only indirectly: religion in the novel is emphasized through its absence. The book borrows from T.S. ELIOT's *The Waste Land;* there are many correspondences between book and poem, and they are handled with great subtlety.

In a *New Yorker* assessment in 1944 Edmund Wilson stated that Waugh was the only first-rate comic and satiric genius to emerge in English literature since SHAW, and praised him for his detachment: he was known to have conservative political, religious, and moral opinions, but these, Wilson said, did not mar his comedy.

However, when Waugh published *Brideshead Revisited* the following year, he made his conservatism so decidedly clear and serious a motive for the new novel's historical realism that Wilson was bitterly disappointed—as were many other critics. *Brideshead* marked a watershed in Waugh's career; as a Book-of-the-Month Club selection, it gained him a much larger following in the United States than he had had, but many of his admirers wished that his novel-writing had remained in the realm of comic or satiric fantasy. Some reviewers claimed that snobbery rather than religion was at the heart of the work; Kingsley Amis ridiculed the deathbed conversion of the novel's Lord Marchmain in an article entitled "How I Lived in a Very Big House and Found God". Like other critics of the book, he overlooked the importance in the story of a representative of simple and ordinary religious faith, Nanny Hawkins.

Religion and satire mingle in a macabre way in *The Loved One,* based on the premise that the decline of Western civilization is first made obvious in the graveyard. A similar mixture of religious feeling, decline, and disillusionment is at the heart of *Sword of Honour,* published as a trilogy in 1965 after appearing in separate volumes. When the war begins, the novel's hero Guy Crouchback views it as a noble crusade through which he can vindicate himself after a life of failure. By the end of the story the crusade too has failed; the sword of Stalingrad, presented to Soviet Russia by Great Britain, has become a symbol of Soviet oppression. In the last volume of the trilogy, *Unconditional Surrender* (*The End of the Battle* in the American edition), the surrender is not just Germany's surrender but Guy's—his surrender to the will of God. He finds vindication, not as he expected, but through his penitent admission that he has been part of "a will to war, a death wish, everywhere".

The novel is especially convincing in conveying the political and moral fog of war, particularly in the narrative of the defeat of the British on Crete. The unifying vision behind *Sword of Honour* is an ironic one, especially in regard to justice in the modern world. Yet the novel concludes that it may still be possible for a Christian to keep his own house in order and to find meaning in life.

Waugh's published letters and diaries—some of which are more fabulous than his novels—provide a picture of the circle in which he moved. On his death his friend GRAHAM GREENE wrote that "A writer of Evelyn's quality leaves us an estate to walk through: we discover unappreciated vistas, paths are left for our discovery at the right moment."

D.J. Dooley

Bibliography

Carpenter, Humphrey. *The Brideshead Generation: Evelyn Waugh and His Friends.* 1989.

Hastings, Selina. *Evelyn Waugh: A Biography.* 1994.

Heath, Jeffrey. *The Picturesque Prison: Evelyn Waugh and his Writing.* 1982.

Stannard, Martin. *Evelyn Waugh: The Early Years 1903–1939.* 1986.

———. *Evelyn Waugh: The Later Years, 1939–1966.* 1992.

Sykes, Christopher. *Evelyn Waugh: A Biography.* 1975.

Webb, Beatrice Potter (1858–1943) and Sidney (1859–1947)

The partnership of Sidney and Beatrice Webb, which formally dates back to their marriage on 23 June 1892, was to develop into an extraordinary fruitful professional and intellectual relationship. The couple became eminent collaborators in a number of fields: in historical research into various social and political institutions (culminating in the publication of such monumental works as *The History of Trade Unionism* (1894); *Industrial Democracy,* 2 vols. (1897); and the multi–volume history of *English Local Government* (1906–29); in social investigation (especially of the problems of poverty and methods of relieving it); in the reform of education at various levels; in local and national politics (mainly, though not exclusively, from behind the scenes); and in the sponsorship of independent journalism (the most notable example of which was their creation of the weekly periodical, the *NEW STATESMAN,* in 1913).

Some of their joint efforts had come to fruition before the end of the nineteenth century. They had already made an enduring contribution to tertiary education with their founding of the LONDON SCHOOL OF ECONOMICS in 1895. By the turn of the century they were busy hobnobbing in top parliamentary circles in order to secure legislative support for the expansion and reorganization of technical and SECONDARY EDUCATION. The government in power at this time was a CONSERVATIVE one, while their own politics were steadfastly socialist, albeit of the non-revolutionary middle-class variety associated with the FABIAN SOCIETY, of which they had become the recognized leaders.

According to their long-serving secretary, F.W. Galton, the Webbs' minds worked "so closely and harmoniously that it is hard to disentangle the parts played by each of them" in their joint writings or other ventures. Their social backgrounds and their personalities were very different, however; and the roles they played, though usually complementary, were never identical.

Beatrice's father, Richard Potter, was a railway magnate, her mother, Laurencina Heyworth, the daughter of a wealthy mill owner. Beatrice herself was educated at her family home in rural Gloucestershire, in the manner of most Victorian upper middle-class girls. Though widely accomplished, articulate, and beautiful, she was never to push herself forward in the political arena, except during her appointment as a member of the Royal Commission on the Poor Laws (1905–9) and in the subsequent campaign—abortive in the short run—to overturn the old legislation and replace it with a cohesive system of state-run welfare services.

Sidney had not been a member of this Commission, though he vigorously assisted Beatrice in the campaign. Up to 1910 the focus of his own political activity, apart from the Fabian Society, was the London County Council, of which had had been an active member since 1892, representing the Progressive Party, a Liberal-Labour alliance. In a sense he was the archetype of the self-made professional who figured so prominently in the Fabian ranks. He had been born into a lower middle-class family in London, though he had enjoyed some unusual advantages: a spell of schooling in Switzerland and Germany; and early exposure to the world of radical politics through some contacts that his father (a hairdresser-turned-accountant) had made when serving on committees supporting the liberal theorist and MP, John Stuart Mill. Sidney went into the civil service soon after leaving school, and it was as a committee man that he was to shine, whether in the Fabian Society, on the London County Council, or during his later years with the LABOUR PARTY. He was chiefly responsible for drafting the "socialist" Clause IV in the party's constitution of 1918, and he served as an effective advocate of the miners' cause when appointed a year later to the SANKEY COMMISSION investigating the condition of the COAL INDUSTRY. Self-effacing in temperament, and physically undistinguished, he lacked the requisite charisma for more public political roles; yet he allowed himself to be thrust into these roles when Labour first came to power in Britain in the 1920s. In the first Labour government of 1924 he served as President of the Board of Trade, and in the second of 1929–31 (having been elevated to the peerage as Lord Passfield) he became Secretary of State for Dominion Affairs and Colonial Secretary.

Following the disappointments of her anti-Poor Law campaign and the calamities of the First World War, Beatrice's usual introspection was to take a more depressive turn for a while. As always, however, she continued to find a creative outlet for such moods in her now-famous diaries (extracts of which were first published in 1926, as *My Apprenticeship,* and in 1948 as *Our Partnership*). By the 1920s she had recovered her spirits sufficiently to play an active, if rather condescending, role as political hostess in Sidney's mining constituency of Seaham Harbour in Durham.

With the collapse of RAMSAY MACDONALD's administration of 1929–31, both partners suffered disillusionment with the Labour Party over its inability to respond in a creative socialist way to the economic crisis of the time. They placed their hopes now in the example of the Soviet Union. A visit there in 1932 helped convert them from the deep skepticism they had been expressing about the communist experiment throughout the 1920s to near-adulation. They published their observations in another joint work, *Soviet Communism: A New Civilisation?* (2 vols., 1935).

This last major work may not have shown them at their sober, steady-sighted best. But for all its more blinkered enthusiasms about Stalinist Russia, it was not entirely oblivious or uncritical of the authoritarian excesses now commonly identified with the regime. And the most impressive qualities of the Webbs' earlier historical and social investigations—intensive research and encyclopedic range—were still clearly in evidence. Whatever their own political achievements, the record of the Webbs as scholarly writers on all manner of issues connected with the labor or socialist movements is far too solid ever to be ignored, even by the most vehement of their detractors.

                                                   Ian Britain

Bibliography

Cole, Margaret, ed. *The Webbs and Their Work.* 1949.

Harrison, Royden. *The Life and Times of Sidney and Beatrice Webb 1858–1905.* 2000.

McBriar, A.M. *An Edwardian Mixed Doubles: The Bosanquets versus the Webbs: A Study in British Social Policy 1890–1929.* 1987.

MacKenzie, Norman, ed. *The Letters of Sidney and Beatrice Webb.* 3 vols. 1978.

——and Jeanne, eds. *The Diary of Beatrice Webb.* 4 vols. 1982–5.

Radice, Lisanne. *Beatrice and Sidney Webb.* 1984.

Welfare State

The term "welfare state", which became part of the everyday British vocabulary after 1945, means a state which defines as an essential part of its role the prevention of absolute poverty and, somewhat more contentiously, the maintenance of an adequate standard of life for all its citizens. It may seek to achieve this goal by a variety of means, including provision of cash benefits and/or services and the regulation of the fiscal system or the labor market in order to maximize incomes.

During the twentieth century such activities have certainly grown in size, range, cost, and complexity. Central and local government expenditure on social welfare services in the United Kingdom was 4.1 percent of GNP in 1913, 10.15 percent in 1921, 9.5 percent in 1929, 11.3 percent in 1938, 17.5 percent in 1951, 23 percent in 1967, 22.5 percent in 1987. This growth has not simply been the result of a benevolent state choosing to levy taxes in order to promote social equality. The objectives of state welfare must be considered in relation to other agencies (the family, voluntary and private institutions, the labor market) which provide support. The state has not necessarily displaced other agencies as providers of welfare; rather their roles have developed complementarily.

At the end of the nineteenth century central and local government were already responsible for a significant range of welfare functions. Apart from a growing state responsibility for education, the Poor Law provided a framework of benefits and services for those in acute need: institutionalized care of increasingly specialized and less punitive character for an expanding range of categories of need—the sick, the elderly, orphaned and abandoned children, and also minimal cash benefits for the "deserving poor", most frequently the elderly and widowed mothers and their children.

The central government came under increasing pressure to extend welfare activities. As institutional provision for such deserving groups as the sick improved, it became less obvious why they should remain within the unpopular framework of the Poor Law. UNEMPLOYMENT was acknowledged to be not always the fault of the unemployed, yet the jobless had no right to assistance other than in the punitive workhouse. The family and voluntary agencies could not meet all needs. Many of the elderly poor in particular had no kin willing to support them because they had never married, were childless, or because their families had emigrated, died, or were simply too poor to help. Throughout the century there is strong evidence that kin have given what they could to those in need. Another striking feature of the early years of the century is the large sums which were redistributed annually through charitable donations, but the demands on charitable funds exceeded the available supply.

Hence the state came under pressure to provide OLD AGE PENSIONS, assist the unemployed, and to support mothers and children by less punitive means. In addition, fears were expressed that appalling urban conditions were leading to degeneration of the national physique. At the same time levels of infant mortality remained high and the birth-rate was falling—fastest among the better off and, it was assumed, physically-fittest specimens. Concern about what were seen as indicators of national decline was the more acute at a time when Britain faced overseas competition economically and militarily from such rivals as Germany. Welfare was seen as desirable not purely for humanitarian reasons but to achieve "national efficiency". The market and private mechanisms could not maintain that efficiency unaided; only the state had the necessary resources and access to information. However, the resulting pressure to improve the health and welfare, especially of infants and children, also faced opposition from those who still believed in minimal state intervention in family life. Poor families themselves often resented official interference in their lives.

Few people at this time, even in the emerging labor movement, favored the state taking complete responsibility for welfare. They believed that voluntary action should be encouraged but supplemented by the vastly greater resources of the state, which would regulate the labor market to ensure full employment and adequate wages. This would enable more people to help themselves and to escape from the low pay and underemployment which the poverty surveys of the period showed to be the main cause of deprivation. Governments were slow to respond to interventionist pressures largely because both major political parties were committed to low levels of taxation. The LIBERALS had a progressive wing and, as the chief beneficiaries of the working-class vote, were induced to enact reform measures which established some of the principles on which the welfare state later developed. These measures, neither costly nor notably redistributive, included free school meals for needy children (1906), medical inspection in schools (1907), a comprehensive Children Act (1908), all stemming from concern about the physical condition of the nation. Old age pensions were introduced in 1908. The first cash benefit to be paid by the state outside the Poor Law, it nonetheless imposed on claimants means and character tests similar in spirit to the Poor Law. The Trade Boards Act (1909) introduced a minimum wage and improved conditions in some of the lowest paid, mainly female occupations. The Housing and Town Planning Act (1909) sought to limit existing and future urban overcrowding and pollution. Successive budgets rendered the system of direct taxation somewhat more progressive. National Insurance, introduced in 1911, provided health and unemployment benefits outside the Poor Law, but mainly for the regularly employed and in return for compulsory weekly contributions. Collectively this was a significant leap in the state's responsibility for welfare. However, there was no underlying intention to establish the state as the permanent primary provider of welfare. It was intended to support self-help and voluntary effort.

These measures were limited and tentative,

and their effects are hard to assess due to the onset of the FIRST WORLD WAR, which greatly extended the range of responsibilities of the state and popular expectations. In general living standards improved because of full employment, and expectations about living standards in the future rose. Fear of political disorder lest these expectations be dashed led the government from 1916 to plan for post-war reconstruction.

Recession and continuous heavy unemployment followed, and the government responded by cutting public expenditure. However the long-term picture of the inter-war years is one of expanded welfare services and mounting expenditure. The government, fearing political unrest, maintained subsistence level payments to the unemployed throughout. Although often subject to humiliating tests of need, for the first time most of the unemployed could be sure of a regular payment, which for some meant a steadier income than they had earned before the war. Large amounts of subsidized COUNCIL HOUSING was built and bad housing pulled down. Local authority health care improved, especially for mothers and children. The main beneficiaries of these improvements were the manual working class. An important force behind the changes was the growing power of the LABOUR PARTY. The inter-war years also saw employers providing on a larger scale such benefits as pensions, especially for their white collar employees, who were largely excluded from state welfare.

Demands for an increased role for the state, already strong in the 1930s, were realized during the SECOND WORLD WAR, when many argued in favor of rewarding the people for their sacrifices in wartime. Despite the sacrifices and loss of life, living standards improved for those who survived, due partly to full employment, partly to effective government planning to ensure adequate supplies of necessities.

The post-war Labour government was committed to full employment and to extending the welfare state. Using modified Keynesian techniques, assisted by high levels of world demand, it achieved full employment which lasted (with occasional mild recessions) until the oil crisis of 1973. This brought significant improvements in the STANDARD OF LIVING for most of the population, but, as social surveys continually revealed, not the abolition of severe deprivation among those excluded from or on the margins of the labor market, such as old people or single mothers.

Economic policy and the operation of the market did more to improve overall living standards than did the development of welfare policies. These made a major contribution to improving conditions even for those on the margins and the quality of life more generally. The Labour government significantly extended welfare provision, introducing the principle that the major benefits and services were available to all social classes. Old age pensions, as well as health and unemployment insurance benefits were much improved, though less generously than as proposed in 1942 by WILLIAM BEVERIDGE. The NATIONAL HEALTH SERVICE, which provided free medical (including hospital) care for all was established, and FAMILY ALLOWANCES were introduced in 1945 for all children other than first children. There were also major improvements in HOUSING, education, and community social services.

An effect of this universalization of services has been that the better off have benefited disproportionately. This was the price that that was paid to encourage taxpayers to fund the new services. It has been argued that this welfare expenditure diverted resources from industrial investment and constrained economic growth. However, it must be noted that higher levels of social expenditure had no such effects on the German economy in this period.

Labour's CONSERVATIVE successors continued the expansion of welfare services, while encouraging the growth of private and business-based forms of welfare—occupational pensions and health care schemes, for example. In the 1950s and 1960s many even in the middle classes felt unable to provide for themselves at the standard provided by the state. The most rapid period of expansion of public expenditure on welfare, in Britain as in most developed countries, came in the 1960s, with large programs of HOSPITAL and house building begun under Conservative governments and continued by Labour.

Conservatives in the 1980s sought to cut state services, to transfer them to the private sector, and to encourage all forms of private insurance and private care (e.g. for the elderly). Legislative protection of lower paid (often female) workers was eroded. In a period of high unemployment, unemployment benefits were less severely cut, except for the very young, because governments still feared the political consequences of unemployment. Also further cuts were restrained by the EUROPEAN COMMUNITY, which sought to set standards of welfare provision throughout the Community higher than those prevailing in Britain in the early 1990s. Pressure from the EC is one reason why public expenditure on welfare did not fall as a percentage of GNP through the 1980s, despite the attempts to reduce it. Difficult as it is to measure precisely, public welfare expenditure absorbed about 22.2 percent of GNP (compared, for example,with 19.4 percent in the United States) at the end of the 1980s. This was also partly due to the costs of supporting the large numbers of the unemployed, elderly people,

and single parents. The major client groups of the welfare state changed somewhat, or reverted to older patterns, while the better off remained heavy consumers of publicly-financed education and health care, though larger numbers of them by this time felt able to provide for themselves independent of the state. The state remained the most efficient available mechanism for remedying the failings of the market and for providing basic minimum standards for all, although not social equality. Statistically it was clear by the early 1990s that one effect of changes in social and economic policies was marked social polarization: the rich grew richer and the poor poorer.

Pat Thane

Bibliography

Crowther, M.A. *British Social Policy 1914–1939.* 1988.

Glennerster, Howard. *British Social Policy Since 1945.* 1995.

Lowe, Rodney. *The Welfare State in Britain Since 1945.* 1993.

Mommsen, W.J., ed. *The Emergence of the Welfare State in Britain and Germany 1850–1950.* 1981.

Thane, Pat. *The Foundations of the Welfare State.* 1982.

Tomlinson, Jim. "Welfare and the Economy: The Economic Impact of the Welfare State, 1945–1951," *Twentieth Century British History.* vol. 6. (1995), pp. 194–219.

Wells, H(erbert) G(eorge) (1866–1946)

H.G. Wells originated most of the themes that have dominated science fiction in this century, including interplanetary warfare, time travel, and genetic engineering. He was also one of the most celebrated novelists and social critics of his day.

Born into the lowest stratum of the middle class, Wells escaped from poverty via a scholarship to the Normal School of Science. There he studied under T.H. Huxley, from whom he absorbed Darwinian theory and some deep forebodings about the evolutionary process. Wells came to fear that humans might regress to their animal ancestors and become the ape-like Morlocks of *The Time Machine* (1895) or the beastmen of *The Island of Dr. Moreau* (1896). But young Wells had also read Plato, and he attended socialist gatherings at William Morris's Kelmscott House: from these influences he developed a passionate faith in a scientifically-planned society. Apocalypse or utopia: Wells spent the rest of his life warning humanity that it had to choose one or the other.

His early novels were pessimistic. *The Time Machine,* which made his reputation, predicted that the upper and working classes would evolve into two distinct species, one preying on the other, while the whole universe descended into entropic decay. Wells admitted that *The War of the Worlds* (1898) was an exercise in wish-fulfillment—he wanted to blast Victorian civilization with Martian heat-rays. *The First Men in the Moon* (1901) conjured up a lunar race of highly evolved social insects as a Swiftean satire on British society.

Wells's mood changed with *Anticipations* (1901), which offered his forecasts for the new century. He now placed his hopes in a dictatorship of technocrats who would establish universal peace and plenty through central planning and eugenics. BERNARD SHAW and SIDNEY AND BEATRICE WEBB were very taken with Wells's elitist socialism, and in 1903 they brought him into the FABIAN SOCIETY.

Wells would attempt to commandeer the Fabians and transform them into a well-funded mass political organization. He might have succeeded, but sabotaged himself through his childish personal attacks on Shaw and the Webbs, whom he later ridiculed in his novel *The New Machiavelli* (1911). That episode set a pattern for Wells: he was always talking up schemes for saving the world, but he habitually provoked quarrels with his friends and lacked the patience for sustained political work.

Nor could Wells commit himself to one woman. He married his cousin Isabel Mary Wells (1866–1931) in 1891, and early in 1894 he took up with Amy Catherine Robbins (1872–1927). His advocacy of sexual liberation in *In the Days of the Comet* (1906) and *Ann Veronica* (1909), as well as his affairs with Amber Reeves and Rebecca West, made him the center of a series of public scandals.

Wells foresaw armored warfare in "The Land Ironclads" (1903), strategic bombing in *The War in the Air* (1908), and nuclear weaponry in *The World Set Free* (1914). Leo Szilard, who worked on the Manhattan Project, claimed that *The World Set Free* led him to the idea of an atomic chain reaction in 1934. Wells's genius lay not so much in predicting gadgetry as in projecting the impact of future technology: he knew in advance how tanks, bombers, and nuclear science would transform warfare.

He was less far-sighted about the FIRST WORLD WAR, which he proclaimed "The War That Will End War." Convinced that the conflict would bring about a technocratic revolution, he fell headlong into war hysteria. In *The Research Magnificent* (1915), *Mr. Britling Sees It Through* (1916), and *God the Invisible King* (1917) he proclaimed his faith in a Wellsian Deity who was somehow leading mankind toward the World State. Wells was an early advocate of the LEAGUE OF NATIONS but was equally quick to become disillusioned with it.

After the war Wells synthesized his whole world view in a grand universal chronicle: *The Outline of History* (1920) sold in the millions and made him wealthy. In collaboration with his son George ("Gip") and JULIAN HUXLEY he produced a similarly popular survey of biology, *The Science of Life* (1930).

Meanwhile, Wells continued to search for a visionary elite that would give his visions reality. In *The World of William Clissold* (1926) he looked to an "Open Conspiracy" of enlightened capitalists, and later he turned hopefully to Franklin D. Roosevelt's New Dealers. In 1934 he went to Russia and tried to convert Stalin; he left disgusted with the Soviet regime and its Marxist dogmatism. In the late 1930s he badgered scientists to assemble a world encyclopedia, but by then Wells was too old and impatient to carry out such a grandiose project. He grew increasingly cranky and scolding, rehashing old ideas, lashing out at politicians and other writers. In disgust with the entire human race, he composed his epitaph: "God damn you all, I told you so."

The younger generation was no longer listening. VIRGINIA WOOLF dismissed him for not being a modernist, Christopher Caudwell denounced him for not being a Marxist. The Art Deco futurama of Wells's film *Things to Come* (1936) looked sterile and chilling in the age of Henry Ford and the Five-Year Plans. E.M. FORSTER's "The Machine Stops" (1908), Evgeny Zamyatin's *We* (1920), ALDOUS HUXLEY's *Brave New World* (1932), and GEORGE ORWELL's *Nineteen Eighty–Four* (1949) all rewrote Wells's dreams as nightmares.

Although Wells was an international cultural celebrity, he has never been admitted to the first rank of novelists. In his 1914 essay "The Younger Generation," Henry James bemoaned Wells's slapdash methods of writing, which only worsened in later years. There is, however, honest workmanship in his novels of lower-middle-class life: *Love and Mr. Lewisham* (1900), *Kipps* (1905), and *The History of Mr. Polly* (1910) have a humorous realism that has been called Dickensian, though they rely less on broad caricature. *Tono-Bungay* (1909) was one of the first novels to confront those twin horrors of the twentieth century, radioactive pollution and mass media advertising. Counterpointing nuclear disintegration with the imminent crack-up of Victorian society, Wells might have had good artistic reasons to ignore Jamesean unities. His rationale—"The splintering frame began to get into the picture"—sounds almost postmodern, coming from a writer who was always straining to leap ahead of modernity.

Jonathan Rose

Bibliography
Hammond, John R. *Herbert George Wells: An Annotated Bibliography of His Works.* 1977.
MacKenzie, Norman and Jeanne. *H.G. Wells.* 1973.
Ray, Gordon N. *H.G. Wells and Rebecca West.* 1974.

Scheick, William J., and J. Randolph Cox. *H.G. Wells: A Reference Guide.* 1988.

Smith, David C. *H.G. Wells, Desperately Mortal.* 1986.

Welsh Nationalism

National feeling in Wales has found expression historically in a variety of ways including cultural, religious, and political movements; these have rarely been exclusively or explicitly nationalist associations, but they have to varying degrees possessed a Welsh national dimension since the early nineteenth century. A more explicit nationalism has made a distinctive impact on Welsh and British politics since the election of the first *Plaid Cymru* (the Welsh nationalist party) member of Parliament in 1966.

It is particularly difficult in the case of Wales to disentangle nationalism from those religious and cultural, especially linguistic, factors which have fed into it. The survival of the Welsh language, still spoken by 44 percent of the Welsh population in 1911, and its distinctive literature combined with a predominant Nonconformity to create a widespread consciousness of a Welsh *gwerin:* a people with a common culture opposed at every point to what was conceived of as an English church and an anglicized, Tory squirearchy. This consciousness found political articulation in an increasingly radical Welsh liberalism, especially after the election of 1868, for which the disestablishment of the "alien" Church of England in Wales was a keynote demand with obvious nationalistic connotations. By the 1890s Welsh politicians such as DAVID LLOYD GEORGE were advocating home rule for Wales and proselytizing in the *Cymru Fydd* movement, a nationalist Young Wales movement founded in 1886 within the LIBERAL PARTY but with ambitions to create a Welsh party in Parliament on the Irish model. This political ferment came to an end effectively in 1896, but it did achieve the establishment of an impressive number of Welsh institutions, including the federal University of Wales. Following the First World War nationalistic liberalism was eclipsed by socialism. There were voices within the LABOUR PARTY, which became, after 1922, the dominant political force in Wales, who argued for devolved Welsh structures, but these were largely overwhelmed by the social struggle of the inter-war years. In the post-Second World War period, however, the Labour Party did accept demands for some degree of devolved government in Wales which resulted, in 1964, in the establishment of the Welsh Office with a Secretary of State for Wales with a seat in the United Kingdom CABINET, a development which was greatly to increase the political visibility of Wales. A Welsh Language Act, granting equal validity to the Welsh language in certain circumstances

was passed in 1967. (In 1981 Welsh was spoken by 19 percent of the Welsh population, over half a million persons.)

However, this Welsh national strategy, which found expression first in home rule liberalism and then in some Labour policies, however, was never nationalist in any explicit sense. That specific political project was to become (following some early ambivalence) associated with the Welsh National Party which later adopted the name *Plaid Cymru* (Party of Wales). The party was launched in 1925, and the key figure in its development until the war was the English-born Welshman, Saunders Lewis, who, in an impressive creative effort, devised an intellectual justification for a self-governing and Welsh-speaking Wales which, surprisingly in such a Protestant country, relied in large measure on a return to a medieval European Catholicism as an escape from the English nationalism of the Reformation and the consequent industrialization of Wales. His appeal to Welsh-speaking intellectuals was profound, but the party made virtually no progress outside such confined circles despite the development of a more socialistic economic policy by D.J. Davies and a celebrated direct action protest and court case in 1936.

During the Second World War the party argued for Welsh neutrality in a conflict which they claimed was of England's making. The party did succeed in broadening its base marginally and in changing to a more pragmatic leadership under Dr. Gwynfor Evans who became president in 1945. The party retained a modest presence in Welsh politics, but its fortunes were transformed by the victory of Evans at the Carmarthen by-election of 1966. This success followed the establishment in 1963 of the Welsh Language Society *(Cymdeithas yr Iaith Gymraeg)* which initiated a direct action campaign for equal status for the Welsh language. Despite the unwelcome publicity attracted by some violent protests and a bombing campaign, Welsh nationalism succeeded in the late 1960s in establishing broad support in some parts of Wales and among certain social groups; the party performed well in a number of further by-elections and, in 1974, succeeded in electing three members of Parliament. This was in part responsible for the devolution legislation and the subsequent referendum of 1979. The referendum result in Wales, however, witnessed a substantial anti-devolution majority.

This was a setback for nationalism but, under the then socialist leadership of Dr. Dafydd Elis Thomas, M.P., the party succeeded in regaining some of the ground during the 1980s. In the April 1992 election it gained only 8.8 percent of Welsh votes but did, nevertheless, succeed in electing four members of Parliament. This phenomenon explains the strength and the weakness of Welsh nationalism—its electoral strongholds have been provided by the still strongly Welsh-speaking west of the country, and the party has found it extremely difficult to break out of the confines of its language base and create a wider nationalist politics in industrialised and urban Wales. In the elections for the European Parliament in 1989 the party adopted a new strongly pro-Europe stance and argued for the creation of democratic institutions to achieve a Europe of the regions.

R. Merfyn Jones

Bibliography

Davies, D. Hywel. *The Welsh Nationalist Party, 1925–45: A Call to Nationhood.* 1983.

Davies, Charlotte Aull. *Welsh Nationalism in the Twentieth Century: The Ethnic Option and the Modern State.* 1989.

Morgan, Kenneth O. *Rebirth of a Nation: Wales 1880–1980.* 1981.

———. *Modern Wales: Politics, Places and People.* 1995.

Wheatley, John (1869–1930)

John Wheatley was Minister of Health (with responsibility also for housing) in the 1924 LABOUR government and is often regarded as that administration's most effective member. More broadly, he was a man of the Labour Left and became a principal critic of RAMSAY MACDONALD's leadership.

He was born in County Waterford in 1869, his family migrated to the west of Scotland, and, probably in 1881, he became a miner. He left the industry in the early 1890s and after a series of business ventures established himself in 1908 as a partner in a printing business which prospered. This social mobility was combined with increasingly radical politics. Early involvement with the United Irish League was followed, probably in 1906, by a move to the INDEPENDENT LABOR PARTY. Wheatley was a devout Catholic whose attempts to demonstrate that Catholicism and socialism could be reconciled led to the founding of the Catholic Socialist Society and to a series of controversies with clerics. Within the labor movement he wrote pamphlets that used his mining experiences to indict capitalism and became a municipal politician. He joined the Glasgow City Council in 1912 and established a reputation as an expert on housing.

Wheatley responded cautiously to the outbreak of war in 1914. He adopted a critical position but concentrated on issues of immediate relevance to the Glaswegian working class. The city's prominence in the munitions' industry intensified the demand for housing, and the labor movement became involved in a campaign of rent strikes and attempts to prevent evictions. This paralleled and sometimes interacted with

the emergence of a strong Shop Stewards Movement concerned to block dilution. The combination produced the image—some would say misleading—of the Red Clyde. Wheatley played a prominent role in the rent agitations and gave advice and support to the Shop Stewards. He was concerned to offer a campaigning alternative to the revolutionary section in the workshops.

The Glasgow ILP emerged from the war with an enhanced reputation, and Wheatley only narrowly missed election to the Commons in 1918. Industrial defeats, the start of the inter-war depression, and the continuing salience of the housing issue all helped to send Wheatley to Westminster in November 1922. At that election Glasgow returned ten Labour MPs. Most were orthodox backbenchers, but a few—most notably Wheatley and JAMES MAXTON—established themselves as left-wing critics and earned the sobriquet the "Clydesiders". In June 1923 Wheatley, Maxton, and two colleagues were suspended from the Commons for unparliamentary behavior. It was a protest, partly instinctive, partly deliberate, against staid parliamentary mores.

Nevertheless, Wheatley was appointed to the first Labour CABINET in January 1924. He achieved prominence because he produced a significant piece of legislation despite the Government's minority status. His Housing Act extended the provision of subsidies for public sector HOUSING projects. This was not innovative; it built upon the earlier legislation by postwar coalition and CONSERVATIVE ministries. Yet for a government concerned to establish Labour's credibility, it demonstrated a reassuring competence. In other spheres Wheatley's record was more ambiguous. He encountered difficulties in reconciling labor movement demands with legal and administrative proprieties. He met vehement opposition from BIRTH CONTROL campaigners over his refusal to allow publicly-funded organizations to give contraceptive advice. It was the one issue on which Wheatley's CATHOLICISM seemingly affected his political judgement.

Following Labour's loss of office in October 1924 Wheatley became increasingly hostile to Labour's leadership. He passionately supported the Miners in their 1926 dispute and attacked their "betrayal" by both party and trade union leaders. His criticism of party policy deepened; he became a somewhat distinctive advocate of the ILP's "Living Wage" policy; he advocated a planned economy and protectionism. When the second Labour government was formed in 1929, he was not considered for office. Instead he and Maxton led a small group of left-wing critics. He died in May 1930, a respected but isolated figure.

Wheatley evades easy categorization—the radical businessman and devout Catholic who was also a Glasgow machine politician, a widely admired minister and eventually a socialist rebel. His contemporaries generally found him an intellectually impressive figure; they also found him elusive. Perhaps this reflected a failure to appreciate the significance of his Glasgow Catholic base, which remained fundamental to his political identity.

David Howell

Bibliography
Howell, David. *A Lost Left: Three Studies in Socialism and Nationalism.* 1986.
McLean, Ian. *The Legend of Red Clydeside.* 1983.
Middlemas, Robert Keith. *The Clydesiders: A Left Wing Struggle for Parliamentary Power.* 1965.
Wood, Ian. *John Wheatley.* 1989.

Whitehead, Alfred North (1861–1947)

Brilliant mathematician, inspirational teacher, gifted philosopher, and unwearying administrator, Alfred North Whitehead was one of Britain's most versatile and admired intellectuals. As close to a Victorian polymath as it was possible to be in the twentieth century, he wrote two dozen books, ranging from the orthodox *A Treatise on Universal Algebra* (1898) to the revolutionary *Principia Mathematica* (3 vols., 1910–13), from the critical *An Enquiry Concerning the Principles of Natural Knowledge* (1919) to the inspirational *Process and Reality* (1929). Revered by his students, esteemed by his colleagues, and worshiped by his disciples, Whitehead became one of Britain's best known and most respected thinkers.

Born to a succession of CHURCH OF ENGLAND clergymen and schoolmasters on the Isle of Thanet, Whitehead was educated at Sherborne School and Trinity College, CAMBRIDGE. An accomplished mathematician—albeit with wide-ranging intellectual interests—Whitehead was elected a Fellow of Trinity in 1884 and quickly established himself as a teacher of uncommon dedication and an academic administrator of rare humility. It was at Trinity that he encountered his most famous pupil, BERTRAND RUSSELL, and proved instrumental in turning Russell's interests to problems of the philosophy of mathematics. Their friendship quickly ripened into a collaboration, culminating in the *Principia Mathematica,* a heroic effort of scholarship aimed at establishing the logical foundations of mathematics.

In 1910 Whitehead stunned his colleagues by resigning his Trinity College fellowship and moving to London. The next year he took up a position at University College and from 1914 to 1924 held a chair of applied mathematics at Imperial College. At Cambridge Whitehead had been almost exclusively a pure mathematician,

writing a series of remarkable papers—such as "On Mathematical Concepts of the Material World" (1906). In London, by contrast, he turned his scholarly energies away from mathematics and towards philosophy and the philosophy of science, publishing many papers and books, most prominently *The Concept of Nature* (1920) and *The Principle of Relativity* (1922).

In 1924 Whitehead again mystified his friends by resigning his London appointment and—at age sixty-three—accepting a position as Professor of Philosophy at Harvard University, a post he held until his retirement in 1937. At Harvard Whitehead once again proved an inspiring teacher and once again shifted his interests, this time towards cosmology and what he termed the "philosophy of organism". Such writings as *Process and Reality, an Essay in Cosmology* (1929) and *Nature and Life* (1934) presented the mature expression of his thought.

Whitehead died—on 30 December 1947—rich with honors: a Fellow of both the Royal Society and the British Academy, a member of the Order of Merit, and the recipient of the Sylvester medal of the Royal Society and the Butler medal of Columbia University. His enduring intellectual reputation rests with his earliest and latest work—with his contributions to the *Principia* and his meditations on the nature of God and the universe. Judged by admirers, skeptics, and critics alike as an estimable man of intelligence, humanity, and wisdom, Whitehead set a standard of personal conduct and intellectual distinction rarely matched in the twentieth century.

Kirk Willis

Bibliography
Kuntz, Paul Grimley. *Alfred North Whitehead.* 1986.
Lowe, Victor. *Alfred North Whitehead: The Man and His Work.* 2 vols. 1985, 1990.
Schilpp, Paul Arthur. *The Philosophy of Alfred North Whitehead.* 1941.

Wilkinson, Ellen (1891–1947)

Ellen Wilkinson was one of Britain's most important female politicians, becoming Minister of Education in ATTLEE's post-war LABOUR government. She was also a trade-union organizer, partly responsible for the JARROW March, a journalist, a brilliant orator, and a prominent member of the Labour national executive.

Wilkinson was born in Manchester on 8 October 1891 into a respectable upper working-class family. She was raised a METHODIST, valued education, and worked her way through school until, winning a scholarship, she entered the University of Manchester in 1910, where she obtained an upper second in History and an M.A. At university she joined the FABIAN SOCIETY and was active in the University Socialist Federation, which brought her into contact with leading socialists of the day, including J.T. Walton Newbold, the first Communist MP, to whom she was briefly engaged, and HERBERT MORRISON. During these years, and subsequently, she gained a reputation for being a fiery personality. The fact that she was red-haired and small led to the epithets "elfin fury", the "Fiery Atom", and later, "Red Ellen". For a time she worked for the National Union of Women's Suffrage Societies, was active in the Women's International League, and, in 1915, became the National Women's Organizer of the Amalgamated Union of Cooperative Employees. She was a powerful and tireless speaker and ubiquitous crusader. Although initially active in the COMMUNIST PARTY, she won her political spurs for Labour when she was returned as a City Councillor for Manchester in November 1923. She lost her first parliamentary contest at Ashton-under-Lyne in 1923 but was eventually returned for Middlesborough East in 1924 and became one of only four women in the House of Commons. She held that seat until the crushing Labour defeat in the 1931 general election but was returned for Jarrow in 1935, holding the seat until her death.

From 1924 until 1939 Wilkinson was very closely associated with the British Left, active in the ill-fated SOCIALIST LEAGUE, involved in PACIFIST and anti-Fascist movements, and contributing to *Tribune*. She also aspired to be a journalist and a novelist. But her claim to fame was the fact that she helped to organize the Jarrow March to pressure the National government to provide jobs for Jarrow, a town suffering mass UNEMPLOYMENT. She later wrote of her experiences and the unemployment and poverty problems of Jarrow in *The Town That Was Murdered* (1939). From 1939 onwards, however, she moved more into the center of Labour politics. In CHURCHILL's wartime coalition government she was appointed Parliamentary Secretary to the Ministry of Pensions in May 1940, Parliamentary Secretary at the Home Office in October 1940, and was made a Privy Councillor at the beginning of 1945. In August 1945 she became Minister of Education in Attlee's post-war Labour government. It was in this capacity that she pressed ahead with free school milk and SECONDARY EDUCATION for all. Unfortunately, her educational work was cut short by her untimely death, of heart failure following bronchitis, on 6 February 1947.

Keith Laybourn

Bibliography

Morgan, Kenneth. O. *Labour People*. 1987.
Rubinstein, David. "Ellen Wilkinson Reconsidered," *History Workshop Journal*, vol. 7 (1979), pp. 161–9.
Vernon, Betty D. *Ellen Wilkinson*. 1982.
Wilkinson, Ellen. *The Town that was Murdered*. 1939.

Williams, Raymond Henry (1921–1988)

Raymond Williams was one of the most important literary and cultural critics of his generation. Born into a Welsh working-class family, he was educated at Abergavenny grammar school and Trinity College, CAMBRIDGE (B.A., 1946). During the Second World War he served in the Guards Armoured Division (1944–5). He worked as an ADULT EDUCATION tutor for fifteen years before joining the Cambridge English faculty in 1961. A fellow of Jesus College, he became a professor in 1974 and taught at Cambridge until his retirement.

In a series of highly influential books, including *Culture and Society, 1780–1950* (1958), *The Long Revolution* (1961), *Modern Tragedy* (1966), *The English Novel from Dickens to Lawrence* (1971), and *The Country and the City* (1973), Williams set forth a new definition of the study of literature for the British tradition by his demonstration of the power of a social-historical analysis at the service of a socialist consciousness. He shared with F.R. LEAVIS an interest in "culture" as a key component of human interaction, and a belief in the power of literature both to embody and disseminate (as well as to critique) the national imagination. But he broke down Leavis's carefully maintained barrier between high culture and mass culture in a radically democratic extension of the franchise; after Williams, every expressive medium, from comics to classics, could be seen to involve a serious imagination and to deserve a careful critical analysis. His pioneering work on POPULAR CULTURE, film, and television, in countless articles and in such books as *Communications* (1962; revised 1968 and 1976) and *Television* (1974), was a major factor in the acceptance of communications research by humanists and historians. Reciprocally, it informed social scientists of the importance of nonquantitative analyses of culture and literature to their own developing disciplines.

In *Keywords* (1976) Williams set out to examine, in dictionary style, the important terms in the vocabulary of modern British culture and society and thereby stimulated an increased awareness, within and well beyond the universities, of the power of words and of their historical and political associations. And in *Marxism and Literature* (1977) he answered those who had accused him of ignoring the European theoretical tradition by producing a masterpiece of literary theory, a field in which he had become more seriously interested after meeting Lucien Goldmann in 1970. Williams kept an untypically clear head throughout the debates for and against Althusser and his brand of theoretical Marxism that dominated the humanities and social sciences in Britain during the 1970s. He never embraced the excesses of what was then called "theory", nor did he endorse the often anti–intellectual extremes of British common sense that were invoked to fend off its challenges. In similar spirit, his interpretations of mass culture avoided both populist celebration, which assumed that whatever was popular was also good, and the equally inflexible critiques mounted by the theorists of the Frankfurt School, who saw in mass culture only the deformed ideological workings of a repressive capitalism.

Williams's life was never that of a mere scholar and university teacher. He wrote several plays and five novels, among them *Border Country* (1960), *Second Generation* (1964), and *The Fight for Manod* (1979), in which he attempted a ficitonal representation of the social and psychological stresses he saw attending the processes of modernization and class struggle in his native Wales. From his earliest years his life was that of a public intellectual. Whether inside or outside the LABOUR PARTY, he was constantly pressuring it toward a socialist agenda. He worked for his local Labour candidate at fourteen and at seventeen spoke out against the MUNICH agreement. In his years as an adult tutor he worked for and edited various magazines and journals, and was an important figure in the foundation and evolution of *New Left Review*. He was only briefly a member of the COMMUNIST PARTY (in 1939–41), and in 1966 he resigned from five years of official membership of the Labour Party, after which he maintained the role of an oppositional socialist intellectual working within the broad Left but with a consistently independent and original perspective. In 1967 he co-edited, with Stuart Hall and E.P. THOMPSON, *May Day Manifesto* (revised and expanded, 1968), in which he and his contributors, many of them at the center of the "New Left," denounced the Labour government as the agent rather than the critic of late capitalism and called for an end to the "deadening language of a false political system."

In his last years Williams remained as energetic as ever in his challenges to the parochialisms and cruelties of the British (and above all the English) establishment, even as he remained immensely loyal to what he saw as the best of the national tradition embodied in a working-class non-metropolitan culture. In *Towards 2000* (1983) he made a major effort to extend and update the analysis begun in *Culture and Society*. His own thoughts and opinions about his long career in criticism and politics can be found in *Politics and Letters* (1979). Since his death, various collections of his essays and reviews have been published, among them *Resources of Hope* (1988) and *What I Came to Say* (1989). In person as in print, he was and continues to be an inspiration for the new generations of oppositional intellectuals in the English-speaking world.

David Simpson

Bibliography

Eagleton, Terry, ed. *Raymond Williams: Critical Perspectives*. 1989.

Gorak, Jan. *The Alien Mind of Raymond Williams*. 1988.

Inglis, Fred. *Raymond Williams*. 1995.

O'Connor, Alan. *Raymond Williams: Writing, Culture, Politics*. 1989.

Prendergast, Christopher, ed. *Cultural Materialism: On the Work of Raymond Williams*. 1994.

Wilson, Angus Frank Johnstone (1913–1991)

Angus Wilson is among the important British novelists to have emerged in the latter half of the twentieth century, not only because of the artistic quality of his fiction but because much of it provides a detailed, shrewd reflection of British society before and after the Second World War in gradual and sometimes painful transition towards a more egalitarian order.

Wilson was born in August 1913 in Bexhill, Sussex, the sixth and last child of a Scottish father and South African mother, both well into their forties. He spent his earliest childhood in England and 1920–4 with his mother's relatives in Durban, South Africa. After three years at a preparatory school run by one of his brothers, Wilson entered Westminster School as a day pupil in 1927, moving from there to Merton College, OXFORD in 1932. He graduated from Oxford in 1935 with a degree in history, and from 1936 to 1955 was employed at the British Museum, first as a cataloguer of books and in 1949 as Deputy Superintendent of the Reading Room. For almost four years of the SECOND WORLD WAR he worked for the Foreign Office at Bletchley Park, in the operations which successfully decoded material transmitted by the German "Enigma Machine." It was the isolation and uncongeniality of his wartime work that led Wilson to his career as a writer. In 1944 he suffered a nervous breakdown, for which writing was suggested as therapy. He did not immediately take up the suggestion, but when in 1946 he started to write, producing his first short story, "Raspberry Jam," in a single weekend, he found he had liberated a fully-formed talent. It was quickly recognized in two prestigious magazines, *Horizon* and *The Listener*.

His first two books were collections of short stories: *The Wrong Set* (1949) and *Such Darling Dodos* (1950). Their mixture of satirical observation and human sympathy established Wilson's reputation, though a third collection, *A Bit Off the Map* (1957), was less successful, and Wilson's only stage play, *The Mulberry Bush*, performed at the Royal Court Theatre in London in 1956, proved to be no match for the new wave of drama inaugurated in the same theater a few weeks later by JOHN OSBORNE's *Look Back in Anger*. Wilson's position as a writer of fiction, however, was by this time incontestable, having been made so by the first two of his eight novels, *Hemlock and After* (1952) and the much longer and Dickensianly-rich *Anglo-Saxon Attitudes* (1956). Each book centers on the self-discovery of an ageing male protagonist, the first a "Grand Old Man" of English letters, the second a distinguished historian. Both novels display acute awareness of the mixed motives of heart and mind in a wide range of characters from recent and contemporary society, and both novels courageously depict HOMOSEXU-ALITY. Wilson's third novel, *The Middle Age of Mrs. Eliot* (1958), presents the slow adjustment to widowhood and reduced circumstances of its middle-class protagonist, and shows Wilson to be a writer as sensitive to the lives of women as to those of men. This empathy is also evident in *Late Call* (1964), set in a post-war British new town, which Wilson presents with his character-istic care for social detail. His two other novels of the 1960s are more technically experimental: *The Old Men at the Zoo* (1961) takes place in a future in which civilized order and liberal values are in the process of breaking down; *No Laughing Matter* (1967) is a panoramic novel covering the lives of six siblings from 1912 to the present, in which the conventions of "realistic" narrative are diversified by interior monologue, dramatic interludes, and functional stylistic parody. Wilson's last two nov-els, *As If by Magic* (1973) and *Setting the World on Fire* (1980), though generally felt to lack the co-gency of their predecessors, nevertheless display considerable vitality in their depiction, respec-tivly, of third-world conditions and of noble risk-taking in artistic enterprise.

In addition to writing his own fiction, Wilson commented on the fiction and the lives of other writers, most notably in *Emile Zola* (1952), *The World of Charles Dickens* (1970), and *The Strange Ride of Rudyard Kipling* (1977). From 1966 to 1973 he was a part-time Professor of English Litera-ture at the University of East Anglia (where he was also Public Orator), and he lectured at many universities in the United States. He chaired the Literature Panel of the ARTS COUNCIL OF GREAT BRITAIN (1966) and the National Book League (1971–4, and was President of the Royal Society of Literature of Great Britain (1983–6). These posts recognized his personal distinction as a writer and his commitment to the cause of literature, as did the many honors awarded him in Britain and abroad, including C.B.E. (1968); Chevalier de l'Ordre des Arts et des Lettres (1972); Honorary Member of the American In-stitute and Academy of Arts and Letters (1980). He was awarded a knighthood in 1980. After hav-ing spent some three decades, from 1955 onwards, living in a cottage in Suffolk, Wilson spent the

later 1980s in St. Remy de Provence. He died, after a long illness, in a nursing home in Suffolk on 31 May 1991.

An inheritor of the realist and liberal-humanist traditions of the English novel—in which capacity he has influenced such younger writers as Margaret Drabble and Malcolm Brad-bury—Wilson was at the same time always aware of "the dangerous edge of things" and of the need for literature to keep pace with the modernist and postmodernist experiment and to encompass fresh and challenging modes of communication.

Averil Gardner

Bibliography
Drabble, Margaret. *Angus Wilson: A Biography*. 1995.
Faulkner, Peter. *Angus Wilson: Mimic and Moralist*. 1980.
Gardner, Averil. *Angus Wilson*. 1985.
Stape, John Henry. *Angus Wilson: A Bibliography, 1947–1987*. 1988.
Wilson, Angus. *The Wild Garden; or, Speaking of Writ-ing*. 1963.

Wilson, (James) Harold (1916–1995)

A dominant figure in British politics for over a decade, Harold Wilson was the first LABOUR PARTY leader to win three general elections and was Prime Minister from 1964 to 1970 and from 1974 to 1976. He became Baron Wilson of Rie-vaulx in 1983. His career attracts mixed assess-ments: although a partial rehabilitation has begun, the balance is unfavorable. While recog-nized as shrewd and tactically adroit, Wilson is also condemned as a mere survivor and political "fixer"; a faint aura of seediness and duplicity sur-rounds his career. He combined a fierce urge for achievement and status with an insecurity which made him constantly suspicious of colleagues and vulnerable to press criticism. Wilson had an agile intelligence but seemed more at home with pro-cesses than outcomes, happier finding short-term solutions than pursuing a political vision.

These characteristics, and his poorly-articulated belief in a roughly-defined set of social-democratic values, can be discerned in his upbringing, education, and early career. Wilson grew up in a lower middle-class family in York-shire. Its strong work ethic and Nonconformist religious faith left an imprint, although critics see more evidence of the former than the latter. At OXFORD he studied hard and competitively: he dabbled in Liberal politics but had no contact with the heady social and intellectual atmosphere of the Labour Club and the Oxford Union, fre-quented by many future colleagues, rivals, and opponents whose loftier social background and assured manner unnerved Wilson throughout his career. As a junior academic he worked with WILLIAM BEVERIDGE, whose ideas influenced the development of the post-1945 WELFARE STATE.

Wilson was attracted to the Labour Party by G.D.H. COLE, one of its foremost intellectuals, perhaps partly because it offered a more plausible route than did the LIBERALS to the political career he already coveted.

The Second World War drew Wilson from academic life into several civil service posts in London; the experience increased his faith in government planning. Elected Member of Parliament for Ormskirk in 1945 (he moved to the Huyton seat in 1950 and retained it throughout his career in the House of Commons), Wilson was quickly promoted to a series of government positions. His resignation from office in 1951 over budgetary priorities coincided with that of ANEURIN BEVAN, a hero of the Left; Wilson exploited or underplayed the association as circumstances required. His ability to manoeuvre among the party's factions sustained his rise through its ranks in the 1950's and secured his election as its leader in 1963. He was seen essentially as a pragmatist; a moderate who did not alienate the party's left wing and who had little time for abstract or electorally damaging ideological debates. He led the party to a very narrow election victory in 1964 (consolidated by another victory in 1966), sidestepping bitter arguments by redefining socialism as the planned management of technological progress and economic efficiency. Although the Wilson government inherited serious economic problems, it began with a self-conscious burst of energy. He appeared committed to modernization, technocracy, and growth, and sought to establish Labour as the more forward-looking, less class-based party. To economic promises were added hopes for an expended welfare state and rejection of establishment values in favor of a more open, dynamic society. However, the government and its 1966 successor offered more than they could deliver. For three years the defense of sterling limited their freedom of action, but this and the restoration of a healthy trade balance were articles of faith to Wilson. The belated decision to devalue the pound in November 1967 constrained growth-oriented policies, while the commitment to planned expansion was also undermined by tensions between the Treasury and the newly-created Department of Economic Affairs. Although Wilson was able to bequeath to his CONSERVATIVE successor a revived trade balance and stable currency, underlying economic problems and patterns of rising public expenditure remained. So did Britain's archaic system of industrial relations; in 1969 an attempt to modernize it was beaten back by the trade unions and much of the rest of the labor movement, despite Wilson's commitment to reform.

It was Wilson's fate to hold office during a difficult period in foreign affairs. Britain was adjusting slowly to its diminishing role in world affairs. The burgeoning EUROPEAN COMMUNITY had previously denied British entry, and did so again in 1967. The "special relationship" with the United States increasingly seemed less special to Washington than to London. Wilson's efforts to act as a mediator in the Vietnam War showed him to be naively optimistic about his personal influence and underlined the decline of British power. The same may he said of the Rhodesian crisis: the white government unilaterally declared independence from the COMMONWEALTH and the Crown. Wilson genuinely disliked racism and had a deep regard for a renewed, post-colonial Commonwealth: he identified himself closely with the issue but could neither prevent independence nor effectively impose punitive measures.

Wilson's overall record as Prime Minister in the 1960s was mixed. For a while the nation seemed reinvigorated and optimistic, although this may have had more to do with changes in POPULAR CULTURE than with politics. The government did, however, introduce or facilitate a series of reforms, in such areas as CAPITAL PUNISHMENT, ABORTION, HOMOSEXUALITY, and DIVORCE, which made for a somewhat mere humane and liberal society. It also entered the fields of RACE RELATIONS, and EQUAL PAY. Wilson's personal style seemed suited to the times; he was witty, informal, and at home on television, in contrast to his recent Conservative predecessors. His manner emphasized rather than disguised his background; it reflected and perhaps helped to quicken something of a thaw of a permafrost of the class structure. Other aspects of Wilson's style drew criticism. He was constantly aware of the need to balance factions in the Labour Party, yet often treated it with disdain. He seemed increasingly to see government in terms of external crises and internal threats. Suspicious of senior colleagues (sometimes with good reason), he kept his cards close to his chest while nervously watching his ministers. His use of small committees to circumvent the full CABINET, his manipulation of the PRESS, and his reliance on a small circle of personal aides and advisers prompted exaggerated talk of a semi-presidential system of "Prime Ministerial government".

Wilson seemed traumatized by Labour's defeat in 1970. He survived as leader of a party which he found increasingly hard to control as its balance tilted leftwards. Particular skill was needed to deal with divisions over European Community membership, which was generally opposed by the Left, favored by the Right, and acted as an ideological litmus-test to both. Wilson's mixture of evasion and compromise was to some observers a necessary display of great dexterity; to others a cynical defense of his own position. It did, at least, take a remarkable politician to paper over the deepening cracks while being attacked from both sides for doing so.

In 1974 Wilson became Prime Minister again at a time of intense industrial unrest and mounting economic problems. The February election produced a Labour government lacking a parliamentary majority; it barely acquired one in October. Wilson's approach differed from that of a decade earlier. He treated the Cabinet as a more collegial body and lacked the restless energy of his earlier years. He described himself disingenuously as the "custodian of the Manifesto", having helped to reduce it to a brief agenda shorn of left-wing items. He strove to sustain the "Social Contract", a grandiose term for the horse-trading between government and unions over wage claims and social policy. He provided one vintage performance, using the unprecedented device of a national referendum to secure continued British membership of the European Community (achieved during the 1970–4 Conservative administration) while preventing an irreconcilable split in the Labour Party, in which a majority favored withdrawal.

In 1976 Wilson unexpectedly resigned as Prime Minister. Rumors then and since link his departure to an alleged longterm campaign by members of the security services, said to believe him to be a Soviet stooge. There had indeed been something of a vendetta, but with no proven justification, and neither this nor a worsening economic situation explains Wilson's departure. He was deeply fatigued and had planned his departure for some time. His final Honors List did not help his reputation; some of its beneficiaries' contribution to national life was hard to identify. Wilson retired to the back benches until 1983; he was then elevated to the HOUSE OF LORDS and largely withdrew from politics. His health failing, he became a somewhat isolated figure, pilloried by the Labour Left for abandoning the party's socialist principles and by the conservative Right for sticking to them.

Wilson was a superb political tactician whose limited strategic view was further diminished by the pressure of events. His achievements may come to look less meager as the record of the THATCHER years becomes clearer. It may also be that the rickety state of Britain's economy, the archaic nature of its institutions, and the divisiveness of the labor movement required a leader best suited to crisis management, the blurring of issues, and postponement of hard decisions.

Steven Reilly

Bibliography
Morgan, Austen. *Harold Wilson.* 1992.
Pimlott, Ben. *Harold Wilson.* 1992

Wilson, Harold. *Memoirs: The Making of the Prime Minister 1916–1964.* 1986.
———. *Final Term: The Labour Government 1974–76.* 1979.
———. *The Labour Government 1964–70.* 1971.
Tiratsoo, Nick. *The Wilson Governments, 1964–1970.* 1993.
Ziegler, Philip. *Harold Wilson: The Authorised Life.* 1993.

Wodehouse, P(elham) G(renville) (1881–1975)

P.G. Wodehouse is one of the masters of the English language, beguiling it into doing improbable things with grace and charm. He enjoyed an equally rare comic genius and commendable industry. These gifts combined to produce ninety-eight books (mostly novels, but including sixteen volumes of short stories, two of collected articles, three of "autobiography", and one posthumous collection of letters); all or part of the book and lyrics for thirty-one produced musicals, mostly smash-hits; seventeen staged plays which he wrote or co-wrote, and a vast amount of journalism. He is best known for creating Bertie Wooster, his valet Jeeves, and the Wodehousian Elysium where it is always glorious summer. But Wodehouse also created a host of other stars in the galaxy of English literature such as Bertie's Aunt Agatha who—her nephew suspects—wears barbed-wire next to the skin, kills rats with her teeth, and sacrifices her young by the light of the full moon. Other notables include Clarence, Earl of Emsworth and his prize pig, The Empress of Blandings; Uncle Fred, fifth Earl of good old Ickenham; Stanley Featherstonehaugh Ukridge; Honoria Glossop whose laugh is like cavalry charging over a tin bridge; Psmith, "The 'p' is silent as in psittacosis," and that wondrous raconteur of golf stories 'The Oldest Member.'

Wodehouse (pronounced Woodhouse) was born into a cadet branch of one of England's great landed families which gave him his knowledge of the aristocracy. He was educated at Dulwich College, which gave him a thorough grounding in Latin and Greek and a deep understanding of the English language.

After Wodehouse left Dulwich there was no money to send him to university, and his father placed him with the Hong Kong & Shanghai Bank in London as a trainee manager. After two years trainees were sent out East, a fate Wodehouse dreaded as all he wanted to do was write. So on evenings and weekends he wrote every sort of journalism for every sort of periodical in a frantic effort to earn enough money from his pen to save him from the luxurious life of a Hong Kong bank manager in Asia. He succeeded.

Wodehouse first came to popular notice as a writer of "schoolstories" such as *Tales of St. Austin's* (1903) and *Mike* (1909), accepted as among the finest of the genre. In 1904 he first visited America, which he instantly loved, and became an Anglo-American author living in, writing for, and selling all his work to, both countries.

If Wodehouse had never written a word of prose he would be remembered, in America at least, as one of the greatest lyric writers for Broadway musicals. His successes, often with Jerome Kern writing the score, included *Oh Boy!* and *Leave It to Jane* (both 1917), although his best known song is "Bill", interpolated into Kern and Oscar Hammerstein's *Show Boat* (1927).

In the late 1920s Wodehouse concentrated on his novels and short stories which became better and better appreciated around the globe and which assure his fame throughout the English-reading world. From 1929 with *Summer Lightning* to 1963 with *Stiff Upper Lip, Jeeves* he produced book after book which had reviewers desperate for new superlatives. Sir Compton Mackenzie gave up and wrote "To criticise him is like taking a spade to a soufflé." Only in Wodehouse's last years did his work become slightly self-derivative and fall below his best.

In 1940 the advancing German armies captured Wodehouse and his wife Ethel at Le Touquet on the North French coast. Later that year, as a civilian internee, Wodehouse made some innocent broadcasts to neutral America. The Nazis rebroadcast these to England, and Wodehouse was subjected to intense obloquy. His knighthood, just before his death in 1975, officially confirmed what had long been recognized: those broadcasts were no more than an unworldly error of judgment.

Wodehouse influenced every subsequent novelist writing in English—whether they realize it or not—and is cited 1,255 times in *The Oxford English Dictionary*. Laymen were amazed when, in a pre-war broadcast in America, Hilaire Belloc described Wodehouse as "The best writer of English now alive. The head of my profession." Fellow writers treated this as no more than a statement of fact. They, at least knew how difficult it was to create such sublime prose.

Barry Phelps

Bibliography
Donaldson, Frances. *P.G. Wodehouse: The Authorized Biography*. 1982.
McIlvaine, Eileen, and others. *P.G. Wodehouse: A Comprehensive Bibliography*. 1990.
Phelps, Barry. *P.G. Wodehouse: Man and Myth*. 1992.
Wodehouse on Wodehouse. 1980.

Wolfenden Report (1957)

In 1954, in the wake of several trials of public figures charged with various homosexual offences, the government appointed a committee, chaired by John Wolfenden (1906–85), Vice Chancellor of the University of Reading, to examine the ex-

isting laws pertaining to HOMOSEXUALITY and prostitution. The committee's report, published in 1957, urged stricter control over public solicitation by prostitutes and recommended that homosexual acts between two consenting adults (over the age of twenty-one) in private should cease to be a criminal offence. The appearance of the report initiated a major public discussion of homosexuality and led to the creation of the Homosexual Law Reform Society, which worked to garner support for legal change. The report's recommendations regarding prostitution were implemented in the Street Offences Act of 1959. However, because opposition to the committee's position on homosexuality was widespread, the government was reluctant to change the laws concerning homosexuality. Only in 1967, with the passage of the Sexual Offences Act, was homosexuality in England and Wales finally decriminalized.

The WOLFENDEN REPORT was a landmark in the struggle for gay rights. By suggesting that it was not the business of the state to act as the guardian of private morality, it prepared the ground for the "permissive legislation" of the 1960s. Nevertheless, although the report called for the decriminalization of homosexual acts, it did not condone homosexuality, and it suggested the need for stricter controls over the public manifestation of what it considered irregular sexual conduct.

Chris Waters

Bibliograpy
National Deviancy Conference, ed. *Permissiveness and Control: The Fate of Sixties Legislation*. 1980.
Wolfenden, Sir John. *Turning Points: The Memoirs of Lord Wolfenden*. 1976.
The Wolfenden Report: Report of the Committee on Homosexual Offences and Prostitution. Cmnd. 247, Parliamentary Papers. vol. xiv (1956–7).

Women

In the first years of the twentieth century there were an unprecedented number of campaigns to achieve for women respect, influence, and independence comparable to that normally accorded to men, and there were changes of fundamental importance for women's lives which occurred independently of any conscious campaigning.

Most significant for most women in the long run was the falling birthrate. Beginning in the later nineteenth century, it eventually affected all social groups, though on a significant class gradient: the fall was greatest among the higher social classes, least, though still observable, among miners. Around 1900 women gave birth to an average of about three children in the highest social class, seven in the lowest. Thereafter family size gradually declined and became increasingly socially homogeneous. Women born in the 1880s and having their children in the early twentieth century had only half as many children as their mothers; their own children in the inter-war years averaged two-thirds as many as themselves (around two). The birth-rate reached its lowest point in the early 1930s (15.8 per 1000 women of reproductive age, compared with 28.7 in 1901), and the trend moved rapidly towards the two-child family norm throughout society. After an upturn during and after the Second World War (to 20.7 in 1947), the birthrate stabilized and then fell again from the mid 1960s.

This change meant liberation from repeated PREGNANCY, miscarriage, CHILDBIRTH, and associated ailments which had been the common lot of women. Throughout the first half of the century working-class women's organizations, such as the Women's Co-operative Guild, and middle-class philanthropic bodies, campaigned for better conditions in pregnancy, childbirth, and child-drearing, especially for poor women. Death in childbirth was the one form of mortality which did not decline from the later nineteenth century; indeed it increased sharply during the First World War, then, after falling back to pre-war levels, rose again during the inter-war depression. The figures did not fall until the introduction of penicillin and the sulphonomide drugs in the later 1930s facilitated the cure of previously fatal puerperal infection. From a little under five maternal deaths per thousand live births in 1911, and a peak of about 7.6 in 1918–9, the rate fell to less than 4 in 1939 and thereafter dwindled to tiny numbers. Tuberculosis was a much more significant cause of female deaths, accounting for 25 percent of deaths of women aged fifteen to forty-four between 1911 and 1930.

Accompanying these changes was a trend to concentrate childbirth into relatively few years of MARRIAGE. By the 1950s most women had completed childbearing by their mid-thirties while still young enough for active involvement in life outside the family, again changing the age-old pattern of most women's lives. At the same time, a higher proportion of women married, at least once. At the beginning of the century about 15 in 100 women did not marry; of women born around 1940 only 5 in 100 have not married at least once. Women have come to have fewer children, but more of them do so.

The reduction in family size appears to have been a result of conscious limitation, although contraceptive devices were hard for any but the prosperous and well-informed to obtain before the 1960s, despite campaigns by women's groups in the inter-war years to make them more readily available. From the 1960s the birth control pill, free BIRTH CONTROL clinics established by the LABOUR government, and access to ABORTION further increased women's control over reproduction.

The partnerships within which children are born have changed. Marriage was a matter of intense debate among women in all classes at the beginning of the century as an institution unduly restrictive of women. DIVORCE was difficult to obtain. The annual average number of divorces was 582 aound 1900, about half of them among working-class people. There were active campaigns by women to give women equal rights with men to end unhappy marriages, resulting in legislation in 1918, 1923, and 1937. Divorce became significantly easier to obtain for both sexes after a further change in the law in 1984.

At the beginning of the century there was still the likelihood that marriage would terminate in middle age due to the death of one of the partners. By the 1930s longevity had changed this pattern and, for a while, the long-surviving marriage became the norm. From the 1950s divorce replaced death as the cause of broken marriages. However, in the 1980s a significant trend towards cohabitation, often stable, to replace marriage began. In 1991 almost one-third of babies in Britain were born to unmarried parents. Many were in stable cohabiting relationships, but large numbers of women were bringing up children alone, and such women were disproportionately poor.

Power to change the law to improve women's position within marriage was one of many reasons why women campaigned for the vote and other political rights. One million women already possessed the vote in local elections in 1900 as legal householders and rate (local tax) payers and several thousand were elected to local authorities. Their effective use of political rights at local level and their active involvement in all political parties made their lack of voting rights at national level the more absurd.

A peaceable but determined campaign for the vote which became more active in the 1900s largely grew out of such political activism. The militant and constitutionalist strands complemented each other more than either realized, putting both public and private pressure upon the government. The concession of the vote in 1918 was much influenced by the fact that the franchise was at the same time extended to all men at twenty-one. Women, however, were initially granted the vote only at thirty. In 1928 the danger of a majority female electorate was judged to have receded, and women were granted the vote on the same terms as men. The women's movement became more active especially in the 1920s in encouraging women to use their new citizenship rights and in campaigning for EQUAL PAY and improved welfare facilities.

The delayed progress of women in elective politics was just one aspect of their slowness to reach the top in any sphere of influence or paid employment. In 1900 women were beginning to be admitted to the professions, but their numbers were small (212 doctors, for example). The FIRST WORLD WAR opened the way for middle class women to undertake paid employment at least until marriage. After the war such women, no longer chaperoned, could lead much freer lives. The SECOND WORLD WAR, which took female labor to the point of limited conscription, extended this process. But in 1946 only 7,198 medical practitioners out of 44,341 were female; 325 out of 9,375 architects and 164 of 17,102 solicitors. By 1961 women represented 15.9 percent of the MEDICAL PROFESSION (concentrated in its less prestigious specialties), 3.5 percent of the LEGAL PROFESSION, 2.3 percent of architects. By 1988 21 percent of lawyers and 22 percent of general practitioners in medicine were female, but only 3.2 percent of surgeons and 0.5 percent of engineers. These changes indicate a new expectation among middle-class families that their daughters might enter professional careers. Accompanying this is a pattern of delayed childbirth and employment of full-time childcare for professional women.

If there is some progress in paid employment of middle-class women, there is much less for lower middle- and working-class women. The range of manual and (especially) lower level white collar occupations open to women has increased, though the prospects of career opportunities, pay, and promotion for women comparable with men have scarcely begun to be realized. At the beginning of the century the largest female occupation was domestic service, but a high proportion of working-class women have continued to be concentrated in low-paid, routinized employment. The First World War created demand for women in paid work, though often in hazardous occupations like making ammunition. After the war working-class women were expected to revert to pre-war occupations, including domestic service, which had sharply diminished during the war and continued to decline down to the 1930s. Although many women suffered in the Depression, some found opportunities in the new light industrial occupations which developed in the inter-war years.

Before 1939 middle-class women would rarely take paid employment after marriage; poorer women were obliged to augment household resources throughout her life-cycle. At the end of the Second World War the government, anticipating a manpower shortage, campaigned to keep women in the labor force. Many left to have or to care for young children, but the total numbers of women in paid employment rose from the later 1940s. Since then a pattern has been established in all social classes for women to cease work for a

few years when children are young and then return to paid work, often part-time. Part-time work is a notable feature of the modern female labor market in Britain, accounting for about one-third of all paid WOMEN'S EMPLOYMENT.

Sexual inequality in paid employment survived a campaign on the part of the trade unions and white collar occupations, from the 1930s, for comparable pay for women, a Royal Commission in 1946 which confirmed the facts of inequality, a revived women's movement, again with complementary moderate and radical wings, the Equal Pay Act (1970), and the establishment of the Equal Opportunities Commission under the Sex Discrimination Act (1975). In the 1980s and 1990s the European Commission and the European Court of Justice have supported some British women's appeals against discriminatory practices. The process, slow and costly, has established valuable precedents.

Unpaid work in the home has been improved by the demographic changes outlined above, by improved HOUSING for working-class people since the 1920s, and generally smaller servantless housing for the better-off. Domestic technology has replaced servants and has filtered down the social scale at increasing speed since the 1950s. The effect has not been to reduce average hours spent on housework, but to eliminate the heavy, debilitating physical labor which housework previously implied.

The experiences of women have differed by class, by age group, and, importantly from the 1950s, by ethnic background. Just as the lives of orthodox JEWISH women among IMMGRANTS early in the century differed from those of the non-orthodox and non-Jewish women, so some Muslim and Hindu women live within the customs of their own cultures, though their experience also varies with age, class, and region of origin, as does that of the large numbers of women of Caribbean origin and the somewhat smaller numbers from Africa.

Pat Thane

Bibliography

Lewis, Jane. *Women in England 1870–1950: Sexual Divisions and Social Change.* 1984.

Meehan, Elizabeth. *Women's Rights at Work: Campaigns and Policy in the United States and Britain.* 1984.

Pugh, Martin. *Women and the Women's Movement in Britain 1914–1959.* 1992.

Reid, Ivan, and Erica Stratta, eds. *Sex Differences in Britain.* 2nd ed. 1989.

Rowbotham, Sheila. *A Century of Women: The History of Women in Britain and the United States.* 1997.

Thane, Pat. "Towards Equal Opportunities? Women in Britain since 1945" in Terry Gourvish and Alan O'Day, eds. *Britain since 1945.* 1991. pp. 183–208.

Women in Wartime (1914–1918 and 1939–1945)

Both world wars have been seen by historians as emancipating for British women. Greater freedom was ostensibly expressed through consumption and personal style: women in war work had their own incomes to spend, wore shorter skirts or even trousers, and smoked cigarettes in public. Enfranchisement in 1918 and the establishment of a Royal Commission on Equal Pay in 1944 appeared to give official encouragement to political and economic equality. But feminist historians have questioned whether women's labor market gains were permanent and whether changes of style indicated a readjustment of the relationship between the sexes. In addition they argued that the vote was granted to women over thirty in 1918 mainly because of suffragist activity and pressure to revise the male franchise, rather than as a reward for war service. They also note that the only outcome of the equal pay debate of 1944–6 was a recommendation that EQUAL PAY might be introduced for a small group of workers in the public services, and this was not acted upon until 1955.

In both wars there were large rises in the numbers of women employed. These were temporary, though they took place in the context of an overall upward trend between 1911 and 1951 in the number and proportion of British women in paid work. Between 1914 and 1918 there was an increase of about 1.5 million women in the industrial labor force, from 5.3 million in 1911 to nearly 7 million in 1918. But numbers then fell to 5.7 million in 1921. UNEMPLOYMENT was rising and there was political pressure to give job preference to ex-servicemen. Women were expected to return to traditional jobs in domestic service and the textiles and clothing industries, or to stay at home. Between the wars, however, the women-employing sectors of some industries, such as electrical assembly, expanded. So did clerical work for women. In 1931 6.2 million women were in paid employment. The SECOND WORLD WAR saw another increase of about 1.5 million women, but once again there was a decrease at the end of the war, from about 7.7 to 6 million between 1943 and 1947. In part this was a temporary post-war readjustment and in part the result of demographic factors. By 1951 the Census recorded 6.9 million women in paid work. The proportion in industries like engineering and transport and in government service was now higher than it had been pre-war. As in the case of the inter-war trend, this was not because women took men's jobs, but because women-employing sectors expanded more than those which employed men.

So the wars themselves contributed to a long term process of enlarging WOMEN'S EMPLOYMENT within gender-stereotyped sectors of the economy. But wartime expansion also appeared to threaten gender boundaries at work and at home. There were four aspects to this problem.

First, in both wars women used the wartime opportunities to obtain relatively well-paid work in industries and occupations which were previously male-dominated, like munitions, engineering, transport, and office work. Most of them had done paid work at some point in their lives before, usually in industries like textiles and clothing, or in services like laundry work, waitressing, shopwork, and personal domestic service. They included married women, who were customarily expected to be supported by a male breadwinner and not to seek paid work. In 1918 40 percent, and in 1943 43 percent of women workers were married, compared with only 15 per cent in 1911 and 16 per cent in 1931. The fact that women rarely did exactly the same jobs as men, and were in the main employed on work which had been simplified, was not as publicly visible as their entry in large numbers into unfamiliar territory. Male workers responded to the influx with varying degrees of hostility. In both wars there were incidents of workplace sabotage by men who opposed women's presence because it meant in the short term that they were likely to be called up into military service, and in the long term that they might lose their jobs to this cheaper workforce. Trade unions endeavored to protect their male members. A Munitions Act, passed in 1915, stipulated that women should be allowed into work from which trade union agreements had excluded them before the war, on the condition that their wages did not undercut those of men, and that they would be removed at the end of the war. In 1940 individual union-employer agreements were signed on the same lines: women should be allowed into men's work for the duration of the war provided they received equal pay after a specified period. In both wars the implementation of these rules was problematic. Women struck for equal war bonus on the LONDON trams and buses in 1918, and for equal pay in a Scottish engineering factory in 1943. Men were prepared to help if they thought it would protect their jobs and pay rates, but did not support women's long-term claims to jobs and fair pay. The unions actively promoted women's redundancies at the end of both wars.

Second, in both wars women were recruited into various uniformed services, an apparent challenge to gender norms that caused considerable public alarm. In 1917 the women's auxiliary services to the Armed Forces (the Women's Army Auxiliary Corps, the Women's Royal Naval Service and the Women's Royal Air Force) were formed on a cautious, experimental basis, recruiting around 40,000 women. A Women's Land Service Corps, later renamed the Women's Land Army, was founded in 1916 and recruited 23,000. In addition a few thousand women joined the Voluntary Aid Detachments as nurses. In the Second World War all these organizations were enlarged and sometimes renamed. The three military services for women were the Auxiliary Territorial Service, Women's Royal Naval Service, and Women's Auxiliary Air Force. They recruited 450,000 women, while 80,000 women joined the Women's Land Army. In addition 500,000 women were employed in civil defence, and a million worked in the Women's Voluntary Services for Air Raid Precautions, established in 1938. Single women aged nineteen to thirty were conscripted into the armed forces, industry, or civil defence following the National Service (Number 2) Act of December 1941. All the same, panic was expressed in the PRESS and in Parliament about the effects a uniform might have on a woman's morals.

Third, steps were taken in both wars to alter the organization of domestic work in order to make women available for war work. In the FIRST WORLD WAR 108 day nurseries attached to large government-run factories, and a small number of municipal and private creches, were established for about 4,000 children of women war workers. Child care was greatly extended in the Second World War when 1,500 nurseries taking nearly 72,000 children were set up by local authorities with subsidies (and regulation) from central government. Fears that nurseries would tempt women to desert their proper role of motherhood in favour of paid work were rife in the First World War. In the Second the Ministry responsible for nurseries (Health) saw them as a temporary necessity when alternative home-based arrangements (such as minding) could not be made, but a mother's place was still perceived to be in the home with her own children. In both wars the goverment responded to food shortages by introducing RATIONING (though not until 1918 in the First World War). But the woman worker faced the problem of missing a meal or absenting herself from work in order to queue for food in short supply. In the Second World War goverment ministries discussed the shopping problem, but the favored solution was to give women unpaid time off to shop, or to introduce schemes of part-time work, rather than to relieve the woman of the work of shopping itself.

Fourth, in both wars there were anxieties that the family was under threat because of the large numbers of women in paid work and of men away from home in the Forces. The illegitimacy rate rose by 30 percent in the First World War and more than doubled in the Second. In 1914

surveillance of servicemen's wives was introduced. If they were drunk or engaging in "irregular conduct", their army separation allowances were stopped. The DIVORCE rate rose between 1918 and 1920 from 0.2 to 0.8 per 10,000 of the population, and between 1938 and 1947 from 1.5 to 13.6 per 10,000. The disruption of the Second World War undoubtedly contributed to this huge increase, but so too did legislation between the wars which made divorce cheaper and easier to obtain. After a rash of "khaki" weddings, there was a slump in the MARRIAGE rate in the middle of both wars, followed by a recovery at the end.

Investigation of these aspects of women's experiences in wartime indicates that the appearance of gender boundaries being under threat may have been much greater than the reality.

Penny Summerfield

Bibliography

Braybon, Gail. *Women Workers in the First World War.* 1989.

———, and Penny Summerfield. *Out of the Cage: Women's Experiences in Two World Wars.* 1987.

Grayzel, Susan R. *Women's Identities at War: Gender, Motherhood, and Politics in Britain and France during the First World War.* 1999.

Gullace, Nicolette F. *The Blood of Our Sons: Men, Women, and the Renegotiation of British Citizenship During the Great War.* 2002.

Summerfield, Penny. "Women, war and social change: Women in Britain in World War II" in Arthur Marwick, ed. *Total War and Social Change.* 1988. pp. 95–118.

———. *Women Workers in the Second World War: Production and Patriarchy in Conflict.* 1984.

Woollacott, Angela. *On Her Their Lives Depend: Munitions Workers in the Great War.* 1994.

Women's Education

The history of women's education in twentieth-century Britain has been a story of progress. Women, as well as men, have benefited from the expansion and democratization of the educational system. On the other hand, gender bias—like class bias and racism—has affected access to equality in education. While there have been some changes since the 1970s, women have experienced the same disadvantages in education that they have had to confront more generally in British society throughout this century.

How did conceptions of gender difference influence the development of PRIMARY and SECONDARY EDUCATION in the period up to 1944? The fact that those with money and power almost invariably selected single-sex schools for their own children reflected the dominant belief that different educational needs of boys and girls should be reinforced through schooling. An ideological commitment to a conception of femininity which encouraged in girls and women not only dependence, but an acceptance of male dominance and masculine privilege affected the curriculum and the mores of elementary education.

The central Board of Education (created in 1899) developed policies and programs designed to ensure that girls would receive training in domesticity through sewing, cookery, and laundry classes. Moreover, as resources expanded, sex segregation within schools increased. Where possible, schools provided separate entrances for girls and boys and separate play areas. The idea that the state school system should be used to train girls to be good wives and mothers, while their brothers were to be trained to be responsible wage-earners, was accepted by the great majority of educational policy makers, men and women alike. Thus, elementary education in the first half of the century was extended relatively equally to girls and boys. However, schooling reflected and reinforced dominant beliefs about the differing roles of women and men explicitly through the formal curriculum (girls and not boys were trained for domesticity) and through less obvious informal mechanisms.

Until the EDUCATION ACT OF 1944, while the numbers of free places in secondary schools were increasing, secondary education was only available to a small minority of working-class children. By 1939 80 percent of the children educated in the state system left school at fourteen. More boys than girls went on the secondary school: 14.5 percent of boys as against 13 percent of girls. Whether secondary school pupils from the state system occupied free places in established schools, or whether they attended secondary schools created by local education authorities, they entered a middle-class milieu. One feature of this milieu was that, in contrast to primary education, secondary education almost invariably meant single sex education. Thus, girls entering secondary schools from the state system were indeed being offered a chance to expand their horizons but not the same opportunities as their brothers. When they entered secondary school, they became part of a *female* middle-class milieu.

The foundations for girls' secondary education were laid by those pioneers of women's education who had established schools for the daughters of the middle classes designed to expand opportunities and prepare women for activities beyond the scope of domesticity. These pioneers, for the most part identified with the conservative wing of the women's movement, had struggled with conflicting objectives. On the one hand, they wished to provide their pupils with sound training, a liberal education, and skills that would allow them to earn their livings in a dignified

manner, should that be necessary. On the other hand, as a group they also wished to develop and reinforce in their pupils the values of Victorian and Edwardian femininity.

Such middle-class girls' schools, whether private proprietary bodies or "public" schools, had developed as independent institutions. After the 1902 Education Act, there was some blurring of boundaries between the state system and the independent schools, as secondary schools serving children from the state system came under the aegis of the Board of Education's Secondary Branch. Its policy makers took the position that while girls, like boys, should be provided with a liberal education, schooling at the secondary level should also reinforce perceived inherent differences between the sexes. A tangible result of this policy was that from 1905, "housewifery" was made compulsory in those girls' secondary schools over which the Board exercised authority.

Thus, the state-supported secondary system created during the first half of the century did incorporate into its structure some significant gender differences. While girls did share in the standard curriculum and were prepared for the School Certificate Examinations introduced in 1917, in crucial ways girls were also taught that their primary purpose was to fulfill their womanly role.

How did girls fare after the passage of the Education Act of 1944? Until the 1960s, when "secondary education for all" meant in practice a two-tier system in which only the 20 percent of children passing the eleven-plus examination were given access to a secondary education that would prepare them for skilled non-manual work or university entrance, clear sex differences in educational opportunity emerged. Although as a group girls did at least as well as boys at 11+, girls' grammar schools were not as successful as those for boys in retaining their pupils. Significantly fewer girls than boys stayed on in school past the age of sixteen: 66 percent of the eighteen-year old school population was male in 1965.

Since the 1970s there has been a marked improvement in the retention rate for girls at the secondary level. By the 1980s girls had overtaken boys in General Certificate of Education "ordinary" level passes achieved, in Certificate of Secondary Education passes, and in the unified General Certificate of Education examination introduced in 1986. Girls are also more likely than boys to attain at least one "A" or Advanced level pass. However, in the late 1980s boys still exceeded girls by a small margin in achieving minimum two "A" levels needed for university entrance.

It is not clear that these improved opportunities for girls at the secondary level can be attributed to the restructuring of the secondary system. More likely they reflect the influence of the partial suc-cess of FEMINISM. It is certainly the case that only since the 1970s have sociologists of education, ed-ucational psychologists, and historians of educa-tion begun to recognize the extent to which the educational system has served to perpetuate in-equalities of gender, and only more recently have serious attempts been made to counteract such inequities.

Although the state system educates the great majority of Britain's children, some 6.7 percent continue to be educated in independent schools and continue to attain a disproportionate number of university places. Some believe that such schools, while offering girls as well as boys un-doubted advantages, reinforce outmoded notions of correct feminine behavior. In contrast, others argue that the academic successes of girls attend-ing independent schools can be attributed to the fact that most of them remain single-sex institu-tions. Such observers believe that state-mandated co-education, a feature of the state secondary school system since the introduction of compre-hensive schools—nearly all of which are co-educational—is in fact damaging to girls, given that the wider culture remains male-dominated. The debate about the relative merits of co-education and single sex education for girls at the secondary level remains unresolved. In the early years of the century post-secondary education was virtually restricted to those educated in the elite, independent stream. Women could attend and receive degrees from most British univer-sities, but a majority of university students were male, and for both sexes UNIVERSITY EDUCATION remained the preserve of an elite minority. With the end of the Second World War a commitment to expand access to higher education became part of social policy. Changes were implemented through an expansion of university and college places and through a program of financial aid to post-secondary students. In the course of this ex-pansion women have made striking advances. Whereas in the 1940s only 20 percent of the post-secondary population was female, by the 1980s this figure had risen to 40 percent. The number of women receiving degrees has increased eight times since the 1940s, whereas the number for men has increased fourfold. However, women still receive slightly fewer degrees than men and hold only a small minority (10 percent) of teach-ing posts at British universities.

Deborah Gorham

Bibliography
Blair, Gage. "Great Britain" in Gail P. Kelly, ed., *Interna-tional Handbook of Women's Education*. 1989. pp. 285–322.
Hunt, Felicity, ed,. *Lessons for Life: The Schooling of Girls and Women 1850–1950*. 1987.
Jones, Carol, and Pat Mahony. *Learning our Lines: Sexu-ality and Social Control in Education*. 1989.
Purvis, June, and Margaret Hale, eds., *Achievement and Inequality in Education*. 1983.
Wilson, Maggie. "England and Wales" in Maggie Wil-son, ed. *Girls and Young Women in Education; A Euro-pean Perspective*. 1989. pp. 41–66.

Women's Employment

Women's economic activity attained a statistical high water mark in the mid-Victorian years, with women working outside the home principally in the textile and clothing industries, domestic ser-vice, and laundressing. Yet women fully engaged at home with domestic chores were also consid-ered to be productively employed and were so tabulated. In the Census of 1881 housewives were still counted, but only as "unoccupied". By the Census of 1911 they were no longer counted at all. Census figures indeed reveal an overall decline in female employment from 1871 to 1911. An increase in real wages in the closing decades of the nine-teenth century fuelled this trend by allowing more married women to remain at home full time.

Prior to the First World War, a good deal of married women's economic activity escaped the official reports. For many working-class women with dependent children, home work done at piece rates away from the workshop provided a means of adding to meager family incomes. Home work constituted sweated labor performed under unregulated and often unsanitary condi-tions; it involved long hours, the frequent use of child labor, and was done for very little pay. Nev-ertheless, home work could be done sporadically, in the event of a financial crisis, by women who could not work outside the home. Sweated occu-pations included cardboard box making, sewing, chain making, carding hooks and eyes, brush making, and fur pulling. Production forces cou-pled with a vigorous public outcry effectively ended most sweated labor by the second decade of the twentieth century.

With the decline of home work, the cleft between the home and workplace was complete. A direct result of this separation was that young single women overwhelmingly comprised the fe-male work force. By the 1920s married women without children increasingly continued their employment until the birth of their first child. But in virtually all events, women considered their jobs to be of short duration. They intended to resign at the first opportunity, usually upon MARRIAGE. Indeed, some occupations such as teaching and nursing enforced a marriage bar compelling a married woman to relinquish her job. This restriction remained in force in a num-ber of fields until the Second World War. Not until 1946 was the marriage bar removed for female CIVIL SERVANTS.

Given the perception of women's employment as transitory by both women and employers, the jobs offered were low-status, low-paying, tedious, and often unskilled or semi-skilled. Job training was minimal. Further, women's participation in trade unions was but a fraction of men's involvement, further reinforcing their low status and pay. Over the decades, the proportion of women to men among trade unionists had remained smaller, despite a solid increase in the absolute numbers of women joining unions.

As the traditional female occupations declined in the twentieth century, other industries sprang up to absorb women workers. Technological advances in many industries made for lighter tasks requiring less skill. As a result, women entered such areas as mining and metallurgy, printing, papermaking, bookbinding, the chemical industry, and food processing. While domestic service continued to employ almost a quarter of the female labor force as late as the 1930s, a significant number of women left service for factory jobs which offered greater freedom, privacy, and higher wages.

Despite women's role in manufacturing, female employment in this century has been characterized by a shift towards white collar work with the development of the distributive and service sectors. Large shops and department stores were established in response to the needs engendered by growing urban populations and the problems of distribution that resulted from new methods of mass production. These large stores replaced smaller family-run businesses and created a sharp demand for shop assistants. The growth of telephone and telegraph services required a large number of semi-skilled and unskilled workers, as did the post office. A series of Education Acts, coupled by the raising of the school-leaving age, increased the demand for teachers as well as providing a higher degree of literacy within the female work force. Clerical work for women received a stimulus with the growth of large offices and the expansion of the insurance and banking industries. Office work evolved into a series of discrete jobs such as typewriting, stenography, filing, and reception, many of which required little or no training. Women entered these occupations on the lower echelons in such numbers that whole segments of these industries became feminized with the attendant depreciation in status and pay.

With the rise of the WELFARE STATE, government bureaucracy increased dramatically, further fuelling the demand for female office personnel. The welfare state is also responsible for the provision of more social services to the public. More vigorous health care demanded more nurses and other hospital personnel. Protective legislation created the need for an army of inspectors. Various public programs required social workers and administrators. Along with elementary school teachers, these occupations were characterized as the low professions (as distinct from the "high professions" of medical doctor, lawyer, and other careers requiring advanced degrees) and were, therefore, considered fit work for women.

The character and composition of the female work force was dramatically influenced by war. Many women were temporarily displaced from their jobs at the start of the FIRST WORLD WAR when a number of industries contracted in the face of economic restrictions. However, they were soon recruited as a reserve army of labor to supply desperately needed workers in munitions and essential industries. The lines between women's and men's work blurred during the war effort as women proved themselves capable of performing more skilled and heavier tasks than they had hitherto been hired to undertake.

The occupational advances made by women during the First World War were short-lived. Trade union agreements to protect men's jobs at the beginning of the war, along with the pressure of public opinion, led to mass resignations of women from the industrial ranks at the war's conclusion. Economic adversity in the inter-war years prevented the reabsorption of many women, particularly married women with children, back into the work force. There continued to be cherished a strong conviction, which most women shared, that mothers should remain at home with dependent children. Married women without young children, however, worked in increasing numbers from the 1920s on, signaling an important shift in the composition of the female labor force.

The SECOND WORLD WAR provided a massive stimulus to women's employment, with 80 percent of married women working. Women with children were also employed on a part-time basis. In contrast to the experience following the First World War, women at the end of the Second World War did not abandon their jobs to the extent that an earlier generation of women workers had done. This was due to a variety of factors operating in the post-war economy. The need to reconstruct the economy, followed shortly by the mobilization for the Korean War, required a constant supply of labor. Attitudes toward women in the workplace were finally revised, with employers and government planners actively encouraging women to remain in industry. The bar to married women in many fields was abolished, and employers, prompted by the government, made some efforts to provide work convenient to the needs of married women. Part-time positions and shift work flourished.

Social changes also contributed to married women taking jobs. By the 1950s over 50 percent of married women were employed. Family planning, labor saving devices in the home, greater literacy levels, and higher economic expectations made work more desirable and respectable. Gradually, more women with children returned to the workplace once their youngest child reached school age.

Despite the transitions that women's employment has undergone in the course of the century, certain elements have been slow to change. Women stay clustered in the lower levels of occupations, and, for most of the century, they have remained concentrated in separate occupations. For much of the period under study, women have received at best 50 to 60 percent of men's pay for equal work. Though much improvement has been wrought by the Equal Pay Act of 1970, the goal of equality in the workplace has yet to be fully realized.

Donna Price Paul

Bibliography

Braybon, Gail. *Women Workers in the First World War: The British Experience.* 1981.

Joseph, George. *Women at Work: The British Experience.* 1983.

Lewis, Jane. *Women in England, 1870–1950: Sexual Divisions and Social Change.* 1984.

Soldon, Norbert C. *Women in British Trade Unions, 1874–1976.* 1978.

Tilly, Louise A., and Joan W. Scott. *Women, Work, and Family.* 2nd ed. 1987.

Women's Social and Political Union (1903–1917)
The Women's Social and Political Union (WSPU) galvanized the WOMEN'S SUFFRAGE movement. Its policy of militant action—"Deeds Not Words"—riveted the attention of the British public, giving the suffrage campaign a visibility and mass base that it had hitherto lacked.

Organized by EMMELINE PANKHURST in 1903, the WSPU burst into prominence in 1905, when CHRISTABEL PANKHURST and Annie Kenney (1879–1953) were bodily thrown out of the Free Trade Hall in Manchester for heckling SIR EDWARD GREY. Seeking imprisonment, Christabel Pankhurst spat on a policeman, was arrested and tried, refused to pay her fine, and went to jail. The publicity aroused the country, and the women's suffrage ranks began to swell.

In contrast to the constitutional tactics pursued by the National Union of Women's Suffrage Societies (NUWSS), the WSPU adopted a policy of spectacular public protest. Until the summer of 1909 militancy remained non-violent. Suffragettes, as WSPU followers were called,

heckled CABINET ministers and obstructed political meetings; they converged on Parliament to meet with MPs who refused to see them. Often, they were met with violence at the hands of the police and civilian bystanders before being arrested. In the summer of 1909 the militants began to throw stones, protesting against politicians who refused their demands by breaking government windows, and—not incidentally—thereby cutting short the sometimes brutal struggles with police before they were arrested.

Upon imprisonment, militant suffragists embarked on hunger strikes, insisting that they be treated as political prisoners and their sentences be reduced to reflect more accurately the nature of their crimes. The authorities responded with forced feedings, a painful and intrusive procedure involving the insertion of a tube through the nasal passage into the stomach.

In 1912 and 1913, in response to the government's repeated refusals to honor its promises of a women's suffrage provision, militancy intensified. Coordinated attacks shattered windows all over LONDON. Christabel Pankhurst, in hiding from British authorities, directed the campaign from Paris, ordering her followers to step up their attacks on windows throughout London, to cut telegraph wires, to pour acid into letter boxes, to slash paintings in public galleries, and to commit arson. DAVID LLOYD GEORGE's country house was set afire, prompting authorities to arrest Emmeline Pankhurst for inciting to commit a felony. She received three years imprisonment. In anticipation of her hunger-striking and thereby cutting short her prison term, the government passed the "Cat and Mouse Act" (1913), which enabled it to release a hunger-striking prisoner and reincarcerate her after she had recovered from her ordeal. On 31 May 1913 Emily Wilding Davison (1872–1913) threw herself in front of the King's horse at the Derby and was trampled to death, providing the militant suffragists with their first true martyr to the Cause.

This kind of behavior could have mixed results. On the one hand, it may have turned many people away from the cause of women's suffrage, perhaps delaying the enfranchisement of women. On the other hand, militancy served to challenge and contest dominant cultural norms of femininity that were mobilized to deny women equality with men and to exclude them from public life. In conjunction with the writings of Christabel Pankhurst in the WSPU's *Suffragette*, the visible and provocative behavior of militant suffragists helped to focus the public spotlight on the grievances of women.

With the outbreak of war in 1914, the WSPU devoted its energies and talents to recruitment for the armed forces. Paradoxically, it did not participate in the negotiations that led to the partial enfranchisement of women in 1918. In 1917 the WSPU renamed itself the Women's Party, but little remained of the FEMINIST agenda that had characterized its pre-war existence. When in 1918 Christabel Pankhurst's bid for a parliamentary seat failed, the Women's Party, too, faded away.

Susan Kingsley Kent

Bibliography

MacKenzie, Midge. *Shoulder to Shoulder*. 1975.

Pankhurst, E. Sylvia. *The Suffragette Movement*. new ed. 1977.

Rosen, Andrew. *Rise Up, Women! The Militant Campaign of the Women's Social and Political Union, 1903–1914*. 1974.

Tickner, Lisa. *The Spectacle of Women: Imagery of the Suffrage Campaign, 1907–1914*. 1988.

Women's Suffrage

The campaign for women's suffrage has generally been considered a purely political and often conservative movement. But women's demands for enfranchisement were understood by contemporaries to constitute a radical challenge to the patriarchal order. Suffragists intended to transform the lives of women and men, to redefine and recreate by political means the sexual culture of Britain.

An important key to understanding the persistence of the demand for suffrage lies in comprehending not only the political, social, and economic developments of the nineteenth and early twentieth centuries, but ideological developments as well. The ideology of separate spheres promulgated during this period assigned women to the household and endowed them with biological characteristics that objectified them as "the Sex." By raising women to the level of angels, Victorian ideology conferred upon them superhuman status; by reducing them to sexual, animal characteristics, it presented them as subhuman. Dehumanization justified women's exclusion from positions of power and legitimated their continued subjugation to men in all aspects of life. The suffrage campaign aimed to change that perception so that women could no longer be objectified or defined essentially in terms of their biology and would no longer be victims of what they identified as male sexual tyranny. Suffragists struggled for over fifty years to obtain votes for women. Their campaign, while continuous, was divided into three phases. During the first phase, from 1866 to 1870, suffrage activity revolved around the Reform Act of 1867, which enfranchised large numbers of working-class men. The women's suffrage campaign emerged in 1866, when Barbara Bodichon (1827–1891), Emily Davies (1830–1921), and Elizabeth Garrett (1836–

1917) began a petition drive to demand votes for women. That same year, in Manchester, Lydia Becker (1827–1890) formed the Manchester Women's Suffrage Committee; soon after suffrage societies in London, Edinburgh, and Bristol were organized. Aware that activities and policy needed to be coordinated, the four independent societies formed the London National Society for Women's Suffrage.

When the effort to enfranchise women failed, however, suffragists tended to direct their attention to other feminist reforms; from 1870 to 1905, the suffrage movement *per se* became somewhat quiescent, though suffragists worked actively to expand educational and employment opportunities to women, to obtain women's property and custody rights, and to end government regulation of prostitution. In 1897, sixteen suffrage societies federated themselves in the National Union of Women's Suffrage Societies (NUWSS), headed by MILLICENT GARRETT FAWCETT.

With the appearance of militancy in 1905, the campaign for women's enfranchisement erupted into public view; the Cause, as it was called by its proponents, took on an intensity and fervor unmatched in earlier years. Adopted by the WOMEN'S SOCIAL AND POLITICAL UNION (WSPU) under the direction of EMMELINE AND CHRISTABEL PANKHURST, militancy had the effect of energizing the entire women's suffrage movement. Between 1897 and 1903, when the WSPU was formed, the NUWSS comprised only sixteen women's suffrage societies. By 1909, fifty-four more societies had emerged and joined the constitutional group, as the NUWSS was called to distinguish it from the militants. In 1911, 305 societies belonged to the NUWSS; that number grew to 400 by 1913. The Women's Freedom League (WFL), headed by Charlotte Despard (1844–1939), broke off from the WSPU when it became clear that Emmeline and Christabel Pankhurst would not permit challenges to their decisions or to their increasingly dictatorial rule, but it continued to follow a militant course. Partially as a consequence of militant tactics, the campaign for votes for women became a mass movement, commanding the attention of the British public and the energies of thousands of men and women.

The creation of a mass movement depended on other factors, however, most importantly the ability of the suffrage campaign to attract large numbers of working-class adherents. While upstaged by the militant organizations, working-class suffrage organizations such as the North of England Society for Women's Suffrage, led by Esther Roper (1868–1938), and the East London Federation of Suffragettes, led by Sylvia Pankhurst (1882–1960), contributed mightily to the growth and vitality of the suffrage campaign. In

1912, responding to the pressures of working-class women for the right to vote and to Prime Minister ASQUITH's betrayal of the women's cause, the LABOUR PARTY overcame its reservations about women's suffrage and joined forces with the NUWSS to establish the Election Fighting Fund; this alliance between labor and suffrage marked the creation of a truly democratic, egalitarian organization. Because women of all classes faced the potential of sexual and economic exploitation within the institutions of MARRIAGE and prostitution, a shared consciousness of women's wrongs enabled suffragists to create an ethos of sexual solidarity among women from diverse backgrounds, and to establish a mass movement.

Christabel Pankhurst's "Great Scourge" articles, published in the WSPU's *Suffragette* in 1913, provide a vivid example of the kind of grievances women's suffrage was intended to end. Pankhurst argued that from 75 to 80 percent of all men in England suffered from venereal disease, and pointed out the consequent dangers of marriage for women. The solution, she asserted, was "Votes for Women, Chastity for Men." Historians have generally dismissed her views with scorn, but her concerns pervaded and informed the entire suffrage movement.

Suffragists maintained that men's monopoly on power extended beyond the economic and political realms into that of the personal, which helps to explain why they focused so much of their attention on sexual issues and self-consciously associated them with their demand for the vote: they were convinced of the intimate connection between their exclusion from political power and their sexual powerlessness and vulnerability. Sexual equality as symbolized by the vote constituted one of the means by which feminists hoped to undermine the power of men in both the public and private spheres, and to challenge the cultural constructions of masculinity and femininity and male and female sexuality that served to justify separate spheres for men and women.

As a badge of civic equality, a symbol of women's humanity and equality with men, the vote had a great deal of appeal. But feminists also intended to use it as a tool to raise the status of women, to increase their welfare, and to protect them from the depradations of men. Their ultimate goal was to effect a profound transformation in the sexual culture and gender hierarchy of Britain, to bring about a society characterized by equality between and respect for men and women.

The outbreak of war in August 1914 brought suffrage activity to a halt. In 1916, when the government became concerned about the need to call a new election, franchise reform once again became an issue. At this point, the NUWSS stepped in, demanding that women be included in any reform that enfranchised new male voters on the basis of service to the country, claiming that women's contributions to and sacrifices for the war effort entitled them, no less than men, to full citizenship. A Speaker's Conference was convened to deal with these thorny issues; its recommendations, issued in 1917, included a measure of women's suffrage.

In 1918 Parliament granted the vote to women over the age of thirty. Contemporary observers attributed the government's willingness to enfranchise women to its appreciation of the work women performed during the war. But other factors influenced the outcome as well. Several Members of Parliament hinted that the militancy of the pre-war years might very well resurface after the war if women were not enfranchised; this contingency persuaded many former anti-suffragists in Parliament to reverse their position. But it was not so much the actual reality of militancy that had so significant and visceral an impact on politicians as what it represented.

A not so subtle undercurrent informed the debates over women's suffrage: that a sex war had, prior to August of 1914, been raging throughout the land, that it had been subsumed in the larger international conflagration, and that failure to resolve the suffrage issue would result in its flaring up again. The conflation of FEMINISM with sex war was not new, but the context in which the equation was made was entirely different now. Feminism soon became linked in the public mind not merely with sex war, but with armed conflict, death, and destruction, and was given greater force by the existence of large numbers of women in uniform. It raised the spectre of combat in the streets of England—combat between men and women.

Fear of renewal of the sex war so characteristic of the pre-war period, but raised now to intolerable levels, determined the terms under which women would be admitted to the franchise. The age requirement ensured that women would not enjoy a majority over men, whose numbers had been greatly reduced in the slaughter of war. Fawcett and other NUWSS leaders explained to their unhappy Labour followers, most of whom would not be eligible to vote because they were under age, that they did not want to jeopardize their chances for partial success by insisting upon full equality with men.

The capitulation of suffragists on so vital an issue as the age restriction resulted from the terms in which the debates over suffrage were framed and conducted between 1914 and 1918: at one level, MPs and suffragists asserted women's right to vote as a function of wartime service, defining them, at least in part, as warriors; on another, feminists' recruitment and relief efforts and debates over peace utilized rhetoric that ultimately served to conflate the suffrage cause with the cause of the war. The National Union's complicity in the war had a distinct bearing on the its cautious stance in the debates over suffrage in 1916 and 1917. Fawcett and the other members of the Executive Committee of the National Union could be held responsible, in holding out for greater representation for women, for perpetuating the war between the sexes. Compromise on the issue of age limitations, by contrast, would reduce the tensions between men and women and help to bring sex war to a halt for good.

In 1928, when women's participation in the political arena no longer seemed to pose a threat to men's power, Parliament gave votes to women on the same lines as for men.

Susan Kingsley Kent

Bibliography

Holton, Sandra Stanley. *Feminism and Democracy: Women's Suffrage and Reform Politics in Britain, 1900–1918.* 1986.

Hume, Leslie Parker. *The National Union of Women's Suffrage Societies, 1897–1914.* 1982.

Kent, Susan Kingsley. *Sex and Suffrage in Britain, 1860–1914.* 1987.

Liddington, Jill, and Jill Norris. *One Hand Tied Behind Us: The Rise of the Women's Suffrage Movement.* 1978.

Morgan, David. *Suffragists and Liberals: The Politics of Women's Suffrage in Britain.* 1975.

Tickner, Lisa. *The Spectacle of Women: Imagery of the Suffrage Campaign, 1907–1914.* 1988.

Woolf, Leonard Sidney (1880–1969)

Although overshadowed by his wife Virginia, Leonard Woolf was an important writer and political activist in his own right as well as a prominent original member of the BLOOMSBURY GROUP. The author of more than twenty books, including a five-volume autobiography published in his eighties, and hundreds of articles, Woolf was also a celebrated publisher, as co-founder with VIRGINIA WOOLF of the Hogarth Press, one of the most innovative small publishers in England.

The son of a JEWISH barrister who died when Leonard was twelve years old, leaving the family in reduced circumstances, Woolf attended St. Paul's School and Trinity College, CAMBRIDGE (1899–1904), where he developed a life-long fascination with classical Greek civilization and came under the influence of the philosopher G.E. MOORE. Elected to the select secret society known as the Apostles, he formed intimate friendships among his university contemporaries, notably with LYTTON STRACHEY, Thoby Stephen (1880–1906), and Saxon Sydney-Turner

(1880–1962). These formative years at Cambridge were perhaps the happiest of his life. From Moore, whose *Principia Ethica* (1903) was published during his student years, Woolf acquired a commitment to duty and moral rectitude that, reinforcing the Jewish ethical values of his childhood, dominated his life; Cambridge gave him not only a classical education, but a belief in rationalism; from his Apostle friends he derived a skepticism towards dogma and disdain for status that became ingrained in his character.

After receiving only second class honors and doing poorly in the civil service examinations, Woolf decided to accept a cadetship in the Ceylon colonial service, where he was to spend seven rewarding, if rather lonely years, promoted rapidly from cadet, to Superintendant, to Assistant Government Agent before returning to London in 1911. An efficient, conscientious, if somewhat rigid administrator, he developed an affection for those under his authority but a strong distaste for imperialism.

In 1912 he resigned from the colonial service, married Virginia Stephen, and launched his career as a writer. His first publications, the novels *The Village in the Jungle* (1913) and *The Wise Virgins* (1914), while interesting autobiographically, proved to be an abortive start and failed to win an audience. Woolf shifted increasingly to political writing, becoming active in the Women's Cooperative Guild and the FABIAN SOCIETY, which commissioned him to write a report on international machinery for the peaceful settlement of disputes. Appearing first as a *NEW STATESMAN* supplement, it was subsequently published as *International Government* in 1916 and had considerable influence on the British proposals for a League of Nations.

In 1917 the Woolfs established the Hogarth Press, publishing not only many of their own works, but also such significant writers as Sigmund Freud, T.S. ELIOT, and Vita Sackville-West. While Leonard was preoccupied with selecting manuscripts, managing the finances of the small company, and, at first, with the actual printing, he was also fully engaged politically by the end of the First World War. A member of the INDEPENDENT LABOUR PARTY, he was appointed secretary to the LABOUR PARTY's Advisory Committee on International Questions and helped to coordinate the reports that were to shape Labour's policy on foreign affairs during the inter-war decades. In addition Woolf wrote extensively on cooperation and on imperialism, producing in rapid succession a series of seminal studies: *Cooperation and the Future of Industry* (1918); *Empire and Commerce in Africa* (1919); *Economic Imperialism* (1920); and *Socialism and Cooperation* (1921). He served as editor of the *International Review*

(1918–19), as literary editor of the *Nation* (1923–30), and as co-editor of *Political Quarterly* (1931–59). During the 1930s and 1940s he was also a frequent contributor, occasional substitute editor, and longtime member of the board of the *New Statesman*.

In his political writings Woolf sought to promote a socialism based on the non-competitive objectives of the COOPERATIVE MOVEMENT, which would enable the community, constituted as consumers, to control production. But if he was concerned to eliminate capitalist exploitation, he was equally concerned to preserve the individuality and tolerance that he cherished in English society as well as in ancient Greek culture. An outspoken opponent of imperialism, striving to accelerate self-government in British dependencies, Woolf broke with many of those on the Left who clung to PACIFISM during the 1930s, like his friend KINGSLEY MARTIN. He became a strong advocate of collective security and of mandatory sanctions and warned Labour against sterile opposition to rearmament in the face of a mounting Fascist threat. By the late 1930s, in books like *Quack, Quack!* (1935) and his LEFT BOOK CLUB selection *Barbarians at the Gate* (1939), Woolf began to criticize the Soviet Union almost as vociferously as he condemned Nazism for creating an irrational tyranny and betraying the civilized ideals implicit in socialism.

After the Second World War Woolf increasingly withdrew from political involvement, devoting himself to the literary estate and reputation of Virginia Woolf and, in his last years, to writing memoirs. After the critical failure of his political *magnum opus,* published in three volumes over twenty-two years—*After the Deluge* (1931, 1939) and *Principia Politica* (1953)—he was both surprised and gratified at the enormous success of his autobiography, written amid the rising tide of popular and scholarly interest in Virginia Woolf and the Bloomsbury Group. Composed in the comparative serenity of his last decade, the five volumes—*Sowing* (1960); *Growing* (1961); *Beginning Again* (1964); *Downhill All the Way* (1967); *The Journey Not the Arrival Matters* (1969)—represent a return to the personal dimension of his earliest works, revealing its author as austere, stoical, rigorous in his moral and political standards, but engagingly human to the end.

Fred M. Leventhal

Bibliography

Leventhal, F.M. "Leonard Woolf, 1880–1969: The Conscience of a Bloomsbury Socialist" in Susan Pedersen and Peter Mandler, eds. *After the Victorians: Private Conscience and Public Duty in Modern Britain.* 1994. pp. 149–68.

Spater, George, and Ian Parsons. *A Marriage of True Minds: An Intimate Portrait of Leonard and Virginia Woolf.* 1977.

Spotts, Frederic, ed. *Letters of Leonard Woolf.* 1989.

Wilson, Duncan. *Leonard Woolf: A Political Biography.* 1978.

Woolf, (Adeline) Virginia Stephen (1882–1941)

Born Adeline Virginia Stephen on 25 January 1882 at 22 Hyde Park Gate, Kensington, London, the daughter of Sir Leslie Stephen (1832–1904) and Julia Jackson Duckworth (1846–95), Virginia Woolf has no letters standing for honored titles after her name. She refused all official honors on political principle, including the coveted Companion of Honour, accepting only the *Femina Vie Heureuse* prize. Though her family was strongly connected to CAMBRIDGE, she was not allowed to attend classes and saw herself as deprived of a university education, a fact which contributed to the development of her concept of the "outsider," most notably in the pacifist, socialist, and feminist polemic *Three Guineas* (1939). Some biographers and critics, however, believe that the private education she received in her father's library was superior to any formal education available to women at the time. Leslie Stephen, Victorian man of letters, founding editor of the *Dictionary of National Biography*, and a leading member of the so-called "intellectual aristocracy", came from a family of public servants remarkable for their reforming zeal and instrumental in shaping British government, education, and the law. Many of the Prinseps and Pattles on her mother's side also served in colonial India, a fact which doubtless served to inspire the writer's insistent critique of imperialism. Her cousin Katherine Stephen (1856–1924) became Principal of Newnham College, Cambridge. Virginia was tutored in languages and continued to read Greek with her tutor, Janet Case, until late in life, believing that knowledge of the classics was necessary for the educated person. She had many close women friends, including Violet Dickinson, Margaret Llewelyn Davies, and the composer Dame Ethel Smyth. Her powerful originality as a writer is often attributed to the fact that she was self-educated and had a chip on her shoulder about her lack of formal education. As a young woman she taught working-class men and women at Morley College in London for three years and also worked in the WOMEN'S SUFFRAGE movement.

Always close to her sister VANESSA (BELL), the painter who was married to art critic CLIVE BELL but lived with painter DUNCAN GRANT, Virginia Stephen married a Cambridge Apostle friend of her brother and a fellow BLOOMSBURY GROUP intellectual, LEONARD WOOLF, in 1912. He is credited both with his wife's successes and her failures in their companionate marriage, caring for her fragile mental health by taking the advice of doctors who advised them not to have children. Her breakdowns and suicide have been attributed alternatively to child abuse, neurasthenia, anorexia, genetic madness, and, most recently, to "bi-polar affective disorder".

In addition to her status as a major twentieth-century English novelist, Virginia Woolf is considered to be one of the most important feminist theorists of what is called the "Second Wave" of the modern movement for women's rights. *A Room of One's Own* (1929), a set of anti-lectures given at Newnham and Girton and written in the style of suffrage pamphlets, is often called the Bible of the women's movement. When university literary canons began to include women writers in the 1970s, *A Room of One's Own*, with its tragic martyr, an imaginary figure of Shakespeare's sister, was the text most often read. Feminist literary criticism began in a struggle over whether Woolf was an exemplary foremother as a feminist critic. The author of several volumes of critical essays on literary and cultural matters, including *The Common Reader* (1925) and *The Common Reader, Second Series* (1932) and the posthumously published *The Death of the Moth and Other Essays* (1942), *The Moment and Other Essays* (1947), *The Captain's Deathbed and Other Essays* (1950), *Granite and Rainbow* (1958), *Contemporary Writers* (1965), and four volumes of *Collected Essays* (1966–7), Virginia Woolf earned a reputation as a formidable modern literary critic. Before her death in 1941 she had also produced many serious reviews for journals like the *Times Literary Supplement*. A new edition of the *Essays* complete in six volumes in chronological order, collects many of these reviews and corrects errors in the earlier editions. Leonard Woolf also published her short fiction as *A Haunted House and Other Short Stories* (1943), now superseded by *Collected Short Stories*, edited by Susan Dick. Leonard Woolf's edition of excerpts from her diaries, *A Writer's Diary* (1953) has been replaced by the five-volume *Diary of Virginia Woolf*, edited by Anne Olivier Bell with the assistance of Andrew McNeillie (1977) and regarded as one of the major personal and autobiographical documents in English literature. The so-called *Early Diaries* and journals were subsequently published in one volume, edited by M. Leaska and including the "1897 Diary", in which the fifteen-year-old Virginia Stephen, upset by the early and tragic death of her mother and her just-married stepsister Stella Duckworth soon afterwards, invented an alter-ego called "Miss Jan". The Diary is notable

for its expression of the wish to mourn her mother in some kind of religious ceremony, a gesture forbidden by Leslie Stephen's aggressive agnosticism and the memory of Julia Stephen's similar views on the subject of religion. Later she showed great interest in the mysticism of her Quaker aunt, Caroline Emelia Stephen, called "Nun." It was this aunt who nursed her after her breakdown after nursing Leslie Stephen on his deathbed (1904), who encouraged her to write, and who got her her first professional paid writing assignments for *The Guardian-Church Weekly*, thereby inaugurating Virginia Stephen's career. Caroline Emelia also left her niece the legacy which allowed her to become independent, famously recalled in *A Room of One's Own* as the "£500 a year" needed for the emancipation of the woman intellectual. Leonard Woolf also published some of the correspondence between Virginia Woolf and LYTTON STRACHEY in 1956. Six volumes of *The Letters of Virginia Woolf* have also appeared, edited by Nigel Nicolson and Joanne Trautmann (Banks) (1975–80) as well as a one-volume edition, *Congenial Spirits: Selected Letters* (1990), establishing Woolf's reputation as one of the finest letter-writers of the twentieth century in her concern to please her correspondents rather than give vent to petty egotistical concerns. The official biography by her nephew Quentin Bell, *Virginia Woolf* (1972), is the standard work.

In addition to the nine novels, five volumes of the *Diary*, six volumes of *Letters*, six volumes of *Essays*, the political pamphlets *A Room of One's Own* and *Three Guineas*, Woolf also published *Flush: A Biography* (1933), a comic spoof about Elizabeth Barrett Browning's dog, and *Roger Fry: A Biography* in 1940.

A brilliant experimental novelist, Virginia Woolf is ranked internationally with JAMES JOYCE, Gertrude Stein, and Marcel Proust as a genius of literary modernism, although the English critic F.R. LEAVIS and his wife Queenie denigrated her writing and her feminism, comparing her unfavorably with D.H. LAWRENCE and undermining her reputation for at least a generation on the false grounds of her alleged "Bloomsbury elitism" and class distance. The style and structure of each of her nine novels is entirely different from the others. *To the Lighthouse* (1927), her much beloved elegy to the Victorian patriarchal family, is regarded as a modern classic. *Mrs. Dalloway* (1925), an evocation of one day in the life of a London society hostess, Clarissa Dalloway, and her spiritual counterpart Septimus Smith, a lower middle class shell-shocked soldier returned from the battlefields of the First World War, is often read in relation to her friend

T.S. ELIOT's modern classic poem, *The Waste Land* (1922), a work for which Virginia Woolf herself hand-set the type and published at the Hogarth Press (founded in 1917 with her husband, Leonard Woolf). *The Voyage Out* (1915), her first novel, a female *bildungsroman* ending with the death of the heroine, and *Night and Day* (1918), the fairly traditional social comedy experimenting with plot structure and reversals as in Shakespeare's plays and Mozart's opera, *The Magic Flute*, were published by Duckworth, her half-brother's press. But her future independence and creativity were assured and protected by the decision to publish the rest of her work, novels, several volumes of literary criticism, and biographies, at the Hogarth Press. *Jacob's Room* (1922), now considered a modernist masterpiece and Woolf's first attempt at long fiction in non-traditional, often called "stream-of-consciousness" style, is an elegy for the lost promise of the youthful generation of elite English boys dead in the war. The novel was inspired, it is said, by the loss of her own brother Thoby.

Orlando (1928), an illustrated fictional "fantastic biography" of her friend and sometime lover, the writer and gardener Vita Sackville-West, and of the historic Sackville estate Knole, which Vita's gender prevented her from inheriting, is a spectacular literary *tour-de-force*, a triumph over the conventions of realism and the limits of historical time in life-writing. The novel extends the actions of its sex-changing man-woman hero-heroine over 360 years of English history, and mocks by imitation and spoof the literary and social conventions of each period traversed by the narrative. Some passages, the description of the skating parties on the Thames during "The Great Frost", for example, are often cited as examples of Woolf's immense powers of "scene-making"; not surprisingly, *Orlando* has been made into a film (Sally Potter, 1993) and dramatized often for the stage. By contrast *The Waves* (1931) is a deeply serious philosophical and historical "play-poem" for six characters conceived of as one. It questions, as Woolf had in *To the Lighthouse*, "the meaning of life," exploring the social meaning of Einstein's theory of relativity and the absence of God in modern life through repeated figures of waves of light and sound. The interior monologues of the characters Ginny, Susan, Neville, Bernard, Rhoda, and Louis take the six friends from childhood through the ignominious death of their common friend Percival who fatally falls from a donkey in India to Bernard's chivalric protest against death. *The Waves* quotes extensively from the Romantic poets, and is read both as a celebration of English culture and an example of the "post-colonial carnivalesque". While critics have traditionally ranked the novel as Woolf's masterpiece and have seen in her Bernard the modern poet as hero, postmodern readings now point to the novel's mockery of the Parsifal myth of the quest for the Holy Grail and to its critique of imperialism and of the role of the English in colonizing India. *The Waves'* chapters of alternating interior monologues during a generation's lifetime, ending in 1930, are surrounded by brief italicized sections describing the movements of the sun from dawn to dusk in the manner of Hindu prayers to the sun. This device suggests the limitations of Western ideologies and English life and culture, at the same time as it celebrates them.

The Years (1937), a great popular success on both sides of the Atlantic, is a family saga which follows an upper-class family and their servants in the social upheavals from the 1880s through the 1930s. It caused Woolf a great deal of trouble, and much of the historical material of the original sections was used in *Three Guineas*. An edition published by the New York Public Library and the Hogarth Press in 1978 contains the original version of Woolf's famous 1931 speech to the National Society for Women's Service, often cited for its invention of that inhibitor of women's creativity "the angel in the house," a figure taken from Coventry Patmore's Victorian poem about ideal womanhood, and used by Woolf to embody the concept of the social pressure on women to sacrifice their artistic creativity and desire to outmoded and destructive notions of propriety, virtue, and chastity, often imposed by mothers on their daughters' lives. The speech urges women to kill the "angel in the house" by throwing their inkpots at her and emancipating their imaginations.

Between the Acts (posthumous, 1941), Woolf's last novel, depicts a village historical pageant during the build-up to the Second World War. The pageant's dramatic form emphasizes the destruction of culture and value in war; its speakers' unfinished sentences and broken bits of dialogue show persons failing to communicate across gender, class, age and religious gaps, which the text calls "scraps, orts and fragments". Charged with sexual violence, the novel connects rape with war and uses the ancient theme of the myth of Procne and Philomel, the swallow and the nightingale, to suggest that sexual violence is the root of war and that the history of imperialism is implicated in twentieth-century European wars.

Who could measure the genius of the artist "when caught and tangled in a woman's heart?" Woolf asks in her classic *A Room of One's Own*, anticipating the day when working class writers would produce Shakespeares from their own

ranks. "For masterpieces are not single and solitary births," but "the product of thinking by the
people," Woolf claims, radically attacking English pride in individualism. Even more radically
her pacifist masterpiece *Three Guineas* argues that
FASCISM did not originate in nationalism or in
Italian or German class ideology, but in the patriarchal family. Increasingly recognized as an important twentieth-century intellectual figure and
as a theorist of FEMINISM and PACIFISM, Virginia
Woolf, always valued by writers for her "difficult"
technical innovations in narrative, has gained
new readers and new popularity as her fiction has
begun to be read from a postmodern perspective.
Jane Marcus
Bibliography
Bell, Quentin. *Virginia Woolf*. 2 vols. 1972.
Briggs, Julia, ed. *Virginia Woolf: Introductions to the
Major Works*. 1994.
Homans, Margaret, ed. *Virginia Woolf: Twentieth Cen-
tury Views: A Collection of Critical Essays*. 1992.
Lee, Hermione. *Virginia Woolf*. 1996.
Marcus, Jane. *Virginia Woolf and the Languages of Patri-
archy*. 1987.
Minow-Pinkney, Makiko. *Virginia Woolf and the Prob-
lem of the Subject*. 1987.
Zwerdling, Alex. *Virginia Woolf and the Real World*. 1986.

Woolton, Earl of [Frederick James Marquis] (1883–1964)

Lord Woolton is best known as a CONSERVATIVE
PARTY politician who restored the party's organization after the 1945 election defeat. However, he
came into mainstream politics only in late-
middle age and not through the usual channels.
He was born Frederick James Marquis in 1883 in
Salford to lower-middle class parents. He attended the University of Manchester, emerging
in 1906 with a combination science degree and an
interest in the causes of social deprivation and
labor mobility. He subsequently published a
number of scholarly articles that established him
as an early yet important social scientist. His
work was recognized by a research fellowship at
the University of Manchester, which earned him
an M.A. degree in 1912. That same year he was
appointed as Warden of the Liverpool University
Settlement, where he continued his social science
investigations.

Following the outbreak of the FIRST WORLD
WAR he was drafted into the CIVIL SERVICE and
took the opportunity to abandon his social science activities. In 1920 he joined Lewis's, a leading Liverpol retailing firm, and soon rose to the
top of the business. He was one of the few businessmen who was alarmed by the rise of Hitler in
Germany, and in 1938 he declared that Lewis's
would not trade in German goods. Before to the

outbreak of the SECOND WORLD WAR he served
on various government committees that were
covertly preparing for war. He was elevated to the
peerage as Baron Woolton in anticipation of
ministerial work and, in 1940, was appointed as a
non-party Minister of Food.

As wartime Minister of Food, Woolton rose to
national prominence, largely through a regular
series of popular radio broadcasts. In these talks
he reassured the British people that they were
being properly fed and looked after by the government, and that the wartime RATIONING
scheme was both equitable and efficient. In 1943
he was appointed as Minister of Reconstruction,
a move that was facilitated by his lack of party
political affiliation. As minister he found that he
had to act as an arbiter between Conservative and
LABOUR interests, and he issued landmark White
Papers on HEALTH, education, social security, and
employment that shaped post-war Britain.

The landslide Labour victory in 1945 alarmed
Woolton because he feared the extension and
consolidation of state controls. In July 1946 he
joined the Conservative Party, and CHURCHILL
quickly named him as Party Chairman. Under his
aegis the party organization underwent what was
called a "Woolton Revolution", which resulted in
its becoming more democratic and more representative of the electorate than it had been previously. Financial burdens upon Conservative candidates were eliminated so that that they were no
longer financially liable to subsidize their consit-
uencies. In 1949 Woolton also successfully completed a £1 million fund-raising drive, which
helped to stabilize the party's finances. At the
same time he successfully pushed for the expansion of active party membership, which peaked at
about 2 million in the period before the Conservatives were returned to power in 1951. By that
time party morale had recovered from the 1945
defeat, and Woolton was largely credited with the
party's organizational revival.

In 1951 Churchill appointed Woolton to one of
the "overlordships" in the new CABINET. He became Lord President of the Council and coordinating Minister of Food and Agriculture. However, in 1952 he suffered serious health problems
and did not return to active government duties
until a year later. At this point Churchill, who
would have preferred to remove Woolton from
his Cabinet team, had to acknowledge Woolton's
continued popularity with the party rank and file
and appointed him as Chancellor of the Duchy
of Lancaster and Minister of Materials. In the
later capacity he wound down many remaining
wartime controls and, to universal acclaim, de-
rationed sugar and sweets. He disliked intensely
the BBC state monopoly over television and

radio broadcasting and threw his weight, both as minister and as Chairman of the Conservative Party, behind the move to establish independent television.

When he retired in 1955, Woolton, one of the most popular Conservative leaders, was raised to an earldom in recognition of his services to the nation and to the party.

Michael David Kandiah

Bibliography

Hoffman, John David. *The Conservative Party in Opposition, 1945–1951.* 1964.

Ramsden, John. *The Age of Churchill and Eden, 1940–1957.* 1995.

Woolton, Earl of. *The Memoirs of the Rt. Hon. the Earl of Woolton.* 1959.

Yeats, William Butler (1865–1939)

William Butler Yeats, one of the finest poets in English during the twentieth century, won the Nobel Prize for literature in 1923. He was born in Dublin in 1865. His father, John Butler Yeats (1839–1922), a brilliant conversationalist and a portrait artist, soon moved the family to London, but in 1881 the family returned to Dublin, where Yeats finished high school and spent two years studying drawing. His first poems were published in 1885. The next year, when his dramatic poem *Mosada* was published as a pamphlet, he began fulltime writing; he returned with his family to London in 1885. London would remain his principal residence until he settled in Dublin in 1919. But he wrote very much as an Irishman, as is apparent from the titles of his first two full volumes of poetry, *The Wanderings of Oisin and Other Poems* (1889) and *The Countess Kathleen and Various Legends and Lyrics* (1892). During the early 1890s Yeats edited collections of Irish folklore and literature, wrote reviews, and he had some success as a fiction writer, with a novella *John Sherman and Dhoya* (1891) and with three short story collections published in 1897: *The Secret Rose,* and *The Tables of the Law,* and *The Adoration of the Magi.* The title of his folklore collection, *The Celtic Twilight* (1893, expanded 1902), has been used to caricature the shadowy remoteness of the Irish folk materials that predominate in Yeats's verse of those years and in his earliest dramas *The Countess Cathleen* (1892; performed 1899) and *The Land of Heart's Desire* (1894).

Yeats was from his early years active in the study of spiritualism and occultism, as a member first of Madame Blavatsky's Theosophical Society (1887–90) and then of the Hermetic Order of the Golden Dawn (1890–1922). The monument of his occultism is *A Vision* (1925, revised 1937), which describes a spirit system that determines cosmic history and individual personality.

In London in 1889 he met and fell in love with Maud Gonne (1866–1953), an ardent Irish nationalist of independent means who lived in Paris and who, unknown to Yeats, maintained until 1898 a secret liaison with a French journalist. Yeats's frustrated courtship of her, which inspired a number of his poems, lasted until 1903 when she married an exiled Irish patriot, Major John MacBride; the courtship revived briefly in 1916 when MacBride was executed for his role in the Easter Rising.

Yeats's support of Irish cultural nationalism intensified when he first visited Lady Augusta Gregory's country home, Coole Park, in County Galway in 1897. He and Lady Gregory collected folklore and provided leadership and plays for the Irish National Theatre Society, which, with generous patronage from Annie E.F. Horniman, an Englishwoman, gained a permanent home at the Abbey Theatre, Dublin, from 1904. The opening production at the Abbey Theatre included plays by Yeats, Lady Gregory, and John Millington Synge, the three directors of the company. Yeats's play was *On Baile's Strand,* one of his finest. It was the first of his several plays about the ancient Irish heroic warrior Cuchulain. During the first decade of the century Yeats was extremely active in the management of the Abbey Theatre, choosing plays, hiring and firing actors and managers, and arranging tours.

Partially as a result of his interest in drama, which requires direct, comprehensible language, and partially perhaps because of the inspiration of the new century, Yeats began a radical simplification of his poetic diction and adopted the rhythms of ordinary speech for his verse. His changes in literary style were cheered on by Ezra Pound, who became a close friend in 1909. When Yeats looked back on those years in which he contributed to the beginning of the modernist reform of poetry, he said, "In 1900 everybody got down off his stilts." His transformation of poetic style developed in *In the Seven Woods* (1903), *The Green Helmet and Other Poems* (1910, 1912), and *Responsibilities* (1914).

Throughout these years Yeats maintained his permanent residence in London, although traveling frequently to Ireland. The 1916 Easter Rising, an unsuccessful, six-day armed rebellion in Dublin by Irish republicans against the British, dramatically reasserted IRISH NATIONALISM in public history and in Yeats's life. His poem "Easter, 1916" eloquently expresses Yeats' complicated reaction, a mixture of surprise, admiration for Irish romanticism, and clear-eyed realism.

In October 1917, at age fifty-two, Yeats married Georgie Hyde-Lees (1892–1968), an occultist twenty-seven years younger than he. Yeats traveled with his bride to Coole Park, where he proudly showed her a nearby medieval stone tower, Thoor Ballylee, which he had purchased along with two cottages in 1916 for £35. The tower became a summer residence for Yeats, his wife, and their two children, Anne (1919–) and Michael (1921–). His next two volumes of poetry, *The Wild Swans at Coole* (1917, 1919) and *Michael Robartes and the Dancer* (1921, title page 1920), show a consolidation of his style into poised, mature works that characterize his "middle" period in the 1920s and the early 1930s.

Although England and Ireland signed a treaty at the end of 1921, bitter controversies erupted within the new Irish Free State over the partition of Northern Ireland and over the wording of a formal oath of allegiance to the British Crown; those issues led to a civil war which ended in 1923 with the Irish Free State's victory over the anti-treaty rebel forces. Yeats emphatically cast his lot with the Irish Free State. In 1922 he bought a house in Dublin, where he took up permanent residence, and accepted a six-year appointment to the Senate of the Irish Free State. He relished the aristocratic overtones of his public role as senator. The Nobel Prize in December 1923 further heightened Yeats' public stature. The energy of the poems written in response to the disturbing times in Ireland and to the aging poet's awareness of his own decrepitude gave astonishing power to his collection *The Tower* (1928), which can justly be considered the best single book of poems in the twentieth century. The high level of accomplishment continued in *The Winding Stair* (1929, 1933) and *Words for Music Perhaps and Other Poems* (1932).

In 1924 Yeats was cautioned about his high blood pressure and told to reduce his pubic speaking and to avoid Irish winters, so he spent eight of his remaining fifteen winters in the Mediterranean. In spite of continuing bouts of serious illness, Yeats's life and writings in his last decade were marked by activity and enjoyment of life. He presided over a circle of young artists, poets, and playwrights in Dublin. He continued to write plays, including two translations of Greek tragedies, Sophocles' *King Oedipus* (performed 1926; 1928) and Sophocles' *Oedipus at Colonus* (performed 1927; 1934), and a full-length play about spiritualism and the eighteenth-century Irish writer Jonathan Swift, *The Words upon the Window-Pane* (performed 1930; 1934).

In 1929 after recovering from illness, he wrote a series of brash poems narrated by "Crazy Jane", a fictitious old Irish peasant woman. His pose as "The Wild Old Wicked Man"—the title of one of his poems from 1938—has at least some basis in the rejuvenation that he felt after a vasectomy in 1934 at age sixty-eight. His poetical vitality was reflected in the title of his 1938 volume, *New Poems*.

In the 1930s Ireland changed in ways that displeased Yeats. His Anglo-Irish Protestant minority no longer controlled Irish society and culture. He turned for inspiration to his eighteenth-century Anglo-Irish predecessors, particularly to Swift, to the philosopher Bishop George Berkeley, and to the statesman Edmund Burke. Their intellectual talent, independence of spirit, and respect for traditional social forms were admired by Yeats. According to his unblushingly anti-democratic views, their greatness contrasted sharply with the undistinguished commonness of contemporary Irish merchants and workmen. He stated his unpopular opinions in the essays of *On the Boiler* (1939) and in his later plays, such as *Purgatory* (performed 1938; 1939).

Yeats's last poems are enriched by conflicting responses to the approach of death. He had courage that was founded partly on a vague hope for reincarnation, and partly on the bold heroism that he admired in Ireland in earlier times. In that courageous mood he could speak in the stern voice of his famous epitaph "Under Ben Bulben": "Cast a cold eye / On life, on death. / Horseman, pass by!" But the stoic coldness is complicated by the terror that distracts the poet's thoughts at the end of another late poem, "The Man and the Echo", and also by the poignantly frivolous desire for life in the closing lines of the poem "Politics", which Yeats placed as the last in his final collection: "But O that I were young again / And held her in my arms."

Yeats's imagination remained very much his own, isolated to a remarkable degree from the successive fashions of modern poetry, despite his extensive contacts with other poets. Literary modernism held no inherent attraction for him except in its general association with vigorous expression. He admired a wide range of traditional English poetry and drama, and he plainly was unconcerned that, during the last two decades of his life, his preference for using rhyme and strict stanza forms would set him apart from the vogue of modernism.

William H. O'Donnell

Bibliography

Adams, Hazard. *The Book of Yeats's Poems.* 1990.

Ellmann, Richard. *Yeats: The Man and the Masks.* 1979.

Foster, R.F. *W.B. Yeats: A Life: vol. I: The Apprentice Mage.* 1997.

Jeffares, A. Norman. *A New Commentary on the Poems of W.B. Yeats.* 1984.

——, and A.S. Knowland. *A Commentary on the Collected Plays of W.B. Yeats.* 1975.

Jochum, K.P.S. *W.B. Yeats: A Classified Bibliography of Criticism.* 1990.

Rosenthal, M.L. *Running to Paradise: Yeats's Poetic Art.* 1994.

Illustrations

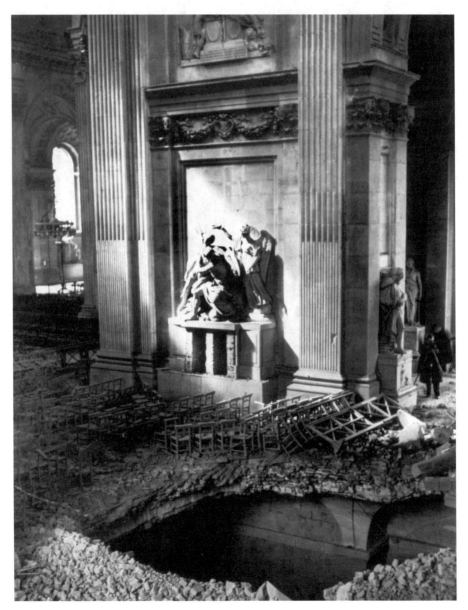

A large crater in the floor beneath the north transept of St Paul's, which was hit by a bomb in the great night raid of April 16, 1941. Cr: Hulton|Archive by Getty Images

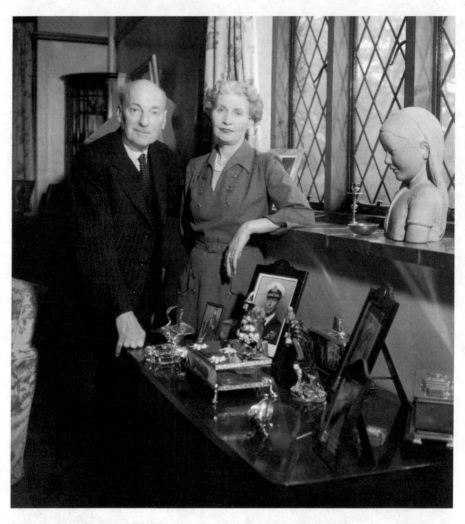

British Labour politician and former Prime Minister Clement Attlee, 1st Earl Attlee and his wife, Violet, at their home, Cherry Tree Cottage in Great Missenden, Buckinghamshire, c. 1955. Cr: Hulton|Archive by Getty Images

The Queen of Great Britain, Elizabeth II on horseback with her two children Princess Anne and Prince Charles, 1956. Cr: Hulton|Archive by Getty Images

Chelsea goalkeeper Robertson watches Tommy Harmer's penalty go past him as Spurs go one ahead in the White Hart Lane match, February 20, 1957. Cr: Hulton|Archive by Getty Images

A young child stands by a donkey cart in front of a whitewashed thatched cottage, August 1964.
Cr: Hulton|Archive by Getty Images

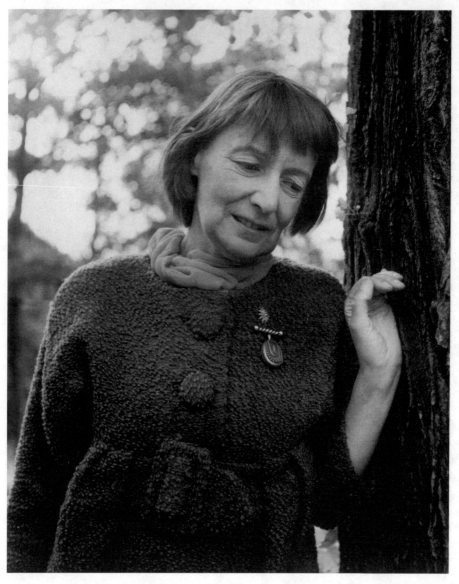

English poet and novelist Stevie Smith (1902–1971), pen name of Florence Margaret Smith, March 1966. Cr: Hulton|Archive by Getty Images

Bernadette Devlin, Independent MP for Mid Ulster, with opposition MP's (left to right), John , Austin Currie and Paddy O'Hanlon, continue their two-day sit-in hunger strike outside 10 Downing Street to press their demand for a public enquiry into the treatment of detainees in Northern Ireland, October 20, 1971. Cr: Hulton|Archive by Getty Images

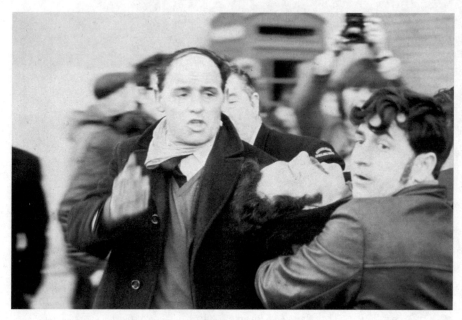

A victim is carried by Irish civilians, Bloody Sunday, Northern Ireland, January 30, 1972.
Cr: William L. Rukeyser/Hulton|Archive by Getty Images

Terraced housing in Leeds, Yorkshire, 1972. Cr: Hulton|Archive by Getty Images

Tony Blair waves to well-wishers after his election as leader of the Labour Party and is photographed by journalists. [21st July 1994] Credit: Hulton|Archive by Getty Images

Early morning outside Kensington Palace with children writing tributes to Diana, Princess of Wales and viewing the flowers left as a tribute to her on the occasion of her death in a car accident, August 31, 1997. Cr: Hulton|Archive by Getty Images

Guide to Further Research

Bibliographies

Catterall, Peter, ed. *British History 1945–1987.* 1990.

Chaloner, W.H., and R.C. Richardson, eds. *Bibliography of British Economic and Social History.* 2nd ed. 1984.

Fraser, A.G.S., ed. *A Subject Bibliography of the First World War: Books in English 1914–1978.* 1979.

Furber, Elizabeth Chapin, ed. *Changing Views on British History.* 1966.

Hanham, H.J., ed. *Bibliography of British History 1851–1914.* 1976.

Havighurst, Alfred, ed. *Modern England 1901–1984.* 2nd ed. 1987.

Howard-Hill, T.H., ed. *Bibliography of British Literary Bibliographies.* 2nd ed. 1987.

Robbins, Keith, ed. *A Bibliography of British History 1914–1989.* 1996.

Schlatter, Richard, ed. *Recent Views on British History.* 1984.

Smith, Harold, ed. *The British Labour Movement to 1970: A Bibliography.* 1981.

Westergaard, John, Anne Weyman, and Paul Wiles, eds. *Modern British Society: A Bibliography.* 2nd ed. 1977.

Labour History Review publishes an annual bibliography of books and articles published in British labour history.

Guides to Sources

Aster, Sidney, ed. *British Foreign Policy: A Guide to Research and Research Materials.* 1984.

Barrow, Margaret, ed. *Women 1870–1928: A Select Guide to Printed and Archival Sources in the United Kingdom.* 1981.

Cook, Chris, ed. *Sources in British Political History 1900–1951.* 6 vols. 1975–85.

    vol. 1: *A Guide to the Archives of Selected Organisations and Societies*

    vol. 2: *A Guide to the Private Papers of Selected Public Servants*

    vol. 3: *A Guide to the Private Papers of Members of Parliament, A–K*

    vol. 4: *A Guide to the Private Papers of Members of Parliament, L–Z*

    vol. 5: *A Guide to the Private Papers of Selected Writers, Intellectuals and Publicists*

    vol. 6: *First Consolidated Supplement*

——, and David Waller, eds. *St. Martin's Guide to Sources in Contemporary British History: vol. I: Organisations and Societies.* 1993.

——, Jane Leonard, and Peter Leese, eds. *St. Martin's Guide to Sources in Contemporary British History: vol. II: Individuals.* 1994.

——, and David Waller, eds. *The Longman Guide to Sources in Contemporary British History.* 1994.

Foster, Janet, and Julia Sheppard. *British Archives: A Guide to Archive Resources in the United Kingdom.* 4th ed. 1999.

Hazlehurst, Cameron, Sally Whitehead, and Christine Woodland, eds. *A Guide to the Papers of British Cabinet Ministers 1900–1964.* 1996.

Kanner, Barbara, ed. *Women in English Social History, 1800–1914.* 3 vols. 1987–90.

Record Repositories in Great Britain: A Geographical Directory. 9th ed. 1991.

Walford, A.J., ed. *Guide to Reference Material.* 3 vols. 4th ed. 1980–7.

Winks, Robin W. ed., *The Oxford History of the British Empire: vol. V: Historiography.* 1999.

Reference Works

Banham, Martin, ed., *Cambridge Guide to Theatre.* 3rd ed. 1995.

Barnes, Philip. *A Companion to Post-War British Theatre.* 1986.

Bergonzi, Bernard, ed. *History of Literature in the*

English Language: vol 7: The Twentieth Century.
1970.
Butler, David E., and Gareth Butler. *British Political Facts 1900–1994.* 7th ed. 1994.
Craig, F.W.S., ed., *British Electoral Facts 1832–
1987.* 5th ed. 1989.
––––––. *British Parliamentary Election Results
1885–1918.* 2nd ed. 1989.
––––––. *British Parliamentary Election Results
1918–1949.* 3rd ed. 1983.
––––––. *British Parliamentary Election Results
1950–1973.* 1983.
––––––. *British Parliamentary Election Results
1974–1983.* 1984.
––––––. *Chronology of British Parliamentary By-
elections 1833–1987.* 1987.
––––––. *Conservative and Labour Party Conference
Decisions 1945–1981.* 1982.
––––––. *Minor Parties at British Parliamentary
Elections 1885–1974.* 1974.
Doughan, David, and Denise Sanchez. *Feminist
Periodicals 1855–1984.* 1987.
Drabble, Margaret, ed. *The Oxford Companion to
English Literature.* 6th ed. 2000.
Farr, Dennis. *English Art 1870–1940.* 1978.
Ford, Boris, ed. *The Cambridge Guide to the Arts
in Britain: The Edwardian Age and the Inter-
War Years.* 1989.
––––––. *The Cambridge Guide to the Arts in Brit-
ain: Since the Second World War.* 1988.
––––––. *The New Pelican Guide to English Litera-
ture.* vols. 7–8. 1983.
Gifford, Denis. *The British Film Catalogue 1895–
1985: A Reference Guide.* 2nd ed. 1986.
Hamilton, Ian, ed. *The Oxford Companion to
Twentieth-Century Poetry in English.* 1994.
Hartnoll, Phyllis, ed. *The Oxford Companion to
the Theatre.* 4th ed. 1983.
Leventhal, F.M., ed. *Twentieth-Century Britain:
An Encyclopedia.* 1995.
Brown, Judith M., and Wm. Roger Louis, eds.
*The Oxford History of the British Empire: vol.
IV: The Twentieth Century.* 1999.
Mitchell, B.R. *British Historical Statistics.* 1988.
Noyce, John, ed. *The Directory of British Alterna-
tive Periodicals, 1965–1974.* 1979.
Ousby, Ian, ed. *The Cambridge Guide to Literature
in English.* 2nd ed. 1994.
Sadie, Stanley, ed. *The New Grove Dictionary of
Music and Musicians.* 20 vols. 1981.
Thompson, F.M.L., ed. *The Cambridge Social
History of Britain 1750–1950.* 3 vols. 1990.

Trussler, Simon., ed. *The Cambridge Illustrated
History of British Theatre.* 1994.

Biography

Banks, Olive, ed. *The Biographical Dictionary of
British Feminists (1800–1945).* 2 vols. 1985, 1990.
Baylen, Joseph O., and Norbert J. Gossman, eds.
*Biographical Dictionary of Modern British Rad-
icals.* vol. 3 in 2 vols. (1870 –1914). 1988.
Bellamy, Joyce M., and John Saville, eds. *Diction-
ary of Labour Biography.* vols. 1–10. 1972–2000.
*Biographical Memoirs of Fellows of the Royal Soci-
ety. 1955–.*
Briggs, Asa, ed. *Dictionary of Twentieth Century
World Biography.* 1992
Dictionary of National Biography. 1908– (with
supplements to 1985). This will eventually be
superseded by the projected *New Dictionary of
National Biography,* H.C.G. Matthew and
Brian Harrison, eds.
Jeremy, David J., ed. *Dictionary of Business Biog-
raphy.* 5 vols. 1984–6.
Robbins, Keith, ed. *The Blackwell Biographical
Dictionary of British Political Life in the Twen-
tieth Century.* 1990.

Dissertations

Comprehensive Dissertation Index. 1973–.
*Index to Theses Accepted for Higher Degrees in the
Universities of Great Britain and Ireland. 1953–.*
Gilbert, Victor F., ed. *Labour and Social History
Theses: American, British and Irish University
Theses and Dissertations in the Field of British
and Irish Labour History Presented Between
1900 and 1978.* 1982.

Periodicals

Contemporary Record: *The Journal of the Insti-
tute of Contemporary History. 1987–1995.* Con-
tinued as *Contemporary British History. 1996–.*
Labour History Review (formerly *Bulletin of the
Society for the Study of Labour History*). 1960 –.
Twentieth Century British History. 1990 –.

Contributors

R.J.Q. ADAMS, *Texas A&M University*
Cliveden Set
Ministry of Munitions
Munich
Simon, John Allsebrook (1873–1954)

ROGER ADELSON, *Arizona State University*
Balfour, Arthur James (1848–1934)
Balfour Declaration
Lawrence, T(homas) E(dward) (1888–1935)

TONY ALDGATE, *The Open University*
Reed, Carol (1906–1976)

NANNETTE ALDRED, *University of Sussex*
Powell, Michael (1905–1990)

ARNSTEIN, WALTER, *University of Illinois*
Monarchy

VICTOR BAILEY, *University of Kansas*
Juvenile Delinquency

STUART BALL, *University of Leicester*
Baldwin, Stanley (1867–1947)
Beaverbrook, Lord [William Maxwell
Aitken] (1879–1964)
Butler, R(ichard) A(usten) (1902–1982)
Churchill, Winston Spencer (1874–1965)
Conservative Party
Major, John (1943–)
1922 Committee

T.C. BARKER, *London School of Economics*
Urban Transport

L. MARGARET BARNETT, *University of
Southern Mississippi*
Defence of the Realm Act (DORA)
Diet and Nutrition
Rationing

GEORGE C. BAUGH, *Victoria History of
Shropshire*
Garden Cities

J.O. BAYLEN, *Georgia State University*
Gardiner, A(lfred) G(eorge) (1865–1946)
Massingham, H(enry) W(illiam) (1860–1924)
Nation (1907–1931)

GORDON BEADLE, *State University College
of New York, Cortland*
Brooke, Rupert Chawner (1887–1915)
Sassoon, Siegfried (1886–1967)
Spender, Stephen (1909–1995)

ALAN J. BEATTIE, *London School of
Economics*
London School of Economics

G.H. BENNETT, *University of Plymouth*
Curzon, George Nathaniel (1859–1925)

VIRGINIA BERRIDGE, *London School of
Hygiene and Tropical Medicine*
Public Health

DONALD S. BIRN, *State University of New
York, Albany*
British Council
League of Nations
Murray, (George) Gilbert (Aimé) (1866–1957)
Peace Ballot

DAVID BLAAZER, *Australian Defence Force
Academy*
Angell (Lane), (Ralph) Norman (1872–1967)
Cripps (Richard) Stafford (1889–1952)
Guild Socialism
Popular Front
Socialist League (1932–1937)
Union of Democratic Control

T.M. BOON, *Science Museum, London*
Haldane, J(ohn) B(urdon) S(anderson) (1901–
1971)
Huxley, Julian Sorrell (1887–1975)

NEWELL D. BOYD, *Houston Baptist
University*
Boer [South African] War (1899–1902)
Milner, Alfred (1854–1925)

SARAH BRADFORD, *London*
Elizabeth II (1926 –)

TREVOR BRAY, *Cardigan, Dyfed, Wales*
Britten (Edward) Benjamin (1913–1976)
Composers
Delius, Frederick Theodore Albert (1862–1934)
Elgar, Edward William (1857–1934)
Holst, Gustavus Theodore von (1874–1934)
Opera
Orchestras
Tippett, Michael Kemp (1905–1998)
Vaughan Williams, Ralph (1872–1958)
Walton, William Turner (1902–1983)

LAURENCE A. BREINER, *Boston University*
Commonwealth Literature

IAN BRITAIN, *Melbourne, Australia*
Webb, Beatrice Potter (1858–1943) and Sidney (1859–1947)

STEPHEN BROOKE, *York University, Toronto*
Attlee, Clement Richard (1883–1967)
Dalton, (Edward) Hugh John Neale (1887–1962)
Labour Party

OLGA R.R. BROOMFIELD, *Mount Saint Vincent University*
Bennett, (Enoch) Arnold (1867–1931)

JAMES M. CAHALAN, *Indiana University of Pennsylvania*
Irish Literature

DAVID CANTOR, *Johns Hopkins University*
Fleming, Alexander (1881–1955)

ROGER CARDINAL, *University of Kent at Canterbury*
Nash, Paul (1889–1946)

DAVID CARLTON, *University of Warwick*
Eden (Robert) Anthony (1897–1977)
Suez Crisis

ROBERT L. CASERIO, *Temple University*
English Novel, 1900–1945
Huxley, Aldous Leonard (1894–1963)

YOUSSEF CASSIS, *University of Geneva*
City of London
Clearing Banks
Merchant Banks

DAVID CHILDS, *University of Nottingham*
Communist Party

IAN CLARK, *Selwyn College, Cambridge*
Nuclear Weapons

ROBERTA A. CLARK, *Chapel Hill, North Carolina*
Birth Control
Stopes, Marie Charlotte Carmichael (1880–1958)

PETER CLARKE, *Trinity Hall, Cambridge*
Hammond, J(ohn) L(awrence) (Le Breton) (1872–1949) and (Lucy) Barbara (1873–1961)
Keynes, John Maynard (1883–1946)
Social Democratic Party
Wallas, Graham (1858–1932)

CATHERINE A. CLINE, *Catholic University of America*
Morel, E(dmund) D(ene) (1873–1924)

RICHARD COCKETT, *Royal Holloway, University of London*
Dawson, Geoffrey (1874–1944)
Garvin, J(ames) L(ouis) (1868–1947)
Observer
The Times

FRANS COETZEE, *George Washington University*
Bonar Law, Andrew (1858–1923)
Tariff Reform

DAVID COHEN, *London, England*
Freud, Lucian (1922–)
Hepworth, Barbara (1903–1975)
Moore, Henry Spencer (1898–1986)
Sutherland, Graham Vivian (1903–1980)

ROBERT COLE, *Utah State University*
Propaganda
Taylor, A(lan) J(ohn) P(ercivale) (1906–1990)

STEPHEN CONSTANTINE, *University of Lancaster*
Emigration

RICHARD A. COSGROVE, *University of Arizona*
Capital Punishment
Judicial System
Legal Profession

ROBERT M. CRAIG, *Georgia Institute of Technology*
Architecture
Lutyens, Edwin Landseer (1869–1944)
Postmodernism in Architecture

DON M. CREGIER, *University of Prince Edward Island*
Carson, Edward Henry (1854–1935)
Irish Land Purchase Act (1903)
Irish Nationalism
Liberal Party
Lloyd George, David (1863–1945)

JAMES E. CRONIN, *Boston College*
Strikes

HUGH CUNNINGHAM, *University of Kent at Canterbury*
Leisure

MARK CURTHOYS, *Christ Church, Oxford*
Oxford, University of

ERYL DAVIES, *London*
Radar

JOHN H. DAVIS, *The Queen's College, Oxford*
London
London Government since 1900

JOAN DEAN, *University of Missouri, Kansas City*
Stoppard, Tom (1937–)

CHARLES DELLHEIM, *Boston University*
Marks and Spencer

DAVID R. DEVEREUX, *Canisius College*
Aviation

FRAM DINSHAW, *St. Catherine's College, Oxford*
Clark, Kenneth Mackenzie (1903–1983)

MICHAEL DINTENFASS, *University of Wisconsin, Milwaukee*
Gold Standard
Mond, Alfred Moritz (1868–1930)

D.J. DOOLEY, *University of Toronto*
Waugh, Evelyn Arthur St. John (1903–1966)

RUTH DUDLEY EDWARDS, *London*
Gollancz, Victor (1893–1967)

BRYAN DYSON, *University of Hull*
Cooperative Movement

DAVID E.H. EDGERTON, *Imperial College, London*
Tizard, Henry Thomas (1885–1959)

DUANE EDWARDS, *Fairleigh Dickinson University*
Lawrence, D(avid) H(erbert) (1885–1930)

CLIVE EMSLEY, *The Open University*
Crime

GEORGE ESENWEIN, *University of Florida*
International Brigade
Spanish Civil War (1936–1939)

T.F. EVANS, *Stone, Staffordshire*
Shaw, George Bernard (1856–1950)

JOHN FERNS, *McMaster University*
Strachey, (Giles) Lytton (1880–1932)

ANTHONY FIELD, *London*
Arts Council of Great Britain

IAN CHRISTOPHER FLETCHER, *Georgia State University*
Haldane, R(ichard) B(urdon) (1856–1928)
Montagu, Edwin Samuel (1879–1924)
Northcliffe, Lord [Alfred Charles William Harmsworth] (1865–1922)

RICHARD FLYNN, *Georgia Southern University*
Children's Literature

AARON FOGEL, *Boston University*
Conrad, Joseph (1857–1924)

MARTIN FRANCIS, *Royal Holloway, University of London*
Benn, Anthony Neil Wedgwood (1925–)
Jenkins, Roy Harris (1920–)

MICHAEL FREEDEN, *Mansfield College, Oxford*
Hobson, J(ohn) A(tkinson) (1858–1940)

AVERIL GARDNER, *Memorial University of Newfoundland*
Wilson, Angus Frank Johnstone (1913–1991)

W.R. GARSIDE, *University of Birmingham*
The Dole
Means Test
Unemployment

KATHY JUSTICE GENTILE, *University of Missouri, St. Louis*
Compton-Burnett, Ivy (1884–1969)

NANCY GISH, *University of Southern Maine*
MacDiarmid, Hugh [Christopher Murray Grieve] (1892–1978)

ROBERT GORDON, *Goldsmiths' College, London*
Actors and Acting
Osborne, John James (1929–1994)
Pinter, Harold (1930–)
Rattigan, Terence Mervyn (1911–1977)

DEBORAH GORHAM, *Carleton University*
Brittain, Vera Mary (1893–1970)
Sayers, Dorothy L(eigh) (1893–1957)
Women's Education

DAVID GULLETTE, *Simmons College*
Joyce, James Augustine Aloysius (1882–1941)

PETER L. HAHN, *Ohio State University*
Anglo-American Relations
Lend-Lease

ANNE HARDY, *Wellcome Institute for the History of Medicine*
Hospitals

CAMERON HAZLEHURST, *Queensland University of Technology*
Asquith, H(erbert) H(enry) (1852–1928)
Campbell-Bannerman, Henry (1836–1908)

TREVOR HERBERT, *The Open University*
Beecham, Thomas (1879–1961)

ANDREW HEWITT, *State University of New York, Buffalo*
Lewis, (Percy) Wyndham (1882–1957)

DAVID LEON HIGDON, *Texas Tech University*
English Novel Since 1945
Greene, (Henry) Graham (1904–1991)

JEFFREY HILL, *Nottingham Trent University*
Cricket
Horse Racing
Tennis, Lawn

DANIEL W. HOLLIS, III, *Jacksonville State University*
Northern Ireland

COLIN HOLMES, *University of Sheffield*
Anti-Semitism
Fascism
Immigration
Mosley, Oswald Ernald (1896–1980)
Refugees

FRANK HONIGSBAUM, *London*
Medical Profession

STEPHEN HOWE, *Ruskin College, Oxford*
Commonwealth

DAVID HOWELL, *University of York*
Hardie, (James) Keir (1856–1915)
Independent Labour Party
Miners Federation
National Union of Mineworkers
Sankey Commission
Wheatley, John (1869–1930)

CHRISTOPHER T. HUSBANDS, *London School of Economics*
National Front

IAN JEFFREY, *Rodmell, East Sussex*
Gill, (Arthur) Eric Rowton (1882–1940)
John, Augustus Edwin (1878–1961)
Sickert, W(alter) R(ichard) (1860–1942)
Spencer, Stanley (1891–1959)

NICHOLAS JENKINS, *Stanford University*
Auden, W(ystan) H(ugh) (1907–1973)

PAUL A. JOHNSON, *London School of Economics*
Hours of Work
Standard of Living

GEOFFREY JONES, *University of Reading*
Multinational Corporations
Nationalization and Nationalized Industries

R. MERFYN JONES, *University College of North Wales, Bangor*
Welsh Nationalism

TUDOR JONES, *University of Coventry*
Crosland, (Charles) Anthony Raven (1918–1977)
Gaitskell, Hugh Todd Naylor (1906–1963)
Labour Revisionism

HEATHER BRYANT JORDAN, *Harvard University*
Bowen, Elizabeth Dorothea Cole (1899–1973)

MICHAEL DAVID KANDIAH, *Institute of Contemporary British History, London*
Powell, (John) Enoch (1912–1998)
Woolton, Earl of [Frederick James Marquis] (1883–1964)

HARVEY J. KAYE, *University of Wisconsin, Green Bay*
Thompson, E(dward) P(almer) (1924–1993)

THOMAS C. KENNEDY, *University of Arkansas*
Allen, (Reginald) Clifford (1889–1939)
Conscientious Objection
No-Conscription Fellowship

CHRISTOPHER A. KENT, *University of Saskatchewan*
Hotels

SUSAN KINGSLEY KENT, *University of Colorado*
Pankhurst, Emmeline (1858–1928), Christabel (Harriette) (1880–1958), (Estelle) Sylvia (1882–1960)
Women's Social and Political Union
Women's Suffrage

FRANK KERSNOWSKI, *Trinity University*
Graves, Robert von Ranke (1895–1985)

LEWIS KLAUSNER, *University of Utah*
English Poetry

JACOB KORG, *University of Washington*
Thomas, Dylan Marlais (1914–1953)

SETH KOVEN, *Villanova University*
Slums

DIANE B. KUNZ, *Columbia University*
Norman, Montagu Collet (1871–1950)

KARL G. LAREW, *Towson State University*
Battle of Britain and Blitz
Dunkirk
El Alamein
Montgomery, Bernard Law (1887–1976)
Second World War: Military

CHRISTOPHER LAWRENCE, *Wellcome Institute for the History of Medicine*
Chemistry
Health of the Population

KEITH LAYBOURN, *University of Huddersfield*
Bevan, Aneurin (1897–1960)
Jarrow
MacDonald, (James) Ramsay (1866–1937)
Morrison, Herbert Stanley (1888–1965)
Snowden, Philip (1864–1937)
Wilkinson, Ellen (1891–1947)

D.L. LEMAHIEU, *Lake Forest College*
British Broadcasting Corporation
BBC Overseas Service
Leavis, F(rank) R(aymond) (1895–1978)
Reith, John Charles Walsham (1889–1971)

VAN MICHAEL LESLIE, *Union College, Barbourville, Kentucky*
Chamberlain, (Joseph) Austen (1863–1937)
Chamberlain, (Arthur) Neville (1868–1940)
Hoare, Samuel John Gurney (1880–1959)

FRED M. LEVENTHAL, *Boston University*
Baylis, Lilian Mary (1874–1937)
Brailsford, H(enry) N(oel) (1873–1958)
Council for the Encouragement of Music and the Arts
Festival of Britain
Henderson, Arthur (1863–1935)
Woolf, Leonard Sidney (1880–1969)

WAYNE LEWCHUK, *McMaster University*
Automobile Industry
Morris, William (1877–1963)

JANE E. LEWIS, *University of Oxford*
Marriage

TREVOR LLOYD, *University of Toronto*
Electoral System
House of Lords

ROGER D. LONG, *Eastern Michigan University*
Decolonization
Partition of India

DAVID C. LUKOWITZ, *Hamline University*
Appeasement
Halifax, Earl of (Edward Frederick Lindley Wood) (1881–1959)
Pacifism
Peace Pledge Union

MARY LYDON, *University of Wisconsin, Madison*
Beckett, Samuel (1906–1989)

RAYMOND N. MACKENZIE, *University of St. Thomas, Minneapolis*
Manchester Guardian
Periodicals

S.P. MACKENZIE, *University of South Carolina*
Codebreaking
Internment of Aliens
Lytton Commission (1931–1932)
Official Secrets Act

JOHN MACNICOL, *Royal Holloway,*
University of London
Beveridge, William Henry (1879–1963)
National Health Service
Old Age Pensions
Titmuss, Richard Morris (1907–1973)

IAN MADELIN, *Bracknell, Berkshire*
Royal Air Force

PETER MANDLER, *Gonville and Caius*
College, Cambridge
Country Houses
Historic Preservation
National Trust
Nicolson, Harold George (1886–1968)
Town and Country Planning

JANE MARCUS, *Graduate Center, City*
University of New York
Woolf, (Adeline) Virginia Stephen (1882–1941)

LARA MARKS, *Imperial College, London*
Pregnancy and Childbirth

JAN MARSH, *London*
Owen, Wilfred Edward Salter (1893–1918)

TONY MASON, *University of Warwick*
Football
Sport

JOSEPH MCALEER, *Stamford, Connecticut*
Popular Fiction

JOSEPH M. MCCARTHY, *Suffolk University*
Army
Falklands War
Home Guard

ARTHUR MEJIA, *San Francisco State*
University
Edward VII (1841–1910)
Edward VIII (1894–1972)
George V (1865–1936)
George VI (1895–1952)

PETER MELLINI, *Sonoma State University*
Punch

ANTHONY MESSINA, *Notre Dame*
University
Race Relations

KENNETH O. MORGAN, *University of Wales*
Devolution, Scottish and Welsh

ELIZABETH J. MORSE, *Oxford, England*
Cambridge, University of
Open University

ALAN Q. MORTON, *Science Museum, London*
Physics
Rutherford, Ernest (1871–1937)

GEORGE H. MOYSER, *University of Vermont*
Church of England
Lang, Cosmo Gordon (1864–1945)
Temple, William (1881–1944)

ELIZABETH MUTHER, *Bowdoin College*
Eliot, T(homas) Stearns (1888–1965)

JOHN F. NAYLOR, *State University of New*
York, Buffalo
Cabinet

BARBARA NEWMAN, *London*
Ballet
de Valois, Ninette (1898–)
Fonteyn, Margot (1919–1991)
MacMillan, Kenneth (1929–1992)

MICHAEL NEWMAN, *University of North*
London
Laski, Harold Joseph (1893–1950)
Left Book Club
Strachey, John (1901–1963)

WILLIAM H. O'DONNELL, *Memphis State*
University
Yeats, William Butler (1865–1939)

WARREN OLIN-AMMENTORP, C*azenovia*
College
Golding, William (1911–1993)

DONNA PRICE PAUL, *Springfield, Virginia*
Women's Employment

BRIAN PEARCE, *Technikon Natal, Durban,*
South Africa
Ayckbourn, Alan (1939–)
Drama

SUSAN PEDERSEN, *Harvard University*
Family Allowances
Feminism
Rathbone, Eleanor Florence (1872–1946)

BARRY PHELPS, *London*
Wodehouse, P(elham) G(renville) (1881–1975)

BRIAN PHILLIPS, *Amnesty International,*
London
Friends, Society of

STEPHEN PRIEST, *University of Edinburgh*
Ayer, A(lfred) J(ules) (1910–1989)

ROBIN PRIOR, *Australian Defence Force*
Academy, Canberra
First World War: Military
Gallipoli
Passchendaele, Battle of
Scott, C(harles) P(restwich) (1846–1932)
Somme, Battle of the

FRANK PROCHASKA, *Yale University*
Philanthropy

JENNIFER RANDISI, *California State*
University, San Bernardino
Spark, Muriel Camberg (1918–)

JOHN RANLETT, *State University College of*
New York, Potsdam
Railways

EUGENE L. RASOR, *Emory and Henry College*
Navy

STEVE REDHEAD, *Manchester Metropolitan*
University
The Beatles
Popular Music

STEVEN REILLY, *University of Kent at*
Canterbury
Callaghan, (Leonard) James (1912–)
Campaign for Nuclear Disarmament
Foot, Michael (1913-)
Heath, Edward Richard George (1916–)
Kinnock, Neil Gordon (1942–)
Thatcherism
Wilson, (James) Harold (1916–1995)

MARILYN REIZBAUM, *Bowdoin College*
Scottish Literature

RICHARD A. REMPEL, *McMaster University*
Imperial Preference

DANIEL RITSCHEL, *University of Maryland,*
Baltimore County
Political and Economic Planning (PEP)

RICHARD RODGER, *University of Leicester*
Council Housing
Housing

JONATHAN ROSE, *Drew University*
Adult Education
Fabian Society
Wells, H(erbert) G(eorge) (1866–1946)

JANICE ROSSEN, *Austin, Texas*
Larkin, Philip (1922–1985)

DAVID RUBINSTEIN, *University of Hull*
Fawcett, Millicent Garrett (1947–1929)

JOHN PAUL RUSSO, *University of Miami*
Literary Criticism
Richards, I(vor) A(rmstrong) (1893–1979)

CHARLES J. RZEPKA, *Boston University*
Detective Fiction

MICHAEL SALER, *University of California,*
Davis
Design
Pick, Frank (1978–1941)

GAIL L. SAVAGE, *St. Mary's College of*
Maryland
Astor, Nancy Witcher Langhorne (1879–
1964)
Civil Service
Divorce and Divorce Law

MARGARET SCANLAN, *Indiana University,*
South Bend
Murdoch, Iris (1919–1999)

RICHARD J. SCHIEFEN, *University of St.*
Thomas, Houston
Roman Catholicism

JONATHAN SCHNEER, *Georgia Institute of*
Technology
Lansbury, George (1859–1940)

MARTHA SCHÜTZ, *London*
Coward, Noel Pierce (1899–1973)
Olivier, Laurence Kerr (1907–1989)
Robbins Report (1963)

KARL W. SCHWEIZER, *New Jersey Institute*
of Technology
Namier, Lewis Bernstein (1888–1960)

PETER SIMKINS, *Imperial War Museum*
Committee of Imperial Defence
Haig, Douglas (1861–1928)
Kitchener, Horatio Herbert (1859–1916)

MADELEINE SIMMS, *Institute for Social*
Studies in Medical Care, London
Abortion

DAVID SIMPSON, *University of Colorado*
Williams, Raymond Henry (1921–1988)

ADRIAN SMITH, *University of Southampton*
Martin, (Basil) Kingsley (1897–1969)
New Statesman
Press

ELTON EDWARDS SMITH, *University of South Florida*
Day Lewis, Cecil (1904–1972)
MacNeice, Louis (1907–1963)

HAROLD L. SMITH, *University of Houston, Victoria*
Equal Pay Movement
Second World War: Homefront

MICHAEL DOUGLAS SMITH, *Germantown, Maryland*
Trevelyan, G(eorge) M(acaulay) (1876–1962)

RICHARD A. SOLOWAY, *University of North Carolina*
Population

PETER STANSKY, *Stanford University*
Bloomsbury Group
Forster, E(dward) M(organ) (1879–1970)
Jennings, Humphrey (1907–1950)
Orwell, George (1903–1950)

SANFORD STERNLICHT, *Syracuse University*
Galsworthy, John (1867–1933)
Masefield, John Edward (1878–1967)
Maugham, W(illiam) Somerset (1874–1965)

STEVEN W. STURDY, *University of Manchester*
Medical Research

PENNY SUMMERFIELD, *University of Manchester*
Mass-Observation
Women in Wartime

BARRY SUPPLE, *The Leverhulme Trust, London*
Coal Mining
Economic Performance

GILLIAN SUTHERLAND, *Newnham College, Cambridge*
University Education

PAUL SWANN, *Temple University*
Documentary Film
Film Industry
Hitchcock, Alfred (1899–1980)

LAURA TABILI, *University of Arizona*
Black People

ANDREW A. TADIE, *Seattle University*
Chesterton, G(ilbert) K(eith) (1874–1936)

LOU TAYLOR, *University of Brighton*
Clothing and Fashion

PAUL TAYLOR, *London School of Economics*
European Union

PAT THANE, *Institute of Contemporary British History, London*
Ageing
Welfare State
Women

DEBORAH THOM, *Robinson College, Cambridge*
Education Act of 1944
Primary Education
Secondary Education

ANDREW THORPE, *University of Exeter*
Blair, Anthony Charles Linton (1953–)

VIRGINIA TIGER, *Rutgers University, Newark*
Lessing, Doris May Tayler (1919–)

TONY TOPHAM, *Leven, North Humberside*
Transport and General Workers' Union

MARINA VAIZEY, *London*
Epstein, Jacob (1880–1959)
Fry, Roger Eliot (1866–1934)

DAVID VAUGHAN, *Cunningham Dance Foundation, New York*
Ashton, Frederick (1904–1988)

JOHN VINCENT, *University of Bristol*
Home, Alec [Alexander Frederick] Douglas- (1903–1998)
MacLeod, Iain Norman (1913–1970)
Macmillan, (Maurice) Harold (1894–1986)
Thatcher, Margaret Hilda Roberts (1925–)

RICHARD A. VOELTZ, *Cameron University*
Baden-Powell, Robert (1857–1941)
Kipling, (Joseph) Rudyard (1865–1936)

MARY WAGONER, *University of New Orleans*
Christie, Agatha Miller (1890–1976)

A. MARTIN WAINWRIGHT, *University of Akron*
Mountbatten, Louis Francis Albert Victor Nicholas (1900–1979)

GRAHAM WALKER, *Queen's University,*
   Belfast
   Labour Representation Committee
   Maxton, James (1885–1946)
   Scottish Nationalism

WESLEY K. WARK, *University of Toronto*
   Spy Novel

KENNETH WARREN, *Jesus College, Oxford*
   Steel Industry

BERNARD WASSERSTEIN, *University of*
   Glasgow
   Jews
   Palestine
   Samuel, Herbert (1870–1963)

CHRIS WATERS, *Williams College*
   Blatchford, Robert Peel Glanville (1851–1943)
   Homosexuality
   Popular Culture
   Priestley, J(ohn) B(oynton) (1894–1984)
   Wolfenden Report (1957)

PETER WEILER, *Boston College*
   Bevin, Ernest (1881–1951)
   New Liberalism

JAMES P. WHITE, *University of Southern*
   Alabama
   Isherwood, Christopher William Bradshaw
   (1904–1986)

JOSEPH WIESENFARTH, *University of*
   Wisconsin, Madison
   Ford, Ford Madox (1873–1939)

KIRK WILLIS, *University of Georgia*
   Moore, G(eorge) E(dward) (1873–1958)
   Russell, Bertrand (1872–1970)
   Whitehead, Alfred North (1861–1947)

T. MERVYN WILLSHAW, *Bromley, Kent*
   Methodism

ANDREW WILSON, *London*
   Bacon, Francis (1909–1992)
   Bell, Vanessa Stephen ((1879–1961)
   Grant, Duncan James Corrowr (1885–1978)
   Hockney, David (1937-)
   Nevinson, C(hristopher) R(ichard) W(ynne)
   (1889–1946)
   Nicholson, Ben (1894–1982)
   Vorticism

TREVOR WILSON, *University of Adelaide*
   First World War: Military
   Gallipoli
   Passchendaele, Battle of
   Scott, C(harles) P(restwich) (1846–1932)
   Somme, Battle of the

GUIL WINCHESTER, *Wellcome Institute for*
   the History of Medicine
   Crick, Francis (1916-)

ANGELA WOOLLACOTT, *Case Western*
   University
   First World War: Homefront

ANTHONY W. WRIGHT, MP, *House of*
   Commons
   Cole, G(eorge) D(ouglas) H(oward) (1889–
   1959)
   Tawney, R(ichard) H(enry) (1880–1962)

C.J. WRIGLEY, *University of Nottingham*
   Citrine, Walter McLennan (1887–1983)
   General Strike (4–12 May 1926)
   Taff Vale Judgment (July 1901)
   Thomas, J(ames) H(enry) (1874–1959)
   Trades Union Congress
   Trade Union Legislation

LYNN ZASTOUPIL, *Rhodes College*
   Government of India Act
   Indian Nationalism

Index